GORE VIDAL GORE VIDAL GORE VIDAL GORE VIDAL

GORE VIDAL

Julian
Williwaw
The Judgement of Paris
Messiah
The City and the Pillar

GORE VIDAL

Octopus/Heinemann

Julian was first published in the United States by Little, Brown & Co in 1964; in Great Britain by William Heinemann Ltd in 1964.
Williwaw was first published in the United States by E P Dutton & Co Inc in 1946; in Great Britain, in hardback form, by William Heinemann Ltd in 1970.
The Judgement of Paris was first published in the United States by E P Dutton & Co Inc in 1953; in Great Britain by William Heinemann Ltd in 1953.
Messiah was first published in the United States by E P Dutton & Co Inc in 1955; in Great Britain by William Heinemann Ltd in 1955.
The City and the Pillar was first published in the United States by E P Dutton & Co Inc in 1948, revised edition in 1965; in Great Britain by John Lehmann Ltd in 1948, revised edition by William Heinemann Ltd in 1965.

This edition first published in the United States of America
in 1979 jointly by

Wiliiam Heinemann Inc
450 Park Avenue, New York, NY 10022

and

Octopus Books Inc
The Olympic Towers, 645 Fifth Avenue,
New York, NY 10022

ISBN 0 905712 39 0

Printed in the United States of America
by R. R. Donnelley and Sons Company.

CONTENTS

JULIAN

BRITAIN
London

GERMANIA

Kellen
Cologne
Bonn
Treves Bingen
Paris
Strasbourg
Sens
Auxerre
Autun Besançon

GAUL

RHINE

DANUBE

Bregentz
RAETIA

NORICUM

Vienna

PANNONIA

Budapest

Vienne
Como
Milan
Turin CISALPINE
GAUL

Aquileia

Mursa

Sirmium

ILLYRICUM

DALMATIA

DACIA

Nish
Succi Pass

Philip

SPAIN

CORSICA

Rome

ITALY

WEST ROMAN

SARDINIA

Tyrrhenian
Sea

EPIRUS

MACED

THESSALY

Delphi

EMPIRE

MEDITERRANEAN

SICILY

ACHAIA

MAURETANIA

Syracuse

LIB

THE ROMAN EMPIRE
In The Fourth Century A.D.

0 50 100   200   300   400
MILES

Sam¹ H. Bryant

SARMATIA

CASPIAN SEA

BLACK SEA

ARMENIA

SIA

CE

Hadrianopolis

Constantinople

Heraclea

BITHYNIA

Nicodomedia

PONTUS

Chalcedon

Nicaea

Acyra

GALATIA

CAPPADOCIA

CORDUENE

Pergamon

Pessinus

ARMENIA

Amida

Bezabde

ASIA

Nazianzus

Caesarea

Resaina

Nisibis

Ninus

Ephesus

LYCAONIA

Edessa

MESOPOTAMIA

Singara

EAST

Tarsus

Mopsucrene

Carrae

CILICIA

Hierapolis

Callinicum

Dura

Anatha

Diacira

Macepracta

Ctesiphon

RHODES

Antioch

Chalcis

Circesium

Thilutha

Achaiachalca

Seleucia

ROMAN

CYPRUS

SYRIA

Baraxmalcha

Pirisabora

Babylon

Ozogardana

Maiozamalcha

Persia

SEA

Tyre

Damascus

Gi

EMPIRE

ARABIA

Alexandria

Pelusium

EGYPT

RED SEA

For Lucien Price

A NOTE

The Emperor Julian's life is remarkably well documented. Three volumes of his letters and essays survive, while such acquaintances as Libanius and Saint Gregory of Nazianzus wrote vivid accounts of him. Though I have written a novel, not a history, I have tried to stay with the facts, only occasionally shifting things around. For instance, it is unlikely that Priscus joined Julian in Gaul, but it is useful to the narrative to have him there.

Julian has always been something of an underground hero in Europe. His attempt to stop Christianity and revive Hellenism exerts still a romantic appeal, and he crops up in odd places, particularly during the Renaissance and again in the nineteenth century. Two such unlikely authors as Lorenzo de' Medici and Henrik Ibsen wrote plays about him. But aside from the unique adventure of Julian's life, what continues to fascinate is the fourth century itself. During the fifty years between the accession of Julian's uncle Constantine the Great and Julian's death at thirty-two, Christianity was established. For better or worse, we are today very much the result of what they were then.

In naming cities, I give the modern rather than the ancient name (Milan, not Mediolanum), except when the original name is more familiar to us (Ephesus, not Selçuk). Dates I put in our fashion, A.D. and B.C. Since Julian's court was a military one, I have used the American army's way of dating, i.e., 3 October 363. Currency is a tricky matter. No one is quite certain what the exact purchasing power of money was in the fourth century, but a gold solidus was probably worth about five dollars. Julian, Priscus and Libanius, the three narrators of this story, all wrote Greek. Their Latin was rather shaky, as they are quick to remind us, but they occasionally use Latin terms, much the way we do. For those readers who will search in vain for Julian's famous last words, 'Thou hast conquered, Galilean!', he never said them. Theodoret must take credit for this fine rhetoric, composed a century after Julian's death.

I should like to thank the American Academy at Rome and the American School of Classical Studies at Athens for letting me use their libraries.

G.V.

YOUTH

I

Libanius to Priscus   *Antioch, March [A.D.] 380*

Yesterday morning as I was about to enter the lecture hall, I was stopped by a Christian student who asked me in a voice eager with malice, 'Have you heard about the Emperor Theodosius?'

I cleared my throat ready to investigate the nature of this question, but he was too quick for me. 'He has been baptized a Christian.'

I was non-committal. Nowadays, one never knows who is a secret agent. Also, I was not particularly surprised at the news. When Theodosius fell ill last winter and the bishops arrived like vultures to pray over him, I knew that should he recover they would take full credit for having saved him. He survived. Now we have a Christian emperor in the East, to match Gratian, our Christian emperor in the West. It was inevitable.

I turned to go inside but the young man was hardly finished with his pleasant task. 'Theodosius has also issued an edict. It was just read in front of the senate house. I heard it. Did you?'

'No. But I always enjoy imperial prose,' I said politely.

'You may not enjoy this. The Emperor has declared heretic all those who do not follow the Nicene Creed.'

'I'm afraid Christian theology is not really my subject. The edict hardly applies to those of us who are still faithful to philosophy.'

'It applies to everyone in the East.' He said this slowly, watching me all the while. 'The Emperor has even appointed an Inquisitor to determine one's faith. The days of toleration are over.'

I was speechless; the sun flared in my eyes; all things grew confused and I wondered if I was about to faint, or even die. But the voices of two colleagues recalled me. I could tell by the way they greeted me that they, too, had heard about the edict and were curious to known my reaction. I gave them no pleasure.

'Of course I expected it,' I said. 'The Empress Postuma wrote me only this week to say that . . .' I invented freely. I have not of course heard from the Empress in some months, but I thought that the enemy should be reminded to what extent I enjoy the favour of Gratian and Postuma. It is humiliating to be forced to protect oneself in this way, but these are dangerous times.

I did not lecture yesterday. I went straight home. I am now living in Daphne, by the way, a charming suburb which I prefer to Antioch proper because of the quiet. As I get older, I find that the slightest sound in the night disturbs me and, once awake, I have difficulty falling asleep again. You can imagine how intolerable my old house in the city became. You remember the house; it was there that I gave the reception for the Emperor Julian when he . . . But I forget. You were not there, and you were much missed! My memory plays me odd tricks these days. Even worse, I tend to mislay the notes I jot down as reminders, or (terrible confession!) when I do find them, I am often unable to decipher my own handwriting. Age spares us nothing, old friend. Like ancient trees, we die from the top.

Except for occasional lectures, I seldom go into town, for the people, though my own, distress me with their loud voices and continual quarrelling, their gambling and sensuality. They are hopelessly frivolous. Nights are made day with artificial light, while nearly all the men now use depilatories, which makes it difficult to tell them from women . . . to think how I once eulogized this city! But I suppose one must be tolerant, recalling that the Antiochenes are the victims of a demoralizingly sultry climate, the proximity of Asia and of course that pernicious Christian doctrine which asserts that a sprinkling of water (and a small donation) will wash away sin, again and again and again.

Now, my old friend, as I sit here in my study surrounded by our proscribed friends (I mean those books of Greece which made the mind of man), let me tell you what thoughts I had last night – a sleepless night not only because of the edict but because two cats saw fit to enliven my despair with the noise of lust (only an Egyptian would worship a cat). I am weary today but determined. *We must fight back.* What happens to us personally is not important, but what happens to civilization is a matter of desperate concern. During my sleepless night, I thought of various appeals that might be made to our new Emperor. I have a copy of the edict before me as I write. It is composed in bad bureaucratic Greek, the official style of the bishops, whose crudity of language is equalled only by the confusion of their thought. Not unlike those celebrated minutes of the council at – where was it? Chalcedon? – which we used to read aloud to one another with such delight! Carefree days, never to come again. Unless we act now.

Priscus, I am sixty-six years old and you are, as I recall, a dozen years older than I. We have reached an age when death is a commonplace not to be feared, especially by us, for is not all philosophy but preparation for a serene dying? And are we not true philosophers who have nothing to lose but that which in the natural course we shall surrender in any case, more soon than late? I have already had several seizures in recent years which left me unconscious and weakened, and of course my chronic cough, aggravated by an unseasonable wet winter, threatens to choke me to death at any time. I am also losing my sight; and I suffer from a most painful form of gout. Therefore let us, fearing nothing, join forces and strike back at the Christians before they entirely destroy the world we love.

My plan is this. Seventeen years ago when you returned from Persia, you told me that our beloved friend and pupil, the Emperor Julian, had written a fragment of memoir which you had got hold of at the time of his death. I have often thought to write you for a copy, simply for my own edification. I realized then, as did you, that publication was out of the question, popular though Julian was and still is, even though his work to restore the true gods has been undone. Under the Emperors Valentinian and Valens we had to be politic and cautious if we were to be allowed to go on teaching. But now in the light of this new edict, I say: an end to caution! We have nothing but two old bodies to lose, while there is eternal glory to be gained by publishing Julian's memoir, with an appropriate biography to be written by either or both of us. I knew his quality best, of course, but you were with him in Persia and saw him die. So between the two of us, I his teacher and you his philosopher-companion, we can rehabilitate his memory and with close reasoning show the justice of his contest with the Christians. I have written about him in the past, and boldly. I refer particularly to the eulogy I composed just after his death when, if I may say so, I was able to bring tears even to hard Christian eyes. Shortly afterwards, I published my correspondence

with Julian. Incidentally, I sent you a copy and though you never acknowledged this gift, I do hope you found it interesting. If by any chance you did not
receive it, I shall be happy to send you another one. I kept all of Julian's letters
to me over the years, as well as copies of my own letters to him. One can never
rely on the great keeping one's letters; and should those letters vanish, one is apt
to be remembered only as the mysterious half of a dialogue to be reconstructed
in the vaguest way from the surviving (and sometimes lesser!) half of the
exchange. Finally, I am at work on an oration to be called 'On Avenging the
Emperor Julian'. I mean to dedicate this work to Theodosius.

Let me know as soon as possible if you concur in my plan. I repeat: we have
nothing to lose. And the world has much to gain. By the way, as a sign of the
times, there is now a *Latin* Academy at Antioch, with a heavy enrolment. It is
enough to chill the blood. The young men are deserting Hellenic studies for
Roman law in the hopes of government preferment. My own classes are still
large but many of my colleagues are literally starving to death. Recently, a
student (Christian, of course) most tactfully suggested that I, Libanius, learn
Latin! At my age and after a lifetime devoted to Greek! I told him that as I was
not a lawyer there was nothing I needed to read in that ugly language, which
has produced only one poem and that a depressing paraphrase of our great
Homer.

I hope after so many years of silence between us that this letter finds you and
your admirable wife, Hippia, in good health. I envy you your life at Athens, the
natural centre of our universe. Do I need to add that I will of course defray any
expenses you might incur in having Julian's memoir copied? The price of copying, luckily, is less at Athens than here at Antioch. Books always cost more in
those cities where they are least read!

Added: An old rumour has just been confirmed. The Great King of Persia,
Sapor, is dead at last. He was over eighty and reigned most of his life. A strange
coincidence that the king who struck down our beloved Julian should die just as
we are about to restore his memory. I was once told that Sapor had read my *Life
of Demosthenes* and admired it. How marvellous books are, crossing worlds and
centuries, defeating ignorance and, finally, cruel time itself. Let us make Julian
live again, and for all time!

Priscus to Libanius   *Athens, March 380*
Yes, the edict is well known here, but the general feeling at the University is
that despite its severe tone we are not apt to be persecuted. The schools are
flourishing. The little Christians flock to us to be civilized, and I find them much
like their Hellenist brothers. But then all young people seem to me more and
more alike. They ask the same questions and they give you the same answers to
the questions they ask you. I despair of teaching anyone anything, least of all
myself. I have not had a new idea since I was twenty-seven. That is why I don't
publish my lectures. Also, too many of us publish out of vanity or to attract
students. At seventy-five (I am nine, not a dozen, years older than you) I am an
empty flagon. Tap me and you will hear an awful hollow sound. My head is a
tomb quite as empty as the one Jesus is supposed to have walked away from. I
incline now to Crates and the early Cynics, less to Plato and the rest. I am not in
the least convinced that there is a Divine Oneness at the centre of the universe,
nor am I susceptible to magic, unlike Julian, who was hopelessly gullible. I often
thought Maximus exploited his good-heartedness. But then I never could en-

dure Maximus. How he used to waste Julian's time with his séances and arcane
gibberish! I teased the Emperor about him once, but Julian only laughed and
said, 'Who knows through what door wisdom will walk?'

As to your publishing project, I am not at all certain that a sympathetic
biography of Julian would have the slightest effect at this time. Theodosius is a
military politician, impressed by bishops. He might of course sanction a biography of his predecessor simply because Julian is much admired to this day,
though *not* for his philosophy. Julian is admired because he was young and
handsome and the most successful general of our century. The people have a
touching admiration for generals who win battles, which is why there are no
heroes today. But if Theodosius did permit a biography, it would have to avoid
the religious issue. The bishops would see to that. And for ferocity there is
nothing on earth to equal a Christian bishop hunting 'heresy', as they call any
opinion contrary to their own. Especially confident are they on that subject
where they are as ignorant as the rest of mankind. I mean death. Anyway, I
don't want to fight them, because I am one and they are many. And though I
am, as you so comfortingly suggest, old and near the end of my life, I enjoy
amazingly good health. I am told that I look no different than I did at forty, and
I am still capable of the sexual act at almost any time. This vitality repels Hippia,
who has aged noticeably in the last few years, but it seems to please various
young women in a certain quarter of Athens which you doubtless have heard of
– in novels of the Milesian school!

Do I make myself clear? I have no wish to be burned alive or stoned or tacked
up to the door of a Christian church, or 'charnel house' as Julian used to call
them. *You* may be as brave as you like and I will applaud you in my heart. But I
have no intention of writing a single sentence about Julian, fond as I was of him
and alarmed as I am at the strange course our world has taken since the
adventurer Constantine sold us to the bishops.

Julian's memoir was written during the last four months of his life. It was
begun in March 363, at Hierapolis. Nearly every night during our invasion of
Persia he would dictate recollections of his early life. The result is a bit helter-
skelter, for both as a writer and as a man he was swift and impulsive. He once
told me that he would like to compose an autobiography of the order of *Marcus
Aurelius to Himself*, but he lacked that writer's discipline. Julian was also influenced by Xenophon's *The March Upcountry*, since Xenophon took much the
same route we did seven centuries later. Julian's interest in history was always
lively, and he was a great sightseer. The resulting memoir is something of a
hybrid; even so, Julian was often an engaging writer, and if he was not better it is
because it is hard to be emperor, philosopher and general all at once. He was
also indiscreet about everyone. I hope you forgive him. I have done so. He
suspected that he had very little time and he wanted to get everything said. As
for his mysterious death, I have a theory as to what happened, which I will
explain to you in due course.

I have never quite known what to do with this work. When Julian died, I took
all his personal papers, suspecting that his Christian successors would destroy
them. I had no right to these papers, of course, but I don't regret my theft. I told
no one about the memoir until I was back safe in Antioch, where I must have
mentioned it to you the day you read us your famous eulogy. I was so moved by
your eloquence that I betrayed my own confidence.

I am now having a fair copy made of the manuscript. You are misinformed if
you think copying is cheaper here than at Antioch. Quite the contrary. The

estimated cost will run to eighty gold solidi, which I suggest you send by return post. On receipt of the full amount, I will send you the book to use as you see fit. Only do *not* mention to anyone that I had any connection with the matter. I have not the slightest desire to endure martyrdom at this time, or ever.

I thought I had written you about your collection of letters. I did get the book and it was very thoughtful of you to send it to me. We are all in your debt for those letters, especially yours to Julian. They are wise. I known of no other philosopher so sensible of posterity as to keep copies of *every* letter he writes, realizing that even his most trivial effusion has, in the context of the large body of his work, an eternal value. Hippia joins me in wishing you good health.

Libanius to Priscus   *Antioch, April 380*
You cannot imagine the pleasure I experienced when your letter was brought to me this evening. So eager was I to hear your voice again, as it were, that I fear I ripped the fastenings and tore the long-awaited page itself. But rest assured, your precious letter will be mended with glue and cherished, since any utterance of your genius is an essential reflection of the Hellenic spirit to be passed on to those who come after.

Let me say right off how pleased I am to learn of your unflagging sexual vigour. It is always inspiring to the rest of us to learn that in certain rare human beings the usual cycle of sad decline does not obtain. You have been indeed favoured by the gods and in your obvious enjoyment of that favour will never sigh at eighty, as did Sophocles, 'At last I am free of a cruel and insane master!' Your master is obviously a good companion, made even more enjoyable by Hippia's acquiescence. Not many wives of philosophers would allow their husbands freedom to consort with those deliciously civilized ladies of Athens whose evening parties used to delight me in my student days. Now of course my life is devoted to philosophy and affairs of state. I leave to younger men the charms of Aphrodite . . . to younger men and now, Priscus, to *you*, who have held at arm's length the villain time! Fortunate man! Fortunate girls to be so loved!

Since I wrote you last, I have not been idle. Through the office of the praetorian prefect at Constantinople, I have proposed myself for an audience with the Emperor. Theodosius has met very few people of our set, coming as he does from Spain, a country not noted for culture. He also belongs to a military family and there is no evidence that he has ever studied philosophy. Outside of politics, his principal interest is breeding sheep. But he is only thirty-three and his character, according to the best information available, is mild. *Though we should not count on this.* How often in the past have we been horrified by princes reputed to be good who, when raised to the throne of the world, have turned monstrous before our eyes! The late Valens for example, or Julian's own brother, the Caesar Gallus, a charming youth who brought terror to the East. We must be on our guard, as always.

The question that now faces us is: how seriously will Theodosius enforce the edict? It is customary for emperors who listen to bishops to hurl insults at the very civilization that created them. They are inconsistent, but then logic has never been a strong point of the Christian faith. The extraordinary paradox is the collusion of our princes with the bishops. The emperors pride themselves on being first magistrates of the Roman imperium, through whose senate they exercise their power; and though in reality we have not been Roman for a century, nevertheless, the *form* persists, making it impossible, one would think, for any prince who calls himself Augustus to be Christian, certainly not as long as the Altar of Victory remains in the senate house at Rome. But confusions of this sort are as inconsequential to the Christian mind as clouds to a day in summer, and as a teacher I no longer try to refute them; since most of my students are Christian, I suppose I ought to be grateful that they have chosen to come to me to be taught that very philosophy their faith subverts. It is comedy, Priscus! It is tragedy!

Meanwhile, we can only wait to see what happens. The Emperor grows stronger in health every day, and it is thought that later this spring he may take the field against the Goths, who as usual are threatening the marches of Macedonia. If he decides to go north, that means he will not return to Constantinople till late summer or autumn, in which case I will have to attend him at Thessalonica or, worse, in the field. If so, I am confident the journey will be my last. For my health, unlike yours, continues to deteriorate. I have coughing fits which leave me weak and longing for the grave. I have also developed a curious rash on the backs of my hands and forearms which may be the result of eating a bad flounder last week (shades of Diogenes and the fatal raw octopus!), or it may be the outward sign of a corruption in the blood. How I wish Oribasius were in Antioch! He is the only physician I ever trusted, in which I follow Julian, who used to say, 'The god Asklepios gave Oribasius secrets known only to heaven.'

Over the years I have made a number of notes for a biography of Julian. I have them before me now. All that remains is the final organization of the material – and of course the memoir. Please send it to me as soon as the copy is ready. I shall work on it this summer, as I am no longer lecturing. I thought it wise to go into seclusion until we know which way the wind blows.

I don't need to tell you that Antioch has ignored the edict. Never in my memory has Antioch obeyed the imperial authority except at sword's point. I have often warned the local senate that emperors do not like disobedience, but our people feel that they are beyond law and reprisal. The folly of the clever is always greater than that of the dull. I tremble for Antioch, even though I am currently a beneficiary of its absence of reverence for the decrees of Caesar.

There have been no incidents so far. My Christian friends come to see me as usual (rather a large number of my old students are now bishops, a peculiar irony). Colleagues who are still lecturing tell me that their classes are much as usual. The next move is up to Theodosius, or, to be exact, up to the bishops. Luckily for us, they have been so busy for so long persecuting one another that we have been able to survive. But reading between the lines of the edict, I suspect a bloodbath. Theodosius has outlawed with particular venom the party of the late priest Arius on the grounds that Galileans must now have a church with a single doctrine to be called universal . . . a *catholic* church, no less! To balance this, we must compose a true life of Julian. So let us together fashion one last wreath of Apollonian laurel to place upon the brow of philosophy, as a brave sign against the winter that threatens this stormy late season of the world. I want those who come after us to realize what hopes we had for life, and I want them to see how close our Julian came to arresting the disease of Galilee. Such a work, properly done, would be like a seed planted in the autumn to await the sun's awakening, and a new flowering.

Apparently, the cost of copying at Athens has gone up incredibly since I had some work done there last year. I find eighty gold solidi exorbitant for what you say is a fragment, or a book of moderate length. Only last summer I paid thirty solidi for a Plotinus which, in length, must be treble that of Julian's memoir. I send now by a friend who embarks tomorrow for Athens thirty gold solidi and this letter. Again my best wishes to the admirable Hippia, and to you, my old friend and fellow soldier in the wars of philosophy.

Priscus to Libanius   *Athens, June 380*

I send you by my pupil Glaucon something less than half of the Emperor Julian's memoir. It cost me exactly thirty solidi to have this much copied. On receipt of the remaining fifty solidi I shall send you the rest of the book. I can only assume that the copying you had done in Athens last summer was the work of an admirer who gave you a cut price as a sign of his esteem for your high contributions to philosophy and rhetoric.

I do not share your pessimism about the new Emperor. He is hardly what *we* would have picked had the choice been ours, but then the choice never has been ours. Julian's accession was the work of Fortune, a deity notable for her absence in human affairs. We can hardly hope to have another Julian in our lifetime. And that is that.

I have studied the edict since I wrote you last, and though it is somewhat sterner in tone than Constantine's, I suspect the only immediate victims will be those Christians who follow Arius. But I may be mistaken. I almost always am in political matters, a weakness no doubt of the philosophic temperament. However, what does give me hope was last year's appointment of the 'poet' Ausonius as consul. Do you know him? I am sure you've read him. If not, you have a treat in store. I have lately become rather an expert on his career. He started life as the son of a well-to-do doctor in Bordeaux. His phenomenal luck began when the Emperor Valentinian made him tutor to his son Gratian. As Ausonius himself puts it, he 'moulded the tiny mind of the infant prince'. When the prince became emperor, he rewarded his old tutor by making him prae-torian prefect of Gaul as well as consul for last year. I mention all this because Ausonius is inclined favourably to us, and he exerts a considerable influence not only on Gratian (who is far too busy hunting wild boar in Gaul to distress us unduly) but on Theodosius as well. He is obviously the man for you to cultivate.

Not long ago I sent round to the library to see what they had by Ausonius. The slave returned with a wheelbarrow full of books. Ausonius must be read to be believed! As poet, no subject is too trivial for him; as courtier, no flattery too excessive. He did write one passable nature poem on the Moselle, but I'm not keen on rivers. The rest of his work is quite marvellous in its tedium. Particularly those verses he wrote at Valentinian's request. Among the subjects chosen by the Emperor were the source of the Danube (Ausonius did not locate it but he made a good try), Easter, and (best of all) four odes to the Emperor's four favourite horses. I had one of these equine odes copied out and Hippia reads it to me whenever I am depressed. It begins 'Oh raven steed, whose fortune it is to spread the golden thighs and Mars-like firm convexities of divine Augustus . . .' I don't know when I have enjoyed a poem so much. I'll enclose a copy. Anyway, I suggest you see Ausonius as soon as possible. And of course you will remember to express admiration for his work! In a good cause hypocrisy becomes virtue.

I never go to evening parties. The quarter I referred to in my letter was *not* the elegant street of Sardes but the quarter of the prostitutes near the agora. I don't go to parties because I detest talking-women, especially our Athenian ladies who see themselves as heiresses to the age of Pericles. Their conversation is hopelessly pretentious and artificial. Their dinners are inedible, and for some reason they all tend to be rather squat with dark vestigial moustaches; no doubt

Aphrodite's revenge on the talking-woman. I live very quietly at home with an occasional visit to the quarter.

Hippia and I get along rather better than we used to. Much of her charm for me has been her lifelong dislike of literature. She talks about servants and food and relatives, and I find her restful. Also, I have in the house a Gothic girl, bought when she was eleven. She is now a beautiful woman, tall and well made, with eyes grey as Athena's. She *never* talks. Eventually I shall buy her a husband and free them both as a reward for her serene acceptance of my attentions, which delight her far less than they do me. But that is often the case with the feminine half of Plato's ugliest beast. But then Plato disliked sexual intercourse between men and women. We tend of course to think of Plato as divine, but I am afraid he was rather like our old friend Iphicles, whose passion for youths has become so outrageous that he now lives day and night in the baths, where the boys call him the queen of philosophy.

I am sorry to hear that your health grows worse but that is to be expected at our age. The rash you refer to *does* sound like bad fish. I suggest a diet of bread and water, and not much of either. On receipt of the money, I will send you the balance of the memoir. It will disturb and sadden you. I shall be curious to see how you use this material. Hippia joins me in wishing for your good – or should I say better? – health.

You will note in the memoir that Julian invariably refers to the Christians as 'Galileans' and to their churches as 'charnel houses', this last a dig at their somewhat necrophile passion for the relics of dead men. I think it might be a good idea to alter the text, and reconvert those charnel houses into churches and those Galileans into Christians. Never offend an enemy in a small way.

Here and there in the text, I have made marginal notes. I hope you won't find them too irrelevant.

2

The Memoir of Julian Augustus

From the example of my uncle the Emperor Constantine, called the Great, who died when I was six years old, I learned that it is dangerous to side with any party of the Galileans, for they mean to overthrow and veil those things that are truly holy. I can hardly remember Constantine, though I was once presented to him at the Sacred Palace. I dimly recall a giant, heavily scented, wearing a stiff jewelled robe. My older brother Gallus always said that I tried to pull his wig off. But Gallus had a cruel humour, and I doubt that this story was true. If I *had* tugged at the Emperor's wig, I would surely not have endeared myself to him, for he was as vain as a woman about his appearance; even his Galilean admirers admit to that.

From my mother Basilina I inherited my love of learning. I never knew her. She died shortly after my birth, 7 April 331. She was the daughter of the praetorian prefect Julius Julianus. From portraits I resemble her more than I do my father; I share with her a straight nose and rather full lips, unlike the imperial Flavians, who tend to have thin hooked noses and tight pursed mouths.

The Emperor Constantius, my cousin and predecessor, was a typical Flavian, resembling his father Constantine, except that he was much shorter. But I did inherit the Flavian thick chest and neck, legacy of our Illyrian ancestors, who were men of the mountains. My mother, though Galilean, was devoted to literature. She was taught by the eunuch Mardonius, who was also my tutor.

From Mardonius, I learned to walk modestly with my eyes to the ground, not strutting or measuring the effect I was creating on others. I was also taught self-discipline in all things; he particularly tried to keep me from talking too much. Fortunately, now that I am Emperor everyone delights in my conversation! Mardonius also convinced me that time spent at the games or in the theatre was time wasted. And, finally, it was from Mardonius, a Galilean who loved Hellenism too well, that I learned about Homer and Hesiod, Plato and Theophrastos. He was a good teacher, if severe.

From my cousin and predecessor, the Emperor Constantius, I learned to dissemble and disguise my true thoughts. A dreadful lesson, but had I not learned it I would not have lived past my twentieth year. In the year 337 Constantius murdered my father. His crime? Consanguinity. I was spared because I was six years old: my half-brother Gallus – who was eleven years old – was spared because he was sickly and not expected to live.

Yes, I was trying to imitate the style of *Marcus Aurelius to Himself*, and I have failed. Not only because I lack his purity and goodness, but because while he was able to write of the good things he learned from a good family and good friends, I must write of those bitter things I learned from a family of murderers in an age diseased by the quarrels and intolerance of a sect whose purpose it is to overthrow that civilization whose first note was struck upon blind Homer's lyre. I am not Marcus Aurelius, in excellence or in experience. I must speak now in my own voice.

I never saw my mother. But I do recall my father. Julius Constantius was a tall imposing man. At least he seemed tall to me then. Actually, from his statues, I reckon him to have been somewhat shorter than I am now, and broader. He was most gentle with Gallus and me on those occasions when we saw him, which was not often for he was always travelling, attending to the various small tasks the Emperor set him. I should mention here that at one time my father was thought to have had a better right to the throne than his half-brother Constantine. But it was never his nature to protest. He was gentle; he was weak; he was destroyed.

On 22 May 337, Constantine died at Nicomedia, to his apparent surprise, since he had just taken the water cure at Helenopolis and all the omens suggested a long life. On his deathbed he sent for our cousin, Bishop Eusebius, to baptize him. Just before the Bishop arrived, Constantine is supposed to have said, rather nervously, 'Let there be no mistake.' I'm afraid that sounds exactly like him. He was not one to leave, as Aristophanes so wittily puts it, a single stone unturned. Constantine was never a true Galilean; he merely used Christianity to extend his dominion over the world. He was a shrewd professional soldier, badly educated and not in the least interested in philosophy, though some perverse taste in him was hugely satisfied by doctrinal disputes; the mad haggling of bishops fascinated him.

According to Constantine's will, the empire was to be divided between his three surviving sons, each of whom had already been raised to the rank of

Caesar. (Every schoolchild knows this but will they always?) To the twenty-one-year-old Constantine II went the prefecture of Gaul. To Constantius, twenty, the East. To Constans, sixteen, Italy and Illyricum. Each was to assume automatically the title Augustus. Surprisingly enough, this division of the world was carried out peaceably. After the funeral (which I was too young to attend), Constantine II withdrew immediately to his capital at Vienne. Constans set out for Milan. Constantius took over the Sacred Palace at Constantinople.

Then the murders began. Constantius maintained that there was a plot against his life, instigated by the children of Theodora, who had been legitimate wife to his grandfather Constantius Chlorus, whose concubine Helena, Constantine's mother, had been discarded when his father was raised to the purple. Yes, it all sounds a muddle to those who read of such matters, but to us, caught in the web, these relationships are as murderously plain as that of spider to fly.

Some say there was indeed such a plot, but I doubt it. I am certain that my father was in no way disloyal. He had not protested when his half-brother Constantine became emperor. Why should he protest the elevation of his son? In any case, during the course of that terrible summer, a dozen descendants of Theodora were secretly arrested and executed, among them my father.

The day of my father's arrest Mardonius and I had been out walking in the gardens of the Sacred Palace. I don't recall where Gallus was; probably sick in bed with fever. For some reason, when Mardonius and I returned to the house, we entered the front door instead of the back, our usual entrance.

It was a pleasant evening and, again contrary to custom, I went to my father where he sat in the atrium with his estate manager. I remember the white and scarlet roses that had been trained to grow in trellises between the columns. And – what else do I remember? The lion-footed chair. A round marble table. The dark-faced Spanish estate manager sitting on a stool to my father's left, a sheaf of papers in his lap. As I dictate these words, I can suddenly remember everything. Yet until this moment – how strange – I had forgotten the roses and my father's face, which was – which is – all clear to me again. What a curious thing memory is! He was ruddy-faced, with small grey eyes, and on his left cheek there was a shallow pale scar, like a crescent.

'This,' he said, turning to the manager, 'is the best part of my estate. Guard him well.' I had no idea what he was talking about. I am sure that I was embarrassed. It was rare at any time for my father to speak to me. Not for lack of affection but because he was even more shy and diffident than I, and not at all certain how to behave with children.

Birds – yes, I can hear them again – chattered in the branches of the trees. My father continued to speak to me, and I listened to the birds and looked at the fountain, aware that something strange impended. He said that Nicomedia was 'safe', and I wondered what he meant by that. The estate manager agreed. They spoke of our cousin, Bishop Eusebius; he was also 'safe'. I stared at the fountain: Greek of the last century, a sea nymph on a dolphin whose mouth poured water into a basin. Remembering this, I realize now why I had a similar fountain installed in my garden when I was at Paris. Can one remember *everything* if one tries this hard? (Note: Have copy of fountain made for Constantinople if original can't be found.)

Then my father dismissed me with an awkward pat; no last word, no mark of undue affection; such is shyness.

While I was having supper, the soldiers came. Mardonius was terrified. I was so astonished by *his* fright that at first I could hardly understand what was happening. When I heard the soldiers in the atrium, I jumped to my feet. 'What's that? Who's that?' I asked.

'Sit down,' said Mardonius. 'Don't move. Don't make a sound.' His smooth beardless eunuch face with its thousand lines like a piece of crumpled silk had gone the colour of a corpse. I broke away from him, in wonder at his fear. Clumsily, he tried to bar me from leaving the room, but now, more alarmed by his fear than by the noise of strange men in the house, I bolted past him to the empty atrium. In the vestibule beyond, a woman slave stood weeping. The front door was open. The porter clung to the frame as if he had been nailed to it. Through the woman's soft weeping, I heard the sound armed men make in a street: creaking leather, dull clank of metal upon metal, and the hollow thud of thick-soled boots on stone.

The porter tried to stop me but I dodged past him into the street. Half a block away, I saw my father walking at the centre of a formation of soldiers, led by a young tribune. Shouting, I ran after him. The soldiers did not halt but my father half-turned as he walked. His face was paler than the ashes of a wood fire. In a terrible voice, stern as Zeus, a voice I had never heard him use before, he said, 'Go back! *Now!*'

I stopped dead in the centre of the street, several yards from him. The tribune stopped, too, and looked at me curiously. Then my father turned on him and said peremptorily, 'Go on. This is no sight for a child.'

The tribune grinned. 'We'll be back for him soon enough.' Then the porter from our house seized me, and though I cried and fought, he carried me back into the house.

Several days later in one of the wine cellars of the Sacred Palace, my father was beheaded. No charges were made. There was no trial. I do not know where he was buried or if he was buried.

It is remarkable how many odd details come back to me as I write. For instance, the tribune's smile, which I had forgotten for twenty years. I find myself suddenly wondering: what ever became of *him*? Where is he today? Do I know him? Is he one of my generals? Could it have been Victor? Jovian? Each is the right age. No, better to let the past go, to preserve it only here upon the page. Vengeance must end somewhere, and what better place to stop than at the prince?

I soon discovered what my father had meant during that cryptic conversation with the estate manager. We were to be sent to our cousin Eusebius, bishop of Nicomedia. He was to be our guardian. The day after the arrest of our father, Mardonius hustled Gallus and me into a wagon with only our personal clothing. Except to change horses, we drove the fifty miles to Nicomedia without rest. Once we were stopped by mounted troops. With quavering voice, Mardonius told them that we were under the personal protection of the Emperor Constantius. They let us pass. We drove all day and all night.

That night! Gallus was suffering from the fever which nearly killed him. In his delirium, tortured by fever demons, he writhed on the pallet set for him on the wagon's floor. Mardonius put linen soaked in vinegar on his face – acrid odour of vinegar – yes, vinegar still recalls that terrible night to me. At one point I touched his face and found it hot as a damp cloth left in the sun to dry. His golden hair was dark with sweat; his arms flailed air; he shouted dream-words and wept.

Wide awake, I sat on the bench beside Mardonius as we jolted over country roads, the warm night as bright as day from a huge yellow moon that shone before us, like a beacon fire set for ships.

I spoke not at all that night. And though I was only six years old, I kept saying to myself: you are going to die; and I wondered what it was like to be dead. I think I became a philosopher that night, for in my youth and ignorance I was more curious than frightened. I suspect that I was even a bit thrilled by this desperate journey across unfamiliar country, with a gold moon blazing and Gallus writhing at my feet, begging me to give him a stick to fight the demons with.

We survived, to our surprise. For five years Gallus and I lived with Bishop Eusebius at Nicomedia and, later, at Constantinople. Eusebius was a grave old man, and though he did not like children he treated us kindly. More to the point, he forbade Constantius to come near us and Constantius obeyed him, for Eusebius was a great power in the Galilean hierarchy. Two years after he became our guardian he was made bishop of Constantinople, where in effect he governed the Eastern church until his death.

Children get used to anything. For a time we missed our father; then we forgot him. Mardonius was always with us, maintaining a link with the old life, and of course my mother's brother Count Julian often visited us. A charming bureaucrat with a taste for intrigue, he kept us informed of what was happening in the world. It was he who explained to us how Constantius was making himself sole master of the state. In the year 340 Constans and Constantine II disagreed. They went to war. Constantine II was ambushed at Aquileia and executed. Constans became sole ruler in the West. Then a general named Magnentius declared himself Augustus and drove Constans from Autun to the Pyrenees, where he was murdered in the winter of 350. The West was in chaos. While Magnentius was desperately trying to hold together his stolen empire, a general on the Danube named Vetranio declared *himself* emperor.

To give Constantius his due, he had a genius for civil war. He knew when to strike and, more important, *whom* to strike. He always won. I have often thought that had he lived he might have destroyed me in the same way that he had dealt with all the others. Faced with two usurpers, Constantius took the field in 350. Vetranio collapsed immediately and, unique in our history, was spared. Magnentius of course was defeated in the battle of Mursa, 28 September 352. This was one of the crucial moments in our history. To this day our army has not recovered from the loss of fifty-four thousand of our best troops.

Needless to say, I knew none of these emperors and usurpers. In fact, I don't recall ever meeting my cousins Constans and Constantine II. For that matter, I did not meet Constantius himself until I was sixteen years old; a meeting I shall presently describe in detail.

While princes schemed and fought, I was educated by Mardonius. He was a strict but inspiring teacher. I liked him. Gallus hated him, but then Gallus hated nearly everyone sooner or later. I recall once when I wanted to watch some chariot races, Mardonius said, 'If you want games, read Homer. Nothing in life can equal what he wrote of games, or of anything else.' Maddening injunction to a child, but wise. As it turned out, I was a grown man before I attended either the theatre or the arena, and then only because I did not want to give offence to others. Yes, I was something of a prig, and still am!

*   *   *

I have but one clear memory of Bishop Eusebius. It was the afternoon he decided to drill me himself in the life of the Nazarene. For hours we sat in a side chapel of the cathedral at Nicomedia while he questioned me. I was bored. The Bishop had a talent for explaining only those things one already knew, leaving mysterious those things one would like to have known. He was a heavy, pale old man, slow of speech and much too easy to follow. Simply for diversion, I stared at the ceiling, which was vaulted and divided into four sections, each dedicated to one of the seasons. In the most brilliant mosaic, flowers and vines, birds and fishes were all intertwined. I knew that ceiling by heart for Gallus and I prayed three times a day in this particular chapel, and during those tedious prayers I used to imagine that I had the power to rise straight up in the air and enter that world of peacocks and palm trees and grape arbours, a gleaming world of gold where there was no sound but that of running water and birds singing – certainly no sermons, no prayers! A few years ago when Nocomedia was shattered by earthquake, my first question concerned the cathedral: did it still stand? Yes, I was told, but the roof had fallen in. And so my childhood's magic retreat is now rubble.

I must have been staring too obviously at the ceiling, for the Bishop suddenly asked me, 'What is the most important of our Lord's teachings?'

Without thinking, I said, 'Thou shalt not kill.' I then rapidly quoted every relevant text from the new testament (much of which I knew by heart) and all that I could remember from the old. The Bishop had not expected this response. But he nodded appreciatively. 'You have quoted well. But why do you think this commandment the most important?'

'Because had it been obeyed my father would be alive.' I startled myself with the quickness of my own retort.

The Bishop's pale face was even ashier than usual. 'Why do you say this?'

'Because it's true. The Emperor killed my father. Everybody knows that. And I suppose he shall kill Gallus and me, too, when he gets around to it.' Boldness, once begun, is hard to check.

'The Emperor is a holy man,' said the Bishop severely. 'All the world admires his piety, his war against heresy, his support of the true faith.'

This made me even more reckless. 'Then if he is such a good Christian how could he kill so many members of his own family? After all, isn't it written in Matthew and again in Luke that . . .'

'You little fool!' The Bishop was furious. 'Who has been telling you these things? Mardonius?'

I had sense enought to protect my tutor. 'No, Bishop. But people talk about everything in front of us. I suppose they think we don't understand. Anyway it's all true, isn't it?'

The Bishop had regained his composure. His answer was slow and grim. 'All that you need to know is that your cousin, the Emperor, is a devout and good man, and never forget that you are at his mercy.' The Bishop then made me recite for four hours, as punishment for impudence. But the lesson I learned was not the one intended. All that I understood was that Constantius was a devout Christian. Yet he had killed his own flesh and blood. Therefore, if he could be both a good Christian and a murderer, then there was something wrong with his religion. Needless to say, I no longer blame Constantius's faith for his misdeeds, any more than Hellenism should be held responsible for *my* shortcomings! Yet for a child this sort of harsh contradiction is disturbing, and not easily forgotten.

In the year 340 Eusebius was made bishop of Constantinople. As a result,

Gallus and I divided our time between Nicomedia and the capital. Of the two, I preferred Constantinople.

Founded the year before I was born, Constantinople has no past; only a noisy present and a splendid future, if the auguries are to be believed. Constantine deliberately chose ancient Byzantium to be the capital of the Roman Empire, and then he created a new city in place of the old, and named the result – with characteristic modesty – after himself. Like most children of the city I delight in its vitality and raw newness. The air is always full of dust and the smell of mortar. The streets are loud with hammering. This confusion should be unpleasant, but it is invigorating. From day to day the city changes. Nearly all the familiar sights of my youth have been replaced by new buildings, new streets, new vistas, and I find it a marvellous thing to be – if only in this – at the beginning of something great rather than at the end.

In good weather, Mardonius used to take Gallus and me on walks around the city. 'Statue hunts' we called them, because Mardonius was passionately interested in works of art and he would drag us from one end of the city to the other to look for them. I think we must have seen all ten thousand of the bronze and marble statues Constantine had stolen from every part of the world to decorate his city. Though one cannot approve his thefts (particularly those from Hellenic temples), the result has been that in and around the various arcades along Middle Street, the city's main thoroughfare, there are more important works of art than anywhere on earth, excepting Rome.

One of our expeditions took us to a Galilean charnel house, close by the Hippodrome. While Mardonius fussed with a map of the city, trying to get his bearings, Gallus and I threw bits of marble at a half-finished house across the street. There are always a satisfying number of things for a child to throw in the streets of Constantinople, chips of marble, splinters of wood, broken tile. The builders never clean up.

'Now here,' said Mardonius, peering closely at the map, 'should be the famous Nemesis of Pheidias acquired some years ago by the divine Constantine, and thought to be the original, though there are those who maintain it is a copy, but a copy made in the same century, in Parian marble, hence not Roman, hence not corrupt.'

Suddenly the door to the charnel house was flung open and two old men ran out into the street, closely pursued by a dozen monks, armed with sticks. The old men got as far as the arcade where we were standing. Then the monks caught them, threw them to the ground and beat them, shouting all the while, 'Heretic! Heretic!'

I turned with amazement to Mardonius. 'Why are they hurting those men?'
Mardonius sighed. 'Because they are heretics.'
'Dirty Athanasians?' Gallus, older than I, was already acquainted with most of our new world's superstitions.
'I'm afraid so. We'd better go.'
But I was curious. I wanted to know what an Athanasian was.
'Misguided fools who believe that Jesus and God are exactly the same . . .'
'When everybody knows they are only similar,' said Gallus.
'Exactly. As Arius – who was so much admired by your cousin the divine Emperor – taught us.'
'They poisoned the priest Arius,' said Gallus, already fiercely partisan. He picked up a rock. 'Murdering heretics!' he yelled and hurled the stone with unfortunate accuracy at one of the old men. The monks paused in their con-

genial work to praise Gallus's marksmanship. Mardonius was furious, but only on grounds of rectitude.

'Gallus!' He gave my brother a good shake. 'You are a prince, not a street brawler!' Grabbing us each firmly by an arm, Mardonius hurried us away. Needless to say, I was fascinated by all this.

'But surely those old men are harmless.'

'Harmless? They murdered Arius.' Gallus's eyes shone with righteousness.

'Those two? *They* actually murdered him?'

'No,' said Mardonius. 'But they are followers of Bishop Athanasius . . .'

'The worst heretic that ever lived!' Gallus was always ecstatic when his own need for violence coincided with what others believed to be right action.

'And it is thought that Athanasius ordered Arius poisoned at a church council, some seven years ago. As a result, Athanasius was sent into exile by your divine uncle. And now, Julian, I must remind you for what is the hundredth – or is it the thousandth? – time, not to bite your nails.'

I stopped biting my nails, a habit I have not entirely broken myself of even today. 'But aren't they all Christians?' I asked. 'Don't they believe in Jesus and the gospels?'

'No!' said Gallus.

'Yes,' said Mardonius. 'They are Christians, too. But they are in error.'

Even as a child I had a reasonably logical mind. 'But if they are Christians, like us, then we must not fight them but turn the other cheek, and certainly nobody must kill anybody, because Jesus tells us that . . .'

'I'm afraid it is not as simple as all that,' said Mardonius. But of course it was. Even a child could see the division between what the Galileans say they believe and what, in fact, they do believe, as demonstrated by their actions. A religion of brotherhood and mildness which daily murders those who disagree with its doctrines can only be thought hypocrite, or worse. Now for the purposes of my memoir it would be convenient to say that at this moment I ceased to be a Galilean. But unfortunately that would not be true. Though I was puzzled by what I had seen, I still believed, and my liberation from the Nazarene was a long time coming. But looking back, I suspect that the first chain was struck from my mind that day in the street when I saw two harmless old men set upon by monks.

In the summer I used to go to my maternal grandmother's estate in Bithynia. It was a small farm two miles from the sea. Just back of the house was a low hill from whose top there was a fine view of the sea of Marmora, while on the horizon's farthest curve to the north rose the towers of Constantinople. Here I spent many hours, reading and dreaming.

One afternoon, lulled by the murmuring of bees, the scent of thyme, the warm salt-laden air, I fell asleep and dreamed that I was having some sort of quarrel with Gallus. I wanted to escape him. So I began to run. As I ran, I took longer and longer steps until I began to bound like a deer. With each leap, I remained higher in the air until at last I was gliding over the countryside while the people below stared with wonder as I sailed over their heads, completely free. There is no dream quite so satisfying as the one of flying.

Suddenly in my pleasant voyage, I was aware that someone was calling my name. I looked about me but there was no one in sight, only pale clouds, blue sky, dark sea. I was gliding over the Marmora, towards Constantinople, when the voice sounded again.

'Who wants me?' I asked.

Then – I don't know how – but I realized that it was the sun who had spoken. Huge and gold above the city, the sun reached out fiery arms to me. And with an astonishingly poignant sense of coming home, I plunged straight into the blazing light. And awakened to find that the setting sun was indeed shining in my face. Dazzled, I got to my feet. I had been overwhelmed by light. I was also bewildered. Something important had happened. But what?

I told no one about this vision. However, some months later when Mardonius and I were alone together in the palace gardens overlooking the Bosphorus, I questioned him about the old religion. I began slyly: was everything Homer wrote true?

'Of course! Every word!'

'Then Zeus and Apollo and all the other gods must exist, because he says they do. And if they are real, then what became of them? Did Jesus destroy them?'

Poor Mardonius! He was a devoted classicist. He was also a Galilean. Like so many in those days, he was hopelessly divided. But he had his answer ready. 'You must remember that Christ was not born when Homer lived. Wise as Homer was, there was no way for him to know the ultimate truth that we know. So he was forced to deal with the gods the people had always believed in . . .'

'False gods, according to Jesus, so if they're false then what Homer writes about them can't be true.'

'Yet like all things, those gods are *manifestations* of the true.' Mardonius shifted his ground. 'Homer believed much as we believe. He worshipped the One God, the single principle of the universe. And I suspect he was aware that the One God can take many forms, and that the gods of Olympus are among them. After all, to this day God has many names because we have many languages and traditions, yet *he* is always the same.'

'What are some of the old names?'

'Zeus, Helios the sun, Serapis . . .'

'The sun.' My deity. 'Apollo . . .' I began.

'Apollo also had many names, Helios, Companion of Mithras . . .'

'Apollo, Helios, Mithras,' I repeated softly. From where we sat in the shady grove on the slope beneath the Daphne Palace, I could just catch a glimpse of my deity, impaled on the dark green bough of a cypress.

'Mithraism was most devilish of all the cults. In fact, there are still some active Mithraists, soldiers mostly, ignorant folk, though a few philosophers (or would-be philosophers) are drawn to Mithras, like Iamblichos . . . I met him once, a remarkably ugly man, a Syrian, from Chalcis, I think, he died a few years ago, much admired by a small circle, but I've always thought his prose unreasonably obscure. He pretended to be a disciple of Plato. And of course he maintained that Jesus was a false prophet and our trinity absurd. Then – utter madness – he invented a trinity of his own, based on Plato.'

Carried away by his passion to explain, Mardonius was now hardly conscious of his rapt listener who understood perhaps every other word he spoke. Yet the general sense of what was being said was perfectly clear: Helios was an aspect of the One God, and there were those, like this mysterious Iamblichos, who still worshipped him.

'According to Iamblichos, there are three worlds, three realms of being, each presided over by the One God whose visible aspect is the sun. Now the first of these worlds is the *intelligible* world, which can be comprehended only by reason. You'll find all this in Plato, when we get to him, *if* you get to him at your present rate. The second world is an intermediary one (this is Iamblichos's invention); a

world endowed with intelligence and governed by Helios-Mithras, with a number of assistants who turn out to be the old gods in various disguises, particularly Serapis to whom our souls return after death, Dionysos the fair, Hermes the intelligence of the universe, and Asklepios who actually lived, we think, and was a famous physican, worshipped by our ancestors as a saviour and healer.'
'Like Jesus?'
'Somewhat similar, yes. Finally, the third world is our world, the world of sense and perception. Between the three worlds, the sun mediates. Light is good; darkness evil; and Mithras is the bridge, the link, between man and deity, light and dark. As you can see – or as you will see – only part of this comes from Plato. Most of it is Persian in origin, based on a Persian hero named Mithras who lived, if he lived, a thousand years ago. Fortunately, with the birth of Jesus and the mystery of the trinity all this nonsense ended.'
'But the sun still exists.'
'To be absolutely precise, at this moment the sun does *not* exist.' Mardonius rose. 'It's set and we're late for supper.'
That is how I became aware of the One God. In a dream Helios-Mithras had called out to me and I had beheld, literally, the light. From that day on, I was no longer alone. The sun was my protector.
I must say that during those years I needed all the solace I could get for I was continually haunted by my predicament. Would I be put to death like my father? One of my recurrent daydreams was that Constantius and I would meet, quite by chance, on my grandmother's hill. In the dream the Emperor was always alone. He was stern but kind. We spoke of literature. He was delighted at my vast knowledge (I liked being praised for my reading). Then we became close friends, and the dream would end with him granting me my freedom to live out the rest of my life on my grandmother's farm, for one look into my eyes had convinced him that I was not worldly, that I wanted neither his throne nor revenge upon him for my father's death. Time and again in my imagination I would convince him with brilliant argument and he would invariably grant my wish, tears in his eyes at my sincerity and lack of guile.
How curious men are! I was indeed sincere at that time. I was exactly as I have described myself. I did not want power, or so I thought. I truly believed that I wanted to live obscurely. And then? I broke Constantius. I took the throne. Knowing this now, were I Constantius and he that dreamy boy on a Bithynian hill, I would have had that young philosopher's life on the spot. But then neither of us realized who I was, or what I would become.

3

When I was eleven years old, my life again changed abruptly. One morning in May I was doing lessons with Mardonius. I was reciting Hesiod and making a good many mistakes, when Gallus came into the room.
'He's dead. The Bishop's dead. In the church. He died. Just like that!'
Mardonius drew a cross on his chest; so did I. A moment later we were joined by clergy, officials, servants. Everyone was stunned, and alarmed, for it is a great event when the bishop of Constantinople dies, and who succeeds him is a matter

of national importance. The emperor – if he is Galilean – always has a hand in the choosing of a successor. But Constantius was a thousand miles away, on the borders of Persia. So for several weeks no bishop was appointed, and no one knew what to do with Gallus and me. Luckily, my uncle Count Julian was in the city, and the day after the funeral he came to see us.

'He's going to kill us, isn't he?' Under stress, Gallus could be reckless.

Count Julian's smile was not very convincing. 'Certainly not. After all, you are the heirs of Constantine the Great.'

'So was our father,' said Gallus grimly. 'And all the others.'

'But the divine Augustus is your friend.'

'Then why are we under arrest?' Gallus indicated the secret police who had arrived only that day; when Gallus and I had tried to go out, we were told politely to stay where we were 'until further orders'.

'They are for your protection.'

'The only protection we need is from Constantius,' said Gallus; but he lowered his voice. Though hot-tempered, he was not suicidal. Count Julian looked very nervous.

'That is not true, Gallus. Now listen to me carefully. Someone close to the Emperor, *very* close, has told me that Constantius believes that the reason he cannot have children is because he – because so many members of his own family were – because they, ah, *died*!'

'Yes, but since he's already committed enough murders to get him into hell, why stop at us? He has nothing to lose.'

'Nothing to gain, either. After all, you are only children.'

Gallus snorted. At sixteen he was physically a man, though in character he was still a child, a fierce destructive child.

'Believe me, you are safe.' Count Julian was soothing. He was in an excellent mood, for he had just been appointed governor of Egypt, and I am afraid that was more on his mind than the fate of his nephews. But he did his best to comfort us, for which I at least was grateful. He left us with the hollow words, 'You have nothing to fear.'

When he was gone, Gallus deliberately smashed the cup he had used. Breaking things always gave Gallus physical relief; shattering this particular cup took on ritual significance. 'He's like all the rest!' Gallus's voice cracked with anger as he stood there in the bright sun of a green May day, his long pale hair tangled across his brow, his startling blue eyes magnified with sudden tears. 'There's no way out of this!'

I tried to say something hopeful but he rounded on me. 'You're no loss, you little ape! But why do *I* have to die?' Why indeed? Everyone asks himself that question sooner or later. No one can ever love us quite so much as we love ourselves. Gallus saw no justice in a world where a beauty and vitality such as his could be pinched out as casually as a lamp wick. Of course fate is cruel. But children cannot accept this, nor men like Gallus who see all things as incidental to themselves. I loved Gallus. I hated him. During the first years of my life I was so entirely absorbed by him that I was hardly aware of myself at all except as I was reflected in those vivid blue eyes, which saw nothing of me nor much of anything else.

But Count Julian was right. Constantius *did* suffer remorse for his crimes. We were safe, for the time being. In due course a message arrived from the Chamberlain Eusebius. Gallus and I were to be sent to Macellum in Cappadocia 'to continue your education'.

'Education for *what?*' asked Gallus when this message had been read us. But Mardonius silenced him. 'The Augustus is merciful. Never forget that he is now your father as well as your lord.'

We departed for Macellum that same day. I was most upset, for Mardonius was not to accompany us. I don't know the motive behind this act of petty cruelty except that as the Chamberlain Eusebius was also a eunuch he might have thought that a fellow eunuch would prove to be too subtle an ally for us. Sniffling wretchedly, I was bundled into a wagon with Gallus.

Mardonius was also grief-stricken but he controlled himself. 'We shall meet again,' he said. 'And when we do, I shall expect Gallus to know as much Hesiod as Julian.' Mardonius stood stiffly in front of the bishop's palace as we drove off, escorted by a cohort of cavalry, just as if we were important princes, which we were, or important prisoners, which we also were. I sobbed. Gallus swore fierce oaths under his breath. In the street a crowd of people were gathered, eager for a glimpse of us. To get a close view one bold burgher thrust his head over the side of the wagon. Gallus promptly spat in the man's astonished face. Then Gallus covered his head with his cloak and would not take it off until we were outside the city gate. No one expected to see us alive again.

All travellers agree that Macellum is one of the beautiful places of the world. I hate it to this day. Macellum is not a town but an imperial residence originally used by the ancient Cappadocian kings as a hunting lodge. Constantine enlarged it so that it is now a complex of many buildings set in lonely woods at the foot of Mount Argaeus, some four hundred miles southeast of Constantinople. When Constantius inherited the principate, he acquired the lodge, along with a number of other properties in the neighbourhood; in fact, our family's private income derives almost entirely from the Cappadocian crown lands.

Tonight when I was telling Priscus about my childhood, he said that it sounded enviable. 'After all, you lived in a palace, with gardens, baths, fountains, a private chapel,' he enjoys teasing me, 'in the very best hunting country with nothing to do but read. You had the perfect life.' Well, it was not perfect. Gallus and I might just as well have been hostages in a Persian prison. We had no one to talk to, except for a series of schoolmasters from near-by Caesarea. None stayed with us very long because of Gallus. He could not resist tormenting them. He got on better with our jailers, particularly the young officers. Gallus could be very winning when he wanted to be, and he soon had them training him in the use of sword and spear, shield and axe. Gallus was a natural athlete, with a gift for weaponry. I would have liked to practise with him but he preferred to keep his military companions to himself. 'You read your books,' he said sharply. 'I'm the one who's to be a soldier.' So I read my books.

We were nominally in the charge of Bishop George of Cappadocia who lived at Caesarea. He visited us at least once a month, and it was he who insisted that our education be essentially Galilean. 'Because there is no reason why *you* should not be a priest.' He pointed a long finger at me. He was a small thin man whose lean face always looked in need of shaving.

While I was respectfully trying to think of a number of reasons why I should *not* become a priest, Gallus with an engaging smile said, 'Julian dreams of the priesthood, Bishop. It's his whole life. He does nothing but read.'

'I was that way myself at your age.' Bishop George looked pleased at finding this likeness.

'But I read philosophy . . .' I began.

'So do we all, of course. But then we come to the story of Jesus which is the beginning and the end of knowledge. But I am sure you have had a good training already from your late cousin, my old friend, the Bishop Eusebius. Those of us who are *true* Christians miss him greatly.' Bishop George began to pace up and down the room, snapping his fingers, a characteristic habit. Gallus grinned at me, very pleased with what he had done.

Bishop George suddenly spun round; the long finger was again pointed at me.

'*Homoiousios*. What does that mean?'

I knew. I rattled my answer like a crow taught to speak. 'It means that Jesus the son is of *similar* substance to God the father.'

'*Homoousios*. What does that mean?'

'That Jesus the son is of *one* substance with God the father.'

'The difference?'

'In the first case, Jesus was created by the father *before* this world began. He is God's son by grace but *not* by nature.'

'Why?'

'Because God is one. By definition singular. God cannot be many, as the late Arius maintained at the council of Nicaea.'

'Excellent.' I received a series of finger-snappings as applause. 'Now in the second case?'

'*Homoousios* is that pernicious doctrine' – I had been well-drilled by old Eusebius – 'which maintains that the father and the son and the holy spirit are one and the same.'

'Which cannot be!'

'Which cannot be,' I chirruped obediently.

'Despite what happened at Nicaea.'

'Where in the year 325 Bishop Athanasius of Alexandria ...'

'A mere deacon at the time ...'

'Opposed my cousin Bishop Eusebius as well as Arius, and forced the council to accept the Athanasian doctrine that the father, son and holy spirit are one.'

'*But* the battle is far from over. We are gaining ground every year. Our wise Augustus believes as we believe, as the late Presbyter Arius believed. Two years ago at Antioch we Eastern bishops met to support the true doctrine. This year we shall meet again at Sardica and, with the Emperor's aid, the true believers shall once and for all destroy the doctrine of Athanasius. My son, you are to be a priest. I can tell. You have the mark. You will be a great force in the church. Tomorrow I shall send you one of my deacons. He will give you religious instruction, both of you.'

'But I'm to be a soldier,' said Gallus, alarmed.

'A God-fearing soldier has the strength of twenty,' said Bishop George automatically. 'Besides, religious training will do you no harm.' And curiously enough, it was Gallus who became the devout Galilean while I, as the world knows, returned to the old ways.

But at that time I was hardly a philosopher. I studied what I was told to study. The deacon who gave me instruction was most complimentary. 'You have an extraordinary gift for analysis,' he said one day when I was exploring with him John 14:25, the text on which the Arians base their case against the Athanasians. 'You will have a distinguished future, I am sure.'

'As a bishop?'

'Of course you will be a bishop since you are imperial. But there is something even more splendid than a bishop.'

'A martyr?'

'Martyr and saint. You have the look of one.'

I must say my boyish vanity was piqued. Largely because of this flattery, for several months I was confident that I had been especially chosen to save the world from error. Which, in a way, turned out to be true, to the horror of my early teachers.

Bishop George was an arrogant and difficult man but I got on with him, largely because he was interested in me. He was a devoted controversialist. Finding me passably intelligent, he saw his opportunity. If I could be turned into a bishop, I would be a powerful ally for the Arians, who were already outnumbered by the Athanasians, despite the considerable help given them by Constantius. Today, of course, the 'pernicious' doctrine of the three-in-one God has almost entirely prevailed, due to the efforts of Bishop Athanasius. Constantius alone kept the two parties in any sort of balance. Now that he is dead the victory of the Athanasians is only a matter of time. But today none of this matters since the Galileans are now but one of a number of religious sects, and by no means the largest. Their days of domination are over. Not only have I forbidden them to persecute us Hellenists; I have forbidden them to persecute one another. They find me intolerably cruel!

Was I a true Galilean in those years at Macellum? There has been much speculation about this. I often wonder myself. The answer is not clear even to me. For a long time I believed what I was taught. I accepted the Arian thesis that the One God (whose existence we all accept) mysteriously produced a sort of son who was born a Jew, became a teacher, and was finally executed by the state for reasons which were never entirely clear to me, despite the best efforts of Bishop George to instruct me. But while I was studying the life of the Galilean I was also reading Plato, who was far more to my taste. After all, I was something of a literary snob. I had been taught the best Greek by Mardonius. I could not help but compare the barbarous back-country language of Matthew, Mark, Luke and John to the clear prose of Plato. Yet I accepted the Galilean legend as truth. After all, it was the religion of my family, and though I did not find it attractive I was unaware of any alternative until one afternoon when I was about fourteen. I had been sitting for two hours listening to the deacon sing me the songs of Arius . . . yes, that great religious thinker wrote popular songs in order to influence the illiterate. To this day I can recall the words of half a dozen of his inane ballads which 'proved' that the son was the son and the father was the father. Finally, the deacon finished; I praised his singing.

'It is the spirit which matters, not the voice,' said the deason, pleased with my compliment. Then – I don't know how it happened – Plotinus was mentioned. He was only a name to me. He was anathema to the deacon. 'A would-be philosopher of the last century. A follower of Plato, or so he claimed. An enemy of the church, though there are some Christians who are foolish enough to regard him highly. He lived at Rome. He was a favourite of the Emperor Gordian. He wrote six quite unintelligible books which his disciple Porphyry edited.'

'Porphyry?' As though it were yesterday, I can remember hearing that name for the first time, seated opposite the angular deacon in one of the gardens at Macellum, high summer flowering all about us and the day hazy with heat.

'Even worse than Plotinus! Porphyry came from Tyre. He studied at Athens. He called himself a philosopher but of course he was merely an atheist. He attacked the church in fifteen volumes.'

'On what grounds?'

'How should I know? I have never read his books. No Christian ought.' The deacon was firm.

'But surely this Porphyry must have had *some* cause ...'

'The devil entered him. That is cause enough.'

By then I knew that I must read Plotinus and Porphyry. I wrote Bishop George a most politic letter, asking him to lend me the books of these 'incorrigible' men. I wished to see, I said, the face of the enemy plain, and naturally I turned to the Bishop for guidance, not only because he was my religious mentor but because he had the best library in Cappadocia. I rather laid it on.

To my astonishment Bishop George immediately sent me the complete works of Plotinus as well as Porphyry's attack on Christianity. 'Young as you are, I am sure that you will appreciate the folly of Porphyry. He was an intelligent man misled by a bad character. My predecessor, as bishop of Caesarea, wrote a splendid refutation of Porphyry, answering for all time the so-called "inconsistencies" Porphyry claimed to have detected in scriptures. I am sending you the Bishop's works, too. I cannot tell you how pleased I am at the interest you are showing in sacred matters.' What the good bishop did not know was that the arguments of Porphyry were to form the basis for my own rejection of the Nazarene.

That same summer, Bishop George suggested that Gallus and I build a chapel at Macellum to be dedicated to Saint Mammas, a local shepherd whose remains were considered particularly potent: skin diseases were promptly cured by applying the saint's shinbone to the afflicted area. Bishop George thought it would be an inspiring gesture if Gallus and I were to build a charnel house for these scraps of dead shepherd. So all one summer Gallus and I worked on this project. I enjoyed laying brick. But Gallus hated prolonged effort of any kind, and I'm afraid he spent a good deal of time cursing Saint Mammas as we sweated in the sun. Shortly after we completed the chapel, the roof fell in. I am told that the Galileans now say that only *my* section of the building collapsed, because I was apostate. This is not true. The *whole* thing collapsed – because of faulty design.

At that time I neither believed nor disbelieved. Yet Porphyry's eloquent case against the Nazarene was now lodged in my head. When I tried to argue doctrinal points with Bishop George, I was swiftly discouraged with this sort of thing: 'The very idea of the trinity is a mystery. Only through faith can it be understood, and then never entirely.' I much preferred Plotinus, who four times in five years achieved that total consciousness of the One which is the ultimate goal of all religious practice. Despite Porphyry's wisdom, he experienced this heightened consciousness only once, at the age of sixty-eight. So far I have experienced it twice. I pray each day for yet another revelation.

Gallus and I had neither friends nor allies. Except for his dogged attempts to make me a priest, Bishop George showed no personal interest in either of us. Everyone else at Macellum treated us with nervous respect. We alarmed people; we reminded them of murder; we were such obvious victims.

I kept to my reading. I took little exercise, though I was naturally strong, particularly in the arms. Gallus continued to surpass me at all games and physical feats. He was taller than I, beautifully made, with the face of a god. The soldiers assigned to guard us were infatuated with him, and he flirted shamelessly with them. They took him hunting whenever he chose and I suppose that he had affairs with some of them, though we were both involved much of the time with the same girl – or rather woman. She was the twenty-five-year-old wife of a civil servant who acted as comptroller to our household. She seduced me first, then Gallus. She was insatiable. Her husband was amenable; not that he had any choice. He used to giggle uncontrollably whenever he saw either of us. He was fat and small, and I remember asking her how she could bear to be touched by him.

'He has gifts,' she said slyly. I can still recall how her black hair glistened as it fell over bare brown shoulders. Never before or since have I felt such smooth skin. I suppose she oiled herself but if she did she was an artist at it, for one's fingers never came away thick with perfumed grease as happens so often with women of her sort. She was Antiochene. What else? Love-making is the only art the people of Antioch have ever taken seriously. She affected to find me attractive, but it was the golden Gallus who really enchanted her. He used to tell me with pride how 'she does everything and I don't move'. His passivity was baffling. But then I never understood Gallus. Later when he turned monster, I was not surprised. He could have been anything at all because at heart he was nothing. Yet when he was in a room, all eyes watched him, for he was physically fascinating; men and women were equally attracted to him and since he felt nothing for anyone, every woman saw him as a challenge who must be made to love. So Gallus was able to take his pleasure as he chose ... while hardly moving!

The Syrian woman was mistress to us both for three years. Though I am now celibate, I often think of her, especially at night. Where is she now? I don't dare inquire. She is probably fat and old, living in some provincial town and paying youths to sleep with her. But for a thousand days she was Aphrodite to my Adonis.

4

Five years passed. Little news of the outside world came to us. Sapor, the Great King of Persia, threatened our Eastern border, while the Germans infiltrated Gaul. That was all we knew. Politics was a forbidden subject. I studied Homer and Hesiod; read Plotinus and Porphyry; made love to the Antiochene; fought with Gallus, until one day I out-wrestled him and he never challenged me again. He was a coward except when he was in a rage; then he would do anything.

As long as I could read, I was never entirely wretched. But I did long to see more of the world than Macellum. It is most unnatural for a youth to be brought up entirely by soldiers and slaves, none of whom dares to be fond of him. Gallus and I had each other for company but we were not true brothers in any but the family sense – and only *half*-brothers at that, for we had different mothers. We were like two potentially hostile animals in the same cage. Yet I was ravished by his beauty, and impressed by his energy. Gallus was always doing something which I wanted to imitate. Sometimes he let me, but more often not, for he enjoyed tormenting me. It gave him particular pleasure to quarrel with me just before we were to go hunting. Then he could exclaim, 'All right! You stay home. This is a day for men.' And the soldiers would laugh at me and I would flee while the exuberant Gallus would ride forth to hunt, as dogs barked and horns sounded through the dark green woods. But when I was allowed to go with him, I was close to ecstasy.

One September afternoon Bishop George arrived unexpectedly at Macellum. We had not seen him for some months, because, according to the deacon, 'It looks as though – now don't repeat a word of this!' (as if we two prisoners had anyone to confide in) – 'Bishop George will be raised to the see of Alexandria. Bishop Athanasius holds Alexandria only because the Emperor Constans of the West insisted upon it. But now the Emperor Constantius is arranging for Athanasius to be exiled again and if he is, *we* go to Alexandria!' The deacon was exalted at the thought.

But Bishop George said nothing to us about church politics when we joined him in the main hall of the hunting lodge. He had other, greater news. His sallow face was dark with excitement while his fingers snapped a sharp continuous accompaniment to his words. 'The divine Augustus will visit you in ten days' time. He is on his way home from Antioch. He is making this side trip for the express purpose of seeing the two of you.' I was too frightened to speak. It was Gallus who asked, 'What does he want?'

The Bishop was impatient. 'He is your cousin. Your guardian. Your emperor. He wants to see you. What else? To see what sort of men you've grown into. To see the result of our education. Now he will be particularly interested in your religious training. Therefore, I shall stay here until he arrives. We will review everything I have tried to teach you. This will mean, Gallus, a great deal of work for *you*. I suggest you put your mind to it, since your entire future may depend on the impression you make.' And so does *yours*, Bishop, I remember thinking to myself, eager to include anyone I could in what I was certain would prove to be a harsh fate.

We studied hard. For hours on end the Bishop drilled us mercilessly. Fortunately I have an excellent memory and can learn – though not always understand! – a page at a glance. Between lessons, we tried to find out all that we could about Constantius's mood. Was he favourably disposed towards us? Were we to remain at Macellum? But the Bishop gave us no comfort. 'The divine Augustus will do what is best, as he always does. You have nothing to fear, *if* you are loyal and obedient.' But of course we had everything to fear. I did not sleep one night through during that time of waiting.

The day before Constantius was due to arrive, the imperial court came to Macellum. Some of the court had been with Constantius at Antioch; but most came directly from the Sacred Palace at Constantinople. All the chief officers of the state were to be lodged in the villa, while in the surrounding fields a hundred tents were pitched to accommodate the thousand clerks and notaries who conduct the business of the government.

At dawn the pageant began. Gallus and I stationed ourselves in the courtyard of the palace and gaped like two bumpkins. Neither of us had ever seen an imperial progress before, and in the general excitement and dazzle of that frosty autumn day we momentarily forgot our terror.

Bishop George stood in the doorway of the villa. He wore a jewelled chasuble, and held a silver crosier in one hand. To his left and right the military garrison of Macellum stood at attention to honour the great magnates of the Roman Empire. Some arrived on horseback, others in litters. Each was accompanied by a retinue of soldiers, clerks, eunuchs, slaves. All wore some variation of military dress, for ever since Diocletian the court has been military in its appearance, symbolic of Rome's beleaguered state.

The courtyard was soon crowded with clerks and slaves, horses and mules; only the area just in front of the door was kept clear. After each official dismounted, he would cross to the doorway, where Bishop George would then greet him with all his titles. The Bishop was a master of protocol. He knew exactly who everyone was and how he should be addressed, an enviable gift, since nowadays there are hundreds of subtle titles and distinctions. Highest in rank are the *clarissimi*. They include the two consuls for the year, all former consuls, the praetorian prefects, much of the senate. Next are the officials who are called *spectabiles*. Then the heads of government departments who are called *illustres*. But it is not easy to keep straight who is what, since an important minister of state like the quaestor (the emperor's legal adviser) is only an *illustris*, while the governor of an insignificant province may be a *clarissimus*. Also, the matter of the counts is confusing. In the old days, 'count' was simply a courtesy title for any official or high-ranking officer who travelled in the emperor's entourage. But Constantine, with his Persian sense of hierarchy, made the title 'count' a reward for important service. So some counts are *clarissimi* while others are merely *spectabiles*. It is amazing how obsessed otherwise sensible people are by these foolish titles. I have sat for hours in the company of grown men who could discuss nothing but who held what title and why he was unworthy of it. Yet a wise emperor can exert considerable pressure on ambitious men by the giving or withholding of these empty titles. Constantius was a master at this sort of thing. Unfortunately, since I find it hard to remember who is what, I call nearly everyone 'my dear fellow', in imitation of Plato. This scandalizes the dignified.

First to arrive was the Count of the Sacred Largesse. It is his task to see that each province pays its taxes promptly on the first of every March. He also administers the government's salt monopoly and the provincial banks, as well as all state-owned factories, mines, and of course the mint. He is never a popular official, but he dies rich. He was followed by the Count of the Privy Purse, who administers the personal property of the imperial family. This official was accompanied by twenty slaves carrying chests of dark wood studded with metal; they contained the large sums of gold and silver the emperor must always travel with. Since Privy Purse is responsible for every coin, he tends to be a nervous, distracted figure, for ever counting boxes. Next, the Count of the East, who governs Syria and Mesopotamia. Then the Master of the Offices, a very great man indeed. He administers the state transportation system and post; he is the head of the bureau of secret agents; he commands the palace guard; he arranges for audiences with the Emperor. Bishop George bowed particularly low to him.

For six years Gallus and I had seen no one except Bishop George and our guards. Now all at once there passed before us the whole power of the state. Our eyes were dazzled by glittering armour and elaborate cloaks, by the din of a thousand clerks and notaries who scurried about the courtyard, demanding their baggage, quarrelling with one another, insisting on various prerogatives. These noisy clerks with their inky fingers and proud intelligent faces were the actual government of Rome, and they knew it.

The last official to arrive was the most important of all: the Grand Chamberlain of the Sacred Palace, the eunuch Eusebius. He was so large that it took two slaves to pull him out of his ivory and gold litter. He was tall, stout and very white. Beneath the peacock blue of his silk tunic one could see the rolls of flesh quiver as he moved. Of all the officers of state, only he wore civilian clothes. In fact, he looked like a winsome lady of fashion with mouth artfully rouged and hair arranged in long oiled ringlets. The gold thread of his cape flashed in the sunlight.

Eusebius looked about him with sharp eyes, and I knew suddenly that he was looking for us. Half hidden by a mound of saddlebags, Gallus and I tried to become invisible, but though the Chamberlain had never seen either of us before, he knew immediately who we were. Gracefully, he motioned for us to join him. Like slaves anticipating a beating, we shuffled forward. Since we were not certain as to how to greet him, I attempted a military salute, which Gallus imitated. Eusebius smiled a tiny smile, exposing small dark teeth; several babyish dimples appeared in his full cheeks. He inclined his head; the neck fat creased; a long curl strayed across his brow.

'*Nobilissimi*,' he said in a soft voice. This was an excellent omen. The title *nobilissimus* is used only for members of the imperial family. Bishop George never used this title with us nor did our guards. Now, apparently, our rank had been restored.

After a long scrutiny, Eusebius took each of us by a hand. I can still recall the soft dampness of his touch. 'I have so looked forward to seeing you both! And how grown up you are! Especially the noble Gallus.' Delicately he felt Gallus's chest. This sort of impertinence would ordinarily have sent my brother into a rage, but that day he was far too frightened. He also knew instinctively that his only protection was his beauty. Complaisantly he allowed the eunuch to caress him as we entered the villa.

Eusebius had the most beguiling voice and manner of anyone I have ever known. I should say something here about the voices of eunuchs. Actors and other people who try to mimic them invariably tend to pitch their voices high, and screech. Eunuchs seldom sound like that. If they did, who would ever find their company tolerable? And at a court one must be particularly pleasing in one's manners. In actual fact, the voice of a eunuch is like that of a particularly gentle child, and this appeals to the parent in both men and women. Thus subtly do they disarm us, for we tend to indulge them as we would a child, forgetting that their minds are as mature and twisted as their bodies are lacking. Eusebius spun his web about Gallus. He did not bother with me. I was too young.

Gallus and Eusebius dined alone together that night. The next day Gallus was Eusebius's devoted admirer. 'He's also a friend,' said Gallus. We were alone together in the baths. 'He told me how he's been getting reports about me for years. He knows everything I've ever done. He even knows about *her*.' Gallus named the Antiochene, and giggled. 'Eusebius says I'll be a great success at court. Not only am I good-looking but I have a well-developed intelligence, those are his exact words. He's positive he can talk the Emperor into letting me go free. He says it may take a little time but that he has some small influence with His Eternity, that's exactly how he put it. He's very interesting, though it's hard sometimes to figure out what he's talking about. He expects you to know all sorts of things you wouldn't have any way of knowing, buried in this damned place. Anyway Constantius does just as Eusebius tells him. Everyone says so. Which means if you have Eusebius on your side, that's half the battle. And I've got him.'

'What did he say about me?' I asked. Gallus seldom strayed very far from his essential interest: himself.

'You? Why should he say anything about you?' Gallus ducked me in the cold pool. I pulled him in after me. He was slippery as a fish, but I managed to hold his head under water for a satisfactory length of time. At sixteen I was as strong as he was at twenty-one. He emerged spluttering and blue in the face. 'He's going to make a monk out of you, that's what. Though if I have anything to say about it, you'll be a eunuch.' He tried to kick me between the legs but slipped on the marble and fell. He cursed loudly, and I laughed. Then we were joined by slaves who helped us dress. Since Gallus was a man, the Master of the Offices had ruled that although he was not technically an officer, he could on this occasion wear the uniform of the household troops. Unfortunately, the *nobilissimus* Julian was merely a student and must dress accordingly. As a result, I looked quite insignificant beside my glittering half-brother. But I was perfectly happy to go unnoticed. Let Gallus shine. I preferred obscurity, and survival.

Constantius had arrived at noon and gone straight to his apartments. That was all anyone knew. He might be with us in a few minutes, a few hours, or not at all. Meanwhile, we waited nervously in the great hall of the villa. The rafters were hung with boughs of evergreen, and the ordinarily musty interior smelled of pine and eucalyptus. At one end of the hall, on a dais, a gold throne had been set. To the right of the throne, but at floor level, was the ivory chair of the praetorian prefect of the East (he had arrived with the Emperor). According to rank the officers of the state were arranged to the left and right of the throne. Just at the foot of the dais stood Bishop George in all his glory with Gallus on his right and me on his left.

Looking more than ever like a huge peacock, Eusebius stood at the door, surrounded by his staff of ushers. No one spoke or moved. We were like statues. Though the room was hot, I was sweating nervously. I glanced at Gallus out of the corner of my eye; his mouth was twitching from the strain.

After what seemed days, we heard trumpets. Then the cry 'Augustus!' which always precedes an emperor began, at first far off and faint; then closer, louder: 'Augustus! Augustus!' My legs began to tremble. I was afraid I might be sick. Suddenly with a crash the double doors were flung open and there in the doorway stood Flavius Julius Constantius, Augustus of the East. With a gentle moan, Eusebius embraced Constantius's knees, melodiously murmuring soft words of ceremony not audible to the rest of us who were now prostrate, as the Lord of the World slowly and with extraordinary dignity crossed the room to his throne. I was too busy studying the mosaic floor to get even a glimpse of my imperial cousin. Not until the Master of the Offices gave the signal for everyone to rise was I able at last to observe my father's murderer.

Constantius was a man of overwhelming dignity. That was the most remarkable thing about him; even his most ordinary gestures seemed carefully rehearsed. Like the Emperor Augustus, he wore lifts in his sandals to make himself appear tall. He was clean-shaven, with large melancholy eyes. He had his father Constantine's large nose and thin, somewhat peevish mouth. The upper part of his body was impressively muscular but his legs were dwarfish. He wore the purple, a heavy robe which hung from shoulder to heel; on his head was a fillet of silver set with pearls.

Constantius sat very still on his throne as the Master of the Offices brought him Bishop George, who welcomed him to Macellum. Not once did the Emperor look at Gallus or me. The occasional ritual responses he made were said in such a low voice that none of us could make out the words.

Then the moment came. Bishop George led Gallus and me to the Master of the Offices, who in turn led us up to the dais and presented us formally to the Emperor. I was terrified. Without knowing how I got there, I found myself embracing Constantius's knees, as court etiquette requires.

From far off I heard the Emperor's voice, measured but rather higher-pitched than I had expected, 'We are pleased to receive our most noble cousin Julian.' A large callused hand reached down, gripped me firmly by the left elbow and helped me to rise.

For an instant I was so close to Constantius that I could make out every pore in his face, which was sunburned dark as a Persian's. I noticed the silkiness of his straight brown hair, only just beginning to turn grey. He was thirty-two, but I thought him ancient. I also remember thinking: what must it be like to be Emperor of Rome? to know that one's face on coins, on monuments, painted and sculptured, is known to all the world? And here – so close to me that I could feel the reciprocal warmth of his skin – was the original of that world-famous face, not bronze or marble but soft flesh and bone, like me, like any other man. And I wondered: what *is* it like to be the centre of the world?

For the first time I experienced ambition. It came as a revelation. Only in communion with the One God have I known anything to equal it. How candid I am! I have never admitted to anyone that in my first encounter with Constantius, all that I could think was how much *I* should like the dominion of this earth! But my moment of madness was brief. I stammered a speech of loyalty, and took my place beside Gallus on the dais. I can remember nothing else that happened that day.

Constantius remained at Macellum for a week. He attended to the business of the state. He hunted. Bishop George had a long interview with him on the day he arrived, but then, to the Bishop's chagrin, Constantius ignored him. Though Gallus and I dined at the Emperor's table every evening, he never spoke to us.

I was beginning to fear the worst. But Gallus, who saw Eusebius every day, said that the eunuch was optimistic. 'He's positive we'll be allowed to come to court this year. At least I will. He also said there was talk in the Sacred Consistory that I be made Caesar for the East.' Gallus glowed with excitement. 'Then I could live at Antioch. I'd have my own court. After all, it's what one was born for!'

Gallus made a good impression on everyone – somewhat to my surprise, for he was always rather sullen with Bishop George and downright cruel to me and his teachers. But set among the great officers of the state, he was a different person. He laughed; he flattered; he charmed. He was a natural courtier, and one by one he enchanted the members of the Sacred Consistory, as the Emperor's council is known. Only with Constantius did he make no headway. Our cousin was biding his time.

During the time the court was at Macellum, the junior officers and lesser officials dined in the main hall of the palace, while the Emperor and the magnates dined in the banqueting hall, which was somewhat smaller. In the hour before dinner everyone used to gather in the main hall to gossip. It was our first experience of a court. I found it bewildering, but Gallus took to it like a swan to water.

One evening Gallus allowed me to tag after him as he moved through that splendid company. Gallus was an excellent politician. He made friends not just with the magnates but also with the clerks and notaries who do the actual work of governing. He was shrewd. I of course was perfectly tongue-tied.

In the large hall, Gallus quickly gravitated to the group of officers with whom he had only that day gone hunting. I remember looking at these young men with wonder, for they had actually killed other men in battle in such far-away places as Germany and Mesopotamia. They were unusually self-contained and rather quiet, unlike the clerks and notaries, who were exceedingly talkative, eager to impress one with their knowledge of secret matters.

Gallus seemed particularly to like one tribune, an officer in his thirties named Victor (who is now one of my generals). Victor was – is – an impressive-looking man who speaks good Greek, though he comes from the Black Sea; he is bandy-legged and pale-eyed like so many Russians. 'Is this the most noble Julian?' he asked, turning to me.

Gallus introduced me in an offhand way to the company. I blushed and said nothing.

'Will you be serving with us in the household troops?' Victor asked.

Gallus answered for me. 'No. He's going to be a priest.'

Before I could deny this, Victor said quite seriously, 'I can think of no life worthier than one in the service of God.' I was struck by the simplicity with which he said this. No irony was intended.

Gallus was somewhat taken aback. 'Not for me,' he said finally.

'Nor for me, unfortunately.' Victor gave me a sympathetic smile. 'You must pray for us,' he said.

Gallus changed the subject. While he talked hunting with Victor, I stood by silently, beginning to feel already like one of those Galilean monks or 'solitaries' as they are called, which is rather a misnomer since no monk is ever solitary. They are the most gregarious set of men in the world, for ever eating, guzzling and gossiping with one another. Most of them retire from the world in order to have a continuous party.

'Are you really going to become a priest?' The voice was low. I turned and saw a young man standing behind me. He had obviously been there for some time. I shook my head. 'No,' I said.

'Good.' He smiled. He had sharp grey eyes beneath brows which met, giving him the look of one continually concentrating on some distant object. He wore civilian clothes, which was odd since at his age anyone of good family wears uniform at court.

'Who are you?' I asked.

'Oribasius of Pergamon, physician to the divine Augustus, who doesn't need me. Your cousin is the healthiest man I've ever met.'

'I am happy to hear that!' I blazed sincerity. One's neck depended on this sort of response.

'It's a matter of diet,' said Oribasius matter-of-factly. 'He's a perfect example of the moderate life. He drinks almost no wine. He never overeats. He'll live for ever.'

'I pray that he does,' I said, my heart sinking. What would *my* life be like, lived in the shadow of a never-dying, always suspicious Constantius?

'But why does your brother say you're going to be a priest?'

'Because I read books. He finds that strange.'

'And he associates strangeness with the priesthood?'

I tried not to smile. 'Something like that. But I should like to be a philosopher or a rhetorician. Apparently I have no gift for soldiering. At least Gallus says I haven't. But then, everything depends on the will of the divine Augustus.'

'Yes,' said Oribasius. He looked at me curiously. I recognized the look. I had seen it all my life. It meant: Are they going to kill this boy? And if they do, how interesting it all is! From birth I had been treated like a character in a tragic play.

'Do you like Macellum?'

'Would you, if you were me?' I had not meant to say this. But his look had irritated me and I suddenly rebelled at being treated like a mere thing, a victim, the dumb sacrifice in a bloody legend.

'No,' said Oribasius evenly. 'I would not.'

'Well, then, you know how it is.' But frightened now that I had said too much, I began to babble about the goodness of my cousin, the kindness of Bishop George, the beauty of Cappadocia. For all I knew, Oribasius was a secret agent. Luckily, one of the chamberlains came to announce the approach of the Emperor, and I hurriedly left the main hall and took my place at table.

I have recorded this meeting with Oribasius, since he was to become my closest friend. But I did not see him again at Macellum or, if I did, I don't remember him. He has told me since, 'I've never seen anyone look so frightened as you.'

When I told him that *my* memory of myself in those days was one of serene self-control, Oribasius laughed. 'I was positive you were on the verge of madness. I even diagnosed you – incorrectly – as an epileptic.'

'And what did you think of Gallus?'

'He was the one who appeared serene. I was quite impressed.'

'And of course Gallus went mad.'

'I don't claim to be infallible.'

People never make the impression they think they make. But Oribasius was quite right in one thing: I *was* terrified.

My interview with Constantius occurred on the last day of his visit. Bishop George spent the morning coaching us in what to say. He was as nervous as we were; his career was at stake, too.

Gallus was admitted first to the sacred presence. During the half-hour he was with the Emperor, I recall praying to every deity I could think of; even then I was eclectic!

At last the Master of the Offices, gorgeous in court robes, came to fetch me. He looked like an executioner. Bishop George rattled out a blessing. The Master gave me instructions in how I was to salute the Emperor and which formula of greeting I was to use. I muttered them over and over to myself as I swam – that was my exact sensation – into the presence of the Augustus.

Constantius was seated on an ordinary chair in the apse of the hall. Eusebius stood beside him, holding a sheaf of documents. On a stool at Constantius's feet sat Gallus, looking well-pleased with himself.

I went through the formula of homage, the words falling without thought from my lips. Constantius gave me a long, shrewd, curious look. Then he did not look at me again during the course of the interview. He was one of those men who could never look another in the eye. Nor should this characteristic be taken, necessarily, as a sign of weakness or bad conscience. I am rather like Constantius in this. I have always had difficulty looking into men's eyes. All rulers must. Why? Because of what we see: self-interest, greed, fear. It is not a pleasant sensation to know that merely by existing one inspires animal terror in others. Constantius was often evil in his actions but he took no pleasure in the pain of others. He was not a Caligula, nor a Gallus.

Constantius spoke to me rapidly and impersonally. 'We have received heartening reports concerning the education of our most noble cousin Julian. Bishop George tells us that it is your wish to prepare for the priesthood.' He paused, not so much to hear what I might say as to give proper weight to what he intended to say next. As it was, I was speechless.

Constantius continued, 'You must know that your desire to serve God is pleasing to us. It is not usual for princes to remove themselves from the world, but then it is not usual for any man to be called by heaven.' I suddenly saw with perfect clarity the prison I was to occupy. Deftly, Constantius spun his web. No priest could threaten him. I would be a priest. 'Bishop George tells me that you have pondered deeply the disputes which – sadly – divide holy church. And he assures me that in your study of sacred matters you have seen the truth and believe, as all Christians ought, that the son is of like substance to the father, though not of the same substance. Naturally, as one of our family, you may not live as an ordinary holy man; responsibilities will be thrust upon you. For this reason your education must be continued at Constantinople. You are already a reader in the church. In Constantinople you can hope to become ordained, which will give us pleasure, as well as making you most pleasing to God who has summoned you to serve him. And so we salute our cousin and find him a worthy descendant of Claudius Gothicus, the founder of our house.' That was all. Constantius gave me his hand to kiss. I never said a word beyond those required by court ceremonial. As I backed out of the room, I saw Gallus smile at Eusebius.

I wonder now what Constantius was thinking. I suspect that even then I may have puzzled him. Gallus was easily comprehended. But who was this silent youth who wanted to become a priest? I had planned to say all sorts of things to Constantius, but he had given me no opportunity. Surprisingly enough, he was nervous with everyone. He could hardly speak, except when he was able to speak, as it were, from the throne. Excepting his wife, Eusebia, and the Grand Chamberlain, he had no confidants. He was a curious man. Now that I am in his place I have more sympathy for him than I did, though no liking. His suspicious nature was obviously made worse by the fact that he was somewhat less in-telligent than those he had to deal with. This added to his unease and made him humanly inaccessible. As a student he had failed rhetoric simply through slow-ness of mind. Later he took to writing poetry, which embarrassed everyone. His only 'intellectual' exercise was Galilean disputes. I am told that he was quite good at this sort of thing, but any village quibbler can make a name for himself at a Galilean synod. Look at Athanasius!

I was relieved by this interview. Of course I did not want to become a priest, though if that were the price I had to pay for my life I was perfectly willing to pay it.

In a blaze of pageantry, Constantius departed. Gallus, Bishop George and I stood in the courtyard as he rode past. Mounted, he looked splendid and tall in his armour of chased gold. He acknowledged no one as he rode out of Macellum. In his cold way he was most impressive, and I still envy him his majesty. He could stand for hours in public looking neither to left nor right, motionless as a statue, which is what our ceremonial requires. It was the Emperor Diocletian who decided that we should become, in effect, if not in title, Asiatic kings, to be displayed on rare occasions like the gilded effigies of gods. Diocletian's motive was understandable, perhaps inevitable, for in the last century emperors were made and unmade frivolously, at the whim of the army. Diocletian felt that if we were to be set apart, made sacred in the eyes of the people and hedged round by awe-inspiring ritual, the army would have less occasion to treat us with easy contempt. To a certain extent, this policy has worked. Yet today whenever I ride forth in state and observe the awe in the faces of the people, an awe inspired not by me but by the theatricality of the occasion, I feel a perfect impostor and want to throw off my weight of gold and shout, 'Do you want a statue or a man?' I don't, of course, because they would promptly reply, 'A statue!'

As we watched the long procession make its way from the villa to the main highway, Gallus suddenly exclaimed, 'What I'd give to go with them!'

'You will be gone soon enough, most noble Gallus.' Bishop George had now taken to using our titles.

'When?' I asked.

Gallus answered. 'In a few days. The Emperor promised. "When all is ready, you will join us." That's what he said. I shall be given a military command, and then . . .!' But Gallus was sufficiently wise not to mention his hopes for the future. Instead he gave me a dazzling smile. 'And then,' he repeated, with his usual malice, *'you'll* become a deacon.'

'The beginning of a most holy career,' said Bishop George, removing his silver headdress and handing it to an attendant. There was a red line around his brow where the crown had rested. 'I wish I could continue with your education myself, but, alas, the divine Augustus has other plans for me.' For an instant a look of pure delight illuminated that lean, sombre face.

'Alexandria?' I asked.

He put his finger to his lips, and we went inside, each pleased with his fate: Gallus as Caesar in the East, George as bishop of Alexandria, and I . . . well, at least I would be able to continue my studies; better a live priest than a dead prince.

For the next few weeks we lived in hourly expectation of the imperial summons. But as the weeks became months, hope slowly died in each of us. We had been forgotten.

Bishop George promptly lost all interest in our education. We seldom saw him, and when we did his attitude was obscurely resentful, as if we were in some way responsible for his bad luck. Gallus was grim and prone to sudden outbursts of violence. If a brooch did not fasten properly, he would throw it on the floor and grind it under his heel. On the days when he spoke at all, he roared at everyone. But most of the time he was silent and glowering, his only interest the angry seduction of slave girls. I was not, I confess, in the best of spirits either, but at least I had Plotinus and Plato. I was able to study, and to wait.

One curious thing happened at this time. At the villa there were a number of Cappadocian youths, free-born country boys who worked in the stables as grooms and trainers. They were a cheerful lot and when I first came to Macellum I was allowed to play games with them. They were the only companions I ever had of my own age. I liked one in particular, Hilarius, a good-looking youth, two years older than I. He had a quick mind, and I remember trying to teach him to read when I was ten and already a pedagogue. But as we grew older, each became aware of his place, and intimacy ceased. Even so, I continued to interest myself in his welfare, and when he told me that he wanted to marry a girl in Caesarea whose father disapproved of the match, I was able to bring the father round. I also made Hilarius my personal groom.

One April morning when I sent for my horse, a strange groom brought it. Where was Hilarius? Out riding with the most noble Gallus. I was surprised.

Gallus had his own groom, and we never used one another's servants. But then I thought no more about it. Quite happy to be alone, I rode towards the foothills of Mount Argaeus, enjoying the cool spring day. New leaves shone yellow-green against black branches, and the earth steamed with a white mist as I rode towards a favourite spot where juniper and cedar grew around a natural spring.

At the approach to the clearing, I heard a sharp cry, like an animal in pain. Then I saw two horses tethered to a bent cedar tree at whose bole were strewn a man's clothes. Close by, hands and feet bound, the naked Hilarius lay on his belly while Gallus beat him with a riding crop. Every time the whip struck, Hilarius would cry out. Most extraordinary of all was the expression on Gallus's face. He was grinning with absolute pleasure, his face transfigured by the other's pain.

'Stop it!' I rode straight up to him. Startled, Gallus turned towards me. The boy called out to me to save him.

'Keep out of this.' Gallus's voice was curiously hoarse.

'He's my groom,' I said, rather irrelevantly, for if the boy had been disobedient then Gallus had quite as much right as I to punish him. 'I said keep out of this! Go back!' Gallus aimed the whip at me but struck the flank of my horse instead. The horse reared. Gallus, alarmed, dropped the whip. In a fury myself, I rode straight at my brother, the way cavalrymen are taught to ride down foot-soldiers. He bolted. I reined in my horse just as he mounted his own. We faced one another for an instant, breathing hard. Gallus was still grinning, his teeth bared like a dog ready to snap.

I tried to be calm. With great effort I asked, 'What did he do?'

To which Gallus answered, '*Nothing!*' Then with a laugh, he spurred his horse and was gone. To this day I can remember the way he said, 'Nothing.' Just as the Pythoness is filled with the spirit of Apollo, so my brother Gallus was possessed by evil. It was horrible.

I dismounted. I untied the boy, who was now sobbing and babbling how he had done nothing – again *nothing!* – when without a word of anger or reproach Gallus had ordered him to dismount and strip. Gallus had meant to beat him to death. I am sure of that.

I rode back to Macellum, ready to do murder myself. But when Gallus and I met that night at dinner, my anger had worn off and in its place I experienced something like fear. I could cope with almost any man. Young as I was, I had that much confidence in myself. But a demon was another matter; especially a demon that I did not understand.

All through dinner I stared at Gallus, who chose to be delightful, playful and charming, and nowhere in his smiling face could I find any hint of that sharp-toothed – I nearly wrote 'fanged' – grin I had seen a few hours earlier. I almost began to wonder if perhaps I had dreamed the whole business. But when I visited Hilarius the next day and saw the scars on his back I knew that I had dreamt nothing. *Nothing.* The word haunts me to this day.

For the remainder of our time at Macellum, Gallus and I contrived never to be alone together. When we did speak to one another, it was always politely. We never mentioned what had happened in the clearing.

A month later a letter arrived from the Grand Chamberlain: the most noble Gallus was to proceed to his late mother's estate at Ephesus; here he was to remain at the Emperor's pleasure. Gallus was both elated and crestfallen. He was free of Macellum but he was still a prisoner, and there was no mention of his being made Caesar.

Gallus said good-bye to his officer friends at a dinner to which I was, surprisingly, invited. He made a pleasant speech, promising to remember his friends if he was ever to have a military command. Bishop George then presented him with a Galilean testament bound in massive silver. 'Study it well, most noble Gallus. Outside the church there can be no salvation.' How often have I heard that presumptuous line!

The next day when it was time for Gallus to say good-bye to me, he did so simply. 'Pray for me, brother, as I pray for you.'

'I shall. Good-bye, Gallus.' And we parted, exactly like strangers who, having met for an evening in a post-house, take different roads the next day. After Gallus left, I wept, for the last time as a child. Yet I hated him. They say that to know oneself is to know all there is that is human. But of course no one can ever know himself. Nothing human is finally calculable; even to ourselves we are strange.

On 1 June 348, almost as an afterthought, orders concerning me were sent to Bishop George. I was to proceed to Constantinople. Though my uncle Julian was in Egypt, his household was at my disposal. I was to study philosophy under Ecebolius, a favourite of Constantius. There was no suggestion of the priesthood, which delighted me if not Bishop George. 'I can't think why Augustus has changed his mind. He was quite positive when he was here.'

'Perhaps he may have some other use for me,' I said tentatively.

'What better use is there than the service of God?' Bishop George was in a bad temper. Athanasius was still at Alexandria, and it now looked as if George was doomed to spend the rest of his life in Cappadocia. With bad grace, he organized my departure.

It was a warm, misty day when I got into the carriage which was to take me to Constantinople. Just as I was about to depart, Bishop George asked me if I was certain that I had returned all the volumes of Plotinus to his library. His secretary had reported there was one missing. I swore that it had been returned only that morning (which was true: I had been hurriedly copying passages from it in a notebook). The Bishop then gave me his blessing and a Galilean testament, bound not in silver but in cheap leather; apparently I was not destined to be a Caesar! Yet I thanked him profusely and said farewell. The driver cracked his whip. The horses broke into a trot. For the first time in six years I was leaving the confines of Macellum. My childhood was over, and I was still alive.

5

'And you like the poetry of Bacchylides, as well? Ah, we have extraordinary taste! No doubt of that.' I was so overcome by Ecebolius's flattery that had he asked me then and there to leap off the top of my uncle Julian's house as a literary exercise, I would have done so gladly, with an appropriate quotation from Hesiod as I fell. I chattered like a monkey as he examined me closely in Hesiod, Homer, Herodotus, Thucydides, and Theognis. For seven hours he listened as I recited from memory the many thousands of lines I had memorized at Macellum. He affected to be amazed. 'I knew Bishop George was a splendid scholar – that enviable library! But I had no idea he was a teacher of such genius!' I beamed idiotically and kept on talking. I had at last found my tongue, and there are those who think I have not stopped talking since.

As a small child, I had studied at the Patricians' School with Ecebolius. So we quickly picked up where we had left off, almost as if nothing had changed, except that I was now a gawky adolescent with a beard thick on the chin, spotty on the upper lip, invisible on the cheeks. I looked frightful but I refused to shave. I am to be a philosopher, I said proudly; and that was that.

In Constantinople I was left largely to myself. I had only one audience with the Grand Chamberlain Eusebius. I say 'audience', for not only did Eusebius exercise the actual power of the Emperor, he imitated his state. In fact, there used to be a joke that if one wanted anything done. Constantius was the man to see because he was reputed to have some influence with the Grand Chamberlain.

Eusebius received me in his suite at the Sacred Palace. He stood up to greet me (although he was the second most powerful man in the empire, he was only an *illustris* and I outranked him). He greeted me in that sweet child's voice of his and motioned for me to sit beside him. I noticed that his fat fingers shone with diamonds and Indian rubies, and he was drenched in attar of roses.

'Is the most noble Julian comfortable in his uncle's house?'

'Oh, yes, very comfortable.'

'We thought he would prefer that to the ... confinement of the Sacred Palace. But of course you are only a few yards away. You can visit us often. We hope you will.' He gave me a dimpled smile.

I asked him when the Emperor would return.

'We have no idea. He is now at Nisibis. There are rumours that he may soon engage Sapor in a final battle. But you know as much as I.' He made a flattering gesture of obeisance to me. 'We have had excellent reports on your progress. Ecebolius tells us that you have a gift for rhetoric which is unusual for your age, though not – if I may say so – for one of your family.' Nervous as I was, I smiled at this hyperbole. Neither Constantius nor Gallus could develop an argument or even deliver a proper speech.

'Ecebolius proposes that you also take a course in grammar with Nicocles. I agree. These things are necessary to know, especially for one who may be raised very high.' He let this sink in. As I gabbled my admiration of Nicocles and my passion for grammer, Eusebius studied me as though I were an actor in the theatre giving a recitation. I could see that he was curious about me. Gallus had obviously charmed him, but then Gallus was neither intelligent nor subtle; he posed no threat to the Grand Chamberlain. He could be governed, just as Constantius was governed. But who was this third prince, this half-grown youth with a patchy beard who talked too fast and used ten quotations where one would do? Eusebius had not yet made up his mind about me. So I did my best to convince him that I was harmless.

'My interest is philosophy. My goal the University of Athens, the lighthouse of the world. I should like to devote myself to literature, to philosophy. "Men search out God and searching find him," as Aeschylus wrote. But of course we know God now in a way our ancestors could not. Jesus came by special grace to save us. He is like his father *though not of the same substance*. Yet it is good to study the old ways. To speak out on every matter, even error. For as Euripides wrote, "A slave is he who cannot speak his thought," and who would be a slave, except to reason? Yet too great a love of reason might prove a trap, for as Horace wrote,

"Even the wise man is a fool if he seeks virtue itself beyond what is enough." '

With some shame, I record the awful chatter I was capable of in those days. I was so uncertain of myself that I never made a personal observation about anything. Instead I spouted quotations. In this I resembled a great many contemporary Sophists who – having no ideas of their own – string together the unrelated sayings of the distinguished dead and think themselves as wise as those they quote. It is one thing to use text to illustrate a point one is making, but quite another to quote merely to demonstrate the excellence of one's memory. At seventeen I was the worst sort of Sophist. This probably saved my life. I bored Eusebius profoundly and we never fear those who bore us. By definition, a bore is predictable. If you think you know in advance what a man is apt to say or do, you are not apt to be disagreeably surprised by him. I am sure that in that one interview I inadvertently saved my life.

'We shall do everything we can to bring to the divine Augustus's attention your desire – *commendable* desire – to be enrolled at the University of Athens. At the moment you must continue your studies here. Also, I suggest . . .' He paused tactfully, his eyes taking in my schoolboy clothes as well as my fingers from which the ink had not been entirely washed. '. . . that you be instructed in the ways of the court. I shall send you Eutherius. Though an Armenian, he is a master of ceremony. He will acquaint you with the niceties of our arrangements twice . . . no, perhaps *three* times a week.'

Eusebius rang a dainty silver bell. Then a familiar figure appeared in the doorway: my old tutor Mardonius. He looked no different than he had that day six years before when he said farewell to us in front of the bishop's house. We embraced emotionally.

Eusebius purred. 'Mardonius is my right arm. He is chief of my secretarial bureau. A distinguished classicist, a loyal subject, a good Christian of impeccable faith.' Eusebius sounded as if he were delivering a funeral oration. 'He will show you out. Now if you will forgive me, most noble prince, I have a meeting with the Sacred Consistory.' He rose. We saluted one another; then he withdrew, urging me to call on him at any time.

When Mardonius and I were alone together, I said gaily, 'I'm sure you never thought you'd see me alive again!'

This was exactly the wrong thing to say. Poor Mardonius turned corpse-yellow. 'Not here,' he whispered. 'The palace – secret agents – everywhere. Come.' Talking of neutral matters, he led me through marble corridors to the main doors of the palace. As we passed through the outer gate, the Scholarian guards saluted me, and I felt a momentary excitement which was not at all in the character I had just revealed to Eusebius.

My attendants were waiting for me under the arcade across the square. I motioned to them to remain where they were. Mardonius was brief. 'I won't be able to see you again. I asked the Grand Chamberlain if I might instruct you in court ceremonial, but he said no. He made it very clear I am not to see you.'

'What about this fellow he told me about, the Armenian?'

'Eutherius is a good man. You will like him. I don't think he has been sent to incriminate you, though of course he will make out regular reports. You must be careful what you say at all times. *Never* criticize the Emperor . . .'

'I know that much, Mardonius.' I could not help but smile. He was sounding exactly the way he used to. 'I've managed to live this long.'

'But this is Constantinople, not Macellum. This is the Sacred Palace which is a . . . a . . . *nothing* can describe it.'

'Not even Homer?' I teased him. He smiled wanly. 'Homer had no experience of this sort of viciousness and corruption.'

'What do they mean to do with me?'

'The Emperor has not decided.'

'Will Eusebius decide for him?'

'Perhaps. Keep on his good side. Appear to be harmless.'

'Not difficult.'

'And wait.' Mardonius suddenly became his old self. 'Incidentally, I read one of your themes. "Alexander the Great in Egypt." Too periphrastic. Also, a misquotation. From the Odyssey 16.187: "No God am I. Why then do you liken me to the immortals?" You used the verb meaning "to place among" rather than "to liken". I was humiliated when Eusebius showed me the mistake.'

I apologized humbly. I was also amazed to realize that every schoolboy exercise of mine was on file in the Grand Chamberlain's office.

'That is how they will build their case for – or against – you.' Mardonius frowned and the thousand wrinkles of his face suddenly looked like the shadow of a spider's web in the bright sun. 'Be careful. Trust no one.' He hurried back into the palace.

I remained the rest of that year at Constantinople. I had a sufficient income, left me by my grandmother who had died that summer. I was allowed to see her just before her death, but she did not recognize me. She spoke disjointedly. She shook with palsy and at times the shaking became so violent that she had to be strapped to her bed. When I left, she kissed me, murmuring, 'Sweet, sweet.'

By order of the Grand Chamberlain I was not allowed to associate with boys my own age or, for that matter, with anyone other than my instructors, Ecebolius and Nicocles, and the Armenian eunuch. Ecebolius is a man of much charm. But Nicocles I detested. He was a short, sparse grasshopper of a man. Many regard him as our age's first grammarian. But I always thought of him as *the enemy*. He did not like me either. I remember in particular one conversation with him. It is amusing in retrospect. 'The most noble Julian is at an impressionable period in his life. He must be careful of those he listens to. The world is now full of false teachers. In religion we have the party of Athanasius, a most divisive group. In philosophy we have all sorts of mountebanks, like Libanius.'

That was the first time I heard the name of the man who was to mean so much to me as thinker and teacher. Not very interested, I asked who Libanius was.

'An Antiochene – and we know what *they* are like. He studied at Athens. Then he came here to teach. That was about twelve years ago. He was young. He was bad-mannered to his colleagues, to those of us who were, if not wiser, at least more experienced than he.' Nicocles made a sound like an insect's wings rustling on a summer day – laughter? 'He was also tactless about religion. All the great teachers here are Christian. He was not. Like so many who go to Athens (and I deplore, if I may say so, *your* desire to study there), Libanius prefers the empty ways of our ancestors. He calls himself a Hellenist, preferring Plato to the gospels, Homer to the old testament. In his four years here he completely disrupted the academic community. He was always making trouble. Such a vain man! Why, he even prepared a paper for the Emperor on the teaching of Greek, suggesting *changes* in our curriculum! I'm glad to say he left us eight years ago, under a cloud.'

'What sort of cloud?' I was oddly intrigued by this recital. Oddly, because academics everywhere are for ever attacking one another, and I had long since learned that one must never believe what any teacher says of another.

'He was involved with a girl, the daughter of a senator. He was to give her private instruction in the classics. Instead, he made her pregnant. Her family complained. So the Emperor, to save the reputation of the girl and her family, a very important family (you would know who they are if I told you, which I must not) . . . the Augustus exiled Libanius from the capital.'

'Where is Libanius now?'

'At Nicomedia, where as usual he is making himself difficult. He has a passion to be noticed.' The more Nicocles denounced Libanius, the more interested I became in him. I decided I must meet him. But how? Libanius could not come to Constantinople and I could not go to Nicomedia. Fortunately, I had an ally.

I liked the Armenian eunuch Eutherius as much as I disliked Nicocles. Eutherius taught me court ceremonial three times a week. He was a grave man of natural dignity who did not look or sound like a eunuch. His beard was normal. His voice was low. He had been cut at the age of twenty, so he had known what it was to be a man. He once told me in grisly detail how he had almost died during the operation, 'from loss of blood, because the older you are, the more dangerous the operation is. But I have been happy. I have had an interesting life. And there is something to be said for not wasting one's time in the pursuit of sexual pleasure.' But though this was true of Eutherius, it was not true of all eunuchs, especially those at the palace. Despite their incapacity, eunuchs are capable of sexual activity, as I one day witnessed, in a scene I shall describe in its proper place.

When I told Eutherius that I wanted to go to Nicomedia, he agreed to conduct the intricate negotiations with the Chamberlain's office. Letters were exchanged daily between my household and the palace. Eutherius was often in the absurd position of writing, first, my letter of request, and then Eusebius's elaborate letter of rejection. 'It is good practice for me,' said Eutherius wearily, as the months dragged on.

Shortly after New Year 349 Eusebius agreed to let me go to Nicomedia on condition that I do not attend the lectures of Libanius. As Nicocles put it, 'Just as we protect our young from those who suffer from the fever, so we must protect them from dangerous ideas, not to mention poor rhetoric. As stylist, Libanius has a tendency to facetiousness which you would find most boring. As philosopher, he is dangerously committed to the foolish past.' To make sure that I would not cheat, Ecebolius was ordered to accompany me to Nicomedia.

Ecebolius and I arrived at Nicomedia in February 349. I enjoyed myself hugely that winter. I attended lectures. I listened to skilled Sophists debate. I met students of my own age. This was not always an easy matter, for they were terrified of me, while I hardly knew how to behave with them.

Libanius was much spoken of in the city. But I saw him only once. He was surrounded by students in one of the porticoes near the gymnasium of Trajan. He was a dark, rather handsome man. Ecebolius pointed him out, saying grimly, 'Who else would imitate Socrates in everything but wisdom?'

'Is he so bad?'

'He is a troublemaker. Worse than that, he is a bad rhetorician. He never learned to speak properly. He simply chatters.'

'But his writings are superb.'

'How do you know?' Ecebolius looked at me sharply.

'I . . . from the others here. They talk about him.' To this day Ecebolius does not know that I used to pay to have Libanius's lectures taken down in shorthand. Though Libanius had been warned not to approach me, he secretly sent me copies of his lectures, for which I paid him well.

'He can only corrupt,' said Ecebolius. 'Not only is he a poor model for style, he despises our religion. He is impious.'

Priscus: That sounds just like Ecebolius, doesn't it? Of course when Julian became emperor, Ecebolius embraced Hellenism. Then when Valentinian and Valens became co-emperors, Ecebolius threw himself down in front of the Church of the Holy Apostles, crying, 'Tread on me! I am as salt which has lost its savour!' I always wondered if anybody did tread on him. I should have liked to. He changed his religion five times in thirty years and died at a fine old age, honoured by all. If there is a moral to his career, it eludes me.

I do recall that story about you and the senator's daughter. Is it true? I always suspected you were rather a lady's man, in your day of course.

Libanius: No, I shall not give Priscus the pleasure of an answer. I shall also suppress Julian's references to that old scandal. It serves no purpose to rake over the past in such a pointless way. I have always known that a story more or less along those lines was circulated about me, but this is the first time I have been confronted with it in all its malice. Envious Sophists will go to any lengths to tear down one's reputation. There was no 'senator's daughter', at least not as described. The whole thing is absurd. For one thing, if I had been dismissed by the Emperor on such a charge, why was I then asked by the court to return to Constantinople in 353? Which I did, and remained there several years before coming home to Antioch.

I am far more irritated by Ecebolius's reference to my 'facetiousness'. That from him! I have always inclined to a grave – some feel too grave – style, only occasionally lightened by humour. Also, if I am as poor a stylist as he suggests, why am I the most imitated of living writers? Even in those days, a prince paid for my lecture notes! Incidentally, Julian says that he paid *me* for the lectures. That is not true. Julian paid one of my students who had a complete set of notes. He also engaged a shorthand writer to take down my conversation. I myself never took a penny from him. How tangled truth becomes.

Julian Augustus

Looking back, I seem to have followed a straight line towards my destiny. I moved from person to person as though each had been deliberately chosen for my instruction. But at the time I had only a pleasurable sense of freedom, nothing more. Nevertheless, the design of my life was taking shape and each wise man I met formed yet another link in that chain which leads towards the ultimate revelation which Plotinus has so beautifully described as 'the flight of the alone to the Alone'.

At Nicomedia I forged an important new link. Like most university towns, Nicomedia had a particular bath where the students assembled. The students' bath is usually the cheapest in town, though not always, for students have strange tastes and when they suddenly decide that such-and-such a tavern or bath or arcade is the one place where they most want to gather, they will then think nothing of cost or comfort.

I longed to go alone to the baths and mingle with students my own age, but Ecebolius always accompanied me. 'The Chamberlain's orders,' he would say, whenever we entered the baths, my two guards trailing us as though we were potential thieves in a market-place. Even in the hot room, I would be flanked by sweating guards while Ecebolius hovered near by to see that no one presented himself to me without first speaking to him. As a result, the students I wanted to meet were scared off.

But one morning Ecebolius awakened with the fever. 'I must keep to my bed "with only cruel pain for handmaid",' he said, teeth chattering. I told him how sorry I was and then, utterly happy, I left for the baths. My guards promised that once inside they would not stick too closely to me. They realized how much I wanted to be anonymous, and in those days it was possible, for I was not well known in Nicomedia. I never went into the agora, and when I attended lectures I always came in last and sat at the back.

Students go to the baths in the morning, when the admission price is cheapest. Shortly before noon I queued up and followed the mob into the changing room where I undressed at the opposite end from my two guards, who pretended to be soldiers on leave. As far as I know, I was not recognized.

Since the day was warm, I went outside to the palaestra; here the athletically inclined were doing exercises and playing games. Avoiding the inevitable group of old men who linger watchfully in the shade, I crossed to a lively-looking group, seated on a bench in the sun. They ignored me when I sat beside them.

'And you took the money?'

'I did. We all did. About a hundred of us.'

'Then what happened?'

'We never went to his lectures.'

'Was he angry?'

'Of course.'

'But not as angry as he was when ...'

'. . . . when all of us went *back* to Libanius!'

They laughed at what was in those days a famous story. Within a year of Libanius's arrival at Nicomedia, he was easily the most popular teacher in the city. This naturally enraged his rival Sophists, one of whom tried to buy Libanius's students away from him. The students took the man's money and continued to attend Libanius's lectures. It was a fine joke, until the furious Sophists applied to friends at court who had Libanius arrested on some spurious charge. Fortunately, he was soon freed.

Libanius: This was the beginning of my interest in penal reform. Over the years I have written a good deal on the subject, and there is some evidence that I am beginning to arouse the conscience of the East. At least our rulers are now aware of the barbarous conditions in which prisoners are held. I had never realized how truly hopeless our prison system is until I myself was incarcerated. But improvements are hard to make. Despite all evidence to the contrary, I do not think human beings are innately cruel, but they fear change of any kind. And now I am digressing.

Is this age? Just yesterday I had a most curious conversation on that subject with an old friend and colleague. I asked him why it was that nowadays whenever I address the assembly at Antioch, the senators cough and talk among themselves. I realize I am not a master of oratory, but after all what I have to say and the way in which I say it is – and I do not mean this immodestly – of obvious interest to the world. I am the most famous living writer of Greek. As quaestor, I am official spokesman for my city. 'So why do people stop listening when I start to speak? And why, when the session is over and I try to talk to various senators and officials in the arcade, do they wander off when I am in mid-sentence, saying that they have appointments to keep, even though it is quite plain that they do not?'

'Because, my dear old friend, you have become – now you asked me to tell you the truth, remember that – a bore.'

I was stunned. Of course as a professional teacher one tends to lecture rather than converse, but that is a habit most public men fall into. 'But even so, I should have thought that *what* I was saying was of some interest . . .'

'It is. It always is.'

'. . . rather than the *way* I say it, which may perhaps be overexplicit.'

'You are too serious.'

'No one can be too serious about what is important.'

'Apparently the Antiochenes think otherwise.'

We parted. I must say I have been thinking all day about what my colleague said. Have I aged so greatly? Have I lost my power to define and persuade? Am I too serious? I am suddenly tempted to write some sort of apologia for myself, to explain my unbecoming gravity. I must do something . . . But scribbling these highly personal remarks on the back of Julian's memoirs is not the answer!

Julian Augustus

As I sat on the bench in the sun, revelling in warmth and anonymity, a dark man approached me. He gave me a close look. Then he said, 'Macellum?'

At first I was annoyed at being recognized. But when I realized that this young man was the physician Oribasius, I was glad that he spoke to me. In no time at all we were talking as if we had known each other all our lives. Together we took the baths. In the circular hot room, as we scraped oil from one another, Oribasius told me that he had left the court.

'To practise privately?'

'No. Family affairs. My father died. And now I have to go home to Pergamon to settle the estate.'

'How did you recognize me? It's been two years.'

'I always remember faces, especially those of princes.'

I motioned for him to lower his voice. Just opposite us two students were trying to overhear our conversation.

'Also,' whispered Oribasius, 'that awful beard of yours is a give-away.'

'It's not very full yet,' I said, tugging at it sadly.

'And everyone in Nicomedia knows that the most noble Julian is trying to grow a philosopher's beard.'

'Well, at my age there's always hope.'

After a plunge in the cold pool, we made our way to the hall of the tepidarium, where several hundred students were gathered, talking loudly, singing, occasionally wrestling, to the irritation of the bath attendants, who would then move swiftly among them, cracking heads with metal keys.

Oribasius promptly convinced me that I should come stay with him in Pergamon. 'I've a big house and there's no one in it. You can also meet Aedesius . . .'

Like everyone, I admired Aedesius. He was Pergamon's most famous philosopher, the teacher of Maximus and Priscus, and a friend of the late Iamblichos.

'You'll like Pergamon. Thousands of Sophists, arguing all day long. We even have a woman Sophist.'

'A woman?'

'Well, perhaps she's a woman. There is a rumour she may be a goddess. You must ask her, since she started the rumour. Anyway, she gives lectures on philosophy, practises magic, predicts the future. You'll like her.'

'But you don't?'

'But you will.'

At that moment we were joined by the two young men from the hot room. One was tall and well built; his manner grave. The other was short and thin with a tight smile and quick black eyes. As they approached, my heart sank. I had been recognized. The short one introduced himself. 'Gregory of Nazianzus, most noble Julian. And this is Basil. We are both from Cappadocia. We saw you the day the divine Augustus came to Macellum. We were in the crowd.'

'Are you studying here?'

'No. We're on our way to Constantinople, to study with Nicocles. But Basil wanted to stop off here to attend the lectures of the impious Libanius.'

Basil remonstrated mildly. 'Libanius is not a Christian, but he is the best teacher of rhetoric in Nicomedia.'

'Basil is not like *us*, most noble Julian,' said Gregory. 'He is much too tolerant.'

I found myself liking Basil and disliking Gregory, I suppose because of that presumptuous 'us'. Gregory has always had too much of the courtier in him. But I have since come to like him, and today we are all three friends, despite religious differences. They were agreeable companions, and I still recall with pleasure that day we met when I was a student among students with no guardian to inhibit conversation. When it was finally time to leave the baths, I promised Oribasius that somehow or other I would join him in Pergamon. Meanwhile, Gregory and Basil agreed to dine with me. They were just the sort Ecebolius would approve of: devout Galileans with no interest in politics. But I knew instinctively that Oribasius would alarm Ecebolius. Oribasius had been at court and he moved in high circles. He was also rich and worldly and precisely the sort of friend a sequestered prince should not have. I decided to keep Oribasius my secret for the time being. This proved to be wise.

In January 350, Ecebolius and I got permission to move on to Pergamon. We made the three-hundred-mile trip in bitter cold. As we rode through the perpetual haze of steam from our own breath, I recall thinking, this must be what it is like to campaign in Germany or Sarmatia: barren countryside, icy roads, a black sky at noon, and soldiers behind me, their arms clattering in the stillness. I daydreamed about the military life, which was strange, for in those days I seldom thought of anything except philosophy and religion. I suspect that I was born a soldier and only 'made' a philosopher.

At Pergamon, Ecebolius insisted we stay at the palace of the Greek kings, which had been made available to me. But when the prefect of the city (who had most graciously met us at the gate) hinted that I would have to pay for the maintenance of the palace, Ecebolius agreed that we were better off as guests of Oribasius, who had also met us at the gate, pretending not to know me but willing, as a good courtier, to put up the Emperor's cousin. In those days Oribasius was far richer than I and often lent me money when I was short of cash. We were like brothers.

Oribasius took delight in showing me his city. He knew my interest in temples (though I was not yet consciously a Hellenist), and we spent several days prowling through the deserted temples on the acropolis and across the Selinos

River, which divides the city. Even then, I was struck by the sadness of once holy buildings now empty save for spiders and scorpions. Only the temple of Asklepios was kept up, and that was because the Asklepion is the centre of the intellectual life of the city. It is a large enclave containing theatre, library, gymnasium, porticoes, gardens, and of course the circular temple to the god himself. Most of the buildings date from two centuries ago, when architecture was at its most splendid.

The various courtyards are filled with students at every hour of the day. The teachers sit inside the porticoes and talk. Each teacher has his own following. Unfortunately when we came to the portico where Aedesius was usually to be found, we were told that he was ill.

'After all, he's over seventy,' said a raffish youth, dressed as a New Cynic. 'Why don't you go to Prusias's lectures? He's the coming man. Absolutely first-rate. I'll take you to him.' But Oribasius firmly extricated us from the young man's clutches. Cursing genially, the admirer of Prusias let us go. We started back to the agora.

'That's how a lot of students live in Pergamon. For each new pupil they bring to their teacher, they are paid so much a head.' Just behind the old theatre, Oribasius pointed to a small house in a narrow street. 'Aedesius lives there.'

I sent one of my guards to ask if the philosopher would receive me. After a long wait, a fat woman with a fine grey beard and spiky moustache came to the door and said firmly, 'He can see no one.'

'But when will he be able to?'

'Perhaps never,' she said, and shut the door.

Oribasius laughed. 'His wife. She's not as nice as she looks.'

'But I must meet him.'

'We'll arrange it somehow. Anyway, tonight I've something special for you.'

That something special was the woman philosopher, Sosipatra. She was then in her forties but looked much younger. She was tall and though somewhat heavy, her face was still youthful and handsome.

When we arrived at her house, Sosipatra came straight to me, knowing exactly who I was without being told. 'Most noble Julian, welcome to our house. And you too, Ecebolius. Oribasius, your father sends you greetings.'

Oribasius looked alarmed, as well he might: his father had been dead three months. But Sosipatra was serious. 'I spoke to him just now. He is well. He stands within the third arc of Helios, at a hundred-and-eighty-degree angle to the light. He advises you to sell the farm in Galatia. Not the one with the cedar grove. The other. With the stone house. Come in, most noble prince. You went to see Aedesius today but his wife turned you away. Nevertheless, my old friend *will* see you in a few days. He is sick at the moment but he will recover. He has four more years of life. A holy, good man.'

I was quite overwhelmed, as she led me firmly by the hand into a dining-room whose walls were decorated with pictures of the mysteries of Demeter. There were couches for us and a chair for her. Slaves helped us off with our sandals and washed our feet. We then arranged ourselves about the table. All the while, Sosipatra continued to talk in such a melodious voice that even Ecebolius, who did not much like the idea of her, was impressed.

'Do you know the beautiful story of Aedesius and his father? No? It is so characteristic. The father wanted his son to join him in the family business. But first he sent him to school at Athens. When Aedesius returned from school, he told his father that it was now impossible for him to go into business. He preferred to become a philosopher. Furious, his father drove him out of the house, shouting, "What good does philosophy do you now?" To which Aedesius replied, "It has taught me to revere my father, even as he drives me from his house." From that moment on, Aedesius and his father were friends.'

We were all edified by this story. Sosipatra was indeed a fountain of wisdom, and we were fortunate to drink of her depths.

Priscus: Did you ever meet this monster? I once spent a week with her and her husband at Pergamon. She never stopped talking. Even Aedesius, who was fond of her (I think he was once her lover), thought her ignorant, though he would never have admitted it. He, by the way, was an excellent man. After all, he was *my* teacher and am I not, after Libanius, the wisest man of our age?

Libanius: Irony?

Priscus: But though Sosipatra was hardly a philosopher, she was a remarkable magician. Even I came close to believing in her spells and predictions. She also had a sense of drama which was most exciting. Julian was completely taken in by her, and I date his fatal attraction to this sort of thing from that dinner party.

Incidentally, a friend of mine once had an affair with Sosipatra. When the act was over, she insisted that he burn incense to her as she lay among the tangled sheets. 'For I am Aphrodite, goddess come among men.' He burned the incense but never went to bed with her again.

Maximus also thought that Sosipatra was divine, or at least 'inhabited from time to time by the spirit of Aphrodite'. Which made her sound rather like an inn. I always found her tedious. But she was often accurate in her predictions. Lucky guesses? Who knows? If the gods exist, which I doubt, might they not be every bit as boring as Sosipatra?

Libanius: As always, Priscus goes too far. But I rather agree with him about Sosipatra. She did talk too much. But then, who am I to criticize her when one of my oldest friends has just told me to my face that I bore all Antioch?

Julian Augustus

When the dinner was over, Sosipatra presented her sons to us. They were about my age. Two of them grew up to be speculators in grain, and most unsavoury. The third, Anatolius, I heard news of only recently. Some years ago he attached himself to the temple of Serapis at Alexandria. After Bishop George destroyed the temple, Anatolius climbed onto a broken column and now stares continually at the sun. How I envy the purity of such a life! But that night at dinner, the future holy man seemed a very ordinary youth, with a slight stammer.

When the sons had withdrawn, Sosipatra sent for a tripod and incense. 'And now you will want to know what the gods advise you to do. Where to go. With whom to study.' She gave me a dazzling smile.

I blurted out, 'I want to study here, with you.' But she shook her head, to Ecebolius's relief. 'I known my own future and a prince is no part of it. I wish it were otherwise,' she added softly, and I fell in love with her on the spot, as so many students had done before me.

Sosipatra lit the incense. She shut her eyes. She whispered a prayer. Then in a low voice she implored the Great Goddess to speak to us. Smoke filled the room. All things grew vague and indistinct. My head began to ache. Suddenly in a loud voice not her own, Sosipatra said, 'Julian!'

I looked at her closely. Her eyes were half open but only the whites showed: she slept while the spirit possessed her. 'You are loved by us beyond any man alive.' That was puzzling. 'Us' must mean the gods. But why should they love a Galilean who doubted their existence? Of course I had also begun to question the divinity of the Nazarene, which made me neither Hellenist nor Galilean, neither believer nor atheist. I was suspended somewhere between, waiting for a sign. Could this be it?

'You will rebuild our temples. You will cause the smoke of a thousand sacrifices to rise from a thousand altars. You shall be our servant and all men shall be *your* servants, as token of our love.'

Ecebolius stirred nervously. 'We must not listen to this,' he murmured.

The voice continued serenely. 'The way is dangerous. But we shall protect you, as we have protected you from the hour of your birth. Earthly glory shall be yours. And death when it comes in far Phrygia, by enemy steel, will be a hero's death, without painful lingering. Then you shall be with us for ever, close to the One from whom all light flows, to whom all light returns. Oh, Julian, dear to us . . . *Evil!*' The voice changed entirely. It became harsh. 'Foul and profane! We bring you defeat. Despair. The Phrygian death is yours. But the tormented soul is ours for ever, far from light!'

Sosipatra screamed. She began to writhe in her chair; her hands clutched at her throat as though to loosen some invisible bond. Words tumbled disjointedly from her mouth. She was a battleground between warring spirits. But at last the good prevailed, and she became tranquil.

'Ephesus,' she said, and her voice was again soft and caressing. 'At Ephesus you will find the door to light. Ecebolius, when you were a child you hid three coins in the garden of your uncle's house at Sirmium. One was a coin of the reign of Septimus Severus. A gardener dug up the coins and spent them. That coin of Severus is now in Pergamon, in a tavern. Oribasius, your father insists you sell the property but hopes you will not make the same mistake you made last year when you leased the lower meadow to your Syrian neighbour, and he would not pay. Julian, beware the fate of Gallus. Remember . . . Hilarius!' She stopped. She became herself again. 'My head aches,' she said in a tired voice.

We were all quite shaken. I most of all for she had practically said that I would become emperor, which was treason, for no one may consult an oracle about the imperial succession, nor even speculate in private on such matters. Ecebolius had been rightly alarmed.

Sosipatra had no memory of what was said. She listened carefully as we told her what the goddess – and the other – had said. She was intrigued. 'Obviously a great future for the most noble Julian.'

'Of course,' said Ecebolius nervously. 'As a loyal prince of the imperial house . . .'

'Of course!' Sosipatra laughed. 'We must say no more.' Then she frowned. 'I have no idea who the dark spirit was. But it is plain that the goddess was Cybele, and she wants you to honour her since she is the mother of all, and your protectress.'

'It also seems indicated that Julian should avoid Phrygia,' said Oribasius mischievously.

But Sosipatra took this quite seriously. 'Yes. Julian will die in Phrygia, gloriously, in battle.' She turned to me. 'I don't understand the reference to your brother. Do you?'

I nodded, unable to speak, my head whirling with dangerous thoughts.

'The rest of it seems plain enough. You are to restore the worship of the true gods.'

'It seems rather late in the day for that.' Ecebolius had found his tongue at last. 'And even if it were possible, Julian is a Christian. The imperial house is Christian. This makes him a most unlikely candidate for restoring the old ways.'

'*Are* you unlikely?' Sosipatra fixed me with her great dark eyes.

I shook my head helplessly. 'I don't know. I must wait for a sign.'

'Perhaps *this* was the sign. Cybele herself spoke to you.'

'So did something else,' said Ecebolius.

'There is *always* the Other,' said Sosipatra. 'But light transcends all things. As Macrobius wrote, "The sun is the mind of the universe." And nowhere, not even in the darkest pit of hell, is mind entirely absent.'

'What is at Ephesus?' I asked suddenly.

Sosipatra gave me a long look. Then she said, 'Maximus is there. He is waiting for you. He has been waiting for you since the day you were born.'

Ecebolius stirred at this. 'I am perfectly sure that Maximus would like nothing better than to instruct the prince, but, unfortunately for him, *I* was appointed by the Grand Chamberlain to supervise Julian's studies and I am not at all eager for my pupil to become involved with a notorious magician.'

Sosipatra's voice was icy. 'We think of Maximus as being something more than a "notorious magician". It is true that he can make the gods appear to him, but . . .'

'Actually appear?' I was fascinated.

'Actors, from the theatre,' muttered Oribasius, 'carefully rehearsed, tricks of lighting . . .'

Sosipatra smiled. 'Oribasius! That is unworthy of you! What would your father say to that?'

'I have no idea. *You* see more of him nowadays than I do.'

Sosipatra ignored this. She turned to me. 'Maximus is no charlatan. If he were, I would have unmasked him years ago. Of course people question his powers. They should. One must not take anything on blind faith. Yet when he speaks to the gods . . .'

'He speaks to them, but do they really speak to *him*? That's more the point,' said Ecebolius.

'They do. I was present once in Ephesus when a group of atheists questioned him, just as you have.'

'Not to believe in Maximus does not make one an atheist.' Ecebolius was growing irritated.

She continued through him. 'Maximus asked us to meet him that night in the temple of Hecate. Now the temple has not been used in years. It is a simple building, containing a bronze statue of the goddess and nothing more, so there was no way for Maximus to . . . *prepare* a miracle.' She looked sharply at Oribasius. 'When we had all arrived, Maximus turned to the statue and said, "Great Goddess, show these unbelievers a sign of your power." There was a moment of silence. Then the bronze torches she held in her bronze hands burst into flame.'

'Naphtha,' said Oribasius.

'But that was not all. The statue smiled at us. The bronze face smiled. Then

Hecate laughed. I have never heard such a sound! All heaven seemed to mock us, as we fled from that place.'

'I must got to Ephesus,' I said.

Sosipatra turned to Ecebolius. 'He has no choice, you know. At Ephesus his life begins.'

The next day I received word that Aedesius would see me. I found him lying on a cot, his bearded wife beside him. Aedesius was a small man who had once been fat, but now because of illness and age the skin hung from him in folds. It was hard to believe that this frail old man had once been the pupil of Iamblichos and actually present on that occasion when Iamblichos caused two divine youths to appear from twin pools in the rock at Gadara. Yet despite his fragility, Aedesius was alert and amiable. 'Sosipatra tells me that you have a gift for philosophy.'

'If a passion can be called a gift.'

'Why not? Passion is a gift of the gods. She also tells me that you plan to go to Ephesus.'

'Only if I cannot study with you.'

'Too late for that.' He sighed. 'As you see, I am in poor health. She gives me four more years of this life. But I doubt that I shall last so long. Anyway, Maximus will be more to your taste. He was my student, you know. After Priscus of Athens, he was my best student. Of course Maximus prefers demonstration to argument, mysteries to books. But then there are many ways to truth. And from what Sosipatra tells me, he was born to be your guide. It is clearly destiny.'

Priscus: It was clearly a plot. They were all in on it. Years later, Maximus admitted as much. 'I knew all along I was the right teacher for Julian. Naturally, I never dreamed he would be emperor.' He did not dream it; he willed it. 'I saw him simply as a soul that I alone could lead to salvation.' Maximus then got Sosipatra and Aedesius to recommend him to Julian, which they did. What an extraordinary crew they were! Except for Aedesius, there was not a philosopher in the lot.

From what I gather, Julian in those days was a highly intelligent youth who might have been 'captured' for true philosophy. After all, he enjoyed learning. He was good at debate. Properly educated, he might have been another Porphyry or, taking into account his unfortunate birth, another Marcus Aurelius. But Maximus got to him first and exploited his one flaw: that craving for the vague and incomprehensible which is essentially Asiatic. It is certainly not Greek, even though we Greeks are in a noticeable intellectual decline. Did you know that thanks to the presence of so many foreign students in Athens, our people no longer speak pure Attic but a sort of argot, imprecise and ugly? Yet despite the barbarism which is slowly extinguishing 'the light of the world', we Athenians still pride ourselves on being able to see things as they are. Show us a stone and we see a stone, not the universe. But like so many others nowadays, poor Julian wanted to believe that man's life is profoundly more significant than it is. His sickness was the sickness of our age. We want so much not to be extinguished at the end that we will go to any length to make conjuror-tricks for one another simply to obscure the bitter, secret knowledge that it is our fate not to be. If Maximus hadn't stolen Julian from us, the bishops would have got him. I am sure of that. At heart he was a Christian mystic gone wrong.

*   *   *

Libanius: Christian mystic! Had Priscus any religious sense he might by now have experienced that knowledge of oneness, neither 'bitter' nor 'secret', which Plotinus and Porphyry, Julian and I, each in his own way – mystically – arrived at. Or failing that, had he been admitted to the mysteries of Eleusis just fourteen miles from his own house in Athens, he might have understood that since the soul *is*, there can be no question of its *not*-being.

But I agree with Priscus about Maximus. I was aware at the time of the magicians' plot to capture Julian, but since I was forbidden to speak to him I could hardly warn him. Yet they did Julian no lasting harm. He sometimes put too much faith in oracles and magic, but he always had a firm grip of logic and he excelled in philosophic argument. He was hardly a Christian mystic. Yet he was a mystic – something Priscus could never understand.

Julian Augustus

Ecebolius was eager to go to Ephesus, rather to my surprise; I had thought he would have wanted to keep me from Maximus. But he was compliant. 'After all, *I* am your teacher, approved by the Emperor. You cannot officially study with Maximus, or anyone else. Not that I would object. Far from it. I am told Maximus is most inspiring, though hopelessly reactionary. But we hardly need worry about your being influenced at this late date. After all, you were taught Christian theology by two great bishops, Eusebius and George. What firmer foundation can any man have? By all means let us visit Ephesus. You will enjoy the intellectual life. And so shall I.'

What Ecebolius had come to enjoy was playing Aristotle to my green Alexander. Everywhere we went, academics were curious to know me. That meant they got to know Ecebolius. In no time at all, he was proposing delicately that he 'exchange' students with them. 'Exchange' meant that they would send him students at Constantinople for which they would receive nothing except the possible favour of the prince. During our travels, Ecebolius made his fortune.

In a snowstorm we were met at the gates of Ephesus by the city prefect and the town council. They were all very nervous.

'It is a great honour for Ephesus to receive the most noble Julian,' said the prefect. 'We are here to serve him, as we have served the most noble Gallus, who has also honoured us by his presence here.' At the mention of Gallus, as though rehearsed, the councillors began to mutter, 'Kind, good, wise, noble.'

'Where is my brother?'

There was a tense pause. The prefect looked anxiously at the councillors. They looked at one another. There was a good deal of energetic brushing of snow from cloaks.

'Your brother,' said the prefect, finally, 'is at court. At Milan. He was summoned by the Emperor last month. There has been no word about him. None at all. Naturally, we hope for the best.'

'And what is the best?'

'Why, that he be made Caesar.' It was not necessary to inquire about the worst.

After due ceremony, we were led to the prefect's house, where I was to stay. Ecebolius was thrilled at the thought that I might soon be half-brother to a Caesar. But I was alarmed. My alarm became panic when later that night Oribasius told me that Gallus had been taken from Ephesus under arrest.

'Was he charged with anything?'

'The Emperor's pleasure. There was no charge. Most people expect him to be executed.'

'Has he given any cause?'

Oribasius shrugged. 'If he is executed, people will give a hundred reasons why the Emperor did the right thing. If he is made Caesar, they will say they knew all along such wisdom and loyalty would be rewarded.'

'If Gallus dies . . .' I shuddered.

'But you're not political.'

'I was born "political" and there is nothing I can do about it. First Gallus, then me.'

'I should think you were safest of all, the scholar-prince.'

'No one is safe.' I felt the cold that night as I have never felt the cold before or since. I don't know what I should have done without Oribasius. He was the first friend I ever had. He is still the best friend I have, and I miss him here in Persia. Oribasius has always been particularly useful in finding out things I would have no way of knowing. People never speak candidly to princes, but Oribasius could get anyone to tell him anything, a trick learned practising medicine. He inspires confidences.

Within a day of our arrival at Ephesus, Oribasius had obtained a full report on Gallus's life in the city. 'He is feared. But he is admired.'

'For his beauty?' I could not resist that. After all, I had spent my childhood hopelessly beguiled by that golden creature.

'He shares his beauty rather liberally with the wives of the local magnates.'

'Naturally.'

'He is thought to be intelligent.'

'He is shrewd.'

'Politically knowledgeable, very ambitious . . .'

'Yet unpopular and feared. Why?'

'A bad temper, occasionally violent.'

'Yes.' I thought of the cedar grove at Macellum.

'People fear him. They don't know why.'

'Poor Gallus.' I almost meant it, too. 'What do they say about me?'

'They wish you would shave your beard.'

'I thought it was looking rather decent lately. A bit like Hadrian's.' I rubbed the now full growth affectionately. Only the colour displeased me: it was even lighter than the hair on my head, which is light brown. To make the beard seem darker and glossier, I occasionally rubbed oil in it. Nowadays, as I go grey, the beard has mysteriously darkened. I am perfectly satisfied with the way it looks. No one else is.

'They also wonder what you are up to.'

'Up to? I should have thought it perfectly plain. I am a student.'

'We are Greeks in these parts.' Oribasius grinned, looking very Greek. 'We never think anything is what it seems to be.'

'Well, I am not about to subvert the state,' I said gloomily. 'My only plot is how to survive.'

In spite of himself, Ecebolius liked Oribasius. 'Because we are really disobeying the Chamberlain, you know. He fixed your household at a certain size and made no allowance for a physician.'

'But Oribasius is a very special physician.'

'Granted, he helped my fever and banished "pain's cruel handmaid . . ." '

'He also has the advantage of being richer than I. He helps us pay the bills.'

'True. Sad truth.' Ecebolius has a healthy respect for money, and because of that I was able to keep Oribasius near me.

We were at Ephesus some days before I was able to see Maximus. He was in retreat, communing with the gods. But we received daily bulletins from his wife. Finally, on the eighth day, at about the second hour, a slave arrived to say that Maximus would be honoured to receive me that afternoon. I prevailed on Ecebolius to allow me to make the visit alone. After much argument he gave in, but only on condition that I later write out for him a full account of everything that was said.

Maximus lived in a modest house on the slopes of Mount Pion, not far from the theatre which is carved out of its side. My guards left me at the door. A servant then showed me into an inner room where I was greeted by a thin, nervous woman.

'I am Placidia, wife of Maximus.' She let go my robe whose hem she had kissed. 'We are so sorry my husband could not see you earlier, but he has been beneath the earth, with the goddess Cybele.' She motioned to a slave who handed her a lighted torch which she gave me. 'My husband is still in darkness. He asks for you to join him there.'

I took the torch and followed Placidia to a room of the house whose fourth wall was covered by a curtain which, when she pulled it back, revealed the mountainside and an opening in the rock. 'You must go to him alone, most noble prince.'

I entered the mountain. For what seemed hours (but must have been only minutes), I stumbled towards a far-off gleam of light which marked the end of the passageway. At last I arrived at what looked to be a well-lit chamber cut in the rock, and filled with smoke. Eagerly, I stepped forward and came up hard against a solid wall, stubbing my toes. I thought I had gone mad. In front of me was a room. But I could not enter it. Then I heard the beautiful deep voice of Maximus: 'See? The life of this world is an Illusion and only the gods are real.'

I turned to my left and saw the chamber I thought I had seen in front of me. The smoke was now gone. The room appeared to be empty. Yet the voice sounded as if the speaker were close beside me. 'You tried to step into a mirror. In the same way, the ignorant try to enter the land of the blessed, only to be turned away by their own reflection. Without surrendering yourself, you may not thread the labyrinth at whose end exists the One.'

My right foot hurt. I was cold. I was both impressed and irritated by the situation. 'I am Julian,' I said, 'of the house of Constantine.'

'I am Maximus, of the house of all the gods.' Then he appeared suddenly at my elbow. He seemed to emerge from the rock. Maximus is tall and well proportioned, with a beard like a grey waterfall and the glowing eyes of a cat. He wore a green robe with curious markings. He took my hand. 'Come in,' he said. 'There are wonders here.'

The room was actually a natural grotto with stalactites hanging from the ceiling and, at its centre, a natural pool of still dark water. Beside the pool was a bronze statue of Cybele, showing the goddess seated and holding in one hand the holy drum. Two stools were the only furnishings in the cave. He invited me to sit down.

'You will go on many journeys,' said Maximus. My heart sank. He sounded like any soothsayer in the agora. 'And I shall accompany you to the end.'

'I could hope for no better teacher,' I said formally, somewhat taken aback. He was presumptuous.

'Do not be alarmed, Julian . . .' He knew exactly what I was thinking. 'I am not forcing myself upon you. Quite the contrary. I am being forced. Just as you are. By something neither of us can control. Nor will it be easy, what we must do together. There is great danger for both of us. Especially for me. I dread being your teacher.'

'But I had hoped . . .'

'I am your teacher,' he concluded. 'What is it that you would most like to know?'

'The truth.'

'The truth of what?'

'Where do we come from and where do we go to, and what is the meaning of the journey?'

'You are Christian.' He said this carefully, making neither a statement nor a question of it. Had there been a witness to this scene, I must have allowed a door in my mind to shut. As it was, I paused. I thought of Bishop George, interminably explaining 'similar' as opposed to 'same'. I heard the deacon chanting the songs of Arius. I heard myself reading the lesson in the chapel at Macellum. Then suddenly I saw before me the leather-bound testament Bishop George had given me: 'Thou shalt not revile the gods.'

'No,' said Maximus gravely. 'For that way lies eternal darkness.'

I was startled. 'I said nothing.'

'You quoted from the book of the Jews, from Exodus. "Thou shalt not revile the gods." '

'But I *said* nothing.'

'You thought it.'

'You can see into my thoughts?'

'When the gods give me the power, yes.'

'Then look now, carefully, and tell me: am I Christian?'

'I cannot speak for you, nor tell you what I see.'

'I believe there does exist a first maker, an absolute power . . .'

'Was it the same god who spoke to Moses "mouth to mouth"?'

'So I have been taught.'

'Yet that god was not absolute. He made the earth and heaven, men and beasts. But according to Moses, he did not make darkness or even matter, since the earth was already there before him, invisible and without form. He was merely the shaper of what already existed. Does one not prefer Plato's god, who caused this universe to come "into being as a living creature, possessing soul and intelligence in very truth, both by the providence of god"?'

'From the *Timaeus*,' I said automatically.

'And then there is the confusion between the book of the Jews and the book of the Nazarene. The god of the first is supposed to be the god of the second. Yet in the second he is father of the Nazarene . . .'

'By grace. They are of similar substance, but not the same.'

Maximus laughed. 'Well learned, my young Arian.'

'I am Arian because I find it impossible to believe that God was briefly a man executed for treason. Jesus was a prophet – a son of God in some mysterious way – yes, but not the One God.'

'Nor even his deputy, despite the efforts of the extraordinary Paul of Tarsus, who tried to prove that the tribal god of the Jews was the universal One God, even though every word Paul says is contradicted by the Jewish holy book. In letters to the Romans and to the Galatians, Paul declared that the god of Moses is the god not only of Jews but also of Gentiles. Yet the Jewish book denies this in a hundred places. As their god said to Moses: "Israel is my son, my first-born." Now if this god of the Jews were indeed, as Paul claimed, the One God, why then did he reserve for a single unimportant race the anointing, the prophets and the law? Why did he allow the rest of mankind to exist thousands of years in darkness, worshipping falsely? Of course the Jews admit that he is a "jealous god". But what an extraordinary thing for the absolute to be! Jealous of what? And cruel, too, for he avenged the sins of the fathers on guiltless children. Is not the creator described by Homer and Plato more likely? that there is one being who encompasses all life – is all life – and from this essential source emanate gods, demons, men? Or to quote the famous Orphic oracle which the Galileans are beginning to appropriate for their own use, "Zeus, Hades, Helios, three gods in one Godhead".'

'From the One many . . .' I began, but with Maximus one never needs to finish sentences. He anticipates the trend of one's thought.

'How can the many be denied? Are all emotions alike? or does each have characteristics peculiarly its own? And if each race has its own qualities, are not those god-given? And, if not god-given, would not these characteristics then be properly symbolized by a specific national god? In the case of the Jews a jealous bad-tempered patriarch. In the case of the effeminate, clever Syrians, a god like Apollo. Or take the Germans and the Celts – who are warlike and fierce – is it accident that they worship Ares, the war god? Or is it inevitable? The early Romans were absorbed by lawmaking and governing – their god? the king of gods, Zeus. And each god has many aspects and many names, for there is as much variety in heaven as there is among men. Some have asked: did we create these gods or did they create us? That is an old debate. Are we a dream in the mind of deity, or is each of us a separate dreamer, evoking his own reality? Though one may not know for certain, all our senses tell us that a single creation does exist and we are contained by it for ever. Now the Christians would impose one final rigid myth on what we know to be various and strange. No, not even myth, for the Nazarene existed as flesh while the gods we worship were never men; rather they are qualities and powers become poetry for our instruction. With the worship of the dead Jew, the poetry ceased. The Christians wish to replace our beautiful legends with the police record of a reforming Jewish rabbi. Out of this unlikely material they hope to make a final synthesis of all the religions ever known. They now appropriate our feast days. They transform local deities into saints. They borrow from our mystery rites, particularly those of Mithras. The priests of Mithas are called "fathers". So the Christians call *their* priests "fathers". They even imitate the tonsure, hoping to impress new converts with the familiar trappings of an older cult. Now they have started to call the Nazarene "saviour" and "healer". Why? Because one of the most beloved of our gods is Asklepios, whom we call "saviour" and "healer".'

'But there is nothing in Mithras to equal the Christian mystery.' I argued for the devil. 'What of the Eucharist, the taking of the bread and wine, when Christ said, "He who eats of my body and drinks of my blood shall have eternal life".'

Maximus smiled. 'I betray no secret of Mithras when I tell you that we, too, partake of a symbolic meal, recalling the words of the Persian prophet Zarathustra, who said to those who worshipped the One God – and Mithras, "He who eats of my body and drinks of my blood, so that he will be made one with me and I with him, the same shall not know salvation." That was spoken six centuries before the birth of the Nazarene.'

I was stunned. 'Zarathustra was a man . . .?'

'A prophet. He was struck down in a temple by enemies. As he lay dying, he said, "May God forgive you even as I do." No, there is nothing sacred to us that the Galileans have not stolen. The main task of their innumerable councils is to try to make sense of all their borrowing. I don't envy them.'

'I have read Porphyry . . .' I began.

'Then you are aware of how the Galileans contradict themselves.'

'But what of the contradictions in Hellenism?'

'Old legends are bound to conflict. But then, we never think of them as *literally* true. They are merely cryptic messages from the gods, who in turn are aspects of the One. We know that we must interpret them. Sometimes we succeed. Sometimes we fail. But the Christians hold to the literal truth of the book which was written about the Nazarene long after his death. Yet even that book so embarrasses them that they must continually alter its meaning. For instance, nowhere does it say that Jesus *was* God . . .'

'Except in John.' I quoted: ' "And the Word was made flesh, and dwelt among us." ' I had not been five years a church reader for nothing.

'That is open to interpretation. What precisely was meant by "Word"? Is it really, as they now pretend, the holy spirit who is also God who is also Jesus? – which brings us again to that triple impiety they call "truth", which in turn reminds us that the most noble Julian also wishes to know the truth.'

'It is what I wish.' I felt strange. The smoke from the torches was thick in the room. All things now appeared indistinct and unreal. Had the walls opened suddenly and the sun blazed down upon us, I should not have been surprised. But Maximus practised no magic that day. He was matter-of-fact.

'No one can tell another man what is true. Truth is all around us. But each must find it in his own way. Plato is part of the truth. So is Homer. So is the story of the Jewish god if one ignores its arrogant claims. Truth is wherever man has glimpsed divinity. Theurgy can achieve this awakening. Poetry can. Or the gods themselves of their own volition can suddenly open our eyes.'

'My eyes are shut.'

'Yes.'

'But I know what it is I want to find.'

'But there is a wall in front of you, like the mirror you tried to walk into.'

I looked at him very hard. 'Maximus, show me a door, and not a mirror.'

He was silent a long time. When he finally spoke, he did not look at me. Instead he studied the face of Cybele. 'You are Christian.'

'I am nothing.'

'But you must be Christian, for that is the religion of your family.'

'I must *appear* to be Christian. Nothing more.'

'You do not fear being a hypocrite?'

'I fear not knowing the truth even more.'

'Are you prepared to be admitted to the secret rites of Mithras?'

'Is that the way?'

'It is a way. If you are willing to make the attempt, I can lead you to the door. But you must cross through alone. I cannot help you pass the gate.'

'And after I pass through?'

'You will know what it is to die and to be born again.'

'Then you shall be my teacher, Maximus. And my guide.'

'Of course I shall be.' He smiled. 'It is our fate. Remember what I said? We have no choice, either of us. Fate has intervened. Together we shall proceed to the end of the tragedy.'

'Tragedy?'

'Human life is tragic: it ends in pain and death.'

'But after the pain? after the death?'

'When you cross the threshold of Mithras, you will know what it is like to be beyond tragedy, to be beyond what is human, to be one with God.'

Priscus: Interesting to observe Maximus in action. He *was* clever. I would have guessed that at their first meeting he would have done tricks. Made the statue of Cybele dance. Something like that. But no. He gives a shrewd attack on Christianity. Then he offers Julian Mithras, a religion bound to appeal to our hero. Mithras was always the favourite deity of Roman emperors, and of many soldiers to this day. Also, Maximus knew that he would be sure of a special relationship to Julian if he were the one who sponsored him during the rites.

There is now no doubt in my mind that at this point in Julian's life almost any of the mystery cults would have got him free of Christianity. He was eager to make the break. Yet it is hard to say quite why, since his mind tended to magic and superstition in precisely the same way the Christian mind does. Admittedly their worship of corpses did not appeal to him, but he was later to find manifestations of 'the One' in even odder places. Had Julian been what he thought he was – a philosopher in the tradition of Plato – one might have understood his dislike of the Christian nonsense. He would have been like you and me. But Julian was concerned, finally, with the idea of personal immortality, the one obsession Christians share with those who are drawn to the old mystery cults.

Despite everything Julian wrote on the subject, I have never understood precisely why he turned against the religion of his family. After all, Christianity offered him nearly everything he needed. If he wanted to partake symbolically of the body of a god, why not remain with the Christians and eat their bread and drink their wine instead of reverting to the bread and wine of Mithras? It is not as if there was anything lacking in Christianity. The Christians have slyly incorporated most of the popular elements of Mithras and Demeter and Dionysos into their own rites. Modern Christianity is an encyclopedia of traditional superstition.

I suspect the origin of Julian's disaffection is in his family. Constantius was a passionate Christian, absorbed by doctrinal disputes. With good reason, Julian hated Constantius. Therefore, he hated Christianity. This puts the matter far too simply, yet I always tend to the obvious view of things since it is usually the correct one, though of course one can never get to the bottom of anything so mysterious as another man's character, and there is a mystery here.

Julian was Christian in everything except his tolerance of others. He was what the Christians would call a saint. Yet he swung fiercely away from the one religion which suited him perfectly, preferring its eclectic origins, which he then tried to systematize into a new combination quite as ridiculous as the synthesis he had rejected. It is a strange business and there is no satisfactory explanation for Julian's behaviour. Of course he claimed that Bishop George's partisanship disgusted him as a boy, and that Porphyry and Plotinus opened his eyes to the absurdity of Christian claims. Well and good. But then why turn to something equally absurd? Granted, no educated man can accept the idea of a Jewish rebel as god. But having rejected that myth, how can one then believe that the Persian hero-god Mithras was born of light striking rock, on December 25th, with shepherds watching his birth? (I am told that the Christians have just added those shepherds to the birth of Jesus.) Or that Mithras lived in a fig tree which fed and clothed him, that he fought with the sun's first creation, the bull, that he was dragged by it (thus symbolizing man's suffering) until the bull escaped; finally, at the command of the sun god, Mithras stabs the bull with a knife and from the beast's body come flowers, herbs, wheat; from the blood, wine; from the seed, the first man and woman. Then Mithras is called up to heaven, after celebrating a sacramental last supper. Time's end will be a day of judgement when all will rise from their graves and evil will be destroyed while the good will live for ever in the light of the sun.

Between the Mithraic story and its Christian sequel I see no essential difference. Admittedly, the Mithraic code of conduct is more admirable than the Christian. Mithraists believe that right action is better than contemplation. They favour old-fashioned virtues like courage and self-restraint. They were the first to teach that strength is gentleness. All of this is rather better than the Christian hysteria which vacillates between murder of heretics on the one hand and a cringing rejection of this world on the other. Nor can a Mithraist be absolved of sin by a sprinkle of water. Ethically, I find Mithras the best of all the mystery cults. But it is absurd to say it is any more 'true' than its competitors. When one becomes absolute about myth and magic, the result can only be madness.

Julian speaks continually of his love of Hellenism. He honestly believed he loved Plato and reasonable discourse. Actually, what he craved was what so many desire in this falling time: assurance of personal immortality. He chose to reject the Christian way for reasons which I find obscure, while settling on an equal absurdity. Of course I am sympathetic to him. He dealt the Christians some good blows and that delighted me. But I cannot sympathize with his fear of extinction. Why is it so important to continue after death? We never question the demonstrable fact that before birth we did not exist, so why should we fear becoming once more what we were to begin with? I am in no hurry to depart. But I look on nothing as just that: *no thing*. How can one fear no thing?

As for the various ceremonies and trials the Mithraic initiate must undergo, the less said the better. I understand that one of the twelve tortures is the pulling out one by one of the pubic hairs, a most spiritual discipline. I was also told that part of the ceremonies are conducted while everyone is roaring drunk and trying to jump over ditches blindfolded, a symbol no doubt of the bewildering life of the flesh. But men are impressed by secret rites, the more gruesome and repellent the better. How sad we are, how terrified to be men!

Libanius: It is not often one finds a philosopher so entirely lacking in the religious sense. It is like being born unable to perceive colours which are plain to everyone else. Priscus does have a logical mind and a precise way of stating things, but he is blind to what truly matters. Like Julian, I was admitted to the Mithraic rites during my student days. The impression the mysteries made on me was profound, though I confess that the effect was not as revealing – for me – as it was for Julian. But I had never been a Christian, so I was not making a dramatic and dangerous break with the world I belonged to. However, for Julian it was a brave thing to do. Had Constantius learned of what he had done, it might have cost him his life. Fortunately, Maximus managed the affair so skilfully that Constantius never knew that at the age of nineteen his cousin ceased to be a Christian, in a cave beneath Mount Pion.

Priscus seems to have missed the point of the Mithraic mysteries, which does not surprise me. Priscus applauds our high ethical standards. We are grateful to him. But he finds the rites 'repellent'. Of course he knows about them only by hearsay, since no one who has been initiated may recount what happens in the cave. But though the 'trials' are often disagreeable, the revelation is worth all the pain that one has borne. I for one cannot imagine a world without Mithras.

Priscus observes with his usual harsh candour that the Christians are gradually absorbing various aspects of the cult. A thought suddenly occurs to me: might not this be the way in which we finally conquer? Is it not possible that the absorber will become so like the absorbed that in time they will be us?

Julian Augustus

In March 351, I was admitted to the mysteries of Mithras. On that day I watched the rising of the sun; and I watched its setting, taking care to be unobserved, for since Constantius had made it illegal to pray to the sun, people had even been arrested for watching a sunset. Spies and informers were everywhere.

I had told Ecebolius that I intended to spend the day hunting on the slopes of Mount Pion. Since he hated hunting, he excused himself as I knew he would. He quoted Homer. I quoted Horace. He quoted Virgil. I quoted Theocritus. Together we used up nearly all of literature's references to hunting.

The next obstacle was the bodyguard. Twelve soldiers and one officer were assigned to my household. At all times I was attended by at least two men. What to do about them? It was Maximus who decided that since Mithras is the soldier's religion, at least two of the soldiers should prove sympathetic. Maximus was right. Of the twelve, five were Mithraists. It was then an easy matter to get two of the five assigned to me for the day. As Mithraic brothers, they were under the seal of secrecy.

An hour before dawn, Oribasius, the soldiers and I left the house. At the mountain's edge we were met by Maximus and nine fathers. In silence we climbed the slope. At a pre-ordained spot, beneath a fig tree, we stopped and waited for the sun to rise.

The sky turned pale. The morning star shone blue. Dark clouds broke. Then just as the sun appeared on the horizon, a single shaft of light struck the rock behind us and I realized that it was not just ordinary rock, but a door into the mountainside. We prayed then to the sun and to his companion Mithras, our saviour.

When the sun was at last above the horizon, Maximus opened the door into the mountain and we entered a small cave with seats carved out of the rock. Here Oribasius and I were told to wait while the fathers of Mithras withdrew into yet another cave, the inner sanctuary. Thus began the most momentous day of my life. The day of the honey and of the bread and the wine; the day of the seven gates and the seven planets; the day of challenges and of passwords; the day of prayer and, at its end (past Raven, Bride, Soldier, Lion, Persian, Courier of the Sun, and Father), the day of *Nama Nama Sebesio*.

Libanius: Of all the mysteries, excepting those at Eleusis, the Mithraic is the most inspiring, for in the course of it one actually experiences the folly of earthly vanity. At each of the seven stages, the initiate acts out what his soul will one day experience as it rises amongst the seven spheres, losing one by one its human faults. At Ares, the desire for war returns to its source; at Zeus, ambition is lost; at Aphrodite, sex, and so on until the soul is purged. Then . . . But *I* can say no more. *Nama Nama Sebesio.*

Julian Augustus

When the day ended, Oribasius and I stumbled from the cave, born again.

It was then that it happened. As I looked at the setting sun, I was possessed by light. What is given to few men was given to me. I saw the One. I was absorbed by Helios and my veins coursed not with blood but light.

I saw it all. I saw the simplicity at the heart of creation. The thing which is impossible to grasp without the help of divinity, for it is beyond language and beyond mind: yet it is so simple that I marvelled at how one could *not* have known what is always there, a part of us just as we are part of it. What happened inside the cave was a testing and a learning, but what happened to me outside the cave was revelation.

I saw the god himself as I knelt among sage bushes, the red slanting sunlight full in my face. I heard that which cannot be written or told and I saw that which cannot be recorded in words or images. Yet even now, years later, it is as vivid in retrospect as it was at the time. For I was chosen on that steep mountainside to do the great work in which I am now engaged: the restoration of the worship of the One God, in all his beautiful singularity.

I remained kneeling until the sun was gone. Then I knelt in darkness for what I am told was an hour. I knelt until Oribasius became alarmed and awakened me . . . or put me to sleep, for the 'real' world ever since has seemed to me the dream while my vision of Helios is the reality.

'Are you all right?'

I nodded and got to my feet. 'I have seen . . .' But I stopped. I could not say what I had seen. Even now, writing this memoir, I cannot describe what I experienced since there is nothing comparable in ordinary human experience.

But Maximus immediately recognized what had happened to me. 'He has been chosen,' he said. 'He knows.'

Silently we returned to the city. I did not want to talk to anyone, not even to Maximus, for I was still enfolded by wings of light. Even the back of my hand where I had received the sacred tattoo did not hurt me. But at the city gate my absorption was rudely shattered by a large crowd which surrounded me, shouting, 'Great news!'

I was bewildered. All I could think was: has the god remained with me? is what I saw visible to all? I tried to speak to Maximus and Oribasius but we could not make ourselves heard.

At the prefect's house, I found Ecebolius with the town prefect and what looked to be the whole council. When they saw me, they fell to their knees. For an instant I thought it was indeed the end of the world and that I had been sent as messenger to separate the good from the bad. But Ecebolius quickly dispelled all thought of apocalypse.

'Most noble Julian, your brother . . .' All about us, men began to repeat Gallus's names and titles. '. . . . has been raised by the divine Augustus to share with him the purple. Gallus is Caesar in the East. He is also to be married to Constantia, divine sister of the divine Augustus!'

There was loud cheering and eager hands touched my robe, my hands, my arms. Favours were requested, blessings demanded. Finally, I broke through the mob and got inside the house.

'But why are they all behaving like lunatics?' I turned on Ecebolius, as though it were his fault.

'Because you are now the brother of a reigning Caesar.'

'Much good it will do them . . . or me.' This was unwise, but it relieved me to say it.

'Surely you don't want them to love you for yourself?' Oribasius teased me. 'You quite enjoyed the attention, until you heard the news.'

'Only because I thought it was the sun . . .' I stopped myself just in time.

'The sun?' Ecebolius looked puzzled.

'Only the son of God should be treated in this fashion,' said Maximus smoothly. 'Men should not *worship* other men, not even princes.'

Ecebolius nodded. 'A relic of the bad old days, I'm afraid. The Augustus of Rome is of course "divine" though not truly a god as men used to think. But come in, come in. The baths are ready. And the prefect is giving us a banquet to celebrate the good news.'

So I beheld the One God on the same day that I learned my brother had been made Caesar. The omen was plain enough. Each was now set in his destiny. From that day on I was Hellenist or, as the Galileans like to call me (behind my back, of course!), apostate. And Gallus reigned in the East.

6

'Naturally the Caesar is concerned.'

'But without cause.'

'Without cause? You are a pupil of Maximus.'

'I am also a pupil of Ecebolius.'

'But he has not been with you for a year. Your brother feels that you are in need of a spiritual guide, especially now.'

'But Maximus *is* responsible.'

'Maximus is not a Christian. *Are you?*' The question came at me like a stone from a sling. I stared a long moment at the black-robed Deacon Aetius of Antioch. He stared serenely back. I was close to panic. What did they know of me at Gallus's court?

'How can you doubt that I am a Christian?' I said finally. 'I was instructed by two great bishops. I am a church reader. I attend every important church ceremony here at Pergamon.' I looked at him, simulating righteousness doubted. 'Where could such a rumour get started? If there is such a rumour.'

'You cannot be seen too often in the company of a man like Maximus without people wondering.'

'What shall I do?'

'Give him up.' The answer was prompt.

'Is that my brother's order?'

'It is my suggestion. Your brother is concerned. That is all. He sent me here to question you. I have.'

'Are you satisfied?'

Aetius smiled. 'Nothing ever satisfies me, most noble Julian. But I shall tell the

Caesar that you are a regular communicant of the church. I shall also tell him that you will no longer study with Maximus.'

'If that is the wisest course, then that is the course I shall take.' This ambiguity seemed to satisfy Aetius. My friends often tell me that I might have made a good lawyer.

As I escorted Aetius to the street, he looked about him and said, 'The owner of this house . . .'

'. . . is Oribasius.'

'An excellent physician.'

'Is it wise for me to see him?' I could not resist this.

'A highly suitable companion,' said Aetius smoothly. He paused at the door to the street. 'Your brother, the Caesar, often wonders why you do not come to visit him at Antioch. He feels that court life might have a . . . "polishing" effect upon you. The word is his, not mine.'

'I'm afraid I was not made for a court, even one as celebrated as my brother's. I resist all attempts to polish me, and I detest politicians.'

'A wise aversion.'

'And a true one. I want only to live as I do, as a student.'

'Studying to what end?'

'To know myself. What else?'

'Yes. What else?' Aetius got into his carriage. 'Be very careful, most noble Julian. And remember: a prince has no friends. Ever.'

'Thank you, Deacon.'

Aetius departed. I went back into the house. Oribasius was waiting for me.

'You heard every word?' I hardly made a question of it. Oribasius and I have never had any secrets between us. On principle, he eavesdrops.

'We've been indiscreet, to say the least.'

I nodded. I was gloomy. 'I suppose I shall have to stop seeing Maximus, at least for a while.'

'You might also insist that he not talk to everyone about his famous pupil.'

I sighed. I knew that Maximus tended – tends – to trade on his relationship with me. Princes get very used to that. I don't resent it. In fact, I am happy if my friends prosper as a result of knowing me. I had learned Oribasius's lesson, and I do not expect to be loved for myself. After all, I don't love others for themselves, only for what they can teach me. Since nothing is free, to each his price.

I summoned a secretary and wrote Maximus asking him to remain at Ephesus until further notice. I also wrote a note to the bishop of Pergamon to tell him that I would read the lesson on the following Sunday.

'Hypocrite,' said Oribasius when the secretary had gone.

'A long-lived hypocrite is preferable to a dead . . . what?' I often have trouble finishing epigrams. Or rather I start one without having first thought through to the end, a bad habit.

'A dead *reader*. Aetius has a good deal of influence with Gallus, hasn't he?'

'So they say. He is his confessor. But who can control my brother?' Without thinking, I had lowered my voice to a whisper. For Gallus had become as suspicious of treason as Constantius. His spies were everywhere.

I blame Gallus's wife Constantia for the overt change in his character. She was Constantius's sister and took it for granted that conspiracy is the natural business of the human race. I never met this famous lady but I am told that she was as cruel as Gallus, and far more intelligent. She was also ambitious, which he was not. He was quite content to remain Caesar in the East. But she wanted him to be the Augustus and she plotted the death of her own brother to achieve this end. As for Gallus, even now I cannot bear to write about his reign.

Priscus: I can. And you certainly can! After all, you were living at Antioch while that little beast was Caesar.

Curiously enough, Julian almost never mentioned Gallus to me, or to anyone. I have always had a theory – somewhat borne out by the memoir – that Julian was unnaturally attracted to his brother. He continually refers to his beauty. He also tends to write of him in that hurt tone one uses to describe a lover who has been cold. Julian professes to find mysterious what everyone else found only too obvious: Gallus's cruelty. Julian was naïve, as I find myself continually observing (if I repeat myself, do forgive me and blame it on our age).

Actually, the member of the family for whom I have the most sympathy is Constantius. He was quite a good ruler, you know. We tend to undervalue him because his intelligence was of the second rank, and his religious mania troubling. But he governed well, considering that he had problems of a sort which might have made any man a monster. He made some of his worst mistakes for the best of reasons, like creating Gallus Caesar.

It is significant that Julian blames Gallus's wife for the reign of terror in the East. I had always thought that they were equally to blame. But you lived through what must have been a terrible time. You doubtless know who was responsible for what.

Libanius: Yes, I do know. At the beginning, we all had great hopes for Gallus. I recall vividly Gallus's first appearance before the senate of Antioch. How hopeful we were. He was indeed as handsome as men say, though that day he was suffering from a heat rash, as fair people sometimes do in our sultry climate. But despite a mottled face, he carried himself well. He looked as one born to rule. He made us a most graceful speech. Afterwards, I was presented to him by my old friend Bishop Meletius.

'Oh, yes.' Gallus frowned. 'You are that teacher-fellow who denies God.'

'I deny God nothing, Caesar. My heart is open to him at all times.'

'Libanius is really most admirable, Caesar.' Meletius always enjoyed making me suffer.

'I am sure he is.' Then Gallus gave me a smile so dazzling that I was quite overwhelmed. 'Come see me,' he said, 'and I shall personally convert you.'

A few weeks later, to my surprise, I received an invitation to the palace. When I arrived at the appointed hour, I was shown into a large room where, side by side on a couch, lay Gallus and Constantia.

In the centre of the room two nude boxers were pummelling one another to death. When I had recovered from my first shock at this indecent display, I tried to make my presence known. I coughed. I mumbled a greeting. But I was ignored. Gallus and Constantia were completely absorbed by the bloody spectacle. As the world knows, I hate gladiatorial demonstrations because they reduce men to the level of beasts – and I do not mean those unfortunates who are forced to perform. I mean those who watch.

I was particularly shocked by Constantia. It was hard to realize that this bright-eyed unwomanly spectator was the daughter of Constantine the Great, sister of the Augustus, wife of the Caesar. She seemed more like an unusually cruel courtesan. Yet she *was* distinguished-looking in the Flavian way – big jaw, large nose, grey eyes. As we watched the sweating, bloody men, she would occasionally shout to one or the other, 'Kill him!' Whenever a particularly effective blow was dealt, she would gasp in a curiously intimate way, like a woman in the sexual act. Constantia was most alarming.

We watched those boxers until one man finally killed the other. As the loser fell, Gallus leapt from his couch and threw his arms around the bloody victor, as though he had done him some extraordinary service. Then Gallus began to kick the dead man, laughing and shouting gleefully. He looked perfectly deranged. I have never seen a man's face quite so revealing of the beast within.

'Stop it, Gallus!' Constantia had noticed me at last. She was on her feet.

'What?' He looked at her blankly. Then he saw me. 'Oh, yes,' he said. He straightened his tunic. Slaves came forward and removed the dead boxer. Constantia approached me with a radiant smile. 'How happy we are to see the famous Libanius here, in our palace.' I saluted her formally, noticing with some surprise that her normal voice was low and musical, and that her Greek was excellent. In an instant she had transformed herself from Fury to queen.

Gallus came forward and gave me his hand to kiss. I got blood on my lips.

'Good, very good,' he said, eyes unfocused like a man drunk. Then without another word, the Caesar of the East and his queen swept past me and that was the end of the only private audience I was ever to have with either of them. I was most unnerved.

During the next few years the misdeeds of the couple were beyond anything since Caligula. To begin with, they were both eager for money. To further her political objectives Constantia needed all the gold she could amass. She tried everything: blackmail, the sale of public offices, confiscation. One of her fund-raising attempts involved a family I knew. It was a peculiar situation. When the daughter married an extremely handsome youth from Alexandria, her mother, an ordinarily demure matron – or so we all thought – promptly fell in love with him. For a year she tried unsuccessfully to seduce her son-in-law. Finally, he told her that if she did not stop importuning him, he would return to Alexandria. Quite out of her mind with rage, the woman went to Constantia and offered that noble queen a small fortune for the arrest and execution of her son-in-law. Constantia took the money; and the unfortunate youth was executed on a trumped-up charge. Then Constantia, who was not without a certain bitter humour, sent the matron her son-in-law's genitals with the brief note: 'At last!' The woman lost her mind. Antioch was scandalized. And the days of terror began.

At times it seemed almost as if Gallus and Constantia had deliberately studied the lives of previous monsters with an eye to recreating old deeds of horror. Nero used to roam the streets at night with a band of rowdies, pretending he was an ordinary young buck on the town. So did Gallus. Caligula used to ask people what they thought of the emperor and if their answer was unflattering, he would butcher them on the spot. So did Gallus. Or tried to. Unfortunately for him, Antioch – unlike early imperial Rome – has the most elaborate street lighting in the world. Our night is like noon in most cities, so Gallus was almost always recognized. As a result, the praetorian prefect of the East, Thalassios, was able to persuade him that not only was it unbecoming for a Caesar to rove the streets at night, it was also dangerous. Gallus abandoned his prowling.

During Gallus's third year as Caesar, there was a famine in Syria. When the food shortages at Antioch began, Gallus tried to fix prices at a level which would make it possible for everyone to buy grain. Even wise rulers from time to time make this mistake. It never works since the result is usually the precise opposite of the one intended. Grain is either held back from the market or bought up by speculators who resell it at a huge profit, increasing the famine. Men are like this and there is nothing to be done about them. The senate of Antioch has many faults, but its members are sound businessmen with an understanding of the market which is their life. They warned Gallus of the dangers of his policy. He ordered them to obey him. When they continued to resist him, he sent his own guards into the senate chamber, arrested the leading senators and condemned them to death.

Antioch has reason to be grateful to both Thalassios and Nebridius, the Count of the East. These two brave men told Gallus that if he went through with the executions, they would appeal to the Augustus and demand the Caesar's removal. It was a brave thing to do, and to everyone's surprise they carried the day. Gallus released the senators, and that was the end of the matter. For some months Antioch was relieved to know that in Thalassios the city had a defender. But then Thalassios died of fever. Of course it was rumoured that he had been poisoned, but I happen to know that it was indeed the fever that he died of, as we shared the same doctor. But I do not mean to write the history of Gallus, which is so well known.

Julian Augustus

After Aetius's visit to me, I met Maximus only in secret. I arranged this by seeing to it that the guards who accompanied me were brothers in Mithras. I don't think I was once betrayed during the three years I lived with Oribasius at Pergamon. I also made a point of becoming a friend of the bishop of the city. With him, I observed every Galilean festival. I hated myself for this deception, but I had no choice.

During these years, I was free to travel wherever I pleased in the East. I could even visit Constantinople, though the Chamberlain's office suggested tactfully that I not live there since it was, after all, the imperial capital *without*, at present, an emperor in residence, which meant that any visit I chose to make could be construed as . . . I understood perfectly and stayed away.

My request for permission to go to Athens was rejected. I don't know why. Gallus sent me several invitations to come to Antioch, but I was always able to avoid accepting them. I think he was relieved not to have me near him. However, he was most conscientious in his role as older brother and guardian, not to mention ruler. I received weekly bulletins from him asking about my spiritual health. He was eager, he said, for me to be a devout and good man, like himself. I think he was perfectly sincere in his exhortations. His fault was a common one. He simply did not know what he was; he saw no flaw in himself, a not unusual blindness and preferable, on the whole, to being unable to find any virtue in oneself.

My friendship with Oribasius is the only intimate one I have ever had – the result, I suppose, of having never known the ordinary life of a family. Oribasius is both friend and brother, even though we are not much alike in disposition. He is sceptical and experimental, interested only in the material world. I am the opposite. He balances me. Or tries to. And I think at times I give him some inkling of what the metaphysical is like. For nearly four years we lived together, travelled together, studied together. We even shared a mistress for a time, though this caused some disturbance since I found, to my surprise, that I have a jealous nature. I had never forgiven the Antiochene at Macellum for preferring Gallus to me. Yet I should have. After all, Gallus was older and handsomer than

I. Even so, I had been resentful. I did not realize to what extent, until I was again put in exactly the same situation. One afternoon I overheard Oribasius and our mutual mistress – a blue-eyed Gaul – making love. I heard their heavy breathing. I heard the leather thongs of the bed creak. Suddenly I wanted to murder them both. I knew then exactly what it was like to be Gallus, and I almost fainted at the violence of my own response. But the moment quickly passed and I was filled with shame.

During those years, Maximus taught me many things. He showed me mysteries. He made it possible for me to contemplate the One. He was the perfect teacher. Also, contrary to legend, he did not in any way try to excite my ambition. We never spoke of my becoming emperor. It was the one forbidden subject.

Priscus: This is simply not true. From certain things both Julian and Maximus said to me, I *know* that they were busy plotting to make Julian emperor. Maximus was not about to waste his time on a minor prince, nor was Oribasius – even though his friendship with Julian was genuine, or as genuine as anyone's relations can be with a prince.

I have been told of at least one séance where Maximus was advised by one of his invisible friends that Julian was destined to become emperor. I also know that Sosipatra and a number of other magicians were secret partisans. Of course after Julian became emperor, every magician in Asia claimed to have had a hand in his success. I can't think why Julian wanted to deny what so many of us know to have been true. Perhaps to discourage others from plotting against *him*, as he plotted against Constantius.

Libanius: 'Plotted' is the wrong word, though of course Julian is disingenuous in his narrative. I agree with Priscus that Maximus and Oribasius were already looking forward to the day when their friend would be, if not Augustus, at least Caesar. I am also perfectly certain that Maximus consulted forbidden oracles, and all the rest. Sosipatra told me as much a few years ago: 'The goddess Cybele always favoured Julian, and said so. We were all so grateful to her for her aid.'

But I strongly doubt that there was any political plot. How could there be? Julian had very little money. He was guarded by a detachment of household troops whose commander was directly answerable to the Grand Chamberlain. Also, I do not believe that Julian at this point wanted the principate. He was a devoted student. He was terrified of the court. He had never commanded a single soldier in war or peace. How could he then, at the age of twenty, dream of becoming emperor? Or rather he might 'dream' – in fact we know that he did – but he could hardly have *planned* to take the throne.

Julian Augustus

In the autumn of 353, Gallus made a state visit to Pergamon. It was the first time we had met since we were boys at Macellum. I stood with the town prefect and the local dignitaries in front of the senate house and watched Gallus receive the homage of the city.

During the five years since we had seen one another, I had become a man with a full beard. But Gallus had remained exactly as he was, the beautiful youth whom all admired. I confess that I had a return of the old emotion when he embraced me formally and I looked once again into those familiar blue eyes. What was the old emotion? A loss of will, I should say. Whatever he wanted me to do I would do. Gallus, by existing, robbed me of strength.

'We are pleased to see once again our beloved and most noble brother.' Gallus had by now completely assumed the imperial manner. Before I could reply, Gallus had turned to the bishop of Pergamon. 'He is, we have heard, a pillar of the true church.'

'Indeed, Caesar, the most noble Julian is a worthy son of holy church.' I was extremely grateful to the bishop. Also, I was rather pleased that my efforts to appear a devout Galilean had been so successful.

Gallus then made a graceful speech to the city fathers, who were so charmed by him that they were obviously puzzled at how this enchanting creature had ever got the reputation of being a cruel and frivolous despot. Gallus could charm anyone, even me.

That night a dinner was given him at the prefect's palace. He behaved himself quite well, though I noticed that he did not cut his wine with water. As a result, he was drunk by the end of the evening. Yet he maintained his dignity and only a slight slowness of speech betrayed his state. Though I sat beside him during dinner, he did not speak to me once. All his efforts were bent on delighting the city prefect. I was miserable, wondering in what way I had managed to offend him. Oribasius, who sat across the room with the minor functionaries of the court, winked at me encouragingly. But I was not encouraged.

The dinner ended, Gallus suddenly turned to me and said, 'You come with me.' And so I followed him as he moved through the bowing courtiers to his bedroom, where two eunuchs were waiting for him.

I had never before seen the etiquette of a Caesar's bedchamber and I watched, fascinated, as the eunuchs, murmuring ceremonial phrases, undressed Gallus while he lolled in an ivory chair, completely unaware of them. He was without self-consciousness or modesty. When he was completely undressed, he waved them away with the command 'Bring us wine!' Then while the wine was served us, he talked to me or rather *at* me. In the lamplight his face glowed red from drink and the blond hair looked white as it fell across his brow. The body, I noticed, though still beautifully shaped, was beginning to grow thick at the belly.

'Constantia wants to know you. She talks of you often. But of course she couldn't come here. One of us must always be at Antioch. Spies. Traitors. No one is honest. Do you realize that? No one. You can never trust anyone, not even your own flesh and blood.'

I tried to protest loyalty at this point. But Gallus ignored me. 'All men are evil. I found that out early. They are born in sin, live in sin, die in sin. Only God can save us. I pray that he will save me.' Gallus made the sign of a cross on his bare chest.

'But it is a fine thing in an evil world to be Caesar. From here,' he indicated a height, 'you can see them all. You can see them at their games. But they can't see you. Sometimes at night, I walk the streets in disguise. I listen to them. I watch them, knowing I can do anything to them I want and no one can touch me. If I want to rape a woman or kill a man in an alley, I can. Sometimes I do.' He frowned. 'But it is evil. I know it. I try not to. Yet I feel that when I do these things there is something higher which acts *through* me. I am a child of God. Unworthy as I am, he created me and to him I shall return. What I am, he wanted me to be. That is why I am good.'

I must say I was stunned by this particular self-estimate. But my face showed only respectful interest.

'I build churches. I establish religious orders. I stamp out heresy wherever I find it. I am an active agent for the good. I must be. It is what I was born for. I can hardly believe you are my brother.' He shifted his thought without a pause. He looked at me for the first time. The famous blue eyes were bloodshot in the full lamplight.

'*Half*-brother, Gallus.'

'Even so. We are the same blood, which is what matters. That is what binds me to Constantius. And you to me. We are the chosen of God to do the work of his church on earth.'

At this point an extraordinarily pretty girl slipped quietly into the room. Gallus did not acknowledge her presence, so neither did I. He continued to talk and drink, while she made love to him in front of me. I suppose it was the most embarrassing moment of my life. I tried not to watch. I looked at the ceiling. I looked at the floor. But my eyes continually strayed back to my brother as he reclined on the couch, hardly moving, as the girl with infinite skill and delicacy served him.

'Constantius will do anything I ask him. That is what blood means. He will also listen to his sister, my wife. She is the most important woman in the world. A perfect wife, a great queen.' He shifted his position on the couch so that his legs were spread apart.

'I hope you marry well. You could, you know. Constantius has another sister, Helena. She's much older than you, but that makes no difference when it is a matter of blood. Perhaps he will marry you to her. Perhaps he will even make you a Caesar, like me. Would that please you?'

I almost missed the question, my eyes riveted on what the girl was doing. Oribasius says that I am a prude. I suppose he is right. I know that I was sweating with nervous tension as I watched the ravishing of Gallus. 'No,' I stammered. 'I have no wish to be Caesar. Only a student. I am perfectly happy.'

'Everyone lies,' said Gallus sadly. 'Even you. Even flesh and blood. But there's very little chance of your being raised up. Very little. I have the East, Constantius the West. You are not needed. Do you have girls in your household?'

'One.' My voice broke nervously.

'One!' He shook his head wonderingly. 'And your friend? The one you live with?'

'Oribasius.'

'Is he your lover?'

'No!'

'I wondered. It's perfectly all right. You're not Hadrian. What you do doesn't matter. Though if you like boys, I suggest you keep to slaves. It's politically dangerous to have anything to do with a man of your own class.'

'I am not interested . . .' I began, but he continued right through me.

'Slaves are always best. Particularly stableboys and grooms.' The blue eyes flashed suddenly: for an instant his face was transfigured by malice. He wanted me to recall what I had seen that day in the clearing. 'But suit yourself. Anyway, my only advice to you, my only warning to you, not only as your brother but as your ruler . . .' He stopped suddenly and took a deep breath. The girl had finished. She got to her feet and stood in front of him, head bowed. He smiled, charmingly. Then he reached up and with all his strength struck her full in the face. She staggered back, but made no sound. Then at a gesture from him, she withdrew.

Gallus turned to me as though nothing had happened and picked up his sentence where he had left off. '. . . under no circumstances are you to see this magician Maximus. There are already enough rumours that you may have lost your faith. I know that you haven't. How could you? We are of the house of Constantine the Great, the equal of the Apostles. We are the chosen of God. But even so . . .' He yawned. He lay back on the couch. 'Even so . . .' he repeated and shut his eyes. I waited a moment for him to continue. But he was asleep.

The eunuchs reappeared. One placed a silk coverlet over Gallus. The other removed the wine. They acted as though what I had witnessed was a perfectly ordinary evening; perhaps it was. As Gallus began drunkenly to snore, I tiptoed from the room.

Priscus: I always thought Julian might have been a happier man had he been a bit more like Gallus. No one can say that Gallus did not enjoy himself. His was an exemplary life of complete self-indulgence. I could not be more envious of him.

Libanius: Obviously Priscus has found his ideal.

Within months of the state visit to Pergamon, Gallus fell. For two years the Emperor had been receiving disquieting reports about Gallus. Nebridius had told him bluntly that if Gallus were not removed as Caesar there would be civil war in Syria. In his last letter to Constantius, Thalassios had said much the same thing.

One final incident brought matters to a head. The food shortage had grown worse. The lower classes were rioting. Having failed at price fixing, Gallus determined to leave Antioch as quickly as possible. As pretext, he announced that he was planning to invade Persia (though he did not have sufficient troops to conquer a mud village on the Nile).

The day Gallus left the city, the senate met him in front of the memorial to Julius Caesar. A considerable crowd had also turned out to see him, but they were not interested in saying farewell to their Caesar. They wanted food, and they said so. They made the most terrible racket. I know. I was there. I have never seen such an angry mob. Behind a row of household troops with drawn swords, the Caesar and the senate exchanged formalities while all around us the mob roared, pressing closer and closer to where we stood. Even Gallus was alarmed.

Then Theophilus, the governor of Syria, came forward to make a speech to the Caesar. Now Theophilus was an excellent official but he was not popular. Why? Who knows? The Antiochenes are completely frivolous in public matters. If a cruel tyrant is witty, they will adore him. But if their ruler is a good man, slow of speech, they will despise him. They despised Theophilus. They jeered his speech. Then the mob began to shout: 'Food! Food!'

During this, I watched Gallus. At first he looked baffled; then alarmed; then – one could observe his very thought – crafty. He raised his hand for silence. But the shouting continued. So Theophilus motioned to the drummers, who set up an ominous rolling. The crowd fell silent.

Gallus spoke. 'My good people, the heart of your Caesar grieves for you. Yet he is puzzled. You say you lack food. But why? There is food in Antioch. There is plenty of grain in the warehouses. Your Caesar put it there for you.'

'Then give it to us!' A voice rang out.

Gallus shook his head. 'But it is yours already. Your governor knows this.' He turned to the stunned governor. 'Theophilus, I have told you to feed the people. Why have you disobeyed me? Why have you been so cruel? Even if you are in league with the speculators, you must take pity on the people. The poor are hungry, Theophilus. Feed them!'

In all my long life I have never witnessed such a vicious scene. Gallus deliberately incited the people against his own governor. Then he rode off at the head of the legions, leaving us to the now violent mob. Like the rest of the senate, I bolted. Fortunately no one was hurt except Theophilus, who was torn to pieces. That day Gallus lost what small support he had among us.

When Constantius received news of the Theophilus affair, he realized at last that Gallus must be recalled. But it is easier to create a Caesar than to destroy one. Constantius knew that if he were to move against Gallus, there would be civil war. So Constantius proceeded cautiously. His first move was to order Gallus's army to rendezvous in Serbia, preparatory to a campaign on the Danube. Inactive troops, said Constantius in a diplomatic letter to the Caesar, are prone to mutiny. So Gallus was left with only his personal guard and a single detachment of targeteers. Then Constantius instructed the prefect Domitian (until recently Count of the Sacred Largesse and a financial expert) to proceed to Syria, as though on a routine tour of the provinces. At Antioch, Domitian was to persuade Gallus to obey the Emperor's order to come to Milan 'for consultation'. Unfortunately, Domitian was vain and overbearing and perfectly confident that no one was so clever as he. I don't know why, but this seems to be a common trait of finance ministers.

Domitian arrived at Antioch to find Gallus again in residence, after a month's campaign on the Persian border. But instead of going first to the Caesar's palace as protocol requires, Domitian proceeded to military headquarters, announcing that he was too ill to come to court. For several weeks Domitian remained at headquarters, plotting against Gallus and sending back highly coloured reports to the Emperor concerning the Caesar's doings. At last Gallus ordered Domitian to present himself at a meeting of the consistory. He did, and in a scene of unrivalled insolence Domitian told Gallus that if he did not immediately obey the Emperor and go to Milan, 'I shall personally order your supplies cut off.' He then marched out of the palace and returned to headquarters, where he thought he was safe.

I was not present at that historic meeting of the Caesar's consistory, but I have been told by those who were there that it was an astonishing confrontation and that for once all sympathy was with the Caesar who had been insulted.

Gallus promptly struck back. He ordered Domitian arrested on a charge of lese-majesty. To give the gloss of legitimacy to this arrest, he sent his legal adviser, the quaestor Montius, to instruct the troops in how to behave. Montius was an elderly man, with a passion for correct procedure. He told Gallus bluntly that the Caesar had no authority over a prefect engaged on the Emperor's business. Gallus ignored this advice.

Montius then appeared before the troops who had been called to assembly, and he told them that what Gallus intended to do was not only illegal but highly dangerous and that any soldier who obeyed the Caesar would be committing treason. 'But should you decide to arrest the Emperor's prefect then I advise you first to overthrow the Emperor's statues, so that your revolt will at least be honest.'

The troops were confused, to say the least. But not for long. When Gallus heard what Montius had done, he rushed to the assembly ground and harangued the troops as only he knew how to do.

'I am in danger. You are in danger. We are all in danger because of would-be usurpers, some of whom sit in my own consistory.' And he turned fiercely on the courageous old Montius. 'Yes, even the quaestor Montius is involved in this conspiracy. He plots against me, as well as against Constantius. He tells you that I may not arrest an insolent prefect because he is on imperial business. But I have the right to discipline any official in the East. I would be untrue to my oath to Constantius if I did not keep order in Antioch.' And so on.

By the time Gallus had finished, the troops were with him. While he stood by, they murdered Montius. Next they marched on military headquarters. No attempt was made to resist them. They found Domitian in the commandant's private office on the second floor. They threw the wretched prefect down the stairs (which are very steep: I once badly twisted my ankle going up them). Then they dragged the bodies of Domitian and Montius side by side through the streets of Antioch.

Gallus was now thoroughly frightened. Though his troops were adequate for controlling Antioch, he was in no position to resist Constantius, and it was perfectly plain that the two would soon be in open conflict. Yet Gallus still pretended to be carrying out the Emperor's orders when he declared martial law and arrested those whom he suspected of plotting against him. This turned out to be half the senate. I withdrew to Daphne during this troubled time.

Gallus set up a military tribunal and arraigned before it all those who had been accused of treason. During the trials Constantia sat behind a curtain listening to the testimony; every now and then she would poke her head into the courtroom to ask a question or to give an opinion. It was a ludicrous display. Hearsay was now accepted as fact, and no one was safe.

In a dyeshop a secret agent noticed a purple robe of the sort only an emperor may wear. It was immediately assumed that the cloak had been ordered by a would-be usurper. The shopowner wisely vanished but they found his files. Although there was no mention of a purple cloak having been ordered, the secret service did come up with a letter from a deacon inquiring when 'the work will be ready'. That was enough. 'The work' was the purple cloak, according to the secret service, which had no other evidence. The guiltless deacon was arrested, tortured, tried, and put to death. This was typical of the 'justice' at Gallus's court.

Having failed to persuade Gallus to come to Milan, Constantius ordered his sister Constantia to attend him. Confident that she could patch up the differences between her husband and her brother, she set out for Milan. But en route the lady died of fever, and that was the end for Gallus. Though he was by now perfectly willing to declare himself Augustus in the East, he lacked the military power to withstand Constantius. He was in a quandary.

Finally a letter arrived from Constantius that was most amiable in tone. The Emperor reminded Gallus that under Diocletian a Caesar *always* obeyed his Augustus, citing the famous case of the Caesar Galerius who walked a mile on foot because the Augustus Diocletian was displeased with him. This letter was delivered by Scudilo, a master diplomatist who told Gallus privately that Constantius wished him no harm.

Did Gallus believe this? It seems impossible. But he was by now a desperate man. He was also completely demoralized by his wife's death. To everyone's amazement, he agreed to go to Milan. However, he insisted on travelling by way of Constantinople, where as the reigning Caesar he presided over the games in the Hippodrome. But Julian describes this scheme.

Julian Augustus

In the late autumn of 354 I learned of the sudden death of Constantia. I wrote
Gallus a letter of condolence which was not answered. He was already having
his difficulties at Antioch, where Constantius had earlier sent him a messenger
who rudely ordered him to return to Milan. Gallus, quite rightly, refused to go.
He knew what his fate would be. Instead he sent Constantia to the Emperor,
hoping that she might make peace between them. But when she died of a fever in
Bithynia, he knew that he must either obey Constantius or begin a civil war.
Tricked by the eunuchs who assured him that he would be safe in Milan, Gallus
set out for the West. On the way he sent me a message, ordering me to meet him
at Constantinople. I obeyed.

Libanius: It is fascinating to observe how a man with Julian's objectivity and
passion for truth can so blandly protect his brother's memory. Not one word
about the murders of Montius and Domitian, nor any mention of the treason
trials. I suspect Julian is more interested in constructing his case against
Constantius than he is in telling what actually happened . . . a human failing.

Julian Augustus

I met Gallus at the back of the imperial box in the Hippodrome. The box is
actually a two-storey pavilion connected by a long corridor to the Sacred
Palace. On the first floor there are rooms for musicians and minor functionaries;
the second floor contains a suite of rooms used by the imperial family.

The horse races were going on when I arrived. Through the curtains which
covered the door to the box, I could hear the crowd cheering its favourite
drivers. Suddenly Gallus flung aside the curtain.

'Stay there,' he said. He let the curtain fall. He was pale. His hands shook. His
voice was low, his manner furtive. 'Now listen to me. I know what people are
saying: that I shall never return from Milan alive. But don't believe them. I am
still Caesar.' He gestured at the curtain. 'You should have heard the way the
crowd cheered me just now. They are with me. Also, I have an army waiting in
Serbia, Theban troops who are loyal. Everything has been carefully planned.
When they join me, I shall be ready to deal with Constantius.' But his face
revealed the uncertainty his words tried to dispel.

'You will go into rebellion?'

'I hope not. I hope for a truce. But who can tell? Now I wanted to see you to
tell you that if anything should happen to me, go into a monastery. Take holy
orders if you have to. That's the only way you will be safe. Then . . .' He looked
suddenly quite lost. 'Avenge me.'

'But I am sure that the Emperor . . .' I started to gabble, but I was interrupted
by a stout red-faced man who saluted me cheerfully. 'Most noble Julian, I am
Count Lucillianus, attached to the Caesar as his . . .'

'Jailer!' Gallus grinned like a wolf.

'The Caesar enjoys making fun of me.' He turned to Gallus. 'The crowd is
waiting for you to give the victor's crown to Thorax. He just won the chariot
race.'

Gallus turned abruptly and drew aside the curtain. For an instant he stood
silhouetted against dazzling blue sky. The mob behind him sounded like a storm
at sea.

'Isn't the most noble Julian joining us?' asked Lucillianus, aware that I had
instinctively stepped back from the harsh light and sudden sound.

'No!' said Gallus. 'He is to be a priest.' Then he let the curtain fall behind him; and that was that.

The rest of the story is well known. Gallus and his 'jailers' took the overland route through Illyria. All troops were moved from the garrisons along the route, and Gallus could call on no one to support him. At Hadrianopolis, the Theban legions were indeed waiting, but Gallus was not allowed to see them. He was now a prisoner in all but name. Then in Austria, he was arrested by the infamous Count Barbatio, who had been until recently the commander of his own guard. Gallus was imprisoned at Histria; here his trial was held. The Grand Chamberlain Eusebius presided.

Gallus was indicted for all the crimes which had taken place in Syria during the four years of his reign. Most of the charges against him were absurd and the trial itself was a farce, but Constantius enjoyed the show of legality almost as much as he disliked the idea of justice. Gallus's only defence was to blame his wife for everything. This was unworthy of him; but then there was nothing that he could say or do which would save him. Also, by accusing Constantius's sister of a thousand crimes (she was guilty of many more), Gallus was able to strike one last blow at his implacable enemy. Furious at the form the defence took, Constantius ordered Gallus executed.

My brother's head was cut off early in the evening of 9 December 354. His arms were bound behind him as though he were a common criminal. He made no last statement. Or if he did, it has been suppressed. He was twenty-eight when he died. They say that in his last days he suffered terribly from bad dreams. Of the men of the imperial family, only Constantius and I were left.

On 1 January 355 a warrant was issued for my arrest. But by then I had joined a religious order at Nicomedia. I am sure that at first none of the monks knew who I was, for I had come to them with head shaved and I looked like any other novice. Oribasius also protected me. When the imperial messenger arrived at Pergamon to arrest me, Oribasius said that I had gone to Constantinople.

I was a monk for six weeks. I found the life surprisingly pleasant. I enjoyed the austerity and the mild physical labour. The monks themselves were not very inspiring. I suppose some must have had the religious sense but the majority were simply vagrants who had tired of the road and its discomforts. They treated the monastery as though it were some sort of hostel rather than a place to serve the One God. Yet they were easy to get along with, and had it not been for the Galilean rituals I could have been quite happy.

I don't suppose I shall ever know how I was discovered. Perhaps one of the monks recognized me or perhaps the secret agents in checking the rolls of the various monasteries for new arrivals had grown suspicious. No matter how it was done, it was done swiftly and efficiently. I was in the kitchen of the monastery, helping the baker to fire his oven, when a detachment of household troops came clattering in. Their commander saluted me. 'The most noble Julian is to accompany us to Milan, by order of the Augustus.'

I made no protest. The monks stared in silence as I was taken from them and marched through the cold streets of Nicomedia to the imperial palace. Here I was received by the city prefect. He was nervous. Under similar circumstances five years earlier, Gallus had been ordered to Milan and *he* had been made Caesar of the East. The same fate might befall me. It was hard for an official to know how to behave.

'Naturally, we regret these security precautions.' The prefect indicated the guards. 'But you will understand that the Grand Chamberlain's office was, as always, most specific. No details were omitted.'

I was polite and non-committal. I was also somewhat cheered to learn that my military escort was to be commanded by Victor, the same officer I had met at Macellum.

Victor was apologetic. 'I don't enjoy this duty. I hope you realize that.'

'Neither do I.'

Victor frowned. 'I particularly dislike taking a priest from a monastery.'

'I am not exactly a priest.'

'Even so, you were prepared to take orders. No one has the right to keep a man from God, not even the Emperor.' Victor is a devout Galilean; at that time he was convinced that I was also one. I said nothing to disabuse him.

The next day we set out for Constantinople. Though I was treated like a prince, not a prisoner, I took it as a bad omen that we were to follow the same overland route to Italy that Gallus had taken a few months before.

As we were leaving Nicomedia, I noticed a head on a pike. I hardly glanced at it, since there is almost always the head of some felon or other on display at the main gate of every town.

'I am sorry,' said Victor suddenly. 'But we were ordered to use this gate.'

'Sorry for what?'

'To lead you past your brother's head.'

'Gallus?' I turned clear round in my saddle and looked again at the head. The face had been so mutilated that the features were unrecognizable, but there was no mistaking the blond hair, matted though it was with dirt and blood.

'The Emperor has had it displayed in every city in the East.'

I shut my eyes, on the verge of nausea.

'Your brother had many good qualities,' said Victor. 'It was a pity.' Ever since, I have respected Victor. In those days when secret agents were everywhere and no man was safe, it took courage to say something good of a man executed for treason. Victor was equally outspoken in my defence. It was his view that the two charges made against me by the Grand Chamberlain's office were not serious (that I had left Macellum without permission; that I had met Gallus in Constantinople when he was already accused of treason). Of the first charge I was innocent. The Grand Chamberlain himself had written Bishop George, giving me permission to go wherever I chose in the East. I had wisely kept a copy of this letter. As for the second charge, I had been summoned to Constantinople by the then reigning Caesar of the East. How could I refuse my lawful lord? 'You have nothing to fear,' said Victor. But I was not optimistic.

Since I was travelling as a prince, I was greeted at each city by the local dignitaries. Concerned as I was about my own fate, I was still able to take some pleasure in seeing new things. I was particularly pleased when Victor allowed me to visit Ilios, a modern city near the ruins of ancient Troy.

At Ilios I was taken round by the local bishop. At first my heart sank: a Galilean bishop was the last sort of person who would be interested in showing me the temples of the true gods. But to my surprise, Bishop Pegasius was an ardent Hellenist. In fact, *he* was the one who was surprised when I asked him if we might visit the temples of Hector and Achilles.

'But of course. Nothing would give me greater pleasure. But I am surprised that you are interested in old monuments.'

'I am a child of Homer.'

'So is every educated man. But we are also Christians. Your piety is well known to us even here.' I could not be sure if he was being ironic or not. My friendship with Maximus was general knowledge and a good many Galileans were suspicious of me. On the other hand, my arrest in a monastery had given rise to a whole new legend: the priest-prince. In this role, I explained to the bishop that it was merely as a student of Homer that I wanted to see the famous temples our ancestors had built to those gods (false gods!) and heroes who had fought in this haunted place.

Pegasius took me first to the small temple which contains the famous bronze statue of Hector, said to be done from life. In the unroofed courtyard which surrounds the temple there also stands a colossal statue of Archilles, facing Hector in effigy as in life. To my astonishment, the altars in the courtyard were smouldering with sacrifice, while the statue of Hector shone from a recent anointing.

I turned to the Bishop. 'What do these fires mean? Do the people still worship Hector?'

Pegasius was bland. 'Of course they do. After all, it would be unnatural not to worship our brave men in the same way that we worship the martyrs who also lived here.'

'I'm not sure it is the same thing,' I said primly.

'Well, at least we have managed to preserve many beautiful works of art.' Then Pegasius proceeded to show me the temples of Athena and Achilles, both in perfect repair. I noted, too, that whenever he passed the image of an old god, he did not hiss and make the sign of the cross the way most Galileans do, fearing contamination.

Pegasius proved to be a marvellous guide to Troy. I was particularly moved when he showed me the sarcophagus of Achilles. 'There he lies, the fierce Achilles.' He tapped the ancient marble. 'A hero and a giant – actually, a giant. Some years ago we opened the tomb and found the bones of a man seven feet tall, and where his heel had been there was the head of an arrow.'

It was awesome to be so close to the legendary past. Pegasius could see that I was impressed. Despite all efforts to the contrary, I am transparent as water. 'Those were great days,' he said softly.

'They will come again,' I blurted out.

'I pray that you are right,' said the bishop of Ilios. Today this same Pegasius is my high priest of Cappadocia. He was never a Galilean though he pretended to be one, thinking that by rising to a position of importance among that depraved sect he would be able to preserve the temples of our ancestors. Now he revels in his freedom.

Priscus: And *now* he revels in life at the Persian court, where, according to gossip, he is a convert to Persian sun worship. Julian took up with the oddest people.

Julian Augustus

At the beginning of February we arrived at Como, a town on a lake about thirty miles north of Milan. Here I remained a prisoner for six months. I was allowed to see no one except the servants who had come with me. Letters from Oribasius and Maximus were not delivered. I might as well have been dead. I consoled myself with reading the complete works of Pliny the Younger, who had lived at Como. I remember with what loathing I read his famous description of 'darling Como'. I hated the place, including the blue-green lake.

During this time I had no idea what was happening in the outside world, which was probably just as well for I was the subject of fierce debate in the Sacred Consistory. According to Eusebius: 'He is another Gallus. He must be put to death.' A majority of the Consistory agreed with the Chamberlain. Surprisingly enough, the opposition was led by the Empress Eusebia. Though she was not a member of the Consistory, she was able to make her views known. 'Julian has committed no crime. His loyalty has never been seriously questioned. He is the last surviving male member of the imperial house. Until such time as we provide the Emperor with a son, Julian is heir to the principate. But should Julian be executed and should the Emperor then – heaven forbid – die without issue, the house of Constantine is at an end and there will be chaos in the empire.' Eusebia finally prevailed. But it took her six months of argument, during which time Constantius said not a word. He merely listened and brooded and waited.

At the beginning of June a court chamberlain arrived at Como. 'The most noble Julian is to wait upon the divine Empress Eusebia.' I was startled: the Empress, not the Emperor? I tried to question the chamberlain but he would say no more than that I was to be given a private audience; no, he could not tell me if the Emperor would receive me; no, he was not even certain that the Emperor was at Milan: he revelled in being uninformative.

We entered Milan through a door in one of the watchtowers. In complete secrecy, I was hurried through narrow back streets to a side entrance of the palace. Once inside the palace I was met by chamberlains who took me straight to the apartment of the Empress.

Eusebia was handsomer than her portraits. The eyes and mouth, which appeared so severe when rendered in marble, in life were not severe at all, merely sad. A flame-coloured robe set off her pale face and black hair. She was not much older than I.

'We are pleased to receive our cousin, the most noble Julian,' she murmured formally. She motioned to one of her ladies-in-waiting, who came forward with a folding stool and placed it beside the Empress's silver chair.

'We hope our cousin enjoyed his stay at Lake Como.'

'The lake is very beautiful, Augusta.' At a gesture from her, I sat on the stool.

'Yes. The Emperor and I enjoy the lake.'

For what seemed an eternity, we discussed that wretched lake. All the while she was studying me carefully. And I must say I was studying her. Eusebia was Constantius's second wife. His first wife had been Galla, the half-sister of Gallus. Galla had the same mother as Gallus, who had the same father as I, but I never knew her, and I don't think Gallus ever met his sister more than once or twice. When Galla died, Constantius promptly married Eusebia. It was said that he had always been in love with her. She came from an excellent consular family. She was a popular figure at court, and on more than one occasion she had saved innocent men from Constantius's eunuchs.

'We have been told that you are planning to become a priest.'

'I was at a monastery, when I was . . . told to come to Milan.' I started to stammer as I often do when I am nervous. The letter 'm' gives me particular trouble.

'But do you seriously want to be a priest?'

'I don't know. I prefer philosophy, I think. I would like to live at Athens.'

'You have no interest in politics?' She smiled as she said this, knowing what my answer must necessarily be.

'No! None, Augusta.'

'Yet you have certain responsibilities to the state. You are imperial.'

'The Augustus needs no help from me.'

'That is not quite true.' She clapped her hands and the two ladies-in-waiting withdrew, closing cedar doors softly behind them.

'Nothing is secret in a palace,' she said. 'One is never alone.'

'Aren't we alone now?'

Eusebia clapped her hands again. Two eunuchs appeared from behind pillars at the opposite end of the room. She waved them away.

'They can hear but they cannot speak. A precaution. But then there are others listening whom one knows nothing about.'

'The secret agents?'

She nodded. 'Everything we say to one another in this room they can hear.'

'But where . . .?'

She smiled at my bewilderment. 'Who knows *where*? But one knows they are always present.'

'They even spy on you?'

'Especially on the Empress.' She was serene. 'It has always been like this in palaces. So remember to speak . . . carefully.'

'Or not at all!'

She laughed. I found myself relaxing somewhat. I almost trusted her. She became serious. 'The Emperor has given me permission to talk to you. He was reluctant. I don't need to tell you that since the Gallus affair he has felt himself entirely surrounded by traitors. He trusts no one.'

'But I . . .'

'He trusts you least of all.' This was blunt. But I was grateful for her candour. 'Against his own good judgement, he raised your brother up. Within months, Gallus and Constantia were plotting to usurp the throne.'

'Are you so certain?'

'We have proof.'

'I am told that secret agents often invent "proof".'

She shrugged. 'In this case it was not necessary. Constantia was indiscreet. I never trusted her. But that is over with. You are now the potential threat.'

'Easily solved,' I said with more bitterness than I intended. 'Execute me.'

'There are those who advise this.' She was as much to the point as I. 'But I am not one. As you know, as the whole world knows, Constantius cannot have a child.' Her face set bleakly. 'I have been assured by my confessor that this is heaven's judgement upon my husband for having caused the deaths of so many members of his own family. Not that he wasn't justified,' she added loyally. 'But justified or not, there is a curse on those who kill their own kind. That curse is on Constantius. He has no heir and I am certain that he will *never* have one, if he puts you to death.'

There it was at last. My sense of relief was enormous, and perfectly visible in my face.

'Yes. You are safe. For the time being. But there still remains the problem of what to do with you. We had hoped you would take holy orders.'

'If it is required, I shall.' Yes, I said that. I am giving as honest an account as I can of my life. At that moment, I would have worshipped the ears of a mule to save my life.

But Eusebia was not insistent. 'Your love of learning also seems genuine.' She smiled. 'Oh, we know whom you see, what books you read. There is very little that has escaped the attention of the Chamberlain's office.'

'Then they know that it is my wish to be a philosopher.'

'Yes. And I believe that the Emperor will grant you your wish.'

'I shall be eternally grateful, and loyal. He has nothing to fear from me, ever
. . .' I babbled on enthusiastically.

Eusebia watched me, amused. Then when I ran out of breath, she said:
'Gallus made him much the same speech.'

On that dampening note she rose, ending the interview. 'I shall try to arrange
an interview for you with the Emperor. It won't be easy. He is shy.' At the time I
found this hard to believe, but of course Eusebia was right. Constantius feared
all human encounters. One of the reasons he was so fond of eunuchs was that,
by and large, they are not quite human.

Two days later, I was visited by the Grand Chamberlain himself. I found it
hard to believe that this enchanting creature with his caressing voice and
dimpled smile was daily advising the Consistory to execute me. He quite filled
the small apartment where I had been confined.

'Oh, you have grown, most noble Julian! In every way.' Delicately Eusebius
touched my face. 'And your beard is now most *philosophic*. How Marcus Aurelius
would have envied you!' For an instant one fat finger rested, light as a butterfly,
on the tip of my beard. Then we stood face to face, beaming at one another; I
with nerves, he with policy.

'I don't need to tell you how pleased I am to see you at court. We all are. This
is where you belong, close to your own kind.' My heart sank: was that to be my
fate? a life at court where the eunuchs could keep an eye on me? A swift death
was almost preferable. 'Now I suggest that when you see the divine Augustus,
you will beg him to allow you to stay always at his side. He needs you.'

I seized on the one fact. 'The Emperor will see me?'

Eusebius nodded delightedly, as though he had been entirely responsible for
my amazing good fortune. 'Of course. Didn't you know? He made the decision
at this morning's Consistory. We were all so pleased. Because we *want* you here. I
have always said that there should be a place for you at the side of the Augustus.
A high place.'

'You flatter me,' I murmured.

'I say only the truth. You are, after all, an ornament to the house of
Constantine, and what better place has such a pure jewel to shine than in the
diadem of the court?'

I swallowed this gravely and replied with equal insincerity, 'I shall never
forget what you have done for me and for my brother.'

Tears came to Eusebius's eyes. His voice trembled. 'It is my wish to serve you.
That is all I ask for.' He leaned forward – with some effort – and kissed my hand.
The rhetoric of hate is often most effective when couched in the idiom of love.
On a note of mutual admiration, we parted.

I was next instructed by one of the eunuchs in the court's etiquette, which was
nearly as complicated as what one goes through during the Mithraic mysteries.
There are a dozen set responses to an emperor's set questions or commands.
There are bows and genuflections; steps to left and steps to right; alternative
gestures should I be asked to approach the throne or merely to remain
where I was. The eunuch loved his work. 'Our ceremonies are among this
world's marvels! More inspiring, in some ways, than the mass.' I agreed to
that.

The eunuch spread a diagram for me on a table. 'This is the great hall where
you will be received.' He pointed. 'Here sits the divine Constantius. And here

you will enter.' Every move either of us was to make was planned in advance like a dance. When I had finally learned my lesson, the eunuch folded his map with an exalted expression on his face. 'We have considerably improved and refined court ceremonial since the divine Diocletian. I am sure that he never dreamed his heirs would be capable of such exquisite style as well as such profound symbolism, for we are now able to beautifully reflect the nature of the universe in a single ceremony lasting scarcely three hours!'

The cutting down of court ceremonies and the removal of the eunuchs was one of the first acts of my reign. It was certainly the most satisfactory.

Shortly after sundown, the Master of the Offices and his many ushers escorted me to the throneroom. The Master of the Offices gave me last-minute instructions on how to behave in the sacred presence. But I did not listen. I was too busy preparing the speech I intended to make to Constantius. It was a masterpiece of eloquence. After all, I had been preparing it for ten years. Face to face, I intended to make Constantius my friend.

The Master of the Offices ushered me into a huge basilica which was once Diocletian's throneroom. The Corinthian columns which line it are twice the usual height and the floor is of porphyry and green marble. The effect is most splendid, especially by artificial light. In the apse at the far end of the basilica stands the throne of Diocletian, an elaborate chair of ivory decorated with gold plaques. Needless to say, I remember everything about that room in which my fate was decided. Torches flared between the columns while on either side of the throne bronze lamps illuminated its occupant. Not counting my childhood encounter with Constantine, this was the first time I beheld an emperor in full state. I was not prepared for the theatricality of the scene.

Constantius sat very straight and still, his forearms resting on his knees in imitation of the Egyptian kings. He wore a heavy gold diadem set with huge square jewels. On one side of him stood Eusebius, on the other the praetorian prefect, while around the room the officials of the court were ranged.

I was officially presented to the Emperor. I paid him homage. Only once did I falter in the course of the ritual; when I did, the Master of the Offices was quick to whisper the correct formula in my ear.

If Constantius was curious about me, he did not betray it. His bronze face was empty of all expression as he spoke. 'We receive our most noble cousin with pleasure.' But there was no pleasure in that high-pitched voice. I felt myself suddenly blushing. 'We give him leave to go to Athens to continue his studies.' I glanced at Eusebius. Though his own grim advice had not prevailed, he gave me a small delighted nod as if to say, '*We've* won!'

'Also . . .' But then Constantius stopped talking. There is no other way to describe what happened. He simply stopped. There were no more words for me. I stared at him, wondering if I had gone mad. Even the Master of the Offices was taken aback. Everyone had expected a full speech from Constantius as well as a response from me. But the audience was over. Constantius put out his hand for me to kiss. I did so. Then with the aid of the Master of the Offices, I walked backward to the entrance, bowing at regular intervals. Just as I was about to leave the presence, two squeaking bats swooped suddenly out of the shadowy ceiling, and darted straight towards Constantius. He did not move, even though one almost touched his face. As always, his self-control was marvellous. I have never known a man quite so deep or so cold.

I returned to my apartment to find a message from the Grand Chamberlain's office. I was to proceed at once to the port of Aquileia. My belongings had already been packed. My servants were ready. A military escort was standing by.

Within the hour, I was outside the walls of Milan. As I rode through the warm night, I prayed to Helios that I never see court or Emperor again.

7

I arrived at Piraeus, the port of Athens, shortly after sunrise 5 August 355. I remember every one of the forty-seven days I spent in Athens. They were the happiest of my life, so far.

It was a windy dawn. In the east, light tore at the dark. Stars faded. The sea was rough. It was like the morning of the world. The ship creaked and shuddered as it struck against the pilings of the quay. I had half expected to see a detachment of troops waiting on the shore, ready to arrest me on some new charge. But there were no troops in sight, only foreign merchant ships and the usual bustle of a busy port. Slaves unloaded cargoes. Officials of the port moved solemnly from ship to ship. Men with carts and donkeys shouted to those just arrived, promising to get them to Athens faster than that youth who ran from Marathon to the city in four hours (and fell dead, one would like to retort, but irony is lost on drivers, even Greek drivers who know their Homer).

Barefoot students in shabby clothes moved in packs from ship to ship, trying to sign up newcomers for lectures. Each student was a proselytizer for his own teacher. There was a good deal of rancour as each of these youths went about trying to convince would-be students (known as 'foxes') that there was but one teacher in Athens worth listening to: his own. Fights often broke out between the factions. Even as I watched, two students actually manhandled a stranger; each grabbed an arm, and while one insisted that he attend the lectures of a certain Sophist, the other shouted that the Sophist was a fool and that only the wisdom of *his* teacher, a Cynic, was worth a student's time. Between them, they nearly tore the poor man in half. Nor would they let him go until he finally made it clear to them in broken Greek that he was an Egyptian cotton dealer and not at all interested in philosophy. Luckily, they did not get as far as my ship; so I was spared their attentions.

Usually when a member of the imperial family travels by sea, the dragon of our house flies at the mast. But since I was technically under 'house arrest', I was in no way identified to the people, which was just as well. I wanted to be free in Athens, to wander unnoticed wherever I chose. But unfortunately a dozen soldiers had been assigned to me as permanent bodyguard (they were, in effect, my jailers) and their commanding officer was responsible for my safety. I felt some obligation to him, though not much.

I made a bold decision. While the servants were busy with the luggage and the men who guarded me were all gathered on the forward deck of the ship in sleepy conference with the officials of the port, I scribbled a note to my head jailer, telling him that I would meet him at the end of the day at the prefect's house. I left the note on one of our travelling chests. Then, student's cloak securely wrapped about me, I swung over the side of the ship and dropped unobserved on to the wharf.

It took a moment to become accustomed to the steadiness of earth. I am not a bad sailor but the monotony of a long voyage and the continual slap and fall of a ship at sea tire me. I am of earth, not water; air, not fire. I engaged a cart and driver after considerable haggling (I was able to bring the driver's cost down to half what he asked: good but not marvellous). Then I climbed into the little cart. Half standing, half sitting on the cart rail, I was borne over the rutted road to Athens.

The sun rose in a cloudless sky. Attic clarity is not just metaphor; it is fact. The sky's blue was painful. One felt one could see straight to the farthest edge of the world if the mountain Hymettos, low and violet in the early light, had not blocked the view. The heat with each instant became more intense, but it was the dry heat of the desert, made pleasant by a soft wind from the sea.

My first reaction was delight at anonymity. No one stared at me. No one knew who I was. I looked a typical student with my beard and plain cloak. There were dozens like me. Some were in carts, most were on foot; all of them moving towards the same goal: Athens and the knowledge of the true.

On every side of me carts rattled and creaked, their drivers cursing and their contents, human or animal, complaining. The Athenian Greek is a lively fellow, though one looks in vain from face to face for a glimpse of Pericles or Alcibiades. As a race, they are much changed. They are no longer noble. They have been too often enslaved, and their blood mixed with that of barbarians. Yet I do not find them as sly and effeminate as certain Latin writers affect to. I think that the Old Roman tendency to look down on the Greeks is no more than a natural resentment of Greece's continuing superiority in those things which are important: philosophy and art. All that is good in Rome today was Greek. I find Cicero disingenuous when on one page he acknowledges his debt to Plato and then on the next speaks with contempt of the Greek character. He seems unaware of his own contradictions . . . doubtless because they were a commonplace in his society. Of course the Romans pretend *they* are children of Troy, but that nonsense was never taken too seriously. From time to time I have had a word or two to say about Roman character, not much of it flattering (my little work on the Caesars, though written much too quickly, has some point, I think). But then one must recall that even as I dictate these lines as Roman Emperor, I am really Greek. And I have been to Athens, the eye of Greece.

Athens. It has been eight years since I rode up to the city gate in a market cart, an anonymous student who gaped at the sights like any German come to town. My first glimpse of the acropolis was startling and splendid. It hovers over the city as though held in the hand of Zeus, who seems to say: 'Look, children, at how your gods live!' Sunlight flashes off the metal shield of the colossal statue of Athena, guarding her city. Off to the left I recognized the steep pyramidal mountain of Lykabettos, a great pyramid of rock hurled to earth by Athena herself; to this day wolves dwell at its foot.

The driver turned abruptly into a new road. I nearly fell out of the cart. 'Academy Road,' he announced in the perfunctory loud voice of one used to talking to foreigners. I was impressed. The road from Athens to the Academy's grove is lined with ancient trees. It begins at the city's Dipylon Gate – which was straight ahead of us – and crosses through suburbs to the green-leafed academy of Aristotle.

The Dipylon Gate was as busy in the early morning as any other great city's gate might have been at noon. It is a double gate, as its name indicates, with two tall towers on the outside. Guards lolled in front, paying no attention to the carts and pedestrians who came and went. As we passed through the outer gate, our cart was suddenly surrounded by whores. Twenty or thirty women and girls of all ages rushed out of the shadows of the wall. They fought with one another to get close to the cart. They tugged at my cloak. They called me 'Billy Goat', 'Pan', 'Satyr', and other less endearing terms. With the skill of an acrobat one pretty child of fourteen vaulted the railing of my cart and firmly grasped my beard in her fist. The soldiers laughed at my discomfort. With some effort I pried my beard free from her fingers, but not before her other hand had reached between my legs, to the delight of those watching. But the driver was expert at handling these girls. With a delicate flick of his whip, he snapped at her hand. It was withdrawn with a cry. She leapt to the ground. The other women jeered us. Their curses were vivid and splendid, Homeric! Then as we passed through the second gate they turned back, for a troop of cavalry had appeared at the outer gate. Like bees swarming in a garden, they surrounded the soldiers.

I arranged my tunic. The sharp tug of the girl's hand had had its effect upon me, and against my will I thought of love-making and wondered where the best girls in Athens might be found. I was not then, as I am now, celibate. Yet even in those days I believed that it was virtuous to mortify the flesh, for it is a fact that continence increases intellectual clarity. But I was also twenty-three years old and the flesh made demands on me in a way that the mind could not control. Youth is the body's time. Not a day passed in those years that I did not experience lust. Not a week passed that I did not assuage that lust. But I do not agree with those Dionysians who maintain that the sexual act draws men closer to the One God. If anything, it takes a man away from God, for in the act he is blind and thoughtless, no more than an animal engaged in the ceremony of creation. Yet to each stage of one's life certain things are suitable and for a few weeks, eight years ago, I was young, and knew many girls. Even now on this hot Asiatic night, I recall with unease that brilliant time, and think of love-making. I notice that my secretary is blushing. Yet *he* is Greek!

The driver indicated a large ruin to the right. 'Hadrian,' he said. 'Hadrian Augustus.' Like all travellers, I am used to hearing guides refer to my famous predecessor. Even after two centuries he is the only emperor *every* man has heard of – because of his constant travelling, his continuous building and, sad to say, his ridiculous passion for the boy Antinoüs. I suppose that it is natural enough to like boys but it is not natural or seemly to love *anyone* with the excessive and undignified passion that Hadrian showed for Antinoüs. Fortunately, the boy was murdered before Hadrian could make him his heir. But in his grief Hadrian made himself and the Genius of Rome look absurd. He set up thousands of statues and dedicated innumerable temples to the dead boy. He even declared the pretty catamite a god! It was a shocking display and permanently shadows Hadrian's fame. For the first time in history, a Roman emperor was mocked and thought ridiculous. From every corner of the earth derisive laughter sounded. Yet except for this one lapse, I find Hadrian a sympathetic figure. He was much gifted, particularly in music. He was an adept at mysteries. He used to spend many hours at night studying the stars, searching for omens and portents, as do I. He also wore a beard. I like him best for that. That sounds petty, doesn't it? I surprise myself as I say it. But then liking and disliking, approval and disapproval depend on many trivial things. I dislike Hadrian's passion for Antinoüs because I cannot bear for a philosopher-emperor to be mocked by his subjects. But I like his beard. We are all so simple at heart that we become unfathomable to one another.

Just inside the wall of the city, I left my driver. Then like one who has gone to sleep over a book of history, I stepped into the past. I stood now on that ancient highway – known simply as The Road – which leads from gate to agora to acropolis beyond. I was now in history. In the present I was part of the past and, simultaneously, part of what is to come. Time opened his arms to me and in his serene embrace I saw the matter whole: a circle without beginning or end.

To the left of the gate was a fountain in which I washed the dust from my face and beard. Then I proceeded along The Road to the agora. I am told that Rome is infinitely more impressive than Athens. I don't know. I have never visited Rome. But I do know that Athens looks the way a city ought to look but seldom does. It is even better planned than Pergamon, at least at its centre. Porticoes gleam in the bright sun. The intense blue sky sets off the red tile roofs and makes the faded paint of columns seem to glow.

The Athenian agora is a large rectangular area enclosed by long porticoes of great antiquity. The one on the right is dedicated to Zeus; the one on the left is of more recent date, the gift of a young king of Pergamon who studied here. In the centre of the agora is the tall building of the University, first built by Agrippa in the time of Augustus. The original building – used as a music hall – collapsed mysteriously in the last century. I find the architecture pretentious, even in its present somewhat de-Romanized version. But pretentious or not, this building was my centre in Athens. For here the most distinguished philosophers lecture. Here I listened three times weekly to the great Prohaeresius, of whom more later.

Behind the University are two porticoes parallel to one another, the last being at the foot of the acropolis. To one's right, on a hill above the agora, is a small temple to Hephaestos surrounded by gardens gone to seed. Below this hill are the administrative buildings of Athens, the Archives, the Round House where the fifty governors of Athens meet – this last is a peculiar-looking structure with a steep roof which the Athenians, who give everything and everyone a nickname, call 'the umbrella'. There used to be many silver statues in the Round House but the Goths stole them in the last century.

Few people were abroad as the sun rose to noon. A faint breeze stirred the dust on the old pitted paving. Several important-looking men, togas draped ineptly about plump bodies, hurried towards the Bouleuterion. They had the self-absorbed air of politicians everywhere. Yet these men were the political heirs of Pericles and Demosthenes. I tried to remember that as I watched them hurry about their business.

Then I stepped into the cool shade of the Painted Portico. For an instant my eyes were dazzled, the result of sudden dimness. Not for some time was I able to make out the famous painting of the Battle of Marathon which covers the entire long wall of the portico. But as my eyes grew used to the shade, I saw that the painting was indeed the marvel the world says it is. One can follow the battle's course by walking the length of the portico. Above the painting hang the round shields of the Persians, captured that day. The shields have been covered with pitch to preserve them. Looking at those relics of a battle fought eight hundred years before, I was much moved. Those young men and their slaves – yes, for the first time in history slaves fought beside their masters – together saved the world.

More important, they fought of their own free will, unlike our soldiers, who are either conscripts or mercenaries. Even in times of peril, our people will not fight to protect their country. Money, not honour, is now the source of Roman power. When the money goes, the state will go. That is why Hellenism must be restored, to instil again in man that sense of his own worth which made civilization possible, and won the day at Marathon.

As I stood there looking up at the tarry shields, a youth approached me. He was bearded; his clothes were dirty; he wore a student's cloak and he looked a typical New Cynic of the sort I deplore. I have recently written at considerable length about these vagabonds. In the last few years the philosophy of Crates and Zeno has been taken over by idlers who, though they have no interest in philosophy, deliberately imitate the Cynics in such externals as not cutting their hair or beards, carrying sticks and wallets, and begging. But where the original Cynics despised wealth, sought virtue, questioned all things in order to find what was true, these imitators mock all things, including the true, using the mask of philosophy to disguise licence and irresponsibility. Nowadays, any young man who does not choose to study or to work grows a beard, insults the gods, and calls himself Cynic. No wonder philosophy has earned the contempt of so many in this unhappy age.

Without ceremony, the New Cynic pointed at the wall. 'That is Aeschylus,' he said. I looked politely at the painting of a bearded soldier, no different from the others except for the famous name written above his head. The playwright is shown engaged in combat with a Persian. But though he is fighting for his life, his sombre face is turned towards us, as though to say: I know that I am immortal!

'The painter was self-conscious,' I said neutrally, fully expecting to be asked for money and ready not to give it.

The Cynic grinned at me. Apparently he chose to regard neutrality as friendship. He tapped the painting. A flake of paint zig-zagged to the ground. 'One day the whole thing will disappear and then who will know what Marathon was like, when this picture's gone?' As he spoke, something stirred in my memory. I recognized the voice. Yet the face was completely strange to me. Confident now that we were friends, he turned from the painting to me. Had I just arrived in Athens? Yes. Was I a student? Yes. Was I a Cynic? No. Well, there was no cause to be so emphatic (smiling). He himself dressed as a Cynic only because he was poor. By the time this startling news had been revealed to me, we had climbed the steps to the temple of Hephaestos. Here the view of the agora is wide and elegant. In the clear noon light one could see beyond the city to the dark small windows of those houses which cluster at the foot of Hymettos.

'Beautiful,' said my companion, making even that simple word sound ambiguous. 'Though beauty . . .'

'Is absolute,' I said firmly. Then to forestall Cynic chatter, I turned abruptly into the desolate garden of the temple. The place was overrun with weeds, while the temple itself was shabby and sad. But at least the Galileans have not turned it into a charnel house. Far better that a temple fall in ruins than be so desecrated. Better of course that it be restored.

My companion asked if I was hungry. I said no, which he took as yes (he tended not to listen to answers). He suggested we visit a tavern in the quarter just back of the temple. It was, he assured me, a place much frequented by students of the 'better' sort. He was sure that I would enjoy it. Amused by his effrontery (and still intrigued by that voice which haunted me), I accompanied him through the narrow hot streets of the near by quarter of the smiths, whose shops glowed blue as they hammered out metal in a blaring racket: metal struck metal in a swarm of sparks, like comets' tails.

The tavern was a low building with a sagging roof from which too many tiles had been removed by time and weather. I bent low to enter the main door. I was also forced to stoop inside, for the ceiling was too low for me and the beams were haphazard, even dangerous in the dim light. My companion had no difficulty standing straight. I winced at the heavy odour of rancid oil burning in pots on the stove.

Two trestle tables with benches filled the room. A dozen youths sat together close to the back door, which opened onto a dismal courtyard containing a dead olive which looked as though it had been sketched in silver on the whitewashed wall behind it.

My companion knew most of the other students. All were New Cynics, bearded, loud, disdainful, unread. They greeted us with cheerful obscenities. I felt uncomfortable but was determined to go through with my adventure. After all, this was what I had dreamed of. To be just one among many, even among New Cynics. The moment was unique, or so I thought. When asked who I was, they were told '*Not* a Cynic.' They laughed good-humouredly. But then when they heard I was new to Athens, each made an effort to get me to attend lectures with his teacher. My companion rescued me. 'He is already taken. He studies with Prohaeresius.' I was surprised, for I had said nothing to my guide about Prohaeresius, and yet Prohaeresius was indeed the teacher of my choice. How did he know?

'I know all about you,' he said mysteriously. 'I read minds, tell fortunes.' He was interrupted by one of the youths, who suggested that I shave my beard since otherwise I might be mistaken for a New Cynic and give them a bad name by my good behaviour. This was considered witty in that room. Others debated whether or not I should be carried off to the baths to be scrubbed, the traditional hazing for new students, and one which I had every intention of avoiding. If necessary, I would invoke lese-majesty!

But my guardian shoved the students away and sat me down at the opposite table close to the courtyard door, for which I was grateful. I am not particularly sensitive to odours, but on a blazing hot day the odour of unwashed students combined with thick smoke from old burning oil was almost too much for me. The tavern-keeper, making sure I had money (apparently my companion was deep in his debt), brought us cheese, bitter olives, old bread, sour wine. To my surprise, I was hungry. I ate quickly, without tasting. Suddenly I paused, aware that I was being stared at. I looked across the table at my companion. Yes?

'You have forgotten me, haven't you, Julian?'

Then I identified the familiar voice. I recognized Gregory of Nazianzus. We had been together at Pergamon. I burst out laughing and shook his hand. 'How did such a dedicated Christian become a New Cynic?'

'Poverty, plain poverty.' Gregory indicated the torn and dirty cloak, the unkempt beard. 'And protection.' He lowered his voice, indicating the students at the other table. 'Christians are outnumbered in Athens. It's a detestable city. There is no faith, only argument and atheism.'

'Then why are you here?'

He sighed. 'The best teachers are here, the best instructors in rhetoric. Also, it is good to know the enemy, to be able to fight him with his own weapons.'

I nodded and pretended agreement. I was not very brave in those days. But even though I could never be candid with Gregory, he was an amusing companion. He was as devoted to the Galilean nonsense as I was to the truth. I attributed this to his unfortunate childhood. His family are Cappadocian. They live in a small town some fifty miles southwest of Caesarea, the provincial capital. His mother was a most strong-willed woman named . . . I cannot recall her name but I did meet her once a few years ago, and a most formidable creature she was. Passionate and proud and perfectly intolerant of everything not Galilean.

Gregory's father was part Jew and part Greek. As a result of his wife's relentless admonitions, he succumbed finally to the Galilean religion. According to Gregory, when his father was splashed with water by the bishop of Nazianzus, a great nimbus shone all round the convert. The bishop was so moved that he declared, 'Here is my successor!' A most generous-minded man, that bishop! Most of us prefer *not* to name our successor. In due course, Gregory's father became bishop of Nazianzus. So his predecessor had the gift of prophecy, if nothing else.

All in a rush Gregory was telling me of himself. '. . . a terrible trip, by sea. Just before we got to Aegina, the storm struck us. I was sure the ship would sink. I was terrified. I'd never been (I still am not) baptized. So if I died like that at sea . . . Well, you must know yourself what I went through.' He looked at me sharply. 'Are you baptized?'

I said that I had been baptized as a child. I looked as reverent as possible when I said this.

'I prayed and prayed. Finally I fell asleep, exhausted. We all did. I dreamed that something loathsome, some sort of Fury, had come to take me to hell. Meanwhile, one of the cabin boys, a boy from Nazianzus, was dreaming that *he* saw – now this is *really* a miracle – *Mother walking upon the water.*'

'His mother or your mother or the mother of Jesus?' I am afraid that I asked this out of mischief. I couldn't help myself.

But Gregory took the question straight. '*My* mother,' he said. 'The boy knew her, and there she was walking across that raging sea. Then she took the ship by its prow and drew it after her to a safe harbour. Which is exactly what happened. That very night the storm stopped. A Phoenician ship found us and towed us into the harbour of Rhodes.' He sat back in triumph. 'What do you think of *that*?'

'Your mother is a remarkable woman,' I said accurately. Gregory agreed and talked at enthusiastic length about that stern virago. Then he told me of his adventures in Athens, of his poverty (this was a thing which I took: I gave him a good deal of money during the course of my stay), of our friend Basil who was also in Athens and was, I suspect, the reason for Gregory's attendance at the University. Wherever Basil went, Gregory followed. At Athens they were nicknamed 'the Twins'.

'I am expecting Basil now. We're both due at Prohaeresius's house this afternoon. We'll take you. You know we live together here. We study together. We argue almost as a team against the local Sophists. And we usually win.' This was true. Both he and Basil were – are – eloquent. I deplore of course the uses to which their eloquence is put. Today they are most active as Galilean apologists, and I often wonder what they think of their old companion who governs the state. Nothing good, I fear. When I became emperor I asked them both to visit me at Constantinople. Gregory agreed to come, but never did. Basil refused. Of the two, I prefer Basil. He is plain, like me. He is misguided in his beliefs but honest. I suspect Gregory of self-seeking.

'Who is this?' Standing over us was a slender girl, with black intelligent eyes and a mouth that was as quick to sneer as to smile. Gregory introduced us; he said that I was from Cappadocia. She was Macrina, a niece of Prohaeresius.

'I like your beard,' she said, sitting down without invitation. 'It comes to a point. Most men's beards are like Gregory's, every which way. Yours suggests a plan. Will you study with my uncle?'

I said that I would. I was charmed by her. She wore her own version of a student's cloak, in faded blue line. Her bare arms were firm and darkened by the sun; strong fingers tore idly at the scraps of stale bread on the table; on the bench our thighs touched.

'You'll like my uncle. He's much the best teacher in this chattering place. But you'll hate Athens. I do! The splitting of hairs. The talk, talk, talk, and everyone trying to make a point, to pretend that all this talk means something.'

'You are now listening to what is known as "Macrina's Lament",' said Gregory.

'But it's true just the same.' She pointed to him like an actress in tragedy. '*They* are the worst: Gregory and Basil, the Twins of argument ...'

Gregory brightened. 'You should have heard Basil's argument yesterday when we were challenged on the virgin birth.' Gregory turned to me. 'As I told you, there are many atheists in Athens. And some of them have the devil's own cleverness. One in particular we despise ...'

'One? You despise everybody, Gregory!' Macrina sipped wine from my cup, without invitation. 'If ever there were a pair of bishops, it's these two. *You're* not a bishop, are you?' she challenged me agreeably.

I shook my head.

'Not even close,' said Gregory, and I detected something sly in his voice.

'But a Christian?' asked Macrina.

'He must be,' said Gregory smoothly. 'He has to be.'

'*Has* to be? Why? It's not illegal to be a Hellenist, is it? At least not yet.'

I loved her deeply then. We were the same. I looked at her with sudden fondness as the fine if rather grubby fingers lifted and drained my cup.

'I mean he cannot be because ...' I frowned at Gregory; he was not to tell her who I was. But he was on a different tack. '... because he is a brilliant student and anyone who truly loves learning loves God, loves Christ, loves the trinity.'

'Well, I don't.' She set the cup down hard. 'I wonder if he does.'

But I evaded. What had been Basil's defence of the virgin birth?

'He was challenged on the University steps, yesterday, shortly before noon.' Gregory spoke precisely as though he were a historian giving the details of a battle all the world would want to know about. 'A Cynic, a true Cynic,' he added for my benefit, 'stopped Basil and said, "You Christians claim that Christ was born of a virgin." Basil said that we do not merely claim it, we proclaim it, for it is true. Our Lord was born without an earthly father. The Cynic then said that this was entirely against nature, that it was not possible for *any* creature to be born except through the union of male and female. Then Basil said – there was quite a large crowd gathered by now – Basil said, "Vultures bring forth without coupling." Well, you should have heard the applause and laughter! The Cynic went away and Basil was a hero, even among those students who have no faith.'

'At least they knew Aristotle,' I said mildly.

But Macrina was not impressed. 'Just because vultures don't mate ...'

'The female vulture is impregnated by the wind.' Gregory is one of those people who must always embellish the other person's observation.

Unfortunately, he is drawn to the obvious. He tells what everyone already knows. But Macrina was relentless.

'Even if vultures don't mate . . .'

'*Even*? But they don't mate. That is a fact.'

'Has anyone ever seen a vulture made fertile by the wind!' Macrina was mischievous.

'I suppose someone must have.' Gregory's round eyes became even rounder with irritation.

'But how could you tell? The wind is invisible. So how would you know which particular wind – if any – made the bird conceive?'

'She is perverse.' Gregory turned to me, much annoyed. 'Besides, if it were not true, Aristotle would not have said it was true and we would not all agree today that it is indeed the truth.'

'I'm not sure of the logic of that,' began Macrina thoughtfully.

'She'll be condemned for atheism one of these days.' Gregory tried to sound playful; he failed.

Macrina laughed at him, a pleasant, low, unmalicious laugh. 'All right. A vulture's eggs are laid by a virgin bird. Accepted. What has that to do with Christ's birth? Mary was not a vulture. She was a woman. Women conceive in only one way. I can't see that Basil's answer to the Cynic was so crushing. What is true of the vulture is not necessarily true of Mary.'

'Basil's answer,' said Gregory tightly, 'was to the argument used by the Cynic when he said that *all* things are conceived by male and female. Well, if *one* thing is not conceived in this fashion – and that was Basil's argument – then another might not be and . . .'

'But "might not" is not an argument. I might suddenly grow wings and fly to Rome (I wish I could!) but I can't, I don't.'

'There are no cases of human beings having wings, but there is . . .'

'Icarus and Daedalus,' began the valiant Macrina, but we were saved by Basil's arrival. Gregory's face was dark with anger, and the girl was beside herself with amusement.

Basil and I greeted one another warmly. He had changed considerably since we were adolescents. He was now a fine-looking man, tall and somewhat thin; unlike Gregory, he wore his hair close-cropped. I teased him about this. 'Short hair means a bishop.'

Basil smiled his amiable smile and said in a soft voice, ' "May that cup pass from me," ' a quotation from the Nazarene. But unlike the carpenter, Basil was sincere. Today he leads precisely the life that I should like for myself: withdrawn, ascetic, given to books and to prayer. He is a true contemplative and I admire him very much, despite his religion.

Macrina, having heard him call me Julian, suddenly said, 'Isn't the Emperor's cousin, the one called Julian, supposed to come to Athens?'

Basil looked with surprise at Gregory, who motioned for him to be still. 'Do *you* know the prince?' Macrina turned to me.

I nodded. 'I know him. But not well.' Solon's famous truth.

Macrina nodded. 'But of course you would. You were all at Pergamon together. The Twins often discuss him.'

I was embarrassed but amused. I have never been an eavesdropper, even in childhood. Not from any sense of virtue but because I really do not want to know what people think of me or, to be precise, what they *say* of me – often a different matter. I can usually imagine the unpleasant judgements, for we are what others need us to be. That is why our reputations change so often and so drastically, reflecting no particular change in us, merely a change in the mood of those who observe us. When things go well, an emperor is loved; badly, hated. I never need to look in a mirror. I see myself all too clearly in the eyes of those about me.

I was embarrassed not so much for what Macrina might say about me but for what she might reveal about Gregory and Basil. I would not have been surprised if they had a low opinion of me. Intelligent youths of low birth tend to resent the intellectual pretensions of princes. In their place, I would.

Gregory looked downright alarmed. Basil's face was inscrutable. I tried to change the subject. I asked at what time her uncle would be receiving but she ignored the question. 'It's their chief distinction, knowing Julian. They discuss him by the hour. They speculate on his chances of becoming emperor. Gregory thinks he *will* be emperor. Basil thinks Constantius will kill him.'

Though Basil knew where the conversation was tending, he was fearless. 'Macrina, how can you be so certain this is not one of the Emperor's secret agents?'

'Because you know him.'

'We know criminals, too. Idolaters. Agents of the devil.'

'Whoever saw a secret agent with that sort of beard? Besides, why should I care? *I'm* not plotting against the Emperor.' She turned to me, black eyes glowing. 'If you *are* a secret agent, you'll remember that, won't you? I worship the Emperor. My sun rises and sets in his divinity. Every time I see that beautiful face in marble, I want to weep, to cry out: Perfection, thou art Constantius!'

Gregory positively hissed, not at all sure how I would take this mockery. I was amused but uncomfortable. I confess it occurred to me that perhaps Gregory or Basil or even Macrina might indeed be a member of the secret police. If so, Macrina had already said quite enough to have us all executed. That would be the saddest fate of all: to die as the result of a joke!

'Don't be an old woman, Gregory!' Macrina turned to me. 'These two dislike Julian. I can't think why. Jealousy, I suppose. Especially Gregory. He's very petty. Aren't you?' Gregory was now grey with terror. 'They feel Julian is a dilettante and not serious. They say his love of learning is just affectation. Basil feels that his true calling is that of a general – if he lives, of course. But Gregory thinks he's far too scatterbrained even for that. Yet Gregory longs for Julian to be emperor. He wants to be friend to an emperor. You're both terribly worldly, deep down, aren't you?'

Gregory was speechless. Basil was alarmed but he showed courage. 'I would deny only the part about "worldly". I want nothing *in* the world. In fact, next month I enter a monastery at Caesarea where I shall be as far from the world as I can be, this side of death.'

Gregory rallied. 'You do have a bitter tongue, Macrina.' He turned to me, attempting lightness. 'She invents everything. She loves to mock us. She is a pagan, of course. A true Athenian.' He could hardly contain his loathing of the girl or his fear of me.

Macrina laughed at him. 'Anyway, I'm curious to meet the prince.' She turned to me. 'Where will you live? With my uncle?'

I said no, that I would stay with friends. She nodded. 'My uncle keeps a good house and never cheats. My father takes some of the overflow and though he's honest he hates all students deeply, hopelessly.'

I laughed. The Twins laughed too, somewhat hollowly. Basil then proposed that we go to the house of Prohaeresius. I settled our account with the owner of 'the tavern. We went outside. In the hot dust of the street, Macrina whispered in my ear, 'I have known all along that you were the prince.'

Priscus: You will be aware of a number of ironies in what you have just read. The unspeakable Gregory is due to preside over the new Ecumenical Council. They say he will be the next bishop of Constantinople. How satisfying to glimpse this noble bishop in his ragged youth! Basil, who wanted only the contemplative life, now governs the church in Asia as bishop of Caesarea. I liked Basil during the brief period I knew him in Athens. He had a certain fire, and a good mind. He might have been a first-rate historian had he not decided to be a power in the church. But how can these young men resist the chance to rise? Philosophy offers them nothing; the church everything.

Julian was more wary of Gregory than I'd thought. But this could be hindsight. When Julian was writing his memoir, he asked me what I thought of Gregory and I assured him that if ever he had an enemy it was that jackal. Julian disagreed. But what I said apparently had some effect. As I have told you before, I want nothing to do with the publication of this memoir. Even so, if it is published, I shall delight in the effect it will have on the new bishop of Constantinople. He will not enjoy public reminder of his pseudo-Cynic youth.

It is also amusing to compare Gregory's actual behaviour in Athens with his own account of those days which he has given us in the Invective he wrote shortly after Julian died. I have this work in front of me as I write. At almost no point is it honest. For instance, Gregory describes Julian's appearance in this way: 'His neck was unsteady, his shoulders always in motion, shrugging up and down like a pair of scales, his eyes rolling and glancing from side to side with an almost insane expression, his feet unsteady and stumbling, his nostrils breathing insolence and disdain, the expression of his face ridiculous, his bursts of laughter unrestrained and coming in noisy gusts, his nods of assent and dissent quite inappropriate, his speech stopping short and interrupted by his taking a breath, his questions without sense or order, his answers not a whit better than his questions . . .' This is not even good caricature. Of course Julian *did* talk too much; he was enormously eager to learn and to teach; he could often be silly. But he was hardly the spastic creature Gregory describes. The malice of a true Christian attempting to destroy an opponent is something unique in the world. No other religion ever considered it necessary to destroy others because they did not share the same beliefs. At worst, another man's belief might inspire amusement or contempt – the Egyptians and their animal gods, for instance. Yet those who worshipped the Bull did not try to murder those who worshipped the Snake, or to convert them by force from Snake to Bull. No evil ever entered the world quite so vividly or on such a vast scale as Christianity did. I don't need to tell you that my remarks are for your eyes alone and *not* for publication. I put them down now in this uncharacteristic way because I find myself more moved than I thought I would be as I recall that season in Athens, not only through the eyes of my own memory but through those of Julian.

Gregory also maintains that he knew even then that Julian was a Hellenist, secretly conspiring against Christianity. This is not true. Gregory might have guessed the first (though I doubt it); he certainly could not have *known* that Julian was conspiring against the state religion, since at that time Julian was hardly conspiring against anything. He was under constant surveillance. He wanted only to survive. Yet Gregory writes, 'I used these very words about him: "What an evil the Roman State is nourishing," though I prefaced them by a wish that I might prove a false prophet.' If Gregory had said this to anyone, it would have been the talk of Athens. It would also have been treason, since Julian was the heir of Constantius. If Gregory ever made such a prophecy, it must have been whispered in Basil's ear when they were in bed together.

I find Julian's reference to Macrina amusing and disingenuous. In the proper place I shall tell you the true story, which you may or may not use, as you see fit. Julian's version is true only up to a point. I suppose he wanted to protect her reputation, not to mention his own.

I see Macrina occasionally. She was always plain. She is now hideous. But so am I. So is all the world, old. But in her day Macrina was the most interesting girl in Athens.

Julian Augustus

Even today, Prohaeresius is a man I greatly admire. I say 'even today' because he is a Galilean and has opposed my edict forbidding Galileans to teach the classics. Though I went out of my way to exempt him from this ban, he has gone into retirement. When I met him, he had been for forty years the city's most famous teacher of rhetoric. His house is a large one near the Ilissos River. At all hours it is – or was – crowded with students asking questions, answering questions.

At first I stood at the back of the crowded dim room and watched Prohaeresius as he sat comfortably in a large wooden chair. He was then eighty years of age: tall, vigorous, with a powerful chest, extraordinary black eyes, not unlike those of his niece Macrina. His hair was white and thick and curled richly upon his brow, like seafoam on a beach. He was in every way a handsome man, with a voice to match. In fact, he was such a master of eloquence that when my cousin Constans sent him on a mission to Rome, the Romans not only admitted that he was the most eloquent speaker they had ever heard, they set up a bronze statue to him in the forum with the inscription: 'From Rome, the Queen of Cities, to Prohaeresius, the King of Eloquence.' I mention this to emphasize his gifts, for the people of the city of Rome are the most jaded and bored in the world. Or so everyone tells me. I have yet to see my capital city.

Prohaeresius was consoling a student who complained of poverty. 'I make no case for poverty. But it is at least bearable in youth. Salt to the day. When I first came from Armenia to Athens, I lived with a friend in an attic, just off the Street of the Slaughter-houses. Between us we had one cloak and one blanket. In winter we broke the day in watches. When he went out, wearing the cloak, I would huddle under the blanket. When he came back, I would take the cloak while he kept warm in bed. You have no idea how good this is for one's style. I would prepare speeches of such eloquence that I brought tears to my own eyes as I declaimed them into that old blanket, teeth chattering from the cold.' There was an amused murmur. I had the sense that this was a favourite story, often told.

Then Gregory spoke to him in a low voice. Prohaeresius nodded and got to his feet. I was startled to see that he was nearer seven than six feet tall.

'We have a visitor,' he said to the others. All eyes were turned to me and I looked nervously to the floor. 'A scholar of some renown.' Despite the irony of this, he said it amiably. 'The cousin of a young friend of mine, now dead. Fellow scholars, the most noble Julian, heir to all the material world, as we are heirs to things spiritual, or try to be.'

There was a moment of confusion. The students were uncertain whether to behave towards me as a member of the imperial family or as a student. Many of those who were seated rose; some bowed; others simply stared curiously. Macrina whispered in my ear, 'Go on, you dummy! Speak to him!'

I pulled myself together and made a speech, very brief and to the point, or so I thought. Macrina told me later that it was interminable and pretentious. Fortunately, now that I am Emperor *all* my speeches are considered graceful and to the point. How one's style improves with greatness!

Prohaeresius then took me round among the students, introducing me to this one and that one. They were shy, even though I had carefully made the point that I intended to come and go at the University like any other student.

Prohaeresius continued his discourse a little while longer. Then he dismissed the students and led me into the atrium of his house. The sun slanted now from the west. From upstairs I could hear the laughter and scuffling of the students who boarded there. Occasionally they would come out on the gallery to get a glimpse of me. But when they caught me looking at *them*, they pretended they had business in someone else's room. I would have given a good deal to have lived anonymously in one of those bare rooms.

I was placed in the chair of honour beside the fountain, as Prohaeresius presented his wife Amphiclea to me. She is a sad woman who has never got over the deaths of two daughters. She spoke seldom. Obviously philosophy has been no consolation to her. I also met Macrina's father, Anatolius, a boorish man who looked like an innkeeper, which he was. Macrina was not fond of him.

Basil and Gregory excused themselves. Gregory was most winning. He offered to take me to all the lectures; he would be my guide. Basil was equally pleasant though he said that he might have to excuse himself from most expeditions. 'It's only a few months before I go back. I have a great deal to do, *if* I'm spared.' And he pressed both hands to his middle, with a look of mock agony. 'My liver feels as if Prometheus's vultures were tearing at it!'

'Stay out of draughts, then,' I found myself saying too quickly, 'or you may conceive and lay a vulture's egg!' Prohaeresius and Macrina both got the allusion and burst out laughing. Basil was not much amused and I regretted the quickness with which I had spoken. I often do this. It is a fault. Gregory shook my hand fondly; then he and Basil left. To this day he is probably afraid that I shall have my revenge on him for what he said about me. But I am not like that, as the world knows.

We drank wine in the garden. Prohaeresius asked me about matters at court. He was most interested in politics; in fact, when my cousin Constans wanted to ennoble him as a sign of admiration, he offered Prohaeresius the honorary title of praetorian prefect. But the old man said that he preferred to be food comptroller for Athens (a significant title Constantius always reserved for himself). Then, exercising the authority that went with his title, he got the corn supply of several islands diverted to Athens. Needless to say, he is a hero to the city.

Prohaeresius was suspicious of me from the beginning. And for all his geniality he seemed by his questions to be trying to get me to confess to some obscure reason for visiting Athens. He spoke of the splendours of Milan and Rome, the vitality of Constantinople, the elegant viciousness of Antioch, the high intellectual tone of Pergamon and Nicomedia; he even praised Caesarea – 'the Metropolis of Letters', as Gregory always refers to it, and not humorously. Any one of these cities, Prohaeresius declared, ought to attract me more than Athens. I told him bluntly that I had come to see him.

'*And* the beautiful city?' Macrina suddenly interrupted.

'And the beautiful city,' I repeated dutifully.

Prohaeresius rose suddenly. 'Let us take a walk by the river,' he said. 'Just the two of us.'

At the Ilissos we stopped opposite the Kallirrhoe Fountain, a sort of stone island so hollowed and shaped by nature that it does indeed resemble a fountain; from it is drawn sacred water. We sat on the bank, among long grass brown from August heat. Plane trees sheltered us from the setting sun. The day was golden; the air still. All around us students read or slept. Across the river, above a row of dusty trees, rose Hymettos. I was euphoric.

'My dear boy,' Prohaeresius addressed me now without ceremony as father to son. 'You are close to the fire.'

It was a most unexpected beginning. I lay full length on the thick brown turf while he sat cross-legged beside me, very erect, his back to the bole of a plane tree. I looked up at him, noting how rounded and youthful the neck was, how firm the jaw line for one so old.

'Fire? The sun's? The earth's?'

Prohaeresius smiled. 'Neither. Nor hell's fire, as the Christians say.'

'As *you* believe?' I was not certain to what extent he was a Galilean; even now, I don't know. He has always been evasive. I cannot believe such a fine teacher and Hellenist could be one of them, but anything is possible, as the gods daily demonstrate.

'We are not ready for *that* dialogue just yet,' he said. He gestured towards the swift shrunken river at our feet. 'There, by the way, is where Plato's *Phaidros* is set. They had good talk that day, and on this same bank.'

'Shall we equal it?'

'Some day, perhaps.' He paused. I waited, as though for an omen. 'You will be emperor one day.' The old man said this evenly, as though stating fact.

'I don't want to be. I doubt if I shall be. Remember that of all our family, only Constantius and I are left. As the others went, so I shall go. That's why I'm here. I wanted to see Athens first.'

'Perhaps you mean that. But I . . . well, I confess to a weakness for oracles.' He paused significantly. That was enough. One word more and he would have committed treason. It is forbidden by law to consult an oracle concerning the emperor – an excellent law, by the way, for who would ever obey a ruler the date of whose death was known and whose successor had been identified? I must say that I was shocked at the old man's candour. But also pleased that he felt he could trust me.

'Is it predicted?' I was as bold as he. I incriminated myself, hoping to prove to him my own good faith.

He nodded. 'Not the day, not the year, merely the fact. But it will be tragedy.'

'For me? Or for the state?'

'No one knows. The oracle was not explicit.' He smiled. 'They seldom are. I wonder why we put such faith in them.'

'Because the gods *do* speak to us in dreams and reveries. That is a fact. Both Homer and Plato . . .'

'Perhaps they do. Anyway, the habit of believing is an old one . . . I knew all your family.' Idly he plucked at the brown grass with thick-veined old hands. 'Constans was weak. But he had good qualities. He was not the equal of Constantius, of course. You are.'

'Don't say that.'

'I merely observe.' He turned to me suddenly. 'Now it is my guess, Julian, that you mean to restore the worship of the old gods.'

My breath stopped. 'You presume too much.' My voice shook despite a hardness of tone which would have done justice to Constantius himself. Sooner or later one learns the Caesarian trick: that abrupt shift in tone which is harsh reminder of the rod and axe we wield over all men.

'I hope that I do,' said the old man, serenely.

'I'm sorry. I shouldn't have spoken like that. You are the master.'

He shook his head. 'No, *you* are the master, or will be soon. I want only to be useful. To warn you that despite what your teacher Maximus may say, the Christians have won.'

'I don't believe it!' Fiercely and tactlessly I reminded him that only a small part of the Roman population was actually Galilean.

'Why do you call them Galileans?' he asked, interrupting my harangue.

'Because Galilee was where *he* came from!'

Prohaeresius saw through me. 'You fear the word "Christian",' he said, 'for it suggests that those who call themselves that are indeed followers of a king, a great lord.'

'A mere name cannot affect *what* they are.' I evaded him. But he is right. The name is a danger to us.

I resumed my argument: most of the civilized world is neither Hellenist nor Galilean, but suspended in between. With good reason, a majority of the people hate the Galileans. Too many innocents have been slaughtered in their mindless doctrinal quarrels. I need only mention the murder of Bishop George at Alexandria to recall vividly to those who read this the savagery of that religion not only towards its enemies (whom they term 'impious') but also towards its own followers.

Prohaeresius tried to argue with me, but though he is the world's most eloquent man, I would not listen to him. Also, he was uncharacteristically artless in his defence of the Galileans, which made me suspect he was not one of them. Like so many, he is in a limbo between Hellenism and the new death cult. Nor do I think he is merely playing it safe. He is truly puzzled. The old gods do *seem* to have failed us, and I have always accepted the possibility that they have withdrawn from human affairs, terrible as that is to contemplate. But mind has not failed us. Philosophy has not failed us. From Homer to Plato to Iamblichos the true gods continue to be defined in their many aspects and powers: multiplicity contained by the One, all emanating from truth. Or as Plotinus wrote: 'Of its nature the sould loves God and longs to be at one with him.' As long as the soul of man exists, there is God. It is all so clear.

I realized that I was making a speech to a master of eloquence, but I could not stop myself. Dozing students sat up and looked at me curiously, convinced I was mad, for I was waving my arms in great arcs as I am prone to do when passionate. Prohaeresius took it all in good part.

'Believe what you must,' he said at last.

'But you believe, too! You believe in what I believe. You must or you could not teach as you do.'

'I see it differently. That is all. But try to be practical. The thing has taken hold. The Christians govern the world through Constantius. They have had almost thirty years of wealth and power. They will not surrender easily. You come too late, Julian. Of course if you were Constantine and this were forty years ago and we were pondering these same problems, then I might say to you:

"Strike! Outlaw them! Rebuild the temples!" But now is not then. You are not Constantine. They have the world. The best one can hope to do is civilize them. That is why I teach. That is why I can never help you.'

I respected him that day. I respect him now. If he is still alive when this campaign is ended, I shall want to talk to him again. How we all long make conversions!

Like two conspirators, we returned to his house. We now had a bond between us which could not be broken, for each had told the other true and dangerous things. Fear defined our friendship and gave it savour.

In the dim atrium, students were again gathered, talking strenuously all at once as students will. When they saw us enter, they fell silent. I daresay the sight of me alarmed them. But Prohaeresius told them I was to be treated as just another student.

'Not that he is, of course, in spite of the beard and the old clothes.' They laughed. 'He is different from us.' I was about to say that even members of Constantine's family have some (if not much) resemblance to the human family, when he said: 'He is a true philosopher. He has *chosen* to be what we *must* be.' This was accepted with some delight. Not until a day later did the irony of what he said occur to me.

Macrina took me by the arm and said, 'You must meet Priscus. He is the most disagreeable man in Athens.'

Priscus sat on a stool, surrounded by students. He is a lean, cold-faced man, nearly as tall as Prohaeresius. He rose when we approached him and murmured, 'Welcome.' I was pleased to meet this great teacher whom I had long known by reputation, for he is as famous for his wit as he is for his ambiguities. He is also completely without enthusiasm, which right off made him a good foil for me since I am often excited by the trivial. We were friends from the start. He is with me now in Persia.

'Try to pin him down,' said Macrina, turning to me, her hand on Priscus's lean arm as though presenting him to me for a bout of wrestling, 'on *anything*. We think of him as the master of evasion. He never argues.'

With a look of distaste which I have come to know so well (and fear when it is turned on me!), Priscus got his arm loose from Macrina's grasp. 'Why should I argue? I known what *I* know. And others are always quick to tell me what *they* know, or think they know. There is no need for confrontation.'

'But surely you must find that new thoughts occur in argument?' I was naïve, of course; I pressed him hard. 'After all, Socrates led others to wisdom through argument and conversation.'

'The two are not quite the same thing. I teach through conversation, or try to. But *argument* is a vice in this city. Glib men can almost always score points off wiser but less well-spoken men. Nowadays style in speaking is everything; content nothing. Most of the Sophists are actors – worse, they are lawyers. And the young men pay to hear them perform, like street singers.'

'Priscus attacks me!' Prohaeresius had joined us. He was amused at what was obviously an old discussion.

'You know what I think.' Priscus was severe. 'You are the worst of the lot because you are the best performer.' He turned to me. 'He is so eloquent that every Sophist in Athens hates him.'

'All but you,' observed Macrina.

Priscus ignored her. 'A few years ago his confrères decided that he was too popular. So they bribed the proconsul . . .'

'Careful,' said Macrina. 'We must not speak of bribed officials in front of what may one day be the greatest official of them all.'

'Bribed the proconsul,' said Priscus as though she had not spoken, 'to exile our host. This was done. But then the proconsul retired and was succeeded by a younger man who was so indignant at what had happened that he allowed Prohaeresius to return. But the Sophists did not give up easily. They continued to plot against their master. So the proconsul held a meeting at the University . . .'

'At my uncle's suggestion.'

Prohaeresius was amused. 'Macrina allows us no secrets. Yes, I put him up to it. I wanted to get my enemies all together in one place in order that I might . . .'

'Dispatch them,' said Macrina.

'*Win* them,' said her uncle.

'Beat them,' said Macrina.

Priscus continued. 'It was a formidable display. Everyone was gathered in the main hall of the University. Friends were nervous. Enemies were active. The proconsul arrived. He took charge of the assembly. He announced that a theme should be proposed for Prohaeresius to argue. Any theme. The assembly could choose it. At first no one said a word.'

'Until my uncle saw two of his very worst enemies skulking in the back. He called on them to set a theme. They tried to escape, but the proconsul ordered his guards to bring them back.'

Priscus looked dour indeed. 'It was the guards, I suggest, that won the day for virtue.'

'The honeyed tongue of Priscus!' The old man laughed. 'You may be right. Though I suspect the bad judgement of the enemy helped most, for they set me a theme of remarkable obscenity and limited scope.'

'Which side of a woman is the most pleasing, front or back.' Macrina grinned.

'But he accepted the challenge,' said Priscus. 'He spoke with such effectiveness that the audience maintained a Pythagorean silence.'

'He also insisted that shorthand reporters from the law court take down every word.' In an oblique way, Macrina was proud of her uncle's prowess. 'He also insisted there be no applause.'

'It was a memorable speech,' Priscus continued. 'First, he presented the argument in all its particulars. Then he took one side . . . the front. After an hour, he said, "Now observe carefully whether I remember all the arguments that I used earlier." He then repeated the speech in all its intricate detail, only this time he took the opposite point of view . . . the back. In spite of the proconsul's order, applause filled the hall. It was the greatest triumph of memory and eloquence heard in our time.'

'And . . .?' Prohaeresius knew that Priscus would not finish without a sudden twist to the knife.

'*And?* Your enemies were completely routed and where before they despised you, now they hate you.' Priscus turned to me. 'They nearly had his life the next year. They still plot against him.'

'Which proves?' Prohaeresius was as curious as I to learn what Priscus was up to.

'That victories in argument are useless. They are showy. What is spoken always causes more anger than any silence. Debate of this sort convinces no one. Aside from the jealousies such a victory arouses, there is the problem of the vanquished. I speak now of philosophers. The one who is defeated, even if he realizes at last that he is fighting truth, suffers from having been publicly proved wrong. He then becomes savage and is apt to end by hating philosophy. I would prefer not to lose anyone for civilization.'

'Well said,' Prohaeresius agreed.

'Or, perhaps,' said the devilish Macrina, 'you yourself don't want to lose an argument, knowing that you are apt to turn bitter as a result of public humiliation. Oh, Priscus, you are vain! You won't compete for fear you might not win. As it is, none of us knows how wise you are. Silence is his legend, Prince. And he is all the greater for that. Each time Prohaeresius speaks he limits himself, for words limit everything, being themselves limited. That's why Priscus is wisest of all: silence cannot be judged. Silence masks all things or *no* thing. Only Priscus can tell us what his silence conceals, but since he won't, we suspect him great.'

Priscus did not answer. Macrina was the only woman I have ever known who could speak with so many odd twistings and turnings. Irony is not usual to woman, but then Macrina was not in any way usual. Before we had an opportunity to see if Priscus could answer her, we were interrupted by the arrival of my bodyguard, as well as an officer of the proconsul's staff. Word had already spread throughout Athens that I was at the house of Prohaeresius. I was again taken into custody.

Priscus: Macrina was a bitch. We all detested her, but because she was the niece of Prohaeresius we endured her. Julian's description of our first meeting is not accurate. That is to say, what he remembers is not what I remember. For instance, he says that his bodyguard arrived *before* I answered Macrina. This is not true. I told her then and there that my silence masked compassion for the intellectual shortcomings of others since I did not wish to wound anyone, even her. This caused some laughter. *Then* the guards arrived.

For the historic record I should give my first impression of Julian. He was a handsome youth, thick in the chest like all his family, and muscular, a gift of nature since in those days he seldom exercised. He was far too busy talking. Gregory was not entirely inaccurate when he described Julian's breathless and continual conversation. In fact, I used to say to him, 'How can you expect to learn anything when you do all the talking?' He would laugh excitedly and say, 'But I talk and listen at the same time. That is *my* art!' Which perhaps was true. I was always surprised at how much he did absorb.

Not until I read the memoir did I know about the conversation with Prohaeresius. I never suspected the old man of such cunning, or boldness. It was a dangerous thing to admit to a strange prince that he had consulted an oracle. But he always had a weakness for oracles.

I never liked the old man much. I always felt he had too much of the demagogue in him and too little of the philosopher. He also took his role as a great old man seriously. He made speeches on any subject, anywhere. He cultivated princes the way bishops cultivate relics. He was a formidable orator, but his writings were banal.

Let me tell you something about Macrina since Julian is not candid and if I don't tell you you will never know. They had a love affair which was the talk of the city. Macrina behaved with her usual clownishness, discussing the affair with everyone in intimate detail. She declared that Julian was a formidable lover, indicating that her own experience had been considerable. Actually, she was probably a virgin when they met. There were not many men of her set who would have made the effort to make her a non-virgin. After all, Athens is famous for the complaisance of its girls, and not many men like to bed a talking-woman, especially when there are so many quiet ones to choose from. I am positive that Julian was Macrina's first lover.

There was a funny story going around at about this time, no doubt apocryphal. Julian and Macrina were overheard while making love. Apparently all during the act each one continued to talk. Macrina is supposed to have confuted the Pythagoreans while Julian restated the Platonic powers, all this before and during orgasm. They were well matched.

Julian seldom mentioned Macrina to me. He was embarrassed, knowing that I knew of the affair. The last time we spoke of her was in Persia when he was writing the memoir. He wanted to know what had become of her, whom she had married, how she looked. I told him that she was somewhat heavy, that she had married an Alexandrian merchant who lived at Piraeus, that she has three children. I did not tell him that the oldest child was his son.

Yes. That is the famous scandal. Some seven months after Julian left Athens, Macrina gave birth. During the pregnancy she stayed with her father. Despite her daring ways she was surprisingly conventional in this matter. She was desperate for a husband even though it was widely known that the bastard was Julian's and therefore a mark of honour for the mother. Luckily, the Alexandrian married her and declared the child was his.

I saw the boy occasionally while he was growing up. He is now in his twenties and looks somewhat like his father, which makes it hard for me to be with him. Stoic though I am, in certain memories there is pain. Fortunately, the boy lives now in Alexandria, where he runs his stepfather's trading office. He has, Macrina once told me, no interest in philosophy. He is a devout Christian. So that is the end of the house of Constantine. Did Julian know that he had a son? I think not. Macrina swears she never told him, and I almost believe her.

A few years ago I met Macrina in what we Athenians call the Roman agora. We greeted one another amiably, and sat together on the steps of the water-clock tower. I asked about her son.

'He is beautiful! He looks exactly like his father, an emperor, a god!' Macrina has lost none of her old fierce flow of language, though the edge of her wit is somewhat blunted. 'But I don't regret it.'

'The resemblance? Or being the mother of Julian's son?'

She did not answer. She looked absently across the agora, crowded as always with lawyers and tax collectors. Her dark eyes were as glittering as ever, though her face has grown jowly and the heavy bosom fallen with maternity and age. She turned to me abruptly. 'He wanted to marry me. Did you know that, Priscus? I could have been Empress of Rome. What a thought! Would you have liked that? Do you think I would have been . . . decorative? Certainly *unusual*. How many empresses have been philosophers in their own right? It would have been amusing. I should have worn a lot of jewellery, even though I detest ornaments. Look at me!' She tugged at the simple garment she wore. Despite her husband's wealth, Macrina wore no rings, no brooches, no combs in her hair, no jewels in her ears. 'But empresses must look the part. They have no choice. Of course I should have had a bad character. I would have modelled myself on Messalina.'

'You? Insatiable?' I could not help laughing.

'Absolutely!' The old edge returned briefly: the black eyes were humorous. 'I'm a faithful wife now because I am fat and no one wants me. At least no one *I* would want wants me. But I'm drawn to beauty. I should love to be a whore! Except I'd want to choose the clientele, which is why I should have loved being empress! History would have loved me, too! Macrina the Insatiable!'

Anyone who saw us on those steps would have thought: what an eminently respectable couple! An old philosopher and a dignified matron, solemnly discussing the price of corn or the bishop's latest sermon. Instead Macrina was intoning a hymn to lust.

'What would Julian have thought?' I managed to interject before she gave too many specific details of her appetite. It is curious how little interested we are in the sexual desires of those who do not attract us.

'I wonder.' She paused. 'I'm not sure he would have minded. No. No. No, he *would* have minded. Oh, not out of jealousy. I don't think he was capable of that. He simply disliked excess. So do I, for that matter, but then I have never had the chance to be excessive, except in food, of course.' She patted herself. 'You see the result? Of course I could still be a beauty in Persia. They revel in fat women.' Then: 'Did he ever mention me to you? Later? When you were with him in Persia?'

I shook my head. I'm not certain why I lied to her, unless dislike is sufficient motive.

'No. I suppose he wouldn't.' She did not seem distressed. One must admire the strength of her egotism. 'Before he went back to Milan, he told me that if he lived he would marry me. Contrary to gossip, he did *not* know that I was pregnant then. I never told him. But I did tell him that I wanted to be his wife, although if Constantius had other plans for him (which of course he did) I would not grieve. Oh, I was a formidable girl!'

'Did you ever hear from him again?'

She shook her head. 'Not even a letter. But shortly after he became Emperor he told the new proconsul of Greece to come see me and ask if there was anything I wanted. I shall never forget the look of surprise on the proconsul's face when he saw me. One look assured him that Julian could not have had any amatory interest in this fat lady. He was puzzled, poor man . . . Do you think Julian knew about our son? It was not the best-kept secret.'

I said I did not think so. And I do not think so. I certainly never told him, and who else would have dared?

'Did you know Julian's wife?'

I nodded. 'In Gaul. She was much older than he. And very plain.'

'So I've heard. I was never jealous. After all, he was forced to marry her. Was he really celibate after she died?'

'As far as I know.'

'He was strange! I'm sure the Christians would have made a saint out of him if he had been one of theirs, and his poor bones would be curing liver complaints at this very moment. Well, that is all over, isn't it?' She glanced at the water clock behind us. 'I'm late. How much do *you* bribe the tax assessor?'

'Hippia looks after those matters.'

'Women *are* better at such things. It has to do with details. We delight in them. We are children of the magpie.' She rose heavily, with some difficulty. She steadied herself against the white marble wall of the tower. 'Yes, I should have liked to have been Empress of Rome.'

'I doubt it. If you had been empress, you would be dead by now. The Christians would have killed you.'

'Do you think I would have minded *that?*' She turned full on me and the large black eyes blazed like obsidian in the sun. 'Don't you realize – can't you tell just by looking at me, my dear wise old Priscus – that not a day has passed in twenty years I haven't wished I were dead!'

Macrina left me on the steps. As I watched the blunt figure waddle through the crowd towards the magistrate's office, I recalled her as she had been years before and I must say for a moment I was touched by the urgency of that cry from the heart. But it does not alter the fact that she was and is a sublimely disagreeable woman. I've not talked to her since that day, though we always nod when we see one another in the street.

8

Julian Augustus

A week later after I arrived in Athens I met the Hierophant of Greece. Since I did not want the proconsul to know of this meeting, it was arranged to take place in the Library of Hadrian, a not much frequented building midway between the Roman and the Athenian agoras.

At noon I arrived at the library and went straight to the north reading room, enjoying as I always do the musty dry odour of papyrus and ink which comes from the tall niches where the scrolls and codices are kept. The high room with its coffered ceiling (for which we must thank Antinoüs's protector) was empty. Here I waited for the Hierophant. I was extremely nervous, for he is the holiest of all men. I am forbidden by law to write his name but I can say that he belongs to the family of the Eumolpidae, one of the two families from which Hierophants are traditionally drawn. He is not only High Priest of Greece, he is custodian and interpreter of the mysteries of Eleusis which go back at least two thousand years, if not to the beginning of our race. Those of us who have been admitted to the mysteries may not tell what we have seen or what we know. Even so, as Pindar wrote: 'Happy is he who, having seen these rites, goes below the hollow earth; for he knows the end of life and he knows its god-sent beginning.' Sophocles described initiates as 'Thrice-happy mortals, who having seen those rites depart for Hades; for them alone is it granted to have true life there; to the rest, evil.' I quote from memory. (Note to secretary: Correct quotations, if they are wrong.)

Eleusis is a city fourteen miles from Athens. For two thousand years the mysteries have been celebrated in that place, for it was at Eleusis that Persephone returned from the underworld to which she had been stolen by the death-god Hades and made his queen. When Persephone first vanished, her mother Demeter, the harvest goddess, sought her for nine days, neither eating nor drinking. (As I tell this story initiates will see the mystery unfold. But no one else may know what is meant.) On the tenth day Demeter came to Eleusis. She was received by the king and queen, who gave her a pitcher of barley water flavoured with mint which she drank all at once. When the king's eldest son said, 'How greedily you drink!' Demeter turned him into a lizard. But then, remorseful over what she had done, she conferred great powers upon the king's youngest son, Triptolemus. She gave him seed corn, a wooden plough and a chariot drawn by serpents; he then travelled the earth teaching men agriculture. She did this for him not only to make up for what in her anger she had done to his brother, but also because Triptolemus was able to tell her what had happened to her daughter. He had been in the fields when the earth suddenly opened before him. Then a chariot drawn by black horses appeared, coming from the sea. The driver was Hades; in his arms he held Persephone. As the chariot careered at full speed into the cavern, the earth closed over them. Now Hades is brother to Zeus, king of the gods, and he had stolen the girl with Zeus's connivance. When Demeter learned this, she took her revenge. She bade the trees not to bear fruit and the earth not to flower. Suddenly, the world was barren. Men starved. Zeus capitulated: if Persephone had not yet eaten the food of the dead, she might return to her mother. As it turned out, Persephone had eaten seven pomegranate seeds and this was enough to keep her for ever in the underworld. But Zeus arranged a compromise. Six months of the year she would remain with Hades, as queen of Tartarus. The remaining six months she would join her mother in the world above. That is why the cold barren time of the year is six months and the warm fruitful time six months. Demeter also gave the fig tree to Attica, and forbade the cultivation of beans. This holy story is acted out in the course of the mysteries. I cannot say more about it. The origin of the ceremony goes back to Crete and, some say, to Libya. It is possible that those places knew similar mysteries, but it is a fact that Eleusis is the actual place where Persephone returned from the underworld. I have myself seen the cavern from which she emerged.

Now: for those who have been initiated, I have in the lines above given in the form of a narrative a clear view of what happens after death. Through number and symbol, I have in a page revealed everything. But the profane may not unravel the mystery. They will merely note that I have told an old story of the old gods.

The Hierophant entered the reading room. He is a short plump man, not in the least impressive to look at. He saluted me gravely. His voice is powerful and he speaks old Greek exactly the way it was spoken two thousand years ago, for in the long descent of his family the same words have been repeated in exactly the same way from generation to generation. It is awesome to think that Homer heard what we still hear.

'I have been busy. I am sorry. But this is the sacred month. The mysteries begin in a week.' So he began, prosaically.

I told him that I wished to be initiated into *all* the mysteries: the lesser, the grreater, and the highest. I realized that this would be difficult to arrange on such short notice, but I had not much time.

'It can be done, of course. But you will need to study hard. Have you a good memory?'

I said that I still retained most of Homer. He reminded me that the mysteries last for nine days and that there are many passwords, hymns and prayers which must be learned before the highest mystery can be revealed. 'You must not falter.' The Hierophant was stern. I said that I thought I could learn what I needed to know in a week, for I do indeed have a good memory; at least it is good when properly inspired.

I was candid. I told him that if I lived, it was my hope to support Hellenism in its war with the Galileans.

He was abrupt. 'It is too late,' he said, echoing Prohaeresius. 'Nothing you can do will change what is about to happen.'

I had not expected such a response. 'Do you *know* the future?'

'I am Hierophant,' he said simply. 'The *last* Hierophant of Greece. I know many things, all tragic.'

I refused to accept this. 'But how can you be the last? Why, for centuries . . .'

'Prince, these things are written at the beginning. No one may tamper with fate. When I die, I shall be succeeded not by a member of our family but by a priest from another sect. He will be in name, but not in fact, the final Hierophant. Then the temple at Eleusis will be destroyed – all the temples in all of Greece will be destroyed. The barbarians will come. The Christians will prevail. Darkness will fall.'

'For ever?'

'Who can say? The goddess has shown me no more than what I have told you. With me, the true line ends. With the next Hierophant, the mysteries themselves will end.'

'I cannot believe it!'

'That alters nothing.'

'But if I were to become Emperor . . .'

'It would make no difference.'

'Then obviously, I shall *not* become Emperor.'

I smiled at this subtlety, for we had got around the law forbidding prophecy.

'Whether you are Emperor or not, Eleusis will be in ruins before the century is done.'

I looked at him closely. We were sitting on a long bench beneath a high latticed window. Lozenges of light superimposed their own designs upon the tiled floor at our feet. Despite his terrible conviction, this small fat man with his protuberant eyes and fat hands was perfectly composed. I have never known such self-containment, even in Constantius.

'I refuse to believe,' I said at last, 'that there is nothing we can do.'

He shrugged. 'We shall go on as long as we can, as we always have.' He looked at me solemnly. 'You must remember that because the mysteries come to an end makes them no less true. Those who were initiated will at least be fortunate in the underworld. Of course one pities those who come after us. But what is to be must be.' He rose with dignity, his small plump body held tightly erect, as though by will he might stiffen the soft flesh. 'I shall instruct you myself. We shall need several hours a day. Come to my house tonight.' With a small bow he withdrew.

During the weeks that followed, we saw each other every day. Yet I came to know the Hierophant no better. On any subject not connected with the mysteries, he refused to speak. I gave up talking to him, accepting him as what he was: a palpable link with the holy past but not a human companion.

I need not describe the celebrations which precede the initiation, since they are known to everyone. Though I may not describe the mysteries themselves, I can say that in this particular year more people took part in the festivities than usual, to the chagrin of the Galileans.

The whole business takes nine days. The first day was hot and enervating. The proclamation was made and the sacred objects brought from Eleusis to the Eleusinion, a small temple at the foot of the acropolis where – among other interesting things – there is a complete list of Alcibiades' personal property, seized when he profaned the mysteries one drunken night by imitating on a street corner the Hierophant's secret rites. The sacred objects are contained in several jars tied with red ribbons. They are put in the Eleusinion, to be returned to Eleusis during the main procession, which is on the fifth day.

On the second day, we bathed in the sea and washed the pig each of us had bought for sacrifice. I chose the beach at Phaleron, and nearly lost the pig I had bought for six drachmae. It is an amazing sight to watch several thousand people bathing in the sea, each with a squealing pig.

The third day is one of sacrifice, and a long night.

The fourth day is sacred to Asklepios; one stays at home.

On the fifth day the procession starts from the Dipylon Gate to Eleusis.

It was a lovely sight. An image of the god Iacchos, son of Demeter, is borne in a wooden carriage at the procession's head. This part of the ceremony is sacred to him. Though all are supposed to walk to Eleusis, most of the well-to-do are carried in litters. I walked. My bodyguards complained, but I was exalted. I was crowned with myrtle and I carried not only the sacred branches tied with wool but also, according to tradition, new clothes in a bundle on a stick over my shoulder. Macrina accompanied me.

The day was cloudy, which made the journey pleasanter than it usually is at that time of the year. All told, there were perhaps a thousand of us in the procession, not counting the curious, which included a number of Galileans who shouted atheist curses at us.

On the outskirts of Athens, just off the main road, Macrina pointed to a complex of old buildings. 'That is the most famous brothel in Greece,' she said with her usual delight in such things. 'The shrine of Aphrodite.' Apparently, people come from all over the world to visit the shrine, where for a price they enjoy the 'priestesses'. They pretend it is religion. Actually, it is mass prostitution. I could not disapprove more.

Just beyond the shrine there is an old bridge. Here the ordeal begins. On the bridge's parapet sit men with faces covered by hoods. It is their traditional function to remind important people of their faults and to condemn their pride. I consoled myself by remembering that Hadrian and Marcus Aurelius had preceded me on this bridge. If they had survived humiliation, so could I.

'It won't be bad.' Macrina tried to be reassuring. 'They're much too frightened of Constantius.' But I recalled how Hadrian had been jeered for his love of Antinoüs, and Hadrian was a reigning emperor, not mere cousin to one. I was sweating as we reached the bridge. All eyes were upon me. The hooded men – at least thirty of them – had just finished tormenting a local magistrate. They turned now to me. Macrina held my arm tight. Heart beating fast and eyes cast down, I walked slowly over the bridge. The jeering and curses were formidable. At first I tried not to listen, but then I recalled that this humiliation is an essential part of the mysteries: to rid oneself of pride. I listened. I was accused mostly of falseness and pretension. I was not a true scholar. I was a *poseur*. I looked like a goat. I was a coward and afraid to serve in the army (this was unexpected). I hated the Galileans. This made me nervous indeed but happily, it was said only once. After all, my tormentors were of the true religion and not apt to hold my dislike of the Galileans against me.

Finally, the bridge was crossed. The ordeal ended. Feeling purged and relieved (the worst is never so bad as one fears), I walked the rest of the way to

Eleusis, with Macrina grumbling at my side. I'm afraid she taunted me quite as much as the men on the bridge. But as I drew closer to the mysteries, I was filled with such a sense of expectancy that nothing could disturb my mood.

It was night when we arrived at Eleusis. The city is a small one on the Saronic Gulf, with a view of the island of Salamis. Like most cities whose principal source of revenue is strangers, Eleusis is full of inns and cookshops and tradesmen eager to sell copies of sacred objects at ridiculously high prices. It is a wonder that any place remains sacred, considering the inevitable presence of those whose livelihood depends on cheating strangers. I am told that Delphi is even worse than Eleusis; while Jerusalem – which is of course 'sacred' to the Galileans – is now a most distressing place to visit.

Torches blazed in every street of the town. Night was like day. Innkeepers solicited us, and at every street corner, men told of places to eat. Even vice was proposed, which shows how debased the local population is, for they should know better than anyone that during the pilgrims' three days in Eleusis, they must fast, remain continent, and touch neither the body of one dead nor that of a woman who has just given birth; eggs and beans are also forbidden us, even after the first day's fast.

Macrina and I followed the crowd to where the mysteries are enacted. Homer has described how the original temple was at the foot of the acropolis, in much the same spot as the present temple, or Telesterion, as it is called. This night everything was illuminated in honour of the Great Mysteries.

The entrance to the sacred enclosure is through a gate, even more noble than the Dipylon at Athens. We entered, passing through a roped-off section where guards and priests made sure that we were indeed initiates, remarkable by our dress and certain signs. The gate is so cunningly arranged that anyone looking through can see no more than a few yards of the sacred way; any further view of the Telesterion is broken by the large blank wall of the Ploutonion, a temple built over the original passage to Hades from which Persephone appeared.

Eyes smarting from torch smoke, Macrina and I ascended the sacred way, pausing first at the Kallichoros Well. I was overcome with awe, for this is the same well described by Homer. It is old beyond memory. It was here in the time when the gods walked the earth that the women of Eleusis danced in honour of Demeter. The opening of the well is several steps below the main terrace, and faced with magnificent marble. Near it stands a large basin containing sacred water. I bathed my hands and began to know Demeter and her grief. I was so moved that I almost neglected to pay the priestess the one drachma for the experience.

Next, we entered the Ploutonion, which is set in a rocky hollow of the acropolis. The elmwood doors were shut to us, but the altar outside, cut in living rock, was illuminated.

Finally we came to the long stoa of Philon, which fronts the Telesterion. Beyond this blue-paved portico the blank façade of the holiest building on earth is set against the acropolis, which provides its fourth wall. There are greater and more splendid temples in the world, but there is none which quite inspires one's reverence in the way the Telesterion does, for it has been holy since almost the first day of man, a creation of that beautiful lost world when the gods, not beleaguered, lived among us, and earth was simple and men good.

Since we were not yet initiates, we could not enter the Telesterion. At this point we were joined by two priests who led us to the house where the Eumolpidae have lived for a thousand years. We were to spend the night there.

The Hierophant, however, did not join us. On this night of nights, he fasted and meditated.

Macrina and I sat up until dawn. 'You must be admitted to the mysteries.' I scolded her, as I had done before.

But she was perverse. 'How can I? I'm not one thing or the other. I don't like the Christians because they are cruel. I don't like the mysteries and all the rest because I don't believe anything can help us when we are dead. Either we continue in some way, or we stop. But no matter what happens, it is beyond our control and there is no way of making a bargain with the gods. Consider the Christians, who believe there is a single god . . .'

'In three parts!'

'Well, yours is in a thousand bits. Anyway, if by some chance the Christians *are* right, then all this' – she gestured towards the Telesterion – 'is wrong, and you will go to their hell rather than to your Elysium.'

'But the Galileans *are* wrong.'

'Who can say?'

'Homer. Thousands of years of the true faith. Are we to believe there was no god until the appearance of a rabble-rousing carpenter three hundred years ago? It is beyond sense to think that the greatest age of man was godless.'

'You must argue with the Twins,' said Macrina; then we spoke of matters which I shall not record.

The next three days were beyond imagination. I was admitted to all of the mysteries, including the final and most secret. I saw that which is *enacted*, that which is *shown* and that which is *spoken*. I saw the passion of Demeter, the descent of Persephone to the underworld, the giving of grain to man. I saw the world as it is and the world that is to come. I lost my fear of death in the Telesterion when, in a blaze of light, I looked upon the sacred objects. *It was true.* More than this I cannot write. It is forbidden to reveal anything that one sees and hears during the two nights spent in the Telesterion. But I will make one general comment, a dissent from Aristotle, who wrote: 'The initiated do not learn anything so much as feel certain emotions and are put into a certain frame of mind.' First of all, one must question the proposition that a new emotion is not something learned. I should think that it was. In any case, I have yet to meet anyone who has been initiated at Eleusis who did not learn new things not only about the life we live now but the one to follow. There is such a logic to what is revealed on those two nights that one is astonished not to have understood it before – which proves to me the truth of what is seen, heard and demonstrated. We are part of a never-ending cycle, a luminous spiral of life, lost and regained, of death to life to . . . but now I begin to tell too much.

Priscus: He tells altogether too much. But that was his charm, except when he goes on altogether too long and becomes tedious. I know that you were initiated at Eleusis and doubtless feel much as he did about what is revealed there. I don't. It is possible that if I had gone through all the nonsense of initiation, I *might* have had a 'revelation'. But I doubt it. There are some natures too coarse to apprehend the mysteries. Mine is one. Nowadays of course we can write with a certain freedom of the mysteries since they are drawing to an end. The Emperor is expected to shut down the Telesterion as soon as he feels the time is politically right. Naturally, the bishops lust for the destruction of Eleusis, which to me is the only argument for preserving it.

I am cool to the mysteries because I find them vague and full of unjustified hope. I do not want to be nothing next year or next minute or whenever this long life of mine comes to its end (of course it does not seem at all long to *me*, not long enough by half!). Yet I suspect that 'nothing' is my fate. Should it be otherwise, what can I do about it? To believe as poor Julian did that he was among the elect as a result of a nine-day ceremony, costing some fifteen drachmae, not counting extras, is to fall into the same nonsense we accuse the Christians of when we blame their bitter exclusivity and lunatic superstition.

I had no idea Macrina was so sensible until I read Julian's account of their conversation at Eleusis. She might have made him a good wife. I had always assumed she only told him what he wanted to hear, like any other woman. She was rare, in her way; but not to my taste.

The remainder of Julian's stay in Athens was uneventful. He was personally popular. The Sophists all tried to curry favour with him. It is remarkable how men supposedly dedicated to philosophy and things of the mind are drawn to power; affecting scorn for the mighty, they are inevitably attracted to those who rule. When the powerful man is as amiable and philosophy-loving as Julian, the resulting attempt to capture him is all the more unseemly.

Libanius: How typical of Priscus! He can hardly restrain his jealousy of me, and his resentment of my influence over Julian. Yet my interest in Julian was *not* self-seeking. How could it be? When I turned down the title of praetorian prefect, I said that the title Sophist was good enough for me. My gesture is still much remembered not only here in Antioch but everywhere philosophy is valued. Those of us who wish to lead others to wisdom respond to any questioning soul, prince or beggar. Sometimes, as in the case of Maximus, Julian showed bad judgement, but by and large he cultivated the best minds of our era. I also find Priscus's remarks about Eleusis distasteful, even atheistic. Cicero, who was hardly superstitious, wrote that if all else Athens had brought the world was swept away, the mysteries alone would be enough to place mankind for ever in Athens' debt. Priscus has got worse with age. Envy festers. He was never a true philosopher. I find myself pitying him as I read his bitter commentary.

Priscus: In any case, when Julian looked with adoration at that sheaf of wheat which is revealed with such solemnity at the highest moment of the ceremony ...

Libanius: This is absolute blasphemy! These things must not be revealed. Priscus will suffer for this in the next world, while whoever betrayed to him our high secret will sink for ever in dung. It is appalling!

Priscus: ... he felt duly elated, believing that as the wheat withers, dies and is reborn, so it is with us. But is the analogy correct? I would say no. For one thing, it is not the *same* sheaf of wheat that grows from the seed. It is a new sheaf of wheat, which would suggest that our immortality, such as it is, is between our legs. Our seed does indeed make a new man but he is not us. The son is not the father. The father is put in the ground and that is the end of him. The son is a different man who will one day make yet another man and so on – perhaps for ever – yet the individual consciousness stops.

Libanius: I hate Priscus! He is worse than a Christian. Homer believed. Was Homer wrong? Of course not.

Priscus: Julian did nothing to offend the Christians in Athens, though it was fairly well known that he tended towards philosophy. But he was discreet. On at least one occasion he attended church.

The Hierophant liked him but thought he was doomed, or so he told me years later. The Hierophant was an interesting man. But of course you knew him for you were admitted to the mysteries during his reign. He realized with extraordinary clarity that our old world was ended. There were times, I think, when he took pleasure in knowing he was the last of a line that extended back two thousand years. Men are odd. If they cannot be first, they don't in the least mind being last.

Julian Augustus

Those marvellous days in Athens came to an abrupt end when an imperial messenger arrived with orders that I attend Constantius at Milan. No reason was given. I assumed that I was to be executed. Just such a message had been delivered to Gallus. I confess now to a moment of weakness. Walking alone in the agora, I considered flight. Should I disappear in the back streets of Athens? Change my name? Shave my head? Or should I take to the road like a New Cynic and walk to Pergamon or Nicomedia and lose myself among students, hide until I was forgotten, assumed dead, no longer dangerous?

Suddenly I opened my arms to Athena. I looked up to her statue on the acropolis, much to the astonishment of the passers-by (this took place in front of the Library of Pantainos). I prayed that I be allowed to remain in Athena's city, preferring death on the spot to departure. But the goddess did not answer. Sadly I dropped my arms. Just at that moment, Gregory emerged from the library and approached me with his wolf's grin.

'You're leaving us,' he said. There are no secrets in Athens. I told him that I was reluctant to go but the Emperor's will must be done.

'You'll be back,' he said, taking my arm familiarly.

'I hope so.'

'And you'll be the Caesar then, a man of state, with a diadem and guards and courtiers! It will be interesting to see just how our Julian changes when he is set over us like a god.'

'I shall be the same,' I promised, sure of death.

'Remember old friends in your hour of greatness.' A scroll hidden in Gregory's belt dropped to the pavement. Blushing, he picked it up.

'I have a special permit,' he stammered. 'I can withdraw books, certain books, approved books . . .'

I laughed at his embarrassment. He knew that I knew that the Pantainos Library never allows any book to be taken from the reading room. I said I would tell no one.

The proconsul treated me decently. He was a good man, but frightened. I recognized at once in his face the look of the official who does not know if one is about to be executed or raised to the throne. It must be cruelly perplexing for such men. If they are kind, they are then vulnerable to a later charge of conspiracy; if they are harsh, they may live to find their victim great and vindictive. The proconsul steered a middle course; he was correct; he was conscientious; he arranged for my departure the next morning.

My last evening in Athens is still too painful to describe. I spent it with Macrina. I vowed to return if I could. Next day, at first light, I left the city. I did not trust myself to look back at Athena's temple floating in air, or at the sun-struck violet line of Hymettos. Eyes to the east and the morning sun, I made the sad journey to Piraeus and the sea.

9

Julian Augustus

It was mid-October when I arrived in Milan. The weather was dry and the air so clear that one could see with perfect clarity those blue alps which separate civilization from barbarism, our world of sun from that melancholy green forest where dwells Rome's nemesis.

Just before the city's gate we were met by one of Constantius's eunuchs, a gorgeous fellow with many chins and an effortless sneer. He did not salute me as is proper, a bad omen. He gave the commander of my guard a letter from the Emperor. When I saw this, I began to recite the first of the passwords I should need when I arrived in the kingdom of the dead. But I was not to be dispatched just yet. Instead I was taken to a house in one of the suburbs. Here I was imprisoned.

Imprisonment exactly describes my state. I was under heavy guard. During the day, I was allowed to stroll in the atrium. But at night I was locked in my bedroom. No one could visit me, not that there was anyone in Milan I wanted to see or who wanted to see me, excepting the Empress Eusebia. Of my household, I was allowed to keep only two boys and two men. The rest were transferred to the imperial palace. There was no one I could talk to. That was the greatest hardship of all. I should have been pleased to have had even a eunuch for company!

Why was I treated this way? I have since pieced the story together. While I was in Athens, a general named Silvanus was proclaimed Augustus in Gaul. I am convinced that at heart he was innocent of any serious desire to take the purple, but the enmity of the court eunuchs drove him to rebellion.

As soon as this happened, Constantius arrested me because he was afraid that I might take advantage of the defection of Gaul to rise against him in Attica. As it turned out, before I reached Milan, Silvanus was dead at Cologne. Constantius' luck in civil war had proved itself again.

But the death of Silvanus did not solve the problem of Julian. While I was locked up in that suburban villa, the old debate was reopened. Eusebius wanted me put to death. Eusebia did not. Constantius kept his own counsel.

I prepared several letters to Eusebia, begging her to intercede with the Emperor that I might be allowed to return to Athens. But I finally decided not to send her any message, for Constantius's suspicions were easily aroused, to say the least, and any exchange between his wife and his heir presumptive would not only be known to him but would doubtless turn him against both of us. I did the wise thing.

At dawn, on the thirteenth day of my captivity, my life altered forever. I was awakened by a slave banging on the bedroom door. 'Get up, Lord! Get up! A message from the Augustus!' Fully clothed, I leapt out of bed. I then reminded the slave that until someone unlocked the door I could hardly receive the imperial messenger.

The door flew open. The commander of my guard was beaming. I knew then that the divine will had begun its work. I was to be spared.

'A messenger, sir. The Emperor will receive you tonight.'

I stepped into the atrium and got my first taste of what it is like to be in favour. The house was now full of strangers. Fat eunuchs in gaudy silk; clerks from various government offices; tailors; sandalmakers; barbers; youthful officers drawn to what might be a new sun and source of honour. It was dizzying.

The messenger from Constantius was no other than Arintheus, who serves with me now in Persia. He is remarkably beautiful, and the army loves him in that fervent way armies have of loving handsome officers. He is auburn-haired and blue-eyed, with a strong, supple body. He is completely uneducated, but brave and shrewd in warfare. His only vice is an excessive fondness for boys, a practice I usually find unseemly in generals. But the men are amused by his sensuality. Also, he is a cavalry man and among cavalry men pederasty is a tradition. I must say that day when Arintheus approached me, blue eyes flashing and ruddy face grinning, I nearly mistook him for Hermes himself, streaming glory from Olympus as he came to save his unworthy son. Arintheus saluted me briskly; then he read aloud the letter summoning me for audience. When he had finished reading (with some difficulty, for he has never found reading easy), he put the message away, gave me his most winning smile and said, 'When you are Caesar, don't forget me. Take me with you. I prefer action.' He patted his sword hilt. I dithered like a fool. He departed.

Then began a new struggle. My beard would have to go, also my student's clothes. I was now a prince, not a philosopher. So for the first time in my life my beard was shaved. It was like losing an arm. Two barbers worked on me while I sat in a chair in the centre of the atrium as the morning sun shone on a spectacle which, looking back, was perfectly ludicrous. There was I, an awkward twenty-three-year-old philosophy student, late of the University of Athens, being turned into a courtier.

A slave girl trimmed my toenails and scrubbed my feet, to my embarrassment. Another worked on my hands, exclaiming at the inkiness of my fingers. The barber who shaved my beard also tried to shave my chest but I stopped him with an oath. We compromised by letting him trim the hair in my nostrils. When he was finished, he brought me a mirror. I was quite unable to recognize the youth who stared wide-eyed from the polished metal – and it *was* a youth, not a man as I had thought, for the beard had been deceptive, giving me an undeserved look of wisdom and age. Without it, I resembled any other youngster at court.

I was then bathed, oiled, perfumed and elaborately dressed. My flesh shrank from the lascivious touch of silk, which makes the body uncomfortably aware of itself. Today I never wear silk, preferring coarse linen or wool.

I have only a vague memory of the rest of that day. I was carried to the palace through crowded streets. The people stared at me curiously, uncertain whether or not it was right to applaud. I looked straight ahead as I had been instructed to do when on view. I tried not to hear conversations in the street. Desperately I tried to recall the eunuch's instructions.

At the edge of the city's main square the palace, grey and forbidding behind its Corinthian colonnade, rose before me like fate itself. Troops were drawn up in full dress on either side of the main door. When I stepped out of the litter, they saluted.

Several hundreds of the people of Milan drew close to examine me. In every city there is a special class whose only apparent function is to gather in public places and look at famous men. They are neither friendly nor unfriendly, merely interested. An elephant would have pleased them most, but since there was no elephant, the mysterious Prince Julian would have to do. Few of them could identify me. None was certain just what relation I was to the Emperor. It is amazing how little we are known to our subjects. I know of places on the boundaries of the empire where they believe Augustus himself still reigns, that he is a great magician who may not die. Of course, the fact each of us calls himself Augustus is a deliberate attempt to suggest that the continuity of power emanating from Rome is the one constant in a world of flux. Yet even in the cities where there is widespread literacy, the average citizen is often uncertain about who the ruler is. Several times already I have been addressed as Constantius by nervous delegations, while one old man actually thought I was Constantine and complimented me on how little I had changed since the battle at the Mulvian bridge!

Inside the palace, curiosity was mingled with excitement and anticipation. I was in favour. I read my good fortune in every face. In the vestibule they paid me homage. Heads bobbed; smiles flashed; my hand was wrung with warmth, kissed with hope. It was disgusting . . . in retrospect. At the time, it was marvellous proof that I was to live for a while longer.

I was delivered to the Master of the Offices, who gave me a final whispered briefing. Then, to the noise of horns, I entered the throne room.

Constantius wore the purple. The robe fell stiffly to his crimson shoes. In one hand he held an ivory staff, while the other rested on the arm of the throne, palm upward, holding the golden orb. As usual, he stared straight before him, unaware of anything except what was in his direct line of vision. He looked ill. His eyes were dark-circled, and his face was somewhat blotchy, as though from too much wine; yet he was abstemious. On a throne at floor level sat Eusebia, blazing with jewels. Though she too played statue, she managed to suggest sympathetic humanity. When she saw me, the sad mouth parted slightly.

To left and right, in full court dress, were the members of the Sacred Consistory. All stared at me as I slowly crossed to the throne eyes downcast. October light streamed through high windows. The odour of incense was heavy in the room. I felt a child again, and this was Constantine. For a moment, the room swam before my eyes. Then Constantius spoke the first line of the ritual greeting. I answered, and prostrated myself at his feet. I kissed the purple, and was raised up. Like two actors we played our scene impersonally until it was done; then I was given a stool next to Eusebia.

I sat very still, looking straight ahead, aware of Eusebia next to me. I could smell the flowery scent of her robes. But neither of us looked at the other.

Ambassadors were received, generals appointed, titles bestowed. The audience ended when the Emperor stood up. The rest of us dropped to our knees. Stiff-legged and swaying slightly from the weight of his robes and jewellery, Constantius marched off to the palace living quarters, followed by Eusebia. The moment the green bronze doors shut behind them, as though from a magician's spell, we were all set free.

Courtiers surrounded me and asked a thousand questions: Would I be made Caesar? Where would I live? Did I need any service? I had only to command. I answered as demurely and non-committally as I could. Then my enemy Eusebius approached, his yellow moonface gravely respectful. Silk robes whispered as the heavy body bowed to me. 'Lord, you are to dine with the sacred family.' An excited whisper went through the court. This was the highest recognition. I was exalted in all eyes. Though my own first reaction was: dinner means poison.

'I shall escort you to the sacred quarters.' Eusebius led me to the bronze doors through which the imperial couple had just passed. We did not speak until we were alone in the corridor beyond.

'You should know, Lord, that I have always, in every way, assured the Augustus of your loyalty to him.'

'I know that you have.' I lied with equal dignity.

'There are those in the Sacred Consistory who are your enemies.' He gestured for a guard to open a small oaken door. We passed through. 'But I have always opposed them. As you know, I had hoped all along that you would take your rightful place here at court. And though there are some who think that the title Caesar should lapse because your brother . . .' He allowed that sentence to go unfinished. 'I have urged his Eternity to make you Caesar.'

'I do not seek such honour,' I murmured, looking about me with some interest. The palace at Milan is a large rambling building. Originally it was a military governor's rather modest headquarters. In the last century when Rome ceased to be a practical centre for the West, the palace was enlarged to become an imperial residence. Because of the German tribes, the emperors had to be close to the Alps. Also, the farther an emperor is from the city of Rome the longer his reign is apt to be, for the populace of that city is notoriously fickle and arrogant, with a long memory of the emperors it has overthrown. None of us stays for long at Rome if he can help it.

Constantine enlarged the palace in Milan, building the state rooms, while Constantius added the second-floor living quarters through which we now walked. These rooms look out on a large inner court. I personally prefer the old-fashioned form of architecture with small private rooms arranged about an atrium, but Constantius was a modernist in architecture as well as in religion. I find such rooms too large, and of course ruinously expensive to heat.

Guards and eunuchs stood at every door, arrogant, yet servile. A court is the most depressing place on earth. Wherever there is a throne, one may observe in rich detail every folly and wickedness of which man is capable, enamelled with manners and gilded with hypocrisy. I keep no court in the field. In residence, I keep as little as possible.

At the final door, Eusebius left me with a deep bow. Guards opened the door, and I stepped into the private dining-room. Constantius reclined on one of the two couches within whose right angle was the table. Opposite him Eusebia sat in an ivory chair. I bowed low to both of them, intoning the proper formula.

Constantius mumbled his response. Then he waved me to the couch beside him.

'You look better without that damned beard.'

I blushed as I took my place on the couch. Eusebia smiled encouragingly. 'I rather liked the beard,' she said.

'That's because you're an atheist, too.'

My heart missed a beat. But it was only the Emperor's heavy wit.

'She likes these high-sounding, low-living Cynics.' He indicated his wife with a knotty ringed hand. 'She's always reading them. Not good for women to read.'

I said something agreeable, grateful to find him in a good mood. Constantius had removed his diadem and outer robes, and he looked almost human, quite unlike the statue he had appeared earlier.

Wine was brought me and though I seldom drink it full strength, this day I drank deep, to overcome nervousness.

'Who does he look like?' Constantius had been examining me curiously, like a new slave or horse. 'Without that beard?'

Eusebia frowned, pretending to be thoughtful. One gives away nothing in dealing with a tyrant, even if the tyrant is one's husband.

The Emperor answered his own question. 'Constans. You look just like him. Just like my brother.' My heart sank. Constantius had always been thought to have had a hand in his brother's death. But there was no significance to this remark, either. Constantius, at his ease, tended to be literal and rather simple.

I said that I had been too young to recall what my late cousin had looked like.

'Much the best of the three of us. Tall. Like our father.' Constantius was much concerned with his own shortness.

An elaborate dinner was served us, and I tasted everything, for to refuse any dish would show that one suspected the Emperor of treachery. It was an ordeal, and my stomach nearly rebelled.

Constantius led the conversation, as emperors are supposed to do – unless they are given to philosophic debate like me, in which case I must speak very fast at my own table to be heard.

I was asked about my studies at Athens. I described them, ending 'I could spend the rest of my life there.' As I said this, I noticed that Eusebia frowned imperceptibly: a signal that I was not to speak of student life.

But Constantius had not been listening. He lay now flat on his back, belching softly and kneading his barrel-like stomach with one hand. When he spoke, he did so with eyes shut.

'I am the first Augustus to reign alone since my father, who was himself the first to reign alone in this century. But he never intended for just one of us to rule. Any more than Diocletian intended for any one of *his* successors to govern alone.' Constantius raised himself on one elbow and looked at me with those curiously mournful eyes which were his most attractive yet most puzzling feature. They were the eyes of a poet who had seen all the tragedy in this world and knows what is to come in the next. Yet the good effect of those eyes was entirely undone by a peevish mouth.

Who could ever know Constantius? I certainly did not. I hated him, but Eusebia loved him – I think – and she was a woman who would not have cared for what was evil. Like the rest of us, Constantius was many men in the body of one.

'The world is too big for one person to govern it.' My heart beat faster for I knew now what was to come. 'I cannot be everywhere. Yet the imperial power *must* be everywhere. Things have a habit of going wrong all at once. As soon as the German tribes get loose in the north, the Persians attack in the south. At times I think they must plan it. If I march to the East, I'm immediately threatened in the West. If one general rises up against me, then I must deal with at least two more traitors at the same time. The empire is big. Distances are great. Our enemies many.' He tore off a roast duck's leg and chewed it, all the time looking at me with those melting eyes.

'I mean to hold the state together. I shall not sacrifice one city to the barbarians, one town, one field!' The high-pitched voice almost cracked. 'I mean to hold the state for our family. We won it. We must maintain it. And that is why we must be loyal to one another.' How that phrase from those cruel lips struck me! I dared not look at him.

'Julian,' the voice was lower now. 'I intend to make you Caesar, and my heir until such time as I have a son.'

'Lord ...' was all I could say. Tears unexpectedly filled my eyes. I shall never know if I *wanted* my fate. Yet when it came to me, a secret line snapped within and the perilous voyage began.

Eusebia congratulated me. I don't recall what was said. More wine was brought and Constantius, in a jovial mood, told me how the astrologers preferred 6 November to any other day in the month. He also insisted that I study military strategy, while assembling a household suitable to my new rank. I was to have a salary. It would not be large, he said, understating the matter considerably: if I had not had a small income from my mother's estate, I would have starved to death that first year. My cousin could never be accused of generosity.

Constantius almost smiled at me. 'Now,' he said, 'I have a surprise for you.' The surprise was his sister Helena. She entered the room with great dignity. I had never met her, though I had seen her at a distance during my first visit to Milan.

Helena was not an attractive woman. She was short, inclined to stoutness, with the short legs and long torso of Constantius. By one of those unlucky chances, her face was the face of her father Constantine the Great. It was most alarming: the same broad cheeks, the thin proud mouth, the large nose, the huge full jaw, an imperial portrait re-created in a middle-aged woman. Yet despite this unfortunate resemblance, she was otherwise most feminine with an agreeable soft voice. (I have always hated women with shrill voices.) She moved modestly, even shyly. At the time I knew nothing about her except that she was ten years older than I, and that she was Constantius's favourite sister.

After formally acknowledging our greetings, Helena took her place in the vacant chair. She was obviously under considerable strain. So was I, for I knew exactly what was going to happen next. I had always known that something like this was apt to be my fate, but I had put it as much as possible out of my mind. Now the moment was at hand.

'We do you the honour,' said Constantius, 'of bestowing our own beloved sister upon you as your wife and consort, a human and tangible link between our crowns.' He had obviously prepared this sentence in advance. I wondered if he had spoken thus to Gallus when he gave him Constantia in marriage.

Helena looked at the floor. I am afraid I turned scarlet. Eusebia watched me, amused but guarded. She who had been my friend and ally could now quite easily become my enemy. I was aware of this, even then. Or do I write now with hindsight? In any case, it was perfectly plain that should Helena have a child and Eusebia remain barren, my child would be Constantius's heir. The four of us were now caught like flies in a spider's web.

I had no clear idea what I said to Constantius. I am sure that I stammered. Helena later said that I was most eloquent, though unable to look at her during my speech of acceptance. Doubtless I was thinking of my conjugal duties. Never did a woman attract me less. Yet we would have to have a child. This sort of burden is the usual fate of princes and I daresay it is a small price to pay for greatness, though at the time it seems larger than it ought.

Helena was a good woman but our moments of intimacy were rare, unsatisfactory, and somewhat pathetic, for I did want to please her. But it was never pleasant, making love to a bust of Constantine. Though I could not make her happy, I did not make her suffer, and I think we became friends.

The dinner ended when Constantius swung his short bowed legs to the floor, and stretched till his bones cracked. Then without a word to any of us, he left the room. Eusebia gave me a half-smile. She put her hand out to Helena and together the two women withdrew, leaving me staring at the pheasant's eggs which an artist-cook had arranged in a beautifully feathered nest as final course. It was an extraordinary moment. I had entered the room a proscribed student. I left it as Caesar and husband. The change was dizzying.

I believe it is true of most courts that the principal figures seldom see one another. This is partly due to choice. The fewer the meetings, the less chance of something untoward happening. But more to the point, it suits the courtiers to keep the great people apart, thereby increasing the importance of inter-mediaries who are then able to hurry from one wing of the palace to another, making mischief and policy as they go.

The court of Constantius was in many ways the worst since Domitian. The eunuchs were all-powerful. They kept everyone from the Emperor. If a man displeased a eunuch, he was doomed and Mercurius, 'the count of dreams', would be called in or Paul 'the chain' (the one so called because he was a genius at finding obscure links to a never-ending chain of treason while the other specialized in the analysis of seemingly harmless dreams which, invariably, upon scrutiny, revealed treasonable intent). Since Constantius would listen only to the eunuchs, injustice flourished. No one was safe, including the great figures themselves, particularly those like myself who were blood heirs to the principate.

I have often felt when studying history that not enough is made of the importance of those intermediaries who so often do the actual governing. We tend to think of courts as wheels at whose centre is the emperor, from whom, like spokes, all those who serve him extend, drawing their power directly from his central presence. The truth is otherwise. Hardly anyone was allowed to come close to Constantius. Only the eunuch Eusebius saw him daily. As a result, factions within the court could form and re-form, irrelevant to the nominal power.

In reading accounts of those weeks at Milan, one would think that Constantius and I saw each other daily, discussing high policy, military strategy and sharing, as it were, a family life. Actually, I saw the Emperor only four times in one month. The first encounter I have described; the second was at my investiture as Caesar.

I was created Caesar 6 November 355, the year when Arbetio and Lollianus were consuls. I will say one thing for Constantius. He had an artist's gift for ceremony. Though I like to think I surpass him in many ways, I know I shall never be able to create the sense of awful majesty he could whenever he chose. One *knew* this was the Augustus when he appeared before a crowd. When I appear, the people are not in the least impressed. I believe they have a certain affection for me, but I don't in the least alarm them. They think I look like a professor of rhetoric. They are quite right. I do.

At the far end of the main square, a high wooden platform had been dec-orated with the eagles of Rome and the dragons of our house. The square itself was filled with soldiers in fully military dress.

As I was led by the generals of the army to the platform, I was conscious that every muscle in my body ached, for I had been practising daily with sword and javelin. I was exhausted, and I'm afraid that my instructors had nothing but contempt for me. They thought me a bookish fool who knew nothing of weaponry and preferred talk to war. Of course they were courteous to my face, but behind my back I often heard soft mocking laughter. Incidentally, I was surprised to discover how little I can endure mockery. One of the best consolations of philosophy is that it supposedly prepares one for the contempt of others. Some philosophers even revel in the dislike of the vulgar. Not I. Perhaps there *is* something to the idea of blood and inheritance. After all, I am descended from three emperors. To be thought weak and womanish by hearty young officers was unbearable to me. Grimly, I made up my mind to surpass them in every way. Unfortunately, at this moment my primacy was more wish than fact. I had done too much too fast. As a result, I was even clumsier than usual.

The moment I reached the base of the platform, horns were sounded. Cheering began. A path opened through the legions, and Constantius appeared in his gilded state carriage; he wore a dragon-shaped gold helmet and the purple. As he passed me, I caught his eye and got a look as blind as Homer's! In public, the emperor does not see mere men.

Slowly Constantius climbed the steps to the platform, his short bowed legs slightly diminishing the majesty of his presence. From the platform, he received the cheer of the legions. Then he motioned for me to join him. With a sense of one going to his own execution, I climbed the steep wooden steps and took my place at the side of Constantius ... I almost wrote at the side of history, for I was now legend. For better or worse, I had become a part of that long chronicle which began with Julius Caesar and whose end none can foresee.

I looked out over the massed troops. This was my first look at an army, and I confess to revelling in the sight. All thought of philosophy went clear out of my head as the dragon pennants fluttered in the autumn wind, and the eagles below us dipped as the salute was given.

Constantius reached out and took my right hand in his. His grip was firm and callused. I glanced at him out of the corner of my eye, conscious something was not right: he was half a head taller than I. I looked down and saw that he was standing on a footstool. Constantius neglected no detail which might enhance his majesty.

Constantius spoke to the legions. His high-pitched voice carried well. The Latin he used was that of the army, but it was easy to understand. He had memorized his speech. 'We stand before you, valiant defenders of our country, to avenge the common cause. How this is to be done, I put to you not as soldiers but as impartial judges. After the death of those rebellious tyrants whom mad fury drove to seize the state, the savages to the north, thinking that this great empire was weak and in confusion, crossed into Gaul. They are there now. Only you and we, in perfect accord, can turn them back. The choice is yours. Here stands before you our cousin Julian, honoured for his modesty, as dear to us for that as for the ties of blood; a young man of conspicuous ability whom I desire to make Caesar if you will confirm him . . . .'

At this point, though in mid-sentence, Constantius was stopped by various voices declaring that it was clearly the will of God, not of man, that I be raised to the rank of Caesar. I quite agreed, though the God they had in mind and the One who did indeed raise me up were not the same. Nevertheless, I admired the skill with which Constantius had staged the scene. The voices rang out as though spontaneous (actually, everything had been carefully rehearsed). Constantius remained very still while they spoke, as though listening to an oracle. My hand in his grew sweaty; but he never relaxed the firm grip. When there was silence again, he nodded gravely to the legions. 'Your response is enough. I see that I have your approval.'

He let go my hand. He motioned for two generals to join us on the platform. One carried a wreath; the other a purple robe. They stood behind us.

'This young man's quiet strength and temperate behaviour' (he emphasized the word 'temperate' to reassure them that I was not Gallus) 'should be imitated rather than proclaimed; his excellent disposition, trained in all good arts, I concur in by the very fact that I have chosen to elevate him. So now with the immediate favour of the God of heaven, I invest him with this imperial robe.'

The cloak was put about my shoulders. Constantius arranged it at the neck. Only once did he look me in the eye as we faced one another, he on his footstool and I with my back to the legions. The look he gave me was curiously furtive and undecided, in sharp contrast to the easy majesty of his movements and the serene power of his voice.

Constantius was a man in terror of his life. I saw it plain in those great eyes. As he put the wreath on my head, he shut his eyes for an instant, like a man who flinches in anticipation of a surgeon's knife. Then he took my right hand again and turned me around that I might face the legions. But before they could salute me, he raised his arm. He had more to say. Though he spoke as though to me, he looked straight at them. Not certain which way to turn, I looked half at him and half towards the soldiers in the square.

'Brother, dearest to me of all men, you have received in your prime the glorious flower of your origin. Yet I must admit you add to my own glory, for I seem to myself more truly great in bestowing almost equal power' (the 'almost' was heavily rendered) 'on a noble prince who is my kinsman than through that power itself. Come, then, to share in pain and perils, undertake the defence of Gaul, relieve its afflicted regions with every bounty. And should it be necessary to engage with the enemy, take your place with the standard-bearers. Go forth yourself, a brave man ready to lead men equally brave. You and I will stand by one another with firm and steadfast affection, and together – if God grants our prayers – we shall rule over a pacified world with moderation and conscientiousness. You will be present with me always in my thoughts, and I will not fail you in anything you undertake. Now go, with haste, with the prayers of all of us, to defend with your honour the post assigned you by Rome herself, and God's appointment! Hail, Caesar!'

This last he said in a loud voice which was immediately echoed by the legions. It was like a burst of thunder. I had sufficient presence of mind to respond: 'Hail, Augustus!' The men repeated this, too. I saluted Constantius. Then I turned and saluted the legions. This was against all protocol. Generals do *not* salute their men. The standards, yes; the legions, no. But my gesture was sincerely tactless. After the first astonishment, the legions roared their approval of me and struck their shields hard against their armoured knees: the highest tribute they may render a man. It is also the loudest. I thought I would be deaf forever as the clatter rang through the square. More terrible, however, is the army's disapproval, when they roll their spears back and forth against their shields, as prelude to mutiny.

I could feel Constantius stiffen beside me. This was more than he anticipated.

I am sure that he was positive that my gesture to the legions had been premeditated. But the deed was done. And I was Caesar.

Abruptly, Constantius left the platform. I followed him. There was a moment of confusion as he got into his carriage. He looked down at me for a long moment. Then he motioned for me to join him. I clambered in beside him and, side by side, we rode through the cheering legions. I felt a sudden affection for them all. We had been united as though in marriage, and like so many arranged marriages, odd though this one was, it proved to be happy.

The carriage moved slowly through the square to the palace. Constantius said nothing to me, and I dared not speak to him, unhappily aware that in this carriage there was no footstool and I was taller than he, a second bad omen. I murmured to myself a line from the Iliad: 'By purple death I'm seized, and fate supreme.' Inside the palace courtyard Constantius and I parted without a word. I did not see him again for several days.

My first act as Caesar was to send for Oribasius, who was at Athens. He had arrived there only a week after my recall. I also wrote Maximus and Priscus, inviting them to join me. Meanwhile, I continued military practice. I also learned as much as possible about the administration of Gaul.

During this time I saw none of the imperial family, including my soon-to-be wife. Yet the day of the wedding had been set and the inevitable documents were brought to me to be studied. I was given a meticulous ground plan of the chapel and my position from moment to moment during the ceremony was precisely traced.

I had but one friend at court, Eutherius, the Armenian eunuch who had taught me at Constantinople. Every evening we would study various documents and memoranda. It was his task, he said, to make an administrator of me.

The night before my wedding, Eutherius came to me with the news that I was to leave for Gaul the first week in December.

'To what city?'

'Vienne. You'll be there for the winter. Then in the spring you will take the field.' He looked at me closely. 'Does it seem strange to you to be a general?'

'Strange!' I exploded. 'Insane!'

He raised his hand in some alarm, indicating the shadows where guards stood and informers listened, always hopeful of catching me at treason.

I lowered my voice. 'Of course it is strange. I've never seen a battle. I've never commanded a single soldier, much less an army. But ...'

'But?'

'But I'm not afraid.' I did not say what I really felt: that I looked forward to military adventures.

'I am relieved.' Eutherius smiled. 'Because I have just been appointed grand chamberlain at the court of the Caesar Julian. I go with you to Gaul.'

This was marvellous news. I embraced him warmly, babbling happily until he was forced to say, 'Roman gravity, Caesar. Please. You are far too Asiatic.'

I laughed. 'It can't be helped. I *am* Asiatic ...'

Suddenly, Eutherius was on his feet. With a speed which I would not have thought possible for one of his age, he darted into the shadowed archway just opposite us. A moment later he reappeared with a dark, richly dressed man.

'Caesar,' said Eutherius with grim ceremony, 'allow me to present Paul, of the secret service. He has come to pay your greatness homage.'

I was hardly startled. I had been under surveillance all my life. The presence of the government's chief secret agent merely reminded me that the higher I rose the more important it was for Constantius to have me watched.

'We are always pleased to receive the Emperor's agents,' I said politely.

Paul was imperturbable. His eyes shone in the lamplight; his hook nose made him resemble some great bird of prey. He bowed. He spoke with a slight Spanish accent. 'I was on my way to the east wing. To report to Rufinus, the praetorian prefect.'

'This is not the usual way to the east wing,' said Eutherius amiably.

'What can I say?' Paul spread his hands, bird's talons ready to seize.

'You *can* say good night, Paul, and report to the praetorian prefect that you heard nothing useful,' I said.

Paul bowed. 'I report only what I hear, Caesar.' He was carefully insolent.

'Stay longer,' I said, 'and you will hear the beginning of your death.'

That shook him, though my boldness was perfect bluff. I had no power. One word from him and I could be brought down. Yet I knew that if I was to be Caesar I would have to assert myself or earn the fatal contempt of eunuchs and spies. Paul withdrew.

I turned to Eutherius. 'Was I too Asiatic?' I teased him, though my heart pounded.

He shook his head. 'Perhaps that is the wisest way to handle him. Anyway, you are safe for the moment.'

'But he is constructing one of his chains.'

'Perhaps he will trap himself.'

I nodded. Paul had been a prime mover in the plot which had destroyed my brother. That night in the palace at Milan I began my own plot.

My wedding day ... what a strange thing for a celibate to write! It seems impossible now that I could ever have been a husband. Yet I became one on 13 November 355. I shall not describe the atrocious Galilean rites. It is enough to say that I endured them, heavy with purple and glittering with state jewels which I later sold in Gaul to buy soldiers.

After the ceremony, there were the usual celebrations and games in our honour. Helena delighted in all the panoply of rank; in this she resembled her brother. I was merely dutiful and did what was expected of me. A few days after the ceremony I was summoned to an audience with Eusebia.

'What do you think of the world now?' Eusebia's eyes gleamed with mischief.

'I owe it all to you,' I said warmly.

'And how do you find Helena?'

'She is my wife,' I said formally; again the conspiratorial look.

'She is very ... handsome,' said Eusebia, with an edge of malice.

'Noble, I should say.' I almost burst out laughing. But there is a rule to these games.

'You will leave soon.'

'I'm glad,' I said. Then added, 'Not that I look forward to leaving ...' I could not say 'you' so I said 'Milan'.

She shook her head. 'This is not your sort of place. It's not mine either, but . . . .' She left what was serious unsaid. Then: 'You will go into winter quarters at Vienne. Money ...'

'Will be scarce.' The Grand Chamberlain had already told me that I would have to maintain myself and household on my salary as Caesar. Additional funds could not be granted at this time.

'Luckily, you are frugal.'

'Helena is not.'

'Helena has her own money,' said Eusebia sharply. 'She should use it. She owns half of Rome.'

I was relieved to hear this, and said so.

'It is my hope,' said Eusebia, 'that you will soon have a son, not only for yourself but for us.'

I admired her boldness. This was the one thing Eusebia did *not* want me to have, since it would endanger her own position. Rather than accept my son as his heir, Constantius was capable of divorcing Eusebia and taking a new wife who could give him what he most desired.

'It is my hope,' I answered evenly, 'that *you* will be blessed with many children.'

But she did not believe me either. The interview now turned painful. No matter what either of us said, it sounded false. Yet I believe she did indeed wish me well, except in that one matter.

Finally, we got off the subject and she revealed to me the state of Constantius's mind. 'I speak to you candidly.' An admission that neither of us had been speaking candidly before. The sad face looked sadder still, while her long hands nervously fingered the folds of her robe. 'He is divided. He cannot make up his mind about you. Naturally, there are those who tell him that you wish to overthrow him.'

'Not true!' I began to protest, but she stopped me.

'I know it is not true.'

'And it *never* will be true!' I believed myself.

'Be tolerant. Constantius has had to face many enemies. It is only natural that he fear you.'

'Then why won't he let me go back to Athens, where I am no danger?'

'Because he needs you more than he fears you.' She looked at me, suddenly frightened. 'Julian, we are in danger of losing all Gaul.'

I stared at her dumbly.

'This morning Constantius had a message from the praetorian prefect at Vienne. I don't know what it said. But I suspect the worst. We have already lost the cities of the Rhine. Should the Germans attack this winter, it is the end of Gaul, unless . . .' She held her hand above the flame of the alabaster lamp. The flesh glowed. 'Julian, help me!' For a stupid moment I thought she had burned her hand. 'You *must* be loyal to us. You must help us!'

'I swear by all the gods, by Helios, by . . .'

She stopped me, unaware that in my sincerity I had sworn by the true gods. 'Be patient with him. He will always be suspicious of you. That is his nature. But as long as I live, you are safe. If something should happen to me . . .' This was the first inkling I had that Eusebia was ill. 'Be loyal to him anyway.'

I forget what I said. Doubtless more protestations of loyalty, all sincere. When I rose to go, she said, 'I have a gift for you. You will see it on the day you leave.'

I thanked her and left. Despite all that Eusebia did to hurt me in the next two years, I still love her. After all I owe her not only the principate but my life.

At dawn on the first of December I left Milan for Gaul. I said farewell to Helena, who was to join me later at Vienne. We both behaved according to the special protocol the eunuchs have devised governing a Caesar's farewell to his new wife as he goes to a beleaguered province. Then, accompanied by the newly arrived Oribasius, I went down to the courtyard of the palace to place myself at the head of my army.

Outside in the frosty air, some three hundred foot soldiers and a score of cavalry were drawn up. I took this to be my personal bodyguard. I was about to ask the whereabouts of the army of Gaul when I was joined by Eutherius. He was frowning. 'I've just spoken to the Grand Chamberlain. There has been a last-minute change in plans. Your legions have been assigned to the Danube.'

I indicated the men in the courtyard. 'Is *this* my army?'

'I am afraid so, Caesar.'

I have never in my life been so angry. Only the arrival of Constantius prevented me from saying the unsayable. I saluted the Emperor; gravely, he returned the salute. Then he mounted a black horse and I mounted a white one. His personal guard (twice the size of my 'army') fell into place behind him. My troops and household brought up the rear. Thus the Augustus and his Caesar launched the power of Rome against the barbarians. It was ludicrous.

The few citizens who were up and around at this hour cheered us dutifully. We made a particularly fine impression at the vegetable market which is just inside the city gate. The farm women waved their carrots and turnips at us, and thought us a brave sight.

Neither Constantius nor I spoke until we were out on the main road, the high Alps visible to us across the Lombard Plain. He had agreed to escort me as far as the two columns which stand on either side of the road midway between Lumello and Pavia. He had obviously decided this would give us sufficient time for a good talk. It did.

Constantius began with, 'We have great confidence in Florentius, our praetorian prefect at Gaul.' This was an announcement; there was no invitation for me to comment.

Of course he has confidence in Florentius, I thought savagely, otherwise he would have had him murdered by now. But I said, 'Yes, Augustus.' And waited. We rode a few more yards. Occasionally, our armoured legs touched, metal striking metal, and each would shrink instinctively from the other. The touch of another man has always disturbed me; the touch of my father's murderer alarmed me.

We passed a number of carts containing poultry; they had pulled off the road at our approach. When the peasants saw the Emperor, they fell flat on their bellies, as though blinded by the sight of that sacred figure. Constantius ignored them.

'We are fond of our sister Helena.' This was also launched upon the dry cool air in an oracular tone.

'She is dear to me, too, Augustus,' I replied. I was afraid he was going to lecture me on my marital duties, but he made no further mention of Helena.

Constantius was constructing a case. His occasional flat sentences, suitable for carving in marble, were all part of an edifice created to contain me. I was to obey the praetorian prefect of Gaul, even though as Caesar I was his superior. I was to remember that Helena's first loyalty was to her brother and ruler, not to her husband. So far, I understood him clearly.

'We have heard from your military instructor that you show promise.'

'I shall not fail you, Augustus. But it was my understanding that I was to go to Gaul with an army, not an escort.'

Constantius ignored this. 'You have come to soldiering late. I hope you are able to learn what you will need to know.'

This was not optimistic, but not unnatural. There was no reason for anyone to suspect that a philosophy student should show *any* talent for war. Curiously enough, I had every confidence in myself because I knew that the gods would not desert me now they had raised me up. But my cousin had no way of knowing my feelings, or judging my capacity. He merely saw a young untried soldier about to go into battle against the fiercest fighters in the world.

'At all times remember that we are divine in the eyes of the people and sacred to heaven.'

I took the 'we' to mean Constantius and myself, though he may have been merely reminding me of his own rank. 'I shall remember, Augustus.' I always called him by his proper title, though he much preferred Lord, a title I despise and do not use for it means that one is the master of other men, rather than simply first among them.

'Control your generals.' Though he still sounded as if he were repeating maxims, I could tell that now he was on the verge of actual advice, if not conversation. 'No officer should be admitted to senatorial rank. All officers must be under strict civilian control. Any governor of any province outranks any general sent to him. No officer must be allowed to take part in civil affairs. Our praetorian prefects are set over all military and civil officials. That is why the administration of the empire runs as smoothly as it does.'

Needless to say, I did not remark that the collapse of Gaul was hardly a sign of smooth administration. But in principle Constantius's advice was good and I tend still to follow it. There is no denying that he had a gift for administration.

'In matters of taxes, take whatever is owing us. Show no mercy to the cities and villages which are delinquent in meeting payments. It is their nature to complain. Assume that your tax-gatherers are honest unless proved otherwise. They are *never* honest, but no one has yet found a way to correct their abuses. As long as they return to you the larger part of what they collect, be satisfied.'

I was later to revise the system of taxation in Gaul, disproving everything he said. But all that in its proper place.

'Control the generals.' He repeated this suddenly as if he'd forgotten he had already said it to me. Then he turned and looked at me for the first time that day. It was startling. No longer was he the sun god on his charger. This was my cousin, my enemy, my lord, source of my greatness and potential source of my death. 'You must know what I mean,' he said, sounding like a man, not an oracle. 'You have seen the state disrupted. Our high place threatened. Provinces wrecked. Cities destroyed. Armies wasted. The barbarians seizing our lands, because we were too busy fighting one another to protect ourselves from the true enemy. Well, Caesar, remember this: allow no general sufficient power to raise an army against you. You have seen what I have had to suffer. Usurper after usurper has wasted our power. Be on your guard.'

'I will, Augustus.'

Then he said, very slowly, his eyes on mine, 'As I am on *my* guard.' He looked away when he saw that his meaning was quite clear. Then he added for good measure, 'We have never yet lost so much as a foot of earth to any usurper, nor will we ever.'

'As long as I live, Augustus, you shall have at least one arm to fight for you.'

We rode until midday. Then at the two columns we stopped. It was a fine brisk noon and, despite the chill in the air, the sun was hot and we were all sweating under our armour. A halt was ordered.

Constantius and I dismounted and he motioned for me to accompany him into a hard stubbled field. Except for our troops, no one was in sight. In every country peasants vanish when they see armed men coming: all soldiers are the enemy. I wish one could change that.

Constantius walked ahead of me towards a small ruined shrine to Hermes which stood at the edge of the field (a favourable omen, Hermes has always watched over me). Behind us, our men watered horses, rearranged armour, swore and chattered, pleased by the good weather. Just as Constantius entered the shrine, I broke a dead flower off its stalk. Then I followed him inside the shrine, which smelled of human excrement. Constantius was urinating on the floor. Even in this, he was grave and majestic.

'It is a pity,' I heard myself saying, aware as I spoke that I was breaking protocol, 'what has happened to these old temples.'

'A pity? They should all be torn down.' He rearranged his clothes. 'I hate the sight of them.'

'Of course,' I muttered.

'I shall leave you here,' he said. We stood facing one another. Though I deliberately stooped, I could not help but look down on him. He edged away from me, instinctively searching for higher ground.

'Whatever you need, you shall have. Call on me. Also, depend on our praetorian prefect. He represents us. You will find the legions of Vienne alert, ready for a spring campaign. So prepare yourself.'

He handed me a thick document. 'Instructions. To be read at your leisure.' He paused. Then he remembered something. 'The Empress has made you a gift. It is with your baggage. A library, I believe.'

I was effusive in my gratitude. I said words but Constantius did not listen. He moved to the door. He paused; he turned; he tried to speak to me. I blushed. I wanted to reach out and take his hand and tell him not to fear me, but I did not dare. Neither of us was ever able to face the other.

When Constantius finally spoke, his voice broke with tension. 'If this should come to you . . .' Awkwardly he gestured at himself to indicate the principate of the world. 'Remember . . .' Then his voice stopped as if a strangler's thumb had blocked the windpipe. He could not go on. Words had failed him again, and me.

I have often wondered what it was he meant to say; what it was I should remember. That life is short? Dominion bitter? No. Constantius was not a profound man. I doubt if he had been about to offer me any startling insight. But as I think back on that scene in the ruined shrine (and I think of it often, I even dream of it), I suspect that all he meant to say was, 'Remember me.' If that is what you meant, cousin, then I have, in every sense, remembered you.

Constantius left the shrine. As soon as his back was to me, I placed the withered flower on the profaned floor and whispered a quick prayer to Hermes. Then I followed the Emperor across the field to the road.

Once mounted, we exchanged formal farewells, and Constantius rode back to Milan, the dragon banner streaming in the cool wind before him. We never saw one another again.

CAESAR

At Turin, as I received city officials in the law court, a messenger arrived from Florentius, the praetorian prefect of Gaul. The prefect thought that the Caesar should know that some weeks ago Cologne had fallen to the Germans, and the Rhine was theirs. The military situation was, Florentius wrote with what almost seemed satisfaction, grave. The German King Chnodomar had sworn to drive every Roman from Gaul within the year. This was the bad news Constantius had not told me.

While the reception continued, Oribasius and I withdrew to the prefect's office to study the report. For some inexplicable reason the only bust to adorn the room was that of the Emperor Vitellius, a fat porker who reigned several months in the year of Nero's death. Why Vitellius? Was the official a descendant? Did he admire the fat neck, the huge jowls of the man who was known as the greatest glutton of his day? To such irrelevances does the mind tend to fly in moments of panic. And I was panicky.

'Constantius sent me here to die. That's why I was given no army.'

'But surely he doesn't want to lose Gaul.'

'What does he care for Gaul? As long as he can have his court, his eunuchs, his bishops, what more does he need?' This was not accurate; in his way, Constantius was a patriot. But in my bitterness there was no stopping me. I denounced Constantius recklessly and furiously. I committed treason with every breath. When I had finished, Oribasius said, 'The Emperor must have a plan. It can't be that simple. What are those instructions he gave you?'

I had forgotten all about the packet I had been given on the road to Turin. It was still in my wallet. Eagerly, I undid the fastenings. I read quickly, with growing astonishment. 'Etiquette!' I shouted finally, throwing the document across the room. 'How to receive an ambassador. How to give a dinner-party. There are even recipes!' Oribasius burst out laughing, but I was too far gone to find any humour in the situation.

'We'll escape!' I said at last.

'Escape?' Oribasius looked at me as if I had gone mad.

'Yes, escape.' Curious ... I never thought I would be able to write any of this. 'We can desert together, you and I. It will be easy. Nothing but a piece of cloth to throw away.' I tugged at the purple that I wore. 'Then we let our beards grow, and back to Athens. Philosophy for me, medicine for you.'

'No.' He said it flatly.

'Why not? Constantius will be glad to see the end of me.'

'But he won't know it's the end of you. He'll think you have gone to plot against him, raise an army, become usurper.'

'But he won't find me.'

Oribasius laughed. 'How can *you* hide in Athens? Even with a new beard and student's clothes, you are the same Julian everyone met a few months ago with Prohaeresius.'

'Then it won't be Athens. I'll find a city where I'm not known. Antioch. I can hide in Antioch. I'll study with Libanius.'

'And do you think Libanius could hold his tongue? His vanity would betray you in a day.'

Libanius: I shall say here that I never found Oribasius particularly sympathetic. Apparently, he felt the same about me. He is of course very famous nowadays (if he is still alive); but medical friends tell me that his seventy-volume encyclopedia of medicine is nothing but a vast plagiarism from Galen. After Julian's death, he was exiled and went to the court of Persia, where I am told he is worshipped by the Persians as a god; he must have enjoyed this, for he was always vain. Also avaricious: he once charged me *five gold solidi* for a single treatment for gout. I could not walk for a month after.

Julian Augustus
'Then I shall find a city where no one has ever seen me or heard of me.'
'Farthest Thule. Wherever you go, officials will know who you are.'
'*Complete* disguise? A new name?'
'You forget the secret agents. Besides, how will you live?'
'I can teach, become a tutor ...'
'A slave.'
'If necessary, why not? In a proper household, a slave can be happy. I could teach the young men. I would have time to write, to lecture ...'
'From the purple to a slave?' He said it with slow cold wonder.
'What do you think I am *now*?' I exploded. I raged. I lamented. When I finally stopped for lack of breath, Oribasius said, 'You will continue into Gaul, Caesar. You will put down the German tribes, or die in the attempt.'
'No.'
'Then be a slave, Julian.' It was the first time he had called me by my name since I had been raised to Caesar. Then he left me alone in the office, where I sat like a fool, mouth ajar, the hog-like face of Vitellius peering at me from above the doorway ... even after three centuries in stone, he looked hungry.

I folded the letter into many squares, each smaller than the other. I thought hard. I prayed to Hermes. I went to the latticed windows and looked for the sun, my peculiar deity. I searched for a sign. At last it came. From the setting sun, light suddenly shone in my face. Yes, out of the west where Gaul was, Helios blazed dark-gold in my eyes. I was to follow my god, and if death was what he required of me, then that would be my offering. If victory, then that would be our glory. Also, it was perfectly plain that I could not escape even if I wanted to. I had indeed been seized by purple death.

I returned to the citizens of Turin as though nothing had happened. As I received their homage, Oribasius looked at me questioningly. I winked. He was relieved.

The next morning we continued our journey. The weather in the mountains was not yet cold, nor was there any snow except on the highest slopes. Even the soldiers, a remarkably complaining lot of Galileans, admitted that God must be with us. He should have been: they prayed incessantly. It was all they were good for.

When we crossed into Gaul, an interesting thing happened. All up and down our route my coming had been excitedly reported, for I was the first legitimate Caesar to be seen in Gaul in many years. I say 'legitimate' because Gaul, traditionally, is the place for usurpers. There had been three in a decade. Each had worn the purple. Each had minted coinage. Each had accepted the oath of fealty. Each had been struck down by Constantius or fate. Now a true Caesar was at last in Gaul, and the people took heart.

Early one evening we entered our first Gallic village, set high in the mountains. The villagers were gathered along the main street to cheer me. As decoration, they had tied many wreaths of fir and pine between the houses on either side of the road. As Hermes is my witness, one of the wreaths broke loose and fell upon my head, where it fitted as close as a crown. I came to a dead halt, not certain what had happened. My first reaction was that I had been struck by a branch. Then I raised my hand and felt the wreath. The villagers were wide-eyed. Even my slovenly troops were impressed. Eutherius who was beside me murmured, 'Even the gods mean for you to be crowned.'

I did not answer him, nor did I remove the wreath. Pretending that nothing had happened, I continued through the village while the inhabitants cheered me with a new intensity.

Oribasius said, 'By tomorrow everyone in Gaul will know of this.'

I nodded. 'And by the next day Constantius will know.' But even this thought could not depress me. I was now in a fine mood, reflecting the brilliant winter day, not to mention the love the gods had shown me.

My passage through the Gallic towns was triumphal. The weather held until we arrived at the gates of Vienne. Then black clouds rolled out of the north and a sharp wind blew. One could smell snow upon the air. Bundled in cloaks, we crossed the winter-black Rhone and entered the city at about the third hour. Cold as it was, the streets were crowded and once again there was the remarkable response. I could not understand it. Constantius inspired awe and fear, but I seemed only to evoke love . . . . I do not mention this out of vanity but only as a puzzling fact. For all these people knew, I might be another Gallus. Yet there they were, cheering me as though I had won some important battle or increased the supply of grain. It was inexplicable but exhilarating.

Just as I came opposite the temple of Augustus and Livia, an old blind woman was thrust forward by the crowd. She fell against my horse. Guards pushed her back; she fell again. 'Help her,' I ordered.

They got her to her feet. In a loud voice she asked, 'Who is this?' Someone shouted, 'It is the Caesar Julian!' Then she raised her blind eyes to heaven and in the voice of a Pythoness proclaimed, 'He will restore the temples of the gods!' Startled, I spurred my horse through the crowd, her words still ringing in my ears.

I met Florentius in the main hall of the palace, which was to be my residence, though 'palace' was hardly the word for this not very large villa. Florentius received me courteously. Yes, he received me, rather than the other way around, and he made it perfectly clear from the beginning that this was his province, not mine, even though I was Caesar and he merely praetorian prefect.

'Welcome to Gaul, Caesar,' he said, as we saluted one another. He had not thought it worth while to call in the city's magistrates or, for that matter, any officials. Several military men attended him, and that was all. Oribasius was my only attendant.

'A warm welcome for a cold season, Prefect,' I said. 'The people at least seem pleased that I have come.' I stressed the 'at least'.

'*All* of us are pleased that Augustus has seen fit to elevate you and to send you to us as a sign of his interest in the matter of Gaul.' Florentius was a small swarthy man with sharp features. I particularly recall his sinewy forearms, which were black with hairs, more like a monkey's than a man's.

'Augustus will indeed be pleased to learn that you approve his actions,' I said dryly. Then I walked past him to where the room's single chair was placed on a small dais. I sat down. I could see this had some effect. The military men exchanged glances. Florentius, however, was imperturbable, even though I was sitting in his chair.

'Present the officers, Prefect.' I was as cold as my disposition ever allows me to be.

Florentius did so. The first officer was Marcellus, chief of staff of the army of Gaul. He saluted me perfunctorily. The next officer was Nevitta, a powerfully built Frank, blue-eyed, loud-voiced, a remarkable commander who serves with me now in Persia. But that day in Vienne, he treated me with such obvious disdain that I realized I would have to respond in kind, or lose all pretence of authority. Either I was Caesar or I was lost.

I turned to Florentius. I spoke carefully. 'We are not so far from Milan that the respect due to the Caesar can be omitted. Field conditions do not prevail in a provincial capital, despite the reverses of our armies on the Rhine. Instruct your officers, Prefect, in their duty to us. Show them by your example what we are.'

Constantius could not have done it better, and in truth I meant every word of this arrogant speech. I was convinced that I had come to Gaul to die, and I meant to die in the most honourable way possible, upholding to the end the great title that was mine.

Florentius looked astonished. The officers looked frightened. Oribasius was impressed ... curious how much we enjoy those rare moments when we can by some public act impress an old friend.

In his confusion, Florentius took too long to react. So in careful imitation of Constantius, I raised my right arm and pointed with forefinger to the floor in front of me, and in a hard voice said, 'We wear the purple.'

The military men with a clatter of armour dropped to their knees. Florentius, with a look of singular venom, followed suit. He kissed the robe. With that gesture, hostilities between us began. They were to continue for five years.

Constantius never meant me to take actual command of the province. I was to be a ceremonial figure, reminding the Gauls by my presence that Constantius had committed, if not a full army, at least his flesh and blood to the task of rallying a frightened people to the defence of the province. Florentius wielded all actual power. He was in direct charge of the army at Vienne and his personal courier service held together the various legions scattered about Gaul. Most of them, incidentally, were trapped in fortresses, for the Germans had laid siege to every sizeable town and military installation from the Rhine to the North Sea.

Only last year, in going through Constantius's secret archives – a fascinating if at times depressing experience, rather like hearing what people say behind one's back – I came across his instructions to Florentius. Now that I have read them I am more tolerant of the prefect; he was merely carrying out orders. Constantius wrote – I am paraphrasing, for the documents are all at Constantinople – that this 'dearly beloved kinsman the Caesar Julian' was to be looked upon as a cadet in the art of war and as a novice in the business of government. Florentius was to be that pupil's dedicated tutor, to instruct, edify and guard him against evil companions and wrong judgements. In other words, I was to be put to school. Military matters were to be kept from me. I was to be watched for signs of *ambitio*, as the Romans say, a word no other language has devised, meaning that sort of worldly ambition which is injurious to the balance of the state.

My first year in Gaul did teach me a good deal, not only in the art of war but also in the arts of concealment and patience. I became a second Ulysses, biding my time. I was not allowed to attend the military council. But from time to time I was briefed on the general military situation. I was not encouraged by what I was told. Though the army of Gaul was considerable, Florentius had no intention of committing it in battle.

We did nothing. Fortunately our enemy Chnodomar did nothing either; his promised offensive never materialized. He declared himself quite pleased to control the Rhine and our largest cities. I was eager to engage him, but I did not command a single soldier, excepting my doughty Italian bodyguard. I was also in need of money. My salary as Caesar was supposed to be paid by the quarter, but the Count of the Sacred Largesse was always late in making payments. I lived entirely on credit my first year in Gaul, and credit was not easily come by when there were daily rumours that I was in disfavour and might be recalled at any moment. I was also irritated to discover that the villa where I lived was *not* the palace of the Caesar but a sort of guest-house where official visitors were housed. The city palace was on the Rhone; and here Florentius and his considerable court were richly housed. He lived like the Caesar, I lived like a poor relation. But there were compensations. I had Oribasius with me, as well as Priscus, who arrived in March from Athens.

Priscus: I should add a bit to Julian's account of his relations with Florentius. The praetorian prefect was avaricious but capable. More to the point, he was following the Emperor's instructions to the letter. I always thought Julian was unduly bitter about him. Of course, on several public occasions the prefect humiliated him. I remember one military review when there was no place for Julian on the dais. So the Caesar was forced to watch 'his' troops from the crowd, surrounded by old women selling sausages. That was probably Florentius's revenge for Julian's behaviour at their first meeting.

To Constantius's credit ... why is one always trying to find good things to say about the bad? Is it our uneasy knowledge that their version of us would be precisely the same as ours of them, from another viewpoint and a conflicting interest? In any case, Constantius was perfectly correct in not allowing a youth with no military or administrative experience to take over the direction of a difficult war which older and supposedly wiser soldiers had nearly lost. No one could have known then that Julian was a military genius, except possibly himself. I almost find myself believing in that Helios of his when I contemplate his Gallic victories.

But at this time he lived much as a student in the villa next to the city wall. His 'court', as it had to be termed, was no more than a hundred people, counting slaves. We dined meagrely. There was never enough wine. But the conversation was good. Oribasius kept us all amused as well as healthy. He was, even then, compiling remedies from every witch he could find, and trying them out on us. Eutherius was also an amiable companion.

I note with some amusement that though Julian mentions specifically my joining him at Vienne, he says nothing of the far more important person who arrived at the new year: his wife Helena. I was not present when she came to Vienne but I am told that she arrived with a luxurious suite of hairdressers, seamstresses, cooks, eunuchs, and wagon-loads of fine clothes and jewels. I don't think she ever got over the shock of that cold depressing villa. But Julian was always very kind to her, though somewhat absent-minded. He would start to leave table without her, or openly make plans for a visit to a near-by town and then forget to include her in the arrangements. I think she liked him a good deal more than he liked her. Not that he disliked her; rather, he was profoundly indifferent. I doubt if he performed his conjugal duties often. Even so, she was twice pregnant in the four years they were married.

My chief memory of Helena is her valiant attempts not to look bored when Julian was talking excitedly about those things which interested him and mystified her. Fortunately, she had learned the royal art of yawning without opening the mouth; but if one watched her very carefully, whenever there was talk of Plato or Iamblichos or you, my dear Libanius (great triad!), one could see her nostrils dilate suspiciously from time to time. I am certain that we literally bored Helena to death.

Libanius: I cannot imagine anyone finding it remarkable that Julian should speak of Plato, Iamblichos and myself as being of a quality. But one can always trust Priscus to be envious. 'Great triad!' indeed! Simply because he has failed as a philosopher and a teacher, he would like to bring down all his contemporaries to his own level. Well, he will fail in that, too.

Julian Augustus

It is not easy to understand the Gauls. Their ways are strange to us, despite their many years as Roman subjects. I think they are the handsomest of the world's people. Both men and women are tall and fair-skinned, often with blue eyes and blond hair. They are forever washing their clothes and bodies. One can go from one end of the province to the other without seeing a man or woman in soiled or ragged clothes. Laundry hangs drying beside every hovel, no matter how poor.

But despite their beauty, they are remarkably quarrelsome. Both men and women speak with curiously loud voices, braying their vowels and sounding hard their consonants. Whenever I gave justice, I used to be deafened by the rival lawyers and claimants, all bellowing like wounded bulls. They boast that in a fight one Gaul is worth ten Italians. I'm afraid this is true. They love battle. They have both the strength and heart for it. And their women love fighting, too. It is not at all unusual for a Gaul in the heat of battle to call to his wife to aid him. When she does, his strength increases tenfold. With my own eyes I have seen Gallic women attack the enemy, teeth gnashing, necks corded with veins, large white arms revolving like the cross-piece of a windmill, while their feet kick like shots discharged by catapult. They are formidable.

The Gallic men take pride in military service, unlike the Italians, who think nothing of cutting off their own thumbs to thwart the state's recruiting officers. Gauls, however, delight in blood-letting, and they would be the greatest of all soldiers but for two reasons: they do not take well to military discipline, and they are drunks. At the most inconvenient moments a commander of Gallic troops is apt to find his soldiers mad with drink, under the excuse that such and such a day is holy and must be marked with a little wine or one of those powerful drinks they brew from grain and vegetables.

I shall not describe my campaigns in Gaul, for I have already published an account of them which flatterers declare is the equal of Julius Caesar's *Commentaries*. I will say that I put more care into writing about the Gallic wars than I did in fighting them! But I shall record some of the things which I could not reveal at the time.

The winter 355–356 was a painful one for me. I had no authority. I was ignored by the praetorian prefect. I had no duties, except to make an occasional progress through the countryside. Yet whenever I did show myself to the Gauls, I attracted large crowds.

Even on the frostiest winter days, the people would come from miles around to look at me, and cheer me on. I was much moved even though I was aware that often as not they hailed me not as Julian Caesar but as *Julius* Caesar. Indeed, there was a legend among the peasants that the great Julius had once vowed that he would return from the grave to protect Gaul from its enemies; many thought the time had now come for the dead general to keep his promise, and that I was he.

Out of these progresses came several unexpected victories for us. One town, besieged by Germans, took heart at the presence of the Caesar, and the towns people drove the enemy from their fields. Another town in Aquitania, defended only by old men, repulsed a German attack, shouting my name as war-cry and talisman of victory.

In Aquitania I fought my first 'battle'. We were passing two abreast through a thick forest, when a band of Germans fell upon us. For a moment I was afraid my Italians would break and run. But they held their ground. That is all one needs when taken by surprise. In those first few minutes of attack an alert commander can rally his troops and strike back, if they hold fast initially.

Fortunately, we were at the forest's edge. I ordered the men at the front to divert the Germans while the men at the rear got through the forest to the open plain. In a matter of minutes, our men were free of the woods. There were no casualties. then, when we began to get the better of the Germans, they prompt-ly fled: first one, then another, then several at a time.

Suddenly I heard myself shouting, 'After them! Cut them off!' My troops obeyed. The Germans were now in full flight, back into the forest. 'A silver piece for every German head!' I shouted. This bloodthirsty cry was taken up by my officers. It was the incentive needed. Roaring with excitement and greed, my troops fell upon the enemy. By the end of the day, a hundred German heads had been brought to me.

I have described this engagement not because it was of military importance – it was not – but because this was my first taste of battle. Unlike nearly all my predecessors (not to mention any conscientious patrician), I was quite without military experience. I had never even seen a man killed in battle. I had always preferred peace to war, study to action, life to death. Yet there I was shouting myself hoarse on the edge of a Gallic forest, with a small hill of bloody human heads in front of me. Was I sickened? or ashamed? Neither. I was excited in a way that men who choose to serve Aphrodite are excited by love. I still prefer philosophy to war, but nothing else. How I came to be like this is a mystery whose origin must be divine, determined by that fierce sun who is the genesis of all men and the protector of kings.

As we rode back to Vienne in the pale winter light, I trembled with an excitement that was close to joy, for I knew now that I would survive. Until that moment, I had not been certain of myself. For all that I knew, I might have been a coward or, worse, too paralysed by the confusion of the moment to make those swift decisions without which no battle was ever won. Yet when the shouting had begun and the blood flowed, I was exalted. I saw what had to be done with perfect clarity, and I did it.

This skirmish was not taken very seriously at Vienne. What was taken seriously, however, was the fact that Constantius had named me his fellow consul for the new year. It was his eighth consulship, my first. I was pleased, but only moderately. I have never understood why men so value this ancient title. The consul has no power (unless he also happens to be emperor), yet ambitious men will spend a fortune to be admitted to consular rank. Of course, one's name will be known for ever, since all dates are figured by consulates. Even so, I am not much drawn to any form which has lost its meaning. Yet at my investiture, Florentius was almost civil, which was something gained. In a private meeting, he told me, 'We plan an offensive in the late spring. You will, if you choose, take part.'

'As commander?'

'Caesar commands all of Gaul.'

'Caesar is most sensible of his high place. But am I to *lead* the armies? Am I to plan the war?'

'You will be our guide in all things, Caesar.' He was evasive. Clearly, he was not about to give up control of the province. But a beginning was made. The wall was breached. Now it was up to me to exploit this small change for the better.

When Florentius had departed, I sent for Sallust, my military adviser. He had been assigned to me when I first arrived in Gaul and I am forever in Constantius's debt for having brought the two of us together. Sallust is both Roman soldier and Greek philosopher. What higher compliment can I give him? When we met, Sallust was in his late forties. He is tall, slow of speech but swift of mind; he comes of an ancient Roman family and like so many Romans of the aristocracy he has never wavered in his allegiance to the true gods. A close friend of such distinguished Hellenists as Symmachus and Praetextatus, he published some years ago a classic defence of our religion, *On the Gods and the World*. As Maximus is my guide to mysteries and Libanius my model for literary style, so Sallust remains my ideal of what a man should be.

Sallust was as pleased as I by the news. Together we studied a map of Gaul, and decided that the best move would be to strike directly at Strasbourg. This large city not only commanded a considerable part of the Rhine; it was also being used as a centre of operations by King Chnodomar. Its recapture would greatly strengthen us and weaken the enemy.

'There is a lesson in this,' said Sallust suddenly.

'In what?'

'Why are the Germans in Gaul?'

'Plunder. Desire for more territory. Why do the barbarian tribes ever move from place to place?'

'They are in Gaul because Constantius invited the tribes to help him against Magnentius. They helped him. And then they remained in Gaul.'

The point was well taken. One must never appeal for help to barbarians. Engage them as mercenaries, bribe them if that is the only way to keep the peace, but *never* allow a tribe to move into Roman territory for eventually they will attempt to seize what is Roman for themselves. Even as Sallust and I were talking, Constantius was on the Danube, fighting two rebel tribes he had once allowed to settle there.

Sallust then told me that there was conclusive evidence that Florentius was dealing secretly with certain of the German chiefs. Some he paid on the sly to remain where they were; others paid him not to disturb their present holdings. Carefully Sallust and I constructed our case against Florentius.

In May the plan to strike directly at Strasbourg was submitted by Sallust and me to Florentius and his general, Marcellus. It was promptly dismissed. We argued. We begged. We promised victory. But they would not listen.

'We are not yet ready to commit the army to a major battle. This is not the time.' Marcellus was provincial commander-in-chief, I was forced to obey.

'At what time,' I asked, looking about the council chamber (we were in the prefect's palace), 'will we be able to obey the Emperor and drive the Germans out of Gaul?'

Florentius was suave. His manner to me, although still condescending, was more cautious than before. Obviously, I was not to fall without careful effort on his part.

'May I propose to the Caesar a compromise?' Florentius played with a delicate purse of deerskin, containing *his* god, gold. 'We have not the men for a major campaign. Until the Emperor sends reinforcements, which he is not apt to do this year since he is already committed on the Danube, we must confine ourselves to holding what we have, and to regaining what we can, without too much risk.'

Florentius clapped his hands, and a secretary who was squatting against a wall sprang to his feet. Florentius was most imperial in his ways, but then, praetorian prefects are important men. At this time Florentius governed Morocco, Spain, Gaul and Britain. The secretary held up a map of Gaul.

Florentius pointed to a town called Autun, just north of us. 'We have received news that the town is besieged.' I almost asked why I had not been told before, but I held my tongue. 'Now if the Caesar chooses, he might – with General Sallust –' Florentius addressed a small crooked smile at Sallust, whose face remained politely attentive – 'relieve Autun. It is an old city. The walls were once impregnable but they are now in considerable disrepair, like nearly all our defences, I'm afraid. There is not much of a garrison but the townspeople are valiant.'

I told him quickly that nothing would please me more. I would go immediately to the relief of Autun.

'Of course,' said Florentius, 'it will take several weeks to equip your troops, to assemble supplies, to ...'

'One good thing,' Marcellus interrupted, 'you won't have to worry about siege engines. Even if the Germans capture the city before you get there, they won't occupy it. They never do.'

'But what about Cologne and Strasbourg?'

'Destroyed,' said Marcellus, with almost as much pleasure as if he personally had done the destroying. 'But not *occupied*. The Germans are frightened of cities. They won't stay in one overnight.'

'Their custom,' said Florentius, 'is to occupy the countryside around a city and starve the inhabitants. When the city finally capitulates, they burn it and move on.'

'How many troops will I be allowed?'

'We are not certain just yet. There are other ... contingencies.' Florentius shifted from hand to hand the purse of gold. 'But in a few weeks we shall know and then the Caesar may begin his first ... Gallic war.' This jibe was crude but I had learned not to show offence.

'Then see to it, Prefect,' I said, as royally as possible, and accompanied by Sallust I left the palace.

As we walked through the city streets to my villa, not even the memory of Florentius's contempt could shatter the delight I took in the thought of action. 'Just one successful campaign and Constantius will give me the whole army!'

'Perhaps.' Sallust was thoughtful. We crossed the square, where carts from the countryside were gathering with the first of the season's produce. Two guards followed me at a discreet distance. Though I was Caesar, the townspeople were by now quite used to seeing me wander alone in the streets and where before they had done me frightened obeisance, they now greeted me – respectfully of course – as a neighbour.

'Only . . .' Sallust stopped.

'Only if I have too great a victory, Constantius will see to it that I never command an army again.'

'Exactly.'

I shrugged. 'I must take my chances. Besides, after the Danube, Constantius will have to face the Persians. He'll have no choice except to trust me. There's no one else. If I can hold Gaul, then he must let me.'

'But suppose he does not go against Persia? Suppose he moves against *you*?'

'Suppose I am struck dead by . . . that cart?' And we both leaped to the side of the road as a bullock-cart rumbled past us while its driver loudly cursed it and us and the gods who had made him late for market. 'It will be all right, Sallust,' I said as we approached the villa. 'I have had signs.'

Sallust accepted this, for he knew that I was under the special protection of Hermes, who is the swift intelligence of the universe.

I I

On 22 June I left Vienne at the head of an army of twelve thousand men – cuirassiers, crossbowmen and infantry. The whole town came out to see us off. Florentius radiated irony, while Marcellus could hardly disguise his amusement. I am sure that they thought this was the last they would see of me. Helena bade me farewell with stoic dignity. She was the essence of a Roman matron, quite prepared for me to return upon my shield.

It was a sunny day as we rode out of the city. On my right was Sallust and on my left Oribasius. Directly in front of me a standard-bearer carried a hideously lifelike image of Constantius, crowned and wearing the imperial robe. My cousin had recently sent me this effigy, with a long set of instuctions on how I was to show it off. He also reminded me that I had not been sent to Gaul as monarch but as a representative of the Emperor whose principal task was to display the imperial robe and image to the people. Despite this small humiliation, I was in high spirits as we took to the road.

We arrived at Autun 26 June. On that same day I defeated the Germans and set the city free. *Note to secretary:* At this point insert relevant chapter from my book, *The Gallic Wars.* It should be that section which covers the campaign from Autun to Auxerre to Troyes to Rheims, where I passed the month of August.

Priscus: As Julian described, Sallust on his right, Oribasius on his left, and myself just behind. His official account of the campaign is generally accurate. From Julius Caesar on, commanders tend to give themselves the best of it in their memoirs, but Julian was usually honest. Of course he tended not to mention his mistakes. He does not tell how he lost the better part of a legion through carelessness: he sent them through a forest where he had been warned that there were Germans ... and there *were* Germans. But in general, Julian was a cautious commander. He seldom committed a man unless he was certain that the odds were in his favour. Or so the experts assure us. I know practically nothing of military matters, even though I served with Julian both in Gaul and Persia. I was not of course a soldier, though I did fight from time to time, with no pleasure. I experienced none of that blood lust he referred to some pages back, a rather surprising admission because in conversation Julian never once admitted to a liking for war.

Sallust took care of all details. He was most capable and in every way an admirable man. Too admirable, perhaps? One often had the feeling that he was playing a part (usually that of Marcus Aurelius); he was invariably demure and diffident and modest and sensible, all those things the world believes it admires. Which is the point. Less self-conscious men invariably have traits we do not admire. The good and the bad are all mixed together. Sallust was all good. That must have taken intense self-discipline as well as the awareness that he was indeed trying to be something he was not. But no matter what his motives, he was impressive, and a good influence on Julian.

Julian lifted the siege at Autun. He then marched north to Auxerre. He rested there a few days. He always took every possible opportunity to refresh his troops, unlike so many generals who drive them past their strength. From Auxerre we moved to Troyes. This was a difficult journey. We were continually harassed by Germans. They are a frightening-looking people, tall and muscular, with long hair dyed bright red, a tribal custom. They dress pretty much like us, wearing armour pilfered from Roman corpses. In open country, they are easily vanquished, but in forests they are dangerous.

At Troyes we spent several hours outside the walls trying to explain to the frightened garrison that we were not Germans and that this was indeed the Caesar. Finally Julian himself, with that 'hideously lifelike' image of Constantius beside him, ordered the people to open the gates.

We stayed at Troyes a day. Then we moved on to Rheims. Julian had previously agreed with Florentius that the main army of Gaul would be concentrated there in August, preparatory to retaking Cologne. So Marcellus was already at Rheims when we got there. Shortly after we arrived, a military council was called. Weary from the long ride and longing for the baths, I accompanied Julian and Sallust to the meeting.

Marcellus was hardly pleased to find Julian so obviously thriving on military life. When Julian inquired if the troops were ready, he was told that they were not. When would they be ready? Evasion. Finally: a major offensive was not possible this year.

Then Julian rose and lied with the genius of a Ulysses. I could hardly believe my ears. He spoke first in sorrow. 'I had hoped to find all of you here eager and ready to fight the tribes. Instead, I find nothing is planned and we are on the defensive, as usual.' Marcellus began to mutter dangerously but Julian was in full flow. You know what he was like when the spirit (often identified as Helios) was upon him.

'I was sent here, General, by the divine Emperor to show his image to the barbarians. I was also sent here to recover the cities *you* have lost. I was sent here to drive the savages back to their forests beyond the Rhine. I have sworn as Caesar to conquer them or to die.'

'But Caesar, we ...' That was all Marcellus was allowed to say. As Julian talked through him, he withdrew a document from his tunic. It was the booklet on etiquette that Constantius had given him. 'Do you see this, General? All of you?' Julian waved it like a standard in the air. No one could tell what it was exactly, but the imperial seal was perfectly visible.

'It is from the divine Emperor. It is to me. It arrived by special messenger at Autun. It contains orders. We are to regain Cologne. Those are his commands and we are his slaves. We have no choice but to obey.'

There was consternation on Marcellus's side of the council table. No one had heard of these instructions for the excellent reason that they did not exist. But the bold lie worked largely because Marcellus was a true politician in the sense that he could not admit that there was anything which he ought to know that in fact he did not know. He gave Julian the army.

Julian Augustus

At Rheims I reviewed the legions as they marched through the city gates, all of us sweating in the hot August sun. It was a lowering day, humid and ill-omened. As I stood on the platform outside the city gate, gnats whirring about my head and sweat trickling down my face, a message from Vienne was handed to me. It was a brief note from Florentius. My wife had been delivered of a boy who had died shortly afterwards. She was in good health. That was all.

It is an odd thing to be the father of a son and the grieving father of a dead son, all in the same instant. I handed the letter to Sallust. Then I turned back to the legions who were marching rhythmically now in Pyrrhic measure to the sound of pipes.

Priscus: The midwife cut too short the child's umbilical cord. We later learned that she had been paid to do this by the Empress Eusebia. Yet I never heard Julian refer to Eusebia in any but the most glowing terms. It is sad how tangled the relations among princes become ... What a ridiculous statement! We are all in the habit of censuring the great, as if we were popular playwrights, when in fact ordinary folk are quite as devious and as wilful and as desperate to survive (if not to prevail) as are the great; particularly philosophers.

Julian skips the rest of that year's campaign with a note that a section from his earlier book will be inserted. That will be your task. Personally, I find his book on the Gallic wars almost as boring as Julius Caesar's. I say 'almost' because a description of something one has lived through can never be entirely dull. But descriptions of battles soon pall. I would suggest – although you have not asked for my literary advice – that you keep the military inserts to a minimum.

Julian's autumn campaign was a success. He fought a set battle at Brumath which strategists regard as a model of brilliant warfare. I wouldn't know. At the time I thought it confusing, but it opened the road to Cologne. That part of the world, by the way, is quite lovely, especially a spot called the Confluence, where – obviously – two rivers join, the Moselle and the Rhine, at a town called Remagen – ours; just past Remagen is an old Roman tower which commands the countryside. Not far from Remagen is Cologne, which to everyone's amazement Julian regained, after a brief battle.

We remained at Cologne all of September. Julian was in excellent form. Several of the Frankish chiefs paid him court and he both charmed and awed them, a rare gift which he apparently shared, if one is to trust Cicero, with Julius Caesar.

A light note of no consequence: Oribasius bet me one gold piece that Constantius would take revenge on Julian for lying to Marcellus. I bet him that he would not. I won the gold piece. We then spent the winter at Sens, a depressing provincial town north of Vienne. It was nearly the last winter for all of us.

Julian Augustus

After the victories described, I went into winter quarters at a pleasant town called Sens whose particular virtue was that it kept me at a proper distance from Florentius at Vienne and Marcellus at Rheims.

During those months Helena kept much to herself. She had several ladies with her from the court at Milan and I think that she was reasonably content, though she was not in good health: because of her age, the birth had been a difficult one. I was always ill at ease with Helena. I could hardly forget that she was the sister of my enemy. For a long time I was uncertain to which of us she was loyal. I do know that she kept up a considerable correspondence with her brother (since destroyed; by whom? very mysterious); as a result, I was careful to say nothing in her presence which might make Constantius suspicious. This self-restraint was a considerable burden for me.

Only once did Helena reveal that she had some idea of what was in my mind and heart. It was in December. We had dined frugally in my office, which was easier to heat than the state apartments. Several braziers gave forth sufficient heat – at least for me; Priscus used to complain bitterly of my meanness in this regard. Helena sat with her ladies at the opposite end of the room, listening to one of the women sing Greek songs, while Oribasius, Sallust, Priscus and I reclined on couches at the other end of the room.

We spoke idly at first, as one does after supper. We touched on the military situation. It was not good. Despite my victory at Cologne, Florentius had left me with only two legions. The rest of my army had been recalled to Rheims and Vienne. I was in the same position I had been my first winter at Vienne, a prince with no principality. Only now I carried a larger burden. But as the old saying goes, 'A pack-saddle is put on an ox; that is surely no burden for me.' It was my task not only to hold Sens but to protect the neighbouring villages from the German tribes who were, even in the dead of winter, moving restlessly from town to town, burning and pillaging. In fact, Chnodomar himself had sworn that he would hang me before the spring thaw. To garrison the near-by towns, I was obliged to give up two-thirds of the soldiers under my command. Added to this, we were faced with an unusual number of desertions, especially among the Italian soldiers.

'Any man who deserts should be executed,' said Sallust, 'publicly, before the legions.'

'It is remarkably difficult, General,' said Priscus in his sly way, 'to execute a deserter. First, you must catch him.'

'The only solution,' I said, 'is victory. If we are successful, the men will be loyal. There are few deserters in a winning army.'

'But we are neither winning nor an army,' said Priscus with unpleasant accuracy.

'Which is exactly what the Emperor wants.' Oribasius spoke too loudly. I silenced him with a gesture. Helena had heard this but she made no sign.

'I am sure the divine Emperor, my cousin and colleague, is eager for us to succeed in driving the Germans from Gaul.' Actually, I had received no word from Constantius since taking up residence at Sens. I assumed that he was angry with me for not returning to Vienne.

Then Priscus asked me to read from the panegyric I was writing on Eusebia. I sent for a notary, who brought me the manuscript. I read a few pages, not liking it at all. The work was rough. I said so.

'Probably,' said the wicked Priscus, 'because it is nearly sincere.'

The others laughed. At Vienne I had written a lengthy panegyric of Constantius which – if I say so myself – was a masterpiece, carefully ordered and beautifully composed. The art of panegyric does not necessarily exclude honesty, though one's true feelings are perfectly irrelevant to the final composition, which is artifice, not truth. Even Constantius realized that I had created something marvellous and wrote me a letter in his own hand, filled with misspellings and errors of syntax. I then tried to write a panegyric on Eusebia, and found it difficult; no doubt, as Priscus suggested, because of my true regard for the subject. Also, I was honour bound not to reveal to what extent she had saved my life. This was limiting.

While we were talking amiably, I heard far off the uneasy neighing of horses, but thought nothing of it. Then Oribasius mentioned those Hebrew books which the Galileans refer to as the old testament. This was a favourite subject with me. So much so that I forgot Helena was in the room. 'I admire the Jews because of their devotion to a single god. I also admire them because of their self-discipline. But I deplore the way they interpret their god. He is supposed to be universal, but he is interested only in them ...'

'Christ,' said my wife suddenly, 'was sent by God to all of us.'

There was an embarrassed silence.

'The issue,' I said finally, with great gentleness, 'is just that: would the One God intervene in such a way?'

'We believe that He did.'

The room was now completely still save for the far-off sound of horses. My companions were on edge.

'Yet is it not written in the so-called gospel of John, that "out of Galilee arises no prophet"?'

'God is God, not a prophet,' said Helena.

'But the idea of the Nazarene's mission, in his own words, is taken from the old testament, which is Jewish, which says that a prophet – a messiah – will one day come to the Jews, but not God himself.'

'That is a difficulty,' she admitted.

'In fact,' and I was stupidly blunt, 'there is almost no connection between what the Galileans believe and what the Nazarene preached. More to the point, I see nothing in the Jewish text that would allow for such a monstrosity as the triple god. The Jews were monotheists. The Galileans are atheists.'

I had gone too far. Helena rose, bowed, and withdrew, accompanied by her ladies.

My companions were alarmed. Priscus spoke first. 'What a gift you have, Caesar, for making the difficult impossible!'

The others agreed. I asked their forgiveness. 'Anyway,' I said, not believing my own words, 'we can trust Helena.'

'I hope so.' Sallust was gloomy.

'One must be true to what is true,' I said, wishing as I so often do that I had held my tongue.

There was a sudden shouting in the streets. We all sprang to our feet. We had hardly got to the door when an officer arrived to report that Sens was being attacked. Elsewhere I describe what happened and I shall not repeat it here.

Priscus: We were besieged for a month. A number of our deserters had gone over to the Germans and reported on our weakness. Encouraged by this, and excited at the thought of capturing a Roman Caesar, King Chnodomar marched on Sens. It was a difficult time and we owed our lives, finally, to Julian's energy and intelligence. Though he could not make us cheerful or even confident, he at least kept us dutiful and modestly hopeful.

That night the call to arms was sounded. Men rushed to their posts on the battlements. The Germans could be seen less than half a mile away, illuminated by burning farmhouses. It had been the neighing of farm horses that had disturbed our after-dinner conversation. Had the Germans been quieter, they might have taken the city. Fortunately for us, every last one of them was drunk.

During the next few days, Julian's mood changed from almost boisterous excitement to grim rage. He was positive that he had been deliberately abandoned. This suspicion was confirmed when a messenger arrived from Rheims to say that Marcellus would not come to our aid; he pleaded weakness. He also insisted that Julian had sufficient men to repulse the Germans.

Our rations were nearly gone when the Germans departed as suddenly as they had arrived. Long sieges bored them. Julian immediately sent to Vienne for supplies. He then recalled all his troops to Sens and the remainder of the winter was passed, if not in comfort, at least without fear of sudden annihilation. Julian also wrote Constantius a full account of Marcellus's refusal to come to his aid. It was a splendid document. I know; Sallust and I helped to write it. So splendid was it, in fact, that unlike most state papers this one had an effect. Marcellus was recalled to Milan and after a short interval Julian finally got what he wanted, the command of the armies of Gaul.

The year 357 was the making of Julian as a world hero. In the spring, when the grain was ripe, he proceeded to Rheims, where he learned that Barbatio, the commander of the Roman infantry, was on his way to Augst with twenty-five thousand troops and seven river boats. He was to assist Julian in a final drive against the Germans. But before a plan could be devised, a tribe called the Laeti passed through our territory and laid siege to Lyon, burning all the countryside around. Julian quickly sent three squadrons of light cavalry to relieve that city. He also set a watch on the three roads radiating from Lyon, in order to ambush the savages when they fled. Unfortunately, Barbatio's troops allowed the Germans to get through because a tribune of targeteers, named Cella, acting under Barbatio's orders, prevented the cavalry commander from attacking. Why? Barbatio was eager for Julian to fail. He was also to some extent in league with the German tribes. Julian ordered Cella and his staff cashiered; only the cavalry commander was let off. He was, incidentally, Valentinian, our future emperor.

By now the Germans were alarmed. They tried to block our progress to the Rhine by felling great trees across the roads. They took refuge on the islands in the Rhine, where they used to bellow all sorts of insults at us, and at night sing the most melancholy songs. When Julian asked Barbatio for his seven ships, they were promptly and mysteriously burned. So Julian, always inventive, ordered the light-armoured auxiliaries of the Cornuti Legion to swim out to one of the islands, using their wooden shields as rafts. This worked. They killed the German defenders and then, using German boats, attacked the other islands. The savages then abandoned the remaining islands and fled into the eastern forest.

Julian next restored the fortress at Savernes, an important installation because it stands directly in the path of anyone intent on the conquest of central Gaul. He then harvested the crops the Germans had planted. This gave him twenty days' rations. He was now ready to face King Chnodomar. His only obstacle was Barbatio. Happily for us, this extraordinary creature was attacked by the Germans just north of Augst. Though Barbatio had a large, well-disciplined army, he fled in a panic back to Augst and promptly announced that he had won a famous victory and, though it was only July, he went into winter quarters. That was the end of him for the year. We were much relieved.

With thirteen thousand men, Julian marched directly on Strasbourg. A few miles from the city, Chnodomar sent Julian an embassy commanding him to quit Gaul since this was now 'German country, won by German arms and valour'. Julian laughed at the king's envoys. But Chnodomar was not a man to be taken lightly. Ever since he defeated the Caesar Decentius, he had been free to come and go in Gaul as though it were indeed his own kingdom. Now, encouraged by the collapse of Barbatio, he was positive he would again be victorious.

The issue was resolved, as we all know, and I am sure you will insert at this point Julian's account of the Battle of Strasbourg. I think it is almost the best of his writings – and you know my prejudice against military commentaries! Only the garrulousness of age makes me go on as I have about these months in Gaul. I do it partly to inform you and partly – to be honest – to see how much memory I have left; more than I thought. One detail which came back to me just as I wrote the word 'memory': while riding outside the walls of a Gallic town, I saw a cemetery where several of the graves were covered with fishnets. I asked one of the native soldiers what this meant. 'It is to keep the ghosts of mothers who die in childbirth from stealing back their children.' There is a lot of interesting folklore in that part of the world and I hope some latter-day Herodotus will record it before the people become so completely Romanized that the old customs are forgotten.

Incidentally, it was at this time that Helena was recalled to Rome, where Constantius was celebrating not only his first triumph but his first visit to the capital. She was again pregnant, and again she lost her baby, this time through a miscarriage brought on by a potion Eusebia gave her.

As for the famous Battle of Strasbourg, I can add very little to what Julian himself wrote.

Libanius: Then why do you? Priscus keeps protesting he can add little and then adds too much. He has aged. He always used to be brief, to the point of being laconic, but now ...!

Priscus: My own memories of that day in August are quite vivid and surprisingly full, considering the fact that I have no memory of what happened last year, or even this morning.

Julian had submitted his plan of battle to Florentius at Vienne and to our surprise it was approved. No one will know what Florentius's motives were. I suspect the fact that Julian had thirteen thousand troops while the German army numbered some thirty-five thousand might have had something to do with it.

On the morning of 14 August we stopped some twenty miles from the Rhine, on whose banks Chnodomar had assembled his army. I recall that day as one of the hottest I have ever experienced. The heat was even worse than Persia, for it was damp. Also, the air swarmed with insects, and I sneezed continually as I always do at that time of year, the result of humours rising from the rank earth.

I was at Julian's side through most of the battle, more as ornament than as soldier, though I did lay about me from time to time simply to avoid being killed. Julian made a good speech to the army. His speeches, though never particularly brilliant, did have the gift of striking precisely the right note with the men. I have often wondered how such a bookish young man could have learned to talk with such ease to some of the most formidably ignorant and prejudiced men on earth. Yet he did. His cultured voice would become harsh, his manner royal; the content modest, the effect inspiring.

Julian sat his horse, with his standard-bearer beside him holding a spear on which the imperial dragon fluttered in the hot wind, purple and ominous. The infantry filled the narrow declivity at the foot of the hill where Julian and his staff were posted, all knee-deep in ripened grain, for we were in the midst of a large farm.

Trumpets blared in unison. Squadrons of cavalry, cuirassiers and archers moved in from left and right until Julian was surrounded. When at last they were all assembled and silent, he spoke to them. He was never more subtle though his manner was vigorous and forthright. He wanted to persuade them to fight immediately, but knowing that they were tired and hot from the sun, he realized that he would have to trick them into wanting what he wanted.

'The thing we most care for is for the safety of our men, and though we are eager to engage the enemy, we also realize that rashness can be dangerous and caution a virtue. Though we are all young men and inclined to be impetuous, as Caesar I must be the one to move warily, though – as you know – I am far from being timid. Now here is our situation. It is almost noon. The heat is terrible. It will get worse. We are all of us tired from a long march. We are not certain of sufficient water this side of the Rhine. The enemy is fresh, and waiting. So I suggest that we erect pickets, that we eat and sleep and make ready for battle tomorrow, when, if it be God's will, we shall strike at first light and with our eagles in the advance, drive the Germans from Roman soil ...'

But the legions interrupted him. They gnashed their teeth, a terrible sound, and struck their spears against their shields.

Then one of the standard-bearers shouted, 'Forward, Caesar! Follow your star!' He turned dramatically to the legions. 'We have a general who will win! So if it be God's will, we shall free Gaul this day! Hail, Caesar!'

This was all that was needed. As the legions cheered, Julian gave the order to prepare for battle. After this, I had him to myself for a moment. We were so close to one another that our stirrups clashed. 'A fine speech,' I said. 'Suitable for history.'

He grinned like a schoolboy. 'How did you like the standard-bearer's speech?'

'Exactly what was required.'

'I coached him in it last night, with gestures.' Then Julian deployed his troops. The Germans were already in battle formation. To left and right as far as the eye could see, their forces lined the river. In their first rank was King Chnodomar, a big man with a great belly who wore a scarlet plume in his helmet.

At noon, Julian ordered the attack. The Germans had dug a number of trenches in our path and there, hidden by green boughs, archers suddenly fired at the legions who halted in consternation. They did not retreat; but they did not advance.

Julian was now in his element. Voice cracking with tension, he darted from squadron to squadron, legion to legion. He drove the men to attack. Those who fell back, he threatened. I cannot remember exactly what he said, but the burden of it was: these are savages, these are the spoilers of Gaul, *now* is the chance to break them, this is the moment we have waited for! He also used a wily approach for those who seemed bent on retreat. 'I beg you, don't follow the enemy too closely! Stop at the Rhine! Let them drown. But you be careful!'

For me, the day was confusion. In the course of that sweltering afternoon, the battle was several times in doubt. At one point our cavalry broke; they would have fled had they not come up against a solid wall of infantry reserves behind them. My most vivid memory is of the German faces. I have never seen anything like them, nor hope to again in this world. Should there be a hell, I am sure that I shall spend it entirely in the company of Germans in battle. Their dyed red hair is worn long, and hangs about the face like a lion's mane. They grind their teeth and shout words which are not words but sounds of rage. Their eyes are quite mad and staring, the veins thick in their necks. I suspect many of them were drunk but not drunk enough to lose their ferocity. I killed several, and was myself nearly killed.

After the Germans had split our cavalry, they turned on the infantry, thinking to overwhelm them by sheer numbers. But they did not reckon with the two best legions of Rome: the Cornuti and the Bracchiati. These men in tortoise formation, heads masked by their shields, steadily advanced into the German horde. This was the crisis of the battle, just as Oribasius maintains that there is a crisis in a fever when all at once it is decided whether the sick man lives or dies. We lived. The Germans died. It was a great – a sickening – butchery. Wounded and dying men lay four and five deep on the river bank; some were suffocated by the bodies above them; some literally drowned in blood. I was never again to see a day quite like that one, for which I am thankful.

Suddenly, as though by some signal (but it was merely instinct; other witnesses of war have noticed this same phenomenon), the Germans broke for the river. Our men followed. It was a lurid sight. The savages desperately tried to swim to the other side. At one point, and this is no chronicler's exaggeration, the Rhine was indeed red with blood.

It was now late afternoon. Aching in every muscle and trembling from what I had seen and done, I found Julian and his staff already encamped on a high bluff beside the river. Julian's tent had been pitched in a gove of ash trees, and though his face was black with sweat and dust, he seemed as fresh as when he began the day. He embraced me warmly.

'Now we're all here!' he exclaimed. 'And still alive.' We drank wine as the shadows of the trees around us lengthened, and Sallust reported that we had lost four officers and two hundred and forty-three men. No one could reckon the German losses but the next day they were figured to be somewhere between five and six thousand. It was the greatest victory for Roman arms in Gaul since Julius Caesar. Difficult though it is for me to delight in military affairs, I could not help but be caught up by the general excitement, which increased when shortly before midnight King Chnodomar himself was brought to us, arms pinned behind him, great belly sagging, eyes white with terror. The Germans lack true pride, as others have so often remarked. In victory they are overbearing; in defeat cringing. The king threw himself at Julian's feet, moaning his submission. The next day Julian sent him to Constantius, who had him imprisoned in Rome's Castra peregrina on the Caelian Hill, where he died of old age. All in all, a better fate than was to befall his conqueror.

Julian records nothing of the rest of the year. He decently buried the Gallic dead. He returned to Savernes. He ordered captives and booty to be taken to Metz. Then he crossed the Rhine into German territory. He seized all livestock and grain; he burned the houses, which are built exactly like ours even though the Germans are supposed to prefer living in forest huts – so much for legend. Then we penetrated those awesome vast woods which fill the centre of Europe. There is nothing like them in the world. The trees are so dense that only a dim green light ever penetrates to the ground. Trees old as time make passage difficult. Here the savage tribes are safe from attack, for what stranger could find his way through that green labyrinth? and who would want to conquer those haunted woods? Except the Emperor Trajan. We stumbled upon one of his abandoned forts, and Julian had it rebuilt and garrisoned. Then we crossed the Rhine once more and went into winter quarters at Paris, a city which the Romans always refer to, with their usual elegance, as Mudtown.

I 2

Julian Augustus

Of the cities of Gaul, I like Paris the best and I spent three contented winters there. The town is on a small island in the River Seine. Wooden bridges connect it to both banks where the townspeople cultivate the land. It is lovely green country where almost anything will grown, even fig trees. My first winter I set out a dozen (jacketed in straw) and all but one survived. Of course the Paris winters are not as cold as those at Sens or Vienne because the nearness of the ocean warms the air. As a result, the Seine seldom freezes over; and its water – as anyone knows who has ever visited there – is remarkably sweet and good to drink. The town is built of wood and brick, with a fair-sized prefect's palace which I used as headquarters. From my second-floor study, I could see the water as it divided at the island's sharp tip, like the sea breaking on a ship's prow. In fact, if one stares hard enough at that point in the river one has a curious sense of movement, of indeed being on a ship in full sail, the green shore rushing past.

As for the Parisians, they are a hard-working people who delight in the theatre and (alas) in Galilean ceremonies. In the winter they are townsfolk, and in the summer peasants. By the most remarkable good luck, they combine the best rather than the worst aspects of the two estates. We got on very well together, the Parisians and I.

Relations with Florentius grew worse. At every turn he tried to undermine my authority. Finally I fell out with him over money. Because of the German invasion, the landowners had suffered great losses. Year after year, whole harvests had been destroyed, buildings burned, livestock stolen. To lessen the burden of men already bankrupt, I proposed that both the poll tax and the land tax be reduced from twenty-five to seven gold pieces a year. Florentius vetoed this, countering with an outrageous proposal that a special levy be raised against all property, to defray the cost of *my* campaign! Not only was this proposed tax unjust, it would have caused a revolt.

Now although Florentius controlled the administration and civil service, as resident Caesar, no measure was legal without my seal. So when Florentius sent me the proposed capital levy, I sent it back to him unsigned. I also enclosed a long memorandum reviewing the financial situation of Gaul, proving by exact figures that more than sufficient revenue was now being raised through the conventional forms of taxation. I also reminded him that many provinces had been wrecked before by such measures as he proposed – particularly Illyricum.

Messengers spent the winter dashing back and forth along the icy roads from Paris to Vienne. The capital levy was dropped, but Florentius was still determined to raise taxes. When he sent me a proposal to increase the land tax, I would not sign it. In fact, I tore it up and told the messenger to return the pieces to the praetorian prefect, with my compliments.

Florentius then appealed to Constantius, who wrote me a surprisingly mild letter. Part of it read: 'You must realize, my dear brother, that it hurts us if you undermine confidence in our appointed officers of state at Gaul. Florentius has his faults, although youthful impetuosity is not one of them.' (I was now quite hardened to this sort of insult.) 'He is a capable administrator with great experience, particularly in the field of taxation. We have every confidence in him, nor can we in all honesty disapprove any effort towards increasing the state's revenue at a time when the empire is threatened both on the Danube and in Mesopotamia. We recommend to our brother that he be less zealous in his attempts to gain favour with the Gauls, and more helpful in our prefect's honest attempts to finance your defence of the province.'

A year earlier I would have bowed to Constantius without question. I would also have been furious at the reference to my victory at Strasbourg as a mere 'defence of the province', but I was learning wisdom. I also knew that if I were to succeed in Gaul, I needed the wholehearted support of the people. Already they looked to me as their defender, not only against the savages but against the avarice of Florentius.

I wrote Constantius that though I accepted his judgement in all things, we could not hope to hold the province by increasing the taxes of ruined men. I said that unless the Emperor directly ordered me to sign the tax increase, I would not allow it to take effect.

There was consternation at Paris. We waited several weeks for some answer. The betting, I am told, was rather heavily in favour of my being recalled. But I was not. By not answering, Constantius condoned my action. I then reduced taxes. So grateful and astonished were the provincials that we obtained our full tax revenue *before* the usual time of payment. Today, Gaul is on a sound financial basis. I mean to make similar tax reforms elsewhere.

I am told that Constantius was shattered by the news of my victory at Strasbourg. He was even more distressed when I sent him King Chnodomar in chains, as visible proof of my victory. But men have a way of evading hard fact, especially emperors who are surrounded by toadies who invariably tell them what they want to hear. The court nicknamed me 'Victorinus' to emphasize the tininess – in their eyes – of my victory. Later in the winter, I was astonished to read how Constantius had personally taken Strasbourg and pacified Gaul. Proclamations of *his* great victory were read in every corner of the empire, with no mention of me. I have since been told by those who were at Milan that Constantius eventually came to believe that he had indeed been in Strasbourg that hot August day and with his own hands made captive the German king. On the throne of the world, any delusion can become fact.

The only sad matter that winter was my wife's health. She had had another miscarriage while visiting Rome, and she complained continually of pain in the stomach. Oribasius did his best for her, but although he could lessen the pain, he could not cure her.

My own health – since I seem never to refer to the subject – is invariably good. Partly because I eat and drink sparingly, and partly because our family is of strong stock. But I did come near to death that winter. It happened in February. As I have said, my quarters in the governor's palace overlooked the river, and my rooms were not equipped with the usual heating through the floor. As a result, I was always slightly cold. But I endured this, realizing that I was hardening myself for days in the field. My wife used to beg me to use braziers but I refused, pointing out that if the rooms were overheated, the damp walls would steam, making the air poisonous.

But one evening I could bear the cold no longer. I was reading late – poetry, as I recall. I summoned my secretary and ordered a brazier of hot coals. It was brought. I continued to read. Soothed by the lapping of the river beneath my window, I got drowsier and drowsier. Then I fainted. The fumes from the coal combined with the steam from the walls nearly suffocated me.

Fortunately, one of the guards, seeing steam escape from underneath the door, broke in and dragged me into the corridor where I finally came to. I vomited for hours. Oribasius said a few more minutes in that room and I would have been dead. So my Spartan habits saved my life; though some, of course, would say it was my stinginess! Curiously enough, thinking back on that night, I cannot help but reflect what a pleasant death it might have been. One moment reading Pindar, the next a pleasant drowsiness, and then the end. Every day I pray to Helios that my death when it comes be as swift and as painless as that night's beginning.

My days were full. I gave justice or, as some say, merely executed the law, since there is no true justice that is man-made. I conferred daily on administrative problems with the various officers of the province, and each month I personally paid the salaries of the high officials. This is an ancient custom and I have always meant to investigate its origins. They date, I suspect, from the early Republic. Among those I personally paid were the secret agents. Though I disapproved of them – and knew that their main occupation at Paris was watching me and reporting on my movements to Milan – I usually concealed my dislike. Except on one occasion.

I sat at a table covered with hides. Gold in various piles was set before me. When it came time to pay the chief agent, Gaudentius, he reached forward and took the gold for himself, not waiting for me to give it to him. Even his fellow agents were startled by this rude gesture, to which I responded: 'You see, gentlemen, it is seizing, not accepting, that agents understand.' This was much quoted.

Evenings were spent, first, in business, then in sleep and, finally, the best part, late at night, talking philosophy and literature with friends, who used to wonder how I could so quickly fall asleep and then awake at exactly the hour I wanted. I don't know myself how this is done but I have always been able to do it. If I tell myself I wish to awaken in the first hour of the night, I shall – to the minute. I attribute this lucky gift to Hermes. But Oribasius thinks it has to do with something in my brain and he wants to take a look at it when I am dead!

Sallust was a considerable historian and drilled me extensively in both domestic and foreign history. We particularly studied the era of Diocletian, for it was he who renewed the empire in the last century and his reforms are still with us.

One of our continuing arguments concerns Diocletian's edict which ordered all men to remain for life at whatever happened to be their craft or labour; also, their descendants must continue in the same way: a farmer's son must be a farmer, a cobbler's son must be a cobbler, and the punishment for changing one's estate is severe. Sallust maintained, as did Diocletian, that this law was necessary for social stability. In the old days, people drifted from city to city, living on doles or through crime. As a result, production of all things was inadequate. Diocletian not only stabilized production but he even tried to set prices for food and other essentials. This last failed, which was a pity. A few months ago I myself tried to set the price of grain at Antioch, and though I have for the moment failed, I think in time this sort of manipulation will succeed.

Priscus took the view that Diocletian's law was too rigid. He thought the people should be allowed to change their lot *if* they showed sufficient capacity. But who is to judge their capacity? He was never able to answer this. Oribasius proposed that the court send out commissions to the main cities to examine the young men to determine which ones showed ability. I pointed out that the corruption involved would be formidable; not to mention the impossibility of judging thousands correctly. Personally, I believe that the lower orders do, on occasion, produce men of ability and I believe that that ability, if it is sufficiently great, will be somehow recognized and used. For one thing, there is always the army. A farmer's son who is ambitious can join the army, which is – in the old Greek sense – the most democratic of institutions: anyone can rise through the ranks, no matter how humble his origins. Priscus responded to this by saying that not every one of ability is inclined to warfare. I was forced to agree that there is indeed some hardship for a man whose talents might be for literature or for the law, but as Sallust was quick to point out, the law schools at Beirut and Constantinople are crowded, and the civil service has more 'capable' candidates than it can find jobs for. We have quite enough lawyers.

Priscus thinks that there should be widespread literacy. Sallust thinks not, on the grounds that a knowledge of literature would only make the humble dissatisfied with their condition. I am of two minds. A superficial education would be worse than none: envy and idleness would be encouraged. But a full education would open every man's eyes to the nature of human existence; and we are all of us brothers, as Epictetus reminds us. I have not yet made up my mind as to this problem. It is doubly difficult because of language. To educate anyone properly he must be taught Greek. Yet in a supposedly Hellenic city like Antioch, less than half the population knows Greek; the rest speak one or another of the Semitic languages. The same is true of Alexandria and the cities of Asia. A further complication is the matter of Latin. The language of both law and army is Latin, while that of literature and administration is Greek. As a result, an educated man must be bilingual. If he were the son, say, of a Syrian tailor in Antioch he would have to be trilingual. Just learning languages would take up most of his time. I know. As much as I have studied Latin, I can still hardly read it. And though I speak the military jargon easily, it bears little relation to Cicero whom I read in Greek translation! So we argued among ourselves in the best of spirits through the winter and a most beautiful spring which covered the banks of the Seine with flowers, and reminded us, in life, what Eleusis shows us in mystery.

At the beginning of June the idyll ended. Constantius transferred Sallust to army headquarters at Milan. He cut off my right arm. My response: grief, rage, and, finally, in imitation of the philosophers, I composed a long essay on the gods, and dedicated it to Sallust.

Insert account of that summer's campaign.

Priscus: That year's campaign was a troublesome one. Constantius had neglected to supply Julian with money to pay his troops. Also, supplies were short and what grain Julian could amass, he was forced to render into hard tack, not the sort of ration calculated to please troops already exhausted from much fighting. Julian was so short of funds that on at least one occasion when a soldier asked him for what the men call 'shave money' or 'the barber's due', he was not able to give the man even one small coin.

Julian moved north to Flanders. In a most guileful way, he conquered a Frankish tribe which occupied the city of Tongres. Then he defeated a German tribe called the Chornevi who dwell at the mouth of the Rhine. After that he marched to the Meuse River and restored three of our ruined fortresses. At this point, the food gave out. The local harvest was late, and the troops were on the verge of mutiny. They jeered Julian in public and called him 'Asiatic' and 'Greekling'. But he comported himself with dignity, stripped the countryside of what food there was, and quelled the mutiny.

Next Julian built a pontoon bridge across the Rhine and we crossed over into the country of the German king, Suomarius ... but all that is in the military history. After this short campaign, we recrossed the Rhine and returned to Paris for the winter.

Julian Augustus

Our second winter in Paris was even more agreeable than the first, though I missed Sallust more than I could say – but then I *did* say it, in panegyric prose! I still had no money. I was watched and reported on by the secret agent Gaudentius. My wife continued to be ill. Yet despite all this, I was content. I had grown used to governing, and I no longer thought wistfully of a private life, teaching at Athens. I was well pleased to be Caesar in Gaul.

The principal event of the winter was the first major trial I was to preside over. Numerius, governor of Gallia Narbonensis (one of the Mediterranean provinces), was accused of embezzling state funds. Enemies had prepared a damning case against him. He was brought to Paris for trial. It was a fascinating experience for me and almost as interesting for the Parisians as their beloved theatre, for I allowed the public to attend the trial.

Day after day the hall of justice was crowded. It was soon apparent that there was no proper evidence against Numerius. He was a striking-looking man, tall and stately. He chose to defend himself against Delphidius, the public prosecutor. Now Delphidius is one of the most vigorous speakers and cunning legal minds in the empire but even he could not make evidence out of air, though he certainly tried, using his own breath.

Numerius had made political enemies, as we all do, and they had trumped up charges against him in the hope that I might remove him. Point by point Numerius refuted every charge against him so skilfully that Delphidius finally turned to me and shouted angrily, 'Can anyone, great Caesar, *ever* be found guilty if all he must do is deny the charge?' To which I answered in one of those rare unpremeditated bursts in which – at least so I like to think – the gods speak through me: 'Can anyone ever be found innocent, if all you must do is accuse him?' There was a sudden silence in the hall. Then a great burst of applause, and that was the end of the trial.

I tell this story out of vanity, of course. I am very pleased with what I – or Hermes – said. But to be honest, I am not the best judge in the world. Often when I think I am making some subtle point, I am actually only spreading confusion. Yet I mention this story because it demonstrates, I believe, the true basis of law. Those of the earth's governors who have been tyrants have always presumed that if a man is *thought* guilty then he must be guilty because why otherwise would he find himself in such a situation. Now any tyrant knows that a man may be perfectly blameless but have powerful enemies (very often the tyrant himself is chief among them), which is why I prefer to place the burden of proof on the accuser rather than on the accused.

Helena was somewhat better that winter. She was particularly animated whenever she discussed her visit to Rome. 'Do you think we shall ever be able to live there?' she asked me one day, when – rather unusually – we found ourselves dining alone.

'That is for your brother to decide,' I said. 'Personally, I like Gaul. I could be quite happy living here the rest of my life.'

'In *Paris?*' The way she said it revealed how much she hated our life.

'Yes, but then who knows what will happen next year, next week?'

'You would love the house in Via Nomentana,' she said wistfully. 'I have the most beautiful gardens ...'

'Better than ours? Here?' We were quite proud in Paris of the many flowers and fruit trees that grew with small effort.

'Infinitely!' she sighed. 'I should so much like to go back.'

'I'm sorry.' This was an awkward moment and I silently cursed whoever it was had contrived for us to be alone together for a meal. I don't think it ever happened again.

'My brother respects you.' This was also unusual. We seldom spoke of Constantius. 'He only fears that you will ... listen to wrong advice.' She put the case tactfully.

'He has nothing to fear,' I said. 'Either from me or my advisers. I have no intention of usurping the throne. I want only to do what I was sent here to do: pacify Gaul. And I may say your brother has not made it easy for me.'

'Perhaps *he* listens to bad advisers.' That was the most she would admit.

I nodded grimly. 'And I can name them, starting with Eusebius ...'

She broke in, 'You have one friend at court.' She pushed her plate from her, as though clearing a place for something new to be set down. 'The Empress.'

'I know ...' I began. But Helena stopped with a strange look; for the first time in our marriage she struck an intimate note. 'Eusebia loves you.' Helena said this in such a way that I could not precisely tell what she meant by that overused and always ambivalent verb. 'Her love is constant,' she went on, adding but not defining. 'While she lives, you are safe. Of course, that may not be long.' Her voice shifted; she became more ordinary, more of a woman telling gossip. 'The night we arrived at Rome, there was a reception for Constantius in the palace on the Palatine. The senate of Rome and all the consulars were present. I've never seen anything quite so splendid. My brother meant it when he said, "This is the great moment of my life!" I suppose it always is when a Roman emperor first comes to Rome. Anyway, Constantius wore the crown, and Eusebia sat beside him. She seemed tired but no one suspected she was ill. Then during the Emperor's reply to the senate's welcome, she turned deathly pale. She tried to rise but her robes were too heavy for her. Since everyone was watching Constantius, hardly anyone noticed her. But I did. I was the first to see the blood flow from her mouth. Then she fell backwards onto the floor. She was unconscious when they carried her from the room.'

I was appalled. Not only at this bad news, but at Helena's pleasure in Eusebia's pain. 'Naturally, my brother – all of us – were concerned. But in a few days she was all right. And of course she was most kind to me when it came *my* turn to ... bleed. All through my labour, Eusebia was beside me. She could not have been more kind. She even arranged for our dead child to be buried in Constantia's mausoleum. She was as thoughtful as though I were her own sister ... instead of her enemy.' Helena flung this last word at me, and got to her feet. I was startled by the quality of her rage.

'Your friend, your protectress, killed both our children.' Helena was now at the door. She spoke with complete calm, like a Sophist who has studied exactly what and how he will say a written speech. 'You pride yourself on your philosophy, your love of harmony and balance. Well, how do you measure *this* in your scales? Two children here.' She held up her left hand. 'Eusebia here.' She held up her right hand and made the scales even.

I did not answer her. How could I? Then Helena left the room. We never spoke of this matter again, but I respected her passion, realizing that one can never entirely know another human being even though one has shared the same bed and the same life.

A month later, we received word that Eusebia was dead.

While I wintered at Gaul, Constantius was a thousand miles away at Sirmium, a large city on the border between Dalmatia and Illyricum. Unlike me, he had a troubled winter. First Eusebia died. Then, though he managed to put down the Sarmatians for a second time, the Danube was far from pacified. The tribes were constantly on the move, causing much damage to us. Constantius, however, issued a proclamation declaring that as victor once again over the Sarmatians, he was for a *second* time taking the title of 'Sarmaticus'. He did not say how he wished to be styled but Priscus thought we should refer to him as Constantius Sarmaticus Sarmaticus.

My own relations with Constantius were no worse than usual. Actually, his reverses tended to keep his mind off me. I do know that he always referred contemptuously to my 'success' in Gaul. In fact, Eusebius used to delight in thinking up epithets for me, knowing that they would amuse his master. Among the ones repeated to me – and it is amazing how much princes are told if they choose to listen – were 'chattering mule', 'ape in purple', 'Greekish pedant', and 'nanny goat' because I had let my beard grow again.

Men are curious when it comes to fashion. Since Constantine and his heirs were clean-shaven, everyone must now be clean-shaven, especially high officials. I always answer those who criticize my beard by pointing out that

Hadrian and *his* successors were all bearded, and that I consider their age superior to ours. Actually, my beard is resented because philosophy is resented. Philosophers wear beards; Julian wears a beard; therefore Julian is a philosopher and may well share with that subversive tribe sentiments hostile to the superstitions of the Galileans.

I have elsewhere described that year's campaign. In brief, I rebuilt seven ruined towns on or near the Rhine, restored their defences, filled their granaries and garrisoned them. The towns were: Fort Hercules, Schenkenschanz, Kellern, Nuys, Andernach, Bonn and Bingen. All were regained without great effort.

At Bingen, I had a surprise. The praetorian prefect Florentius, whom I had not seen for more than two years, suddenly appeared at the head of his army to assist me in my task. Since the campaign was nearly over, I could do no more than thank him for the graciousness of his gesture and extort as much grain and gold as I could from him. We had an amusing interview.

Both our camps were pitched outside Bingen. I chose to live in my tent since the town was in considerable turmoil with rebuilding, while the praetorian prefect's army was encamped to the south of me, close to the river. Florentius requested audience the day after our armies had converged. I granted it to him, noting with some pleasure that Florentius now came to me instead of insisting that I attend him.

Florentius arrived at sundown. I received him inside my tent, alone. He saluted me with unusual ceremony. He was noticeably changed. There was no ironic reference to my Spartan quarters. He was plainly nervous. But why?

We sat in folding chairs near the opening of the tent through which came the golden light of a summer evening. Birds sang. The noise of the army about us was constant but soothing. In the distance one could see, just above the green of woods, the grey walls of Bingen. Florentius began the dialogue. 'You know, Caesar, that Persia is now in arms against us.'

I said that I knew only what was common knowledge, that an embassy Constantius had sent to Sapor had failed.

'I'm afraid it's worse than that.' His nervous gaze flitted here and there like a bird searching for a branch to light on. His hands trembled. 'Several months ago Sapor marched on Mesopotamia. He laid siege to Amida.'

I was surprised, not so much that Sapor had attacked us as I was that the news had been kept from me. Ordinarily not a head can fall in the empire that word of it does not circulate thousands of miles in an instant, like the wind – no, swifter, like the sun's rays. No one knows how it is that news travels faster than men and horses, but it does. Yet this news had not. I said as much.

Florentius gestured. 'The Augustus,' he said. 'He has kept the matter as secret as possible. You know how he is.'

It was part of Florentius's task in dealing with me to make subtly derogatory remarks about Constantius, hoping to lure me into expressing treasonable sentiments. But I never fell into this trap, and he knew that I never would; yet we continued to play the familiar game, rather like those old men one sees in the villages who sit hour after hour, year after year, playing draughts with one another, making the same moves and countermoves to the end of their lives.

I was puzzled. 'Why would he want to keep the matter secret?'

'Because, Caesar, it is a disaster.' Florentius withdrew his purse of doeskin and fingered his gold. 'Amida has been destroyed.'

I could not have been more affected if he had said that Antioch or even Constantinople had fallen to the barbarians. Amida was the most important of our border cities, and supposedly impregnable.

'The city was besieged for twenty-three days. I have a full account for you, if you want to study it. There were seven legions inside the city walls. Those troops, plus the inhabitants, meant that one hundred and twenty thousand people were crowded in a single small space. They suffered from plague, hunger, thirst. Sapor himself fought in the first ranks. Fortunately, we fought better, and Sapor lost thirty thousand men.'

'But we lost Amida?'

'Yes, Caesar.'

'What now?'

'The Augustus plans to move to Antioch for the winter. Next spring he will launch a major offensive against Persia. He has sworn to recover Amida.'

'And Sapor?'

'He has withdrawn to Ctesiphon to prepare ... who knows for what?'

We sat in silence as the light fell behind the trees. The warm air was full of the smell of cooking. Men laughed. Metal struck metal. Horses whinnied; a soldier's dog barked. I thought of Amida, destroyed.

'Naturally, the Augustus will want all the troops he can muster.' I said this first, knowing that was why Florentius had come to see me.

'Yes, Caesar.'

'Has he specified *what* he will want from me?'

'No, Caesar. Not yet.'

'I have, all told, twenty-three thousand men, as you know.'

'Yes, Caesar. I know.'

'Most of my men are Gallic volunteers. They joined me on condition that they fight only in Gaul for the protection of their own country.'

'I am aware of that, Caesar. But they are also Roman soldiers. They have taken the oath of allegiance to the Emperor. They must obey him.'

'Even so, I cannot guarantee how they will act if the word I gave them should be broken.'

'Let that be my responsibility, Caesar.' Florentius put away the purse.

'Nothing in Gaul can be done without me, Prefect. *All* responsibility is mine.' I let that hard statement fall between us like a slab of marble dropping into place.

'Such is the will of Caesar,' said Florentius politely, with only the slightest trace of his usual irony. We both rose. At the opening to the tent, he paused. 'Might I see the agent Gaudentius?'

'Haven't you already talked to him?' I was as bland as he. 'But of course you may. Ask my chamberlain. He'll know where to find him. I'm sure you will find Gaudentius in excellent health, and informative, as always.'

Florentius saluted me. Then he disappeared into the twilight. I sat alone for a long time. It was my duty to let Constantius have whatever troops he wanted; yet if I sent the Gauls to Asia I would have broken my word to them. I would also be fatally weakened as a commander. What to do?

In the next few days, every detail of the fall of Amida was known to the army. We also learned that Constantius had dispatched Paul 'the chain' to the Orient to conduct treason trials. It was Constantius's inevitable reaction. Any defeat must be the work of traitors. For a season, Paul wreaked havoc in Asia, and many blameless men were exiled or executed.

The remainder of that summer I spent on the Rhine, treating with the German kings, sometimes severely, sometimes generously. The Germans are innately treacherous, and their word means nothing. They are unfathomable. If we had taken their forest-country away from them, I might understand their constant duplicity: love for one's own land is common to all, even to barbarians. But it was not *their* land and cities we took from them, but our own, held by us for centuries and ravaged by them. Yet whenever a treaty could be broken, they would break it. Whenever any dishonourable thing might be done, it was done.

Why are the Germans like this? I don't know. They are difficult to understand, even those who have been educated by us (ever since Julius Caesar we have taken kings' sons as hostages and civilized them, but to no avail). They are wild by nature. They love fighting as much as Greeks and Romans hate it.

To govern at all, it was necessary for me to obtain a reputation for strictness. I achieved it. I executed kings who broke their word. I crossed the Rhine whenever I chose. I was hard. I was just. Slowly it dawned upon the Germans that I meant to keep them to their side of the Rhine and that any man who chose to rise against me would be struck down. When I left Gaul, the province was at peace.

13

My third and last winter at Paris was crucial. I had heard nothing from Constantius directly or indirectly since the meeting with Florentius. The prefect preferred to stay at Vienne while I remained at Paris. We did not meet, though documents continually passed between us. Aware that there might soon be a crisis in our affairs, I proposed at one point that Florentius join me for the winter at Paris. But he declined. Obviously he wanted to keep what authority he could. In principle I was the master of Britain, Gaul, Spain and Morocco. In fact Florentius administered that part of Gaul which is south of Vienne, as well as Spain and Morocco. I controlled Britain. For the time being, we had tacitly agreed not to interfere in each other's territories.

Helena's health grew worse, and when the cold weather came, she took to her bed. The pains increased. I sent for Oribasius. He was not hopeful. 'I'm afraid the best I can do is keep her out of pain. She has a tumour of the stomach. There is nothing to be done.' And he told me of a new herb he had discovered which causes the flesh to lose sensation.

Oribasius was a comforting companion. So was Priscus, though he kept threatening to go home. His wife Hippia had sent him several angry letters, and he longed for Athens, though he denied it. Priscus always likes to appear more unfeeling than he actually is. Eutherius was a constant source of intelligence. But except for these three friends, I was quite isolated. My chief of staff Lupicinus, who had replaced Sallust, was arrogant and ignorant, while Sintula, the cavalry commander, was hardly company. Nevitta, that splendid officer, I kept at Cologne, to guard the Rhine.

Rather desperately, I wrote letters to old friends, inviting them to Paris. To those who liked to hunt I promised whole packs of deer and a clement season. To philosophers I praised the delights of Parisian intellectual life, though there was

none except for the Galilean bishop and his entourage, from whom I kept my
distance. But no one came. Even Maximus was unable to make the journey,
though he wrote me often, in a code of his own devising.

At about this time, November or December, I had a prophetic dream. In the
third watch of the night I fell asleep, tired from dictating the notes which later
became my commentary on the Battle of Strasbourg. As often happens when I
have something specific on my mind, I dreamed first of the battle. Then the
battle vanished, as things do in dreams, and I found myself in a large room at the
centre of which grew a tall tree; at the time this seemed perfectly natural. But
then the tree fell to the floor, and I noticed that a smaller tree was growing
among its roots, and that the smaller tree had not been uprooted by its parent's
fall. 'The tree is dead,' I heard myself say. 'And now the smaller one will die,
too.' And I was filled with a pity all out of proportion to the event. Suddenly I
was aware of a man beside me. He took my arm. But though I could not make
out his face, he did not seem strange. 'Don't despair.' He pointed. 'See? The
small tree's root is in the ground. As long as it is there, it will grow, even more
securely than before.'

Then the dream ended, and I knew that I had spoken to my patron deity,
Hermes.

When I told Oribasius of this, he interpreted it as meaning that Constantius
would fall while I would flourish, my roots in the All-Seeing One. Needless to
say, we kept this dream a secret. Men were regularly executed for innocent
dreams and mine was hardly innocent. It was prophecy.

In December our quiet court was interrupted by the news that the Picts and
Scots who inhabit the north of Britain were menacing the border. Our governor
begged for reinforcements. I was in a quandary. I had few enough troops as it
was and I knew that my chances of keeping even those were slim for it was
everywhere rumoured that the Caesar at Gaul was to be stripped of his army the
day Constantius took the field against Persia. But Britain was of great economic
importance to us. Since so many Gallic farms had been ravaged by the
Germans, we were forced that year to rely on British grain to feed the people.

I took counsel and it was decided that Lupicinus must go immediately to
Britain. He was a good commander, though we used often to wonder whether he
was more covetous than cruel, or more cruel than covetous.

On the day that Lupicinus arrived in Britain, the tribune Decentius, an
imperial state secretary, arrived at Paris with a considerable retinue of lawyers
and fiscal agents. Before coming to me, he had spent several days in Vienne with
Florentius. I did not take this well, since it is usual to pay homage first to the
Caesar.

Decentius was an exhausted man when he arrived. So I allowed him to sit
while he read me the Emperor's letter. The tone was friendly, but it was absolute
in its demands. I was to send Constantius the Aeruli, the Batavians, the Celts
and the Petulantes – the best of my legions – as well as three hundred men from
each of the remaining legions. They were to start for Antioch without delay, in
time for a spring offensive against Persia.

When Decentius finished, I said as calmly as I could, 'He wants slightly more
than half my army.'

'Yes, Caesar. It will be a difficult war in Persia. Perhaps a decisive one.'

'Has the Emperor considered the effect this will have upon the Germans? My
army is small enough to begin with. If I am allowed less than twelve thousand

soldiers – and those the worst – the German tribes are sure to rise again.'

'But the Augustus was led to understand by your own reports that Gaul has been pacified for a generation, because of your great victories.' I wondered whether Decentius had thought of this on the spur of the moment or whether Constantius had instructed him ever so gently to prick me.

'No province is ever entirely pacified. As long as there is a German alive, we are in danger.'

'But no *immediate* danger, Caesar. You would agree to that?'

'No, Tribune, I would not. Also, at this moment, there is serious trouble in Britain.'

'There are always troubles, Caesar. Nevertheless, in the prosecution of the war against Persia, the Augustus feels he must have the best of all *his* armies with him. He feels ...'

'Is he aware of the vow I made the Gallic soldiers: that they were not to fight outside the province?'

'Your vow to them is superseded by the oath they took to the Augustus.' This was stated with a sharp legality.

'True, but I must warn you, Tribune, there is a chance of mutiny.'

He looked at me intently. I knew what he was thinking. Will this supposedly unambitious Caesar now see his chance to stage a mutiny and usurp the West? Courtiers never take things at face value. When I said the troops *might* mutiny, he took this as a threat that I would, if provoked, incite them to revolt.

'I am,' I said carefully, 'loyal to Constantius. I shall do as I am told. I merely warn you that there may be trouble. Meanwhile, we must wait at least a month before the troops can be sent to the East.'

'Augustus has said immediately ...' Decentius began.

I interrupted. 'Tribune, as we sit here, the legions he asked for are now at sea, bound for Britain.' And I told him about Lupicinus. But then to demonstrate my good faith, I allowed him to listen as I dictated a letter to Lupicinus ordering him back from Britain. This done I sent Decentius to Sintula and gave orders that the Tribune was to be obeyed in every way. By the end of the week, some of my best soldiers had departed for Antioch. The subtle Decentius must have promised them various bounties, for they left in better humour than I thought possible.

Now there are those who believe that at this point I planned to disobey Constantius and set myself up as the Augustus of the West. This is not true. I will not deny that I did not *think* of it as a possibility – it would have been impossible not to. After all, through my efforts, the Rhine was secure and I governed a third of the world. Even so, I was not eager to break with Constantius. He was stronger than I. It was as simple as that. Also, I had no desire to challenge my cousin in that one field where he was pre-eminent: keeping his throne.

But I was considerably shaken when Decentius insisted that I order all the remaining troops in Gaul to come to Paris so that he might choose the best for the Persian campaign. We argued several days about this. Not until I threatened to abdicate did Decentius agree to maintain the Rhine garrisons at full strength. I then ordered the army of Gaul to converge on Paris. All obeyed me, except Lupicinus, who wrote to say that he could not possibly return to Paris before April. Decentius complained bitterly, but there was nothing to be done.

By the second week in February when the legions were encamped on both sides of the river, Decentius dropped his courtly mask. He no longer wheedled; he ordered. Eutherius was with me when the Tribune finally pounded the table and shouted, 'If you won't speak to the legions, I will, in Constantius's name!' I told him mildly that there was no need for him either to shout at me or to do my work. I then dismissed him. Eutherius and I were left alone in the council chamber. We looked at one another; he concerned, I wretched.

'Well, old friend,' I said at last, 'what do I do?'

'As you are told. Unless ...' He paused.

I shook my head. 'No, I won't go into rebellion.'

'Then tell the men that you have been ordered to send them east. The rest,' he said this slowly, with emphasis, 'is up to them.'

The next day was 12 February. I was up at daybreak. I gave orders to my household that a dinner be prepared for all officers that evening. It was to be a sumptuous affair. I ordered the best wine from the palace cellars. All sorts of fowl and livestock were to be prepared. Though I pride myself on the austerity of my table, this time I chose to be lavish.

I then set out to make the rounds of the army, accompanied only by my standard-bearer. Our breaths were frosty as we clattered across the wooden bridge to the left bank. Slowly I made my way through the camp. I spoke to the men, singly, in groups. It was good-humoured talk, and I soon had an idea of their mood. They were well-disposed towards me, and suspicious of Constantius. There are no secrets in an army.

When I came to the encampment of the Petulantes, my own favourite among the legions, I paused to talk to a large group. We chatted lightly but guardedly. Finally, one of them stepped forward, with a letter in his hand. He saluted me. 'Caesar, none of us can read.' There was some laughter at this broad deception. Well over half the Petulantes are reasonably literate. 'When we got here, we found this on the door to the church.' He pointed to a nearby charnel house, a temple of Vesta converted by Galileans. 'Read it to us, Caesar.'

'If I can,' I said amiably. 'It's Latin, and I'm only an Asiatic, a Greekling ...' Mention of two of the pleasanter nicknames they have for me made them laugh. The letter was in soldier-Latin. I started to read. 'Men of the Petulantes, we are about to be sent to the ends of the earth like criminals ...' I stopped, blinded for a moment by the pale sun to which I had turned almost instinctively, as though for guidance. The men shouted grimly, 'Go on, Caesar!' They already knew the contents of the anonymous letter. I shook my head and said firmly, 'This is treason against the Emperor.'

I threw the letter to the ground and wheeled my horse about. 'But not against *you!*' shouted the man who had given me the letter. I spurred my horse and with the standard-bearer lagging behind, I galloped back to the island. To this day I do not know who wrote the letter; naturally, I have been accused of having written it myself.

Shortly after noon the officers arrived at the palace. I received them in the great banqueting hall which had been made to look quite festive on such short notice. Evergreen boughs festooned walls and rafters while coal-burning braziers cut the chill. It was the most costly banquet of my career thus far. Helena was too ill to join us, so I did the honours alone. Decentius sat on my right, watching me carefully. But I neither said nor did anything remarkable.

When the officers had begun to grow boisterous with wine, Decentius said, 'Now is the time to tell them that they must leave within the week.'

I made one last attempt, 'Tribune, in April the legions from Britain will be here. If we wait until then ...'

'Caesar,' Decentius shifted from presumptuousness to guileful reasonableness, 'if you wait until then, people will say that the British legions forced you to obey the Augustus, but if you carry out your orders *now*, they will say it was of your own choice, and that you are indeed master of Gaul, not to mention loyal to the Augustus.'

There was no doubting the truth of this. I felt the trap spring. I surrendered. I agreed to make the announcement at the end of the dinner. Did I have any secret design? I think not. Yet at important moments in one's life there is a tendency to do instinctively the necessary thing to survive.

During the banquet, I was saluted repeatedly by minor officers, in violation of etiquette. At one point, Eutherius murmured in my ear, 'You have broken every rule governing Caesar's table.' I smiled wanly. This was an old joke between us. 'Caesar's table' was a euphemism for the restrictions put on me by Constantius.

At the end of the dinner, I said a few words to the officers, who were now in a mood for anything from riot to battle. I told them that I had never known better troops. I told them that for the first time in my life I envied Constantius, for he was about to receive the world's best soldiers into his own army. There was muttering at this, but no more. I was careful not to play too much on their emotions. I chose not to provoke them.

Priscus: Yet.

Julian Augustus

After many tearful embraces, the banquet ended. I accompanied the officers as far as the square in front of the palace. Just to the right of the main door, there is a high stone tribunal from which proclamations are read. I stood at the foot of it, while the officers milled somewhat unsteadily about me. As I said good-bye to this one and that one, I noticed that a large crowd had gathered in the arcades which border the square on two sides. When the people recognized me, they rushed forward. Quickly my guards drew swords and made a ring about me. But the crowd was not hostile. They were mostly women with children. They implored me not to send their husbands away. One woman waved a baby in front of me like a screaming flag. 'Don't send his father away! He's all we have!'

Others shouted, 'You promised us, Caesar! You promised!'

Unable to bear their cries, I turned away. At the door to the palace, Decentius was deep in conversation with the secret agent Gaudentius. They broke off guiltily when they saw me approaching. 'An old friend,' said Decentius.

'I am certain of that,' I said sharply. I motioned to the crowd. 'Do you hear them?'

Decentius looked at me blankly for a moment. Then he looked towards the square. 'Oh, yes. Yes. That's quite usual in the provinces. The women always complain when the men are ordered away. When you have been in the army as long as I have, you won't even notice them.'

'I am afraid I find it hard *not* to notice. You see, I did promise them ...'

But Decentius had heard quite enough of my famous promise. 'My dear Caesar,' he said, and his tone was that of a father, 'these women will each have found a new man by the time the warm weather comes round. They are animals. Nothing more.'

I left him in the square and went straight to my study on the second floor. I sent for Priscus, Oribasius and Eutherius. While waiting for them to arrive, I tried to read but I could not concentrate. I counted the tiles in the floor, I paced up and down. Finally, I opened the window on the Seine and looked out. The cold air was refreshing. My face burned as though I had the fever. My hands trembled. I took deep breaths, and started to count the blocks of broken ice as they floated downstream. I prayed to Helios.

Eutherius was the first to come. I shut the window. I motioned for him to sit in my chair. Because of his size no other chair would hold him and he tended to break stools.

'It is a plot,' he said. 'Constantius has an army of nearly a hundred thousand men in Syria. Your Gauls will hardly make much difference.'

'But they will to me, if I lose them.'

'They will to you. And that is the plot. He wants you destroyed.'

I was surprised at Eutherius. Of all my friends and advisers he was the one who invariably preached caution. He loved good form, justice, the orderly processes of the state at peace. He was not made for treason. But he had changed.

'You believe this?'

Eutherius nodded, the small black eyes glittered like the eyes of an Egyptian statue.

'Then what shall I do?'

At this point Oribasius and Priscus entered. They heard my question. Oribasius answered for Eutherius. 'Rebel,' he said promptly. That was, I swear by Helios, Mithras and my own Hermes, the first treasonable word that had ever passed openly among us. There was dead silence. Priscus sat on the edge of my heavy wood table. Oribasius stood at the room's centre, staring intently at me. I turned to Priscus.

'What do you think?'

'You must consider everything. Can you remain in Gaul without those troops? If you can, what is Constantius apt to do? Will he remove you? Or will he be too occupied in Persia to do anything at all? I suspect,' and Priscus answered his own question, 'that you have heard the last from Constantius for some time. He must retake Amida and defeat Sapor. That may be his life's work. Meanwhile, you are master of the West and, should he die, emperor.'

Eutherius nodded. 'That is the *sensible* point of view, of course.' He smiled. 'Because it has been my own point of view all along. Yet I think the situation is a good deal more serious than that. You forget Florentius. My agents tell me that he is to be given full authority in Gaul as soon as Caesar loses his army. When that happens, there is nothing we can do but submit. Frankly, I think it better to resist now than to wait and be destroyed by Florentius.'

While they talked among themselves, I retreated again to the window and watched the sun, a bitter winter orange, fall in the west. Night fires blossomed on the river banks. What to do? There was a sudden pounding at the door. Angrily, I opened it, declaring, 'No one is to disturb us ...'

But there stood Decentius, pale and distressed. 'A thousand apologies, Caesar,' he saluted hurriedly. 'I should not have disturbed you, but they are here!'

'*Who* is *where?*'

'Can't you hear them?' Decentius was chattering with fright. We all fell silent and listened to the far-off sound of men shouting and women wailing.

'Mutiny!' said Oribasius. He ran to the window and looked out. Though one ordinarily sees only the river and the tip of the island from my window, by craning one's head it is just possible to see the wooden bridge to the north. 'It's the Celtic Legion. They're crossing to the island!'

As I joined him at the window, there was a shout from just below us. 'Caesar!' I looked down and saw a squad of infantry with swords draw. They waved to me cheerfully but their voices were threatening. 'Don't let us go, Caesar. Keep us here!'

One of the men, a tall fierce Celt with a blond moustache and a blind white eye, thrust his sword towards me and in a voice hoarse from many battles roared: 'Hail, Augustus! Hail, Julian Augustus!' The others took up the cry. I stepped back from the window. Decentius turned to me. 'This is treason! Arrest those men!'

But I pushed him to one side and hurried to one of the rooms which look out on the square. I peered through a crack in the shutter. The square was filled with troops and they were by no means all drunk, as I had first suspected. This was indeed rebellion.

In front of the palace, my personal guard stood with drawn swords and levelled spears, but the mob seemed in no mood to do violence. Instead, they shouted my name, demanded my presence, declared their loyalty. Then, as if by signal – who knows how these things suddenly start? I suspect Hermes – they began to chant, first one group, then another, then the entire crowd: 'Augustus! Augustus! Julian Augustus!'

I turned from the window.

'Attack them!' said Decentius. 'Show them the Emperor's image. They won't dare defy that.'

'We have four hundred troops in the palace,' I said. 'There are some twenty thousand men out there. Even an inexperienced soldier like myself avoids such odds. As for the imperial image, I'm afraid they will hack it to bits.'

'Treason!' was all Decentius could say.

'Treason,' I replied reasonably, as though identifying a particular star for one who wishes to know the nature of the heavens. Decentius rushed from the room.

We looked at one another, the word 'Augustus' falling regularly on our ears like surf upon the beach.

'You will have to accept,' said Eutherius.

'You who always preach caution tell me this?'

Eutherius nodded. Oribasius was even more emphatic. 'Go on. You have nothing to lose now.'

Priscus was cautious. 'My interest, Caesar, is philosophy, not politics. If I were you, I would wait.'

'For what?' Oribasius turned on him indignantly.

'To see what happens,' said Priscus ambiguously. 'To wait for a sign.'

I accepted this in the spirit Priscus meant it. He understood me. He knew that unless I believed I had heaven's revealed blessing, I could not act with full force.

'Very well,' I motioned to the door. 'Oribasius, see to the guard. Make sure no one is admitted to the palace. Eutherius, keep an eye on our friend the Tribune. Don't let him out of your sight. Priscus, pray for me.' On that we parted.

In the main corridor, one of my wife's ladies was waiting for me. She was close to hysteria. 'Caesar, they're going to kill us, all of us!' I took her by the shoulders and shook her till her teeth chattered; in fact, she bit her lower lip, which had a most calming effect. She then told me that my wife was asking for me.

Helena's bedroom was dimly lit and unbearably warm. Her illness made her crave heat. A heavy odour of incense and musk filled the room, yet it could not disguise the sweet-sharp odour of the dissolution of the flesh. I hated visiting Helena, and thought myself contemptible for this aversion.

Helena lay in bed, a prayer book on the coverlet. Beside her stood the bishop of Paris, a solemn charlatan who was her closest friend and adviser. He saluted me. 'I dare say that the Caesar will want to speak to the Queen alone . . .'

'You have dared say it, Bishop. And it is true.' The bishop withdrew in a swirl of splendid robes, chanting loudly, as though we were a congregation.

I sat beside the bed. Helena was pale and she had lost much weight. Her eyes had grown large, as eyes appear to do when the face thins. She was a sickly yellow in the lamplight, and yet in a way she looked more appealing in her illness than ever she did in health. She no longer resembled the vigorous, hard-jawed Constantine. She was a woman now, delicate and melancholy, and I felt a sudden surge of feeling as I took her hand, hot with fever and delicate as a dead bird's wing.

'I am sorry I was too ill for the reception . . .' she began.

I cut her off. 'It was of no importance. How is the pain?'

Her free hand touched her stomach reflexively. 'Better,' she said, and lied. 'Oribasius finds me a new herb every day. And I take whatever he finds. I tell him he must make me his collaborator when he writes his encyclopedia.' I tried not to look at her stomach, which curved large beneath the coverlet as though she were in the last month of pregnancy. For a moment neither of us spoke; then the silence was broken by the rhythmic chanting: 'Augustus!' She turned towards me.

'They have been shouting that for hours.'

I nodded. 'They are angry because the Emperor wants them to fight in Persia.'

'They call you Augustus.' She looked at me very hard.

'They don't mean it.'

'They do,' she said flatly. 'They want you for Emperor.'

'I've refused to show myself to them. Anyway, now it's dark, they'll soon get cold and bored and go away, and tomorrow they will do as they're told. Sintula has already gone, you know. He left yesterday with two legions.' I talked fast, but she would not be put off.

'Will you take what they have offered?'

I paused, uncertain what to say. Finally, neutrally, 'It would be treason.'

'Traitors who prevail are patriots. Usurpers who succeed are divine emperors.'

I still could not tell what she wanted me to do. 'Emperors are not made,' I said at last, 'by a few thousand troops in a small provincial city.'

'Why not? After all, it is God's will that raises us up, as it is God's will that . . . throws us down.' She looked away and again her hand strayed to the seat of her mortality. 'Those few soliders are enough, *if* it is meant to be.'

'What do you want me to do?' For the first and only time I asked her a direct question, as one person to another; and I did wish to know her answer.

'Tonight? I don't know. This may not be the moment. You must judge that. But I do know that you are meant to be Emperor of Rome.'

Our eyes met and we studied one another as though the face of each was new and unexplored. I responded with equal candour. 'I know it, too,' I said. 'I have had dreams. There have been signs.'

'Then *take* it!' She said this with unexpected force.

'Now? An act of treason? Against your brother?'

'My brother and his wife killed our two children. My loyalty has ... shifted to my cousin, who is my husband.' She smiled on the word 'shifted' but her great eyes were solemn.

'Curious,' I said finally. 'I always thought you preferred him to me.'

'I did. I did. Until that last visit to Rome. You know, he tried to keep me there after the baby died. He said that there might be difficulties for you in Gaul.'

'But you came back.'

'I came back.'

'Leaving your beloved villa?'

'Leaving that was hardest of all!' She smiled.

Then she indicated the window and the city beyond. 'Now the difficulties he promised have begun. You must decide very soon.'

'Yes.' I rose.

'Decentius was here,' she said suddenly.

I was startled. 'When?'

'Just before the reception for your officers. He wanted to know if I would like to return to Rome. He said the Gallic legions would escort me as far as Milan.'

'He is sly.'

'Yes. I told him I chose to stay. He was disappointed.' She laughed softly. 'Of course even if I wanted to go, I cannot travel ... again.'

'Don't say that. One day we shall go to Rome together.'

'I want that more than anything,' she said. 'But be quick about it ...'

'I will be quick,' I said. 'I swear it.'

I kissed her brow, holding my breath so as not to catch the scent of death. She clutched at me suddenly with all her strength, as though she were suffering a sharp spasm of pain. Then she let me go. 'What a pity I was so much older than you.'

I did not answer. I grasped her hands in silence. Then I left.

The Bishop was in the anteroom with the ladies. 'The Queen is improved, don't you think, Caesar?'

'Yes, I do.' I was curt. I tried to get past him. But the Bishop had more to say.

'She is of course concerned by that mob outside. We all are. Most frightening. A terrible lapse of discipline. One hopes that the Caesar will dismiss this rabble with stern words.'

'The Caesar will do what the Caesar must.' I pushed past him into the main gallery. Servants rushed here and there, as though on urgent business. The ushers kept to their posts, but even they had lost their usual aplomb. All eyes were on me, wondering what I would do. As I crossed to the room which overlooks the square, I nearly stumbled over Gaudentius, lurking in the shadows. I was pleased to see that he was frightened.

'Caesar! The Tribune Decentius asks for audience. He is in the council chamber. They are all there. They want to know what you intend to do. We are completely surrounded. No one can escape ...'

'Tell the Tribune I am going to bed. I shall be happy to see him in the morning.' Before the agent could recover himself, I was halfway down the gallery to my own room. Outside my door stood the chief usher. I told him I was not to be disturbed unless there was an attack on the palace. I then went to my room and bolted the door after me.

It was a long night. I read. I prayed. I thought. I have never before nor since been so undecided. Everything seemed to me to be premature; events were pushing me faster than I chose to go. Yet would a moment like this come again? How often is an emperor spontaneously made? We all know of ambitious generals who have staged 'popular' coronations for themselves; yet these seldom occur without the general's active collusion. I am sure that Julius Caesar very carefully instructed his friend to offer him the crown in public, simply to see what the reaction might be. Now that same crown had come to me, without my asking.

Still undecided, I slept. I dreamed and, as often happens, I found in dreaming what I must do awake. I was seated in my consular chair, quite alone, when a figure appeared to me, dressed as the guardian spirit of the state, so often depicted in the old Republic. He spoke to me. 'I have watched you for a long time, Julian. And for a long time I have wished to raise you even higher than you are now. But each time I have tried, I have been rebuffed. Now I must warn you. If you turn me away again, when so many men's voices are raised in agreement with me, I shall leave you as you are. But remember this: *if I go now, I shall never return.*'

I awakened in a cold sweat and leapt from my bed; my own room was suddenly strange and menacing, as sometimes happens when we have dreamed deeply. Was I awake or not? I opened the window; icy air restored me. The stars were fading. The east was pale.

The mob was still gathered in the square. They had built bonfires. From time to time they chanted 'Augustus!' I made up my mind. I summoned my body-servant. He dressed me in the purple. Then I went out into the gallery.

Apparently I was the only one who had slept that night. Men and women still scurried through rooms and corridors, like mice seeking holes. In the council chamber I found Decentius and most of my advisers. As I entered, Eutherius was saying in his most calming voice, 'Everything rests now with the will of Caesar. There is nothing we can do to affect that ...'

'Precisely,' I said. The room came to attention. Decentius, haggard, needing a shave, crossed to me and declared: 'Only you can stop them! You must tell them to obey the Emperor. They will listen to you.'

'I intend to speak to them now.' I smiled at Eutherius. 'You may all attend me on the tribunal ... if you like.'

Decentius seemed not to want this honour. But my friends did. Together we went to the main door of the palace.

'Be prepared,' I said, 'for anything. And don't be startled by anything I say.' Then I motioned to the frightened guards to slip the bolt and open the gate.

With a deep breath, I stepped out into the square. When the mob saw me, they began to cheer. Quickly I climbed the steps to the tribunal, my companions close behind me. Then my personal guard, swords drawn, surrounded the tribunal. The mob drew back. I waved for silence; it was a long time coming. When at last I spoke, I was temperate.

'You are angry. You have reason to be. And I take your side in this matter. What you want, I promise to get for you. But without revolution. You prefer service in your native land to the dangers of a foreign country and a distant war. So be it. Go each of you to his home and take with you my promise that none of you shall serve beyond the Alps. I assume full responsibility for this decision. I shall explain it to the Augustus, and I know that he will listen to me, for he is reasonable and just.'

With this speech, I dispatched my duty to Constantius. Honour was satisfied. Now what would happen? There was an instant of silence, and then shouts of

'Augustus!' began again; also, insults to Constantius – and a few to me for weakness. The mob pushed closer and closer to the platform. I remained absolutely still, looking across the square to the place where day was coming, grey and cold above the houses of the town.

Eutherius whispered in my ear. 'You must accept. They'll kill you if you don't.' I made no answer. I waited. I knew what was to come. I saw what was about to happen as clearly as I had seen the spirit of Rome in my dream. In fact, that whole morning was like a continuation of the night's dream.

First, my guards broke and scattered as the mob pushed against the tribunal. One soldier climbed on to the back of another and seized me by the arm. I made no effort to resist. Then – again as in a dream but that pleasant sort of dream where one knows one is dreaming and has no fear – I fell into the mob. Hands, arms, shoulders broke my fall. All around me the deafening cry 'Augustus!' sounded; strong in my nostrils was the smell of sweat and garlic, as hard bodies forced me up from the ground where I lay, lifted me up high above them all like a sacrifice to the sun.

In full view of the mob, the fiercest of the men seized me. 'Accept!' he shouted, sword's point held to my heart. I looked him in the face, saw red broken veins on the nose, smelled wine on his breath; that one glance was like a lifetime's acquaintance. Then in a matter-of-fact voice I said, 'I accept.'

The roar was tremendous. An infantryman's shield was placed under me and I was borne around the square like a Gallic or a German king. Thus was I made Augustus not by Romans nor according to Roman custom, but by barbarians, and according to their ritual.

I was returned to the tribunal. Then someone shouted that I must wear the diadem. Now I did not possess a crown of any sort. It would have been worth my life to have owned one. I told the mob this.

'Get one from your wife!' shouted a cavalryman. The mob laughed good-naturedly. Worried that my life's great moment might turn unexpectedly into low foolery, I answered quickly, 'You don't want an emperor who wears a woman's jewels.'

This went down well enough. Then a tall fellow named Marius, standard-bearer to the Petulantes, clambered on to the platform. He took from his neck the ring of metal which supports the chain that holds the regimental eagle in its place. He jerked the circlet free of the chain; then, holding the ring of metal high over my head, he shouted: 'Hail, Julian Augustus!' As the mob repeated the phrase, Marius placed the battered circlet on my head.

The thing was gone. I motioned for silence, and got it. 'You have this day made a solemn choice. I promise you that as long as I live you shall not regret it.' Then recalling the usual form in these matters, I said, 'To each man here today I give five gold pieces and a pound of silver. May heaven bless this day, and what we have together done.'

Then I descended the steps of the tribunal two at a time and darted into the palace.

14

Julian Augustus

I went straight to my wife's room. She had already been told what had happened. She was sitting up in bed, attended by several women. Her hair had been combed and her sallow face was cruelly mocked by rouge. The women withdrew.

'It is done,' I said.

'Good.' She held my hands and for a moment I felt strength in her fingers. 'Now there will be war.'

I nodded. 'But not immediately. I shall tell Constantius that this was none of my doing, and it was not. If he is wise, he will accept me as Augustus in the West.'

'He won't.' She let go my hands.

'I hope he does.'

She was staring at me with eyes half shut (her vision had never been good and to see things clearly she was forced to squint). At last she murmured, 'Julian Augustus.'

I smiled. 'By grace of a mob in the main square of a provincial town.'

'By the grace of God,' she corrected me.

'I think so. I believe so.'

She was suddenly practical. 'While you were in the square, one of my officers came to tell me there is a plot to murder you. Here. In the palace.'

I did not take this too seriously. 'I am well guarded.'

She shook her head. 'I trust this man. He is my best officer.' Like all ladies of the imperial house, Helena not only had her own servants and attendants but her own bodyguard.

'I shall look into it.' I rose to go.

'Decentius is behind the plot.'

'Naturally.'

As I crossed to the door, she said in a loud voice, 'Hail, Augustus!' I turned and laughed, and said, 'Hail, Augusta!' Helena smiled. I had never seen her as happy as she was at that moment.

Next I went to the council chamber, where all of my court was assembled, including Decentius.

I came straight to the point. 'You are all witnesses that I did not in any way arouse the soldiers. Nor did I ask for this honour they have done me – illegally.' There was a murmur of disappointment in the chamber. Decentius began to look hopeful. I gave him a friendly smile; I continued. 'I shall report all of this to the Augustus, describing exactly what happened, and I shall pledge him, as always, my loyalty not only as a colleague but as a kinsman.' Everyone was now quite puzzled. Decentius stepped forward.

'If that is ... Caesar's decision.' He was very bold to call me 'Caesar', but I respected his loyalty to his master. 'Then Caesar must discipline his own troops. He must do as the Augustus wants, and send them to the East.'

'My dear Tribune ...' I sounded even to myself like the most honey-tongued of lawyers. 'I am willing to give my life for the Emperor in any battle against barbarians. But I will not give it in this way. I have no intention of being murdered by an army I have devoted five years to training, an army which loves me perhaps too much and their Emperor too little. No, I shall not take back what they have given me.' I suddenly recalled that I still wore the metal circlet. I took it off and held it up. 'A piece of military equipment, no more.' I let the circlet drop on the table in front of me. 'Nor do I have any intention of sending them East. For one thing, Tribune, they will not go. No matter what I or anyone says.'

'Then, Caesar, do you mean to go against the Augustus?' Decentius was stony.

I shook my head. 'I shall try to obey him. But that may not be possible. We shall write Constantius today. But even better than our writing will be your own description of what happened here in Paris. I am sure that once you have explained to him our true situation, he will be sympathetic.' There was a murmur of laughter.

'Very well, Caesar. Have I your permission to go?'

'You have it,' I said.

Decentius saluted and left the chamber.

Then tired as I was, I called a meeting of the consistory. We spent the morning dictating a long letter to Constantius. In brief, I said that I had not incited the troops, that they had threatened me with death if I did not take the title Augustus, that I had accepted for fear they might select someone else, another Magnentius or Silvanus. I then requested that the legions be kept in Gaul. I promised, however, to send Constantius all the Spanish horses he needed (there had been some correspondence already on this subject), as well as a number of targeteers from the tribe of Laeti on the Rhine: good soldiers, eager for war. I requested that a new praetorian prefect be appointed; the other officers of state would be selected by me, as is usual. I ended with the hope that only harmony prevail between us, and so on.

There was a good deal of discussion as to how I should style myself. My own view prevailed. I signed the letter 'Caesar', not 'Augustus'.

Eutherius offered to take the letter himself to Constantinople. Since he was my best advocate, I let him go.

The next few days were turmoil. Decentius left for Vienne. Eutherius departed for Constantinople. I sent Gaudentius packing. During this period, I did not show myself in public, nor wear the diadem, nor style myself Augustus. This was a time for caution.

Though I had sent several messages to Florentius, I had heard nothing from Vienne except conflicting rumours: Florentius planned to take the field against me in the spring. Florentius had been recalled. Florentius was withdrawing to Spain, to Britain, to Morocco. In the absence of any word from the praetorian prefect himself, I replaced every governor in Gaul with men of my own choosing, and thus assured the loyalty of the cities.

Priscus: Julian skips that spring and summer. I suppose because much of it is covered in his military history.

That spring, while we were at Paris, Constantius moved to Caesarea. There he assembled an army for the campaign against Persia. He was very good at assembling armies. His problem was that he never quite knew what to do with

an army once he'd got it all together. He was joined at Caesarea first by
Decentius, then by Florentius who had fled to Gaul, leaving his family to shift for
themselves. To everyone's surprise, Julian later allowed the family to join
Florentius, transporting them at state expense. Julian was determined to be
merciful. He saw himself in the line of Marcus Aurelius. Actually, he was greater
than that self-consciously good man. For one thing, he had a harder task than his
predecessor. Julian came at the end of a world, not at its zenith. That is
important, isn't it, Libanius, my fellow relic? We are given our place in time as
we are given our eyes: weak, strong, clear, squinting, the thing is not ours to
choose. Well, this has been a squinting, wall-eyed time to be born in.
Fortunately, when most eyes see distortion as a matter of course, nothing bizarre
is thought out of the way, and only a clear vision is abnormal.

Poor Eutherius had a most difficult embassy. Everything went wrong for him
on the road. Because of his rank as chamberlain to the Caesar he was necessarily
accompanied at many stages by other important officials. You know how it is
when one travels at state expense. It is marvellous of course because it costs
nothing, one gets the best horses, there is always a place to spend the night, and
brigands seldom assault guests of the state. *But* one must contend with the highly
placed bores (who are contending with us!). There is always the general who
recalls old battles. The bishop who sputters at the thought of his colleagues'
'heresies'. The governor who was honest and can prove it as he returns home
with a retinue of several hundred heavily burdened pack-horses.

Eutherius was taken over by officials. By now the world knew what had
happened, and Julian's chamberlain was wined and dined so much en route
that he lost many days' travel. Finally, braving storms at sea and the snows of
Illyricum, he crossed to Constantinople only to learn that the Augustus was at
Caesarea. So the embassy wearily pressed on. The chamberlain was received in
late March.

Julian told me that Eutherius told him that he had never seen Constantius in
such a rage. He fully expected to be slaughtered on the spot. But – luckily for
Julian – Constantius was trapped. Though his every instinct (and his political
cunning was always astute) told him that he must strike at Julian as soon as
possible, he could not because Sapor was in Mesopotamia. Constantius was
forced to stay in Asia. So he dismissed Eutherius non-committally; he also gave a
letter to the tribune Leonas to be delivered to Julian personally.

As luck would have it, the day Leonas arrived in Paris, Julian was to take part
in some sort of festival which was to be heavily attended not only by the troops
but by the Parisians. Now Julian dearly loved showing off in front of a crowd, an
unexpected trait in a philosopher. Knowing pretty much what was in the letter,
Julian presented Leonas to the mob, telling them why he was in Paris. Then, in
front of thousands, Julian read the letter aloud from beginning to end. When he
came to the part where he was ordered to remain in his rank of Caesar, the
crowd roared back as though rehearsed. 'Augustus! Julian Augustus!'

The next day Julian gave Leonas a letter for Constantius; I gather it was
conciliatory; among other things, he accepted Constantius's appointment of the
quaestor Nebridius as praetorian prefect, and he signed himself 'Caesar'. One
ought to have all his letters at hand. I suppose they can be found in the archives
at Constantinople, although I am not sure what the current policy is as to his
papers. Some years ago when a student of mine – a Christian – wanted to
examine certain of Julian's state papers, he was not allowed to see them. In fact,
the chamberlain's office was most suspicious, which *is* suspicious. But that was in

Valens's time. Maybe things have changed. You will doubtless find out when you edit these papers.

In June Julian took the field against those Franks who live near Kellen; they were the last of the tribes to molest Gaul. Despite the bad roads and thick forests that protected their home across the Rhine, he defeated them easily. But I was not with him. Just before he took to the field, I departed for Athens.

The day I was to leave, I went to say good-bye to Julian in his study, a room always referred to by his friends as the Frigidarium. I have never known a room to be so cold. But Julian seemed not to mind it. And of course after he nearly suffocated that first winter, he never heated the room properly again. In warm weather, however, it was pleasantly cool, and the last I saw of him at Paris was on a fine June day. I found Oribasius also waiting outside the study door.

'He has a bishop with him,' said Oribasius.

'No doubt converting him.'

'No doubt.'

Then the door opened and a scowling, red-faced man sailed past us.

Julian came to the door and pulled us inside. His eyes gleamed. He had obviously been enjoying himself. 'You should have heard him!'

'What sort of bishop is he?' I asked. 'Arian or Athanasian or . . .'

'Political. That was Epictetus, bishop of Civitavecchia. His interests, I suspect, are secular rather than religious. Constantius sent him to me, with a most extraordinary message.' Julian threw himself on the military cot by the window. (Though he nowhere in his memoir mentions it, he often dictated while lying down; after reading some of his late-night essays, I used to accuse him of talking in his sleep. To which he would answer, 'In sleep the gods speak to us, so what I say in my sleep must be divine.')

'My colleague, the Augustus, proposes that if I step down as Caesar, abandon the army of Gaul, return to Constantinople as a private person, my life will be safe.'

Both Oribasius and I laughed; but I was uneasy. 'It's absurd, of course,' I said, 'yet what is the alternative if you don't?'

'The bishop was not specific. The implication is that sooner or later Constantius will deal with me.'

'Much later,' said Oribasius. 'He is having his difficulties in Persia. It will be at least a year before he can march against us.'

Julian shook his head. 'I'm not sure.' He swung his legs over the cot and reached over to a near-by folding table on which lay the usual sheaf of agents' reports. 'All sorts of news.' He tapped the papers. 'Here is an order we intercepted from Constantius to the prefect of Italy: gather three million bushels of wheat, have them ground at Bregentz – that's on Lake Constance – and store the grain in several cities, all on the border of Gaul. Then here's another order for wheat to be stored on the Italian side of the Cottian Alps. He means to invade Gaul. There's no doubt of that.'

'But when?' Even though I was leaving and would soon be safe (not being a hero, my constant interest is the preservation of my own life), I did care what happened to my friend.

'Who knows? We can only hope Sapor involves him in a major campaign. Meanwhile, *I* have all that grain.' He grinned like a boy. 'I've ordered it confiscated and held for my own use.' He paused; then: 'All I need is a year.'

'And after that?' I looked at him closely, for Julian had never before spoken of any time other than the immediate future. As well as we all knew him, none of us had any idea of the extent of his ambition, or the nature of his long-range plan.

He answered cautiously, again flat on his back, one hand tugging at his youthful beard, which glinted gold as fox fur in the bright June night. 'In one year I shall be secure in Gaul, *and* in Italy.' Now it was out. To cross the Alps would indeed mean war.

'I have no choice,' he said. 'If I stay here, if I remain as I am, he will have my head.' He indicated the papers on the table. 'There is a report here that he is negotiating with the Scythians to come into Gaul. Typical, of course. To destroy me he'll wreck Gaul a second time, fill it again with savages and *never* regain it.' He sat up. 'Next spring, my friends, I take the field against Constantius.'

All that I could think to say, finally, was, 'He has ten times the army you have. He controls Italy, Africa, Illyricum, Asia . . .'

'I know.' Julian was unexpectedly calm. Ordinarily, such a conversation would have had him on his feet, arms waving, eyes flashing, words tumbling over one another in his excitement. I think I was more impressed by his unusual gravity than by what he said. 'But if we move swiftly, gathering strength as we go, I can take all of Europe in three months.'

'Then you must face the largest army on earth, at Constantinople.' Oribasius looked unhappy.

'I believe I shall win. Anyway, better to die at the head of an army than perish here and be known to history as the *fourth* usurper Constantius put down. Besides, this contest is between the Galileans and the true gods, and we shall win it because I was chosen to win it.' He said this so quietly, so lacking in his usual exuberance that there was nothing left for us to say; sooner tell the rain to stop on a spring morning in Gaul.

Then he was his old self. 'So now Priscus deserts us! Just as the battle lines are drawn, he retreats to Athens.'

'Cowardice is my prevailing characteristic,' I said.

'And uxoriousness,' said Oribasius slyly. 'Priscus longs for the powerful arms of Hippia . . .'

'And the company of my children, who are now at an age to embarrass me not only intellectually but financially.'

'Will you need money?' Julian, even at his poorest – and at this point he was unable to pay his household expenses – was always generous to friends. Maximus took him for a considerable fortune . . . and Maximus was one of the reasons I was leaving Gaul: he was rumoured to have accepted Julian's offer to join him in the spring. I could not face that.

I told Julian I had all the money I needed. He then gave me his personal medallion, or *tessura*, which allowed me to travel free of charge anywhere in the West. We made a most warm farewell. He seemed perfectly certain of his own victory, although in the memoir he betrays an anxiety which one would never have suspected from his behaviour, proving that our Julian had at last grown up. For one he kept his own counsel.

Julian and Oribasius saw me off in the afternoon carriage which left from the palace door for Vienne. As I got into the wagon with its usual complement of bishops and secret agents, Julian whispered in my ear, 'We shall meet in Constantinople.' That was the last I saw of him until we did indeed meet in Constantinople, to my surprise. I thought he would be dead before the autumn.

Julian Augustus

I should here sum up what I did in Gaul during the four years I was actively

Caesar. Three times I crossed the Rhine. One thousand persons who were held as captives on the farther bank I took back. In two battles and one siege I captured ten thousand prisoners, men in the prime of life. During those years, I sent Constantius four levies of excellent infantry, three more of infantry (not so good), and two very distinguished squadrons of cavalry. I recovered every place held or besieged by the barbarians, some fifty towns.

After strengthening our defences as far as Augst, I proceeded late in the summer to Vienne by way of Besançon. All told, I spent three months in the field that summer.

I had hoped to find Maximus at Besançon. There was a rumour that he was there, waiting for me. But though I had the agents look everywhere, he was not to be found. I did have a curious experience in Besançon while strolling about the city, quite alone, enjoying the sights. There is a fine view from the citadel, which is situated on a high rock. The place is well protected, not only by its eminence but by the River Doubs which circles it like a moat.

Besançon is a small town now, but it was once an important city and there are many abandoned temples, relics of a better time. Standing in front of the ruined temple of Zeus, I saw a man dressed as a Cynic. I was so positive that it was Maximus that I came up behind him – as boys do, I'm afraid – and clapped him on the shoulder to startle him. I succeeded. He turned about and to my embarrassment it was not Maximus at all but a fellow I had once met at Prohaeresius's house. Both of us blushed and stammered. Then he saluted me, and said, 'How great is Caesar to remember the friend of his youth, a humble philosopher, a mere seeker of truth ...'

'Welcome to Gaul,' I said, not letting on I had mistaken him for another. 'You must dine with me.' And thus I attached to my court for several months one of the most extraordinary bores I have ever known. Oribasius teases me about it to this day. But I never had the heart to dismiss the man, so he sat with us night after night, ruining all conversation. Why do I find it difficult simply to say, 'No!' Why am I so timid? I envy the tyrants. Also, why do I tell this story when it is my purpose to describe only crucial events? Because I am reluctant to describe the state of my own mind that winter at Vienne when, like Julius Caesar before me, I decided to cross the Alps. I have always said that I acted in self-defence, that I did not want to usurp the throne, that I wanted only to be recognized by Constantius as legitimate Augustus in the West. Yet I must say I find it impossible to describe what I really felt. Only historians can ever be certain of one's motives! Nevertheless, I do mean to record the truth, no matter how painful or in what a bad light it puts me.

I entered Vienne about 1 October. I moved into the praetorian prefect's palace. I now had a personal retinue of nearly a thousand men and women, slaves and soldiers. Heaven knows how these households expand, but they do, and they are ruinously expensive even for emperors .... even? *Especially* for emperors! I installed Nebridius, the new praetorian prefect, in my old villa by the wall. He was a good enough fellow who wisely kept to himself.

At this time I made an important decision. In all public places it is the law that the image of the Emperor, either painted or in the round, be displayed. Oaths are sworn to it. No legal decision is binding unless made in the sight of his image. And so the ubiquitous face of Constantius, with its soulful eyes and pinched mouth, looked down on every official in the West, including me. My first day in Vienne, I ordered that my own portrait, *as Augustus*, be placed beside his. Now the two of us stared, side by side, at litigants and lawyers. I am told that we were known as 'man and wife', since I looked the man with a beard and he, with his jewellery and smooth face, seemed the woman.

I was bombarded all through the summer with letters from Constantius. Why had I detained Lupicinus? Why had I stolen grain belonging to the prefecture of Italy? Where were the troops I had promised? The horses? Why did I style myself Augustus? I was ordered to report immediately to Constantius at Antioch. He even prescribed the household I might bring with me: no more than a hundred soldiers, five eunuchs ... he delighted in making lists. Yet to every denunciatory letter I made soft answer, always signing myself 'Caesar'.

While I was assembling the army of Gaul, Constantius was having his difficulties with Arsaces, that most unreliable king of Armenia, who was suspected of dealing with the Persians on the sly. I have since read the secret transcript of the meeting between Arsaces and Constantius. It was shocking. Arsaces got everything he asked for in exchange for remaining as he ought to be in the first place: loyal to us who support not only his throne but his country's independence. Constantius was hopeless at negotiations. To seal this 'reunion' (there is no word to describe holding an ally to a course to which honour and treaty have already committed him), Constantius gave Arsaces as wife the daughter of the old praetorian prefect Ablabius. Her name is Olympia, and she was once supposed to marry Constantius, which made her the nearest thing he had to an unmarried female relation. She is now queen of Armenia, a devout Galilean and hostile to me.

During this exchange between the Emperor and the Armenian, there was much talk of me. It is a strange experience to read literal transcripts of conversations in which one is discussed like a character in an epic.

Arsaces brought up the subject: would Julian march against the Emperor? Constantius thought it unlikely. If I did, at a signal from him the German tribes would attack me on the Rhine. Then, should I survive them, Scythians would bar my way to the East, not to mention the loyal armies of Italy and Illyricum.

Arsaces wanted to know if it was true that Julian's victories in Gaul surpassed those of Julius Caesar. Constantius responded angrily: 'All that was done in Gaul was done by my generals, acting on the orders of my praetorian prefect, who obeys me.' Constantius then went on to declare that he himself had achieved every victory, despite my hopeless muddling. In fact, I was so incompetent that Constantius was himself forced to take personal command of the army in order to win the famous victory of Strasbourg!

I must say I trembled with rage when I read those lines. Yes, I am vain. There is nothing to be done about it. I want credit. I want honour. I want fame. But I want only what is mine. I was amazed at Constantius's boldness. How could he lie with such recklessness? Arsaces must have known that Constantius was on the Danube becoming Sarmaticus Sarmaticus, while I was freeing Gaul. I rather suspect that Arsaces *did* know the Emperor was lying, for in the transcript he swiftly changed the subject.

I was particularly struck by one passage about myself (how hungrily we read about ourselves!). Constantius said that I had no gift for soldiering; I was a pedant who should have been left at the University of Athens. Arsaces remarked that the pedant seemed to have made a remarkable court of fellow pedants for himself at Paris. He even named them. Constantius said that he approved of the company I kept for schoolteachers would keep me so occupied with books and idle dispute that I would not have time to ponder treason. He offered to show Arsaces the 'cringing' letter in which I declared my loyalty to him, while rejecting the title 'Augustus'. Arsaces said that he would indeed like copies, and they were prepared. I wonder if Constantius showed him *all* the correspondence? I still blush when I think of that Armenian reading my highly politic and conciliatory (but hardly 'cringing') letters.

Then Arsaces said, 'I mention the men at Julian's court because there is a rumour that they are all of them atheists.' Surprisingly, Constantius seemed not at all interested in this. He merely remarked that schoolteachers tend to be unreliable, dirty, greedy, impious, beard-wearing ... all of them Cynics, he said largely. But Arsaces was obviously concerned; he hoped that Julian was a true Galilean. Constantius said that he was certain I was but that it made little difference, since after the Persian campaign I would cease to exist. They then talked of other matters.

Constantius next proceeded south to Melitena, Locatena and Samarath. He crossed the Euphrates and made for Edessa, a large city of Mesopotamia, sixty miles west of the ruins of Amida, now Sapor's by right of conquest. Daily Constantius's army grew larger and larger, but he did nothing with it. Finally, as autumn began, he marched to Amida. In sight of the troops, he wept; not a particularly helpful gesture in a war. That was the same day that Ursulus, the Count of the Sacred Largesse, made his much-quoted remark, 'See how bravely our citizens are protected by those soldiers, whose pay is bankrupting us!' This sardonic remark later cost him his life. One sympathizes with treasurers, but one must honour soldiers, especially those who fought at Amida against impossible odds.

From Amida, Constantius crept some thirty miles south-east to Begabde, a Persian town on the Tigris. He laid siege to the town, but because of the ardour of the Persians and his own incompetence, Begabde withstood every sort of assault. Then came the rainy season. Those who were there have since told me that the thunder and lightning was appalling. Our men were demoralized by what they took to be heaven's anger – and perhaps it was, directed at Constantius. Also, there were innumerable rainbows, which means that the goddess Iris has been sent down from heaven to effect some important change in human affairs. Constantius abandoned the siege and withdrew to Antioch for the winter.

Meanwhile, I was getting my own affairs in order at Vienne. I sent for various wise men and prophets, including the Hierophant of Greece. I consulted oracles and sacred books; I made sacrifices to the gods ... in secret, of course, for Vienne is a city dominated by Galileans. All signs agreed that I would prevail and that Constantius would fall. Yet I did not neglect the practical. Every prophecy is always open to interpretation and if it turns out that its meaning was other than what one thought, it is not the fault of the gods but of us who have misinterpreted their signs. Cicero has written well on this. I particularly credit dreams, agreeing with Aristotle that important messages from heaven are often sent to men as they sleep, though to dream meaningfully it is necessary for the eyes beneath the lids to be turned neither to left nor right but set straight ahead, often difficult to arrange.

At the end of October, during consistory, Oribasius sent me a message. I must go straight to my wife. She was dying.

Eyes shut, Helena lay in her bed. She was emaciated except for her stomach, which was grotesquely large beneath the coverlet. Oribasius was at her side while the bishops of Vienne and Paris chanted and prayed. I took Helena's hand, now cool, soon cold. It is a grisly miracle when the soul leaves the body, taunting us with the unimportance of that flesh which in life so entirely enslaves us, since it *is* us, or seems to be.

'Julian.' She spoke in an ordinary voice.

I found I could say nothing, only murmur sounds of compassion. Yet I suffered with her even though I hardly knew her. We were royal animals, yoked by the same master to pull a golden carriage. Now one animal had fallen between the traces.

'They tell me I am dying.' Before I could give ritual comfort, she said, 'I don't mind. I'm not afraid. Only do remember that the new wing on the east has only a temporary roof. There wasn't time to have the right sort of tiles made. You know the ones I mean. They are called, I think, Patrician tiles. Anyway, the steward knows what to buy. The temporary ones will have to be replaced *before* the spring rains. I have had estimates made of the cost. It will be expensive, but we can take it out of my private account in Rome. The new mosaic work could be spoiled should there be a great deal of rain, which there is apt to be this time of year in Rome.' With those words, Helena died, thinking of her beloved villa in the Via Nomentana.

The bishops looked at me furiously as though I had in some way spoiled their fun. Then they set to praying, very loud. I left the room. In the outer hall I found Helena's women.

'The Queen is dead.' I felt nothing. They began to wail.

'Prepare her,' I said sternly, 'and save your tears.'

They went inside the bedroom. Oribasius put his hand on my shoulder. I looked about me at all the things Helena had owned, worn, touched.

'I don't know,' I said at last, with wonder, '*what* I feel.'

'You should feel relief. She suffered. Now it's over.'

I nodded. 'We are toys, and a divine child takes us up and puts us down, and breaks us when he chooses.'

So my marriage ended. Helena's body was sent to Rome and she is buried in the same mausoleum as her sister Constantia and our son. I also remembered to give orders to replace the tiles in the villa. Helena was forty-two when she died. I was twenty-eight. The day after her death, I took the vow of calibacy, as an offering to Cybele for her continued favour.

15

On 6 November 360, I celebrated my fifth year as Caesar, my 'quinquennial', as the Romans call it.

I thought it wise to make a great event of this occasion. It is well known that I detest what goes on in hippodromes, whether games, fighting or the slaughter of animals. But there are certain things one must do in a high place and the giving of games is one of the most important. If the games are a success, one enjoys popularity with the mob. If not, not. It's as simple as that. Though I have many times cursed those consuls of the old Republic who started this boring and costly business, I always do what is expected of me as well as I can with the means at hand.

I am told that the games at Vienne were a success. I cannot judge. I attended them as little as possible. But when I did appear, it was as Augustus. I wore a heavy gold crown which I am now quite used to, justifying it to myself as a symbol of the sun, which is God. I looked quite imperial that year. Even Oribasius was satisfied; he could never endure the old purple fillet I usually wore in public. 'You look like a gymnasium director,' he would complain.

Constantius and I exchanged polite letters on the death of Helena. Then in December I received the announcement that Constantius had married a lady of Antioch called Faustina. I sent him congratulations. Meanwhile, each of us prepared for civil war.

A number of significant things happened in December. One afternoon while I was practising with shield and sword (I do this nearly every day, because I came late to soldiering and must work harder than most to toughen muscles and learn the subtleties of combat), my shield broke loose from both the handle and the strap, and fell to the ground with a crash in full view of the Petulantes with whom I took exercise. Before anyone could interpret this as an ill omen, I said loudly, 'Look!' And I held up the handle which I still clutched. 'I have what I was holding!' This was taken to mean that I would hold Gaul, no matter what happened. But I was puzzled until that night when I dreamt that I saw again the guardian deity of Rome. He came to my bedside, and he spoke very plainly, in verse:

> *When Zeus the noble Aquarius shall reach*
> *When Saturn come to Virgo's twenty-fifth degree,*
> *Then shall Constantius, K. of Asia, of this life so sweet,*
> *The end attain with heaviness and grief.*

This was as clear a statement as one could hope for from the gods. The next morning I told Oribasius, and he in turn called in Mastara, the best of the Etruscan astrologers. He cast Constantius's horoscope and found that the Emperor would indeed be dead within a few months. He even set the date as some time in June 361. But in spite of this celestial assurance, I took no chances. I continued to prepare for war.

I liked the praetorian prefect, Nebridius, though he did not like me, for the very reason I liked him: he was faithful to his master and I honoured him for that. Yet despite his loyalty to Constantius, he did not conspire against me. Because of this, I allowed him to carry out the ceremonial functions of praetorian prefect, though nothing more. Yet despite our cordial relations, he was always on the lookout for ways to trap me. He devised an excellent embarrassment.

On 6 January, the Galileans celebrate something called the feast of the Epiphany. It is the day the Galilean is supposed to have been baptized. Suspecting my dislike of the Galileans, Nebridius announced to the city that I would attend the feast of the Epiphany at the Vienne charnel house, a brand-new basilica paid for by Helena's numerous gifts to the bishops. I was furious but dared not show it. I am sorry to say Oribasius was amused at my predicament.

Grimly, I did what I had to do. I spent two hours meditating on the thighbone of some villain who had been eaten by lions at Rome, while the bishop delivered a considerable sermon to me, praying that I would throw the weight of my majesty against the enemy Arians. He even turned political by suggesting that as Constantius was Arian and I *possibly* Athanasian, the line might then be drawn between us in all things, and the side of 'truth' (also the side of the majority, he added pointedly) would prevail, supporting my throne like columns, I believe was his metaphor, or it may have been holy caryatids. When it came time to pray, my words were addressed to the Galilean but my heart spoke to Zeus.

The winter was a time of waiting. I was now ready to march. All that I needed was a sign from heaven. Though the prefect at Rome would not allow my emissaries to consult the Sibyline books, a friendly priest of the old order was able to look at a part of that book which describes our period. According to his secret report, I would indeed be the next emperor. My reign would be stormy but long. That is all I ask for: time. Time to make an old world young again, to make winter spring, to free the One God from the triple monster of the atheists. Give me twenty years, O Helios, and I will fill the earth with praise for your light, and illuminate the dark windings of Hades' kingdom! Even as Persephone returned to Demeter, so shall our time's living-dead return to your arms, which are light, which is life, which is all!

In April I learned that the German tribe of King Vadomar had crossed the Rhine and was devastating the area near Raetia. This was particularly puzzling news because two years before we had negotiated a 'final' peace with Vadomar. He had no grievance against us. He was a cultivated man, educated at Milan. He was by nature cautious. To any show of force he always responded with a thousand apologies and a quick withdrawal to his own side of the river. That Vadomar was now actively in the field against me could mean only one thing. He was acting on Constantius's orders.

I sent Vadomar one of my counts, a man called Libino. He was a good soldier and negotiator, or so I thought. I sent him with half a legion and orders to reason with Vadomar. Should reason fail, threats of extinction were in order. Libino got as far as Sechingen on the Rhine. There the Germans surrounded him. Unfortunately, Libino was eager for battle, even though his mission was only to negotiate. Like a fool, he ordered his men to attack. Five minutes later, Libino himself was hacked in two by a German sword, and his men, outnumbered five to one, were massacred.

I then dispatched the Petulantes to the Rhine only to find that the savages had faded into their forests, as mysteriously as they had appeared. For the moment all was peaceful on the Rine. Now ordinarily I would have taken this for what it seemed to be: a single raid by restless tribesmen, conducted without the knowledge of Vadomar, who all the while was writing me long and eloquent letters, offering to punish his own people, *if* of course the guilty ones were his. He even sent a gift of money to the family of the dead Libino.

I did not believe Vadomar, but I was willing to forget the matter until one of the border guards intercepted a German messenger bound for the East. The messenger was found to be carrying a letter from Vadomar to Constantius. I quote from it: 'Your will is being done, Lord, and your Caesar who lacks discipline will be chastened.' That was all I needed. I promptly sent one of my notaries, a clever chap named Philogius, to join the Petulantes who were still at Sechingen, close to the country of Vadomar.

Libanius: I feel compelled to note that this same 'clever chap named Philogius' has just been appointed Count of the East by Theodosius. He is a dedicated Christian and no one knows how we shall fare under his rule. If only Julian had sent *him* instead of the long-forgotten Libino to that fatal rendezvous on the Rhine! But then, were it not he, fate would no doubt find us a worse Philogius. The Count arrived in Antioch early this month. I saw him for the first time yesterday in the senate. He moved amongst us like a swan who has found himself in a particularly small and distasteful pond. Do I dare mention Julian to him?

Julian Augustus

I gave Philogius sealed instructions. If he encountered Vadomar on *our* side of the Rhine, he was to open the letter and do as he was told. Otherwise, the letter was to be destroyed. I was fairly certain that he would see Vadomar, who often travelled in our territory, visiting Roman friends. Like so many German nobles, he was in some ways more Roman than the Romans.

Philogius met Vadomar at a reception given by a local contractor. Philogius invited the king to dinner the next day at the officers' mess of the Petulantes. Vadomar said that he would be delighted to dine with such distinguished men. When he arrived for dinner, Philogius excused himself, saying that he had forgotten to give certain instructions to the cook. He then read my letter. In it I commanded him to arrest Vadomar for high treason. Philogius did so, to the astonishment of his guest.

A week later, Vadomar was brought to me at Vienne. I received him alone in my study. He is a handsome, blue-eyed man, with a face red from hard drink and cold winters. But his manners are as polished as any Roman courtier's. He speaks excellent Greek. He was very frightened.

'You have made a bad choice, King,' I said.

He stammered: he did not know what I meant. I gave him the letter we had intercepted. The red face became blotchy.

'I did as I was told, Augustus ...'

'In the letter you call me Caesar.'

'No, no, Augustus. That is, I *had* to when I wrote to him. He'd ordered me to attack you. What could I do?'

'You might have honoured your treaty with me. Or your might have made a better choice, as I suggested originally. You might have chosen me instead of Constantius as your master.'

'But I do, great Lord. I do *now*! I always have. Only . . .'

'Don't!' I stopped him with a gesture. I take no pleasure in seeing another man grovel before me. 'Actually, you – and your correspondence – have been very useful to me.' I took the letter back from him. 'I now have proof that not only does Constantius mean to destroy me, he incites the barbarians against his own people. Now I know what to do, and how to do it.'

'But what will you do, Augustus?' Vadomar was momentarily distracted from his own fate.

'Do? I shall exile you to Spain.' He fell on his face in gratitude, and it was with difficulty that I extracted myself from his embrace, and turned him over to the guards.

I sent for Oribasius. I have never been so elated in my life. 'We're ready!' I shouted when he joined me. 'Everything is ready!' I don't recall now what else I said. I suppose I 'babbled', as Priscus calls my talk during seizures of enthusiasm. I do remember that Oribasius, always the most conservative of advisers, agreed entirely with me. It was now or never. There remained only one possible obstacle, the mood of the legions. Some were still adamant about leaving Gaul.

Together we studied the military roster. Those units prone to mutiny we sent as permanent garrisons to the farther cities of Gaul. The remainder would assemble at full strength on 25 June, when it would be my task to rouse them for the war against Constantius. Never was an orator given greater challenge. I rehearsed my speech every day for three weeks. Oribasius coached me until he too knew every word by heart.

At dawn on the 25th, Oribasius and I met with several officers of like mind in a small chapel off the council chamber. There I made special offering to Bellona, goddess of battles. The omens were propitious. Then, nervous at the thought of the speech ahead, I went forth in full regalia to review the legions who were gathered in a field outside the city, just beyond the gate through which I had arrived in Vienne five years before, a green boy with a handful of troops who knew only how to pray. I thought of this as I made my way to the stone tribunal, my neck rigid beneath its burden of gold.

I do not have a copy of this speech with me. In fact, my chief secretary seems to have packed none of my personal files though I *especially* asked that they be brought with us, knowing that I would be composing this memoir in Persia. Nevertheless, I recall most of what I said, even down to the gestures which I find myself reproducing as I repeat the words I said two years ago. I will not weary the reader with a catalogue of gestures, nor every word of the peroration. I will only say that I was at my best.

First, I addressed the army as 'Noble soldiers'. This is an unusual way to style an army, and it caused much comment. Yet I wanted to emphasize to them their importance to me and my respect for them. I spoke of all that we had done together against the Germans and the Franks. 'But now that I am Augustus, I shall, with your support and that of the Deity – should fortune honour us – aim at greater things. To forestall those in the East who wish us ill, I propose that while the garrisons of Illyricum are still small, we take possession of all Dacia and then decide what more must be done. In support of this plan, I want, under oath, your promise of a lasting and faithful accord. For my part, I will do all that I can to avoid both weakness and timidity. I also swear that I will undertake nothing that does not contribute to us all. I only beg you: do nothing to hurt private citizens, for we are known to the world not only as the victors of the Rhine but as men whose right conduct in victory has made half a world prosperous and free.'

There was more in this vein. At the end, by various cries and loud oaths, they swore that they would follow me to the end of the earth, something of an exaggeration since their immediate interest was the spoils to be got as the result of what they knew would be an easy campaign in Dacia.

When I asked them to swear the oath of allegiance to me as Augustus, they did so, swords to their throats. Then I turned to the officers and officials gathered about the stone tribunal:

'Will you, too, swear allegiance to me, in God's name?' I asked according to ritual. All swore, except Nebridius. There was a menacing growl from the troops.

'You will not swear allegiance to me, Prefect?'

'No, Caesar. I have already sworn an oath to uphold the Emperor. Since he still lives, I cannot swear again without jeopardizing my soul.' His voice trembled, but not his will.

Only I heard his whole speech, for on the word 'Caesar' the men roared their anger. Swords were drawn. A legionnaire grabbed Nebridius by the neck and was about to throw him in the dust when I quickly stepped down from the tribunal and put myself between the soldier and the prefect. Nebridius, pale as death, clung to my knees. I removed my cloak and threw it over him: the ancient gesture which means a man has the protection of the emperor. Then I shouted to the legions, 'He will suffer quite enough when we are masters of Rome!' This bit of demagoguery distracted the men, and I ordered Nebridius taken under guard to the palace.

I then reviewed the troops. It was a fine sight, and all the doubts which had tormented me in the night were dispelled by the blue-green summer day and the sight of twenty thousand men marching in rhythmic unison to the Pyrrhic measure. It is at such moments that one realizes war is an essential aspect of deity, and that the communion of an army is a mystery in its way quite as beautiful as that of Eleusis. For a moment all hearts beat to the same music. We were one and there was nothing on earth we could not do!

When I returned to the palace, I sent for the stubborn Nebridius. I exiled him to Tuscany. He had expected death. With tears in his eyes he said, 'Caesar, give me your hand. Let me . . . in gratitude . . .' But I pulled back.

'There would be no honour nor sign of affection for me to give to my friends, if I gave *you* my hand.' That was the end of Nebridius in Gaul.

On 3 July I took the field against Constantius. The omens were excellent and the weather fair.

We moved east to Augst, where I called a staff meeting. As usual, I had kept my plans to myself; not even Oribasius knew what I intended, though we rode together, ate together and chattered like schoolboys.

With me as commanders were Nevitta – the great Frank whom I come to admire more and more as I know him; Jovinus, a competent officer; Gomoarius, a man I did not trust, for he was the one who betrayed his commander Vetranio when he rebelled against Constantius; Mamertinus, a good secretary; Dagalaif, perhaps the best commander of cavalry in the history of the Roman army. I began with the announcement that Sallust was now on his way to Vienne to act as praetorian prefect; he would govern in my place. This was well received. Sallust is admired not only by me but by all men.

'I now have certain appointments to make.' I did not have to consult the sheet of paper before me. I got the disagreeable task over with first. 'Gomoarius, I remove you as commander of cavalry. That post goes to Nevitta.' There was silence. Gomoarius said nothing. All knew my motive. We are a small family, the military, despite the size of the empire. We all know one another's faults and virtues. 'Jovinus, I make you quaestor; Mamertinus, treasurer; Dagalaif, commander of the household troops.'

Then I went over the map on the folding table. 'We are outnumbered ten to one by the combined armies of Illyricum and Italy. Fortunately, those armies are not combined. They consist mostly of garrison troops, while ours is an aggressive army, used to swift attack. Now, what is our best course of action?' I paused. They took my question for the rhetoric it was. 'When in doubt, imitate Alexander. Whenever his army was seriously outnumbered, he would disperse his troops in such a way as to give the impression that he had far more men than anyone knew. Therefore I mean to split the army in three sections. We shall seem to be attacking from every direction.

'Jovinus will take the direct route to Italy.' I pointed to the map. 'You will notice I have marked the main roads for you. Spread out along them. I want everyone to see you. Nevitta, you take the middle course, due west through Raetia. I shall take the remainder of the army and go north through the Black Forest to the Danube. Then west and south along the Danube, straight to Sirmium. Whoever holds Sirmium controls Illyricum and the approach to Constantinople.' I turned to Nevitta. 'You and I will rendezvous at Sirmium, no later than October.'

None objected to my plan. Incidentally, for those who may get the impression from history that divine emperors are never contradicted by those who serve them, I should note that such is not the case in the field. Though the emperor's word is final, any commander is free to argue with him as much as he likes until the war plan is actually set in motion. Personally, I have always encouraged debate. Often as not it deteriorates into quibbling, but occasionally one's strategy is improved. This time, however, there was little discussion, only the usual arguments as to who got what legion. The next day the army was divided, and the conquest of the West began.

The Black Forest is a strange and ominous place. Seeing it from within made me understand the Germans better. The place is haunted; perverse demons lurk in every shadow . . . and what shadows! Even at noon, the forest is so dim that it is like being drowned in a deep green whispering sea. As we rode over quiet trails, the legions, two abreast, wound like some slow sea-serpent on the ocean floor. Fortunately, we had reliable guides who knew every twist and turn of the forest. I cannot think how, for there were no markers of any kind; yet they knew their way through the green maze. For days on end we never saw the sun, until I despaired of ever seeing my god again.

By the middle of August we were in the wild but beautiful valley of the Danube. Though the river is not as impressive to look at as the Rhine, it is far less treacherous to navigate. So I decided to make the rest of the journey by water.

At a village on the south bank, we halted and I ordered boats built. While this was being done, I received the fealty of the local tribes. They were amazed to see a Roman emperor (even a not quite legitimate one!) so far north. When they discovered that I meant them no harm, they were most co-operative and offered to act as river pilots. They are a handsome, fair-skinned people, somewhat shy.

Meanwhile, messengers from Jovinus arrived, with good news. Milan had fallen. He also wrote me the latest news of Constantius. Sapor had advanced to the Tigris. Constantius had then withdrawn to Edessa, where he was now holed up, avoiding battle. I was amused to note that he had appointed Florentius praetorian prefect of Illyricum. I was obviously poor Florentius's nemesis. I had sent him out of Gaul; soon I would drive him from Illyricum. I believe of all those who hate me, he must hate me the most. He certainly has the best reason!

We sailed down the Danube through a golden country, rich with harvest. We paused at none of the towns or fortresses which became more numerous the farther south we went. There was no time to waste. If I took Sirmium, all these towns would be mine by right, but if I paused to lay siege to each I should never be done fighting. Most of the natives were well disposed towards us; but then none was put to the test.

In early October, at night, with the moon waning, we reached Bonmunster, nineteen miles north of Sirmium. It is a small town, with no garrison. Late as it was, I ordered all men ashore. We pitched camp on the bank of the river.

I do not know if it is common to all in my place, but it was my experience as a usurper (and one must call me by that blunt name) that everywhere I went well-wishers and informers flocked to me like bees to honey, until I was forced to devise a screening process to examine each would-be ally and determine if he could be used. Most proved to be sincere; but then I proved to be victorious!

Before the moon had sent, I had learned that Count Lucillianus was at Sirmium, with a considerable army and orders to destroy me. However, Lucillianus did not expect me in the vicinity for another week, and so he slept now at Sirmium.

As soon as I had heard these reports, I sent for Dagalaif. I ordered him to go straight to Sirmium with a hundred men; he was to seize Lucillianus and bring him back. This was a considerable assignment, but I knew from spies that the city was no more than usually guarded and that the palace where Lucillianus was staying was close to the gate. At night our men would look no different from any other imperial troops; there would be no problem entering the city. For the rest, I counted on Dagalaif's boldness and ingenuity.

After Dagalaif had left, Oribasius and I strolled together on the river bank. It was a warm night. In the black sky a misshapen moon, like a worn marble head, made all the country silver. Behind us the fires and torches of the camp burned. The men were quiet; they had orders to make no unnecessary noise; only the horses occasionally disobeyed me, with sharp sudden whinnies. At the top of the river bank we stopped.

'I like this,' I said, turning to Oribasius, who was seated now on a rock, staring at the bright diagonal the moonlight made across the slow deep water.

Oribasius looked up at me. The moon was so bright that I could make out his features. 'This?' He frowned. 'Do you mean the river? or war? or travel?'

'Life.' I sat on the damp ground beside him and crossed my legs, muddying the purple I wore. 'Not war. Nor travel. Just this. Right now.' I sighed. 'I can hardly believe we have crossed nearly half the world. I feel like the wind, without a body, invisible.'

He laughed. 'You are probably the most visible man on earth, and the most feared.'

'Feared,' I repeated, wondering if I would ever take satisfaction from the knowledge that men's lives and fortunes could be taken from them at a nod of my head. No, I cannot enjoy that sort of power; it is not what I want.

'What *do* you want?' Oribasius had divined my mood, as he so often does.

'To restore the gods.'

'But if they are real and do exist . . . .'

'They are real! There is no "if"! They do exist!' I was fierce.

His laughter stopped me. 'Then they exist. But if they exist, they are always present, and so there's no need to "restore" them.'

'But we must worship what God tells us to.'

'So the Christians say.'

'Ah, but theirs is a false god, and I mean to destroy them.'

Oribasius stiffened at the word 'destroy'. '*Kill* them?'

'No. I shall not allow them the pleasure of martyrdom. Besides, at the rate they kill one another, it would be gratuitous for me to intervene. No, I shall fight them with reason and example. I shall reopen the temples and reorganize the priesthood. We shall put Hellenism on such a footing that people will choose it of their own free will.'

'I wonder.' Oribasius was thoughtful. 'They are rich, well-organized. Most important, they educate the children.'

'We shall do the same!' I was thinking as I spoke; I had no plan. 'Even better, we could take the schools away from them.'

'If you could . . .'

'The Emperor can.'

'It might work. Otherwise . . .'

'Otherwise?'

'You would have to reign as a bloody tyrant and even then you'd lose.'

'I am not so pessimistic.' But Oribasius had put an idea into my head, one which will save us all. Curiously enough, though we had often spoken of what it would be like when I became emperor, none of us had ever really considered in much detail what form the contest between Hellenism and the Galileans would take. We agreed that when I could I would publicly repudiate the Nazarene, but none of us had thought what the reaction might be, particularly from the common people of whom perhaps half are Galilean. Only the army is truly religious. The men worship Mithras. There are few Galileans in the ranks, though a third of the officers believe in the triple monster.

We talked until it was morning. Just as the sun appeared over the world's edge, like an omen, Dagalaif returned to camp with Count Lucillianus as prisoner.

I hurried to my tent. There on the ground in his nightclothes was Lucillianus, trussed like a chicken. He was terrified. For a moment I looked down on the shivering body, recalling that the last time I had seen him he had been my brother's jailer. Then I loosened his bonds and raised him to his feet. This friendly gesture somewhat relieved his anxiety. He is a large man, given to peculiar diets. For years he would eat only udder of sow; at least that is the story one hears.

'We are happy you could attend us on such short notice, Count.' I was formal but agreeable.

'If only I had known, Caesar . . . I mean Augustus . . . I should have met you myself . . .'

'And put me to death, like Gallus?'

'Those were my orders, Augustus, but you may depend on my loyalty to you in this dispute. I have always been loyal. I have always preferred you to the Emp— to *him* at Antioch.'

'We accept your loyalty, your troops, your city of Sirmium, and the prefecture of Illyricum.'

He gasped but bowed. 'Such is the will of Augustus. All these are yours.'

'Thank you, Count.' I was in an excellent mood. Lucillianus is the sort of man who does not think ahead – witness his failure to anticipate my arrival – and men who do not think ahead tend to accept what is; they never conspire.

I said, 'Now swear your oath to me.' He swore; and kissed the purple, getting a bit of Danube mud on his face. 'You will retain your rank, Count, and serve in my army.'

Lucillianus's recovery was swift. 'If I may say so, Lord, it is a very rash thing you have done, coming here with such a small army in the midst of someone else's territory.'

'Reserve, my dear Count, your wisdom for Constantius. I have given you my hand not to make you my counsellor but less afraid.' I turned to Mamertinus. 'Give the word to the army. We march to Sirmium.'

Sirmium is a large city, highly suitable for an imperial capital, standing as it does upon the border between the prefecture of Illyricum and the diocese of

Trace – the westernmost country of the prefecture of the East. I was now at the beginning of the territory traditionally assigned to the Augustus of the East.

I had warned my officers that there might be incidents. I did not expect the city to surrender without token resistance, even though its commander was now with us, riding at my side.

But to my astonishment, we were met outside the gates by a vast crowd of men, women and children, carrying chains of flowers, boughs of trees and numerous sacred objects. I was hailed as Augustus with the most extraordinary enthusiasm.

I turned to Lucillianus and shouted to him above the din, 'Did you arrange this?'

He shook his head. He was too stupid to lie. 'No, Augustus. I don't know who arranged it . . .'

'Legend!' said Oribasius. 'They know you'll win. They always do.'

A large bouquet of flowers hit me in the face. Eyes stinging, I swept it aside; a blood-red poppy caught in my beard. Men and women kissed my robe, my legs, my horse. Thus was I escorted into the capital of Illyricum while the grapes were still green. It was the first great city ever to fall to me, twice the size of Strasbourg or Cologne or even Treves. The date was 3 October 361.

I went straight to the palace, and to business. I received the senate of the city. I allayed their fears. They swore loyalty to me, as did the legions within the city. I ordered a week of chariot races next day to amuse the populace, one of the burdens the conquered invariably put upon the conqueror. With great pleasure I received Nevitta who, true to his promise, arrived at Sirmium after a victorious passage through Raetia. The West was ours.

I called a staff meeting, and we discussed our next move. Some favoured marching straight to Constantinople, two hundred miles distant. Dagalaif argued that with Constantius in Antioch, Constantinople would fall to us without a battle. Nevitta was not so certain. He was afraid that Constantius was probably already on the march from Antioch to the capital. If this were so, we were hardly a match for what was in fact, the largest army on earth. I agreed with Nevitta. We would remain where we were for the winter.

I entrusted to Nevitta the defence of the Succi Pass, a narrow defile in the high mountains that separate Thrace from Illyricum. Whoever holds this pass is safe from attack by land. I then sent two of the Sirmium legions to Aquileia, to hold that important seaport for us. With the main part of the army I withdrew some fifty miles north-west to Nish (where Constantine was born); here I went into winter quarters.

The weeks at Nish were busy ones. Every night I dictated until dawn. I was determined to present my case against Constantius as clearly as possible for all to read and comprehend. I sent a lengthy message to the Roman senate. I also composed separate letters for the senates of Sparta, Corinth and Athens, explaining what I had done and what I intended to do. Heavily but justly, I placed the blame for all that had happened on Constantius. Then – though Oribasius warned me not to – I assured the various senates that I intended to restore the worship of the old gods, making the point that I personally imitated them in order that, by having the fewest possible needs, I might do good to the greatest possible number. These letters were read at every public gathering. They made a profound and favourable impression.

During this period I planned an amphibious attack on Constantinople to take place as soon as the winds favoured us. We were in a good position militarily. At

Succi we controlled the land approach to the West. At Aquileia we controlled the sea approach to northern Italy. I felt reasonably secure, and was confident that before civil war broke out, Constantius would come to terms with me. But my sense of security was rudely shattered when I learned that the two legions I had sent to Aquileia had promptly gone over to Constantius. The port was now his, and I was vulnerable to an attack by sea. Since I was not able to leave Nish and Nevitta could not leave Succi, my only hope was Jovinus, who was in Austria en route to Nish. I sent him a frantic message: proceed immediately to Aquileia. My situation was now most precarious. Constantius could at any time land an army at Aquileia and cut me off from Italy and Gaul. I was in despair, confident that the gods had deserted me. But they had not. At the last moment, they intervened.

On the night of 20 November I was working late. Lamps filled with cheap oil smoked abominably. The three night secretaries sat at a long table, mountains of parchment stacked in front of them. At a separate table I was writing a letter to my uncle Julian, trying to reassure him – and myself – that victory was certain. I had just finished the letter with one of those postscripts which even old friends say they cannot decipher, when I heard footsteps quickly approaching. Without ceremony the door flew open. The clerks and I leapt to our feet. One never knows if assassins are at hand. But it was Oribasius, out of breath, a letter in his hand.

'It's happened!' he gasped. Then he did something he had never done before. He dropped on his knees before me, and offered me the letter. 'This is for you . . . Augustus.'

I read the first line. Then the words blurred together and I could read no more. 'Constantius is dead.' As I said those extraordinary words, the clerks one by one fell to their knees. Then, as in a dream, the room began to fill with people. All knew what had happened. All paid me silent homage for I had, miraculously, with the stopping of one man's breath, become sole Augustus, Emperor of Rome, Lord of the world. To my astonishment, I wept.

AUGUSTUS

16

Priscus: That is the way it happened. At least that is the way Julian *says* it happened. As you must gather, he omits a number of details. To read his account one would think that there had been no resistance at all to him, other than from the wicked Constantius. This was hardly true. I should say that a majority of the 'responsible' men in the empire preferred Constantius to Julian, nor was this on religious grounds, since Julian's passion for Hellenism was not generally known as of November 361. I am sure you will want to state matters as they actually were. Your famous balance would be seriously deranged if you were to record that Julian's success was the result of a popular uprising against Constantius. It was not – despite the impression you gave in your justly celebrated oration at the time of Julian's death. But then the great wings of a memorial, like those of a panegyric, are not expected to be clipped by tedious fact.

Libanius: How typical!

Priscus: Julian notes in passing that he sent various messages to different cities. Indeed he did! He must have composed at least a dozen lengthy harangues, addressed variously to the senates at Rome and Constantinople – a not unnatural precaution – but then an equal number of *apologias* were sent to such cities as Corinth and Sparta, as if they still mattered in the scale of power. Their poor backwoods town councils must have been astonished to receive an emperor's homage.

I was present at the senate in Athens when the message to us was read. Since I know that you want only the truth, I must tell you that the letter was not well received, and of all cities Athens was most inclined to Julian.

I sat beside Prohaeresius while the message was read. The old man was amused, but cautious. So was I. Of course, everyone in Athens was aware that I had only recently come from Julian; even so, I was firm in saying that I knew nothing of his plans. I even praised Constantius on several public occasions. After all, Constantius might have lived. Julian might have been defeated. *I* might have been executed for treason. Like everyone else, I prefer to avoid undue distress at the hands of tyrants.

We were all quite nervous at the beginning of the message. (If you don't have a copy of this address, I will send you mine, free of charge.) Naturally, we were flattered by Julian's references to our ancient past, as well as respectful of his quite skilful mastery of rhetoric, even though he was prone to clichés, especially when he was tired or writing too fast. He could seldom prepare a message without 'Xerxes defying nature', or trotting out that damned 'oak tree' which no contemporary writer seems able to avoid.

But after a good beginning, Julian then denounced Constantius. He named all the murders. He made a point of Constantius's infertility (not knowing that Constantius's new wife Faustina was pregnant). He denounced the eunuchs, particularly Eusebius. He gave us a considerable autobiography, generally accurate, ending with the statement that he was now in the field because no one could trust the word of Constantius, since it was, he declared (relying again on a familiar phrase), 'written in ashes'. At this point the senators of Athens began to clear their throats and scuff their sandals on the floor, always a bad sign.

At the end of the message there was no discussion. The senate, wisely, went on to other matters. No one had the courage to behave as the senate at Rome did when they were read their letters, and Tertullus, the city's prefect, shouted, 'We demand reverence for Constantius, who raised you up!'

When the senate adjourned, Prohaeresius and I left the chamber together. No one spoke to anyone else. Then – as now – the secret service was ubiquitous. We knew nothing except that Julian was somewhere in the Balkans, that the West *appeared* to be his, and that Constantius was moving against him with a superior army. It was not easy to know how to behave. Our sort is for ever courted by usurpers and asked to join in this or that undertaking. Since no one can know the future, it is quite easy to pick the wrong side. The death of Maximus was instructive, wasn't it, old friend?

But of course we are all so used to these sudden changes in government that there is almost an etiquette in how one responds to invitations which could as easily turn out disastrous as advantageous. First, one appears to ponder the request with grave attention; then one pleads a personal problem; finally, one does nothing. That is how you and I have managed to live to be so old in such a stormy time.

I recall vividly my walk with Prohaeresius. It must have been some time in the second week of November. The weather was cold, the wind sharp, the afternoon clouds more thick than usual. Absently, Prohaeresius put his arm through mine. We hurried through the crowd which had gathered outside the senate house. Not till we were past the temple of Hephaestos did he speak. '*You* know him. What will happen?'

'I think he will win.'

'How can he? Constantius has the army. The people are with him. They're certainly not with your . . . *our* young student. The senate's mood was perfectly plain.'

'I think he will win, that's all.' But I was by no means as confident as I sounded.

'The oracles . . .' But the old man stopped. He was not about to give himself away to me. 'Come home with me.'

I accepted, not yet eager for Hippia's company. My marriage, always unhappy, was at this time unbearable: Hippia was still furious at me for having spent nearly three years in Paris, despite the money I had been able to send her. Today, however, after fifty years of mutual loathing, we are quite dependent on one another. Habit is stronger than hate.

I was surprised to find Macrina at Prohaeresius's house. She had not been much in evidence since the birth of her child (ostensibly sired by the businessman husband). She had gained a little weight, which was attractive.

Macrina greeted us in the inner court. She was ecstatic. 'It's happened! He's all right!'

'What has happened? Who is all right?' Prohaeresius was irritable.

'Julian is Emperor!'

That is how we got the news at Athens. Apparently, the formal message to the senate had been delayed. But Julian had written Prohaeresius and me, taking it for granted that we had already heard the news. We were both invited to attend him at Constantinople.

Macrina was exultant. 'We must all go to the court. Every one of us. We'll all live in Constantinople. No more Athens. No more grubby students ...'

'No more grubby husband?' I could not resist this. She stopped talking.

Prohaeresius, who had been studying the letter, frowned. 'He says, "I worship the true gods openly and all the troops with me worship them. I have offered the gods many oxen as thank-offerings for my victory, and I shall soon restore their worship in all its purity."' The old man looked at us grimly. 'So he means to do what he said he would do.'

'Why not?' Macrina was sharp. 'He can't be worse than the bishops.'

'Except that now he's Emperor there won't be an ox left in the world!' I believe I was the first to make what was soon a universal joke: Julian's sacrifices were so rich that he was nicknamed 'Bull-Burner'.

Unlike Macrina and me, Prohaeresius was in a dark mood. 'I see only trouble for us,' he said.

'Trouble? When you are the man the Emperor most admires?' Macrina was unbelieving. 'Nonsense. It'll be the making of all you schoolteachers. He'll be another Marcus Aurelius. Well, Septimus Severus, anyway.'

'Julian is better than Marcus Aurelius,' I said, and I meant it. Marcus Aurelius has been enormously overrated as a philosopher. People – especially scholars – are so thrilled that an emperor can even write his own name that they tend to exaggerate the value of his literary productions. If you or I had written those *Meditations*, they would not, I am certain, be considered of any great value. They are certainly inferior to your own superb *pensées*.

Not for several weeks did we know the details of Constantine's death, or in what manner the succession had been assured. Julian gives his version of what happened.

Julian Augustus

As far as I can make out, Constantius had been in poor health for some months. He had chronic stomach trouble, a family weakness from which I alone seem to be exempt (so far!). As soon as I had been given the news, I sent everyone out of the room except Oribasius. Then the two officers from the Consistory were brought to me. My first question was the obvious one: 'How did he die?'

'Of a fever, Augustus.' The older officer, Aligildus, did most of the telling.

'Had there been omens?' I particularly wanted to know because I had myself received a number of mysterious signs during the previous weeks. It is good to be scientific about these things. Might not an omen observed to be malign by Constantius appear simultaneously to me as benign?

'Many, Augustus. For several weeks in the field he had been disturbed by waking-dreams and nightmares. On one occasion, he thought he saw the ghost of his father, the great Constantine, carrying in his arms a child, a handsome, strong child which Constantius took and held on his lap.'

I turned with wonder to Oribasius. 'Is Constantine *my* creator?' For it was plain enough that I was the child in the dream.

'Then the boy seized the orb Constantius held in his right hand ...'

'The world,' I murmured.

'... and threw it out of sight!' Aligildus paused.

I nodded. 'I understand the dream. Did *he?*'

'Yes, Augustus. Shortly afterwards, when we came to Antioch, the Emperor told Eusebius that he had a sense that something which had always been with him was gone.'

'The Spirit of Rome. These are the signs,' I said to Oribasius. Like so many who deal too much in the material world, Oribasius puts little stock in omens and dreams. Yet I think even he was impressed by what he had heard. I quoted Menander, 'A spirit is given each man at birth to direct his course.' Then I asked about my cousin's last days.

'He spent most of the summer at Antioch, assembling an army to . . .' Aligildus paused, ill at ease.

'To use against me.' I was amiable. Why not? Heaven was on my side.

'Yes, Lord. Then in the autumn, after many dreams and bad omens, Constantius left Antioch for the north. Three miles outside of the city in a suburb . . .'

'Called Hippocephalus,' said Theolaif, the other officer, reminding us that he too was messenger and witness. 'We saw, on the right-hand side of the road, at noon, the headless corpse of a man *facing west.*'

A chill ran through me. I hope that when my star falls I shall be spared the torment of such signs.

'From that moment on, Lord, the Emperor was not himself. We hurried on to Tarsus, where he came down with a fever.'

'But he could not stop,' said Theolaif, suddenly inspired: the deaths of princes and the malignity of Fate obsess us all. 'I know. I was with him. I rode beside him. I said, "Lord, stop here. Wait. In a few days you will be well." But he looked at me with glazed eyes, his face dark with fever. He swayed in the saddle. I steadied him with my hand and felt *his* hand, hot and dry. "No," he said, and his tongue was dry, too. He could hardly speak. "We go on. We go on. We go on." Three times he said that. And we went on.'

Aligildus continued, 'When we came to the springs at Mobsucrene, he was delirious. We put him to bed. In the night he sweated and the next morning he seemed better. He gave orders to leave. We obeyed, reluctantly. But when the army was ready to move, he was delirious. Constantius was ill three days, his body so hot that it was painful to touch him. Yet he had moments of clarity. In one of those moments, he made his will. This is it.' Aligildus handed me a sealed letter which I did not open.

'How was he, at the end?'

'When he was conscious, he was angry.'

'At me?'

'No, Lord, at death, for taking him in his prime, for taking him from his young wife.'

'It is bitter,' I said formally. Who is so inhuman as not to feel *something* at a man's death? even that of an enemy.

'Then shortly before dawn on 3 November, he asked to be baptized, like his father. After the ceremony, he tried to sit up. He tried to speak. He choked. He died. He was forty-five years old,' added Aligildus, as though he were making a funeral address.

'In the twenty-fifth year of his principate,' I noted, in the same style.

'Pray, Augustus,' said Oribasius suddenly, '*you* reign as long.'

We were silent for a moment. I tried to remember how Constantius looked and failed. When a famous man dies one tends to remember only the sculpture, especially when there is so much of it. I can recall Constantius's monuments but not his living face, not even those great dark eyes which are to my memory blank spaces cut in marble.

'Where is the Chamberlain Eusebius?'

'Still at the Springs. The court waits upon your orders.' Aligildus for the first time sounded uncertain. 'You Augustus, are the heir legitimate.' He pointed to the letter that I held in my hand.

'There was no . . . objection in the Consistory?'

'None, Lord!' The two men spoke as one.

I rose. 'Tomorrow you will return to the Springs. Tell the Consistory that I shall meet them as soon as possible at Constantinople. See that the body of my cousin is brought home for a proper burial, and that his widow is treated with all the honour due her rank.' The officers saluted, and departed.

Then Oribasius and I opened the will. It was short and to the point, unlike the usual imperial prose. One knew that a man had dictated it, not a lawyer.

'The Caesar Julian at my death is raised legitimately' (even on his deathbed he could not resist this jab) 'to the principate of Rome. He will find my stewardship has been faithful. Despite much treason within the empire and formidable enemies without, the state has prospered in my reign and the borders are secure.'

I looked at Oribasius, amused. 'I wonder how they feel about that in Amida.'

I read on. 'We entrust to our most noble cousin and heir our young wife Faustina. She is provided for in a separate testament, and it is our final prayer that our most noble cousin and heir will respect the terms of that will and carry them out as befits a great prince who can afford to show mercy to the weak . . .'

I paused. 'Once I tried to make that same speech to him.'

Oribasius looked at me oddly. 'He spared *you*,' he said.

'Yes. To his regret.' I hurried through the rest of the document. There were a number of bequests to retainers and friends. One particularly struck me. 'I cannot recommend to my most noble cousin and heir a wiser counsellor or one more loyal than the Grand Chamberlain Eusebius.' Even Oribasius laughed at this. Then, at the very last, Constantius spoke directly to me. 'We have had differences, the Caesar Julian and I, but I think that he will find when he fills my place that the earth seems not so big as he thought it was from his previous place or from any other place, saving this summit where there can be but one man and a single responsibility for all men, and great decisions to be made, often in haste and sometimes regretted. We are not to be understood by any except our own kind. My most noble cousin and heir will know what I mean when he takes up the orb I have let go. Now in death I am his constant brother in the purple and from whatever place God sees fit to put my soul I shall observe his deeds with fellow-feeling and hope that as he comes to know the singularity of his new estate – and its cruel isolation – he will understand if not forgive his predecessor, who wanted only the stability of the state, the just execution of the law, and the true worship of that God from whom come all our lives and to whom all must return. Julian, pray for me.'

That was it. Orabasius and I looked at one another, unable to believe that this crude and touching document was the work of a man who had governed the world for a quarter century.

'He was strong.' I could think of nothing more to say.

The next day I ordered a sacrifice to the gods. The legions were most enthusiastic, not only at my accession (and the avoidance of a civil war), but at being allowed to pray to the old gods openly. Many of them were fellow brothers in Mithras.

Priscus: This is quite untrue. In actual fact there was a near-mutiny when the sacrifices were ordered, especially among the officers. At this time Julian was very much under the influence of a Gaul named Aprunculus, who had foretold Constantius's death by discovering an ox liver with two lobes, which meant that . . . et cetera. As a reward for having found that double liver, Aprunculus was made governor of Gallia Narbonensis. It was said at the time that a *quadruple* liver might have got him all of Gaul.

Aprunculus persuaded Julian to place the images of the gods next to his own image so that when each man came to throw incense on the fire as homage to the emperor, he also did reverence, like it or not, to the gods. This caused a good deal of bad feeling, none of which Julian notes.

Julian Augustus

Less than a week later, I gave the order to proceed to Constantinople. I will not dwell on the elation of those days. Even the cold winter – and it was the coldest in many years – did not depress us.

In a blizzard, we filed through the pass of Succi and descended into Thrace. From there we proceeded to the ancient city of Philippopolis where we stayed overnight. Then we moved south to Heraclea, a town fifty miles southwest of Constantinople where, shortly before midday, to my astonishment, most of the senate and the Sacred Consistory were gathered in the main square.

I was hardly prepared for such a greeting. I was tired, dirty, and I desperately needed to relieve myself. Imagine then the new emperor, eyes twitching with fatigue, hands, legs, face streaked with dust, bladder full, receiving the slow, measured, stately acclamation of the senate. Looking back, I laugh; at the time I was hard pressed to be gracious.

I dismounted at one end of the square and crossed to the prefect's house. The Scholarian Guards made an aisle for me. They are called Scholarian because their barracks are in the front portico – the 'school' – of the Sacred Palace. I studied my new troops with a cold eye. They were smartly turned out; most were Germans . . . what else? They studied me, too. They were both curious and alarmed, which is as it should be. Too often in the past emperors have been frightened of the guard.

I climbed the steps to the prefect's house. There, all in a row, were the officers of the empire. As I approached, they fell to their knees. I asked them to rise. I hate the sight of men old enough to be my grandfather prostrate before me. Recently I tried to simplify the court's ceremonies but the senate would not allow it, so used are they to servitude. They argue that since the Great King of Persia keeps similar state, I must, too, or appear less awesome in men's eyes. Nonsense. But there are too many important changes to be made to worry about court ceremonial.

The first official to greet me was Arbetio, who had been consul in the year I was made Caesar. He is a vigorous, hard-faced man of forty; born a peasant, he became a soldier, rising to commander of cavalry and the consulship. He wants my place, just as he wanted Constantius's place. Now there are two ways to handle such a man. One is to kill him. The other is to keep him near one, safely employed, always watched. I chose the latter for I have found that if someone is reasonably honest and well-meaning – though he has treated one badly – he should be forgiven. When men are honest in public life we must be on good terms with them, even though they have treated us badly in a private capacity; while if they are dishonest in public affairs, even though they are personally devoted to us, they must be dismissed.

Arbetio welcomed me in the name of the senate, though he was not its chief officer.

'We are here to do as the Augustus wills.' The proud loud voice belied the words. 'In everything.'

'. . . and to prepare for his entering the city as our Lord!' I turned when I heard those words and there, approaching me from a crowd of senators, was Julian, my uncle. He was trembling with excitement (and infirmity, for he suffered from a recurrent fever, souvenir of his days as governor of Egypt). I embraced him warmly. We had not seen each other for seven years, though we had corresponded as regularly as we dared. My uncle had aged alarmingly; his face was haggard, the yellow skin loose, eyes deep-set, but even so, this day he was transfigured with delight. I kept my arm through his as I addressed the crowd.

'I am moved at your gesture, since it is not usual for the senate to leave their city to meet the first citizen. Rather it is the first citizen who must come to you, to his peers, who share with him the task of governing, and I shall be with you shortly in your own house to do you the homage you deserve. Meanwhile, I make only one announcement: I shall accept no coronation money from the provinces, imitating in this Hadrian and Antonius Pius. The Empire is too poor at present to make me a gift.' There was applause. Then after a few more ungraceful remarks, I pleaded fatigue, and excused myself. The town prefect bowed me into the building, stammering, stumbling, getting in my way, until at last I shouted, 'In Hermes's name, where do you piss?' Thus graciously did the new Emperor of Rome come to the East.

The prefect's house had a small private bath and while I soaked in the hot pool, taking deep breaths of steam, my uncle Julian discussed the political situation.

'When Constantius died, Eusebius sounded out several members of the Consistory to see if they would accept Arbetio as emperor, or Procopius . . . or me.' My uncle smiled shyly at this. He wanted me to hear this from his own lips rather than from an informer.

'Naturally,' I said, watching the dust from my beard float like a grey cloud into the centre of the pool where a Negro slave stood, ready to scrub me with towels and sponges, unaware that I never let bath attendants touch me.

'What did the Consistory say to all this?'

'That you were the Emperor, by blood and by choice.'

'As well as being only a few hundred miles away.'

'Exactly.'

'Where is Eusebius?'

'At the palace, preparing for your arrival. He is still Grand Chamberlain.' My uncle smiled.

I submerged for a moment, eyes tight shut, soaking my head. When I came to the surface, Oribasius was sitting on the bench beside my uncle.

'That is no way to approach the sacred presence,' and I splashed Oribasius very satisfactorily. He laughed. My uncle Julian laughed, too, for I had soaked him as well. Then I was alarmed. In just this way are monsters born. First, the tyrant plays harmless games: splashes senators in the bath, serves wooden food to dinner guests, plays practical jokes; and no matter what he says and does, everyone laughs and flatters him, finds witty his most inane remarks. Then the small jokes begin to pall. One day he finds it amusing to rape another man's wife, as the husband watches, or the husband as the wife looks on, or to torture them both, or to kill them. When the killing begins, the emperor is no longer a man but a beast, and we have had too many beasts already on the throne of the world. Vehemently, I apologized for splashing my uncle. I even apologized for splashing Oribasius, though he is like my own brother. Neither guessed the significance of this guilty outburst.

Oribasius told me that the Consistory wanted to know whom I intended to appoint as consuls for the coming year.

'Uncle, what about you?'

'I can't afford the consulship.' It was sign of my uncle's wealth that he always complained of poverty. Actually, the consulship is not so expensive as it used to be. Nowadays, the two consuls pool their resources for the games they must sponsor, while the emperor usually helps them from the Privy Purse.

'I don't think *you'd* like it, Oribasius.'

'No, Augustus, I would not.'

'Mamertinus,' I said, swimming to the far side of the pool.

Both my uncle and Oribasius approved. 'He's a distinguished rhetorician,' said my uncle. 'Of good family, a popular choice . . .'

'And Nevitta!' I dived under the water as I said this. When I came up for air, I could see that Oribasius was amused and my uncle horrified.

'But he . . . he is . . .'

I nodded. 'A Frank. A barbarian.'

I got out of the bath. The slave wrapped me in a large towel. I broke away from him before he could start pummelling me. 'He is also one of our best generals. He will be a continual reminder to the East that my power rests securely in the West.'

'No one will ever accuse you of consistency.' Oribasius grinned. Only the month before at Nish, I had denounced Constantius for appointing barbarians to prefectures. Now I was making one consul. There is nothing harder politically than to have to reverse yourself publicly. But where Constantius would rather die than ever admit to a mistake, I was quite willing to look a bit foolish, and do the right thing.

'We shall deny,' I said with much grandeur, 'that I ever criticized the appointment of barbarians to high office.'

'Your letter to the Spartan senate was a forgery?'

'In every detail.'

Oribasius and I laughed but my uncle looked pained. 'At least,' he said, 'name only Mamertinus today. Besides, it's the custom to name one consul at a time, so name him for the East. Later you can announce the . . . the other man for the West.'

'So be it, Uncle!' And together we went into the dressing-room where I put on the purple.

The Consistory was almost at full strength, some forty officers of state, who received me ceremoniously at the town hall. Arbetio escorted me to my ivory chair. To my left and right were the empty consular chairs. One for Florentius, who had – has – vanished from the face of the earth; the other for Taurus, who fled to Antioch when I first came into Illyricum.

I greeted the Consistory politely. I noted the absence of the consuls, remarking that as a new year was about to begin, there would soon be two new consuls. One would be Mamertinus. This was received with every appearance of satisfaction. I then made a number of additions to the Consistory. When I had finished, Arbetio begged to address me. Heart sinking, I granted him leave.

Slowly, solemnly, as though *he* were the Augustus, Arbetio moved to the centre of the room, just in front of my chair. He cleared his throat. 'Lord, there are those who have plotted against you.' A sharp intake of breath was heard all round the room. After all, there was hardly a man present who had *not* conspired against me. It had been their duty. 'Those men are still are large. Some in high places. Lord, there are also those who conspired against your most noble brother, the Caesar Gallus. They, too, are at large. Some in high places.'

I looked about the room and saw several men 'in high places' look most uneasy. There was the stout Palladius, chief marshal of Constantius's court. He had brought charges against Gallus. Next to him stood Evagrius, Count of the Privy Purse; he had helped prepare the case against Gallus. And Saturninus, Steward of the Household . . . A dozen conspirators looked back at Arbetio and me. The question in every face was: Will this reign begin in blood?

It was Ursulus, Count of the Sacred Largesse, who spoke up boldly. 'Augustus, are those of us who served the emperor *you* served so well, to suffer for having done our duty?'

'No!' I was firm.

But Arbetio turned his bleak, pale gaze upon Ursulus. 'Yet, Augustus, those who have by *deed* hurt you and your brother, by *word* and by deed, must be condemned.'

There was an uneasy murmur in the room. Yet Ursulus stood his ground. He was a handsome fleshy man with a quick wit and quicker tongue. 'The Consistory are relieved, Lord, that only those who are truly guilty will be charged.'

'They shall be charged,' said Arbetio, speaking for me, which I did not like, 'if it be our Lord's will.'

'It is our will.' I said the traditional phrase in Latin.

'Who shall compose this court, Lord? and where shall it sit?'

Now I should have stopped Arbetio at that moment. But I was tired from the long journey and languorous from a hot bath (*never* try to do any business immediately after bathing). I was unprepared for a strong will with a plan, and Arbetio had a plan, alas. Meanwhile, Ursulus proposed: 'Since the Emperor Hadrian, the Consistory has been our highest court. So let the guilty be judged here, by us who are responsible for the business of the state.'

'But, Count,' and Arbetio's voice was cold in its correctness, 'the Consistory is still that of the late emperor, *not* of our new lord. I am sure the Augustus will want his own tribunal, as he will in time want his own Consistory.' This was undeniable.

I motioned to one of the secretaries to pay close attention as I spoke. 'The court will be headed by Salutius Secundus.' This went over very well. As praetorian prefect of the East he is known for his sense of justice. I then named Mamertinus, Agilo, Nevitta, Jovinus, and Arbetio to the court. It was, in short, a military tribunal. I then ordered them to meet at Chalcedon, across the Bosphorus from Constantinople. Thus began the treason trials. I shall – sadly – refer to them later.

On 11 December 361 I entered Constantinople as Roman Emperor. Snow fell at slow intervals and the great flakes turned like feathers in air so still that the day was almost warm. The sky was low and the colour of tarnished silver. There was no colour that day in nature, only in man, but what colour! It was a day of splendour.

In front of the Golden Gate, close to the sea of Marmora, the Scholarians in full-dress uniform stood at attention. On each of the brick towers at either side of the gate, the dragons were unfurled. The green bronze gates were shut. As custom demanded, I dismounted a few yards from the wall. The commander of the Scholarians gave me a silver hammer. With it I struck the bronze gate three times. From within, came the voice of the city's prefect. 'Who goes there?'

'Julian Augustus,' I replied in a loud voice. 'A citizen of the city.'

'Enter Julian Augustus.'

The bronze gates swung open noiselessly and there before me in the inner courtyard stood the prefect of the city – and some two thousand men of senatorial rank. The Sacred Consistory was also there, having preceded me into the capital the night before. Quite alone, I passed through the gate and took possession of the City of Constantine.

Trumpets sounded. The people cheered. I was particularly struck by the brightness of the clothes they wore. I don't know whether it was the white setting which made the reds and greens, the yellows and blues almost unbearably vivid, or the fact that I had been away too long in northern countries where all colours are as muted and as dim as the forests in which the people live. But this was not the misty north. This was Constantinople, and despite the legend that we are the New Rome (and like that republican city, austere, stern, virtuous), we are not Rome at all. We are Asia. I thought of this as I was helped into the gold chariot of Constantine, recalling with amusement Eutherius's constant complaint, 'You are hopelessly Asiatic!' Well, I am Asiatic! And I was home at last.

As flakes of snow settled in my hair and beard, I rode down Middle Street. Everywhere I looked I saw changes. The city had altered completely in the few years I had been away. For one thing, it has outgrown the wall of Constantine. What were once open fields are now crowded suburbs, and one day I shall have to go to the expense of building a new wall to contain these suburbs, which, incidentally, are not carefully laid out in the way the city was but simply created helter-skelter by contractors interested only in a quick profit.

Colonnades line Middle Street from one end to the other. The arcades were crowded with people who cheered me ecstatically. Why? Because they loved me? No. Because I was a novelty. The people tire of the same ruler, no matter how excellent. They had got bored with Constantius and they wanted a change of programme and I was it.

Suddenly I heard what sounded like thunder at my back. For a moment I took it as an omen that Zeus had approved me. Then I realized it was not thunder but my army singing the marching song of Julius Caesar's troops: '*Ecce Caesar nunc triumphat, Qui subegit Gallias!*' It is the sound of war itself, and of all earthly glory.

The prefect of the city walked beside my chariot and tried to point out the new buildings, but I could not hear him for the noise of the mob. Even so, it was exhilarating to see so much activity, in contrast to old cities like Athens and Milan where a new building is a rarity. When an old house collapses in Athens, the occupants simply move into another one, for there are far more houses than people. But everything in Constantinople is brand-new, including the population, which is now – the prefect shouted to me just as we entered the Forum of Constantine – close to a million people, counting slaves and foreigners.

The colossal statue of Constantine at the centre of the oval forum always gives me a shock. I can never get used to it. On a tall column of porphyry, my uncle set up a statue of Apollo, stolen I believe from Delos. He then knocked the head off this masterpiece and substituted his own likeness, an inferior piece of work by any standard and so badly jointed that there is a dark ring where head and neck meet. The people refer to this monument as 'old dirty neck'. On the head there is a monstrous halo of seven bronze rays, perfect blasphemy, not only to the true gods but to the Galilean as well. Constantine saw himself as both Galilean and as incarnation of the sun god. He was most ambitious. I am told he doted on this particular statue and used to look at it every chance he got: he even pretended that the Apollonian body was his own!

We then entered that section of Middle Street which is called Imperial Way and leads into the Augusteum, a large porticoed square which was the centre of the city when it was called Byzantium. In the middle of the Augusteum, Constantine set up a large statue of his mother Helena. She is seated on a throne and looks quite severe; in one hand she holds a piece of wood said to have been a part of the cross to which the Galilean was nailed. My great aunt had a passion for relics; she was also infinitely gullible. There was not a charnel house in the city to which she did not give some sliver of wood, shred of cloth, bit of bone said to have been associated in one way or another with that unfortunate rabbi and his family.

To my astonishment, the entire north side of the square was taken up by the basilica of a charnel house so new that the scaffolding had not yet been removed from the front. The prefect beamed cheerfully at me, thinking I would be pleased.

'Augustus may recall the old church that was here? the small one the Great Constantine dedicated to Holy Wisdom? Well, the Emperor Constantius has had it enlarged. In fact, only last summer he rededicated it.'

I said nothing but immediately vowed to turn the Saint Sophia into a temple to Athena. It would never do to have a Galilean monument right at my front door (the main entrance to the palace is on the south side of the square, just opposite the charnel house). To the east is the senate house to which the senators were now repairing. The senate's usual quorum is fifty, but today all two thousand were present, elbowing one another as they hurried up the slippery steps.

The square was now jammed with people, and no one knew what to do next. The prefect was used to being given his orders by the palace chamberlains, who were, if nothing else, masters of pageantry. But today the chamberlains were in hiding and neither the prefect nor I knew what to do. I'm afraid between us we made rather a botch of things.

My chariot had stopped at the Milion, a covered monument from which all distances in the empire are measured. Yes, we counterfeit Rome in this, too; in everything, even to the seven hills.

'The senate waits for you, Lord,' said the prefect nervously.

'*Waits* for me? They're still trying to get inside the senate house!'

'Perhaps the Augustus would prefer to receive them in the palace?'

I shook my head, vowing that never again would I enter a city without preparation. No one knew where to go or what to do. I saw several of my commanders arguing with the Scholarians, who did not know them, while ancient senators slipped and fell in the slush. It was a mess, and a bad omen. Already I was handling matters less well than Constantius.

I pulled myself together. 'Prefect, while the senate meets, I shall make sacrifice.'

The prefect indicated Saint Sophia. 'The bishop should be inside, Augustus. If he's not, I can send for him.'

'Sacrifice to the true gods,' I said firmly.

'But ... *where?*' The poor man was bewildered, with good reason. After all, Constantinople is a new city, dedicated to Jesus, and there are no temples except for three small ones on the old Byzantine acropolis. They would have to do. I motioned to those members of my entourage who had got through the guards and together we made a small ragged procession to the low hill where stood the shabby and deserted temples of Apollo, Artemis and Aphrodite.

In the dank filthy temple of Apollo, I gave thanks to Helios and to all the gods, while the townspeople crowded round outside, amused by this first show of imperial eccentricity. As I sacrificed, I swore to Apollo that I would rebuild his temple.

Libanius: A few weeks ago the Emperor Theodosius gave the temple of Apollo to his praetorian prefect, as a coach house!

Julian Augustus

I then sent Mamertinus, as consul-designate, to tell the senate that I should not address them until 1 January, out of deference to my predecessor, whose body was already on its way to the city for interment. Through a now gusty blizzard, I made my way to the palace, entering through the Chalkê Gate, whose vestibule is covered with a bronze roof. Just over the gate, I noticed a new painting of Constantine. He is shown with his three sons. At their feet, a dragon, javelin in its side, sinks into the pit: the true gods slain. Above the emperor's head is a cross. A nice coat of whitewash should do the trick.

On either side of the gate, the Scholarian Guards are quartered. They saluted smartly. I ordered their commander to house and feed my military retinue. Then I crossed the inner court and entered the main part of the palace. In the great hall I found Eusebius with his eunuchs, notaries, slaves, secret agents, at least two hundred men and half-men, all waiting for me in a room which was as bright and as warm as a summer's day. I have never seen so richly dressed a group in my life, nor smelled so much expensive perfume.

I stood in the doorway and shook snow from my cloak as a dog shakes water from his back. All present fell to the floor with exquisite grace, and Eusebius humbly kissed the hem of my robe. I looked down for one long moment at that large body which resembled one of those African beasts Egypt sends us for the games. Eusebius glittered with jewels and smelled of lilies. This was the creature who had tried to destroy me, as he had destroyed my brother.

'Get up, Chamberlain,' I said briskly. I motioned for the others to do the same. With some difficulty, Eusebius got to his feet. He looked at me shyly, with appealing eyes. Though he was terrified, years of training at court and a consummate skill at negotiating served him well; not once did his voice falter nor his poise desert him.

'Lord,' he whispered, 'all is in readiness. The bedrooms, the kitchens, the rooms of assembly, the robes, the jewels . . .'

'Thank you, Chamberlain.'

'An inventory will be presented to the Lord of the World tomorrow.'

'Good, and now . . .'

'Whatever he wishes, our Lord need only command.' The voice that whispered in my ear was confiding and intimate.

I stepped away from him. 'Show me my apartments.'

Eusebius clapped his hands. The hall emptied. I followed the eunuch up white marble stairs to the second floor, where, through latticed windows, one can see the splendid gardens which descend in shallow terraces to the sea of Marmora. Off to the right is the mansion of the Persian Prince Ormisda who defected to us in 323, as well as the group of small buildings or pavilions known as the Daphne Palace; here the emperors hold audience.

It was strange to be in Constantius's rooms. I was particularly moved when I saw the inlaid silver bed where my cousin had slept, and no doubt dreamed uneasily of me. Now he is gone and the room is mine. I wonder: who will sleep here after me? My reverie was interrupted by Eusebius, who cleared his throat nervously. I looked at him blankly. Then I said, 'Tell Oribasius I want to see him.'

'Is that *all*, Lord?'

'That is all, Chamberlain.'

Face grave and perfectly controlled, Eusebius withdrew. That evening he was arrested for high treason and sent to Chalcedon to stand trial.

Together Oribasius and I explored the palace, to the consternation of the staff, who had never before seen an emperor stray from the strict round prescribed for him by ceremonial. I was particularly interested in seeing the palace of Daphne. So Oribasius and I, escorted by no more than a dozen guards, pounded on the door of the little palace. A nervous eunuch opened it and showed us into the throne room where, years before, I had seen Constantine on a day when all our family was together; now all are dead but me. The room was as splendid as I remembered, including, I'm afraid, the jewel-encrusted cross which covers the entire ceiling. I should like to remove it, but traditionalists argue that no matter what the state's religion it should be kept simply because my uncle put it there. Perhaps they are right.

The old eunuch who had shown us into the room said that he remembered the day I was presented to my uncle.

'You were a handsome child, Lord, and we knew even then that you would be our master.' Naturally!

We also explored the banquet hall, with its arched triklinos at one end where, on a dais, the imperial family dine. The floor is particularly handsome, inlaid with different-coloured marbles from every province of the empire. While we were gaping like countryfolk, the Master of the Offices appeared, accompanied by a tall lean officer. After gently chiding me for having escaped him, the Master indicated the officer, a commander of cavalry named Jovian. 'He has just arrived, Augustus, with the sacred remains of the Lord Constantius.'

Jovian saluted me; he is a good-humoured unintelligent man who serves with me now in Persia. I thanked him for his efforts and assigned him to temporary duty with the Scholarians. I then called a Consistory where, among other matters, we planned the funeral of Constantius. It was the last ceremony the eunuchs conducted and I am happy to say it went off without a hitch. He had loved them; they loved him. It was fitting that their last task at court should have been the funeral of their patron.

Constantius's funeral was held in what the Galileans call the Church of the

Holy Apostles, which is situated on the fourth of the city's hills. Just back of the basilica, Constantine had put up a round mausoleum, much like the one of Augustus at Rome. Here lie his remains, and those of his three sons. May the earth rest lightly on them.

To my surprise, I was quite moved at the funeral of my life's enemy. For one thing, since I am celibate, our line ends with Constantius. But that's not quite true: his widow Faustina was then pregnant. I saw her at a distance, heavily veiled among the mourners. Several days later I granted her an audience.

I received Faustina in Constantius's dressing-room, which I use as an office because it is lined with cupboards originally built to hold his many robes and tunics. I now use the cupboards for books.

When Faustina entered, I rose and greeted her as a kinswoman. She knelt. I raised her up. I offered her a chair. We both sat.

Faustina is a vivacious woman, with a high arched Syrian nose, blue-black hair and grey eyes, testament to some Gothic or Thessalian ancestor. She was clearly frightened, though I did my best to put her at her ease.

'I hope you don't mind my receiving you here.' I indicated the row of tailor's dummies which still lined one wall, mute reminder of the body they were intended to represent.

'Wherever my Lord chooses,' she said formally. Then she smiled. 'Besides, I have never been inside the Sacred Palace before.'

'That's right. You were married at Antioch.'

'Yes, Lord.'

'I am sorry.'

'It was the will of heaven.'

I agreed that indeed it was. 'Where will you live, Princess?' I had decided to style her thus. 'Augusta' would have been out of the question.

'If it pleases my Lord, at Antioch. Quietly. In retirement. With my family. Alone.' She dropped each phrase like a coin at my feet.

'You may live wherever you please, Princess. After all, you are my last kinswoman and . . .' As tactfully as possible, I indicated her swelling stomach beneath black robes, '. . . you bear the last child of our house. That is a great responsibility. Were it not for you, the Flavians would come to an end.'

For a moment, I saw fear and suspicion in the grey eyes; then she lowered her head and faint colour rose in her neck. 'I hope, Lord, you will have many children.'

'None,' I said flatly. 'Your son – or daughter – alone must continue the line.'

'When my husband was dying, he said that you would be just and merciful, Lord.'

'We understood each other,' I said. But then I could not help adding, 'Up to a point.'

'I am free to go?'

'You are perfectly free. Constantius's bequests to you shall be honoured.' I rose. 'Let me know when the child is born.' She kissed the purple; and we parted.

I get regular reports on her from Antioch. She is thought to be proud and difficult but not given to conspiracy. She dislikes me for not allowing her the title of Augusta. Her child, incidentally, turned out to be a girl, much to my relief. She is named Flavia Maxima Fausina. It will be interesting to see what happens to her.

Libanius: Flavia – or Constantia Postuma as we call her – is a lady of the greatest charm, very like her mother, and a most intimate friend of mine. She of course married the Emperor Gratian and they reside now in Treves. So the daughter became what her mother did not, a reigning Augusta. Faustina is extraordinarily proud of her daughter, though when I saw her last month she was somewhat hurt at not having been invited to join the Empress in the West. Apparently the thoughtful child felt that the journey would be too taxing for her mother. Also, as I told Faustina: children *do* tend to live their own lives and we must be tolerant. I even loaned her the only copy I have of my little essay on 'The Duty to Parents'. Which reminds me that she has not returned it.

As for the Emperor Gratian, he is everyone's hero, although (alas!) he is a devout Christian. When he was raised to the principate, he refused the title of Pontifex Maximus, the first emperor in our history to do so, a most ominous sign. As a matter of record, last year when Gratian selected Theodosius to be Augustus of the East, he gave his mother-in-law the honorary title Augusta. We were all tremendously pleased.

Julian Augustus

When Faustina left, I sent for a barber. My hair had not been cut since Gaul, and I was beginning to look quite savage, more Pan than philosopher. I was studying the palace roster when what looked like the Persian ambassador entered the room. I nearly got to my feet, so awed was I by the spactacle: gold rings, jewelled brooch, curled hair. But this was not an ambassador. This was the barber. My response was weak. 'I sent for a barber not a tax collector,' I said. But the man took this serenely, as an imperial pleasantry.

He chattered freely. He told me that he had an annual salary, paid by the treasury; he also earned twenty loaves of bread a day, as well as fodder for twenty pack animals. Yet he felt himself underpaid, he said, as he trimmed my beard, gracefully deploring the fact that I like it to come to a point. I held my tongue until he had left; then I dictated a memorandum dismissing all barbers, cooks, and other supernumeraries from my service.

I was engaged in this pleasant task when Oribasius joined me. He listened with amusement while I roared and waved my arms, getting more and more upset as I thought about the court I had inherited. When I had finally run out of breath, Oribasius reported that he had been exploring the barracks of the Scholarian Guards. It seems that the men slept on *feather mattresses*! Their mess was sumptuous, and their goblets were a good deal heavier than their swords. As a sideline, some conducted a traffic in jewels, either stolen or extorted from rich merchants whom they regularly terrorized, demanding protection money. As if this were not bad enough, the guardsmen had formed a glee club and regularly hired themselves out to private parties where they sang *love songs*!

I'm afraid I was screaming with anguish by the time Oribasius had finished. He always takes pleasure in arousing me, deliberately adding detail to detail just to watch the veins in my forehead throb. Then after he has roused me to a blind rage, he takes my pulse and tells me that if I'm not careful I shall have a stroke. I will, too, one day.

I was all for clearing out the barracks at once. But he thought it would be better to do it gradually. 'Besides, there is far worse going on in the palace.'

'Worse!' I raised my eyes to Helios. 'I didn't expect soldiers to be philosophers. I know they steal. But singing love songs, feather mattresses . . .'

'It's not the soldiers. It's the eunuchs.' But he said nothing more, indicating the secretaries. Sworn though they are to secrecy, one must always be careful what one says in front of any witness.

'Later,' Oribasius whispered.

We were suddenly aware of a great babble from below. The Master of the Offices entered, breathing hard. 'Lord, the Egyptian delegation begs your presence, humbly, graciously . . .' At this point the noise below began to sound like a riot.

'Is this usual, Master?'

'No, Lord, but Egyptians . . .'

'. . . are noisy?'

'Yes, Lord.'

'And the praetorian prefect is unable to handle them?'

'Exactly, Lord. He told them you could not see them and . . .' There was a noise of breaking pottery, and a few high-pitched screams.

'Are the Egyptians always like this, Master?'

'Often, Lord.'

Much amused, I followed the Master of the Offices downstairs to the praetorian prefect's audience chamber. Just as I was about to enter the hall, a half-dozen attendants appeared from nowhere. One arranged my hair; another my beard; my cloak was redraped; a diadem was set on my head. Then the Master of the Offices and what was now a considerable retinue opened the doors and, feeling rather like Constantius, I entered the prefect's chamber.

I should explain that Egyptians are easily the most tiresome of my subjects, if one wishes to generalize . . . and who does not? Their bad reputation was not gained for nothing. They particularly delight in litigation. Sometimes a family will conduct a lawsuit for a century, simply for the pleasure of making trouble. This particular delegation had come to see Constantius in Antioch, but he was gone before they arrived. They pursued him to the Springs, where death mercifully saved him from them. Then, hearing that a new emperor would soon be in Constantinople, they had come straight to me. Their complaint? A thousand suits against our government in Egypt.

They swarmed about me – they were of every colour, from pale Greek to black Numidian – and they all talked at once, quite unimpressed by my greatness. The praetorian prefect looked at me across the room; hopefully, he made the sign of the knife. But I was more amused than offended.

With some difficulty, I got their attention. 'Justice,' I shouted, 'will be done each of you!' This occasioned both cheers and groans. Apparently, some felt things were going much too easily. 'But,' I said firmly, 'no redress can be given here. Only at Chalcedon, across the Bosphorus. That is where the treasury is, where such matters are decided.' I was now improvising quite freely, to the amazement of the prefect, 'You will all be taken there at my expense.' A rapturous sigh from the delegation. 'And tomorrow I shall join you and examine in detail each suit. If I find any of you has been injured, I shall know what to do.' There was a pleased response, and I slipped out of the room.

The Master of the Offices was distressed. 'But tomorrow is impossible! And the treasury is here, not there.'

'Get the whole lot of them to Chalcedon. Then tell the boatmen that no Egyptian is to be brought back to the city.'

For the first time I felt that I had earned the respect of the Master of the Offices. The Egyptians stayed at Chalcedon a month, annoying the local officials. Then they went home.

Priscus: You will note that though Julian referred some while back to the treason trials at Chalcedon and promised to discuss them, he never mentions the subject again. Of course he did not have the chance to go over any of these notes, but I am not sure that even if he had caught the omission he would have been at all candid. The whole business was shameful, and he knew it.

Arbetio arrested a dozen of Constantius's high officials. They were all friends of Arbetio, but that did not prevent him from charging each with high treason. Why? Because any one of these officers of state might have compromised him. Arbetio wanted to be emperor; he had tried to persuade Eusebius to recognize him as Constantius's heir. As a result, he was now a man with a purpose; the covering of his own tracks.

Although Salutius Secundus was officially president of the court, Arbetio was in charge. He was a tiger among sheep. Palladius, a blameless official who had been chief marshal to the court, was charged with having conspired against Gallus; on no evidence at all, Palladius was exiled to Britain along with Florentius (a chamberlain, not our friend from Gaul). Also exiled – again on no evidence – were Evagrius (former Count of the Privy Purse), Saturninus (former Steward of the Sacred Household), Cyrinus (a private secretary). Even more shocking was the exile of the consul Taurus, whose only fault was that he had joined his rightful lord Constantius when Julian marched into Illyricum. Public opinion was particularly scandalized to read a proclamation which began, 'In the year of the consulate of Taurus and Florentius, Taurus was found guilty of treason.' That sort of thing is not done, except by the most reckless of tyrants.

The praetorian prefect Florentius was condemned to death, properly, I think. He did indeed try to destroy Julian, though if one wanted to be absolutely just (and who does in political matters?), he acted only upon Constantius's orders. Fortunately for him, his trial was conducted *in absentia*. He had wisely disappeared the day Constantius died and he did not reappear until some months after Julian's death. He lived to a great age and died at Milan, rich and contented. Some live to be old; some are struck down too soon. Julian of course would have said it was inexorable Fate, but I know better. It is nothing, absolutely nothing. There is no design to any of it.

Paul 'the chain', Mercurius 'the count of dreams' and Gaudentius were all put to death, as was proper. Eusebius also was executed, and his vast property reverted to the crown from which he had stolen it.

Then the outrage occurred. Of all the public men in our timorous time, Ursulus alone had the courage always to say what he thought was right, despite consequences. He understood Arbetio perfectly. He deplored the trials. He said so. To everyone's amazement, Arbetio had Ursulus arrested.

The trial was an abomination. I am told by those who were present that Ursulus tongue-lashed Arbetio, mocked his ambition, dared the court to find him either disloyal to Julian or in any way connected with Gallus's death. I say that I was 'told' this because I was not able to read about it: the records of the trial have vanished. But I *was* able to talk frankly to Mamertinus, who had been a horrified witness of this grim farce. He told me what happened, making no excuse for himself. Like all the rest, including Julian, he was led by the wilful Arbetio, and must share in the guilt.

Forged testimony was prepared against Ursulus, but the forgeries were so clumsy that he was able to have them thrown out as evidence. At this point even Arbetio might have given up, but he had one last weapon in reserve. The trial was a military one, held in the camp of two legions. Now Ursulus was supremely unpopular with the army because of the bitter remark he made when, surveying the ruins of Amida, he said, 'See how bravely our citizens are protected by those soldiers, whose pay is bankrupting us!'

Suddenly Arbetio threw this quotation in Ursulus's face. Immediately the officers and men who were present at the trial made a loud racket, demanding Ursulus's head. They got it. He was executed within the hour.

This was the talk of the city when I arrived in January. I questioned Julian about the trial; he was evasive. 'I didn't know what was happening. I put the whole thing in Salutius's hands. I was as surprised as anyone.'

'But they acted in your name . . .'

'Every village notary acts in my name. Am I responsible for all injustice?'

'But surely you had to give permission for the execution. Under Roman law . . .'

'The military court acted on its own initiative. I didn't know.'

'Then every member of the court was guilty of treason for using your power of life and death illegally.'

'The court was not illegal. They were duly constituted by imperial edict . . .'

'Then they *must* have informed you before the execution and if they did . . .'

'*I did not know!*' Julian was furious. I never mentioned the subject again. But when we were in Persia he brought up the matter, on his own. We had been talking about the idea of justice when suddenly Julian said, 'The hardest thing I ever did was to allow a court to condemn an innocent man.'

'Ursulus?'

He nodded. He had quite forgotten he had once told me that he had known nothing of the Chalcedon proceedings. 'The army wanted him dead. There was nothing I could do. When the court found him guilty of high treason – even though he was innocent – I had to let the sentence stand.'

'To appease the army? or Arbetio?'

'Both. I was not sure of myself then. I needed every bit of support I could get. But if the trial were today, I would free Ursulus and indict Arbetio.'

'But yesterday is not today, and Ursulus is dead.'

'I'm sorry,' said Julian, and that was the end of that chapter. It is one of the few instances I know where Julian was weak and in his weakness bad. But how might *we* have acted in his place? Differently? I think not. One good thing: Julian did not confiscate Ursulus's estate as law requires in the case of a traitor. The property all went to the dead man's daughter.

Libanius: Priscus seems unduly sentimental in this matter. As he himself admits, he did not study the transcript of the trial, so how could he know what sort of evidence was presented against Ursulus? Unlike Priscus, I should never predict my own behaviour in any circumstance until I knew precisely what the given facts were. Is not all conduct based on this sort of empiricism? or have I misled three generations of pupils?

Julian Augustus

I had heard all my life about what went on in the eunuchs' quarters of the Sacred Palace. But I tend to discount gossip, having been myself the subject of so much, most of it fantastic. I confess I did not really want any rumours confirmed, but Oribasius insisted that we see for ourselves. So I got myself up in a hooded robe while Oribasius disguised himself as a Syrian merchant with oiled ringlets and glossy false beard.

Shortly before midnight, we left my apartment, by way of a private staircase. Outside the palace we found ourselves in a small courtyard, bright with moonlight. Like shadowy conspirators, we crossed to the opposite wing of the palace where the eunuchs and minor officials lived. We slipped inside the portico. At the third door from the south, Oribasius stopped, and rapped three times. A muffled voice said, 'What is the time?'

'The time is ours,' said Oribasius. This was the correct password. The door opened just wide enough for us to enter. A dwarf greeted us and pointed to the dimly lit stairs. 'They're just starting.'

Oribasius gave him a coin. On the second-floor gallery deaf-mute slaves showed us into what had been Eusebius's dining hall. It was almost as splendid as my own! Against the walls of the room some fifty eunuchs reclined on couches. They were so gorgeously dressed that they looked like bales of silk on display. In front of each couch a table was set, piled with food. Even for an evening of what (in my innocence) I took to be music, the eunuchs needed their food.

At one end of the room there were chairs and benches for what were known as 'friends of the court'. Here sat a number of Scholarian officers, drinking heavily. I was completely mystified but dared not speak for fear someone would recognize my voice. As Mardonius – that *good* eunuch – used to say: 'Julian has no lyre, only a brazen trumpet.'

We sat down in the front row, next to a centurion of the Herculani. He was already quite drunk. He nudged me in the ribs. 'Don't look so gloomy! And take that hood off, makes you look like a dirty Christ-y!' This was considered high wit, and there was a good deal of laughter at my expense. But the glib Oribasius rescued me. 'Poor fellow's from the country, doesn't dare show his patched tunic.' Oribasius's accent was pure Antioch. I was most impressed.

'He part of the show?' The centurion pushed his face close to mine, his breath like the last dregs from a skin of wine. I pulled back, hand to my hood.

'No,' said Oribasius. 'A friend of Phalaris.' This impressed the centurion, who left me alone. Oribasius whispered in my ear. 'Phalaris is our host. He's there. In the centre.' Phalaris was large and sullen, with a pursed mouth. I knew that I had seen him before, but I could not place him. Oribasius explained. 'He's in charge of the kitchen. Which makes him – now that Eusebius is dead – the richest man at court.'

I sighed. The emperor is hugely robbed by his servants.

Cymbals were struck. A long line of Scholarians filed into the room. They halted before Phalaris and gave him a parody of the imperial salute. I started angrily to my feet, but Oribasius held me back. With a gesture quite as majestic as any of Constantius's, Phalaris acknowledged the salute. The soldiers then took their places against the wall and, at a signal from their leader, they sang a love song! But there was worse to come.

Fifty shabbily dressed youths entered the hall. They moved awkwardly and seemed not to know what to do until a Scholarian shoved one of them to his knees in front of Phalaris; all followed suit. The eunuch then motioned for them to sit on the floor directly in front of us. I was completely baffled. These youths were obviously not entertainers. They looked like ordinary workmen of the sort one sees in every city, hanging about the arcades, eyeing women.

Next, the same number of young girls were herded into the room. All around me the 'friends of the court' breathed satisfaction. The girls were uncommonly pretty, and terrified. After a slow tour of the hall, they were ordered to sit on the floor beside the young men. They too wore ordinary clothes, which meant that they were neither prostitutes nor entertainers. I saw that the eunuchs were studying the girls with almost as much interest as were the men about me. I thought this surprising, but Oribasius assures me that the desire for women remains cruelly strong in eunuchs, especially in those gelded after puberty. Incapacity does not prevent lust.

Musicians appeared and played while a troupe of Syrian cotylists danced. I suppose they were good. They moved violently, made astonishing leaps in the air, did lewd things with the cups which are a part of their 'art'. While all eyes watched them, I tapped the shoulder of the boy who sat just in front of me. He gave a nervous start, and turned around, pale with fright. He had the fair skin and grey eyes of Macedonia. His hands were large and callused, the nails black with soot. I took him to be a metal-worker's apprentice, at the most eighteen years old.

'Sir?' His light voice cracked with tension.

'Why are you here?'

'I don't know, sir.'

'But how did you get here?'

'They . . .' He motioned to the Scholarians. 'I was coming home from the silver market, where I work, and they stopped me and made me go with them.'

'Did they tell you why?'

'No, sir. They won't kill us, will they?' There is no terror to equal that of the ignorant in a strange place.

'No,' I said firmly. 'They won't hurt you.'

The Syrian dancers were followed by what looked to be priestesses of the Egyptian cult of Syra. Though I recognized many of the ritual gestures, I suspect that these women were not actually priestesses but prostitutes, imitating the sacred erotic dances. It was, after all, a night of travesty. Every stage of the mysteries was acted out, including the ceremony of abundance with its wooden phalluses. This last brought loud applause from the 'friends of the court', and ecstatic sighs and giggles from the eunuchs. Though the cult of Syra does not much appeal to me, I was offended to see its mysteries profaned.

After the 'priestesses' had finished their dance, several burly Scholarians motioned for the girls and youths to parade in pairs before the reclining eunuchs, much the way young people stroll on feast days in provincial towns. For some minutes they moved, tense, self-conscious, trapped. Then Phalaris motioned for a particular girl and youth to approach him. This was a signal for the other eunuchs to choose pairs. They did so, hissing like angry geese.

Suddenly Phalaris reached up and tore the girl's dress at the shoulder; it fell to her knees. Those about me gasped with excitement. I was too stunned to move. When the girl tried to pull her dress back in place, Phalaris tugged at it again and this time the cheap material split and came away in his hand. Like a sacrifice, she stood, naked, arms crossed on her breast. Phalaris then turned to the boy and lifted up his tunic as far as the belly. Loud laughter; the youth wore nothing underneath. Phalaris then pulled both girl and boy, the one pale and the other red with embarrassment, on to the couch, his fat arms girdling each.

Meanwhile, the other eunuchs had stripped their terrified prey. None resisted, although one young man, inadvertently shying from a eunuch's grasp, was cracked hard across the buttocks by the flat of a Scholarian's sword. The rest submitted.

As I watched, I had the sense of having witnessed something similar. This monstrous scene contained a bafflingly familiar element. Not until days later did

I recall what it was: children opening presents. The eunuchs were like greedy children. They tore the clothes off their victims in the same way children tear wrappings from a gift, passionately eager to see what is inside. Stubby eunuch fingers explored the strange bodies as though they were toys; they were particularly fascinated by the sex, male and female. Imagine fifty huge babies allowed people for playthings and one can begin to apprehend what I saw that night.

I might have sat there for ever, turned to astonished stone, if I had not noticed the boy I had talked to earlier. He was stretched across a eunuch's lap while a frightened girl poured dippers of honey over his belly, the eunuch fondling him all the while, preparatory to heaven alone knew what vice. That was enough.

I had got as far as the centre of the room when one of the Scholarians grabbed me roughly by the shoulder. The hood fell back from my head. One look at my face was enough. The music stopped, instrument by instrument. No one moved. No one spoke. Only the young people stared at me dumbly and without interest. I motioned to a tribune who sat on the first row. He was the highest-ranking officer present. Trembling, he saluted me. I indicated the boys and girls and in a low voice that only he could hear, I said, 'Send them home.' Then I pointed to Phalaris. 'Arrest the eunuchs. Confine all Scholarians present to barracks.' In a silence as complete as any I have ever heard, Oribasius and I left the banquet hall.

Oribasius feels that I took the entire thing too seriously because I am celibate. But that is not the reason. It is the basis of a lawful society that no man (much less half-man) has the power to subject another citizen to his will. If the young people had been voluntary prostitutes, I would have forgiven the eunuchs. But what was done that night – and many other nights, I discovered – was lawless and cruel.

Priscus: Julian often used to talk about that night in the eunuchs' quarters. He was naïve to be so upset. Palace eunuchs are distressing in their habits and what he saw was hardly a revelation. Naturally, it is not pleasant to think of such things going on in the Sacred Palace, but then there are perhaps twenty thousand people associated with the court, which makes the palace a world in itself, and like the world. But nothing could stop Julian when he had made up his mind. He sacked the lot and as a result, life in the palace was quite unbearable. For one thing, no one knew where anything was. Every day search parties were sent out to explore the cellars and attics, and of course a number of new scandals came to light, including a sizeable counterfeiters' mint which had been set up in the cellar of the Daphne Palace by several enterprising Scholarians.

There were certain aspects of life which Julian never faced if he could help it. The sexual impulse was one. He pretended to be shocked at the way the eunuchs commandeered ordinary citizens for their pleasure. Of course this is a bad thing, contrary to the laws and customs of a decent society. It should not be allowed. Naturally. But is it *astonishing*? Julian writes – and used to talk – as though the evil he had witnessed was some sort of unparalleled horror, which it was not.

I finally asked him if he had any idea what his own armies did in the German and Frankish villages. Wasn't he aware that no man, woman or child was safe from their lust? Julian responded vaguely, deploring the brutality of war in general. But I pressed him until he admitted that though he had *heard* of such things happening (I know of at least a dozen cases of rape he was forced personally to punish), he had always accepted them as a concomitant of war. Though this was disingenuous, Julian was often surprisingly innocent. His celibacy after Helena's death was not a pose, as so many (including myself) suspected at the time. He was quite genuine in his mortification of the flesh, which explained his dislike of being touched and his avoidance of any place where the human body was revealed, particularly public baths.

I think what most distressed him about the behaviour of the eunuchs was the knowledge that not only had he the power to do the same but that he *wanted* to. This recognition of his own nature horrified him. Note that as he lingers over the scene, what most strikes him is not so much the demonstration of lust but the power to do what one likes with another, and that other not a slave but free. Our Julian – like all of us – had a touch of Tiberius in him, and he hated it.

For twenty years now I have been haunted by one detail, the pouring of honey on the genitals of the smith's apprentice. What exactly *was* the eunuch's plan? What was the girl supposed to do? And why honey? I have theories of course, but I shall never know for certain since Julian ended the party much too soon. I am confident of one thing: the eunuch was a cook and accustomed to basting game birds with honey. He was obviously reverting to habit.

Libanius: The lechery of Priscus is an unexpected development of his senescence. I am not aware of any 'touch of Tiberius' in myself, rather the contrary.

17

Julian Augustus

Constantius seldom addressed the senate for the excellent reason that he could not speak for any length of time without stammering or making some error in logic or grammar. As a result, he almost never set foot in the senate house. He preferred to summon the senate to the throneroom in the Daphne Palace where he could address them informally, on those rare occasions when he dealt with them at all.

I returned to the old ways, imitating Augustus, who was content to be first citizen. On 1 January I walked across the square to attend the senate merely as a member. The conscript fathers affected to be pleased by my gesture, and for the remaining months that I was in the city I often attended their sessions. I don't need to add that whenever I did, I always spoke!

It is customary for new consuls taking office to sponsor games and entertainments. Mamertinus gave us three days of chariot races in the Hippodrome which I attended as a courtesy to him. I found the races interminable but I enjoyed the crowds. They always greeted me with an ear-splitting roar, and I was told that not once in twenty-five years had Constantius evoked such an affectionate response. Since several people told me this perhaps it is true and not mere flattery.

While attending the first day's races, I examined with some interest the various works of art Constantius had placed along the centre of the track: obelisks, columns, bronze memorials. One of them is particularly beautiful:

three bronze snakes intertwine to form a tall column upon which a golden tripod supports a golden bowl dedicated by the Greeks to Apollo at Delphi as a thanksgiving for their victory over Persia. Constantine stole even the holiest of relics to decorate his city. One day I shall send them all back to their original homes. But thinking of Delphi gave me an idea. I turned to Oribasius. 'We should consult the oracle.'

'Which oracle?' Oribasius maintains that between soothsayers, oracles and sacrifices, I have terrified the future into submission.

'Delphi. The only oracle.'

'Does it still exist?'

'Find out.'

Oribasius laughed. 'Shall I go now, before the games are over?'

'No. But you want to visit Greece anyway. If you do, visit the oracle and consult the Pythoness.'

So it was agreed. We were wondering what form my question to the oracle should take, when a number of slaves were brought forward to receive their freedom. This is an ancient custom, to celebrate the new year and the accession of new consuls. The slaves lined up before the imperial box and I eagerly said the legal formula which made them free. There was a startled gasp from the crowd. I was bewildered. Mamertinus who sat on my right was much amused. 'Augustus, the consul is supposed to free the slaves, just as the consul gives the games.' Greatly embarrassed, I shouted to the people, 'I hereby fine myself ten pounds of gold for usurping the consul's function!' This was received with much laughter and cheering, and I think it made a good impression.

On 4 February 362 I declared religious freedom in the world. Anyone could worship any god in any way he chose. The cult of the Galileans was no longer the state's religion, nor were Galilean priests exempt from paying taxes and the usual municipal duties. I also recalled all the bishops who had been sent into exile by Constantius. I even allowed the terrible Athanasius to return to Alexandria, though I did not mean for him to be bishop again. Among those who returned from exile was Aetius, who had given a good report of me to Gallus. I shall always be grateful to him.

Soon after I had taken possession of the capital, I was faced with a most disagreeable crisis. My old teacher Bishop George had finally succeeded Athanasius as bishop of Alexandria. Not surprisingly, George proved to be an unpopular prelate. He was high-handed and arbitrary with everyone. Matters came to a head when he destroyed a Mithraeum, saying that he intended to build a charnel house on its foundation. When our brothers rightfully protested this sacrilege, he retaliated by displaying all sorts of human skulls and bones as well as obscene objects, declaring falsely that he had found these 'proofs' of human sacrifice buried in the Mithraeum. It was an ugly business.

George also incurred the wrath of the Athanasians by his single-minded persecution of all those who had followed the teachings of the bishop. The Alexandrians could not endure him. When word finally came that his protector Constantius was dead, the mob stormed the bishop's palace and murdered George; his body was then tied to a camel and dragged through the city to the beach, where it was burned and the ashes thrown into the sea. This happened on 24 December. When I heard about it, I wrote the people of the city a harsh letter, threatening reprisals. Their officials were most apologetic and promised to keep the peace. Not long after, Athanasius appeared in the city with a great mob of fanatics and resumed his old place as bishop. Almost his first gesture was to 'baptize' the wife of my governor. This was too much. I banished Athanasius, making it clear that a return from exile did not mean a return to power for deposed bishops, especially those who are resourceful enemies of Hellenism.

At about this time I acquired George's library, easily one of the best in Asia. I am rather sentimental about that library, for his were the actual books which had shaped my own mind. I am travelling at this moment with George's set of Plotinus. The rest of the books I left at Constantinople as a nucleus for the Julian library.

The Edict of 4 February had a good effect, though there was much complaint from the Arian bishops, who felt that by allowing their Athanasian brethren to return, I was ensuring doctrinal quarrels which would inevitably weaken the Galilean organization. Exactly! They are now at one another's throats. I have also insisted that all lands and buildings which over the years the Galileans seized from us be restored. I realize that this will cause some hardship, but there is no other way of getting the thing done. I am quite prepared for trouble.

On 22 February I issued another edict, reserving to myself alone the right to use the public transport. The bishops, hurrying here and there at the state's expense, had wrecked the system. *Note:* At this point list all edicts for the year, as well as government appointments. They are of course on permanent file at the Record Office, but even so one must be thorough. Meanwhile, I want only to touch on the high points of those six months in Constantinople.

Late in February I learned, quite by accident, that Vettius Agorius Praetextatus and his wife were in the city. He is the leader of the Hellenist party at Rome while his wife, Aconia Paulina, has been admitted to every mystery available to women as well as being high priestess of Hecate. I was eager to meet them.

Praetextatus is a slight, frail man, with flowing white hair and delicate small features. His wife is somewhat taller than her husband and as red-faced and robust as a Gaul, though she is of the purest Roman stock. They are most enthusiastic at what I am doing, particularly Aconia Paulina. 'We have had a remarkable response at our temple of Hecate. Truly remarkable. And all due to you. Why, last year in Rome we could hardly get anyone to undergo initiation but now . . . well, I have received reports from Milan, Alexandria, Athens . . . *everywhere*, that the women are flocking to us! We are second only to Isis in enrolment, and though I am devoted to the Isis cult (in fact, I am an initiate, second degree), I think Hecate has always drawn a better class of women. I only hope we shall be able to open a temple right here.'

'You shall! You shall!' I was delighted. 'I want every god represented in the capital!'

Aconia Pauline beamed. Praetextatus smiled gravely. 'Every day,' he said softly, 'every waking hour, we pray for your success.'

For at least an hour the three of us celebrated that unity which only those who have been initiated into the mysteries can know. We were as one. Then I got down to business.

'If we are to defeat the Galileans we must, very simply, have a comparable organization.'

Praetextatus was dubious. 'We have often discussed this at Rome, and until recently we thought we were at least holding our own. At heart, Rome is anti-Christian. The senate is certainly Hellenist.' He paused and looked out of the window, as though searching for Zeus himself in the rain clouds rolling in from the sea. 'You see, Augustus, we are not one organization like the Galileans. We are many. Also, we are voluntary. We do not have the support of the government . . .'

'You do now.'

'. . . *now*, yes, but is now too late? Also, our appeal is essentially to the individual, at least in the mysteries. Each man who is initiated undergoes the experience *alone*. At Eleusis it is the single soul which confronts eternity.'

'But there is also the sense of fellowship with other initiates! Look at us! You and I are brothers in Mithras . . .'

'That is not the same thing as belonging to an open congregation, our conduct governed by priests who are quite as interested in property and political power as they are in religion.'

'I agree.' I tapped the papers in front of me. 'And I suggest we fight them on their own ground. I plan a world priesthood, governed by the Roman Pontifex Maximus. We shall divide the world into administrative units, the way the Galileans have done – and each diocese will have its own hierarchy of priests under a single high priest, responsible to me.'

They were impressed. Aconia Paulina wanted to know if *all* cults would be represented in the priesthood. I said yes. Every god and goddess known to the people, no matter in what guise or under what strange name, would be worshipped, for multiplicity is the nature of life. We all believe – even the Galileans, despite their confused doctrine of trinity – that there is a single Godhead from which all life, divine and mortal, descends and to which all life must return. We may not know this creator, though his outward symbol is the sun. But through intermediaries, human and divine, he speaks to us, shows us aspects of himself, prepares us for the next stage of the journey. 'To find the father and maker of all is hard,' as Socrates said. 'And having found him it is impossible to utter him.' Yet as Aeschylus wrote with equal wisdom, 'men search out god and *searching* find him.' The search is the whole point to philosophy and to the religious experience. It is a part of the Galilean impiety to proclaim that the search ended three hundred years ago when a young rabbi was executed for treason. But according to Paul of Tarsus, Jesus was no ordinary rabbi nor even messiah; he was the One God himself who rose from the dead in order to judge the world *immediately*. In fact, Jesus is quoted as having assured his followers that some of them would still be alive when the day of judging arrived. But one by one the disciples died in the natural course and we are still waiting for that promised day. Meanwhile, the bishops amass property, persecute one another, and otherwise revel in this life, while the state is weakened and on our borders the barbarians gather like winter wolves, waiting for us to stagger in our weakness, and to fall. I see this as plainly as I see my hand as it crosses the page (for this part I do not entrust to any secretary). To stop the chariot as it careers into the sun, *that* is what I was born to do.

I explained my plans to Praetextatus. Some I have already put into effect. Others must wait until I return from Persia.

The failure of Hellenism has been, largely, a matter of organization. Rome never tried to impose any sort of worship upon the countries it conquered and civilized; in fact, quite the contrary. Rome was eclectic. All religions were given an equal opportunity and even Isis – after some resistance – was worshipped at Rome. As a result we have a hundred important gods and a dozen mysteries. Certain rites are – or were – supported by the state because they involved the genius of Rome. But no attempt was ever made to co-ordinate the worship of Zeus on the Capitol with, let us say, the Vestals who kept the sacred fire in the old forum. As time passed our rites became, and one must admit it bluntly, merely form, a reassuring reminder of the great age of the city, a token gesture to the old gods who were thought to have founded and guided Rome from a village by the Tiber to world empire. Yet from the beginning, there were always those who mocked. A senator of the old Republic once asked an augur how he was able to get through a ceremony of divination without laughing. I am not so light-minded, though I concede that many of our rites have lost their meaning over the centuries; witness those temples at Rome where certain verses learned by rote are chanted year in and year out, yet no one, including the priests, knows what they mean, for they are in the early language of the Etruscans, long since forgotten.

As the religious forms of the state became more and more rigid and per-functory, the people were drawn to the mystery cults, many of them Asiatic in origin. At Eleusis or in the various caves of Mithras, they were able to get a vision of what this life can be, as well as a foretaste of the one that follows. There are, then, three sorts of religious experiences. The ancient rites, which are essentially propitiatory. The mysteries, which purge the soul and allow us to glimpse eternity. And philosophy, which attempts to define not only the mat-erial world but to suggest practical ways to the good life, as well as attempting to synthesize (as Iamblichos does so beautifully) all true religion in a single comprehensive system.

Now into this most satisfactory – at least potentially – of worlds, came the Galileans. They base *their* religion on the idea of a single god, as though that were a novelty: from Homer to Julian, Hellenes have been monotheist. Now this single god, according to the largest of the Galilean sects, sent his son (conceived of a virgin, like so many other Asiatic gods) to preach to the world, to suffer, to rise from the dead, to judge mankind on a day which was supposed to have dawned more than three hundred years ago. Now I have studied as carefully as any bishop the writings of those who knew the Galilean, or said they did. They are composed in bad Greek, which I should have thought would have been enough to put off any educated man, while the story they tell is confused, to say the least (following Porphyry I have discovered some sixty-four palpable con-tradictions and absurdities).

The actual life story of the Galilean has vanished. But I have had an interest-ing time trying to piece it together. Until thirty years ago, the archives of Rome contained a number of contemporary reports on his life. They have since disappeared, destroyed by order of Constantine. It is of course an old and bitter joke that the Nazarene himself was not a Christian. He was something quite else. I have talked to antiquarians who knew about the file in the archives; several had either read it or knew people who had. Jesus was, simply, a reforming Jewish priest, exclusive as the Jews are, with no interest in proselytizing outside the small world of the Jews. His troubles with Rome were not religious (when did Rome ever persecute anyone for religious belief?) but political. This Jesus thought he was the messiah. Now the messiah is a sort of Jewish hero who, according to legend, will one day establish a Jewish empire prior to the end of the world. He is certainly *not* a god, much less the One God's son. The messiah has been the subject of many Jewish prophecies, and Jesus carefully acted out each prophetic requirement in order to make himself resemble this hero (the messiah would enter Jerusalem on an ass; so did he, et cetera). But the thing went wrong. The people did not support him. His god forsook him. He turned to violence. With a large band of rebels, he seized the temple, announcing that he had come with a sword. What his God would not do for him he must do for himself. So at the end he was neither a god nor even the Jewish messiah but a rebel who tried to make himself king of the Jews. Quite correctly, our governor executed him.

We must never forget that *in his own words,* Jesus was a Jew who believed in the Law of Moses. This means he could not be the son of God (the purest sort of blasphemy), much less God himself, temporarily earthbound. There is nothing in the book of the Jews which prepares us for a messiah's kinship with Jehovah. Only by continual reinterpretation and convenient 'revelations' have the Galileans been able to change this reformer-rabbi's career into a parody of one of our own gods, creating a passion of death and rebirth quite inconceivable to one who kept the Law of Moses . . . not to mention disgusting to us who have worshipped not men who were executed in time but symbolic figures like Mithras and Osiris and Adonis whose *literal* existence does not matter but whose mysterious legend and revelation are everything.

The moral preachings of the Galilean, though often incoherently recorded, are beyond criticism. He preaches honesty, sobriety, goodness, and a kind of asceticism. In other words, he was a quite ordinary Jewish rabbi, with Pharisee tendencies. In a crude way he resembles Marcus Aurelius. Compared to Plato or Aristotle, he is a child.

It is the wonder of our age how this simple-minded provincial priest was so extraordinarily transformed into a god by Paul of Tarsus, who outdid all quacks and cheats that ever existed anywhere. As Porphyry wrote so sharply in the last century, 'The gods have declared Christ to have been most pious; he has become immortal and by them his memory is cherished. Whereas, the Christians are a polluted set, contaminated and enmeshed in error.' It is even worse now. By the time Constantine, Constantius and the horde of bishops got through with Jesus, little of his original message was left. Every time they hold a synod they move further away from the man's original teaching. The conception of the triple god is their latest masterpiece.

One reason why the Galileans grow ever more powerful and dangerous to us is their continual assimilation of our rites and holy days. Since they rightly regard Mithraism as their chief rival, they have for some years now been taking over various aspects of the Mithraic rite and incorporating them into their own ceremonies. Some critics believe that the gradual absorption of our forms and prayers is fairly recent. But I date it from the very beginning. In at least one of the biographies of the Galileans there is a strange anecdote which his followers are never able to explain (and they are usually nothing if not ingenious at making sense of nonsense). The Galilean goes to a fig tree to pick its fruit. But as it is not the season for bearing, the tree was barren. In a fit of temper, the Galilean blasts the tree with magic, killing it. Now the fig tree is sacred to Mithras: as a youth, it was his home, his source of food and clothing. I suggest that the apologist who wrote that passage in the first century did so deliberately, inventing it or recording it, no matter which, as a sign that the Galilean would destroy the worship of Mithras as easily as he had destroyed the sacred tree.

But I do not mean here in the pages of what is supposed to be a chronicle to give my familiar arguments against the Galileans. They may be found in the several essays I have published on the subject.

Praetextatus and I worked closely together all that winter in Constantinople.

I found both him and his wife enormously knowledgeable on religious matters. But whenever I spoke of practical matters, Praetextatus would lose interest. So quite alone, I set about reorganizing ... no, organizing Hellenism. The Galileans have received much credit for giving charity to anyone who asks for it. We are now doing the same. Their priests impress the ignorant with their so-called holy lives. I now insist that our priests be *truly* holy. I have given them full instructions on how to comport themselves in public and private. Though Praetextatus lacked inspiration, he worked diligently with me on these plans. But Aconia was no help at all. She does not, as the saying goes, grow on one. I am afraid that her only interest is her own salvation. She regards religion as a sort of lottery, and if she takes a chance on each of the gods, the law of averages ought to favour her to pick the right one who will save her soul. Though what eternity would want with Aconia Paulina, I don't know.

Priscus: Bravo Julian!

Though Julian makes no mention of it, at about this time our old friend Maximus made his triumphant entry into Constantinople. I was not there when he arrived, but I certainly heard enough about it. When he became emperor, Julian invited every philosopher and magician in the empire to court. And just about all of them came. Only his Christian 'friends' stayed away. Basil was being holy in Cappadocia; I don't think Gregory was invited. It might be interesting the check the Record Office about Gregory because I seem to recall a most flattering letter he wrote Julian at about this time, but perhaps I dreamed it . . . Only last week I called Hippia by my mother's name, after half a century of marriage! I am of course losing my mind. But why not? When death comes, it will have nothing to take but a withered sack of bones, for the memory of Priscus, which is Priscus, will long since have flown.

Several times, Julian tried to get Maximus to leave Ephesus and come to Gaul, but the omens were never right. I'm sure they weren't! Maximus was not about to ally himself to what most people though would be the losing side of a rebellion. But when an invitation finally came from the Sacred Palace, Maximus was ready. He arrived in Constantinople while Julian was at the senate house. Incidentally, Julian was in his element with that body, though I'm not sure they enjoyed him as much as he did them. The senate usually cannot master a quorum. But with an emperor present, the senate chamber threatened to burst. The conscript fathers sat on one another's laps while Julian joked, prayed, exhorted and, all in all, got quite a lot of work done, for there was nothing which he did not concern himself with.

During the six months he was at Constantinople, Julian built a harbour at the foot of the palace. He exempted all men with thirteen children or more from paying taxes: he was much concerned at our declining birthrate. I can't think why. It is not as if there were not too many people on earth as it is and to make more of them will simply dilute the breed. But he was disturbed by the fact that the barbarians increase in numbers while we decrease. He also confirmed our old friend Sallust as praetorian prefect of Gaul, though he clearly would have liked to have him close by. He made this personal sacrifice because there was no one else he could trust to protect the West, and he was right, as each year confirms. Today Gaul is still secure while the Goths are now just a few days' march from this house in Athens where I sit, writing of old things, and re-membering more than I thought.

Julian was in the middle of an impassioned speech when Maximus appeared in the door of the senate chamber. The great 'philosopher' was dressed in green silk robes covered with cabalistic designs; his long grey beard was perfumed and his shaggy eyebrows were carefully combed – I've actually seen him comb them to give the effect of two perfect arches. He carried his magic staff carved from dragon's bone, or some such nonsense. The senators were shocked, for no one but a senator may enter during session; certainly, no one may enter when the emperor is speaking. But Julian, seeing Maximus, stopped in mid-sentence and ran, arms outstretched, to embrace that old charlatan. I'm glad I was not there.

Julian then presented Maximus to the senate, calling him the world's wisest and holiest man and stressing what an honour it was for all present to do homage to such a man. Needless to say, everyone was scandalized. Maximus and his wife were given an entire wing of the Sacred Palace for their own court; and there were now two emperors in Constantinople. Maximus's wife did a considerable business on her own as a sort of unofficial Master of the Offices, arranging audiences with the Emperor and granting petitions. They made a fortune in those months. They were a rare couple.

Though I am not in the habit of laughing at anyone's death, I still chuckle to myself when I think of *her* death. Do you know the story? After the Persian campaign when Maximus was first in trouble, he decided to commit suicide. His wife agreed that this was the correct thing to do. She also insisted on killing herself. With her usual brisk efficiency, she put their affairs in order; bought poison and composed farewell letters of enormous length. Then, gravely, they said good-bye to one another. She drank first and promptly died. Maximus lost his nerve, and survived. To this day I find myself smiling whenever I think of that preposterous couple.

Julian Augustus

At the beginning of April, for my own amusement, I summoned the bishops to the palace. After all, I am Pontifex Maximus and all religion is my province, though I would not have the temerity to say to any priests what Constantius said to the bishops at the synod of Milan in 355: 'My will shall be your guiding line!'

I received the Galileans in the Daphne Palace. I wore the diadem and I held the orb. (Galileans are always impressed by the ritual show of power.) It was a remarkable occasion. Nearly a thousand bishops were present, including those whom I had recalled from exile. As a result, there are often two bishops for one see. This makes for much bitter wrangling. They are not gentle, these priests of the Nazarene.

At first the bishops were afraid of me, but I put them at their ease. I told them that I was not a persecutor, though others before me had been, not all of them emperors. This was directed at several militant bishops who had, by violence, destroyed their enemies.

'No one,' I said, 'shall ever be hurt by me because of his faith.' There was a general easing of tension. But they were still wary. 'Of course I should like to convince you that I am right. But since what is true is as plain as the sun, if you will not see it, you will not see it. But I cannot allow you to hurt others, as you have done for so many years. I will not list the crimes you have committed, or permitted. The murders, the thieving, the viciousness more usual to the beasts of the field than to priests, even of the wrong god.'

I held up a thick sheaf of documents. 'Here are your latest crimes. Murders requested, and property requested . . . oh, how you love the riches of this world! Yet your religion preaches that you should not resist injury or go to law or even hold property, much less steal it! You have been taught to consider nothing your own, except your place in the other and better world. Yet you wear jewels, rich robes, build huge basilicas, all in *this* world, not the next. You were taught to despise money, yet you amass it. When done an injury, real or imagined, you were told not to retaliate, that it is wrong to return evil for evil. Yet you battle with one another in lawless mobs, torturing and killing those you disapprove of. You have endangered not only the true religion but the security of the state whose chief magistrate I am, by heaven's will. You are not worthy even of the Nazarene. If you cannot live by those precepts which you are willing to defend with the knife and with poison' (a reference to the poisoning of Arius by Athanasius), 'what *are* you then but hypocrites?'

All through this there had been mumbling. Now there was a fine Galilean eruption. They began to shout and rant, shaking their fists not only at me – which is treason – but at one another – which is folly, for they ought to be united against the common enemy. I tried to speak but I could not be heard, and *my* voice can be heard by an entire army out-of-doors. The tribune of the Scholarians look alarmed, but I motioned to him to do nothing.

Finally, like the bull of Mithras, I bellowed, 'The Franks and the Germans listened when I spoke!' This had a quieting effect. They remembered where they were.

I was then all mildness. I apologized for having spoken harshly. It was only because I had such respect for the words of the Nazarene, as well as for the strict law of the Jews which he – as a Jew – sought only to extol. This caused a slight but brief murmur. I then said that I was willing to give the Nazrene a place among the gods between Isis and Dionysos, but that no man who had the slightest reverence for the unique creator of the universe could possibly conceive that this provincial wonder-worker could have been the creator himself. Before they could start their monkey-chatter, I spoke quickly and loudly, 'Yet I am willing to believe he is a manifestation of the One, a healer, much like Asklepios, and as such, I am willing to honour him.'

I then repeated what I had written in the Edict of 4 February. There was to be universal toleration. The Galileans could do as they pleased among their own kind though they were not to persecute each other, much less Hellenists. I suggested that they be less greedy in the acquiring of property. I admitted that I was causing them hardship when I asked for the return of temple lands, but I pointed out that they had done *us* considerable hardship when they had stolen them. I suggested that if they were less contemptuous of our ancient myths – Kronos swallowing his children – we might be less rude about their triple god and his virgin-birth.

'After all, as educated men, we should realize that myths always stand for other things. They are toys for children teething. The man knows that the toy horse is not a true horse but merely suggests the idea of a horse to a baby's mind. When we pray before the statue of Zeus, though the statue contains him as everything must, the statue is not the god himself but only a suggestion of him. Surely, as fellow priests, we can be frank with one another about these grown-up matters.

'Now I must ask you to keep the peace in the cities. If you do not, as chief magistrate I shall discipline you. But you have nothing to fear from me as Pontifex Maximus, *if* you behave with propriety and obey the civil laws and conduct your disputes without resorting, as you have in the past, to fire and the knife. Preach only the Nazarene's words and we shall be able to live with one another. But of course you are not content with those few words. You add new things daily. You nibble at Hellenism, you appropriate our holy days, our ceremonies, all in the name of a Jew who knew them not. You rob us, and reject us, while quoting the arrogant Cyprian who said that outside your faith there can be no salvation! Is one to believe that a thousand generations of men, among them Plato and Homer, are lost because they did not worship a Jew who was supposed to be god? a man not born when the world began? You invite us to believe that the One God is not only "jealous", as the Jews say, but evil? I am afraid it takes extraordinary self-delusion to believe such things. But I am not here to criticize you, only to ask you to keep the peace and never to forget that the greatness of our world was the gift of other gods and a different, more subtle philosophy, reflecting the variety in nature.'

An ancient bishop got to his feet. He wore the simple robes of a holy man rather than those of a prince. 'There is but One God. Only one from the beginning of time.'

'I agree. And he may take as many forms as he chooses for he is all-powerful.'

'Only one form has the One God.' The old voice though thin was firm.

'Was this One God revealed in the holy book of the Jews?'

'He was, Augustus. And he remains.'

'Did not Moses say in the book called Deuteronomy that "You shall not add to the word I have given you, nor take away from it"? And did he not curse anyone who does not abide by the Law God gave him?'

There was a pause. The bishops were subtle men and they were perfectly aware that I had set some sort of trap for them, but they were forced to proceed according to their holy book, for nothing in this part of it is remotely ambiguous.

'All that you say Moses said is not only true but eternal.'

'Then,' I let the trap snap shut, 'why do you alter the Law to suit yourselves? In a thousand ways you have perverted not only Moses but the Nazarene and you have done it ever since the day the blasphemous Paul of Tarsus said "Christ is the end of the Law"? You are neither Hebrew nor Galilean but opportunists.'

The storm broke. The bishops were on their feet shouting sacred texts, insults, threats. For a moment I thought they were going to attack me on the throne, but even in their fury they kept within bounds.

I rose and crossed to the door at the back, ignored by the bishops who were now abusing one another as well as me. As I was about to leave the room, the ancient bishop who had challenged me suddenly barred my way. He was Maris of Chalcedon. I have never seen such malevolence in a human face.

'You are cursed!' He nearly spat in my face. The Scholarian tribune drew his sword but I motioned for him to stand back.

'By you perhaps, but not by God.' I was mild, even Galilean.

'Apostate!' He hurled the word at me.

I smiled. 'Not I. You. I worship as men have worshipped since time began. It is you who have abandoned not only philosophy but God himself.'

'You will burn in hell!'

'Beware, old man, you are the one in danger. All of you. Don't think that the several generations which have passed since the Nazarene died count for more than an instant in eternity. The past does not cease because you ignore it. What you worship is evil. You have chosen division, cruelty, superstition. Well, I mean to stop the illness, to cut the cancer, to strengthen the state . . . Now step aside, my good fellow, and let me pass.'

He stepped not aside but directly in my path. The tribune of the Scholarians said suddenly, 'He is blind, Augustus.'

The old man nodded. 'And glad that I cannot see you, Apostate.'

'You must ask the Nazarene to restore your sight. If he loves you, it is a simple matter.' With this, I stepped around him. As I did, he made a hissing noise, the sort old women make when they fear the presence of an evil demon. He also made the sign of the cross on his forehead. I responded to this gracious gesture by making the sign which wards off the evil eye, but it was lost on him.

Spring came early to the city. It was an exciting time, full of new things accomplished. I attended the senate regularly. I was the first emperor since Augustus to act simply as a member of that body rather than as its lord and dictator. Priscus thinks they detest me for my taking part in their debates; perhaps he's right, but even if they do, it is always good to restore meaning to ancient institutions.

I made many reforms. I removed all Galileans from the Scholarian Guard. I refused to allow any Galilean to be governor of a province. There was some outcry at this. But I am right. A governor who sympathizes with the Galileans can hardly be expected to carry out my edicts, particularly those which have to do with the rebuilding of temples. Several senators took me to task in debate: why if I was so tolerant of all religions did I persecute Galilean officials? For obvious reasons my answer was more sophistic than honest.

'Do the conscript fathers agree that a governor must uphold the laws of the state?' There was agreement. 'Are not there certain crimes – such as treason – which carry with them the death penalty?' Again agreement. 'Would you also agree that no man could be an effective governor who did not have the right to sentence the guilty to death?' A few had now got the drift to my argument. 'Well, then how can a Galilean be a Governor when he is expressly enjoined by the Nazarene never to take another man's life, as you may read in that book which is said to be by Matthew, Chapter XXVI, verse 52, and again in the work of the writer John?' Always use their own weapons against them; they use ours against us.

I removed the cross from all military and civil insignia, as well as from the coins I minted, substituting instead images of the gods. I addressed everyone as 'my good fellow', imitating Socrates. Finally, I took direct charge of the army. The emperor of course is commander-in-chief, but if he is not an experienced soldier he can never be more than a sort of totem or sacred image, the actual business of war being left to the field commanders. But with my own Gallic troops as core, I was able to dominate the army, aided by the officers I had brought with me from Gaul, particularly Nevitta, Dagalaif, and Jovinus; from the old army of the East, I retained Victor, Arintheus and my cousin Procopius.

Curiously enough, I heard nothing directly from Sapor when I became Emperor. This was a serious breach of etiquette, for the Roman and Persian rulers always exchange ritual greetings upon the accession of one or the other. Yet there was only silence from Ctesiphon. But I did learn something about Sapor when a most opulent and curious embassy arrived in the city at the beginning of May. The ambassadors were a brown-skinned, delicate little people from Ceylon, an island off the coast of India. They brought rich gifts. They wished to establish trade with us, and we were most receptive. Their ambassador told me that Sapor had followed closely my campaigns in Gaul and feared me. How strange to think that an Oriental king at the edge of the world should know all about my conquests three thousand miles away! But then I know quite a lot about him. Sapor and I have more in common with one another than we do with our own intimates, for we share the same sort of responsibility and the same awesome power. If I take him captive, we should have much to talk about.

I planned a winter campaign, recalling the old saying that in cold weather 'a Persian won't draw his hand from his cloak'. Unfortunately, as it turned out, I was several months off schedule. But meanwhile, Nevitta trained the troops and their spirits were high; even the Celts did not mind the East as much as they thought they would.

During this time, I got to know the Persian Prince Ormisda. He is a half-brother of Sapor, and the Persian throne is rightfully his. But when he was a boy Sapor exiled him. After a brief stay at the court of Armenia, Ormisda attached himself to us. For forty years (he is sixty) he has dreamed of only one thing, a Roman conquest of Persia that would place him on the throne. Constantine, Constantius and myself have all used him as a soldier and as a source of information. But of the three I am the first to try and make his dream a reality. Meanwhile, he is invaluable to me. He has many secret partisans at the court of Ctesiphon; he is a fine soldier who fought with Constantine in Europe; and of course he always used to accompany Constantius whenever that bold warrior would assemble the Eastern army for a march to the Euphrates. Once at the river's edge, the Emperor would make camp and wait until Sapor and the Persian army appeared. As soon as the enemy was in view, Constantius would then withdraw with superb dignity to Antioch or Tarsus and go into winter quarters. These military pageants got to be a most depressing joke. Ormisda was in despair, until I became emperor. Now he is content. As I write these lines, he is almost Great King of Persia.

In my leisure time – there was no leisure! – I sat up late with friends and we talked of a thousand things. I was particularly close to Maximus; in fact, it was like old times in Ephesus. As always, he was the link between the gods and me. I recall one evening as being particularly significant; even revelatory.

A number of us were gathered on the garden terrace of the Daphne Palace. It was a warm night, and there was a splendid view of the sea of Marmora, glittering in the full moon's light. Flowering trees and shrubs filled the air with fragrance. Far off the lights of the city flickered at the sea's edge. The night was still, except for us and the cry of an occasional guard as he challenged strangers.

Ormisda seemed eager to speak to me; I motioned for him to come with me to the far end of the terrace. Here we sat on a ledge among roses in their first bloom.

'Sapor does not want a war, Augustus.' Ormisda still speaks with a heavy Persian accent despite a lifetime among us.

'So the Singhalese embassy tells me.' I was non-committal; I beat a war-tattoo with my heels on the ledge.

'Do you know what the Persians call you?'

'I can imagine.' I sighed. It is amazing how one's intimates enjoy repeating the terrible things said of us. In ancient times those who brought bad news were promptly put to death: one of the pleasures of classical tyranny!

'The thunderbolt.'

'Because I am the agent of Zeus?'

'Because of the speed with which you crossed Europe and surprised the army at Sirmium.'

I was pleased. 'It's as good as a battle won to be feared by your enemy.'

'They fear "the thunderbolt".'

'But then Constantius's army fears Sapor. So the fears are now balanced.'

Ormisda came to the point. 'They will do everything possible to placate you. I am told by . . .' He gestured delicately with his rose. He knew that I knew he maintained close connections with the dissident party in Persia. '. . . that Sapor is willing to withdraw from the border, to leave Mesopotamia. Almost anything you ask, he will do.'

I looked at him gravely. He looked at me. A long moment. Then I smiled. 'I promise you to listen to no embassy.'

'But I did not suggest that, Augustus.'

'No embassy. No treaty. Only war to the end. That is the holy vow.'

'I believe you, Lord. I thank you.' He spoke softly, in his curiously accented Greek.

'And if the gods are with us, I shall crown you myself at Ctesiphon, with Sapor as . . .'

'Footstool!' Ormisda laughed, referring to a particularly gruesome custom of the Persian kings, who skin captured rulers and stuff them for cushions. Then Praetextatus joined us on the ledge. As much as I esteem him, I find his company sometimes burdensome. He has no lightness in him, only a constant noble gravity. Yet in religious matters, I could not manage without him.

'Are we making progress?' That was my usual greeting to him.

'I hope so, Augustus. I believe so. Only last week my wife initiated a hundred local ladies into Hecate's mysteries.'

'Wonderful!' And it was, for women are the operatives of religion and though they seldom possess the true religious sense, they are excellent at getting things done and making converts. The early Galileans devoted much time to flattering slave-women in order to win over their mistresses. Even at Rome today, it is not uncommon for senators to uphold fiercely the old gods in the senate only to come home to a house filled with Galilean women, singing Galilean songs.

'When I leave for the south, Praetextatus, I shall want you to fill an important post for me.'

'What is that, Augustus?' Noble as he was, I detected that sudden alertness in the face which I have come to recognize as the premonitory look of one who hopes to be raised up.

'If it suits you, I mean to make you proconsul of Greece.' It suited him beautifully, and at great length he thanked me. I then gave him instructions to be as useful as he could to such old friends as Prohaeresius and his niece Macrina.

After this, I left the ledge of roses and walked down a flight of shallow steps, breathing the night air with some delight, aware how little opportunity I now have, simply, to be. For one whose essential interest is philosophy I have managed to be almost everything else: soldier, administrator, lawyer . . . whatever is *not* contemplative I am it!

Maximus was standing at the foot of the steps in the shadow of a tall cypress. He was looking at the moon. In his hand he held a small staff which, from time to time, he held up to the sky, shifting it this way and that, the shadow crossing his face, drained now of colour in the pale light.

'What are the omens?' I stayed outside the circle of the tree, not wanting to disturb what could have been a spell. Maximus did not answer for some minutes as he continued to study the staff and the moon from various angles.

'Good,' he said at last, stepping outside the circle of the tree's shadow. 'At almost any time this year the omens are good. No matter what you attempt, you will succeed.'

'We have come a long way,' I said idly, looking down at the city, and the sea beyond. It is awesome to think that everything is one's own, at least for the brief space of a life – which is why I have always the sense I must hurry to get things done, that there is hardly any time at all for a man to impress his quality and passion upon a world which will continue after him, as unconcerned as it was when it preceded him. Each day that I live I say to myself: the visible world is mine, use it, change it, but be quick, for the night comes all too fast and nothing is ever entirely finished, nothing.

'You have made Praetextatus proconsul of Greece.'

Once again Maximus knew what – until a few minutes before – only I had known. Does he read my mind, the way the Chaldeans do? or does he get instruction from his private genius? No matter *what* his method, he can always anticipate not only my mood but my administrative appointments!

Priscus: Julian was often wilfully gullible. Maximus had been standing just below the ledge when the announcement was made. He did not need to consult 'his private genius', just his ears. As a matter of fact Maximus's ears *did* resemble those of a fox: long, pointed and slightly bent forward. He was a notorious eavesdropper, proving that nature is always considerate in putting together a man. Though as philosophers, we might argue that a man born with the ears of a fox might then be impelled to become an eavesdropper.

Julian Augustus

'I saw something interesting tonight.' Maximus took me by the arm and led me along the terrace to a bench which faces the sea. Several small ships were making for the new harbour I am building just to the north. We could hear the long cry of sailors across the waters, and the response from the harbour. 'Safe landing,' I prayed to Poseidon out of habit. We sat down.

'All the signs for several weeks have pointed to a marvellous victory for you – for us.' He indicated my star, which shone at that moment in the west.

I nodded. 'I have had good signs, too.'

'Yesterday – while praying to Cybele – the goddess spoke to me.'

I was impressed. Maximus speaks often to gods of the lower rank (and of course to demons of every sort) but very seldom does he hear the voice of Cybele, the Great Mother; Earth herself.

Maximus was excited, though he tried to disguise it. He had every reason to be exultant, for to speak with Cybele is an extraordinary feat. No, not feat, for one cannot storm heaven; rather, a beautiful sign that the prime movers of the universe now thought him ready and worthy to receive their messages.

'I was praying in her shrine. Down there.' He pointed to the makeshift temple I had built near the Daphne Palace. 'The chapel was dark, as prescribed. The incense heavy. Her image dim by the light of a single lamp. I prayed as I always pray to her . . .'

'The full verses? to the seventh power?'

He nodded. 'Everything, as prescribed. But then, instead of the usual silence and comfort, I felt terror, as if I had strayed to the edge of a precipice. A coldness such as I had never felt before came over me. I thought I might faint, die. Had I offended her? Was I doomed? But then she spoke. The light from the lamp suddenly flared and revealed her image, but it was no longer bronze, *it was she!*'

I murmured a prayer to myself, chilled by his account.

' "Maximus," she called my name and her voice was like a silver bell. I hailed her by her titles. Then she spoke. "He whom you love is well loved by me." '

I could hardly move or breathe while Maximus spoke. It was as if I myself were now listening to the voice of this goddess.

' "He whom the gods love as their true son will be Lord of all the earth." '

'Persia . . .?' I whispered. 'Did she mean Persia?'

But Maximus continued in the voice of the goddess.

' ". . . of all the earth. For we shall send him a second spirit to aid him in the long marches." '

'Hermes?'

' "One who is now with us shall be with him until he reaches the end of the earth and finishes the work which that spirit began, for our glory." ' Maximus stopped, as though he had come to the end of a page.

There was a long silence. I waited, then Maximus turned to me, eyes flashing, beard like water flowing in the moonlight. 'Alexander!' He breathed the name. 'You are to finish his work.'

'In Persia?'

'And India and all that lies to the farthest east!' Maximus took the edge of my cloak in his hand and held it to his lips, the gesture of a suppliant doing homage. 'You are Alexander.'

'If this is true . . .'

'*If!* You have heard her words.'

'Then we shall break Sapor.'

'And after that nothing shall stand in your way from Persia to the eastern ocean. She asks only that you restore her temple at Pessinus.'

'Gladly!'

Maximus made a secret and holy gesture to my star. I did the same. Then we were interrupted by Priscus, who said in his loud clear voice, 'Star-gazing again?'

Priscus: If I had known that they were up to, I should have had a good deal more to say in my 'loud clear voice'. From certain things Julian let slip during the Persian campaign I did get the impression that he believed he was in some spectacular way supported by the gods, but I had no idea that he actually thought he was Alexander, or at least had the ghost of Alexander tucked inside of him, located somewhere between the heart and the liver. This particular madness explains a good deal about the last stages of that campaign when Julian-Alexander began to act very peculiarly indeed. Personally, if I were a general, I would not like to be inhabited by another general, especially one who went insane! But Maximus was capable of anything; and Julian never doubted him.

This is all there is to the Constantinople section of the memoir. Julian intended to give a full account of all his edicts and appointment, but he never got round to it. You can doubtless obtain this material from the Record Office.

In May, Julian left Constantinople, to tour Galatia and Cappadocia, en route to his winter quarters at Antioch. Though he said nothing publicly, everyone knew that the Eastern army would assemble at Antioch, in readiness for the invasion of Persia.

I stayed on in Constantinople because I was hard pressed for money at this time. Unlike Maximus and his wife, who were making a fortune out of their imperial protégé, I asked for nothing and I got nothing. Julian never thought of money unless you did. Then he was generous. Fortunately, I was able to give a series of lectures at the University. Old Nicocles was most helpful in getting me pupils. You knew him, didn't you? But of course. He forced you to leave the city back in the 40s. A sad business. But Nicocles was a good friend to me and I was soon able to send Hippia quite a large amount of money. Also, Julian allowed me to live at the Sacred Palace while I taught, so my personal expenses were slight.

One interesting detail: just before Julian left for Antioch, Oribasius returned from Greece. He was significantly silent and there was no longer any talk of restoring Apollo's temple. It was not until many years later that Oribasius told me what had happened at Delphi, the so-called 'navel of the earth'.

Oribasius found modern Delphi very sad indeed. The works of art which had once decorated the numerous shrines are all gone. Constantine alone stole 2,700 statues. There is no sight quite so forlorn as acres of empty pedestals. The town was deserted except for a few tattered Cynics, who offered to show Oribasius about. I've never visited Delphi myself, but one has always heard that the people who lived there were the most rapacious on earth, even worse than the tradesmen at Eleusis. I cannot say that I feel particularly sorry for them now. They had a thousand years of robbing visitors. It was unreasonable to think that this arrangement would last for ever.

I suspect Oribasius disliked all religion, much the way I do. But where I prefer the mind of man to any sort of magic, Oribasius preferred the body. What he could not see and touch did not interest him. He was an unusual friend for a prince. His only passion was medicine, which I have always regarded as a branch of magic, though his approach to it was blessedly matter-of-fact. Have you noticed that whenever a physician prescribes such-and-such a treatment, and one follows it and is cured, he is always slightly surprised? Everything a doctor does is guess-work. That is why he must be as good at acting as any Sophist; his cures depend entirely upon a convincing show of authority.

At the temple of Apollo, Oribasius called out, 'Where is the priest?' No answer. He went inside. Part of the roof had fallen in: dust was everywhere. Just behind the pedestal where the god's statue had been, he found a sleeping priest with a half-empty skin of wine beside him. It took Oribasius some minutes to wake the man. When told that Oribasius was the Emperor's envoy, he became quite nervous. 'It's been a bad season for the temple, very bad. Our revenues are gone. We don't even get the few visitors we had last year. But you must tell the Augustus that we still go about our holy tasks, even though there's no money to fix the roof, or to pay for sacrifices.' He got to his feet, swaying from drink.

Oribasius asked about the oracle.

'Oh, we're still functioning. We have an excellent Pythoness. She's rather old but she gets good results. Apollo talks to her all the time, she says. We're quite pleased with her work. I'm sure you'll find her satisfactory. Naturally, you'll want to talk to her. I'll go and ask when she can receive you. She has bad days, you know . . .' He gestured vaguely. Then he disappeared down a steep flight of steps.

Oribasius examined the temple. All the famous statues were gone, including the one of Homer which used to be by the door. Incidentally, Julian found this particular statue in a storeroom of the Sacred Palace, and had it set up in his library. I've seen it myself: a fine work, the face full of sadness, Homeric in fact.

The priest returned to say that the Pythoness would consult the oracle the following day. Meanwhile, the usual propitiatory ceremonies must be enacted, particularly the sacrifice. The priest salivated at the word.

Next day, Oribasius and the priest sacrificed a goat on the altar outside the temple. As soon as the animal was dead, the priest sprinkled it with holy water and the legs trembled, supposedly a good sign. After this, they entered the temple and descended the steep steps to the crypt. Against his will, Oribasius found the whole nonsense most impressive.

They sat in a sort of waiting-room cut in rock. Opposite them was a door which led into the cell of the god. Here, from a fissure in the earth, steam rises; here, too, is the navel of the world – the omphalos – a round stone said to have been flung to earth by Zeus.

The priestess entered from the temple. She looked at neither priest nor visitor. According to Oribasius, she was immensely old and shrunken and tooth-less.

'She is now pure,' whispered the priest. 'She has just bathed in the Kastalian spring.' The Pythoness threw a number of laurel leaves and barley meal on a brazier; the room filled with an acrid smoke. 'Now she is making the air pure,' said the priest. Then Oribasius, eyes streaming with tears from the smoke, followed the Pythoness into the inner cell where, for a thousand years, Apollo has spoken to man. Just beside the omphalos was a tripod, on which the Pythoness sat, cross-legged, her face bent over the steam as it escaped from the earth below her. She muttered incantations.

'All right,' whispered the priest. 'She is ready to hear you.'

In a loud voice Oribasius said: 'I come from Flavius Claudius Julianus, Augustus and Pontifex Maximus. He does homage to the god Apollo, and to all the true gods.'

The Pythoness sang softly to herself during this, her attention fixed on the steam at the foot of the tripod.

'The Augustus wishes guidance from the god Apollo. He will do whatever he is commanded.'

'The question?' The old voice was thin and indistinct.

'Shall the Emperor restore the holy temple of Delphi?'

For a long moment the only sound in the shrine was the faint hissing noise steam makes escaping rock. That sound is possibly the origin of the legend that the earth goddess Ge had a son who was a serpent called Python. The serpent controlled the oracle until Apollo killed him and threw the body down a crevice. The steam is supposed to come from the corpse. The hissing sound is the serpent's dying voice.

At last the Pythoness stirred. She took several deep breaths of steam. She gasped; she coughed; she rolled her eyes; she clung with claw-like hands to the top of the tripod, rocking back and forth. Then she was motionless. When she finally spoke, her voice was firm and distinct despite the absence of teeth.

'Tell the King: on earth has fallen the glorious dwelling, and the water-springs that spoke are still. Nothing is left the god, no roof, no shelter, and in his hand the prophet laurel flowers no more.'

That was all. The Pythoness shut her eyes. She seemed to sleep. Oribasius and the priest departed. The priest was distraught. 'I don't believe it,' he said. 'Of course Apollo wants his temple rebuilt. I can't think what got into her. Of course these messages are always open to interpretation. Sometimes they are de-liberately perverse, and obscure . . .' But it was no good.

I asked Oribasius what Julian said when he was told the oracle. 'Nothing,' said Oribasius. 'Except to ask me to mention it to no one.'

Personally, I am certain that the priestess was in the pay of the Christians. They knew what importance Julian set by oracles, especially this one. Why do I think they had a hand in the prophecy? Because if the priestess was genuine she would have done everything possible to see that Delphi was restored. She would not have admitted in so many words that the game was up. And to speak *against* the interests of her own establishment meant that she had been made a better offer. Of course I do not believe – as Julian did – that Apollo speaks to us through a succession of ladies who have fits from breathing steam. The whole thing was always a fake. But this time I am positive it was a double fake. Oribasius rather agreed with me when I told him my theory.

As I said, Julian left Constantinople in high spirits and I did not see him again for some months. When I did, I noticed a great change in his mood. The euphoria of Constantinople was gone. He was uneasy and touchy and of course he hated Antioch, which he describes.

18

Julian Augustus

On 10 May I left Constantinople for Antioch. All omens were favourable. The weather was good, though far too dry for that time of year. Instead of going straight south to Syria, I swung to the east, passing through Phrygia and Galatia. I pretended that I wanted to see for myself what these territories were like so that I might have some firsthand knowledge of their problems when it came time for the tax reforms the new Count of the Sacred Largesse, Felix, insisted that I make. But my actual motive was to visit the temple of Cybele at Pessinus and there make solemn offering to my patroness.

I was accompanied by the Petulantes and Scholarians. The remainder of the army of the East was to gather at Antioch in the autumn. For a number of reasons, I had decided to postpone the invasion of Persia to the following spring. This would give me half a year at Antioch to train the troops and to put in effect various civil and religious reforms. Of my close friends only Maximus accompanied me on this progress. Priscus remained in Constantinople, while Oribasius preferred to make his own way to Antioch, stopping at out-of-the-way villages to look for cures – and he accuses *me* of liking magic!

It was good to be on the move again, even though, try as I might to reduce my retinue, it was still large and cumbersome. Half the Sacred Consistory attended me, as well as most of the administrative staff of the Sacred Palace. I was particularly bored – yet impressed – by Count Felix, who was acknowledged to be the most brilliant juggler of figures in the empire, a reputation he never allowed me to forget, since his vanity was boundless. Whenever I would rather timidly try to recall my own experiences with the finances of Gaul, he would point a long finger at me and, in the tone of master to schoolboy, define the extent of my ignorance, the folly of my instincts, and the need I had of his advice which was invariably: never forgive tax arrears. I came to dread his tall crane-like figure as it approached me after each Consistory, the long dour face set primly in a mask of false patience. But Felix was remarkable in his grasp of detail and, like it or not, I learned a good deal from him.

We crossed the Bosphorus on a fine spring day. The countryside was yellow with wild flowers and the warm air smelled of honey. We passed by Chalcedon but did not enter the city. At Libyssa, I paused to look at the grave of Hannibal. Like my predecessors, I honour him. I particularly admire him as a soldier, for his campaigns in Italy were perhaps the most remarkable of all time, excepting always those of Alexander. No one will ever know why Hannibal failed to take Rome – which is proof to me that the gods on that occasion intervened to save Rome from its most resourceful enemy. The grave is shabby: only a plain marble *stele* records the death of the exile.

We then proceeded to Nicomedia. This was a sad occasion, for Nicomedia is now in ruins. On 24 August 358 earthquakes destroyed half the city. It was the worst natural disaster in our time.

We reached the outskirts of Nicomedia in the late afternoon. Here I was met by the senate of the city, all in darkest mourning. As we passed through streets filled with rubble, I nearly wept; so many familiar sights were gone or altered beyond recognition. Along the street to the palace the people stood, intent and watchful. Every now and then one would step forward to kiss my hand or touch the purple. Some I recognized as fellow students from the University, others as people I had observed in the forum. It was a wretched day.

I granted Nicomedia a considerable sum of money for rebuilding. Felix thought I was setting a bad precedent, but I pointed out to him that this was not just any city but a former world capital, made memorable by that fact that it was here on 24 February 303, Diocletian launched his edict against the Galileans, ordering their charnel houses razed and their communities dissolved. Unfortunately, Diocletian retired two years later and his work was not completed. If it had been . . . but that is wishful thinking. To me has fallen the same task, now doubly difficult, for the enemy have had half a century in which to establish themselves not only among the ignorant but in the Sacred Palace itself.

I could not wait to get away from Nicomedia. As soon as it was decently possible, I bade farewell to the senate. I should note here that everywhere I went I set about restoring the temples, and it was not easy. Most of them are in ruins or occupied by Galileans. To make matters worse, the priesthood in many places has completely died out. Provinces like Cappadocia are now entirely atheist.

Yet I forced no one. Instead, I argued. I reasoned. Occasionally, I confess, I bribed the people to honour as they ought to honour their constant deities. I was criticized for this, particularly by Count Felix, who has no interest in religious matters and thought it folly to give anything to local temples, much less to the people themselves. But I felt it was worth doing. No matter what impels a man to pray to a god, the fact that he performs the ritual act is itself an act of worship and a beginning, even though his heart is false. I do not delude myself that I made many converts. Though I spoke at length to many groups in Galatia, Cappadocia, Cilicia, I convinced only a few. I am perfectly aware of this. Yet one must begin somewhere, even if it means talking to stones. I now realize that the business of restoration will be slow, but it will be sure. Meanwhile, the Galileans are hopelessly divided, and in their division is our hope.

At Pessinus I went straight to the temple of Cybele, at the foot of the town's acropolis. The temple is very old and very impressive, but in disrepair. It has been a holy place ever since the statue of the goddess fell from heaven. This was

about the time she gave birth to her son, the legendary King Midas, who built
the first sanctuary, in honour of his mother. The myth that everything Midas
touched turned to gold, though symbolically fascinating – and certainly caution-
ary! – was probably based on the fact that the countryside around Pessinus is
rich in iron. Midas was one of the first to make and sell weapons of iron and this
made him fabulously rich. What he touched indeed turned to metal, but the
metal was iron. In the side of the acropolis, next to Midas's tomb, I saw with
my own eyes the world's first foundry, given to the king by his mother.

I offered a great sacrifice to Cybele, but the townspeople would not take part
in the ceremonies even though I offered them a bounty, to the horror of Count
Felix. More than ever I relied on Maximus, who is in constant communication
with the goddess. It was he who found me Arsacius, a Hellenist whom I
appointed High Priest of Galatia. Arsacius is old and garrulous, but he gets
things done. In less than a week he had enrolled some twenty priests in the
service of Cybele. On several occasions I lectured them at length on the
necessity of proving themselves to be as virtuous in all their dealings as the
Galileans *claim* to be in theirs. I particularly forbade them to attend the
theatre, enter taverns, or involve themselves in shady business deals. I also
ordered them to set up hostels for the poor and to be particularly generous
to those who are Galilean. I then assigned to the diocese of Galatia an
annual allowance of 30,000 sacks of corn and 60,000 pints of wine, one-fifth
to be used for the poor who serve the priests, and the rest to be given to
strangers and beggars, since 'from Zeus come all strangers and beggars, and a
gift, though small, is precious'. That quotation is *not* from the Nazarene, but
from our own Homer!

My last night in Pessinus, I sat up late with Maximus, discussing the nature of
the Great Mother Goddess. He was more than usually eloquent and I was more
than usually inspired by him, and of course by her spirit. Cybele is the first of the
gods, the mother of all; and though I do not approve of eunuchs in politics, I
have only veneration for those of her priests who, imitating Attis, castrate
themselves in order to serve the goddess completely. After Maximus left me, I
was so keyed up that I began to dictate a hymn to the Mother of the Gods. I
completed it before morning. Maximus thinks it easily my best work in that vein.

Next we moved on to Ancyra. Here I was besieged by a thousand litigants. It
was like a visit to Egypt. I did my best to give justice, but my temper was getting
short. Reports of religious dissension were coming in from all sides. Some of our
own people, excessively zealous, were damaging Galilean property, while the
Galileans were doing everything possible to prevent us from reopening the
temples. Sooner or later I knew that I would have to make a stand and by some
harsh gesture convince the Galileans that I meant to be obeyed. But for the
moment, I reasoned and argued. I promised Pessinus funds for public works, *if*
the townspeople would support the temple of Cybele. I refused to visit Nisibis
until they became less hostile to Hellenism. I deposed several bishops and
warned the remainder that there was to be no interference with my plans. I
don't know what I should have done without Maximus. He was always at my
side; his energy never flagged; he was always a source of consolation, and I
needed consoling.

At Ancyra I lost my temper. I had spent three days in the courthouse,
listening to men lie about one another. The creative lengths to which human
malice will go quite inspire awe. One man, determined to destroy a business
rival, came to me every day bringing new charges against his enemy. Each was

promptly dismissed. Finally, the accuser declared in a ringing voice, 'He has committed high treason, Augustus. He aspires to your place.'

This got my full attention. 'What evidence do you have?'

'Two weeks ago he ordered a silk robe, of *purple*!' Everyone gasped with horror at this lese-majesty. I could stand it no longer. I pulled off my red shoes and flung them as hard as I could at the idiot's head. 'Then give him these shoes! They go with the purple.' The terrified rogue fell prone in front of me. 'And then remind him – and yourself – that it takes more than clothes to be an emperor!' I was not particularly pleased with myself for this outburst, but I was under great tension.

From Ancyra I moved west and south. At what they call the Gates, a mountain pass connecting Cappadocia and Cilicia, I was met by Celsus, a governor of Cilicia. I had known him slightly in Athens, where he had been a fellow student. He was also a disciple of Libanius. I'm afraid that I was so overjoyed to see a friendly Hellenic face that I kissed him in full view of the Petulantes. Then I let him ride beside me in my carriage as far as Tarsus. In a strange country, surrounded by hostile people, one clings to mere acquaintances as though they were brothers. That day I would gladly have made Celsus praetorian prefect of the East, simply to show my pleasure in talking to someone who believed as I did.

On the road to Tarsus, Celsus told me many things. He was not optimistic about my revival of Hellenism, but he felt that, given time, we might prevail. He did agree with me that the Galileans would eventually kill one another off.

We also discussed the most important political problem in the empire: the town councils or senates.

Everywhere I have travelled as emperor, I am met by crowds of well-to-do citizens begging me to exempt them from serving in their local councils. What was once the highest honour a provincial might aspire to is now a cruel burden, because the councils are responsible for raising taxes. This means that in a year of poor harvest when the people are unable to pay their taxes, the members of the local council must make up the tax deficit out of their own pockets. Not unnaturally, no one wants to serve on a town council. The only alternative would be to govern directly through imperial decree, and that is not practical for obvious reasons. The whole thing is a mess and no emperor has known how to handle it. I don't. Like my predecessors, I give rousing speeches to those concerned. I tell them that it is a great honour to govern a city and that the state would perish without the co-operation of its worthiest citizens. But the burghers still beg for exemption from public service and I can't blame them. One solution of course is *not* to hold the councils responsible for the collection of taxes. But that would cut the state's revenue in half, which we cannot afford. Someone must see to tax-collecting and who should be better qualified than the leading citizens of the community? So I have chosen to reinvigorate the councils rather than change the system drastically. One way to distribute the responsibility more fairly is to allow no exemptions from service in the councils. Under Constantius both the Galilean priests and the military were exempt, I have changed this, making more rather than fewer citizens available for service. There have been a good many repercussions, but I think in time the communities will be strengthened. It is certainly an intolerable state of affairs when men of property refuse to be senators in a famous city like Antioch.

I stayed a number of days at Tarsus, a pleasant town on a lake, connected by canal with the sea. Celsus assembled an interesting group of philosophers to meet me, and we had several enjoyable discussions. The modern Tarsians are quite worthy of their predecessors, the great Stoics of six centuries ago. I even went swimming one afternoon in the Cydnus River, despite the fact that Alexander was almost killed after *his* swim in that river. Although Tarsus is predominantly Galilean (there are innumerable memorials to the devilish Paul who was born here), I found the inhabitants reasonable and simple in their ways. I was almost sad when it came time to leave. But I consoled myself with the thought that I was exchanging Tarsus for Antioch, the Queen of the East. I shudder now when I recall my excitement.

I arrived at Antioch in the last week of July, on a hot humid day. Just outside the city I encountered a large crowd of men and women. Naturally, I thought they had come to welcome me, and I was about to make them a speech of thanks. But they ignored me, calling out strange words, while waving branches in the air.

I looked about for my uncle Julian, but there was no official in sight, only this mob which kept singing rhythmically that 'a new star had risen in the east'. I'm afraid that I took this to be a reference to myself. One gets used to all sorts of hyperbole. But when I tried to speak to them, they ignored me, their eyes on heaven. At the North Gate the praetorian prefect, Salutius Secundus, my uncle and the senate welcomed me officially. The instant the formal exchanges were finished. I asked, 'What is this crowd?'

My uncle was apologetic. Of all days to come to Antioch, I had arrived on that of the festival which commemorates the death of Adonis, the lover of Aphrodite. Adonis is one of the principal gods of Syria, and Maximus and I should have known that this was the day sacred to him. But the mistake was made and there was nothing to be done about it. So I made my entrance into Antioch amid cries and groans and funereal keening, quite spoiling my first impression of the city which, after all, is a beautiful place inhabited by scum. No, that is not fair. They have their ways and I have mine. I am dog to their cat.

The North Gate is a massive affair made of Egyptian granite. Past the gate, one's first view of the city is dazzling, for the main street is two miles long and lined with double porticoes built in the reign of Tiberius. Nowhere else in the world can you walk beneath a portico for two miles. The street itself is paved with granite and so laid out that it always gets a breeze from the sea, twenty miles away. Always a breeze . . . except on this day. The air was stifling. The sun oppressive. Sweat streaming from beneath my helmet, I rode grimly towards the forum, while the people remained within their shady porticoes, occasionally moaning that Adonis was dead.

As I rode I looked about me curiously. To the left is Mount Silpius, which rises abruptly from the plain. Most of the city is contained between the Orontes River on the west and Silpius on the east and south. The finest villas are on the mountain's slopes, where there is morning shade, luxurious gardens, and a fine view of the sea. One of the Seleucid kings, during a year of plague, carved a colossal head in the rock just above the city. It is called the Charonion and it broods over the city like some evil spirit. One sees it from almost every quarter. The natives admire it. I don't, for it represents to me Antioch.

The forum of Tiberius contains a large statue of the emperor as well as an elaborate marble and mosaic nymphaeum built over a spring whose waters Alexander claimed were sweeter than his mother's milk. I drank from it and found the water was good, but then I was extremely thirsty, as Alexander no doubt had been. I cannot recall the taste of my mother's milk, but since Alexander's mother was bitter in all things, no doubt her milk was, too.

Then, accompanied by city officials, I entered the main square of the island in the river where, just opposite the impressive façade of the imperial palace, stands a brand-new charnel house, begun by Constantine and finished by Constantius. It is octagonal in shape and capped with a gilded dome. The building is known as the Golden House and I must confess that it is a most beautiful example of modern architecture. Even *I* like it, and I am no modernist. In front of the charnel house stood Bishop Meletius and his fellow priests. We greeted one another politely. Then I entered the palace, most of which was built by Diocletian, who invariably reproduced the same building wherever he was: a rectangle based on a military camp. But in recent years my family has added so much to the old palace that the original austere design has been completely obscured by new buildings and elaborate gardens. Within the palace compound there are baths, chapels, pavilions and, best of all, an oval riding track surrounded by evergreens, a great convenience for me.

I was greeted by the palace chamberlain, an ancient eunuch who was terrified that I would do to him what I had done to the eunuchs in Constantinople. But I put his mind at rest. All that I demanded, I said, was decent behaviour. If I was well served, I would make no changes. Needless to say, I was looked after superbly, an improvement over my last weeks in Constantinople when my bed was often not made and dinner was never on time. There is something to be said for being comfortable, at least when one is not in the field.

I chose an apartment for myself high above the river, with a roofed terrace where I could sit or stroll in the open air, and look across the western plain to the sea. Here I spent most of my time. During the day, I received visitors and worked; in the evening, I was joined by friends. Close to the palace is the Hippodrome, one of the largest in the East. Yes, I did my duty. I attended the games when I had to, though I never stayed for more than six races.

There was much ceremonial. I received the senate. I listened to testimonials. I attended the theatre. I made graceful speeches, though Priscus claims that no matter how secular the occasion, sooner or later I get on to the subject of religion! I reviewed the troops who were already there, and made plans for the reception of the legions which had not yet arrived. To the horror of Count Felix, I remitted one fifth of all tax arrears in Syria, on the reasonable grounds that since we did not stand much chance of getting these revenues anyway, why not do the popular thing? And I was most popular – for about three months.

In August during a meeting of the Sacred Consistory I received word that Sapor had sent me a messenger with an important letter. I turned to Ormisda who happened to be attending the Consistory that day. 'Will he want peace or war?'

'My brother always wants both. Peace for himself. War for you. When you are disarmed, he will arm. When you are armed, he will . . . write you letters.'

The messenger was brought before the Consistory. He was not a Persian but a well-to-do Syrian merchant who had business dealings with Persia. He had just come from Ctesiphon. He knew nothing of politics. He had been asked to deliver a letter. That was all. But a Persian had accompanied him, in order to take my answer back to the Great King. I asked for the Persian to be brought to us. He turned out to be a tall gaunt nobleman, with a face as composed as statuary.

Only once did he betray emotion: when Ormisda addressed him in his native tongue. Startled, he answered. Then when he realized who Ormisda was, his mouth set. He was silent. I asked Ormisda what he had said to him. 'I inquired about his father. I know his family,' said Ormisda mildly.

'He seems not to admire you. Perhaps we can change that.' I gave Ormisda the letter and he read it rapidly in the soft sibilant Persian tongue. Then he translated. Briefly, Sapor wished to send me an embassy. Nothing more; but the implication was plain. 'He wants peace, Augustus,' said Ormisda. 'He is afraid.' He handed me the letter. I let it drop to the floor, an affront to a fellow sovereign. I turned to Ormisda.

'Tell the Persian that there is no need for Sapor to send us an embassy, since he will see me soon enough at Ctesiphon.'

The war was now officially resumed.

At Antioch I dictated ten, even twenty, hours at a stretch, until my voice gave out; then I would whisper as best I could. Still there was not enough time to do what I had to do. The reaction to the two February edicts has not been good. The Galileans in Caesarea set fire to the local temple of Fortune. I fined the city and changed its name back to Mazaca; it does not deserve the title of Caesarea. I received private information from Alexandria that my enemy, Bishop Athanasius, has not left the city, though I had expressly banished him from Egypt. Instead he is living hidden in the house of an extremely rich and beautiful Greek woman who, my informant suggests, is his mistress. If this is so, we have a splendid weapon to use against him, since much of his authority derives from the so-called holiness of his life. I have given orders that he be kept under surveillance until the right moment comes for us to expose his venery. When Athanasius was told that I had exiled him, he is supposed to have said, 'It is a little cloud which soon will pass.' He is remarkably confident.

I also ordered the Serapion at Alexandria rebuilt, and I restored to it the ancient Nilometer which is used to record the levels of the Nile. The Galileans had moved the Nilometer to one of their own buildings. I moved it back. During this time I strengthened the Antioch senate by adding to it (despite their piteous protests) two hundred of the richest men in the city.

In September, with Maximus's help, I composed the most important edict of my reign so far: concerning education. I have always felt that much of the success the Galileans have had was due to their mastery of Hellenic writing and argument. Skilled in *our* religion, they turn our own weapons against us. Now we never ask our priests to teach the writings of Matthew, Mark, Luke and John, and not merely because they wrote bad Greek. No. Our priests do not believe in the Nazarene-god. Therefore why should we offend those who do believe in him by teaching the work of his apologists? But Galileans teach our classics in every university in the world. They teach them as models of style and wit, while discarding what they say as untrue. This is intolerable. I therefore decreed that no Galilean be allowed to teach the classics. Naturally, the sternness of this law has been resented and I am sorry for the hurt it has caused certain admirable men. But I had no choice. Either the line is clearly drawn between the gods of Homer on the one hand and the followers of the dead Jew on the other, or we shall be quite absorbed in the general atheism of the day. Friends of mine disagree with me; Priscus, in particular. But Maximus and I stood firm. At first I made no exceptions to the law, but then I modified it to allow Prohaeresius at Athens and Marius Victorinus at Rome to continue teaching. Both accepted gladly. In

Constantinople my old teacher Ecebolius forsook the Galilean madness, and in a most eloquent declaration returned to the true gods.

Priscus: Julian is here misrepresenting everything. Ecebolius we know about. Whatever the reigning emperor worshipped, Ecebolius adored. Now I was not at Athens when the edict took effect, but Prohaeresius told me later that he himself promptly stopped teaching. Later, when his personal exemption arrived, he still refused to teach, declaring that though the edict was highly unjust, if it was to be law, it must at least be consistent. This sounds rather braver than in fact, it was, for the day the edict was published Prohaeresius paid a visit to his old friend the Hierophant. I don't know how the Hierophant did it, but he had a genius for guessing the future. He was the only soothsayer who ever impressed me. By the way, he has just predicted the destruction of all the temples in Greece within *this* decade. I don't know whether he means by Theodosius or by the Goths. From the way the tribes are gathering on our borders, I suspect the latter.

Anyway, Prohaeresius had a chat with the Hierophant. Now obviously he could not ask him directly about Julian's life expectancy. That was treason. But he could ask about one of Julian's pet projects: the reassessment of all Achaian real estate in order that the land taxes might be lowered. Prohaeresius pretended to be worried about some property his wife owned. Should she sell it now? or wait until the tax went into effect? Sell it now, said the Hierophant (no breathing from a steaming rock or magic spells), the tax cut will not take place. Prohaeresius then knew that Julian's reign would be short.

Julian was quite right when he said that I opposed the Edict on Education. I thought it cruel, as well as impossible to regulate. At least half the good teachers in the universities are Christian. Who could replace them? But Julian at this period was more and more showing the strain of his huge work. In a way, it was a pity that he was not a Tiberius, or even a Diocletian. Had he turned butcher, he might have got his way. Though the Christians declare that their blood is semen, an emperor whose sole intent is their destruction might succeed through violence, especially if he were at the same time creating an attractive alternative religion. But Julian had made up his mind that he would be a true philosopher. He would win through argument and example. That was his mistake. One has only to examine what the Christians believe to realize that reason is not their strong point. Only the knife might have converted them to Julian's beliefs. But, good man that he was, his blade was sheathed.

Despite Julian's resolve to be serene, the continual bad news from the provinces affected him. He grew irritable and began to retaliate. The Edict on Education was, he thought, a terminal blow. If he had lived, it *might* have worked, though I doubt it. At heart he was too mild to have made it stick. In all of this he was constantly egged on by Maximus, who was at his most insufferable those months in Antioch.

Libanius: For once Priscus and I are in complete agreement. Maximus was neither Sophist nor philosopher, neither lawyer nor teacher. He was a magician. Now I have never *not* believed in magic (after all, there is so much that is familiar which we cannot comprehend), but the magic of Maximus was obvious fakery and the influence he exerted over Julian was deplorable.

Julian Augustus
There was one amusing sequel to the Edict on Education . . . the only one, as

far as I was concerned. Two literary hacks, a father and son named Apollinaris, immediately rewrote the testaments of the Galilean and the old book of the Jews as Greek tragedies and plays! In this way they hoped to get around the edict and be able to teach classic Greek. I read several of these monstrous works and I must say, crude as they were, they read rather better than the originals. The new testament they rewrote as a series of Socratic dialogues, imitating Plato (but in anapaests!), while the old book of the Jews was compressed into twenty-four chapters from Alpha to Omega, rendered in deadly dactyl.

The works of the Apollinarises were sent me for comment by a very nervous bishop at Caesarea . . . I mean Mazaca. I sent him back a letter of one sentence: 'I read; I understood; I condemn.' Just before I left Antioch I got a reply to this letter from my old friend Basil (I have several times asked him to court but he will not come). Basil's letter was also one sentence: 'You have read but you have not understood, for if you had understood you would not have condemned.' No one can accuse Basil of time-serving!

I shall not describe at any length the people of Antioch. Their bad character is too well known. They are quarrelsome, effeminate and frivolous; they are devotees of horse races, gambling and pederasty. The city is of course beautiful and well favoured by climate and geography. There is a large Syrian population which lives in its own quarter down by the river, just opposite the island. To visit that quarter is like going to Persia, so Oriental are the people in costume and appearance. There is also a considerable Jewish population in the south section of the city and along the road to Daphne; the Jews are mostly farmers who received land as a reward for military service. I shall have more to say about them later.

During my first 'popular' weeks, I made all the usual appearances. I presided at the Hippodrome, and was laughed at for my beard. But the laugh was good-natured. I also attended the theatre which is built into the side of Mount Silpius, following a natural curve in the hill. The performance was Aeschylus so I did not feel my time wasted. Generally, I am required to attend comedies. Since most of the emperors have been rather light-minded, theatre managers tend to save their most idiotic farces for imperial patrons. Constantine loved Menander. Constantius probably liked farce though no one knows since it was his policy never to laugh or smile in public. But I suspect that the fast-spoken old Greek of the comedies with its many puns and plays on words probably bewildered him. My uncle Julian, as Count of the East, was at least able to spare me comedies. I enjoyed the Aeschylus very much. It was his *Prometheus*.

A good part of my time was passed in the law courts. There was the usual log-jam of cases, aggravated by my presence. When litigants know that an emperor is coming to their city, they all try to get him for judge, believing that he is impartial (rightfully) and tending to leniency because he wishes to curry favour with the mob (in my case, wrongfully).

Though emperors tend to be more merciful than local magistrates, a few lawyers inevitably press their luck too hard and at one time or another we all make some angry judgement we later wish we hadn't. Aware of this tendency in myself, I instructed the city prefect to stop me whenever he thought I was becoming too emotional or irrelevant. After he overcame his first shyness, he was very useful to me, and kept my prow to the course, as the saying goes.

As a matter of private curiosity, I did ask each litigant what his religion was, and I believe most of them answered honestly. Quite a few admitted to being Galilean when it would have helped their case (so it was believed) to lie to me.

But since it was soon known that I never allowed my own religious preferences to affect my judgement, many of those who appeared before me declared themselves Galileans in the most passionate way, demanding I persecute those not of their persuasion.

In Antioch the Galileans are divided between blind followers of Arius and semi-blind followers; they quarrel incessantly. There are of course good Hellenists in the city, but they are ineffective. *Potentially* there are many who agree with us, but we make no headway, for the Antiochenes cannot be bothered with serious religion. They like the Nazarene because he 'forgives' their sins and crimes with a splash of water . . . even though there is no record of this water having cured even a wart! One interesting paradox I mentioned to Bishop Meletius. We met only twice; once cautiously, once angrily. On the first and cautious occasion, Meletius told me that the city was devoutly Galilean not only because Paul of Tarsus himself had converted so many of the people but also because it was at Antioch that the presumptuous word 'Christian' was first used to describe the Galileans.

'Then, why, Bishop, if your people are so devoted to the Nazarene, does the entire city celebrate the death of Adonis? one of *our* Gods?'

Meletius shrugged. 'Old customs are hard to break.'

'So is an ancient faith.'

'They regard it merely as a festival.'

'Yet they break the law the Nazarene preaches: Thou shalt have no other god but me.'

'Augustus, we do not condone what they do.'

'I cannot believe it is possible for a Galilean to worship both Adonis and the dead man you call god.'

'One day we hope to persuade them to forsake *all* impious festivals.'

'Unless of course I have succeeded in persuading them to worship the One God.'

'The many gods of paganism?'

'Each is an aspect of the One.'

'Ours *is* the One.'

'But isn't it written in the book of the Jews – which you believe to be holy because the Nazarene thought it holy . . .'

'It is holy, Augustus.'

'. . . written that the most high god of the Jews was a jealous god . . .'

'It is written and so he is.'

'But was he not also by his own definition the god only of the Jews?'

'He is all embracing . . .'

'No, Bishop. He was the *particular* god of the Jews, as Athena was the goddess of Athens. He did not claim to be the One God, only a particular and jealous god, limited to one unimportant tribe. Well, if he is limited then he cannot, by definition, be the One God, who, you will agree with me, can have no limitation, since he is in everything and all things comprise him.'

I was particularly vehement at this period, for I was doing research for my book *Against the Galileans*, in which, following Porphyry, I make a considerable case against the atheists. The bishops of course tend to dismiss the many contradictions in their holy books as signs of a divine mystery rather than plain proof that theirs is a man-made religion, suitable for slaves and uneducated women.

Right to the end of my stay in Antioch I was popular in the law courts, if nowhere else. The people often burst into applause at my decisions. Now I realize that I am in some ways very vain. I enjoy applause. Of course most men are like this, excepting perhaps the greatest of philosophers. But I think I am capable of discerning true admiration from false. The people of Antioch like making a noise, and they are guileful flatterers. One day I decided to let them know that I was on to them. After I had given a lengthy judgement on a peculiarly difficult case, the courtroom burst into frantic applause, and there were many cries of 'Perfect justice!'

To which I answered, 'I ought to be overjoyed at your praise for my good judgement. But I am not. For I know – sadly – that though you can praise me for being right, you have not the power to blame me for being wrong.'

When I was first in Antioch, I was not able to do anything I wanted to do. My time was taken up with administrative tasks, and the settling in of the court. It was not until October that I was able to go to the suburb of Daphne and worship at the temple of Apollo. I had made several attempts to go there but urgent business always kept me in the city. At last all preparations were made. The schedule called for a dawn sacrifice at the temple of Zeus Philios in the old quarter of Antioch; then, to the amazement of the Antiochenes, I announced that I would walk the five miles to Daphne, like any other pilgrim.

When the day came, I was awakened before dawn. Accompanied by Maximus and Oribasius (who grumbled at the early hour), I crossed the bridge to the Syrian quarter. I was accompanied only by archers, as though I were a simple city magistrate. I had hoped to escape notice, but of course the whole quarter knew that I was to give sacrifice at dawn.

We entered the Syrian quarter, with its crowded narrow streets. Here on the river bank the original Antioch was founded almost seven hundred years ago by a general of Alexander's. The temple of Zeus Philios is one of the few remaining from that time. It is small and completely surrounded by a market whose thousand carts beneath awnings make it a colourful, if unholy sight. Luckily, the temple has never been entirely abandoned. Even the Galileans respect it because of its associations with the founding of the city.

As the archers made a path for me through the crowded market, I carefully kept my hands under my cloak; since they had been cleansed according to ritual, I could not touch anything. The market people ignored me. Not even an emperor could disturb the important work of selling.

But at the temple a large mob was gathered. They cheered me gaily. Brown hands reached out to touch me. It is the thing I hate most about my place: hands for ever grasping at one's clothes. Sometimes it is done merely for the thrill of having touched the purple, but usually the hands belong to those who are diseased and believe that the living body of an emperor is a powerful cure. The result is that emperors are peculiarly prone to contagious diseases. So if the knife does not end our progress in this world, the hand of a sick subject will. Diocletian and Constantius never allowed the common people to come within a dozen feet of them. I may yet imitate them, on hygienic grounds!

The altar in front of the temple was already garlanded and ready. Of the two priests who held the white bull, one looked suspiciously like a butcher. We are short of priests. On the steps of the temple, just back of the altar, the leading Hellenists of the city were gathered, with my uncle Julian at their head. He looked quite cadaverous and coughed almost continuously, but otherwise, he was in excellent spirits. 'All is ready, Augustus,' he said, joining me at the altar.

The crowd was noisy, good-humoured and perfectly oblivious to the religious significance of what was happening. Be calm, I murmured to myself, betray nothing. The archers arranged themselves in a semicircle about the altar, making sure that I would not be touched during the ceremony. Behind us the market continued about its business, as noisy as a senate discussing taxes.

I turned to Maximus and asked him in ritual phrases if he would assist me. He responded that he would. The bull was brought forward. I looked at it with a most professional eye. I suppose I have performed ten thousand sacrifices and there is little I do not know about auguries. Everything is significant, even the way the bull walks as it is led to the altar. This bull was unusually large. He had obviously been drugged, a practice most priests tolerate though purists argue that drugging makes the pre-sacrifice movements meaningless. Yet even drugged, one can tell a good deal. The bull moved unsteadily. One leg was weak. He stumbled. A bad omen.

I took the ritual knife. I said what must be said. Then I cut the bull's throat in a single clean gesture. At least that went well. The blood gushed. I was covered with it, and that was also good.

Through all of this, the priests made the appropriate gestures and responses and I repeated the formula of offering as I had done so many times before. The mob was now quiet, interested, I suppose, in an ancient ceremony which many of them had never seen before.

When it came time for the augury, my hand hesitated. Some demon tried to prevent me from seizing the bull's liver. I prayed to Helios. Just as I did, the sun rose behind Mount Silpius. Light streamed on either side of the mountain, though its shadow still fell across the morning city. I plunged my hand into the entrails and withdrew the liver.

The omen was appalling. Parts of the liver were dry with disease. I examined it carefully. In the 'house of war' and in the 'house of love' death was the omen. I did not dare look at Maximus. But I knew he had seen what I had seen. Entirely by rote, I continued the ceremony, held the sacrifice aloft to Zeus, studied the entrails with Maximus, repeated the old formulas. Then I went inside to complete the ceremonies.

To my horror the temple was crowded with sightseers; worse, they applauded as I entered. I stopped dead in my tracks at this impiety and said, 'This is a temple not a theatre!' I had now made a complete hash out of the ceremony. If even one word is misplaced in a prayer, the entire ritual must begin again from the beginning. By speaking to the crowd, I had broken the chain that links the Pontifex Maximus with the gods. Cursing under my breath, I gave orders to clear the temple, and to begin again.

The second bull – undrugged – tried to bolt just as I raised the knife, again the worst of omens. But at least the liver was normal, and the ceremony was completed satisfactorily. Nevertheless, in the worst of moods, I began my walk to Daphne not in the cool of early morning as I had planned but in the full heat of noon.

Maximus and Oribasius walked beside me. My uncle, pleading illness, was carried beside us in a litter. The archers cleared a way for us and though crowds occasionally gathered along the route, they did not try to touch me; nor was there much importuning, though as always there was that man who suddenly throws himself at one's feet and begs for imperial favour. I don't know how he manages it, but no matter whether one is in Gaul or Italy or Asia, he always breaks through every guard and lands at one's feet. Patiently, I take his name and try to do something for him – if he is not, as so many are, merely mad.

Depressed and nervous as I was, the walk to Daphne was a lovely distraction. The road follows more or less the course of the Orontes River. The earth is rich and because there is an abundance of water the gardens along the way are among the most beautiful in the world. In fact, their owners hold an annual competition to see whose garden is the most various and pleasing. This year, despite practically no rainfall, the gardens were as dazzling as ever, watered by underground springs.

There are of course many fine villas along the way, and an unusual number of inns, built originally for the thousands of pilgrims who used to come from all over the world to worship at the temple of Apollo. But now there are few pilgrims and the inns are devoted almost entirely to providing shelter for lovers. Once holy, Daphne is now notorious for the amorousness of its visitors.

Halfway to the suburb, my uncle suggested we stop at an inn kept by a former slave of his. I must say it was an attractive place, set back from the road and hidden from view by a hedge of laurel.

We sat outside at a long table beneath a vine trellis heavy with dusty purple grapes whose thick scent attracted humming bees. The innkeeper brought us earthen jugs of fruit juice mixed with honey, and we drank thirstily. It was the first pleasing moment in a bad day. Only my uncle's health disturbed me. His hands shook as he drank. From time to time he would grimace in pain. Yet he never allowed his body's discomfort to interfere with his conversation, which was, as always, lucid and courtly.

'You will find the temple in fairly good condition,' he said. 'The old priesthood was disbanded some years ago, but there is still a high priest in residence. Naturally, he is most excited at your coming.'

Maximus shook his head sadly and tugged at his beard. 'When I was here as a boy there were a thousand priests, daily sacrifices, crowded inns . . .'

I am always amazed at how much Maximus has travelled. There is hardly a holy place in the world he has not visited, from that Paphian rock where Aphrodite came from the sea to the precise place on the bank of the Nile where Isis found the head of Osiris.

'I'm afraid you'll find Daphne changed,' said my uncle. 'But we should be able to get things going again. After all, everyone wants to visit Daphne, if only for the waters and the beauty of the place. It is perfect except for one thing . . .'

I finished his sentence, a bad habit of mine. I interrupt everyone, including myself. 'Except for the charnel house my brother Gallus saw fit to build to contain the bones of . . . what was that criminal's name?'

'The late Bishop Babylas, executed by the Emperor Decius.' My uncle's hand shook and he spilled fruit juice on his tunic. I pretended not to notice. But Oribasius, who had been carefully dissecting a large honey bee with a fruit knife, reached across the table and felt my uncle's wrist. 'Drink the waters today,' said Oribasius at last.

'I have not been well,' said my uncle, apologetically, death in his face. I have noticed that the eyes of men who are dying of natural ailments tend to be unnaturally brilliant. They have a kind of straining look as though they want to see everything there is to see before they go. I liked my uncle, and wanted him to live.

As for Daphne, I can only say that it is quite as beautiful as one has always heard. The town is set among gardens and springs. Near by is the famous grove of cypresses planted centuries ago by Seleucus, at the command of Apollo. The trees are now so tall and dense that their branches form a roof against the sun, and one can walk for hours on end in the cool shade. Daphne has always been sacred; first to Hercules, then to Apollo. It was here that Apollo pursued the nymph Daphne. When she appealed to Zeus to save her, Zeus changed her into a laurel tree. I have seen this tree myself. It is incredibly old and gnarled, yet each spring it puts forth new shoots, reminding us that held by magic within its ancient grasp a girl sleeps, always young. One may also visit the grove where Paris was required to judge which of the three goddesses was the most beautiful.

I went quickly through the ceremony of welcome in the town square. Then instead of going straight to the palace, I went sightseeing with Maximus and Oribasius while my uncle went on to the temple of Apollo to prepare for the sacrifice.

I was particularly impressed by the variety of limestone springs. They flow freely in every weather. Hadrian – yes, he was here, too – built a large reservoir at the Saramanna Spring with a colonnade; here one can sit on a marble seat and enjoy the cool air that spring-water brings with it from the earth below. I also saw the famous Kastalian Spring which was once an oracle of Apollo. When Hadrian was a private citizen he inquired about his future by dropping a laurel leaf into the water. The leaf returned to him a moment later marked with the single word 'Augustus'. When Hadrian eventually became the Augustus, he had the spring sealed with marble on the reasonable ground that others might learn what he had learned and this was not in the best interest of the state. I plan to reopen the spring, *if* the omens are propitious.

The town prefect tactlessly showed us the basilica which contains the remains of the criminal Babylas. I was saddened to see quite a long line of sightseers waiting to be admitted. They believe the bones of this dead *man* have a curative power, yet they will not go near Apollo's springs! Next to the charnel house there is a large factory manufacturing Galilean curios. Apparently, this business is run at a considerable profit. How superstitious people are!

It was late afternoon when we arrived at the temple of Apollo. A large crowd had gathered outside, but none had come to do homage to the god. They were all sightseers.

I went inside. It took my eyes a moment to accustom themselves to the shadowy interior. At last I could make out the marvellous colossus of Apollo. I could also see that no preparations had been made for a sacrifice. Just as I turned to go, two figures hurried towards me from the far end of the temple. One was my uncle. The other was a stout man carrying a cumbersome sack.

According to my breathless uncle, this was the high priest of Apollo. High priest! He was a local handyman who had been entrusted by the town council to keep the temple swept and to make sure it was not used as a home for the poor, or as a convenience for lovers, or for those with a full bladder. Lacking any other attendant, *he* was the god's priest.

'Naturally, Lord, we have no money. I wasn't able to get us a proper white bull or even a goat . . . and a goat does just as well, I always say, if it's not old and stringy. But knowing you'd be here, I brought you this from home. She's the last I've got. Not too tough, I'd say.' With that he removed a furious grey goose from the sack he was holding.

Aware that I was ready to roar, my uncle spoke quickly. 'This will do nicely, high priest. For now. But tomorrow we'll have a proper ceremony. You must see how many former priests you can find. I'll take care of all expenses. We can rehearse them in the morning. Then . . .' He chattered on until I had controlled myself. I thanked the oaf politely for his efforts, said a prayer to the god and departed, the goose unsacrificed.

Fortunately, I found prompt distraction at the palace. The great Libanius had arrived from Antioch. This was our first meeting and I must admit that I was thrilled. He is a noble-looking man, with a grey beard and eyes pale with cataracts. He is going blind, but like the philosopher he is, he makes no complaint. We had a long talk that night, and almost every night that I was in Syria. I was only too pleased to appoint him quaestor, an office which he very much wanted.

Libanius: It is curious how people's memories err. I *never* requested the post of quaestor. What I did request – at the insistence of the senate of Antioch – was the right to be able to argue the city's case before the Sacred Consistory. I had done a good deal of this in the past, trying to justify the deeds – often misdeeds! – of my fellow citizens. Even before the awful 22 October, I sensed that there would be serious trouble between emperor and city, and since my love for each was as equal as two things can be, I felt that I might be able to keep the peace. My fellow senators agreed. Julian agreed. And I take some credit for saving Antioch from what, under any other emperor, might have been a bloodbath. In any case, Julian made me quaestor on *his own initiative*. I did not ask for the post, nor for any post. After all, I later turned down the title 'praetorial prefect', a fact the world knows. I have never coveted titles or official honours.

In my dealings with Julian I was precisely the opposite of Maximus. I made no attempt to win favour. I never once asked for an audience, except when I was acting as spokesman for the city. Julian has not recorded how we met, but I shall, for my behaviour at the beginning permanently set the tone of our personal relationship, doomed to be so short.

When Julian first came to Antioch, I confess that I expected to be sent for immediately. We had corresponded for years. At Nicomedia, he had had my lectures taken down in shorthand. He had based his prose style on my own, and there is no higher compliment than that. But weeks passed and I was not sent for. Later he apologized by saying that he had been much too distraught to see me. I understood of course. Yet I confess I was like a proud father who wanted more than anything else to delight in the success of his gifted son. Naturally, I saw him when he addressed our senate, but we did not meet, though he referred to me in his speech as 'principal ornament of the crown of the East'! I was thought to be in high favour after this, but there was still no summons to the palace.

Not until late October did I receive an invitation from Julian, asking me to dine with him that day. I replied that I never lunch because of fragile health, which is true: a heavy meal during the heat of the day invariably brings on headache. He then invited me to join him the following week at Daphne, and I accepted.

As the record plainly shows I did not 'run after' him; rather, *he* ran after me. He mentions the cataracts in my eyes. I had not realized they were so noticeable. In those days I could see fairly well. Now of course I am practically blind.

I was enchanted with Julian, as most men were. He flattered one outrageously, but there was always enough good sense in his flattery to make it more agreeable than not.

Unfortunately, he enjoyed sitting up all night and I don't; as a result, I was for ever excusing myself just as he was getting a second wind. Even so, we still found time to discuss my work in considerable detail and I was gratified to discover how much of it he had memorized. We also discussed Iamblichos and Plato.

Julian Augustus

I finally made a proper sacrifice to Apollo, offering up a thousand white birds. This occupied most of one day. Then I entered the temple to consult the oracle. I asked certain questions, which I may not record, but the priestess would not answer. She was silent for nearly an hour; then she spoke with the god's voice: 'Bones and carrion. I cannot be heard. There is blood in the sacred spring.' That was all. That was enough. I knew what had to be done.

As I left the temple, there was a crowd gathered in front of it. They applauded me. I paused and looked across the way to the charnel house, the cause of the pollution. I turned to my uncle. 'Tomorrow I want the bones of that Galilean, Babylas, removed.'

'Babylas, removed?' My uncle looked distressed. 'But this is one of their most famous shrines. People come from all over Asia to touch the remains of Saint . . . of the bishop.'

'They can still touch them all they like. But not here. Not in Daphne. This place is sacred to Apollo.'

'There will be trouble, Augustus.'

'There will be even more trouble if Apollo is not obeyed.'

Glumly my uncle bowed, and crossed to the charnel house across the square.

As I was about to get into my litter, I noticed a group of Jewish elders standing on the edge of the crowd. I signalled for them to come forward. One proved to be a priest. He was an old man, and I teased him. 'Why didn't you join me in the sacrifice?'

'Augustus knows we may not.' The priest was stiff; his companions were nervous. In the past emperors had often slaughtered Jews for not observing the rituals of state.

'But surely you prefer Apollo to . . . that!' I pointed to the charnel house across the square.

The old man smiled. 'Augustus must know that this is one of the few choices we have never been forced to make.'

'But we have at least a common enemy,' I said, quite aware that since my voice could be heard by those near by, every word I said would soon be repeated from the Tigris to the Thames. The old man did not answer, but he smiled again. I continued, 'You should at least make occasional sacrifice. After all, your High God is a true god.'

'We may sacrifice in only one place, Augustus. At the temple in Jerusalem.'

'But that temple has been destroyed.'

'So we no longer make sacrifice.'

'But if the temple were rebuilt?'

'Then we should offer up thanksgiving to our God.'

I got into my litter, a plan half-made. 'Come and see me at Antioch.'

The Nazarene predicted that the temple of the Jews would be for ever destroyed; after his death the temple was burned by Titus. If I rebuild it, the Nazarene will be proved a false prophet. With some pleasure, I have given orders that the temple be restored. Also, what better allies can one have against the Galileans than the Jews, who must contemplate with daily horror the perversion of their holy book by the followers of the man-god?

Priscus: Julian does not again refer to this matter, but when he gave orders for the Jewish temple to be rebuilt, there was consternation among the Christians. They hate the Jews, partly because they feel guilty for having stolen their god from them, but mostly because they realize that the Jews know better than anyone what perfect nonsense the whole Christian mishmash is. Now if the Jewish temple were rebuilt, not only would Jesus be proved a false prophet but the Christians would again have a formidable rival at Jerusalem. Something had to be done. And it was.

I got the true story from my old friend Alypius, who was in charge of the project. He had been vice-prefect in Britain when Julian was Caesar. Looking for a new assignment, Alypius came to Antioch and we saw a good deal of one another, for he was as much given to the pleasures of the flesh as am – as *was* – I. One night we visited every brothel in Singon Street. But I shall spare you the idle boasting of an old man.

Libanius: For this small favour, I thank heaven.

Priscus: Julian sent Alypius to Jerusalem to rebuild the temple. He had *carte blanche*. With the help of the governor, they started work, to the delight of the local Jews, who agreed to raise all necessary money. Then the famous 'miracle' happened. One morning balls of flame flared among the stones and a sudden fierce north wind caused them to roll about, terrifying the workmen who fled. That was the end of that. Alypius later discovered that the Galileans had placed buckets of naphtha in the ruins, so arranged that if one was lit all the others would catch fire, too, giving the impression of fire-demons scurrying about.

The north wind was not planned; it is of course possible that Jesus sent the wind to ensure his reputation as a prophet, but I think coincidence is more likely. Plans were made to start rebuilding in the spring, but by then it was too late.

Julian Augustus

The next day was 22 October. At dawn, a thousand Galileans assembled to remove the pieces of the late Babylas from the shrine Gallus had built for them. It was all carefully planned. I know because on that same day I too returned to the city and saw the procession.

The Galileans – men and women – wore mourning as they reverently escorted the stone casket which contained the criminal's remains. None looked at me. All eyes were cast down. But they sang ominous dirges for my benefit, particularly, 'Damned are they who worship graven images, who preen themselves in idols.' When I heard this, I spurred my horse and cantered past them, followed by my retinue. We kicked up a gratifying amount of dust, which somewhat inhibited the singers. In good spirits I arrived at Antioch.

The next day I learned what had happened in the night. My uncle was delegated to inform me. Everyone else was too frightened.

'Augustus . . .' My uncle's voice cracked with nervousness. I motioned for him to sit, but he stood, trembling.

I put down the letter I had been reading. 'You should see Oribasius, Uncle, you look quite ill.'

'The temple of Apollo . . .'

'He's got a herb the Persians use. He says the fever breaks overnight.'

'. . . was burned.'

I stopped. Like so many who talk too much, I have learned how to take in what others are saying even when my own voice is overriding them. 'Burned? The Galileans?'

My uncle gestured wretchedly. 'No one knows. It started just before midnight. The whole thing's burned, gone.'

'The statue of Apollo?'

'Destroyed. *They* claim it was a miracle.'

I controlled myself. I have found that one's rage (which in little things is apt to make one quite senseless) at great moments sharpens the senses. 'Send me their bishop,' I said evenly. My uncle withdrew.

I sat a long time looking out across the plain. The sun hung in the west, red as blood. I allowed myself a vision of perfect tyranny. I saw blood in the streets of Antioch, blood splattered on walls, arcades, basilicas. I would kill and kill and kill! Ah, how I revelled in this vision! But the madness passed, and I remembered that I had weapons other than the sword.

Bishop Meletius is an elegant ironist, in the Alexandrian manner. For a Galilean prelate his Greek is unusually accomplished and he has a gift for rhetoric. But I gave him no opportunity to employ it. The instant he started to speak, I struck the table before me with my open hand. The sound was like a thunderbolt. I had learned this trick from an Etruscan priest, who not only showed me how to make a terrifying sound with one's cupped hand but also how to splinter solid wood with one's bare fingers held rigid. I learned the first trick but have so far lacked the courage to attempt the second, though it was most impressive when the Etruscan did it and not in the least magic. Meletius gasped with alarm.

'You have burned one of the holiest temples in the world.'

'Augustus, believe me, we did not . . .'

'Don't mock me! It is not coincidence that on the day the remains of your criminal predecessor were taken from Daphne to Antioch, our temple which has stood seven centuries was burned.'

'Augustus, I know nothing of it.'

'Good! We are making progress. First, it was "we". Now it is "I". Excellent. I believe *you*. If I did not, I would this day provide a brand-new set of bones for your followers to worship.' His face twitched uncontrollably. He has a tic of some sort. He tried to speak but no sound came. I knew then what it was the tyrants felt when they were in my place. Fury is indeed splendid and exhilarating, if dangerous to the soul.

'Tomorrow you are to deliver the guilty ones to the praetorian prefect. They will be given a fair trial. The see of Antioch will of course pay for the rebuilding of the temple. Meanwhile, since you Galileans have made it impossible for us to worship in our temple, we shall make it impossible for you to worship in yours. From this moment, your cathedral is shut. No services may be held. What treasures you have, we confiscate to defray the costs of restoring what you have burned.'

I rose. 'Bishop, I did not want this war between us. I have said it and I have meant it: all forms of worship will be tolerated by me. We ask for nothing but what was ours. We take nothing that is lawfully yours. But remember, priest, when you strike at me, you strike not only at earthly power – which is terrible enough – but at the true gods. And even if you think them not the true, even if you are bitterly atheist, by your behaviour you disobey the teachings of your own Nazarene, whom you pretend to follow. You are hypocrites! You are cruel! You are ravenous! You are beasts!'

I had not meant to say so much, as usual. But I was not displeased that I had spoken out. Trembling and speechless, the Bishop departed. I dare say he will one day publish a long vitriolic sermon, claiming that he had spoken it to my face. Galileans take pride in acts of defiance, especially if the enemy is an emperor. But their reckless denunciations are almost always the work of a later date and often as not composed by another hand.

I sent for Salutius and ordered him to shut down the Golden House. He already had theories about the burning and was confident that in a few days he would be able to arrest the ringleaders. He thought that Meletius was ignorant of the whole affair. I was not so certain; we shall probably never know.

A week later, there were a number of arrests. The man responsible for the burning was a young zealot named Theodore, who had been a presbyter in the charnel house at Daphne. While he was tortured, he sang that same hymn the Galileans sang to me on the road to Antioch. Though he did not confess, he was clearly guilty. Salutius then held a board of inquiry, and to everyone's astonishment the so-called priest of Apollo (the one who had brought me the goose for sacrifice) swore by all the gods that the fire was indeed an accident and that the Galileans were not responsible. As watchman of the temple he has always been in their pay, but because he was known to Antioch as 'priest of Apollo', his testimony managed to obscure the issue.

So far I have not had the heart to go back to Daphne. After all I was one of the last to see that beautiful temple as it was. I don't think I could bear the sight of burned walls and scorched columns, roofed only by sky. Meanwhile the Golden House in Antioch will remain closed until our temple is rebuilt. There is much complaint. Good.

19

Priscus: I arrived not long after the fire. My season of teaching ended with the old year, and I travelled from Constantinople to Antioch in eight days, which is excellent time. Julian so completely reformed the state transportation system that travel was a pleasure. Not a bishop in sight, though there were several newly appointed high priests in the carriages and I confess I began to wonder if they were any improvement over the Christians. I suspect that had Julian lived, matters would have been just as they were under Constantius, only instead of being bored by quarrels about the nature of the trinity we would have had to listen to disputes about the nature of Zeus's sex life . . . rather an improvement, come to think of it, but essentially the same thing.

I found Julian much changed. You of course were seeing a great deal of him then, but since you had not known him before, you could not have realized how nervous and ill-humoured he had become. The burning of the temple was not only a sacrilege in his eyes, it was a direct affront to his sovereignty. He always did have trouble keeping in balance his two roles of philosopher and king. The one might forgive and mitigate, but the other *must* be served, if necessary with blood.

My first day in Antioch, Julian insisted I go with him to the theatre. 'At least we can talk if the play is too foolish.' Now it happens that I very much like comedy, particularly low farces. No joke is so old that it cannot delight me, if only by its dear familiarity. The comedy that night was *The Frogs* by Aristophanes. Julian hated it, even the rather good jokes about literary style which ought to have amused him. Julian was not without humour. He had a lively response to bores; some gift of mimicry; and he enjoyed laughing. But he was also conscious every moment of his sacred mission, and this tended to put him on guard against any form of wit which might turn against himself; heroes cannot survive mockery and Julian was a true hero, perhaps the last our race shall put forth.

I was delighted to be in Antioch that day. I enjoy the languorous weather, the perfumed crowds, the wide streets . . . As you can gather, I like the luxurious and 'depraved' ways of your city. If I had the money, I would be living there right now. How I envy you!

I was in a fine mood when we arrived at the theatre. We all were. Even Julian was like his old self, talking rapidly, waving with good humour to the crowds that cheered him. But then from the cheaper seats came the ominous cry, 'Augustus! Augustus!' And a chant began, 'Everything plentiful, everything dear!' This kept on for half an hour, the voices growing louder until it seemed as if everyone in the theatre was bellowing those words. At last Julian motioned to the commander of the household troops, and a hundred guards appeared so swiftly that they gave the impression of being part of the programme as they gathered about the Emperor with drawn swords. The chanting promptly ceased, and the play, rather dismally, began. The next day the food riots started, but then you, as quaestor, know far more about all this than I.

Libanius: One curious aspect of human society is that preventive measures are seldom taken to avert disaster, even when the exact nature of the approaching calamity is perfectly plain. In March when the rains did not fall, everyone knew that there would be a small harvest; by May, it was obvious that there would be a food shortage; by June, famine. But though we often discussed this in the senate – and the people in the markets talked of little else but the uncommon dryness of the season – no plans were made to buy grain from other countries. All of us knew what was going to happen, and no one did anything. There is a grim constant in this matter which might be worth a philosopher's while to investigate.

It was Julian's bad luck to come to Antioch just when the shortages began. But though he could in no way be blamed for either the dry weather or the city fathers' lack of foresight, the Antiochenes (whose emblem ought to be the scapegoat) immediately attributed the famine to him.

They claimed that the quartering and provisioning of his considerable army had driven up prices and made food scarce. This was true in a few commodities but not in grain, the essential food: corn for the army was imported directly from Egypt. Yet the people of the city were eager to abuse Julian. Why? Bishop Meletius had declared that Julian's fate was decided when he removed the bones of St Babylas from Daphne. That strikes me as a rather special point of view. Meletius also maintains that the people of the city turned against him the day he shut down the cathedral. I doubt this. Some were shocked of course, but the Antiochenes are not devout Christians; they are not devout anything, except voluptuaries. Not wanting to blame themselves for the famine, they blamed

Julian, who had made himself ridiculous in their eyes by his continual sacrifices and grandiose revivals of archaic ceremonies.

I confess that even at the time I felt Julian was overdoing it. On one day at Daphne, he sacrificed a thousand white birds, at heaven knows what expense! Then a hundred bulls were sacrificed to Zeus. Later, four hundred cows to Cybele. That was a particularly scandalous occasion. In recent years the rites of Cybele have been private affairs, involving as they do many ceremonies which are outrageous to ordinary morality. Julian decided to make the ceremonial public. Everyone was shocked at the ritual scourging of a hundred youths by the priestesses. To make matters worse, the youths had agreed to take part in the ceremony not out of faith but simply to curry favour with the Emperor, while the priestesses were almost all of them recent initiates. The result was unhappy. Several young men were seriously hurt and a number of priestesses fainted at the sight of so much blood. The ultimate rites were a confused obscenity.

But Julian grimly persisted, on the ground that no matter how alarming some of these rites may appear to us, each is a part of our race's constant attempt to placate the gods. Every ancient ceremony has its own inner logic, and efficacy. The only fault I find with Julian is that he was in too great a hurry. He wanted everything restored at once. We were to return to the age of Augustus in a matter of months. Given years, I am sure he could have re-established the old religions. The people hunger for them. The Christians do not offer enough, though I must say they are outrageously bold in the way they adapt our most sacred rituals and festivals to their own ends. A clear sign that their religion is a false one, improvised by man in time, rather than born naturally of eternity.

From the beginning, the Christians tried to allay man's fear of death. Yet they have still not found a way to release that element in each of us which demands communion with the One. Our mysteries accomplish this, which is why they are the envy of the Christians and the enduring object of their spite. Now I am perfectly willing to grant that the Christian way is *one* way to knowing. But it is not the only way, as they declare. If it were, why would they be so eager to borrow from us? What most disturbs me is their curious hopelessness about *this* life, and the undue emphasis they put on the next. Of course eternity is larger than the brief span of a man's life, but to live entirely within the idea of eternity is limiting to the spirit and makes man wretched in his day-to-day existence, since his eye must always be fixed not on this lovely world but on that dark door through which he must one day pass. The Christians are almost as death-minded as the original Egyptians, and I have yet to meet one, even my old pupil and beloved friend Basil, who has ever got from his faith that sense of joy and release, of oneness with creation and delight in what has been created, that a man receives when he has gone through those days and nights at Eleusis. It is the meagreness of Christian feeling that disconcerts me, their rejection of this world in favour of a next which is – to be tactful – not entirely certain. Finally, one must oppose them because of their intellectual arrogance, which seems to me often like madness. We are told that there is only one way, one revelation: theirs. Nowhere in their tirades and warnings can one find the modesty or wisdom of a Plato, or that pristine world of flesh and spirit Homer sang of. From the beginning, curses and complaints have been the Christian style, inherited from the Jews, whose human and intellectual discipline is as admirable as their continuing bitterness is limiting and blighting.

I see nothing good ever coming of this religious system no matter how much it absorbs our ancient customs and puts to use for its own ends Hellenic wit and logic. Yet I have no doubt now that the Christians will prevail. Julian was our last hope, and he went too soon. Something large and harmful has now come into the life of this old world. One recalls, stoically, the injunction of Sophocles: 'And ever shall this law hold good, nothing that is vast enters into the life of mortals without a curse.'

It is also significant that this death cult should take hold just as the barbarians are gathering on our borders. It is fitting that if our world is to fall – and I am certain that it will – the heirs of those who had originally created this beautiful civilization and made great art should at the end be art-less and worship a dead man and disdain this life for an unknown eternity behind the dark door. But I have given way to my worst fault! Prolixity! I have delivered myself of a small oration when I should have kept to the task at hand, Julian in Antioch.

Not only did the people regard Julian's continual round of sacrifices wasteful and ridiculous; they were alarmed by the Gallic troops who used to attend every sacrifice, pretending to do honour to the gods but really waiting for the banquet of smoking meat which followed. The moment Julian left the temple, the soldiers would devour the sacrificed animals and guzzle wine until they became unconscious. Whenever a drunken legionnaire was carried like a corpse through the streets, the people would say, 'The Emperor has been praying again.' This did Hellenism little good in the eyes of the Antiochenes, who are so adept at vice that they never get drunk, and have the greatest contempt for those who do.

The trials of those supposedly responsible for the burning of the temple of Apollo also turned the city against Julian. As quaestor, I looked into the matter perhaps more closely than anyone. Now Julian honestly thought that the Christians had set the fire, but for once they were (probably) innocent. I talked many years later to the so-called priest of Apollo and he told me what he had *not* told the Board of Inquiry.

On 22 October, shortly after Julian left the temple precinct, the philosopher Asclepiades arrived, hoping to see the Emperor. Finding him gone, Asclepiades went inside and placed as an offering a small silver statue of the goddess Caelestis at the feet of Apollo, just inside the wood railing. He also lit a number of tapers and arranged them about the statue. Then he left. That was at sundown. Just before midnight, sparks from the expiring candles set fire to the railing. The season was dry; the night windy; the cedar wood ancient. The temple burned. Now if this fool had only told Julian the truth *before* the arrests, nothing would have happened, but he was almost as afraid of the Hellenic Emperor as he was of the Christians.

The whole episode was sad. Fortunately, no lives were lost. The Christians suffered nothing more serious than the shutting down of the cathedral. Later a number of bishops came to Julian to complain that he was causing them great hardship, to which he replied with some humour, 'But it is your duty to bear these "persecutions" patiently. You must turn the other cheek, for that is the command of your God.'

Julian Augustus

Late in the autumn a large crowd appealed to me in a public place by chanting that though everything was plentiful, prices were far too high. This was a clear indictment of the wealthy class of Antioch, who will do anything to make money, even at the risk of starving their own people. Just seven years ago they had taken advantage of the same sort of situation, and the people had rebelled. Lives were lost, property destroyed. One would have thought that the burghers might have learned something from such recent history; but they had not.

The day after the demonstration, I sent for the leading men of the city. Before the meeting, I was briefed at length by Count Felix. We sat in the empty council chamber, a pile of papers on a table between us. A bronze statue of Diocletian looked disdainfully down at us. This was very much the sort of problem he used to enjoy wrestling with. I don't.

'These figues, Augustus, show a century of corn prices as they fluctuate not only from year to year but month to month.' The count beamed with pleasure. He got from lists of numbers that same rapture others obtain from Plato or Homer, 'I have even – as you will notice – made allowances for currency fluctuations. They are listed here.' He tapped one of the parchments, and looked at me sharply to make sure I was paying attention. I always felt with Count Felix that I was again a child and he Mardonius. But Felix was an excellent guide to the mysterious underworld of money. He believed, as did Diocletian, in the fixing of prices. He had all sorts of proof from past experiments that such a system would increase the general prosperity. When I was with him, he always convinced me that he was right. But then in matters of money anyone can, momentarily at least, convince me of anything. After a brilliant, yet to me largely unintelligible, discourse, Felix advised me to set the price of corn at one silver piece for ten measures, a fair price in Antioch. We would then rigorously hold the price at this level, preventing the merchants from taking advantage of the season's scarcity.

In principle I agreed with Felix. 'But,' I asked, 'shouldn't we allow the senate to set the price themselves? to restrain their own people?'

Count Felix gave me the sort of pitying look Mardonius used to when I had made some particularly fatuous observation. 'You cannot ask a wolf *not* to eat an unprotected sheep. It is his nature. Well, it is their nature to make as much profit as they can.' I thought not. As it turned out, Felix was right.

At the appointed hour some three hundred of the leading burghers of Antioch were admitted to the council chamber. I kept Felix close beside me, as well as Salutius. As Count of the East my uncle Julian should have presided, but he was ill. The Antiochenes were a handsome ceremonious, rather effeminate, crew who smelled – though the day was hot – like three hundred gardens of Daphne; in that close room, their scent made my head ache.

I came straight to the point. I quoted that morning's price for corn. 'You ask the people to pay three times what the corn is worth. Now food is scarce but not so scarce as that, unless what I've been told is true, that certain speculators are keeping their corn off the market until the people are hungry and desperate and will pay anything.' Much clearing of throats at this, uneasy glances exchanged. 'Naturally, I don't believe these stories. Why would the leaders of any city wish to exploit their own people? Foreigners, yes. Even the imperial court.' Dead silence at this. 'But not your own kind. For you are men, not beasts who devour their weaker fellows.'

After thus soothing them, I carefully outlined Count Felix's plan. While I spoke, his lips moved, repeating silently along with me the exact arguments I had learned from him a few minutes before. The burghers were distraught. Not until I had thoroughly alarmed them, did I say, 'But I know that I can trust you to do what is right.' There was a long exhalation of breath at this. They were all relieved.

I was then answered by the city prefect. 'You may depend on us, Lord, in all things. We shall – and I know I speak for every man here – hold the price of grain at its usual level, though it must be taken into account that there *is* a shortage . . .'

'How many bushels?' I broke in. The prefect conferred a moment with several hard-faced men.

'Four hundred thousand bushels, Lord.'

I turned to Salutius. 'Send to Chalcis and Hierapolis. They have the grain. Buy it from them at the usual cost.' I looked up at Diocletian; the heavy face was majestic yet contemptuous; how he had despised the human race!

When the burghers of Antioch departed, Felix rounded on me. 'You have done exactly the wrong thing! I know them better than you. They will hold the grain back. They will create a famine. Then they will sell, and every time you reason with them they'll tell you: but this is the way it is always done. Prices *always* find their proper level. Do nothing. Rely on the usual laws of the market-place. Well, mark my words . . .' Felix's long forefinger had been sawing the air in front of me when suddenly he froze, an astonished look on his face.

'What's wrong?' I asked.

He looked at me vaguely. Then he touched his stomach. 'The fish sauce, Augustus,' he said, turning quite pale. 'I should never touch it, especially in hot weather.' He ran quickly to the door, in much distress. I'm afraid that Salutius and I laughed.

'My apologies, Augustus,' he said. 'But one greater than you calls!' On that light note Felix left us. An hour later he was found seated on the toilet, dead. I shall never have such a good tax adviser again.

Two weeks later I had a most unsettling vision. I had gone to pray at the temple of Zeus on Mount Kasios, which is in Seleucia, not far from Antioch. I arrived at the temple just before dawn. All preparations had been made for a sacrifice, and there was none of the confusion I had met at Daphne. I was purified. I put on the sacred mantle. I said what must be said. The white bull was brought to the altar. As I lifted the knife, I fainted.

My uncle attributed this to the twenty-four-hour fast which preceded the sacrifice. No matter what the cause, I was suddenly aware that I was in danger of my life. I was being warned. No, I did not see the face of Zeus or hear his voice, but as a black green sea engulfed me, I received a warning: death by violence was at hand. Oribasius brought me to, forcing my head between my knees until consciousness returned.

That night, two drunken soldiers were heard to say that no one need worry about a Persian campaign because my days were numbered. They were arrested. Eight more were implicated. They were all Galileans who had been incited to this action by various trouble-makers, none of whom was ever named. I was to have been killed at the next day's military review, and Salutius made emperor.

Salutius was most embarrassed by this, but I assured him that I did not believe he was responsible for this hare-brained plot. 'You could kill me so easily in far subtler ways,' I said quite amiably, for I respect him.

'I have no desire to kill you, Augustus, if only because I would kill myself before I ever allowed anyone to make me emperor.'

I laughed. 'I felt that way once. But it is curious how rapidly one changes.' Then I said to him with perfect seriousness, 'Should I die, you might well be my personal choice to succeed me.'

'No!' He was fierce in his rejection. 'I would not accept the principate from Zeus himself.'

I think I believe him. It is not that he is modest or feels himself inadequate, quite the contrary. But he does feel (and this I gather by what he does not say) that there is some sort of – I cannot find any but a most terrible word to describe his attitude – 'curse' upon the principate. As a man, he would be spared it. Perhaps he is right.

The ten soldiers were executed. I used the military review where I was to have been murdered as an occasion to announce that I would not make any further inquiry into the matter. I said that unlike my predecessor I was not afraid of sudden death by treachery. Why should I be when I had received a warning from Zeus himself? 'I am protected by the gods. When they decide that my work is done then – and not until then – will they raise their shield. Meanwhile, it is a most dangerous thing to strike at me.' This speech was much cheered, largely because the army was relieved to discover that I was not one of those relentless tyrants who wish to implicate as many as possible in acts of treason.

But while this matter ended well, my relations with the magnates of Antioch were rapidly deteriorating. Three months after our meeting, they had not only not fixed prices, they had kept off the market the corn I had myself imported from Hierapolis. Prices were sky-high: one *gold* solidus for ten bushels. The poor were starving. Riots were daily. I took action.

I set the price of corn at one silver piece for fifteen bushels, though the usual price was one for ten. To force the merchants to unload their hoarded grain, I threw on the market an entire shipment of corn sent me from Egypt for the use of the troops. The merchants then retreated to the countryside, forcing up the price of grain in the villages, thinking that I would not know what they were doing. But they had not counted on thousands of country people flocking to the city to buy grain. Their game was fully exposed.

I was now ruling by imperial decree and military force. Even so, the burghers, confident of my restraint (which they of course took to be weakness), continued to rob the poor and exploit the famine they had themselves created.

I again sent the senate a message, ordering the burghers to obey me. At this point several of the wealthier members (my own appointees) saw fit publicly to question my knowledge of the 'intricacies of trade'. A report of this rebuke was sent me while the senate was still in session. I had had enough. In a rage, I sent troops to the senate house and arrested the entire body on a charge of treason. An hour later, thoroughly ashamed of myself, I rescinded the order, and the senators were let free.

Criticism of me now went underground. Rude songs were sung and anonymous diatribes copied and passed around. The worst was a savagely witty attack, composed in elegant anapaests. Thousands were amused by it. I read it, with anger. These things always hurt no matter how used one is to abuse. I was called a bearded goat (as usual), a bull-butcher, an ape, a dwarf (though I am above the middle height), a meddler in religious ceremonies (yet I am Highest Priest).

I was so much affected by this attack that on the same day that I read it I wrote an answer in the form of a satire called 'Beard-Hater'. This was written as though it were an attack by me upon myself, composed in the same style as the unknown author's work. Under the guise of satirizing myself, I made very plain my quarrel with the senate and people of Antioch, pointing out their faults, much as they had excoriated mine. I also gave a detailed account of how the speculators had deliberately brought on famine.

My friends were appalled when I published this work, but I do not in any way regret having done so. I was able to say a number of sharp and true things. Priscus thought the work ordinary and its publication a disaster. He particularly objected to my admitting that I had lice. But Libanius felt that I had scored a moral victory against my invisible traducers.

Libanius: I do regard 'Beard-Hater' highly. It is beautifully composed and though there are echoes in it of many other writers (including myself!) I found it altogether impressive. Yet Julian somewhat misrepresents me in suggesting that I approved of the work and thought its effect good. How could I? It was an unheard-of gesture. Never before had an emperor attacked his own person with a *pamphlet!* The sword and the fire, yes, but not literature. Nor had any emperor ever before written a satire upon himself.

Antioch laughed. I remonstrated with friends and fellow senators, reminding them that the patience of even this unusual emperor could be strained too far. But though the arrest of the senate had certainly frightened them, the subsequent countermanding of the order had convinced them that Julian was mad, but in a harmless way. There is of course no such thing as a harmlessly mad emperor, but my constant exhortations were ignored. Luckily, I was able to save Antioch from Julian's wrath, for which I was credited at the time. All this, naturally, has been forgotten or twisted by malice into something other than the truth. There is nothing so swiftly lost as the public's memory of a good action. That is why great men insist on putting up monuments to themselves with their deeds carefully recorded, since those they saved will not honour them in life or in death. Heroes must see to their own fame. No one else will.

I should note – I *will* note when I assemble this material for the final edition – that the senate did have a case against Julian. Though a few senators were speculators, most of them had not taken advantage of the famine. Their only fault had been negligence in not preparing for the scarcity, but if negligence in statesmen were a capital offence there would not be a head left in any senate in the world. When Julian's message was read to us, it was received most respectfully. Yet everyone agreed that his abrupt underpricing of grain would result in a worse shortage than the overpricing of the speculators. As it turned out, the senate was right. The grain which had been sold so dramatically below cost was soon gone, and the shortage was as bad as before.

I suspect Julian of wanting to make himself popular with the mob. He had hoped to win their support against the wealthy Christian element, but he failed. Our people can be bought rather cheaply, but they are far too frivolous to remain bought. Also, he neglected to hold down the price of other commodities, and it is the luxuries, finally, that are the key to the Antiochene heart. So his attempt at price-control was a failure, just as Diocletian's had been. Perhaps if Count Felix had lived the thing might have worked, for he was most brilliant in these matters and all his life had searched for a prince who could put into effect his quite elaborate system of economic controls. Myself, I tend to believe with the conservative element that inflation and scarcity must be endured periodically and that in time all things will come more or less to rights. But then I am neither trader nor fiscal agent . . . merely Stoic!

Count Felix, incidentally, had literary ambitions, and I once spent a pleasant afternoon with him at Daphne in the house of a mutual friend. The count read us a most entertaining set of verses on – I believe – the pleasures of agriculture. Odd because he was very much a city man. I remember his saying that my essay 'For Aristophanes' had opened his eyes to a whole new view of that superb writer.

Julian Augustus

Shortly before noon on 2 December, a messenger came to me with the appalling news that once again Nicomedia had been struck by earthquake. Everything that had been rebuilt was thrown down.

As soon as I heard the news I went outside. The day was dark and cold, and a thin rain fell. I walked to the garden just north of the riding ring, and there I prayed to Zeus and to Poseidon. All day I prayed, while the rain continued to fall and the cold wind to rise. Not until sundown did I stop. Two days later I learned that the tremors ceased at exactly the moment I began my prayers in the garden. So what had been the worst of signs became the best: the gods still look favourably upon me, and answer my prayers.

A week later I was deeply saddened, though not surprised, to learn that my uncle Julian had died in his sleep. The Galileans promptly declared that he had been struck down by the Nazarene for having removed the treasure from the charnel house in Antioch. But of course his illness preceded this act by some years. Actually, I am surprised that he lived as long as he did, considering the gravity of his illness. I can only assume Asklepios must have blessed him.

I was fond of my uncle. He was a good and loyal functionary; he was also the last human link with my parents. His only fault was the common one of avarice. He could never get enough money. In fact, our last meeting was spoiled by a small quarrel about the Bithynian farm my grandmother had left me. He was furious when I gave it to a philosopher friend, even though the land was not worth one of the gold vases he used to display in his dining-room. I seemed to have missed the fault of avarice. I have no desire to own anything. No. On second thought, I am greedy about books. I do want to own them. I think I might commit a crime to possess a book. But otherwise, I am without this strange passion which seems to afflict most men, even philosophers, some close to me.

Priscus: An allusion to our friend Maximus. He was at this time buying real estate in Antioch with the money he obtained from selling offices and titles. Looking back on those days, I curse myself for not having feathered my own nest. Unlike Julian, I *am* rather greedy, but I am also proud and the excessiveness of my pride prevents me from asking anyone for anything. I cannot easily accept a gift. Yet I could steal, if I thought I would not be caught.

Julian's uncle was an amiable man, though overzealous as an official. He once told me that his sister Basilina, Julian's mother, had been extraordinarily ambitious. When she was pregnant with Julian, he asked her what sort of life she wanted for her child, and she replied, 'There is only one life for a son of mine. He must be emperor.'

Julian used to describe his mother (from hearsay) as having been quite blonde. She was indeed. According to her brother, she was an albino. I once made love to an albino girl in Constantinople. She had the most extraordinary blood-red eyes, like an animal's. The hair of course was absolutely white, including the pubic hair. I believe she was called Helena.

Libanius: How interesting!

Julian Augustus

On 1 January 363, I became consul for the fourth time in association with Sallust. Naturally, there were many complaints, since Sallust was not of senatorial rank. But I ignored custom. Sallust is my right arm at Gaul. I also appointed Rufinus Aradius as Count of the East and filled a number of other offices, mostly in the West. I was now ready for the Persian campaign. I waited only upon the weather.

On the Kalends of January I went to the temple of the Genius of Rome to make sacrifice. Here, on the steps, were assembled most of the city's priests and high officials. As I was completing the ritual, I happened to look up just as one of the priests fell the length of the steps. Later I learned that the priest who had fallen was not only the oldest but he had fallen from the highest step, dead of a heart attack.

By nightfall all Antioch had interpreted this to mean that he who is highest (oldest) in the state will fall from his great place (the top step), dead. So my days are supposed to be numbered. But I interpret the omen another way. The dead priest was on the top stair. Our highest rank is consul. There are two consuls. The dead priest was the *oldest* priest. Sallust is many years my senior. If either of us dies, the omen suggests it will be Sallust, not I. Of course the whole thing might possibly have no significance at all. Perhaps I should listen more to Priscus, who does not believe in signs.

Priscus: Indeed I don't! I am sure that if the gods (who probably don't exist) really wanted to speak to us, they could find a better messenger than the liver of a bull or the collapse of an old priest during a ceremony. But Julian was an absolute madman on this subject. And I must say, even though I don't believe in omens, I was impressed by the number of disasters reported. Among them: the second earthquake at Nicomedia, the first in the Jewish temple, the burning of the temple of Apollo, and as if all these 'signs' were not bad enough, Julian sent to Rome for a consultation of the Sibylline books. As we all know, these 'books' are a grab bag of old saws and meaningless epithets, much rewritten at moments of crisis. But bogus or not, their message to him was clear: Do not go beyond the boundaries of the empire this year. I never heard him reinterpret that sentence. I can't think why I am recording all this. *I* don't believe any of it, but then Julian did, which is the point. True or false, these signs affected his actions.

There was one more bit of nonsense. The day that Julian left Antioch for Persia, an earthquake shook Constantinople. I told Maximus that if he told Julian what had happened, I would kill him. As far as I know, he never said a word.

Julian Augustus

Late in February I completed plans for the Persian campaign. Word was sent the legions that we would start moving east during the first week of March. I also sent a message to Tarsus, instructing the governor that his city would be my winter quarters, as I would not return to Antioch. My private letter to the governor was immediately known to the senate of Antioch, and they were most contrite. Would I not reconsider? I would not. And so I was ready to depart, in good spirits, except for the fact that Oribasius, suddenly ill of fever, was not able to accompany me. This was a blow. But I shall see him later in the year at Tarsus.

The day before I left Antioch, I had a final meeting with Libanius. Getting to know this wise man was perhaps the only good experience I had in that terrible city. He had been unable to attend a dinner I had given the night before, because of gout. But the next day he felt somewhat better and was able to join me while I was exercising at the riding ring.

It was the first spring-like day. Air warm, sky vaporous blue, first flowers small but vivid among winter grass. I was practising sword-play with Arintheus and though we had both started the exercise in full winter uniform, by the time Libanius had joined us, we were half-stripped and sweating freely in the sun.

Libanius sat benignly on a stool while we banged at one another. Arintheus has the body of a god and is far more agile than I, but my arms are stronger than his, so we are well matched. Besides it is not humanly possible for a mere army commander to defeat an emperor, even in mock combat.

Finally, Arintheus, with a mighty cry, struck my shield a fierce blow which caused me to stagger back. He was almost upon me with his blunt practice sword when I raised my hand majestically and said, 'We must receive the quaestor Libanius.'

'As usual, when I'm winning,' said Arintheus, throwing his weapons to the nearest soldier to catch. Then, wearing only undershorts, he sauntered off.

'The young Alcibiades,' said Libanius, appreciatively, watching the muscular figure as it disappeared into the barracks.

I wrapped myself in a cloak, breathing hard. 'Let's hope he doesn't take to treason like the original.' I sat in my folding chair. There was a long pause. Aware then that Libanius had something private to say to me, I motioned for the guards to fall back to the edge of the riding ring.

Libanius was unexpectedly nervous. To put him at his ease, I asked him a question about philosophy. Answering me, he recovered his poise. Even so, it was some time before he got the courage to say, 'Augustus, I have a son. A boy of five. His mother . . .' He stopped, embarrassed.

'His mother is a slave?'

'A freedwoman. She *was* my slave.'

I was amused by this unexpected sign of vigour in one in whom I had thought such things had long since been forgotten. But then Libanius had rather a scandalous reputation when he first taught at Constantinople. He was often in trouble with young girls of good family (and young boys, too), if one is to believe his envious rivals. I do and I don't. There is usually *some* truth to gossip, except when it concerns me!

'This child – his name is Cimon – cannot of course be made my legal heir. Up till now I've been able to provide for him. But when I die, he'll be penniless, no better than a slave. In fact, he could be sold into slavery if he were not protected.'

'You want me to recognize him as your legal heir?'

'Yes, Augustus. The law of course . . .'

'. . . is quite clear. It cannot be done. But *I* can get round it by special decree. Make out a deposition, and I'll present it myself to the Consistory.' He thanked me profusely. I had never before seen Libanius humanly moved; it was most impressive. Usually, he is entirely the philosopher, serene and explicit, his only passion that for ideas. But now he was a father, and I was touched.

We then spoke of the coming campaign. I asked him to come with me but he pleaded infirmity and I was forced to agree that a man with failing sight and severe gout would find life in the field torture.

'But I do wish, my dear friend,' (now that Libanius was no longer a subject asking a favour of his ruler, he reverted to being teacher with pupil) 'you would reconsider this military adventure.'

'Reconsider? I have no choice. We are at war.'

'We have been at war for many years with Persia. But war does not necessarily mean invasion this year.'

'But the omens . . .'

'The omens are not good. I have heard about the Sibylline books.'

There are no secrets. I cursed silently to myself, wondering who had betrayed me. I had expressly forbidden the priests from Rome to tell anyone what the books advised. 'I have reinterpreted the prophecy,' I said flatly. 'Besides, both Delphi and Delos are favourable.'

'Augustus.' He was now solemn. 'I am sure that you will defeat Persia. I have perfect faith in your destiny. I only wish that you would put off going until next year. You have set in motion a hundred reforms. Now you must see to it that they take effect. Otherwise, the Galileans will undo everything the moment you are out of sight. You cannot control them from the field or even from the ruins of Ctesiphon.'

Libanius is right of course and I continually worry, particularly now, at what is happening in my absence. But I told him what I believe to be true: that as conqueror of Persia I would be more than ever awesome to the Galileans, who would see in my victory a clear sign of heaven's favour to me. This useful end is worth a few months' confusion at home.

Libanius was not convinced, but he said no more and we talked of other matters. I find him inspiring, though somewhat long-winded, a traditional fault of great teachers. I am sure that I would be long-winded, too, except for the fact that in conversation I can never sustain any subject for very long. I shift rapidly from point to point, expecting those who are listening to fill in the gaps. They often don't. But in talking with Libanius there are no gaps or incompleted sentences. Listening to him is like being read to from a very long book, but what a splendid book!

Since I am writing these notes as history as well as for my own amusement, I should perhaps set down the reasons for this present war with Persia. One of the faults of most historians is that they take too much for granted. They assume that the reader must know the common things they know; therefore, they tell only the *un*common things, details ferreted out of archives and from private conversations. It is frustrating to read most history, because so many times one can see the author hovering on the verge of explaining some important fact and then shying away out of fear of dullness; everyone knows *that*, the author says to himself, and I won't bore the reader (and myself) by telling him what he already knows.

But if one is writing to be read a hundred years from now or, with luck (and a continued interest in one's period), even a thousand years, like great Homer, then all those things we take so much for granted today will be quite unknown to those who come after. So we must explain things that every schoolboy now living knows. For instance, everyone knows that Constantius would not eat fruit, but is it likely that anyone will know – or care – in the next century? Yet it is a point to be made about him, and worth exploring on religious grounds.

I confess that I do have some hope of being read by the future, not because of my negligible literary art nor because of my deeds (though I hope they will be great), but because I am an emperor and I mean to be candid. Such autobiographies cannot help but be interesting. Marcus Aurelius is the supreme example. But the other memoirs which have come down to us are also interesting, especially the commentaries of Julius Caesar and the fascinating if calculated memoirs of Octavian Augustus. Even Tiberius's clumsy autobiography is interesting, particularly his attack on Sejanus . . .

There! I have strayed from my point. I ask the pardon of my poor secretary, who can barely keep his eyes open as I talk, faster and faster, for in my fatigue I often have the most extraordinary bursts of clarity. At such moments the gods are near; my beloved Hermes hovers at my side. But in the interest of good form, I shall of course revise all that I have dictated, cutting out those parts where I tend to ramble.

The future will want to know why I am invading Persia. I am quite sure that there are many at this very moment who do not understand what I am trying to do. It is of course taken for granted that we must protect our boundaries and occasionally annex new provinces. Though Salutius and the literary men who are with me know how this war started, I am confident that neither Nevitta nor Arintheus has the slightest idea why I have taken the field against Sapor. Nor do they care. They think I want plunder and military glory, because that is what *they* want. Well, I am not without a certain love of worldly glory – though I deplore it in myself – but that is not why I must prosecute this war. Persia (or Parthia as we ceremonially call it in imitation of our ancestors) has always been the traditional enemy of Rome. There have been occasional generations of peace, but for the most part we have been in conflict ever since the wars against Mithridates brought Rome to Parthia's border four centuries ago.

The present war began in an almost frivolous way. Some thirty years ago an adventurer named Metradorus made an expedition to India. He was received generously by the king of India, who presented him with a number of gifts from the king to the Emperor Constantine. As I piece together the story, this Metradorus was a singular liar and schemer. When he returned home he gave Constantine the Indian presents but claimed that they were his own gifts to the emperor. Then, afraid that Constantine might wonder why there was no gift from the king of India, Metradorus declared that there had indeed been many rich gifts, but that the Persians had confiscated them en route, in the name of Sapor.

Constantine, partly out of greed, partly out of policy, wrote Sapor, demanding that he return the gifts. Sapor did not deign to answer him. Constantine sent another angry letter (copies are to be found in the Sacred Archives). Finally, Sapor answered: he demanded Mesopotamia and Armenia as rightful territories of the Persian crown; there was no mention of the presents. Constantine declared war on Sapor, but before he could take the field he was dead.

For most of Constantius's reign, Sapor was relatively inactive. He had political problems in his own country. But then in 358, he sent Constantius a most arrogant embassy, again demanding Mesopotamia and Armenia. Much alarmed, Constantius sent an embassy to Ctesiphon, headed by Count Lucillianus and my cousin Procopius. Our ambassadors were duly alarmed by Sapor, and they advised Constantius to maintain the *status quo*. But even this was not possible when Sapor laid siege to the border city of Amida, leading his army in person; an innovation, by the way, for in the old days the Great King never appeared in battle, his life being considered too sacred to risk in combat.

Amida fell. It was a terrible defeat for Rome. Sapor was surprisingly merciful to the inhabitants. Even so, we have lost an important city, and our border defences are dangerously weakened. When I succeeded Constantius, I looked through all his military papers and talked with his commanders, but I could not find what if any plan he had for defeating Sapor. I was forced to start from the beginning. Now I am ready.

It is my plan to conquer Persia in three months. I have no alternative. For if I fail none of the reforms I have proposed will ever come to pass, nor can our state long survive between the continual harassment of the Goths on our borders to the north and the Persians to the east. Also, and I confess it honestly, I want the title *Parthicus* after my name and an arch to my memory in the forum at Rome. Not since Alexander has a Greek or Roman commander conquered Persia, although some, like Pompey, pretended to, after small victories. I dream of equalling Alexander. No, I must be honest: I dream of surpassing him! And are we not one, in any case? I want India. I want China beyond. Upon the shore of that blood-dark sea to the farthest east, I would set the dragon standard and not simply for the glory (though the very thought of it makes me dizzy . . . oh, where is philosophy now?), but to bring the truth about the gods to all those lands bending towards the sun, the god from whom all life flows. Also, Persia is to me a holy land, the first home of Mithras and Zarathrustra. It will be, for me, a homecoming.

I always keep a biography of Alexander at my bedside. It is remarkable how many of us have used the deeds of that extraordinary youth as a standard of measurement for ourselves. Julius Caesar wept at Alexander's tomb because, already older than the boy was at his death, he had not yet begun a conquest of the world. Octavian Augustus opened the tomb and looked a long time at the mummy's face. The body was well preserved, he tells us in his autobiography, and he says that he would have recognized Alexander from his portraits. Withered and brown in death, the face was set in an expression of such rage that despite all the centuries which separated the living politician from the dead god, the cool Octavian knew for the first time what fear was, and he ordered the sarcophagus sealed. Years later, it was reopened by the beast Caligula, who stole the shield and breastplate from the tomb and dressed up as Alexander, but there all likeness ceased. Each of my predecessors longed to equal this dead boy. None did. Now I shall!

Priscus: There it is. The memoir of Julian. You were present of course when he left the city on 5 March. I can still hear in memory your witty citizens chanting 'Felix Julian *Augustua*', meaning that after Count Felix and his uncle Julian, the Augustus was next to die.

The army marched east across the Euphrates to Carrae. Here Julian split it in two. Thirty thousand men under his cousin Procopius and Duke Sebastian were sent on to Armenia. There they would rendezvous with King Arsaces. Then with the Armenian troops as auxiliaries, they would seize Media, and strike for Ctesiphon where they would meet us. With the remaining thirty-five thousand troops, Julian started to go south along the Tigris. But he was wily. In a surprise manoeuvre, he retraced his steps to Callinicum on the Euphrates and then moved directly towards Ctesiphon, the Persian capital, some four hundred miles south. Sapor was demoralized by this feint. But all that is military history. It is generally agreed that Julian moved armies faster than any general since Julius Caesar.

Though Julian never had the chance to shape the memoir. I suspect he would have left it just the way it was. He hated rewriting. *He* never filled a gap if he could help it. I could fill quite a few about those days in Antioch, but I refrain since you were there, too, and can rely on your own excellent memory. He was by no means finished with the chronicle of his life, any more than he was finished with living it. He intended to write an account of his Persian campaign and the notes he made during those last months are fascinating.

I hope my occasional commentary has not been too burdensome. I think it is always good to get as many viewpoints as possible of the same event, since there is no such thing as absolute human truth. You should be pleased at Julian's final reference to you. He admired you tremendously. I cannot think what he meant when he called you 'long-winded'. You are merely thorough. But then Julian was often like a child whose span of attention is capricious. I shall be very curious to see what you do with this memoir.

By the way, whatever happened to your son Cimon? Did Julian make him your legal heir? Naturally, one has heard of Cimon's exploits as a lawyer, but I never realized he was a child of yours. You are full of surprises.

Libanius to Priscus   *Antioch, July 380*

I have been working for some weeks on my preface to the memoir of Julian, which will, I hope, set this work in its proper historical frame. May I say that your notes have been of the greatest – perhaps even decisive – value to me? Just this morning as I was reviewing the last pages of the work, so tragically cut short, I noticed a phrase of yours which had escaped my attention. You say that Julian was planning to write an account of his Persian campaign. You then add: 'the notes he made during those last months are fascinating'. Is there more text? I had thought the memoir was all that was left. Do let me know, for I am impatient to start a final 'shaping' of the work.

Yesterday I paid a call on my old friend Bishop Meletius. You recall him I am sure, from your visit here. He is much aged and rather fragile, but he has kept all his wits. I intimated that I might be doing a new work on Julian, using previously unpublished material. He thinks this might be a mistake. 'Theodosius is a Spaniard,' he said, meaning, I suppose, that the Emperor has all the stern uncompromising violence of that race. 'It is one thing to send him a graceful essay "On Avenging Julian", whose merit was literary rather than political,' (I thought my work highly political) 'but it is quite something else to challenge the Church, especially now that the Emperor has been saved by Christ.' I never know if Meletius is serious or not. His tendency to be ironic has so increased with age that he seems never to mean what he says.

Meletius also told me that the Emperor expects to be in Constantinople this autumn. So I shall wait until then to see him. I also learned that the poisonous Gregory, now a bishop, is urging that a new Ecumenical Council meet next year, probably in the capital. There is also talk that he is angling to be made bishop of Constantinople. No doubt of it, his career has been a success. But then those people usually do well. I extend my best wishes to your wife Hippia, and of course to yourself.

Added: Julian died before he was able to legitimize my son. Due to religious bigotry and the continuing perseverance of academic enemies, none of Julian's successors was willing to do the humane thing in this matter. I now pin my hopes – without much hope – on Theodosius.

Priscus to Libanius   *Athens, September 380*

You must forgive me for not answering your letter earlier, but I have been ill. A mild stroke has drawn down the side of my mouth in a peculiarly sinister way. I now look like one of the infernal deities and country folk make the sign to ward off the evil eye when they see me tottering along the road to the Academy. Happily, my mind is not affected. If it is, then – equally happily – I don't know it. So all's well.

It is now definite that Theodosius will spend the winter at Constantinople and you ought to go see him. It's only a ten-day journey. He is reasonable, I am told, but much impressed by his miraculous recovery. Whether he would sanction your project is another matter, but you can lose nothing by trying. He won't eat you. Also your being a friend of the Empress in the West will do you no harm. She is most active politically and, some say, had a hand in her husband's raising Theodosius to the purple. Use her name freely. But then I hardly need advise the famous quaestor of Antioch in how to put a case!

Yes, Julian left a considerable journal describing the day-by-day campaign. I have been annotating it with a thought *perhaps* of publication, though I should need at least some of your courage to go through with it, for this work is far more dangerous than the memoir. Julian knew all about the plot against his life; as did I. I also know what he did not, the identity of his murderer.

I have nearly finished the work of annotation. I have been slowed up recently as a result of my stroke, but I hope to get at it soon again. If I decide not to publish, I should of course be pleased to sell you the work at the same price you paid for the memoir. The cost of copying is still what it was here at Athens. If anything, it has gone up.

I hope your vision is not any worse; at our age nothing gets better. My student Glaucon was delighted to meet you last spring when he delivered the manuscript, but saddened to find your sight so greatly impaired. Oribasius used to have a non-surgical cure for cataract, but I have forgotten it. Look in his encyclopedia. It should be in the latest edition, but if you don't have that, look it up in Galen. That's probably where *he* got it from.

Hippia sends you her best wishes, as always. She is eternal. She will bury us all. She certainly looks forward to burying me. We spend quite a lot of time eyeing one another, each speculating on which will outlast the other. Until this stroke, I thought I had a clear edge. Now I'm not so sure. She was quite thrilled when I was sick, and gay as a girl for several days 'looking after' me.

Libanius: On top of everything else, Priscus is a thief. Our agreement was plain. I was to get everything Julian left for the original price. Then he holds back the most important work of all and there is nothing I can do but submit to this robbery and pay the price! I must say I hope Hippia will soon be a widow. Priscus is a terrible man!

Priscus to Libanius   *Athens, October 380*

Here is the journal, as I promised. I have done extensive notes, which you are free to use in any way you like. I have been somewhat weakened as a result of my stroke, but so far neither my memory nor the ability to string together sentences seems to be affected. Some of these notes have been dictated, as you will notice when you see Hippia's childish handwriting. I pay her to be my secretary. She will do anything for money. To this day she denounces me for not having made us a fortune when, as a friend of Julian's, it would have been so easy, as you well

know. Though of course *your* fortune was made long before Julian became
Emperor. I was much impressed the first time I visited you at your Antioch
mansion and you told me, with perfect casualness, that you had just sent a cargo
ship to Crete. Fortunate Cimon to have such a wealthy father! I am sure
Theodosius will legitimize him for you.

I have talked – very discreetly – to several people close to the court and they
agree that the Emperor would *probably* stop publication of any work which
showed Julian in too favourable a light. Needless to say, I did not mention that
there was both a memoir and a journal in existence. But it is perfectly plain that
if Theodosius and his bishops knew about these works they would do everything
possible to destroy them, just as they labour so devotedly to distort the history of
Julian's reign. It is the perquisite of power to invent its own past. Julian must be
obliterated or at least made monster before the Christian Empire can properly
be born. I don't mean to sound discouraging, but there it is.

I must confess that I'm relieved to have got Julian's papers out of my house
and into your most capable hands. I tell you these things simply to put you on
your guard, for one of those I talked to at some length was the celebrated
Ausonius, who is very much in favour at court. I flattered him unmercifully
when he visited here last month.

Ausonius is a small stately man who gives an impression of great dignity and
power until he starts to speak. Then one knows he is simply one of us, a nervous
clerk, embarrassingly anxious to be admired. He also stammers. He was pleased,
he told us in his speech at the proconsul's reception, to be in such a distinguished
assemblage of intellectuals and magistrates, particularly because he liked to
think of himself as a 'sort of bridge between the two'. We wagged our tails
fiercely at this to show that we loved him and wanted favours. When he finished,
he nicely took my arm and told me how much he admired me. What could I do
but quote his own poetry to him?

'I have always admired you, P-P-Priscus, and I am g-g-glad to find you still
alive and well.'

'So am I, Consul.' I beamed down at the absurd figure in its consular robe. I
then praised his many books, and he praised my many silences. The acad-
emicians all about us watched me with a quite satisfying envy. Then, rather
skilfully I think, I brought Julian into the conversation.

Ausonius frowned. 'We aren't very happy with him of course. Not at all. No,
not at all.'

I murmured the ancient saw about the rarity of human happiness. Almost
any quotation from Sophocles has a soothing effect.

'Theodosius is most displeased about the body. Most unhappy. But she
insisted.'

'What body? Who insisted?' I was at sea.

'His. Julian's. It's been m-m-moved. From Tarsus to Constantinople. The
Emperor Gratian ordered it, or to be p-p-precise, his w-w-wife.' P's, W's and
M's are Ausonius's main obstacles. Having told you this, I shall no longer try to
dramatize his speech.

After much spluttering, I learned that your friend the Empress Postuma, last
of the Flavians, suddenly realized that her blood was also Julian's and that the
new dynasty's legitimacy rests upon that frail fact. So Postuma got her husband
Gratian to move Julian's remains from Tarsus to the Church of the Holy
Apostles at Constantinople. At this very moment Julian's body is lying beside
Constantine's mother Helena. How each would have hated that proximity!

Though Ausonius did not mention it, I suspect that both Postuma and Gratian are aware for the first time what a great man Julian was. They live in Gaul, and for the Gauls Julian is the only emperor since Augustus. I am told by everyone who comes from there that he is still spoken of with awe and affection, and that the common people believe that he is not really dead but sleeping beneath a mountain, guarded by the dragon of his house, and should the West ever be in danger, Julian will awaken and come to the defence of the Rhine. It will take some doing to destroy his legend in Europe.

We spoke of you. Ausonius admires you. Who does not? He told me that Theodosius admired your 'graceful' (!) essay 'On Avenging Julian', but took it as a rhetorical exercise. I am sure that is not how you intended it, but I suggest you allow the imperial adjective to be your own.

'What would be the feeling in court if *I* were to publish a book about Julian, covering, say, the Persian campaign?'

Ausonius picked a word beginning with 'm' and nearly choked to death. Finally, in bursts, he told me, 'Never! Theodosius and Gratian both regard him as the devil. Only out of courtesy to Libanius, who is old, did Theodosius accept the essay. But nothing more. Ever! We don't mean to persecute pagans of course,' (the 'we' reminded me of Maximus; do all busy friends of princes use 'we' in that awful way?) 'but we shall make it as disagreeable as possible for them to worship in the old way. You've read the two edicts? There will be others. I can give no details of course. Premature.'

'But Libanius *was* able to write a defence of Julian.'

'Once. Only. We've also heard he's planning a book about Julian.' (No, I did not tell him.) 'Discourage him, as a friend. Also, there is a private matter he would like attended to. I'm not free to say what it is, but he has already sent us a request. Well, one hand washes the other, as they say. Do tell him.' I suppose this refers to the matter of your natural son Cimon. Anyway, that is the gist of my talk with Ausonius. Perhaps you can do better yourself face to face with the Emperor.

Here then is the journal. Some of it is cryptic. There are many lacunae. I have tried to provide as many missing pieces as possible. For weeks now I have been reliving that tragic time and I am amazed at how much I was able to recall when I set what is left of my mind to the task.

My mouth is still ominously twisted but vision and speech are unimpaired, to the surprise of my doctor. I almost wrote 'disappointment'. Doctors like for one's decline to be orderly and irrevocable. How is your gout? Your eyesight? Hippia, whose exquisite penmanship you have been reading, sends you her respects (she has given me such a sweet smile!), as do I.

20

The Journal of Julian Augustus
Callinicum on the Euphrates,   *27 March 363*
Waiting for the fleet. They should have been here when we arrived. Callinicum is a rich city, strongly fortified. Morale is good. Dictating this while riding in a carriage to the river. Today is the festival of the Mother of the Gods.

There is a great ceremony at Rome. I hold a small one here. The sun is hot. People crowd about the carriage. I dictate to the secretary. I wave to the crowd. I am in ceremonial vestments. Maximus and Priscus are with me. The local priests are waiting at the river bank. The people who crowd around are dark-skinned with long thin arms that reach towards me like the tentacles of some twisting vine. They chatter, shrill as Egyptians.

Priscus: This is the first entry. Most of the journal is written in Julian's own hand. He usually wrote late at night, after he had finished dictating his memoir. I recall this particular day in Callinicum as one of the 'good days'. They were so few that each is relatively vivid in my mind.

Several thousand people lined the Euphrates when we arrived for the ceremony. A few were pious, most were merely curious. The Euphrates is a broad muddy river set in rolling country, at this season green.

Julian handled the ceremonies with his usual efficiency. This particular bit of nonsense involved the immersion and ritual washing of the carriage in which the image of the goddess is carried. Julian was thoroughly soaked but happy as he carried out his duties as Pontifex Maximus. Later he gave us dinner (if mashed beans, native bread and fresh tough venison can be called dinner) in the prefect's house. We were all in excellent spirits.

As I wrote you in one of my letters (at least I *think* I wrote you: I often don't remember nowadays whether something I meant to say I did say or not), the generals were seldom a part of Julian's inner circle. For one thing, they don't stay up late; while Aristotle, as the beautiful Arintheus so often used to say, makes the military head ache. Nevertheless, these particular officers were superior men; and of course three of them became emperors.

The generals fell in two categories. The Christian–Asiatics and the Hellenist–Europeans. The first group had been loyal to Constantius; the second to Julian.

For the record, I give you my impression of the principal commanders.

The Asiatics

Count Victor: In appearance, a typical Sarmatian, short, bandy-legged, with a large head, pale eyes slanted like a Hun's. He spoke both Greek and Latin with a barbarous accent. A devout Christian, he was profoundly contemptuous of Julian's philospher friends. I always mistrusted him.

Arintheus: Julian has described him. Once his beauty has been noted, there is not much else to say. He and Victor led the Christian party.

Jovian: An extraordinarily tall man, even taller than I – or would have been had he ever stood up straight. He tended to eat and drink too much, though he never gained weight. He had the reputation for being stupid, and I see no reason for altering this common judgement. Jovian was well connected, which largely explains his later moment of glory. His father was the famous general Varronian, and his wife was the daughter of the egregious Count Lucillianus. I am told that Jovian had a monstrous childhood, living under 'field conditions' until he was seventeen. Old Varronian was an insufferable martinet. Jovian commanded the household troops.

The Europeans

Nevitta: He was a large man, red-faced, blue-eyed, perhaps forty years old at the time. He was an illiterate boor but a fine soldier and completely loyal to Julian. Even so, we all hated him. To his credit *he* hated no one. We were beneath his contempt.

Dagalaif: He was an amiable sort. Stocky and fair (are all good soldiers blond? shall we offer this as a topic of debate for our students?), Dagalaif spoke excellent Greek and Latin. He was a marvellous cavalry man and much of Julian's legendary swiftness was due to Dagalaif's ability to manoeuvre men and horses. He used to ask me for reading lists. He longed to be civilized. Three years later, when he was made consul, he wrote me a panegyric, with surprisingly few mistakes.

Salutius Secundus: A mild, elderly man. We got on famously, though he had almost no conversation. In that sea of youth our grey hairs and ageing muscles called out to one another, like to like. As praetorian prefect he spared Julian many tedious details. He was an excellent administrator who would have made an admirable emperor.

Among others of the court, I should mention the chief marshal, Anatolius, a nice fat little man who managed to create quite a lot of confusion in a position where one is supposed to make order. Also, the notary Phosphorius, whose family forced him to enter the civil service. Solely through merit and hard work he rose to a place on the Consistory; his career was unique. I have never known another like it. As for Julian's philosopher friends, you met them all at Antioch. The only new addition was the Etruscan high priest Mastara. He was exactly what you might think.

On the march, we would usually make camp at sundown. As soon as Julian's tent was raised, we would dine with him, Maximus and I, and sometimes one or another of the commanders. At first Julian was in marvellous spirits. He had every reason to be. Sapor was demoralized at the speed of our attack. The weather was good. The countryside was rich in grain that soon would come to harvest. All things promised well, except the omens.

Julian's tent was a plain affair, necessarily large but simply furnished, not half so comfortable as the tent of any of his generals. As I recall, there were two large folding tables, a number of folding chairs, stools, and several large chests containing state papers and the small library Julian always travelled with. There were several tripod lamps, although seldom was more than one lit at a time. Julian wondered if he was mean: yes, he *was* mean, but compared to the lavish waste of his predecessors this was a virtuous fault. In a corner, his black lion-skinned bed was screened by a woven Persian rug.

Julian was invariably dictating when we presented ourselves. He would smile at us and indicate that we sit down without once breaking the flow of his thought. He did an amazing amount of work, nearly all of it necessary. He conducted a lot of business usually left to notaries or eunuchs. When he had completely exhausted one set of secretaries, he would send for another. All complained that he dictated too fast. And he did, as if he suspected there was hardly time to put on paper all the ideas he had in his brain. We know his famous postscripts. No sooner was a letter sealed than he would have it opened again so that he could scribble some afterthought in his own hand, apologizing with his usual phrase, 'I write fast, without taking breath.' His fingers were always black with ink by the time we arrived for supper.

Before we ate, Maximus or I would read him Homer and he would wash his hands in a plain earthen jug, listening all the time. The meal was always simple.

But then you know his crotchets about food. I usually had another dinner later that night. I am sure Maximus ate before. Sometimes we would be joined by Salutius, an intelligent man for a general, or by Arintheus, whom I always thought a bore. Incidentally, Arintheus was in Athens several years ago. I was shocked to see him. He is now stout and bald, and though he was no favourite of mine, I nearly wept at what time had done. But tears were stopped by his conversation, which had undergone no change. When he saw me at the proconsul's reception, he gave a loud empty laugh and shouted across the room in a voice hoarse from battle and wine, 'That Aristotle of yours *still* makes my head ache!' And that I'm afraid is all that passed between us after so many years and so much history.

As I have said, the philosophers and warriors seldom mingled. That night in Callinicum was one of the few occasions when Julian's two worlds confronted one another.

I sat in a corner and watched Julian play his various roles. Up to a point, we all tend to assume different masks with different people. But Julian changed completely with each person. With the Gallic soldiers, he became a harsh-voiced, loud-laughing Gaul. With the Asiatics, he was graceful but remote, another Constantius. Not until he turned to a philosopher friend was he himself. *Himself?* We shall never know which was the true Julian, the abrupt military genius or the charming philosophy-mad student. Obviously he was both. Yet it was disquieting to watch him become a stranger before one's eyes, and an antipathetic one at that.

I was joined in my corner by Victor. He asked if he could sit down. I beamed fatuously. Why are we all so physically awed by soldiers? 'By all means, Count,' I dithered. He sat down heavily: he smelled of wine but he was not drunk.

'You're a long way from the Academy at Athens,' he said.

I agreed. 'But then Gaul was a long way, too, and the Battle of Strasbourg.' Silently I cursed myself for having boasted of a military career. The ideal philosopher would have conducted the conversation entirely in his own terms; he would *never* compete in an alien field. But then I am not the ideal philosopher. Everyone says so.

'Yes . . . Gaul,' he said, as though that were enough. I could not divine his mood or attitude. We were both silent, watching Maximus as he held a number of the young officers spellbound with some nonsense or other. His flowing beard was exquisitely combed and he wore a robe of saffron-yellow silk, the gift of a magician in China, or so he said. He probably found it in the market at Antioch.

'Can you make your gods appear?' asked Victor suddenly, 'the way *he* does?' Because Victor would not dignify Maximus by giving him a name, my heart went out to him, briefly.

'No,' I said. 'The gods rather leave me alone. But then I make no effort to talk to them.'

'Do you believe?' He spoke with such passionate urgency that I turned to look at him. I have never seen such cold eyes as those which stared at me beneath thick pale brows. It was like coming face to face with a lion.

'Believe in *what?*'

'Christ.'

'I believe that he existed.' I was myself again. 'But I don't think of him as a god.'

Victor was again the Roman commander. 'It will be a long campaign,' he said, as though speaking of the weather. 'But we shall win it.'

We are at Circesium, ninety-eight miles south of Callinicum. We have been here two days. All goes well.

On 28 March while I was still at Callinicum, four tribes of Saracens appeared at the city's gate. Their princes wished to speak to me. Now the Saracens are among the most savage and unreliable of this world's races. They live in tents in the desert. They never build so much as a hut nor till an acre of ground. Restlessly, they roam through the deserts of Assyria, Egypt, Morocco. They live on game, wild birds, whatever grows of itself. Few have tasted grain or wine. They love warfare, but on their own terms. They are good at striking swiftly (their ponies and camels are especially bred for fleetness), but since they fight only for plunder, they are useless in a formal engagement. They are best at scouting and harassing an enemy.

Salutius did not want me to see them. 'They will offer to help you. Then they will make the same offer to Sapor – if they haven't already – and betray you both.'

'So we shall be on our guard.' I was not in the least disturbed.

I received the Saracen princes. They are small, sinewy, dark from the sun. They wear full cloaks to their knees. Beneath their cloaks, they wear only leather drawers. Of the dozen princes, only one could speak Greek.

'We come, Lord, to pay homage to the ruler of the world.' The Saracen then motioned to one of his fellows, who gave him an object wrapped in silk. The prince removed the silk to reveal a heavy gold crown. Hermes knows what king lost it to them. I took the crown and made them a little speech, to which the prince replied, 'Lord, we wish to fight beside you in your war against Sapor. Our courage is known to all the desert. Our loyalty to our ruler is so far beyond that of the merely human that it partakes of the divine . . .' Salutius cleared his throat but I did not dare look at him. 'Therefore, Lord, with us beside you in the desert, you need never fear . . .'

At that moment Nevitta broke into the meeting, to the horror of Anatolius. 'Caesar, the fleet is here!' I'm afraid we all behaved like excited children. I turned the Saracens over to Salutius. Then, followed by the entire Consistory, I made my way to the docks where, as far as the eye could see, the river was filled with ships. 50 W.S., 64 P.B., 1403 C.S., Ct. Luc.

Priscus: This entry breaks off here. The abbreviations mean that there were 50 ships of war, 64 pontoon boats used for making bridges, 1403 cargo ships containing food, weapons, foundries, siege engines; Count Lucillianus was in charge of the fleet. As you will recall, he was the commander at Sirmium whom Dagalaif captured in the middle of the night. Though he was a ridiculous creature, Julian used him because he was an important strand in that web of men and families which governs the world. Despite the vastness of the empire, the actual rulers are a small, close-knit family. Every general knows or has heard of every other general, and they talk of nothing else except, 'How is old Marcellus? still with the same wife? got a different post?'

Lucillianus was waiting at the river bank when Julian and the Consistory arrived. He greeted Julian with meticulous ceremony and formally turned the fleet over to him. Suddenly Dagalaif said, 'Lucillianus, where's your nightshirt?' Everyone laughed except Julian, who muttered, 'Shut up, Dagalaif.' I noticed that Lucillianus's son-in-law Jovian scowled. He was less than amused.

Julian Augustus   *4 April*

I have been working for three hours on my memoir. It is nearly dawn. My voice is hoarse. The secretaries have just gone. I scribble these random notes. We are still at Circesium. It is a large city, well fortified by Diocletian. The city occupies a promontory between the Euphrates River and the place where the Abora River empties into the Euphrates. The Abora is the traditional border between Rome and Persia. Circesium is our last important outpost. From now on we shall be in enemy country.

All night the troops have been crossing the river. The engineers are complaining because the river is swollen with spring rains. But engineers always complain. So far their pontoon bridge is holding. Scouts report no sign of the Persian army. The Saracens tell me that Sapor is astonished at the suddenness of our attack. Apparently, he did not expect us until May. That means he has not yet assembled his army. All of this is marvellous for us. Yet I am not so energetic and hopeful as I ought to be. For one thing, I have just received a long letter from Sallust at Paris. He is unimpressed by the good omens. He begs me not to cross into Persia. Like Libanius, he wishes I would remain at Constantinople and execute the reforms I have proposed. As usual he puts his case superbly, and I am thoroughly depressed.

Tonight I sent away everyone except Maximus. I showed him what Sallust had written, remarking that since Sallust was seldom wrong when it came to politics, we ought at least to consider his advice. Maximus agreed. He praised Sallust at extraordinary length and I wonder how I had ever got the impression they were not friends. For almost an hour Maximus and I discussed the pros and cons of the Persian campaign. We agreed it must continue; although Maximus pointed out that there were any number of precedents for assembling an army and then not using it. Constantius used to do this every year, maintaining that the assembling of an army is in itself a deterrent; perhaps it is.

'But then of course Sallust does not know what we know,' I said at last, referring to Maximus's vision of Cybele.

'There is something else he does not know.' Maximus fixed me with those luminous eyes which have looked upon so many secret and forbidden things. 'Something I have not told even you.'

There was a long silence. I knew Maximus well enough not to hurry him. I waited, heart's blood pounding in my ears.

Maximus got to his feet. The robe of yellow silk fell about him in hieratic folds. In the wavering lamplight he cast a huge shadow on the wall. I felt the imminence of some extraordinary force, that premonitory chill which signals the approach of deity. To ward off demons, Maximus drew a circle around us with his staff. Then he spoke.

'Last night, at the darkest hour, I summoned from the depths of Tartarus, Persephone herself, the Queen of all the Dead that are and ever shall be.'

The lamps flickered; his shadow danced upon the wall; though the night was warm, I shivered with cold.

'I asked her the one question that must not be asked, but since the question concerned not me but you, not you but Rome, not Rome but the worship of the gods, I believed that I could ask this awful question without incurring the wrath of the Furies, or tangling the web of Fate.'

I knew the question. I waited. I could hardly breathe. Maximus drew precautionary symbols on the floor, murmuring spells as he did.

'I asked: "Dread Queen of Tartarus, tell me the place where your loyal son Julian will meet his death." '

Maximus suddenly stopped. His hand went to his throat. He choked; he stumbled; only by clutching at his staff was he able to keep from falling. Something invisible wrestled with him. I did not move to help him for fear of breaking the power of the circle he had drawn. At last he was free. 'Demons,' he whispered. 'But we have the highest power. Helios is our shield. . . . Persephone said, "While all men mourn and all gods rejoice at a new hero come to Olympus, our beloved son Julian will die in Phrygia." '

Maximus's voice faded as though from great weariness. I sat very still, cold as my own Phrygian death. Then Maximus clapped his hands and said in a matter-of-fact voice, 'We are quite a long way from Phrygia, my dear fellow.'

I laughed weakly, from relief. 'And if I have my way, I shall never set foot in that province again.' I then told Maximus that I had been told the same thing by Sosipatra. He was most surprised. He had not known.

'In any case, you see now why I am not concerned by Sallust's letter. Persephone has spoken to us. You know what few men have ever known, the place of your death.'

'And the hour?'

'. . . impossible, for that would be an affront to Fate herself. But we do know that you will survive the Persian campaign. If you survive it, that means you will have conquered.'

'Like Alexander!' In a rush my confidence was restored. Am I not Alexander come again to finish the great work of bringing to the barbarous East the truth of Hellas? We cannot fail now.

Priscus: That was Maximus at his very best, and further proof that Sosipatra and Maximus were in league together. Maximus should have been an actor. But then he *was* an actor, and Julian was his devoted audience.

I don't remember much else about Circesium except that a supply master was executed because the grain barges he had promised for 4 April did not arrive. An hour after the wretch was put to death, the barges were sighted. It was an unpleasant business and Salutius, who had ordered the execution, was most unhappy at what he had done.

At dawn the next day, unable to sleep, I walked to the river bank where Salutius sat in his praetorian prefect's chair, while the army laboriously crossed the pontoon bridge into Assyria, as that part of Persia is called. I remember that cool dawn as though it were today's. A pale pink light in the east, the Abora River muddy and swollen, the cavalry on the bridge, horses shying, men cursing, armour rattling. As far as the eye could see men waited, their armour gleaming like stars in the first light, their voices unnaturally subdued, even apprehensive, for it had been many years since a Roman army had pursued the Great King into his own land.

I sat on a stool beside Salutius while aides came to him at regular intervals: could the Tertiaci Legion cross before the Victores, who weren't ready? in what order were the siege engines to be moved? were the Saracens to cross now with the cavalry or later with the infantry? Patiently, Salutius kept all things in order.

In between messengers, we chatted. I asked him bluntly what he thought of the campaign. He shrugged. 'Militarily, we have nothing to fear from the Persians.' He indicated the legions about us. 'These are the best soldiers in the world, and the Emperor is the best general. We shall beat them in every battle.'

'But they avoid battles. And this is their country. They know how to harass an enemy.'

'Even so, we are the superior force. Only . . .'

'Only?' Salutius studied the list of legions which rested on his lap. 'Only?' I repeated.

But at that moment a centurion rode up, cursing the Saracens, who insisted on crossing at the same time as the cavalry 'with those damned wild horses of theirs!' Salutius soothed the man, effected a compromise, by which time a notary had come to tell me that the Emperor wished me to attend him. As I left, Salutius said, 'Be on your guard, Priscus. We are not safe.' An understatement, as it turned out.

Julian Augustus   *6 April*

I crossed the Abora River yesterday afternoon. As Highest Priest I made sacrifice to Zeus. All omens were good except one: my horse nearly rode over the body of a quartermaster who had been executed by order of the praetorian prefect. Luckily, one of my aides pulled the horse to one side, nearly unseating me in the process.

We then rode some fifteen miles to a village called Zaitha, which means 'olive tree' in Persian. The day was cool, and our spirits were high. Miles before we got to Zaitha we could see its principal monument, the tall circular mausoleum built for the Emperor Gordian. In 242 Gordian conducted a successful campaign against the Persians. Two years later he was murdered by his own men, who had been incited to mutiny by an Arab named Philip who became – briefly – emperor. A sad story, and typical. How often have emperors won great victories and saved the state only to be struck down by an unsuspected rival! Gordian decisively defeated the Persian king at Resaina, only to be murdered by Philip. As a result, a lasting victory over Persia was promptly thrown away by that pusillanimous Arab who wanted only to loot an empire gained by murder.

We stopped for an hour at the tomb, which is in good repair since the Persians respect monuments to the dead, while the roving Saracens fear all buildings. I offered a sacrifice to Gordian's spirit and prayed that I be spared his fate. I must get a biography of him. I know almost nothing of his life, except of course that he was a friend of Plotinus. Maximus says Gordian still haunts this part of the world, demanding vengeance. Unhappy spirit!

While we were still at the tomb, Nevitta got me to one side. He was troubled because, 'The men believe this is the first time Romans have ever invaded Persia. They believe that . . .' he gestured to include all the south . . . 'this country has a spell on it.'

We were standing in the shadow of the tomb. I reached out my hand and touched the rough-hewn tufa. 'Here is the proof that we have been in Persia before.'

'Exactly, Emperor. They say that this old emperor was killed by Persian demons because he dared to cross the Abora River. They say lightning struck him dead. They say Persia is forbidden to us.'

I was astonished. Nevitta, who fears no man, is frightened of demons. I spoke to him as teacher to child. 'Nevitta, Gordian defeated the Great King in a battle one hundred and twenty years ago. Then he was killed by his own men. The Persians had nothing to do with his death. They are not demons. They are men. Men can be defeated, especially Persians. We have defeated Persians many times before.'

Nevitta almost asked 'when?' but then he thought better of it. After all, as a Roman consul he is expected to know something of Roman history. Yet as far as I know, he has never read a book of any kind, though in preparation for this campaign he told me, quite seriously, that he was studying Alexander. When I asked which biography he was reading, he said, *Alexander and the Wicked Magician,* a popular novel!

I reassured Nevitta. I told him about the victories of Lucullus, Pompey and Ventidius, Trajan, Verus and Severus. Apparently, these names had a some- what familiar ring and he looked relieved. I did not of course mention our defeats. 'So tell the soldiers that their fear of the Persians is the result of Constantius's fear of war.'

'You tell them, Emperor.' Nevitta is the only man who addresses me by that military title. 'They don't know these things. And there's a lot of talk about how bad things are going to be.'

'The Galileans?'

Nevitta shrugged. 'I don't know who starts it. But there's talk. You'd better give them one of your history lectures.' That is the closest Nevitta ever comes to humour. I laughed to show that I appreciated his attempt.

'I'll speak to them when we get to Dura.' Nevitta saluted and started to go. I stopped him.

'It might be useful . . .' I began. But then – I don't know why – I chose not to finish. 'Tomorrow, Nevitta.'

He left me alone in the shadow of the tomb. I had meant to ask him to find out who was spreading rumours. But I thought better of it. Nothing destroys the spirit of an army more quickly than the use of secret agents and midnight interrogations. Even so, I have been warned. I must be on guard.

We set out for Dura. We were only a few miles south of Zaitha when two horsemen appeared from the east, carrying something in a sling between them. At first I thought it was a man, but when they came close I saw that it was a dead lion of great size. Maximus whispered excitedly in my ear, 'A king will die in Persia!' But I had already got the point to the omen quite on my own. I also refrained from making the obvious retort: '*Which* king?' But as this Persian lion was killed by Roman spears it seems likely that the Persian King Sapor will be killed by Roman arms.

This lion, incidentally, was the first I'd ever seen close to; even in death, he was terrifying, with teeth long as my thumb and yellow eyes still glaring with life's hot rate. I ordered the lion skinned. I shall use its pelt for my bed.

As we continued towards Dura, the sun vanished, the sky turned grey, lightning flashed. A violent thunderstorn broke. We were all soaked and chilled by the rain, but we continued our march.

Shortly before evening, Victor rode up to me. 'Augustus, a soldier has been killed by lightning.' Though Victor is a Galilean he has the usual military man's interest in omens. 'The soldier was watering two horses by the river when the storm broke. He was just about to lead them back to his cohort when he was struck by lightning. He was killed instantly.'

'What was his name?'

'Jovian, Augustus.' I pretended to take this merely as an added detail. 'Bury him,' I said, and rode on. Maximus was the first to speak. 'The sign is ambiguous. The fact he is named after the king of the gods, the thunderer Jove himself, does not necessarily mean that a king is involved.' But I did not listen. This was a matter for the Etruscans.

We made camp on the outskirts of Dura, a long-deserted town whose houses of brick are slowly returning to the dust from which they were shaped by dead hands. The streets were empty except for herds of deer. I allowed the men to kill as many as they could for food. It was an amusing sight to see our best archers and cavalrymen careering through muddy streets in pursuit of the deer, who promptly fled to the river and, like seasoned troops obeying an agreed-upon plan, swam to the other side. In midstream the bargemen killed many of them with their oars.

That night Maximus, Priscus and I dined on fresh venison in my tent. Afterwards we were joined by the Etruscan priests. Their chief is an elderly man named Mastata. He is held in high regard at Rome, where he used to be consultant to the senate. I record here, privately, that Mastara has been against this campaign from the beginning. He even interpreted the killing of the lion as unfavourable to me.

In general, the Etruscan religion is well known; in particular, it is obscure. From the beginning of time, the genius of the Etruscan religion has been its peculiar harmony with the natural forces of creation. The first revelation is known to all. Tages, a divine child, appeared in the field of a peasant named Tarchon, and dictated to him a holy book which is the basis of their religion. Later Vegoia, a young goddess, appeared during a ceremony to the thunder god and gave the priests a second book which contained instructions on how to interpret heavenly signs, particularly lightning. According to this book, the sky is divided into sixteen parts, each sacred to a particular god (though the same god may at times influence a section not his own). One can discover which god has manifested himself by the direction from which the lightning comes, the angle at which it strikes, and of course the place where it strikes.

Mastara wasted no time. He had already analysed the death of the soldier Jovian. 'Highest Priest, the lightning came from the ninth house.' I knew what this meant even before he interpreted it. 'The house of Ares. The house of war. At the eleventh hour Ares struck down the soldier Jovian beside the river to our west. That means a soldier from the west, a king, will be killed late in a war. We are now making projections as to the exact day and hour of this king's death. By tomorrow we should be able to tell you when this . . . warning shall become fact.'

There it was. We were all quite still for several moments. Maximus sat opposite me, hand wound in his beard, eyes shut as though listening to some voice within. Priscus shifted his long frame uneasily on a hard bench. The Etruscans were motionless, their eyes downcast.

'The king,' I said at last, '*could* be Sapor.'

'Highest Priest, Sapor does not come from the west.'

'Nor do I, to be exact.' I was ready to quibble as people always do when a prophecy has gone against them. 'I come from the north. The only kings hereabout who are from the west are the Saracen princes. My own interpretation is that one of them will die in battle.'

'Then shall we continue with our projection, Highest Priest?' Mastara did not show emotion. He was a priest speaking to his superior, correct, demure, obedient.

'No,' I said firmly. 'I see no need. But to the extent that the army is apt to hear of your first interpretation, I must ask you to allow the second – and correct – interpretation to be generally known.'

Mastara bowed. He and his priests departed. Priscus gave that dry chuckle of his. 'I see now why the early emperors always insisted on being Highest Priest, too.'

'I don't think I misinterpreted the sign.' But realizing this sounded weak, I turned to Maximus for help. He opened his eyes. Then he leapt to his feet and turned first west then east then north then south. 'Not even a Saracen!' he said abruptly. 'Africa. Mauretania. *There* is the doomed king.'

At first I wondered if perhaps Maximus was not trying deliberately to raise my spirits, but as he was in such an exuberant mood for the rest of the evening I now believe him. I have just written a letter to Sallust, asking him to send me news of the Mauretanian kings.

It is daybreak. I have not slept in twenty-four hours, nor will I sleep for another twelve. We must be on the march within the hour. I hear my servant Callistus outside the tent, giving the guard the password. I must now make notes for the speech I give to the troops today. My head is empty. My eyes burn. How to begin?

Priscus: The speech was a success. If Julian was tired, he did not show it. Incidentally, in his description of that séance with the Etruscans he omits my remark to him, 'What is the point of listening to soothsayers, if you won't believe what they tell you?' But Julian was very like the Christians who are able to make their holy book endorse anything they want it to.

Julian's speech had a good effect. In the briefest but most convincing way, he explained to the men how often Roman armies had won victories in this country and he warned them against listening to defeatists, particularly those who had been set among us by the Persians, whose cunning and treachery he emphasized. When he finished, there was a great racket of approval. The Gauls were vociferous, but the eastern legions were unenthusiastic, particularly Victor's cavalry. I mentioned this later to Julian. Yes, he had noticed it, too. 'But they don't know me. The Gauls do. When they've won a few battles and looted a few cities they will love their leader.' Julian the practical soldier, not the Hellenic humanist!

Julian Augustus   14 *April*

L. Arin., Orm., Cav.; R. Nev. Tert., Pet., C.; C. inf. J . . . Dag., Vic.; Van. 1500 sc.; Pyrr.; Luc. fleet; Anatha island: Luc. 1000? Waiting. Cyb. Mith. Her.

Priscus: I think I can interpret this entry. Julian is noting for himself our military order during the march south. On the right, skirting the river bank, Nevitta commanded the Tertiaci, Petulantes and Celts. In the centre Julian commanded the main part of the infantry – the baggage and the philosophers were also in the centre. On the left – or east – Arintheus and Ormisda commanded the cavalry. Though Ormisda was an infantry general, in the field there is a good deal of shifting back and forth of high-ranking officers. Dagalaif and Victor brought up the rear, while 1,500 mounted scouts ranged the countryside before us. Lucillianus commanded the fleet which accompanied us downriver.

'Anatha island: Luc. 1000?' refers to the first Persian stronghold we came to, a heavily fortified island in the middle of the river, four days' march from Dura. Julian sent Lucillianus with a thousand light-armed troops to make a night landing under the walls of the fortress. As there was also a heavy mist that evening, Julian hoped to take the island by surprise. But at dawn the mist suddenly lifted and a Persian soldier went out to draw water, seeing

Lucillianus's men, shouted a warning and that was the end of Julian's surprise attack.

A few hours later, Julian crossed over to the island. One look at those huge walls decided him against a siege. He would have to take the fort by other means. Incidentally, this was to be his policy during the whole campaign. Between the Roman border and Ctesiphon – a distance of more than three hundred miles – there were a dozen fortresses and walled cities. Julian had the power to take any one of them but at the cost of weeks' or even months' delay. He could not afford this. So he chose to isolate the fortresses, knowing that once the Great King fell all the cities would be his.

Julian sent word to the governor of Anatha that he would spare the lives of the garrison if they surrendered. The governor asked for a parley with Ormisda. Julian describes this in the next entry.

'Waiting.' These notes were made late in the night of the fourteenth when Lucillianus was still hidden on the island.

'Cyb. Mith. Her.' A prayer: Cybele, Mithras, Hermes.

Julian Augustus   *15 April*

Anatha has surrendered! Our first victory on Persian soil. At noon the governor of the island, Pusaeus, asked me to send him Ormisda to work out the details of the surrender. I confess I was nervous while awaiting the outcome of the conference. Pusaeus could so easily murder Ormisda. But less than an hour after Ormisda entered the fortress, the gates swung open and a garlanded ox was led forth by a Persian priest as sign of peace. There was a great cheer from our legions. Then Ormisda and the governor appeared. Pusaeus is a dark intense man, reputedly a good soldier (why else would he have been entrusted with this important fort?). He saluted me as he would have saluted the Great King, flat on his belly. Then, face full of dust, he asked me what I intended to do with the inhabitants of the town.

I motioned to Anatolius and his notaries to join us. Then I said, 'Governor, since you have shown yourself friendly to us and honourable in your dealings, we shall, at our own expense, move your people to Syria, to the city of Chalcis, where they will be able to live as they have lived here.'

He thanked me warmly, his head rolling about in the dirt until I told him to get up. Pusaeus then asked me if I would take him into the Roman army. I turned to Ormisda. 'Should I?'

Ormisda's face is a sea of delicate responses; by the slightest quiver of a brow or the flaring of a nostril he is able to communicate without words. The face said: beware! The voice said, 'Yes, but perhaps not here, perhaps with a garrison in Spain or Egypt.' So I made Pusaeus a tribune and posted him to Egypt.

All this took place in the main square of Anatha, a town of wood and thatch and mud brick, exactly like every other town, Persian or Roman, in this part of the world. While we talked, the people passed by us. The women balanced rolls of bedding and clothing on their heads while the men carried weapons and cooking utensils. Suddenly a frail old man, supported by two women, approached us. He gave me the Roman salute and said in soldier-Latin: 'Maximanus, foot soldier with the Ziannis, reporting for duty.' He stood shakily at attention. I looked at him with wonder. 'Where are you from? Who are you?'

'A Roman soldier, General. In the army of Galerius Augustus.'

Salutius said flatly. 'That's impossible. It's a hundred years since Galerius died.'

'No, Prefect,' said the old man (he still knew a praetorian prefect when he saw one), 'Galerius was here sixty-six years ago. And I was with him. I was eighteen years old. I'd enlisted at Philippopolis in Thrace. We won great victories here.'

'But why are you *still* here?' Easily the most fatuous question one could ask a man in his eighties. But I was quite overwhelmed by this relic of another age.

'I fell ill with the fever. My tribune, Decius – never got on with him – thought I was going to die. So he left me here with a family who said they'd bury me properly when the time came. Then the army left.' He laughed, an old rooster cackling. 'Well, they haven't buried me yet. You can see that, I guess! And *they're* all gone: Galerius, Decius, Marius . . . he was a good friend, but got the pox . . . he's gone, too. So the family here that was willing to bury me took me in and I married two of their daughters. Both good girls. Dead now. These are later wives.' He indicated the women who stood, ready to support him should he stumble. 'General, I beg one favour.'

'Whatever I can grant,' I said.

'I have sworn that I would die on Roman soil and be buried in Roman earth. Send me back to Thrace.'

'So be it, soldier.' I motioned for Anatolius to arrange the matter. The old man then kissed my hand and I looked down with wonder at the back of his shrivelled neck, lined as old parchment and burned dark by the fierce suns of nearly a century. What must it be like to have lived so long? With some difficulty, his wives got him to his feet. He was breathing hard from the exertion. He looked at me curiously.

'You *are* the Emperor of Rome, aren't you?'

I nodded. 'Do you doubt it?'

'No, no, Lord. They told me that the Roman general was also the Emperor and that's when I advised the town council to surrender. "You haven't a chance," I said, "not when there's an Emperor on the loose and the Great King out there, hidden in the desert, frightened out of his wits. Better surrender," I said. Didn't I, Pusaeus?'

'Yes, Augustus, he did say so.'

'This Pusaeus is married to a grandchild of mine, which makes him part-way to being Roman. They're a good people, you know, the Persians. I hate to see them hurt.'

'We shall be as merciful as we can.'

'I've had a good life here.' He looked about him vaguely. Then his eye caught on the standard of the Ziannis. 'There's my legion! I must talk to those boys. I knew their fathers, *grandfathers* anyway. Yes . . .' He started to walk off but then, recalling me, he stopped. 'Thank you, General.'

'Thank you, soldier, for remaining loyal to Rome all these years.'

'You know, General . . . Lord, I don't follow too much what happens in the world outside of the province here because there's so little news and what there is makes no sense because they're capital liars, the Persians. They can't help it, you know, they don't mean any harm by it. It's just their way. But I did hear word of a great emperor who they call Constantine. That's not you, is it?'

'No, but there was such an emperor and he was my uncle.'

'Yes, yes.' The old man was not listening. He frowned, trying to recall something. 'There was also this young officer who was with us in 297 . . . well-connected, he was, *his* name was Constantine, too. I often wondered if it was the same fellow. Do you know if he was?'

Constantine had indeed served one year with Galerius in Persia. I nodded. 'It could have been the same,' I said.

'He looked a bit like you, only he was clean-shaven. A nice enough young chap, though we none of us thought he'd ever make a soldier, liked the girls and the soft life too much, but who doesn't?' He sighed contentedly. 'So now I've seen three emperors, and I'll die on Roman soil. And where's the tribune Decius, I ask you? who used to give me such a hard time and left me here to die? Where is he? who remembers him, after all these years? But I'm alive and I've been talking to the Emperor, to Julius himself! Now that's a great thing, isn't it? So if you'll excuse me, General, I want to go chat with those Thracian lads; maybe one is a grandchild to Marius, though they say when they get the pox it makes the children stillborn or worse. He was a lovely friend, Marius.'

The old man saluted me and, helped by the two old wives, he slowly crossed the square to the place where the standard of the Ziannis had been set up. I was much moved by this encounter, even though I had been called Julius!

When all the inhabitants had left Anatha, we set fire to the town. Then I returned to our camp on the river bank to be greeted by the Saracens, who had just captured a number of Persian guerrilla fighters in the act of raiding our supplies. I gave the Saracens money to show my pleasure, and told them to continue to be on the alert. I also asked if the Saracen princes were safe. Yes.

It is late at night. I am pleasantly drowsy. Our first encounter with the enemy has been all that I could have wished it. If it were not for the rain which is falling and turning the floor of my tent to mud, I would be perfectly content.

Priscus: The rain that night was accompanied by winds. The next day, 16 April, at about the third hour, we were struck by a hurricane from the north. Tents were ripped by the wind, while the river, already swollen from spring rains, overflowed and several grain barges were wrecked. The dikes which control the flow of river water into irrigation ditches broke and some suspected the Persians of deliberately shutting the sluice gates in order to flood our camp. We shall never know if they did or not. Anyway, after two wet wretched days, we moved on.

Julian was in good spirits. We all were. The first Persian stronghold was ours and the Great King's army had vanished. It was too good to be true.

Our army was stretched out over ten miles, much the same trick Julian used when he came from Gaul, to give the impression of a mighty host. Julian rode either at the head or at the rear of the army, the two places most apt to be harassed by guerrillas. But we did not come up against the Persians for some days. They kept to the opposite side of the river, watching us. Whenever we made as though to cross, they would disappear in the thickets of wormwood. Yet they were very much on the alert. When one of the Gauls – for reasons of his own – crossed over, he was butchered and his head placed on a long pole in full view of our army.

Incidentally, I lost my tent in the storm and for three nights I was forced to share quarters with Maximus. We were not happy with one another. Among other bad habits, he talked in his sleep. The first night we slept together, I found his mumbling so unbearable that I woke him up.

'I? Talking in my sleep?' He looked at me blearily, silver beard tangled like fleece wool before carding, face stupid with sleep. Then he remembered himself. 'But of course I was talking. It is in sleep I converse with the gods.'

'Then could you perhaps *whisper* to them? You're keeping me awake.'

'I shall do my best.' He later complained to Julian that my coughing had kept him awake! But I coughed hardly at all considering that I had caught a very bad cold as a result of being soaked in the storm. Julian was much amused at the thought of our sharing the same quarters.

Julian Augustus   *22 April*
17 April. Thilutha, Achaiachalca. 18 April, abandoned fort burned. 20 April. Baraxmalcha, cross river 7 miles to Diacira. Temple. grain. salt. bitumen springs. deserted. burned. to Ozogardana. deserted. burned. monument to Trajan. two days in camp. 22 April, attempt to ambush Ormisda. Warning. Persian army gathering tonight.

Priscus: Between 17 April and 20 April we passed three island fortresses. The first was Thilutha, a mountain peak jutting out of the water with a stronghold on the top of it. Julian sent a messenger demanding surrender. The commandant sent back a most courteous answer. He would not surrender, but he swore to abide by the outcome of the Emperor's war with the Great King. Since we could not waste time in a siege, we accepted the commandant's reply. In return, the garrison saluted our fleet as it passed beneath the walls of the island. The same thing happened at Achaiachalca, another island fortress.

On 20 April we came to a deserted village called Baraxmalcha. At Ormisda's suggestion we then crossed the river and marched seven miles inland to Diacira, a rich market centre. The city was deserted when we arrived. Fortunately, the warehouses were filled with grain and, most important, salt. Outside the town wall, Nevitta's soldiers found several women and put them to death. This did not sit well with me. I don't know if Julian knew about these murders or not. He was ruthless when it came to punishing disobedience and treachery, but was not cruel, unlike Nevitta and the Gauls, who liked blood for its own sake.

Diacira was burned, as was the near-by town of Ozogardana where, incidentally, we found the remains of a tribunal of Trajan. Julian made this relic centre to the camp that was pitched. We remained there for two days while the grain and salt taken from Diacira was loaded onto barges. During this time, Julian was busy with his generals and I did not see him at all.

I contented myself with the company of Anatolius (who was quite amusing, particularly about his failures as marshal of the court), the admirable Phosphorius, and Ammianus Marcellinus, whom I had met earlier at your house in Antioch. I liked him very much. He told me that we had first met at Rheims where he'd been on duty with one of Ursicinus's legions, though I'm afraid I don't recall that meeting. As you know, Ammianus is writing a history of Rome which he plans to bring up to date. Brave man! Some years ago he sent me an inscribed copy of the first ten books of his history, *in Latin!* Why he has chosen to write in that language, I don't know. After all, he comes from Antioch, doesn't he? And I seem to have got the impression that he was of good Greek family. But looking back, I can see that he was always something of a Romanophile. He used to spend most of his time with the European officers, and he rather disliked the Asiatics. As a historian, he has deliberately put himself in the line of Livy and Tacitus rather than that of Herodotus and Thucydides, showing that there is no accounting for taste. He wrote me recently to say that he is living at Rome where, though he finds the literary world incredibly arid and pretentious, he means to make his mark. I wish him well. I haven't read much of his history but he seems to write Latin easily, so perhaps he has made the right choice. But what a curious old-fashioned thing to want to be, a *Roman* historian! He tells me that he is in regular correspondence with you. So I dare say the two of you will join forces when the time comes to publish the memoir.

The night of 22 April Ormisda was about to go reconnoitring when he was nearly ambushed by a cohort of the Persian army. Nobody knows how the Persians knew the exact hour he was to leave the camp, but they did. Ormisda was saved by the unexpected deepness of the river at that point. The enemy could not ford it owing to the rains.

'Warning.' I don't know what Julian means by this. Perhaps a counterspy warned Ormisda at the last moment. Or someone warned Julian of a plot against *his* life.

'Persian army gathering tonight.' The next morning (23 April) we finally saw the Persian army. Several thousand horsemen and archers were assembled a mile from our encampment. In the morning's light their glittering chain mail made our eyes water. They were under the command of the Grand Vizier, who is second only to the Great King himself, a position somewhere between that of a Caesar and a praetorian prefect. Associated with the Vizier's army was a large band of Assanatic Saracens, a tribe renowned for cruelty.

At the second hour, Julian engaged the enemy. After much manoeuvring, he got his infantry into position some yards from the Persian archers. Then before they could fire, he gave the order for an infantry charge at quick march. This manoeuvre startled the Persians just long enough for our men to neutralize their archers. Infantry shields were thrust against archers in such a way that the Persians could not take aim to fire. They broke and ran. The field was ours.

Julian was delighted. 'Now our soldiers know the Persians are men just like ourselves!' He looked the perfect war god: face flushed, purple cloak stained with the blood of others, eyes bright with excitement. 'Come along,' he shouted to Maximus and the philosophers who were now coming up to what had been the front line. 'Let's see the walls of Macepracta!'

None of us knew what Julian meant until he led us to a deserted village near the battlefield. Here we saw the remains of an ancient wall. Julian consulted a book. 'This,' he said, 'is part of the original Assyrian wall. Xenophon saw it when he was here 764 years ago.' Happily, our victorious general clambered over the stones, reading at the top of his voice from Xenophon's *March Upcountry*. We all looked dutifully on what had been a ruin even then, so long ago, but I'm afraid that after the stimulus (and terror) of battle, no one was in a mood for sightseeing. Finally, Julian led us back to the river.

On the outskirts of the encampment, a legion of household troops were gathered around a rock on which stood their tribune, haranguing them. He was tall, thickly muscled, with fair hair. '. . . you fear the Persians! You say they are not men like us but demons! Don't deny it! I've heard you whispering at night, like children afraid of the dark.'

The tribune's voice was strong. His face was ruddy and his eyes were – what else? blue. We dark-eyed people have lost the world to those with eyes like the winter ice. He spoke with a slight German accent. 'But now you've seen these demons close to. You beat them in battle. Were they so fierce? So huge? So terrible?'

There was a low murmur from the men about him: no, the Persians had not been superhuman. The tribune was a splendid demagogue. I looked at Julian, who had bundled his cloak about his face as momentary disguise. He was watching the man with the alert interest of an actor or rhetorician studying a rival's performance.

'No. They are men like us. But *inferior* men. Look!' The tribune motioned for one of his officers to step forward. The man was holding what looked at first to be a bundle of rags. But it was a dead Persian. The officer tossed the body to the tribune. He caught it easily. The men gasped, impressed at the strength of these two men who handled a corpse as though it were a doll.

The tribune with one hand held up the body by the neck. The dead Persian was slight, with a thin black moustache and a fierce display of teeth. His armour had been stripped away and the remains were clad only in a bloody tunic. 'There he is! The Persian deveil! *This* is what you were afraid of?' With his free hand, the tribune tore the tunic away, revealing a slight, almost childlike body with a black crescent beneath the breast-bone where a lance had entered.

The tribune shook the body, as a hunting dog will shake a hare. 'Are you afraid of this?' There was a loud response of 'No!' Then great laughter at the sight of the hairless smooth body, so unlike us. The tribune tossed the remains contemptuously to the ground. 'Never again do I want to hear anyone whisper in the night that the Persians are devils! *We* are the men who will rule this land!' To loud cheering, the tribune stepped down from his rock and walked straight into Julian. He saluted smartly, not at all taken aback. 'A necessary speech, Augustus.'

'An *excellent* speech, Valentinian.' For as you have doubtless guessed, the tribune was our future emperor. 'I want all my commanders to give their troops the same . . . demonstration. First-rate.'

The soldiers promptly vanished, as soldiers tend to the moment they realize the Emperor is among them.

Julian and his successor exchanged a few soldierly words. Then as we were about to move on, Valentinian motioned to a young cavalry officer who was standing near by, wide-eyed at the sight of the Emperor. 'Augustus, may I present to you my brother Valens?'

I often wonder what Julian would have thought if he had known that in less than a year those brothers, sons of an Austrian ropeseller turned general, would be co-emperors of East and West. I suspect he would have approved of Valentinian, but Valens was a disaster. And the fact that both were Christian would hardly have pleased him. It certainly did not please us, did it? I nearly lost my life because of Valens. Maximus did lose his.

Then Julian left his successors, none aware of the future. If the gods exist, they are kind. Despite oracles and flashes of lightning, they tell us nothing. If they did, we could not bear it.

The next day we came to a place where the water of the Euphrates was drawn off into a network of irrigation canals. Some of these canals are a thousand years old and without them Persia would not be the rich country it is. There were those who wanted to divert the waters and cause the fields to dry up but Julian would not allow this, pointing out that we should soon be living off the produce of these same fields. At the beginning of the largest canal was a tall tower, marking the source of the Naharmalcha (Persian for 'the king's river') which flows into the Tigris below Ctesiphon. This river or canal was unusually swift from the rains. With difficulty, pontoon bridges were constructed. The infantry got across safely, but a number of pack animals were drowned in the current. As I recall, there was some harassing of the cavalry by Persian scouts, but they were soon driven off by our Saracen outriders.

On 28 April, after an uneventful march, we came to Pirisabora, a large city with impressive high walls and towers burned by the sun to the buff colour of a lion's skin. The river surrounds the city naturally on three sides. On the fourth, the inhabitants have dug a canal so that they are, in effect, an island and hard for an enemy to approach. At the centre of the city on a high hill was a formidable inner fortress. I must say my heart sank when I saw it. The siege of such a place could take months.

Julian sent his usual message to the city: if they surrendered, he would spare the lives of the inhabitants. But Pirisabora was one of the important cities of Persia, and the answer of its commandant, Mamersides, was arrogant indeed. The city would not surrender. But Mamersides would speak to Ormisda (apparently they had been in secret correspondence with one another).

I was present when Ormisda, tall and glittering and very much a Persian king, rode to the moat which separated city from mainland. He reined in his horse at the water's edge. When the Persians on the wall recognized him, they began a loud jeering and hissing. They called him 'traitor' and worse. I was close enough to Ormisda to see his sallow face set in harsh lines, but he did not move or in any other way show that he had heard. For a full half-hour he endured their insults. Then, seeing that there was to be no dealing with these men, he motioned for his standard-bearer to join him. This caused an even louder tumult. Ormisda's standard was that of the Great King of Persia. Majestically, Ormisda withdrew, and Julian ordered a siege.

Unfortunately, Julian did not describe the siege and I don't remember much about it. Perhaps our friend Ammianus will record it. Military history is not really my forte. My chief memory of this siege was a series of quarrels with Maximus. I shall spare you the quarrels, since I've completely forgotten what they were about.

The city of Pirisabora fell on the second day, after much fighting. But the matter was not yet finished, for the army and the governor promptly took refuge on their mountain top and there, behind walls of bitumen and brick, strong as iron, they held fast. Julian himself led the first attack on the citadel, and was repulsed.

On the third day, Julian ordered a helepolis built. This is a tall wooden tower which is used to scale even the highest walls. There is no defence against it, not even fire, for it is covered with wet hides. The helepolis was not needed. No sooner was it half assembled than Mamersides asked for a truce. He was lowered from the citadel by a rope which broke a few yards from the ground; he fractured both legs. Julian was merciful. All lives would be spared if the citadel was surrendered.

At sundown, some 2,500 Persians, men and women, issued forth, singing a hymn of thanksgiving to the Great Lord who had spared their lives and would now reign mercifully over them. Then Pirisabora was burned to the ground. By this time, I was no longer speaking to Maximus.

Julian Augustus   *3 May*
3 squ. cav. Trib. killed. Viz. command. Standard lost! 2 Trib. cash. dec. Stand. regained. speech. 100 p. silv.

Priscus: I recall '3 squ. cav. Trib. killed, etc.,' vividly. The day after the burning of the city we all dined at midday with Julian. It was a pleasant meal and he was refighting the siege, as soldiers like to do, the 'what-might-have-happened-if'

kind of thing, when Anatolius came into the tent with the news that the Grand
Vizier had personally put to flight three of our cavalry squadrons, killing one of
the tribunes and capturing the regimental standard.

I thought Julian would have a stroke. He hurled his plate to the ground and
rushed from the tent, shouting for a call-to-arms. Within the hour, the Vizier's
force had been located, and our standard regained. Within three hours, the two
surviving tribunes were cashiered and, of those who had fled before the enemy,
ten were executed, according to the old law of decimation. I had never seen
Julian so angry nor so much the classic general. He ordered the entire army to
watch the execution. When it was done, he made a speech, warning against
disobedience and cowardice, and reminding the army that should anyone
surrender to the enemy, the Persians would hamstring him and leave him to die
in the desert. Then he praised the troops for the victory at Pirisabora, and he
gave each man a hundred pieces of silver.

Poor Julian! Having so little interest in money himself, he could never get
sums right. He never knew the correct price of anything, including the common
soldier's loyalty. At the mention of such a small sum, the army roared its
displeasure and I was afraid they would mutiny right then and there. But Julian
was not intimidated. He told them sharply that he himself was a poor man and
that the Roman nation was in straitened circumstances because so many of his
predecessors had used gold to buy a false peace rather than iron to fight
necessary wars. But he promised them that soon they would be at Ctesiphon and
the treasure of all Persia would be theirs. This put them in a good humour, and
they cheered him and clattered their shields.

Julian Augustus   *4 May*
   14 miles. Floods. Halt. Bridges.

Priscus: The Persians broke the river dikes to the south of us and we lost a day
while boats and rafts were used to get across the many pools the river water
made. The countryside had become a giant swamp. My chief memory is of giant
blood-sucking leeches clinging to my legs as I waded through muddy waters.

Julian Augustus   *7 May*
   Maiozamalcha. Camp. Prepare siege. Ambush. Treason?

Priscus: Three days later we came to Maiozamalcha, another important city
with great walls. Here Julian set up camp.

'Ambush' refers to what happened that evening. Julian and several scouts
made an inspection of the outer walls, to look for points of weakness. While they
were passing under the walls, ten Persians slipped out of the city through a
porter's gate and, crawling on their hands and knees, took Julian and his scouts
by surprise. Two of them set upon Julian. He killed one, protecting himself from
the other with his shield. In a matter of minutes the Persians were dead and
Julian returned to camp, happy as a boy with the dead Persian's weapons for
trophy.

'Treason?' How did the Persians know about this scouting party? Julian was
aware that his army was full of spies, not to mention those who wished him
harm. He suspected treason, and he was right.

The inhabitants of Maiozamalcha refused to surrender. So Julian settled in
for a siege. He was now fearful of the Persian army which was supposed to be

gathering just south of Ctesiphon. For added protection, he erected a double palisade around our camp.

Julian Augustus   *8 May*

Cavalry under the Grand Vizier attacked pack animals in the palm groves. No casualties for us. Several for them. Persians driven off. Countryside is heavily wooded and full of streams and pools. I always thought Persia was desert. How I should like to have the leisure to turn Herodotus and describe this part of the world! It is so beautiful. Date palms and fruit trees abound. Fields are yellow-green with new grain. This year's harvest will be a good one, and ours!

I find particularly interesting the pools of naphtha, an oily flammable substance which bubbles up from the ground. This morning I ordered one of the pools lit. A column of fire leapt to heaven. The only way it can be put out is to smother the pool in sand; otherwise, it may burn for years. I left the pool afire as an offering to Helios.

Several prisoners from this morning's raid were brought to me. They are curious-looking creatures and I examined them with some attention, recalling one of the tribunes who recently showed his troops a Persian corpse, saying: 'See what you feared? This is the Persian devil, all of seven feet tall with arms of bronze and breathing fire!' Then he showed them the remains of a fragile creature more like a boy than a man.

Priscus: Traditionally the reporting of speeches in historical texts is not meant to be literal. But my version of Valentinian's comments was accurate because I kept a few notes at the time, which I am using now in making this commentary. Yet here is Julian less than a week later already altering the text. History is idle gossip about a happening whose truth is lost the instant it has taken place. I offer you this banality for what it is: *the truth!*

Julian Augustus   *8 May*

The Persians I examined were cavalrymen. They are small, wiry, leaden-complexioned. Ormisda acted as interpreter. Though they expected immediate death, they seemed without fear. One spoke for all of them, a flood of words. When he was finally out of breath, I asked Ormisda what he had said.

Ormisda shrugged, 'Typically Persian.' Ormisda was in his Greek mood. 'He hopes we choke in our pride and that the moon will fall on our army and crush it and that the tribes of the desert will rise up from as far away as India and China to butcher us. The Persian style of address is always a bit exaggerated, particularly the metaphors.'

I laughed. I have always been more amused than not by Persian rhetoric. It is characteristic of eastern peoples to talk always with a mad extravagance. Even their diplomatic letters are often unintelligible because of Pindar-like excesses.

Ormisda replied in kind. The Persians listened contemptuously. They are handsome men with pointed smooth beards and eyebrows which tend to grow together. Their eyes are particularly expressive, black and deep. They are quite slender because of their austere diet. They eat only when they are hungry, and then very little. They seldom drink wine. Their only excess (aside from their conversation!) is women. Each man has as many concubines as he can afford. They do not like boys. They are most modest about their persons and it is considered shameful for a man to be seen by another relieving himself in a natural way. I rather wish our army would imitate their physical modesty. Yet for all their virtues, they are not a likeable people. They are arrogant and boastful and revel in cruelty. The nobles terrorize the lower classes as well as the slaves, torturing or killing them as they please, and there is no law to protect the helpless, nor any idea of charity. Their laws are savage. For instance, if a man is guilty of a capital crime, not only is he executed but all of his family as well.

'They are hopeless,' said Ormisda wearily when the captives were taken away. 'The most foolish race on earth.'

'But *you* are their Great King,' I teased him. 'Therefore the most foolish of all.'

'I've lived too long among you,' he said sadly.

'But as a ruler you should be all the better for that. You can change them.'

'No change.' He shook his head. 'That is the point to Persia. As we were, we are; as we are, we shall be. When I am Great King (the Sun and Julian willing), I shall be Greek no longer. Plato will be forgotten. I shall be like Darius and Cyrus, like Xerxes and ... yes, like my brother Sapor.'

'An unreliable ally to Rome?' I asked this jokingly, but I was serious.

'What else? I am the heir to the Sassanides kings. We are cruel and extravagant.' Then he smiled, winningly. 'You'd be well advised, Augustus, to kill *all* the Persians, including me.'

'Impracticable,' I said, and changed the subject. But I was impressed by what Ormisda said, and uneasy. Should I keep a Roman army at Ctesiphon and govern through a proconsul? Or would we fail in this the way our ancestors failed with the Jews? I wish Sallust were here.

We spent the rest of the day with the staff, preparing for the siege of Maiozamalcha. The town is on high ground with a double wall. It is well garrisoned. I have ordered a mining of the walls. This is a good exercise we have not yet tried. Nevitta and Dagalaif are at this moment digging tunnels beneath the walls. At dawn, Victor and a number of cavalry scouts will reconnoitre as far as Ctesiphon. There is a rumour the Great King's army is on its way to us from the east, but it is only rumour.

Everything goes too easily. Yet why should I be surprised? The gods are with me and the spirit of Alexander whispers: advance, to the farthest edge of the world!

Priscus: As usual the spirit of Alexander was over-ambitious. We had enough troubles taking Maiozamalcha, much less India and China. But at this time Julian was not mad, despite Maximus's best efforts. There was no immediate plan to conquer farthest Asia. Julian anticipated a short campaign in Persia, winter at Tarsus, and *then* an expedition to India.

Julian does not describe the siege and fall of Maiozamalcha and neither shall I. As I recall, the city was on a high bluff overlooking the river. To get to it one had to climb steep cliffs, eminently suited for defence. The first day a frontal assault was attempted. It failed. Meanwhile, tunnels were being dug beneath the walls.

The second day the siege engines were brought up. The air was filled with the roaring sound of rocks being catapulted against the walls. The sun burned fiercely. Defenders and attackers were soon exhausted. But Julian drove the men to the limit of their strength, for he had no time to waste in a siege so near Ctesiphon and the Great King's army. Finally, word came from the tunnel builders that they were ready to break into the city. That night, Julian attacked the walls with his army while the troops below ground entered the city through the floor of the back room of an empty tavern. The city surrendered.

Julian Augustus   *11 May*

We have had excellent luck. Maiozamalcha fell with few casualties for us. I have just received Nabdates, the Persian commander. He hailed me as Lord of the World and I have spared his life. This should make a good impression. If the Persian lords believe that I am merciful, they will be more apt to surrender when overwhelmed. I hope so, since there is nothing so demoralizing for an army as to fight long sieges for unimportant cities.

Nabdates swears that he does not know where the Great King is, and I believe him. He suspects that Sapor is not at the capital but somewhere to the south. In any case, we shall soon meet, the Great King and I.

I write this in my tent beside the river. On its high hill the city of Maiozamalcha burns like a torch in the black night. With difficulty I prevented a slaughter in the city. The Gauls regard Persian resistance as an affront; they always do. Incidentally, they discovered several hundred women hidden in the citadel. They promptly drew lots for them. At such times, the officers vanish and the men take over. Quite by accident, I happened to be near the square during the lottery.

The women were huddled together, along with the city's treasure: gold coins, ornaments, bolts of silk, whatever had been found in the ruins had been brought together for a fair division. One of the Petulantes, seeing me, shouted, 'Something for Julian!' So I joined the men on foot, like a legionnaire.

The centurion in charge of the lottery indicated one of the piles of gold. 'That's your share, soldier,' he said, using the traditional phrase. I thanked him and took a single piece of gold. Then the men began to shout that I should take one of the women. They know of course that I am celibate, and find this fact infinitely comic. I refused amiably. But they kept pressing me. So I looked at the crowd of wretched women, thinking to take a child and set her free. But there was none, only a very handsome boy of about ten. So I pointed to him. The men were delighted. Better a boy-lover than a celibate on the throne!

The boy turned out to be a deaf-mute of great intelligence. The signs he makes with his hands are swift and graceful and I find that I can understand him easily. I have made him my personal servant and he seems happy.

I am depressed tonight. Ordinarily, I would be exhilarated by victory. I can't think what is wrong. Perhaps it is the memoir. I have been dictating memories of my childhood at Macellum and remembering those years always puts me in a bad mood.

Interesting note: One of the men of the Herculani reports that at the height of the battle today he saw a huge man in strange armour climbing one of the siege ladders. Later he saw this same warrior in the thick of the fighting, but he could not identify him nor could any of the others who saw him. They are all certain that this warrior was the war god Ares himself. I must ask Maximus to find out.

12 May

It is afternoon. I am seated in the throne room of one of the Great King's palaces, a fine building in the Roman style, more like a country villa than a formal palace. Next to it is a fenced-in game preserve. Here all sorts of wild animals are kept in a wooded area . . . lions, boars and that truly terrible beast, the Persian bear. The men have just broken down the fences and are now hunting and killing the animals. I should have preferred for them not to indulge in this slaughter but they must be kept in a good mood, for we are close to Ctesiphon and the decisive battle.

Jovian has just come and gone. He brought me the skin of a lion he killed, quite a large beast. 'A match for the one on your bed.' I thanked Jovian warmly. Of the Galilean officers, he is the one I trust the most, possibly because he is the stupidest. I gave him some wine we had found in the cellar of the palace. He drank it so greedily that I gave him two more flagons to take with him when he left. He was most pleased and slightly drunk.

Priscus and I explored the palace together. It is both beautiful and comfortable, a combination Roman emperors are not used to. Apparently the servants fled shortly before we arrived, leaving a dinner still warm in the kitchen. I was about to taste the contents of one of the pots when the deaf-mute boy struck the ladle from my hand. Then *he* tasted the mess, indicating that I should beware of poison. I never think of such things. No, that is not true. I do occasionally wonder if my evening bowl of polenta contains my death, but I never hesitate to eat it. If that is to be my end, there is nothing I can do about it. Fortunately, the dinner the Persians left us was not poisoned.

I have set the secretaries to work in the throne room, a cool dim room with latticed windows and a red lacquered throne on which I now sit scribbling. The Great King lives far more luxuriously than I. In one of the rooms we discovered hundreds of his silk robes . . . Priscus insists that I give them to Maximus.

Tonight I have planned a large dinner for the military staff. I have the beginnings of a plan for this last phase. Contrary to what historians may think, wars are mostly improvisation. One usually has an ultimate goal, but the means of attaining it cannot be determined in advance. That is why the favourite deity of generals – and of Rome – is Fortune.

16 May

Encamped for three days now at Coche. This is a village near the site of the now vanished city of Seleucia, built by Alexander's general. Farther on are the ruins of yet another city, destroyed in the last century by the Emperor Carus. I thought it good policy to show this to the men, demonstrating yet again how victorious Roman arms have been in Persia.

I am still struck by the beauty of the countryside. Flowers bloom; fruits ripen; there are many forests; much water. This is an idyllic part of the world and I am sad that so many of its cities must be put to the torch. But what men build they can rebuild. I am with the Stoics, who regard all life as an infinite series of growth and decline, each temporary terminus marked with the clean impartiality of fire.

Near the city Carus destroyed, there is a small lake which empties into the Tigris. Here we beheld a gruesome sight. Impaled on stakes were the entire family of Mamersides, the officer who surrendered Pirisabora to us. Thus cruelly does the Great King punish those who disobey him. It was horrible to see not only women but children put to death in this painful way.

While we were at the lake, Ormisda and his Persian court (he now has over a hundred Persians in attendance on him) appeared, with Nabdates, the governor of Maiozamalcha. Ormisda saluted me formally. Then he said, 'Augustus, I have passed sentence of death on Nabdates.'

I asked him why.

Ormisda was grim. 'Before the siege, we had a private understanding. He was to surrender the city to us. It was all arranged. Then he broke his oath to me, the highest oath a Persian can swear. Therefore, as Great King, I *must* put him to death, by fire.' I was impressed by Ormisda's manner. The closer we come to Ctesiphon, the more imperial and Persian he becomes. So I gave my assent, and the wretched man with his broken legs was dragged to the stake. I left before the burning began. I dislike all executions except those done with the sword.

I write these lines seated on a bench in what looks to be some nobleman's park. It is a beautiful day; the sun is warm but not hot; as far as the eye can see the countryside is green and blooming. I am certain now of success. A messenger from Arintheus has just come and gone. A fortress some twenty miles to the east will not surrender.

I shall have to go there to determine whether or not there should be a siege. Now another messenger approaches. I feel lazy and comfortable. I would like to sit in this park for ever. A warm south wind suddenly brings me the scent of flowers: roses?

Priscus: The second messenger probably brought him the bad news that three of Dagalaif's cohorts were set upon by the Persians at a town called Sabatha. While the cohorts were thus engaged, guerrillas sneaked up behind the army and slaughtered most of the pack animals and their attendants. This was a severe blow and Julian was furious with Dagalaif, who had left the beasts unguarded.

As for 'the fortress some twenty miles to the east', which would not surrender, Julian rode too close to its walls and was nearly killed; his armour-bearer was wounded.

That night Julian ordered the siege engines to be put in place. Unfortunately, the moon was nearly full and night was like day. While the mantlets and turrets were being placed against the walls, the Persians suddenly threw open their gates and charged our siege troops with sword and javelin. They killed the better part of a cohort, as well as the tribune in command.

How do I remember all this so clearly? Because I have just received by post a rought draft of Ammianus Marcellinus's account of Julian's Persian campaign. I wrote him months ago to ask him if he had written anything about those days. In a covering letter, he says that he kept 'untidy notes in Persia, as usual'. I assume that his account is reliable. He is particularly good at describing military action. He ought to be. As a professional soldier, he served from Britain to Persia. I would send you his history, but since it is in Latin you won't be able to read it and I am sure that you wouldn't want to go to the expense of having it translated. By the way, he says that he intends to write the history of Julian's reign 'just as it occurred'. I suppose he means 'deadpan', as though Julian's reign took place a thousand years ago and were not of any contemporary interest. I wish him luck.

Where was I? The mauling of one of our cohorts by the Persians. As soon as the Persians had done their bloody work, they escaped inside the fortress. The next day Julian threw the full force of his army against the fortress. After fierce fighting, it fell. Julian was physically exhausted by this engagement. I am told that he led the siege himself, fighting for thirteen hours without a break. I don't know because our camp was pitched ten miles away. We of the court rested comfortably while the soldiers fought.

What do I remember of that particular time? Not much. I used to play draughts with Anatolius. We would sit in front of his tent and play on a portable table whose top was inlaid with squares like a game board. Inside the tent, the clerks laboured incessantly. The Emperor's correspondence is always kept up just as though he were at the palace in Constantinople. No matter how desperate the military situation, he must answer his mail.

Once when Anatolius and I were busy at draughts, Victor swept through the camp at the head of a column of light cavalry. We were nearly blinded by the dust. Anatolius was furious. 'He does that deliberately! He knew we were sitting here!' He dabbed the dust from his eyes with the edge of his cloak.

'He behaves rather as the Gauls are supposed to.' I said this to be challenging. Anatolius was usually close-mouthed about the various factions at court.

'He is a good deal worse than any Gaul. More ambitious, too.'

'For the purple?'

'I can't say.' Anatolius pursed his small mouth.

'What *do* you know?'

'Augustus knows what I know.' He said no more. I then won four silver pieces from him, which he never paid me. That is the sort of historian I am.

Julian Augustus   *19 May*

We are again spending the night in one of the Great King's palaces. This one is even handsomer and more luxurious than the hunting lodge. It is surrounded by a large park of cypresses in a countryside rich with vineyards and orchards. We are now at high summer. What a fine season to be at war!

Victor reports that he was able to ride up to the walls of Ctesiphon and no one stopped him. The gates were shut. The guards on the walls made no move to fire at his men. According to rumour, the Great King's army is still some miles to the south. We must now be ready to move fast. Once the capital falls, the war is over. Sapor will sue for peace. At the worst, he will risk everything in one set battle, and the Persians are not noted for their ability at conventional warfare. They are by nature marauders, like the Saracens.

I gave dinner to Maximus, Priscus, Anatolius and Ormisda. The dining room is particularly splendid with painted frescoes showing Sapor hunting lions and boars, all very realistic, the sort of painting I like, though I have not much taste for these things. Even so, after two months of staring at the wall of a tent, one enjoys beauty.

I was surprised to find that Maximus is rather a connoisseur of art. This morning he made a careful tour of the palace, recommending to Anatolius what should be packed up and sent back to Constantinople. 'But have you noticed, Augustus, how the paintings have only one subject? Killing. Animals in the chase. Men at war. Beast against beast.' I hadn't noticed this, but it was quite true.

'That is because we regard killing as a necessary and sacred part of life,' said Ormisda.

'So do we,' said Priscus. 'Only we pretend to abhor it.'

I chose not to correct him. I was – am – in much too good a mood. I had bathed in the Great King's marble bath, and put on one of his fine linen tunics. Apparently we are the same height. I also found a strongbox containing a number of Sapor's personal ornaments, among them a gold ram's head helmet with the imperial ensign on it. I gave it to Ormisda.

'You may as well get used to wearing this,' I said. He took it from me. Then he dropped to his knees and kissed my hand. 'The House of Persia is grateful to you for all eternity.'

'A generation of peace will do,' I said dryly, wondering how long it would be before the Great King Ormisda would prove disloyal to Rome. Men are without gratitude, particularly kings. Ormisda does not know it, but I have decided to maintain an army at Ctesiphon indefinitely.

While the philosophers amused themselves in debate, Ormisda and I met the generals in an adjoining room. On the table was a map of Ctesiphon which Ormisda had found in the Great King's library. He believes it reliable. Victor, Nevitta, Dagalaif, and Arintheus were present; also the chief engineer.

I came straight to the point. 'There is no way for us to approach Ctesiphon by water.' I pointed to the map. 'We are within a triangle. Above us the King's River; behind us the Euphrates; in front of us the Tigris. The Euphrates and Tigris Rivers meet here, just south of Ctesiphon. But we can't sail from the Euphrates to the Tigris because Ctesiphon commands the Tigris at the natural juncture. Also, we would be downstream from the city. As you know, we'd hoped to use the King's River, which joins the Tigris *above* Ctesiphon, but that section of the channel is dry. We are left only one choice, to open up Trajan's canal.' I pointed to a dotted line on the chart. 'When Trajan was here, he dug a deep channel from the Euphrates to the Tigris, following the bed of an old Assyrian canal. The chief engineer has been studying this canal for the past two days. He believes it can be reopened.'

The chief happily listed the many difficulties involved in opening the canal, the principal being a stone dam the Persians had built across the channel to prevent invaders from using it as Trajan had. But once the dam was breached, the chief engineer was positive the canal would be navigable. After a brief discussion, I gave orders for the dam to be broken.

The generals are in a good humour. Dagalaif and Victor are particularly eager for a decisive battle. Ormisda is nervous: so close to the fulfilment of all his dreams. I then dismissed everyone except Nevitta, who asked to stay behind. Disturbing. Ch.

Priscus: What did they talk about? I think Nevitta must have warned him that there was a plot against his life. 'Disturbing' suggests this. 'Ch' means the Christians. Put the two together and the meaning is plain.

On 24 May the channel was opened and the fleet crossed the three miles from the Euphrates to the Tigris, anchoring half a mile north of the city of Ctesiphon, which rose from the green valley of the Tigris like a mountain of brick whose massive weight seemed quite enough to cause the earth itself to bend. From our side of the river we could see nothing of the city except the walls, which are half again as high as those of Constantinople. At regular intervals, semicircular towers support the thick masonry. Between the Tigris and the city there is an open plain where, during the night of 25 May, the army of the Great King gathered.

Anatolius woke me at sunrise and together we left the camp and went to the river bank, where half our army was already gathered to observe the enemy. It was a splendid sight. The Persian army numbered almost a hundred thousand men. Or so we now claim. No one ever knows how large the enemy's army is, but we always say that it is three times the size of ours. I think this one probably was. Behind a wooden palisade on the steep river bank, the Persians were drawn up in battle formation. A crossing seemed madness.

All around us soldiers talked worriedly among themselves. It did not take a skilled veteran to realize how difficult it would be to cross that river under fire and, even worse, to climb the slippery river bank and assault the barricade.

I turned to Anatolius, who looked as worried as I felt. 'We can't cross here.'

'Perhaps the Emperor means to move upstream. To cross a few miles to the north then, circling round – you know, the classic Constantine manoeuvre ...' But in spite of his amateur's passion for strategy, Anatolius mumbled into silence. For almost an hour we stared gloomily at the Persians who stared right back. Then one of Julian's heralds appeared, calling the men to assemble. The Emperor would give the day's orders in person.

'Nothing short of complete retreat will satisfy me,' I said, while Anatolius wondered what would happen if we simply ignored Ctesiphon and turned south to the Persian Gulf 'where the pearls come from. Very rich country, too, from all accounts.'

Julian appeared to the assembled troops. He was exuberant: his eyes shone; his cloak for once was clean; his nose was only slightly peeling from sunburn.

'Men, you have seen the army of Persia. More important, they have seen us!' He paused for cheering. There was none. He cut the silence short. Generals who allow an unfortunate pause to last too long are apt to find the silence filled with that one rude phrase which sets off mutiny.

But Julian had a surprise for us. 'We are all tired today. It has been a difficult week, clearing the channel, moving the fleet, setting up camp. So today we shall have games. I propose horse racing, with gold prizes for the winners. The betting will be your affair since there are, I understand, a few Petulantes who know about racing odds. I'm sure they'll help the rest of us. Have a good time.' He dismissed the men with a wave, like a schoolteacher giving his pupils an unexpected holiday.

Everyone was stunned. If it had been any other general, the men would have thought him mad. But this was Julian who had never lost a battle. After the first gasp of surprise, the men delightedly cheered their young leader who could, with such aplomb, order games while the entire army of the Great King of Persia was drawn up only a mile away. To a man they trusted Julian's luck and skill. If *he* was this confident, who were they to worry? So the army did as he told them, and spent the day in races and games.

That night Julian ordered a surprise crossing of the Tigris. The army was divided into three sections. When the first had secured a footing on the far side, the second would embark, and so on. The generals opposed this plan. Victor pointed to the thousand Persian campfires which filled the horizon. 'They have every military advantage.'

'Not *every*,' said Julian ambiguously. 'You'll see that I'm right. Tell your men to board ship. I want everyone across by morning.'

Four thousand men boarded five empty cargo ships, under the reluctant command of Victor. I've never seen soldiers so frightened. Just before they left, Victor quarrelled with Julian on the river bank. None of us heard what was said, but Victor departed in a rage and Julian was uncharacteristically quiet.

The ships disappeared into the darkness. Silence. An hour passed. Julian paced up and down, pretending to be interested only in the remaining ships which were to take the rest of the army across the river once the Persian side had been secured. The army waited.

Suddenly flaming arrows pierced the black night. Victor's men were landing. The Persians were attacking them. First one, then two, then all five of the boats were set afire by Persian arrows. Far off, we could hear Victor's men shouting to one another as they clambered up the slippery river bank by the flickering light of burning ships. On our side of the river, panic was beginning.

Julian saved the situation with one of his inspired lies. Just as we were all positive the landing had failed and the men were lost, Julian pointed to the five burning ships and shouted, 'That's it! The burning of the ships. That's the signal, Victor's signal. The landing's a success! To the boats! To the boats!'

I don't know how he did it, but he made the men believe him. He raced up and down the river bank, shouting, pushing, coaxing the men onto the landing craft. Then he himself leapt into the first boat just as it was about to leave the shore. The men were now as excited as he. They crowded on to the remaining boats. Some even floated across the river on their shields. Convinced of total disaster, I watched the Roman army disappear onto the black river.

By dawn, to my amazement, we held the river bank.

The next day Maximus and I, along with the priests and other timid folk, sat comfortably at the river's edge and watched the Battle of Ctesiphon as though we were at the theatre. When we complained of the heat, umbrellas were brought us, and wine. Never have philosophers watched in such comfort two empires collide so fatefully.

I sat between Maximus and the Etruscan Mastara. Anatolius was not with us, for he had bravely chosen to fight beside Julian that day, even though court marshals are not expected to be warriors. We teased him a good deal as he got ready for battle, his tiny mouth a firm military circle in his hopelessly soft face.

'Many years with the cavalry,' he said casually. His round stomach jiggled beneath ill-fitting armour as he motioned imperiously for the groom to bring him his horse. With a flourish, Anatolius mounted the horse and fell off the other side. I'm afraid we clerks laughed at our impetuous brother. But Anatolius had his way; he followed his Emperor into battle.

At first we saw everything plain. The Persians were spread out in an arc between the walls of Ctesiphon and the river. Cavalry first; then infantry; then against the wall, like a range of mud hills, a hundred elephants each with an iron tower on its back, containing archers.

The Persian cavalry wear an extraordinary form of armour which consists of hundreds of small iron plates sewn together in such a way that not only is the soldier completely covered by armour but he is able to move easily, the iron fitting the contours of his body like cloth. Their horses are protected by leather blankets. In the hands of a capable general, the Persian cavalry is a remarkable weapon. Fortunately for us, there were at this time no Persian generals of any distinction. Also, the Persian army is not a permanent institution like ours but a haphazard collection of conscripts, mercenaries, noblemen and slaves. At times of national crisis every able-bodied man is impressed into service, hardly the best of systems.

Behind the cavalry, the Persian infantry advanced in close order, protected by oblong wicker shields covered with rawhide. Among the elephants at the rear was the Grand Vizier, while on the walls of Ctesiphon the Great King and his court observed the battle in much the same way we philosophers watched it in our folding chairs on the river bank. We were too far away to recognize Sapor, though Maximus, as usual, claimed he saw him quite clearly.

'I am extraordinarily far-sighted, you know. Sapor is to the left of that tower by the gate. You see the blue canopy? Well, he is just under it, wearing scarlet. Those must be his sons with him. They look quite young . . .' And on he babbled. Actually, all any of us could see was a faint blur of colour on the battlements.

But Julian was most visible, riding restlessly along the front line as our army advanced. He was easily identified not only by his white horse and purple cloak but by the dragon standard which always accompanied him.

Our trumpets sounded the advance. The infantry then began its curious stylized march, based on that of ancient Sparta's army: two short steps, a pause, two short steps, a pause, all in perfect unison while the drums beat the tattoo. It is ominous both to hear and to see. Even Maximus was silent as the Roman army advanced. Then with a shout, our skirmishers in the front rank threw their javelins into the Persian cavalry. And the two armies vanished. For an instant I almost believed in Maximus's magic. Where a hundred and thirty thousand men had been perfectly visible to us in the bright sun, there was now nothing but an oppressive cloud of dust. We could see nothing. But from the heart of the cloud we heard trumpets, drums, war cries, metal striking metal, the hiss of arrows.

The battle began at sunrise and continued until sundown. After an hour or two of watching dust, the Etruscans grew bored, and withdrew 'to pray for victory'. Instead, they settled down in a near-by grove of date palms for a drinking party. They were prodigious drinkers. One of my few happy memories of the Persian campaign was the night when all five Etruscans were dead drunk during an important religious ceremony. It was a splendid debacle. They kept dropping sacred vessels and books, while Mastara solemnly assured the furious Julian that 'the god has possessed us'.

Maximus and I watched the wall of dust all day. The only sign we had of how the battle was going was the position of the dust cloud as, hour by hour, it shifted closer to the walls of Ctesiphon. The Persians were giving ground.

'On 15 June we shall return to Tarsus,' said Maximus suddenly; he had been making signs in the dust at our feet with his magician's staff.

'In three weeks?'

'Three weeks? Is that three weeks?' He looked at me blankly. 'Why so it is! Amazing to think we shall conquer Persia in such a short time. Alexander hardly did as well. Perhaps I've made a mistake.' He studied the dust at his feet. I wanted to break his stick over his foolish head.

'No. The calculation is correct. 15 June. Plain as day. We must tell Julian. He'll be so pleased.' He looked vaguely towards the battlefield.

'How do you know that the Emperor . . .' I emphasized the title. No one but Maximus ever referred to Julian by name. '. . . is still alive?'

'He has to be. 15 June. I just showed you. Look, in the Sun's Fourth House . . .'

'And how do you know we shall win this battle?'

'Sometimes you amaze me, Priscus. It is all so plain. Sapor is about to fall, and we shall go home victorious. It is pre-ordained. And frankly I look forward to a return to private life. I'm here only because Julian insisted . . .'

While Maximus chattered, I stared at the walls of Ctesiphon, waiting for the battle's end. Shortly before sunset, a soft breeze thinned the cloud of dust until we were again able to see the two armies, now in a hopeless tangle at the city's gate. The elephants were running amok, trunks curled, tusks flashing. I am told the Persians use them to intimidate their own men quite as much as the enemy's. Persians as well as Romans were trampled by those hideous beasts.

As the red sun set, the gates of the city opened to receive the Persian army. Our men pursued them. In a matter of seconds, the Persian army ceased to be an army and became a mob of frightened men, all trying to get within the gates. Then it was dark.

Julian Augustus   *27 May*

I cannot sleep. Within my tent, I walk up and down. I am exhausted from twelve hours of fighting – but too excited to sleep, to do anything. I can barely write these lines. My hand shakes with tension.

I have defeated the Great King's army! Twenty-five hundred Persians dead, and only seventy-five Romans! We could have taken Ctesiphon. Our infantry could have entered when the Persians did but Victor stopped them. He was afraid they might be outnumbered inside a strange city. I am not sure that he was right. Had I been at the gate, I would have ordered the men to go through. We should have taken the chance. The Persian army was in flight. That was our opportunity. But Victor is cautious. He was also wounded – an arrow in the right shoulder, not serious. Now we shall have to lay siege to the city. A long business.

I saw the Great King today, and he saw me. Sapor was seated on the wall, beneath a canopy. I was only a few yards away. Though nearly seventy, Sapor looks much younger. He is lean and black-bearded (Ormisda says that his hair is dyed: Sapor is vain about his appearance, also his potency . . . no one knows how many children he has). Sapor wore a gold crown with a scarlet plume. As a gesture of disdain, he wore court dress! He looked like a peacock, glaring down at me.

I waved my sword arm. 'Come down!' I shouted, but in that tumult I doubt if he heard me. But he saw me and he knew who I was. The Great King saw the Emperor of Rome at the gate to his city! The courtiers around him looked terrified. No one made a move. Then I was distracted by the battle around me. The next time I looked at the wall, Sapor was gone.

Before we returned to camp, we buried our dead and stripped the Persian corpses. Many nobles were killed and their armour is much prized by us. Unfortunately, none of the Gauls and Germans can wear Persian armour. It is too small for them. So the best armour in the world goes to our worst soldiers, the Asiatics!

We had a victory dinner in my tent. The generals got drunk. But I could eat· and drink nothing. I am too tense. Maximus says the war will be over in three weeks. Soldiers have been serenading me all night. Many of them are drunk but I do not scold them. I go outside and embrace them and call them by name, telling them what fine fellows they are, and they tell me the same thing. Tomorrow I give out war crowns to those who showed unusual valour. I shall also sacrifice to the war god Ares.

Why didn't Victor go into the city?

Priscus: The next day was marred only by the sacrifice. After the men had been given their decorations, Julian tried to sacrifice a bull to Ares on a newly built altar. But for one reason or another, nine bulls were found wanting by the Etruscans. The tenth bull, acceptable, bolted at the last minute. When it was finally caught and sacrificed, the liver indicated disaster. To everyone's amazement, Julian threw down the sacrificial knife and shouted to the sky, 'Never again will I sacrifice to you!' Maximus looked quite alarmed and even I was taken aback. Flushed and sweating from the hot sun, Julian disappeared into his tent. I can only attribute his strange action to the fact that he had not slept in two days.

The same day Anatolius took me on a tour of the battlefield. He was very soldierly. 'Here the Herculani made a flanking movement to allow for the light-armed cohorts of Petulantes to break through . . .' That sort of thing. Anatolius was so pleased with his own military expertise that I did not have the heart to laugh at him as he led me over the dusty ground, still littered with Persian dead. I noticed one interesting phenomenon. Persians do not putrefy in the hot sun the way Europeans do. After two days of this climate, a dead European is in an advanced state of decay. But not the Persians. They simply dry up and become hard as leather. I once asked Oribasius about this and he said it was due to diet. According to him, we drink too much wine and eat too much grain while the Persians eat sparingly, preferring dates and lentils to our rich fare. Yet I have observed the dead bodies of lean Gauls – yes, there are some – and though their owners lived austere lives, they decayed as swiftly as their corpulent brothers. It is very puzzling.

The Persians had been stripped of their armour and valuables, except for one who still wore a gold ring. I decided to take it as a souvenir. Even now I can remember the feel of that cold, hard hand as, with great effort, I bent straight the fingers which had been drawn into a brown fist. I stared at the dead man's face. He was young; he wore no beard. I looked at him. He looked at me, eyes glazed as though with fever. Flies buzzed about his head.

'Spoils of war,' said Anatolius comfortably.

'Spoils of war,' I said to the dead Persian, letting him drop back on the ground with a thump. He seemed unconvinced. The flies settled on his face. I wore the ring until a few months ago when I lost it at the baths. I have become thin lately and the ring fell off in the hot room. Naturally, the attendants never return anything they find.

Two days later, on 29 May, Julian moved the army to Abuzatha, a Persian fort on the Tigris three miles from Ctesiphon. Here we made camp. For several days none of Julian's friends saw him. He was closeted with his military staff. There was disagreement among the generals. Some wanted to lay siege to Ctesiphon. Others preferred to isolate the city and continue the conquest of Persia. A few advised returning to Roman teritory. None of us knew what Julian's plan was or even if he had a plan. Nor did any of us know that while we were in camp, he had received a secret embassy from Sapor. I confess that even if I had known, I would not have cared much. Like half the camp, I was ill with dysentery.

Julian Augustus   *30 May*

The Persian envoys have just left. Ormisda is with them. I sit alone in my tent. Outside, Callistus is singing a mournful song. It is very hot. I am waiting for Maximus. If I withdraw from Persia, the Great King has promised to cede me all of Mesopotamia north of Anatha; also, at his own expense, he will rebuild our city of Amida, and pay in gold or kind whatever we ask to defray the cost of this war. Persia is defeated.

The ambassadors came to me secretly. They wanted it that way. So did I.

They were brought to me as though they were officers taken captive in a Saracen raid. No one except Ormisda and myself knows that this was an embassy. The chief ambassador is a brother of the Grand Vizier. He maintained a perfect dignity while proposing a treaty which, if I accept it, will mean that I have gained more of the East for Rome than any general since Pompey. Realizing this, the ambassador felt impelled to indulge himself in Persian rhetoric. 'Never forget, Augustus, that our army is more numerous than the desert's sand. One word from the Great King and you and all your host are lost. But Sapor is merciful.'

'Sapor is frightened,' said Ormisda, to my irritation. I prefer to seem in-different while envoys talk, to give them no clue as to what I intend to do. But Ormisda has been unusually tense the last few days. Despite his age, he fought like a youth at Ctesiphon. Now he sees the crown of Persia almost in his hands. He is terrified it will slip away. I am sympathetic. Yet my policy is not neces-sarily his policy.

Ormisda taunted the ambassadors. 'I know what happens in the palace at Ctesiphon. I know what is whispered in the long halls, behind the ivory doors. Nothing that happens among you is kept from me.'

This was not entirely bluff. Ormisda's spies are indeed well placed at the Persian court and he learns astonishing things. Also, as we conquer more and more of Persia, there is a tendency among the nervous courtiers to shift from the old king to what may be the new. But the ambassador was not one of those whom Ormisda could win.

'There are traitors in every palace, Prefect.' He used Ormisda's Roman title. Then he turned to me. 'And in every army, Augustus.' I did not acknowledge this dangerous truth. 'But the Great King is merciful. He loves peace . . .'

Ormisda laughed theatrically. 'Sapor wears rags, taken from a beggar. His beard and hair are full of ashes. He dines off the floor like an animal. He weeps, knowing his day is ended.' Ormisda was not exaggerating. During the last few hours we have had several harrowing descriptions of Sapor's grief at my victory. He has every reason to be in mourning. Few monarchs have been so thoroughly humiliated.

The ambassador read me the draft of the treaty. I thanked him. Then I told Ormisda to take the embassy to Anatolius's tent, which is next to mine. They will wait there until I have prepared an answer. Ormisda wanted to stay behind and talk to me but I made him go. He is not Great King yet.

I now sit on the bed. The treaty is before me: two scrolls, one in Greek, one in Persian. I have placed them side by side on the lion skin. What to do? If I accept Sapor's terms, it will be a triumph for me. If I stay, I am not entirely certain that a siege of Ctesiphon would be successful. It will certainly take a long time; perhaps a year, and I cannot be away from Constantinople that long. Today the Persian army is no threat, but who knows what sort of army Sapor might put in the field next week, next month?

Everything depends, finally, on Procopius. He is in the north, at Bezabde in Corduene. Or so I hear. There has been no direct word from him.

Maximus was brilliant just now. As always, he went straight to the heart of things.

'This treaty is a triumph; a province gained, peace assured for at least . . .'

'. . . a decade.'

'Perhaps longer. Amida rebuilt. A fortune in gold. Few emperors have accomplished so much. But then . . .' He looked at me thoughtfully. 'Was it just for *this* we have come so far, to gain half a province? or to conquer half a world?'

He paused. I waited. Like a true philosopher, he then turned the matter round, first to one side, then to another. 'There is no denying this is an excellent treaty, better than anyone would have dreamed . . . except us, who know what no one else knows. Cybele herself promised you victory. You are Alexander, born again, set on earth to conquer Asia. You have no choice.'

Maximus is right. The gods have not brought me this far simply to have me turn back as though I were some Saracen chief raiding the border. I shall reject Sapor's treaty and begin the siege of Ctesiphon. Once Procopius arrives, I shall be free to order a march straight into the morning sun. Yes, to the house of Helios himself, the father from whom I came and to whom I must return, in glory.

Priscus: Have you ever read such nonsense? If only I had known! But none of us knew what Maximus was up to, even though he was for ever dropping hints about 'our plans'. But since those plans were never revealed, we were all equally in the dark. When the rumour that Sapor had sued for peace swept the camp, Julian firmly denied that there had been an embassy, and we believed him. I am certain that if the generals had known the terms of the treaty, they would have forced Julian to accept. But Julian and Maximus lied, as did Ormisda, who was not about to end his last hope of reigning in Persia. All three wanted the war to continue.

From the moment of this decision, I trace the rapid decline of Julian. Nothing went right again. In retrospect his actions are those of a madman. But since he seemed so entirely normal at the time, none of us seriously questioned his orders or thought anything he did unusual. We merely assumed that he had information we did not. Also, up until the last day of May, everything he had attempted had proven successful. Even so, the generals were becoming critical. And treason was in the air.

22

Julian Augustus   *31 May*

Midnight. The deaf-mute sits cross-legged at my feet, playing a Persian instrument much like a lute. The melody is unfamiliar but pleasing. Callistus is arranging my armour on the stand beside the bed. Ormisda has just left. He is pleased at my decision, but I am somewhat uneasy. For the first time I find myself in complete disagreement with my officers. What is worse, I cannot tell them why I *know* that the course I have embarked upon is the right one. At this evening's staff meeting, Victor challenged me openly.

'We have not the force, Augustus, to attempt a long siege. Nor the supplies. We also have many wounded.' He touched his own bandaged shoulder.

'And no hope of reinforcements.' Arintheus automatically follows Victor's lead.

'There is the army of Procopius and Sebastian,' said Ormisda. He sat on my right at the conference table, on which our only map of this part of Persia was unrolled. So far, the map has proved completely unreliable.

'Procopius!' Nevitta said the name contemptuously, concentrating in that one word a lifelong contempt for all things Greek. 'We'll never see him here. Never!'

'I've sent Procopius orders . . .' I began.

'But why hasn't he obeyed you?' Victor led the attack. 'Why is he still in Corduene?'

'Yes, why?' One is never certain whether Dagalaif is naïve or subtle.

'Because he is a traitor,' said Nevitta, the Frankish accent growing harsh and guttural, the words difficult to understand. 'Because he and that Christian king of Armenia, *your* friend,' he turned malevolently on Ormisda – 'want us all dead, so that Procopius can be the next *Christian* emperor.'

There was a shocked silence at this. I broke it, mildly. 'We can't be sure that that is the reason.'

'*You* can't, Emperor, but I can. I know these Asiatics. I never trusted one in my life.' He looked straight at Victor who returned the hard gaze evenly.

I laughed. 'I hope you trust me, Nevitta. I'm Asiatic.'

'You're Thracian, Emperor, which is almost as good as being a Frank or a Gaul. Besides, you're not a Christian, or so I've heard.'

Everyone laughed; the tension was relieved. Then Victor expressed the hope that we obtain as good a treaty as possible from Sapor. Ormisda and I exchanged a quick glance. I am sure that Victor knows nothing. I am also glad we kept the embassy a secret, especially now that I know Nevitta and Dagalaif are eager to go home. Except for me, no one believes Procopius will join us. I am certain that he will. If he does not . . .

Salutius proposed a compromise. 'We should all assume that Procopius intends to obey his Emperor. Having recently executed a man whom I'd falsely accused of not doing his duty, I favour giving Procopius every opportunity to prove himself loyal. After all, we don't know what difficulties he may have encountered. He may be ill, or dead. So I suggest that the Augustus wait at least a week before beginning the siege, or making any other plans.'

This compromise was accepted. Like most compromises it solves nothing while prolonging – perhaps dangerously – the time of indecision. But I said nothing beyond agreeing to delay the siege. I wanted to appear reasonable because I was about to propose what I knew would be a most unpopular action.

'Our fleet requires twenty thousand men to man and guard it. As long as we keep close to the river, the men can do both. But if we enter the interior – either to go home or to pursue the Great King's army – those men must go with us. If they go with us, the Persians will seize our ships. To prevent that, we must burn the fleet.'

They were stunned. Nevitta was the first to speak. He wanted to know how I expected to return to our own country without ships. I explained that whether we returned by way of the Euphrates or by way of the Tigris, we would have to go upstream, a slow and laborious business. The fleet would be an encumbrance. This point was conceded to me; even so, I was opposed by the entire staff except Ormisda, who realized that only by burning the fleet will I be able to get the legions to follow me into the interior.

Yes, I am determined now to secure all of the provinces of Persia as far as the border of India, a thousand miles to the east. Alexander did as much. I am convinced that I can do it. Sapor's army is no match for ours. With the harvest at hand, we shall not have to worry about supplies. Only one things holds me back: Procopius. If he were here, I could set out confident that with Ormisda's help Ctesiphon would fall and there would be no enemy at my back. But I cannot leave until I know where Procopius is. Meanwhile, I must burn the fleet.

Patiently, I answered the arguments of the generals. I convinced none but all acquiesced. As they were leaving my tent, Salutius took me to one side. I could feel the unpleasant heat of his breath on my skin as he whispered close to my ear the single word 'Mutiny'.

'Who?'

Though the last of the generals had left the tent, Salutius continued to whisper. 'The Christians.'

'Victor?'

'I don't know. Perhaps. My reports are vague. The men are singing a song that they will soon be home but *you* will not be.'

'That is treason.'

'The way the words run, the thing sounds innocent enough. Whoever wrote it was clever.'

'Who sing it? Galileans?'

Salutius nodded. 'The Zianni and the Herculani. Only a few are involved so far. But if you burn the fleet . . .'

'Salutius, believe in me.' I took his hand. 'I know things that others don't.'

'As you command, Lord.' Salutius bowed and left me.

I have spent this night alone except for the deaf-mute and Callistus. I pray. I study Alexander's campaign in Persia. I examine maps and read histories. Helios willing, I shall spend the winter on the border of India. No Roman emperor has ever annexed so great a territory to our world.

Julian Augustus   *1 June*

The fleet is burned. Twelve ships were spared, suitable for making bridges. We shall transport them on wagons. I have just sent Arintheus with the light-armed infantry to wipe out the remnants of the Persian army in hiding near by. I have also ordered him to fire the surrounding fields and slaughter the cattle. Once we are gone it will take the inhabitants of Ctesiphon many months to get sufficient food. That will give us time. No word from Procopius.

Priscus: On a hot and windy morning, the fleet was set afire. Flames darted swiftly from ship to ship until the brown Tigris itself seemed to burn. As the sun's heat increased, all objects were distorted by heatwaves. Creation seemed to be ending exactly as Stoics teach, in a vast, cleansing, terminal fire.

I watched the burning with Anatolius. For once I almost believed in Nemesis. The men, too, sensed that this time their Emperor had reached too far, plunging himself and them into the sun's fierce maw. Ordinarily, any order Julian gave was promptly obeyed, and the more puzzling it was the more certain were the men of his cleverness. But that day he was forced to fire the first ship himself. No one would do it for him. I saw fear in the faces of the men as Julian offered the fleet to Helios.

'Of course we are not generals,' said Anatolius tentatively, knowing what was in my mind. 'The Emperor is a master of war.'

'He can still make a mistake.' Neither of us could take our eyes off the fire. What is there in the burning of man-made things which so thrills us? It is like Homer's image of the two rivers in Hades: one of creation, the other of destruction, for ever held in uneasy balance. Men have always enjoyed destroying quite as much as building, which explains the popularity of war.

We were still gaping at the fiery river when a group of officers rode past us. One of them was Valentinian, his face scarlet with heat and rage. 'Stupid! Stupid! Stupid!' he snarled. Anatolius and I exchanged nervous glances. Was there to be a mutiny of officers? But there was none, despite the grumbling of the tribunes. Incidentally, I have never forgotten that brief glimpse I had of Valentinian, his face swollen with the same rage that was to kill him years later when he died of a stroke while bellowing at a German embassy.

By nightfall, the fleet was gone. In the distance one could see the Persians gather on the walls of Ctesiphon to watch this extraordinary sight. No one will ever know what they made of it. The Roman Emperor burning the Roman fleet must have seemed to them perfectly incomprehensible. I could hardly believe it myself.

Julian Augustus   *3 June*
We have broken camp and are moving southeast, into the interior. The countryside is rich; there is plenty of water. The men are less apprehensive than they were. They see now that we do not need the river to survive.

Julian Augustus   *4 June*
All goes well. Nevitta: on guard. Victor. Ch. Close? How? Days grow hotter. May begin night marches.

Priscus: Nevitta again warned Julian of a Christian plot. This time Victor was directly involved. I know. I rode beside Julian that same afternoon. He spoke frankly of what Nevitta had told him.

'But if they kill me, who will take my place? There's no one except Salutius and he is hardly a friend to them.'

'There is Victor.'

Julian smiled coldly. 'He would be butchered by the Gauls.' Then he frowned. 'Nevitta says they have put someone close to me to . . . to do their work. Is it you?' He turned on me and I saw that though his voice was light and playful his face was not. He stared at me with sun-dazzled eyes. Like all of us, his face was burned dark and his eyes were red from sand and sun, the lids suppurating. He had lost weight and one could see the working of the cordlike muscles of his forearms as he grasped the reins. He was a boy no longer, nor even young.

'No, not I.' I tried but could not think of a joke to make.

'You'd make a very poor emperor.' He was his old self again. We rode on. Before and behind us, the army wound through bright country, rich with coming harvest.

Salutius joined us, wearing a headcloth.

'Look at that! A classic Roman consul!' Julian teased him. But Salutius for all his intelligence had no humour. He explained to us at solemn length why he could not wear a helmet in the sun because the heat made his forehead break out in a rash. Then he handed Julian a letter. 'From the senate at Constantinople. To congratulate you on your victory.'

Julian sighed. 'Too soon,' he said, giving the letter back. I recall how the sun shone on the back of his hand and the blond hairs glittered against sun-darkened skin. I also noticed what large nails he had (now that he'd ceased biting them). Curious the clarity with which one remembers the shape of a hand glimpsed years ago, while so many things of importance are lost.

Midnight: Fire. Trenches.

Priscus: That night the Persians set fire to the harvest. For miles around fields, vineyards, orchards, villages . . . everything caught fire, and night was like day. Although Julian ordered protective trenches dug around the camp, a number of our tents burned, as well as several wagons.

For three days and three nights the fire continued. Whenever I think of those weeks in Persia, I see fire in my mind, smell smoke, feel the terrible heat of sun blazing while fire burns. Luckily, there were springs in the camp and we had sufficient water. We also had food for perhaps a week. But after that, famine. As far as the eye could see, there was black desert. Nothing green survived.

I now shared a tent with Anatolius. This meant that I was more than usually involved in the business of the court. Ordinarily I kept out of such things, for I have always been bored by politics, but now I was very interested in what was going on. We all were. Our lives were at stake. It seemed that everyone had a plan to save us, except the Emperor.

The army was now almost evenly divided between Julian and Victor, between the Europeans and the Asiatics, between the Hellenists and the Christians, Julian of course was strongest because his adherents were, quite simply, the best soldiers. Yet as each day passed in that burnt-out wilderness, the party of Victor became all the louder and more demanding, insisting that the Emperor act. But Julian gave absolutely no hint of what he intended to do. In fact, without this journal we might never have known what was in his mind.

Persian cavalry raided our supply depot just before dawn. Several of them killed. No casualties for us. We must expect more of this.

At noon I prayed to Helios. I sacrificed a white bull. The augury was not decisive. What to do?

A sharp encounter with Victor at this afternoon's staff meeting. My quarters are stifling. None of us wore armour. The generals were arranged about me on stools. At my feet sat the deaf-mute; he watches my every move with the alert, loving eyes of a pet dog. I have only to think I am thirsty for him to read it in my face and bring me water.

No sooner had I greeted the generals than Victor took the initiative. 'Augustus, we must go back the way we came, through Assyria.' Arintheus promptly agreed with him. The others waited to see what I would say.

'That is always a possibility. Of course. Always.' I assumed the Mardonius manner: maddeningly reasonable yet perfectly evasive. 'But perhaps, Count, you will tell us, first, why you believe we must go back now and, second, why you prefer that route.'

Victor looked more than ever like the village bully trying to control himself in the presence of the schoolmaster. 'First, as the Augustus knows, we shall soon be short of food. My scouts report that for twenty miles to south and east there are only ashes. To the north there is desert. That leaves us the west, where we came from.'

'Have you forgotten that we ourselves burned the fields around Ctesiphon?'

'Yes, we made that mistake, but . . .'

Nevitta made a threatening noise, deep in his throat, like a bull preparing for attack. One may not accuse the Emperor of making mistakes. But I motioned for Nevitta to keep silent. I tried to sound amiable. 'But since this "mistake" was made, what is the point of going from one devastated region to another?'

'Because, Augustus, there are still some regions which we did not burn. We can live off the country. We can also use those forts we captured ...'

'... and burned? No, Count, those forts are of no use to us and you know it. So I ask you again: *Why* do you want to go back the way we came?'

'Because we know that country. We can live off it, somehow. The men will be reassured.'

'May I speak, Lord?' Ormisda has ceased to be Great King and is once more Greek courtier, a bad sign. 'The army cannot return up the Euphrates because there is no longer a fleet. Nor have we the means to make bridges.'

'We can use the ships that were saved,' said Victor.

This time Salutius answered him. 'Twelve small ships are not enough to cross the Tigris. Like it or not, we are now confined to this side of the river. If we set out for home it must be by way of Corduene.'

'Can't we get ships from the Persians?' asked Dagalaif suddenly. 'There must be hundreds in the river ports.'

'They'll burn them first,' said Ormisda.

'I have been making inquiries,' Salutius began, sounding as if he were sitting comfortably in his praetorian prefect's chair at Constantinople, surrounded by notaries, instead of sweating in an airless test with a cloth wrapped about his sunburned head. 'And it appears that what ships the Persians have are well out of range. Our only hope would be to build new ones, but of course we lack the materials.'

Ormisda finished the matter. 'Even if we could cross the Tigris, we would have the same difficulties returning north we have had here. Sapor means to starve us out. He will burn all Persia if he has to. Also, the rains have now begun in Mesopotamia. The winter ice in the mountains has melted. The road that brought us to Ctesiphon is a fever-swamp, swarming with insects. But of course we shall go wherever the Augustus bids.'

'So shall we all,' said Victor, 'but *what* is his plan?' I looked into the bright eyes of my enemy and saw that he means to kill me. I have known it from the start.

I answered quietly. 'Augustus means to consider every possibility before he comes to a decision. He also reminds the council that we have yet to hear from Procopius. There are rumours that he is even now on his way to us here. If he arrives, we shall lay siege to Ctesiphon.'

'Using what for food?' Victor challenged me.

'Procopius will bring supplies. Also, to get here, he will have to open up a line of communications from our province of Corduene. That's only three hundred miles away. We don't need to worry about supplies if Procopius comes.'

'But if he does not?' Victor leaned forward, a hunting dog who has got the quarry's scent.

'Then we are where we are now. It seems agreed that we cannot return the way we came.'

'Because the fleet was burned.'

This was too much. I turned on Victor. 'Count, you will not speak again until I give you leave.' As if struck, Victor blinked and sat back.

I continued. 'We can always take our chances in the desert to the north. But it will be a hard march to Corduene.' I could see that Ormisda wanted to speak. I nodded.

'The Augustus should know that there are no maps of that territory. We shall have to rely on guides. They may not be reliable.'

'Can't we follow the course of the Tigris?' Dagalaif fanned himself with the frond of a date palm.

'Not easily,' said Ormisda. 'There are many strong fortresses . . .'

'And we shall be a retreating army, not a conquering one. We would be unable to lay siege to the cities.' I let this sink in. Until now no one has mentioned the possibility of our defeat. After all, we have broken the Great King's army; half Persia is ours. Yet now we must talk of retreat because we have been burned out by Persian zealots. It is tragedy. I should have anticipated it. But I did not. The fault is mine. It is hard to believe that without the loss of a single battle one can so swiftly cease to be a conqueror and become the chieftain of a band of frightened men who want only to go home as fast as possible. Is this the revenge of Ares for what I said to him during the sacrifice at Ctesiphon?

Arintheus took my challenge. 'We're not retreating, Augustus. How could we be? Why, old Sapor will make a treaty with you tomorrow, giving you anything you want if only we go home.' News of the Persian embassy has been in the air for a week. Nothing is secret for long in an army. I suspect the Persians themselves of spreading the rumour, to create discord: why is your Emperor driving you so hard when we are willing to give you gold and territory and a safe passage home? The Persians are expert at this sort of thing.

'Victor seems to feel that we have been defeated,' I said. 'I don't. I think we must wait a few days longer for Procopius. If he does not come, we shall consider whether to go north to Corduene or keep on south to the Persian Gulf.' I said this casually. It was the first time I have suggested such a thing to the generals. They were astonished.

'The Persian Gulf!' Victor momentarily forgot my ban of silence. He quickly muttered an apology.

Salutius spoke for what, I am afraid, is the majority. 'It is too far, Augustus. We are only three hundred miles from Roman territory and it seems like three thousand miles. If we continue any deeper into Persia, we'll be swallowed up.'

'The men won't go.' Nevitta was abrupt. 'They're already frightened. Order them to go south and you'll have a first-class mutiny on your hands.'

'But the cities of the Gulf are rich and unprotected . . .'

'They won't go, General. Not now. But even if they would, what's to keep the Persians from burning everything in our path? They're crazy enough to. We'd starve to death before we ever saw the Gulf.'

So I have abandoned this dream. For now, I dismissed the council.

I sit on my cot, writing this on my knees. Callistus is preparing the sacrificial robes. The deaf-mute plays the lute. In a few minutes Maximus joins me. In an hour I pray first to Zeus, then to the Great Mother. Where have I failed? Is this the revenge of Ares?

Julian Augustus 7 *June*

The omens are bad. The auguries inconclusive. They advise against returning home by way of Assyria, they also advise against going north to Corduene. One indicated that I should go south to the Gulf! But the troops would not obey. They are already close to mutiny. I must bring Victor to heel or face rebellion.

Julian Augustus 8 *June*

I have not slept for days. The heat at night is almost as bad as the heat by day.

It is like having the fever. We all resemble dried-up cadavers. I lose my temper with everyone. I struck Callistus when he fumbled with the fastening of my robes. I quarrelled with Salutius over a trivial matter, and he was in the right. Tonight Maximus was with me. We were alone together because Priscus is sick with dysentery and Anatolius nurses him. While I was having supper, Maximus tried to cheer me up. He achieved the opposite.

'But it's so simple. Give the order to march south. They must obey. You are the Emperor.'

'I shall have been the Emperor. They'll kill me first.'

'But Cybele herself has told us that you must complete your work. After all, you are Alexander.'

I erupted at this. 'No, I am *not* Alexander, who is dead. I am Julian, about to die in this forsaken place . . .'

'No. No! The gods . . .'

'. . . misled us! The gods laugh at us! They raise us up for sport, and throw us down again. There is no more gratitude in heaven than there is on earth.'

'Julian . . .'

'You say I was born to do great things. Well, I have done them. I conquered the Persians. I conquered the Germans. I saved Gaul. For what? To delay this world's end for a year or two? Certainly no longer.'

'You were born to restore the worship of the true gods.'

'Then why do they let me fail?'

'You are Emperor still!'

I seized a handful of charred earth from the tent's floor. 'That is all that's left to me. Ashes.'

'You will live . . .'

'I shall be as dead as Alexander soon enough, but when I go I take Rome with me. For nothing good will come after. The Goths and the Galileans will inherit the state, and like vultures and maggots they'll make clean bones of what is dead, until there is not even so much as the shadow of a god anywhere on earth.'

Maximus hid his face in his hands while I raged on. But after a time I stopped, ashamed of having made a fool of myself. 'It's no use,' I said finally, 'I am in Helios's hands, and we are both at the end of the day. So good night, Maximus, and pray for me that it will indeed be a *good* night.

But I can't believe it is over yet. Our army is intact. The Persian army is broken. We can still go north to Corduene. If Helios deserts me now, there will be no one to restore his worship.

But this is madness! Why am I suddenly in such despair? Why should I die now, at the height of my reign, at the age of . . . I had to stop to count! I am thirty-two.

Julian Augustus   *10 June*

Afternoon. We are still encamped. Food is running low. No word from Procopius. Yesterday and again this morning, Persian cavalry attacked us. They strike at the outskirts of the camp. Then when we sound the call to arms, they vanish. This is the most demoralizing kind of warfare.

I must soon decide what to do. Meanwhile, I make daily sacrifice. The omens are not good. The auguries confused. I want to put Victor under arrest. Salutius thinks I should wait.

Julian Augustus   *14 June*

During this morning's staff meeting, there was a sudden racket outside my tent. I heard the tribune who commands my bodyguard shout, 'Stand back! Stand back!'

I went outside. A thousand men, mostly Asiatics, surrounded the tent. They begged me to lead them home by way of Assyria. They had been well coached. They shouted and whined, wept and threatened. It took me some minutes to silence them. Then I said, 'We shall start for home only when our work is done.'

Several jeered at this. I pretended not to hear.

'When we do go home, it cannot be by the way we came. Your general Victor will tell you why.' This was a pleasantly ironic move. Victor was now forced to placate the men he had himself incited. He did it very well, explaining why the Euphrates route was no longer open to us. He was plausible, and the men listened to him respectfully. When he had finished, I assured them that I was as eager as they to return to safety. At the proper time we would go; meanwhile, I asked them not to take seriously the Persian-inspired rumours which I knew were going about the camp. They dispersed. I turned to Victor.

'This is *not* the way to force us,' I said carefully.

'But, Augustus . . .'

I dismissed him. He has been warned.

Later, I spoke privately to each of the generals. Most are loyal. For instance, Jovian sat on a stool in my tent, his tunic wet with perspiration, his face flushed from the wine as well as heat. 'Whatever Augustus commands, I will obey.' His voice is deep and somewhat hoarse, for he drinks those harsh German spirits which burn the throat.

'Even if I say go south to the Persian Gulf!'

Jovian squirmed uncomfortably. 'That is far away. But if the Augustus orders us . . .'

'No, I shall not order you. Not now.'

He was relieved. 'Then that means we'll be going back soon, won't we?'

I said nothing.

'Because the longer we stay here, the more difficult it will be. What with the heat, the Persians . . .'

'The Persians are defeated.'

'But the Great King still has a good many soldiers and this is their country, not ours.'

'Half of it is ours, by right of conquest.'

'Yes, Lord. But can we hold it? I'm for getting out. They say demons ride with the Persians, especially at night.'

I almost laughed in his foolish face. But instead I proposed: 'Pray to your man-god to make them go away.'

'If demons haunt us, it is because Christ wills it,' he said piously.

I smiled. 'I prefer a god who protects those who worship him.'

'I don't know about these things, Augustus, but I say let's make terms with the Persians and leave this place. Not that it's for me to decide.'

'No, it is not for you to decide. But I shall bear in mind your advice.' I dismissed Jovian, more depressed than ever.

I make sacrifice in a few minutes.

Julian Augustus   *15 June*

Mastara sees great peril no matter what I do. I sacrificed yesterday and again this morning. There is still no sign. The gods are silent. I prayed more than an hour to Helios. I looked straight at him until I was blind. Nothing, I have offended. But how? I cannot believe that my anger at the war god would turn all heaven against me. Who else will do their work?

Nevitta brings me word that the Asiatic troops already speak of my successor 'who will save them'. But apparently there is no popular choice. They follow Victor but do not love him. Arintheus? Emperor? No. Not even his boys would accept that. Salutius? He is loyal to me and yet . . . I grow suspicious. I am like Constantius now. I suspect treason on every side. For the first time I fear the knife in the dark. I make Callistus sleep on the ground beside my bed while the deaf-mute remains awake most of the night, watching for the assassins's shadow to fall across the door to my tent. I never believed that I would become like this. I have never feared death in battle, and I never thought that I feared murder. But I do. I find it hard to sleep. When I do, my dreams are of death, sudden, black, violent. What has gone wrong?

Beside my bed there is a book by Aeschylus. Just now I picked it up and read this at random: 'Take heart. Suffering when it climbs highest lasts but a little time.' Well, I am near the peak. Will it be swift? or slow?

Priscus and Maximus spent most of the evening with me. We talked philosophy. No one mentioned our situation and for a time I was able to forget that the gods have abandoned me. Yet why do I think this? Merely because the Persians have burned the countryside? Or because of the treachery of Procopius, which does not come as a surprise? Although things are not so bad as I feel they are, the fact that I have this sense of foreboding is in itself a message from the gods.

Maximus wanted to stay behind after Priscus left. But I would not let him pleading fatigue. I suspect even him. Why should he be in league with Victor? Everyone knows he has influence over me, and certainly anyone could buy him if they met his price. This is insane. Of course Maximus is loyal to me. He has to be. The Galileans would have his head if I were not here to protect him. I must stop this brooding or I shall become as mad as those emperors who feared the long night of death more than they loved the brief living day. I am still alive; still Augustus; still conqueror of Persia.

Tomorrow we start for home. I gave the order at sundown. The men cheered me. They don't know what a long jorney it is from here to Corduene. All they know is that we are leaving Persia. All *I* known is that the goddess Cybele revealed to me that I was Alexander born again, and I have failed both her and Alexander, who is once more a ghost, while I am nothing.

I should have agreed to Sapor's treaty. Now that we are withdrawing, we shall get worse terms.

Priscus: As well as I knew Julian, I never suspected that he was in such despair. The exhausted man who scribbled the journal, and the proud laughing general Maximus and I used to dine with are two different creatures. Naturally, we knew that he was worried. But he never betrayed to us that morbid fear of assassination he writes about. He joked occasionally about the succession, saying that if Rome were to have a Christian emperor he hoped it would be Victor because in a year there would be a million converts to Hellenism. But that was all. He talked as he always talked: rapidly, enthusiastically, late into the night, reading aloud to us from the classics, quarrelling with me over Plato's meanings, teasing Maximus for his ignorace of literature. The great magician, having always been in such close communion with the gods, seldom condescended to read the reports of those who could only guess at the mysteries he *knew*.

On 15 June Julian gave the order to go north along the Tigris to Corduene and Armenia. The thing was finished. Even Ormisda now realized that he would never rule in Persia.

At dawn 16 June we broke camp. Julian asked me to ride with him. I did not realize until I read the journal what a good actor he was. That day he was the exuberant, legendary hero, hair and beard burned a dull gold by the sun, arms and legs dark, face as clear and untroubled as a child's; even the constant nose-peeling had finally stopped and his head looked as if it had been carved from African wood. We were all quite black except for the pale Gauls, who turn painfully red in the sun and stay that way. There was much sunstroke among them.

As we rode through fire-blackened hills, Julian seemed unusually cheerful. 'We haven't done too badly. The campaign has been a success, though not exactly what I had hoped for.'

'Because Ormisda is not Great King?'

'Yes.' He did not elaborate.

We were interrupted by the tribune Valens. It was the only other time I recall seeing him in Persia. He was not bad-looking, though physically rather dirty, even as soldiers go. He was profoundly nervous in Julian's presence. 'Augustus, the scouts report an army approaching. From the north.'

Julian dug his heels into his horse's ribs and cantered down the road to the head of the army, two miles distant. Within half an hour, the sky was dark with swirling dust. The rumour went about quickly: Procopius has come. But Julian took no chances. We made a war camp on the spot, with a triple row of shields placed around us. Then we waited to see whose army it was, Procopius's or Sapor's.

We were on battle alert all day. I bet Anatolius five silver pieces at three-to-one odds that the army was Sapor's. Neither of us won. The 'army' turned out to be a herd of wild asses.

But that night the Great King's army materialized.

Julian Augustus   *17 June*

Sapor's army still exists. They are encamped a mile from us. Cannot tell what their numbers are but not so many as were assembled at Ctesiphon. Our troops eager for battle. Had to restrain them all morning. At noon Persian cavalry attacked one of our battalions. General Machameus killed. Though wounded, his brother Maurus fought his way to where the body was lying and carried it back into camp.

The heat is beyond anything I have ever before endured. Though we are all of us giddy from too much sun, I ordered the march to be continued. At first the Persians fell back; then they rallied and tried to stop us. We butchered them. By afternoon they were all of them gone except for a band of Saracens who follow us even now, waiting for the right moment to raid our baggage train.

I write this sitting on a stool beneath a date palm. Everywhere I look I see green circles before my eyes. I am dazzled by Helios. The air is so hot it scorches the lungs. My sweat mingles with the ink on the page. The letters blur. Few casualties.

Julian Augustus 20 *June*

For two days we have been encamped at Hucumbra, the estate of a Persian nobleman who, luckily for us, did not burn his crops and orchards. Food and water are plentiful. The men are almost happy. I have ordered them to take all the food they can for we must burn this place as soon as we leave it. We shall not find so much food again until we reach our own territory, twenty days' march from here.

Julian Augustus 21 *June*

On the march. The country is hilly and barren. We are about twenty miles to the west of the Tigris, moving north. Early today the Persian cavalry attacked our infantry rear-guard. Fortunately, the cavalry of the Petulantes was near by and drove them off. One of the Great King's counsellors, Adaces, was killed and his armour brought me by the soldier who struck him down. As I gave the usual reward, Salutius suddenly said, 'We were good friends, Adaces and I.' He then reminded me that the Persian had once been Sapor's envoy to Constantius.

An ugly business tonight. Instead of attacking the Persians at the same time as the Petulantes, the cavalry of the Tertiaci gave way. As a result, what might have been a complete rout of the Persians became only a skirmish. I broke four tribunes but took no other action. We shall soon need every man we have, coward or brave.

We are no longer certain where we are. We move in a line north, but there are no maps to show us where water and villages are. But two days ago, at Hucumbra, an old Persian who knows the province well offered to lead us to fertile country. Ormisda talked with him at length and believes he is not a spy. The old man says there will be three days of barren country and then we shall be in the rich valley of Maranga.

Julian Augustus 22 *June*

Battle. Execution. Vetranio. Victory. Where?

Priscus: The old Persian was of course a spy who led us straight into an ambush at Maranga, which was not a 'rich valley' but a stony place where we were exposed on all sides to the Persian army. Julian was just able to form the army into a crescent when they attacked. The first rain of Persian arrows did little harm. There was no second flurry. Julian was able to resort to his favourite tactical exercise, throwing his infantry at the enemy's archers before they could get proper range.

The fighting went on all day in ovenlike heat. I remained with the baggage and saw very little of what happened. My principal memory is of heat, of blood on white rocks, of the hideous trumpeting of elephants reverberating through the narrow valley.

'Execution.' The old Persian was crucified when it was discovered that he had deliberately led us into this trap.

'Vetranio.' He was commanding officer of the Zianni; he was killed.

'Victory.' The Persian army disappeared at nightfall. Their casualties were three to our one. But the men were frightened. The business of the Persian spy had particularly alarmed them. How far out of the way had he taken us? Wouldn't it be better – if riskier – to follow the crooked Tigris north? All these questions were addressed to Julian whenever he appeared among the troops. But he seemed confident as always.

'Where?' Where indeed!

Julian Augustus   *23 June*

We are now eight miles from the Tigris. I have decided to follow the river north, though that is the longest and most dangerous route, since we shall have to pass many fortresses. Even so, I am alarmed by this wilderness. We have no idea where we are. The advantage is entirely the enemy's. We are short of food. I have ordered my own supplies given to the men. Ormisda tells me that the Great King is again ready to make peace on terms still favourable to us. Ormisda advises me to accept the treaty. This alarms me most. If Ormisda has given up his dream of the Persian throne, the war is lost.

Julian Augustus   *25 June*

There seems to be a tacit truce between the Persians and us. They have completely vanished. We are remaining in camp, tending to the wounded, repairing armour, getting ready for the long journey north. I feel like Xenophon, who also went this way.

A while ago I fell asleep while reading *The March Upcountry*. So deep was my sleep that I did not realize I was dreaming (usually I do). I thought I was wide awake. I was even aware of the oil lamp sputtering as insects passed through its flame and burned. Suddenly I felt someone watching me. I looked up and there at the door to the tent was the tall figure of a man with head veiled; in one hand he held the horn of plenty. At first, I tried to speak, but could not – tried to rise but could not. For a long moment the spectre looked at me sadly. Then without a word the figure turned and left my tent, and I awakened, cold as a corpse. I leapt to my feet and crossed to the tent opening. I looked out. Except for the sleepy sentry no one was in sight. Small fires glowed in the darkness. I looked up just as a star fell in the west; it came from on high, flared briefly, then vanished.

I awakened Callistus. 'Fetch me Maximus. And Mastara. Quickly.'

When they arrived, I told them about the star. I showed them exactly where it had fallen in the sky.

Mastara interpreted. 'According to the book of Tages, when a meteor is seen to fall in time of war, no battle must be undertaken for twenty-four hours, nor a move of any kind.'

I turned to Maximus. 'Well, at least it was not *my* star.'

Maximus was reassuring, but Mastara was firm. 'One thing is certain. You must remain here in camp another day.'

'But I have given orders. Tomorrow we cross to the Tigris.'

'You asked me, Highest Priest, for the word of Tages and I have given it.'

I allowed Mastara to go. Then I told Maximus of the dream. He was troubled. 'Are you so certain the figure was Rome?'

'Yes. I saw him once before, in Paris, when he ordered me to take the purple.'

Maximus frowned. 'It could of course be a demon. They are everywhere in this cursed land. Why, even as I walked here tonight, I felt them all about me, tugging at my beard, my staff, testing my power.'

'This was not a demon. It was the Spirit of Rome. And he abandoned me.'

'Don't say that! After all, in three weeks we shall be home. You can raise a new army. Then you shall complete Alexander's work . . .'

'Perhaps.' Suddenly I found myself tired of Maximus. He means to be helpful, but he is not always right. He is not a god; nor am I. Much against his wish, I sent him away. Before he left, he begged me not to break camp tomorrow. But I

Callistus is polishing my armour. He says the breast plate straps are broken, but he will have the armourer fix them before we leave tomorrow. The deaf mute sits at my feet. He plays a Lydian song, very old and very strange; yet one can recognize the voice of Dionysos in the melody. To think, the god sings to us still, though the golden age is gone and the sacred gloves deserted.

For an hour I walked among the tents, unobserved by the men. I gather strength from the army. They are my life, the element in which I have my being. That is the final irony. I who wanted to live at Athens as a student have been eight years a general. Such is fate.

I paused at Anatolius's tent. Through the flap, I could see Anatolius and Priscus playing draughts. I nearly spoke to them. But then I realized that I am hardly the best of company tonight. So instead I sat in front of my tent, watching the sky. My own star burns bright as ever. If it were not for tonight's troubling dream, I would be content. Without reinforcements, we have done all that we could do in this place. But what's to be done with Victor and the Galileans? Nevitta tells me that I am not safe. Yet what can they do to me? If I am openly murdered, the Gauls and Franks will slaughter the Asiatics. If secretly . . . but when an emperor dies suddenly in his youth it is not secret. No, they do not dare strike at me, yet. Curious, as I lie here on the lion bed, I think of something Mardonius once told Gallus and me.

Priscus: That is the last entry, broken off by sleep, and then by death.

23

Priscus: The next morning Julian gave the order to march west to the Tigris. We were in a dry desolate country of sand and stone. Our slow passage made clouds of white choking dust as we rode towards a series of low hills where waiting Persians watched us, like so many scorpions among the rocks.

I was with Julian in the vanguard. He wore no armour. His servant had not yet repaired the leather straps. 'Just as well,' he said. Like all of us, he was soaked with sweat, even at dawn. Flies clung to our lips and eyes. Most of us suffered from dysentery. Yet despite the heat and the discomfort, Julian was in excellent spirits. For one thing, he had finally interpreted the dream to his own liking. 'The Genius of Rome deserted me. There's no denying that. *But* he left by the tent door, which was to the west. That means this campaign is finished, and we must return home to the west.'

'But you said the face was grieving.'

'So is mine when I think of what we might have done here. Even so . . .' As we talked, messengers came to him at regular intervals. Persians sighted in the valley ahead. Skirmishing on the left flank. Count Victor fears an attack.

'No attack,' said Julian. 'They won't meet us again in battle. They will harass us, but nothing more.' He gave rapid orders. The left flank to be reinforced. The

Saracens to go to the rear. Count Victor to be soothed. Suddenly a courier arrived from Arintheus: Persian cavalry was attacking the rear-guard. Julian promptly turned his horse about and rode to the rear, followed by Callistus.

Some thirty minutes after Julian left us, the van was attacked by Persian archers hidden in the cliffs to the right of the trail. Nevitta called for battle formation. I quickly joined my fellow non-combatants at the centre.

Safe among the baggage, I found Maximus calmly combing his beard, unaware we were being attacked. When I told him what was happening, he was not in the least alarmed. 'No more set battles,' he said, echoing Julian. 'Only guerrilla warfare. Nothing to fear.'

But Anatolius was roused by this information. 'I must join the Tertiaci. They count on me.' Then the absurd creature was off, the plump little body kept astride his horse only by the weight of armour. It should be noted that if one is at the centre of an army whose vanguard is ten miles from its rear-guard, a considerable battle can take place and one not know it. Huddled among the wagons, Maximus and I might just as well have been travelling from Athens to Sirmium as in the midst of a Persian war.

Now this is what happened to Julian. Halfway to the rear, he was stopped by a second courier, who told him that the vanguard was also under attack. Julian started back. He had gone perhaps a mile when the Persians attacked our centre. Elephants, cavalrymen, archers swept down from the hills so suddenly that the left flank momentarily gave way. Julian rushed into this action, his only armour a shield. He rallied the troops. They struck back at the Persians. With swords and axes they hacked the trunks and legs of the elephants.

The Persians retreated. Julian rode after them, waving to the household troops to follow him. Suddenly he and Callistus were caught up in a confused mêlée of retreating Persians. For some minutes both men were lost to view. Finally the last of the Persians fled and Julian was again visible. He rejoined the household troops, who cheered him, relieved that he was safe. Not until he had come quite close did they notice the spear that had penetrated his side.

'It is not much,' said Julian. But when he tried to draw the spear, he gave a cry, for the shaft was razor-sharp and cut his fingers. I am told that he sat a long moment staring straight ahead. Then suddenly he hurled his own blood straight at the sun. 'It is not much,' he said again, and pitched headlong to the ground.

Julian was carried in a litter to his tent. At his own insistence, he was completely covered by a cavalryman's cloak so that no one might know the Emperor had fallen.

When I saw the litter approaching the tent, I thought stupidly: Someone has killed a deer and they're bringing it for our supper. When I realized that it was Julian in the litter, I felt as if I had been struck very hard in the chest. I looked at Maximus. He too was stunned. Together we followed the litter into the tent. Julian was now conscious.

'There is a lesson in this,' he murmured, while Maximus leaned over him, as though to hear the words of an oracle.

'Yes, Julian.' Maximus whispered prayerfully.

'Always, in war – no matter what – wear armour.' Julian smiled weakly at us. Then he turned to the frightened Callistus. 'Are the straps fixed yet?'

'Yes, Lord. Yes.' Callistus began to sob.

The surgeons meanwhile had cut away Julian's tunic. The head of the spear had entered just below the rib cage, penetrating the lower lobe of the liver. There was almost no blood on the white skin. Julian glanced down at his wound with an air of distaste, like a sculptor who detects a flaw in the figure he is shaping. 'Only my hand gives me pain,' he said. Then he turned to Salutius who had joined us. 'How is the battle?'

'We are turning them back.'

'Good. But even so, I'd better show myself. The men must see that I'm still alive.' Though the surgeons tried to restrain him, he sat up. 'It's all right. I feel no pain. The wound's not deep. Callistus, my armour.' He turned to the surgeons. 'If you can't draw the spear, at least cut it short so I can hide it under my cloak.' He swung his legs over the bed; blood gushed from the wound; he fainted. I nearly did, too. Swiftly, the surgeons worked to stanch the flow.

It was Salutius who asked the surgeons, 'Will he die?'

'Yes, Prefect, he will die, very soon.' We looked at one another like idiots, amazed, unbelieving.

Nevitta appeared at the tent's opening. 'Emperor!' he shouted to the pale unconscious figure on the lion bed.

Salutius shook his head and put his fingers to his lips. With a howl like an animal in pain, Nevitta fled the tent. Salutius followed him. That day the Gauls and Franks, the Celts and Germans slaughtered half the Persian army to avenge their Emperor.

The fighting did not end until nightfall. But I saw none of it. With Maximus, I sat in that stifling tent and watched Julian die.

He was conscious most of the time. He did not become delirious. His mind never wandered. He suffered little pain. For a long time he pretended that all he had suffered was a flesh wound.

'But how?' I asked. The javelin in his side looked absurd, like a long pin stuck in a child's doll.

'I don't know. How?' Julian turned to Callistus, who sat on the ground like a terrified dog, close to the armour stand. 'Did you see how it happened?'

'No, Lord. I was behind you. The Persians were all around us. I lost sight of you. Not until we were free of them did I see what had happened.'

'At the time I hardly felt it; a light blow, as if I'd been struck by a fist.' Julian motioned to the deaf-mute boy to give him water. But at the surgeons' request, he did not swallow.

News of the battle was brought us regularly. When Julian learned that the Persian generals Merena and Nahodares were dead, he was delighted. 'They were the best of Sapor's officers. This *is* the last battle. I'm sure of it!'

I confess that for once I was grateful for Maximus's logorrhoea. There were no silences that day as he told us endless anecdotes of the various gods he had spoken to. Apparently, all Olympus delighted in his company.

At sundown, the bleeding started again. When it was finally stopped, Julian's face was ashy beneath sunburned skin. 'Will you be able to draw the spear?' he asked the surgeons.

'No, Lord.' That was the death sentence, and Julian knew it. He nodded and shut his eyes. He seemed to sleep. I sweated nervously. Maximus drew designs on the sandy floor. From far off, the sound of battle grew fainter. Just as Callistus was lighting the lamps, Salutius and Nevitta entered the tent. Julian opened his eyes. 'How goes it?' His voice was low but firm.

Salutius placed an ornate bronze helmet at the edge of Julian's cot. 'This belonged to General Merena. The Persian army is defeated. So far we have counted fifty of their greatest lords among the dead.'

'We won't see that army soon again,' said Nevitta.

'You fought well.' Julian touched the Persian general's helmet with his good hand. 'This war is over.'

'But we nearly lost Salutius.' Nevitta attempted heartiness. 'They had him surrounded. Because of the purple cloak, they thought he was you. So he had to fight just like a Frank to get away. Never thought such an old man could have so much energy.'

Julian smiled dimly. 'The old man won't be able to walk tomorrow, from stiffness.'

'He can hardly move now.' Salutius kept up the badinage.

Julian gave a sudden quick gasp. He gripped his sides as though the chest were about to burst. Sweat glistened on his body. The muscles of his stomach contracted in pain.

'Helios,' he muttered. Then he added, 'Where are we? What is this place called?'

It was Maximus who answered, 'Phrygia.' And dully Julian said, 'Then the thing is done.'

Incidentally, I have always wanted to know whether or not that patch of desert was indeed called Phrygia. Knowing Maximus, I suspect him of lying; after all, his reputation as a prophet was at stake. But true or false, it is now a matter of historic record that the Emperor Julian was struck down in Phrygia, as foretold by Maximus and Sosipatra.

Julian turned to the surgeons. 'Will I die soon?'

'Lord, we cannot say. The liver is pierced. A few hours . . .' Callistus began to weep again. Nevitta clenched and unclenched his huge hands as though ready to break to bits bony death himself. Salutius sat limply on a stool, weak from the long day's battle.

'So I have seen the sun – living – for the last time.' Julian said this in a matter-of-fact voice. 'I should have made sacrifice. Now of course *I* am the sacrifice.'

'Augustus.' Salutius was urgent. 'You must determine the succession. Who is to be our emperor when the gods take you back?'

Julian was silent. For a moment it seemed as if he had not heard. Then he said, 'I must add certain things to my will, personal bequests. Send for Anatolius.'

It was Salutius who said, 'He is happy, Lord.' The classic expression which means that a man has died honourably in battle. I was particularly upset by this.

Julian was startled. 'Anatolius dead?' Tears came to his eyes. Then he laughed. 'Here I am a dying man mourning the dead! That, Priscus, should appeal to your sense of the incongruous.' He became businesslike. 'There is a will at Constantinople, Salutius, you know where it is. See that it is honoured. Nevitta, summon the generals. Maximus, my friends. I am ready to say good-bye.' He grinned and looked suddenly like a schoolboy again. 'You know, most of our emperors died too swiftly to be able to prepare a final speech. While the ones who were allowed sufficient time proved disappointing. Vespasian made a bad joke. "Dear me," he said, "I seem to be turning into a god." Augustus rambled. Hadrian discussed astronomy. None took advantage of the occasion. Well, I mean to be an exception.'

Julian nodded to Callistus, who brought him a small chest from which he withdrew a scroll. 'As always, the gods have been kind to me. I shall die unique: the first emperor to deliver himself of a well-written (if I say so myself) farewell.' He smiled at me. 'Yes, I wrote my last words in Antioch, just in case. So no matter what happens to my reputation, I shall always be remembered for this departure.' He spoke with such a delicate self-mockery that even Salutius smiled and said, 'You have surpassed Marcus Aurelius.'

'Thank you,' said Julian. Then he shut his eyes and waited. In a matter of minutes the tent was crowded with friends, priests, generals. Almost as if by design, the Asiatic generals stood at one side of the bed, while the Europeans were ranged at the other.

When all were present, Julian motioned for the surgeon to prop him up, a physical effort which caused him some pain. Breathing hard, he ordered Callistus to light more lamps, remarking, again to me, 'At the end, Priscus, we can be extravagant.' I of course could think of nothing to say.

Julian opened the scroll. 'Friends,' he began. He looked about him. Victor did not stir when Julian's gaze fell on him. 'Friends,' he repeated. Then he read rapidly, as though he might not live long enough to get to the end. 'Most opportunely do I leave this life which I am pleased to return to Creation, at her demand, like an honourable man who pays his debts when they come due. Nor am I – as some might think . . .' he paused once more and looked about the tent at the faces of his generals, curiously shifting and grotesque in the uneven lamplight . . . 'sad' – he stressed the word oddly – 'at going.'

He returned to the text. 'For I have learned from philosophy that the soul is happier than the body; therefore, when a better condition is severed from a worse, one should rejoice, not grieve. Nor should we forget that the gods deliberately give death to the greatest of men as the ultimate reward. I am confident that this gift was given me so that I might not yield to certain difficulties, nor ever suffer the humiliation of defeat. After all, sorrow can only overwhelm weakness; it flees before strength. I regret nothing I have ever done. I am not tormented by the memory of any great misdeed. Both before and after I was raised to the principate, I preserved my own god-given soul and kept it without grievous fault, or so I think. I conducted the business of the state with moderation. I made war – or peace – only after much deliberation, realizing that success and careful planning do not necessarily go hand in hand, since the gods, finally, must determine the outcome. Even so, believing as I did that the purpose of a just rule is the welfare and security of the people, I was always – as you know – inclined to peaceful measures, never indulging in that licence which is the corruption of deeds and of charity.' He stopped. He took several long deep breaths, as though he could not get enough air in his lungs.

I looked about me. All eyes were on Julian. Nevitta and Jovian wept openly; the one from emotion, the other from drink. Victor stood on tiptoe at the edge of the bed, like some predatory bird ready to strike. Of that company, only Maximus was his usual self, muttering spells and crumbling dried herbs onto the nearest lamp, no doubt sending messages ahead to the underworld.

Julian continued, his voice weaker. 'I am happy that the state like an imperious parent so often exposed me to danger. I was forced to be strong, to hold my own, to resist the storms of fate, even though I knew what the end would be, for I long ago learned from an oracle that I would die by the sword. For this good death, I thank Helios, since it is the fear of those in my place that we die ignobly by secret plots or, even worse, by some long illness. I am happy that I die in mid-career, victorious, and I am honoured that the gods have found me worthy of so noble a departure from this world. For a man is weak and cowardly who wants not to die when he ought, or tries to avoid his hour when it comes . . .' These last few words were said almost in a whisper. The scroll dropped from his hand. He seemed to have difficulty in concentrating his thoughts.

'There is more,' he said at last. 'But I cannot . . . I am . . . I will *not* ramble.' An attempt at a smile failed. Instead a muscle in his cheek began to twitch spasmodically. Yet his next words came out clearly. 'Now as to the choice of an emperor.' Instinctively, the generals moved closer to the bed, the scent of power exciting them much as blood draws wolves to a wounded deer.

Even in his pain, Julian understood precisely the nature of the beasts who encircled him; he spoke slowly and carefully. 'If I select someone as my heir and you reject him, as you might, I shall have put a worthy man in a fatal position. My successor would not let him live. Also I might, through ignorance' – this time he did manage a faint smile – 'pass over the worthiest man of all, and I would not want *that* stain on my memory, for I am a dutiful child of Rome and I want a good ruler to succeed me. That is why I leave the choice to you. I propose no one.'

There was a long sigh in the room. The generals stirred restlessly. Some were disappointed; others pleased: now *their* moment might come.

Julian looked at me. 'Did I read that well?'

'Yes, Lord.'

'Then I have made the departure I intended.' He turned to the generals. 'Now let us say good-bye.' One by one, the generals kissed his hand for the last time. Many wept. But he ordered them not to. 'I should weep for *you*. I am finished with suffering while you, poor devils, are still in the midst of it.'

When the last of the generals had gone, Julian motioned for Maximus and me to sit beside his bed. 'Now we talk,' he said, employing the phrase he always used when he was alone at last with his friends.

Then Julian engaged us in a discussion of the *Phaedo*. What is the precise nature of the soul? What form does it take? In what way does it return to Serapis? I talked philosophy; Maximus talked mysteries. Julian preferred Maximus to me at the end and I could not blame him, for I am bleak and Maximus was hopeful. Together they repeated Mithraic passwords to one another and made cryptic references to the Passion of Demeter. Julian derived a good deal of comfort from Maximus. As usual, I was quite unable to express my affection for him; instead, like a village schoolmaster, I quoted Plato. I was never more inadequate.

Shortly before midnight, Julian asked for cold water. Callistus brought it to him. Just as he was about to drink, black, clotted blood suddenly gushed from his side. He gave a sharp cry and clutched the wound as though with his bare hand he might keep the life from leaving. Then he fainted. The surgeons tried to close the wound. But this time it was no use; the haemorrhage when it finally stopped did so of its own accord.

For some minutes Julian lay with eyes shut, hardly breathing. To this day I remember how the hair on his chest was matted with dried blood, like the pelt of some animal newly killed. I remember the sharp contrast between his sun-darkened neck and the marble white of his torso. I remember that foolish sliver of metal stuck in his side, and I remember thinking: such a small thing to end a man's life and change the history of the world.

At last Julian opened his eyes. 'Water,' he whispered. Callistus held up his head while he drank. This time the surgeons allowed him to swallow. When he had drained the cup, he turned to Maximus and me, as though he had just thought of something particularly interesting to tell us.

'Yes, Julian?' Maximus leaned forward eagerly. 'Yes?'

But Julian seemed to have a second thought. He shook his head. He closed his eyes. He cleared his throat quite naturally. He died. Callistus, feeling the body in his arms go limp, leapt back from the bed with a cry. The corpse fell heavily on its back. One limp brown arm dangled over the edge of the bed. The lion-skin covering was now drenched with blood. No one can ever use it again, I thought numbly as the surgeon said, 'The Augustus is dead.'

Callistus wept. The deaf-mute moaned like an animal by the bed. Maximus shut his eyes as if in pain. He did not need to exert his gift for seeing into the future to know that the days of his own greatness were over.

I sent Callistus to fetch Salutius. While we waited, the surgeons drew the spear from Julian's body. I asked to see it. I was examining it when Salutius arrived. He glanced briefly at the body; then he turned to Callistus, 'Tell the staff to assemble immediately.'

Maximus, suddenly, gave a loud but melodious cry and hurried from the tent. Later he told me that he had seen the spirits of Alexander and Julian embracing in the air several feet above the earthen floor of the tent. The sight had ravished him.

After covering the body with a cloak, the surgeons departed, as did the deaf-mute, who was never seen again. Salutius and I were alone in the tent.

I showed him the lance that I was still holding. 'This is what killed him,' I said.

'Yes. I know.'

'It is a Roman spear,' I said.

'I know that, too.' We looked at one another.

'*Who* killed him?' I asked. But Salutius did not answer. He pulled back the tent flap. Outside the generals were gathering by the light of a dozen torches guttering in the hot night wind. Resinous smoke stung my eyes. As Salutius was about to join them, I said, 'Did Julian know it was a Roman spear?'

Salutius shrugged. 'How could he *not* have known?' He let the tent flap fall after him.

I looked at the figure on the bed. The body was shrouded in purple, except for one brown foot. I adjusted the cloak and inadvertently touched flesh: it was still warm. I shied like a horse who sees a shadow in the road. Then I opened the box from which Julian had taken his deathbed speech. As I had suspected, the memoir and the journal were there. I stole them.

What else? The meeting that night was stormy. Victor and Arintheus wanted an emperor from the East. Nevitta and Dagalaif wanted one from the West. All agreed on Salutius. But he refused. He is the only man I have ever heard of who really meant it when he declared that the principate of this world was not for him.

When Ammianus insisted that Salutius at least agree to lead the army out of Persia, Salutius was equally firm. Under no circumstances would he take command. At a complete impasse, the two factions agreed to meet again the following day.

During the night, Victor took action. Realizing that he himself had no chance of becoming emperor, he decided to create an emperor, one easily managed. His choice was Jovian. In the early hours of 27 June, Victor got the household troops drunk. He then incited them to proclaim their commander Jovian as Augustus.

At dawn, the frightened Jovian was led before the assembly by a hundred young officers with drawn swords. The thing was accomplished. Rather than risk bloodshed and civil war, we swore the oath of allegiance to Jovian. Then the new Emperor and his guards made a solemn progress through the army. When the men heard the cry 'Jovian Augustus!' they thought at first it was '*Julian* Augustus', and so they began to cheer the miraculous recovery. But when they saw the clownish figure of their new lord, red-eyed, nervous, stooped beneath ill-fitting purple like some exotic African bird, the cheers turned to silence.

That same day, I myself buried poor Anatolius. I found him lying at the bottom of a steep ravine. Until now I have never had the heart to tell anyone that he was not killed by the Persians. He was thrown from his horse and broke his neck. He was a terrible horseman but a delightful companion. I kept his draughtboard, which I lost – naturally – on the trip from Antioch to Athens. Nothing is left to me. Well . . .

The rest is familiar history. Jovian made a thirty years' peace with Sapor. He was so eager to get out of Persia and begin a round of parties in Constantinople that he agreed to all of Sapor's demands. He ceded Persia five provinces, including our cities of Singara and Nisibis! It was a disastrous treaty.

We then proceeded to Antioch. En route, Procopius and Sebastian joined us. To this day no one knows why Procopius did not join Julian in Persia. He must have given some excuse to Jovian, but it never filtered down to us. Happily, he himself was put to death, some years later, when he tried to seize the East. So there is a rude justice in our affairs, at least in this case.

Seven months later the Emperor Jovian was also dead. The official report said that he died in his sleep from breathing the fumes of a charcoal stove. To this day, many believe that he was poisoned by Victor, but I have it on good authority that he died naturally. In a drunken sleep, he vomited and choked to death, the perfect end for a glutton. Rather surprisingly, Valentinian was declared Emperor, and that was the end of Victor as a political force. Remember how pleased we all were when Valentinian made his brother Valens Augustus for the East? Such a mild young man, we thought. Well, Valens nearly had my head. He did have Maximus's, and even you had a most difficult time of it. But now the brothers are also dead, and we live on under Valentinian's son Gratian and his appointee Theodosius, who in turn will die, to be succeeded by . . . I sometimes feel that the history of the Roman principate is an interminable pageant of sameness. They are so much alike, these energetic men; only Julian was different.

Towards the end of your justly admired funeral oration at Antioch, you suggested that Julian was killed by one of his own men, if only because no Persian ever came forward to collect the reward the Great King had offered the slayer of Julian. Now I was one of the few people who knew for certain that Julian had been killed by a Roman spear, but I said nothing. I had no intention of involving myself in politics. As it was, I had quite enough trouble that year when Maximus and I were arrested for practising magic. I a magician!

Fortunately, I was acquitted. Maximus was not. Even so, the old charlatan did manage to have the last word. During his trial, he swore that he had never used his powers maliciously. He also prophesied that whoever took his life unjustly would himself die so terribly that all trace of him would vanish from the earth. Maximus was then put to death by the Emperor Valens, who was promptly killed at the Battle of Adrianople by Goths who hacked the imperial corpse into so many small pieces that no part of him was ever identified. Right to the end, Maximus was lucky in his predictions.

When I was finally released from prison (I wish you luck in your campaign for penal reform), I went straight home to Athens. I locked up Julian's papers in one of Hippia's strong-boxes and thought no more about them until this correspondence begun.

Lately I have found myself thinking a good deal about Julian's death. You were right when you hinted that he was killed by one of his own men. But by whom? And how? I have studied the last entries in the diary with particular care. From the beginning Julian knew that there was a plot against his life, and it is fairly plain that he suspected Victor of conspiracy. But was Julian right? And if he was right, how was the murder accomplished?

About ten years ago Julian's servant Callistus wrote a particularly lachrymose ode on the Emperor's death. We were all sent copies. I'm afraid I never wrote to thank the author for his kind gift. In fact, Callistus had completely dropped from my memory until I reread the diary and realized that if anyone had known how Julian died, it would be the servant who was with him when he was wounded.

Callistus of course had sworn that he did not see who struck the blow. But at the time there was good reason for him to lie: the Christians would very quickly have put him to death had he implicated any of them. Like so many of us, Callistus chose silence. But might he not be candid now, with all the principals dead?

It took me several weeks to discover that Callistus lives at Philippopolis. I wrote him. He answered. Last month I went to see him. I shall now give you a full report of what he said. Before you use any of this, I suggest that you yourself write to Callistus for permission. His story is an appalling one, and there is some danger in even knowing it, much less writing about it. *I must also insist that under no circumstances are you to involve me in your account.*

After a tedious trip to Philippopolis in the company of tax collectors and church deacons, I went straight to the house of an old pupil who kindly offered to put me up, a great saving since the local innkeepers are notorious thieves. The only advantage to having been a teacher for what seems now to have been the better part of a thousand years is that no matter where I go, I find former students who let me stay with them. This makes travel possible.

I asked my host about Callistus (I myself could remember nothing about him except the sound of his sobbing at Julian's deathbed). 'One never sees your Callistus.' My old student is a snob. 'They say he's quite rich, and there are those who go to his house. I am not one of them.'

'Where did his money come from?'

'Trade concessions. Imperial grants. He is supposed to be quite clever. He was born here, you know. The son of a slave in the house of a cousin of mine. He returned only a few years ago, shortly after the Emperor Valentinian died. They say he has important friends at court. But I wouldn't know.'

Callistus is indeed rich, his house far larger and more lavish than that of my former pupil. A Syrian steward of breathtaking elegance led me through two large courtyards to a small shady atrium where Callistus was waiting for me. Here I was greeted most affably by a perfect stranger. I don't recall how Callistus used to look, but today he is a handsome middle-aged man who looks years younger than he is. It is obvious that he devotes a good deal of time to his appearance: hair thick and skilfully dyed; body slender; manners a trifle too good, if you know what I mean.

'How pleasant to see you again, my dear Priscus!' He spoke as though we had been the most intimate of friends, even equals! I returned his greeting with that careful diffidence poverty owes wealth. He took my homage naturally. He asked me to sit down while he poured the wine himself, reverting to at least one of his old functions.

For a time we spoke of who was dead and who was living. To people our age, the former category is largest. Nevitta, Salutius, Sallust, Jovian, Valentinian, Valens are dead. But Victor is still on active duty in Gaul and Dagalaif serves in Austria; Arintheus, recently retired to a suburb of Constantinople, has taken to drink. Then we spoke of Persia and the days of our youth (or in my case the halcyon days of my middle age!). We mourned the dead. Then I got the subject round to Julian's death. I told Callistus of your plans. He was non-committal. I told him that you were in possession of the memoir. He said that he had known at the time that the Emperor was writing such a work and he had often wondered what had become of it. I told him. He smiled. Then I said, 'And of course there was the private journal.'

'A journal?' Callistus looked startled.

'Yes. A secret diary which the Emperor kept in the same box with the memoir.'

'I didn't know.'

'It's a most revealing work.'

'I am sure it is.' Callistus frowned.

'The Emperor knew about the plot against his life. He even knew who the conspirators were.' Something in Callistus' manner prompted me to add this lie.

'There were no conspirators.' Callistus was bland. 'The Augustus was killed by a Persian cavalryman.'

'Who never collected the reward?'

Callistus shrugged. 'Perhaps he himself was killed.'

'But why was this Persian cavalryman armed with a Roman spear?'

'That sometimes happens. In a battle one often takes whatever weapon is at hand. Anyway, I should know. I was with the Augustus, and I saw the Persian who struck him.'

This was unexpected. With some surprise, I asked, 'But why, when Julian asked if you had seen his attacker, did you say you saw nothing?'

Callistus was not in the least rattled. 'But I *did* see the Persian.' He sounded perfectly reasonable. 'And I told the Augustus that I saw him.'

'In front of Maximus and me, you said that you did *not* see who struck the blow.'

Callistus shook his head tolerantly. 'It has been a long time, Priscus. Our memories are not what they were.'

'Implying that *my* memory is at fault?'

He gestured delicately. 'Neither of us is exactly young.'

I tried another tack: 'You have doubtless heard the rumour that a Christian soldier killed the Emperor?'

'Of course. But I was . . .'

'. . . there. Yes. And you know who killed him.'

Callistus' face was a perfect blank. It was impossible to tell what he was thinking. One can see why he has been such a success in business. Then: 'How much *did* the Emperor know?' he asked, the voice flat and abrupt, very different from the easy, rather indolent tone he had been assuming.

'He knew about Victor.'

Callistus nodded. 'I was almost certain he knew. So was Victor.'

'Then *you* knew about the conspiracy?'

'Oh, yes.'

'Were you involved in it?'

'Very much so. You see, Priscus,' he gave me a most winning smile, 'it was I who killed the Emperor Julian.'

There it is. The end of the mystery. Callistus told me everything. He regards himself as one of the world's unique heroes, the unsung saviour of Christianity. As he talked, he paced up and down. He could not tell me enough. After all, for nearly twenty years he has had to keep silent. I was his first auditor.

A cabal had been formed at Antioch. Victor was the ringleader. Arintheus, Jovian, Valentinian and perhaps twenty other Christian officers were involved. They vowed that Julian must not return from Persia alive. But because of his popularity with the European troops, his death must appear to be from natural causes.

Victor assigned Callistus to Julian as a bodyguard and servant. At first he was instructed to poison the Emperor. But that was not easily accomplished. Julian was in excellent health; he was known to eat sparingly; a sudden illness would be suspicious. Finally, an ambush was arranged with the Persians. Julian has described how that failed. Then it was decided that Julian must die in battle. But he was an excellent soldier, highly conspicuous, always guarded. The conspirators were in despair until Callistus hit upon a plan.

'After the Battle of Maranga, I broke the straps of his breastplate.' Callistus' eyes sparked with delighted memory. 'Luckily for us, the Persians attacked the next day and the Emperor was forced to go into battle without armour. He and I got caught up in the Persian retreat. He started to turn back but I shouted to him, "Lord, this way!" And I led him into the worst of the fighting. For a moment I thought the Persians *would* kill him. But they were too terrified. When they recognized him, they fled. It was then that I knew that God had chosen me to be the instrument of his vengeance.' The voice lowered; the jaw set. 'We were hemmed in. The Emperor was using his shield to try and clear a path for himself through the tangle of horses and riders. Suddenly he twisted to his left and stood in his stirrups, trying to see over the heads of the Persians. This was my chance. I prayed for Christ to give me strength. Then I plunged my spear into his side.' Callistus stopped, obviously expecting some outcry at this. But I merely gave him that look of alert interest with which I reward those exceptional students who succeed in holding my attention.

'Go on,' I said politely.

Somewhat deflated, Callistus shrugged. 'You know the rest. The Augustus didn't realize he was wounded until after the Persians fled.' He smiled. 'The Augustus even thanked me for having stayed so close to him.'

'It was a good thing for you that he suspected nothing.' But even as I said this I wondered whether or not Julian had known the truth. *That* remains the final mystery.

'But what is death?' asked Callistus, promptly losing all the respect I had come to have for him as a villain. He is an ass. He talked for another hour. He told me that Victor wanted to be emperor, but when he saw that this was impossible, he raised Jovian to the purple. Then the notoriously strong-willed

Valentinian took Jovian's place and that was the end of Victor. Meanwhile, Callistus was paid off handsomely by everyone. He has invested his money wisely and today he is a rich man. But he will not be a happy man until the world knows his secret. He suffers from what he feels to be an undeserved anonymity.

'By all means tell Libanius the truth. One did what one was born to do.' He looked pious. 'I am proud of the part I have played in the history of Rome.' He turned his face to me left-three-quarters, in imitation of the famous bust of the second Brutus. Then he came off it. 'But we'll have to get permission from the palace before Libanius can publish, and I have no idea what the policy is now. Under Valentinian, I was sworn to secrecy.'

'Did Valentinian know about you?'

'Oh, yes. He even gave me the salt concession for Thrace. But he ordered me to keep silent. And I have. Until today. Naturally, I hope that we can make the whole matter public, in the interest of history.'

Callistus offered me dinner but I chose to take nothing more from him. I said I must go. He accompanied me to the vestibule. He was all grace and tact, even when he chided me for never having acknowledged the 'Ode to Julian' he had sent me.

I apologized for my negligence. But then I said, 'How could you write such an affectionate work about the man you murdered?'

Callistus was perfect in his astonishment. 'But I admired him tremendously! He was always kind to me. Every word I wrote about him was from the heart. After all, I am a good Christian, or try to be. Every day I pray for his soul!'

I doubt if Theodosius will allow you to publish any of this. But one never knows. Anyway, *I* am finished with the whole thing and I ask you, please, to keep me out of it.

24

Libanius, Quaestor of Antioch, to the
Lord Theodosius, Augustus of the East   *Antioch, May 381*

May it please Your Eternity, I have it in mind to compose a biography of your famous predecessor the Augustus Julian, employing certain of his private papers which have only recently come into my possession.

Since Your Eternity expressed pleasure in my ode, 'On Avenging the Emperor Julian', I need hardly mention that I intend to pursue my labour of vindication in precisely the same discreet style as the ode which you so graciously admired. Realizing as I do the religious and political implications of this work, I am impelled not only to remind the Augustus of my perfect (and obvious!) loyalty to his sacred person and sagacious policies but to assure him that I intend to relate this marvellous tale with the conscious delicacy which the subject inspires and the times require.

Lord, those of us who cherish the old ways (yet mean to obey to the letter your just and necessary edicts) will be for ever beholden to your magnanimity in allowing me to write with love and candour of a hero whose deeds once blazed upon an astonished and fortunate earth like the sun itself and whose fame in its day (though as nothing compared to Your Eternity's) was Rome's shield against the barbarian. It is my humble wish to reflect that remembered glory in the pages of my own dim but faithful prose.

My cherished friend, the Bishop Meletius, who is now at Constantinople, has told me that he will put my case to Your Eternity with the same high eloquence with which he has for so many decades enlightened the congregations of the East. Accept, then, oh Lord, the homage of one who is old and close to death, and wants nothing for himself but truth, and its telling.

Eutropius, Master of the Offices, to
Libanius, Quaestor of Antioch   *Constantinople, June 381*

The Augustus has read your letter with the interest anything you write deserves. He has commanded me to tell you that it is not possible at this time to publish a life of the late Augustus Julian.

You refer to Bishop Meletius. He is dead. He was stricken last week during a session of the Ecumenical Council. His remains have already been sent to Antioch for burial. I am, however, at liberty to tell you that before the Bishop died, he asked the Augustus to recognize as legitimate your natural son Cimon. The Augustus is pleased to comply with this holy man's request. The documents are now being prepared by my office and will be forwarded in due course to the Count of the East, who will in turn deliver them to the governor of Syria, at which time you will be officially notified.

It would not be remiss, Quaestor, were you to send the Augustus a complete edition of your works. He would value them.

Libanius to himself

I have just come from the funeral of Bishop Meletius, which was held in the Golden House on the island. I don't think I would have been able to cope with the mob in the square if I had not been with Cimon. It seems that all Antioch was on hand to say farewell to their bishop.

The crowd recognized me, as they always do, and they made way for my litter. There was a certain amount of good-humoured comment about 'pagans' (a new word of contempt for us Hellenists) attending Christian services, but I pretended not to hear. Just inside the arcade Cimon lifted me out of the litter. I have been suffering lately from gout not only in my right foot, as usual, but also in my left. Though I use both a crutch and a staff, I can barely hobble without assistance. Fortunately, Cimon, good son that he is, got me safely inside the church. He was also able to provide me with one of the chairs which had been reserved for the governor's party (the Christians stand during their services and only great visitors may sit).

Of course I saw nothing. I can distinguish light and dark, but little else. I do have some sight out of the corner of my left eye, and if I hold my head at a certain cocked angle I can see well enough to read for a short while, but the effort is so great that I prefer to spend my days in the cloudy subaqueous world of the blind. My impression of the church interior was one of pale circles (faces) and dark columns (cloaks of mourning). The air was thick with incense and the inevitable heavy odour of people massed together on a summer day.

Prayers were said and eulogies delivered, but I am afraid that I wool-gathered during the service. I could think of nothing but that curt letter from the

Sacred Palace. I am not to publish. Not even the legitimizing of Cimon can compensate for that cruel blow.

As I sat in the hot octagonal church, the altar to my left and the tall marble pulpit to my right, I was suddenly conscious of the voice of the priest officiating. Like most blind or near-blind people, I am acutely sensitive to voices. Some delight me; others (even those of friends) distress me. This particular voice, I noted with some pleasure, was deep and resonant, with that curious urgency which I always find appealing. The speaker was delivering a eulogy of Meletius. I listened attentively. The words were gracefully chosen; the periods artful; the content conventional. When the priest had finished, I turned to Cimon and whispered, 'Who is that?'

'John Chrysostom, the new deacon, appointed last month by Meletius. You know him.'

'Do I?'

But the service had continued and we kept silent while the new bishop blessed the congregation. Who was this John 'Golden-Mouth'? Where did I know him from? Had he been a pupil? And if he had, would I be able to recall him? My memory is not what it was; also, I have taught literally thousands of men and no one could remember them all. Finally, when the ceremonies ended, Cimon got me to my feet just as the governor of Syria passed us. I recognized him by the colour of his robe. The governor paused when he saw me.

'Ah, Quaestor, how good to see you in such blooming health.'

The governor is an ass, who means well. 'The old tree survives,' I said. 'But it does not bloom.'

However, he had turned to my son. 'It is not premature, I hope, to congratulate you on the Emperor's favour.'

Cimon was delighted; he craves honour, the way some men crave truth.

'No, Governor, not premature at all. Many thanks. My father and I were both delighted at the Emperor's kindness.'

'You must give me some advice, Cimon.' And the governor took my son by the arm and led him away, leaving me stranded in the church, blind as Homer and lame as Hephaestos. I confess to a moment of anger. Cimon should have remained with me. He could have made an appointment to see the governor at another time. But Cimon is a lawyer, and one must be tolerant. Even so, I found it difficult to forgive him when I realized that I was now alone in the Golden House, unable to see and hardly able to walk. Leaning heavily on my stick, like some night-creature dazzled by day, I crept towards what I hoped would be the door. I had taken no more than a step when a firm hand took me by the arm.

'Thank you,' I said to the vague shape beside me. 'I seem to be deserted, and I do need help. I cannot see.'

'Any help I give you is nothing compared to the help you have given me.' I recognized the voice of the deacon John Chrysostom.

I pretended to remember him. 'Oh, yes, John . . .'

'They call me Chrysostom. But you remember me as the son of Anthusa and . . .'

I did remember him. I knew exactly who he was. 'My best student!' I exclaimed. 'Stolen from me by Christians!'

He laughed. 'Not stolen, *found*.'

'So my John is the famous Chrysostom the people listen to.'

'They listen. But do they understand? After all, I am strange to them. For ten years I have been in the desert, alone . . .'

'And now you've come back to the world to be a bishop?'

'I have come back to the world to preach, to tell the truth, the way my old teacher does.'

'We hold a different view of what is true,' I said more sharply than I intended.

'Perhaps not so different.' We had paused near the door. With an effort, I could just make out the lean face of my old pupil. John has begun to grow bald, and he wears a short beard. But I confess that even were my sight better I should not have recognized him; it has been nearly twenty years since he studied with me.

'Before he left Antioch, Bishop Meletius told me of your plan to write about the Emperor Julian.' I wondered if John could see into my mind. Why else would he mention the one thing which most concerned me yet could hardly interest him?

'Unfortunately, it is no longer a plan. The Emperor has forbidden me to publish.'

'I'm sorry. I know what Julian meant to you. I saw him once. I must have been about fifteen. It was just before I came to you, to study. I saw him the day he left the city for Persia. I was in the crowd, in the forum, standing on the rim of the Nymphaeum when he rode by. I remember the people were shouting something rude . . .'

'Felix Julian *Augustus*,' I murmured, hearing again the chanting of that malicious crowd.

'Yes. I was so close to him I could have touched his horse. And though my mother had told me I should hate him, I thought he was the most splendid man I ever saw, and when he looked my way, his eye suddenly caught mine, and he smiled as though we were friends, and I thought to myself: this man is a saint, why do they hate him? Later of course I realized why they hated him, but I have never understood why he hated us.'

I burst into tears. I have never been so humiliated, or felt so ridiculous. The most famous philosopher of his time, if I may say so, was weeping like a child in front of a former pupil. But John was tactful. He said not a word until the storm had passed, and then he made no reference to my senile outburst. He took my arm and led me to the door. Then he turned round and indicated a high place on the opposite wall. 'New work,' he said. 'I think it quite beautiful.' I twisted my head so that I could see – just barely – what appeared to be the giant figure of a man with arms outstretched.

'Can you see him clearly?'

'Oh, yes,' I lied. The gold mosaic glowed like the sun itself in the afternoon light.

'It is Christ Pantocrator, come to redeem us. The face is particularly fine.'

'Yes, I see the face,' I said flatly. And I did: the dark cruel face of an executioner.

'But you don't like what you see?'

'How can I, when what I see is death.'

'But death is not the end.'

'It is the end of life.'

'*This* life . . .'

'Life!' I turned on him fiercely. 'You have chosen death, all of you . . .'

'No, not death. We have chosen life eternal, the resurrection of the . . .'

'That is a story to tell children. The truth is that for thousands of years we looked to what was living. Now you look to what is dead, you worship a dead man and tell one another that *this* world is not for us, while the next is all that matters. Only there is no next world.'

'We believe . . .'

'This is all we have, John Chrysostom. There is nothing else. Turn your back on this world, and you face the pit!'

There was a silence. Then John said, 'Do you see no significance in our victory? For we have won. You must admit that.'

I shrugged. 'The golden age ended. So will the age of iron, so will all things, including man. But with your new god, the hope of human happiness has ended.'

'For ever?' he taunted me gently.

'Nothing man invents can last for ever, including Christ, his most mischievous invention.'

John did not answer. We were now outside the church. The day was pleasantly warm. People I could not see greeted me. Then my son hurried up and I said good-bye to John and got into my litter. All the way home to Daphne, Cimon babbled about his interview with the governor. He has hope of 'governmental preferment'.

I am alone in my study. I have already put away Julian's papers. The thing is finished. The world Julian wanted to preserve and restore is gone . . . but I shall not write 'for ever', for who can know the future? Meanwhile, the barbarians are at the gate. Yet when they breach the wall, they will find nothing of value to seize, only empty relics. The spirit of what we were has fled. So be it.

I have been reading Plotinus all evening. He has the power to soothe me; and I find his sadness curiously comforting. Even when he writes: 'Life here with the things of earth is a sinking, a defeat, a failing of the wing.' The wing has indeed failed. One sinks. Defeat is certain. Even as I write these lines, the lamp wick sputters to an end, and the pool of light in which I sit contracts. Soon the room will be dark. One has always feared that death would be like this. But what else is there? With Julian, the light went, and now nothing remains but to let the darkness come, and hope for a new sun and another day, born of time's mystery and man's love of light.

April 1959–6 January 1964, Rome

A SELECTED BIBLIOGRAPHY

Julian, *The Works of the Emperor*.

Ammianus Marcellinus, *The History*.

Libanius, *Orations:* 'In Praise of Antioch', 'To Julian', 'Monody on Julian', 'Epitaph on Julian', 'On Avenging Julian', et cetera.

Gregory Nazianzen, 'Oration Against Julian'.

Sozomen, *Ecclesiastical History*.

Socrates, *Ecclesiastical History*.

Theodoret, *A History of the Church*.

Eunapius, *Lives of the Philosophers*.

Pausanias, *Description of Greece*.

Edward Gibbon, *The Decline and Fall of the Roman Empire*.

Jacob Burckhardt, *The Age of Constantine the Great*.

R. A. Pack, *Studies in Libanius and Antiochene Society under Theodosius*.

T. R. Glover, *Life and Letters in the Fourth Century*.

J. Bidez, *La Vie de l'Empereur Julien*.

J. B. Bury, *History of the Later Roman Empire*.

Franz Cumont, *The Mysteries of Mithra*.

Norman Baynes, 'The Early Life of Julian the Apostate', *Journal of Hellenic Studies*, Vol. XLV, pages 251–254.

G. E. Mylonas, *Eleusis and the Eleusinian Mysteries*.

M. J. Vermaseren, *Mithras: The Secret God*.

Glanville Downey, *Ancient Antioch*.

Glanville Downey, *Antioch in the Age of Theodosius the Great*.

Stebelton H. Nulle, 'Julian Redivivus', *The Centennial Review*, Vol. V, No. 3, summer.

WILLIWAW

For Nina

Note: Williwaw is the Indian word for a big wind peculiar to the Aleutian islands and the Alaskan coast. It is a strong wind that sweeps suddenly down from the mountains towards the sea. The word williwaw, however, is now generally used to describe any big and sudden wind. It is in this last and more colloquial sense that I have used the term.

C.V.

CHAPTER ONE

I

Someone turned on the radio in the wheelhouse. A loud and sentimental song awakened him. He lay there for a moment in his bunk and stared at the square window in the wall opposite him. A seagull flew lazily by the window. He watched it glide back and forth until it was out of sight.

He yawned and became conscious of an ache behind his eyes. There had been a party, he remembered. He felt sick. The radio became louder as the door to his cabin opened. A brown Indian face looked in at him.

'Hey, Skipper, chow's ready below.' The face vanished.

Slowly he got out of his bunk and onto the deck. He stood in front of the mirror. Cautiously he pressed his fingers against his eyelids and morbidly enjoyed the pain it gave him. He noticed his eyes were bloodshot and his face was grimy. He scowled at himself in the mirror. From the wheelhouse the sound of Negro music thudded painfully in his ears.

'Turn that damn thing off!' he shouted.

'O.K., Skipper,' his second mate's voice answered. The music faded away and he began to dress. The second mate came into the cabin. 'Quite a party, wasn't it, Mr Evans?'

Evans grunted. 'Some party. What time is it?'

The mate looked at his watch. 'Six-twenty.'

Evans closed his eyes and began to count to himself: one, two – he had four hours and thirty minutes of sleep. That was too little sleep. The mate was watching him. 'You don't look so good,' he said finally.

'I know it.' He picked up his tie. 'Anything new? Weather look all right?'

The mate sat down on the bunk and ran his hands through his hair. It was an irritating habit. His hair was long and the colour of mouldering straw; when he relaxed he fingered it. On board a ship one noticed such things.

'Weather looks fine. A little wind from the south but not enough to hurt. We scraped some paint off the bow last night. I guess we were too close to that piling.' He pushed back his hair and left it alone. Evans was glad of that.

'We'll have to paint the whole ship this month anyway.' Evans buttoned the pockets of his olive-drab shirt. High-ranking officers were apt to criticize, even in the Aleutians. He pinned the Warrant Officer insignia on his collar. His hands shook.

Bervick watched him. 'You really had some party, I guess.'

'That's right. Joe's going back to the States on rotation. We were celebrating. It was some party all right.' Evans rubbed his eyes. 'Have you had chow yet, Bervick?'

The mate, Bervick, nodded. 'I had it with the cooks. I've been around since five.' He stood up. He was shorter than Evans and Evans was not tall. Bervick was lightly built; he had large grey Norwegian eyes, and there were many fine lines about his eyes. He was an old seaman at thirty.

'I think I'll go below now,' said Evans. He stepped out of his cabin and into the wheelhouse, glancing automatically at the barometer. The needle pointed

between Fair and Change; this was usual. He went below. At the end of the
companionway, the doors to the engine room were open and the generator was
going. The twin Diesel engines were silent. He went into the galley.

John Smith, the Indian cook, was kneading dough. He was a bad cook from
southeastern Alaska. Cooks of any kind were scarce, though, and Evans was glad
to have even this bad one.

'What's new?' asked Evans, preparing to listen to Smitty's many troubles.

'The new cook.' Smitty pointed to a fat man in a white apron gathering dishes
in the dining saloon.

'What's wrong now?'

'I ask him to wash dishes last night. It was his turn, but he won't do nothing
like that. So I tell him what I think. I tell him off good, but he no listen. I seen
everything now . . .' Smitty's black eyes glittered as he talked. Evans stopped
him.

'O.K. I'll talk to him.' He went into the dining saloon. Here two tables ran
parallel to the bulkheads. One table was for the crew; the other for the ship's
officers and the engineers. The crew's table was empty; only the Chief Engineer,
Duval, sat at the other table.

'Morning, Skipper,' he said. He was an older man. His hair was grey and
black in streaks. It was clipped very short. His nose was long and hooked and his
mouth was wide but not pleasant. Duval was a New Orleans Frenchman.

'Good morning, Chief. Looks like everybody's up early today.'

'Yeah, I guess they are at that.' The Chief cleared his throat. He waited for a
comment. There was none. Then he remarked casually, 'I guess it's because
they all heard we was going to Arunga. I guess that's just a rumour.' He looked
at his fork. Evans could see that he was anxious to know if they were leaving.
The Chief would never ask a direct question, though.

The fat cook put a plate of eggs in front of Evans and poured him some black
coffee. The cook's hand was unsteady and the coffee spilled on the table. The
cook ignored the puddle of coffee, and went back into the galley.

Evans watched the brown liquid drip slowly off onto the deck. Dreamily he
made patterns with his forefinger. He thought of Arunga island. Finally he said,
'I wonder where they pick up rumours like that?'

'Just about anywhere,' said the Chief. 'They probably figured we was going
there because that's our port's headquarters and the General's Adjutant is here
and they say he's breaking his back to get back fast and that there aren't no
planes flying out for a week. We're the only ship in the harbour that could take
him to Arunga.'

'That sounds pretty interesting,' said Evans and he began to eat. Duval
scowled and pushed back his chair from the table. He stood up and stretched
himself. 'Arunga's a nice trip anyway.' He waited for a remark. Again there was
none. 'Think I'll go look at the engines.'

Evans smiled as he left. Duval did not think highly of him. Evans was easily
half the Chief Engineer's age and that meant trouble. The Chief thought that
age was a substitute for both brains and experience; Evans could not like that
idea. He knew, however, that he would eventually have to tell the Chief that
they were leaving for Arunga.

Evans ate quickly. He noticed that the first mate's place was untouched. He
would have to speak to him again about getting up earlier.

Breakfast over, he left the saloon by the after door. He stood on the stern and
breathed deeply. The sky was grey. A filmy haze hung over the harbour and

there was no wind. The water of the harbour was like a dark glass. Overhead the seagulls darted about, looking for scraps on the water. A quiet day for winter in these islands.

Evans climbed over the starboard side and stepped down on the dock. There were two large warehouses on the dock. They were military and impermanent. Several power barges were moored near his ship and he would have to let his bow swing far out when they left; mechanically, he figured time and distance.

Longshoremen in soiled blue coveralls were loading the barges, and the various crews, civilians and soldiers mixed, were preparing to cast off for their day's work in the harbour.

A large wooden-faced Indian skipper shouted at Evans from the wheelhouse of one of the barges. Evans shouted back a jovial curse; then he turned and walked across the dock to the shore.

Andrefski Bay was the main harbour for this Aleutian island. The bay was well protected, and, though not large, there were no reefs or shallow places in the main part of the harbour. No trees grew on the island. The only vegetation was a coarse brown turf which furred the low hills that edged the bay. Beyond these low hills were high, sharp and pyramidal mountains, blotched with snow.

Evans looked at the mountains but did not see them. He had seen them many times before and they were of no interest to him now. He never noticed them. He thought of the trip to Arunga. A good trip to make, a long one, three days, that was the best thing about going. He had found that when they were too much in port everyone got a little bored and irritable. A change would be good now.

Someone called his name. He looked behind him. The second mate, Bervick, was hurrying towards him.

'Going over to the office, Skipper?' he asked, when he had caught up.

'That's right. Going to pick up our orders.'

'Arunga?'

'Yes.' They walked on together.

The second mate was not wearing his Technical Sergeant's stripes. Evans hoped the Adjutant would not mind. One could never tell about these Headquarters people. He would warn Bervick later.

They walked slowly along the black volcanic ash roadway. At various intervals there were wooden huts and warehouses. Between many of the buildings equipment was piled, waiting to be shipped out.

'It's been almost a year since we was to Arunga,' remarked Bervick.

'That's right.'

'Have we got some new charts?'

'We got them last fall, remember?'

'I guess I forgot.' A large truck went by them and they stood in the shallow gutter until it had passed.

'You seen the sheep woman lately?' asked Evans.

The sheep woman was the only woman on the island. She was a Canadian who helped run the sheep ranch in the interior. She had been on the island for several years, and, though middle-aged, stout, and reasonably virtuous, the rumours about her were damning. It was said that she charged fifty dollars for her services and everyone thought that that was too much.

Bervick shook his head. 'I don't know how she's doing. O.K., I suppose. I'm saving up for when we hit the Big Harbour next. I don't want nothing to do with her.'

Evans was interested. 'Who've you got in mind at Big Harbour?'

'Olga.'

'I thought she was the Chief's property.'

Bervick shrugged. 'That's what he says. She's a good girl.'

'I suppose so.'

'I like her. The Chief's just blowing.'

'None of them are worth much trouble.'

A light rain began to fall. The office was still a half a mile ahead of them. All the buildings of the port were, for the sake of protection, far apart.

'Damn it,' muttered Evans, as the rain splattered in his face. A truck came up behind them. It stopped and they climbed into the back. Evans told the driver where they were going, then he turned to Bervick. 'You better pick up the weather forecast today.'

'I will. I think it'll be pretty good.'

'Hard to say. This is funny weather.'

The truck let them off at the Army Transport Service Office. The office was housed in a long, one-storeyed, grey building.

The outer room was large, and here four or five enlisted men were doing clerical work beneath fluorescent lights. The walls were decorated with posters warning against poison gas, faulty camouflage, and venereal disease.

One of the clerks spoke to Evans. 'The Captain's waiting for you,' he said.

'I think I'll go check with Weather,' said Bervick. 'I'll see you back to the boat.'

'Fine.' Evans walked down a corridor to the Captain's office.

A desk and three neat uncomfortable chairs furnished the room. On the walls were pictures of the President, several Generals, and several nudes. The nudes usually came down during inspections.

The Captain was sitting hunched over his desk. He was a heavy man with large features. He was smoking a pipe and talking at the same time to a Major who sat in one of the three uncomfortable chairs. They looked up as Evans entered.

'Hello there, Skipper,' said the Captain and he took his pipe out of his mouth. 'I want you to meet an old friend of mine, Major Barkison.'

The Major stood up and shook hands with Evans. 'Glad to know you, Mister . . .'

'Evans.'

'Mister Evans. It looks as if you'll be pressed into service.'

'Yes it does . . . sir.' He added the 'sir' just in case.

'I hope the trip will be a calm one,' remarked the Major with a smile.

'It should be.' Evans relaxed. The Major seemed to be human.

Major Barkison was a West Pointer and quietly proud of the fact. Though not much over thirty he was already bald. He had a Roman nose, pale blue eyes, and a firm but small chin. He looked like the Duke of Wellington. Knowing this, he hoped that someone might someday mention the resemblance; no one ever did, though.

'Sit down here, Evans,' said the Captain, pointing to one of the chairs. The Major and Evans both sat down. 'We're sending you out on a little trip to Arunga. Out west where the deer and submarines play.' He laughed heartily at his joke. Evans also laughed. The Major did not.

The Major said, 'How long will the trip take you?'

'That's hard to say.' Evans figured for a moment in his head. 'Seventy hours is about average. We can't tell until we know the weather.'

Barkison nodded and said nothing.

The Captain blew a smoke ring and watched it float ceilingward, his little eyes almost shut. 'The weather reports are liable to be pretty lousy,' he said at last.

Barkison nodded again. 'Yes, that's right. That's why I can't fly out of here for at least a week. Everything's grounded. That's why I can't get out of here. It is imperative that I get back to Headquarters.'

'The war would stop if you didn't get back, wouldn't it, Major?' The Captain said this jovially but Evans thought there was malice in what he said.

'What do you mean, Captain?' said the Major stiffly.

'Nothing at all, sir. I was joking. A bad habit of ours here.' Evans smiled to himself. He knew that the Captain did not like regular army men. The Captain had been in the grain business and he was proud that he made more money than the men in the regular army. They did not understand business and the Captain did. This made a difference. The Major frowned.

'I have to get my reports in, you know. You understand that, of course. You know I would never have a boat sent out in weather like this unless it were important. This weather precludes air travel,' he added somewhat pompously, enjoying the word 'preclude'. It had an official sound.

'Certainly, Major.' The Captain turned to Evans. 'From what I gather the trip shouldn't be too bad, a little rough perhaps, but then it usually is. You had better put into the Big Harbour tomorrow and get a weather briefing there. I got some cargo for them, too. I told the boys to load you up today.' He paused to chew on his pipe. 'By the way,' he said in a different voice, 'how do you feel after our little party last night?'

Evans grimaced. 'Not very good. The stuff tasted like raisin jack.'

'You should know.' The Captain laughed loudly and winked. Barkison looked pained. He cleared his throat.

'I guess you people have a hard time getting liquor up here.' He tried to sound like one of the boys and failed.

'We manage.' The Captain chuckled.

The door opened. A young and pink-faced Lieutenant looked doubtfully about the room until he saw the Major.

'Come in, Lieutenant,' said the Major.

'Lieutenant Hodges, this is Mr Evans.' The two shook hands and sat down. The young Lieutenant was very solemn.

'Is there anything new on our leaving, sir?' he asked.

'Yes,' said Barkison. 'Weather permitting, we'll leave tomorrow morning. We should be back . . . how long did you say?'

'Maybe three days, maybe less,' Evans answered.

'Isn't that awfully long, sir? I mean we have to be back day after tomorrow.'

The Major shrugged. 'Nothing we can do about it. There are no planes going out for an indefinite period.'

'Well,' the Captain stood up and Evans did the same, 'you had better check on the weather and take water and do whatever else you have to do. You'll definitely leave tomorrow morning and you'll stop off at the Big Harbour. See you later today.' He turned to the Major. 'If you'd like to move aboard tonight . . .'

'Oh no, never mind. We'll move on tomorrow.'

'O.K., be seeing you, Evans.'

Evans muttered that he had been pleased to meet them and left the room. As he walked down the corridor he wondered if Bervick would be able to understand the weather chart. He decided not.

Outside, the rain had stopped. The wind was cooler and more brisk. Evans walked towards a half-barrel-shaped hut: the weather office. Ravens glided heavily around him, their black feathers glistening bluely in the pale light. High above him he could make out an eagle flying northward.

Inside the weather office a Master Sergeant was handling the maps and charts. The weather officer had not come in yet.

'Hello, Mr Evans.'

'Hello, has Bervick been here?'

'Yes, he just now left. I think he's gone to get some paint over to Supply.'

'I see. What's the deal on the weather?'

The Sergeant shuffled his papers. 'It's hard to say. If the wind shifts around to the north, and it looks like it will, you'll be fine.'

'Is there much wind outside the harbour?'

'There's some.'

'Much wind? Thirty mile an hour? It is more?'

'Damned if I can tell. You're leaving tomorrow, aren't you?'

'That's right.'

'Well, I'll check with the Navy boys and get in touch with you later. This isn't a good month for travelling the Chain.'

'I know. Is that the weather chart you got there?'

'Yes.' The Sergeant pushed the chart at him. Evans pretended to study it. Actually he knew very little about reading these charts. He knew from practical experience, though, that they were often wrong.

'It'll probably be rough, Mr Evans.'

'That's nothing new. You say Bervick's at Supply?'

'I think so.'

'O.K., and thanks a lot. I'll see you when you have some more dope.' Evans went out. He stood for a while watching the power barges, blunt-nosed and slab-like, move back and forth across the harbour. There were rumours that the port of Andrefski was to be closed soon and only the inland air base would be kept going. Many men had already been moved out, only a few hundred were left now. On the rocky, moonstone and agate littered beach, lumber was piled, waiting to be loaded on the Liberty ship, edged greyly against the main dock. This ship was the largest in the harbour and it made the other boats look like toys in a bathtub.

A jeep, with an awkward plywood body tacked onto it, rode by and splashed him with mud from the side of the road. Evans swore at the driver. Then he walked along the road, keeping close to the pebbled embankment. There was quite a lot of traffic at this time of day.

The Supply warehouse was large and gloomy and empty-looking. He walked around to the side of the building and went inside. He could hear Bervick's voice. 'Come on, you can give us six gallons. Christ, you have the stuff piled up all around.'

Another voice answered, 'Sorry, three's all you get.'

'Why that's . . .' Evans walked up to them. Bervick was holding three gallon cans of paint.

Evans grinned. 'That'll do us fine, Bervick. Are you through here?'

'I guess so.'

'Well, let's get on back to the ship.' Bervick picked up two of the cans and Evans took the other.

A thin drizzle was beginning to cloud the air.

'Nice day,' said Bervick.

'Yes, nice day. All days are nice here. We go to the Big Harbour tomorrow.'

'And from there to Arunga?'

'That's right. We got some rank to carry.'

'Who? I heard the Captain might come.'

'That's a new one. I hadn't heard about him. We've got a Major who is the Adjutant at Arunga, and a Lieutenant.'

'Any cargo?'

'Some for the Big Harbour. That's all.'

They walked along the road, their feet grinding the wet cinder-like surface. Seagulls circled high above them, a sign of bad weather according to the Indians. Among the sharp rocks the ravens croaked drearily. Silently they walked back to the ship.

Two of the men were hosing down the deck. The sea water from their hoses made a drumming sound as it shot across the decks.

Evans was surprised. 'The first time they've ever done this without being told.'

Bervick laughed, 'The crew knew we were going before you did.'

'They usually do.'

They climbed aboard. Bervick went aft with the paint. Evans opened the door to the dining saloon and stepped inside.

The Chief, sitting on one of the tables, was smoking a cigar. Down the companionway, Evans could see the two assistant engineers working on the auxiliary.

'What's new, Skipper?' asked Duval.

'Hello, Chief. Your boys pretty busy?'

'Yeah, getting ready for the big trip. Lucky we took fuel last week.'

'It was.'

'When we leaving?' The Chief asked one of his few direct questions.

'Tomorrow morning.'

'Straight to Arunga, I suppose.'

'No, we're going to the Big Harbour first. We go on from there.'

'I guess I'll be able to see Olga then.' The Chief grinned.

Evans looked at him. 'What about Bervick?'

'What about him?' The Chief was not interested and they said nothing for a few moments. Then he said, 'I hear the Chaplain'll be with us.'

'So I've heard. I guess the Captain will tell me about it later.'

'Probably. I got to get to work.' The Chief slid off the table and walked towards the engine room. Evans could hear the sound of his voice as he talked with his assistants. Evans knew he was telling them that they were going west to Arunga as he had said they would. Evans walked into the galley. The cook, John Smith, was scrubbing pans. He was alone in the galley.

'How's it going, Smitty? Where's your helper?'

Smitty put down the kettle he was scrubbing. 'Gone,' he said with suppressed drama. 'I seen everything now. What does this guy do? Does this guy help in here? No. He go down and lay on his fat butt. I'm going to get off this boat. I seen everything. He won't work, won't do nothing . . .'

'I'll talk to him, Smitty.' That was always a good promise to make. Smitty would be mad at something else the next day anyway. 'By the way,' he added, 'have you got enough rations to get us to Arunga? We're going to have three passengers.'

Smitty gasped. His lean ugly brown face was contorted with grief. 'I seen *everything* now.' He spoke softly as if he were praying. 'I got no bread. I got no meat. I got no nothing now. How,' his voice rose to a wail, 'how am I going to feed the crew? I make no bread on the water. They eat out of cans, that's all.'

'Well, you work it out and get what you need. We'll leave tomorrow at eight.'

Smitty muttered to himself. Evans went up to the wheelhouse.

Bervick was standing over the chart table: a chart of all the islands in the Aleutian Chain before him. He was squinting thoughtfully and carefully measuring out a course.

'Think you can get us there?' asked Evans.

'What? Oh sure, I was just checking the old course. Last time we ran too close to shore off Kulak.'

'I remember. We'll work out a course over at the Big Harbour.' The salt spray from the hoses splattered the wheelhouse windows. 'That reminds me, you better get some water. We're pretty low.'

'O.K.' Bervick put the chart in a drawer under the table and left the wheelhouse.

Evans looked out the window. He could think of nothing very important to be done before they sailed. They had fuel. Smitty would get rations. The charts were up to date. He rubbed his face to see if he needed a shave. He did.

Evans went into his cabin and turned on the water in his basin. He noticed that his eyes looked a little better, though they still hurt him. He sighed and tried to look at his profile in the glass. This he knew would exercise his eyes, also in the back of his mind he wondered if he might not be able to see his profile. He had seen it once in a tailor's three-way mirror. He had been greatly interested, and he hoped vaguely that he might see it again sometime. Strange things like that obsessed people who had been to sea for a long time.

Someone turned on the radio. A deep sterile radio voice staccatoed in the air for a moment and was gone. The air was filled with static, and then the voice came back again. Evans could not make out what the voice was saying but he could guess from the tone that our 'forces were smashing ahead on all fronts': the usual thing. He was bored by the war.

Methodically he shaved himself. He wondered who had turned on the radio. Probably Martin, his first mate.

A light wisp of fog came into the room through the half-open window; quickly Evans shut it. He shivered. The cold was penetrating.

'I'm cold as gold is old,' he muttered to himself. It was a jingle that went occasionally through his mind. For several years he had known it. Queer phrases and jingles often came to him when he had been too much alone. Sometimes they worried him. Evans often wondered if he might not be a little crazy. They say, though, that when you are crazy you never know it, he thought. There was consolation in that and he murmured again to himself, 'I'm as cold as gold is old.' Then he finished shaving.

He looked much older than twenty-five, he noticed, looking at himself intently in the mirror. When he was eighteen he has worked alone in a lighthouse. He used often to look at himself in the mirror then. He felt less alone when he did that and the habit had stayed with him. He yawned and turned away from the mirror. Neatly he put his shaving equipment away, then he sat down at his desk and looked at the papers on it. Most of the papers were memorandums from the Headquarters. He pushed them to one side.

In his desk drawer was a quart of bourbon. He wondered if he should take a swallow, a small one, enough to take away the ache behind his eyes. Evans reached for the drawer. Before he could open it, Martin walked into the cabin. Martin never knocked.

'Good morning,' said Evans and he tried to sound sarcastic.

'Hail to the Chief,' said Martin, eying Evans' hand on the liquor drawer. 'Starting in early, aren't you?'

'What do you mean? Oh, this,' Evans withdrew his hand quickly. 'I was just looking for something.'

'So I see.' The first mate smiled, showing all his teeth. He was a year younger than Evans, but looked even younger than he was. He had a carefully studied collegiate manner though he had never been to a college. John Martin had been one of the numerous unpromising young actors in a New England stock company. He was dark and nearly handsome. His voice was deep, interesting and mocking. He knew nothing about being a mate.

'Did you just get up?' Evans asked, knowing that he had.

'Why yes – the party, you know. I felt I should sleep. The ravell'd sleave, you know.' He spoke with a pseudo-British accent which he knew irritated Evans.

'Well, go get on down below and make sure they take water,' Evans snapped.

'Right you are, sir.'

'Can the funny stuff. We're going to the Big Harbour tomorrow.'

'Any passengers?'

'Yes, the Adjutant at Arunga, a Lieutenant and the Chaplain.'

'That sounds gay. When're we going to haul another group of USO girls?' Martin winked in what he would have called a roguish manner. Evans had once become too interested in a USO girl on tour.

Evans murmured. 'Not for a while.' He turned away and played with the papers on his desk. He tried to think of something for Martin to do. 'You might,' he finally said, 'go see the Chaplain and find out when he's coming aboard. Also, you'd better get hold of a copy of the special orders with his name on them. The Captain forgot to tell me he was going.'

'Fine.' Martin started to go. 'By the way,' he said, and Evans knew and dreaded what he was going to say, 'how do you feel after the party last night? You don't look so good.'

'I feel awful. Now go get to work.'

Martin left and Evans rested his head on his arm. He felt tired. The ship was unusually still. Far away he could hear the rasping croak of a raven. He opened the desk drawer.

II

John Martin walked into the galley.

'What's on your mind, Smitty?' he asked. Martin was always polite with the men and Evans was not. The men liked Martin better and that was the main reason why Evans did not like him, or so Martin thought.

'Nothing on my mind. You want to eat something?'

'No thanks. I'll just take a little of this.' He poured himself some pineapple juice from a large can. Smitty watched him drink it.

'What's on for chow tonight?'

The Indian's eyes gleamed. 'Vienna sausage and that's all I got. I have to go get rations for a whole week now. I haven't got no time to make bread or nothing. That guy,' he pointed upward, 'he tell me just today to get this stuff.'

'Well, that's O.K., Smitty,' Martin murmured soothingly, as he left, 'it'll be all right.'

On deck he found two of the crew coiling the long black water hose.

'Pretty empty, wasn't she?'

One of them nodded. He was a heavy blond fellow, a professional seaman. 'Are we going out west?' he asked.

'That's right. Leaving tomorrow.'

'That's what Bervick said. We didn't know what he was bulling or not. Weather don't look bad.'

Martin looked at the pale sky. 'You can't ever tell,' he said.

'No, you can't.' They went on coiling the hose.

Martin walked across the dock. He watched lumber being loaded onto the Liberty ship by sailors with heavy fantastic beards. The port was slowly closing down and he, for one, was not sorry. For a year now he had been at Andrefski as a first mate. He had fought constantly with Evans and he had known all the time that Evans was right: that he was no seaman. Martin had drifted into boat work in the army. After two years he had been made a Warrant Officer and assigned to this Freight-Passenger ship. The whole thing was unreal to him, the Bering Sea, these boats, the desolate stone islands. He wished he were in New England and the thought that he would be at least another year in these islands was maddening.

Thinking of these things, he walked to the warehouse where the mail was delivered. A door in the warehouse opened and Bervick came out. He carried a bundle of letters in his hand. 'Hello, Johnny,' he said. 'You up so soon?'

Martin smiled. There was no formality between them. Living together in the same small stateroom they understood each other well. 'I thought a run in the fog would be just what I needed. Got something for me?'

Bervick thumbed through the bundle and handed Martin a letter. 'How does it smell?' he asked.

Martin inhaled the perfume that had been sprinkled on the envelope. 'Like magnolias,' he said.

Bervick sniffed. 'Smells like a Ketchikan whore to me.'

'Careful,' said Martin, 'speak softly when you speak of love. Which reminds me, when are they going to load cargo?'

'Right after lunch, I suppose. That's if the longshoremen can get together long enough to do some work.'

'Then you'd better move the boom over.'

'O.K.' Bervick walked away.

Martin stepped inside the warehouse. Standing close to the door – there was almost no light in the building – he read the perfumed letter. She thought a lot about him. She wondered how he was. She did not go out much. She wished he were back. She did not go out much, she repeated that. She wondered if he remembered when . . . Martin folded the letter and put it in his pocket. Her letters were always the same but she was a nice girl and he would probably marry her and be bored. He felt sorry for himself. He looked at the bleak sky and saw that it suited his mood.

A blast of damp air came through the door and he buttoned his parka at the throat. Then, remembering his errand with the Chaplain, he walked out into the grey light.

A mile away on a slight mound was the post chapel. It was like all other army chapels: box-shaped, with a short square tower and spire. The building was brown and looked dingy from camouflage. He walked towards it.

The wind blew at his back. The wind was rising and there were whitecaps in the bay. Gulls flew worriedly in the bedrizzled air.

A jeep went by him on the road. It stopped and he climbed in. The Captain was sitting at the wheel, his pipe firmly between his teeth.

'How's the boat business, Martin?' he asked cheerfully.

'Fine as ever.'

'Good.' He started the jeep. 'Where are you headed?'

'Over to see the Chaplain. I hear he's coming with us.'

'Damn! I knew I forgot to tell Evans something. The Chaplain's going with you people. They're having a meeting at Arunga and he's already on orders. Does Evans know?'

'Yes, he heard about it.'

'Grapevine,' the Captain muttered. 'I'm going as far as the Post Exchange. You want out there?'

'That'll be fine.'

The Captain drove deliberately and in silence over the road. After a few minutes he stopped in front of a long low building and they both got out. They walked into the Post Exchange.

'You getting on all right with Evans?' the Captain asked.

'Sure, we're coming along fine,' Martin said trying to sound sincere and succeeding.

'That's the way things should be. I'm glad to hear it.'

The Post Exchange was not yet crowded. A long counter ran the length of the building and behind the counter there were shelves of candy, stationery, toilet articles, magazines . . . At one end of the building was a barber's chair and a soldier barber, and at the other end was a Coca-Cola machine. Everything was neatly arranged beneath hard bare electric lights.

Martin bought a lurid Love magazine. Nothing else caught his eye and he left.

He was out of breath when he reached the top of the mound where the chapel was. A few enlisted men were wandering about near by, getting up enough nerve to go in and see the Chaplain and ask for help. This Chaplain had a reputation for being able to get things done for the men. The religious aura, however, was unmanning to most of them.

The inside of the chapel was quiet and dim and warm. There was little ornament here, only an altar and plain, large-windowed walls without colour or design. In a small office to the right of the door, Martin found O'Mahoney, the Chaplain.

He was a short squat Irishman with a red-veined nose, plump cheeks and nearsighted blue eyes. His hair was thick and dark and looked like a neat wig. His manner was awkward and friendly. He had been a monk in a Maryland monastery, and now, in the army, he acted as if he were playing a part in a bad dream, which perhaps he was.

'Hello, Father,' said Martin respectfully.

'How do you do . . .' O'Mahoney paused with embarrassment. Martin was not a churchgoer and he did not recognize him.

'John Martin, sir,' he said quickly. 'I'm the first mate on the boat that's taking you to Arunga.'

O'Mahoney smiled. 'Do sit down, Mr Martin,' he invited. Martin arranged himself with a sigh in a large armchair. He was tired from his walk. For a moment he breathed the musty leather smell which all churches seemed to have. O'Mahoney offered him a cigarette. He refused and said that he did not smoke.

'A good habit not to have,' said the Chaplain in his light Irish voice. There was a pause.

'I wanted to know,' began Martin in a loud voice which he quickly lowered. He was always conscious of wrong tones. A loud voice was wrong in a church. 'I was wondering,' he said softly, 'when you were planning to move aboard, tonight or in the morning.'

'Tomorrow, if that's convenient.'

'It will be.' Martin smiled. 'You'll be ready for bad weather, won't you?'

'Bad weather? Is that the report?'

'Well, yes, but it's also a joke of ours that whenever we haul a Chaplain we have bad weather.'

O'Mahoney chuckled uneasily. 'Well, that's the way those things go, I suppose.'

'Yes, it's probably just an invitation for you to walk on the water.'

'What? Oh, yes.' O'Mahoney was not quite sure if this was blasphemy or not. He decided it was not. 'Are you Catholic, Mr Martin?' he asked. He usually asked that question.

Martin shook his head. 'I'm not much of anything,' he said. He could see that the Chaplain was tempted to inquire further. He did not, though. Instead he changed the subject.

'The Captain at the Transport Office did tell me that the weather might be unreliable at this time of year.'

'That's right, but it shouldn't be bad.' Martin spoke as if the sea and the weather had no secrets from him. Often he marvelled at how professional he sounded.

'I'm certainly glad to hear that. I suffer terribly from *mal de mer*.' He spoke the French self-consciously and Martin wondered if he was going to translate it or not. He decided to save him the trouble.

'I'm sure you won't be sick, Father.' Martin got to his feet. 'If you want to send any stuff down tonight, we'll stow it for you.'

'Thank you, but I'll bring my gear down with me in the morning.'

Martin turned to go, then he remembered the orders he had come to get. 'Do you think I could have an extra copy of your orders? We have to have one, you know.'

'Certainly.' O'Mahoney handed him a paper from his desk.

'Thank you. See you tomorrow.'

'Aren't you going to the Captain's party tonight, Mr Martin? He's giving one in his quarters for the Major.'

'Why, yes, I suppose I will.'

'See you then.' The Chaplain walked with him to the door.

III

Bervick and Duval were arguing again. Supper had been finished and Evans had gone to the wheelhouse. Martin sat quietly in a corner while the Chief and Bervick insulted each other. Their arguments were thought very funny by the rest of the crew. No one took them seriously except Martin, and he was not sure if they were serious or not.

Olga, a Norwegian girl at the Big Harbour, was the cause of their trouble. The year before she had come to work in a restaurant. Because she had let Bervick sleep with her for nothing, he had decided that it must be love and he had almost decided to marry her. Then one day he discovered that she was also seeing Duval and accepting his money and a great many other people's money, too. He had asked her to stop but she was a thrifty girl, supporting her mother in Canada. She had told him that it was none of his business. Duval had laughed at him because of this and he had come to hate Duval and feel that it was his fault that Olga had changed.

Somewhat drowsily Martin listened to them talk. This time they were arguing whether the knife should be set on the table edge of the blade towards the plate or away from it. Duval claimed the edge should be away from the plate and Bervick claimed it was towards the plate.

'I don't suppose you'd know where it went anyway,' said Duval bitingly. 'You probably always ate with your hands.'

This was a hard blow and Bervick countered, 'I don't guess you ever used anything but a knife to eat with. I've seen *cajuns* like you before.'

Duval was proud of his pure French ancestry. He came from a long-settled New Orleans family and he was sensitive about being thought a *cajun*.

'*Cajun*, hell,' he said, trying not to sound irritated. 'You wouldn't know one if you saw one.'

'I guess I'm talking to one.'

This was too much. The Chief Engineer remembered his rank. He stood up. 'That's enough, Sergeant,' he said with dignity.

Bervick stood up also. Martin could see he was pleased. It was always a victory when the Chief fell back on his rank. 'Yes, Warrant Officer Junior Grade Duval,' he said.

'Better not get so fresh, Sergeant.' The Chief turned to Martin and said, 'Just a little squabble.' Bervick left the saloon, laughing, 'Fresh bastard,' muttered the Chief.

'Oh, he's all right,' said Martin smoothly. 'Just a little hot-tempered at times.'

'Maybe that's it.' Duval sat down on the bench beside Martin. They looked out the window at the pale grey of evening. The day was over and the wind had died down.

'Probably be a strong southwest wind tomorrow,' remarked Duval.

'Can't tell, really.'

'Thank God we've only a few passengers. Every time it's rough we have at least forty.'

'That's the way it goes.'

At the other table five deckhands were playing Hearts. Martin watched them. His thoughts drifted and he saw stages and heard speeches and listened to the sea. The sea was becoming a part of himself, and whenever he relaxed, his mind seemed to be caught up in the restless tempo of the water and he would become uneasy: at sea he was always uneasy. He yawned abruptly and cleared his mind.

Evans came into the saloon. 'Say, Mate,' he said, 'the Captain's giving a party over at his quarters. You and the Chief want to come?'

Martin nodded. 'I always like free beer.'

'So do I.' The Chief got to his feet. 'I hope he's got some bourbon. I haven't had any good stuff for quite a while. It gets used up so fast because I always share it.' The Chief knew of Evans' liquor and he also knew that Evans never shared it. Evans looked away.

'We'd better get started then. The dispatcher's waiting outside. He's going to take us over in his jeep.'

The Captain's quarters consisted of two huts knocked together. Normally three officers lived there, but at the moment he was alone and had the whole place to himself.

Several men were already in the room when they entered. The Captain was fixing drinks behind a bar made out of a packing case. He grunted at them, his pipe moving slightly as he greeted them.

Evans and Duval were jovial in their greetings. Martin merely smiled. The Chief was on particularly good terms with the Captain. They were of the same age and had had many parties together.

'How does it go, Old Chief?' inquired the Captain, speaking out of the side of his mouth.

'Great. We keep the army on the waves.'

'That's something. What'll it be, gentlemen?' While the others told what they wanted, Martin looked about him. He had not been in the Captain's quarters for a long time. He never liked to seem too close to higher ranking officers. He was always afraid someone would think he wanted something.

The walls were decorated with large paintings of nudes. They had been done for the Captain by a soldier. A lamp, several chairs, and a bookcase with a few books and a great many rocks in it furnished this end of the room.

A Major and a Lieutenant were standing before one of the paintings. Martin, who did not recognize them, decided that they must be the passengers for Arunga. In one corner beside a radio the Chaplain sat, a pale bourbon and water beside him. He was turning the dial of the radio. Three officers from the Harbour Craft Detachment made up the rest of the party.

'What'll it be, Martin?' asked the Captain.

'Beer, if you have it.'

'Beer! O.K., suit yourself. I'm always glad to save the real stuff.' He handed Martin a bottle of beer.

Loud music startled them. The Chaplain looked about him apologetically and quickly lowered the volume. 'Finally got some music,' he announced. 'The static isn't so bad tonight.'

The Major agreed, 'Yes, the static's not bad at all tonight.'

The Lieutenant remarked that the static had been bad the night before.

That, thought Martin, takes care of the static. He often wondered why people spoke so inanely.

'These are very interesting works of . . . of art, you have here,' remarked the

Major somewhat archly. Martin could see that he was trying to be a good fellow.

'Like them?' The Captain came out from behind the bar. 'Had a soldier do them for me. Very talented fellow he was, too. Quite lifelike, aren't they?' He winked at the young Lieutenant, who blushed and looked away. Martin chuckled and noticed that the Major was smiling, too.

The Major said, 'Lieutenant Hodges doesn't care for modern art.'

The Captain laughed, 'Oh, to be young! Wouldn't it be nice, Major, if we were young again.'

The Major winced slightly. He was not old and did not like to be thought old, but because he was bald and his face was lined, people took him to be older than he was. He did not like that.

'Youth is very important,' he murmured, paying no attention to what he was saying.

'Most important for the future,' agreed the Chaplain.

Martin was bored by this. He took his beer and sat down in an easy chair. He drank the beer slowly. It was green and tasted bitter. He watched Evans and Duval draw near to the Major. Both were good politicians.

'It looks as if the war will be over soon,' remarked Evans, a half-question in his voice.

'Yes,' said the Major. He always said 'yes' first, even when he meant 'no'.

'Yes, it should be over soon, but of course we have no effective way of gauging the enemy's rate of attrition. The attrition rate is important. Attrition can decide wars.' Martin wondered if he would repeat this last: it sounded like a maxim. He did not. He continued. 'There are only a few good strategists in the enemy's army. They could be named on the fingers of one hand. Most of them know nothing but frontal attacks.'

'I guess bombings are messing them up,' suggested Evans.

'Wars,' said the Major, 'cannot be won by aviation. No matter what the Air Corps says.' He sounded bitter. Martin wondered if the Major might not be jealous of the quick promotions in the Air Corps.

'I guess that's right,' Evans agreed.

Everyone began to talk at once. Evans and the Major discussed the latest movies. The Chief, who was Catholic, discussed moral issues with the Chaplain. One always seemed to discuss such things with Chaplains. The Captain talked about women and the Lieutenant listened to him gravely.

Cigarette smoke was becoming thick in the room. Blue veils of it floated upward from each smoker. Martin's eyes watered. He finished his beer. The radio played on. Music of every sort swelled in the room. The room was too hot. The oil-stove in the centre was giving off heavy waves of heat. Martin felt a little drowsy. He wondered if they would notice it if he shut his eyes for a moment.

Lieutenant Hodges was standing beside his chair, when he opened his eyes again.

'Must have been asleep,' Martin mumbled. His eyes felt heavy. He looked around and saw that the others obviously had not noticed he had gone to sleep. They were talking and singing and drinking. There was a strong barroom odour in the hut. The Chaplain, he noticed, had gone.

'Sorry to bother you,' said the Lieutenant. 'I didn't mean to wake you.'

'That's all right. I don't know what happened to me. I was just tired, I guess. I've had a pretty hard day,' he lied.

'You're on the boat that's taking us west, aren't you?'

'Yes. I'm the mate. Martin's the name.'

'My name is Hodges. I'm the Major's assistant.' They shook hands in the self-conscious manner of people who have already met.

There was not much to say. They stood there watching the others move about. Almost everyone was drunk. Martin got slowly to his feet. 'What time you got?' he asked.

Hodges looked at his watch carefully. 'Eleven fifty-seven.'

'That's pretty late for me to be up. I guess I better get a move on. See you in the morning.'

'Sure thing. Good night.'

Martin went over to the corner where Evans, the Major, and the Captain were singing.

'I think we'd better head back,' he said, catching Evans between songs. Evans shook his head. He was drunk.

'Hell no,' he said. 'You go back if you want to. You go back.'

Martin shrugged and turned away. The Chief was in a crap game with an Indian skipper.

'Can't leave now,' the Chief said, his eyes on the dice.

Martin picked up his parka and put it on.

'I think I'll walk back,' he announced. Hodges was the only one who heard and he nodded as Martin turned to go.

The Major was talking of strategy when he left.

'Wellington, of course, was the perfect general. Wellington understood attrition. Attrition . . .' The Major talked ,on.

Outside Martin breathed the deep night air gratefully. It was good after the heat and smoke. There were no stars out yet and that was not good. With a shiver he turned and walked quickly towards the docks.

CHAPTER TWO

I

'It's seven o'clock, Mr Evans.' The man on watch looked into his room.

'O.K., be right down,' Evans mumbled. The door was slammed shut and he opened his eyes. It was another morning. His bed was warm and the room, lit greyly by the morning sun, was cold. He closed his eyes and imagined that he was out of bed and already dressed. He imagined this clearly; so clearly that he began to fall asleep again. The sound of dishes being dropped startled him awake. He sat up in bed and put on his shirt. Then, quickly, so as not to feel the cold, he sprang out of bed and finished dressing. He was brushing his teeth when Bervick came in the room.

'Morning, Skipper, nice party? I heard you come in this morning.' Evans wondered why his second mate always seemed pleased when he had a hangover.

'It was pretty good. Is the Mate up yet?'

'He's getting up. What time we sailing?'

'Eight o'clock if everyone's aboard. They won't be, of course.'

Bervick disappeared. Evans straightened his tie. Then he went below. The Chief and his assistants were at the table when he came into the saloon. The Chief seemed cheerful.

'Looks like smooth sailing weather,' he observed. He pointed at the window and at the still harbour beyond.

'I hope so.' Evans was noncommittal. He had seen too many days when the sea was calm in the harbour and rough outside. They would know the weather soon enough.

Martin and Bervick walked in together.

'Did you get home all right?' Martin asked.

'It looks like it, doesn't it?' Evans spoke sharply. He did not like to be thought a heavy drinker. He noticed Martin was scowling. Evans, deciding that he had spoken too roughly, added, 'Yes, the Captain took the Chief and me home. It was some fracas.'

Duval laughed loudly. 'It sure was! We almost ended up in the ditch a couple times.'

'The perils of drink,' murmured Martin, his mouth full.

'Not much else to do in these islands,' said Evans. He did not really hate the islands, though. They had been home to him before the war when he had fished in these waters. He could not admit to the others, however, that he liked the Aleutians.

'I've got a bad egg,' said Bervick. 'I guess this was a pre-war egg.' He pushed the plate away from him. 'I think I'll go get the eight o'clock watch up.' He left.

'It takes one to know one,' said the Chief, referring back to the eggs.

They ate in silence. The two men on watch entered yawning. They sat down at the other table and started their breakfast. Evans finished his own quickly.

A few minutes before eight, a jeep drove down the dock and stopped at the ship. The three passengers and the Captain climbed out and unloaded their baggage on the dock.

Evans went out on deck. 'Good morning,' he said.

'It's a hell of a morning,' said the Captain. The passengers stood about sheep-like, waiting for guidance. Evans shouted to one of the deckhands inside. Together they got the baggage aboard. Then the passengers and the Captain climbed onto the deck.

The Captain hoped that he would not be sick. They all said they hoped they would not be sick. The Major remarked that he had never been seasick in his life; he added, however, that there was a first time for everything. Evans guided them to the dining saloon and Martin volunteered to show them to their state-rooms. Evans and the Captain went back on deck.

'What's the new report on the outside?' Evans asked.

'According to the man over at Weather and the Navy people, you'll have a ten-foot sea and a thirty-mile wind in gusts from the southwest. That's as far as the Big Harbour. From there you'll have to get another forecast.'

'Pretty good news. No planes flying yet?'

'No, no planes. Bad weather beyond the Big Harbour, too.' The Captain reached in the coat of his parka and brought out a brown envelope. 'Here's your clearance. You can take her away now. Don't spend too much time at Arunga. I don't go for none of that, you know.'

Evans smiled, 'I know,' he said. 'We'll be back in a week.'

'Fine. Give my love to the Big Harbour girls.'

'I sure will.'

'Good sailing then.' The Captain climbed back on the dock. He stood beside his jeep and waited for them to cast off. Several longshoremen stood by their lines on the dock. The Major and the Chaplain came out to watch and Evans went to the wheelhouse. Martin and Bervick were waiting for him there.

'Cast the bow and spring lines off first. We'll drift out, then let go the stern.' He rang the telegraph to the engine room, setting the markers at Stand By. A minute later the engine room rang back. Rather quick for the Chief, he thought. Martin and Bervick went below. Evans could see them, with two deckhands, moving about on deck.

He opened one of the wheelhouse windows. 'Let her go,' he shouted. Quickly they began to pull in the lines. The bow swung out from the dock.

'Let the stern go, Bervick,' he shouted again from the window. A second later they were free of the dock. Evans rang both engines Slow Ahead. Cautiously he manoeuvred the ship away from the dock. Then he rang Full Ahead. He could feel the engines vibrate as the ship shot ahead. She would do twelve knots easily.

Martin came up to the wheelhouse. His face was flushed from the wind and cold and his nose was running. He sniffed as he spoke.

'All squared away. Anything you want done?'

'Nothing I can think of.' Evans kept his eyes fixed on the nets that guarded the narrow neck of the harbour a mile away. He steered with the small electrical steering gear. He preferred it to the larger wooden wheel which he insisted that his crew use: it was more seaman-like.

'Guess I'll go to bed then,' said Martin, and he went into his cabin. His watch did not begin until noon.

The door opened again and one of the men on Evans' watch entered. He took the wheel and Evans gave him the course from memory. He knew the courses to the Big Harbour by heart.

Ahead he could see the entrance to the nets. He rang Slow Speed as they went through them. The Navy detachment on the near-by point always watched the boats as they passed through, making sure that they were at least at half-speed.

Five minutes later they were abeam Andrefski point. The sky was still grey and he could feel the swell of the waves increase beneath them. In a few minutes he would be able to tell how rough the trip would be. He rang Full Speed again.

Bervick came into the wheelhouse. 'How's it look to you?' he asked.

'Fair so far,' answered Evans. They both looked through the windows at the waves crashing whitely on the black rocks of the point. A haze hung in the air and the wind was not strong or direct. Then they swung around the point and into the open sea. The ship rocked back and forth as she dipped between the swells.

'Just about a ten-foot sea,' remarked Bervick.

Evans nodded. 'Looks like the forecast is going to be right. Sea striking on the port bow but it doesn't seem so bad. In fact it's pretty good.'

'It'll be a good trip.' Bervick went into his cabin. Evans stood by the window and watched the bare sharp mountains of the island move slowly by.

'Rather rough, isn't it?'

Evans looked around and saw the Major standing beside him. The Major was holding onto the wooden railing beneath the window.

'A little bit. We'll make good time, though.'

'That's important.' The Major looked old this morning Evans thought. His sallow face showed the signs of heavy drinking. He would probably be sick and say that he had indigestion.

The Major squinted at the mountains. 'How far off shore are we?' he asked.

'About two miles. That's our usual running distance.'

'It looks closer than that.' He contemplated the shifting water and the stone hills and the steel colour of the birdless sky. 'It looks very close.'

'It does,' said Evans. The ship was dipping now from sea-valley to sea-mountain with monotonous regularity. Evans was exhilarated by the ship's motion. He felt at home now. This was where he belonged. He began to whistle.

The Major laughed. 'I thought that was bad luck – for old mariners to whistle in the wheelhouse.'

Evans smiled. 'I'm not superstitious.'

'Just an old custom, I suppose. Let's hope there's nothing to it.'

'There isn't.'

They were approaching another cape and Evans gave the man at the wheel a new course.

'Have you been in this business long, Mr Evans?'

'Been at sea long? Well, most of my life, since I was sixteen.'

'Really? It must be fascinating.' The Major spoke without conviction.

'Yes, it's been a pretty good deal. Sometimes, though, I wish I'd gone to West Point.' On an impulse he added this, knowing that it would interest the older man. It did.

'Did you have the opportunity?' he asked.

'In a way. You see the Congressman from our district was a good friend of my uncle who was married to my mother's sister, and I think he could have swung it. I know I used to think about it, but I went to sea instead.'

'You made a great mistake,' said the Major sadly, 'a very great mistake.' He looked out the window as if to behold the proof of the mistake in the rolling sea. Mechanically he made his profile appear hawk-like and military . . . like Wellington. Evans smiled to himself. He had seen a little of the regular army people and he thought them all alike. To parade around in uniform and live on an uncomfortable army post, to play poker and gossip; that was all of the world to them, he thought. The life wasn't bad, of course, but one was not one's own boss and there was not, naturally, the sea. The life seemed dull to him.

'I suppose it was a mistake,' said Evans, knowing it was not.

The Major sighed, 'I can't say that I care very much for the water.' His face was drawn and tired and there were greyish pouches under his eyes.

'It's something you have to have in you, I guess. With me it was being a sailor or a farmer. Farming was hard work and so I got to be a sailor.'

'Sometimes one shouldn't run away from the hard things,' said Major Barkison tightly. 'The easy way is not always the best way,' he added with infinite wisdom.

'I guess you're right at that.'

'Well, I think I shall go downstairs now.' The Major walked unsteadily across the rocking wheelhouse deck. He opened the door and went below.

'Quite a guy, the Major,' the man at the wheel remarked.

'Yes, he seems to be O.K. At least he's not chicken like some of the ones we've carried.'

'No, he seems to be a good guy.'

Evans looked out the window. The weather was consistent. The wind was blowing around twenty miles an hour. There was a thick snow flurry a few miles ahead. He would go by the clock through the snow.

The wheelhouse was quiet. From other parts of the ship he could hear voices, and from the galley came the occasional sounds of breaking china.

The clock struck three bells. Snow began to splatter on the window glass and whiten the decks. He could see only a few yards ahead. The sea had gotten no rougher, though, and the wind was dying down. He looked out into the whiteness and thought of nothing.

Martin came out of his cabin. 'How's it going?' he asked.

'Pretty good. Some snow just came up. We'll be off Point Kada in five minutes.'

'That's good time. Want me to take over for a while?'

Evans was surprised. Martin usually slept until his watch began at noon. It was unusual for him to be helpful. 'Sure. Fine. Thanks,' he said, and he went below.

The cook was swearing at the stove. The pots slid dangerously back and forth over the stove. Evans passed quickly through the galley.

In the saloon the Chaplain and the young Lieutenant sat. There was an open book on the Chaplain's lap, but he did not seem to have been reading. He appeared ill. Lieutenant Hodges on the other hand was enjoying himself. He was watching the waves hit against the stern.

The saloon was lighted by one electric bulb. Everything looked shapeless in the sickly light: the rack where the tattered library of the ship was kept, the wooden chairs piled on the two tables, the two men sitting in one corner, all this looked gloomy and strange to him. He flipped on another light and the place became cheerful.

'Quite unpleasant, isn't this?' Chaplain O'Mahoney remarked. He closed the book on his lap.

'Beginning to feel it?'

'Oh my no, certainly not. I've been sitting here reading. I feel very well.'

'Where's the Major?'

Lieutenant Hodges answered, 'He's asleep in his stateroom. I think he's pretty tired after last night.'

'So I gather. You went home early, didn't you, Chaplain?'

'Yes, yes, I had to get my eight hours, you know,' he said lightly. 'I had so many things to do before our departure.'

Evans turned towards the galley. 'Hey, Smitty!' he shouted. 'When you going to have chow?'

'In about an hour.'

'See you then.' Evans nodded to the two men and went back to the wheel-house. Martin was looking out the window and singing softly to himself. Evans stood beside him. They watched the snow swirling over the water; they watched for signs of change. That's all this business was, thought Evans. Watching the sea and guessing what it might do next. The mist was thinning, he noticed. He could make out a familiar cape ahead of them. They were on course.'

'How's your buddy, the Major?' asked Martin.

'He's in his sack.'

'I thought he was up here for a while.'

'He was.'

'I guess you'll make Chief Warrant now.'

Evans flushed, 'That's your department, polishing the brass.'

'You do it so much better.' Martin chuckled. Evans bit his lip. He knew that Martin often tried to irritate him and he did not like it when he succeeded. He turned away from him. The man at the wheel had been listening and was grinning.

Evans looked at the compass without seeing the numbers. 'Keep on your course.'

'But I am on course,' the man said righteously.

Evans grunted. Martin walked away from the window and back into his cabin. Evans cursed slightly. Then, relieved, he stood, looking out the port window, his arms and legs braced as the ship plunged from wave to wave, slanting the wheelhouse deck.

At five bells Smitty shouted that chow was ready.

Evans went into the mates' cabin. Both were asleep. He shook Bervick, who was in the top bunk.

'Lunch. You'd better get up.' Bervick groaned and Martin rolled out of the lower bunk.

'You take over,' Evans said, speaking to Martin. 'You can eat when I get back. I'll take part of your watch for you.' He went below.

The crew was using the galley table. The officers and passengers used one of the saloon tables. The three passengers were walking about aimlessly.

'All ready for some of our wonderful hash?' Evans spoke the words gaily, but even to his own ears they sounded flat. He did not have Martin's light touch with words.

'I feel quite hungry,' said the Major, rubbing his hands together briskly.

'I seem to have no appetite,' said the Chaplain sadly. They sat down at the table. The Major on Evans' right, the Chaplain on his left. Hodges sat next to Duval, who had come up from the engine room.

'Engines running smoothly, Chief?' Evans asked.

Duval beamed, 'They've never been better. We're making good time.'

'Good.' Evans helped himself to the hash. It looked pale and unnourishing. The Major frowned.

'This is that new canned ration, isn't it?'

'Yes. We have this when we're travelling. It's usually too rough to have anything else fixed.'

'I see.' The Major took some. The Chaplain decided that he was not hungry at all.

'You had better have some crackers,' Evans remarked. The Chaplain refused with a weary smile.

There was little conversation. Bervick and the Chief disagreed on the expected time of arrival. For a moment Evans was afraid they would begin an involved argument. Luckily they had enough sense not to. Evans wondered why people could never get along with each other. Of course living in too close quarters for a long time had a lot to do with it. On these boats people saw too much of one another.

After lunch Evans went back to the wheelhouse. Silently he relieved Martin who went below. There was another snow flurry ahead. It looked as if the rest of the trip would be by the clock. Evans watched the water and waited for the snow to come.

At noon Martin returned.

'Where are we?' he asked.

Evans studied the pale snow-blurred coast. 'Almost abeam Crown rock. We'll be in Big Harbour in about two hours. Don't get any closer to shore than we are and wake me up when you think you're near the nets.'

'O.K.' Martin checked the compass and the logbook and then he stood by the window and looked out. Evans went into his cabin and stretched out on his bunk. The rocking of the boat he found soothing. He slept.

'We're about two miles from the nets,' said Martin, when Evans came back into the wheelhouse. Outside the snow was thick and they could see nothing but a blinding whiteness. The outline of the shore was gone. Evans checked the time and the chart. He figured that they were less than two miles from the entrance buoy. In another ten minutes they should be able to see the nets. He rang Stand By. Martin went below and Evans waited for a thinning of the snow.

At last it came. Dimly he could see the great black mass of mountain that marked the entrance to the Big Harbour. He felt much better seeing this. He had never lost a ship in the fog or snow, but he knew that far better sailors than he had gone on the rocks in similar weather.

He directed the man at the wheel to pull in closer to shore. Just ahead of him, only somewhat hazed by the thinning snow, he could make out a red buoy off his starboard bow. Beyond this buoy were the nets. He rang for Half Speed. On the deck below he could see the Major standing in the wind. The Major thought Evans looked quite nautical, as he gazed sternly into the snow. Spray splashing over the bow sent him quickly to cover.

At Slow Speed, Evans glided the ship between the nets. For five minutes they vibrated slowly ahead. Then, in the near distance, he suddenly saw the spires of the old Russian church, rising above the native village.

To the right of the village were the docks. Evans took the wheel himself and the ship moved slowly around the harbour's only reef. With a quick spin of the wheel Evans took the ship in closer to shore. The water was deep up to within a few feet of the black abbreviated beach. A hundred yards ahead of them were the docks.

Two deckhands stood on the bow and attached heaving lines to the bow and spring lines. Martin stood by the anchor winch, his eyes on the dock where they would tie up. No other ships were on the face of this dock. They would have it to themselves.

Evans stopped both engines. They drifted ahead. The wind was off their port bow, which was good. He pointed the bow towards the centre of the dock and then he waited.

Ten feet from the dock he began to swing the bow away from shore. He swore loudly as the ship turned too slowly. He had mistimed the speed. Quickly he gave the off shore engine Slow Astern. The bow pulled out more quickly, while the stern swung in. They hit lightly against the pilings. A man on shore had already taken their spring line. Evans stopped the off shore engine and waited to see if the lines were under control. They were and he rang off the engine room. The landing had been good. His heart was fluttering, he noticed, and the sweat trickled down his left side. These landings were a strain.

II

Martin was in his bunk; handling the lines had tired him. His eyes were shut but he was not asleep. He listened to Bervick moving about the cabin. 'Going up town?' he asked.

'That's right.' Bervick adjusted his cap.

'You going to see Olga?'

'I might. Haven't had much to do with her lately.'

'That's right, you haven't.'

Bervick pulled on his parka. Thinking of Olga excited him. He still liked her, and the thought of the Chief with her, bothered him. The Chief would not be with her tonight; for some reason he was sure of that. Tonight was his night.

'I'll be seeing you,' he said to Martin, and he went out onto the forward deck.

The tide was going out and the wheelhouse was now level with the dock. With an effort he pulled himself up to the dock. To his left was the native village and to his right were more docks and warehouses. Men from the various boats walked about on shore, dim figures in the twilight. Pale blue smoke circled up from the galley smokestacks. There was a smell of cooking, of supper, in the cool air. Bervick turned and walked into the village.

The main street of the settlement curved parallel with the beach for half a mile. Most of the houses were on this street. Bars and restaurants and one theatre, all wooden, also lined the street. The buildings had been painted white originally; they were many weathered shades of grey, now. On a small hill, behind two bars and a former brothel, the old Russian Orthodox church rose straightly against the evening. Its two onion-shaped cupolas were painted green; the rest of the church was an almost new white.

On several lanes, running inland from the main street, were the homes of the two hundred odd pre-war residents. Most of the houses had been vacated at the beginning of the war. The windows were boarded up and the privies leaned crazily in the back yards. Seven trees, which had been imported, were withered now, and their limbs had been made grotesque by the constant wind.

A mile inland from the shore and the village was the army camp. It had been erected early in the war and its many barracks and offices duplicated the military life of the distant United States.

Soldiers from the post and sailors from the Navy ships in the harbour wandered about the crooked lanes and along the main street. They were looking for liquor and women. There was much of one and little of the other in the Big Harbour. Prices were high for both.

Bervick walked very slowly down the main street, proving to himself that he was in no hurry to see Olga. He would see her later in the evening.

He stopped at a building somewhat larger than the rest. It was the Arctic Commercial Store, the main store in the village. Almost anything could be bought here. It was said that the store had made over a million dollars since the war.

Bervick went inside. It was warm and crowded and cheerful. Sailors with beards in various stages of development walked about. Some wore gold earrings in their ears. Bervick grimaced. Earrings were an old sea custom recently revived. He did not like them.

The shelves of the store were stocked with canned goods and souvenirs; upstairs was a clothing store. Bervick looked around at the counters. In the corner where souvenirs were sold, he saw several bright pink and blue silk pillow covers. On them were printed, in gay colours, maps of Alaska and various endearments.

'How much is that one there?' Bervick asked the bearded man behind the counter.

'What one?'

'That one over there.' Bervick flushed and pointed to a pink one, inscribed *To My Sweetheart*.

'You mean the Sweetheart one?' Bervick wondered if the man were deaf. For some reason he felt a little foolish. He nodded and said, 'Yes, that's the one.'

The bearded man chuckled and handed it to him. Bervick paid him. The price was too high but that was not unusual here.

He stuffed the fake silk cover in his pocket. When he saw Olga he would give it to her casually. The Chief had more money, but sometimes sentiment was much more important. His breath came shorter when he thought of Olga. He controlled himself. He would not go to her yet. She had probably already heard that his ship was in. He would make her wait for him. Bervick hoped the Chief would not try to see her tonight. The Chief had said that he planned to work on the engines. Bervick hoped that he would. The Chief wasn't really much competition, though, thought Bervick.

He walked down the street. Drunken sailors in groups went grimly from bar to bar. The Shore Patrol men stood warily on the wooden sidewalk, waiting for trouble. Fights would begin later in the evening.

The Anchorage Inn was a popular bar. It rambled for a hundred feet or less on the main street, a few buildings from the Arctic Commercial Store. Bervick decided to have a drink.

A blast of heat and light engulfed him as he entered. The smell of liquor, food, and too many people was strong in the room. It took him several minutes to get used to the light and heat.

A long counter extended across one end of the building. Through the open kitchen door, behind the counter, he could see a fat woman cooking at a greasy stove; clouds of smoke and steam sizzled up from the stove. Two women and one man were serving at the counter and tables. Soldiers and sailors crowded the place. A half-dozen women were unevenly distributed. They worked in the shops and restaurants and bars. They made a lot of money.

Sitting at a table with two sailors was a large woman who immediately recognized Bervick. 'Hey, Joe,' she yelled. 'You come over here.'

'Hello, Angela. How're you doing?' Bervick sat down at the table. The two sailors were young and seemed frightened by Angela. They looked relieved to see him.

Angela was a huge and heavy breasted woman. She wore a green dress of thick cloth. Her eyes were narrow puffy slits and her face was painted carelessly. There was no reason for her to take pains up here, thought Bervick. Any woman was a beauty to men who had been without women for many months and occasionally years. Her hair was a bright brass red, dark at the roots. Angela was several years older than the forty she claimed to be.

'What's new, Joe?' she asked when he had made himself comfortable.

'Not a thing. We just got in a little while ago.'

'Yeah. I heard.'

'News travels fast, I guess.'

'It sure does.'

The two young sailors mumbled something and moved away. Angela winked, 'There they go . . . my admirers.'

'I guess you still got a lot of them.'

'Oh, I don't do so bad. When you going to visit me? I live over the store now, you know.'

'So I heard.'

'News travels fast.' They laughed.

'How's little Olga?' Angela asked.

'I suppose she's O.K. I don't see her so much any more.'

'That's just as well. I don't like to talk much about the other girls, you know I don't, but that Olga is just plain loose. I'm not saying the rest of us are any the better, I mean I know I'm not such a pure . . . well, you know, but after all I don't take on more than one . . .'

'For Christ's sake!' Bervick snapped at her. He was disgusted by this corrupt mass of a woman saying such a thing of Olga. 'That's hard to believe,' he added more calmly.

'What? That I don't go with more than one? Why you know perfectly well I don't. My only fault is that I'm just too affectionate.' She purred this last, and under the table her knee was pushed against his.

'I guess that's right.' You couldn't be angry with Angela, he thought. He wondered if Olga would be waiting for him.

'Then of course you know about her . . . Olga, I mean . . . two-timing that Frenchman off your boat. What's his name?'

'I know about that. That's old.' Bervick spoke with authority, and Angela was impressed as he intended her to be.

'Well, maybe she's through with him.' She sighed and her great breasts rippled. Bervick wondered if Olga might marry him if he asked her. That would certainly cut the Chief out, he thought viciously. He frowned.

'What's the matter, darling?' asked Angela, leaning over the table, her face close to his. Cheap perfume floated up from her in heavy waves; it made him want to cough.

'Not a thing, Angela, not a thing.' He moved back in his chair.

'Well, don't frown so,' she said peevishly, and then more brightly, 'What about a drink? They've got some good stuff here. Hey, Joe,' she yelled at the waiter. He came over to their table.

'Two shots, Joe.'

The man went behind the counter and returned a moment later with two jiggers of whisky. Bervick started to pay.

'Never mind.' Angela pushed his money aside. 'This is on the house, isn't it, Joe?'

'Sure.' Joe walked away.

'I know so many things about Joe, you see.' Angela giggled. They gulped the whisky. A tall blond sailor across the room caught her eye. She smiled and winked at him. The sailor came over to their table.

'Hello, beautiful,' he said.

'Hello, handsome.' Angela made fluttering feminine movements. Bervick stood up.

'I think I'll go now,' he said. He noticed the sailor wore a gold earring in one of his ears.

'Bad luck, soldier,' said the sailor, leering and putting his arm around Angela. Bervick turned away.

'Give my best to Olga,' said Angela. He did not answer. He walked outside into the cold air of the Arctic night. The whisky had warmed him and he did not feel the cold. He was glad he had taken it.

The street was crowded with sailors. They were becoming more noisy. Bervick walked on the extreme edge of the road in the shadow of the buildings. He wanted no trouble tonight.

The restaurant where Olga worked was called the Fall Inn. It was owned by a man named Fall who had a great sense of humour. Olga used to laugh a lot with Bervick when she thought of the funny name Mr Fall had thought of. She liked to explain to customers why the name of the restaurant was so funny.

The Fall Inn was a large, well-lighted frame house on one of the lanes that went back from the main street. Near it was a withered evergreen tree surrounded by a picket fence. This had been Mrs Fall's idea.

Bervick stepped inside. He stood in the doorway, accustoming his eyes to the light. Behind the counter, stood Olga. She was waiting on a dozen or so customers. Olga was a tall girl with a slim figure. Her features were rather flat and without distinction, but her eyes were a beautiful shiny china blue. Her hair was silver-gold, long and untidy, and her complexion was white and smooth. She had thick legs and graceful hands.

She saw Bervick when he came in. She looked away quickly and busied herself with the cash register.

He went over to her and sat down at the counter. 'How are you?' he asked, not knowing anything else to say.

'What do you want?' She spoke nervously.

'I just wanted to see you,' he said. 'I guess it's O.K. for me to sit here.'

'Go ahead, it's a public place.' Still she did not go away. A man across the room shouted for some coffee. Slowly she went back into the kitchen. She seemed frightened.

'Not making any headway with her, are you?' Bervick looked behind him. Duval was standing there. He had been there for some time.

Bervick felt sick to his stomach. For a moment he said nothing. Then he asked easily, 'What are you doing here?' He was careful to control his voice.

'Just what do you think, Sergeant?' Duval grinned. 'I'm just here having some coffee and maybe having Olga later on. I haven't made up my mind yet.' Duval sat down beside him.

'I thought,' Bervick spoke slowly, 'that you weren't going to see her tonight.'

'I never said I wasn't. Besides it's her and my business. She don't want nothing to do with you anyway.'

'That's where you're wrong.'

'Well, you just go ask her, sucker.' Duval played with the sugar container.

Olga came back from the kitchen. She was frowning. Her light brows almost met.

'What are you doing tonight? Are you going to see this guy?' Bervick asked. Olga flushed and thought a moment. Bervick knew already what she would answer. Olga liked money too well. But, knowing this, he still wanted her.

Olga decided to be angry. 'What makes you two think you're so good you can tell me what to do? I think you're both conceited. Maybe I ain't interested in neither of you.'

'Maybe you're right,' said Duval. 'I guess I'll just pay for some coffee and get on out.' Then he opened his wallet and let her see the thick sheaf of bills. Her eyes narrowed.

'What you in such a hurry to go for? My gracious, you'd think I was poison or something.' A customer yelled for food and she went back into the kitchen.

'I'd like to break your back,' said Bervick very deliberately, making each word a curse.

'Don't get upset, Sergeant. I just got more than you. I been keeping Olga ever since she got tired of you. You know that, so why do you keep hanging around? What you want to do? Marry her?'

Bervick felt sick. He watched the Chief's wide mouth move as he spoke. He noticed the Chief had a bright gold upper tooth. It gleamed cheerfully as he spoke.

Duval went on talking. 'There're some other girls around here. What about that fat girl who's so stuck on you? What's her name? Angela?'

'Angela!' exclaimed Olga. She came back from the kitchen in time to hear the name 'Angela'. 'Why she's just a big fat you-know-what. So you been seeing her.' She turned on Bervick, glad at last of an excuse to be rid of him. 'Well, you got your nerve to want to do anything with me after you been with her. Why I bet she's got everything wrong with her.' A customer wanted to pay for his meal. She went to the cash register.

'Too bad,' said Duval. 'You aren't much of a lover, are you? You go see Angela. She's just your speed.'

Unsteadily Bervick got to his feet. He buttoned his parka. Olga did not look at him; she pretended to be busy figuring change. The Chief absently twirled the sugar container between his broad hands.

Bervick walked out of the Fall Inn. He did not shiver when the cold hit him. Some men from the boats were urinating beside one of the buildings. They did it all the time, all over the place. It was unpleasant, he thought, Someone should put a stop to it. Thinking of this and not of Olga, he walked back to the Anchorage Inn.

Angela was not surprised to see him. The blond sailor with the gold earring was sound asleep in the chair beside her. On the table was a half empty bottle of whisky. Wearily Bervick walked over to her.

'Hello, darling,' she said brightly. 'Was Olga mean to you?'

'That's right,' he said. He sat down beside her. The sailor stirred sleepily. His long hair fell in his face.

'Nice, isn't he?' commented Angela, with a motherly air.

'Yeah. What are you doing tonight?'

She looked at him. The playfulness left her face. She was strictly business now. 'Sure, darling, sure,' she said. 'But you know how it is.'

'I know just how it is. I only got ten dollars,' he lied.

Angela sighed. Then she smiled, her fat face creased with kindness. 'I'll lose my reputation for this,' she said with a chuckle, 'but for an old pal, that's a deal.' Bervick thanked her. He wondered to himself how these wrecks of women would ever be able to adjust themselves to peacetime when no man would look at them. 'Of course you might take me to the show first,' she added coquettishly: a female elephant trembling at the thought of love.

'I suppose I could. What's on tonight?'

'*Saturday Magic*. I hear it's real good. I saw it advertised when I was in Frisco ten years ago.'

'That sounds good to me.' Bervick helped her up. The sailor was still asleep. Angela took the bottle of whisky and slipped it in her coat pocket.

'He'll never miss it. Besides we might want some in the movie,' she said cosily. They pushed their way through the crowd of soldiers and sailors. Standing outside the door were two Shore Patrol men waiting gloomily for the eventual riot.

'Nasty bunch them SP's,' remarked Angela, and then, 'Jesus but it's cold.' She pulled her coat tight about her neck. Quickly they walked to the small theatre at the end of the street.

The theatre held about two hundred people. It was almost filled now and the show had begun. They found seats at the back. A shot was being fired on the screen and Angela, hearing it, squealed with gay terror. Two rows in front of them a man vomited. Bervick shuddered.

'That's all right, dear. You'll be warm in a minute,' whispered Angela. He put his arm around her thick shoulders. She giggled and let her hand rest on his knee. Together they watched the figures on the screen and thought of each other.

III

Morning came whitely over the harbour. The water was oily calm. A small Navy boat went through the channel and the crews of the different boats began to stir about on the docks.

Bervick walked down the deserted street of the village. The houses looked unlived in. There was no sign of life away from the docks. His footsteps sounded sharp and clear in the emptiness of the morning.

He thought of Angela and felt sick at the memory of her making love in a torn silk dressing gown, her frizzled red hair hanging stiffly down her back. Olga was so much cleaner. He would not think of Olga, though.

The ship was already awake. The crew was straggling up out of the fo'c'sle. He could see Evans moving around in the wheelhouse. Martin was out on the forward deck.

'Have a good time?' yelled Martin when he saw him.

'Sure. Don't I always?'

'Sure.'

Bervick climbed aboard and stood beside Martin who was adjusting the hatch cover.

'Who were you with last night? Olga?'

'No. I was with Angela.'

'That pig?'

'I know it.' Bervick sighed and began, for the first time, to recall Angela's large torso. 'She's got a nice personality,' he said absently.

'Don't they all?' said Martin. He kicked the edge of the canvas into place. 'Let's have chow.'

Evans was sitting alone at the table when they came in. He muttered a good morning. They sat down.

Bervick was hungry. He ate even the cold-storage eggs, which Smitty invariably served them and which they seldom ate.

Martin looked up. 'Say, Evans,' he said, 'what's this story I hear about John Jones? You know, the Indian guy from Seldovia.'

'He killed himself.' Evans pushed himself back from the table and teetered his chair on the deck.

'What went wrong?' Bervick was interested. He had been on a power barge with Jones.

'He drank a bottle of methyl alcohol last night.' Evans made himself appear bored. He always did when anyone they knew died.

'Well, what did he do that for?' Evans irritated Bervick sometimes. Evans always wanted to be asked things, as if he were an authority.

'The girl he had back in Seldovia, an Indian girl, she left him and gets married. She writes him about it and he locks himself up in the head and drinks this stuff. They found him around midnight. He looked pretty awful they said. I guess he took the girl too seriously.' Bervick knew the last remark was intended for him and he did not like it. He would not kill himself for a woman, not himself, that was certain.

'That's life,' said Martin helpfully. The Chaplain and the Major entered the saloon. Both were cheerful and both looked rested. They announced that young Hodges was still asleep.

'We played poker for a little while last night. Where were you, Sergeant? We needed an extra man.' The Major spoke genially to show that aboard ship he was not conscious of rank.

'I was visiting friends in the village, sir.' Bervick shifted uneasily in his chair.

'They have a fine old Russian church there, don't they?' asked the Chaplain.

'Yes, they do.'

'Very interesting, these old churches. I suppose one can't go in the church here.'

'I think it's locked until the war's over,' said Evans. 'The priest was evacuated.'

'Such a pity,' the Chaplain complained. 'I should like to have seen it.'

Duval and his assistants came up from the engine room. The first assistant, a short heavy man, was splattered with grease.

'What's the matter?' Evans asked.

'Just a little trouble with the auxiliary again. It'll be O.K. I think. Just go easy on them winches. I been up since five working on this damned thing.' Duval gestured with his hands. Bervick wondered when he had left Olga.

'Good morning, Bervick,' said Duval genially. 'Did you sleep well last night?'

Without answering Bervick left the saloon and went in the galley. He could hear the Major murmur words of surprise and he could hear Evans change the subject.

Martin joined Bervick in the wheelhouse. 'What's bothering you?' He asked. 'You aren't still sore at the Chief because of that Norwegian animal?'

'Maybe I am. That's my business.'

'You're acting like a half-wit. Before you know it, the Chief'll get Evans to throw you off the boat.'

'That's fine by me. I don't know if I want to be around that guy.' Bervick gave the bulkhead a vicious poke.

'You're getting a little crazy in the head.'

Bervick shrugged. 'I'm not the only one, I guess.'

'Well, you better not bother the Chief very much or there'll be some real trouble one of these days. Anyway I can't see how you managed to get so hot and bothered over Olga.'

'That's my business.'

Martin looked at Bervick and saw that there were harsh lines about his mouth. He was fingering his long hair.

'I guess it is,' said Martin finally.

Evans came whistling into the wheelhouse. He was followed by a Captain, the Assistant Superintendent of the harbour.

'Are we sailing?' asked Martin.

Evans nodded. 'Just as soon as the Captain here gives us clearance.'

'The weather ... ?'

'According to the Navy,' said the Captain, examining some papers in his hand, 'according to the Navy you will encounter heavy weather near the Agan cape. Twenty-foot sea at the worst. Fair visibility and not too much wind. Of course you realize at this time of year anything can happen.'

'There are no planes leaving, are there?' asked Evans.

The Captain shook his head. 'Not for a week anyway. This is about the quickest trip for the Major.' He handed Evans an envelope. 'Here's your clearance and the weather report in detail. See you on your way back.' The Captain left.

'We're off,' said Martin. He looked out over the still harbour. 'I guess it will be a good trip. Hope so, anyway.'

Evans looked at the grey sky. 'There's a lot of snow up there. Go tell the Major that he can't fly. He wanted to know.'

Martin and Bervick went below together. They found the Major in the saloon, filing his nails. He looked inquiringly at them.

'No planes leaving, sir,' said Martin. 'They're still weathered in.'

'Well, that *is* too bad.' The Major seemed cheerful. Bervick decided that Major Barkison liked the idea of a three-day trip. 'Will we leave soon?'

'Right away.'

'Good.'

Bervick and Martin met the Chaplain in the companionway. The Chaplain was not particularly pleased at the idea of a boat trip, but he decided to be hearty and take it like a good sport. 'Well, that will be nice. I have always wanted to do this sort of thing. We never were near the ocean in Maryland. That is, Maryland was near, or rather on, the ocean, but we weren't. This'll be quite an experience for a landsman.'

'It will,' said Martin.

'I hope I shan't have a repeat performance ...'

'Not if you eat plenty of crackers. Will you excuse us, Chaplain?'

'Of course.'

They could hear Evans ringing Stand By. Together they went out on deck. The men on watch were already there.

'How do you want to go?' Martin shouted to Evans in the wheelhouse. Evans put his head out the window.

'Let everything go at once!'

Two seamen from one of the power barges stood by their lines on the dock. 'O.K.,' said Martin. 'Cast off.' The crew began to pull in the lines. Bervick went aft and helped handle the stern. Martin waited while the men coiled the lines. Then he yelled to Evans, 'All free!' He could see Evans nod and go to the telegraph.

The ship swung slowly away from the dock. The wind blew damply and gently in their faces. The seagulls circled high overhead.

Bervick joined Martin on the forward deck. They watched the bow of the ship cut with increasing speed through the dark and rippled water.

'It looks awful quiet, don't it, Martin?'

'Does look quiet. I hope it stays that way. The weather didn't look too good in the report.'

'Didn't look bad?'

'No.'

'I wish to hell I'd stayed in the Merchant Marine.'

'It's tough all over.'

'Yeah.'

'We better see what Evans wants. He'll probably want to hose down the decks.'

'Yeah.'

As they turned to go, Bervick reached in his pocket and brought out a bundle which he tossed quickly overboard.

'What was that?' asked Martin curiously.

'Some old rags.'

'Oh.' They went below.

The bow of the ship cut more and more swiftly through the harbour and toward the nets. The gulls wheeled higher and higher in the sky, and on the crest of one wave floated a pink piece of cloth, decorated with the words *To My Sweetheart* . . . and a map of Alaska.

CHAPTER THREE

I

Major Barkison contemplated the sea and was pleased by it. Today the water was smooth and only occasionally disturbed by gusts of wind. The Major stood alone on the forward deck. A few miles to his left was the vanishing entrance to the Big Harbour; before him was the Bering Sea.

Dreamily the Major thought of the sea: of the great masses of moon-guided water, constantly shifting: of sunken ships; of all the centuries that people had gone out on the water, and of all those, like Evans, to whom the sea was a part of living. He enjoyed thinking of these large vague things as the ship moved steadily ahead, causing sharp small waves of its own, waves which shattered themselves into the larger ones.

The water of the Bering Sea was a deep blue-black, thought the Major, and he watched carefully the ship-made waves: black when with the sea mass, then varying shades of clear blue as they swept up into the large waves, exploding at last in sudden whiteness. When he had the time, Major Barkison appreciated beauty. He had three days now in which to be appreciative.

Several sea lions wallowed fearlessly near the ship. Their black coats glistened in the pale morning light. For a moment they dove and splashed near the ship, and then, quickly they went away.

He heard the sound of wings behind him. He turned and saw the Indian cook throwing garbage overboard. The air was filled with seagulls, fighting for scraps on the water. He watched them as they glided in the air, their wings motionless, their heads rigidly pointed. They seemed reptilian to him. For the first time, noticing their unblinking black beady eyes, he saw the snake in these smooth grey birds. The Major did not like snakes.

Visibility was good. They seemed even closer than two miles to shore. In the distance, towards the end of the island, he could see one of the active volcanoes. At regular intervals a column of smoke and fire came up out of it. The island was a cluster of volcanoes, tall and sharp, their peaks covered with snow. Clouds hung over the peaks and the stone of the mountains was black and grey.

Overheard the sun made an effort to shine through the clouded sky; the sun seldom did, though. This was the place where the bad weather was made, according to the Indians, and the Major agreed. He yawned and was glad that he had not flown. He did not like flying over hidden peaks. He hoped this trip would be uneventful.

Major Barkison had a sure method of foretelling weather, or anything else for that matter. He would, for instance, select a certain patch of sky and then count slowly to three; if, during that time, no seagull crossed the patch of sky, the thing he wanted would come true. This method could be applied to everything and the Major had great faith in it.

He looked at a section of sky above a distant volcano. Slowly he counted. At the count of two a gull flew across his patch of sky. The Major frowned. He had a way, however, of dealing with this sort of thing. He would use the best two out of three. Quickly he counted. No gull appeared. The trip would not be bad. In his mind, though, he wondered if it might not be cheating to take the best two out of three. One had to play fair. Not that he was superstitious, of course.

The Major began to feel the cold of the wind. The cold came gradually. He did not realize it until he found himself shivering. Carefully, holding onto the railing, he walked aft to the galley.

Inside he stood by the range and warmed himself. He shivered as the cold left. Steam came up from his hands.

Hodges and the Chaplain were sitting at the galley table drinking coffee. The Indian cook was arranging some canned rations in a cupboard. Major Barkison took off his parka and sat down at the galley table.

'Pretty cold, isn't it?' remarked the Chaplain.

'Yes, it is. Very penetrating, this cold. Goes right through to the bone.'

'I suppose so. Actually this isn't half so cold as Anchorage or Nome. The Chain isn't much worse than Seattle.'

'I'll take Seattle,' said Hodges. 'Who was it who said this place was the chamber pot of the gods?' The Major laughed.

'I hear,' said the Chaplain, 'that you are going to be promoted, Major.'

'How did you hear that?'

The Chaplain giggled. 'Through the grapevine. You hear all sorts of things that way, you know.'

Barkison nodded. 'It looks like it'll be coming through any time now.'

'That'll be nice for you. Your career and all that.'

'Yes, it will be nice.' The Major poured himself a cup of coffee from the pot on the stove. Then he sat down again. He poured some canned milk into the coffee.

'They say that the natives think that's where milk comes from, out of a can,' Hodges remarked.

'You can get to like condensed milk,' said the Major. 'I never used to like it before I came up here.' He stirred his coffee and thought of Fort Lewis where he had been stationed for many years before the war. As he remembered, he missed the trees and green fields the most; large leafy trees and green smooth clover pastures. He wondered how long it would be before he went back.

'Where is your home?' asked the Chaplain, turning to Hodges.

'Virginia, the northern part.'

'Oh, really. That's quite near to me. You know the monastery of Saint Oliver?'

Hodges shook his head. 'Well that's where I was, near Baltimore, you know. When I was a child I used to visit relatives in Pikefield County. You didn't know anyone in Pikefield, did you?'

'I'm afraid I never did. I was never in the southern part of the state much. I was mostly in Fairfax.'

'Great country,' commented the Major. 'I've been in many horse shows around there, around Warrenton. Beautiful country, I've always liked it.'

'I never knew you rode, sir,' said Hodges.

'Why yes. I was in the cavalry when I first got out of the Point. Changed over later. Cavalry was a little bit too much wear and tear for me. You see,' and he lowered his voice and spoke rather wearily, 'you see, I have a heart murmur.'

'Really?' The Chaplain became interested. 'Isn't that odd, but you know I've got the same thing. As a matter of fact the doctor up at Anchorage told me I might drop dead at any moment. You can imagine how surprised I was to hear that.'

'I can imagine.' The Major spoke drily. The Chaplain's heart did not interest him. He was a little annoyed that the Chaplain should have mentioned it.

'Yes, I might drop dead at any moment.' Chaplain O'Mahoney seemed to enjoy saying those words.

The Major looked out the porthole and watched the grey water shifting under the still sunless sky.

'I like Anchorage,' said the Chaplain absently.

'The best place in Alaska,' agreed Hodges. 'You can get real steak there. You got to pay high for it, though.'

'Sure, but they're a lot more civilized than some places I could mention. It certainly does get cold up there.' The Chaplain shuddered at the thought.

'That's why war is hell,' said the Major. He wondered how long it would be before his promotion came through. Almost without thinking he used his method. If the Chaplain blinked his eyes within the count of three, he would not get his promotion for at least six months. He looked at the Chaplain's eyes and he counted to himself. The Chaplain did not blink. Major Barkison felt much better. He would be a Lt Colonel in less than six months. O'Mahoney was watching him, he noticed.

'Do you feel well, Major?' the Chaplain asked.

'Never better. Why?'

'I thought you looked odd. You were staring so. It must be my imagination.'

'It must be. I was just staring, daydreaming, you know.'

'Yes, I do it often myself. Once I had an unusual revelation that way.'

The Major changed the subject. He spoke to Hodges. 'Are you going to stay with the Adjutant General's department after the war?' Lieutenant Hodges was regular army like the Major.

Hodges shook his head. 'I don't think so. I'm going to try to get in Operations.'

'It's quite interesting, these revelations; I suppose one would call them that . . .' O'Mahoney began again.

Major Barkison interrupted hurriedly. 'I am certain they are.' He turned to the Lieutenant. 'Of course, Hodges, the work's quite different from what you've been doing.'

'I know. I think I'd like it though.'

Barkison could see that O'Mahoney was trying to decide whether to tell of his revelation or not. He decided not to. They sat without speaking, and the Major listened to the sounds of the ship. Distant voices from the saloon and the wheelhouse and, nearer them, the soft curses of Smitty, the Indian cook, as he prepared lunch. The ship, Barkison noticed, was rocking more than usual. Evans was probably changing course.

The Major excused himself and walked into the almost dark saloon and stood by the after door, looking out. In shallow ridges the wake of the skip foamed on the sky-grey water: grey when you looked at its surface but obsidian-dark beneath. A slight wind blew, troubling only the gulls, who floated uneasily on it.

Martin came and stood beside him in the doorway.

'Ah, Mr Martin. Smooth sailing, isn't it?'

'Yes, very.'

'I'm certainly glad it is. Certainly glad it's calm. I had thought we might have rough weather according to the report, but it doesn't seem so.'

'Might be bad yet, Major. This is pretty unusual. In fact this isn't at all what we expected.'

'Weather's incalculable here, I suppose. That's true of all the Aleutians, I suppose.'

'You're right there. You can't tell much till it's almost too late.'

'What sort of work did you do before you came in the army, if I may ask?'

'I was an actor.'

'Is that so?' At one time the Major had been interested in the theatre. He was still fascinated by the business. 'Were you in the pictures?'

'No, on the stage. Up around New England.'

'Indeed? This,' the Major pointed at the water, 'this seems quite different from that sort of work.'

'In a way I suppose so. That's what the army does. It's just one of those things, I guess.'

'Just one of those things,' echoed the Major. He thought of himself on a stage. In his mind he could see himself playing Wellington. The uniforms would be flattering. He would look martial in them Major Barkison was a romantic, a frustrated romantic perhaps, but still a romantic. Before the war, when the army could wear civilian clothes, Major Barkison had worn very bright ties. 'Must be interesting work.'

'Yes, I guess I'll do it again if I can.'

'You must certainly. One should always do the thing one does best.' The Major spoke with the firmness of the master of the platitude.

'That's right, sir.'

Major Barkison toyed with the thought of himself as Wellington. The thought was pleasant and he examined it from all angles. He dreamed for several moments.

'I understand,' said Martin at last, 'that they are going to rotate to the States all men who've been here two years or more.'

'What? Oh, yes, that's our policy. It's a little hard to do, naturally. There aren't many replacements so far. How long have you been here?'

'Fourteen months. I've got another ten months to go.'

'I know how you feel. How long has Mr Evans been here?'

'Over three years, but then he's practically a native. He lived in Seward. He probably likes Alaska.'

'He must, to stay here that long. For some people, it's a good place.'

'He used to fish in these waters.'

'Really? He seems to want to go back now. I can't say I blame him.'

'Neither do I.'

Major Barkison wondered if his own request to join a certain General in another theatre would be granted. He hoped it would be. There were times when he felt his whole career was being blocked in this, now inactive, theatre of war.

'Arunga's getting to be quite big, isn't it, Major?'

'Yes, it's about the best developed island here. Probably be quite a post-war base. Key to the northern defence.'

'So I hear.'

'Yes, the General was wise to build up Arunga.'

'I hear he's got a big house there with a grand piano and all that sort of stuff.'

Barkison laughed. 'He lives in a shack.'

'I guess somebody just started talking too much once.' Martin looked about him. 'I got to go up top now,' he said. 'Will you excuse me?'

'Certainly.' Martin left through the galley.

Major Barkison sat down on a bench in the saloon. He looked at the books in the rack. Most of them looked dull.

He sat quietly and studied the linoleum of the deck. The cracks in the linoleum formed interesting patterns, rather like lines on a battle map. He wondered just what battle these lines looked the most like. Probably Gettysburg. All maps looked like Gettysburg.

Bored, he examined the books again. One of them caught his eye: a book of short biographies. He picked it up and thumbed through the pages. The last biography was about General Chinese Gordon. Interested, he began to read. In his subconscious Wellington, for the time being, began to fade. A stage appeared in the mind of the Major, and he saw himself, the frustrated romantic, surrounded by Mandarins; dressed as General Gordon, he was receiving a large gold medal for his defeat of the Wangs. Major Barkison could almost hear the offstage cheers of a crowd. He began to frame a speech of thanks in his mind. He could hear his own inner voice speaking brilliantly and at length of attrition. As Chinese Gordon he thought of these things.

II

At ten o'clock, two hours after they had left the Big Harbour, Evans noticed that the barometer had dropped alarmingly.

He called Bervick over. Together they figured how much the barometer had fallen in the two hours. Evans was worried; Bervick was not.

'I seen this sort of thing before,' said Bervick. 'Sometimes it's just the chain inside the barometer skipping a little, or maybe it's just for the time being. I seen this sort of thing before.'

'Sure, so have I.' Evans lowered his voice, he was afraid the man at the wheel might hear them. 'I seen it blow all to hell, too, when the barometer dropped like this.' Evans was nervous. He did not like to be nervous or seem nervous at sea, but lately some of the most trivial things upset him. A falling barometer, of course, was not trivial. On the other hand, it was not an unusual thing.

'Well, the weather don't look bad, Skipper. Take a look.'

They opened one of the windows and looked out. The sky, though fog-ridden and dark, was no more alarming than ever. The sea was not high and the wind was light. The seagulls were still hovering about the ship.

'I still don't like this,' murmured Evans. 'It's just the way it was the time the williwaw caught us off Umnak, remember that?'

'Sure, I remember. We been hit before. What you so hot and bothered about? You been sailing these waters a long time. We seen the barometer drop worse than this.' Bervick looked at him curiously.

Evans turned away from the window. 'I don't know,' he said finally. 'I just got the jumps, I guess. This weather gets under my skin sometimes.'

'I know, it's no good, this crazy weather.'

Evans took a long shaky breath. 'Well, we're near enough to a lot of inlets if anything blows up.'

'That's right.'

'Tell the quartermaster to steer a half mile nearer shore.'

'O.K.' Bervick talked to the man at the wheel a moment. Evans looked at the chart of the islands. Bervick joined him and together they studied the chart and an old logbook which had been used on their last trip.

Evans rechecked the courses and the running times around the different capes. The stretches of open sea, while more vulnerable to the big winds, were generally safest. The capes and spits of rock were dangerous. One had to deal with them every fifteen minutes or so.

He checked the bays and inlets that they would pass. He also figured the times they would be abeam these openings. At the first sign of danger he would anchor inside one of these sheltered places. In the open sea they would have to weather any storm that hit them, but there would be no rocks in the open sea and that was a help.

'There's some good harbours on Kulak,' said Bervick, examining that island on the chart.

'That's right, we'll be there early tomorrow morning. We'll leave this island around four in the afternoon. We'll coast along by Ilak for around six hours and then we hit open sea.'

'It's about a hundred miles of open sea; it'll take us over nine hours. Then we reach Kulak.'

'I'll feel O.K. there. Weather's good from there on.'

'Sure the weather's always good from there on. It's always wonderful here.' Bervick went back into his cabin. His watch did not begin until four.

Evans put away the charts. Then he stood by the window and watched the sky. Towards the southwest the clouds were dark, but the wind, which was faint, was from almost the opposite direction. The wind could change, though. When it was not strong and direct anything could happen.

Martin came into the wheelhouse. He looked at the barometer and whistled.

Evans was irritated. 'Don't whistle in the wheelhouse. It's bad luck.'

'You always do.'

'That's different.'

Martin chuckled, then, 'Barometer's mighty low. How long she been dropping?'

'For almost two hours.' Evans wished his first mate would not talk so loudly in front of the man on watch.

'That doesn't look . . .'

'No, it doesn't.' Evans interrupted sharply. He looked warningly at the wheelsman. Martin understood. He walked over and stood beside Evans at the window.

'The sky looks all right.'

'Sure. Sure. That's the way it always is.'

'What's all the emotion for?'

'None of your damned business. Why don't you crawl in your sack?'

'I think I will.' Grinning, Martin went into his cabin.

Gloomily Evans looked at the sky again. He knew that he must be acting strangely. He had never let them see him nervous before. Weather was beginning to get on his nerves after all his years in these waters.

The wheelhouse was getting a little warm, he noticed. He opened one of the windows and leaned out. The cold damp air was refreshing as it blew in his face.

At eight bells Smitty announced lunch. Martin took Evans' place on watch. Bervick and Evans went below to the saloon.

The passengers were already seated. Their morale, Evans could see, was quite high. Duval, oil streaks on his face and clothes, looked tired.

'Engines going smooth?' asked Evans sitting down.

'Just like always. Little bit of trouble with a valve on the starboard, but that's all. The valve isn't hitting quite right.'

'You got a spare part, haven't you?'

'Sure.'

'Well, let's not worry.'

Smitty brought them hash and coffee and crackers. He slammed the dishes down on the table.

'I feel as if I could eat a horse,' said the Chaplain.

'You come to the right place,' said Smitty. They laughed at the old joke.

'Any new developments?' asked the Major.

Evans shook his head. 'No, nothing new. We're making about twelve knots an hour. That's nice time.' He looked at Bervick. 'Weather's fine,' he added.

'Splendid,' said the Major.

'What was that you were reading, Major, when we came in?' asked the Chaplain.

'A piece about General Gordon. A great tragedy, Khartoum, I mean. They were most incompetent. It's a very good example of politics in the army.'

'Yes, I know what you mean,' said O'Mahoney.

'Are there many seals in these waters?' asked Hodges.

Evans nodded. 'A good many. If we see any salmon running you'll see a lot of seals chasing them. Sea lions hang around all the time.'

'I saw some this morning,' commented the Major. 'I understand they're the fastest fish in the water.'

'I believe they are classed as mammals,' corrected the Chaplain, looking at Bervick who nodded.

'That's right, sir, they are mammals.'

'You heard the Major,' Duval suddenly said. 'They are just big fish.'

'A lot you know about fish,' said Bervick coolly.

'I know enough about these things to know a fish when I see one swim in the water.'

'Anybody with any kind of sense knows that sea lions aren't fish.'

'So you're calling the Major and me dumb.'

Bervick caught himself. 'I'm sorry, Major, I didn't mean that, sir.'

Major Barkison agreed, a little puzzled. 'I'm sure you're right, Sergeant. I know nothing about these things.'

Bervick looked at the Chief triumphantly. He murmured, 'That's like I said: they aren't fish.'

The Chief was about to reply. Irritated, and a little worried that the Major might get the wrong impression of them, Evans said firmly, 'I've heard all I want to hear about sea lions.' Duval grumbled something and Bervick looked at his plate. The silence was awkward.

'When,' asked the Chaplain helpfully, 'do we get to Arunga?'

'It's about eight hundred miles. I always figure about seventy hours or more,' Evans answered, glad to change the subject.

Evans thought of the falling barometer and the stormy sky. For some reason, as he thought, the word 'avunculus' kept going though his head. He had no idea what it meant but he must have heard or read it somewhere. The desire to say the word was almost overpowering. Softly he muttered to himself, 'avunculus'.

'What was that?' asked Bervick who, sitting nearest him, had heard.

'Nothing, I was thinking, that's all.'

'I thought you said something.'

'What tonnage is this boat?' asked Hodges.

'Something over three hundred,' answered Evans. He had forgotten, if he had ever known, the exact tonnage.

'That's pretty big.'

'For a small ship it's average,' said Evans. In the past he had sailed on all types of ships. He had been an oiler and a deckhand and finally master of a fishing boat outside Seward. Of all the ships he had been on, he liked this one the best. She was easy to handle. He would like to own a ship like this when the war was over. Many changes would have to be made, of course. The ship was so expensive to run that only the government could afford the upkeep. He could think of at least a dozen changes that should be made.

The others discussed the ship, and Duval told them about the engine room. He was proud of his engine room. Evans knew Duval was a fine engineer.

Evans looked at his empty plate and remembered that the hash had been good today. Smitty had put garlic in it and he liked garlic. The others seemed to like the hash, too, and he was glad. He always felt like a host aboard his ship. Ships were his home; this one in particular.

Before the others had finished, Evans motioned to Bervick and they excused themselves.

In the wheelhouse Evans took Martin's place on watch. There had been no change in the barometer.

'I want you to cut that stuff out,' said Evans abruptly.

Bervick, who was playing with the dividers at the chart table, looked surprised. 'Cut what out?'

'You know what I mean. All this arguing with the Chief. I don't like it and you better not let it happen again. You got more sense than to fight with him in front of some rank like the Major.'

Bervick set his jaw. 'No fault of mine if he wants to argue all the time. You tell him to keep out of my business and I won't say nothing.'

'I'll talk to him, but you better remember too. I can't take much more of this stuff. You been at each other for months now.'

'He gets in my hair. He gets in my business.'

'For Christ's sake!' Evans exploded. 'Can't you forget about that bitch? Can't you figure that there're a lot more where that one came from? What's wrong with you anyway?'

Bervick gestured. 'I guess I just been up here too long. I guess that's what's the matter.'

Evans was tired now. 'Sure, that's it. That's what's wrong with all of us. We been to sea too long.' Evans knew as well as Bervick the truth of this. After living too long in close quarters with the same fifteen or twenty men, one began to think and do irrational things. Women were scarce and perhaps it was normal that Bervick should feel so strongly. He watched Bervick as he fiddled with the dividers on the chart. He was a good man to have around. Evans liked his second mate.

'How's the barometer doing now?' asked Evans.

Bervick looked at it, twisting his hair as he did. 'About the same. Bit lower, maybe.'

Evans grunted. A mile ahead he could make out a long black spit of rock and stone and reef. As they approached it he changed the course. First five degrees to port, then ten, then they were around the point. The end of the island, some fifteen miles away, came clearly into view. This island was a big one and mountainous. In the clear but indirect light he could see the white peaks that marked the westernmost cape. Because of the size of the volcanic peaks the shore looked closer than it was.

'Sky's still dark,' said Bervick. Evans noticed his mate's eyes were the colour of the sea water. He had never noticed that before. It was an unusual thing, Evans thought, but having lived so long with Bervick he never really looked at him and probably could not have described him. Evans looked back at the sky.

'Still bad looking. I don't like it so much. Still we're keeping pretty close to shore. We can hide fast.'

'Sure would delay us if something did blow up.'

'It always does.'

'You might,' said Evans after a moment, 'check the lifeboat equipment.'

Bervick laughed. 'We're being real safe, aren't we?'

Evans was about to say, 'Better safe than sorry,' but he decided that it sounded too neat. Instead he said, 'You can't ever tell. They haven't been checked for a while.'

'O.K., I'll take a look.' He left through the door that opened onto the upper deck where the two lifeboats and one raft were kept.

Evans watched the dark long point they had just passed slowly fade into a harmless line on the water.

Martin returned from the galley. He glanced at the barometer as he came in. He did not comment on what he saw.

'What's the course?' he asked.

Evans told him.

'Where did Bervick go? Is he in the sack?'

'He's out on deck.'

'He and the Chief were really going to town at lunch.'

'Yeah, I don't like that stuff. I told Bervick to stop it.'

'You better tell the Chief, too; a lot of this mess is his fault. You know the whole story, don't you?'

'Sure, I know the story. Bervick's been weeping over it long enough. I'm talking to the Chief, don't worry.'

A gust of wet wind swept through the wheelhouse as Bervick came back in.

'Cold outside?' asked Evans.

Bervick shook his head. 'Not bad. The boats are in good shape. Water's still fresh in the tanks.'

'Good.'

Bervick walked towards his cabin, 'I think I'll turn in,' he said.

'So will I,' Evans wrote down the course and the time and a description of the weather in the logbook. 'Get me up,' he said to Martin, 'if you see a ship or something. You got the course straight?'

'I got it.'

Evans went into his cabin. He took the papers off his desk so that they would not fall on the deck if the ship should roll. He looked at himself in the mirror and said quite loudly, 'Avunculus'.

III

Major Barkison found the Chief to be good, if not particularly intelligent, company. In the middle of the afternoon Duval had joined the Major in the saloon. They talked of New Orleans.

'I have always felt,' said the Major, recalling in his mind the French Quarter, 'that there was no other place like New Orleans. It's not like New York. It is nothing like Paris.' Major Barkison had never been to Paris but that was not really important.

'It sure is a fine place,' said Duval. 'Those women there are something.' He winked largely at the Major who quickly agreed.

Duval continued, 'Yes, I think of those women up here all the time; anywhere, in fact, because there's just nothing like them anywhere.'

'Yes,' said the Major. He changed the subject. 'Of course the food is wonderful down there; marvellous shrimp there.'

'So do I like it. You know I used to know a girl down there who was pretty enough to be in the pictures, and she was some lay, too. I was just a young fellow at the time and she was maybe seventeen, eighteen then, and we sure played around together. She was sure some woman. I bet you can't guess what she's doing now?'

'No,' said the Major, making a good mental guess. 'No, I can't guess what she's doing.'

'Well, she's got a big bar in New York and some girls on the side. I bet she makes more money than all of us put together. I got a picture of her here. I always carry her picture around with me. You can bet my wife don't like it.' The Chief pulled a worn leather wallet from his pocket. He opened it and showed the Major a picture.

Major Barkison smiled stiffly and looked at the heavy mulatto nude. 'Very nice,' he said.

'You bet she is. She's some woman.' He put away the wallet. 'I'd sure like to see her again sometime. She is some woman.'

'She seems to be,' said the Major.

Duval looked into space. A distant expression came over his harsh and angular features. Barkison coughed. 'Do you put into the Big Harbour often?' he asked.

Duval nodded, returning slowly to the present. 'We stop in there once, twice a week. That's our regular run. It's the most civilized place on the Chain.'

'Yes, I know. There seems to be an unusual number of civilians there. What's their status? I've never really looked into the problems of the civilian population up here, that's another department.'

The Chief scratched himself thoughtfully. 'Well, they're just here. That's all I know. They work in the stores. Some were pre-war residents. A lot of them are middle-aged women. We aren't supposed to have nothing to do with them. The army's real strict.' The Chief laughed. 'But there are all kinds of ways to operate. Them girls get pretty rich.'

'I suppose they do. They seemed an awful-looking lot.'

'Most of them are. There's one that isn't, though. She's Norwegian. You know the type, real blonde and clean-looking. She's real good. We been operating for some time now.'

'Is that so?' The Major wondered how, as an upholder of army regulations, he should take this. He decided he would forget it after a while.

'She's gotten around a lot, of course. You know the mate. The squarehead, Bervick.'

The Major said he did.

'Well, him and this girl were hitting it off pretty well until I came along. So I give her some money and she's like all the rest and quits him. He acts like a big fool then. He hasn't caught on that she's the kind that'll carry on with any guy. He's dumb that way and I got no time for a damn fool.'

'It seems a shame that you two shouldn't get along better.'

'Oh, it's not bad. He just shoots off his mouth every now and then a little too much. He's a little crazy from being up here so long.'

'I can imagine he might be. It's hard enough on shore with a lot of people. Must be a lot worse on a small ship.'

Duval agreed. 'It is,' he said, 'but you get used to it. When you get to be our age you don't give much of a damn about things. You do what you please, isn't that right, Major?'

Barkison nodded. He was somewhat irritated at being included in the same age group with the Chief. There was almost twenty years' difference in their ages. Major Barkison tried to look youthful, less like Wellington. He looked too old for thirty-one.

'Well, I think I'll go below and see if the engines are going to hold together.' Duval gestured cheerily and walked out of the saloon, balancing himself, catlike, on the rolling deck.

The Major got to his feet and stretched. He felt lazy and at ease. This was the first real vacation he had had since the war began. It was good not to be writing and reading reports and making inspections.

He had enjoyed his visit to Andrefski Bay, though. The ATS Captain had been a bit hard to take but the officers had been most obliging. He had finally made out a report saying that the port should be closed except for a small housekeeping crew. This report had naturally made him popular with the bored men of Andrefski.

The Major walked about the empty saloon, examining the books. They seemed as dull as ever to him. He decided he would finish reading about Gordon. He had read little more than a page when Hodges strolled into the saloon and sat down beside him. The Major closed the book.

'A little rougher,' commented Hodges.

'Yes. I suppose they've changed course again. Have you been up in the wheelhouse?'

'No, I was down in the fo'c'sle. I was talking with some of the crew.'

'Really?' Major Barkison was not sure if this was such a good thing; as experience, however, it might be rewarding. 'What did they have to say?'

'Oh, not so much. They were talking about an Indian who drank some methyl alcohol the other night.'

'Yes, I heard about that.'

'Well, they were just talking. Same thing, or rather something very like it, happened to his brother down in Southeastern Alaska.'

'Is that right?' The Major played with the book on his lap.

'He was working on a wharf on one of those rivers and he fell in. They said he never came up again. There was a lot of thick mud under the water and he just went down in it. People just disappear in it.'

'Is that right?' The Major wondered if he would be sick again. The ship was beginning to roll almost as badly as it had on the trip to the Big Harbour.

'I guess that must be awful,' said Hodges frowning, 'to fall in the water like that and go right down. They said there were just a few bubbles and that was all. Must have been an awful sensation, going down, I mean.'

'I can imagine,' said the Major. He remembered the time he had almost drowned in the ocean. His whole life had not passed in review through his head; he remembered that. The only thing he had thought of was getting out of the water. A lifeguard towed him in.

'You know they were telling me,' said Hodges, 'that there's an old Indian belief that if a dying man recognizes you, you will be the next to die.'

'That's an interesting superstition. Did this fellow, the one who died last night, did he recognize anyone before he died?'

'No, as a matter of fact he was unconscious all the time.'

'Oh.'

Hodges tied one of his shoes thoughtfully. The Major could see he was still thinking of the Indian.

'What else did you hear?' asked the Major. He was always interested to know what the men thought of their officers. Sometimes their judgements were very shrewd.

'Not much, they talked a lot about Evans.'

'Do they like him?'

'They wouldn't really say, of course; probably not, but they think he's a fine seaman.'

'That's all that's really important.'

'That's what I said. They say he married a girl in Seattle. He'd only known her a week.'

'How long did they live together?'

'Around a month. He was up in Anchorage last month getting a divorce from her.'

'Did she ask for it?'

'I don't guess they know. I gather he hadn't heard from her in the last three years.'

'People should be more careful about these things,' said the Major. He, himself, had been when he married the daughter of his commanding officer. She was a fine girl. Unfortunately her father had died soon after they were married. They had been happy, nevertheless.

Hodges got to his feet and said he thought he would go to the wheelhouse. He left. The Major put his book down on the floor. He was sleepy. There was something restful in the rocking motion of the ship. He yawned and stretched out on the bench.

Major Barkison awoke with a start. The ship was pitching considerably. The saloon was in darkness. Outside evening and dark clouds gave a twilight colouring to the sea and sky.

He looked at his watch. It was four-thirty. In the galley he could hear Smitty cursing among the clattering pots and pans. He turned on one of the lights in the saloon. The saloon looked even more dismal in the pale light.

He picked the book up from the deck and tried to read it, but the motion of the ship was too much for him.

Hodges came into the saloon from the after door. His face and clothes were damp from spray; there was salt matted in his hair. His face was flushed.

'I've been out on deck, Major,' he said, slamming the door shut. 'She's really getting rough. The Skipper told me I'd better come back inside.'

'Yes, it seems to be getting much rougher.'

'I'll say.' Hodges took off his wet parka and disappeared into the galley. A few minutes later he was back, his face and hair dry.

'What did Mr Evans have to say about the weather?'

'I don't know. He yelled to me out the window, that's all. I was on the front deck. So I came back in. The waves are really going over the deck.'

'Oh.' The Major was beginning to feel sick.

Chaplain O'Mahoney walked into the saloon from the galley.

'Isn't this rolling dreadful?' he said. The Major noticed that the Chaplain was unusually pale.

'It's not so nice,' said Major Barkison. O'Mahoney sat down abruptly. He was breathing noisily. 'I certainly hope these waves don't get any larger,' he said. He ran his hand shakily over his forehead.

'It couldn't be much of a storm,' said the Major. 'Mr Evans would have said something about it earlier. They can tell those things before they happen. There's a lot of warning.' The Major was uneasy, though. Hodges, he noticed, seemed to enjoy this.

Major Barkison went to one of the portholes and looked out. They were in open sea now. The island was five or six miles behind them. Waves, grey and large, were billowing under the ship. On the distant shore he could see great sheets of white spray as the waves broke on the sharp rocks. A light drizzle misted the air.

Very little wind blew. The sky was dark over the island mountains behind them. No gulls flew overhead. A geenish light coloured the air.

'What does it look like to you?' asked Hodges.

'Just bad weather, I guess. We're in the open now, I see.'

'Yes, we left the island a little after four. We'll be near Ilak around seven tonight.'

'I wonder which is best in a storm: to be near shore or out like this?'

Hodges shrugged, 'Hard to tell. I like the idea of being near land. You don't suppose we're going to have one of those big storms, do you?'

'Heaven forbid!' said the Chaplain from his seat on the bench.

'Well, if it is one I have every confidence in the Master of the ship,' said Major Barkison, upholding vested authority from force of habit. The idea of a storm did not appeal to him.

'I think we should go see Evans,' said Hodges.

The Major considered a moment. 'Might not be a bad idea. We should have some idea of what he plans to do. We might even go back to the Big Harbour.'

'Let's go up, sir.'

Hodges and the Major went into the galley. The Chaplain did not care to go. In the galley they found Smitty groaning in a corner. He was very sick.

They went up the companionway to the wheelhouse. Evans, Martin and Bervick were standing together around the chart table. Only Evans noticed them as they entered.

'Bad weather,' Evans announced abruptly. 'The wind's going to blow big soon.'

'What's going to be done?' asked the Major.

'Wait till we've figured this out.' Evans lowered his head over the chart. Together with his mates he talked in a low voice and measured distances.

Major Barkison looked out the windows and found the lurid view of sky and water terrifying. He wished that he had flown. He would have been in Arunga by now.

The Chief came into the wheelhouse. He spoke a moment with Evans who waved him away. Duval came over to the Major. 'Bit of a storm,' said Duval.

'Doesn't look good. You know about these things, does this look particularly bad to you?'

'I don't know. All storms are different. You don't know until it's over just how bad it was. That sky looks awful.'

'Quite dark. This greenish light is new to me.'

They watched the ink-dark centre of the storm, spreading behind the white peaks of the island they had recently passed. Evans turned around and spoke to the Chief. 'Engines in good shape?'

'That's right.'

'Could you get up any more speed, say thirteen knots?'

'Not if you want to keep the starboard engine in one piece.'

In a low voice Evans talked with Bervick. He spoke again to the Chief. 'Keep going just as you are, then. Keep pretty constant. I'm heading for Ilak. The wind probably won't be bad until evening.

'If it holds off for a dozen hours or so, or if it isn't too strong, I'll take her into Kulak Bay tomorrow morning. We'll be safe in there.' Evans spoke with authority. The Major could not help but admire his coolness. He seemed to lack all nervousness. The Major was only too conscious of his own nerves.

Hodges was listening, fascinated, his dark eyes bright with excitement. Major Barkison wished he could be as absorbed in events as young Hodges. I have too much imagination, thought the Major sadly. He would have to set an example, though. His rank and training demanded it.

'What would you like us to do, Mr Evans?' he asked.

'Keep cool. That's about all. Stay below and stay near the crew. If anything should go wrong, they'll get you in the lifeboats. The chances of this thing getting that bad are pretty slight, but we have to be ready.'

'I see.'

'Is the Chaplain in the saloon?'

'Yes. I think he's sick. Your cook is, too.'

'I can't help that. I'd appreciate it, Major, if you and the Lieutenant would go below. The mate who is not on duty here will stay in the saloon with you. I'll have him keep you posted on what's happening.'

'Right.' Major Barkison was relieved to see Evans had such firm control of the situation. 'We'll go down now,' he said to Evans.

In the saloon the Chaplain was waiting for them. 'What did they have to say?' he asked.

'Going to blow pretty hard,' the Major answered.

The Chaplain groaned. 'I suppose we must bear this,' he said at last in a tired voice. 'These things will happen.'

Duval walked in; he looked worried. 'I don't like this so much,' he said.

'It does seem messy,' the Major answered, trying to sound flippant.

'Looks like the start of a williwaw. That's what I think it looks like. I could be wrong.' Duval was gloomy.

'What,' asked the Chaplain, 'is a williwaw?'

'Big northern storm. Kind of hurricane with a lot of snow. Just plain undiluted hell. They come and go real quick, but they do a lot of damage.'

'I hope you're wrong,' the Major said fervently.

'So do I.' Duval hurried off towards his engine room. Chaplain O'Mahoney sat quietly on the bench. Hodges watched the big waves through the porthole.

Major Barkison said, 'I think I'll go to my cabin. If anybody wants me, tell them I'm there. I'm going to try to sleep a little.' This was bluff and he knew it sounded that way, but somehow he felt better saying it.

He opened the after door and stepped out on the stern. The ship was rocking violently and he had trouble keeping his footing. The wind was damp and cold. He waited for the ship to sink down between two waves, then, quickly, he ran along the deck towards the bow and his cabin.

A wall of grey water sprang up beside him, then in a moment it was gone and the ship was on the crest of a wave. He slipped on the sea-wet deck, but caught himself on the railing. As they sank down again into another sea-valley, he reached the door to his cabin. He went inside and slammed the door shut as spray splashed against it.

He stood for a moment in the wood-and-salt-smelling darkness. Great shudders shook him. Nerves, he thought. He switched on the light.

Water, he noticed, was trickling in through the porthole. He fastened it tight. More water was trickling under the door from the deck. He could do nothing about that.

Major Barkison took off his parka and lay down on his bunk. He was beginning to feel sick to his stomach. He hoped he would not become sick now.

If the ship went up on the crest of a wave within the count of three. . . .

Outside the wind started to blow, very lightly at first.

CHAPTER FOUR

I

Bervick sat on a tall stool by the window, his legs braced against the bulkhead. The ship groaned and creaked as she was tossed from wave to hollow to wave again.

Evans stood near the wheelsman. He watched the compass. They were having trouble keeping on course, for with each large wave they were thrown several degrees off.

'Keep her even,' said Evans.

'It's pretty hard ...' A wave crashed over their bow, spray flooded the windows for a moment. They were swung ten degrees to starboard.

'Hard to port,' said Evans, holding tightly onto the railing.

The man whirled the wheel until they were again on course.

'Pretty hard, isn't it?' Bervick looked over at Evans.

'Not easy. Pitching like hell.'

'Why not get her on electric steering?'

'Might break. Then where'd we be?'

'Right here.'

Evans stood by the compass. He knew they could not afford to be even a few degrees off their course. Ilak was a small island, and if they should miss it ... Evans did not like to think of what might happen then.

He wished the storm would begin soon if it were going to begin at all. Waiting for the big wind was a strain, and there was no sign of the wind yet. Only the sea was becoming larger.

The sky was still dark where the heart of the storm was gathered. Dirty white snow clouds stretched bleakly in the damp almost windless air. The strange green light was starting to fade into the storm and evening darkness. Grey twenty-foot waves rolled smoothly under them, lifting them high and then dropping them down into deep troughs.

Evans noticed the man at the wheel was pale.

'What's the matter?' he asked. 'You feeling the weather?'

'A little bit. I don't know why.'

'You been drinking too much of that swill at the Big Harbour.'

'I didn't have so much.' The man spoke weakly. There were small drops of sweat on his forehead.

'You better get some air,' said Evans. 'I'll take her.'

Quickly the man went to one of the wheelhouse windows, opened it, and leaned out. Evans took the wheel. He could get the feel of the ship when he was steering. He liked to take the wheel. Each time they descended into a trough they would be thrown several degrees off course. He would straighten them out as they reached the next wave-crest, then the same thing would happen again. It was not easy to keep the ship even.

'How's it feel?' Bervick asked.

'Fine. We're going to be knocked around a bit before we're through. May have to lash the wheel in place.'

Spray splattered the windows of the wheelhouse. Salt water streamed down the glass making salt patterns as it went. Evans tried to make out land ahead of them, but the mist was too thick on the water. They were in the open sea now. Somehow Evans felt very alone, as though he were standing by himself in a big empty room. That was a favourite nightmare of his: the empty room. He would often dream that he had walked into this place expecting to find someone, but no one was ever there. Then he would dream that he was falling; after that he would wake up. Once in Anchorage a girl he had spent the night with told him that he had talked in his sleep. He told her his dream; she never dreamed, though, and could not understand.

Evans let his mind drift. Anything to keep from thinking of the coming storm. That was a bad thing about storms: you could not really get ready for one. Once you knew a storm was coming all you could do was wait and deal with it when it came.

He wondered what would be said if he lost the ship. He could hear the Captain at Andrefski saying, 'I knew all along that guy Evans would crack up. I told him not to go.' People were all alike that way. Make a mistake, or even have some bad luck and they'll say that they knew it was going to happen all along. People were all like, thought Evans gloomily. He felt like a drink. He would not let himself have one, though. He would have to be able to think quickly. His stomach was already fluttering as he waited.

Evans looked over at the man on watch. He was still leaning out the window, his shoulders heaving. At last he turned around. He was pale but seemed relieved. 'I guess I'm O.K. now,' he said.

Evans stepped away from the wheel. 'You sure you're not going to get sick again?'

'Yeah, I'm all right.' The man took the wheel. Evans gave him the course. Then Evans walked to the port side where Bervick sat watching the water. He was daydreaming. His eyes were fixed on the sea.

In silence they looked out the windows. Except for an occasional sound of creaking from the bow, there was no sound to be heard in the ship. The wheelhouse was getting too warm, Evans thought. He unbuttoned his shirt. His hands shook a little as he did. This annoyed him.

'Getting warm, Skipper?'

'It's too hot in here. The Chief's really got the heat going fine. When we really need it in port he breaks something.'

'Engine rooms are always like that. I'm glad I'm not an engineer.'

The clock struck three bells. Evans looked at his watch. He always did that when the clock struck.

'When do you figure we'll be off Ilak?' Bervick asked.

'Just about two hours. Just about seven-thirty.'

Bervick scratched his long hair thoughtfully. 'I don't think this thing's going to blow up for a while.'

'I don't either. We better just hope that we're near a good bay when it does. I expect we'll get the big wind tonight. It's taking a long time getting here.'

'That's what I like.' Bervick looked at the black unchanging storm centre. 'Maybe we'll miss the whole thing.'

Evans smiled. 'No chance, bucko, we'll get all of it. Right in the teeth, that's where we're going to get it.'

'I wish I never left the Merchant Marine.'

'You got a hard life.'

'That's what I think.'

'Don't we all.' Evans made his mouth smile again. He tried to be casual.

His ex-wife would get his insurance, he thought suddenly. He remembered that he had not changed it from her name to his family's. He chuckled to himself. Everyone would be surprised. She would be surprised to get it; his family would be furious for not getting it. His father had four other sons and an unproductive farm. The insurance would be useful to them. He had not seen his family for seven years but sometimes they wrote to him. His mother always wrote. She was an educated woman but his father had never learned to read or write. He never felt there was much advantage in it. Evans thought of his family. His mind raced from person to person. He tried to recall how each of them looked. This was a good game that he often played with himself. It kept his mind off things that were bothering him, off storms, for instance.

Evans thought of his wife. She was a nice girl. If he had met her at any other time than during a war they might have been happy. He did not know her very well, though. He could not decide whether their marriage would have been any good or not. He wondered what she was doing now and where she was. He felt rather sad that he had not had time to know her better. There were others, of course. There was consolation in that.

A wave, larger than the rest, hit violently across their bow. Evans staggered and almost fell. Bervick and his stool were upset and Bervick was thrown heavily on the deck. He stood up swearing.

'How did it feel?' asked Evans.

'Guess.' Bervick limped across the wheelhouse and got the stool again. He placed it in one corner under the railing. He did not sit down again. 'Waves getting larger,' he said.

'We haven't seen nothing,' said Evans. He looked at the compass. 'Get on course,' he said sharply. They were a dozen degrees off.

'O.K., O.K.,' the wheelsman was beginning to sound a little desperate. He had not been at sea long.

Evans went back to his corner. He tried to recall what he had been thinking about, but his train of thought had been shattered. Only fragments were left to trouble him.

He looked at the forward deck. It had never looked so clean. The constant spray had made the grey-blue deck glisten. The door to the fo'c'sle opened and a swarthy face appeared. The fat cook looked out at the slippery deck. Carefully the fat cook stepped up on the deck. A small wave hit the bow. He tried to get back in the fo'c'sle but he was too slow. The wave threw him against the railing. Struggling, he was floating aft. Evans could see him, soaking wet, get to his feet at last and disappear in the direction of the galley.

'Some sailor, the cook,' remarked Bervick.

'He's some cook, too. He can burn water.'

The wheelhouse door opened and Martin joined them. His face showed no particular expression. He seemed to be unaware of the storm. He glanced at the barometer.

'A little lower,' he remarked.

Evans looked at it, too. 'Yes, the thing's fallen some more.' He went to the chart table and recorded the barometer's reading in the logbook.

'When's the wind going to start?' Martin asked.

'Can't tell yet, John,' Bervick said. 'Around midnight, that's my guess.'

'How're the passengers?' asked Evans.

'They're pretty bothered. The Chaplain's sick as a dog.'

'Where'd the Major go when he left here?'

'He went to his cabin. I guess he's in the sack.'

Evans frowned. 'I wanted them to stay in the saloon. You should have kept them there. Suppose he comes walking down the deck and a wave knocks him overboard?'

'That's an act of God,' snapped Martin. For some reason Evans was pleased to have irritated his Mate. 'Besides,' Martin added, 'he'd already gone when I went below.'

'Well, when you go down again get him back in the saloon. What's Hodges doing?'

'He thinks it's a game.'

'I'm glad somebody's having a good time.' Evans leaned against the bulkhead. The ship was not pitching quite so much now. The wind, what there was of it, was probably shifting. He remembered his insurance again. He wished he had taken care of it before they left. 'Leave nothing undone and nothing begun,' a Warrant Officer in Anchorage had told him. The words had a nice sound to them. They were also true.

'I've never been in a williwaw,' remarked Martin.

Evans glanced at him. He did not like to hear a storm described aloud in advance. Evans had a complicated system of beliefs. If some things were mentioned before they happened they would take place exactly as mentioned. He never said much about bad weather before it broke. He would never have said this was going to be a williwaw. That was predicting, not guessing.

'Weren't you aboard that time we was off Umnak?' asked Bervick.

Martin shook his head. 'I was having some teeth fixed. I missed that show.'

'I guess you did at that. You'll make up for that now.'

'I suppose I will.'

A thirty-foot wave swept them amidships. The wheelhouse creaked as the salt water cascaded over them. Martin stumbled. The stool rolled across the deck. The man at the wheel lost his grip; the wheel spun around. Evans grabbed it quickly. His right arm felt as if it had been ripped off. With a great deal of trouble he got the ship on course again.

'You hang on this,' he said to the wheelsman. 'When you being relieved?'

'In a half-hour.'

'Well, keep holding it tight. We don't want to wander all over this damned ocean.'

'Pretty good-sized wave,' said Bervick.

'Yeah, and there're more where that came from.' Evans was breathing hard. The struggle with the wheel had tired him. His arm ached. He flexed it carefully.

'Get your arm?' Bervick was watching him.

'Just about pulled the thing off.' Evans went to the window and leaned on the sill. The wave that had just hit them was a freak one, for the sea was not as high as it had been. The wind definitely seemed to be shifting. The sky was becoming darker. There was snow ahead.

Martin left them, and went below. Absently Evans rubbed his arm; it hurt him. He watched the water and waited for the big wind to come.

II

Duval walked into the galley. He was hungry and, bad weather or not, he did not like to miss too many meals.

Several members of the crew were playing cards at the galley table. They were taking the storm casually. They pretended not to be interested in what was happening outside.

The ship rocked violently. Heavy coffee mugs slid back and forth on the galley table. Smitty sat in a corner of the galley, his chin on his knees. From time to time he would groan. The fat cook, in salt-soaked clothes, opened cans.

Duval took a can of hash out of the locker. The ship rolled suddenly, slanting the deck. He stumbled across the galley and sat down on the bench with the others.

'Lousy, isn't it?' commented one of them.

'Just a little blow, that's all. You've never seen nothing till you've seen a tropical hurricane. This stuff up here is nothing like that. This is a breeze.'

'Sure, we heard that one before, Chief.'

'That's the truth.' The Chief put food into his mouth. He had not realized how hungry he was. The fat cook poured him coffee.

The men talked about the Big Harbour and other things. They did not speak of the storm which was beginning. They spoke of the Indian who had died at the Big Harbour. Everyone told the story differently and Duval was bored to hear the story again. He had never liked Aleuts anyway. He looked at Smitty in the corner.

'What's the matter with you?' he asked.

'This water.' Smitty cursed for several moments. 'This the last trip I ever make. I seen everything now. I'm getting off this boat, I'm going back fast. We ain't never getting out of this.' His dirt-coloured hands gestured limply. The others laughed.

'Take it easy, Smitty,' said the Chief. 'You going to live forever.' Smitty said nothing.

Duval chuckled. He was not frightened by bad weather. He had seen so many storms and he did have confidence in Evans. Duval was not worried.

The men talked of the Big Harbour and of all the things they had done.

'Say, Chief,' said one, 'did you see Olga?'

'Sure I saw her. I always see her. Anybody with money can see her.'

The man laughed. 'I guess Bervick isn't feeling so good today.'

'He takes life too seriously,' said the Chief and that was all he would say.

Hodges came into the galley from the saloon.

'What've you been up to, Lieutenant?' asked Duval, genially.

'I've been wandering around the boat. I've never seen waves as big as they are outside. They must be over fifty feet.'

'Not quite that big but they will be pretty soon.' Duval closed his eyes for a moment. He had found that closing his eyes for a moment or so was very restful. It soothed him to do this. He was not at all worried, of course.

The light from the electric bulb overhead shone on his eyelids, and he could see nothing but red with his eyes shut, a warm clear red. He thought of the colourful bayou land of Louisiana. Usually he did not care where he was, but he did like colour and there was no colour in the Aleutians, only light and shadow on rock and water. The Chief opened his eyes.

Hodges was biting his thumbnail. The Chief watched him. He wondered what he might have done if he had been as well educated as Hodges. Probably the same things. Life was about the same for all people; only the details varied.

'I hear they expect the big wind around midnight,' said Hodges.

'That's what Evans says. He don't know, though. He guesses just like the rest of us do. We guess, we all guess and most of the time we're wrong.' The Chief enjoyed discrediting Evans occasionally.

'Well, it should be some sight. I'm glad I'll be able to see it.' One of the deckhands laughed.

'You won't like it so much,' said Duval. 'Even though these blows up here aren't nothing compared to what we used to have in the Gulf.' The crew laughed. Anything that could keep their minds away from the coming storm was good.

'What's happened to the Chaplain?' asked Duval.

'He's in the saloon. I expect he's feeling bad. He doesn't take to this sea business at all.'

'I suppose I'd better go see how he is.' Carefully Duval got to his feet and walked across the deck. He slipped once and swore to himself as he did. His balance wasn't as steady as it had once been.

Chaplain O'Mahoney was sitting at the galley table, his jaw set and his face white. He was playing solitaire. He looked up as they came in and he managed to smile.

'I suppose it will be worse,' he said.

Duval nodded.

'That's what I expected.'

'This'll really be something to tell our grandchildren,' said Hodges cheerfully. The Chaplain laughed.

'Something to tell *your* grandchildren,' he said.

'If you ever live to have any,' remarked Duval.

They sat together around the table, each thinking of the storm. Duval watched the Chaplain's hands. They were white and plump and helpless. The Chaplain, Duval thought, could not have fixed a valve or even changed a sparkplug in a car. Of course the Chaplain knew many things. He could speak Latin, and Duval was impressed by Latin and the Church rituals. O'Mahoney's soft hands could give blessings and that was an important thing. Perhaps it made no difference that his hands were not practical.

'Are you Catholic?' asked O'Mahoney, turning to Hodges.

The Lieutenant shook his head. 'No, we're Episcopal down home.'

'Indeed? I have known some very fine Episcopal ministers, very fine ones.'

'We've got a lot of them down home, ministers I mean.'

'I should suppose so. I knew some before I went into the monastery.'

'What's a monastery like, sir?'

'Just like anything like that would be. Just the way you'd expect it to be. Perhaps a little like the army.'

'It must be queer, being so out of things.'

'One's not so far out of the world. There is certainly nothing harder than living in close quarters with a group of people.'

'I thought it was supposed to be a kind of escape.'

'Certainly not. We have more time to think about the world. Of course, we do own nothing, and that makes life much simpler. Most people spend all their lives thinking of possessions.'

'I suppose you're right,' said Hodges. Duval did not listen as they talked. Instead he walked restlessly about the saloon.

Through the after door he watched the white wake foaming. The wind appeared confused: blowing from first one direction and then shifting to another. There was snow in the clouds overhead.

The ship was tossed about like a stick in a river current. But somehow they managed to keep on course. The Chief tried not to think of this. He thought instead of a gauge on the starboard engine, but even that was too close to the storm. He turned and went back to the Chaplain and Hodges. Religious talk was soothing if nothing else.

He asked O'Mahoney about his monastery. O'Mahoney was happy to talk of it.

'A very simple place. There's really not much to tell. We all have our different jobs.'

'What sort of work did you do?' asked Hodges.

'Well, I was in charge of the novices. Those are the beginners, the apprentices.'

'Sounds like a First Sergeant's job,' said Hodges.

'Very much the same. I wish,' said the Chaplain wistfully, 'that I was back in Maryland now.'

'So do I,' agreed Duval. 'In New Orleans, I mean. I'm tired of this place.'

'We all are, but here we are. You have a wife, I suppose, in New Orleans?'

'Yes, I got a wife and two kids. We lost a new one two years ago. I guess she was too old to be having kids.'

'Such a pity, your child dying.'

'One of those things, they happen all the time. I saw the kid only once so it wasn't so bad.'

The Chief sat down beside the Chaplain. Duval reached in his pocket and took out a knife. Carefully he whittled his fingernails. He concentrated on what he was doing. He would think of nothing else for a while.

Suddenly the ship lurched and Duval was thrown off the bench. His knife clattered on the deck.

He got to his feet quickly. The Chaplain was holding onto the bench with both hands, his face very white. Hodges was braced against a table. Duval looked down at his hand, conscious of a sharp pain: he had cut one of his fingers and it was bleeding. He waved his hand in the air to cool away the pain. Bright red blood in a thin stream trickled down his hand. The waving did not help. He stuck his finger in his mouth.

'You'd better get a bandage on that,' said O'Mahoney helpfully.

'Yes,' agreed Hodges. 'That's dangerous, cutting yourself.'

'I know, I'll fix it. You people better hang around here until Evans decides what to do. You might get the Major up.' Holding his finger in the air, Duval went quickly down the companionway and into his engine room.

His two assistants were sitting beside the engines. They wore dirty dungarees and thin shirts; it was hot in the engine room. One of the oilers crouched in a corner. He had come aboard only the week before. Fumes from the oil, as well as the motion of the ship, had made him sick.

The two assistants, however, had been in this engine room in all sorts of weather for several years. They sat now under the bright electric lights and read much-handled magazines about Hollywood.

The Chief went aft to his stateroom in the stern. Carefully he wrapped a piece of gauze about his finger and then he tied the ends of the gauze into a neat bow. When he had finished he sat down on his bunk. He had always hated the sight of blood. He closed his eyes and took a deep and shaky breath. His heart was pounding furiously.

The first assistant came into the cabin.

'What's the matter, Chief?'

'Not a thing.' Duval sat up straight and opened his eyes. 'Cut my finger, that's all. How's that starboard engine sounding?'

'She sounds O.K., she's going to be O.K.' The man leaned against the bulkhead. He was stout and red-headed and a good mechanic. He came from Seattle.

'Say, what's this I hear that there's going to be a big wind soon? Is that right?'

'I expect so. Evans don't seem so bothered but the barometer's gone down low. Going to have a williwaw.'

'It must be blowing hard outside. We been feeling it rock pretty bad but that's not new on this run. Maybe I ought to go up and take a look.' The assistants seldom left the engine room. Several times they had gone through bad storms and had not known it until later. Even violent pitching and tossing did not alarm them.

'The wind ain't too bad yet. Blowing maybe sixty, maybe more. It's not coming from anywhere certain yet. The sea's big, though.'

'Think we'll anchor somewhere?'

'I don't know. That guy Evans never tells us anything and I'm sure not going to ask him anything. Yes, I guess we'll anchor in Ilak.'

'Well, it won't be the first time we had to anchor in like that.'

'No, it won't be the first time.'

Duval fingered the blue and white bedspread his wife had made for him and, fingering it, he thought of Olga. He hoped they would spend more time in the Big Harbour on the trip back.

'What did you do last night?' he asked.

His first assistant shrugged. 'I didn't do so much. Got tight, that's all.'

'Too bad. Did you see that squarehead Bervick last night?'

'I saw him for a little while. He was in the Anchorage Inn. He was with old Angela. She's sure a fat woman.'

Duval chuckled. 'Serves him right. He was trying to sew up Olga. He wasn't so smart about it. She'd come running if he didn't keep bothering her about the others she sees. After all she's got to make some money, like everybody else.'

'I heard that one before.' His assistant laughed. 'She's a fair looking girl, Olga is.'

'She certainly is.' Duval looked at his finger. He examined the bandage closely to see if the blood was seeping through. He was relieved to see it was not. 'Let's take a look around,' he said.

'O.K., Chief.'

They went back to the engine room. The other assistant was reading his magazine. He sat, teetering his chair with each lunge of the ship. Duval walked between the engines, checking the gauges and listening for trouble. Everything appeared in order. He switched on the hold pumps. When they were in a big sea the hold leaked badly; there was a leak somewhere but no one had ever found it.

Duval was pleased. If anything should happen to the ship now it would be Evans' fault. The Chief did not like to take the blame for anything and in that he was quite normal.

He glanced at the oiler in the corner. For a moment he wondered if he should get him some ammonia or something because he looked so ill. He decided not to; when you were seasick you liked to be alone.

'Everything looks fine,' he said to his assistants. Then he went aft again to his stateroom, carefully examining his bandage for signs of fresh blood.

III

The night was dark. Off the port side Martin could barely make out the coastline of Ilak. Since seven-thirty they had been searching for the place where Evans intended to anchor.

Martin stood close to the window. He could hear waves crashing loudly on the near-by shore. The wind was increasing and the sea was becoming larger. He held tightly to the railing, his stomach fell dizzily as they sank into an unusually deep trough.

Evans had taken the wheel himself and the man on watch stood beside him ready to help in case the wheel should get out of control. Bervick stood by the chart table. From time to time he would call out their position.

The wheelhouse was dark except for dimmed lights in the binnacle and over the chart table. Martin could hear the wind howling around the corners of the wheelhouse. It sounded seventy or eighty miles an hour, and this, according to Evans, was just the start.

Martin made a quick dash for the chart table.

'When'll we get there?' he asked.

Bervick did not look up. 'Ten minutes and we should be abeam.'

'What's that?' Evans asked, his voice pitched high above the wind.

'We're getting close, that's all. That inlet you're looking for. Two miles away, as I figure.'

'Good.' Evans motioned to the man on watch who quickly took the wheel. Then Evans opened a window on the port side. A tremendous roar of wind and breaking water exploded into the wheelhouse. Spray splattered in Evans' face as he watched the coastline.

Martin and Bervick went over and stood near him. Less than a mile ahead Martin could see a long spit of high rock pointing out into the sea. 'That it?' he asked.

Bervick nodded. 'Just around the corner there. Nice deep bay.'

'All right,' said Evans, speaking to the man at the wheel. 'Bring her to port, five degrees. Ring Stand By, Mate.'

Martin skidded across the deck. He rang the engine room several times on the telegraph. Then he set the markers on Stand By.

They waited for the Chief to answer. Two minutes passed and then the Chief rang back. He was ready.

'Half Speed Ahead,' said Evans.

Martin set the markers on Half Speed. The ship's vibration changed. Waves which had once crashed against them now lifted the ship easily onto their crests.

Evans turned to Martin.

'Go below and get some of the crew. Be ready to anchor when I give the word. When we get out of the wind you and your men go out on the forward deck and stand by.'

'Right.' Martin went quickly below. The idea of going out on deck in this weather did not appeal to him. Someone had to do it, though.

He gathered two deckhands in the galley. They cursed loudly but he knew they were glad to be anchoring.

Then, the ship having rounded the point, they went outside on the forward deck. Martin was almost thrown off his feet by a gust of wind. Though somewhat protected by the hills, they were not yet completely out of the storm. The wind was cold and penetrating. It chilled him, even through his heavy parka. Water whipped their faces. The deck was dangerously slick and the ship still pitched badly. On hands and knees, their eyes barely open and smarting from the salt, they wormed their way forward to the bow and the anchor winches.

They reached the bow. Martin got to his feet, holding tightly onto the tarpaulin which covered the winch. The other two did the same. Luckily they knew their job so well that he would not have to make himself heard over the sea-thunder.

The deckhands swiftly slipped the tarpaulin off the winch. Martin stood beside the lever which operated the anchor. The other two stood ready to knock the brakes from the chain.

He watched as the ship skirted the teethlike rocks and headed into a small bay. Dark mountains stood large against the sky. The bay itself was less than a mile wide and perhaps a little more than a mile deep. Mountains rimmed it on three sides.

Abruptly the ship stopped pitching. They were out of the wind at last. Inside this bay there was neither wind nor a large sea.

Evans leaned out of the wheelhouse window and waved.

'Let her go,' said Martin.

There was a loud clanging and then the metallic sound of falling chain as the freed anchor dropped into the water. The ship drifted slowly. Evans had stopped the engines.

Patiently Martin waited for the tug which would tell them the anchor was secured in the sea-floor. The ship glided ahead softly, cutting the small waves as it moved shoreward: a slight jolt and the ship stopped; rocking slightly, she began to circle about.

'Anchor's holding,' shouted Martin. Evans waved and shut the wheelhouse window. Martin and the deckhands went back to the galley.

Martin stood before the galley range and tried to warm himself. Water had seeped through his shirt to his skin and he was completely wet. He could not remember when he had been so cold. The two men who had been out on deck with him were also shivering.

He slipped off his parka and shirt and then he rubbed himself in front of the stove. His teeth chattered as he began to get warm again.

'Going to be here long, Mate?' asked one of the men.

'We'll probably leave at dawn. Wind should let up then.'

'Getting better then?'

'Yes,' said Martin, knowing it was not getting better. 'Storm should be over by morning.'

'That's good.' The men talked a while longer. Then they went to the fo'c'sle. In his corner Smitty began to stir. Groaning, he got to his feet and walked over to the range and poured himself some coffee.

'You feel bad?' Martin asked.

'You bet I feel bad.' Smitty walked unsteadily away.

Martin sat down for a moment. He was tired, more tired than usual. Lately it seemed that he was always tired. He wondered if something was wrong with him. Perhaps he should see a doctor and get sent back to the States.

Everything was quiet, he noticed gratefully. It seemed that there had been nothing but noise since they left the Big Harbour that morning.

'Say, Martin.' He turned around and saw Evans standing in the door. 'Come on out and help me nest the boom. Somebody didn't do a very good job when we left.' This remark was meant for him and if he had not been so weary he would have snapped back; the effort, however, was too great.

'Sure, sure,' Martin said.

On the forward deck the wind was direct but not strong. Small waves slapped the sides of the ship. The hills seemed peaceful and only a faraway roar reminded them of the storm.

They stood beside the mast, Evans absently twisting a wet rope. 'I'll go up top,' he said finally. 'You let the boom down.' He walked away. A few moments later Evans appeared on top of the wheelhouse.

'Let her down easy,' he shouted.

Martin let the boom descend slowly into place. He had to admire the quickness with which Evans lashed the mast secure.

'O.K.,' said Evans and he disappeared.

Bemused by the quiet, Martin walked back to the stern. He stood a while watching the mountains. He noticed that the side of one sharp peak seemed oddly blurred. It was the snow being ripped off the mountains by the wind. In the daylight it was a wonderful sight.

He walked slowly into the saloon. His watch started at midnight. He would sleep on one of the salon benches until then. He was tired.

A few minutes after twelve Martin was awakened by Evans.

'Your watch,' said Evans. 'I'm going to get some sleep. If anything looks bad, get me up.'

'Sea still high outside?'

Evans nodded. His eyes looked sunken, Martin noticed, and his lids were red.

'We'll leave around sunup if we do leave, that right?'

'That's right,' said Evans. 'We'll leave in the morning.'

They went up to the wheelhouse. Evans went to his cabin. Martin and the men on watch stood silently in the pale light of the wheelhouse. They listened to the sea.

'Think the radio will work, Mate?'

'We can find out.' Martin turned the radio on. A blast of static thundered out at them. 'I guess not,' said Martin and he turned it off.

He noticed the barometer was still low. He recorded the time and the barometer reading in the logbook.

'I'm going below for a while,' he said.

Outside on deck there was little wind and the dark night was serene. He glanced at the higher mountains; the wind was still violent, for snow was blurring the peaks. He went towards the bow and down into the fo'c'sle.

It was warm inside the fo'c'sle and the lights were burning brightly. Bunks in two tiers lined the bulkheads. Some of the men were sleeping; others sat on their bunks and talked. In the middle of the deck the ship's dog was licking a bone.

The men who were awake looked up as Martin came down the ladder.

'How's it going, Mate?'

'Fine. The bulkheads sweating much?'

'I'll say they are.' The man who spoke brushed his hand over the wood. 'Look,' he said. Beads of water clung to his fingers.

'That's pretty lousy,' said Martin. 'At least it's not cold in here.'

'Well, if it was we'd all be dead. This is the dampest boat I was ever on.' The others agreed. Martin sat down on an empty bunk and looked around. The fo'c'sle was even sloppier than normal. It was, of course, bad most of the time and nothing could be done about it. Evans had tried to do something with no success. He had only made himself unpopular with the men.

Clothes littered the deck and the bunks were unmade. Old shoes and much-gnawed bones had been hidden in the corners by the dog. Martin could see why Evans hated dogs, especially on ships.

None of these things were important now, though. Nothing, except getting out of the storm, was important.

'I wonder how she's blowing outside?' remarked a deckhand.

'Ought to be hitting a hundred about now,' answered another. 'What do you think, Mate?'

'I hope it's a hundred. If it is that means the storm'll be over by morning. They don't last so long, these storms.'

'That's what I say.'

The men spoke together in low voices. Martin examined the pin-up pictures that plastered the bulkheads. Whenever he thought of his army career he thought of these pictures first. Somehow they almost never changed no matter where he was. These pictures and the radio, those were the two constant things. Occasionally there was no radio but the pictures were always there: half-dressed girls, in mysteriously lighted bedclothes, promising sex.

He thought of the three years he had spent in the army, and, of those years, only a few things stood out in his memory: certain songs that were popular when he had left for overseas, the waiting in line for almost everything . . . The rest of his army career came to him only as a half-feeling of discomfort.

The dog, he noticed, was chewing his shoe. He grabbed the animal by the muzzle and pushed it away.

He got up. 'See you,' he remarked at large and he began to climb the ladder that led to the forward deck.

'See you, Mate.'

Major Barkison sat at a table in the saloon, a stack of writing paper in front of him.

'Good evening, sir,' said Martin.

'Good evening. Things seem a bit quieter now.'

'Yes, we'll be able to get some sleep.'

'I'm glad to hear that. I never thought the sea could get so rough.' The Major contemplated the fountain pen in his hand. 'I was,' he confided, 'quite sick.'

'I'm sorry. You should have let us know, we've got some stuff to take care of that.'

'Have you really? I felt so terrible that I couldn't get out of my bunk. I've never seen such jumping around. Does this sort of thing happen often?'

'Not too often, thank God.'

'It was quite enough.' The Major stroked his bald brow. The veins stood out on his hand. Martin hoped the Major had nothing seriously wrong with him. It was one of Martin's nightmares that someone should have appendicitis or something like that aboard ship when they would be unable to help. Such things had happened before on other ships.

'I've been doing a little letter writing,' the Major explained, pointing to the papers. 'I can really get caught up on a trip like this.'

'Would you like some coffee, Major?'

'Why yes, very much.'

Martin went into the galley and poured two cups from the pot which always sat, warming, on the stove. He brought the cups back into the saloon and set them down on the table.

The Major grunted his thanks. They drank the dark and bitter liquid. Martin warmed his hands on the coffee mug. His hands were cold and stiff from climbing the fo'c'sle ladder without gloves.

'Tell me, Mr Martin,' said the Major finally, 'do you feel . . . I know it's a tactless question, in fact an unethical question to ask . . . but do you feel that Mr Evans is . . . well, quite capable of handling this situation?'

Martin smiled to himself. 'Yes, Major. I have a lot of faith in Evans; when it comes to sailoring he's one of the best seamen up here.'

'I'm very glad to hear you say that. I should never have asked, of course. But the situation being as it is, well, I thought it best to get your opinion.'

'I quite understand.'

'I hope you'll regard my question as confidential, Mr Martin.'

'I certainly shall.'

'Thank you.' The Major sighed and sketched cartoons of sinking ships on a piece of paper.

'The Chaplain gone to bed?' asked Martin.

'I expect so. I haven't seen him for several hours.'

'It looks like the old jinx is at work again.'

'What do you mean?'

'Well, every time we carry a Chaplain we have a bad storm.'

'O'Mahoney must be a potential Bishop if one goes by results,' commented the Major.

Martin laughed. 'He's done pretty well so far.'

The Major played with his pen a moment. 'Where,' asked Martin, 'do you expect to be stationed after the war, sir?'

'Well, I should like Tacoma, naturally, but I think I'll be sent to Washington, D.C. A tour of duty there is worth more than a lifetime of field work.'

'I've always heard that.'

'It is not,' said the Major wisely, 'what you know, it is who you know.'

'You certainly are right.'

'Yes, that's the way it is.' They pondered this great truth in silence. Martin finally got to his feet.

'I hope you'll feel better tomorrow, Major. We'll leave in the morning; it should be calm by then.'

'I hope so, good night.'

'Good night.' Martin walked slowly through the galley. The lights were still on. He snapped them off. Then he walked out on deck.

A pleasant breeze cooled his face. Water lapped quietly against the sides of the ship. The night sky was black. In another forty-eight hours, if all went well, they would be in Arunga.

As he stood there many dramatic speeches came to Martin. Plays he had read or had seen on the stage, came to him. The rolling periods of the Elizabethans flowed through him like water in a rock channel. He always enjoyed these moments when he could think of words and voices speaking words.

He walked about on the deck. He stood by the railing on the port side and breathed the clean air. In these islands there was no odour of earth and vegetation in the wind, only the scent of salt and stone. He raised his head and looked at the mountains. The snow still whirled seaward.

CHAPTER FIVE

I

Morning.

Evans walked into the wheelhouse. He had slept unusually well. As a rule he stayed awake during bad weather, but this time he had really slept and he was glad that he had.

Bervick, whose watch it was, stood looking at the barometer.

'What do you think, Skipper?'

Evans looked at the barometer: still low, there had been almost no change overnight.

'I think there must be something wrong with the thing. You seen them act up before, haven't you?'

Bervick agreed. 'They can be wrong. It looks fine outside.' Evans went over to the window. There was little light in the sky, but the pre-sunrise stillness was good. Even in the mountains there was no wind.

'What do you think, Skipper?'

'I don't know. I'll have to think about it. I don't know.' Evans felt suddenly inadequate. He wished that he did not have to make this decision. He wondered for a moment what would happen if he got into his bunk and refused to get out. When he was very young he had often had a feeling like that: to lie down somewhere and not move and let unpleasant things take care of themselves.

'I suppose,' he said finally, 'seeing as how the wind has died down, I suppose we should take a chance.'

'We'll make a dash for Kulak if anything goes wrong.'

Evans went to the chart table. Mentally he computed distances and positions. 'We'll take a chance,' he repeated. 'Get Martin up.'

Bervick went into his cabin; he came out, a moment later, with Martin.

'Bervick,' said Evans, 'you take some men out on deck and get ready to weigh anchor. Martin, you go on down and see how the passengers are doing. Talk to the Chief and tell him we're leaving right away. We want to get to Arunga tomorrow night.'

Martin and Bervick left together. Evans looked at the compass; he looked at the barometer, and then he looked at the chart. He walked out on deck and watched morning move slowly into the east. The day looked peaceful; there was no way, though, to tell what might happen. There never was any way to tell.

He watched Bervick and several deckhands as they walked on the forward deck, testing the winches, preparing to weigh anchor. Evans went to the telegraph and rang the engine room. He set the markers on Stand By. Almost immediately the Chief rang back.

Evans took a deep breath. Then he opened the window and yelled, 'Pull her up!'

Bervick pushed a lever. There was much clanging and rattling. The anchor chain came up easily. Evans let the ship drift slowly with the tide. At last, satisfied that the anchor was free, he gave the engine room Slow Speed Astern.

The ship, vibrating strongly, drew away from shore. Evans twirled the electri-

cal steering gear hard to starboard and headed the ship for the opening and the
sea beyond.

At Slow Speed Ahead they moved through the channel, neatly cutting the
still water. The uneven rocks of the point moved by them. A raven, the first he
had seen since they left Andrefski, flew warily among the rocks. A damp breeze
came to him through the window. Snow clouds hung over the mountains.

Bervick came back. 'All squared away. We left the tarpaulin off. Just in case
we might need the anchor again.'

'Good.' Evans motioned to the man on watch who had been standing by the
door. 'You take over.'

Evans examined the blue-green paint of the wheelhouse. It was too dark. He
had thought so when they first used it, but this dark colour was the only paint he
could get. A lighter colour would have been much better. He would have
everything repainted when they got back to Andrefski.

Without warning the ship was lifted several feet in the air by a long wave.
They were out of the inlet. The rocks of the point receded in the distance.

'Bring her to port,' commanded Evans. The bow swung parallel to shore.
They were headed west again.

'So far so good,' said Bervick.

Evans agreed. There was quietness in the morning. There would be snow
flurries but the big wind seemed to have gone. Evans was glad. He began to
whistle.

Bervick looked at him. 'We're not in the clear yet,' he said.

Evans laughed, 'I guess you're right. I just feel good. I wish I knew what was
the matter with that damned barometer, though.'

'Maybe that little chain's stuck, like I said.'

'Might be.'

Martin joined them. 'The passengers look fine today,' he said.

'The Chief say everything's working in his department?'

'That's what he said. Smitty's got breakfast ready. They're eating now.'

Evans remembered that he had had nothing to eat for almost a day. 'I think
I'll go below,' he said.

'O.K., Skipper.' Bervick went over to the chart table and Martin went into
his cabin.

The galley, Evans saw, was much more cheerful today. Smitty had cleaned
the deck and straightened the unbroken china. Several deckhands sat at the
galley table talking loudly. You could tell, thought Evans, how long a man had
been up here by the way he talked. The longer a man was in the islands the
longer his stories were. Talking was the only thing to do when there was no
liquor.

The passengers were eating heartily.

'Good morning,' said Evans, entering the saloon.

'Good morning,' said the Chaplain, giving the phrase its full meaning. 'There
is practically no rocking,' he observed happily.

'This may be a quiet trip yet,' said Evans. He sat down and Smitty brought
him breakfast. The Major was in a good mood. He was not even pale today,
Evans noticed.

'I hear we may be in Arunga tomorrow night,' said the Major.

'That's what we hope,' said Evans. Breakfast tasted better than it ever had
before.

'I shall really be glad when this trip is over,' said the Chaplain. 'Not of course that I haven't every confidence ... But, you know, I just wasn't designed for ocean-going. You don't think it will rock much, do you?'

Evans shook his head. 'I don't think so.'

Duval and his assistants arrived and sat down at their end of the table.

'Didn't blow up after all, did it, Skipper?' said Duval.

'We're not there yet,' Evans could not resist saying this. Duval liked to be positive. Especially about things which were none of his business.

'Well, it looks to me like clear sailing.' Duval spoke flatly. He stirred his coffee.

'How fast are we going?' asked Hodges suddenly.

'Nine, maybe ten knots,' Evans answered.

'Nearer twelve, I'd say,' commented the Chief.

'Engineers are all the same,' said Evans. The Chief said nothing.

'You people should be going home shortly,' Major Barkison announced. Evans looked up and the others were interested, too.

'Yes,' the Major continued, 'we're going to close down Andrefski, as you've probably gathered. That's why I was out there. When it closes down those of you who are due for rotation will probably get it. We don't need any more sailors here.'

'That's good news,' said Evans thoughtfully. The Chief and his assistants questioned the Major further and Evans thought of Seattle. He would get married again. That would be the first thing he would do. After that he would get a second mate's berth on some liner. He would come back to these islands again. Someday, perhaps, he might get a fishing boat and live in Seward. There were many things that he would do.

'If you'll excuse me,' said the Major, rising, 'I think I'll write some more letters.' The other passengers also left the table.

'Martin tells me,' said Duval, 'that the barometer's still low. What do you think's wrong?'

Evans shrugged. 'I don't know. We'll have to wait and see what happens.'

'We were going to do that anyway,' said the Chief sourly and he left the table, his assistants close behind.

Evans wondered why he had so much trouble getting along with his crews. When he had been a second mate on a cargo ship he had had no trouble, in fact he had even been popular. Somehow things just didn't work as easily aboard this ship. He wondered if he might not be too much of a perfectionist. People didn't like to live with that sort of thing. He spun his coffee mug between his hands. Finally he stood up. 'Smitty,' he said loudly. 'You can clear the table now.'

Bervick had the case off the barometer, when Evans returned to the wheelhouse. Bervick and Martin were examining the mechanism.

'Find anything wrong?' asked Evans.

Bervick shook his head. 'There's nothing wrong with it. The thing's in good order.' Evans frowned. He did not like to think of what would happen if this reading were correct. He went to the chart table.

They would be off Kulak around one o'clock in the afternoon. Between his present position and Kulak there was open sea and no protection. He felt suddenly sick. Without a word to the others he walked out on deck.

The air was cool and moist. There was no wind and no sign of wind. Dark clouds hung motionless in the air. He felt the vastness of this sea and the loneliness of one small boat on the dividing line between grey sky and grey water. They were quite alone out here and he was the only one who realized it. This was very sad, and feeling sad and lonely he went back into the wheelhouse.

Martin and Bervick had gone below, he was told by the man at the wheel.

Evans stood by the window on the port side and watched Ilak disappear. Snow, coming from the west, he noticed, was bringing wind with it. He closed the windows.

Martin returned silently. He looked at the snow clouds. 'We won't be able to see so well,' he said.

Evans nodded. 'We got the times figured out pretty well. I don't like coming so near to Kulak, sailing blind.'

They waited then for the snow to start.

At a few minutes to nine whiteness flooded them. Snow splattered softly on the window glass. Luckily there was enough wind to keep it from collecting on the windows. Below them Evans could see the deck being covered with snow. The sea had increased in size but was not yet large.

Bervick joined them.

'Just a little snow,' said Evans.

'That's the way a lot of them start.'

'A lot of what?'

'Williwaws.'

'Sometimes, maybe.' Evans thought of the low barometer.

'Remember that one off Umnak?' asked Bervick.

'Sure, I remember it.'

'That one started this way.'

'Not with snow. It started with a little wind.'

'A little wind like this and a lot of snow. You remember the snow, don't you?'

'Yes, I guess I forgot about it. That was a year ago.'

'That was a lousy thing.'

'We got out of it fine.' Evans' hands were cold and his stomach kept being flooded with something.

'Sure, we got out of it. Our luck should hold.' Bervick sounded cheerful.

'It had better,' said Evans and he blew on his hands to warm them.

II

'Not much change,' said Martin. Evans had been in the engine room with Duval since lunch. It was two o'clock now and snow still swept over the water.

Evans looked gloomily at the whiteness. Martin watched him closely to see what his reactions were. Evans only frowned.

To the south the snow flurries were thinning a little and they could see the dark outline of Kulak. They had been abeam the island for over an hour.

'Kulak,' remarked Evans.

'We've been in sight of it since one.'

'A lot of good harbours there,' said Evans.

'Thinking of anchoring, maybe?'

'I'm always thinking of anchoring.' Evans walked over to the compass and watched it.

Martin yawned. The monotony of waiting was beginning to get on his nerves.

Evans walked slowly about the wheelhouse. 'That wind's a lot stronger outside,' he said suddenly.

Martin was surprised. 'I don't think so. I think you're wrong.'

'Don't tell me I'm wrong,' Evans flared. Martin said nothing; he had seen Evans upset before. Sometimes he acted oddly. 'Weather's changing,' said Evans more quietly. 'I can feel it. Look,' he pointed to the island, 'the snow's thinning. That means the wind's picked up. Besides, feel the sea.'

Martin noticed for the first time that the ship was tossing much more than it had an hour before. He had been daydreaming and had not noticed the gradual change.

Evans opened one of the windows and the familiar roar of wind and water filled the wheelhouse. Snowflakes flew in and melted quickly, leaving wet marks on the deck.

The snow flurries were disappearing and every moment the shores of the island became clearer. The sea was large though not yet dangerous.

'I don't like it,' said Evans.

'Barometer's still low,' said Martin helpfully.

'I know. Did we nest that boom, the one on the port side?'

'We did it last night, remember?'

'That's right. The hatches are pretty well battened down ...' Evans' voice trailed into silence.

A wave crashed over the bow and the whole ship shook. Martin slipped on the linoleum-covered deck; he caught himself before he fell. Evans was holding onto the wheel and did not lose his balance. The man at the wheel swung them back on course.

Through the open window blasts of wind whistled into the wheelhouse. Martin slammed the window shut. It was almost quiet with the window shut.

'You didn't want that open, did you?'

'No. Go write up our position and the barometer reading in the logbook.'

Martin obeyed. When he had finished he stood by the telegraph.

'What do you think's happening?' he asked.

'I don't know. I haven't got any idea. Where's Bervick?'

'I think he went to the fo'c'sle to get one of the men.'

Evans swore loudly. 'Why did you let him go up there? He should have stayed here. Why didn't he have sense to stay here?'

'What's the matter with you?' Martin was irritated. 'What's so bad about his going there? It's none of my business.'

'How,' said Evans tightly, 'do you think he's going to get back if the wind gets any worse? He's going to be stuck there and no damned use at all.'

'That certainly's too bad,' snarled Martin. 'You want me to send out a carrier pigeon?'

Evans started to say something. He thought better of it, though. He walked across the slanting deck without speaking.

Martin, still angry, looked at the sea. He was surprised to see that the snow had almost stopped, and that black clouds hung in the sky and a strong wind was lashing the waves.

He turned around to speak to Evans and at that moment the williwaw hit the ship.

Martin was thrown across the wheelhouse. There was a thundering in his ears. He managed to grasp the railing and, desperately, he clung to it.

The wheelhouse hit the water with a creaking smack. For a minute the deck of the wheelhouse was at a right angle with the water. Then, slowly, the ship righted herself.

Evans, he saw, lay flat on the steep deck. The man who had been at the wheel was huddled near the companionway. The wheel was spinning aimlessly.

The ship shuddered as tremendous waves lifted her high in the air. Martin, confused and helpless, shut his eyes and wished that the huge sound of the wind would go away.

When he opened his eyes again he saw Evans crawling on hands and knees across the deck. Martin watched him move closer and closer to the wheel. A sudden lunge of the ship and Evans was thrown against it. Quickly he caught the wheel. Martin watched as Evans fought grimly to keep on course.

Through the windows, Martin could see what was happening. They were being driven towards the island. Evans was trying to hold them on any course away from shore.

Another jolt; a mountain of water swept over the wheelhouse. Evans was thrown against the bulkhead on the port side. Water streamed into the wheel-house from new-made cracks.

Again the ship righted herself and again Evans started his slow crawl over the deck, only now the deck was slick with water. As the ship reached the crest of a wave Evans got to his feet and made a dash for the wheel. But this time he was flung against the door of the companionway. The man who had been at the wheel lay beside him.

Evans shouted something to Martin. The noise was too much and his voice did not carry. Evans gestured furiously with his hands. Martin understood him finally. Evans wanted the engines stopped.

Martin ran to the telegraph and, before a new wave hit them, he rang the engine room. Even in that moment he wondered what good it would do. He got back to his railing.

Luckily, Martin noticed, they were headed at an angle for the shore. They would not hit for a little while. He looked at Evans and saw that he was vomiting. He had never seen Evans sick before.

The wind, howling more loudly than ever, pushed them almost sideways at the island. The ship's side was held at a forty-five-degree angle. Once again, as Martin watched, Evans tried to get his hands on the wheel.

He got safely across the deck. Distantly, as though he were only an onlooker, Martin watched Evans struggle with the whirling wheel. Then there was a crash that shook the whole ship and Martin lost his grip on the railing.

He felt surprised, and that was all, as he was flung lightly to the other end of the wheelhouse. There was an explosion in his head and the last thing he saw was the dark blue-green of the bulkhead.

Duval was sitting in the salon. Major Barkison, the Chaplain and Hodges were playing cards. Smitty was clearing away the lunch.

Duval was about to get up and go to his engine room when the whole ship seemed to turn upside down. He was pinned between the bench and the table.

Across the saloon he saw the deck of cards scatter into the air. The Major, who had been sitting in a chair, was thrown heavily on the deck.

Hodges had fallen against one of the bulkheads. He was trying to find something to hold onto.

The Chaplain, like Duval, had been pinned between the bench and the table. His eyes were closed and his face very white. His lips were working quickly.

Slowly the ship righted herself. Duval thought of his engine room. He would have to get back to it. He started to move from behind the table but another gust of wind flattened the ship on the water. He relaxed and waited.

He was surprised at the force of the wind. It must be over a hundred ten miles an hour, he thought. He tried to think calmly. They would, of course, ride it out and then anchor somewhere.

Major Barkison staggered to his table and grasped it firmly. In the galley Duval could hear, even over the roar of the wind, the sound of crashing china. He noticed Smitty in the companionway, his feet braced against the bulkhead.

Hodges ran across the deck and sat down on the bench behind the Chaplain's table. The Chaplain's eyes were still closed, his face still pale.

The ship creaked and groaned and shuddered as the wind, almost capsizing her, pressed the port side to the sea.

Duval got to his feet. Holding the table tightly, he went towards the companionway. Then, when he was as close as he could get without letting go of the table, he jumped.

For a second he wondered if he had broken anything. He had tripped over Smitty and had fallen on the deck. He flexed his arms and legs. Nothing seemed to be wrong. Smitty, he could hear, was praying loudly.

Carefully the Chief worked his way down the companionway and into the engine room.

Each assistant was holding onto one of the engines. They were frightened. Duval pointed to the engines and raised his eyebrows in question: were they all right? The two men nodded.

He worked his way, without falling, back to his cabin. Everything that could have been broken was broken. Clothes were scattered over the deck. He sat on his bunk.

For the first time he noticed a pain in his knee. He felt the kneecap. Waves of pain shook him. He wondered if it was cracked and if so what he should do.

A sudden lurch of the ship and he forgot about his knee. He went back to the engine room. His assistants were still standing by.

The oiler who had been sick lay quietly on the deck. He had passed out.

Duval stood close to his first assistant. 'No ring yet?' he yelled, pointing to the telegraph.

The man shook his head.

'Stop her O.K.?'

The man nodded.

There was a loud crash. Duval looked around and saw water trickling down the companionway. A porthole must have broken in the saloon.

The Chief waited for Evans to ring instructions; he wondered if this was to be the way he would die. He had thought about it, often, dying up in the islands. Everyone had thought about it. He had never thought, though, that he would come this close. New Orleans was a much better place to die.

The loud ring of the telegraph startled him. He nodded to his assistants. They spun the mechanism which stopped the engines. This done, the real wait began.

'Where we heading?' the man next to him shouted.

Duval thought a moment. He had not noticed and he did not know. He shook his head.

The same question was in each of their minds: were they heading for the island and the rocks? Those sharp tall rocks, much pounded by the sea.

He cursed himself for not having noticed. Just to know where they were going, without being able to do anything about it, was better than knowing nothing.

From above there came a loud splintering and a crash. He wondered what had happened. He wondered if he should go up on deck, but his knee was bothering him. He might not be able to get back.

The Chief held tightly to the engine as the ship rocked in the wind. He and his assistants waited. That was all they could do.

Bervick had gone into the fo'c'sle to get the fat cook.

Smitty had complained that he could not take care of lunch alone with the ship pitching.

Several men were in the fo'c'sle. The fat cook was asleep in his bunk. Bervick shook him. 'Come on and get up. You got to help out in the galley.'

The fat cook yawned and swore. Slowly he hoisted himself out of the bunk. Bervick played with the dog.

'Hey, Bervick,' said one of the men, 'anything new going on? We're jumping around quite a bit. I thought the Skipper said there wasn't going to be no more storm.'

'Looks like he's wrong. The sea's a lot bigger.'

'You're telling me.'

The fat cook was finally ready. They climbed the ladder to the main deck. Bervick looked out the porthole. He could not believe what he saw. A high hill of grey-black water was sweeping down on them.

'Get down,' he shouted to the cook who was below him on the ladder. They were too late. Both were thrown back into the fo'c'sle.

The lights went out and in the darkness there were shouts from the surprised men. Bervick reached into his pocket and lit a match. Mattresses and blankets had been thrown against the port side. The men were clinging to the bunks. The match went out.

Guided by the pale grey light from the porthole above the ladder, Bervick climbed up against and looked out at the deck. The wind had blown the rigging loose from the mast and the ropes twisted in the air; many of them had been blown out to sea.

The ship was pressed close to the sea on the port side. The wheelhouse slapped the water with each new gust of wind. Waves, higher than he had ever seen before, swept over the decks. Water streamed over him from cracks in the deck.

Then Bervick saw that they were being driven towards the shore. The ship was out of control. No one could control her now.

Wind, almost visible in its strength, struck at the ship. One of the booms became loose. Horrified, Bervick watched it swing back and forth.

Quite easily the boom knocked the signal light off the top of the wheelhouse.

For a moment Bervick considered what his chances were of reaching the wheelhouse in this wind. He dismissed the thought.

There was nothing he could do. If they hit the rocks there was little chance of any of them living. A person might last five minutes in the cold water. But the wind and waves would dash one to pieces faster than that.

He wondered what Evans was doing: probably trying to get control of the ship. When the wind was over a hundred miles an hour there was not much anyone could do but wait. That was what Evans would do. Stop the engines and wait.

The wind became more powerful every minute. The big wind was at its height. Great streams of wind-driven water battered the ship.

A large wave hit across their bow. Bervick stumbled and fell off the ladder. He rolled helplessly in the dark. There was a sudden snapping sound, louder than the wind. Then there was a crash. Bervick knew what had happened: the mast had been broken off. In the dark fo'c'sle the dog began to whine.

The mast was gone.

Evans had seen it splinter as the wind-rushed waves went over the ship.

The man on watch crouched near the wheel. He was trying to hold it, to stop it from spinning. Martin lay unconscious on the deck. As the ship rolled, his limp body skidded back and forth.

Only eight minutes had passed since the williwaw struck. To Evans it seemed as if the wind had been shouting in his ears for hours.

His mind was working quickly, though. He tried to figure what would be the best way to go aground if he got control of the ship. The best thing would be to hit at an angle.

He looked at the approaching shore. Ten minutes, perhaps a little longer: that was all the time he had and the wind was not stopping.

On the rocks the giant waves swirled and tumbled. A white mist rose from the shore, a mist of sea spray hiding the mountains behind the rocks. His stomach fluttered when he saw these rocks, black and sharp, formed in a volcanic time.

He wished Bervick was with him. He even wished that Martin was conscious. His mind raced to many things. He thought of a number of things. They came to him in quick succession, without reason.

Evans wondered if the fire was out in the galley range. If the electric generator was still working. What, the ship's dog, whom he hated, was doing. Whether Duval still had his bandage on his finger and if not what the possibilities of blood poisoning were. He wondered what blood poisoning was like. His mother had died in childbirth; he thought of that.

The deckhand caught at the wheel and held it a moment. Then he had to let go. They could not even lash it secure. The ropes would break.

But the fact that the deckhand had managed to stop the wheel, even for a moment, gave Evans some hope.

Outside the sea was mountainous. Grey waves pushing steeply skyward, made valleys so deep that he could not see sky through the windows.

Evans hopped across the deck and grabbed the wheel. With all his strength he struggled to hold it still. The deckhand helped him hold the wheel. With both of them straining they managed to control the ship.

Ahead of them the shore of Kulak came closer. A long reef of rock curved out into the sea. Inside this curve the sea was quieter. They were running towards the end of the reef. They would strike it on their port bow.

Evans decided quickly to get inside the reef. It was the only thing to do.

'Hard to port,' yelled Evans. The man helped push the wheel inch by inch to the left. Evans slipped but did not fall as a wave struck them. The deck was wet from the water which streamed in under the bulkheads.

Bits of rigging from the now vanished booms clattered on the wheelhouse windows. Luckily the windows had not been broken.

A gust of wind threw the ship into a wave. Both Evans and the deckhand were torn loose from the wheel.

Evans was thrown into the chart table. He gasped. He could not breathe for several moments.

When he had got his breath back, Evans went to the window. Controlling the wheel was out of the question now. But they were inside the reef and that was good.

Evans held tightly to the railing. He watched the shore as they approached it.

Two tall rocks seemed to rush at him. Evans ducked quickly below the windows. They crashed into the rocks.

The noise was the worst thing. Breaking glass, as several windows broke. The almost human groan of the ship as the hull scraped on the rocks. The wind whistling into the wheelhouse and the thundering of water on the shore.

And then there was comparative quiet.

The wind still whistled and the sea was loud but the ship had stopped all motion.

Evans walked across the angled deck, and he was surprised at what he saw. The ship had been wedged between two rocks on the reef. The starboard side was somewhat lower than the port. The sea was deflected by one of the rocks and waves no longer rolled over the deck.

Martin, pale, his nose bleeding, walked unsteadily over to where Evans stood.

'We hit,' he said.

'We hit,' said Evans.

'How long I been out?'

'Maybe fifteen minutes.'

'What're you going to do?'

'Wait till the storm stops.'

Evans looked about him. The ship was securely wedged between the rocks. There did not seem to be much chance of being shaken loose. Evans shivered. He realized that he was very cold and that the wind was blowing through the two broken starboard windows.

He went into his cabin and put on his parka. His cabin, he noticed, was a tangled heap of clothes and papers and furniture.

He went back into the wheelhouse. 'You stay here,' he said to the deckhand. 'Don't do anything. I'll be below for a while.'

The galley was much the way he had expected it to be. Broken dishes on the deck and food and ashes littering the table and benches. Smitty sat silently amid the wreckage. He did not speak as Evans passed him.

The saloon was in better shape: there had been fewer movable articles here. Still, chairs were scattered around in unlikely places and books were heaped on the deck.

Major Barkison sat limply on one of the benches. There were blue bruises on his face. He was flexing his hand carefully as though it hurt him.

Chaplain O'Mahoney sat very stiffly behind the table. His dark hair was in his eyes and sweat trickled down his face. He managed to smile as Evans entered.

Hodges, looking no worse for the storm, was peering out one of the portholes.

'Everyone all right?' Evans asked.

'I believe so,' said the Chaplain. 'We three aren't very damaged.'

'Is it going to sink?' asked the Major, looking up.

'This ship? No, we're not going to sink. Not today anyway.'

'What happened?' asked Hodges. 'What did we hit?'

'We're stuck between two rocks inside a reef. We've been lucky.'

'When are you going to get us out of here?' The Major was frightened. They were all frightened but the Major showed it more than the others.

'Just as soon as the wind lets up.'

'Is that long?' asked Hodges.

'I don't know. There's a first aid kit in the galley locker.' Evans went down the companionway and into the engine room.

Everything looked normal here. The two assistant engineers were checking their numerous gauges and the Chief was oiling a piece of machinery.

'What the hell did you hit?' asked the Chief. He did not seem bothered by what had happened and this annoyed Evans.

'We hit a rock, that's what we hit. How are the engines?'

'I think they're all right. The propellers aren't touching bottom and you can thank God that they aren't.'

'Will she be able to go astern?'

'I don't see why not. Is that what we're going to do?'

'Yes.'

'When do you want to push off?'

'When the wind stops.'

'We'll have it ready.'

Evans met Bervick in the saloon. Bervick was wet from his dash across the open deck.

'What's the fo'c'sle doing?' asked Evans. 'Leaking?'

'No, we was lucky. We're hung up just under the bow. We've lost our guardrail and that's about all.'

'Good.' Evans looked through the after door. The sea crashed all around them, the white sea spray formed a cloud about them.

'Should be over soon,' remarked Bervick. 'I think it'll be over soon.'

'Yes, it should be over,' said Evans and he turned and walked back towards the wheelhouse.

III

Bervick walked on the forward deck.

Since sundown the wind had almost died away. Water rippled about them and the ship creaked as she moved back and forth between the two rocks.

There was only a sharp stump where the mast had been. A few bits of rigging were scattered on the deck; for the most part the deck was clean of all debris.

One of the ventilators was gone and someone had covered up the hole where it had been with a piece of canvas. The other ventilator was slightly bent; otherwise, it was in good shape.

To his left rose the mountains of Kulak. They were like all the other mountains in the islands. The closer one was to them the more impressive they were.

He walked to the railing and leaned over and touched the hard wet rock that shielded them from the last gusts of the wind.

Martin came slowly towards him. He walked unsurely. The knocking he had taken had weakened him.

'Here we are,' he said.

Bervick nodded. 'We got real messed up. It's the dry-dock for us if we get back.'

'Hope we're sent to Seward. I like Seward.'

'Nice town for Alaska. Maybe we'll get sent down to Seattle.'

'My luck's not that good.' Martin leaned over the railing and ran his hand over the shattered guardrail. 'You think we'll get off these rocks all right?'

'I think so. Maybe we knocked a hole in the bottom. If that happened we got no chance.'

'Maybe we didn't get a hole.'

'That's the right idea.'

They walked on the deck, looking for damage.

The cover to the anchor winch had blown away; the winch itself was not damaged.

'Let's go up top,' said Martin. 'Evans wants us to check the lifeboats.'

The top of the wheelhouse was much battered. One of the two lifeboats was splintered and useless. Martin laughed.

'Those things aren't any use anyway, not up here they aren't.'

'Sometimes you can get away.'

'In a lifeboat like that?'

'Sure, it's been done.'

'I wouldn't like to do that.'

'Neither would I,' Bervick tested the broken hull of the lifeboat with his hand. The wood creaked under the pressure.

'Let's go below,' said Martin. 'That's no good any more.'

'I guess you're right.'

They crossed the bridge and went into the wheelhouse. Evans was at the chart table. 'What did you find?' he asked.

'One lifeboat knocked up and one ventilator on the forward deck gone,' said Bervick.

'I saw the ventilator go,' said Evans. 'You say the lifeboat's out of commission?'

'That's right.'

'Shipyard for us,' said Evans and that was all. He turned back to his charts. Evans put on an act sometimes, thought Bervick.

'We're going below, Skipper,' said Bervick and he and Martin left the wheelhouse.

Duval was in the saloon. His coveralls were smeared with grease and he looked gaunt. He was sitting at the table, alone.

'When're we leaving this place?' he asked.

'Pretty soon,' answered Bervick. 'How're your engines?'

'I guess they'll be all right. You'll find out soon enough.'

Bervick looked at the Chief's grease-stained overalls. 'You have some trouble?'

'One of the pumps stopped working. I think we got it fixed. The boys are testing it now.'

'You look beat,' commented Martin.

'You would be too. How did Evans manage to get us on the rocks, I wonder?'

'He didn't,' said Bervick. 'Just fool's luck that we got out of this thing this well.'

'You mean so far,' said the Chief sourly.

Bervick looked at him with dislike. Usually when they were working together there was no enmity but now, even on the rocks, he could not keep from disliking Duval.

'What's happened to the passengers?' asked Martin.

'Damned if I know. They've probably gone out on deck or hit their sacks. That Major certainly got excited.'

'They all seemed excited,' remarked Bervick.

'I suppose you weren't.' The Chief stood up and sighed deeply. 'I think I'll talk to Evans and see what's going to happen.' He had started to leave when Evans came into the saloon.

'When we going?' asked the Chief.

'Right away. Say, Martin, you take some men and go on deck and stand by while we go astern.'

Martin left the saloon. 'Are you going to be able to handle the engines all right?' asked Evans, turning to the Chief.

'I think so. What're you going to do, go half speed astern?'

'Full speed, I think. Depends how tight we are. Come on, Bervick.'

Someone had tacked pieces of canvas over the broken windows in the wheelhouse. 'Handle the telegraph for me,' said Evans.

'O.K.' Bervick looked out the window and saw Martin with several deckhands. They were standing on the bow, waiting. Lieutenant Hodges was also on the forward deck.

Evans manoeuvred the wheel for several moments. 'Ring Stand By,' he said at last. Bervick set the markers on Stand By. The Chief rang back quickly.

'Slow Astern,' said Evans.

Bervick rang the engine room again. The regular throbbing of the engines began. The ship creaked and shifted slightly.

'Half Speed Astern,' said Evans, his hands clutching the wheel tightly.

Bervick rang for Half Speed. The ship trembled. There was a ripping sound as they began to move from between the rocks. 'There goes the guardrail,' said Bervick.

'Full Speed Astern,' said Evans.

Bervick set the markers on Full Speed. 'Here we go,' he said.

The ship, with much groaning as pieces of wood were torn from the bow, moved away from the rocks.

Evans swung the wheel hard to port. There was a suspended instant and then the bow splashed off the rocks. The ship rolled uncertainly for a moment. Then they were free.

'Cut the engines,' said Evans.

The ship drifted away from shore. 'So far so good,' said Evans. 'Give her Slow Ahead.' As the ship moved ahead Evans swung the bow out to sea.

'Now we can wait,' he said.

'For the leaks to start?'

'For the leaks.'

'Maybe I ought to go see the Chief, see how the pumps are working,' suggested Bervick.

'Sure, go below.'

The engine room was hot. Fumes from the engines made the air almost unbreathable. Duval was watching the gauges. His assistants stood beside the engines.

'Evans wants to know if the pumps are working.'

'Tell him I think so. Got good pressure.'

'I guess the engines weren't bothered at all.'

'You can be glad of that.'

Bervick went up to the saloon. Martin was looking out the porthole at the island shore.

'We made it,' said Bervick.

'Yes, we got off the rocks. I was afraid for a while we weren't going to be able to. We were really jammed in there. Took the whole guardrail off.'

'Did you look in the fo'c'sle to see if there were any leaks?'

'No. You think we should?'

'Yes. You take the fo'c'sle and I'll go down in the hold.'

On deck the wind was brisk but not strong. The air was clearer but the sky was still overcast. With night coming the weather might yet be good.

Bervick slipped the covering off one end of the hatch. Carefully he went down the narrow ladder. The hold was dark and damp and smelled of salt and wood. When he got to the bottom he turned on a light.

There were several crates of machinery on the deck of the hold. They had not been given much cargo to carry on this trip. Pieces of tarpaulin and lengths of line were strewn over the deck. Ammunition for the ship's gun rolled about the hold. They had dismantled most of their gun and had stored the pieces. No one ever saw the Japanese in these waters.

Bervick examined the damp bulkheads carefully. They seemed to be sound. He walked over the deck and could not find any sign of a leak.

He turned off the light and climbed out of the hold. Martin was standing by the railing.

'Find anything?' Bervick asked.

Martin shook his head. 'Everything fine. You find anything?'

'No.' They went aft to the saloon. Martin went above to tell Evans about their inspection.

Major Barkison was in the saloon when Bervick entered. He was nervous; his fingers played constantly with his belt buckle.

'Do you think it's over for good?' he asked.

'I expect so. The heat of the storm's gone by us.'

'I hope so. That was really dreadful, the rocks and all that wind. Does this happen often?'

'Occasionally it happens.'

'It was awful. We'll get back all right now, though. Won't we?'

'I hope so. Evans is good, he knows his business. I wouldn't be too worried.'

'No, I suppose it's all over.' The Major shuddered. 'That wind, I've never seen anything like it. It was terrible, all that wind.' The Major sat down heavily.

Evans came into the saloon. He seemed cheerful. He was smiling.

'Martin tells me there aren't any leaks.'

Bervick nodded, 'That's right.'

'We'll get there then. I'm hungry. Is Smitty around?'

'I think he's below. I'll get him.'

'Fine.'

'I gather,' said the Major slowly, 'that the storm is over.'

'Well, it looks like it. Never can tell, of course. We may have some more but the worst is over.'

Major Barkison was relieved. 'You know,' he said, 'I must admire the way you've handled this. I'm going to recommend you for a citation.'

Evans laughed, 'Send me back to the States, that's what I want.'

'I'm serious,' said the Major. 'You've done a remarkable job and we are all, naturally, most grateful.'

There was an embarrassed silence. Bervick looked at Evans and saw that Evans was at a loss to say anything. Evans did not know how to say the right things.

'I'll get Smitty up,' said Bervick.

'Fine,' said Evans. 'Go get him up. I'm hungry.'

Bervick found Smitty in his bunk. 'Come on and get up,' he said. 'We want some chow.'

Smitty swore loudly, 'I seen everything now,' he said and he got out of his bunk.

Bervick went back to the saloon.

CHAPTER SIX

I

They had steak for supper. Smitty, in a mood of thanksgiving, had cooked an unusually good meal. He served it himself, almost cheerfully.

'Such a nice quiet evening,' exclaimed the Chaplain.

'It's a real relief,' said the Major. 'A real relief. I thought for a while that . . . well, that that was it, if you know what I mean.'

'It was pretty close,' said Evans, smiling. His passengers looked much better. The Chaplain especially seemed happy.

'Yes,' said the Major, 'I think we've been lucky. Of course, we have Mr Evans here to thank. If it hadn't been for his . . . his efforts, I suppose, we'd be dead now.'

'That's right,' said the Chaplain, looking fondly at Evans. 'You really did a remarkable job.'

'Pass the sugar,' said Duval and he took the sugar when it was passed to him and put several spoonfuls of it in his coffee. Evans could see that he did not like to hear his Skipper praised.

'By the way,' said Evans, 'I think we should really compliment the Chief. He sure did a good job. If his engine room hadn't been operating I don't know where we'd be.'

'That's right,' said the Major, 'we mustn't forget Mr Duval.'

'We've been extremely fortunate,' said the Chaplain. 'Not of course that we all weren't quite ready to . . . to meet our Maker, as it were.'

'I wasn't,' said Hodges abruptly. The others laughed.

'Tell me, Mr Evans,' said the Major, 'when do you expect to get to Arunga?'

'Tomorrow sometime, afternoon, I guess. Depends on what kind of time we make.'

'Excellent.'

'By the way,' said the Chief, 'that ventilator, the one over the starboard engine; water and everything else's been coming down it. You get someone to fix it?'

Evans nodded; he looked at Bervick, 'You want to take care of that?'

'Sure.'

Evans sat down on one of the long benches that lined the bulkheads. Martin was in the wheelhouse. They were on course and the barometer was rising.

He shut his eyes and relaxed. The rocking of the ship was gentle and persistent. He had had an operation once and he had been given ether. There were terrible dreams . . . All through the dreams there had been a ticking, a heartbeat rhythm, and a floating sensation much like the sea. He began to recall the dream. He was happy, and when he was happy he enjoyed torturing himself in a subtle fashion. He pretended that he was under the ether again, that the rocking of the ship was the dream. He recalled objects that looked like straws set in a dark green background. Lights shone from the tops of the straws and deep deep voices speaking in a Negro manner came out of the tips of the straws. He began to sink into the vastness of the ether dream. There was a struggle and then a sense of being alone, of being overcome. The deep voices kept throbbing in his ears. Then there was quiet.

'Did you have a nice nap?' asked the Chaplain.

Evans opened his eyes and tried to look alert. 'Just dozing.' He sat up. The Chaplain and he were the only ones in the saloon. He looked at his watch: it was after ten.

'I cannot,' said the Chaplain, 'get over the great change in the weather.'

'In the williwaw season weather does funny things.'

'I had what you might call a revelation of sorts, if you know what I mean, during the storm.'

'Is that right?' Evans wondered who was on watch. It was supposed to be his watch until midnight. Bervick had probably taken over while he slept.

'I had a sort of vision, well not quite a vision, no, not a vision, a presentiment, yes, that's what I had, a presentiment of something.'

'Did you?' Evans was not sure that he knew what a presentiment was.

'This vision, presentiment I should say, was about the ship.'

'Well, what was it?'

'Nothing much at all. It's really quite vague to me now. It was only that we'd all get out of this, that no one would be hurt on the trip, that's all. That's why I suppose one would call it a presentiment. It was just a feeling of course. A kind of instinct.'

'Is that right? I've had them too.' Evans wondered if the ventilator was still leaking.

'Have you really? I know there's a sort of intuition, a sort of sixth sense I would suppose you'd call it.'

'Sure, that's what I'd call it.' Evans wondered if there was anything to religion. Probably not, at least he himself had gotten along without it. He tried to recall if he'd ever been inside a church. He could not remember. In the back of his mind there was a feeling of great space and peacefulness which might have been the memory of a childhood visit to a church. He had seen some movies, though, that had church interiors in them. Churches where grey-haired men in long black robes stood in what appeared to be upright coffins and talked interminably about large resonant things. He had learned about religion from the movies and from the Chaplains he had met.

The Chaplain, his sixth sense at work, guessed what he was thinking. 'You are not particularly, ah, religious, are you, Mr Evans.'

'Well, I wouldn't say that,' said Evans, who would have said just that if he had not disliked being thought different from other people.

'Oh, no, I can tell that you're a . . . a pagan.' The Chaplain chuckled to show that this epithet was not serious.

'I hope not.' Evans was not too sure what 'pagan' meant, either. He wished that people would use simple familiar words. That was the main thing he disliked in Martin: the long words that sounded as if they meant something very important.

'Well, there are many, many people like you in the world,' said Chaplain O'Mahoney sadly, aware suddenly of the immensity of sin, the smallness of virtue.

'I guess there are.' Evans wondered if Martin had recorded the rising barometer readings regularly.

'Did you ever feel lost?' asked the Chaplain in an almost conspiratorial tone.

'What? Well, I don't know.'

'I mean did you ever feel lonely?'

'Certainly, haven't you?'

The Chaplain was a little startled; then he answered quickly, 'No, never. You see I have something to fall back on.'

'I suppose you do,' said Evans and he tried to sound thoughtful and sincere but he managed only to sound bored.

The Chaplain laughed. 'I'm being unfair, talking to you like this when your mind's on the ship and . . . and things.'

'No, no, that's all right. I'm very interested. I once wanted to be a preacher.' Evans added this for the sake of conversation.

'Indeed, and why didn't you become one?'

Evans thought a moment. Pictures of grey-haired men in black robes and grey-haired men advertising whisky in the magazines were jumbled together in his inner eye. He had never become a minister for the simple reason that he had never been interested. But the thought that was suddenly the most shocking to him was that he had never wanted to *become* anything at all. He had just wanted to do what he liked. This was a revelation to him. He had thought about himself all his life but he had never been aware that he was different from most people. He just wanted to sail because he liked to sail and he wanted to get married again because it seemed like a comfortable way to live. Chaplains and Majors wanted to become Saints and Generals respectively.

'I guess I never really wanted to be a minister very much.' Evans ran his hand through his hair. He noticed it was getting long. He would have a haircut when they got to Arunga.

'Some, I suppose,' said the Chaplain philosophically, 'are chosen, while others are not.'

'Isn't that the truth?' said Evans with more emphasis than was necessary.

The Chaplain squinted his eyes and took a deep breath and Evans could see that he was going to be lectured. He stood up and the Chaplain, looking surprised, opened his eyes again and exhaled, a slight look of disappointment on his face.

'If you'll excuse me I'm going up top. My watch's now.'

'Of course, certainly.'

Bervick was standing by the windows, looking out. Evans stood beside him and they watched the sea together. The dark water shifted lazily now, gusts of wind occasionally ruffling the surface of the water. The night sky was black.

'You been asleep?'

Evans nodded.

'That's what I thought. Martin hit the sack.'

'Barometer's up.'

'That's nice. I don't like low barometers.'

'Nobody likes them.'

Evans looked at the stump where the mast had been. 'She really tore off hard, didn't she?'

'Glad I wasn't under it.'

'I guess the boys'll really talk about us now, the guys on the other boats.'

'Sure, they're just like women. Talk, talk, that's about all they do.'

'I guess they'll say it was my fault. Harms would say that. He'd want to cover his own hide for sending us out.'

'Well, you didn't have to go if you didn't want to. That's sea law.'

'That's true.'

'But I don't think they're going to say it was your fault. Worse things've happened to a lot of other guys.'

'It wasn't my fault, this thing, was it?'

'I don't think so. You ain't no weather prophet.'

'There wasn't any way for me to tell that there'd be a williwaw.'

'Well, this is the season for them.'

'But how could I know that it was going to happen? We were cleared at the Big Harbour.'

'It's on their neck then.'

'I hope so, it'd better be. I couldn't help it if we got caught like that, got caught in a williwaw.'

'Sure, sure, it was no fault of yours.'

Evans looked out of the window. He was getting a little worried. The thought that he might be held responsible for taking a boat out and getting it wrecked in williwaw weather was beginning to bother him. Bervick was soothing, though.

'You taking over now?' he said.

Evans nodded, 'Yes, I'll take over. You got a couple of hours, why don't you get some sleep?'

'I think I'll go below and mess around. I'm not so sleepy.'

'By the way, did you fix that ventilator, the one over the Chief's engine room?'

Bervick frowned, 'No, I forgot all about it. I'll go now.' Bervick left the wheelhouse. Evans checked the compass with the course. Then he opened one of the windows and let the cool air into the wheelhouse. In a few minutes he would go to his cabin and take a swallow of bourbon; then he would come back and feel much happier as he stood his watch and thought.

II

Major Barkison and the Chaplain were in the saloon when Bervick entered. The Chaplain was putting on his parka.

'Hello, Sergeant,' said the Major. 'We thought we might take a stroll on deck before turning in.'

'It's pretty windy still.'

'Well,' said the Chaplain, 'I wouldn't want to get a chill on top of all this excitement.'

'Well,' said the Major, 'maybe we'd better just go to our cabins.' The Chaplain thought that was a good idea and Bervick was glad to see them go.

He walked around the saloon, straightening chairs and arranging the books which were still scattered about. The saloon was quiet, now that the big wind had stopped. Even the bare electric lights seemed more friendly than usual.

The after door opened and Hodges came into the saloon. He slammed the door and stood shivering as the heat of the saloon warmed him.

'What were you doing out?' asked Bervick.

'Walking around. I think we'll be able to see stars soon. Looks like it's clearing up.'

'Going to be quite a while before she clears that much.'

'Well, it looked pretty clear to me.'

'Clouds thinning maybe. I'll be on deck myself soon.'

'You'll see nice weather, at least that's what I saw.' Hodges sat on the bench and scratched his leg thoughtfully.

'Hope so.' Bervick tried to think why he had come below. He looked up and saw that Duval was standing near him; he remembered.

The Chief was angry, 'Say, Bervick, I thought you was going to fix that ventilator.'

'What's the matter with it now, we ain't rocking much.'

'Well, it's leaking all over my engine, that's what's the matter. I thought Evans told you to get that fixed long time ago?'

'He certainly did. You heard him, too, I guess,' Bervick tried to irritate Duval.

'Damn it then, what're you going to do, just stand there like a stupid bastard?'

Bervick frowned. 'You watch what you say, Chief.'

'Who do you think you are telling me what I should say, anyhow?'

'Let's take it easy,' Hodges, remembering his superior rank and deciding that things were getting out of hand.

Bervick and the Chief ignored him. 'I don't want you calling me a bastard,' said Bervick. He enjoyed himself, fighting with Duval like this. Somehow Duval had begun to represent everything that he hated.

'I'll call you anything I like when you sound off like that. You think you're pretty smart, don't you? Hanging around Evans all the time. You and he think you're mighty superior to everybody else.'

'We sure in hell are to you.'

Duval flushed a dirty red. 'Shut up, you thick squarehead.'

'*Cajun!*' Bervick snarled the word, made an oath of it.

Duval started towards him. Hodges stood up. 'By the way,' said Hodges quickly, 'where are the Major and the Chaplain?'

'What?' Duval stopped uncertainly; then he remembered himself. 'I don't know.'

'They've gone to bed,' said Bervick. He was sorry that the Chief had not tried to fight with him.

Hodges, pleased that he had stopped what could have been serious trouble, tried to think of something else to say. He asked, 'Do you get into the Big Harbour often, Mr Duval?' This was the first thing that came into his head and it was the wrong thing to say.

'Yeah, we go there once, twice a week,' said Duval.

'A lot of nice people there,' said Bervick, looking at Duval.

'All you got to have is money,' said the Chief softly, 'money and technique, that's all you've got to have. Some people ain't got either.'

'You're right there,' said Bervick. 'Some people got just one and not the other. Some people that I could name are just like that.'

'Some people,' said Duval, beginning to enjoy himself, 'haven't got nothing to offer. I pity those people, don't you, Lieutenant?'

Hodges, somewhat puzzled, agreed that he pitied those people.

'Of course,' said Bervick, 'there are some guys who sneak around and get other people's girls and give them a lot of money when they get too old to give anything else.'

This stung Duval but he did not show it. 'Sure, sure, then there're the big snow artists. They talk all the time, that's all they do is talk. That's what Olga said someone we know used to do all the time, talk.'

'You must've made that up. Maybe she meant you. Yes, that's who she meant, she meant you.'

'I don't think so. She knows better. This guy was a squarehead, the guy she was talking about.'

'I think,' said Hodges, worried by the familiar pattern of the argument, 'I think maybe you better take care of that ventilator, like you said.'

'That's right,' said Bervick, 'we can't let the spray get on the Chief Engineer. That's getting him too near the water.'

'I been on boats before you was born.'

'Sure, they have ferries where I come from, too.'

There was silence. Bervick felt keen and alive and strangely excited, as though something important was going to happen to him. He looked at the Chief in an almost detached manner. Hodges was frowning, he noticed. Hodges was very young and not yet able to grasp the problems of loneliness and rivalry.

'Someday,' said the Chief at last, 'somebody's going to teach you a lesson.'

'I can't wait.'

'I think it would be a good idea,' said Hodges, 'if you went and fixed whatever you have to fix. You're not getting anywhere now.'

'O.K.,' said Bervick, 'I'll fix it.'

'You going to do it alone?' asked Hodges.

'Sure, it's too late to get anybody else to help. I couldn't ask the Chief because he's too high-ranking to do any work.'

'Shut up,' said the Chief. 'I could do it alone if I wanted to.'

'Then why don't you?'

'Why,' said Hodges, 'don't you do it together?' At Officers' School they had taught him that nothing brought men closer together than the same work.

'That's a fine idea,' said Bervick, knowing that Duval would not like it.

'Sure,' said the Chief, 'sure.'

They walked out on deck. Hodges stayed in the saloon, playing solitaire.

There was a cold wind blowing and the ship was pitching on the short small waves. Spray splattered the decks from time to time. The sky was beginning to clear a little. Hodges had been right about the weather.

The ventilator was dented and slightly out of position. When spray came over the side of the ship it eddied around the base of the ventilator and water trickled through to the engine room.

Duval and Bervick looked at the ventilator and did not speak. Bervick pushed it and felt it give slightly. Duval sat on the railing of the ship, opposite the ventilator.

'I suppose,' said Bervick, 'we should hammer the thing in place.'

'You go get the hammer then.'

Bervick walked to the afterdeck. He leaned down and raised the lid of the lazaret. A smell of tar and rope came to him from the dark hole. He climbed down inside the lazaret and fumbled around a moment in the dark. Then he found a hammer and some nails.

'What took you so long?' asked the Chief. He was standing by the ventilator, smoking.

'You forgot about blackout rules, huh? You making your own smoking rules now?'

'You just mind your business.' Duval went on smoking calmly.

'I'm going to tell Evans,' said Bervick.

'You do just what you please. Now let's fix that ventilator and stop talking.'

Bervick got down on his knees and tried to wiggle the ventilator in place. It was too heavy. He stood up again.

'What's the matter? Can't you get it in place?'

'No, I'd like to see you try.'

The Chief got down on his knees and pushed at the ventilator. Nothing happened. In the darkness Bervick could see the lighted tip of the Chief's cigarette blinking quickly as he puffed. Duval stood up.

'You have to move these things from the top, that's what you have to do.'

'Well, why don't you?'

'That's what you're on this boat for, to take care of them things like that. You're a deckhand and this is deck work. This isn't my job.'

'You're the one that's complaining. It don't make no difference to me if your engine gets wet.'

Duval tossed his cigarette overboard. 'Take care of that.' He pointed to the ventilator.

Bervick slowly pushed the ventilator over the opening it was to cover. Then he picked up the hammer and stared to nail the base of the ventilator into the deck.

'How's it coming?' asked a voice. Bervick looked up and recognized Hodges. He was standing beside the Chief.

'Don't know yet. Trying to nail this thing down.' He was conscious that his knees were aching from the cold damp deck. He stood up.

'What's the matter now?' asked Duval.

'Knees ache.'

'You got rheumatism, maybe?' asked Hodges with interest.

'Everybody has a little bit of it up here,' said Bervick and he rubbed his knees and wished the pain would go away.

'I never had it,' said the Chief as though it were something to be proud of.

'Why, I thought I saw you limping around today,' said Hodges.

'That was a bang I got in the williwaw. Just bruised my knee.'

'Well, I'll see you all later.' Hodges walked towards the forward deck. The ship was pitching more than usual. The waves were becoming larger but overhead the sky was clearing and there was no storm in sight.

'Let's get this done,' said Duval, 'I'm getting cold.'

'That's too bad. Maybe if you did some work you'd warm up.'

'Come on,' said Duval and he began to wrestle with the ventilator. It was six feet tall, as tall as Duval.

'That's no way to move it,' said Bervick. He pushed the Chief away and he grasped the ventilator by the top. Slowly he worked it into place again. Duval watched him.

'See how simple it is,' said Bervick.

Duval grunted and sat down on the railing again. Overhead a few stars began to shine very palely on the sea. Bervick hammered in the dark. Then, working too quickly, he hit his own hand. 'Christ!' he said and dropped the hammer.

'Now what's wrong?' asked Duval irritably, shifting his position on the railing.

'Hit my hand,' said Bervick, grasping it tightly with his good hand.

'Well, hurry up and get that thing nailed.'

Anger flowed through Bervick in a hot stream. 'Damn it, if you're in a hurry, do it yourself.' He picked up the hammer and threw it at Duval.

The hammer, aimed at Duval's stomach, curved upwards and hit him in the neck. The Chief made a grab for the hammer and then the ship descended into a trough.

Duval swayed uncertainly on the railing. Then Duval fell overboard.

There was a shout and that was all. Bervick got to his feet and ran to the railing. He could see the Chief, struggling in the cold water. He was already over a hundred feet away. Bervick watched him, fascinated. He could not move.

His mind worked rapidly. He must find Evans and stop the engines. Then they would get a lifeboat and row out and pick the Chief up. Of course, after five, ten minutes in the water he would be dead.

Bervick did not move, though. He watched the dark object on the water as it slipped slowly away. The ship sank into another deep trough and when they reached the crest of the next wave there was no dark object on the water.

Then he was able to move again. He walked, without thinking, to the forward deck. A wet wind chilled his face as he looked out to sea. The snow clouds were still thinning. In places dim stars shone in the sky.

He walked back to the stump where the mast had been. He felt the jagged wood splinters and was glad that he had not been under the mast when it had fallen.

Slowly Bervick walked to the afterdeck. He had left the lazaret open; he closed it and then he went into the saloon.

Hodges was building a house of cards. His hands were very steady and he was working intensely. When Bervick shut the door the house of cards collapsed.

'Damn,' said Hodges and smiled. 'Get it fixed all right?' he asked.

'Yeah, we got it fixed.'

'I thought I heard a splash a minute ago. You drop anything over?'

Bervick swallowed hard. 'No, I didn't throw nothing overboard.'

'I guess it was just waves hitting the boat.'

'Yeah, that was it, waves hitting the deck.' Bervick sat down on a bench and thought of nothing.

'Where'd the Chief go?' asked Hodges.

Bervick wished that Hodges would shut up. 'I think he went below. He went around outside.' Once the lie was made things became clearer to Bervick. They wouldn't know what had happened for hours.

Hodges began to build his house of cards again.

Light glinted for a moment on Hodges' gold ring. That reminded Bervick of something. He was puzzled. It reminded him of something unpleasant and important. Then he remembered: the Chief's gold tooth which always gleamed when he laughed, when he laughed at Bervick. Duval was dead now. He realized this for the first time.

The saloon was very still. Bervick could hear the careful breathing of Hodges as he built his house of cards. Bervick watched his fingers, steady fingers, as he worked.

No one would be sorry Duval was dead, thought Bervick. His wife would be, of course, and his family, but the men wouldn't. They'd think it was a fine thing. They would talk about it, of course. They would try to guess what had happened, how Duval fell overboard; they would wonder when it had happened.

'You and the Chief were really arguing,' commented Hodges, putting a piece of the roof in place.

'We're not serious.'

'You sounded serious to me. It's none of my business but I think maybe you sounded off a little too loud. He's one of your officers.'

'We didn't mean nothing. He talked out of line, too.'

'That's right. That's dangerous stuff to do, talk out of line. There can be a lot of trouble.'

'Sure, a lot of trouble. Sometimes guys kill each other up here. It's happened. This is a funny place. You get a little queer up here.'

'I suppose you're right.' Hodges added a third storey to his house.

'Me and the Chief, we don't get along so well, but I ain't got any hard feelings against him, know what I mean?'

'I think so. Started over a girl, didn't it?'

'There're not many up here. The ones they've got there's a lot of competition for. We were just after the same one.'

'He got her?'

'Yeah, he got her.'

Hodges began to build an annex on the left side of the house. Bervick hoped he would build one on the right side, too. It looked lopsided the way it was.

'That's too bad,' said Hodges.

'I didn't like it so much, either.'

'I know how you feel.'

Bervick doubted that, but said nothing.

Hodges decided to build a fourth storey. The house of cards collapsed promptly. 'Damn,' said Hodges and he did not rebuild.

Bervick looked at his watch. 'I'd better get some sleep,' he said. 'See you in the morning.'

'Yeah, see you.'

Evans was singing to himself when Bervick came into the wheelhouse. The man at the wheel looked sleepily out to sea.

'Fix the ventilator?'

'Yes.'

'Have much trouble with it?'

'Not so much.'

'Hammer it?'

'We hammered it.'

'Who helped you? Not the Chief?'

'Well, he stood by and watched.'

'Was he sore you hadn't already done it?'

'He's always sore about something.'

'I thought I heard you and him arguing below.'

Bervick played with his blond hair. 'We had a little argument about fixing the ventilator.'

'I'll bet you sounded off right in front of the Major.'

'No, just Hodges.'

Evans groaned, 'What the hell's matter with you? Can't you get along any better than that with people?'

'Doesn't look much like it.'

'He's going to try get you off this boat, you know that?'

'I don't think he will,' said Bervick and he was sorry he had spoken so quickly.

'What do you mean?'

'Oh, you know, I don't think he's that kind of guy.'

'I never heard you say that before.'

'Well, he's not so bad, when you get to know him.'

'Is that right?' Evans laughed. 'You don't make much sense.'

Bervick laughed. It was the first time that he had really felt like laughing in several months. The surface of his mind was serene: only in the back of his mind, the thoughts he was not thinking about, only there was he uneasy.

'Martin taking over at eight bells?'

Evans nodded. 'You better get him up.'

Bervick went into the small dark cabin. Martin was asleep and breathing heavily. Bervick shook him.

'Get up,' he said.

'Sure, sure,' said Martin wearily. He rolled out of his bunk; he was already dressed.

'Afraid we might sink?'

'Sure, sure,' said Martin and he moved unsteadily to the wheelhouse.

Bervick sat down on his bunk and looked at the darkness. Duval was dead. He imagined how it must have felt: the cold water, the numbing sensation, desperation, and then the whole elaborate business of living ended.

Evans opened the door of his cabin. 'You asleep?' he asked.

'No.'

'I'm going below now. Which ventilator did you fix? I've forgot.'

'The starboard side. The one amidship.'

'That's what I thought.'

'You going below now?'

'I thought I'd look around before I turned in. Chief still up?'

Bervick controlled his breathing very carefully. 'No. He said he was going to hit the sack.'

'I won't bother him then. Good night.'

'Night.' Evans closed the door.

Bervick lay in the darkness. He rolled from side to side in his bunk as the ship lunged regularly on the waves.

It was not his fault. He was sure of that. He had handed Duval the hammer. Well, he had thrown the hammer to him. He had not thrown it very hard, though. The Chief had lost his balance, that was all. Perhaps the hammer had hit him and thrown him off balance, but that was not likely. The ship had been hit by a wave and he was on the railing and fell off. Of course, the hammer might have been thrown much harder than he thought, but Duval had caught it all right. Well, perhaps he had not quite caught it; the hammer had hit him in the neck, but not hard enough to knock him overboard.

Then Duval was in the water and Bervick had tried to get help but it was too late. No, that was not right, he had not tried to get help: he had only stood there. But what could he have done? Fifteen minutes would have passed before they could have rescued him. Duval would have been frozen by then. Of course, he should have tried to pick him up. They couldn't lose time, though. Not in this weather. He had tried throwing Duval a line; no, that wasn't true at all. He had done nothing at all.

They would find he was gone by morning, or sooner. Then they would talk. Hodges would try to remember when Duval had left and he would remember hearing a splash: the hammer falling overboard. The Chief had gone back to the engine room or some place like that.

Bervick slept uneasily. From time to time he would awaken with a start, but he could not remember his dreams. That was the trouble with dreams. The sensation could be recalled but the details were lost. There were so many dreams.

III

'I don't see how it happened,' said the Major. 'It's been so calm.'

'I know, it's been very calm,' agreed the Chaplain.

Major Barkison, the Chaplain and Hodges were in the saloon. A half-hour before, at three-thirty in the morning, Evans had told them that Duval was missing.

In the galley the crew was gathered. The passengers could hear their voices as Evans questioned them.

Hodges sat at the galley table playing solitaire. He had been asleep when one of the crew had come and asked him to see Evans in the saloon.

Hodges was sleepy. He hoped that Evans would finish his questioning soon and let them go back to bed. It was exciting, of course, to have a man disappear, and he wondered what had happened. Hodges could not believe that Duval had fallen overboard. That was too unlikely. That couldn't happen to anyone he had talked to such a short time before.

'The decks are quite slick,' commented the Major. 'It's easy to slip on them; all you have to do is slip and that's the end.'

'I can't believe it happened that way,' said the Chaplain. 'He must be somewhere around the ship. There must be a lot of places where he could be.' The Chaplain, like Hodges, could not grasp sudden death.

'This isn't a big ship,' said the Major serenely. 'They must've looked everywhere.'

'That water must be awfully cold,' said Hodges, beginning to feel awake.

The Chaplain shuddered and muttered something under his breath.

'Almost instant death,' said the Major. 'Almost instant death,' he repeated softly. The Chaplain crossed himself. Hodges wondered how the water must have felt: the killing waves.

Evans and Martin walked in from the galley. Evans looked worried.

'Did any of you people see Duval tonight?' he asked.

The Major and the Chaplain said they had not.

'I did,' said Hodges.

'About when?'

'Around ten or eleven, I guess, I haven't kept much track of time lately.'

'What was he doing?'

'Well, he and Bervick were arguing about fixing the ventilator or something.'

'I know all about that. Did you see him around later?'

'No. He and Bervick went outside to fix this thing. Bervick came back in alone. He said something or other about the Chief going below.'

Evans sat down on the bench. The lines in his face were deep now. He seemed to Hodges to have stood about all he could. First the williwaw and then this.

'Go get Bervick,' said Evans, turning to Martin.

Martin left.

'I guess he fell off, if he did fall off, after Bervick came in,' said Hodges.

'Could be,' said Evans.

'I can't really believe this has happened,' said the Chaplain. 'He must be somewhere on the ship.'

'I wish he were,' said Evans. 'I wish he were.'

'There will probably be an investigation,' said the Major.

Evans nodded. 'They'll be running all over the ship.'

Bervick and Martin joined them. Bervick looked surprised.

'Chief's missing. That right?'

'Yeah, he's gone. The Lieutenant here didn't see the Chief after you and him went out to fix the vent.'

Bervick nodded. 'We went out and when we finished the Chief said something about going up forward. I went on back to the saloon. I guess he went on below later.'

'Or else he fell overboard after you left,' commented Evans. He turned again to Martin, 'Get the assistants, will you?'

The assistant engineers were as surprised as the rest.

'I don't know nothing about it,' said the heavy-set one. 'Chief, he went on up top around ten o'clock and he didn't come back down, or at least I didn't see him again.' The other assistant had not seen him either.

'Well, there's the story,' said Evans. 'On his way back he must have slipped.'

'But it wasn't rough at all,' said the Major. 'I wonder how he managed to fall over.' The Major carefully made his large-nosed profile appear keen and hawklike.

'Well, he'd been sitting on the railing when I was fixing the ventilator. He might have sat on the forward railing after I left,' said Bervick.

'He could lose his balance then?'

Bervick nodded, 'Easiest thing in the world.'

'I see.'

'We had a deckhand fall off that way once.'

'Of course, that's what I feel must have happened. The decks are so slick.'

'And you can lose your balance on a railing.'

'I suppose so.'

The Chaplain was calm now. He remembered his duty as a priest. 'There will have to be some sort of service,' he said, looking at Evans.

'That's right,' Evans agreed. 'I'm supposed to give it but if you wouldn't mind I'd rather have you take care of it.'

'That's perfectly all right. I should be glad to give the service.'

'What kind is it?' asked the Major dubiously.

'The Burial at Sea one,' said Evans. 'Masters of ships are supposed to read it when one of the men dies at sea.'

'Do you have a copy somewhere?' asked the Chaplain. 'I'm afraid I don't know it. Not quite in my line, you know.'

'Yeah, I've a copy up top.' Evans looked into the galley. 'Hey, Jim,' he said, 'go up and get that Manual, the grey one on my desk.'

There was loud grumbling from Jim as he obeyed.

'Will you make a sermon?' asked the Major.

'No, I don't think so. Well, perhaps.'

Hodges could see that the Chaplain was rising to the occasion with considerable gusto.

'Perhaps a short prayer after the service. Something very simple, something to describe our, ah, thankfulness and so on.'

'That will be nice,' said Major Barkison.

'Yes, after all it's our duty to do this thing right.'

'I'll bet the Chief would get a kick out of this,' commented Martin.

Bervick, who was standing beside him, nodded. 'Chief would really like all this attention.'

Hodges sat beside Evans on the bench. 'What kind of report you going to make, Mr Evans?'

Evans shrugged. 'The usual one, I guess. Lost at sea in line of duty, accident.'

'That's the simplest, I suppose.' Hodges looked at the others. They were very solemn. Death had a sobering effect on people: reminded them that they were not immortal.

The Chaplain sat muttering to himself. Hodges wondered if the Chaplain enjoyed this sudden call on his professional services.

Major Barkison, whom Hodges admired, was indifferent, or at least he seemed indifferent. His face was cold and severe. Hodges tried to look cold and severe, too.

Martin was excited. His face was flushed and his eyes unusually bright. He talked with Bervick who seldom answered him.

Hodges tried to remember something. He was reminded of this thing by the sound of waves splashing on the deck. He scowled and thought and concentrated but the thing floated away from his conscious mind.

Evans was talking to one of the assistant engineers. 'I want you to get the Chief's stuff together. I'll have to inspect it and then we'll send it back.'

'I'll get the stuff together.' The two engineers were less moved than any of the others.

Evans turned to Martin, 'You better make out that usual notice, you know the one about all people owed money by the Chief, that one.'

'I'll write it up tomorrow.'

The deckhand named Jim returned and gave Evans a flat grey book.

'Here's the book,' said Evans.

'Oh, yes.' The Chaplain stood up and Evans handed him the book. The Chaplain thumbed through the pages muttering, 'Fine, fine,' to himself. 'A very nice Burial,' he announced at last. 'One of the best. I suggest you call the men together.'

Evans nodded at Bervick and Bervick went into the galley. The Chaplain took his place at the head of one of the tables. Evans stood beside him. Hodges joined Martin and the Major at the far end of the saloon.

The crew wandered in. There was a low growl of voices as they talked among themselves. Bervick assembled them in front of the Chaplain. Then he stood beside Evans.

'Everybody's here except the man on watch.'

'O.K.,' said Evans. 'You want to start, Chaplain?'

The Chaplain nodded gravely. 'I wish,' he said in a low voice, 'that I had my, ah, raiment.'

'It's in the hold,' said Evans. 'I don't think we could get it.'

'Perfectly all right.'

Hodges strained to remember the thing that hovered in the back of his mind; the thought that made him uneasy.

The Chaplain was speaking. He was saying how sad it was that Duval was dead.

Hodges watched the Chaplain. He seemed to expand, to become larger. His voice was deeper and the words came in ordered cadences.

He began to speak:

'Unto Thy Mercy, most Merciful Father, we commend the soul of our brother departed, and we commit his body to the deep; in sure and certain hope of the resurrection to eternal life through our Lord Jesus Christ.

'I heard a voice from Heaven saying . . .'

Hodges looked at Bervick. His face was tired. A wave hit over the ship; there was a splashing sound.

The Chaplain began to speak Latin and Hodges looked at Bervick again.

CHAPTER SEVEN

I

'Snow's starting to clear,' said Martin.

Evans looked up from the chart table. 'We'll see Arunga when the snow clears.'

A high wind had sprung up during the afternoon and snow flurries swept by them constantly. For a while Martin had been afraid there would be another williwaw, but now that they were so near to Arunga it made no difference. A williwaw near port was much different from one at sea.

Martin watched Evans as he measured distances on the chart with a pair of dividers. Already he was relaxed. He was whistling to himself.

'Looks like we're going to make it,' said Martin.

'I guess so.' Evans did not look up from his chart.

'That williwaw, that was pretty close, wasn't it? I mean we were almost knocked out.'

'I'll say.' Evans stood up straight and stretched himself. He looked at the barometer and smiled. 'We'll have sunshine soon,' he said.

'That'll be the day.'

'It could happen.'

Evans walked over and looked at the compass. 'Five degrees to port,' he said. The man at the wheel began to swing the ship over.

Martin looked out the window at the whiteness. He thought of Duval. His name had not been mentioned since the service early that morning.

'What's the procedure when somebody dies aboard ship, when somebody disappears?'

'An investigation.'

'Just a routine one?'

'Usually. It's different if they disappear and nobody sees them.'

'What happens then?'

'Still an investigation; a little more so, maybe.'

'What are you going to tell them?'

'Just what I know. Last anybody heard the Chief was out on deck. Then he fell overboard.'

'I wonder what they're going to think happened.'

'Nothing happened except that. What makes you think anything else happened?' Evans spoke sharply.

'I don't think anything different happened,' said Martin. 'It's what they'll think, that's all.'

'This thing's happened before. They know what to do. They'll be routine.'

'I hope so.'

Evans looked at him a moment. Then he looked out the window.

Martin yawned and watched the small grey waves splatter against the bow. Then the snow was suddenly gone. Weather was like that here. A snowstorm would stop in several minutes. A gale could blow up and be gone in five minutes.

'There it is,' said Evans.

'What?'

'Arunga, off the port bow.'

Martin looked and saw, for the first time, the black bulky coastline of Arunga.

'See that cape?' asked Evans.

'Yes. That the port?'

'That's the port,' Evans said happily. 'Go down and see what shape the lines are in.'

'How long before we'll dock?'

'Couple of hours.'

'Fine.' Martin went below. Outside on deck the wind was cool and direct. The air was clear and he could make out details of the island mountains.

One of the deckhands came out of the fo'c'sle, the ship's dog with him. The dog sniffed the air suspiciously and then, satisfied, headed for the galley.

'Is that Arunga, Mate?' asked the deckhand.

'That's Arunga.'

'I guess we really made it. I guess it was pretty close some of the time.'

'I'll say. We had luck.'

'That's no lie.' The deckhand walked back to the galley. Martin examined the lines. They seemed to be in good shape. He walked to the afterdeck and checked the stern line: undamaged. He walked into the saloon.

The passengers were talking loudly. Their baggage was piled on the deck of the saloon and they were ready to go ashore.

'Somebody would think you people wanted to get off this boat,' said Martin.

The others laughed. 'We've enjoyed it, of course,' said the Chaplain charitably. 'But, we are, ah, land creatures, if you know what I mean.'

'I thought it was pretty interesting,' said Hodges. 'Not everybody sees a wind like that.'

'At least not many people get a chance to tell about it,' agreed Martin.

Hodges and the Chaplain began to talk about the trip. Major Barkison, looking almost as young as he actually was, turned to Martin. 'I hope there'll be no trouble about the accident.'

'You mean Duval?'

'Yes. If I can be of any help at all just let me know. Tell Evans that, will you? I feel sure that nothing happened for which any of you could be held responsible.' Having said this, the Major joined the Chaplain and Hodges.

Martin sat down. He knew what the Major thought. He knew what some of the crew thought, too: that Bervick had had something to do with Duval's death. No one would say anything about it, of course. The crew would be loyal to Bervick. Evans would pretend that the thought had never occurred to him. Of the passengers only the Major appeared to suspect anything. The Chaplain would never think of it. Hodges might.

'When are we docking?' asked Hodges.

'Around an hour or so.'

'Isn't that marvellous,' exclaimed Chaplain O'Mahoney. 'I'm sorry,' he added quickly. 'We've all appreciated what you've done.'

'I know how you feel,' said Martin. 'It's too bad we had to have so much excitement.'

'That,' said the Chaplain, 'is life.' There was no answer to this. Martin went into the galley and watched Smitty fixing supper.

'We going to Seward next, Mate?' asked Smitty.

'Some place like that. We'll have to go to drydock somewhere.'

'Well, I want to get off somewheres. I don't like this stuff.'

'That's too bad.' Martin was getting tired of Smitty's complaints. He went slowly up the companionway to the wheelhouse.

Bervick and Evans were talking. They stopped abruptly when Martin entered.

'How're the lines?' asked Evans.

'Good shape.'

'We'll be docking soon.'

Martin looked out the window. Ahead of them he saw the string of tombstone-like rocks that marked the entrance. They were a little over five miles from the rocks.

Bervick opened one of the windows and the wind cooled the hot wheelhouse.

'Look,' said Bervick, pointing at the sky.

'What do you see?' Martin asked.

'Gulls, lots of gulls. Can't you see them?'

Martin strained his eyes and with much effort he was able to see dark specks moving in the cloudy sky.

Evans looked at the sky, too. 'Well, here we are,' he said, almost to himself.

They drew closer and closer to the rocks of the entrance.

'We'll dock in about fifteen minutes,' said Evans. 'We'll be inside the harbour then anyway. You two go below and get the crew together. Remember we haven't got a guardrail.'

'O.K., Skipper,' said Martin. He and Bervick went below to the galley. The crew was gathered about the galley table. They were talking casually of the williwaw and somewhat less casually of Duval.

'Let's hit the deck,' said Martin. 'We going to tie up soon. Stand by on the lines.'

The deckhands went out on deck; Martin and Bervick followed them.

Bervick took a deep breath. 'When the weather's good it's really good here.'

'It's appreciated anyway.' They watched the men move about the deck, uncoiling lines, arranging the lines for the landing.

They entered the bay of Arunga.

The bay was several miles long. Mountains sloped down to the water. On the steep slopes were the buildings of the port and the army post. They were spaced far apart along the water edge. There were many brown, rounded huts and large olive-drab warehouses. There were cranes on the shore for unloading ships and there were many docks.

'Looks good,' said Martin, 'looks good. I never thought I'd be glad . . .'

'Neither did I,' said Bervick.

The ship glided at half speed through the nets. They were still over two miles from the docks.

'Is the radio out?' asked Martin.

'What? No, I don't think so. I don't think it is. No, I heard Evans tell the signalman to contact the shore.'

'I'll bet they're plenty curious on shore.'

'Because we haven't got a mast?'

'Sure, what did you think I meant?'

'I don't know. We're pretty late arriving.'

'They know there was a williwaw. They probably knew it here all along.'

The windows of the wheelhouse were opened. Evans leaned out of one.

'All ready to land?' he yelled.

Martin nodded.

'We're going to the East dock. Tie up on this end. Port landing.'

Martin nodded. Evans disappeared from the window.

Bervick went aft to handle the stern lines. Martin walked forward to the bow. He turned on the anchor winch.

'We'll put the bow line on the winch,' he said to the deckhand who was handling that line.

The man tossed one end of his line over the revolving winch. When they docked he would draw the bow into shore with the winch.

A crowd was gathered on the dock. They were pointing at the ship and talking. Martin felt suddenly important. He always did when he was at the centre of things. Every eye was on their ship. What had happened to them would become one of the many repeated stories of the islands. They were part of a legend now. The ship that had been smashed in a williwaw and had lost her Chief Engineer in a mysterious fashion.

Evans slanted the ship hard to port. They were headed for the dock. Martin saw that he was going to do one of his impressive landings. For a moment he hoped that Evans would foul up the landing. He didn't, though.

Just as they seemed about to hit the dock Evans swung the ship hard to starboard. Easily, gracefully she glided along parallel to the dock.

One of the crew threw the heaving line onto the dock. A man caught it and pulled their bow line out of the sea. Then he threw it over a piling.

Evans cut the engines off.

'Pull the bow in,' Martin shouted to the deckhand beside the winch. Quickly the man obeyed. The ship stopped moving. Several officers who had been standing on the dock climbed aboard. Martin walked slowly towards the after-deck. The seagulls began to circle about the ship.

II

'Handle that carefully, please.' The Chaplain was worried about his baggage and he did not like the looks of the man who was placing it on the dock.

'O.K., O.K., Chaplain. I got it all right. Nothing's going to get broke.'

'Thank you.' Chaplain O'Mahoney shuddered as his duffel bag fell wetly into a puddle on the dock. Undisturbed, the man began to load the other passengers' baggage on top of his duffel bag.

The Chaplain buttoned his parka tightly at the throat. It was not particularly cold but he did not like the thought of being chilled.

He walked up and down the forward deck while the longshoremen began to unload cargo. Men were walking all over the ship, examining the stump of the mast and the other scars of the storm. Up in the wheelhouse he could see Evans talking with a group of officers.

He looked up at the dock from time to time. Chaplain Kerrigan was supposed to meet him at the dock. In the morning there was to be a meeting of all Chaplains; they were to discuss something or other, O'Mahoney was not sure what. He wished that Kerrigan would arrive soon.

Hodges and Major Barkison came out on deck.

'All ready to go ashore?' asked the Major.

'Just as soon as they get unloaded,' said the Chaplain. 'This is the first time I've been on Arunga.'

'Is that right? Would you like me to give you a lift? My staff car'll be here soon.'

'No thank you. Someone's supposed to meet me.'

'Fine.' The Major climbed up on the dock and Hodges followed him. O'Mahoney watched them take their baggage off his now-soaked duffel bag.

'Chaplain O'Mahoney?' a voice asked.

He looked to his left and saw a long thin person coming towards him.

'Hello, Kerrigan,' O'Mahoney said, and with great care he pulled himself up on the dock. He tried not to strain himself because of his heart.

'We were almost afraid we weren't going to have you for our meeting,' said Kerrigan as they shook hands.

O'Mahoney laughed. 'Well, I almost didn't get here.'

Kerrigan looked at the ship. 'No mast, I see. We were told that one of the nastiest williwaws they've ever had hit you people.'

'Is that right? It was really terrifying, if you know what I mean. Wind all the time. Waves so big you couldn't see over them. Oh, it was dreadful.'

'How long did the storm last?'

'Two days at least. It was bad most of the time, of course.'

'Well, we had a prayer meeting of sorts for you.'

'With good results, even from a Protestant like yourself.' They laughed.

'You all ready to go?' asked Kerrigan.

'Well . . .' O'Mahoney stood undecided. He looked at his duffel bag, blotched with water. 'I'd better check with the Master of the ship before I go.'

He looked around for Evans. Finally he saw him standing with a group of officers near the edge of the dock. They were talking seriously. O'Mahoney walked over to Evans.

'I'm about to go,' he said. 'I wondered if . . .' Evans looked at him blankly. Then he seemed to remember.

'That's O.K., Chaplain. Go right ahead. They may get hold of you for this investigation tomorrow, but that's all.'

'They know where to get me.'

'I don't suppose you'll be travelling back with us?'

The Chaplain shook his head. 'I think I'll fly,' he said.

Evans smiled. He was really a pleasant young man, thought the Chaplain suddenly. He appeared a little abrupt at times but then he had many responsibilities. They shook hands and said good-bye and murmured that they would see each other again at Andrefski.

Some twenty or thirty people were on the dock now, examining the ship. Officers and enlisted men and sailors from the navy boats crowded about the ship.

The Chaplain found Major Barkison talking to a grey-haired Colonel.

'On your way, Chaplain?'

'Yes. My friend just met me. I'm going to be out near Chapel Number One, I think.'

'Well, you know where I am, Adjutant's Office. Drop by and see me.' The Major was cordial and distant.

'I certainly will. Good luck.'

'Good luck, Chaplain.' They shook hands. Then the Chaplain shook hands

with young Hodges who had been standing near by. The Chaplain walked back
to where Kerrigan stood waiting.

'Come on,' said Kerrigan. 'It's getting cold, standing around like this.'

'Be right with you.' The Chaplain picked his duffel bag up out of the puddle.
He looked at the black water marks.

'What a shame,' said Kerrigan. 'I'll help you.' Together they put the duffel
bag in the back of Kerrigan's jeep.

O'Mahoney climbed into the front seat of the jeep and Kerrigan got in beside
him, carefully shutting the plywood door. Kerrigan started the engine and
slowly they drove down the dock.

The Chaplain took a last look at the ship as they drove by her. The crew was
hosing down the decks and the longshoremen were closing the hatch.

'I'll bet you're glad to be off that boat.'

O'Mahoney nodded. 'You know, that trip took years, literally years off my
life. I don't think that I'm the same person now that I was when I left
Andrefski.'

'How come?'

'Oh, the wind and all that. Fear, I suppose you'd call it. Somehow all the little
things that used to bother me don't seem important now, if you know what I
mean.'

'That right?' Kerrigan looked at him with interest. 'There must be something
purging about being so near to death.'

'I think so.' The Chaplain sighed. 'Jealousy and things like that. Being afraid
to die and things like that. They seem unimportant now.' The Chaplain said
these things and meant them.

'It must have been a great experience. I understand one of the men was
lost.'

'That's right. Poor fellow fell overboard. He was a Catholic.'

'That doesn't follow, does it?'

'What? Oh, no,' the Chaplain laughed. 'Just an accident.'

'You know Worthenstein, the rabbi who was up here?'

O'Mahoney nodded, 'Fine chap.'

'Well, he got himself stationed in Anchorage.'

'No!' The Chaplain was indignant. 'I wonder how he arranged that. I don't
like to be unkind but . . .'

Kerrigan nodded, 'I know what you mean.' A truck came suddenly around a
corner. Quickly Kerrigan pulled the jeep out of its way.

'My gracious!' exclaimed Chaplain O'Mahoney. 'Watch where you're
going.'

Major Barkison went out on deck just before the ship docked. He did not like
to admit it but he could barely wait to get off. He stood watching as they drew
near to shore.

He felt slightly sick when he saw the bow of the ship heading straight into the
dock. He saw a group of men standing on shore. If the one on the left moved
within the count of three they would smash into the dock . . .

He was forced to admire the way in which Evans swung the ship over.

Hodges joined him with the baggage. 'I got everything here, Major.'

'Good, good. You might toss it up on shore.' A deckhand came, though, and
took the baggage for them.

'Looks like everybody's down to see us.'

The Major nodded. Several officers were waving to him. His friend, the Chief of Staff, an old army Colonel, was waiting for him on the dock.

Impatiently Major Barkison watched the deckhands as they made the ship fast. When they were at last securely moored to the dock, he looked up at the wheelhouse and asked, 'Is it all right to go ashore, Mr Evans?'

'Yes, sir,' said Evans, who was standing by one of the windows.

The Major and Hodges climbed onto the dock. They were immediately surrounded by a group of officers.

Major Barkison was quite moved at the concern they showed. It seemed that the ship had been reported missing and that they had given up all hope of seeing him again. It was only an hour before that they had heard the ship had been sighted off the coast of Arunga.

The Colonel was especially glad to see him. 'We were pretty bothered. You know how it is. I hadn't any idea who we could make Adjutant if anything happened to you. Joe, here, he applied for the job.' The Colonel pointed to a short, stout Captain and everyone laughed except Joe. Major Barkison smiled to himself: Joe probably *had* asked for his job.

'You get seasick?' asked the Colonel.

'Certainly not,' said the Major. 'You know my iron stomach.' The junior officers laughed at this bit of esoterica, and Major Barkison began to feel more normal.

'They tell me they lost one of the men.'

'Chief Engineer. He fell overboard.'

'What a shame. We heard a garbled report about it. I suppose it was too late to do any good when they picked him up.'

'Well, they never did find out when he fell over.'

'Really?' The Colonel was surprised. 'That's a new one. Those things happen, of course.'

'They certainly do.' All the officers began to ask questions about the trip.

'I don't see how you had the nerve to take a boat out at this time of year,' commented Joe admiringly.

'Well.' The Major frowned and made his profile look like Wellington. 'There were no planes flying,' he said. 'I had to get back. The General wanted my report and this was the only way I could come. It could have been worse,' he added and he knew as he said it that he was sounding foolish to Hodges, if not to himself.

'We certainly appreciate that, Barkison. Not many people would have done it,' said the Colonel.

Major Barkison was about to say something further when the Chaplain walked up to him to say good-bye. The Major spoke with the Chaplain for a few minutes. He liked O'Mahoney but Chaplains generally did not appeal to him. They exchanged good-byes.

'Got some good news for you, Barkison,' said the Colonel when the Chaplain had left.

'What is it?'

'You've been promoted, Colonel.'

Major Barkison was very happy. The congratulations which flowed in around him made up for the fear in which he had spent the past few days.

'When did it come through?' he asked finally.

'Day before yesterday. I got something for you.' The Colonel searched in one of his pockets and brought forth two silver Lt Colonel's leaves. 'I'll pin them on,' he said. He managed to get the Major's insignia off but his hands got cold before he could pin the new insignia on.

'Oh, hell,' said the Colonel, handing the leaves to Barkison. 'Put them on later.'

'Thank you,' said Barkison.

'Let's get out of here,' said the Colonel. 'We got two cars.' He waved to two staff cars which were parked on the other end of the dock. Their drivers got into them and in a moment the cars were beside the ship.

'Here's Evans,' said Hodges as Barkison was about to get into one of the cars.

'Oh yes, Mr Evans. Do you think you can come to my office sometime tomorrow? We'll talk over that investigation business.'

'I certainly will, sir.'

'And thank you for everything, Mr Evans. You did a fine job.'

'Thank you, sir.'

Barkison nodded and Evans walked away.

Barkison sat between the Colonel and Hodges in the back seat. For the first time he noticed the difference between being on land and on the sea. The steadiness of the land soothed him. He felt safe.

'You're giving us a party, aren't you, brother Barkison?'

'Certainly, Colonel. I've been saving up some liquor for a moment like this.'

The Colonel laughed. 'You dog, you knew all along you were going to get this. I bet you were counting the days.'

'Oh, not quite,' said Barkison. He was thankful now that he was still alive. He felt like making a dramatic speech. He began to think of General Gordon and this made him think of his own immediate General.

'I hope the old man doesn't think I'm too late in getting back.'

The Colonel shook his head. 'Don't give it a second thought. He was glad to hear that you're still with us. The report could have waited.'

'That's a relief,' said Lt Colonel Barkison and he relaxed in his seat as the staff car took them quickly over the black roads to the Headquarters.

Hodges helped put the baggage on the dock. Then he stood with the Major while the other officers asked questions. Hodges, as much as he admired the Major, could not help thinking that he was a bit of a poseur. He watched the Major as he talked of the storm. The Major was much too assured. From the way he talked one would have thought that he had brought the ship in.

Evans came over to say good-bye and Major Barkison was rather patronizing. Hodges wondered if he should be patronizing, too. He decided not.

'Good-bye, Mr Evans,' he said. 'We really appreciate what you did for us.'

'Thanks. I'll probably see you around tomorrow.'

'I hope so.'

Evans walked back to the ship and Hodges joined the Major in the staff car.

'Well, Lieutenant,' said the Colonel, 'what do you think of your boss here getting promoted?'

'I'm certainly glad, sir.'

'That's the spirit. Maybe you'll be, too.' The Colonel chuckled.

Barkison was quiet, Hodges noticed. He seemed to be dreaming about something. Hodges could always tell when Barkison was daydreaming because his mouth would become very stern and he would look straight ahead, his lips occasionally moving.

'How was this guy,' the Colonel nodded at Barkison, 'how was he on the trip? I'll bet he was sick all the time.'

'Oh, no, sir. I don't think he was sick at all.' Hodges disliked higher ranking officers being playful.

The Colonel and Barkison began to talk about various things and Hodges looked out the window.

It was several miles to the Headquarters. It was several miles to everything around here.

The countryside, if it could be called that, was bleak and brown. There was no vegetation, only the spongy turf. Low hills sloped down into the water and beyond them the white mountains disappeared into the clouds.

Ravens and gulls were everywhere. Some of the younger officers had caught ravens, slit their tongues, and occasionally had taught them how to talk. Ravens made good pets.

'I wonder how the Chaplain's going to get back to Andrefski?' asked Hodges.

'I haven't any idea,' said Barkison. 'He'll probably fly. Are planes flying out of here now, Colonel?'

'Certainly. They have all along. Well, except for a few days last week.'

Barkison smiled tightly. 'Just when we wanted one, they stopped flying.'

'It must have been a great experience for you,' said the Colonel. 'I'd give anything to have been in your shoes. That ship was really busted up.'

'Yes, we took quite a knocking.' Barkison looked away dreamily as though he were reliving those daring hours when he had stood on the bridge shouting orders to the men. Hodges thought this was very funny.

'I know the General thinks a lot of you for this. I heard him say so this morning at a staff meeting, which reminds me we've got a new Colonel in the Headquarters.'

'Who is it?'

'Jerry Clayton. He was at the Point before your time.'

'The name's familiar. What's he going to do here?'

'Well, this is just between us, Barkison, but I suspect . . .' The Colonel lowered his voice and Hodges looked out the window.

The staff car drove up to a long building, rather complicated-looking because of its many wings. Hodges opened the door and they got out.

'I'll see you later, Hodges,' said Barkison. 'I've got to go in and see the old man. You'll be over at the club for supper, won't you?'

'Yes, sir. I'm going over there right now.'

'I'll see you then.' Barkison and the Colonel walked down a long dimly lit corridor to a door marked Commanding General.

Hodges went to his own office. This was a large room which he shared with three clerks and two Lieutenants. Only one of the Lieutenants was in the room when Hodges entered.

'Well, what do you know, here's the boy again,' said the Lieutenant, grinning and shaking hands. 'You don't look so bad. A little pale, but nothing that a dose of raisin jack won't cure.'

'Well, you look plenty lazy.' They insulted each other good-naturedly for several minutes. The other Lieutenant was in his middle twenties and a close friend of Hodges. They had gone to Officers' School together. The other Lieutenant was dark and handsome and constantly shocked at Hodges' desire for a military career. A desire which he usually referred to as 'crass' or 'gross'.

'How's the office been?'

'Just about the same. I think our friend the Chief of Staff is going to get moved out.'

'How come?'

'Well, they sent a new Colonel in and it looks like our politician friend is on his way out.'

'I guess that's why he was down to meet us.'

'Sure, he's winning friends all the time.'

'Say, I'm hungry. Let's go over to the club.'

'O.K., wait till I take care of this.' The Lieutenant put some papers in his desk. 'I wonder where that damn CQ is? Well, we'll go anyway.'

They went outside and Hodges saw that his baggage was gone. The driver had probably taken it over to his quarters. He was glad that he wouldn't have to carry it.

They walked silently along the black roads. Jeeps and trucks clattered by them. Men on their way to the theatres or cafeterias or recreation halls walked along the road. The twilight was almost as dark as the night.

The club was another long low complicated building.

Inside, it was warm and comfortable. There was a large living room with a fireplace and comfortable chairs. In here it was almost possible to forget that one was in the Aleutians.

Next to the living room was a bar and beyond that a dining room. Hodges and the Lieutenant went to the bar.

'Beer.'

'Beer.'

They got beer.

'Those little ships are pretty light, aren't they? I mean even in good weather they jump all over the place.'

Hodges took a swallow of the bitter liquid. 'I wouldn't know,' he said at last. 'I've never been in a boat like that in good weather.'

'I guess that's right. Say, did you stop off at the Big Harbour?'

'We were there for a night.'

'How was it? I never been there but I've heard a lot about the girls there. Got a lot of Canadians there.'

'Well, they're all over fifty.'

'That's not what I heard.'

'That's what I saw anyway.'

They drank their beer. 'Come on,' said Hodges when they had finished, 'let's go in the dining room. I'm starved.'

'Didn't they have food on that boat?'

'They had it but it was pretty hard to get down when you were jumping about like we were.'

The dining room smelt of steak. They took a table in a corner, and a man took their order.

Barkison, wearing his new silver leaves, entered the dining room with the Colonel. They nodded to the Lieutenants who nodded back.

'Is that what you want to be? A guy like Barkison: more brass than brains?'

'Oh, he's not so bad. You just have to get to know him. He's done pretty well. He might even be a General before this is over.'

'No war could last that long.'

The waiter brought them their dinner. Hodges ate hungrily.

'By the way,' said the Lieutenant, 'I heard that a guy got killed on your boat. Mast hit him or something?'

'That's not quite right. He fell overboard.'

'How did that happen?'

'I don't know. Nobody knows. He went out on deck to fix something and he never came back.'

'You think he got the old push, maybe?'

'No, I don't,' said Hodges and he spoke more sharply than was necessary.

'Well, don't get so excited. It wouldn't have been the first time. Was he a popular guy?'

'No, I don't suppose he was.'

'That sounds mighty familiar to me.'

'I think it was an accident, though,' said Hodges and he said the words lightly, not making the mistake of sounding too interested as he had before.

'This is the toughest steak I ever ate,' complained the dark Lieutenant.

'That's one of the horrors of war.'

'It sure is.' They finished their dinner.

Hodges thought of the night that the Chief had disappeared. He could remember himself building a house of cards. He could hear the Chief and Bervick arguing. Then they went out together and he had stayed inside building his house of cards. He had gone out on deck once. Duval had been sitting on the railing and Bervick was fixing the ventilator. Then he had gone back inside.

'Want some water?' asked the waiter, filling his glass and Hodges thought of the splashing sound and of Bervick coming back into the saloon alone.

'What's the matter with you?' asked the dark Lieutenant.

'Nothing's the matter with me. What's on at the show tonight?'

III

Bervick came into Evans' cabin. It was seven o'clock and Evans was still asleep.

'Hey,' said Bervick, and he shook him.

'What's the matter?' Evans sat up in bed.

'Nothing's the matter. Just thought I'd see if you were up.'

'Well, I'm not up.' Evans stretched out again in his bunk. For a moment he lay there quietly, his eyes half shut. He enjoyed the gentle rocking of the ship.

'Get me a cigarette,' he said finally. Bervick felt in his pocket and brought out a crumpled pack. He took out a cigarette, lit it, and handed it to Evans.

'Thanks,' grunted Evans. He inhaled the smoke comfortably. Then he began to think. When he awakened in the morning he always knew if something pleasant or unpleasant was supposed to happen to him. Today he felt would be a pleasant day.

'What you got on your mind?' Evans asked.

'Nothing, nothing at all.'

'That's what I thought. What're you doing up so early?'

'Just messing around, that's all. I couldn't sleep.'

'You never do sleep in the morning. You've probably got a guilty conscience.'

'What do you mean?'

'Well,' Evans looked at him a little surprised, 'well, I don't know what I mean, do you?'

'How should I?'

'This isn't making much sense.'

Bervick agreed. Evans looked at him thoughtfully. He had been acting strangely lately, ever since the Chief had disappeared. Evans wondered absently if Bervick might not have had something to do with Duval's death. He examined the idea with interest. Bervick might have hit him on the head with a hammer and then he might have dropped him overboard. That was not at all unlikely. Evans smiled.

'What's so funny?'

'Nothing, nothing at all. I was just thinking.'

'What about?'

'I was thinking what a funny thing it would be if you'd knocked the Chief on the head and tossed him overboard.'

'Well, I didn't,' said Bervick. His voice was even. 'Don't know that I wouldn't have liked to.'

'It doesn't make much difference one way or the other,' said Evans, quite sure now that Bervick had killed Duval. 'It doesn't make no difference at all. He was better off out of the way. Guys've been knocked off before. Nicer people than the Chief have been knocked off.'

'I thought about doing it a lot, but I didn't do anything to him. He just lost his balance.'

'You saw it then?'

Bervick nodded slowly. 'Yeah, I saw him fall off.'

'Well, don't tell me any more about it. I don't want to know.'

'What're you going to tell the investigating people?'

'That I don't know nothing about what happened, and that's what you're going to tell them, too.'

'You think I should?'

'I sure do.' Evans made smoke-rings. He was surprised at how easily he was able to take all this. He felt certain that Bervick had been responsible for the Chief's death. He should report what he knew but he would not. He would rather protect Bervick. Duval was dead now and he saw no reason why anyone else should be hurt.

'You know I didn't push him,' said Bervick. He looked strained, Evans thought.

'O.K., then you didn't. I don't care.'

'I just want you to get that clear. I didn't push him or do anything else. He just lost his balance.'

'I believe you,' said Evans, and he almost did.

'I don't want to talk about this any more. Is that all right with you?'

'Sure it is. You know what my report's going to be. Let's forget about it.'

'Fine.' Bervick looked better already, and Evans wondered if perhaps Bervick was telling the truth. Evans puffed on his cigarette. He was not curious to know what had happened and he would probably never know. It was Bervick's business, not his.

'Going to see the Major this morning?'

Evans groaned. 'I suppose I have to.' He got out of bed and shivered in the cold room. He always slept naked, even in winter. Quickly he dressed himself. Then he looked at himself in the mirror. He looked scrofulous. Evans was not sure what the word meant, but it had been going through his mind for several days and the sound of it was most descriptive. From time to time he would mutter the word to himself. Evans combed his hair and reminded himself again that he would have to get a haircut soon.

'Are you ready?' asked Bervick, who had been watching him impatiently.

'All ready.' Evans put on his cap and they left the cabin and the wheelhouse.

One of the deckhands was out on deck trying to tack another piece of canvas over the hole where one of the forward ventilators had been. As Evans and Bervick went by him, he asked, 'Say, Skipper, do you know what happened to the hammer? The one we keep in the lazaret.'

'No, I don't. It was in there last I heard. You know anything about it, Bervick?'

'I used a hammer to fix the ventilator the other night. I stuck it back in the lazaret.'

'Well, it ain't there now.'

'You better look again,' said Evans.

'It ain't there.' The man turned back to his work and Evans and Bervick climbed up on the dock.

Evans chuckled and Bervick said nothing.

They walked past the warehouses and the docks. Bervick was very quiet and Evans did not bother him.

He looked at the sky and saw that grey clouds were beginning to thin. Perhaps they would have a good day, one of those days when the sky was blue and the sun shone clearly. He watched the seagulls dart and glide in the windless air.

Evans wondered what the Major would have to say about the investigation. He hoped there would not be too many questions. He was afraid Bervick would say the wrong thing.

A truck stopped for them and they got into the back.

'I don't think Barkison's going to be too much bother,' said Evans. 'I think he'll help us out.'

'I hope so. Not that we've got anything to hide from him, much.'

'Sure, that's right. We haven't got anything to hide.'

The truck stopped at the Headquarters and they jumped out.

They entered a large well-lighted room, full of clerks and typewriters and file cases and all the necessary impedimenta of waging war.

Evans asked an effeminate-looking Corporal where he might find the Adjutant's office.

'Right down the hall, sir. First door on the left, sir.' The man emphasized the 'sir' in an irritating manner.

Evans and Bervick walked down the corridor. The anteroom to the Adjutant's office was smaller than the room they had just left. Several clerks and several Lieutenants had desks here. On the walls were charts of as many things as it was possible to chart or graph.

Evans noticed that one of the empty desks had the sign 'Lt Hodges' on it.

'Can I help you, sir?' asked a clerk.

'Yes, I'd like to see Major Barkison.'

'You mean *Colonel* Barkison.'

'When was he promoted?'

'Well, he got it yesterday. You're the Master of the boat he was on, aren't you?'

'That's right.'

'I think he's expecting you. Wait here please.' The man went into the adjoining office and came out a moment later. 'Colonel Barkison is busy right now. He'll see you in a few minutes. Why don't you sit down?'

'O.K.' Evans sat in Hodges' chair and Bervick sat on the desk.

'Quite an office Barkison's got here,' commented Bervick.

'Yeah, I'd go crazy in a job like this, though. He sits on his butt all day long.'

'I'd sure like to make the money he makes.'

'You could make more fishing.'

'Could be.' They waited for fifteen minutes. Then Lt Hodges came out of Barkison's office.

'How are you?' he greeted them. 'You can go in now.'

'Thanks.'

Lt Colonel Barkison was sitting behind his desk, his mouth firm and his jaw set as he shuffled some papers. He looked up as they came in. Evans and Bervick did not salute and Evans was not quite sure whether Barkison was disappointed or not.

'Good morning, Evans, Bervick. How's your boat today?'

'Just fine, Colonel.'

'Good.' Barkison did not invite them to sit down and that irritated Evans.

'About this investigation . . .' Barkison began. He paused and seemed to be thinking. Then he said, 'I've been appointed Investigating Officer.'

'Is that right, sir? I thought they would hold the investigation at Andrefski.'

'Normally they would, but you're not going back there. We just got word from Andrefski that you're to proceed straight to Seward for repairs.' Barkison smiled. 'Maybe you'll even get to Seattle.'

'That's the best news I've heard,' said Evans, delighted. Bervick agreed with him.

'So,' Barkison frowned, 'I've been made Investigating Officer.' He paused again, then he confided, 'I'll tell you what I'm going to do. I'll take statements from you two and some others who might have seen Duval. We'll do all that tomorrow. From what I've already gathered I feel that nothing new will turn up. So I can tell you *now* that I'm going to report plain accident in line of duty.'

'I'm glad it'll be as simple as that,' said Evans, not knowing what else to say.

'I feel you've had enough trouble without an unpleasant investigation,' said Barkison and Evans noticed that he was careful not to look at Bervick.

'Thank you, sir.'

'Don't mention it. I'm quite appreciative of what you, ah, did. I'm not quite sure in my mind, however, that it was a wise thing to do, to take a ship out in such bad weather.'

Evans was surprised and a little angry. 'What do you mean, Major, I mean Colonel?'

'Nothing at all, except that some might say, now mind you I don't, but some might say you showed bad judgement.'

'I don't know what you're talking about, sir. You insisted on the trip. I said that we were taking a chance, that was all.' Evans tried to keep the anger out of his voice.

'I quite understand, Mr Evans,' said Barkison coldly, beginning to shuffle his papers again. 'I shall see you tomorrow.'

'Yes, sir.' Bervick saluted and Evans did not as they left Barkison's office.

'Well,' said Bervick when they were outside the Adjutant's office, 'there goes that medal of yours.'

'I'd like to knock that little bastard's head in,' said Evans with feeling. 'Did you hear him say I showed bad judgement?'

'Well, he had to pass the buck; I mean, it would look bad if people heard he insisted on taking this trip in such bad weather. He just wants to cover himself.'

'That man sure changed from what he was on the boat.'

'He's just acting natural.'

Hodges came into the outer office as they were about to leave.

'What's new?' he asked.

'Not a thing,' said Evans.

'How long you going to be around?'

'A few more days, maybe. We're going to Seward.'

'So I heard. That's a good deal.'

'I'll say.'

'Well, I'll be seeing you around,' said Hodges. He looked at Bervick a moment and he seemed about to say something. Then he decided not to. 'See you,' he said.

They said good-bye and went outside.

'What's the matter with Junior?' asked Evans. 'He looked at you sort of queerly.'

'He's got too much imagination, I guess.'

'Is that it?'

'That's it.' Bervick smiled.

The sky was blue and clear now and the sun shone on the white mountains. They walked back to the ship.

THE
JUDGEMENT
OF PARIS

For John Latouche

PART ONE

'But what are kings, when regiment is gone,
But perfect shadows in a sunshine day.'
Marlowe: *Edward the Second*

CHAPTER ONE

She wore her trauma like a plume. When she was seven an elderly man attempted to have his way with her in a telephone booth at Grand Central (her mother had been buying a ticket to Peekskill). Although she was in no way defiled, the shock was great and, to this day, she was so terrified of the telephone that she was forced always to compose innumerable messages on pale blue paper for the instruction and pleasure of those acquaintances whom she might otherwise, in a less perilous era, have telephoned.

That was all there was to it, he thought sadly, studying this one paragraph typed neatly at the top of a sheet of fine white paper: there would be no more; he was confident of that. 'She' was lost to the world, trauma and all, and the contents of those messages on blue paper would never be known. She had emerged in his mind one day, clear and precise, a lady of the highest, most Meredithean comedy, with just a trace of something more racy, vulgar even, to give her a proper contemporary relevance, but he had lost her for good after that first paragraph, watched with helpless resignation as she sank back into a limbo of unarranged words, convincing him that he would never be a man of letters: not, of course, that he had ever thought too seriously of becoming one; rather, it had seemed a pleasant way to spend a life, composing sentences day after day with a tight smile on his lips and a view of mountains, or the sea, from a study window.

His failure was complete, however, and he knew with a sad certainty that his lady of the blue notes (not a bad title, he thought, wondering if there might not be a double meaning in it: something to do with music) would remain unrevealed forever, this paragraph her *alpha* and *omega*. But that is that for now, he thought, and he gave up literature as he had given up painting and music the year before, having composed one art song to a three-line Emily Dickinson poem, and painted one nonobjective painting in the style of Mondrian. 'I am not an artist,' he murmured to himself with some satisfaction, putting the paper back into his suitcase and ending forever a never too urgent dream of creativity.

The problem of what to do with his life still existed, of course; but time undoubtedly would arrange all that, he decided, removing the Hotel Excelsior, Napoli, tag which had only this morning been stuck on his new suitcase by a hotel porter whom he had never seen until that moment and who expected, but never received, a large tip for this superfluous service, thus further darkening the none too bright reputation of Americans in post-war Italy. There had been a scene as he got into the taxi but he carried it off well and at the station, as an act of contrition, he gave the cab driver a thick pile of torn and dirty *lire*.

He hated scenes, he thought, looking out the train window at the green countryside rippling uncertainly beyond the solid fact of glass, shimmering in the heat of a white spring sun.

Philip Warren sighed happily. He was here at last: Italy, Europe, a year of leisure, a time for decision, a prelude to the distinguished fugue his life was sure to be, once he got really to it, once the delightful prelude had been played to its conclusion among the foreign cities.

He glanced out the window again, looking instinctively for modern ruins which he hoped would not be there: the way one reluctantly examines the remains of a dead dog on a country road. Fortunately, there were no ruins in sight, except the ancient, the respectable ones. Bits of an aqueduct arched over the plains of Latium, brown-brick against the Apennines . . . The Apennines, he murmured the name aloud, with reverence. Yes, he was on the march to Rome.

'This is your room,' said the clerk, showing him a room as scrubbed and neat as the young clerk himself, a fresh-faced Swiss. A big balconied window looked out onto a quiet Roman street of tall trees against the baroque façades of seventeenth-century houses – all embassies now, remarked the clerk, opening the window and letting in the sunlit air. Then after a quick briefing on the meaning and the uses of the various bells, Philip was left alone in this handsome room with its feather bed and numerous pillows, its old-fashioned bathtub hidden, along with a bidet, behind curtains. Very happy, he unpacked.

Now then: what does he look like? What sort of man or boy or youth is Philip Warren? Well, it is much too early to draw any conclusions about his character since he is hardly yet revealed. On the other hand, there is something to be said about his appearance. His face, certainly, must be described before he ventures out into the Roman afternoon and as he has not yet looked into a mirror (the usual device for describing one's protagonist), let it be noted that Philip Warren is twenty-eight and fairly handsome, slim, unembarrassed by overdeveloped muscles, flat-bellied (could one ever have a protagonist who was young and stout?) and though not tall, not short (all things to all men obviously); he is, then, of middle height, his face more square than oval, his cheekbones prominent. His nose is unheroic, small and stubby, making him look even younger than he is. His eyes are a dark blue, not very interesting but, as one writer once said of another writer's eyes, interested. His skin is still boyish and taut and except for a deep line between fair brows he has no outward marks of age or experience or character in his face.

His body, for those who are interested in such things, was well formed and greatly admired by the not inconsiderable company which had, at one time or another (and on some occasions at the same time) enjoyed it. On the inside of his left thigh, near the groin, a small butterfly had been tattooed, a memento of the war when he had been a junior Naval officer on leave in Honolulu. His speaking voice was manly but marred by the faintest lisp, a defect which he hated although, unknown to him, it was his greatest charm for, instead of sounding sissy as he imagined, it made him seem very boyish and charming: a puzzled youthful man in need of a woman's protection. As a result his success with women was quite remarkable not only because of his boyishness but also because he genuinely liked them in an age and nation where, generally speaking, they were less admired than usual.

'Do you play bridge?'

'Why yes,' said Philip, turning, as a stout bald man moved apologetically into the room from the hall.

'I'm so glad. I do hope you'll excuse my dropping in like this but your door was open and I live right down the hall and we do have so few people in Rome who even *play* bridge, much less *want* to play it. You do want to play?'

'Yes, not now, though. Some other time perhaps.'

'Of course, of course . . . I was thinking of the future, not the present. You play it decently, I hope?'

'Rather,' said Philip, meaning 'rather decently' but, in the excitement of the moment, he found himself parodying the other's British accent.

'I'm so glad. Are you from home?'

'No,' said Philip, already alerted. 'I'm from America.' He blushed as he said this unaccustomed phrase, as though he had begun suddenly to unfurl and snap, all red and white and blue in a chauvinistic breeze.

'Yes? Well, one never knows any more. The world is becoming one at last, is it not? Pleasant thought, or is it? Ah well, soon it will be a *fait accompli* and no concern of ours. My name, if I may introduce myself, is Clyde Norman.' Information of this sort was formally exchanged and Mr Norman gave him a card, a very proper sort of card which declared that Mr Norman was a director of the Fabian Trade Mission, otherwise undefined. 'I've lived in Rome almost all my life, you know. Stayed here all through the war. Very risky. Quite a story in all that, I suppose. If one likes stories, eh? But now I'm sure you have many things to do . . .'

They agreed, then, that it might be a good idea to have a drink together, to celebrate Philip's arrival.

Mr Norman was splendidly knowing, decided Philip, as they strolled from the hotel to the Via Veneto, the fashionable street of Rome. He was able to say something amusing about almost everything mentioned, or at least he spoke as though what he said might prove amusing if one fully understood the various references.

Dingy youths stood on street corners, peddling blackmarket cigarettes, candy bars and currency. The streets otherwise were discouragingly familiar. The buildings were either severe and formal or baroque and formal, their stucco façades a weathered grey-gold, the colour of Rome. The day was so very fine, however, that this momentary disappointment was succeeded by a sudden elation, a blitheness which he had seldom experienced since childhood. He controlled a sudden impulse to slip away from Clyde Norman, to run as fast as he could until he had reached the Forum, where he would sit among the broken marble and recall Horace and Keats and think how good it was to live, or to die, for both seemed equally desirable, the dark and the light, one meaningless without the other, twins and opposites. But he dared not mention this to Mr Norman who was, he gathered, more concerned with details than with abstractions.

'In thirty years one picks up quite a bit, you know. One comes to know the city *behind* the city, if you get what I mean.'

'I certainly do.'

'England is like a foreign country to me now. I hardly know how to act when I'm there, and the climate . . . do you know English weather?'

'By reputation.'

'Damp, very damp. And from September to May everyone has a cold . . . ah, here we are, the Via Veneto.'

They paused for a moment, surveying this celebrated thoroughfare. Mr Norman was somewhat proprietary while Philip found it not strange at all. The street reminded him of a minor avenue in Washington, D.C., except that it curved up a slight hill to a massive brick arch and fissured wall behind which could be glimpsed the rich green of gardens. The gardens of the Villa Borghese, according to his companion, who indicated various other sights of interest: the Excelsior Hotel, an outdoor café called Doney's where, presently, they sat in iron chairs at iron tables, the sidewalk between them and the main part of the café.

'This is the centre,' said Mr Norman. 'So many cities have no centre. London for instance has none, or rather too many: the Strand, Westminster, Piccadilly Circus, but no place where one can go and see everybody. No cafés like this one where, sooner or later, those one wants to see will come. I have always thought London must have been like this in the days of the coffeehouses.' He ordered apéritifs with unfamiliar names. They they sat back to watch. Philip felt as though he were sitting in a theatre just as the lights had begun to dim, that expectant moment before the discordancies of an orchestra trying its instruments become an overture. Mr Norman, with a smile, figuratively tapped his music stand with an imaginary baton and the curtain rose as one of the late dictator's mistresses, a plump little woman in black, walked slowly between the crowded tables of chattering people, accompanied by a plump little chow, its sad face a doggish facsimile of her own.

'I always thought mistresses were beautiful,' said Philip who had thought nothing of the kind but, having been trapped in a role – naïve, youthful, American – had the good manners not to confuse the other by assuming a character closer to his own.

'They say she used to be,' said Mr Norman, watching her as she nodded to numerous acquaintances who nodded back and then, when she was out of earshot, discussed her eagerly, her health, morals and current fortune.

'But then . . .' said Mr Norman, solemnly, pausing as though expecting an epigram on the nature of courtesans to spring sharp and original to his thin bluish lips; but as none came he took a sip of his apéritif instead. He was, Philip decided, one of those charming men whose way of speaking is so ceremonious and shrewd that they seem to be scoring one linguistic hit after another on the all too vulnerable target of human character while, actually, they do little more than repeat the clever sayings of other men . . . which takes a good memory, decided Philip tolerantly, not to mention a sense of timing and, finally, a style which was set if not by Dr Johnson then by Horace Walpole in the great days of aristocracy, after the perfect pearl of the Renaissance was misshapen by a rigid manner and the baroque was born of that tension between nature and artifice. Philip wondered if he would have an opportunity to tell Mr Norman that the word 'baroque' came from the Portuguese *barroco*, which meant a misshapen pearl. Later, perhaps, if they spoke of architecture (Philip was good at guiding conversations into home waters where, with infinite skill, he could scuttle the barks of others with some torpedo of esoterica, some bit of knowledge, properly timed; it was, he knew, the surest way to total unpopularity in a pretentious age).

'There are of course many different sets in Rome. The Church, the government (which isn't much these days), and the old nobility which is very fine and very distant, set apart. One hardly ever sees them. They live the way they've always lived in those *palazzi* and they are quite scornful, I suspect, of the rest of the world, of people whose ancestry does not go back to the Republic, as they maintain their own does, to the Republic and even further in some cases, to the gods.'

'But then doesn't everyone go back that far?'

'Yes, but the descent is not recorded.'

'Caesar traced his family back to Venus, didn't he?'

'Fully documented, too. Which proves I think that all genealogy is myth,' said Mr Norman smiling, displaying two rows of British teeth in a state of only partial repair. 'But tell me why you are here, Mr Warren, if I may ask.'

'You certainly may,' said Philip cordially. Then he paused awkwardly, destroying the illusion of cordiality with this ill-timed hesitation. Discreetly Mr Norman began to murmur, to back away from the personal until Philip, the reason for his hesitation still not clear to him, said at last, 'To travel. I have a year, you see.'

'A year? Is that all? I mean a year for what?'

'A year to travel in, to make up my mind.'

'About your future?'

'Yes, about the future.'

'I wonder if one can ever do precisely that.'

'You mean come to a decision about life in a given period?'

'Yes, to make a positive, irrevocable decision. I shouldn't think it could be done, or should be done.'

'I would like to try, even so,' said Philip vaguely, distracted by the sight of a well-known American actor who strode quickly by, scowling like Cato and carrying under one arm a new and shiny book with its provocative title in bold black letters on red: *Decadence.* The actor disappeared into the door of the Excelsior Hotel.

'Accept the moment: there is nothing else.'

'Perhaps not. Still, I am nearly thirty and . . .'

'You look so young! I thought you were a college boy.'

'Thank you. And I feel I must decide what to do with the rest of my life.'

'Even though, terrible thought, it might be, considering the state of the world (and pardoning the impertinence of my gloom), very short?'

'Or, considering my natural cowardice and cunning, longer than the average.'

'Ah, now you exaggerate. I only suggested that your life might be shortened to convince you of the very real folly of making long-range plans: they are just *not* the thing to do nowadays.'

Philip appeared to ponder this pronouncement while the waiter brought them more apéritifs, pronouncing their name 'Cinzano' as he slopped the glasses before them on the table.

The day, Philip decided, was perfect in every way: clouds burdened the west, preceding the golden globe of the afternoon sun as it sank rapidly through the blue to the seven hills of the city, to the sea and to the new world beyond that. The day was warm, without wind but not hot, not the way he had been warned it would be in the spring. Conscious of weather and bemused, he said yes and he said no as his pleasant companion advised him to accept what was, since there would be, for all he knew, no more. As he had already planned to do precisely that, to live as he pleased for a year, he found that he could agree with the older man and, by agreeing, could establish a tentative friendship.

'What precisely do you plan to do with this year of yours . . . this climacteric in your life?'

Philip smiled. 'I haven't the slightest idea. Sit at this café, perhaps. Or go and walk in those gardens over there. Or journey up the Nile, to its source.'

'You have no plan?'

'None.'

'Wise! Very wise . . . and then you're so fortunate.'

'In what way?'

'To be young.'

'One doesn't realize it at the time. I'm not conscious of any serious blessing. Perhaps I will be one day.'

'You will. How extraordinary though that you should feel that way. Are you really so detached? Or like so many of the politic young men nowadays, have you merely learned the proper responses?'

'You're too quick,' said Philip, taken aback, not prepared for the other's shrewdness, for of course it was true: he had learned to say many things which got him easily and with no exertion the respect of his elders, statements which he knew well in advance would amuse or shock or please and which had little or no relation to what he actually thought. It was a schoolboy's trick and he felt a sudden shame to be playing again the brightest boy with the headmaster, as though he were still fourteen and ruthless, without a heart.

Mr Norman had the grace not to pursue his advantage; instead he remarked, 'And then you are fortunate because you have money.'

Philip laughed. 'I have none,' he said.

'But you are able to travel well . . . That's what I mean by having money. You are not caught like me in a web of chicanery, trying to make your few pounds support you by doing all the squalid black-market things.'

'In that sense, yes, I'm fortunate . . . I have the correct nationality.'

'Indeed you have.' Mr Norman drank his Cinzano moodily and Philip watched the street become more crowded as the golden light darkened and the evening star shone silver over the gardens. He was aware, after this discussion of currency, that he would be called upon to pay for the apéritifs and this thought did not sadden him for he was, after all, a young man with an income, a small one but sufficient for the traveller's purpose and he knew that he would entertain many strangers before he was done and though none of them might prove to be angels in disguise they had, he knew, a right to his hospitality since he had come among them to learn what he could.

Mr Norman suddenly got to his feet and shook the hand of a stooped middle-aged man with a fire-red face in which, shadowed by a bird's-beak nose, two watery blue eyes danced about seemingly unable to focus (although Philip was aware that he himself had been immediately comprehended by the newcomer in one quick intense glance).

'Sit with us, Ayre,' said Mr Norman. 'I want you to meet a young friend of mine, a new friend, only just arrived from America. His name is Philip Warren.'

'How do you do?' said the older man in a curiously accented British voice, most of the stresses falling in unexpected places, a mock-Welsh voice as Philip later learned. 'I can sit just a moment. I'm expecting Guido. I said I'd meet him here. He's late. Why is he always late? Why?'

'That's just his way.'

'There is of course a possibility that *I* am late. I never know.'

'I'm sure he'll be along presently,' said Mr Norman with quiet authority and then he turned to Philip and said in a voice from which every trace of pride had been resolutely banished to accord harmoniously with a Stoic attitude: 'This, Mr Warren, is Lord Glenellen.' Since they were now all seated, Philip could only incline his head respectfully at the peer who was now insulting the waiter in faultless Italian, or what sounded to Philip (and to the waiter) like faultless Italian. Mr Norman watched his countryman with some satisfaction, smiling at the more colourful epithets and frowning furiously when the waiter attempted a mild insult or two on his own.

'About the coffee,' said Glenellen finally, as the waiter walked away, 'coffee I had yesterday. It made me ill.'

'What will you have now?'

'Not a thing. I think perhaps I'll go to the Excelsior for some decent coffee.'

'And not wait for Guido?'

'He could wait for me, you know. There *are* worse fates.'

'Of course, Ayre, of course.'

'You're an American, aren't you?' The blue eyes, milky as though filmed by cataracts, turned on him disconcertingly, avoiding his eyes, though, concentrating instead on the line of his chin, the curve of his mouth.

'Yes, from New York, the state . . .'

'Ah, I know. I know. Don't tell me. There's a state named that as well as a city. I was there, you see. Long, long ago. I adored Harlem. Is it still going?'

'Very much so.'

'Do you visit there much?'

'No, almost never.'

'Well, times change. Where do people go?'

'Nowhere in particular. There seems to be little difference now between one part of the city and another. The East Side is no different from Greenwich Village.'

'Ah, I had forgotten the Village! Has it changed much? Is it still amusing?'

'I expect so, I don't live in the city, though. I live up the Hudson River, at a town called Hudson.'

'All great civilizations,' announced Mr Norman, checking in, 'have flourished on the banks of rivers. There has never been a civilization of any importance on a lake, for instance.'

'Is that so?' Philip was polite.

'Do you plan to stay here long?' asked Glenellen.

'I have no plans.'

'A gentleman of leisure,' said Mr Norman, with a father's smile.

'Fortunate boy . . . to have no plans. Now I, on the other hand, am burdened with plans. I have every day and every hour of every week outlined for months ahead. Dinner with this person and tea with that one. A week end at Ischia; a week in Vienna. I think sometimes I am over-organized because, in spite of all my activity, I have no time for work.'

'Work?'

'Oh my goodness, yes.'

'He composes,' said Mr Norman, giving a brother's smile this time at the lean figure beside him. 'He composes music,' he added, 'chamber music.'

'When I have time,' said Glenellen uneasily. 'Tell me: where are you stopping?'

'He's at my hotel,' said Mr Norman. 'Isn't that a coincidence? I barged right in on him this afternoon and asked him if he played bridge. He does. Aren't you pleased?'

'I am pleased that he is here, Clyde,' said the other courteously. 'Besides, you know perfectly well that I seldom play cards.'

'Ah, your barren life, Ayre. I had forgotten.'

'I have my compensations.'

'Yes, yes, indeed yes. Innumerable.'

'And unmentionable!' They both laughed loudly and Philip looked from one to the other, puzzled as one always is by the private references of acquaintances newly met, the jokes which suggest vast unexplored areas of vice and virtue unrevealed to the outsider.

'But to consider you: you intend to follow your instinct, obey your whims, travelling here and there without a plan?'

'Exactly. I shall look at buildings I have heard about, absorb as much scenery as I can . . . I'm just a tourist, you know, not even a student like the rest. Then when I've had as much as I can take, I will go home and do something.'

'Do something? Do what?' Glenellen leaned forward as though suddenly eager to know truth, to attend at a revelation.

But Philip was not equal to the moment nor for that matter was he in the mood to be examined, to speak of himself when for once there was so much outside himself that he wanted to see and to know: he suddenly resented the attentions of these two odd Englishmen who, for all he knew, were mocking him.

'Whatever I can,' he said with a heavy attempt at lightness. 'Take a job . . . I'm a lawyer, you know. I graduated from law school last June, from the one at Harvard.'

'A lawyer?' Glenellen pronounced the word as though not quite sure what it meant. 'How peculiar. No, I don't mean peculiar: I mean to say it seems so strange to find a personable young American who is not trying to be a painter or some such romantic thing among the ruins of our old Europe. I suppose, Clyde, that we see only the romantic ones, the ones who have got away for a time.'

'I think it most impressive, his being a lawyer. Original even.'

'But, my dear Clyde, does one *want* to be impressed by young men? Isn't it far more agreeable to be *pleased* by them, charmed by their freshness and impracticality?'

'*I* am charmed,' said Mr Norman, patting Philip's knee as the sun unexpectedly set: the light going from gold to grey, the air from warm to cool.

'Will you go into politics?' asked Glenellen.

'I may, yes. I've thought about it. My family is in politics, back home.'

'You find it interesting?'

'Oh yes . . . but for a career, I don't know.'

'And what are your politics?'

'Darkly reactionary, I suppose. In practice, however, I should, if ever in office, devote my time to staying there.'

'No convictions . . . wonderful youth!' exclaimed Mr Norman, drinking the rest of his Cinzano. 'How different you are from the young men of my day. How much more sensible. Tell me, would you like an ice or something? a little cake?'

'I don't think so . . . thanks.'

Glenellen looked at him thoughtfully. 'I would like very much to have a chat with you one day about European politics. I have certain insights which may interest you, certain schemes which . . . but more I cannot say, for now. Though let me add that when I was your age, I, like you, was interested primarily in the progress of my own life, my time given to hobbies . . .'

'Hobbies?'

'A joke of Lord Glenellen's, Mr Warren,' said Clyde Norman quickly, too quickly thought Philip, and he wondered what was not being said for his benefit.

'A joke, Mr Warren, yes, a joke . . . and here is the wicked Guido. Late! You're late! Hear me?'

The wicked Guido heard and he smiled a smile like polished bone. He was a slender well-proportioned Italian boy with a head like a Michelangelo and a body, as much as could be seen through his suit (a great deal), as fine as a Donatello.

'This is Guido,' said Mr Norman urbanely as he and Philip rose and shook hands, while the high clear voice of the seated peer inveighed against the boy's character, accused him in English and Italian of monstrous crimes, denunciations which were received by the youth with a lovely smile.

'I was on my way stopped,' he said, finally, when the querulous voice had paused for an instant; his English was good if original. 'I find my brother has taken the only white good shirt of mine and so I went to my brother to receive the shirt once more for me. I want to look nice,' he added simply, expressing his philosophy in five words.

'Shirts, suits, shoes, watches . . .' Glenellen sighed and turned to Philip. 'Those are the only things that really matter to these people.'

'I like the motorcars, too,' giggled Guido. 'I like to drive very fast in *Alfa Romeo*. Oh good car, good car. I take cars apart. I know about things inside. Were you a soldier?' he asked all in one breath, noticing Philip as though for the first time.

'A sailor, for several years.'

'In the war? In Italy?'

'In the war . . . in the Pacific.'

'I knew many soldiers here. You might know some of them maybe. Nice men . . . very kind. I was fourteen years old so they gave me presents. A camera was given to me by one captain but it was stolen from me by one thief I know and he sells it.'

'Come, Guido,' said Glenellen, rising. 'You can tell your stories to Mr Warren another time.' He turned to Philip. 'I would like to see you again one day soon, if I may.' They shook hands. 'Do you know the Baths of Nero?'

'I'm afraid not. I've only just arrived.'

'That's so. Of course you wouldn't have had a chance . . . Well, should you have a moment to spare, do drop by tomorrow afternoon around four. I always arrive at four and leave at five, like clockwork . . . Marvellous for the figure, I've found. Not that you need to think of that quite yet, but we could talk. I have a plan which might interest you. Now I'm off. Many thanks, my dear Clyde, for introducing this young man to me.'

Farewells were made and Glenellen hurried away, followed at a more leisurely pace by Guido, immaculate in his good white shirt.

'Splendid fellow,' said Mr Norman as they watched the older man and the youth turn the corner beyond the Excelsior Hotel. 'Difficult of course . . . one of the last of those eccentric peers my country used to produce with such abandon in the old days. The supply seemed inexhaustible but now of course, with currency restrictions and so on, Ayre is the last, the very last of a great line . . . and under a cloud, too.'

'A cloud? But why?'

'Oh, for so many reasons. His life has been too colourful for one thing, too many hobbies. Then there was the scandal about his wife. I suppose you were too young to remember that.'

'What happened to her?'

'I'm afraid he set fire to her at a party in the British Embassy at Berlin. There was the most terrible fuss made . . . relations were strained at the time and this was added fuel to the blaze, as it were. They got him out of Germany as quickly as possible. The Ambassador was furious and the party, needless to say, was ruined.'

'And his wife?'

'Lady Glenellen was burned to a crisp. Fortunately they were able to get the Glenellen diamonds back . . . she had been wearing a good many of them at dinner, a number of quite important pieces too. The settings were badly melted, I believe, but Ayre had them remounted later in the Etruscan fashion, a stroke of genius as it later developed, for he started an Etruscan vogue in jewellery which lasted a number of years.'

'Was he never prosecuted?'

'For making Etruscan art the vogue? Heavens no! He received a decoration from the Pope.'

'I meant prosecuted for burning up his wife.'

'Ah well,' Mr Norman gestured vaguely, 'she was an unpopular woman, a great hypochondriac and a bit of a religious maniac, too. Then of course there was some question as to whether the fire was his fault or hers.'

'Who *was* responsible?'

'Who can say? All I know is that, as the ladies were getting up from dinner to go into the drawing room, he picked up the candelabra and hurled it at her, shouting, "Be Joan of Arc, *if you dare!*" It was the addition of the "if you dare" which saved him from more stern consequences since the phrase implied, you see, a certain choice in the matter. That she elected of her own free will to *be* Joan of Arc demonstrated a deliberate choice on her part and, as a result, he could hardly be held responsible for an act in which she so obviously concurred, perhaps even precipitated since it was well known that she had always expected some sort of martyrdom . . . ever since the day she married Glenellen, in fact, fully aware of the extent and the nature of his hobbies. Her life was one long expiation for the original sin, as Catholics say, of having been born.'

'You must tell me about his hobbies one day.'

'I should be glad to, but best of all observe him yourself. He will tell you all; show you everything . . . he has no discretion, alas. You should go, by the way, to the Baths of Nero tomorrow.'

'Are they interesting?'

'I have always thought so. It depends upon one's taste, of course.' Mr Norman looked at him furtively and Philip experienced a sudden weariness as he recognized the ancient pattern, traditional and obvious, revealed perfunctorily, with little hope and less ceremony. He gave it back to Mr Norman: gently, firmly, he folded it up and placed it on the table before him; then, wiping the dust from his hands, he guided the conversation to an end.

Mr Norman sighed. 'I shall see you at the Baths then. I often go there for the health's sake . . . to lose weight. I get stout in the summer and slim in the winter, unlike the rest of the world.'

'Does Lord Glenellen live in Rome or England?'

'In Rome. He isn't allowed to enter England.'

'Why not?'

'They disapprove of him. At least the Home Office does. Being officials, they have no humour. They don't recognize his very real value.'

'Why do they disapprove?'

'Hobbies. But now it's getting very late. Where do you plan to have dinner?'

'I hadn't thought.'

'Then try the hotel. The food is very good there. I should like to dine with you

but I have a function I must attend . . . dull sort of affair, part of my job, I fear.'
When the waiter came there was a struggle for the check which Philip won, as
both knew from the beginning he would.

'Awfully good of you, really, but now of course you must allow me to take you
to dinner one night this week. Until tomorrow then . . . the Baths of Nero. The
hotel will direct you.'

They parted and Philip made his way alone through the darkening streets to
the hotel, elated and curious, aware not only of himself but of the city, too. For
an instant, he was no longer separate but a part of it: an airy and fantastic bridge
across the gulf challenged him and, deliberately, he moved across it, above the
dark division, to the other side where strangers were.

CHAPTER TWO

His first dinner in Rome was as good as Mr Norman had predicted it would be. He had dined alone with a volume of Byron's *Don Juan* before him on the table and as he ate antipasto and minestrone and chicken and drank chianti (the sort of Italian dinner that was served in America but seldom in Italy except at the better hotels, for tourists), he read of Don Juan's shipwreck and the hilarious account of the famished mariners who ate one another, beginning with Don Juan's tutor Pedrillo.

> 'Part was divided, part thrown in the sea,
> And such things as the entrails and the brains
> Regaled two sharks, who followed o'er the billow –
> The sailors ate the rest of poor Pedrillo.'

Excellent, he thought, murmuring the couplet to himself. Then feeling somewhat stuffed, he left the dining room, receiving the respectful bows of the maître d'hotel with a bemused expression which he hoped would be thought dignified but gracious. In the lobby the pink-cheeked desk clerk gave him a dolorous cocker-spaniel look and wished him a good evening.

A good evening? It was more than that: a splendid evening! warm and star-scattered. There was no moon, but he was too happy to object to this one omission as he strode down the Via Veneto in the direction of the *piazza* where he had been assured the Colosseum might be found. He hummed the only aria he knew from *Tosca* as he followed the curving Street of the Tritons towards the *galleria*. On the way he passed restaurants and *trattorias* all open, bright with undiffused light and loud with the noises of people eating and laughing and singing sad songs. Then he turned into the *galleria*, a massive arcade, not unlike a Gothic cathedral except, instead of a groined ceiling, it had dirty glass panels high overhead. Shops and bars like profane chapels edged the nave. Young boys and girls stood about soliciting buyers, older youths sold drugs and *lire* and lovers with a sharp good humour, very different from the manner of such salesmen in other cities. Nothing was sordid here. The pimps, though shabby, were not at all sinister, and the boys and girls were cheerful, obviously more pleased than not to be making money in such an easy way. The young Swiss at the hotel had already instructed Philip in the current prices for girls, for virgins, for women and, with a blush or two, he had even quoted (from hearsay only, of course) the price for boys, and the one for men – there was a distinction, Philip had been amused to discover, but when he had pressed the young Swiss to define that difference he had only blushed all the more deeply and said that really he didn't know, he'd only heard tell, as everyone had.

But tonight Philip was not interested in finding a companion. He was on a mission of the spirit: to behold certain of the more profound Roman symbols by starlight. So, spiritually mighty, he paused in silence before the dark and rather unimpressive palace where, on a balcony, the fallen dictator had made so many appearances, burdening the newsreels of Philip's boyhood with a rock-jawed, insensitive face tilted with boundless assurance to a classic disaster. Few people frequented the square at night as though in deference to that battered ghost which still seemed, Philip felt, to brood over the palace, arm raised forever in a facsimile Roman salute; dwarfed, however, in death as in life by the fantastic marble monument across the square, the pillared white temple of the first modern Italian king, Victor Emmanuel, now a resident with the dictator in that limbo which some clever god has no doubt devised with the express purpose of maintaining the onetime great men of our world in a state of eternal discomfort, of perpetual desire and thwarted will. Philip, meditating comfortably on the folly of human enterprise, crossed the square, dodging the occasional cars which darted about, lights blazing and horns shrieking. He paused and asked a policeman where the Colosseum might be. Having had this one sentence already prepared for several weeks, he was confident that the other would be able to understand. The young policeman, with a gravely stupid frown, shook his head wonderingly and Philip said '*Grazie*' and turned down the street which seemed most likely to lead him to his goal.

It was the right street. He sensed that instinctively and he toyed with the idea of pretending to himself that he had been here before, that some atavistic memory was leading him on to the centre of the ancient city, over paths which in another life he had walked many times: a general returned from Parthia followed by his legions. He chuckled at the thought . . . more likely a prisoner from the island of Britain, a fair-skinned oaf with shaggy beard who'd probably fetch a better price at the slave market than an African, but not so good a one as an Asiatic.

Suddenly the modern buildings ceased and on either side he saw dark canyons a dozen feet lower than the street, and he could see dimly by starlight the ruins of the Forum, pale familiar shapes of broken buildings, shattered columns and arches, an occasional dark massive section of some government building still intact, reminiscent in style of nearly every railroad station in every American city. He walked slowly, quite alone. There were no other pedestrians and he wondered if perhaps the Romans had some feeling against frequenting ruins at night, the fear of ghosts, of all the bloody happenings which had taken place among this broken stone, the centre once of a world of fine law and some order, an age of silver untarnished by that Christian blight which had coincided, somewhat suspiciously he'd always thought, with the dark ages.

The avenue widened and there before him, illuminated by several floodlights, was the Colosseum, far higher than he'd ever imagined it to be, solemn in its age. He paused, awaiting revelation. None came, however . . . he was aware only that his legs were rather tired from walking and that his left shoe was pressing too tightly against his little toe. There it was, though, precisely as he'd imagined it would be from the various photographs he had studied years ago in school, in the days when he had read with excitement the stories of Livy and the *Lives of Plutarch* and the splendid, trimming letters of Cicero. Now by the floodlights which managed to diminish rather than enhance this relic, he was able to regain in a rush that youthful fascination with the past which, like a sudden tide in the blood, returned: a love of the old not merely because the old was in itself romantic nor because the worst of the dull sad moments had long ago been winnowed out by chroniclers too busy describing great deeds to note that the human condition (how he loved this echoing phrase: the human condition!) was constant in its confusion, in its vulnerability to pain. No, he loved the past for another reason: continuity, that was it. He'd always known instinctively that when he died the poignant progress of one Philip Warren would end for good.

He had known this from the day he'd first been told about death: when he was four years old and his grandfather had died in the room next to his. War had only confirmed him in this knowledge. Men whom he knew became after an air attack so many torn limp carcasses to be put in canvas bags and dropped into the sea, their personal belongings sent home to a faraway family (equipment gone through carefully beforehand, however, to make sure that no unusual letters, lewd photographs or contraceptive devices would be sent on to shock the grieved family). Nothing remained of these warriors but fast-blurring images in the minds of friends whose primary interest is never the devout recollection of the good dead but survival. Somewhere Thomas Hardy had written a poem on this theme, he recalled. But Philip, though he acknowledged change, valued the past, his own and the world's. He became, as he pondered, all the more impatient with detail, more curious about the whole design of which only tantalizing fragments had been revealed by scholars, men not unlike himself, in temperament at least, all haunted by the fact of change, which they attempted, in the only way they knew, to define, by fixing the near-true moment in the careful prose of history.

' "O, call back yesterday, bid time return," ' Philip whispered as he descended a deep flight of steps and approached the crypt-like building, eroded by weather and scarred by all the visiting Northern warriors. With a sense of one about to make a discovery, he entered a dark archway, pausing midway through the building, suddenly alert, as he realized there were people all about him in the dark. He could see no one but he heard breathing, an occasional whispered word. Finally the lighting of a match revealed a pair of lovers while, behind them, stepping hastily into the shadows, thieves and murderers forgathered to contemplate acts of violence. Although conscious of danger, he was unafraid, protected by his own conception of this battered place: no one is murdered in a dream, he knew, and like a dreamer he walked out into the open and observed with nostalgia and delight the tiers of seats which circled an arena whose floor had been torn up by archaeologists to reveal the complicated passageways beneath. This was Rome.

'Do you think the ruins of Madison Square Garden will look as impressive?'

He started. The voice, a woman's, laughed pleasantly. He turned and saw that she was behind him, seated on a fallen column.

'Perhaps,' he said evenly, moving towards her. 'Have you been here long?'

'On this column? No, not very, a few minutes . . .'

'How could you tell I was an American?'

'Only an American would come here at night and walk out into the arena. An Italian would have hid beneath the arches, doing business.'

'Are we the only romantics?'

'It would seem so.'

Was she young or old, he wondered, pretty or beautiful or plain? He could not tell. He moved beside her and caught the odour of her perfume.

'You're a student, aren't you?' she asked.

'In what sense?' he parried, remembering this stylized phrase so often used in intellectual debate when one warrior of the word, needing time to compose a new strategy, invites the other to lose his way in definition.

She laughed again, mockingly. 'Now I know you must be a student. Scholarly young men always want to know "in what sense" any question is intended.'

He laughed, too. 'I was stalling,' he said, wondering whether he should tell her a lie or not. If she were old or plain he would not for a moment have hesitated to make himself sound as romantic as the occasion and the setting insisted that he be. If she were desirable he would of course be romantic about *her* and stick only to the facts, favourably arranged. Which should he do? What should he be? He paused, knowing that his decision would be irrevocable, that, if she were to be one day a lover, it would never do to begin by telling her that he was one of the heroes of the Air Force, now doomed to travel feverishly about until the cancer which had already begun to spread to his nerve centres (explaining that tiresome lisp) finally, and in great agony, brought him Icarus-like to earth. No, he would play it safe, he decided; and moving closer to her, he said: 'I graduated from law school a month ago.'

'How young you must be,' she said, and his heart sank: he was positive now that she must be sixty with a strong resemblance to his mother. He backed away, wondering if it was too late to speak of his fatal disease.

'No, not so young,' he said.

'Then you are one of the veterans who went back to school.'

'Yes.' He waited for an opening.

'What was it like, going back? Didn't you feel too wise to be taught?'

'I always felt too wise to be taught,' he said, stumbling into an epigram, 'but not, I hope, too wise to learn.'

'Oh, I hope not.' And again he caught the mocking note in her voice. Well, I earned it that time, he thought, grimly. 'You're a lawyer now?'

'Yes . . . believe it or not.'

'It doesn't seem so incredible. There have been other lawyers.'

'But I never thought *I* should be one.'

'Why not? what would you have rather been?'

'I don't know . . . probably nothing at all. I would have made a very fine dilettante in the eighteenth century . . . the sort that had theories on everything and wrote long careful letters to friends.'

'You were born too late for that. Everyone must struggle now.'

'A pity, isn't it?'

'I don't think so.' She was now going to become serious, he could see, and the advantage would all be his. He had been on the defensive as long as she questioned or mocked him; but now she was vulnerable and he felt very much better. She said: 'I suppose it's fashionable now to avoid responsibility, to speak lightly of Armageddon as though it were really of no concern.'

'What can one man do, or fifty men, or even a million . . . if you could imagine a million men, or fifty of them for that matter, being united on any policy. What *can* they do? How can they alter the direction of life?'

'You sound so fatalistic.'

'Not really,' said Philip, wishing to get the conversation back to earth again, to himself and to the story he had planned to tell her of the sanatorium where he had spent the last year, and of this final fling before the end (had he not been warned that if he came down to sea level before the five years of his cure were up he would die?).

'Have *you* any interest in politics?'

'Only a spectator's.'

'But you're a lawyer.'

'What has that to do with it?'

'You know perfectly well what that has to do with it . . . the law is the first step in most political careers.'

'So?'

'Have you money? Aside from what you earn?'

'I have enough. I've never earned anything yet . . . except my Navy pay.'

'Are you married?'

'No, and I'm not likely to be.' This was better. He was about to inquire into her status but she gave him no opportunity.

'Then obviously you have everything . . . and how you could enjoy yourself if you wanted to, in politics too.'

'Talking to dull people all day? Smiling at my cretinous constituents and promising them all the things they have never had? It doesn't sound like fun to me.'

'But can't you imagine yourself the head of state? making important decisions? striking an admired pose for your . . . cretinous public?'

'Too easily . . . I fight against the temptation.'

'Then you *are* tempted?'

'Of course, but the fact that I'm reasonable now doesn't mean I should act reasonably if placed in a different situation.'

'Then you *could* imagine yourself involved in politics?'

'I can imagine myself involved in anything . . . the one virtue of having served in a war is that one quickly learns nothing is unlikely. I can do anything.'

'But would you like it?'

'I would have a real contempt for the whole business.'

'But would you like it?'

'Probably.' He qualified, partly from conviction, out of a desire to be as nearly accurate as words would allow and partly to see what she would say next, to determine, if he could, the reason for her curious urgency.

'Ah . . .' She had got her way and for a moment she did not speak. Both stared across the trenched arena towards the tiers of seats on the other side. Stars shone large and white in the black sky. Beneath the dark arches of the building, struck matches, for brief instants, glowed like fireflies on a summer lawn. The air was still. There was no wind and, though he tried, he could not hear the sounds of the modern city which he knew must be all about them, outside this much-scarred oval of antique marble. An occasional voice, muffled and secret, came to him from the archways but, excepting those near-by voices, the rest was silence. What would she say? She asked him where he was from and when he told her, she laughed and asked him his name. He told her this, too, and she said, 'I know your family.'

'Oh no! I'll never escape, I see.'

'Why escape? You have so much to do . . . Philip, and there isn't much time.'

His name sounded odd to him, spoken like this in the warm Roman dark by a stranger, by a woman who apparently knew all about him though he knew nothing of her.

'What do you mean, not much time? Are you speaking prophetically?'

'Oh no . . . just relatively, I suppose. I was thinking how short lives are at best, and since you are thirty . . .'

'Not quite.'

'Not quite . . . and presuming you live to be seventy, your life at this moment is half gone.'

'Nearly half.'

She laughed and repeated, 'Nearly half.'

'Then, of course, you could so easily be killed in a new war. But somehow I feel you will survive it.'

'So do I. But how did you guess I'd planned to avoid it?'

'I'm intuitive, I suppose.'

'You must be. Yes, I've very elaborate plans for keeping out of the trouble. First, I shall have all my teeth taken out . . .' He paused; then: 'Where did you know my family?'

'In Hudson. My husband knows your father very well.'

'And your husband, what's his name?'

'Rex Durham . . . my name is, as you probably know, and a poor joke it is after all these years, Regina.'

He said nothing for a moment. He was surprised and amused and, against his will, more than a little impressed. All his life he had heard of Rex Durham and he still remembered, years ago, when Durham had married Regina: Rex and Regina. For fifteen years he had heard stories about them. Their parties, their deeds (both amatory and political). Durham was the boss of the party which was the boss of their state and the state, often as not, was the boss of the country. Philip's father had always been proud that he knew Rex well enough to call him by his first name, while his mother had always thought Regina lovely, 'in a hard sort of way.'

'No wonder,' said Philip at last, 'you're so interested in politics.'

'No wonder,' she echoed. 'But tell me, have we ever met before? I must be honest and say I remember almost no one I meet, unless I've been briefed in advance.'

'No, we've never met. But I was thirteen when you were married . . . I remember that very clearly. My parents were at the Albany reception.'

'I remember, too. I mean, I remember your mother and father that day. I was twenty then,' she added self-consciously.

'I know.'

'Time passes,' she said. 'Shall we go?' She stood up, facing him in the dark. She was taller than he had suspected, not much shorter than himself, and her body was indeed slim. Her face he had imagined from the many photographs he'd seen of it: dark hair drawn severely back, thin mouth, arched nose, and black eyes with thick brows. He knew all the details, knew they made handsome photographs. He was curious to see how those familiar features looked in life.

Beyond the Colosseum, they both stopped as though by mutual consent beneath the first lamppost and examined one another with, he thought uneasily, that shameless eagerness which in the past had meant only one thing; and that one thing, he'd already decided, was out of the question for a number of reasons, all good.

As he looked at her he wondered if, perhaps, electric light was not in its way as false as photography. For this light was stark and dramatic and it made her face deathly white. It made the features bold as it cast dark shadows in all the hollows, emphasizing her large deep-set eyes. She wore no hat and her hair seemed pale and rather dull, not grey nor yet blonde but somewhere in between; not dark like the newspaper photographs, nor as severe. She seemed very young to him or, rather, ageless; a woman with handsome features and a tranquil expression.

'I thought you would look older,' she said, smiling.

'I thought you would, too,' he said, without thinking.

She laughed at this. Yet, suddenly self-conscious, she stepped out of the light. 'You're not very gallant,' she said.

'I'm sorry. I didn't think ... one of those unfortunate sentences that don't mean what they say.'

'Don't make too many of them or we'll never get you elected.'

'Am I running for office?'

'Of course. Let's go back to the hotel ... you must meet Rex, you know.'

'Now? this very minute?'

'Why not? Are you afraid?'

'No, just uncertain. I never know what to say to politicians.'

'He isn't like a politician. Besides, you'll have to learn how to talk to everyone easily. There's a trick to it.'

'You'll really teach me all those things?' He was careful to disguise his amusement.

'Of course.'

'Why?'

'For reasons of state,' she said evenly, as though the phrase had been long prepared in her mind awaiting the proper moment to be spoken, to disguise, he was quite sure, her true intentions whatever they might be.

'I haven't consented yet,' he said lightly as they approached the mammoth white confection which contained the martial spirit of that dull king who fathered the no less dull and now, thought Philip, fortunately defunct royal house of Savoy. A bat suddenly swooped across their path, circled in front of them and doubled back to the vast ruins of the Forum behind them.

'But you will,' she said seriously. 'You'll see, I think, that you must. For many, many reasons that I will give you one day, if you like.'

'I should like to hear them.'

'I should like to tell them to you. I wonder why you seem so much younger than you really are.'

'Because I lisp, I suppose. It's my cross ... before my voice changed I was considered the sissy of all time. After it changed I was considered very sweet and everyone wanted to protect me.'

'The way I do?'

'I don't know. By the way, how am I to succeed in politics if I can't talk straight?'

'Stop finding difficulties.'

'Tell me, do you know Lord Glenellen?'

'No, I don't think so. Why?'

'I only wondered.'

It was almost midnight when they arrived at the Excelsior. The lobby was nearly empty as they turned to the right of the desk and walked downstairs to a crowded bar. As they walked between the red damask walls, he caught a glimpse of her in the mirror and saw her, he realized, for the first time. Among glass and damask and well-dressed people, she moved with purpose, pale and strange, foreign not only to this room, to these people, but in a sense to all that was familiar. He wondered with some amusement how she managed to please her husband's political friends, for she was abrupt in a way sure to be resented. But then, too, it occurred to him that she might after all be a good actress and that the figure he saw crossing the room was an actress hurrying from her dressing room to the wings, mumbling lines to herself, oblivious of the supers who stepped aside, making way for the star.

Philip stepped forward like Ganymede prepared to meet Jove and, with a smile, he shook the hand of Rex Durham who had risen to greet them. The introductions were quickly and skilfully made and before the first Scotch and water had been brought, Rex had been told all that he would ever need to know of the past life and deeds of Philip, who said nothing while his protectress (or temptress, he was not sure which) instructed her lord.

Rex Durham was a tall man, heavily built, with a great head and large grey eyes, which, Philip noticed, could look either commanding or stupid, and nothing else. The brow was massive and deeply lined and his hair was a thick chrome-silver, while the square strong face was ruddy and healthy. He was just fifty, powerful, admired, and married to a remarkable woman, a combination of good things which, Philip reflected, might combine to destroy a lesser man. But Rex was in no sense a lesser man. He was a major one. He was, at this moment in his history, leader of the party and in rank a member of Congress. He believed, like all good bosses, that it was wiser to remain out of important office, away from the direct influence of the frivolous ballot box which could occasionally (though, he saw to it, not often) upset the most reasonable of combinations for the most irrelevant of reasons. He represented, Philip recalled, his own district on the melancholy-green banks of the Hudson River.

'Been waiting for you for half an hour, Regina,' said Rex clearing his throat oratorically, trumpeting.

'I lost my way,' she said. 'Then, when I finally got there, I met this young man and we talked for a long time. He walked me back.' Rex looked at Philip with the large grey eyes empty, not seeing. 'He's one of your constituents,' she added, 'that's why I've been so nice to him. He's Judge Warren's son.'

'Judge Warren! Old friend of mine, young man. I'm very fond of your father, very fond indeed. Do remember me to him when you write him next. We've been through a lot of campaigns together, the Judge and I. Wonderful old devil.'

Rex's manner had changed and his eyes glittered as he reminisced. 'But isn't that remarkable, Regina,' he said, turning to his wife with an ingenuous air, 'your finding a boy from our own backyard right in the middle of the Colosseum . . .'

'In the middle of the night, too,' she added. 'I thought you would be pleased.'

'Certainly am. So you're Judge Warren's son. You were in the war, weren't you?'

The catechism was then read through with a degree of simulated interest and vigour on both sides; Philip impressed by the older man's legend, while the older man, used from habit to flattering others, conducted the questioning with ease. It was soon done and they drank Scotch thoughtfully as the room suddenly filled with noisy young Americans, cheerful and handsome and a little drunk. The boys had crewcuts and wore seersucker suits. Their innocent faces were tanned from long drives through the golden countryside with short-haired, full-skirted girls. They filled the bar, four couples, collegiate and simple.

'They're really enjoying themselves,' commented Regina with an inexplicable neutrality; he was disappointed that she did not share his pleasure.

Rex talked politics. He mentioned great names, many great names. He did not drop them to impress, the way an ordinary man might have done. No, he fired them in volleys. He was discreet for all his bluffness, and Philip knew the other was trying deliberately to appear frank while saying nothing that a reasonably dedicated reader of *Time* magazine might not have known. But the effect was all that could be desired and Philip listened with pleasure to a description of the Pope's views on the world's state.

'Grave, very grave.'

Then he reported to Regina on his day and they spoke over Philip's head as though he were not there or were a child.

'Saw Jim this afternoon, after I left you.'

'And he said?'

'Wouldn't be able to play ball with us . . . going to handle the whole thing through State . . . regardless.'

'But didn't you tell him . . .'

'How could I? As long as they have confidence in him, I'm helpless.'

'But not quite.'

'No, not quite . . . the President . . .'

Their conversation at this moment became so very grand that Philip wondered if he should not tiptoe out of the room which had, with only a magic word or two, become, somewhat incongruously, a residence of majestic intrigue, despite the boisterous young people at the next table who were debating whether or not they should drive to Ostia that night and go swimming.

Rex Durham predicted a major war within thirty-six months.

'Let's not talk about that,' said Regina uneasily.

'We must, though. It would never do to be unprepared again.'

And here we go again, thought Philip: all his life there had either been talk of a war just ended or one about to begin or, and in a way best of all, a war in progress. Somehow the fact was never so terrible as the anticipation, as the gloomy predictions which his family in particular had indulged in all his life, confident as they were that they would some day be swept away by a common catastrophe, a major war or, failing that, a popular uprising. They belonged to that small class in America which regards itself as aristocratic, a wealthy class, nicely educated and as old in a tradition as the people of a new country can be . . . which is old enough, thought Philip, trying to recall the origins of the Durham family, deciding at last as he recalled some half-forgotten bit of gossip that Rex must have belonged to one of the new families, a self-made man or the son of one. But soon it would make no difference if his own father's prediction were to come true or not: the old man believed their days were numbered and that the old freedom their class had enjoyed was, with each year, being surrendered bit by bit as the taxes increased and the business of the government became larger and more oppressive, more concerned with the details of its citizens' lives in an effort, partly benevolent and mostly political, to sustain a majority of the voters in the grey and uniform security of a nursery where the eccentric and the private would not be permitted; and their own society, for the most part as stolid and as nearly virtuous as any reformer could wish, would vanish and their lawn-circled houses would serve to house girls' schools and asylums for the insane (the latter drawn more and more, Philip was certain, from the wise and the senisitive and the formerly free).

Rex had got to his feet. Rex was going to bed. Rex was tired.

'It's been a pleasure, young man. I hope we'll see a lot of you now that we're all here in Rome together. Far from home.'

Tall elms, only somewhat blighted, black twisted locust trees, glittering copper beeches, green lawns and silver river: home was the same place for all of them. Philip bade the Durhams good night or, as it turned out, only Mr Durham, for Regina said that she was not yet sleepy and that she would like to sit up a few minutes longer.

'Regular night owl,' commented Rex, as Philip knew he would.

Then he was alone in the bar with Regina. The young people had, with a good deal of noise, departed just before Rex, their destination as far as Philip could determine still undecided.

'It's late,' said Philip.

'Yes,' said Regina, 'very late.'

Contemplating the lateness, they looked at one another across the table, aware of the silence in the room, empty except for a sleepy waiter on a high stool behind the bar.

'Do you like it?' she asked.

'Yes, very much,' he said, not sure what she meant, willing to match her ambiguousness with his own.

'I do, too, very much. You'll spend a year in Europe, then? A year travelling?'

'So I've planned.'

'Afterwards you'll come home?'

'I may come home, yes.'

'But you may not.'

'It's possible. The year has only begun.'

'Only begun,' she repeated thoughtfully, then: 'You will be coerced, you know, by all of us.'

'Am I as valuable as all that?'

'Of course . . . don't you think you are?'

'Naturally, but I wasn't aware that the world valued me as much as I do.'

'But it does.'

'A great responsibility.'

'Of course. You *are* responsible . . . that is the meaning of the whole business.

'What business?'

'Being alive. Responsibility, action, to live usefully.'

'For others?'

'Why not? Wherever the greater glory lies.'

'One wants glory?'

'Oh, more than anything else! To live grandly, to shape the world!'

He laughed. 'It's too rich a diet for me. In any case, I've already given you my opinion of politics.'

'Shallow, smart opinions. You didn't mean what you said.'

'But I did. Besides, I'm a shallow person. That's why I've come to Europe, to grow deep.'

'You're making fun of me.'

He smiled. 'No, not at all. Only I don't think it's worth the trouble. You're wasting too much interest on me. Let's talk of something else . . . Mr Durham.'

'My husband? What of him?'

'An unusual man.'

'I think so. A political genius, if politicians can be said to have genius. I respect him.'

'Will he be President?'

She looked at him without expression; as though she had not heard or had not understood. She answered elliptically, 'Is he the sort, do you think?'

'I don't know. I mean, after all, he's your husband.'

'Yes, he is. Would you like to be President?'

'I don't think so.'

'It could happen.'

'Nonsense.'

'You don't know, you don't know,' she repeated, shaking her head. The bartender, who had been asleep, fell off his stool. He got to his feet, blinking.

'Tell me something else,' said Regina.

'What do you want to know?'

'Tell me . . .' she paused; then changed the question, 'Tell me a story,' she said.

'Any sort?'

'Yes please.'

'Once upon a time there was a mother who had five children. She was very proud of them in her way, but her way was very severe for she was ambitious. She made up her mind that she would make them the most successful children in the world and so every day she beat them until she had taught them how to fly. In time they got so they could fly very well indeed. They could glide and soar and do arabesques five thousand miles up; naturally, people thought very highly of them.'

'Then what happened?'

'Oh, they flew away from home and joined a circus and became very rich.'

'And their mother?'

'They never saw her again.'

'Do you like that story?'

'Not very much.'

'I don't like it either.'

'It's getting late.'

'Is it late?' She looked at a small diamond watch.

'Is there time?' he asked.

She nodded.

CHAPTER THREE

The ultimate moment. The splendid act. The joining of body and spirit in one breathing centre about which the earth and stars revolve, counter to all the established laws of the empiricists who know only detail, and that partly, while lovers know truth wholly. Or, to put it less grandly, it is great fun indeed for the lighthearted, solemn and emotionally edifying for the rest, the ones who are aware of the tradition involved in the long duet, and who approach it reverently, even fearfully, if the Puritan spirit has by chance spoiled them as it has spoiled so many, even now in these relatively enlightened days when most of the fear has gone out of the act.

Union. An end of loneliness, exaltation, a moment compared to which all other moments are tedious and unbearable. What more can one say? Since Pindar, it has been said all in a rush (and presumably before that in Babylon, China, Egypt and the gnomic land of Crete), and so nowadays one must confine oneself to the peripheral rather than to the central aspects of the business, the splendid game in which we are all, to the best of our capacities, engaged.

Now, part of the pleasure one gets from reading novels is the inevitable moment when the hero beds the heroine or, in certain advanced and decadent works, the hero beds another hero in an infernal glow of impropriety. The mechanical side of the operation is of intense interest to everyone. Partly, of course, because so few of us get entirely what we want when it comes to this sort of thing and, too, there is something remarkably exciting about the sex lives of fictional characters. For one thing, there is so much clear and precise talk both before and after the act. So much talk that one feels far more clearly engaged than one does in life where the whole thing is often confused and clumsy. Also, there is a formidable amount of *voyeurism* in us all and literature, even better than pornographic pictures, provides us at its best with an excitation occasionally more poignant than the real thing.

I have, of course, overstated the case, and Philip presents something of a problem at this point. Like most young Americans of his age and class, he has a tendency towards promiscuity, towards 'emotional brashness,' as an eminent English critic once remarked, rather sternly, of contemporary novels and their faithless, aimless protagonists. Philip is not, of course, aimless but his approach to sexual matters lacks the solemnity which those of us who care deeply for man's highest emotion demand of that most intimate union between man and woman. Taking all of this into account, it would, I know, be wisest to avoid the subject altogether and begin this new chapter as though nothing untoward had happened that evening in the Excelsior Hotel. One could indicate, perhaps, that the relationship between Regina and Philip had somehow magically deepened or, better yet, a fistful of asterisks tossed over the page might solve everything; and one would be praised for reticence since there are always a great many American ladies (of both sexes) who tell one that there are enough unpleasant things in the world without reading about them in books, lovemaking, significantly enough, being considered very nearly the most unpleasant activity of all.

But, nevertheless, I feel obligated to reveal as candidly as I think proper what happened between Philip and Mrs Durham on the fourth floor of the Excelsior Hotel in a room separated from Mr Durham's by a sitting room and a locked door.

First, despite the essential beauty of the act, the union was not well made. There were a number of small frictions, tiny annoyances, which almost always occur between two people who are not yet properly attuned to one another and who are also overexcited by the novelty and the danger of what they are doing.

Philip had only half his mind on what he was doing. The other half was listening, somewhat frantically, for the sound of Mr Durham rattling the locked door and demanding entrance. Philip had placed his clothes on a chair in such a fashion that he could get into them with a speed which always did credit to his military training (shirt inside jacket, drawers inside trousers). Regina did her best, however, to put him at his ease, remarking that Mr Durham seldom demanded his marital rights, his energies, as far as she knew, being devoted to the greater business of controlling Presidents.

Now, one hardly knows how far to go in describing precisely what happened. There is the brutal school, which uses the blunt words to get to the point. Then there are the incredibly popular lady novelists who titter and leer, describing the hero's great, rough (yet sensitive) hands and the back of his bronzed neck (for some unaccountable reason, the back of the neck has become, for the female at least, an erotic symbol of singular fascination). Then there are the sort to whom the business is very beautiful and very fine, the centre of the book, tender and warm and serious, very serious. Much is described, as much is left to the imagination. One is moved and, should the novelist be a good one, the scene can have a remarkable immediacy. Yet, in this particular case at least, we must attempt another method. For Philip is not brutal nor is the back of his neck bronzed nor is he in love with Regina. He finds her attractive and desirable and it seems to him like a very pleasant way to spend his first night in Rome. In the words of that English critic, he is 'emotionally brash,' though it is to be hoped that in the year of self-discovery he has so wisely elected to embark upon he will come into a proper relationship with another human being, thus giving a certain emotional richness to the deed which, in Regina's cool arms, he lacks.

Cool arms. Now we come to it. At seventeen minutes after two o'clock they entered the bedroom. Regina turned on the light, took her rings and bracelets off and accepted his embrace. By two-thirty, more or less, they were both undressed and investigating one another with some pleasure. Regina's body was very fine. She was not too heavy. Her waist was slim and taut. Her hips were somewhat large but handsomely curved. Her breasts were not in the least unusual; they did not sag while, on the other hand, they did not point skyward like mounds of ice cream, the way the glands of girls in magazine advertisements are supposed to point. Her skin was rather brownish and quite smooth.

Philip has been described already in some detail. It should be noted here, however, that he had very little hair on his body, a characteristic which seemed to appeal enormously to Regina who caressed his chest and belly with some intensity. Genitally, he did not in the least resemble those lewd markings on the walls of public conveniences. He was properly and sturdily endowed, normally shaped and without any peculiarities. He was capable of a spirited performance, guided by an intuition of the other's rhythm which often bordered on the miraculous. Tonight, however, because of nerves, his performance was violent and boyish rather than sensible and manly. Conscious of this tension, Regina helpfully murmured an occasional direction, but the stars were not right and the act, which lasted seventeen minutes, counting preliminaries of course, was not epoch-making in either of their lives. On the other hand, it afforded each some relief and the previous atmosphere of tension was succeeded by a state akin to euphoria.

The final details are not particularly relevant. Needless to say, Philip was anxious to leave, afraid of that locked door opposite the bed through which at any moment he expected to hear the rumbling of the husband's querulous voice. Regina turned on the light and they looked at each other with considerable interest, even critically now that desire was for a time allayed. Happily, they found that even under these somewhat exacting circumstances they were still charmed by one another and it was immediately apparent to both that they would, with some pleasure, repeat the act whenever in the future an opportunity should present itself.

Regina gave a number of dates and times when she felt opportunities would arise. They decided that, all in all, late afternoon was the best time to meet and his hotel the best place in which to reaffirm their passion. After a few more remarks (all whispered) they parted and Philip returned through darkened streets to his hotel where he slept without dreaming until noon the next day.

He was awakened by a gentle but insistent rapping at the door. 'Come in,' he said, sitting up, still half asleep.

'I can't,' said a faraway British voice. 'The door is locked.'

'Wait a minute.' Philip grabbed an enormous bath towel and wrapped it about himself like a cloak; then he opened the door and admitted Clyde Norman.

'Ah, you were bathing,' said Mr Norman, rather pleased. 'You Americans bathe every day, I'm told. Go ahead. Don't let me interrupt you.'

'Oh, that's all right,' said Philip vaguely, 'come on in.' Now that he was awake he did want to take a bath but modesty prevented him: there was no bathroom, only the curtained alcove which contained the bathtub and the bidet, this last an object of considerable fascination to Philip who thought it wicked.

'Don't you find it terribly unhealthy, bathing I mean? Doesn't it open up the pores dreadfully? I have a weak chest and so I take no chances. I never bathe.'

'I'm afraid I've never thought about it,' said Philip, getting back into bed. Clyde Norman went to the window and pulled back the curtains, admitting a flood of yellow light. In the street Philip could hear a newsboy shouting.

'You don't mind, do you? It's quite warm out.'

'No, not at all. I've only just got up. I was very tired, you know . . . the train and all that.'

'I should think so. Your first morning in Rome! How wonderful for you!'

Mr Norman sat down in the room's only armchair, crushing Philip's trousers beneath him. 'I come,' he said, making himself comfortable, 'from Lord Glenellen, who would like you to play bridge with us tonight at his place. There will be only four people, counting yourself, should you come. Ayre, myself, you and Ayre's secretary, a pleasant Welsh boy named Evan Morgan who can't sing a note.'

'Sing?' Philip was beginning to wake up at last.

'The Welsh all sing,' said Mr Norman easily, 'like your Negroes.'

'Do they?'

'Of course they do. All except Evan, who doesn't sing one note properly though Ayre likes to listen to him. Ayre claims he's the only real interpreter of the Bardic songs . . . a minor peculiarity of his Lordship's and, to my mind, the only really insupportable one. The poor child is often called on to render a song or two after dinner and once every season there is a recital . . . all very sad, but then one must allow for human nature.'

'I suppose so. Yes, I should like to play bridge. What time?'

'After dinner, at ten. I'm afraid we won't be invited to dinner . . . Ayre hates to serve food though he's one of the richest men in England . . . or, I should say, *out* of England.'

'He seems unpleasant,' said Philip sharply.

'Yes, doesn't he?' Mr Norman was bland. 'It's very strange how unsympathetic people seem when described by a good friend. But of course in life all the unpleasant characteristics are blended in such a way that, to the friend at least, the result is most agreeable. To an outsider, Ayre must seem a monster. His reputation is not only frightful, it's frightening. Yet I find him one of the dearest people in the world.'

Mr Norman paused sentimentally and Philip looked away uncomfortably, afraid he would find a tear on the other's sallow cheek.

Fortunately Mr Norman changed the subject. 'What did you do last night?'

'I went to the Colosseum.'

'But there was no moon.'

'I know. I wanted to see it anyway.'

'And did you? Could you?'

'Oh yes. It's lit up on the outside at least. Inside it was dark.'

'Rather aangerous, too. You should be careful.'

'I met an American couple while I was there.'

'Of course. I should have known that the Colosseum at night would attract all sorts of Americans, as well as murderers and thieves and pimps. Who were they?'

'The couple? A Mr and Mrs Durham.'

'Not the politician?'

'The same. Friends of my family.'

'How very interesting! I've already met them, or rather I've seen them at the Embassy. There was a garden party given for them last week. It rained. Do you know them well?'

'No. I'd never met either of them before.'

'How strange they'd be sightseeing in the middle of the night. He seemed such a hard, shrewd man . . . so very American.'

'Anyway, we all went back to the Excelsior for a drink.' Philip had a natural inclination to cover his tracks, an instinct which was at the same time usually undone by a need to discuss at length everything which had happened to him or might yet happen to him. He was sufficiently wise, however, to include Mr Durham in the starlight meeting, to allay any possible suspicion on the part of Mr Norman who, fortunately, had none at all along these lines but perhaps a suspicion along another, or at least a hope, faint but persistent.

'Then you must know them quite well by now.'

'Not even Americans work that fast.'

'But you'll see them again.'

'Very likely, yes.'

'I see.' Mr Norman shut his eyes. It was a trick he had when he was about to make an announcement or to change the subject. Philip, wanting now to have his coffee and a bath, wished he would make his pronouncement quickly and go. Mr Norman was capable of a mild surprise or two, however, for instead of some vague observation he asked a question. 'You care much for politics?'

Philip moaned softly.

'I've heard nothing but politics for the past twenty-four hours. No, I'm not interested in them at all. I have decided that I'm going to be a water-colourist,' he said inventively, surprising even himself with this choice of profession.

'How nice. Whom will you study with?'

'A Russian who lives in Paris. You probably don't know him.'

'I see. Well, isn't that nice?'

'It's what I've always wanted,' said Philip softly, gathering the towel about his neck and pointing his bare feet like a ballet dancer. Mr Norman watched the toes, an unpleasantly rapt expression on his ordinarily serene face. Philip wondered absently if perhaps Mr Norman liked boots.

'Do you approve of the Communist Party?' asked Mr Norman at last, with an effort removing his somewhat febrile attention from Philip's toes to his face, unshaven for two days now and covered with a golden stubble.

'No,' said Philip.

'Do you approve of monarchy?'

'Why?'

'I should like to know. If I seem to pry, do tell me and I won't ask you any more questions.'

'Yes, I like kings very much. In a decorative sense.'

'I see I . . . I had to know.'

Mr Norman laughed apologetically. 'Fortunately, you said what I thought you would. You see, we've already looked into your history. Rather thoroughly, if I say so myself.'

'We? Who's we? And why are you interested in what I think?'

'I can't answer either question yet,' said Clyde Norman smoothly, enjoying the mystery.

'I'm not sure I like this at all,' said Philip, sitting up and swinging his legs over the side of the bed, the towel falling about his body in toga-like folds.

'Don't be alarmed. It's just that both Ayre and I were quite impressed with you yesterday and we may ask you to help us in something.'

'In what?'

'I'm afraid I can't say. Ayre may tell you tonight. In fact, I can say almost certainly that he will tell you tonight, ask you to become one of us.'

'Oh no . . . none of that,' said Philip a little harshly, causing a blush to come to Mr Norman's usually pleasant face.

'I am speaking of a political movement,' said Mr Norman evenly, retaining some but not all of his usual dignity.

'I know,' said Philip, confused and embarrassed. 'I meant . . .'

'I'm sure you will be interested in it. The fact that you know Rex Durham makes you all the more necessary to us . . . if you will but help us.' He paused impressively, once again master of the dialogue.

'I'd like to hear all about it,' said Philip contritely, eagerly, willing to do anything to erase the memory of his ungraciousness.

'Good,' said the conspirator, getting to his feet. 'I shall call for you at eight. We will dine in a *trattoria* I know and then on to our bridge game.' He chuckled and, with the noise of Philip's good offices and protestations of friendship in his long hairy ears, he departed, well pleased.

Philip bathed. Then he had coffee sent up and he drank it thoughtfully. Finally dressed, with a minor anthology of major poetry under one arm, he set out for the Forum to commune with that splendid age to which he had always been mystically drawn, as though to a point of origin until now too obscured by distance to be more to him than a dream of home, a ghost or a shadow of a time of splendour. And so he came to the great pit which contained the squares and streets, the monuments and office buildings of that age, and after buying the inevitable ticket, he passed under a triumphal arch and walked solemnly down the grass-grown, moss-decked Sacra Via towards the hill where Capitoline Jove once sat in his temple and where today the tower of a building of state, the work of Michelangelo, dominates this marble wreck of a world which still contained for Philip, despite the shattered walls and broken arches, a certain grandeur divorced from reality perhaps but, in effect, in essence, no less valid for that reason: a world which he wished to absorb directly, the way he had, years ago, read the stories of Livy and the poems of Horace, with the aid of a trot.

It was both more and less than he had expected. He had not anticipated such vastness: the ruins of the various basilicas and public baths startled him with their unaesthetic massiveness. They seemed too ponderous, too calculated to overawe. He wondered what a savage must have thought, coming from the foggy green forests of Germany to this stern behemoth of a city, this centre of the world. He stood looking up at a dome still intact, the work of the penultimate and gentlest dynasty, and he tried to think of it the way it had been. He failed completely, as he always did. He had no visual imagination, only an emotional one; he could simulate attitudes and re-create forgotten moods but he could not with any success people the past with figures that seemed to him visually convincing. His Forum was altogether too much like Times Square on a Saturday night when he stared at it very hard, trying to imagine it as it was, Cicero and Brutus, Catullus and Julius, but he got only a double exposure of the jostling, noisy, sinister New York crowd against these delicate columns which contained only sky and summer air; tall umber walls emerging from green unexcavated hills and cliffs where coins and urns and marble heads lay buried in subterranean rooms, smothered in the fine brown earth of violent and unremembered days.

Tourists wandered in and out of the Temple of the Vestal Virgins, remarking upon their reflections in an oblong pool of stagnant water greener than the Tiber, like a pea soup which has sat too long and gathered on its surface an iridescent scum. Thinking of the Vestal Virgins, Philip crossed the atrium of their house, past a series of statues which looked for all the world like a conclave of club ladies, serious and benign; at the first bench, an austere one of marble, he sat down between a pair of Corinthian-capped columns which supported a solid fragment of pediment on which a frieze had once been chiselled, a design now lost except for a man's shoulder and arm, preceded by the tail and buttocks of a prancing stallion.

He looked about him. The day was cool and the sky was clear and yet, in spite of this total realization of an old wish, he was neither excited nor content. He felt lethargic, the way he had always imagined a man who has come suddenly into a long desired place in the world must feel: this is it; the rest will be repetition. He shut his eyes and the sun was warm on his eyelids. He breathed deeply, wanting to absorb all this, to be all this. But he was himself, he knew, opening his eyes suddenly very wide and staring straight into the sun, going blind for a moment, lost in a green-gold world of Catherine wheels.

And then, as several American ladies, well dressed and confidently equipped with Baedekers, studied reverently the remains of the Ministry of Colonies, under the impression it had once housed the god Dionysius and his erotic mysteries, Philip read:

'Oh rose thou art sick!
The invisible worm
That flies in the night,
In the howling storm,

'Has found out thy bed
Of crimson joy,
And his dark secret lover
Does thy love destroy.'

This suited his mood, he decided gloomily, reading it again.
'Do you really think that's what they did?'
'Of course, Claire. I have read all about them.'
'Just think, it happened right here, right where we're standing!'
Philip glared at them, imagined satyrs sweeping them up in hot goatish embraces and bearing them off to catacombs, their hats, handbags and Baedekers scattered among the ruins as final witness to their impiety. But they moved on, unmolested, and he repeated, ' "Oh rose thou art sick!" '
Feeling a little ill himself, though not much like a rose bewormed or not, he wandered off towards Capitoline Hill and its memory of Caesar's death and of Jove and of *his* slow death at the hands of that Eastern mother and her mortal son.

There was a telephone message from Regina when he got back to his hotel. He called her, and after some trouble with a non-English- and possibly non-Italian-speaking operator, he got through to her at her hotel. She sounded very far away.
'What did you do today?' she asked as they made awkward conversation, behaving like strangers who have contacted one another reluctantly and at the insistence of a mutual friend. He told her where he had gone and what he had seen.
'Real sightseeing,' he added, obscurely ashamed at not having been more like the other Americans here, the worldly ones who spent their days in the cafés talking and their evenings practising hobbies with the cheerful and ever amenable Romans who, for money, were available for any activity.
'Are you free this evening?' she asked.
'No, I'm afraid that . . .' He told her where he was going, pleased that he could at least claim a certain social success for himself in this strange city where he had had letters to no one, except that unofficial one, a large draft on youth and charm which, in proper proportion and for a time at least, can buy the vitiated heart of the world.
'Perhaps another time then?'
'Tomorrow at five?'
'The day after at five.'
'I should like that.'
'So would I.'
'Shall we meet here?'

'If you like. I have so many things to tell you.'

'So many things,' he repeated. And then, since neither could think of anything else to say, made shy by the intimacy of their short acquaintance, they said good-bye to one another and the two tiny mechanical clicks emphasized the distance between them.

Philip went down to the bar of the hotel at seven o'clock, only to find Mr Norman was not yet there. Two cherubic American ladies were drinking orangeade in one corner of the rather bleak clean little room with its tile floor and odour of antiseptic: a 'sincerely Swiss room' had been Mr Norman's comment on it and, perversely, he liked it and made it, after Doney's of course, his club.

One of the ladies said to the other, 'Would you like a straw, dear?'

'No. No thanks.'

'Oh . . . I *like* a straw.'

Mr Norman wore a handsome dark blue suit with unusually narrow lapels which made him seem quite foreign, while the striped shirt with plain white detachable collar only added to his quaintness in Philip's eyes. He apologized for being late, allowed Philip to pay for a quick round of Cinzanos. Then they went to Mr Norman's *trattoria*, a small dirty place with a great many electric-light bulbs and an accordion-playing tenor who sang 'Catalina' with a ghastly tenderness which cloyed Philip but pleased Mr Norman, who asked for a number of other songs all having to do with the fate of Italian maidens who love unwisely in Amalfi, Sorrento and Venice.

A very fine *pasta con burro* was followed by an entree which Mr Norman claimed was the specialty of the house: lumps of pink meat containing unexpected bits of bone served in a tepid white cream sauce.

'What is it?' asked Philip as he felt a filling loosen, his teeth having come down hard on a bit of bone.

'Goat,' said Mr Norman with a happy smile. 'It *is* good, isn't it?'

The Palazzo Mettelli was a large building covered with buff-tinted stucco and roofed with tile. The façade, as presented to the Square of the Mettelli, was as shabby and inexpressive as the fountain in the centre of the square which was attributed to one of Michelangelo's students, the one who failed the course, according to Mr Norman, as they paused to stare at the dirty water which trickled from a number of unusual outlets placed frivolously in various parts of several marble ladies who were oddly imvolved with bowls of fruit and a dolphin.

The interior, however, was much more impressive, thought Philip, as they were led by an Italian youth across the long entrance hall whose ceiling was encrusted with gold decorations and paintings of heaven where various members of the Mettelli were prominently displayed, chatting with the higher-ranking personnel of the heavenly host.

'There is no electricity in the Palazzo,' said Mr Norman as the boy led them through the great hall which, though handsomely tapestried, was not furnished. At the end of the hall they paused while their guide lit a new candle. 'Ayre has never liked electricity.'

'Why not?' asked Philip as they followed the boy up a wide marble staircase which curved into darkness, a place of unexpected drafts of air which made the candle flicker crazily. 'I don't know. I never asked him,' said Mr Norman. 'I don't think he minds it in other people's houses. I'm glad you mentioned it, though. I shall remember to ask him.'

They followed the will-o'-the-wisp flame down a long corridor to a massive door of carved oak. Bowing theatrically, the boy opened the door to reveal a small brilliantly lighted chamber with walls of carved wood and heavy brocade curtains. A table and four chairs were in the centre of the room beneath a chandelier which glittered with many candles. A fire roared in the pink marble fireplace and before it, in leather armchairs, sat Glenellen and a plump young man with blue eyes and dark curly hair. Both rose as the newcomers entered.

'Behold the young American!' exclaimed Glenellen, moving forward in a stately glide and taking Philip by the hand; then, still ignoring Mr Norman, he led him to the fireplace where he was introduced to Evan Morgan, '. . . my secretary. An invaluable assistant. Invaluable,' he repeated, looking at the young man solemnly. 'When the truth is known one day, as it must be, he will be made a Chevalier of the Order of St Jerome of Padua. Mark my words and recall then at the proper time,' he added, deepening the mystery by putting his forefinger to the side of his nose and winking.

'Did the meeting go well today?' asked Mr Norman by way of reminding the other of his so far unremarked presence.

'I don't know what you mean,' said Glenellen blankly; then he smiled, revealing terrible teeth. 'Ah, Clyde. You came after all. I was just saying to Evan here, I wonder if Clyde will come tonight and play a rubber or two of bridge with his old friends, and here you are. Do sit down by the fire. And you too, young man. I like a fire this time of year; these old palaces get so awfully damp. Fire dries them out. Dries me out, too, though I doubt whether that's such a good idea. Eh, Evan? Well, let's have a drink. Evan, ring for Guido, will you? And tell him to bring ice. Dreadful boy. You met him the other day, I think.' Philip nodded. 'If he doesn't learn to concentrate, I'm afraid I shall have to lock him up again.'

'Lock him up?' asked Philip.

'Oh yes, often . . . with chains. He likes that best, he tells me.'

Guido appeared with a tray of glasses, bottles and a silver bowl of ice. Philip studied him carefully but the boy's face revealed nothing at all. No scars attested to Ayre's grim reference and when he had set the tray down on a console he left the room. Evan mixed the drinks. Glenellen was disappointed to hear that Philip preferred Scotch to absinthe.

'I suppose I have the best absinthe in Europe,' he said proudly, 'guaranteed to make a weak head dissolve. But then nothing that is good is for the weak, is it, Clyde?'

'An interesting idea, Ayre,' said the other noncommittally, turning to Evan. 'Did you have a good day?'

'I think so,' said the young man, glancing uneasily at Glenellen. But the peer was daydreaming, staring into the blue-gold flames of the fire as though anticipating the birth of the Phoenix or recalling his wife's death, thought Philip, suddenly remembering Mr Norman's story of the Embassy dinner.

'Did you hear from the Vatican?'

'Yes, the Monsignor came.'

'The Polish?'

'No, the Austrian, the old one.'

'And he felt . . .'

'That we would get considerable help at the proper time.'

'From whom?'

'The Cardinal.'

'Which one?'

'The fat one ... you know, the River Po.'

'Ah yes. But no news from above?'

'None. *He* must remain aloof.'

'I suppose so, but perhaps at the proper time ...'

'The proper time, and all will be forthcoming, or so the Monsignor indicated.'

Evan turned to Philip and asked, 'Mr Norman tells me that you're a friend of Mr Durham's?'

'I know him slightly.'

'He'll be in Rome another month, I hear.'

'I'm seeing them day after tomorrow.'

'Ayre,' said the young man, nudging his employer who had so identified himself with the flames that his face had turned a sympathetic scarlet and his gaze was as abstracted and as flickering as the fire itself. But he responded to the nudge, his eyes focused on Evan. 'Yes, my boy?'

'The Durhams. He knows the Durhams.'

'And *who* are the Durhams?'

'You know perfectly well, Ayre,' said Mr Norman. 'He is the President's right hand.'

'Which President?' His eye might be focused but his mind was not, thought Philip, wondering if this was the work of the absinthe he had drunk.

'The American one,' said Mr Norman patiently. 'Mr Durham is here on a mission to the Italian government. The President is relying on him. Our young friend has Mr Durham's ear. Isn't that enough?'

'Why didn't you tell me this before, Clyde?' said Glenellen, suddenly brisk and businesslike. 'I could have made preparations. If I had only known I could have told the Monsignor when he was here today. Why, why didn't you tell me?'

'I did tell you, Ayre. Yesterday we discussed the entire thing and you suggested Mr Warren be brought here tonight ... to play bridge.'

'Bridge?' said Glenellen hopefully, clutching at the one reference which seemed most concrete. 'I haven't had a good game of bridge in four years, since the German occupation.'

'Ayre was here during the war,' explained Mr Norman quickly.

'He was opposed to the Nazis ...' began Evan.

'*Parvenus!*' interrupted Glenellen, throwing his glass into the fire. It shattered among the flames.

'But he had some friends from the old days, from the old German court. They protected him,' finished Evan.

'You have influence with this Durham?' asked Glenellen suddenly, his foggy blue eyes on Philip's.

'No, none at all.'

'He is being modest,' said Mr Norman. 'His family is politically very close to Mr Durham.'

'How do you know that?' asked Philip, surprised.

'Oh, I know a lot of things about you.'

'Clyde, this isn't the young man you told me about yesterday, is it?'

'The same,' said Mr Norman wearily, appealing to Evan who was now at the other end of the room fixing drinks.

'I sometimes think, Clyde, that you try deliberately to confuse me. Young man, how do you stand politically?'

'Nowhere at all,' said Philip.

'But you disapprove of chaos?'

'I suppose so.'

'You recognize the importance of human affairs?'

'Yes and no,' said Philip, not understanding what this meant.

'Have you an adventurous nature?'

'Oh yes, yes,' said Philip. Why else would he be here? he added to himself, intrigued though still confused.

'Do you play good bridge?'

'Fairly . . . I don't know. It depends.'

'In that case, Clyde had better be your partner. I usually play with Evan anyway. He understands my bidding. The only other good player in Rome.'

They rose and went to the card table and for two hours they played while hot wax from the chandelier overhead dripped on the table, and got in their hair, and Glenellen cursed but made no move to move the table somewhere else. Finally, when the game was over and the eccentric playing of Glenellen and Evan had triumphed over the more conservative game of their opponents, Ayre rose from the table and turned to Mr Norman. 'It was good of you, Clyde, to bring this young man here tonight. We must remember, however, that discretion is of the greatest importance and that it is altogether too soon to admit him to our Order. Watch him, Clyde. Study him. Question him and if he seems trustworthy and valiant bring him to me next week.'

'But the Durhams, Ayre . . . they won't be here forever.'

'The Durhams can keep,' said Glenellen sharply. He turned to Philip with a smile. 'You must not mind being tested, my boy. We all are, every day, in one way or another, if not by man by God. I am sure you will not be found wanting.'

'But will he *want* to serve us?' asked Evan reasonably. But this question was ignored. Clyde Norman sighed. 'Very well, Ayre. It's your organization. Where shall we meet next week? And when?'

'Thursday will be the best day,' said Glenellen. He frowned. 'Not here, though. This place is being watched twenty-four hours a day. The Baths.'

'The Baths?'

'Yes, Clyde. The Baths of Nero, at five o'clock.'

'But, Ayre, I don't think . . . I mean.' He gestured futilely in Philip's direction. But Glenellen was already ringing the bell for Guido to show them out.

Regina arrived on time, simply dressed, and Philip, when he met her in the lobby, thought her most desirable, more attractive even than she had been the night of their first meeting. They decided to take a walk in the near-by gardens of the Villa Borghese for both were a little shy at first and he hesitated about inviting her up to his room: he was not yet free of that American fear of desk clerks which has rendered the great game so depressing in his own country.

The day was fine, cool and at this hour golden, elegiac in mood, with rococo clouds arranged above the rolling meadows and dark woods of ilex trees which comprised the gardens, contained in part, along the Via Veneto, by a fragment of the wall of Rome and by a most heroic arch where, on either side, families lived like cave dwellers in the thick masonry. They paused by a silver pond beneath the dark green ilex trees. Priests strolled up and down; lovers sat together on the benches, silent and passive, watching with self-conscious eyes the children of others as they sailed little boats on the water and played tag between the trees.

'What can they mean?' he asked at last. He told of his evening with Glenellen. He had wanted to amuse and interest her without becoming too personal and since their supply of mutual reference was seriously limited, it was best, he decided, to stick to anecdote until they had known one another long enough to have a language in common, a world of easy familiar reference in which they could meet without resorting to the neutral or to the irrelevant.

'I'm not sure,' she said with a frown. 'It's a mystery. They all sound quite mad.'

'I thought that, too, but amusing.'

'I wonder if it's wise . . . you seeing them, I mean?'

'What harm could it do?'

'Well, one never can tell. The present government here isn't having an easy time of it, you know. Some think there may even be a revolution this year.'

'But I'm just a visitor. I'm not interested in their politics . . . I'm not even interested in our own.' He smiled at her to see if she would take up the challenge as she had at such length the first night. But today she was in a different mood; she turned away and walked to a bench near by. They sat down. A soldier with one leg and a face bristled like the back of a black boar came up to them and successfully begged a hundred *lire* from Philip.

'Be careful,' she said, looking at him, her blue eyes serene; no matter what her mood, they never changed expression.

'I'll see them once again . . . I promised Mr Norman I would . . . and that will be the end.' He chuckled. 'Well, at least I haven't got in with the usual group.' Philip was suddenly conscious that his head was aching terribly. He shut his eyes and pressed his hand against the lids; inside his head the universe was definitely and brilliantly exploding outward, infinitely, and he with it. He opened his eyes and blinked.

'What on earth is the matter?' Regina was staring at him, alarmed. 'Are you sick?'

'I don't know,' he said weakly. The light hurt his eyes and he half shut them. 'I have a headache. That's all. Came on me all of a sudden.'

'Do you have them often?'

'Never.'

'We'd better go back then.'

'No, not yet. Let's sit here. It'll go away. I probably ate something that . . . Oh!' He groaned, recalling the dinner the night before. 'Goat!' he exclaimed, and he told her of the dinner. Then, when the pain was less acute, they got up and slowly, as though he were an invalid only just arisen from bed, they walked down avenues of ilex to the Via Veneto and to his hotel where, at his insistence, she went up to the room. He ordered tea and aspirin and then, after this had arrived, sick though he was and in spite of her cautioning, they made love, the afternoon sun imprisoning the room with bars of light.

This time, it should be noted, all went well in spite of the fact the phone rang at the most important moment and continued to ring irritably for some time, as though the caller suspected he was being ignored deliberately. Then, when they were through, each knew (though neither was indelicate enough to mention it) that, in spite of his headache, it had gone very much better than the first time. Philip especially enjoyed it and he felt relaxed and easy when, finally, exhausted, they lay side by side on the bed and he smoked and she drank tea and the conversation turned once again to Glenellen.

'I'll find out about him, if you like,' she said.

'I wish you would. And by the way, why should he be so interested in your husband?'

'I don't know. But the fact that he is means that he's up to something politically. If you want to do anything in this country you have to go to the Americans.'

'And your husband is the American to go to?'

'So they think.'

'I see.' He blew a series of elliptical smoke rings. They watched the pale rings distend and vanish in the golden mote-scattered light of the room. When the last one had vanished, she sat up in bed and propped a pillow behind her head. He looked at her with interest and pleasure, relieved in a way that the novelty was gone (usually it went in the first five minutes) and that he could regard her without that distorting of perspective lust caused. What he saw now he liked and he could, he knew, in time and if all went well, love or at least grow accustomed to her in such a way that he might think himself in love: that grand nineteenth-century passion which had never, at this moment in his life at least, touched him with its burnished wing . . . although, if questioned, he would no doubt insist with some severity that he had loved and suffered in his day, adding as all philanderers do that the promiscuity of his more recent years had in no way atrophied his power to love one person wholly, should that person by some miracle materialize in his arms after the usual dalliance with a responsive stranger. Thus did he believe love would come, quickly, suddenly, utterly transforming some stranger into a creature as desirable and as unique as those goddesses who, in ancient days, would for love of a mortal become temporary exiles from the heroic beds of heaven.

But the transformation was not destined to be made that day. Regina, sensing no doubt what he was thinking, suddenly pulled the sheet about her and said, 'Rex thought you very charming.'

'I'm glad. But I prefer you.'

'But he can do more for you.'

'Oh no, not that.'

'For someone who professes to hate politics you've got rather involved all on your own.'

'You mean the Glenellen business? That's just idle curiosity. He makes me laugh.'

'Do I make you laugh?'

'No. No, you don't, not at all. Should you?'

'I'm not sure.' She sighed. 'I must go now. Rex is waiting.'

'When shall I see you?'

'Anytime you like. Tomorrow?'

'Tomorrow. The same time?'

'I'll be here. How do you feel now?'

'Rather odd.'

'I wonder if you should see a doctor.'

'No. I'll be all right. I'll sleep it off.'

But the next day he was worse. The night had been terrible. He now had a fever as well as a headache and he tossed about unable to sleep until, shortly after dawn, he took a shot of brandy and at last slept fitfully, tormented by nightmares, by all the childhood monsters of the fever world. When he tried to sit up he grew dizzy, his head throbbed and his eyes ached, dazzled by the morning light. Convinced that he was going to die, he rang for some tea and some brandy to hasten the end. He wondered if they would bury him in the Protestant Cemetery, near Keats and Shelley. He could imagine the fuss his mother would make: his body would be shipped back at great expense and deposited with the other Warrens on the banks of the Hudson where he had, he thought lugubriously, played as a child. The idea of his own premature death, complicated by the very real discomfort he was in, so moved him that he was tempted to cry, not noisily but softly, in a manly way. The arrival of the waiter, however, immediately lessened the pain and brought him again into a proper relationship with the living as they exchanged greetings. Then Philip drank the tea and the brandy and felt somewhat better. He was considering whether to get up and take a bath, to try and draw the fever out of his aching joints, when Mr Norman entered the room, a friendly smile on his face.

'Do excuse me for barging in like this but I'm to tell you of a little change in our plans. Ayre has been called to Milan on business and so the meeting will be postponed for a week. I hope that's all right with you.'

'Anything is all right with me,' said Philip gently, beginning to die now that he had an audience.

'What *is* the matter with you?' Mr Norman was alarmed. 'You look perfectly frightful.'

'I am sick,' Philip whispered and shut his eyes, feeling rather better for having drunk the brandy.

'Ah, you've caught it,' said Mr Norman with some satisfaction, proud of his adopted city's treachery.

'Caught what?'

'We call it Roman fever, and everyone gets it. It lasts about a week. Possibly it's from the water, or perhaps it's just because the city is so low . . . used to be malarial, you know. There was a time when no one could stay here during the summer.'

'But what do I do?'

'I'll get you a doctor. Nice chap I know, a German. He'll fix you up in no time. Meanwhile, you'll have to stay in bed and miss this splendid weather.'

'I don't care. I don't care about anything.'

'By the way, I telephoned you yesterday afternoon but there was no answer.'

'I wasn't here. I was walking in the park.'

'Now that's odd because the manager said you were in your room.' Mr Norman chuckled maliciously.

'I take long walks up and down the corridor,' said Philip, wishing Mr Norman would go away. His wish came true, for Mr Norman, after this final indication that he knew precisely what the other was up to, departed with the promise to send him the doctor immediately.

Illness becomes the young, in moderation, of course. It makes them pause in the midst of their physical euphoria and contemplate mortality. For young men like Philip the body is unobtrusive, something to be fed and washed like a motorcar and, from time to time, relieved in different ways. It gives no trouble and, served properly, can be the best of all possible toys. Philip's was no exception. He was vaguely fond of his body. He admired it dispassionately, without vanity though not without some complacency when he compared it to others and found it not only decorative but useful, equal to the admittedly not very rigorous tasks he set for it. But now after twenty-eight years of loving care, something had gone wrong. He had had the childhood illnesses but none had been severe, while his maturity had been marked by the most resolute health. Yet now, in an instant, he had been laid low and at first he wished he were dead; then, suddenly aware of what it would be like to die, he wished he were well and thousands of miles away from this city which had so gratuitously returned his passionate admiration with a well-aimed blow in the most unexpected quarter.

He convalesced slowly. He read. He sat on his balcony in the cool sunshine and surveyed the life of the street with a detached eye, aware that he was set apart from the busy men and women out of doors who did not know, as he did, that man is vulnerable and the flesh, after a certain age, corrupt and festering, preparing for its final dissolution. The morbidity of such conjectures appealed to him hugely and once the pain left he found that he almost missed the knowledge of the body it gave him, the sense of the secret actions and counteractions of the flesh which caused him to live and to be, which would cease all too soon when the mechanism, unbalanced at last, would degenerate into dust to be rearranged in time into other less sentient forms.

Regina came to see him every day. They talked of many things and she spoke often of politics, of his natural gift for them (though how she knew he had such a gift was never apparent to him). She tempted him in every way she could to go home when she did and to prepare for a great career. He was touched that she had such faith in him. Her calm assurance, however, was bewildering: she spoke of the winning of future elections as a fact. It all seemed easy when she spoke of it, so definite. She told him how elections could be won, which person could do what for him. Knowing her power, he could not, at least when it came to detail, doubt what she said. In his weakened state he found himself more receptive to this gaudy dream of dominion than ordinarily he would have been. And she, seeing that her companion was making some progress, pressed on until at last he was almost ready to agree to go back in two months' time and begin the ascent: wondering always what it was that she wanted from him, what he must give her in exchange. He did not like to ask and so he held back from the final declaration she so much wanted to hear.

One morning he awakened to find that he was well again. He stretched and unsuccessfully tried to recall what the pain had been like; but he could not remember, even the memory of the fever was gone.

Mr Norman, who had kept careful watch over him during his illness (he had even encountered Regina briefly in his room), arrived shortly after breakfast.

'You look very well, very well indeed.'

'I'm going to go out today.'

'By all means. Get more air . . . won't do you a bit of harm. Summer is here and the day is fine. I've been up since seven.'

'It'll be nice to get out of this room.'

'Has Mrs Durham called you yet?'

'No, I'm seeing her tonight.'

'A lovely woman,' said Mr Norman, looking in the mirror and combing his thin hair straight back. 'She's quite a nurse, too, isn't she?'

'She's been very kind,' said Philip, pulling the blanket about him and getting up. He felt strong and confident, ready for almost anything. Which was fortunate, for Mr Norman had, as usual, a plan to which Philip, with a number of unexpressed doubts, finally agreed. At four o'clock that afternoon he arrived, alone, at the Baths of Nero.

The Baths were in a small side street. A large, soiled plaster head of Nero hung above the door through which he passed into a dingy reception room. A man who spoke no English indicated the price, which Philip paid, wondering, as always, whether or not he was being cheated. He was then led down a spiral staircase to a large well-lit room full of cubicles with wooden numbered doors. Men dressed in sheets or towels padded up and down the corridor; when he entered several stopped their patrolling and stared at him.

Now, it should be remarked at this point that Philip was neither naïve nor innocent. He had had a varied and interesting life which had included a thorough indoctrination in almost every human activity. His own tastes were set when, at thirteen, he seduced a high-school senior, a much admired girl of eighteen and the object of his older brother's less virile attention. The excitement of this conquest had gone to his head and so, for fifteen years now, he had untiringly repeated that first experience with various partners, his enthusiasm and pleasure increasing rather than lessening as he grew older. Over the years, however, he had been offered any number of opportunities to explore other ways in the company of excited strangers. When he was fifteen an older woman, a respectable family friend, had tried to get him to beat her with the silken cord of her dead husband's dressing gown. He had refused her sternly. A year later, at prep school, he was invited to indulge in certain erotic ceremonies conducted by the school's leading athlete, a strong passionate boy who died in the fire of a bomber the year the war ended. In spite of his adulation for this young hero, Philip's natural modesty, combined with a precocious love of his own pleasure, caused him, with great politeness, to refuse the invitation. Later, in uniform, seldom a day went by without some form of adventure presenting itself. Elderly men bought him drinks and invited him up to their rooms for a nightcap. He refused them all, even though on occasion he would accept a drink or two at a bar. The lavatories of various railroad and bus terminals of the country were brilliant with generous invitations which he always declined pleasantly as he continued his own quiet and orderly progress. He was never outraged. In fact, everything interested him in the abstract, and several times when friends of his had tried to sell him on this or that variation he had admitted that it all sounded very interesting and that perhaps at some other time he might give it a try. But that other time never came and meanwhile Philip covered the field like a quarterback with good interference.

From time to time, however, he had become involved in situations which had he been less of a traveller, less curious, he might never have known about, much less become involved in – proving, perhaps, that he had an inclination towards forbidden vice; a very slight one, however; certainly not enough of one to render enjoyable this visit to the Baths of Nero where, after tying a small white apron about his loins, he timidly opened the door of his cubicle and stepped out into the hall.

Slowly, barefoot, not liking the thought of the dirty coarse matting under his feet, he walked down the hall towards a small sitting room where a number of middle-aged gentlemen were smoking and chatting and drinking apéritifs provided by the management. They paused in their conversation and looked at him very carefully. Several were noticeably aroused and one sighed audibly as Philip, blushing furiously, walked past them to the thick glass door of the steam room. He caught the words '*Inglese, Americano.*' He wished he had not come. He had known perfectly well what it would be like: the world of the Turkish bath was no secret to him nor, for that matter, was the character of Mr Norman. Idle curiosity had brought him here, and now, he decided grimly, he would have to go through with it.

Hanging his apron on a peg beside the other aprons, he stepped into the hot room.

It was a large room with stained-glass clerestory windows which gave it a faintly ecclesiastical air. On three sides of the room a broad white marble shelf had been built and here, in Roman fashion, a number of figures reclined or sat. Off to the right was another door of glass, the door to the steam room. A fountain decorated the centre of the hot room and cold water trickled from the fountain's mouth into a basin where the clients dipped their hands from time to time and cooled their faces. The most remarkable feature of the establishment was a number of unusually handsome Italian boys, with deep chests and velvet skins, who wandered about the room with pre-occupied expressions, stopping here and there to say a few words to this or that person. They were, Philip could see, the quarry, the central attraction of the Baths.

The men on the marble benches were for the most part middle-aged though there were some very young ones, Philip noticed, as well as several incredibly old ones not yet free of Sophocles' cruel and insane master, though very nearly free of the flesh itself. They talked in all languages, laughing and joking like club-men. There was a significant pause when Philip entered, and as he walked across the room to a vacant place on the bench he was aware that he was being judged, point by point, like a prize bull. Simulating indifference, he swung himself onto the bench and modestly crossed his legs. The conversation resumed, although there were many glances in his direction and one young man, a lean American with a crewcut, came over and asked him if he would like to go back to his room with him. Philip shook his head politely and smiled. 'I'm meeting somebody,' he said. Sadly the young man went away and Philip rubbed himself until he began to sweat, trying not to notice the various odd duets about the room.

In a great burst of sound, talk and laughter, Glenellen, red and leathery as a salamander, entered from the steam room, a towel arranged about his head in the fashion of the Pharaohs. He was accompanied by Evan, who looked handsome with his clothes off, and Mr Norman, who did not.

'Ah, there you are, my boy. Hardly recognized you. Hardly recognized you, indeed,' hummed Glenellen, inspecting him quickly, professionally. 'May we join you on the slab?' They arranged themselves like corpses around him; Glenellen sighed voluptuously. 'The heat, the heat,' he murmured, 'ah, the darling heat.'

'We come here every day,' said Evan, who looked as though he would rather have been anywhere else: he was sweating profusely, unlike the two older men who seemed to absorb the heat greedily.

'Good for the soul,' said Mr Norman, hesitantly patting Philip's calf. Philip moved out of range.

'I should think you'd all get very thin,' he said, for want of anything else to say. He had never felt so out of place and already he had begun to plan his escape.

'Source of life,' intoned Glenellen, sitting up and looking at the youths who stood in decorative attitudes around the fountain, showing their wares to the would-be purchasers and talking in low voices among themselves. 'Give me young lips that taste of fruit,' said Glenellen, smiling, revealing his carious teeth. 'What say you, young man?'

'Oh, by all means,' said Philip distractedly.

'Aren't they lovely? Like young gods. Commercial young gods, but still divine.'

'Very nice,' said Philip, not wishing to give offence or to be thought gauche.

'Which would you pick?'

'I don't really know,' said Philip beginning to blush, aware that Mr Norman was watching him with great amusement.

'You can have any one you like,' said Glenellen with a royal gesture. 'I will treat you to one.'

'I . . . I'm afraid I'm not in the mood today.'

'Nonsense. A healthy boy like you is always in the mood. Come now, don't be shy. Take your pick . . . my party, you know.'

'Are they very expensive?' Philip stalled.

'Five hundred *lire*, that's all . . . *prix fixe*. Here, at least. On the street you have to pay more. Well . . . what about that dusky Venetian blond? Wonderful type! How Titian would have loved that skin, and Michelangelo that torso. I almost want him for myself . . . but after you. I will be generous. You are my guest today.'

Philip did not know whether to reveal himself as a womanizer and a tourist, or to dodge the whole thing gracefully by going off with the boy for a polite length of time. Mr Norman, a mound of white dimpled flesh, saved him by remarking, 'Before we play, Ayre, I suggest we do our business. Besides, you must remember that our young friend has been very sick these last few days. He may not be in the mood for games.'

'He looks all right to me,' said Ayre suspiciously, 'but you're right, we must set to work.' He sat cross-legged on the marble. The heat, Philip decided, was good for him. Glenellen was far more alert than usual, even rational. 'Evan, go take one of the boys and cool off. You look like a weeping willow.'

Evan, obviously pleased, scrambled off the bench and walked over to the fountain, where he engaged a small sinewy Sicilian in conversation. They came to terms immediately and with a wave to the others, Evan followed the young man out of the room.

'He always likes those small muscle-bound boys,' said Ayre peevishly. 'He has no taste. No love of beauty. Poorly educated, that's the trouble, like all the Welsh. Where were we, Clyde?'

'Business. Mr Warren.'

'Ah, yes. Mr Warren, we need you.' His voice was urgent. He looked about furtively to make sure that no strangers were listening. 'We've examined your record carefully, both of us, Clyde and myself, and we've decided that you can be of great use to us in our movement. But before I go into detail, I must impress upon you the need for secrecy. If you feel that you cannot for any reason respect my confidence, I wish you would say so now and I will not continue . . . my lips will be sealed.'

'Well,' began Philip uncertainly, torn between curiosity and a fear of involvement.

'I accept that, then, as your pledge,' said Glenellen, rearranging his red, loose body upon the marble. 'We know that politically you are in sympathy with us. Your comments on politics have been duly noted and interpreted. In short, Mr Warren, we recognize you as a fellow royalist and we wish for a short period to utilize your talents in our movement to restore the House of Savoy to its rightful place here in our adopted land.'

It was out at last. Philip, who had long ago decided that Glenellen was the head of an international opium combine, gave a sigh of relief; pleased to know what it was all about, a little disappointed that the more glamorous alternative had not materialized.

'What do you think Philip?' asked the suet-white lump on his other side, a flaccid, breathing shape which contained a soul as passionate as any other's.

'I don't know. I mean, I haven't any idea what you want me to do.' Philip was immediately furious with himself for having taken the wrong line, for not having immediately opposed any suggestion that he join the cabal. He realized, however, that it was now too late, at this moment anyway, to back out; he had indicated interest and he was partly committed.

'Two things,' said Glenellen promptly. 'We need a courier to go to Amalfi next week. Most of our people are already known to the police and are being watched. We must send someone they cannot suspect and someone they don't dare touch. The fact that you are an American and new to Rome is all in your favour. You have never been seen with me. This place is safe, by the way. My own house, of course, is watched but if you remember, there was no moon the night you came. The second thing is the more difficult and the more important: we want you to try to enlist Mr Durham on our side. We feel that if he could present the true facts of the case to your President he would intervene and restore the monarchy. The Republic is a fiasco. Everyone knows it. Any day now the Communists will take over and that will be the end of Italy. We have great resources behind us ... great men are helping us ... but we must proceed cautiously and not force an issue too soon. Above all, we must get the American government on our side. Naturally, we have any number of people at work in Washington but it has not been easy to interest your government. Since you are on the best of terms with Mrs Durham, you could, if you chose, exert considerable influence in that quarter, adding immeasurably thereby to the total effort in which we are all engaged.' He paused, the foggy blue eyes beneath the Egyptian headdress alert, the usual vagueness replaced by an unfamiliar concentration which impressed Philip, against his better judgement.

'I'm afraid,' he said at last, 'that there isn't much I can do about the Durhams. They both know what they think and I'm sure they wouldn't take any advice from me on foreign affairs. After all, that's his specialty, you know. And, to be practical, even if I could influence him, that still doesn't mean it would be any help to you. The President and Congress don't respond to that sort of influence when it comes to a national policy ... at least, I don't think they do,' he added, suddenly appalled by the unexpected pedantry of his reply; it was not as if he knew what he was talking about. He persevered, however, covering up his involuntary expression of doubt by several more dogmatic remarks on American foreign policy.

'But that doesn't mean,' said Mr Norman smoothly, 'that one can't try. Every little bit helps, you know. Mr Durham can supply us with information either directly or indirectly. We can discover what his government is thinking, learn how to change, if possible, that thinking. Oh, there are many ways to accomplish our ends, many ways, and there are many of us at work on different levels. You could try, at the very least. If you wanted to.'

'Perhaps,' said Philip doubtfully, already intrigued.

'Will you deliver the papers for us?' asked Glenellen.

'What are they?'

'Very important documents. I can tell you no more. In any case, they must never fall into the government's hands. If there is any danger you must destroy them.'

'Where are they being sent?'

'You will take them?'

'Depends on where you want me to go. I'm travelling for pleasure and I have only a year and many things to see. I don't want to waste any time.'

'Waste any time! Young man, do you realize that at this very minute Umberto, our martyred king . . .'

'Amalfi,' said Mr Norman quickly. 'I'm sure you will like it . . . one of the loveliest old cities in Italy, and the bathing is excellent.'

In a reckless mood, Philip accepted the commission. Both Mr Norman and Lord Glenellen profusely complimented him on his wisdom and thanked him for his wise partisanship to their high cause. Mention was made of several decorations which would be given him when a grateful king once more adorned the Quirinal Palace. Although Philip questioned them further about the movement, he received no new information. They would not tell him whether Umberto himself was involved or what stand the Vatican was taking. They suggested darkly that they had powerful friends who would, at the right moment, declare themselves king's men. As for his own role, instructions on how to proceed would be given him in a few days, said Mr Norman. He would not have to leave Rome before another week, in which time it was hoped he would have made some headway with Mr Durham. Philip agreed, dubiously, to much of this: he could already imagine himself in front of a firing squad of Republican soldiers.

This grim vision was cut short by the return of Evan, breathless but otherwise cheerful. The Sicilian youth also returned a moment later, unruffled and businesslike. He joined his confreres at the fountain and they conversed seriously, like a group of brokers on the exchange. It was obvious, even to Philip, that they were discussing the price of their commodity.

'Good?' asked Mr Norman.

Evan nodded, catching his breath at last. 'Awfully.'

'Better than Guido?'

'Well, Guido is Guido. I mean, there could hardly be another.'

'No, I suppose not.'

'We have forgotten our friend!' cried Glenellen, sitting up. 'We've done nothing for him. Shown him no hospitality. Evan, go get that blond one over there, the Venetian beauty. I'm sure he will provide Mr Warren with a fine welcome to the Baths of Nero.'

'But . . .' Philip got no further, for Glenellen then proceeded to celebrate in extravagant phrases the virtues of the baths and how, on more than one occasion, their existence had saved civilization. Even today, he implied, the serious work of Rome would be tragically affected if the lawyers and businessmen could make an occasional visit to the baths on their way home to their wives and children. According to Glenellen, every Roman would be hopelessly frustrated and neurotic without this marvellously organized release.

Evan returned without the blond. 'He won't come,' he said, upsetting Glenellen's entire system.

'Won't come? And why not?'

'He says that our friend here is too young and too good-looking, that he only likes older men. He asked me to introduce him to you instead.' They all laughed: Philip with relief and Glenellen with almost childish pleasure. Then the boy was brought over and presented to Glenellen who quickly, and in Italian, made the necessary arrangements. Philip, who only a moment before had congratulated himself on his narrow escape, was not yet safe, for Glenellen, with all the insistence of his monomania, summoned a powerfully built adolescent, with a body like the David and the face of a stupid angel, to be Philip's companion.

'A gift!' exclaimed the peer warmly.

It was too late for Philip to retreat. He submitted without a word, aware that Mr Norman was especially enjoying his discomfort. Led by Glenellen, they left the room for their various cubicles and those transports of commercial bliss which have ever engaged the highest talents of the finest poets but will not for once concern us here.

After making a date to see Philip in two days' time, Glenellen disappeared with his Venetian. Mr Norman, too, had engaged the services of a temporary friend, while the satiated Evan ordered wine.

When the others were gone, Philip turned rather hopelessly to the youth and told him, first in English and then in French, that he would get his money all right but that because of some fundamental perversity in his own nature he would rather forgo the pleasures of the couch. The youth knew neither French nor English. He smiled charmingly and said, '*Si?*' Then he followed Philip to his room.

It would be startling to report that the stalwart Philip succumbed to pagan vice, that the habits of his maturity were in an instant undone by this classic figure which, against his will, he found himself admiring. But we must remain true to the fact of Philip's character and report, truthfully, that nothing happened. When they got into the cubicle the boy removed his apron and hung it on a peg. Then he looked down at himself and smiled with an ingenuous vanity, as though to say: 'Isn't this handsome?' Philip smiled back. They stood facing one another for a moment. Then, a little bewildered that no move had been made, the boy sat down on the edge of the bed. Philip, feeling silly, sat down too, several inches away from the smooth olive-skinned flank. The boy then asked for a cigarette. Each had a cigarette. The boy felt Philip's arm muscle and nodded admiringly; then he flexed his own arm and Philip gingerly touched the other's biceps with a forefinger. Another silence. The boy changed his position on the bed several times and Philip sat bolt upright beside him. Finally, the boy frowned and, indicating himself, suggested by signs that perhaps he was not Philip's type. Philip quickly put the lie to this by demonstrating with gestures that the young man's body was all that could be desired, but that (and here he made certain universal signs in the air) it was not a woman's body. This revelation astonished the other. He talked a great deal, stating, as far as Philip could tell, that all Americans, English and Germans liked Italian boys and even Italian boys, though they didn't make too great a thing of it, liked Italian boys.

He then demonstrated graphically that he was all a woman could desire and that women were all that he desired even though he came every day to the baths not only for money but for the companionship of his friends, the other youths about the fountain. How could Philip understand all this? Never mind. He did. One of the first things one learns in travelling is that people understand one another if they want to, no matter how great the language barrier. And so, on a friendly note, their brief encounter ended. The boy put his apron back on, borrowed another cigarette, shook hands and left the room with, Philip knew, a hell of a funny story to tell the boys in the hot room.

'It is the most absurd thing I've ever heard.'

'I suppose so . . . but then to me anything that has to do with politics is absurd.'

'Well, you certainly won't go.'

'I'm not so sure,' he said stubbornly, waving to a waiter who responded as waiters do by distractedly going off in the opposite direction. They were seated in the open at Doney's, their backs to the street, facing the sidewalk and the afternoon display of new alliances and costumes, all rosy in the light of the setting sun.

'But Philip, you can get into trouble. Just remember the Communists may take over Italy any day now. There isn't a chance in the world of the monarchy being restored and even if there were, that madman Glenellen wouldn't be involved in it.'

'So you do know who he is.'

She grimaced. 'I found out after you mentioned him the other day. Do be careful. He's really bad news, and mad as a hatter.'

'But I want to see Amalfi.'

She sighed. 'That's another thing, of course.'

'Is it really lovely?'

'Oh yes. I went there with Rex once, years ago, when we were first married.'

Finally, a treaty was made after many speeches, border disputes, hostages surrendered and compliments exchanged; their affair was, at the end, no longer the same, weakened by policy but like a fracture that has healed, strongest at the point where the break occurred. When two people are fond of one another the first quarrel, the first sign of wills in opposition, comes as a shock, destroying the vain illusion that two can be one: a knowledge that is saddening but, happily, soon obscured if the new alliance is intelligently refashioned, defined by sensible treaty. The covenant to which they both agreed was that he go to Amalfi, that he not mix in politics, that he await with mounting impatience her arrival some ten days later in a small English car called a Riley, very fast with a convertible top and room for only two people in it.

CHAPTER FOUR

'I don't know why, but I can hardly believe that this is the room where Ibsen wrote *Ghosts*.'

'Probably because this is *not* the room. It's over there, across the hall.'

'But the manager said distinctly that it was the first room to the left.'

'Well, dear, this is the first room to the right.'

'So it is, Bella. I'm sorry. I was hasty.'

'And there seems to be someone in it.'

'Why, so there is. I wonder who.'

'Not so loud, dear, he's asleep.'

'Do you think it's an American?'

'Good heavens, how can I tell? I mean, he's asleep.'

'Now *you* are talking loud.'

'Come along, May. Let's look in the *right* room now.'

'It's really terribly thrilling! I love Ibsen, don't you?'

'Oh yes, yes.'

'What was *Ghosts* about, by the way? I've forgotten.'

'Tuberculosis.'

Philip waited until he heard them withdraw; then he rolled over and opened his eyes, unpleasantly aware that as usual in the heat he sweated more asleep than awake. Slowly he got to his feet and like an old man enjoying his discomfort, he crossed the room and shut the door, wondering why he had accepted this ridiculous mission. Pondering bleakly the House of Savoy, he put on bathing trunks and a dressing gown; then he left the room.

The hotel was a rambling, odd sort of structure on top of a steep cliff at the town's edge. In the centre of a Moorish-style patio with delicate carved arches of yellowed plaster, ancient tiles, cracked and smooth from age, were arranged in oriental patterns about a lily pond, shadowed by a single orange tree.

He stood a moment blinking in the hot sun. Below him was the town of Amalfi, surrounded by steep cliffs and green hills, cut by a narrow ravine through which a slender foaming river ran, curving down through terraced stone houses to the luminous blue sea which sparkled a hundred feet below him, vivid in the noon light.

He crossed the street and descended the steps which had long ago been cut in the rock of the cliff.

He had had a brief recurrence of the fever coming down the day before on the train and now, today, he felt tired and irritable, obscurely despondent, without direction, conscious of no real centre to his life. The thought of his secret mission depressed him further and he wondered if it might not solve everything if he drowned himself in that warm blue sea beside which he now sat in his bathing trunks, one foot in the water and his face turned blankly to the scorching sun, like a tired love offering to the occupant of the far-ranging golden car.

Then, bored with sunlight, he looked about him at the sharp brown rocks which edged the peninsula at this point; there were no beaches here, only cliffs and rocks. At the town's centre, the ravine and the river were contained by wharves, the focus of Amalfi which, like some great pink amphitheatre, fanned out over the green and umber hills at whose summits dead castles rose in solemn silhouette.

It was all very lovely, he decided sourly, giving up the idea of suicide for the moment.

'Are you American?'

'Yes.'

'How nice, Bella. We were right . . . at least, I was.'

He recognized the voices: the two ladies who had awakened him in search of Ibsen's *Ghosts*. They stood now before him in white dresses and wide hats, with cameras over their shoulders, each holding a great handbag containing pills and lotions, guidebooks and expensive cameos. They were American, plump, no longer young, resolutely cheery; mannerisms and costumes so alike they seemed identical twins, although he was sure that, examined carefully, there must be any number of differences easily remarkable to their friends.

Introductions. Bella and May Washington were sisters, teachers of English and Social Science, respectively, in the Bigelow Clapp High School, Council Bluffs, Iowa. Both were unmarried, they hastened to say, both virginal, he decided.

'Isn't it nice?' said Bella, sitting on the rock to his left.

'So lovely and warm,' said May, perching on a rock to his right. He pivoted to face them, the sun on his back now.

'We saw Pompeii, did you?'

'Not yet. But I passed near it on the bus from Naples this morning.'

'Then you only got here today.'

'A few hours ago.'

'We've been here a week.'

'We must really apologize for breaking in on you like that but May had been reading about Amalfi in the guidebook when lo and behold! she discovered that Ibsen had stayed at our hotel and that he had written *Ghosts* there so we hastened to discover which had been his room and the manager very kindly told us. By mistake we got into your room. May's mistake.'

'Yes. Silly of me, wasn't it? I never seem able to follow directions. But it was so interesting, seeing the room. I asked the manager all about Mr Ibsen and he said that he remembered seeing him years ago when he was a little boy, when the manager was a little boy.'

'Tell Mr Warren what he said about him.'

'He said that he had whiskers and that he refused to eat *pasta* . . . isn't that interesting?'

'It certainly is,' agreed Philip.

'Will you be here long?'

'About two weeks,' said Philip, imagining those two weeks: A sun-scorched time of dazzling seas, of restless nights until Regina came. '*Dies irae*,' he murmured to himself as he was told what to see in Amalfi, which churches were lovely and which were tacky, which stores were expensive and which were reasonable and full, yes full! of fine cameos, old and rare. Would he like to see one? Yes? He was shown a large yellow cameo of Minerva, or was it the goddess of liberty? No, more likely Minerva. 'I mean, after all in those days the Goddess of Liberty was rather *de trop*, as the French say. Not at all proper to reproduce in a monarchy like Italy,' which reminded him again of his mission and thinking of it, he shuddered suddenly in the hot sun.

'And then he was killed by the Count's servants and eaten by wolves.'

What on earth was she talking about? he wondered, aware that he'd missed an entire anecdote.

'How terrible!' he exclaimed. Then, to show interest: 'Where did the wolves come from?'

'The forest, naturally. The castle was surrounded by a forest in those days and there were wolves everywhere. Certainly proves the legend, doesn't it?'

'I should say so.' Philip was now ready to go swimming but they had other plans for him: they wanted to take his picture. So he posed for them against a rock, looking out to sea like a tired Hermes prepared for flight.

'Thanks so much. That's our hobby, you know, taking pictures. We have seventeen scrapbooks now.'

'We travel a great deal. This is our fourth trip to Europe . . . the first since the war.'

'Bella likes Italy. I like France.' Their views were presented to him and he passed judgement as tactfully as possible and then, before they could draw him out, he rose and excused himself and with some style dived into the warm sea, narrowly missing a sharp rock which might have split his head, providing the sisters Washington with an unusual snapshot.

He left the hotel through a back door, wondering whether or not he should have worn a cape. In his coat pocket, fastened with a safety pin, was the document which he was to deliver to the 'organization.' But before he could meet the 'organization' he would first have to present himself at midnight at a certain antique shop where the proprietor, according to Glenellen's verbal instructions, would receive him warmly if he remembered to say '*O lente, lente currite, noctis equi.*' He had been drilled in this one sentence by Clyde Norman and as he walked down the narrow street murmured it over and over to himself.

The street fascinated him: steep and only a few feet wide, a cobbled path between the windowless façades of buildings, broken here and there by deep-set bolted doors. The only light came from the fragment of moon overhead and from the lights of the town at the foot of the street. Feeling disembodied and faintly unreal, he walked like a ghost through the warm wine-odoured darkness, the stale heat of the day lingering in the quiet air, and he wondered what would happen if, irrationally, he began to shout and batter on one of those metal-studded doors.

His mood changed when he stepped into the circle of dim electric light which illuminated the level part of the town, stage to the amphitheatre. Men and youths stood about on the wharves in groups talking, their shadows long upon the sea. In open cafés men and women were singing loudly and, Philip thought, melodiously on pitch. He was aware of curious glances as he walked in front of the main café. Tourists were still a curiosity in this country so recently con-quered by the foreign armies.

In front of a pool hall he asked a policeman where the antique shop he wanted was and the policeman, an affable man, was able to tell him, in English. After thanking the man, he strolled up the main street of the town.

The farther he walked away from the sea the narrower the streets became, while the long dark shapes of the mountains on either side grew more oppressive by moonlight as they converged and the town continued on up the hillside, almost to the castle-crowned summits. Near the fast and narrow river, contained by masonry and spanned by medieval bridges, was the shop of Signor Alberto Guiscardo. A sign in Gothic script announced Signor Guiscardo's name and business. Philip pulled the bell; there was a loud jangling.

After a long wait the door was opened by a young boy who spoke rapid Italian until, seeing that Philip did not understand, he stopped abruptly and made a motion for Philip to come into the house.

The first room was the shop, large and musty, crowded with furniture and mirrors and paintings all jumbled together like a looted museum. The next room they entered was a modern drawing room, small, well lighted and airless. The windows were all shut and Philip wondered if he would be able to stand the heat and the odour of incense which burdened the torpid air. He was invited to sit down; then the boy disappeared. Philip had just picked up a book which someone had left open on a coffee table when the tinkling noise of a Mozart quartet filled the room. He put the book down nervously and looked about for some sign of life; there was none. The phonograph was in another room. He was about to pick up the book again when *it* appeared. Philip started with dismay. *It* was a fat middle-aged man in a Sulka dressing gown (mulberry with gold figurings) who wore over his face a rubber mask like the ones sold in American drugstores. This particular mask depicted, in the most lifelike manner, the rosy features of a plump somewhat vacuous hog.

'How do you do. How do you do. Please don't get up. Sherry? Yes? I always drink sherry, too. I've nothing stronger, in any case.' A glass of sherry was produced from the sideboard. Philip took it, still staring at the pig's face of his host.

'Now let us chat,' said Signor Guiscardo, settling comfortably into an armchair. 'You wonder at how well I speak English? So do I. I have never had a single lesson. I've never been out of Italy, in spite of my numerous . . . I repeat, numerous . . . friendships with Americans and English people. You are American?'

'Yes . . . just visiting.'

'Have you been to Capri?'

'No.'

'Do you plan to go there soon?'

'No. I shall probably go back to Rome when I leave here.'

'You must under no circumstances miss Capri,' said the Pig solemnly, taking the sherry through a slit under the snout.

'If it's very interesting, perhaps I will go there.'

'Do, by all means.'

There was a long pause as they sipped sherry and Philip sweated in the heat and looked longingly at the sealed windows. It did no good, however, for his host obviously had no intention of opening them. Finally, when the silence got too oppressive for him to bear, Philip said the magic words Ayre had drilled him in before leaving Rome. '*O lente, lente currite, noctis equi.*'

No sooner had he pronounced the incantation than the Pig stood up abruptly, spilling sherry all over its mulberry dressing gown. Hands to his head, as though the piggish jowls might burst, he rushed from the room leaving Philip bewildered and a little frightened. He was nearly ready to make a run for it himself when his host reappeared. This time the dressing gown was of stiff brocade, dark green with a *mille-fleurs* design. On his face he wore a new mask, that of a goat, a pale astonished-looking goat with haggard features and unhealthy red eyes.

'I think this is more becoming,' said the Goat quietly, returning to his chair and folding his hands in his lap.

Philip half expected to see cloven hoofs instead of hands. 'So do I,' said Philip, refusing to betray the very real alarm he felt.

'So much more in keeping with the tone of our discussion.'

'I couldn't agree more.'

'What were we discussing?'

'I had made a Latin reference. I had quoted a line of Ovid.'

'Of course. In the excitement it had slipped my mind. Do you like the classics?'

'Very much. Especially Horace.'

'Superb, superb poet. But I must say Catullus is more me.'

'I'm not surprised.'

'You're not despised?'

'No. I said that I am not surprised.'

'Oh.' There was a pause. The Goat looked at him thoughtfully; then it said: 'How is milord Glenellen?'

'Very well. He sends you his regards.'

'Send him mine, when you see him.'

'I shall.' Philip was relieved that the conversation had begun to take an anticipated turn. 'Shall I give you the papers now?'

The Goat threw up its hands as though in terror. 'Under no circumstances, my dear young man, are to to give me anything. Ever! Do you understand?'

'But I thought . . .'

'I don't care what you thought. You are not to give me anything. Do you realize that I am watched every minute? I can take no chances. There are a number of people who await with eagerness my downfall. I wish to disappoint them.'

'Well, of course, if you . . .' The Goat had rushed to the window and was looking out into the darkened street, presenting, Philip thought, a dreadful vision to any passerby, civilian or spy.

'I can advise, however,' said the Goat suavely, satisfied that at the moment the street was empty, the enemy in hiding. 'Not only can I advise, I will, with your permission, suggest.' He looked inquiringly at Philip who nodded gravely. 'In five days the moon will be full. You will proceed to the ruined Church of St Elmo on the slope above the St Elmo Bridge . . . you can't miss it . . . and there (you must arrive at midnight precisely, not earlier, not later) the committee will await you in front of what was formerly the high altar. Deliver your papers to them.'

'Are you sure you don't want them?'

'As sure as I am that the House of Savoy will return to its proper place among us,' said the Goat with an intense piety, in keeping with its sacerdotal features.

'In that case, I had better go. I hadn't planned to stay in Amalfi quite so long.'

'You're not going to leave without delivering the papers?' The Goat was anxious.

'No, I am going to leave you . . . I mean. I don't want to impose myself on you any longer tonight. You have been very kind.'

'Not at all. I'm only sorry I couldn't have been of more help to you. But I'm sure that you appreciate my position in all of this.'

'Of course. You must be careful.'

'Not for myself, either,' said the Goat with dignity, like a martyr discussing an *auto-da-fé*, 'but for Italy and for our king.'

The silence that followed this pronouncement was so long, so reverent, that Philip was tempted to steal quietly away. The Goat, however, was not finished. 'Are you by any chance interested in antiques?' he asked in a different voice.

'No,' said Philip cruelly, 'not at all.'

The Goat appeared to be depressed. 'That's a pity. I have some exciting bits and pieces, you know.'

'You see, I have no place to put them,' explained Philip, relenting.

'I know how it is. In case you know of anyone who might care for some rather unusual items, do send him to me.'

'I certainly will.'

'I am sure you will enjoy yourself in Amalfi,' said the Goat. 'We have everything a gentleman needs.'

'I haven't been well,' said Philip. 'I plan to rest here, to get some sun.'

'We have quite a number of fair-haired people in this section . . . where do they come from? Ah, who knows? From those great barbarian armies that once ranged up and down this ancient realm, taking their pleasure where they chose, clothed in the rough skins of beasts like so many forest gods. Then, later, the Normans came, from whom I am descended on both sides, the blood of Plantagenets like some heady tide in my veins, pulled this way and that by the waxing and waning of the silver moon; and from the Normans a new vitality infused the old stock, and the kingdom of the Two Sicilies flourished for many years until it came under foreign dominion and corrupt houses reigned; at last, under a mongrel Bourbon, God willed that it cease to be and Italy accepted Savoy, as I do, until that glad day when my own nation is free again and I, my dear sir, am restored to my rightful place as the first prince of Europe, as the rightful King of Naples.' The Goat stopped, one arm stretched out before him, upraised as though awaiting the anointing and the orb.

'May that day be soon,' said Philip quietly, now very alarmed.

'It will come,' said the Goat, arising and peering once again out the sealed window at the dark street. 'It will come. In the meantime, I devote my days to the restoration of Savoy, knowing that once they have returned the task of Plantagenet will be more easy, that our day must surely come.'

Philip rose. 'Now I must really go, sir,' he said, adding the 'sir' as he'd always been told one must with royalty. The Goat-King got to its feet, too.

'We've enjoyed your visit. You must come back to see us soon, by daylight, on a mission of less state.'

'I will, if I may.'

'And should you perhaps want an interesting object or two, or know of a friend who does, why, bear my little shop in mind.'

'I will, sir, I will indeed.'

'I shall show you out myself.' He led Philip down the dark hall of the dimly lit shop. Here they paused for a moment and the Goat rummaged through an antique Renaissance chest. At last he found what he wanted. 'It is from Pompeii,' he said. 'Keep it as a little memento of our agreeable meeting.'

'Thank you very much. I will,' said Philip, pocketing the small metal object. Then he was led to the door, which was opened after a good deal of unbolting and unchaining, like a fortress Philip thought; he turned to say good night to his host who had, in the meantime, somehow managed, between the shop and the front door, one final metamorphosis. The altogether too realistic face of a grey wolf stared at Philip, its green eyes glowing savagely in the dark.

'We must meet again. Remember your rendezvous: the Church of St Elmo the first night of the full moon.' The wolf's teeth glittered.

'It has been a great pleasure,' said Philip, backing out into the street with an agility which would have done credit to Little Red Ridinghood.

Two days later, at lunch with Bella and May Washington, he felt in his pocket for a handkerchief (the day was hot, the meal was a heavy one and all three were uncomfortably damp). The handkerchief was not there but the present from the King of the Two Sicilies was. He had forgotten all about it. While the two ladies were devouring chunks of hot fried veal, he examined the object. Then he tried unsuccessfully to hide it under his napkin but he was not quick enough, for the beady eyes of Bella Washington, like an eager raven's, had caught the shine of metal.

'A present someone gave me the other night. Nothing of importance.'

'Oh, do let us see it.' And there was nothing for him to do but hand them the small bonze phallus, executed in perfect detail by some long-dead Roman as an amulet to inspire fertility.

'What on earth is it?' asked Bella. 'Is it very old?'

'Very. Roman, or so I was told.'

'Let me see.' May took it and after a quick glance she blushed, betraying a knowledge of mysteries denied the virgin. She looked at Philip accusingly, as though he had this on purpose to reveal her secret, to taunt her with memories, no doubt still vivid, of past events never to be repeated in this bleak world. She gave it back to Bella who asked what it was.

'An amulet, dear,' said her sister, recovering her composure.

'Isn't it meant to be anything at all? It looks like something.'

'A tree,' said Philip helpfully, May glared at him.

'Do you know the Church of St Elmo?' asked Philip quickly, changing the subject, guiltily avoiding Bella's eyes.

'Oh yes,' said Bella. 'We loved it. So ruined.'

'One of the most interesting examples of Romanesque,' said May, her manner still constrained. 'We recommend it very highly. Or have you already seen it?'

'No, not yet. Someone told me it was quite interesting. An antique dealer, a man named Guiscardo. Have you met him yet?'

Bella nodded. 'We liked him,' she said. 'He sold us the marvellous cameo you saw your first day here. I thought it was a real bargain.'

'Did he seem in any way unusual?'

'Oh heavens, no . . .'

'Of course he did,' said May. 'His English – why, I've never heard an Italian speak such correct English. He was a most fluent conversationalist and his grasp of the idiom was firm. His remarks, too, were cogent and well expressed on nearly every topic we discussed.'

'On *every* topic,' said Bella benignly.

'You are correct, Bella, as always. On every topic. And he kissed our hands when we left.'

The sisters Washington went to a near-by castle after lunch and Philip, left to himself, wandered disconsolately about the hotel bowing gravely to the other guests, a dozen or so Europeans from the prosperous north of the continent, red-faced and long-haired, demoralized by the heat.

Then Regina, all in green, joined him on the terrace. 'Here I am,' she said.

'At exactly the right moment, too,' said Philip, standing up, but not taking her hand or kissing her. 'I was just this moment thinking of the flesh.'

'How flattering! A woman my age always enjoys being thought of as flesh, a decorative cushion for the lust of men. I knew that it was wise of me to come before I was expected.'

He pulled up a chair for her and they both sat down. She was extraordinarily handsome, he thought . . . her face darkened by the sun and her hair beginning to bleach.

'Has anything happened?' asked Philip, wondering how long it would take to reconstruct their affair, for the days that had separated them had provided each with a different memory of what had been at other meetings; memories which had been further distorted by separate ponderings: what one forgot the other treasured until at last they met on a hotel terrace overlooking Amalfi, and they were strangers.

She had come away from Rome sooner than planned, for Rex had suddenly gone on a tour of factories in western Austria and she had used this trip of his as an excuse to get away, to come to the seaside for a little bathing, to escape the heat of Rome which reminded her, she said, of that famous hymn by St Francis written during a terrible medieval summer and bedecked with sun images still vivid centuries later.

They spent the long days together, bathing in the warm salt water, boating, exploring caverns and listening to legends as old as the gods and as remote. At night, avoiding Bella and May Washington, who watched with eyes too interested to be disapproving, they strolled about the town visiting the waterfront cafés, drinking with the sailors and whores until, tired at last, they returned to the hotel and made love with an intensity that diminished as the moon grew great until, by the time the moon was full, Philip found his passion succeeded by a solicitousness which was more good manners than tenderness. Yet they needed one another and both knew that although there would soon be a change, this was not the time. He tried not to consider the future, unlike one of his idols, Stendhal, who always imagined the end of every love affair at the moment it began.

The afternoon of the day he was to go to the Church of St Elmo to fulfill his mission, he and Regina rented a rowboat and they rowed from the town to a grotto which could only be approached from the sea. They moored the boat to a large flat rock at the grotto's mouth; then they took off their clothes and swam nude into the cool dark blue of the cavern, away from the glare of the June day.

The water was warm and the air cool. For a time they paddled in and out among the stalagmites which supported, church fashion, a central nave from which dark forbidden-looking passageways extended into a watery darkness, sacred to old forgotten deities, terrible and proud. Finally, bored with swimming, they climbed up on a rock off to one side of the central nave and lay side by side together in the dim blue light and stared at the groined odd ceilings and Philip saw bats, hanging like furry fruit from stone branches, asleep, fearful of even this pale light. Regina took her bathing cap and let her long dark hair fall free upon the stone.

'It's lovely, isn't it?' she said at last, her words echoing through the nave, repeated endlessly from wall to wall like the talk of gossips. They both laughed; they talked in whispers, not wishing to be overheard by the guardians of the grotto.

'If one could only prolong this,' said Philip, wishing he had said something more spontaneous, less trite. But insincerity seemed more and more to be his way in love affairs as he tried always to please the other, to say what the other expected him to say, his own true feelings sacrificed in the process: perhaps because I do not feel at all, he thought gloomily, turning on his side to face Regina, aesthetically pleased by the sight of their bodies side by side, prototypical of their sex, the first man and the first woman, or the last. He wondered what it would be like to have no consciousness, to be, just that, a half with no other function than to become, easily and blissfully, a whole.

'But we can,' she said, still on her back, her eyes shut and her dark hair gathered under her head like a cushion. 'You can come on to Paris with us next month. We could see each other every day . . .'

'What about Rex?'

'What about him? He has his own philandering to do.'

'I thought you said he wasn't interested in such things.'

'No . . . or at least I should have said he isn't interested in me any more. He likes young silly creatures and I'm just as pleased with the arrangement. I have no false pride about my role in his life. You see, we're very happily married. We have the same interests. We enjoy politics. He'd be quite helpless without me, professionally at least.'

'Does he know about me?' Philip, like all young men, was eager to know everything everyone thought of him, the more uncomplimentary the better. He liked to think of himself as a ruthless buccaneer who strode across the world shattering sensibilities and conventions with the fury of his progress but he knew, of course, at the same time, that most people thought him rather a lamb . . . a conception based on his small nose and his babyish lisp.

'Of course not.' Regina laughed. 'Why should he? We never discuss our infidelities. As a matter of fact, he thinks you're a promising young man.'

'Promising what?' Philip was disappointed.

'A great career.'

'In politics?'

'What else? Is there any other?'

'Of course, but since I probably won't pursue any of them either, I can't throw an easel or a violin at you . . . Give me time,' he said, suddenly serious.

'How long a time?' She sat up and looked at him. Her body upon the dark rock was smooth and fine as the white marble statue of that girl-saint who lies sprawled on the floor of the catacombs near Rome, martyred beneath the cross and the fish.

'Give me my year. Then I'll know.'

'You promise?'

'I promise. I must have the year first, no matter what I do.' Then feeling the tug of sex, he took her and they made love on the hard rough surface as lovers before them had done since the days when the gods in human form wandered about the earth seducing mortals and rewarding them with curious gifts, with crowns and genius, with constellations in their image spangled across the black fields of night; or, if the mortals refused to yield to these passionate gods, they were struck down, destroyed, transformed to winter shadows or to summer flowers, their beloved forms becoming green laurel on the slopes of hills or wildflowers in the fields where the thunder sounded.

'Must you go?'

'I said I would. I promised Glenellen.'

'But you promised me you wouldn't.'

'I didn't really promise. I said I would try to get out of it. But it was too late. Besides, what harm can come of it? They are all perfectly harmless lunatics.'

'I'm sure they are but you don't want to get into any trouble with the police.'

'Why not? You can get me out.'

'That's no reason to do anything foolish. Suppose they shoot you.'

'Oh, for God's sake! and suppose I get run over by a taxicab? There's more danger of that happening, you know.'

'Do as you please,' she said. And he did.

He left her at eleven o'clock that night. They had dined with Bella and May Washington whose curiosity had finally got the best of them. May especially was eager to ferret out if possible the nature and the enormity of their sin. But Regina handled her beautifully, and, when dinner was over and Philip excused himself, the sisters Washington were fawning on Mrs Durham, eager to win her favour.

In the middle of the sky the white moon rode among black and silver clouds, blown north by the dry desert wind of Africa tempered with sea's salt but not much cooled from the long journey. The townspeople seemed more exuberant tonight than usual, as though celebrating unconsciously some old festival of the moon's fullness.

Philip paused a moment before the largest waterfront café. Inside men and women were singing and dancing. One tigerish, black-frizzy-haired woman (descendant of some Moorish or Carthaginian sailor) was doing a wild dance for the men, her skirt pulled up to her fat thighs, her legs moving like fleshy pistons in time to the music.

Philip, as unobtrusively as possible, slipped into the café and watched until, amid laughter and curses and cheering, the dancer stopped and the usual sentimental laments were wrung stickily from the fiddle and the accordion. Everyone was hot, sweating, flimsily dressed and happy, all that he'd ever imagined the joyful peasant to be. Yet he knew that if he looked close he would see what the outsider never saw: fear, antagonisms, envy, all the usual human characteristics accentuated by this summer land, the violence checked by pleasure in the evening, by piety and labour during the bedazzled day. Feeling much better, Philip left the café and turned into the street which led to the Bridge of St Elmo.

Even these ordinarily dark streets were well lighted, for the doors that were usually sealed against the night were open and townspeople sat on their own doorsteps or lounged about the cobbled streets beneath the full moon which hung, now rich and golden, swollen with summer, among its clouds, like a lantern in the dark.

On the other side of the bridge, all was quiet. A few houses were set back against the hill on terraces above the town, accessible only by foot. Set apart from these houses was the ruin of the Church of St Elmo, surrounded by olive trees and ilex, by giant cypresses, black and mourning in the moon's light.

But before he could get to the church he first had to climb many steps, each, it seemed to him, more steep than the one before and he was thankful for the south wind when he finally arrived, breathing heavily, at the top of the steps, where he paused a moment to rest. Amalfi was below him, its yellow light gleaming in a pattern as inscrutable as that of the white stars which shone everywhere, one beyond another, in the midnight sky. Far out to sea, a ship with blinking lights was making its way to Africa and, as he stared at the ship on the dark horizon, a star fell in the west, a delicate sudden arc of light.

He turned and walked slowly down a narrow flagstone path to the grove of trees where the church, now black and silver, stood like a ship wrecked on a sandbar, roofless, its windows empty as idiot's eyes and its towers gone. He stood for a moment looking up at the cracked stone towers. Insects whirred drily in the trees and, far far away, he heard the faint tinkle of music, the echo of laughter in the town below.

Conscious of his danger, dreading ghosts more than police or Communists, he entered the church and stood in the roofless nave surveying the shattered arch beneath which the high altar, now a mound of rubble, had once been. As he moved down the nave the noise of the cicadas abruptly ceased. He stopped then, waiting for the ordinary sounds of the night to resume, but they did not; the silence persisted. He looked up at the moon, now bone-white, no longer golden, sailing through the black and silver clouds which separated solid earth from empty sky like an antique shawl from Spain thrown over that one-half world beneath.

He waited, trembling, before the mound where the altar had been. Minutes, hours, years, eras passed and still he waited, frozen by moonlight into a pallid facsimile of his living self. He saw the church as it once was: stained glass, wine-red and cerulean, filled with empty windows and translated clear sunlight into rainbows, while figures in vivid costumes moved about in ritual attitude and celebrated the ancient Mass. Then windows shattered and the roof fell; the towers crashed down the hillside and, as he stood there, even those walls which still stood buttressed all around him fell at last and he was alone in the dust, the burnt stumps of cypress and ilex and olive around him, and the sea where the town was.

He moved. The cicadas resumed their monotonous whirring and the moon was hidden by clouds. He looked at his watch and saw by its luminous dial that he had been there ten minutes, that it was now fifteen minutes past twelve and neither conspirator nor policeman had shared with him the ghosts and the constant shadows.

'Hello!' he said in a loud voice, which frightened him; but no one answered. Resolutely, he explored the church, pushing his way past the fallen masonry into chapels where wild grapes grew. He went everywhere except down into the dark hole behind the high altar where, he knew, the illustrious dead had once been buried in ice-cold crypts, the earth of their bodies now holding, indiscriminately, nests of scorpions and the roots of flowers, in decay, as in life, the fine balance between good and evil kept. Satisfied at last that no one lving was in the church, he left.

As he stepped across the stone threshold he noticed something gleaming on the lintel. He picked it up, but since the moon was hidden he could not identify it in the dark; it felt like an empty balloon or a bag. He put it in his pocket, and went down the steps to the world again, his vision lost already.

Regina listened with amusement to his story of the empty church and his moment of vision.

'Then your time wasn't entirely wasted . . . you at least had a revelation.'

'But of what?' Philip was irritable, conscious obscurely that he had been made a fool of in a way he did not understand.

'It would seem obvious from your description. I've always suspected, though, that revelations are valuable only in themselves, not for what, if anything in particular, they reveal. It would seem that you saw the life of one building from its beginning to its end, when not only the ruin will be destroyed but Amalfi as well. Nothing remarkable about that. Since nothing endures it's quite logical to conclude that Amalfi is not eternal, that one day the sea will make a bay of what is now a town. But since the exact date of this phenomenon was withheld, you do not qualify as a prophet.'

'It all seems quite pointless, including your analysis,' said Philip, tired and angry. 'I'd like to get my hands on that antique dealer.'

'Forget about it, darling. Why bother? Now we can go back to Rome. You've had your moment as a courier, a conspirator . . .'

Philip, remembering something, reached in his pocket and pulled out the rubber bag which, upon examination, proved to be a mask of a grey wolf's head, quite realistic, with green eyes which reflected light the way the taillights of automobiles do.

'This must have been Guiscardo's,' said Philip.

'Do you think he was there all the time?'

'Perhaps. If he was, I wonder why he didn't speak to me.'

'He wanted to see what would happen.'

'Yet, what did happen?'

'You will never know now.'

'I suppose not. Shall I return the mask to him?'

'No, keep it as a souvenir.'

'Of what?'

'Of your monarchist days.'

He snorted and shoved the mask into a wastebasket. They were in his room, seated in front of a tall window which overlooked the sea.

'Shall we go back to Rome?' asked Regina at last.

'I suppose so. I would like to see more of this country first.'

'We can drive slowly.'

'We might even go to Capri,' suggested Philip.

She nodded. 'It's lovely there this time of year. Crowded, though.'

'I don't mind.'

'You will see nothing but Americans.'

'I've a feeling the best way to get to know them is to see them in Europe.'

'You're right. But do you want to know them?'

'No, but for a budding politician I thought it the right thing to say.' They laughed at one another. Then he took his jacket off. As he did, he noticed the safety pin which fastened Glenellen's documents to his inside pocket. He undid the pin and held the plain white envelope under the lamp.

'Do you think I should open it?'

'Of course. How will you ever know what's inside?'

'But I shouldn't really.'

'Why not? Your mission is over. You'll have to destroy it anyway. Open it. I can't wait.'

He tore the envelope open and took out a single sheet of paper on which had been written one word in Greek letters, a language he had not studied in school.

'What on earth does it mean?' he asked, bewildered.

'Let me see.' Regina took the paper for a moment; then she handed it back to him, smiling.

'Well, what does it mean? Can you really read Greek?'

'Oh, yes. There's no end to my talents,' she smiled.

'What does it say?'

'I can only tell you what the word means. You'll have to interpret it.'

'Why?'

'Because it's a message, for you I think.'

'But that's ridiculous. I was supposed to deliver it to the royalists here.'

'Then perhaps it wasn't intended for you. In any case, *you* must decide. The word is *Asebia.*'

'And it means?'

'Failure to worship the gods . . . a capital crime in ancient Greece. It was the principal charge brought against Socrates.'

'I am very confused,' said Philip.

'A confusing age,' said Regina with a sigh. 'How lucky none of us knows what will happen.'

The vulgarity of Mrs Helotius was one of the few really perfect, unruined things in Europe; it was a legend and unlike most highly publicized phenomena, never a disappointment to the eager tourist who (properly sponsored) had got himself into any one of those five villas which decorated the spas of fashionable Europe like rough diamonds, bases for her considerable operations.

Officially she had never been born. That area of the world where she had first appeared fifty-two years ago had changed nationality so many times that all records had long since disappeared. But, as she freely admitted to her intimates (those creatures to whom she accorded precedence either because of birth or well-rewarded talent), she had started from scratch, as had Helotius, a Greek who had made more money than any honest man should out of figs in Asia Minor. Later, when he became British, he married Mrs Helotius whose family name had never been revealed to her intimates though all of them called her by her first name, Zoe.

Helotius was thirty-seven years older than Zoe at the time of their marriage. After twenty years together he died, leaving her the figs and a lust for position which until that moment had gnawed secretly at her vitals ever since, as a child, she had scrubbed the floors of her under-privileged home in that part of the world which, even then, was in the throes of being torn from one nation by another. Yet money itself was not important to her; clothes and servants and houses had, in themselves, no charm for her. She always said that a bit of horsemeat and a cold boiled potato was the best meal in the world and little did her fine friends know that she meant what she said. But Position was something else and fortunately she now had the money to achieve it. Her career began two months after Helotius died. She had gone to the finest couturier in Paris and ordered a wardrobe which would knock everybody's eyes out. It did.

There were those of course who laughed and thought her in bad taste but everyone else followed her activities in *Vogue* and *The Tatler* with feverish interest, aware that money was beng spent and that something must be done about it.

She was vulgar. But she was rich, and the villas were being bought at the rate of one a year. At the end of five years she was a Papal Countess and her implacable design was now fully displayed across the ravaged old world of

Europe as everyone came to her lunches, her dinners, her ballet parties and her fêtes. The birthday of the British king was always the occasion of her greatest effort: it usually took place at night on the Eiffel Tower which was acquired for the occasion. Unkind people said that her observance of this particular day was because George VI was the last holdout. She had never been presented at his Court. The time she had invaded the Royal Yacht Squadron at Cowes with a bouquet of roses, thistles, shamrocks and leeks was not considered cricket, although she did get one glimpse of alarmed majesty before the guards led her away.

But even her enemies were now forced to admit that she had won through and that, very likely, her vulgarity had been more of an asset than not. Had she been more sensitive she could never have endured the contempt of the established figures of this world; the fact that she had ignored their hostility in the end gave her a certain moral dominion over them. If she was really so sure of herself, they reasoned, perhaps there *was* something to her after all and certainly she entertained richly. Finally, almost everyone came around; the ones who did not were considered stuffy and not in the fashion.

For Mrs Helotius the world was an enormous jungle full of lions to be bagged and no one, not even a woman as well equipped and devoted as herself, could hope to assemble more than a fraction of them under her roof. To add to her frustration new lions appeared every season, and how was she to know if they were to reign for a number of seasons and become legitimate or be devoured in the first months of their maturity? Yet she did not make many mistakes. She never read books but she was able to skim reviews and study the authors' biographies on the dust jackets and determine with remarkable accuracy whether the gentleman in question was 'there' or nearly there, or gone. She did not handle lionesses unless they were either royal or very noble. In science she was guided by *Time* magazine and the various selections of the Nobel Prize Committee. In politics and religion she was infallible. As for society, she had every Register, every Peerage and Almanac available while her secretary-companion, Lady Julia Keen, an impoverished daughter of a bankrupt Earl, presided over a portable filing case where everyone was neatly indexed according to age, general appearance, income, connections, with comments on the number of times they had been entertained at the five villas and the number of times they had entertained her at *their* villas. She was, as one ill-natured editor who had failed to be invited a second time to her house remarked, the Havelock Ellis of the social world.

Now she was in residence at Capri, and Regina and Philip lunched on the terrace of her house in the company of twenty brilliant creatures, the best to be had on Capri at that moment: a British Field Marshal, a Spanish Marquis, four American novelists (they were everywhere that season), a number of politicians, and a dozen men and women whose names are known to everyone who reads about the doings of the international set.

The house and the terrace, the day and the island were, Philip thought, marvellous. He'd never seen such vivid colours: burning green and blinding blue, flashes of flame-red and flame-yellow flowers among the green, stirred gently by the south wind, and by the more drunken guests who wandered off the flagstone terrace to look down the steep rock cliff at the sea below.

The house itself was not large: a dozen bedrooms, half as many baths, and the usual offices. Of the five villas it was the smallest but because of its setting, Mrs Helotius always spoke of it as her 'jewel'.

'You will so enjoy meeting the Field Marshal, Mrs Durham . . . and there are a number of people from your Embassy whom you must know. They will know *you*, certainly, and be so thrilled to meet you if they haven't already. Do come to lunch, both of you.' She had said this last with a sharp rather puzzled glance at Philip. 'The Field Marshal is so sweet.'

And so they came to the lunch and the Field Marshal was his famous self, not sweet at all. Regina knew a number of the Americans and all the Italians. It was a good way to spend his first day on Capri, thought Philip, who was thoroughly impressed, much more so than he'd been that morning in the main square of the town when Zoe Helotius, dressed in a Swiss dirndl and wearing dark harlequin-shaped glasses, swooped down on Regina, a hairy-legged Italian Duke in tow.

She was more elegant now. She wore one of her couturier's creations, a gossamer grey affair with emeralds the size of egg yolks at her throat. Her hair was a dark red, streakily dyed to give it the illusion of authenticity. She was a short lean woman, with no waist at all. Her features were tiny, except for the chin which was slightly undershot. She was always carefully painted and her face was lifted once a year until now it was almost totally expressionless, as though fixed for all time by some Medusa, in a mood midway between surprise and doubt. Her voice was harsh, very English, seldom betraying her obscure foreign birth.

They had dined at a buffet. Then, drinking champagne, the guests moved about a dainty gazebo which, banked by flowers, overlooked the sea below.

'Shall you be here long, Mrs Durham?' inquired Mrs Helotius, gazing over Regina's shoulder at the Field Marshal who was grimly tearing one of her finest yellow roses apart.

'I'm going back to Rome tomorrow. Then on to Paris.'

'With your husband?'

'Oh yes. He has a job to do, you know.'

'Indeed I do. All Europe knows. All Europe awaits his report with bated breath,' she said dramatically, averting her eyes from the Field Marshal who was now heading purposefully towards a bush of white roses with much the same expression he'd undoubtedly worn on his face the day he had ordered one of his divisions into the worst ambush of the last European war, for which he had been raised to the peerage and sent to New Zealand to mobilize the Maoris in defence of those islands.

'I am sure his report isn't that earth-shaking,' Regina said with a smile.

'Nonsense. He has the President's Ear,' said Mrs Helotius intensely, betraying her near-Oriental origin by an exotic overemphasis which was very un-British and certainly not American.

'You must let me give a party for you next month in Paris,' she said at last, gracefully accepting the fact that she would learn nothing of Durham's mission from his wife.

'We should like that very much.'

'You come too, Mr . . .'

'Warren,' said Philip, who was wondering just how Regina was going to explain him.

'. . . met him just yesterday in Naples. His father is one of my husband's very good friends . . . a judge . . .'

'Ah, the Law,' intoned Mrs Helotius, surveying the gazebo, wondering who was drunk and who was not. Lady Julia marked a minus after each name in the filing cabinet to denote one instance of drunkenness or bad behaviour. Three minuses excluded all but the most eminent from the hospitality of the villas and the Eiffel Tower.

'Well, what do you think of her?' asked Regina as Mrs Helotius hurried away to defend her rosebush from the Marshal.

'Much better than I'd imagined.'

'Quite up to expectations. I'm glad we came.'

'To Capri? Or here?'

'Both. Aren't you?'

'I think so. I must go back to Rome soon.'

'When?'

'Tomorrow, I think.' For a week now they had been together growing dark in the sun and easy in one another's arms. Neither had referred to her plans or to his or to whether those plans would, after this week, coincide or not. It had been his idea to visit Capri. They had connecting rooms at the hotel and as she had predicted, everyone she knew was on the island. There were no secrets here, which did not disturb Philip much. He had nothing to lose and he was more pleased than not to be known as Regina's lover.

'Will you stay on here?' she asked, not looking at him, smiling pleasantly as a young American presented himself to her.

'A little while. I'll be in Rome before you go,' said Philip quickly: then he said how-do-you-do to the young man whom Regina introduced to him as Robert Holton, of the State Department.

The three chatted amiably. Holton was one of those smooth well-educated youths Philip particularly disliked, not objecting to their smoothness or the fact they had gone to Harvard as he himself had, but rather to the way they mixed opportunism, charm and earnestness in such a fashion as to render (to him at least) their every remark suspect. Young men dupe older and wiser men but never their own contemporaries with whom they must compete for the good places of this world. And Holton, carefully dressed, beginning to go bald, cautious, no doubt sensed the other's hostility for presently he went away.

'He used to be in Wall Street,' said Regina, as though anxious not to talk of themselves now that, in a moment, the plan had been made for the next meeting, a promise exacted, 'but he got into the State Department this year. I used to see him at Mrs Stevanson's in New York. You know her, don't you? Blue hair? That one. He had an affair with a charming Italian girl whose name I can never remember. He treated her badly or she treated *him* badly. I've forgotten which. Oh, here comes the Field Marshal: the dullest man in Europe!'

And smelling of all the roses he had that afternoon destroyed, the warrier bored them for twenty minutes until Lady Julia Keen, under orders from their hostess, led him away.

'It seemed that Mrs Helotius was staying at Antibes many years ago at the house of some very grand friends, when some less grand friends at Cannes invited her to lunch. She wired them she couldn't possible make it. She then received a card from them saying how sorry they were that she couldn't come to lunch since the P. of W. would be there. Lunch was nearly over, when Zoe arrived, dusty and dishevelled, her Daimler boiling in the hot sun. "Where is he" she said to the startled host. "Where is who?" "Who? Why the Prince of Wales, of course." "Oh, the Prince isn't here. Just us and the Provost of Worcester." '

Robert Holton was full of stories about Mrs Helotius and Philip enjoyed them. Since Holton was staying at his hotel they saw a great deal of one another after Regina's departure and Philip's first unfavourable impression had been succeeded by an amused neutrality. He did not like young men. He'd never had a close friend among his contemporaries and he thought it unlikely that he would begin to care for one of them now. He enjoyed the company of older men if they were civilized (his standards were precise) and he liked women. Young men, however, always brought out the worst in him, made him irritable and competitive.

But Holton was very nearly as neutral as he himself and they were able to spend the days together blandly, eating and drinking and bathing in the sea. At night there were various parties, expeditions to bordellos where everything was handled blithely and gracefully. The Italian pleasure in the natural communicated itself to these two Puritan youths who, nevertheless, felt all pleasure was evil and that only pain was good. Consequently neither could exact more than a temporary physical satisfaction from any act. Each would have been far more exalted by some calculated frustration and its attendant anguish. But the young and the unengaged in these fiery last days of the Christian era of which I write were not allowed the excuse of faith nor the rare delight of conscious martyrdom, rather, they were allowed to play any game they wanted, to invent the rules as they went along, to do exactly what they pleased as their culture approached its diffuse end and they themselves, though liberated from the arbitrary ways of the old church, from its superstition and dogma and bloody intolerance, had not yet managed to exorcise the mean devil of guilt, the sense of sin nurtured for two thousand years. Now though the churches themselves had died of their own victory long before the last of the wars of religion began, the fear of pleasure and the hate of loving persisted, a withering frost at the heart of summer, and all the martyrs, clinging upside down like bats from the rafters of heaven, no doubt felt that their work had survived the vicissitudes of knowledge better than even they might reasonably have suspected. Perhaps, though one must not look too far into the irrelevancies of the future, their great monument, that core of gleaming ice in each man's heart, might yet become once more the focal point of a new, more savage orthodoxy in which the dream of the martyrs would at last be fulfilled in the vast design of some new dogma from which there could be no deviation since the mind, as the late Christian scientists have discovered, can now be controlled: drugs will extract a truth or a fact from any man and no matter how strong he may be, he will recant on schedule with apparent calm, while virtue becomes the province of the state and the hero vanishes.

Does Philip know this? All men know it or rather feel it, in different ways. Were he examined he would say perhaps that he disliked the cold but whether he would choose the fire is doubtful. Yet neutrality bores him and, unconsciously, he does await the thawing of that spirit which was frozen by a long accretion of laws of conduct, empiric and mystical; to be unfrozen, if at all, by some act of loving outside the jungle that the flesh is, that the mind is, too. The beloved shrine of the false saints shattered at last by some central force, the glacier exploding into a million particles of ice, brilliant in the light of the fire outside, as the flow resumes, like a wide river in the spring or like those myriad galaxies of burning stars which, they tell us, are eternally flowing outward from some dark cold centre to the void where nothing was before.

CHAPTER FIVE

Philip arrived in Rome on a hot grey day, windless and enervating. The Via
Veneto was crowded with tourists who seemed very nearly as depressed as he
himself. The chatter at Doney's was more subdued than usual and from time to
time, anxious glances were turned skyward as though a storm of the Second
Coming was imminent. Far away, beyond the Alban hills, thunder rolled. He
told Clyde Norman that he wished it would rain.

Mr Norman had been sitting alone at a table gloomily chewing a meringue
glacé, the whites of his eyes a liverish gold. He had greeted Philip cordially but
without enthusiasm. He, too, wished it would rain.

'I haven't been well,' he observed briefly as Philip sat down.

'What's the matter?' Philip tried not to sound as unsympathetic as he felt. The
Amalfi adventure still rankled.

'Liver. And, for some reason, when I'm having a liver attack I eat all the
wrong things. A demon drives me to larger and larger meringues, more and
more curries and heavy veal . . . until at last I'm forced to go to the hospital for a
few days and live on bread and water. The body! How I loathe it.'

'I'm sure that mess you're eating will do the trick.'

'Send me to the hospital? Very likely. But I can't stop. I just can't stop. By the
way, have you tried the nougat here? It's splendid, but be sure to take the little
bits of paper off – otherwise it has rather a nasty taste. Will you have something
to eat?'

'I don't think so. A drink, perhaps.' A drink was ordered.

'I went to Amalfi.'

'I wondered. I didn't want to ask.'

'Why not?'

'Well, Ayre is the one you must report to. I'm only a small cog in the
organization. Did you enjoy Amalfi?'

'I liked the bathing . . .'

'Excellent water, so warm. I shouldn't mind going down there myself but the
sun is the worst thing in the world for a liver complaint.'

'But everything else went wrong.'

'Wrong? In what sense?'

'In every sense. I wasn't able to deliver the message.'

'Oh.' Mr Norman sighed and looked distractedly about, as though for
succour.

'And Guiscardo was no help at all.'

'I don't know him.'

'You know who he is.'

'Who who is?'

'Guiscardo.'

'Oh . . . I do wish you'd talk to Ayre about all this. I'm sure he'll make much
more sense than I will.'

'I can hardly believe that,' said Philip, growing angry. 'Of all the people
involved in this idiocy, he is the one who has consistently made no sense at all.'

'Hobbies,' murmured Mr Norman.

'What are they, by the way?' asked Philip, deflected for a moment from his calculated denunciation.

'Oh, one thing and another.'

'Such as?'

'Can't you tell?'

'The young men?'

Mr Norman blushed. 'That too, of course. No, I meant the vagueness you referred to.'

'What about it?'

'Narcotics, my boy. He takes heroin at the moment. But don't ever think he isn't making sense. He is. The difficulty is that when he's under the influence his tempo is somewhat different from that of a . . . civilian and consequently he tends to skip certain details in a conversation which, were they supplied, would make him very easily understood, even admired, for he has an excellent mind, you know.'

Philip decided to postpone his scene. Obviously there would be no point in dissipating his wrath on Mr Norman who was not, so far as he knew, directly involved in the Guiscardo business.

'I suppose I'd better report to him, then.'

'I think it would be a good idea.'

'I shall also tell him that the House of Savoy can be restored without my assistance.'

'Oh . . . I'm sorry.' Mr Norman looked as concerned as it is possible for anyone to look with a mouth full of meringue. He swallowed noisily and repeated, 'I'm sorry. I had so looked forward to our working together.'

'My connection with the movement wasn't intended to continue after Amalfi anyway.'

'What about Mrs Durham?'

'Mrs Durham?'

'Yes. I thought you were going to approach her about our cause. I thought that was why she went to Amalfi.'

'How did you know she was there?'

'One hears things.'

'She came to Amalfi, and we did talk once or twice about your party and she was all against it.'

'I was afraid of that. You weren't able to change her mind at all?'

'Not at all. As a matter of fact, I never tried. We only talked about it.'

'Oh dear. This *is* discouraging. Well, I suppose everything will work out properly in the end. By the way, what did you think of Zoe Helotius?'

'How did you know I met her?'

'Someone saw you at a party she gave on Capri.'

'You know everything.'

'If only I did! But how did you like her?'

'She was pleasant enough, I suppose. I only met her once.'

'Fabulous woman. I remember such a funny story they used to tell about her. It seems she was staying with some rather distinguished people at Antibes . . .'

Philip listened for the third time to this story, idly comparing its delivery to earlier accounts, finally awarding the prize for recitation to Mr Norman. When they had done laughing, an appointment was made for Philip to wait upon Lord Glenellen at his palace on the following day, to report the failure of his mission in the south. Refusing nougat and another Helotius story, Philip left Doney's and walking quickly, he got to his hotel before the rain in quick warm drops fell on the dusty streets, and thunder clapped above the gardens of the Villa Borghese.

Raindrops were in her hair and on her face. She had worn no hat. 'Why wear a hat when the rain will ruin it?'

'I'll dry you off.'

He took a towel and partly dried her hair and face, liking the familiar scent of rain on woman's hair, recalling once how he had made love on the banks of the Hudson during a summer storm and how, when the moment came, lightning had struck a near-by tree.

'I'm glad you're back,' she said, when he had finished and they lay side by side on the bed.

'I got tired of Capri.'

'I thought you would.'

'I don't like that sort of thing.'

'What sort of thing?'

'People who are interested only in people . . . or is that what I mean?'

'I don't know, my darling. *You* must know what you mean.'

'Yes, I suppose I do. It's not that I object to malice and gossip. I'm capable of both myself, I know, but it isn't my principal interest.'

'What is?'

He grunted. 'Here we go again.' He arranged the pillow behind his head. 'Myself,' he said at last, 'but it's awful to admit.'

'No one else?'

He paused. Then he repeated, not looking at her, 'No one else.'

'Sad,' she said, with no inflection.

'Should there be someone else?'

'That's not what I mean, Philip,' she said. 'I'm not really very romantic either. I've had affairs. I have a husband. I've liked some men, adored others. But I will admit to you now that I have never loved anyone either, nor have I ever once put someone else's interest before my own.' She laughed softly. 'We're a fine pair, aren't we?'

Illogically, this hurt him. He did not care a great deal about her but for either to admit this truth to the other when their bodies had so recently been joined was a form of brutality which he had never before encountered. Seeing his momentary dismay, she kissed his hand.

'But I adore you,' she said lightly. 'Don't look at me as though I'd done you an injury.'

He recovered. 'I was just startled to hear you say something so frank.'

'You don't think I'm ordinarily frank?'

'No . . . it's just that I've never known a woman to say anything like that, so soon after making love.'

'Perhaps I merely said what you were thinking.'

'No. That would have been childish. But then I'm not so sure anyone ever really sacrifices his comfort for another person . . . which is, I suppose, the ultimate test and definition of love.'

'Oh, many people do.'

'What do you want from me, then?'

Regina sat up and faced him.

'A great deal.'

'But not love.'

'Not what we usually call love, no. I don't want self-sacrifice, no grand gestures or frenzies. What I want is something else again. Something which has to do with our discussion that first night.'

'But how could all that help you or, should I say, gratify you?'

'That is my business.' She spoke more sharply than she had intended and for an instant Philip had a glimpse of another Regina, one like her name, cold, unfeeling, indifferent to everything but power and its impersonal logic; but the vision was brief. She was herself again. She apologized for the sharpness with which she had spoken but as she resumed her early role, he sensed with some uneasiness that the Regina he had seen so briefly might be, after all, the real one. And so, in that one instant of doubt, the affair ended. What might come after would perhaps seem unchanged and though they could still make love, talk intimately, affectionately, he was withdrawn, no longer committed or sympathetic, a stranger with all the privileges but none of the demands of the lover. If Regina was aware of his withdrawal, she did not show it. She talked of other matters.

'Did you see much of Zoe before you left Capri?'

'A quick and poignant meeting in the square,' he said, selecting a number of artificial phrases to disguise his confusion, to give him time to recover. 'She was guiding the Field Marshal about the town with a look of terrible triumph. I believe she thought I had written a book for when I said hello to her she told the warrior that he should read it. Unfortunately, the book must not have done very well because, before I could indentify myself, they were gone.'

'So like her.'

'Why does everyone say "so like her"?'

'Philip.' He looked at her then.

'What's the matter?' She seemed puzzled, even defensive.

'Nothing's the matter,' he said weakly. 'Nothing at all. I'm just rather put out by the whole damned trip.'

'I thought you enjoyed it.'

'I did, parts of it.' But he could not add the sentence she wanted to hear. He went off in another direction. 'It got on my nerves, that's all.'

'Have you seen Glenellen?'

'I go tomorrow for dinner.'

'What will you tell him?'

'What happened, what I think of the whole thing.'

'Do be careful.' Then she got up and dressed. Philip put on a dressing gown and sat down in an armchair by the open window. Monotonously, the rain fell.

'Where's your husband?' asked Philip suddenly.

'Rex?' She paused, his hairbrush in one hand. 'He's gone to Florence for a few days. I have to meet him there.' She brushed her dark hair back, her eyes watching not her own reflection in the mirror but his.

'How does he feel about your . . . trip?'

'We never discuss those things.'

'Have there been so many?'

She turned around, smiling, and faced him. 'Now, Philip, for some reason you want to quarrel with me. Heaven knows why. But I'm not going to quarrel with *you*. If I've done something you don't like, then tell me what it is. But please don't be disagreeable.'

Since there is no way to handle reasonableness when one is in a bad temper,

Philip was forced, rather foolishly, to apologize, to say a number of things he didn't mean while Regina, the calm mistress of the situation, continued to arrange her hair.

'The rain is almost over,' he said at last, examining the broken lines the drizzle made, as it slanted palely against the dark wet trees across the street.

'Would you like to drive with me to Florence next week?'

'I thought you said Rex was there.'

'That's right. I'm joining him. We're going on to Paris the first of next week.'

'I don't think it's such a good idea, my seeing him. Do you?'

'Why not? He likes you.'

'But – well, after all . . .'

'Don't be silly. Besides, it's no concern of his what I do when I take a trip. I thought I'd explained all that to you. In any case, should he have been suspicious, he won't be if he sees us together. Obviously I would not travel to Florence with my lover.'

'I don't understand.'

'Oh . . .' She came over to him where he sat and looked down at him for a moment, smiling; then she said, 'It's my plot, don't you see? Our going to Florence is part of it, the most important part. Do humour me. It's for you, after all.'

'For me?'

'And for me too, in a way. But that's my problem.'

'I'm not sure if I'll be able to get away,' he said.

When the rain stopped, she left. He had given her no definite answer and he had been, he realized sadly, childish and hostile; this depressed him as all weakness in himself did, for as a rule he was at ease with everyone, especially lovers. But Regina was different; how different he could not tell, and because she puzzled him he felt, quite correctly, that he was at a disadvantage and he was undecided as to what course to follow: whether to break with her at once and for good or to go to Florence and examine the mystery close-to.

He stood in the window looking down at the street. He saw Regina get into a taxicab and drive away. The boys who bought and sold black-market money reappeared as the grey sky broke and the sun shone.

'You will find Ayre somewhat changed,' said Mr Norman, as they crossed the dusty parquet of the great hall and Philip noticed for the first time the threadbare ensigns of ancient battles which hung from the walls at regular intervals, between cracked and flaking portraits which stared darkly at him; the Mettelli in solemn conclave expressed their contempt for the dust and the new age.

'I always find him changed,' said Philip. 'Each time I see him he's a different person.'

'Yet always the same Ayre, devoted . . .'

'To what?'

'Life,' said Mr Norman grandly. The Mettelli looked aghast, while somewhere in the palace a large piece of plaster (or a body) fell crashing to the floor. Philip started, but the servant who was their guide smiled reassuringly and showed them into Ayre's study, the same room in which Philip had been received before.

A table had been set for lunch. Four places, Philip noticed, wondering who the fourth would be. Ayre greeted him effusively.

'So good to see you again, young man. We've missed you here in Rome.

Missed you very much. Just the other day at the baths I turned to Clyde and said, "Where could that nice young American be?"'

'I was in Amalfi, part of the time,' said Philip precisely.

'I remember,' said Ayre, and an expression which could only be called furtive passed over his lizard face. 'We'll go into that in good time. But now let us dine, my dears.' Fussing and chattering, he put first Clyde then Philip on his right. After that, the seating arrangement determined, they sat down.

'Is Mr Morgan coming?' asked Philip, indicating the empty place across from Glenellen.

'Of course not. He's in Wales, where I hope he'll stay.'

'He *did* leave?' asked Mr Norman, interested.

'Yes, several days ago. I must say, too, that I feel well out of it. When I think of the sacrifices I've made, I could do someone an injury.' He looked balefully at Philip as though he were an accomplice of the villainous Morgan. Then, collecting himself, he smiled. 'You must excuse the outburst. I've been on edge lately. Very. Very on edge. But now here comes dinner.'

A white-jacketed boy brought them caviar and blinis. A feast, Philip decided; his resolve to be stern and intractable wavered. Vodka was served in small chilled carafes and it was not until he'd finished the blinis and two glasses of vodka that he noticed Glenellen was wearing a fawn-coloured tunic without pockets or tie. He was allowed no opportunity, however, to comment for between them Mr Norman and Glenellen controlled the conversation, moving easily if eccentrically through history, literature, medicine and finally politics. He was forced to wait until both Glenellen and Clyde were out of breath. Then, quickly taking advantage of this unusual hiatus, he said, 'I saw Guiscardo.'

Glenellen stared at him, his pale eyes glassy in the candlelight and his face red and shining from the vodka. 'Oh.' He looked at Mr Norman, who looked away, worrying a pickled beet with his fork. 'Guiscardo, eh?' Glenellen cleared his throat. 'Charming, didn't you think?'

'No.'

'Trouble of some kind?'

'Yes. I wasn't able to deliver the papers.'

'The papers? Oh.' Glenellen looked puzzled. 'I was under the impression that you did deliver the papers.'

'Who told you that?'

'Guiscardo himself. He sent a message to me by a mutual friend, a man of the highest integrity.'

'I went to the antique shop and Guiscardo was wearing a mask . . .'

Glenellen chuckled. 'Just like the old days, Clyde, isn't it?' Clyde agreed.

'He told me to take the papers to a certain church a few nights later. He refused to touch them.'

Glenellen's eyes opened very wide at this. He blinked furiously and a tear glittered in the corner of one eye. 'But he said that you gave them to him.'

'Are you positive?'

'Of course I'm positive. Not only do I have his word for it but later events, unhappily, proved that he *had* received my message. You see, he gave it to the police.'

'The police?' Philip was frightened. 'I thought he was one of your most important people.'

'He entertained Republican sentiments in secret,' said Glenellen primly. He poured himself more vodka. 'Never trust a Plantagenet.'

'What did the police do?'

'The sold me the papers. What else? Isn't all business done that way?'

'I'm afraid I don't know.' Philip hardly knew what to say or do. 'You didn't have any trouble, did you? With the police, I mean?'

'Of course I did. You don't think I enjoy giving them money, do you? I denounced the police captain to his face, told him a thing or two, but in the end I paid. One must, after all.'

'And Guiscardo?'

'I am no longer in communication with him. I felt he'd let me down.'

'I should think so.'

'He sold me a bronze which he swore he'd authenticated, an Augustan piece. Well, of course, he hadn't. I don't know how well you know him but he is very nearly the laziest man I have ever known, and slovenly in business matters. I sent him a wire saying that one of the Vatican curators had proved this piece a forgery. Well, would he give me my money back? No. He sent me another bronze, a companion piece which was also fake. The man's perfidy is endless.'

'But you are still fond of him,' said Clyde sweetly.

'Of course I am. It's not his fault he is badly organized.'

'But how did he get the papers?' Philip was dogged.

'You gave them to him.'

'I did *not* give them to him.'

'Then how did he get them?' Glenellen's voice was growing irritable.

'I don't know,' said Philip, wondering if perhaps he had drunk too much vodka.

'What makes you think you *didn't* give them to him?' asked Clyde suddenly.

'First, because I didn't. I still can remember most things that have happened to me in the last month. And, second, because I broke the seal and read the message.'

'You should not have done that,' said Glenellen, unexpectedly mild. 'It would have been much better to have dropped the whole business. After all, Guiscardo did have the real message.'

'Which I could not deliver and so, having failed, I read what you had written.'

'And what was that?'

'One word,' said Philip, astonished at his own boldness. 'A Greek word, *Asebia.*'

'I don't know a word of Greek,' said Glenellen flatly.

'It would seem,' said Clyde, 'that you either delivered the message and forgot it (somewhat farfetched but possible) or Guiscardo got it from you without your knowledge.'

'*Asebia* wasn't your message?'

Glenellen shook his head, his eyes bulging with indigestion, his hand on his stomach.

'It looks as though someone were playing a joke on you,' said Clyde with his usual reasonableness. 'Perhaps Guiscardo had a servant at the hotel substitute his message for the one Ayre intended you to deliver. There are any number of possibilities . . .'

'And none quite plausible,' said Philip.

'Let's forget about it, shall we?' Glenellen motioned to the boy to take the plates away, to bring in the dessert. 'I have a good reason for not wanting to remember.'

'A very good reason,' agreed Mr Norman.

'Things are not as they were in Italy,' said Glenellen. 'Situation fluid – how fluid, none can say. There have been certain realignments which I believe you should know.'

'There has been one particular alignment which may come as a surprise to you,' added Mr Norman uneasily. 'You see, Ayre has . . .'

'Seen the light! I have abandoned the House of Savoy to its fate. Yes, I have made the plunge. It wasn't easy, believe me. I weighed the pros and I weighed the cons. I went through the entire section on Italy in the Encyclopaedia Britannica and when I finished I knew that I had been wrong all these years, lulled to sleep by the decadent music of a dying order. But the awakening came; and not a moment too soon, for I can see that had I continued much longer to wander in the morass of reactionaryism I might have ended by losing all touch with the People, who are, we must admit, the only reason for political action, both here and abroad. On a Wednesday morning I realized with horror what I had so narrowly missed becoming. By afternoon I had acted. I cancelled all my engagements for the next two months. Letters were sent to old friends and acquaintances, giving them fair warning of the change, allowing them, if they chose, to sever their relations with me. Many did. Some few did not, among them Clyde. Others I have not heard from. Their silence I interpret as a tacit disapproval, and so I have been forced to accept, stoically I hope, an abrupt yet necessary end to involvements which, in this perilous and exacting time, did afford me some pleasure. The Pope, among others less illustrious, did not acknowledge my letter, to my great surprise considering all that I've done for the Church. But I will not be petty. I want no one ever to say that Ayre Glenellen was petty in good times or bad.'

'You see, Philip, Ayre became a member of the Communist Party last Wednesday.' Mr Norman's voice betrayed not only melancholy but a certain pride in his friend's ability to do the unexpected.

'Sweet Jesus!' said Philip.

In one of the tall towers a thousand candles gleamed and flickered in the soft wind, as though alive, in contrast to the fixed constellations of electric lights which circled this old tower and defined the limits of the hill-rimmed city of Florence, crossed by a winding grey river, reflecting city lights and many stars.

Philip stood alone in the window looking down on the city, wondering whether the pleasant scent of the warm night was from orange or from lemon, from mimosa or from the rich gardens which had been carved in terraces out of the hills of Fiesole where he was now, in a villa, at a party, shortly before the moonrise and the end of the green summer, the beginning of the burning autumn, bright, intense and withering. A new season.

'I though I'd lost you,' said Regina, crossing the darkened library and coming out onto the balcony where Philip stood. 'Oh, it is lovely. Look, the tower! They've lit all the candles. I wonder why? It must be some saint's day or rather the day of one of the old gods. The people are still faithful, you know . . . quite unchanged.'

'They gave the gods new names?'

'Names change from age to age but the gods are constant . . . Are you a Christian?'

This shattered him. He lived in a period where it was not polite for well-bred people to discuss their spiritual convictions or speculations, and for Regina, the great materialist, to ask him suddenly whether or not he subscribed to the official religion of his culture was almost as shocking as it would have been, a generation earlier, for her to have asked him if he had ever enjoyed sexual congress.

He laughed nervously and wondered what to answer. To say he was an agnostic sounded too much like everyone else and to say that he was an atheist would place him, socially, in the same class with undergraduates who had only just discovered to their horror that the rules of conduct they had always been taught were heavenly inspired were, after all, only a makeshift convenience, broken by everyone including their stern guardians. Yet the truth was somewhere between those two worn words. Philip said: No, he was not a Christian.

Regina leaned against the railing of the balcony, the party within forgotten. 'Something will happen soon.'

'What? A new messiah?'

'I'm afraid so.'

'Has he already come, do you think? Marx? Freud? Lenin?'

'I don't know. But I feel it in my bones and I'm never wrong about such things.'

Philip laughed. 'You could hardly have had much experience. It's been a long time since the last one, you know.'

'That isn't what I mean. I . . . but it's too hard to explain. I only hope the new one will respect the old gods.'

'You prefer them, don't you?'

She nodded. The moon rose from behind the hills, red as blood, like a cold sun in the east. 'They are different from the messiahs. They have nothing to do with philosophic systems. They are facts. Some are simple: the sea, the sun, the air. Some are more complex: violence, love, the mother, the father. It makes no real difference which is Queen of Heaven, Mary or Isis or Juno, as long as the idea of the mother exists, as it always will. Sometimes the mother dominates. Sometimes she does not and her son reigns. There are periods when war is regnant, or justice . . .'

'Or love?'

'Can you see to the end already?' She looked at him oddly, as though he had frightened her, but she had no reason to be alarmed for he had not understood. He shook his head in bewilderment.

'I see nothing. Do you mean . . .'

'I meant only that there's a conflict between the natural gods who are, for the race at least, constant, and the messiahs who wish to rearrange the hierarchy of heaven, banishing this god, elevating that one, transforming some and murdering others, or attempting murder, for in the end it is the messiah who dies, a victim of the same forces he attempted to govern. No matter how appealing or ruthless his dogma, the old gods defeat him in the end; they change their names: Saint This-One, pray for me, give me wealth. Saint That-One, pray for me, give me strength. Hail Mary, full of grace – as indeed she was, and is.'

He nearly saw the design, but a shadow before the moon hid the pale face beside him and the warm flower-burdened wind lulled him and he forgot what in an instant he had almost known.

'We'd better go in to the party. Your husband . . .'

'Is indifferent. But we'll go in. Are you enjoying yourself?'

'Yes, I think so. It's the first really Italian party I've been to. Something of a novelty.'

'The host is very powerful in the government, behind the scenes. Rex says that when he wants anything done he goes to him rather than to the ministers.'

In the drawing room, Philip stared a long time at this powerful man, wondering what it was that made him so different from other men. But the problem was insoluble, as he had already discovered this last week in Florence in constant attendance upon Rex Durham who had, during all that time, not made an original or profound observation on any subject. Philip wondered if perhaps a certain type of energetic mediocrity might, after all, be politically more useful in a republican society than brilliance or wit or passion. Pondering the nature of power and earthly dominion from one age to the next, Philip sat in a chair between two sofas. Several decorative ladies and gentlemen shifted easily from Italian to English, and included him in their talk.

'We were discussing the Church,' said one gentleman, with a brilliant smile, glossy moustache, and sporting in his buttonhole (as the late E. Phillips Oppenheim used to say) the discreet ribbon of some knightly order.

'And we were being so anti-American,' said a thick vivacious lady.

'*You* were. Not I.'

'We were talking Church gossip.'

'What is the gossip?' asked Philip politely, pretending to listen, his eyes on Regina.

'The Roman hierarchy has come to a secret decision. I have this on the best authority. If the Russians conquer Europe they will make an agreement with Stalin that if he leaves the Church alone the Church will not oppose him. The alternative, the Romans feel, would be far more terrible.'

'Alternative? What do you mean?' asked Philip, his eyes shifting from Regina to the white teeth and gleaming black moustache.

'Flight. The removal of the Church to America and an American Pope. The Romans consider the boorish Irish-American hierarchy more dangerous to the faith than an atheist tyrant who will fall, in time. The Church has survived worst catastrophes than communism. She might not, the Romans feel, survive the Irish-Americans.'

'Suppose Stalin persecuted the Church?'

'Then there would be new catacombs and more saints in heaven.'

On a signal from Regina, Philip excused himself and joined her and Rex.

'Enjoying yourself, Mr Warren?'

'Very much, sir.'

'Good boy. We'll see a lot of you when we get back home.'

Philip could never determine whether Rex's continual omission of the pronoun 'I' was the result of modesty or merely a trick to make himself seem precise, direct, without fuss or frills.

'Regina, here, tells me you might want to take a fling at the great game. Think you'd like it?'

'Why . . . yes.' He tried to get Regina's eye but she was smiling at someone across the room. 'You're your father's son all right.' Rex chuckled deeply and Philip recalled his father's contempt for politics.

'We've enjoyed seeing you these last few days. Glad to find someone Regina likes. Most people bore her to death and I'm tied up all the time.'

'I've enjoyed . . .'

'She's shrewd. Never makes a mistake. Always take her advice when it comes to people. Thinks you've got a career. So do I. You're young. Unmarried.

That's good at this point. You're a lawyer; a veteran; a judge's son. Can you make a good speech?'

'I ...'

'It's a trick. You'll pick it up. Remember: tell 'em only what they want to hear.' In short staccato sentences Durham outlined a political career for him. Then he stared at Philip with his small grey eyes, bloodshot beneath heavy brows.

'Give it a whirl?'

'I think so,' said Philip, trapped.

'Leaving tomorrow, you know.'

'Yes. Reg ... Mrs Durham told me.'

'Farewell party tonight as you gathered. Off to Paris first. Salt mines. Don't look forward to it. Can't do business with the French. Talk all the time about *la Patrie*, think all the time about money. Americans just the opposite. Will you be in Paris?'

'Not right away.'

'Regina may stay over. I'm going back to Washington in a few weeks. Probably won't see you till fall.'

'Or winter.'

'That's right. Your year. Come see me in Washington, or on the river if we're there.'

'I will.'

'Good boy.' Politicians swept him away from Philip and, for the moment, he and Regina were alone together.

'You see,' she said, 'how easy it will be?'

'Why did you tell him I was interested?'

'Because you are.'

'You know I'm not and yet you insist I must be. Why?' He looked at her frowning. 'I can't see why it should concern you so.'

'But it does,' she said lightly. 'So there.'

'And what do you want from me in exchange?'

'Nothing,' she said evasively, not looking at him.

'I can't believe that.'

'Is it so strange? Must every motive be selfish?'

'Yes and no. The word means nothing. I only feel ...'

'What?'

'That you are not candid.'

'When you tell me that you want a career I will tell you what you want to know.'

'And name your price?'

'And name my price.' She laughed. 'Now I've confused you and I didn't mean to. I hate people who are mysterious, don't you?'

'I won't be able to answer you until my year is up.'

'There's no hurry. I can wait.'

'Where shall we meet?'

'Any place you like.'

Addresses were exchanged and various geographical positions charted as they compared itineraries; then the party ended. The guests went home, carrying with them all the anxieties of the age: a beleaguered church, intellectuals in search of dogma, a barbarian horde poised upon the eastern marches, a materialistic giant beyond the western sea, neither civilized nor barbarians. Each age has its tyrants, thought Philip, preparing for bed. He was soothed by this knowledge as are all properly educated Americans when they come to Europe and visit ancient rooms in which all the fears of other days have been resolved by time or superseded by equivalent crises. He turned out the light and thought of what Regina had said about the old gods, and he wondered if she were right: were they constant after all? Would they reappear now that the last messiah's work had been undone? The son giving way to his mother and the father lost in heaven? He hoped so, knowing that when men are wise they love the natural more than dogma, more than revelation.

For an instant Philip was nearly convinced, as he hovered between waking and sleep. The Gods were alive again, for him at least; but then he recalled the solemn humourless religion of the barbarians, both Eastern and Western, and he saw with Virgilian clarity a new, more monstrous figure appear, furiously denouncing the body and the spirit, refashioning history, casting a long shadow upon the future.

The moon set and the stars were drowning in the pale dawn when finally he slept. Near by, the wind put out those of the tower's candles which had burned all the night.

PART TWO

'The life of the world is only play,
And idle talk, and pageantry.'
The Koran

CHAPTER SIX

Philip stood on the river bank looking down at the water gliding from south to north through the dry land. A solemn bloody sun was setting opposite him, its circle bisected already by the chalky mountains across the river. As he watched, the sun sank quickly, pulling the day after, bleeding the sky of light until when the sun was gone, the day was too. There was no time of twilight in this place, only day and night.

He lit a cigarette. The familiar brief glow of match fire reassured him as he turned away from the river and walked towards the colonnade beyond the row of dark palms. He wondered, as he walked, if those dead Egyptians had felt the same wonder in the presence of their new buildings as he experienced among the ruins of the same temples, cluttered still with all the debris of faith and glory. He decided not, for discounting their official preoccupation with death and the attendant details of dying, they must have been, all in all, more cheerful than not, too much preoccupied with family life and the never-ending struggle for political preferment, to brood too much upon that last journey from the east bank to the west bank of the river.

He thought of his own river, cold and broad, stately in summer, gleaming with ice fragments in the winter, as unlike this muddy turgid river as possible and yet, like it, a source of life. It soothed him to walk by a river, made him feel less strange, more at home, as if he were closer to the centre of the world.

He entered the roofless temple and stood between two thick high columns. In the darkness he could just make out various shrines, some still roofed, others shattered by weather and the wars. He stepped down onto the old pavement of the temple and proceeded to the centre of the main court where he stood, awed by the dark and by the immensity of acanthus-crowned columns. Then far away, he heard the sound of automobiles and the shouts of street vendors. Thinking of dinner, he left the temple, crossed a field and walked several yards down a palm-edged road to the hotel where he was staying, a rambling stucco building on the edge of a town of whitewashed mud with tall striped minarets and narrow haphazard streets, a town oppressed, obsessed by the ruins on which it perched, like a living weed in a bone heap: the remains of the palaces and temples, markets and quais of what had been the greatest city in the world three thousand years before. Too long a time, thought Philip wearily, with a sense of having strolled out of time altogether.

The manager of the hotel, fortunately, recalled him to the present. Mr Koyoumdjian got not only his conversation but his love of America from the movies which he attended zealously, often seeing, he confessed, the same movie four or five times, each time learning new some expression he could add to his ever-lengthening American line.

No sooner had Philip entered the lobby than Mr Koyoumdjian was upon him, his face scarlet with crisis.

'He has done it! While you were out. Just after you left.'

'Who has done what?'

'Your friend Mr Willys – with a gat. He tried to take his life. Such a caper!'

'What happened?'

'Shot himself. Except he missed – just nicked the top of one ear. The sawbones came and gave him something to make him sleep.'

'But that's terrible.'

'Real excitement! You can bet your life. I've got his rod in my safe. Want to see it?'

'No, thanks. Is he awake now?'

'Yes. I sent one of the bozos in with some tea and toast. Though why a man has just shot himself should be fed tea and toast I couldn't know. Maybe you'd better see him. Cheer him up.'

The would-be suicide lay inert on his bed, a mountain of flesh behind the white mosquito netting; purple pyjamas with white piping contained those rolls of flesh which composed the wretched Briggs Willys. A bed lamp was turned on and the night table was cluttered with medicine bottles. There was a strong odour of iodine in the room.

'I hear you've had an accident,' said Philip, attempting cheeriness. 'How do you feel?'

'It was *not* an accident,' said a thin voice, emerging from the still, fat centre of the large iron bed.

'But I thought . . .'

'I tried to kill myself and I failed, as I have in everything else.' A plump starfish of a hand pushed aside the netting and the bandaged head and shoulders of Mr Willys were revealed. He was not an ugly man nor was he old; he was just very fat. His features were small and rather indistinct, since one's examination of them was distracted by the full shining cheeks, the ripe tiers of chins, the splendid ruddy colouring which the white bandage emphasized.

'Now that's no way to talk,' said Philip, sitting down in a chair near the bed.

'It may be no way to talk but it's the way I feel. Next time I won't fail.'

'You're not going to try to shoot yourself again?'

A crafty expression rippled across the vast face and the tiny eyes disappeared altogether, until they resembled twin navels. 'No, not shoot. Poison may be my next weapon.'

'Surely you don't really want to die.'

'And why not?'

'You have so much to live for.'

'*What* have I to live for?'

There was no immediate answer to this. Looking at the matter dispassionately, Philip could see very little reason for Mr Willys to continue living with such an outlandish body, one that not only set him apart from the rest of mankind but one which gave him continual anxiety; for him to walk across a room was a physical effort not unlike a decathlon for someone of more ordinary proportions. But Philip was conscience-bound to be life's advocate.

'Any number of things. I don't know you well enough to be able to mention your pleasures . . .'

'Sleep,' sighed the thin voice. 'I love only sleep.'

'Food, perhaps,' hazarded Philip, tactlessly.

'Certainly not. I eat like a bird. I loathe food. A cup of consommé and a cracker is all I ever need. Just because . . .'

'I was only making a guess,' said Philip, quickly. Mr Willys fell back against his five pillows with a gentle moan of exhaustion, his eyes shut.

'Still, there are so many things to do when you're alive that you can't do dead,' he continued, becoming more and more inane. Mr Willys was not listening. 'You can travel, for instance. You don't have to work for a living. Think how other people envy you being able to travel anywhere you like . . .'

'I came to Egypt to die,' said Mr Willys suddenly. 'I was afraid I wouldn't have the courage to kill myself anywhere else so I decided to come up the Nile to the hottest town with a decent hotel and even if I lost my nerve, I should die of the heat. I can't stand the heat. My heart is not strong. My kidneys are bad. My liver is swollen out of shape. Yet I have been here in Luxor in this hotel for two months, unable to move, unable to sleep, unable even to shoot myself for my hand shook so I only scratched an ear. Oh, it's too terrible.' Sobs convulsed the purple mountain like an earthquake. The bed creaked.

'There now,' said Philip over and over again until the crisis had passed. 'What you should do is go on a nice trip to the mountains, someplace where it is cool, like Switzerland, and take a cure . . .'

'Altitudes make me dizzy, and there is no cure. None at all. It's either wait until the heat kills me or else take poison.'

'When?'

'When what?'

'When do you plan to take poison?'

'Well, I haven't picked a date yet. But soon. Very soon. Then it will be over.'

'Have you thought what sort of poison you would take?'

'No,' said the fat man dreamily, 'I haven't. Something with a pleasant taste, I hope. Something quick.'

'Will you do it sober or drunk?'

'Well, I'd planned it sober but now that you mention it, it might be easier to do if I had been drinking. Yes, that *is* a good idea. Thanks very much. I'd probably never have thought of it.'

'That's all right. I just want to make it easy for you.'

'I appreciate that, Mr Warren.'

'Do you know much about poisons?'

'Not a thing. I did consider swallowing some iodine this evening but I'm sure it would burn like fire.'

'No, iodine is out. What you need is something like strychnine.'

'How do you happen to know so much about these things?'

'I used to read a great many detective stories,' said Philip, quite carried away by the situation. He was alarmed, however, when Mr Willys asked him if he would bring him some strychnine the next morning.

'I suppose you can get it without a doctor's prescription?'

'Oh, I doubt that,' said Philip. 'But I'll see what I can do.'

'That will be splendid: to be out of this mess for good! By the way, I shall want to be cremated.'

'Awful mess for the hotel, though, your taking poison in one of their rooms.'

'Won't do them a bit of harm. The legal end of it shouldn't take more than a few hours. Besides, it will give that despicable manager something to talk about. He took my gun away, you know.'

'You could hardly blame him.'

'But I do.' A barefoot servant appeared at the door and informed Philip his dinner was ready. After promising to go first thing in the morning to buy poison, Philip said goodnight and went downstairs.

He had the large airy dining room to himself. French doors opened onto a garden. Flies buzzed about the electric light and fans suspended from the ceiling slowly twirled, hardly disturbing the hot air. A white-coated Negro, wearing a dirty fez, brought him a number of dispiriting courses of simple food, badly cooked.

The manager came by for a little chat as Philip was drinking the thick muddy black coffee.

'Did you see him? Was he green about the gills?'

'No, he was in the pink,' said Philip, getting into the spirit of the manager's conversation.

'Why do you think he did it?'

'He seems to be tired of life and so he tried to kick . . .'

'The bucket,' finished Mr Koyoumdjian with a smile of one Mason meeting another in the Libyan Desert. 'I suppose it never occurred to him how disagreeable it would be for us if he killed himself.'

'It was my impression that he didn't really care, that he was more interested in his own problems.'

'Problems!' exploded Mr Koyoumdjian. 'He has money, hasn't he?'

'A great deal, I think.'

'Then what problems does he have? He can go anywhere he likes, do anything he wants. Buy any doll . . .' The manager paused. 'He isn't impotent, is he?'

'I didn't ask. But I wouldn't be surprised, with that weight.'

'Weight has nothing to do with it. There's an old man here in town who weighs twenty stone and he's the busiest cat in Luxor in regard to the frails. He has a couch specially tilted so . . .'

'I don't think that would help Mr Willys,' said Philip, not wanting to hear any more details.

'Maybe not. I wonder if I should have him moved to the Mission hospital, it'd be their lookout then, not mine.'

'I'd leave him alone. There isn't much he can do without a gun and I don't suppose he has a knife long enough to penetrate all that flesh.'

Mr Koyoumdjian laughed heartily at this grim conceit. 'You got something there.'

'Are there any more guests coming this month?' The last party, a group of cotton scientists from the United States, had left that morning and there was no one in the hotel but Mr Willys and Philip.

'Not for ten days.'

'How on earth do you make enough in summer to keep a place like this running?'

'We don't. But the owner decided not to shut up this year. We usually close in May.'

'Do you like having to stay here in this heat?'

Mr Koyoumdjian shrugged. 'It's a living, Buster.'

But the manager was wrong. The next morning after an early breakfast, Philip took a stroll in the garden and discovered that another guest had arrived in the night. She was seated on an iron bench at the end of a lane of magnolias or what Philip took to be magnolia trees: this garden was a strange one with flowers and trees he had never seen before, mysteriously set out in cabalistic designs, a maze of heavily scented green.

'Lovely morning,' he said, approaching her.

'Yes. The only cool time of the day.'

'May I sit down?'

'Certainly.' She moved over and he sat beside her, conscious of the green world all about them. There was a hedge behind the bench and a sudden right-angled turn of the path in front of them gave the illusion of a roofless green-walled room, oblong and carpeted with grass, while flowers still damp with night broke the solid areas of green with their bright colours.

'Did you just arrive in Luxor?' he asked.

'This morning.' He liked her voice, which was cool and even, an educated American or perhaps British voice. He moved about on the bench so that he could see her more clearly. She was handsome, though not pretty in a con-temporary sense for her nose was large, like a Julian portrait bust, and her skin was white and unpainted. Yet her eyes were extraordinary, pale grey with long dark lashes, and her hair was a fine auburn, drawn softly back from her face and gathered in a bun at the back. She was not forty, he decided; she wore no wedding ring.

'Not the best time of year to visit Egypt,' he commented.

'I like Egypt any time of year,' she said.

'You've been here before?'

'Many, many times. In fact, my father's family used to live here a long time ago.'

'Then it must be like home.'

'Yes, like home. Have you been here long?'

He told her he had been in Egypt for a month, in Luxor for a week, and that he was seeing everything there was to see in the company of an old dragoman named Said.

'I envy you, coming to it fresh like this even in the heat.'

'I don't mind hot weather. The rest of course is wonderful. I've never felt so relaxed before. For the first time, nothing matters.'

'The ruins,' she said. 'That's what does it, of course. It's very hard to dream of the future when the past is all around one, reminding one that what is has been before and will be again, over and over and over.'

'Are you staying here?' asked Philip.

She nodded. 'I always stay here when I am in Luxor.'

'The manager told me he was expecting no one for a few days.'

'We're old friends, Mr Koyoumdjian and I. He's never surprised when I appear without notice.'

'Have you some business here?' asked Philip tentatively, realizing it was none of his business and that she appeared to be quite capable of reminding him that it was not. But she only smiled and said that she was interested in archaeology: 'Disproving, perhaps, my own theory that all is forgotten since I for one am devoted to seeing that nothing is forgotten, that every second of history is accounted for.'

'History or, rather, legend is seldom wholly forgotten,' said Philip with the studied diffidence of a man making an epigram. 'Men always are.' When this was said, as though by common assent, made reverent by pompousness, they rose and walked silently down the green path to the hotel.

'I see you've met Miss Oliver,' said the manager, coming over to their table later that day at lunch, as Philip was toying with a number of vivid stewed fruits, all poisonous-looking and tasteless.

'Yes, we met in the garden,' said Miss Oliver, whose first name Philip had already been informed was Sophia.

'A surprise visitor,' said Mr Koyoumdjian. 'You could have knocked me over with a feather when she walked in the hotel this morning as cool as a cucumber and asked for her old room. More investigations, eh?'

'Just one more,' she said, removing a half-drowned fly from her coffee. 'I may have to go out to the desert for a few days. I'm not sure.'

'What's the desert like?' asked Philip, hoping this would lead to an invitation; it did not. He was lectured for several minutes on life in the desert, and by the time she finished an interesting account of the Arab method of divining the presence of water, the fly, which had been moribund, pulled itself together and flew away, heading directly, Philip noticed, for a coil of flypaper already nasty with the corpses of its fellows.

'Have you seen Mr Willys this morning?' he asked suddenly when Miss Oliver had concluded her remarks and was thoughtfully sipping coffee, her thoughts far away, no doubt in some distant *wadi*, her eyes narrowed as though against the glare of bright sun on sand.

The manager had indeed seen Mr Willys. 'He seems in good spirits, keeping his pecker up. I think he'll be all right now. He spoke of coming down to dinner tonight. He asked to see you, by the way. Said you had something for him.'

'Who is this?' asked Miss Oliver, the desert fading like a mirage as Philip explained the details of Mr Willys's obsession. She had, however, no comment to make on the situation other than a conventional word or two and a perfunctory expression of sympathy for the trouble the manager had been put to. Then she turned to Philip and, discovering that he was to go to Karnak that afternoon with his dragoman, asked if she might go along. Making a date for five o'clock when the sun would be less violent, they parted.

Philip found Mr Willys still in bed, but now quite nude, without even a mosquito netting to diffuse the horror. 'Good morning,' said Philip from the door, giving the other a chance to cover himself but Mr Willys did not have the energy or the desire. Instead he pulled himself up so that his stomach with its mottled pink flesh covered his genitals, giving him the curiously sexless look of a celluloid Kewpie doll. Philip found it difficult not to stare fascinatedly at this unusual display of one of nature's more bitter jokes.

'Good morning, Philip. Did you bring it?'

'Bring what?'

'The poison. You promised.'

'Ah, the poison.' Philip had no lie ready. He stammered. 'I – I haven't been to town yet.'

'You will remember it?'

'I'll see what I can do. I'll have to get a doctor's prescription, you know; and that may be difficult.'

'You're not trying to get out of this, are you?' Mr Willys was suspicious.

'I'll do my best ... but now I have to go out. I'll see you tonight. Mr Koyoumdjian said you were coming down to dinner.'

'I have no intention of ever leaving this room alive. I only said I'd get up to put him off the scent. I was afraid they might try to move me to the Mission hospital. But now, if you'll do as you promised, I shall be asleep by dinnertime ... forever!' And with a gusty sigh, Mr Willys began to turn over; the bed creaked; he groaned; the flesh sagged alarmingly and Philip fled.

*   *   *

'Yonder wall,' said the dragoman, in his King James Biblical English, 'was builded by the children of Israel before their liberation by Moses. You see, some of the bricks are made with straw; others not with.'

'This tree was brought back from the land of Punt by Queen Hatshepsut's fleet,' said Miss Oliver. Philip was bombarded with information from all sides; some of it he absorbed, most of it he did not hear for he was too occupied with his own reactions. Like a man feeling his own pulse, he tried to define what he felt as he walked through the rooms and dusty gardens of three thousand years before.

When they came to the small Temple of Ptah, they sat down in its shade, out of the terrible light of the sun which scorched the temple walls and parched the earth as it rode like a disc of bronze in the harsh blue sky.

It is difficult to know how to deal with well-known landscapes when one is writing a novel. There is an impulse to describe everything literally, enthusiastically, giving dimensions, dates, distances and other pertinent information. This is the guidebook approach and the dangers are numerous: for instance, should one care to describe the Sphinx, one would have to record those dimensions which are available to any owner of an encyclopedia. Should one rely on memory there will inevitably be angry comments to the effect that the left paw is not worn away, that one haunch is higher than the other, that the bridge of the nose is still intact if one observes the face from the east, and so on. The impressionistic manner is somewhat better: to use the celebrated object as a point of departure, like Pater describing the Mona Lisa, or Henry James describing the Capitol at Washington, or rather Henry James describing Henry James describing the Capitol at Washington. Then there is the contemporary fashion of keeping away from celebrated objects altogether. In Paris the story, if it concerns artists, will all take place within a few blocks of the rue du Bac or if of high life, around the Crillon and the Ritz. While in a book about Egypt most of the action will take place either in a wealthy suburb of Cairo or else in a desert village with goats and lice-infested children running about, eating dates and drinking stagnant water. It would be pleasant to make some sort of compromise, to be able to give a thorough instructive tour of Karnak, the Valley of the Kings, and so forth, soaring every now and then with burnished wings into a paradise of lyric metaphor, getting around the object, as it were, translating its aura into a few balanced melodious sentences. But, reader, you will be spared even this. The movies have already made us so familiar with foreign countries that the novel, for its own good I am sure, can no longer be usefully employed in cataloguing details of well-known landscapes and so, except for an occasional odd glimpse of this place or that, travelogues and the monthly *Geographic* must still be our source material. But it might be useful to quote at this point what a well-known authority on Egypt had to say in 1887 of the country in general. After first remarking on the monotony of the scenery, the authority adds: 'The monotony is relieved, however, in two ways, and by two causes. Nature herself does something to relieve it. Twice a day, in the morning and in the evening, the sky and the landscape are lit up by hues so bright and so delicate, that the homely features of this prospect are at once transformed as by magic, and wear an aspect of exquisite beauty . . . The orb of night walks in brightness through a firmament of sapphire; or, if the moon is below the horizon, then the purple vault is lit up with many coloured stars. Silence profound reigns around. A phase of beauty wholly different from that of daytime smites the sense . . .' A beautiful style, alas, is not enough, while generalities are always treacherous; for as we have seen only the night before, the sun set quickly without one single bright hue in evidence.

'The Arab women bring their babies here to bless them,' said Sophia, as they stood in the close dark room, a life-sized statue of a woman with a lion's head in front of them, partly lighted by a shaft of light coming from a square opening directly overhead.

'She has great power,' intoned the dragoman, an untidy old man with a grizzled beard and wearing the national sheet-like robe, a fez on his head, sandals on his feet. He was a true Egyptian, he assured Philip when they first met, not like one of those God-damned Arabs in the north. Proudly, he had shown Philip a blue cross tattooed on his arm. 'I am a Christian, a Copt,' he had said.

'All the gods have power if one believes,' said Sophia firmly.

Philip, though he liked her, found her positive assertions a little trying; she advanced every opinion as a fact of nature. The dragoman, seeing his own position as an Egyptologist endangered, had spent most of the morning attempting politely but tenaciously to disprove her observations and theories. She, in her turn, was far more direct; she contradicted him flatly until Philip was afraid there might be trouble but they got through the day without unpleasantness, and it was in a friendly mood that they rode back to the hotel in a horse-drawn carriage, the top up against the evening sun.

Men sat sleepily in doorways as they drove into Luxor. Even the big-bellied, naked children sat or lay in the fly-buzzing shade of acacias, hardly moving. Only the women worked, preparing food, bringing water from the fountains, nursing the children, cursing the men and the flies in their deep harsh voices, cursing the fine dust which the foreigners' carriage turned up in clouds as Philip and Sophia drove through the dusty streets of the village to the highway which led to their hotel, to fine modern bathrooms and cool rooms.

'You failed me.'

'But I tell you the doctor refused to give me a prescription.'

'I counted on you. All day I've been happy. Happier than I've ever been before, thinking that never again would I have to open my eyes to see the morning, to look at this aching wreck and to realize that I must endure it for yet another day . . . Oh, it's too terrible!' And he groaned piteously, the sheet which covered him rippling like a sea effect in an old-fashioned play.

'I did my best,' said Philip firmly. 'It's up to you from now on.' And so, having divorced himself from Mr Willys's project, he left the room, ignoring the pleas, the anguished entreaties from behind the mosquito netting: 'Oh, come back! I'm sorry. I didn't mean it. You *must* help me!'

In the lobby, Mr Koyoumdjian met him. 'We have a surprise for you!' he said, smiling, his face breaking into a number of geometric shapes. 'Another lady has just arrived – an American from New York City. You probably know her, Mrs Fay Peabody.'

'No, I don't think I've met her. You see . . .'

'New York's a big town. I know. Babylon on the Subway, that's what they call it. I'm not green. What I meant is you probably know her books. She writes detective stories – hard-boiled. Seen some of them myself, but I have no time to read.'

'Where is Miss Oliver?'

'In the dining room with Mrs Peabody. They're waiting for you.'

Sophia was stately and cool in a pale blue evening dress which flattered her well-formed body, and yet, recognizing dispassionately all her physical attractions, he was in no way attracted to her; she was like one of those voluptuous figures carved in ice at a winter carnival in New England. Usually he had a difficult time explaining to himself why this person or that person appealed to him but now he was amused to find himself wondering why he was not attracted to this handsome, apparently available woman. When he tried to think of her in erotic terms, he experienced the same sort of embarrassment when, as an adolescent, he had speculated on the private behaviour of his parents. He had concluded that it was the enervating heat which had done this to him, heat combined with the mood of the place and a new knowledge of the ebb and flow of all of those generations whose debris, solemn and dusty, surrounded that garden which he now glimpsed, pale and shadowy, through the French windows of the dining room.

Sophia introduced him to Mrs Fay Peabody. The famous mystery-story writer was plump and soft, elderly, and though she had a slight speech defect (the result of ill-fitting dentures) she managed, nevertheless, to speak with very nearly as much authority as Sophia herself; she was limited however to fewer fields: the underworld, publishing and the law.

'Well, here we all are,' she observed, after the introductions had been made and an American canned fruit cocktail was set before them. 'Probably the only Americans in Upper Egypt.'

'No, there are quite a few over at the Ponsoonah Laboratories outside of town.'

'I mean, not counting professional people,' clicked Mrs Peabody. 'Although, perhaps, I don't quite mean that either since I, too, am a professional, *on a job*.' There was a pause. Philip, aware that it was up to him to ask Mrs Peabody who she was, did so, neatly. She told him that she was Fay Peabody and he told her that he enjoyed her books. Sophia remained silent.

'I believe in doing my research on the spot, Mr Warren. None of this secondhand business for me ... Looking things up is all very well for most writers but, if I say so myself, I have quite a large body of readers who look to me for *the real thing* and that's what I give them. When I describe the inside of Leavenworth it means that I have been inside Leavenworth, as a *prisoner*.'

'You must be joking,' said Sophia mildly.

'I never joke about my work, Miss Oliver. Yes, I arranged with the warden and he allowed me to reside three days in a cell, just like any other prisoner, wearing man's apparel. You perhaps remember the prison scenes in *Red, White and Blue Murder?* well, those are *authentic* scenes based upon my personal experience.' There was an awed silence after these remarks. Philip, toying with a bit of cold fried fish, wondered what to say next. He glanced at Sophia. She asked Mrs Peabody what she was doing in Egypt.

'I believe, Miss Oliver, that a *change of pace* is good for all of us. Even the best. I was never one to rely on formula, although the Fay Peabody method may be considered, perhaps, to be a *kind* of formula. Yet I have been aware for some time now that there were certain limitations to the method. Not that I lack readers! No, bless them! each books sells more than its predecessor. Yet, in spite of such encouragement, one does have a duty to oneself and though I have written exclusively of crime in Philadelphia with, of course, related minor scenes elsewhere, I have never *thrown down the gauntlet*, you might say, and tackled a really big job elsewhere.'

'Like Agatha Christie,' said Philip innocently. The storm broke. Mrs Christie was flayed before their eyes and her corpse, like Hector's, pulled after Mrs Peabody's triumphal car from one end of publishers' row to the other. Sales were compared down to the last twenty-five-cent copy sold. Mrs Peabody had at her tongue's tip the exact sales of every mystery novel published since Conan Doyle, and while they are the dry grey flesh of some mysterious beast, it became apparent to them that not only in quality but in sales, too, Mrs Peabody was tops. No, she was not going to do the Christie sort of thing in Egypt. She was going to do the Fay Peabody sort of thing in Egypt and, her jaw set, she looked from one to the other of her companions, challenging them to compare her with anyone, living or dead. Philip was impressed.

'Will it have J. R. Snaffles in it?' he asked, recalling the name of her detective, an ex-prizefigher with an aquiline profile and an appeal which reputedly drove women wild, not only in fiction but the ones in life who bought every book about Snaffles Mrs Peabody was good enough to write for them.

'Yes, Snaffles will be in it. I can't make too large a break with my fans. I mean, if you buy a Fay Peabody mystery you expect Snaffles. Isn't that right, Miss Oliver?' Sophia nodded and the denture-clicking words of Mrs Peabody continued, a thin trickle of saliva glistening at the corner of her mouth. 'I can only give you the barest hint of my plot. To do more would be unfair to my other fans. Suffice it to say, Snaffles has been hired by the wealthy Greta Preston of the Main Line to accompany her and her brother on a tour of Egypt to ascertain, if possible, the whereabouts of her father who disappeared in Twenty-nine with most of his bank's available cash. (She has independent means from her mother.) Of course, *he* did not take the cash . . .'

By the time coffee was brought, they knew a good deal more about the next adventure of Snaffles than any Fay Peabody fan in the world, or at least in Upper Egypt.

'What a nasty taste!' exclaimed the authoress, after swallowing with difficulty one sip of the thick Turkish coffee.

'Oh, it's wonderful,' lied Philip.

'You must get used to it,' said Sophia. '*Everyone* drinks it here. Even your Mr Snaffles will have to drink it,' she added maliciously.

Mrs Peabody sighed. 'In that case, I'd better swallow it all, like medicine. Research! Never let anyone tell you it's easy. Take my word for it.'

It was not until they were seated on the screened-in porch overlooking the garden that Philip had his marvellous idea.

'Tell me, Mrs Peabody, have you ever known a man who wanted to be murdered?'

'Certainly not, Mr Warren. The whole point to mystery stories is that people do *not* want to be murdered.'

'Perhaps I should put it another way. A man wants to kill himself but he's afraid to.'

'I presume you are speaking of suicide. I do not wish to sound intolerant, Mr Warren, but I do not approve of suicide. It is *unfair to the reader*. I know, of course, that you are a great admirer of Mrs Christie . . .' And that poor lady's body was once more dragged the length of publishers' row.

'All I meant,' said Philip, when she had stopped for breath, 'is that there's a man staying here who wants to kill himself but hasn't the nerve. He tried to shoot himself a few days ago, but missed. Now he's been begging me to get him some poison.'

'Good heavens!' exclaimed Mrs Peabody, for the first time interested in anything either Philip or Sophia had said that evening. Then, briskly: 'Why doesn't he buy his own *lethal dose*?'

'He is very fat. He can hardly get out of bed.'

'I see. You refused, of course, to do as he requested?'

'Yes, as a matter of fact I did, but I thought you might be able to help him.'

'How could *I* help him?'

'I thought perhaps you might murder him, Mrs Peabody,' said Philip blandly.

Mrs Peabody snorted dangerously. 'If that is your idea of a joke, Mr Warren, then I must tell you I think it in poor taste.'

'But you said yourself that you are always authentic,' remarked Sophia, joining the game. 'How can you write about murders if you've never committed one?'

Mrs Peabody glared at her. 'I don't think that follows at all. Besides, my novels are primarily concerned with the *detection* of the murderer, not the murder itself.'

'In any case, Mrs Peabody, you could give him some advice on what poison to take – you know, some of the little tricks of the trade a layman might not know.'

'But I wouldn't dream of such a thing!' She was outraged. 'I can only hope that you're not serious, that this is some sort of private joke between you and Miss Oliver.'

'I'm afraid he means what he says,' said Sophia. 'I haven't seen Mr Willys but I've heard all about his attempts at suicide not only from Mr Warren but also from the manager who took his gun away from him.'

'What sort of weapon was it?' asked Mrs Peabody, in a voice suddenly precise and businesslike.

'A revolver,' said Philip.

'You have no idea what make? Type bore?'

'I suppose Mr Koyoumdjian will let you look at it if you want to.'

'No. It's not important. I'm always curious, however, about weapons. In my last book I had a murder committed with a sash weight attached to a medieval crossbow. Rather an original touch, I thought, since the murderer was able to prove he was next door at a party when the victim's skull was crushed by the weight. Fay Peabody books are noted, if I say so myself, for their *unusual weapons*.'

'I think you should meet Mr Willys,' said Philip, taking advantage of the authoress's change of mood. 'I mean, it's really an interesting case.'

'But I'm quite sure that in his present state he wouldn't want to meet me . . .'

'Nonsense. In his present state he'd be thrilled.'

Philip put his head in the door to make sure that Mr Willys was still covered by the sheet; he was. The would-be suicide was propped up in bed, modestly tented, drinking Scotch and doing a crossword puzzle. Philip introduced him to the ladies.

'I've read a lot of those books of yours,' said Mr Willys. 'I've a great deal of time on my hands, you know, and since I've nothing better to do, I read.'

'Many great men read books,' said Mrs Peabody gently, her ruthless material-gathering eye taking in everything: the whalelike body, the whisky, the bottles of medicine. 'As a matter of fact, my most prized possession is a letter from the late President of the United States of America, Franklin Delano

Roosevelt, saying that he thought *Red, White and Blue Murder* "a swell yarn", to use his expression.' She talked on hypnotically, her eyes narrowed as though estimating a bullet's trajectory from different angles of the room, as well as places where a crossbow might be secreted, a sash weight dropped. 'And I've heard that Mr Churchill also enjoys an occasional tale of detection when his mind is not occupied with the multifarious activities of state in which his high office involves him, not to mention his own *not inconsiderable literary activities*,' she said, moving over to the night table and, as though against her will, picking up the bottles and reading their labels as she talked. She was still talking when Philip and Sophia tiptoed out of the room.

'I wonder if I should have done that,' said Philip, as they stepped out of the French windows and into the warm moonlit garden.

'I don't think much harm will be done. If what you say about Mr Willys is true, they have a great deal in common.'

'You don't think she'll murder him?' He was half serious. Sophia laughed. 'Don't be absurd. She's an idiot and he is a neurotic who'll never kill himself as long as he has someone to talk suicide to.' Philip had almost forgotten about people who used such words as 'neurotic' in conversation; he'd been under the impression that the private language of the mental therapists was becoming unfashionable, and that the cleverest people no longer talked about their psychoanalyses; but then Sophia would not bother to be fashionable; she would use whatever words she chose to make her point.

He often felt that he was with a foreigner when he was with her, someone who used the language intelligently but with no great facility or, rather, personal colour: no tone, no habits of speech, no peculiar phrases or repetitions. It was all so clear and direct. For the first time, he asked her where she lived.

'I live in Paris now. But I travel a great deal.'

'Why? Any purpose?'

'I like it. No other purpose. I have "means," as Mrs Peabody would say.'

'That monster.' Philip chuckled. They sat down on the tile edge of a small fountain. The light in Mr Willys's second-floor room burned brightly, a warm and yellow oblong in the dark wall of the hotel.

'Were you born in Paris?'

She shook her head but then instead of answering, she scooped up a handful of water and let it trickle back into the fountain. Water struck water with an unmusical sound. 'Why are you in Egypt?' he asked.

'You ask so many questions,' she said: observation, not complaint. 'Why are *you* in Egypt?'

'To see it. I've never been here.' He explained to her about his year.

'Well, I'm here to see it, too.'

'You've been here before.'

'I like the ruins,' she confessed. 'I'm interested in archaeology and I've occasionally put a little money into expeditions.'

'Is there an expedition on now, one of yours?'

'Yes, in a way. I'm involved in the digging over at El Farhar.'

'What are they digging?'

'They seem undecided. As far as I know it's a small temple built in the time of Seti the Second, an amiable young man who was deposed early in life, possibly because he was the son of Merneptah, the unfortunate bureaucrat who followed Moses into the Red Sea.'

'How far away is this place?'

'About sixty miles to the south. We might go there, if you care to.'

'I'd like to very much.'

'El Farhar is a good-sized town. The excavations are near by. A group from the University of Berne are doing the work; thankless of course, since the Egyptian government confiscates everything of value, but then it's a mania, like any other, a passion for knowledge. Much more admirable than a passion for money or for position. I actually know of people whose principal interest it is to interfere in the lives of others, for their own good, of course.'

Philip felt very close to her at that moment: two pure non-interventionists, seated in the jasmine-scented darkness of an Egyptian garden, each pursuing his own solitary way, paragons of human virtue and as just as gods. He could not help but compare her with Regina. He even asked her if she had met Mrs Durham.

'Regina? Of course. I've known her for years. When did you meet her?'

'A few months ago. In Rome.'

'Did you like her?'

This was a dangerous question obviously.

'Yes, I liked her,' said Philip, deserting policy for a relative truth. 'But she does answer your description: she's one of those people who want to govern others for their own good.'

'I don't like her,' said Sophia flatly. Philip changed the subject. They spoke now of the expedition to El Farhar.

'There's another reason for going there,' she said; then she stopped suddenly, as though she had been indiscreet.

'Another reason? What?'

'I'm not sure I should tell you yet. I'm not sure myself what it is or, rather, if the rumour I've heard is true or not true. We'll find out soon enough.'

Then she said that she was tired, that the sun had been very hot that day, that perhaps they should go in.

As he passed the door to Mr Willys's room, Philip looked in to say good night. Mrs Peabody had drawn her chair close to the bed and was saying excitedly, 'There are four methods of making a hangman's noose. I always favoured the traditional "double coil and slip" nose . . .' Neither Mr Willys nor Mrs Peabody heard Philip's good night.

CHAPTER SEVEN

The car that they hired to take them to El Farhar ran out of water first, then oil, then gasoline, all of which Sophia patiently paid for even though the price for the services of the car was to have included everything. Fortunately, none of the tyres blew out and they arrived at El Farhar in the late afternoon. They were taken to the town's only brick building, the Fuad I Hotel, and here they signed a register which was printed in French and they were welcomed by a manager who addressed Sophia in Italian, a language she spoke well.

Then they walked out into the glare of the day where not one sign implored them to drink Coca-Cola. A battered jeep parked before the house of the local administrator provided the only contemporary note in this hot dusty world of whitewashed mud houses and minarets with wooden balconies from which the faithful were summoned to regard the northeast and to comtemplate the mercy of Allah and his dead Prophet's wisdom. The long-robed people stared at the two foreigners as they crossed the dung-littered market place where animals and their owners milled about, kicking dust into market stalls which were sheltered from the sun by a candy-pink and white striped arcade.

'I don't think they're very friendly,' said Philip uneasily as they finally got through to the far side of the square, displacing a group of villainous-looking *fellahin.*

'No, I don't suppose they are,' said Sophia, quite composed, her sensible heels clicking on the broken cobbles of a broad sycamore-lined street.

'But why? What have the Americans done to them?'

'They don't know we're Americans. All they know is that we're white and from the north, that we have money and eat pork. They don't dislike us enough to be dangerous yet,' she added, comfortably.

The half-uncovered temple was at the end of a lane on the town's edge, not far from the dull snake-green river. To the west Philip could see the limestone mountains which separated the Nile Valley from the Libyan Desert, dead-white lunar mountains without water or vegetation. To the east, open country, dusty green where it had been irrigated and, where it had not, only dust and stone, broken here and there by clusters of slender date palms grown up about desert wells or, as Philip's authority, the Victorian George Rawlinson, M.A., Camden professor of Ancient History in the University of Oxford and corresponding member of the Royal Academy of Turin, in collaboration with Arthur Gillman, M.A., once wrote: 'Egypt is a land of tranquil monotony. The eye commonly travels over a waste of waters, or over a green plane unbroken by elevations. The sky is generally cloudless. No fog or mist enwraps the distance in mystery; no rainstorm sweeps across the scene; no rainbow spans the empyrean; no shadows chase each other over the landscape. There is an entire absence of picturesque scenery.' Egypt was not much like England and Mr Rawlinson missed the grey damp days, the homely pleasures of the common cold, the soft dampness which, as Mrs Woolfs Orlando discovered, stole over England shortly after Prinny's death, diffusing the bright sun of a more heroic age with veils of coal-smoke and fog, while high spirits gave way to probity and all the poets departed, following the sun to Italy.

But Philip, a child of the sun, was perversely attracted to Mr Rawlinson; especially now, while he sweated on the banks of the Nile, the foggy tones of Mr Rawlinson were a breath of cool northern air. He could almost hear a phlegm-ridden voice intone that one bright sentence in *The Story of Ancient Egypt*, 'Silence profound reigns around.'

But there was no silence here, profound or superficial. The workmen chatted noisily as they went about their various jobs: some digging, others dusting blocks of stone with brooms.

Sophia and Philip walked slowly about the pit. The top of the temple just appeared above the surface of the ground. The excavators had dug down to the original level in front of the main colonnade. They were now engaged in completing a wide trench about the entire building. The roof of the temple had long since fallen in but the pillared façade was unbroken and although it lacked the familiar grace of Greek columns, it had a fineness of its own, despite squat proportions and dull earth colour. Thinking of the bas-reliefs inside, hidden by earth and sand, he experienced some of the excitement which he knew archaeologists must feel when they finally enter rooms where no one for centuries has been.

You see? Quite against one's will the grey shadow of Professor Rawlinson falls across this discussion of Egyptian ways, making one almost agree with that contemporary English poet who once remarked that Hoboken not only has an evocative name but that just as interesting things happen there as in more exotic locales. Nevertheless, Philip has come to Egypt and there is a good reason not only for his sightseeing among the ruins but for this uncomfortable visit to El Farhar in the middle of the summer as well. For Sophia had a plan. There was a prophet in El Farhar. He had strange news.

That night after dinner, accompanied by an interpreter from the hotel, Philip and Sophia walked through the eccentrically twisted streets of the town. The moon had not yet risen but the stars were large and bright and in the open doorways lanterns shone, dull and yellow, flickering in the darkness. The high noise of Arab talk sounded in the streets as the sun-oppressed village of the day became secret in the warm darkness and lovers met and thieves fell out and murderers went about their bloody business, more like the slim shadows of palm trees than men by starlight, close to that shrunken summer river which was parent to them all.

Several children were playing a game of tag in the Street of the Date Palm. They stopped their game and stood back in the shadows, silent, as the three strangers passed them. In the Street of the Dead Camel, they paused before a tearoom where the men sat about inside, smoking water pipes, chewing hashish and drinking numerous hot cups of tea. But then one looked up and saw the foreigners standing in the doorway; he scowled and turned to his companion. The foreigners moved on, walking more quickly. 'I always have a sense of danger when I walk about an Arab town at night,' said Philip in a low voice to Sophia, not wanting their grim-faced, elderly interpreter to hear.

'It *is* dangerous, I suppose,' she said equably, betraying no anxiety. 'But I always feel nothing will happen to me.'

'And I always feel something will happen to me,' said Philip, realizing unhappily that the traditional attitudes of the two sexes were being reversed.

'I suppose I have the white man's guilt,' he said nervously, as a man suddenly crossed the street in front of them, his robe making a rustling noise as he vanished into a dark doorway.

'Wait here,' said the guide, stopping suddenly before a building like every other in the Street of the Dead Camel. He knocked on the door. After a long wait, it was opened by a small boy who stared suspiciously at them. The guide asked him a question in a low voice and the boy, impressed by his gravity and the presence of the two white people in the street, opened the door and told them to enter.

They were left alone in a long room with an earth floor, lit by a single dim lantern. Sandals filled the room. Some were carefully arranged in pairs on crude racks while others were piled haphazardly on the floor. The unpleasant odour of imperfectly tanned leather filled the air.

'Is the prophet a cobbler?' asked Philip.

'I don't think so,' said Sophia, puzzled. 'I can't think where we are.' They were not left long in doubt. The guide and the boy returned with a message that the prophet would see them, that he lived next door, that they were in the house of his brother-in-law, Marouf the cobbler.

The boy was then paid off and they followed the guide across a courtyard where a goat was tethered, a rank, still figure in the yard. Behind the goat was a door through which they passed into a room where several silent veiled women sat playing dice. They did not look up as the strangers walked through their quarters to the next room. Here they sat cross-legged on a worn dirty rug, the only furniture in the room except for a battered lantern which sputtered and flickered, threatening to go out.

'He will join you shortly,' said the guide, sitting a few feet away from his temporary employers, as though to disassociate himself from them.

'I hope he puts on a good show,' said Philip, with a spurious casualness.

'I'm very curious about him. His claims, or so I've heard, are the most rational of all.'

'And how many others have you visited?'

'A dozen. Some were Christ come again. Others were Israfel, trumpet and all. Still others were without precedent.'

'Do you seriously believe a man can predict the future?'

'No. That would be granting too great an importance to the human race. But I think there's a significance in the *fact* of a prophecy. One often knows intuitively when one is in personal danger. Or one often knows that there is something seriously wrong with the body even when there's no pain, and a doctor can find no trace of the cancer whose presence the body instinctively knows. Well, I have a theory it is the same with prophecy. Some men feel more sensitively than others that some great event is pending. Usually the less educated, more simple man is better able to divine what the world wants than the educated man who relies too much upon logic, unaware of the simple need of the race which creates the messiah.'

Before Philip could dispute this, the prophet entered the room. He was a small wiry little man, dressed in desert rather than town fashion, his head bare and his beard wild and tangled. His face was more Arabic than Egyptian, with a large beak of a nose and black eyes; the skin was dark and wrinkled and the only modern touch to this Biblical austerity was a pair of steel-rimmed spectacles through which the bright black eyes, somewhat magnified, stared at the visitors.

His name was Abu Bekr.

'The prophet greets you,' said the guide, equalling the solemnity of their host, who made a salaam and then seated himself before them on the rug, in the centre, Philip noticed with some interest, of a cabalistic design on the carpet. At first he was not sure if this was intentional or not but, when the prophet carefully pulled his robe within the circle, Philip was quite prepared for the carpet to ascend gently with all of them on it and float out the door to the land of Oz.

'We would like to hear the exact prophecy Abu Bekr has made,' said Sophia firmly to the interpreter, who repeated this sentence with various ceremonial flourishes to the old man who mumbled a brief reply.

'Abu Bekr would like to know *which* prophecy you want to hear.'

'Do you think he wants money?' asked Sophia of the interpreter.

'Certainly not. He is a holy man, inspired by Allah.'

'I wasn't sure. Ask him what prophecies he has made.'

The holy man's answer was a little longer than the preceding response. 'He wants to know why you've come to see him and what you want to hear.'

'We want to hear the truth and we have come to him to know the future. We have been told that he has had a revelation, that a new teacher is born.'

The prophet answered at length, his voice growing louder, more excited as he talked, gesturing with his hands, moulding the air as though creating out of nothing the figure of a divine child. When he finished, the interpreter began his translation, haltingly, confusedly.

'The world is an evil place today, more evil than ever before. The men kill each other with machines and the women go without veils and act like men in the streets and bazaars, while both men and women have deserted the faith and the angel of Allah stands at the gate of heaven looking down upon the earth, ready to blow the trumpet which will put out the sun and shake the stars from the night and level mountains, cities in a sea of flame. But the angel's moment has not come, for a new token of Allah's mercy has appeared in a land to the west, a village by the sea. He will grow up a holy man and he will teach the word of Allah to all the world. The people shall hold him in reverence and call him great for he will teach them not to fear death.' The interpreter stopped and looked expectantly at Sophia.

'*Why* will they not fear death?' she asked, looking directly at Abu Bekr, ignoring the interpreter. 'What will he teach the people that will make them unafraid?'

The older man's answer to this was mumbled and he stared at the design in the rug while he talked, one hand wound in his beard. 'Abu Bekr says he does not know, that he is not the teacher but only a man to whom part of the future has been revealed. He says the Koran says: a true believer need not fear hell.'

'When was the saviour born?'

The answer was prompt: 'Two months and nine days ago when the moon rose he was born and, the same night, an angel came to Abu Bekr in a dream and told him what had happened so that he might prepare himself and the men of his tribe for the cleansing.'

'Will he be a king or a warrior or a priest?' asked Sophia.

'He will be a man,' said Abu Bekr, rising. The audience was over.

All the way back to the hotel Sophia and Philip quarrelled. The interpreter was silent as he led the way down the Street of the Dead Camel to the town's centre and their hotel.

'You don't really believe such nonsense,' said Philip, obscurely angry at what they had heard.

'Of course I do.'

'But how can you? He's just an ignorant old man living in a godforsaken village on the Nile. He obviously knows the New Testament and he's made up his mind that it might lessen the monotony of daily life if he were to become John the Baptist and attract as much attention as possible, which he seems to have done.'

'He knows the Koran, too,' said Sophia mildly. 'The first speech he made us was a paraphrase of Mohammed.'

'I'm still not impressed. I think it amusing and all that, like palmistry, but I refuse to take any of it seriously.'

'But he gave us an opportunity to check what he had said. He told us the exact day of the birth.'

'But didn't mention the place.'

'We can find out easily enough. I don't think he knew himself where the place was.'

'How can you find out?'

'There aren't too many sections of the world where the new moon rose in a country to the west, on the sea, on a day that we know.'

'A line of longitude is several thousand miles long. I'm sure that a town on that line will be easy to find. Yet even if you should discover that the old man meant Tacoma, Washington, it will probably be thirty years or more before the mission becomes known.'

'It's something to look forward to in our old age,' said Sophia, laughing in the dark.

'Why do *you* care so much?' asked Philip suddenly. 'Even if every word the old man said were true, what difference would it make?'

'A great deal to everyone.'

'There's nothing you can do to affect it, is there?'

'No. Of course not.'

'What would you do, if you *could* do something?'

'I would kill the child at birth,' said Sophia. 'But like Herod, I should fail. These things happen. No one can stop them from happening. We can only endure.'

CHAPTER EIGHT

'Welcome home, young man,' said Mr Willys cheerily. 'How were the ruins? Hot work, isn't it? Archaeology, I mean.'

He was sitting up in bed, his thin grey hair combed, the head bandage removed and the torn ear nearly healed. He wore a Chinese dressing gown of white silk with a blue dragon picked out in it.

'Very hot, and I'm glad to be back: the food was terrible. How have *you* been?'

'On top of the world.' Mr Willys beamed. 'I can never thank you enough for introducing me to Mrs Peabody. I never imagined any woman could be so wonderful. She knows everything, literally everything – in her field, that is. It's been a real education, I can tell you.'

'Is she getting on with her book?'

'Oh, she's not *writing* here. She's just doing field work. Collecting data, that's all. She will later dictate the entire work in five days into a tape recorder.'

'Prodigious,' said Philip, sitting down beside the bed in such a way that the afternoon sun was not in his eyes. 'Then you're taking a more cheerful view of things, I suppose.'

'I certainly am,' said Mr Willys. 'I feel better than I have in years.'

'You've stopped all that nonsense about wanting to kill yourself?'

'Well – yes and no.' Mr Willys suddenly looked as crafty as his open pudding face would allow. 'If you mean have I given up hope of being able to kill myself, I will say yes, I have. I just don't have the courage to do it.'

'That's good news. And that means you probably won't be staying here much longer.'

'No. Not much longer.' He smiled craftily.

'I'm afraid I don't understand you.'

'Can I trust you?' Mr Willys narrowed his tiny eyes until they disappeared.

'Of course you can.' Philip was curious.

'You'll try not to interfere in any way, if I tell you?'

'I promise.'

'I know I shouldn't let on but I can't help it. I *must* talk to someone and you're the logical person since without knowing it, of course, you brought the whole wonderful thing about.'

'What wonderful thing?'

'Fay Peabody.'

'Well? *Is* she a wonderful thing?' Philip had a vision of Mr Willys and Mrs Peabody being married in a Hollywood chapel full of lilies of the valley. But his guess was wrong.

'You can take it from me, young man, that she's a mighty bright little lady, with her heart in the right place. She's consented to do it.'

'To marry you?' Philip did not want immediately to give up this dream.

'No, to administer the poison. We've had a number of long talks and she's consented to do for me what no other person of my acquaintance would do and what, as you know, I couldn't do for myself. As a matter of fact, she's quite thrilled by the whole thing.'

'You had no trouble in persuading her?'

'A great deal, especially at first. She had all sorts of scruples but when she saw how serious I was and how much I needed help she took pity on me. She has a heart as big as all outdoors.'

'And she isn't afraid?'

'At first she was. But since then she has steeled herself to the task. Especially when I reminded her who she was: the greatest murder-mystery writer in America. You know what President Roosevelt said about her book *Red, White and Blue Murder.*'

'He said it was a swell yarn.'

'That's right. I never cared much for him, by the way. Did you?'

'I hate all politicians,' said Philip. 'But how is she going to do . . . what you want her to do?'

'I don't know.' He sighed. 'Isn't it wonderful? I don't know how or when. Only why. The motive, as Mrs Peabody would say.'

'You must be scared to death,' said Philip tactlessly, carried away by the novelty of the situation.

'I've never enjoyed life more. If that doesn't sound inconsistent. To know that any day now it will be over for good . . . Well, it's far more than I bargained for, believe me. There was a spell last week when I was going to go on forever like this, without relief.'

'Is it to be a perfect crime, or will it resemble suicide?'

'She hasn't told me and I haven't asked. I don't want to pester her. I mean, what if she should suddenly refuse? No sir, I'm not asking any questions. I wouldn't interfere for a million! I figure that little lady has done pretty well in this field, the writing end of it anyway, and I don't want to put my oar in.'

Philip wondered whether or not Mr Willys was quite sane. Perhaps the heat and the fat and the near-suicide had made him subject to hallucinations, made his dream of death seem nearly realized. Presuming that not a word of what he had said was true, Philip decided to humour him.

'I should think Mrs Peabody would be nervous, even if *you* aren't. After all, you want to die. But she, I suppose, wants to live and she is, you know, risking her very valuable life to satisfy a whim of yours.'

'I should hardly call my wish to die a whim and although I may not have been very much in my life I think I should tell you that, as a citizen, there was a time when I was very highly regarded in Philadelphia: I was a director of the Quaker Greeting Card Company, before the Depression.'

'I didn't imply your death was a matter of no importance. I only meant that it would be a real tragedy if Mrs Peabody were to be caught.'

'Fay Peabody caught? Never! Even though this is her first attempt at this sort of thing she is a complete master of both method and theory. I wouldn't worry about her.'

'But I do,' said Philip. 'For all her competence she is still only a theoretician.'

'Well, have no fear, Mr Warren. *I* have none.'

'I hope she pulls it off.'

'I'm sure she will.'

'When do you think – *it* will happen?'

'Sometime during the next week, I suppose. I haven't given it much thought.'

'Poison?'

'I believe so. The only stipulation I made was that it should happen so quickly I wouldn't be aware of it until it was all over.'

'Sounds like poison then.'

'I should think so. To help her, I've taken to ordering enormous meals – all my favourite dishes: not that I have much appetite, but I was something of a gourmet in my younger days so I've got that manager working his tail off. Tonight he's promised a *sauce béarnaise* made with his own hands. He's an amateur chef, he tells me . . . Yet who knows *what* may be in that sauce?'

'Who knows, indeed?' said Philip, rising. 'I hope everything works out for you.'

'Thank you very much. You realize, what I've told you is in the strictest confidence? You won't repeat a word of it, will you? Not even to Mrs Peabody?'

'Of course not.'

He did not see Sophia that evening until they joined Mrs Peabody for dinner.

Sophia was in a good mood. She had spent the day across the river near the Valley of the Kings and she had bought a contemporary cartoon of Ikhnaton which one of the natives had found the week before in the wreckage of an incompleted tomb. She showed them the fragment of plaster on which a cruelly sophisticated artist had, in a few strokes, sketched the long head and heavy-lidded eyes, the full mouth and sharp chin of the great monotheist, gratuitously adding whiskers, revealing Pharaoh as he looked when he had not shaved for a week.

'What a fool he must have seemed to his contemporaries,' said Sophia, putting the sketch back into her purse.

'What a fool he was,' said Philip. 'From a practical point of view. He was given a first-rate country to govern and he wrecked it, all for the love of God.'

'What did you say his name was?' asked Mrs Peabody, liverish in a gown of fever-red with garnets at her throat.

'Ikhnaton,' said Sophia. 'He ruled over three thousand years ago.'

'Such a long time!' mused Mrs Peabody, toying with her fork. 'You say he was a Christian?'

'No, Mrs Peabody. He tried to replace the old religion with a form of sun worship which various authorities have, ever since the nineteenth century at least, found singularly prophetic and attractive; actually, he was a mystic and he did the usual amount of harm those people do. His theology was soon forgotten but the damage survived him, as it always does.'

'"And the good is oft interred with their bones",' quoted Mrs Peabody, under the impression she was reciting from the Bible. 'How sad it all is! I am sure he must have been very fine. That face you showed us was sensitive. I can tell. I know a thing or two about faces. When I was doing field work for *The Dark Pullman Car Murder* . . .' As she told them about her research, Philip examined her narrowly for any sign of anxiety or guilt, but she seemed much as ever and he decided that Mr Willys had indeed gone mad with the heat. In fact, the authoress was uncommonly animated tonight and dressed with more than usual care; she had even given her hair a fresh rinse and it was now a startlingly frizzled maroon by artificial light. When she had finished discussing faces, Philip asked her how her work was coming.

'Very well, all things considered: I don't care too much for the heat, you know. So I've taken to wearing an old picture hat with a heavy muslin veil, stuffy, but at least it protects me from the harsh rays of the sun.'

'But you've done a good deal of work?'

'Ah, Mr Warren, that is something I can never tell until the moment I start to dictate. Then, if I have done my task well, the book takes form splendidly and another Fay Peabody work is born. But if I make a false start, I know that I have failed of my goal, that I have done insufficient spade work and so, willy-nilly, I am driven back into the field. At the moment, my guess is that my rate of progress has been average. I spent the morning with the manager studying the train schedules. That sort of thing is important, very important. How many a work of imagination has failed because of *faulty verisimilitude!*'

'How many indeed,' echoed Philip and Sophia, in excellent humour.

'Get the facts, I tell you people who are contemplating a career in the field of detection writing. That and plenty of elbow grease *spell success.*'

There was very little to say after this until the dessert, an elaborate Arab affair of crushed nuts and thin pastry, was put before them. Then just as Fay Peabody, eyes glistening, had brought a large forkful halfway to her thin lips, Philip asked her how Mr Willys had been. She was obviously caught between delaying her answer for several awkward, perhaps even suspicious, moments while she chewed the longed-for confection, or disappointing her salivary glands by delaying the anticipated treat to answer him. She exercised her will. She put the fork down, swallowed hard and said, 'Poor Mr Willys. I fear he is *morbidly inclined.*'

'He has very little to live for,' said Sophia.

'Is not life itself enough, a precious gift?' Mrs Peabody chewed contentedly now, her dentures making odd little clicking noises.

'I should have thought that you, of all people, Mrs Peabody, might have sympathized with Mr Willys's attitude,' said Philip, watching her face. She was admirably controlled.

'Come, come, Mr Warren. Merely because I have devoted my life to the problems of detection does not mean that I have, along the way, jettisoned that moral code which I learned long years ago at my mother's knee in Cleveland. Quite the contrary. My field work has dramatically demonstrated to me that *crime is bad.*'

Philip waited a moment before he answered, not sure whether she had completed her statement or not; she had.

'I have never looked at it that way,' he said humbly. 'But I'm sure you're right. Still, a suicide is not precisely a crime.'

'It is considered a major crime by both State and Church, far worse, morally, than murder. As a device in novels of detection, it is only to be deplored. It is not fair to the reader. Fortunately, most authors do not use it as a device, recognizing that it is not Fair Play.'

'But I should say that Mr Willys could only hope for death to come quickly of its own accord or else to pray that someone will murder him.'

The effect of this statement convinced Philip that Mr Willys had been rational after all; Mrs Peabody was indeed contemplating murder. A startled expression fluttered across her soft, ordinary face. Then she declared herself guilty when she said, 'I shouldn't imagine he was in very good health, *with all that weight.*'

'He might have apoplexy any day,' said Philip, wondering whether to interfere or not.

'He has a bad heart, I believe,' said Mrs Peabody, finishing her dessert.

'Perhaps nature will take care of him soon and solve his problems once and for all.'

'I pity him,' said Fay Peabody, as they left the table. She then excused herself, murmuring that an authoress's work *was never done*. Sophia and Philip wandered out into the garden where they discussed his discovery.

'Now the problem is what to do.'

'But why do anything?' Sophia sounded surprised. They stopped walking and stood in the middle of the path; palm trees hid the hotel.

'I think she should be stopped.'

'Why? For one thing it's no business of yours and, for another, she's doing a good deed. If I were tempted to do a good deed, which I am not usually, I might have taken on the assignment myself.'

'I'm afraid I must seem conventional to you,' said Philip more from a sense of duty than from any real conviction.

Sophia laughed. 'It's also the funniest thing I've ever heard! I could have sworn that woman wouldn't have been able to kill a fly.'

'That bothers me too. Suppose she's caught?'

'Who will catch her? The authorities here aren't going to bother about the death of a fat man whom no one knows, a semi-invalid.'

'Your attitude seems rather cold-blooded.'

'Then let's go and tell the police.'

'We can't do that either,' said Philip.

'Let's wait and see,' said Sophia. 'Perhaps she won't go through with it. She may give up, you know.'

But Fay Peabody did not give up. She did not lose her nerve. And even when the situation looked darkest, she was able to draw strength from the knowledge that she was, after all, the incomparable Fay Peabody, peerless in the world of detection writing, a woman whose field work was a legend throughout the civilized world.

The first attempt on the life of Mr Willys was made at breakfast the next day. Philip first heard of it when, somewhat late, he came downstairs to find Mr Koyoumdjian despondent, in what he called 'a blue funk.'

'That guy Willys ought to be in an institution like a hospital.'

'What's the matter? Has something happened?' Philip's hands grew cold, as though he himself were the murderer.

'He got sick to his stomach after breakfast. The local sawbones is upstairs giving him the word. I told him I wanted Willys moved to the hospital but the doc said no dice. He stays here. Next thing he'll probably die on me.'

Philip thought this very likely but he did not say so. 'Where is Miss Oliver?'

'Up early and gone across the river for the day.'

'And Mrs Peabody?'

'She's out in the garden. Says she wants to do some flower arrangements for the dining room. The gardener will be fit to be tied but the customer is always right, like they say.'

Mrs Peabody, wearing her picture hat, gave a start when Philip came up behind her as she was leaning over some purple blossoms with a pair of garden shears.

'You startled me!' she said, dropping the shears. Philip got them for her. She sat down heavily on a near-by bench. 'The heat,' she sighed.

'Mr Willys is sick this morning.'

'I should really look in on him. I plan to take him some of these gorgeous blooms after I do the downstairs arrangements. I hate untidy bouquets.'

'Mrs Peabody, do you think it wise? Do you really feel you should risk your own life just to oblige Mr Willys?'

Mrs Peabody, now very pale indeed, dropped the shears again; neither made a move to pick them up. 'What do you mean?' she asked, in a voice so tiny that had he not been sitting beside her, he might have thought a bee had sounded, or a cicada had whirred somewhere in the green foliage.

'I'll be frank with you, Mrs Peabody. Mr Willys once made me the same proposition he made you. Only I refused to help him. You, on the other hand, were taken in. Whether it was out of curiosity or out of a real desire to help him makes little difference. The facts are the same in either case. You agreed to murder him.' Philip paused.

'Mr Willys told you this – fantastic story?' She got a grip on herself again. The panic of the moment was now succeeded by nonchalance. She picked up the shears and put them back into the half-filled flower basket.

Philip pressed his last bit of advantage. 'And I also know that you poisoned him this morning at breakfast, but that something went wrong.'

Mrs Peabody rose with great dignity and said, 'Follow me.' She led him to the far end of the garden where, in the shade of a gnarled eucalyptus tree, she said, 'Since we are now completely alone and there are no witnesses, I will be candid, even though I vowed my lips would remain sealed until the day I died, but as the plot is already getting tangled, and you, whether you like it or not, are involved quite deeply, I will confess to you that I took on this perilous job and that I mean to see it through, *come hell or high water!* My motives were, and are, of the highest. My method has, to my own amazement, been faulty. I erred. I blundered. I took a hypodermic needle early this morning and filled it with a colourless, tasteless poison of local origin which I inserted into the soft-boiled eggs he had ordered for breakfast. The chemist had informed me, prior to my purchase, that the dose was not only lethal but that it would kill a host of rats. It failed, however, to kill Mr Willys. From my room I could hear the doctor talking to him and I gather he was only mildly nauseated.'

'Which is probably just as well for you, Mrs Peabody.'

'Let me tell you, Mr Warren, that should you attempt to go to the police you would only be laughed at since, obviously, I would deny having confessed to you while Mr Willys himself would never testify against me.'

'I have no intention of going to the police. I was just reminding you of the risk involved, should you try again.'

'I will take that risk, Mr Warren. Rome was not built in a day. I am not discouraged. *I shall strike again.*'

'I don't see how you have the nerve,' said Philip, wonderingly; but then one look into the bright little eyes of Fay Peabody convinced him that she was a fanatic, and an artist. She would not be stopped by anyone until her demon was satisfied, until Mr Willys was dead.

'It proves,' she said, in an ordinary voice, 'that one can't rely on foreign products. If I'd had more time, I'm sure I would have been able to try the poison out on some creature to see if it were efficacious but, as you can see, I was forced to rely on the word of a native chemist and all my plans "gang aft agley" as Bobbie Burns would say – like a false start on my dictaphone – yet when I fail to get the beginning right, I go back into the field with renewed vigour and I have never, never failed to *bring home the bacon,*' she said slowly, fixing Philip's eyes with her own serious ones, a loose flap of the muslin veil now shadowing her left cheek and eye, giving her a somewhat slovenly air.

'Well, I won't interfere, Mrs Peabody, beyond saying that I think that what you're doing is dangerous and that the morality of the thing is confused, to say the least.'

'I will do my duty as I see it and though I appreciate your concern . . .' Suddenly she stopped talking and for a moment Philip was afraid she was going to faint. Quite pale, she made for the bench; with one last spurt of strength, she got to it and crumpled, her hand to her heart and her eyes wild with fear.

'What in God's name is the matter?' asked Philip, startled, positive that she was having a heart attack.

'*The hypodermic,*' she whispered, growing paler by the instant. 'I left in the pantry.'

'Good Lord!' Then: 'You must get it back immediately. Perhaps they haven't found it yet.'

'It's been there several hours. How *could* I? How could I have blundered so? The plan was perfect. Oh!' She moaned into the muslin veil which now completely covered her face.

'There's no use in your losing your nerve now, Mrs Peabody. Go to the pantry and see if the needle is there. After all, Mr Willys isn't dead yet.'

'That's right.' This thought comforted her and she emerged for a moment from behind the veil. 'We must hide the evidence.'

'*You* must hide the evidence, not I. I'm not going to be one of your – what do you call them? – accessories?'

'After the fact. Only there's no fact yet. Come to the pantry.'

The hypodermic was where she had left it and since there were no servants in sight, she hid the weapon in the flower basket; then with something of her old assurance, she went into the lobby, accompanied by Philip.

'Ah, flowers,' exclaimed Mr Koyoumdjian brightly. 'I hope you'll take some up to Mr Willys. Cheer him up. He's been asking for you.'

'Poor dear man! Has the doctor gone?'

'He just now left. He's getting to know Mr Willys very well . . . it was him who patched him up after he tried to take a powder.' Philip was pleased to find that the manager could make an occasional mistake in his well-loved vernacular.

'What did he say was wrong with our Mr Willys?'

'Nothing much, just stomach trouble. He picked up a bug in Cairo, I wouldn't be surprised.'

'I have just the medicine for him,' said Mrs Peabody, marching off, her flower basket swinging jauntily on her arm.

The second attempt on the life of Mr Willys was made during the night when his bed collapsed; the iron crosspiece that held up the mosquito netting missing his head by several inches. Philip, when he heard the noise, thought to himself: 'That's done it' and went back to sleep, refusing to be even a witness to Mrs Peabody's plot.

In the morning, on his way to breakfast, he looked in to see what damage had been done. The room was the same as ever, however, and Mr Willys was sitting up in bed, glumly sipping water through a straw.

'What was all the racket last night?'

'The bed,' said Mr Willys. 'It collapsed. Gave me quite a shock. My heart's pounding so I can barely breathe.'

'Mrs Peabody?'

'Mrs Peabody.'

'She's failed twice.'

'I know,' said Mr Willys. 'It's getting on my nerves. I had no wish to be hurt, you know. I can't bear pain. The thought makes me quite ill. And now the suspense! It's horrible. I tell you I don't know when or where she'll strike next.'

'Make her stop.'

'Oh, I couldn't do that. She's gone to such trouble. It would hardly be fair.'

'I don't see that fairness has anything to do with it.'

'But I still want her to pull it off. Only she's so damned sloppy. First of all, I knew those eggs were poisoned. She left enormous holes in the shells and they tasted god-awful but I ate them anyway and got sick. Then last night, the bed caved in. How she managed that, I'll never know. I suppose she loosened the top piece while I was taking a bath. I must say she's ingenious. What a mind that little lady has – like a steel trap!'

'A trap which won't close. If you weren't a willing victim, she'd be in jail now.'

'Well, we must remember that this is all quite new to her: there's a lot of difference between writing about something and actually doing it.'

'I could do a better job,' said Philip scornfully. 'Anybody could.'

'You wouldn't take it on, would you? I'd be very grateful. I could make it worth your while. You can name your price, within reason.'

'No, I'm afraid you're stuck with Mrs Peabody. It's a little like the medical profession. You engaged her and until *she* consents to call in a consultant it would be most unethical for you to replace her.'

'This is *not* a joke.'

'I realize that it isn't but there's nothing I can do about it except tell the police you want Mrs Peabody to kill you and that she's trying to, without much success. No, I'm afraid you will just have to trust to luck and the Fay Peabody Method.'

'You're not very encouraging.'

'Now, why don't you be sensible and tell her to stick to her writing while you go to Switzerland and lose weight.'

'I can't. Glands.'

'Then take shots.'

'They don't work on me. No, my mind is made up. Yet I keep wondering *what* will she do next.'

'Probably drown you in your bath.'

Mr Willys shuddered. 'I hate the idea of drowning: strangling to death, that's all it is. Well, I'll keep the bathroom door locked. She won't be able to get in. Bolts on the inside. Besides, we have an agreement to the effect that the business must be done in an instant.'

'But she's a desperate woman. Remember that. She's failed twice. Rather than fail a third time, she's quite capable of losing her head and setting fire to you.'

'Oh, she wouldn't do that.' He was alarmed, and Philip hoped that the fear of pain might yet force him to change his mind. 'I'm sure the next time she'll be able to do it, easily, without any fuss.'

'I think you're optimistic,' said Philip darkly, and he left the room and went downstairs to join Sophia and Mrs Peabody who were already at breakfast.

'Did you hear the noise last night?' asked Sophia, cool in green, unlike Mrs Peabody who looked more dowdy than ever, her eyelids red and granulated from fatigue. Her hands shook as she drank the bitter black coffee.

'Mr Willys told me his bed collapsed on him in the middle of the night.'

'Poor Mr Willys,' said Sophia maliciously. 'So many things seem to happen to him.'

'He's very unlucky, poor man,' said Philip, watching the murderess *manquée* out of the corner of his eye. She appeared not to be listening.

'One could almost believe in a malignant destiny. How could one man have so many things happen to him?'

'Foul play?' suggested Philip.

'It's possible. But who would want to hurt poor, harmless Mr Willys?'

'Mr Willys himself.'

'Possible. But no one else. The whole thing is so strange.'

Then having made Mrs Peabody suffer for her projected sin, they changed the subject and spoke of the trip they were to make that day to some tombs near the Valley of the Kings and, to their great surprise, Mrs Peabody asked if she might accompany them that afternoon because 'I've never done those tombs.' Since there was no polite way to refuse her, she was allowed to join the expedition.

After leaving the hotel, they went down the steps to the river where a rowboat and their dragoman were waiting. A number of naked boys stared curiously at the women who refused, pink-faced, to stare back. Then crossing the slow, warm river, they passed a sand island where donkeys were being raced to the delight of a large group of men. How the donkeys had got there and why they were racing one another Philip could never learn, for the dragoman, though he spoke English fluently, invariably expressed himself in such cryptic phrases that Philip preferred not to ask him questions.

The day passed pleasantly. They visited many tombs, small cheerful rooms cut in stone with bright wall paintings. The colours were new and fresh, preserved by the dry heat. They read in pictures of the lives of the dead and looked at representations of country houses, children, friends, all the activities of three thousand years before.

Mrs Peabody took many notes. She spoke very little but what she did say was to the point. They were, Philip decided, seeing the true Fay Peabody, the tireless master craftswoman giving her fans the best that was in her.

Once when Sophia and the dragoman were quarrelling over a figure of Osiris, Philip got Mrs Peabody off in one corner of the tomb of the Second Chief Accountant to the Royal Household and asked her in a low voice why the last attempt on the life of Mr Willys had failed.

'A miscalculation. I miscalculated the position of the crosspiece,' she said bitterly.

'But it was clearly in the centre of the bed. I don't see how you could have expected it to drop anywhere except in the middle of the mattress or on his stomach.'

'It was weighted,' she said, looking at him with undisguised malevolence. 'It was so arranged that when he turned over the entire thing would drop, from a considerable height, onto his head. Had it done so, he would no longer be with us. I had not counted, however, on his head being at *the very edge* of the bed. The odds were ten to one it would be close to the centre where the weight *did* fall, missing him.'

'I think it's getting on his nerves, these false attempts of yours.'

'Getting on *his* nerves!' She glared at him. 'Do you think it a picnic for me? Do you? Do you imagine I enjoy making a fool of myself before all the world? Or at least before you and Mr Willys. You seem to forget that I embarked on this project for completely selfless reasons. I have twice failed of my object. I admit that. But I hardly feel that others should criticize me for not being able to do easily what they would never dare attempt to do in the first place. I want it clearly understood, by both of you and Mr Willys, that I will brook no criticism of my methods *and* if I do not have the fullest co-operation and confidence of Mr Willys, I may be forced to withdraw altogether. Do you understand?'

'Perfectly.'

'You will repeat this to Mr Willys?'

'I will.'

'What time is it, by the way?'

'Four o'clock.'

'Ah! Then you will probably be spared the onerous task of repeating what I have said for, unless some unforeseen contingency has again arisen, Mr Willys is dead.'

Here, among the tombs, the announcement lost much of its inherent awfulness.

'But how?'

She would not answer his question. Instead, she unpinned her veil, shutting out the world with muslin.

Mr Koyoumdjian was in a rage. 'I'm going to have him moved today. I won't have him here another minute. The servants are thinking somebody has got the evil eye and they won't go near him. He's jinxed.'

'Has . . . something happened to Mr Willys?' asked Fay Peabody, one hand on the corner of the desk as though to steady herself.

'Asthma!' Mr Koyoumdjian said with a moan. 'He nearly choked to death. The doctor's with him. I'm going to get him out of this hotel if it's the last thing I do.'

Sophia looked at Philip and smiled. Mrs Peabody, without a word, went to her room.

'What do you think she could have done to him?' murmured Philip, as he and Sophia followed Mrs Peabody up the stairs.

'I haven't any idea. Do you think she tried again?'

'Oh yes. She told me so this afternoon. She intimated that he would be dead when we got back.'

'Poor woman. She must be desperate. Let's hope she doesn't lose her head and blow up the entire hotel.'

Mrs Peabody did not lose her head. That night she came down to dinner even more carefully dressed than usual, her garnets complemented by a double strand of pearls which were dingy enough, small enough, to be real. She was obviously aware that both Philip and Sophia knew her scheme and she carried the dinner off as well as possible under the circumstances, discussing fluently and instructively the large world of detective writers and readers among whom she was still a figure of the greatest magnitude, a thought which obviously sustained her now in her hour of defeat.

During dinner, the manager entered with the latest bulletin: 'He's going in the morning. The doctor says he shouldn't be moved but when I told him I couldn't have any more of this monkey business in my hotel he said they'd send a car over tomorrow and take him to the hospital. I've never seen anythng like it. My staff is just about ready to leave. They say a demon is loose in the hotel.'

'Is he feeling better?' asked Mrs Peabody with an air of gentle concern.

'I think so. He stopped choking. But he looks green about the gills. Doesn't want to leave, of course, but I had the doctor tell him he would have to go in the morning.'

'He's certainly an unlucky creature,' said Sophia.

'I sure wish he'd be unlucky somewhere else,' said the manager.

In the lobby, after dinner, Philip had another chance to talk with Mrs Peabody. She tried to avoid him, but he was too quick for her. 'What went wrong?' he asked.

'I would rather not discuss it.'

'You won't try again, will you?'

'It's no business of yours,' she snapped. 'But to satisfy your curiosity, no, I *won't* try again. Now, if you'll excuse me . . .'

'Do tell me what you did this time.'

'I placed a certain deadly, air-polluting poison in the pistils of a large number of flowers which I then set about his room so that, in a few hours, the atmosphere would be completely malignant. I had not, however, taken into account the fact that Mr Willys had an allergy to all flowers and that he nearly choked to death before they could be removed.'

'Frankly, Mrs Peabody, I'm astonished you failed. I can't imagine anything simpler than killing someone who wants to die in a country where there probably would never be an investigation.'

'I should like to see *you* try it.'

'People do it every day. How can you explain that? Thousands of murders go undetected every year. I don't understand why you, with every advantage, can't do as well.'

'Perhaps because *I* am not a criminal,' said Mrs Peabody; and she went upstairs.

'How did she do it this time?' asked Sophia.

Philip told her and she laughed. 'If only her fans could see her now.'

That night before going to bed, Philip visited Mr Willys. He looked the same as ever but his thin voice was more weak than usual and talking seemed to tire him.

'It's all over with me,' he said. 'She won't try again.'

'Just as well. I was always against the idea.'

'I can't imagine her quitting now. After wrecking my nerves and health she refuses to finish the job! It isn't fair. It just isn't fair.'

'I'm sure you'll be well in no time.'

'I expect to be an invalid for the next twenty years. I can hardly move as it is. The strain of getting out of bed and going to the bathroom gives me such palpitations that I can hardly bear it. Oh, it's so terrible,' and he moaned plaintively, his eyes tight shut, as though to blot the world out forever.

'Anyway it nearly worked last time,' said Philip, illogically, hoping that this would please him, this reference to the plan which had failed; it did not.

'The fool! The incompetent fool!' Mr Willys turned on his former idol with a ferocity made all the more frightening because his voice was too weak to bear the passion of a denunciation. 'Any half-wit Arab could have done better, if he thought there might be a plugged nickel in it for him. But the brilliant Fay Peabody, given every chance in the world, flops. She could have asked me about the flowers. But no, she waited until I'd gone to the bathroom, then she put them all around the room like a funeral parlour. It was half an hour before I could get enough breath to shout for help.'

'Do you think that anyone suspected the flowers were poisoned?'

'How? They were thrown out right away, while I was strangling. I suppose if she had put a few more in the room, nature might have done the trick.'

'Did she have any excuse to make?'

'She attacked *me* for having an allergy. Said it was the most ridiculous thing she'd ever heard of, that if she'd put it in a story nobody'd believe it.'

'I hope you told her off.'

'Don't worry! I said that if she'd ever . . .' He began to wheeze alarmingly, shaking the bed, fat rippling dangerously as he gagged, tried to get his breath. When finally he did, he was pale and exhausted, too sick to acknowledge Philip's sympathy.

The next morning, refusing the litter which the doctor had sent over, Mr Willys dressed himself and slowly descended the stairs, supported on each side by a fragile native boy. It was the first time that Philip had seen Mr Willys on his feet and he was surprised to find that he was a short man, broader than he was tall, with ludicrously small hands and feet. He wore a crumpled white suit and a loud tie decorated with reindeer, a souvenir no doubt from his greeting-card days. He was very pale and breathing hard when, against the doctor's advice and the manager's wish, he insisted on joining the others at breakfast.

'Good morning,' he puffed, as a place was laid for him.

'It's nice to see you up,' said Sophia politely.

'I'm vertical, if that's what you mean. I am hardly *up*. I can hardly breathe in this weather. But a large breakfast does seem in order.' And he had them bring him sausages, eggs and potatoes, as well as toast and coffee. 'A real American breakfast,' he said, eating as quickly as he could, his white face glistening with sweat.

'Do you think you should eat so much in this heat?' asked Philip, somewhat sickened by the other's unnatural appetite.

'I need a hearty breakfast,' mumbled Mr Willys.

'I believe that toast and coffee is all *anybody* needs,' said Fay Peabody. 'Except, of course, working men who must *labour with their hands*.'

Mr Willys snorted but made no answer as he speared a fried potato.

Philip looked out the French windows at the green gardens flickering in the heat. For several moments the only sound at the table was the wet noise of Mr Willys chewing and swallowing food.

Sophia mercifully broke the silence: 'Where do you intend to go next?'

'Switzerland, if I can survive the altitude. Start taking glands and things. See if maybe they can do something. Doubt it, though.'

This speech was dragged out to an inordinate length by long stops for breath and nourishment. Philip could not take his eyes off him, much as he would rather have looked anywhere else than at that grey shapeless face with the loose lips which quivered as Mr Willys gasped and talked and chewed, all at once. Philip almost wished, if only on aesthetic grounds, that Mrs Peabody had succeeded.

'Will you be in Europe long?' asked Sophia, who, of them all, was the only one not officially in on the conspiracy which had failed.

'Can't tell. May go back to Philly. Though it's hot there, too. Waiter, bring me some more toast. One place pretty much like another to me, except some are hot and some are cool. Want a cool place now.' Then he did things to a soft poached egg which Philip never wanted to see done again.

'Did you get to see much of Egypt?' Sophia was intent on being polite.

'Saw the Sphinx my first day in Cairo. Then had a heat stroke and I've been laid up ever since. First there; now here.'

'I'm sure you'd have enjoyed Karnak.'

'Don't think so. I did want to see the Sphinx but outside of that I'm not so keen on sightseeing. It's hard on a man my size.'

'Why did you want to see the Sphinx?' asked Sophia.

'Always heard about it.'

'Did you like it?'

'Not much. Face all gone.'

'At least you're able to get a bit of reading done,' said Philip helpfully; only a few minutes to go.

'Don't read much. Eyes can't take it. I used to like detective stories.' He put down his fork, swallowed noisily and stared at Mrs Peabody who had the grace not to stare back.

'I'm sure Mrs Peabody is pleased to hear that,' said Sophia. 'I've never read a detective story, I'm afraid. A terrible confession to make in front of you,' she said, turning to the authoress.

'Not at all. I am aware that the vineyard in which I have for so long toiled produces nothing more than a good table wine. At least so the connoisseurs in these matters seem to think; but it is good enough for me and for a great many other people as well, *both at home and abroad.*'

Mr Willys looked at her with loathing, but he said nothing while the others talked about Mrs Peabody's vineyard.

The manager came in just as Mr Willys was debating whether to have more coffee. 'The car's waiting for you outside, sir. I've also got the bill for you and some other things out in the lobby if you'll be so kind as to take care of them for me.'

'Let us go then,' said Mr Willys, pushing back from the table; the two frail native boys moved forward, got him to his feet and escorted him out of the dining room and into the lobby. Mrs Peabody, with a bleak little smile, excused herself and left the room for the morning-fresh garden.

'Well, that's the end of that,' said Philip.

'She seems rather crushed by it all.'

'And he doesn't, which is suspicious. He seems almost cheerful.'

'A great deal of attention sometimes has a good effect on people who are often alone. I don't suppose Mr Willys has ever been the centre of attention before in his life, except as a minor curiosity in public places.'

'All that food!' Philip shuddered.

'He could hardly walk.'

'Let's go see him off,' said Philip, and they went into the lobby where Mr Willys stood unsupported in the doorway, his baggage, all about him and Mr Koyoumdjian, beaming with relief, was wishing him a quick recovery.

'Ah, there you are,' said Mr Willys, as they approached. 'This is it. I'm off at last.'

'Have a good trip,' said Philip, shaking the cold damp hand. 'Are you going to stay at the hospital long? Are you going down to Cairo?'

'Cairo. Tomorrow. Then I'm leaving this goddamn country for good.'

'I was going to say if you were at the hospital for any length of time, we would come visit you.'

'Very kind of you, I must say. You've been wonderful about the whole thing

... very kind. But now I must be off. Good-bye, Miss Oliver. Been a pleasure.' Then, unaccompanied, he walked into the sunlight where he collapsed, a few feet from the automobile which was to have taken him to the hospital. His last recorded words were: 'Get a doctor.'

The sudden death of Mr Willys shocked them all. To Philip it seemed, somehow, grossly unfair while to the manager it was The End: he did not believe anyone could be as jinxed as he was. Several servants resigned on the spot while the remaining ones gave him a vote of no confidence but did not press for any immediate action, either on his part or theirs. The body was removed the moment the doctor announced that the anguished, flesh-burdened soul of Mr Willys had departed this vale of tears. Philip told the doctor that the deceased had wanted to be cremated and his ashes cast into the Nile. This last touch was Philip's own. The doctor thought they might have trouble finding a large enough oven for this purpose but that there was a possibility the brick kiln on the edge of town could be hired to do the job. Fortunately, Mr Willys had had sufficient cash in his pocket to make a fine cremation possible. Other details, such as the disposition of personal effects and the writing to the next of kin, were assigned to Mr Koyoumdjian.

That night at dinner the two ladies wore black and Philip wore a blue serge suit.

'What did the doctor say he died of?' asked Sophia, after a long, lugubrious silence.

'A heart attack,' said Philip, in a low reverent voice. 'Excitement, the heat, and all that food he ate finished him off.'

'What were his last words?' asked Mrs Peabody, softly, her hands folded before her on the table, as though in prayer.

'He asked for a doctor,' said Philip; a sudden suspicion crossed his mind.

'It doesn't sound as if he was very *sincere*,' said Mrs Peabody, unaware of the suspicion in which she was held by Philip. 'All that talk about wanting to die and then when he *does* get his wish, he is frightened. *A lack of moral fibre*, I should say.'

'You . . . you weren't responsible?' asked Philip, forgetting that Sophia was not supposed to know about the attempt on Mr Willys's life.

'No, I wasn't,' said Mrs Peabody. 'I debated whether or not to give it one last whirl. His rudeness to me at breakfast, however, restrained my essentially kind impulse and I allowed him to depart for what I hoped might have been a long life of physical distress and melancholia. Fortunately, for him, nature intervened.'

The next day the manager brought Philip a shoe box which contained all that was mortal of Mr Willys. 'You go throw them in the Nile,' said Mr Koyoumdjian, 'and do it quick because if the boys find out that even that guy's ashes are in the hotel, they'll leave me pronto.'

Philip said that he would conduct the last rites immediately and so, accompanied by Sophia, he walked to the bank of the Nile and climbed down the rocky embankment to the water's edge. Sailboats glided across the water. Philip opened the box which contained some grey-black lumps of bone and ash.

'Who would have thought he could have been compressed to this?' he said, in an unconscious paraphrase.

'Give me the box,' said Sophia, and she took it from the bemused Philip and emptied its contents into the green water. 'You see how easy it is?' she asked, throwing the box away.

'How easy what is?'

'Dying.'

'No, I don't.'

CHAPTER NINE

He pressed his eyelids and saw two black suns, two eclipses in the red darkness. His head ached from the glare and heat of the day which, fortunately, was very nearly over. He opened his eyes again and looked across the desert at the near-by pyramids: large buff-coloured objects as meaningless as a child's toys upset in a sandbox. The sky was a pale luminous pink, cloudless and now, as the red disc slipped over the desert's edge, sunless as well. To his left was Cairo and to his right the desert. The green Nile Valley ended abruptly at his feet. One foot touched grass; the other brown desert: the line between was unnaturally precise, as though drawn by a giant. He turned and looked at the city, coral pink and white, divided by the Nile, edged by dusty green which was, in its turn, circled by the wide flat desert at whose edge he now stood, a few yards from Mena House where he had been entertained that day with lunch and a swim in the hotel's new pool. Thinking of his host, wondering if he should go back into the lobby and look for him, Philip strode slowly up the steep road which led to the pyramids. He was nearly at the top when he heard someone call his name. He stopped until, out of breath, his host and new friend Charles de Cluny joined him.

'I had things to do. The manager wanted to know about a party some friends of mine were giving. How I hate this hill! It's so steep. I'm quite out of breath. The sky. Isn't it a fine colour? This is the time of day when I find myself really loving Egypt. Rose. Wonderful rose colour, the sky, and cool without the sun. Here we are.'

They were now at the top of the sand hill near the base of the great pyramid. Below them in the roseate distance was Cairo while across the desert, indistinct by twilight, were set the other pyramids, like so may broken metronomes.

'Magnificent sight. I never tire of it. I'm always staggered when I recall the age of these buildings. Think what they must have seen. Think!'

Philip thought and then de Cluny, shifting from contemplation of the past to the scandal of the present, pointed to the only house in the desert, a small cube of a building with great windows and a soldier standing guard in front of it.

'His,' he whispered. And from his tone Philip knew that he meant the King, a plump young Albanian, successor to those austere Pharaohs who had reigned before him over the same green valley.

'He brings his women here,' his guide whispered as they moved towards the great pyramid. 'A gloomy-looking place,' said Philip, as they passed the sentry. 'No trees, no garden, just sand.'

'But the view! Think of it! Having the pyramids in front of you on a starlit night, with a beautiful woman beside you!'

'Do you think he enjoys it?' said Philip who often, in self-defence, liked to take the popular American view that the rich and powerful were hopelessly miserable with no whims left to be granted, no use at all of their wealth and even less for their power which was, of course, invariably attended by guilt and shame.

The old woman who dies in a tenement house with fifty thousand dollars sewed in her mattress or the Texas millionaire who lives on cornflakes and weak tea are recurrent American folk types. But even Philip had to agree that the King of Egypt probably never suffered from much more than an occasional hangover or a moment's anguish at the lithe figure he had sacrificed to a robust appetite.

They stopped on the edge of a valley where, handsomely silhouetted against the sky, was, yes, the inevitable attraction, the Sphinx. To our authority, Professor Rawlinson, it is 'among the marvels of Egypt, second to none. The mysterious being with the head of a man and the body of a lion is not at all uncommon in Egyptian architectural adornment, but the one placed before the Second Pyramid (The Pyramid of Shafra) and supposed to be contemporaneous with it, astonishes the observer by its gigantic proportions. It is known to the Arabs as *Abul-hôl*, the father of terror.'

Philip stared into the mild, faintly smiling face and saw nothing at all, only an ancient monument; and yet, though what he saw was not in itself impressive, the associations of thousands of years affected him as strongly as it had at Luxor and he experienced once again that grave serenity, that secret knowledge of the endless flow of life, of generation and regeneration, never-ending, never-constant, the endless structure which contained all time and matter, the waking dream behind his own blue eyes, eyes which could if briefly hold it all.

Then the sky turned grey and silver specks appeared overhead; the ruddy-faced Sphinx turned the colour of slate and Philip muttered that frightening name 'Abul-hôl' to himself as he and de Cluny walked back to Mena House.

Later he sat in the dark rose-smelling garden of the hotel and drank whisky with Charles de Cluny, his friend of several days now, a traveller like himself but a knowing traveller, one who had been here often before. He was French. He had lived everywhere: in Central America, in Europe, in Africa. Now, for this month at least, he was in Cairo.

'When does she arrive, this friend of yours?' asked Charles suddenly.

'Miss Oliver? Next week, I think. She's in the desert now. I have no idea where; but I suppose she'll be here when she said she would.'

'She sounds like a very intelligent woman,' said Charles, disapprovingly.

'Very,' said Philip. 'She's good company. That's all.'

'Ah. Then you're *not* in love?'

'Good Lord, no! She's the last woman in the world I'd be interested in.'

'Do you think *she* knows that?'

'I doubt if she's ever given it a thought,' said Philip, who sometimes wondered whether she had or not. His vanity often insisted that she *did* love him. Fire beneath cold surface, but his reason thought it unlikely.

'Is she wealthy?'

'I expect so.'

'I wonder if she might want to buy some jewels. I have an impoverished cousin – as a matter of fact, I have dozens of impoverished cousins – but the one I have in mind has some exquisite pigeon's-blood rubies which she'd sell for nothing. Do find out if Miss Oliver's interested. It would be such a help if she were. My cousin, by chance, happens to be right here in Cairo.'

'I'll ask her,' said Philip, wondering how de Cluny himself earned a living.

'I should appreciate that.'

After a long silence, de Cluny asked Philip if he knew Zoe Helotius.

'Only slightly. Is she here?'

'Just for the week. Out of season, too. But then there's to be a great party and wherever there's a great affair, Zoe's on hand. Amusing woman. When did you know her?'

Philip told him. A number of names were then exchanged. They had several acquaintances in common whom they had not, until that moment, bothered to discuss. They had met as strangers and neither had made the effort to fix the other's place in the world since the identity of each was so clearly apparent: a young American of apparent leisure and a French adventurer with a taste, but not a flair, for philosophy and a flair, but no taste, for a fashionable life on an income whose origin was obscure.

'If you care to,' said de Cluny, when Philip's attitude and position had become more clearly defined after the naming of the names, 'I will get you invited. It might interest you. A real Cairo affair to celebrate the wedding of. . .' And here he named both the host and the bridegroom, two Egyptian men so highly placed that they could have touched the throne itself if they had been so minded. 'It will be a Western party, although we won't see the bride. Both gentlemen are enlightened, but not that much. Other women will be there, however . . . despite the Prophet.'

There was too much of everything at the reception: too many people, too many flowers, too much food and champagne, and more jewels than Philip had ever seen before. The non-orthodox Egyptian women were especially gaudy in lace and damask with huge yellow diamonds, square emeralds, rubies like gouts of blood; their glossy black hair coiled and contorted by Paris hairdressers, dusted with gold and bright with diamond moons and stars. Philip had never before seen such display, as he walked from one large, airy room to the next, through Moorish arches while servants in white Western-style jackets served wine.

De Cluny was an excellent guide. He saw to it that they never remained too long with the very dull or missed meeting the occasional odd or interesting citizen of Cairo who stood, usually, at the centre of a large group, receiving homage, constructing epigrams or diatribes or platitudes or whatever his specialty, applauded by the distinguished and decorative audience which moved from one point of interest to the next, like tourists in a museum.

The host, a large imposing man in a morning coat, welcomed them gravely in French, declaring that his house was theirs. That was the last they saw of him.

'And there,' said de Cluny, as they crossed the largest of the rooms, 'is a Russian spy, under the chandelier . . . calls herself Princess.'

The spy was a small pretty woman in her forties, wearing an Indian sari. She smiled engagingly at de Cluny. 'How are you?' she said in French, as he kissed her hand. Then, to Philip: 'And how are *you*? I've seen you in Shepheard's, haven't I?'

Philip said that she had.

'Oh, let's find some chairs. Everyone stands. It just makes me wilt, standing in the heat.' She went over to one corner where three gilt chairs were placed against the wall. Two of them were empty; the third was occupied by a small Egyptian. The spy gave a dazzling smile. 'Princess would like to sit down,' she said.

The small Egyptian looked puzzled.

'I said, *Princess* would like to sit down,' repeated the spy, more sternly. The little man got to his feet and fled.

'That's better, isn't it?' They sat down. 'They have such bad manners, Egyptians.'

'Are you from India?' asked Philip, naïvely, not realizing that in Cairo no one asked the spies direct questions for fear of seeming gauche.

'My mother is Indian,' she said, repeating the same dazzling smile that so confused the former occupant of the chair; then she began a long involved story about the peregrinations of her family and herself, a mélange of nationalities and resounding titles.

'But I am talking only of myself,' she exclaimed, when both de Cluny and Philip were afraid she might never talk of anything else again all evening, holding them close to her with her brilliant smile and tiny gesturing hands which, every now and then, touched Philip's sleeve as she named yet another country in which she had lived. 'Tell me about you.'

'I'm an American,' said Philip. 'There isn't much more to tell.'

'Come now. Princess doesn't believe that! I'm sure you must be a wonderful businessman building oil wells and making dollars all over the world.' For a moment he was afraid that this might be a preface to an attack on capitalism but she meant it literally.

'No, I'm a tourist, just out of school,' he said; her interest waned perceptibly.

'How wonderful for you to come see our old countries. To breathe the same air that Cleopatra did! Oh, history is my passion! How I should love to have lived in those times and gone to the sources of the Nile in a pleasure barge. Princess would like some champagne.'

It took him a moment to separate the request from the rhapsody; by the time he did, de Cluny had clapped his hands and a boy came with champagne for them.

'Aren't you drinking, Charles?' she asked, noticing that de Cluny refused the wine.

'I'm a good Moslem today.'

'Now you're making fun of me. Princess is a *real* Moslem but she believes the Prophet would not mind too much since he has promised us all the wine that we can drink in Heaven.'

'Only the men were promised that,' said de Cluny with a smile.

'You *are* old-fashioned! How are your cousins? I was at a dinner not long ago with one of them but I forgot her name.'

'There are so many.'

'How wonderful it must be to have distinguished relatives all over the world!'

'And all struggling to survive,' said de Cluny.

'The old ways change,' said the Princess gravely, and she walked off.

'I don't believe she's a Russian spy,' said Philip, as they moved towards another large room where an orchestra was playing waltzes.

'I'm sure she's not either,' said de Cluny agreeably, 'but she's just like the ones they used to have here during the war. *That* was a time! Everyone was a spy and . . . Oh, look! There *he* is.'

They stopped in the doorway of the ballroom where a dozen couples were dancing to the music of an orchestra which was hiding behind potted palms. The parquet floor had been newly waxed and from time to time the dancers slipped and stumbled, amusing those spectators who stood chatting, all eyes discreetly centred on a short burly figure in a tuxedo who was, de Cluny murmured to Philip in a low voice, the King of Egypt. Philip immediately recognized the curiously stiff figure and immobile face, half hidden now by dark glasses which made him look, more than ever, like an interesting experiment in taxidermy. The blonde with whom he was dancing was a head taller than he and very beautiful.

'He's incognito,' said de Cluny. 'In other words, no one is allowed to fuss over him. But, on the other hand, no one can approach him without *his* consent. A happy arrangement. But here are the guards.' Philip looked and saw that in each corner of the room stood a man in a business suit, hand in pocket, revolver barrel pointed.

Then they came to the last of the suite, a small Chinese room with carved teakwood furniture and crimson silk banners on the walls. Here a group of sedate Westerners were gathered, talking politics. De Cluny knew them all and he introduced Philip, saying the names rapidly and precisely. As there was no place farther to go, their journey ended, they sat down and de Cluny promptly talked politics with the severest and greyest of the men and listening to him, Philip could not help but feel that he was perhaps too fluent, too affable, too ready to see the other person's point of view and to argue it with even greater eloquence than the other person was capable of, at the expense of his own convictions, assuming he had any.

Zoe Helotius entered the room like some predatory bird of prey with white leather face, sharp beak, blood-red lips stretched in a vulture's smile. She attacked, surrounded by equerries, advisers, friends and enemies who spread out like an army, flanking the room, rounding up and sorting its contents until a series of concentric circles had been arranged, the lesser figures close to the periphery, important ones at the small centre where Zoe herself stood, talking quickly, casting febrile glances around the room to see if she was missing anything. She was not. She was now the centre of attraction; the main event.

'Ah, Charles, my dear. It's been a long time.'

'Five years, madame.'

'Too long a time. And how is X? and Y? I love them. I never see them. You must come pay me a call. Afternoon. At five. I'm staying with Z.' A shudder of delight went through the circles, like waves from a stone cast in water, the circles ever widening until at last they spent themselves against the silk-hung walls.

'Mr Warren? Have we met? In Capri? Ah, Regina's friend. I remember now. You were attached to the Embassy at Rome. I love your Ambassador. Tell him I look forward to that dinner in Venice. He'll know what I mean. Is Regina here in Cairo? But of course not. I saw her in Paris a week ago. So much more like a queen than any of the queens one knows, if you follow me. Do you know her, Charles? Yes? No? Ah, you would love her. She has style and *he*, well, one defers to the most powerful man in the world, which he is nowadays. But,' and she lowered her voice and opened her eyes very wide, her onyx irises circled now by white, 'I hear *he* is going to divorce *her*.' Philip was by now sufficiently used to the varying degrees of emphasis with which people in Cairo mentioned otherwise unidentified pronouns to establish the intended reference: *he* was Farouk; *she* was the heir-less Persian he had married.

'I hope not,' said Charles, neutrally.

'It is what *they* say. But here is Anna Morris. Where have you been hiding? This is Charles de Cluny, Mr Warren.'

Charles kissed the lady's hand. Philip bowed to the newcomer, a dark-haired girl, of his own age, with large hazel eyes and a husband who joined them a moment later, a burly, rough-voiced man with a limp. An industrialist, Philip gathered. In steel.

'Some party,' said Mr Morris, in a tone which could easily have been hostile. 'Never seen so much jewellery in my life. Build the Aswan Dam with one roomful of it.'

'You have no love of beauty,' said Mrs Helotius, who had, and who told them all about it while Philip talked to Anna, learning that she was originally European of mixed nationality and that she was now married to the industrialist with whom she was touring Europe and North Africa for her pleasure as well for his business: he had come to Egypt to sell steel. Philip was charmed by her voice which was low and melodic, faintly accented and appealing. He was also overawed by the bull-necked husband in whose broad shadow she now stood.

'It is too much,' she said, in answer to a remark of Philip's about the reception. 'Too heavy. I prefer lightness.'

'The Petit Trianon?'

'Oh, I'm sure I would have loved that. So delicate, so false. Have you been there?'

He shook his head. 'I've never been in France. Next month I'll be there, in Paris.'

'I lived there a long time.'

'Is it . . .?'

'It is.' She smiled. 'You'll never want to leave.'

'I'm sure of that.'

'But when you do leave you'll not be the same.'

He laughed. 'Now, that's an exaggeration. I've known hundreds of people who've gone there, been enchanted, and returned the same as ever.'

'But not you. I can tell.' She looked at him gravely while he looked not at her serious, shining eyes but at her mouth instead, wondering at its Botticelli shape, like a bird gliding.

'I can believe anything,' he said. 'This is my year of belief. Until recently I doubted everything and trusted no one. Now the wilder, the more improbable the story I am told, the more eager I am to believe it. Tell me there are serpents in the sea and I will believe you; the next time I travel by ship I will see one a mile long, attended by mermaids with seaweed in their hair.'

'There *are* serpents in the sea,' she said, smiling, one hand touching the odd-shaped bit of crystal she wore about her neck on a silver chain.

'Then I shall see one.'

'Mermaids, too?'

'A platoon of them, all wearing naval officers' caps.' She laughed and then, aware that her husband was saying farewell to Mrs Helotius, she turned to Philip and gave him her hand. 'Perhaps I'll see you when you come to Paris. Where will you stay?'

'I've no idea. Where do *you* stay?'

'We,' and the pronoun was suddenly forbidding, 'always stay at the Ida, a quiet place. We'll be there for several months, I think – this autumn. Or at least *I* will stop there while Vane is travelling about.' The 'I' was a promise; on that they parted.

Mrs Helotius looked about the conquered room. Each person had been drained of information, catalogued and filed. She raised one arm slowly as though to adjust her hair. But this was no spontaneous gesture, Philip saw: it was a military signal, a cavalry officer's command to charge. Led by Lady Julia, made in green watered silk, her cohorts assembled about her and swiftly the invaders withdrew, in a flood of sound.

'Did you ever hear the story about Zoe Helotius and Bernard Shaw . . .' began Charles.

'Many times,' said Philip, sternly. 'I have vowed never to hear it again.'

'In that case I shall respect your wishes. There are too many stories about her anyway. Shall we move on?'

Not until they had regained the ballroom, now crowded with dancers, did Charles mention Anna Morris.

'I could see you liked her,' he said.

'Why? Did I stare? Turn red with excitement?'

'You did indeed! I don't blame you. She's an attractive woman.'

'Got a bad character, hasn't she?'

'Not as far as I know. Why do you say that?'

'I don't know. Isn't that what one always says about beauties?' asked Philip, wishing the orchestra would play no more Strauss waltzes, hoping Charles would have more to say; he did.

'You mean is she faithful to her husband? In that case, I can tell you, to your great delight, that she has been unfaithful on occasion; but she has good taste.'

'In lovers?'

'In everything. Not that I know her especially well but I have followed her career with some interest these last few years. She has quite a vogue in Paris, you know. Less of one in America, I should expect. Too fine for them. That doesn't offend you?'

'Nothing offends me,' said Philip, happily. But he spoke too soon. The Russian spy, her somewhat crumpled sari floating behind her, approached them, smiling stonily, like the Gorgon confronting two doomed mortals. 'Princess has been looking for you,' she said.

Philip was not surprised to find that Sophia and Charles had everything in common except mutual sympathy and so, after one grim dinner together, he kept them apart, devoting most of his time to Sophia who had arrived early in the week from her journey into the desert where she had inspected a newly discovered city of the Twelfth Dynasty and interviewed yet another holy man who had gloomily predicted the end of the world next spring, in the first week of Ramadan.

They kept mostly to Shepheard's, for Philip, once he had seen the great museum and a few of the mosques, had no real desire to explore Cairo, not liking the heat or the filth or the men and boys who followed them everywhere they went, begging and selling, their voices alternating between intimate whines and shrill cries of anger. He usually pushed past them, striking out at the brown hands which tugged at his coat: he hated being touched by anyone.

One afternoon he had tea with Sophia in the garden at the back of Shepheard's and he asked her what had become of Abu Bekr and his prophecy.

'I never saw him again,' she said, her grey eyes lovely, almost compensating for the thin mouth and square jaw. The wind rustled the branches of the tree overhead, scattering lozenges of sunlight across the white tablecloth. A Negro servant wearing a fez, tight jacket and bloomers leaned against the wall of the hotel, lazily trying to catch flies with one hand. An English family sitting at a table with a striped awning were the only other people in the garden. They looked red and hot, in white crumpled linen.

'I suppose he will stay there all his life, making prophecies as long as people will listen.'

'They will always listen. Whether they believe or not is another question.'

'Do you?'

'I'm not sure. In general, yes. Something is about to happen. Where and when and how . . . not to mention *what*, are a puzzle. I look for keys.'

'The keys are at Rome,' said Philip obscurely.

'Rusty keys,' said Sophia, pouring herself more tea. Philip put a whole scone in his mouth and chewed thoughtfully. Still leaning against the wall, the servant caught a fly; smiling happily, he dried his palm on the bloomers.

Then Philip told her that he would leave for Paris in a week's time. By plane, he added, assembling details as he spoke, pleased with the suddenness of his own decision.

'Oh, I'm sorry. I had hoped you would stay here another month. I thought you might be interested in some Ptolemaic things they've come across near Alexandria.' If she was in any deeper way distressed or put out, she did not show it. She talked of ruins until the fact of his going had been accepted as immutable, a day of sure departure at last selected, a time of change.

'You'll be coming to Paris, too?' asked Philip politely yet not hypocritically, for he did like her.

'I'm not sure. My plans are seldom definite. How long do you think you'll be there?'

'A few months. Perhaps most of the winter. I'm not sure. I shan't know until I've tried it.'

'If you're there several months, we shall see one another again.' And the sentence came out cold and formal, which was obviously against her will for she smiled and tried, unsuccessfully, to be spontaneous. Her failure both surprised and embarrassed him. He covered it quickly, volubly, agreeing that they would see one another, pouring himself tea and inquiring quickly, irrelevantly about Mrs Peabody.

'Mrs Peabody? Ah, I'd almost forgotten that nightmare. She's gone back to America, I think. I saw very little of her after you left. She avoided me, too, for that matter. I think she was suddenly rather horrified at what she'd very nearly done. Last I saw of her she was going down the Nile to Alexandria on a freight ship. The regular passenger ships have been discontinued since the war but, undaunted, she found a place for herself aboard a terrible little freighter and, if she manages to survive that phase of her field work, she's probably at the very minute sitting, dictaphone in hand, composing *The Karnak Corpse*.'

'That is *not* the title.'

'Indeed it is. She told me so herself the day she left. Suggested I look for it when it was published next spring.' They laughed. A bird chattered in the branches of a tree near by while another, like a scarlet shuttlecock, swooped in an arc from sky to flowers.

'Poor Mr Willys,' said Philip, thinking back on those weeks at Luxor as though three years instead of three weeks had passed since they had stood on the edge of the Nile and scattered the ashes.

'Poor? He got his wish, didn't he? That's more than most of us get.'

'What a terrible wish. What a terrible life!'

'I agree that the life was a piece of misfortune, a bad trick of chance but the wish was something else again.'

'I don't want to die,' said Philip exactly recalling vividly the horror of certain death dreams he had had from time to time all his life. When he was a child, he had often awakened alone and desperate in the impersonal night, trying to visualize what nothing must be like. The dream had changed very little over the

years; the terror and the despair remained as he realized that one day he would
die and *not* be. He shivered in the warm flower-scented wind and he touched the
table, the cups, as though to prove to himself that he was still alive and that the
present was all.

'Why should you want to, now? But one day —'

'I'm more interested in how to live than how to die,' said Philip, feeling silly at
the heroic ring of this statement: how often had he found a moment of true vision
become, when reduced to words, a dusty bromide.

'There is only one way to live,' said Sophia, pushing a strand of hair out of her
eyes. 'To do as you want, making of course the obvious allowances for the rules
your neighbours in place and time have established.'

'And live according to the body,' said Philip, wondering if he should accept
de Cluny's invitation to visit a brothel that evening.

'That is part of it. But one comes closer to the way through contemplation. I
feel a greater affinity to those men who built the temples of Luxor than I do to
living men. The idea of the dead is pure and unconfused by the senses; we cannot
see or hear or touch them . . . the irrelevant flesh has been swept away and only
the idea of Thutmose or Amenhotep, Socrates or Plato, endures.'

'I haven't the vocation to spend my life among the ruins.'

'Then spend it with the shadows of men. Their books or attitudes which are so
much purer than they themselves.'

'But I've done that most of my life. I hate involvement in other people's lives.
My serene disposition is a result of childhood vow that I would keep my distance
from all the trouble in the world . . . let no one touch me.'

'And yet the further you seem to withdraw from the world of the living, the
closer you come to life itself,' she said urgently. 'You see it dispassionately and,
as they say, you see it whole. You see not a man but the idea of a man.'

Philip looked at his watch. 'I'm afraid I'd better go in and shave. I'm going
out for dinner.'

'Oh, I'd forgotten. With Charles?'

Philip nodded. 'I believe we're going to the French theatre afterwards.'

'Give him my regards,' she said, too wise to state her disapproval of the
volatile Frenchman.

'I shall,' said Philip; and he did, just as he and Charles entered the narrow
dim alley which led to the brothel of the Three Sisters of Fatima from Beirut.

PART THREE

'And I wish that all times were April and May, and every month renew all fruits again, and every day fleur-de-lis and gillyflower and violets and roses wherever one goes, and woods in leaf and meadows green, and every lover should have his lass, and they to love each other with a sure heart and true, and to everyone his pleasure and a gay heart.'

An anonymous student,
Thirteenth Century, Paris

CHAPTER TEN

'It usually happens at twelve,' said Glenellen. 'Seldom later than twelve-thirty. Well worth seeing, you know. People come from all around but very few of us get this close. Takes a lot of managing, believe me.'

'I certainly do,' said Philip, remembering the four locked doors and the villainous *concierge* at the gate.

'You see the great thing is: *what* shall it be?'

'Does it vary?'

'Continually, from day to day. One never knows what to expect.'

'What will it be today?'

'How should I know? That's one of the reasons I came. In any event, it's one of the seven wonders of Paris, if not of the world.'

'And the other six?'

'I was speaking rhetorically. I don't think you properly appreciate the situation.'

'I was only joking. I'm sorry.'

'Americans always joke,' said Glenellen, sulking. Philip sighed and looked about the room. It was a cube, large and shabby with a dusty gold throne at one end and a number of scallop-shell Venetian chairs on two of which the visitors sat while the chamberlain, a small dour gentleman wearing the rusty striped trousers and morning coat of a minor French civil servant, sat on a frayed wart-like, salmon-coloured pouf. A door covered with green baize and studded with rusty nails led into the Presence, the shrine.

'Is there anyone else coming?' asked Philip, oppressed by the room's silence, by the lonely faraway sound of the traffic in the street below, muffled by heavy plush curtains which shut out light and air, made the cool morning a lowering twilight.

'How should I know?' Glenellen was petulant. 'With considerable effort I have arranged this audience and now you sit and make jokes.'

'I'm sorry,' repeated Philip, tired of Glenellen, wishing that he had not accepted the invitation.

The chamberlain on the pouf answered him, however, in French. 'We never know how many will attend the levée . . . seldom less than five. Occasionally as many as a hundred, in times of national crisis.'

'It is also an expensive thing to arrange,' muttered Glenellen. 'One could dine at Maxim's for the cost.'

'If you'll let me, I'll gladly . . .'

'But you're my guest,' said Glenellen, recovering his usual equanimity. 'I wouldn't hear of such a thing.'

There was a tinkling at the door and the chamberlain opened it to admit a beautiful young woman with short hair, wearing a shirt, necktie, tweed skirt and a pair of sensible shoes; under one arm she carried a swagger stick. 'On the scene yet?' she inquired in a blurred English voice. 'No? Not yet? I'll wait then.' She sat down, ignoring Philip, who had risen at her entrance, and Glenellen who had not.

'She comes here every day,' said the chamberlain in a low proud voice. 'She . . .' but the tinkling of the bell sent him back to the door: this time a slim blond boy, unmistakably American with a crewcut and saddle shoes, entered, accompanied by an older man with steel-grey hair brushed carefully back from a smooth baby-fat face . . . the sort of man who had his nails manicured, thought Philip intolerantly, not moving as the newcomers were led by the chamberlain to chairs only a few feet away. The older man looked first at Philip with an expression which he had long since learned to interpret and not to resent; then, seeing Glenellen, he waved one of his well-tended paws and exclaimed: 'Ayre! Why aren't you in Capri?'

'Edmond! My God!' retorted Glenellen, as though stunned; he rallied, 'Haven't seen you since . . .'

'The Baths of Nero . . . small world.' He looked uneasily at the girl in tweed, as though unsure whether it was safe to speak out; obviously encouraged by the severe lines of her tailored back, he said, 'But I hardly expected to find you here. You don't come regularly, do you?'

'No, this is the first time.'

'Many, many friends of ours come here religiously, all the time. They find it soothing and I must say I have to admit that I do, too. I mean one shouldn't be ashamed of one's pleasures . . . And is this the charming Mr Morgan I've heard so much about?'

'No,' said Glenellen, 'it isn't.'

'But do introduce me. I like to know *all* the young Americans in Paris. My name is Edmond Twill,' he said, warmly shaking hands with Philip, both leaning far out of their chairs, neither getting up. 'And this is Jim, an American, too,' said Mr Twill. The handsome youth with the crewcut nodded distantly at Philip, not speaking. 'As a matter of fact, we're all Americans here today except Ayre . . . quite unusual, too, because as a rule Americans seldom come here . . . I can't think why, can you?' he asked Philip, with a smile which revealed very even white false teeth, as clean and neat and expensive as his pearl cuff links, as well cared for as the round pink fingernails which now tapped out restless messages on the arms of his chair.

'I wouldn't know,' said Philip. 'I've never been here before.'

'I'm sure you'll come again and again, the way many of us do. Would you like a cigarette?'

'Cigarettes are forbidden at this time,' said the chamberlain who was now sitting cross-legged on the pouf.

'I must have lost my head,' giggled Mr Twill. 'I wonder why I haven't seen you around town, Phil. I thought I knew nearly everyone.'

'I don't know,' said Philip who knew perfectly well why they had not seen one another before. 'I've been here since the first of August.'

'A whole month! Well, we must do something about that. You and Ayre must come and have dinner with me one evening this week. Will Tuesday be all right . . . at seven?'

Philip shook his head, amused. 'No, I'm afraid I'm tied up that night.'

'Mr Warren has his *own* world,' said Glenellen, in a warning voice which Mr Twill, recklessly, chose not to understand.

'But how *special!* So few people have their own world any more. I had one but I gave it away . . . traded it in for the great one. But then we're none of us twenty, are we, Ayre?'

'Speak for yourself, Edmond,' said Glenellen irritably, making various decisive gestures as though he could, with a wave of his hand, dismiss Mr Twill forever. But Mr Twill was not that easily discouraged. He renewed the siege. 'In any event, you and Ayre must stop by my house one day this week for a drink. You'll love the place . . . only a few blocks from here. Used to be the hôtel of the Duc de Lyon et Grénoble. I have a floor in it . . . a really fine set of rooms.'

'That would be very nice,' said Philip noncommittally.

'Do see he comes, Ayre . . . like a good fellow.'

Glenellen glanced at him, not answering. The ringing of the doorbell put a temporary stop to Mr Twill's offensive. This time nine thin young men of various heights and exotic arrangments of facial hair entered; the chamberlain ordered them to stand out of the way, against the wall opposite the bookcase where the girl in tweed now stood, reading the titles of the books to herself like a rosary, her mouth half open.

'*Messieurs, mesdames*,' said the chamberlain, climbing on top of the pouf, both hands raised to silence the room. 'The moment approaches. Those of you who have never before been presented should take cognizance of the following ceremony. At the moment of Entrance, all must rise to their feet and bow very low until The Seating, after which you, too, may sit down, in absolute silence, however, until The First Statement of the Day. Is that understood by everyone? Are there any questions? Good.' He jumped to the floor and paused for a moment, as though straining to hear some celestial melody. No one spoke. Then, from behind the Baize Door, came the unmistakable sound of an alarm clock going off, followed by the tolling of a dinner bell. Slowly the door opened and, preceded by the chamberlain, who backed into the room, a tall figure, with head erect, moved as though sleepwalking across the room to the throne. Philip who was standing like the others, his head bowed, caught a glimpse of the man, a tall pale creature with dark red hair, shoulder-length; and wearing a white undecorated gown which touched the floor. When he was seated, the worshipers sat down and waited silently for the First Statement.

The figure on the throne looked straight ahead, the unseeing eyes glassy. Philip wondered if he was drugged. Then suddenly, remarkably, the eyes became focused, the pupils dilated and in a high toneless voice the man said, 'Augusta.' There was a round of applause.

'Oh, I'm so glad!' exclaimed Mr Twill. 'I like her best, don't you, Ayre? But I forgot, this is your first time. Believe me, when I say it's a real treat you're getting. You just happened to hit it right. You'll adore her as much as we do.'

Throughout the room there was a murmur of approbation following the applause. Everyone seemed pleased and there was a curious atmosphere of good fellowship to which Philip responded with some wonder, not understanding yet what it was these people were experiencing as they moved excitedly around the throne, making remarks about (but not to) the now smiling figure. The chamberlain disappeared into the sanctum behind the Baize Door; he returned a moment later with a large box which was placed on the floor to the left of the throne . . . a chair which looked to Philip like a discarded theatrical property, the gold paint mostly gone and the red tassels torn.

'Now comes The Robing,' said Mr Twill delightedly. 'The best part. I always lose my head during The Robing, don't I, Jim?' But Jim, too, was part of the vast conspiracy to snub Edmond Twill for he made no answer, only sat passively in his chair watching the others as they opened the large box and reverently removed a number of articles of women's apparel.

'What happens now?' asked Philip.

'Augusta is to be dressed,' answered Mr Twill, eyes glistening. '*We* do that. It's part of the ritual.'

'Who's Augusta?' asked Philip.

'She's sitting on the throne, silly.'

'Oh,' said Philip, his masculine pride suddenly pricked at being called 'silly' by Mr Twill. He let it go, however. The ritual was now under way. The habitués were crowding about Augusta, each carrying some part of the ceremonial costume. Mr Twill had seized upon the hat, a toque somewhat similar to that affected by the stately dowager Queen of England. The young woman in tweed held a large frivolous-looking brassiere, ready to snap it in place at the proper moment . . . which soon came for, at a signal from the chamberlain, Augusta stood up, only to vanish in a sea of clothes and chattering worshippers. All participated in this rite except Glenellen, Philip and the silent American boy.

It was soon over, to the sorrow of the worshippers who were now dangerously excited, shouting to one another in French and English, touching reverently the figure which they had robed with such speed and accuracy: Augusta now stood magnificent, if slightly rumpled, in a floor-length tea gown of apple green, a feather boa about her shoulders and numerous coral and amber beads attached to her person like decorations on a Christmas tree and with much the same logic and cheerful effect. Over one eye, at a jaunty angle, was the toque, Mr Twill's triumph.

'The Robing is completed,' announced the chamberlain and the devotees withdrew slowly, admiringly, their eyes upon Augusta who stood for a long moment staring at the floor; then she sat down.

'Now wasn't that wonderful?' exclaimed Mr Twill, joining the non-participants.

'Very fine,' said Glenellen, sincerely, his pale eyes interested. Could this be a new hobby? wondered Philip.

'Did you see me manage the *chapeau*? I do it the best, the chamberlain says, and he should know. I mean people do it every day yet on the occasions when I do it I add a little something, a nuance, or so he thinks.'

'What does Augusta think?' asked Philip.

'Who can tell? I believe she appreciates it. One can tell a lot from the way she holds her head. When it is thrust slightly forward you had better watch out . . . she's on the warpath. When it's to one side, she is nervous . . . when the chin is held high, however, that means all is well . . . like now. She's always in a good mood when I officiate at The Robing.'

'That's a very great honour,' said Glenellen. 'You should be proud.'

'I am indeed. You must take part in the next one, Ayre. Tell the chamberlain you want to. He can fix it.'

'How much?'

'Don't pay more than a thousand francs. That's all *I* ever paid. Some people, Americans mostly, pay as high as ten or fifteen thousand, which is outrageous.'

'Does the money go to Augusta?' Philip was curious about the details.

'Who knows? It certainly goes into the establishment; then of course there are the missions.'

'What missions?'

'Oh . . . missions,' said Mr Twill vaguely.

'Is he booked up, do you think, for the next Robing?' asked Glenellen. 'I would like to attend, you know.'

'Oh, nothing could be easier, if you're properly sponsored and I would be very, very happy to sponsor you, Ayre. You know that.'

'That's awfully kind,' said Glenellen warmly, his former frosty manner quite thawed by the other's generosity as well as by the vision of Augusta seated on her throne, head back, eyes blissfully closed, absorbing the devotion of her worshippers like a lizard in the noonday sun.

'I suggest you come Friday. It is always Augusta without fail.'

'When is it *not* Augusta?' asked Philip.

'Well, yesterday it was not Augusta. And it probably won't be tomorrow.'

'What was it yesterday?'

'Augustus,' said Mr Twill. 'That's the whole point of the Hour of Meditation and the First Statement which precedes The Robing. During the hour, the First Statement is decided upon behind the Green Door. No one knows what agony of spirit racks that frail body during the lonely hour of decision. But always the choice is made; the facts are faced and the First Statement is delivered, calmly and unequivocally, no matter how difficult, how painful the decision behind the Green Door has been. Such courage!'

'Very real courage,' murmured Glenellen, admiringly, 'real character.'

'Such mysticism, too!'

'Obviously. One can see that.'

'The only functioning hermaphrodite in Paris, France,' said the young man named Jim in a low Southern voice which, though the message was heard by no one except his immediate companions, sent a ripple of unanticipated sound through the room; hostile glances were turned upon them and even Augusta was seen to move uneasily, as though aware of a disturbing and unharmonious presence.

'Now, now, Jim,' said Mr Twill, anxiously, smiling, looking about the room feverishly, exonerating himself, neutralizing with apologetic smiles the effect that that low voice had had on the Post-Robing Assembly. 'You must not say such things here, not in the presence of Her. You are entitled to your opinion like everyone else but you must have the courtesy, not only to Augusta but to me, to refrain from outbursts like that.'

Jim only grinned, pleased with himself. Philip rather liked him for this unexpected honesty. He wondered idly what he was doing here with Mr Twill. The obvious explanation seemed unlikely but then Philip never knew. His attention was distracted by Mr Twill who was discussing the lineage of Augusta. 'You mustn't think that the influence Augusta has and the reverence so many intelligent and unsuperstitious people do her are entirely the result of the unusual condition to which Jim just now alluded. No, indeed! Augusta is directly descended from the goddess Venus and those volumes in that bookshelf prove it . . . and not on the male side (which is never accurate, due to the frailness of women) but through the female line so that there can be no doubt of her legitimacy.'

'How do you know this?' asked Philip, squinting, trying to read the titles on the spines of the books.

'We know it because her genealogy has been traced back to Julius Caesar who, in turn, traced his own ancestry to Venus. Look, she even has the Julian nose.'

And so she had, Philip saw, recalling those busts he had seen which were reputed to be of Caesar.

'Then she is Italian,' said Philip.

'No, she is Augusta,' said Mr Twill, bowing slightly in the direction of the throne. 'But now comes the Naming of the Names.' And, to Philip's horror, the names of every eldest daughter of the house of Julius in the one hundred generations since that great man's murder were pronounced, slowly and distinctly, by the chamberlain, to the obvious pleasure of the worshippers who grew more and more excited as the chamberlain passed from the Middle Ages into the sixteenth century, until, by the time the nineteenth century was reached, they were singing and cheering so loudly that they almost drowned out the final name which the chamberlain, in a religious ecstasy, shouted so that all might hear: 'Augusta!'

'Wonderful, wonderful!' said Glenellen, mistily, his eyes tearful with excitement. 'Wonderful! Absolutely wonderful.'

'It is our best moment,' said Mr Twill simply, wiping his own eyes with the back of a shaking hand. Philip and Jim looked at one another dry-eyed; then Philip looked quickly away as though he was in danger of being detected in a conspiracy.

After the last cheers had died away, Augusta rose and, attended by a profound silence, left the room, the Green Door closing noiselessly behind her. The levée was over and the chamberlain went to the door through which the visitors had originally entered and opening it with a flourish, he bade them all farewell.

In the street, Philip and Glenellen left Mr Twill and his companion in a flurry of plans; dates and places were still being discussed when a taxi carried off Mr Twill and the silent Jim.

'What did you think?' asked Glenellen, as they left the rue des Saints-Pères and crossed the tree-lined Boulevard St Germain.

'Very unusual,' said Philip, not wanting to dampen the other's enthusiasm. 'I liked The Robing very much.'

'Oh, it was magnificent! Really so! I must look into the possibilities of bringing all this to the attention of the world.'

'I suppose their missions do that, don't they?'

'I am speaking on a grand scale. Do you realize that this could catch on? Like wildfire! Something the world has been waiting for: workers, intellectuals, everyone.'

'I thought you were a Catholic.'

'That has nothing to do with it. The two don't conflict, as I see it. One will complement the other splendidly. I shall wire the Vatican tomorrow.'

'And the party?'

'What party?'

'The Communist Party. You were a member when I saw you last spring in Rome.'

'Ah, the party . . . but that was Italy. This is France. Can't you tell the difference? The air is different. None of us is the same: even *you* are changed, in Paris.'

'How am I changed?'

'Well, for one thing you had dark hair in Rome. You are now a blond; that is the principal physical change.'

'I had blond hair in Rome, too,' said Philip sharply.

'Oh, come now, you don't expect me to believe that, do you? Besides, you look very nice with blond hair . . . no reason to be ashamed. Many boys dye their hair these days.'

Philip made no comment and in silence they walked down the rue du Bac to the river. In front of the white gleaming Pont Neuf they parted as casually as they had met the day before in the street. Glenellen hoped that they would see a great deal of one another; then he disappeared into the Metro while Philip crossed the bridge, enjoying the warm sun and blue sky, the design of the green gardens on the other side of the river.

One pleasant, aimless day followed another. The summer grew dry and dusty and the leaves darkened on the trees. Here and there, in the Tuileries gardens, an occasional vivid red leaf suggested autumn: the southerly flight of birds, the return of the tourists to the west, a cold time when Paris would become French again, the trees bare-branched and the winter skies as grey as the nineteenth-century façades of the buildings that lined the wide avenues the last Napoleon had carved out of the confusion of narrow medieval streets, avenues still green and gentle with the waning summer.

Neither Anna nor Regina was in Paris. He had inquired after both of them but no one knew when Regina would return. Anna, however, would arrive in six weeks, or so the desk clerk at the Ida Hotel had assured him that first day in Paris when he had moved in a happy dream through a silver afternoon, so different from the harsh hot country he had left behind early that morning.

He had been fortunate in finding a hotel for himself, a dark congenial place on the rue de l'Université, a block from the rue du Bac. Here he spent his time reading, when he was not sightseeing or meeting old friends from America who had come over to drink a great deal of cheap wine and to see night clubs where the girls took off most all of their clothes, so exciting the American boys that Philip almost believed the remark of a French brothel keeper who had once told him, quite seriously, that all Americans were *voyeurs*, except for the aviators who liked to be beaten.

But these old friends of his were in the minority that year for the city had been conquered by his homosexual countrymen, and he watched with wonder as the scandal grew, as mask after mask fell from familiar and ordinary faces to reveal the unexpected Grecian visage. Businessmen from Kansas City, good Rotarians all, embraced bored young sailors on the streets at night or paid high prices for slim Algerian boys at those bordellos which catered to such pleasures. College boys, young veterans, the ones Philip had always known in school or in the Navy, athletes and aesthetes both, ran amok among the bars and urinals in search of one another, the nice girls back home forgotten, as they loved or tried to love one another in this airy summer city.

Like most of his generation, Philip was tolerant of everything. It was an age in which, as a reaction to the horrors of the various European pogroms and experiments with genocide, his countrymen had been driven, somewhat hysteri-cally, into the opposite direction, until the intolerance of intolerance had be-come so remarkably virulent that one Jew or one Negro or one Italian not admitted to certain residential districts in America caused more disturbance in the newspapers than the gas chambers at Belsen. Fortunately, those people who must always have someone to hate could, if they chose not to be intolerant of intolerance, attack one another on grounds of sexual behaviour. But this last cherished area for intolerance was suddenly declared out of bounds by a cele-brated statistical report which revealed that one third of the nation's men had, at one time or another, committed a homosexual act. This survey promptly lessened everyone's guilt and, if only by the weight of the numbers given, it made the idea of pederasty much less remote, no longer exclusively associated with managers of flower shops or with a fearful fumbling in the back row of a darkened movie house. Those sturdy youths who had been ashamed of their secret practice now took much pleasure, at least in Paris, in openly doing what they pleased and with all the enthusiasm of zealots, they proselytized furiously.

It amused Philip to think that his own puritan nation of Baptists and Methodists and good sound Americanism should, in its moment of empire, become so gaudily Roman, so truly imperial in one generation. Yet he disliked feeling out of things. The groups that gathered on the landing of his hotel would stop their intense conversations when he walked by and he was aware, or thought he was aware, of their real contempt for a countryman who, because of some basic duplicity or sexual inadequacy, refused to play the game. Nor did he enjoy being treated like a pretty young girl who could be rolled into bed at a moment's notice by a properly aggressive man. The tragic novel of the age, he decided irritably, would not be about the anguish of the sensitive neurotic youth who wanted to make ladies' hats but about the confusion of the undistinguished womanizing youth who came to the big city to make his fortune only to find that everywhere he turned men desired him and that the ill will his refusal to surrender his virtue created was so great that he was forced either to adapt himself to a life of pederasty or to go back home, not returning to the big city until age had so lessened his physical attractions that he was rendered safe from attack.

He had, however, two allies who felt the same as he did: apostates, for they had been lovers for seven years, first in high school, then in the Army, then in college and finally here in Paris, in a room next to his own. They were both twenty-five, robust, and charmingly simple. The following June, when they graduated from college, they were to be married to two girls they had known for a long time in their home town, Spartanburg, South Carolina, and their future was to be as simple and as well directed as their past, living next door to one another, working in the same business. They would even, they confided to Philip, name their children for one another.

'What will the wives think of all this?' asked Philip, putting his feet up on the bed. He was in their room, a small one with two big beds, an old bureau and a bidet hidden by a torn curtain. The single window was tall and the room was cool and full of light. Clothes were scattered everywhere: as well as tennis racquets, bathing trunks, even a pair of boxing gloves, for they were obsessed with their bodies, eating carefully, drinking very little, keeping their bellies flat with exercise. He could hear them every morning, doing pushups, puffing and straining. He had never heard them make love, however, even though the walls were thin . . . not that he had wanted to, quite the opposite, yet the idea had a real fascination for him, a morbid appeal, like the time when once, at a resort, he had slept in the room next to his parents and had heared everything until he could stand it no longer and had covered his head with a pillow. Unlike the other occupants of the hotel, these young men were quiet and well behaved. Regularly, often in Philip's company, they picked up girls and brought them back to the hotel, increasing rather than diminishing their love for one another on these occasions when, side by side on the same bed, they possessed the women, to use a good Victorian verb, an applicable one, thought Philip, since their devotion and respect for each other was essentially nineteenth-century: neither would have dreamed of humiliating the other, unlike most American combinations, orthodox or not. He was continually beguiled by the Southern courtliness with which they treated one another.

'I don't suppose they'll think anything about it at all,' said the taller one, a fair-haired, dark-eyed boy named Stephen. 'I mean, they've known we've always been good friends. They'd think it was unnatural if we stopped seeing one another after we got married.'

'Besides, the girls get along,' said Bill, a stocky young man with a boxer's figure and dark curly hair which grew low on his forehead. 'I guess it would be impossible if they didn't like each other.'

'You seem to have it all worked out,' said Philip, not concealing his admiration for a long-range plan which had, so far at least, worked.

'We figured the whole thing out in high school,' said Stephen with gentle pride, scooping up all the dirty clothes and tossing them into a corner.

'How do you plan to get away? I mean . . . see each other?'

'We'll be living in the same block and everybody knows we like to go hunting on week ends, when the weather's good. And the girls, they never go hunting. We'll have a lot of week ends together. Oh, there'll be plenty of time for everything.'

'Well, you've done a good job,' said Philip, sighing, thinking of his own loveless, aimless life which, though it usually pleased him, was obscurely incomplete: he could hear the beast in the jungle so clearly that he felt he knew what it would be like when, finally, at the end of a long difficult chase, he captured it. But he envied these lovers for having stumbled across it at an age when he had not even suspected that the jungle contained another living creature besides himself.

'I think so, too,' said Bill, leaning back on the bed, stretching his legs till they cracked, his head against Stephen's thigh.

Philip was both envious and depressed. The trail had never before seemed so dark to him, or the quarry so elusive. He hated them for one ungrateful instant.

The evening was warm and windless when they arrived at the Café Flore and took their places at a table outside, close to the street where the curious and the fantastic stared at one another solemnly. Bearded young men wearing blue jeans and open red-checked shirts contrived to look more like Iowa than Murger, while the young women, their hair long and tangled, also wore open shirts and blue jeans, as dirty as the boys and quite as happy, as they too pursued the grand grim business of expressing themselves, imitating the French of that quarter who, with no effort at all, managed to be far dirtier, far more dishevelled . . . in every way fine models for these children of the new world who had temporarily forsaken ice cream, Coca-Cola and the linoleum-floored new high schools of the West.

The two Southerners were amused, pointing out the various freaks to one another, without malice or condescension, examining with wonder the superficial variety of which man is capable. Every now and then a murmur went through the crowded café as a celebrity of some sort passed by or the rumour of a celebrity who might have passed by, and immediately all eyes turned in the same direction and two camps, one friendly, one hostile, discussed the poor creature freely, to his face if he was unwise enough to linger.

'Did *you* ever try writing anything?' asked Stephen, turning to Philip.

'Not seriously,' said Philip, recalling Cyril Connolly's protest that he never again wanted to read a novel where, referring to a character who was an artist, another character asked, 'How's his stuff?'

'I'm surprised,' said Stephen. 'You always struck me like you might be a writer or something.'

'Just my pedantic manner,' said Philip who had himself often been struck with the superficial resemblance he, on occasion, bore to those who fashioned the one bright book of life.

He was about to give them his considered views on contemporary literature in America when a slim familiar figure walked past their table, paused, and then came back. It was the boy who had been with Edmond Twill at Augusta's levée. He was very handsome, thought Philip looking at the golden hair and dark blue eyes. He was dressed like a conservative schoolboy in dark grey trousers and a sports coat. 'You're Philip, aren't you? I met you last week ... at that place.'

'I remember,' said Philip. 'Stephen, Bill, this is Jim.' It was like the Navy, he thought, the old anonymous days of first names. The three Southern boys gravely shook hands. 'Want a drink?' asked Philip.

Jim shook his head. 'I've got to go,' he said, in his low expressionless voice. 'You want to meet me here tomorrow at six?'

'Why ... all right,' said Philip, suddenly, surprised not only at the invitation but at his own prompt acceptance.

'I'll see you then ... at six. Good-bye.' He nodded to the others and walked away.

Bill chuckled. 'Looks like you got yourself a buddy.'

'Do you a world of good,' said Stephen.

'I'm sure it will,' smiled Philip, who saw no reason to protest.

Under a violet summer sky, they met at six. A storm threatened and the leaves of the trees along the boulevard fluttered white and green in the sudden wind. The air smelled of sun and stone but there was a wet sharp edge to the hot wind which came from the northwest where night and the thunder were. An awning had been unfurled over the outdoor tables; here a few quiet tourists sat, waiting for Sartre.

'Let's get out of here,' said Jim. 'It's going to rain.'

Philip, surrendering himself to the other's care, followed him across the square to the church of St Germain de Prés behind which was a narrow street, damp and shadowy, where above a restaurant Jim lived. 'We can have a drink there,' he said. 'If it rains, we can eat downstairs.'

Philip agreed, wondering a little uneasily what was expected of him.

'This is the dump,' Jim opened a door, revealing two high-ceilinged rooms furnished haphazardly. A large carved bed of dark wood with four posters but no canopy stood in the centre of the second room whose windows looked out on a grey court, littered with broken tile and discarded furniture. Unframed drawings by Tchelichew and Picasso were propped on the grey marble mantelpiece, a relic of the house's onetime splendour. To Philip's surprise, the drawings were originals and one of them, the head of a lean Picasso boy, was familiar to him and presumably of great value. There were no books anywhere except for a beautifully bound set of Balzac scattered carelessly on a plain kitchen table, as though placed there on arrival and never touched again.

'I've even got a bathroom,' said Jim, as the storm broke over Paris with a sudden roar. 'Oh ... there she goes.' They went to the window and looked out at the grey diagonals of rain which splattered in the street below. Gutters became rivers while the rain made sudden coronets of water in the puddled streets; men and women ran for cover with newspapers and umbrellas unfurled. The day was over and evening, dark and secret in the rain, moved across the wet city.

'I like the rain,' said Philip, aware that someone always said that.

'I don't give it much mind.'

'That's a Southern expression,' smiled Philip, as they turned away from the window and went back into the dark room. Philip stumbled against a chair, Jim turned on a single lamp.

'I am Southern,' he said. 'Sit down and I'll get you some wine. Or do you want Pernod? I got both.'

'Pernod. Where did you come from originally?' Philip found himself for some reason fearing silence, not wanting to be alone in the room with Jim with only the sound of rain against the windows; he was ill at ease, without words.

'From Virginia.' He brought two wineglasses out of a cupboard and carefully filled them both. 'Here you go.' The apéritif slopped onto Philip's hand. 'I'm sorry,' said Jim. 'Need a handkerchief?'

'I've got one.' Philip wiped the stickiness off his fingers, slowly, deliberately, wanting to prolong the operation, to delay the moment of revelation which, he was sure, resided in the baroque clock on the mantelpiece: when the long and short hands came to a predestined conjunction he would be forced to handle with tact and severity his companion's suggestion. A moment later, Philip saw he had made a mistake: the clock was broken; both were spared. Relieved, he said, 'I like Virginia, what I've seen of it . . . around Warrenton. I come from New York.'

'I figured you were a Northerner.'

'Have you been in Paris long?'

'Three years.'

'A long time.'

'A real long time. I like it here.'

'You don't want to go back?'

'No, I can't go back, even if I wanted to.'

'Oh . . . I'm sorry.'

'Nothing to be sorry about. I got into trouble. Lot of people get into trouble. So I left. I've had a good time.'

Philip was puzzled by the other's bleakness. He was curious about the trouble but his own years in the Navy had taught him not to inquire too closely into the lives of others, partly from fear of embarrassing them, partly because they might embarrass him with too complete an account of their lives. Mystery was often best.

'Are you working now? In Paris?' This was tactless, Philip knew, but he persisted.

Jim smiled at him, a slow engaging smile and with the first show of warmth either had displayed that evening, he said, 'I don't work. You know that.'

'Oh.' Philip was stopped. Not knowing what to answer, he grinned foolishly and drank his Pernod in two long fiery swallows.

'I just drift along. It's easier.'

'Do you . . . like Twill?' asked Philip.

'I don't like any of them.'

'They like you.'

'Yes . . . funny, isn't it? I've often wondered why.'

'You're good-looking.' This was not the sort of remark Philip liked to make to another man but having accepted the other's line, he was bound to it.

Jim made a face. 'They can get a better-looking piece of flesh with a bigger thing for a dollar in any street in this town.'

'Maybe they're attracted by your hostility.'

'I've thought of that. But then I'm always very quiet when I'm around them . . . a real good boy who doesn't say much.'

'And you get money?' Philip sounded to himself like a college boy talking to his first prostitute, asking her how she could possibly have become so degraded.

'I get everything.' He waved his hand briefly at the apartment, the drawings, the set of Balzac. 'One old guy settled a hundred a month on me for life.'

'For his life, or yours?'

Jim laughed. 'For mine. Get property . . . that's the thing. So many kids, when they start in, just go around chiselling drinks until they get fat and nobody wants them any more. But I get cash if I can . . . or jewellery or pictures: I've learned a lot about painting these last few years. I once spotted a phoney Degas some old guy tried to get me to take.'

'You make the deal in advance?'

'I'm not that crude. I get things without asking. That's what I mean when I say I don't know what it is that they see. I've often thought that if I knew what it was, I'd really be able to cash in.'

'I suspect,' said Philip, 'that the fact you don't know may be your charm. Self-consciousness often produces great art but I doubt if many find it a lovable trait, in others. The secret to wide popularity is a kind of mysterious negativity . . . something that can't be imitated. Not that I mean you're actually negative, or mysterious (though you may, for all I know, be both), but you give that appearance.'

'How do you figure that out?'

Philip, halfway through his spurious character analysis, suddenly realized the implication of his blunder. He had started talking nervously, affected by the rain and the dark, by the Pernod gulped too quickly on an empty stomach, and carried away by his own solemn attempt at analysis, he had managed to create a false impression on several levels at once, a considerable trick, he thought wryly, undoing the damage, reorganizing what he had said.

'I was putting it more in terms of the president of a high-school class,' he said glibly. 'When I was in school the handsomest and quietest boy in the class was always elected president. No one envied him, no one feared him; he was admired because of the strength of character his pleasing silence obviously hid. Boys who boasted were always thought liars; it never occurs to simple people that a loud, conceited person may be more competent than a modest quiet one.'

They were now a long way from the centre and Philip examined the idea of popularity until, sick of it himself, he stopped suddenly in the middle of a sentence and stared at the Picasso sketch, the monotonous noise of the rain succeeding the equally monotonous sound of his own voice in the room.

'We'd better have another drink,' said Jim, filling their glass. Halfway through the second glass of Pernod, Philip's unease vanished and he talked about himself freely, and Jim seemed nearly as interested as he himself was. Yet the pleasures of egotism were brought to a rude halt when Jim suddenly asked him if he liked boys.

'No,' said Philip, freezing, aware that a misstep would distress them both. 'I never have.'

'Not even once, in school?'

'Not even then. I have all the earmarks of a pederast, I suppose . . . or so a friend of mine at Harvard used to say; but I've never done anything about it.'

'Would you like to?'

'No, I don't think so. I'm too old to change my habits . . . and they tell me it's mostly habit.'

'You wouldn't like to try?' The invitation was abrupt.

'No, I wouldn't. I'm sorry.'

Jim sighed, but not sadly. 'You might have liked it.'

'I wouldn't know what to do.'

'You wouldn't have to do anything.'

'I'm not that passive. I could never enjoy lying still while somebody else thrashed around.'

'But you'd give me pleasure,' said Jim, smiling, some of his early abruptness gone; he was almost gentle.

'That's the worst of it,' said Philip, a new idea occurring to him; one which might be very significant. 'I don't want to give anyone pleasure, especially a man.'

'You want to give a woman pleasure.'

'Yes . . . no. Consciously I do, for the usual selfish reasons; unconsciously, I want to take care of myself and go home.'

'Even when you're in love?'

'I've never been in love.'

'I'm one up on you.'

'Did you like it?'

'That's a stupid question.' Jim's voice was unexpectedly sharp. He apologized quickly. 'I'm sorry. I didn't mean that.'

'Forget it,' said Philip, his curiosity aroused. But then, remembering his new idea, he worried it a bit. 'I think maybe that's the difference between men and women, between men and certain kinds of pederasts; the man's instinct is to take his pleasure, the woman's to give it, to receive the man.'

'That could explain the old guys in the latrines, looking for sailors. They get a charge out of that.'

'Of course I know women who wanted men the same way men ordinarily want women, but there don't seem to be too many of them . . . yet who knows? Perhaps the difference in attitudes is only a social one.'

'I don't think you know very much about it,' said Jim, nicely.

'Am I wrong?'

'Damned if I know. I haven't got any theory. All I know is that it's one thing to love somebody and another thing to have sex with somebody you don't know or don't care about, the way I do all the time.'

'Women, I know, often get their greatest pleasure out of the man's excitement. They ignore him. He's just so much sweating, heavy bone and flesh on top of them but when they realize that it is their own desirable body which has made an animal out of him, they are quite carried away by this vision of their own desirability and they reciprocate, loving themselves being loved in his arms.' This very nearly said it, thought Philip, not wanting to see any cracks in the dike of his reasoning, pleased with the area he had rescued, if only for a moment, from the floor of a confused sea.

'You make it sound like acrobatics,' said Jim mildly.

'Isn't it? It's often that in . . . well, in the other world.'

'I don't think so. I suppose I've been mauled as much as anybody can be but in spite of all that I think it's possible to care about one person and to forget the acrobatics and think just of him and not the two bodies. But I suppose I'm romantic because I'm just a whore and know how little sex has to do with loving.'

I got a theory that the more you do it, the more likely you are to love somebody when the time comes.'

'When is that?'

'Only once for me, so far . . . maybe again. I hope so.'

'Never for me, so far. But then, how can one tell? What's love for me may just be an ordinary experience to another person . . . or a leap into the abyss for still another.'

'I've . . . It's stopped raining,' said Jim, who apparently disliked theorizing as much as Philip enjoyed it. 'Shall we go across the street and have dinner? It's better than the place downstairs.'

'I'd like to. I didn't have lunch today.'

'They got wonderful snails across the street.'

'I don't like snails.'

'Have you ever tried any?'

'No.'

'Well, how do you know?' They both laughed and Philip realized the crisis had passed. He was relieved. He was also surprised how callow and inexperienced he felt beside this youth whose life had been, or so he would have supposed, so much less than his own, so differently balanced.

He thought of Henry Miller's rhetorical title, 'The Wisdom of the Heart,' and, while he ate snails with Jim in the dingy restaurant, he wondered what, if anything, the phrase might mean: intuition? Possibly. And what was that? Accuracy in emotional matters achieved by chance, quickly, illogically, without recourse to any deliberation. That was intuition, he thought, not liking the snails. But what then was accuracy? Emotion was not a logic and one person's definition of a state of being or of a situation which involved himself and a lover, say, might not be remotely like his partner's: the wisdom of one man's heart could very easily seem like shocking ignorance to another's. Without ultimates it was impossible to define anything except in immediate and relative terms. Perhaps, he thought suddenly, the heart's wisdom was the knowledge that two people in a certain relationship *together* possessed, for that moment at least, in that one place, a special joint knowledge of mysteries which, separately, was denied them. He looked curiously at the snail-eating Jim, and wondered if he *knew*, if he had really *been* . . .

After dinner, somewhat against Philip's will, they went back to Jim's apartment. 'Just for a moment,' he said, as they climbed the damp-smelling stairs. 'I have to practice my vice.'

When they got to the front room, Jim turned on a lamp, an orange and black Japanese lantern; then he placed what looked to Philip like a Bunsen burner from a chemistry class in the middle of the table. A blue flame blossomed at the end of a lighted match.

'Have to be careful,' said Jim, lighting the burner. 'I don't want to set the place on fire.' From a cabinet he took out a yard-long wooden pipe, brightly decorated with Moorish designs, and a thin metal spoon in which he placed a single dark pellet. 'This is the tricky part . . . the cooking. Have to have a steady hand.' Holding the spoon in one hand over the flame, he prodded the melting pill with the end of a safety pin. A strong odour like incense, like medicine, filled the room. 'Now,' said Jim, 'here it goes.' The hot viscous remains of the pellet were poured into the chimney of the pipe and quickly, all in one integrated movement, Jim turned off the blue flame, put down the spoon and raised the pipe to his lips and inhaled so deeply and so long that his face grew red and his eyes stared. Then, slowly, he exhaled a pale cloud of smoke. 'Oh, that's good stuff,' he said happily, smiling at Philip. 'That's better than anything I know.' He took several more lungfuls of the smoke before he offered the pipe to Philip who declined on the unusual but accurate grounds that, since he did not smoke tobacco, he wouldn't know how to inhale.

'Well, it won't work if you can't inhale,' agreed Jim. 'Anyway you ate the snails. That's enough for one night.'

'How do you feel?' asked Philip, curiously.

'Like I'm dreaming . . . a little like a dream of flying.'

'Better than love?'

'Wouldn't you rather fly than make love?'

'Any day.'

'This way I feel like I'm doing both.'

'Shall I go?'

'Oh, no . . . not yet. Stay with me until I'm way gone. It won't be long.' He walked over to the carved bed and carefully, like a figure in a motion picture at half speed, he lay down, the pipe still clutched in his hand. 'Sit over here,' he said, pointing to the edge of the bed. Philip did, both of their faces in shadow now, the dull orange lantern far away in the other room, like daylight at a tunnel's end. 'Take my shoes off. I don't like to move when I get this far.'

Philip untied the scuffed schoolboy shoes and put them neatly side by side on the floor, scrupulously careful not to touch the other's body, to avoid receiving the sensual shock of warm flesh against warm flesh, no matter what one's habit was. 'Now I feel better,' said Jim softly. 'I can't think of anything unpleasant when I'm like this. Can't think about you.'

'About me?'

'About the ones like you I've known . . . but it all seems fine now I'm flying.' He inhaled again and again. The sweet heavy odour was making Philip sick; he wanted to go.

'I don't eat the dregs,' said Jim suddenly. 'Some people do, but not me. It's the worst of all. When you start to do that, you can't ever walk again, never touch the ground until they bury you in it . . .' His voice grew softer and softer as he talked, now in flight, now of a river and one green day long ago in June. For a time Philip sat beside him in the shadowy room and listened to him talk. But then when he was sure that the other was no longer conscious of him, he got quickly to his feet and, blowing out the paper lantern, he left the apartment.

In the street, he paused. A thin grey rain was falling now and he was grateful for its coolness and for the fresh night air which he breathed in great gulps until he could no longer taste or smell the smoke on which, far away, Jim drifted, momentarily beyond the gravity which would, Philip knew, pull him back one day to the hard inevitable earth beneath that pale cloud which now maintained him, for one eternity at least, safe and dreaming above the land. The rain was cold in Philip's face, as he hurried down the rue de l'Université to his hotel.

'We were picked up,' said Stephen, when Philip got back to the hotel.

'That's right,' Bill chuckled. 'Friend of yours, too. He said to send you his love.'

'Who was that?'

'An old queen named Edmond Twill. We didn't know you were handling the carriage trade.' They laughed, mockingly.

'I met him once,' began Philip, feeling suddenly guilty.

'At a religious ceremony,' said Stephen. 'He told us all about it.'

'I wish he'd told *me* all about it. I'm still confused.'

'Perhaps he will tomorrow. There's a party and we're invited . . . you too.'

'What kind of a party?'

'Can't you guess?' said Bill.

'We're going,' said Stephen. 'For the hell of it.'

'He said he wanted some men for a change . . . I thought that was real flattering.'

'Are you sure he wants me to come?' asked Philip.

'Sure,' said Stephen. 'He wants you special. He told me so. He also said that you were being kept by Lord Somebody-or-other, but that you had stolen his car and sold it.'

Philip whistled. 'That's a wild one.'

'You didn't sell it, did you?' asked Bill.

'Never knew he had a car. I've only seen him once since I've been in Paris. I wonder who started that story.'

'According to Mr Twill, everybody knows it. He said the only reason you weren't in jail because you had too much on him, on Lord What's-his-name.'

'That's quite a story,' said Philip, more amused than angry.

'Anyway,' continued Bill, obviously enjoying himself, 'he's going to have the old guy at the party just to see what will happen . . . only I'm not supposed to tell you that he'll be there. Mr Twill wants a scene.'

'I told him you weren't one of the boys,' said Stephen. 'But he wouldn't believe me.'

'They never do,' said Bill.

Mr Twill occupied a floor of one wing of the former Hôtel of the Duc de Lyon et Grénoble, a Marshal of Napoleon, who had grandly renovated the former town house of an aristocrat whose head had fallen into the basket during the Terror, to the cheers of the blood-minded women of Paris, one of whom had stolen it, according to legend, and rolled it all the way to the aristocrat's house, where, in a fit of poetic justice, she heaved it through a window, frightening the clerks in the government bureau which occupied the house at that time. A generation later, the Duc de Lyon et Grénoble, having robbed the quarter-master corps of a great many golden napoleons, restored the house to a point considerably beyond its original splendour. Traces of the Marshal's private vision of elegance were everywhere in the suite Mr Twill now ornamented, although two Watteau fans and a heavenly stole occupied the place of honour over the mantelpiece where once the portrait of the Emperor had hung, beneath two sabres crossed by the baton of a Marshal of France.

Money was as much in evidence now as it had been during the years the Duc had lived in these high-ceilinged rooms with their white and gold walls, marble floors, resplendent (if dusty) chandeliers which were suspended like inverted frozen fountains from ceilings where cherubs and Napoleonic deities consorted archly with one another against a cerulean sky.

Mr Twill received them in the first of two drawing rooms. He looked much as ever, thought Philip, in spite of the feathered hat he wore and the white flowing gown which sparkled with brilliants.

'Do you like it?' he asked, giving Philip his hand. 'I have the most wonderful little man who can copy anything. I don't suppose you recognize it, do you? It's from a Winterhalter portrait of the Empress Elizabeth. She was my ideal, you know.' He turned to Stephen and Bill who were staring at him with alarmed eyes. 'My two Southern lambs! How sweet of you to come. I've always said Southern boys are the loveliest. Don't you think so, Phil? But what have I said? You're not Southern!'

'South of Albany,' said Philip, pleased with his own *sangfroid*; he was now prepared for anything. But anything proved only to be several middle-aged gentlemen in evening gowns and twenty or thirty young men in Brooks Brothers suits. They were gathered, for the most part, in the second drawing room, seated on Louis Quinze gilt chairs and fauteuils. On one wall a tapestry depicted Sebastian receiving, with a certain smugness, the arrows of his fate. Two Japanese boys in white jackets served champagne and brandy.

It was superficially like almost any party, thought Philip, yet in essence it was radically different, unfocused, even if one were to disregard the presence of the monsters in their elaborate gowns. In the other world, when men without women were together in the same room, an entirely different atmosphere was evoked: one that was louder, more fraternal, dull but easy, not like this decorous group of watchful creatures whose eyes never for a second ceased to shift from person to person, judging, calculating, comparing. Cats and dogs, thought Philip grimly, following Stephen and Bill into the room, aware of the excited interest which burst over them like waves over the bow of a ship leaving calm harbour for high seas.

Stephen and Bill were immediately separated by three young Frenchmen with narrow shoulders and pink healthy faces who moved between the lovers with all the cunning of a star basketball team in a classic manoeuvre. Philip, in his turn, was borne to the still centre of the party by a nervous, hairy-chested Frenchman in a low-cut crimson gown slashed with gold, a large cameo about his neck.

'*Joli gosse, n'est-ce pas?*' he commented to two older conventionally dressed men who sat side by side on the largest couch in the room, a number of young men arranged around them, some speaking English, others French, their sibilants cracking like whips across the room no matter which language they spoke. Philip was introduced to everyone and he smiled amiably, taking his place on the couch between the two older men, one of whom was Clyde Norman.

'My dear Philip. It's been an age.'

'Half a year.'

'Ah, the year . . . the precious year. I see you haven't forgotten, have you? *Toujours fidèle.*'

'To whatever it is.'

'But don't you know?'

'Three hundred sixty-odd days . . . no more.'

'You still haven't decided?'

'No. I'm afraid you were right. It's not so easy. Nothing short of a Major revelation will do it now. If anything, I'm more confused than I was. Too much experience is worse than too little.'

'It wasn't experience you lacked, only conviction . . . and conviction takes a lifetime to come by.'

'I hope not. I don't want to go on forever like this.'

'Why not? Aren't you enjoying yourself? You're young and pretty . . . why live in the future?'

'Why live at all is the question I ask myself,' said Philip, wanting to change the subject which, fortunately, a Japanese bearing champagne interrupted; when he withdrew, Philip was able to ask Mr Norman where he had summered.

'Torquay, of all places . . . the British Riviera. I stayed with a sister I'd forgotten all about. Now I'm on my way back to Rome.'

'Is Glenellen here?'

'Not yet. He told me he'd seen you. He's got a new interest, you know. Augustus, or whatever his name is.'

'I know,' said Philip. 'By the way, I understand I've been accused of stealing his car.'

'First I heard of it,' said Mr Norman. 'But now, tell me all about Egypt.'

Philip told him, his eyes as watchful as all the others, sizing up each newcomer, commiserating with Stephen and Bill who were being devoured alive by the bright-eyed little Frenchmen.

'What, by the way, are you doing here?' asked Mr Norman, after he had swallowed his third glass of champagne and could dare to be less delicate than usual. 'You haven't by any chance . . .' But three glasses of champagne were not sufficient to give him the courage to finish that sentence; so he merely gestured weakly with one hand and frowned.

'Oh, no,' said Philip. 'I'm just a tourist.'

'I thought so. But, with Americans, it's often hard to tell . . . with the young especially.'

'I met Mr Twill at Augusta's levee, a place Glenellen took me to,' said Philip carefully. 'Then I ended up here.'

'In the secret shrine of the lodge, as it were.'

'Where are the articles of worship?'

'There's only one . . . the sacred totem which each man carries with him and to which our *laus perennis* is addressed.'

'There are, of course, deviationists,' said Philip.

'Worse . . . schism! Since the very beginning there have been interventionists.'

'Better to give than to receive?'

'Their philosophy precisely. But there is a movement afoot, not organized of course, to bring the two groups closer; for one to complement the other.'

'Don't they do that now?'

'Often in individual practice but since the initial heresy, various interdicts have been hurled back and forth and the gap has widened terribly in certain countries. I must say, however, that we look to America for that third way which both of the traditional Western parties could accept . . .'

'And the third way?'

'All Americans know it,' said Mr Norman roguishly. 'It is the practice of the young nation . . . no matter what your interests, whether you belong or not, you know instinctively *the way*. That is a rule. I've known many Americans and all accepted, even if they did not *live*, the third way.'

'I knew something fine and spiritual would one day come out of America,' said Philip who was fast losing track of the conversation. 'I never thought it would be that.'

'Neither did any of us. One's first reaction to the idea of America is: look at all that money! those vigorous pioneers! uncouth fathers of thousands of children! But when they came over here during the last war, ah! we were surprised. Since the last century of course we have been used to the American exquisites, the careful New Englanders, the opulent New Yorkers who collected our paintings with the same energy that their daughters collected our titled men. They were too gentlemanly, too civilized to be endured, especially the bachelors who accompanied their mothers obediently from spa to spa, entranced by each new dowager, revelling in our old world of manners which might have expired sooner than it did had it not been for the heady and unexpected applause of our Western cousins. But the war . . . *that* was something else. Those lovely golden youths without guilt, like an Athenian army come to save an outlying province from the Persians. It was not until I'd come to know those youths that I realized what the frontier had been like. We'd forgotten in Europe what a world without women could be like. We grew up in rebellion against an old society, the organized world of our mothers, the elaborate conventions which contained, with remarkable success, the native exuberance of the young. We turned away from what we knew, not loving the other but rather hating what we had known. Then, suddenly, the children of that last frontier descended on us and showed us what it was, traditionally, to love one another: not out of hate or inadequacy but spontaneously, like the Moslems, like those Asiatics whom we call inscrutable. It was a refreshing experience, believe me. The third way . . . Such a relief after the accretion of attitudes and fetishes which have so long burdened both our camps that our activities have become as formalized and as ritualistic as a ballet. *Le vice anglais*, that sort of thing was unknown to those frontiersmen who lived without women and who loved one another, men who needed men in every sense.'

'We're several generations removed from the frontier,' said Philip gently, thinking of the nervous pederasts on the beaches of Southern California, descendants of the forty-niners, their dyed hair carefully arranged as they searched continually for those lusty youths who would tolerate them for a price, who often in a neurotic frenzy beat them, to their great delight: O pioneers! 'We have our rebels, too,' said Philip, 'but our world is almost as rigidly stratified as yours. The frontier is gone, its myth ignobly preserved by Wild West movies.'

'Where the hero never kisses the girl.'

'Where the hero kisses the horse's ass,' said Philip. 'And speaking of horses, there is Glenellen.'

The peer, wearing a plum-coloured smoking jacket and a gold chain about his neck, the sort wine stewards in the better restaurants affect, approached the couch where Philip and Mr Norman were seated, the bleeding Sebastian behind them and the youths in a semicircle before them. 'There you are. I'm exhausted, absolutely shattered.' And he sat down heavily. 'Such a day . . . there were a hundred this morning.'

'Where? A hundred what?' asked Mr Norman.

'A hundred in attendance on Augusta at The Robing . . . you've never seen such a madhouse! Then I spent all afternoon at the new mission. We now have an abbot and eleven monks there. I am following the medieval church in my reorganization of the various missions. Such a task! Absolutely Augean! Doubt if I shall survive it.'

'Where will it end, Ayre?' asked Mr Norman, no longer an ally.

'In a world conversion . . . I demand nothing less. I've been entrusted by Augusta with The Chain.' He fingered the chain about his neck which, Philip saw, was indeed a wine steward's badge of office, for the small cup which was pendant to it bore the legend 'Ritz Hotel' in a handsome engraved script.

'A very great responsibility,' said Mr Norman.

'It makes one, somehow . . . humble, to feel the weight of such a responsibility on one's shoulders. I sometimes feel myself hardly equal to the task.'

'About the car,' said Philip, interrupting.

'What car?'

'I don't know. I heard some crazy story that I'd been accused of stealing your car.'

'I don't think I *accused* you.'

'But you're not sure?'

'Not entirely. I vaguely recall having drawn up a list of suspects for the *Sûreté*. Your name might possibly have been on that list.'

'Even though I didn't know you had a car? that I had seen you only once, briefly, since I'd been in Paris.'

'One can never tell.'

'I would appreciate it if you told Mr Twill that I didn't steal it . . . told him right now.'

'My dear fellow, you're taking much too pedantic an attitude about this. Besides, the police discovered I'd left it myself on a side street; *they* didn't make a scene . . . took it very well, as a matter of fact.'

'You should exonerate Mr Warren,' said Clyde. 'It is only fair.'

'Later,' said Glenellen. 'By the way, Clyde, I've arranged for you to attend the Friday levée. It's always the best.'

'I'll be there. Any special costume?'

'We like a morning coat but, alas, so few people have them nowadays. Only the English Lesbians dress properly . . . vigorous crew: backbone of our missions, both here and abroad.'

'Abroad?' Mr Norman's eyebrows arched. 'Has it spread so far?'

'Indeed it has. Nicaragua, Germany and Norway all boast Missions, while we have Conveyors of the Word in England, Italy, Spain and Switzerland.'

'Not in America?'

'Potentially our largest plum. I am leaving for New York September first, a trip which may change the history of the world . . . you realize that, Clyde?'

'It is possible. So many things are continually changing the history of the world that your journey could very easily be one of them.'

Mr Twill slept over and they made room for him on the couch, between Philip and Glenellen. 'Ayre, my darling, where did you get that ghastly thing about your neck?'

'If you'd been at the services for the last month, you would have known that it was presented to me by Augusta herself when I was made Guardian of the Green Door.'

'But I had no idea! Do forgive me! That was nearly blasphemous, wasn't it?'

'Very nearly. Why haven't you been in attendance?'

'The crush,' said Mr Twill, adjusting his white elbow-length gloves. 'There are too many people there nowadays . . . too many of the wrong sort. But, although I may not be there in person, my heart is with Augusta.'

'You are a backslider.'

'Oh, Ayre, don't be cruel! I tried, God knows I tried to get there but I have so many appointments . . . and I don't get up till noon nowadays anyway.'

'There is a story that you are ashamed to go back because of the time you dropped the toque.'

'You are merciless, Ayre,' said Mr Twill, genuinely if briefly wretched.

'It is only for Augusta,' said Glenellen gently. 'We must do everything for *her*. We must not let *her* down.'

'I'll be there tomorrow. I'll move all my appointments up an hour so that I can attend. You are absolutely right: I've been selfish, headstrong, and I *was* upset when someone knocked the toque out of my hand. I confess now that I swore I would never go back . . . I was in such a pet. But you're right, this is no time to be small.'

'You have made us very happy, Edmond, very happy indeed.'

'Will I . . . be able to handle the toque?'

'You will indeed. And should it be Augustus instead of Augusta I think I might be able to get you assigned the Privilege of the Braces.'

'Ayre!' Too moved to say any more, Mr Twill managed a high whinny of pleasure.

'By the way,' said Philip, 'I didn't steal Lord Glenellen's car.'

Mr Twill looked puzzled. 'But isn't this the one, Ayre, who was at the levée?'

'The same one . . . but it seems that I lost the car. No one took it after all; my suspicions were groundless.'

'Oh, what a pity! I so hoped he had. I like a bold reckless boy!' He squeezed Philip's thigh; once out of sheer exuberance, a second time to corroborate the favourable impression of the first squeeze. Philip moved away. 'Such a solid boy, isn't he? I love that combination, blond hair and violet eyes.'

'He looked better in Rome,' said Glenellen. 'He had dark hair then.'

Philip sighed but said nothing.

'Well, I'm glad he changed it.' And he cast a sidelong flirtatious glance at Philip, his eyes small and bloodshot behind artificial beaded lashes.

Then, as though a stage manager had given a command, everyone changed his position: groups dissolved, reassembled in new combinations, presenting all sorts of possibilities. Large quantities of brandy and champagne were consumed and the lights had been so dimmed that Sebastian had quite faded away, only the golden arrows still visible against the wall. In the next room the phonograph played the songs from the latest of Mr Cole Porter's musicals, and the doors to two bedrooms were already locked.

For one brief moment Philip found himself with Stephen and Bill, both bewildered and far less amused than he. 'Don't take it so seriously,' he said. 'It's not so vicious, after all.'

'I don't think it's very funny,' said Bill, his face flushed and his dark curls sweaty from the room's heat and the brandy he had drunk.

'He's a big hit,' said Stephen, the less outraged of the two. 'That joker in the red dress has been goosing him all night. Just now he offered to take him on a Mediterranean cruise; then when Bill told him we were buddies, he said he would give us each a hundred dollars if we'd let him watch some time.'

'Easy money,' said Philip, enjoying himself.

Bill snorted and then, seeing the fat figure of the red-gowned man moving towards him, he walked quickly to the next room. Stephen close behind him.

'You're not so bad, either,' said Red Dress, drunkenly, pausing in front of Philip, his breath hot and unpleasant with wine and garlic. 'You want to take a little trip with me? Moonlight . . . Mediterranean. We could have a swell time, you and me. We could . . .' But Philip was gone before Red Dress had finished telling him what they might do together.

He crossed the room and stood for a moment between the ghost of Sebastian and the couch where Glenellen still sat, surrounded now by a group of young belles. Voices were growing louder and there were now over fifty people in the two dimly lit rooms. Amorousness in dark corners warned Philip that it was time to go.

'Excuse me,' said a dignified grey-haired man, a Frenchman who spoke excellent English and looked exactly like Philip's idea of a Quai d'Orsay man, with the rank of minister at least. 'You're American, aren't you?'

'This is my first trip to Paris.'

'This is a part of the grand tour now, isn't it?' He indicated the room with a scornful gesture of his long white hand.

'A very interesting part.'

'For a young man, yes, but not for me. I've seen too much, I suppose. I'm bored with this sort of thing . . . so obvious, so feverish, so pointless.'

'But worth seeing once.'

The Frenchman raised his dignified brows. 'This is not your *métier?*'

Philip shook his head. 'I'm here under false pretences . . . incognito, a spy.'

'But how charming! You dabble, of course?'

'No. I don't dabble.'

'But surely you plan to one day, don't you? You're not fighting that hard against it.'

'I'm not fighting it at all,' said Philip blandly. 'I'm a grown man, perfectly contented.'

'How rare! How refreshing! But then my instinct is always infallible in these matters. Placed in a room with twenty men who all look alike, who all share the same tastes except one, I will, unerringly, go to *that* one, to the incorruptible . . . my fate, alas.'

'Isn't that rather sad for you?'

'Fortunately I live in Europe, where a gentleman can buy very nearly anything he wants, including the incorruptible.'

'That is fortunate.'

'Indeed, yes, but tell me, have you found a comfortable hotel?'

Philip told him where he was staying.

'How very nice, so Bohemian. Young people live that way, for a time at least, even though the facilities are not always of the best. Do you have a bath? That's lucky. So many of those places have no hot water. In which case I should have offered you my own place for bathing . . .' He laughed and added, 'Quite legitimate, as you people say. I never force myself on people. What about the laundry situation, though? That's always so difficult this time of year.'

Philip, a little bored, said that he had had no trouble in getting his laundry done.

'I see. If you cared to, however, you could give it to my woman to do . . . she's quite marvellous, no starch . . . the way Americans like their shirts.'

'Thank you very much but . . .' Philip declined his offer, looking around the room in search of Mr Twill; he was ready to leave.

'Tell me,' asked his companion, 'do you wear what the Americans call "jockey shorts"?'

Philip looked at him startled. 'Why on earth do you want to know?'

'But do you?' The other was insistent.

'I do.'

'Are you wearing a pair now?'

'Yes, but why . . .'

'I will give you ten thousand francs for them.'

Philip fled. In the black marble foyer he found Jim who was just arriving.

'What the hell are you doing here?' asked Jim, surprised.

'I'm beginning to wonder myself. I was just getting out while I could.'

The Judgement of Paris

'Good idea.' The boy's face was very pale and his eyes were half shut. 'Can't stand the light,' he murmured.

'Are you flying?' asked Philip gently.

'And how! I'm real gone. I'm never going to touch the ground again. Why, I can't even see you from where I am.' He smiled at Philip, opening wide his silver eyes and Philip saw the tears.

CHAPTER ELEVEN

She looked exactly the way he had remembered her that day in Cairo when Zoe Helotius introduced them in the room with the silken banners on the wall. She was sitting with Charles de Cluny at a table opposite the door. Philip looked at his watch: twelve-thirty at the Ritz. He was on time. With a smile, he went over to her table, suddenly self-conscious, aware that he needed a haircut, that his shoes were not shined.

'I'm so happy we found each other,' she said warmly as he greeted her and Charles, and sat down.

'So am I,' said Philip. 'It's nice to see you too, Charles. How long've you been here?'

'Just a few days.'

'Oh, do you know each other?' asked Anna.

'We're old friends,' said de Cluny. 'In Cairo.'

She nodded. 'Now I remember ... at the party. This is an unexpected meeting, isn't it?'

'It certainly is,' said Philip. 'I checked with your hotel every week until they finally told me you were here.' This was indiscreet, he thought, aware suddenly of de Cluny's knowing glance; but he carried it off. 'They must have got tired of me.'

'On the contrary, I was told that a gentleman with a very nice American voice had inquired for me and the manager was extremely solicitous, hoping, I am sure, that he would be allowed to assist at an intrigue. He couldn't have been more disappointed when I told him what a great friend Mr Warren is of my husband's. We saw each other quite often in Cairo,' she said, turning to de Cluny; Philip admired her for the clear and sensible way she arranged the facts, confirming all de Cluny's suspicions.

'Are you in the steel business now?' asked Charles maliciously, his cigarette holder pointed at Philip like a conductor's baton.

'I'm *very* interested in steel,' said Philip, suggesting by his tone innumerable secret committee meetings where wars were decided upon and governments broken, all for the love of steel.

'Mr Morris is a giant among men,' said de Cluny, placing the cigarette holder between his teeth, smoke for an instant hiding his narrow face.

'He'll be in Paris soon,' she said as the waiter brought the cocktails.

'I hope you will all do me the honour of dining at my house.'

The invitation was accepted with a friendly vagueness.

'Will you have lunch with us today, Charles?' she asked.

'If only I could! But I have to be with Hélène de Lyon et Grénoble. She's deaf and blind but she has an uncanny gift for divining whether one is talking to her or not. I don't know how she does it but when one is not at her house, she knows it and, though most of her faculties are gone, she is not yet mute. What a tongue! So, if you'll excuse me, dear lady, and you, Philip, I shall make my way to the Faubourg ... regretfully. Don't forget about our dinner when Mr Morris has returned. Philip, I'll call you tomorrow.'

More graceful words and then, with several bows and flourishes of the cigarette holder, he was gone.

'I like Charles,' she said, not looking at Philip, as though she were suddenly shy at finding herself alone with him. 'He's been acting the part of the courtier so long he has finally become one. The role has swallowed up the man.'

'The courtier with no court?'

'That's his charm: he makes each of us the centre of the world . . . he has a hundred *reines-lunaires* and though they realize how absurd he is they love him for his attentiveness, for his good manners. And where would we be without the snobs, without the people who value tradition?'

'Where would we be?' repeated Philip. 'Well, I'm afraid we'd be exactly where we are now since all the old traditions are gone and new ones are still aborning.'

'It's a pity, I suppose,' said Anna, watching the bartender shake a cocktail so hard that the eye was confused and his hands and the silver shaker became a single blur in space, reflected by many mirrors. 'But perhaps there is an advantage to living in a time of great change . . . though every time is one of change . . .' They looked at each other for the first time and he saw his own face twice reflected in her hazel eyes.

'I called your hotel,' she said, suddenly personal, her voice changing as she discarded the eternal manner which became her not at all.

'Today?'

'Yesterday when I arrived. But you were out and I didn't leave a message. I wasn't sure you'd remember me.'

'You knew I'd remember.'

'Perhaps. I have a good memory, too. I remember your telling me that you would get your mail through the Embassy. I called them and they gave me your address.'

'Would you have called today if I hadn't telephoned you?'

She nodded. 'Yes . . .'

'I'm glad,' he said and then to bridge the awkward moment, this time of shy and difficult declaration, he ordered two more cocktails. 'I drink too much in Paris,' he said. 'I don't know why. I go for months at a time without taking anything; then, all at once, I find that I want to be amiable and relaxed and sentimental like other people . . . like some other people at least.'

'I'm sure it's good for you,' she said, hardly touching her own glass. 'I don't need it, I'm afraid. Nature made me sentimental from the very start. I think that if I drank I should be maudlin.'

'Or perhaps the opposite . . . very hard and aloof.'

'Never . . . even though there are times when I should like to give that impression.'

'But not with me, I hope.'

'No, not with you.'

They lunched in a small restaurant around the corner from the Crillon, a place with Chinese red walls, lacquered and gleaming and decorated with banks of roses and ferns not yet wilted, still fresh with morning.

'I see why you chose it,' said Philip. 'The Chinese room . . . with all the banners.'

'The same mood, without Zoe.' She laughed.

The day went easily, carefully. Each deferred to the other and their conversations alternated between a delicate formality and a loverlike intimacy:

usual prelude to an affair. But Philip for once could not determine the nature of the work to come.

He was often able to see at the very beginning the end of an affair, with a painful clarity which had, in recent years especially, done much to diminish the intensity of his own emotions. Too fine an understanding was far worse, he knew, than the confusion with which most young men blundered into love affairs. He had always known, for instance, not only how far he would commit himself with Regina but also at what point his withdrawal would, imperceptibly, commence, and though his prescience was saddening, it gave him a sense of security, of power which made the affairs, at least while they lasted, singularly agreeable, lacking in the usual dissensions, the blind misunderstandings; then, too, as he grew older, he had become more kind; he prided himself now on having become an adept at the art of separation, the gradual retreat which left neither anguish nor rage behind. But, being a child or the grandchild of the Romantic Movement, living in a culture still dominated on a vulgar level by the high romantic poets of the nineteenth century, he longed instinctively for the flames, for the one attachment: 'my last and only love,' the love which increased from moment to moment until the lovers strangled for lack of air among those peaks which touch the edge of heaven, close to the consuming sun in whose fire, united at last, they perish to the accompaniment of French horns and frenzied woodwinds, the voice of Isolde, strong and pure, lingering in the vast golden dome of heaven where angels, out of sympathy, deluge the earth below with their pity. And in the back of his mind, each time he began the intricate ritual, he hoped that his own knowledge would be proved false by the unexpected conquest of that suspected but never before attained dimension in which he could indulge not only his secret passion for romance, for immolation, but also achieve that instant which each man awaits as though it were his due, inevitable, the moment of recognition that there is someone else in the world with whom the mortal's loneliness can be shared and finally overcome, the last of the fluttering moths from Pandora's box, caught and speared.

But I am a realist, said Philip to himself, disliking this self-estimate, aware that it was true: he was not a romanticist or a visionary.

Yet for Philip, for the realist who recognizes the more obvious limitations of both flesh and spirit, the hope of a great romantic experience is tempered always with the grim knowledge that nothing is constant and that even though a certain height might, temporarily, be attained, descent from it is inevitable and painful, unless one chooses to perish at the grand moment, a gesture which did not attract Philip although the rich, dark tragedy at Mayerling had fascinated not only him but others of his generation, as directionless as he, all of them like compass needles gone awry, awaiting the pull of some magnet to set their courses for them, true north no longer the centre it had once been. But Mayerling or not, he had no wish to die. He would, he knew, go as far as his temperament would permit into a separate world with one other person but since it would not be his only world, since he was possessed by other demons, the pure expression he dreamed of seemed unlikely although, as he talked to Anna, he thought it would be difficult ever to become bored with her and that was more than he could ever have said of any other woman he had known, at this point at least in the ceremony of union. As he talked he recalled the loveliest of the *Minnesänger's* songs: '*Unter den Linden, an der Heide, da unser zweier Bette.*' A bed for us on the heather would be very fine, he thought and, as it always had before, his desire drowned his love and he could only think of the act, the excitement, the mysteries revealed, a new conquest and as he succumbed to the familiar itch, Anna ceased to be, her face and character were veiled, only the body was real and immediate. But she countered him, to his surprise, for just when the moment seemed very nearly achieved, the way clearly indicated, she withdrew, leaving him staring angrily into his half-empty coffee cup.

'I promised to meet some people. I ran into them yesterday and they made me promise.'

'Tonight . . .'

'A silly dinner. But tomorrow why don't we get Charles to give us dinner at his house. He has a lovely one, or rather some rooms in one, opposite the Isle de la Cité.'

'I've always thought there was a happy symbolism in the choice of St Germain's name for our left bank boulevard. He was a remarkable man, a Bishop of Paris at the end of the sixth century and having that rarest of maladies, ancient or modern, a Christian conscience, he went about Europe raising funds for the liberation of slaves. By the time he died, he had very nearly shattered that barbarous practice in Europe. Now the young people come from all over the world to live here on his boulevard, to lose their superstitions, to become emancipated. It is very touching.' But nothing de Cluny said ever sounded as though he quite meant it, thought Philip critically: Charles had cultivated the ironic manner to such an extent that his most casual words were redolent with self-mockery and double meaning. Yet he talked well enough, Philip conceded to himself, content with the dinner they had just eaten, with the view from an open balconied window of Notre Dame against the stars, with Anna who wore Chinese red like a Chinese bride, the curious fragment of crystal about her neck.

The evening had been perfect and they now sat in a book-lined study, neither shabby nor elegant, made unique by the view. Philip and Anna had talked little, pleased with the moment, not wanting to upset the delicate balance with irrelevant words. De Cluny, aware of this happy situation, seized the opportunity to speak of himself and while his guests looked at one another, he talked of his recent sojourn in a country of Central America.

'An incredibly lifeless place, all things considered . . . and in my dozen years there I did consider nearly everything, including suicide. Not that my job wasn't interesting . . . I was adviser to the President, Alvarez Asturias. You may have heard of him.'

Philip and Anna murmured in unison that they had not.

'He was a dictator, one of the better ones. But he was deposed and I followed him into exile. Had he remained in private life all might have been well. We were very snug in New Orleans but he attempted a revolution in which I took part, a ghastly affair and disastrous for everyone concerned, except me: it galvanized me into a feverish literary activity. I had lain fallow for so long that I thought it unlikely I should ever bloom again. But I did. We escaped by helicopter . . . an exciting time, I might add, with government troops firing on us. Fortunately we got as far as Guatemala where we fell, for some reason no one has ever been able to determine, in the middle of Lake Atitlán . . . on a clear day, mind you. I have a theory that the pilot was drunk but we shall never know for he was knocked unconscious when we crashed, and sank like a stone. The rest of us were rescued by a fishing boat and I went back to France as soon as I could, where I had certain properties saved from the deluge.'

The moment had come when the dinner must be paid for. Philip and Anna looked at one another. It was agreed silently that she request the reading. She did, graciously, with an air of real sincerity.

'I know what an ordeal it is to be read to, especially in French, but of course you, dear lady, *are* French and Mr Warren speaks it beautifully.' And he shuffled papers on his desk, assembled a staggering number of manuscript pages from which he read in a loud ringing voice, the cadence as regular and as monotonous as the alexandrines at the Comédie-Française, without benefit of scenery or of entr'actes or of talent.

Gently, Philip dropped off to sleep. He awakened with a start, aware that a question had been asked, that the others were looking at him intently, awaiting an answer.

'Fine.' He croaked; then, clearing his throat, he sat up and said, with as much resonance as his light voice would permit, 'Very fine.'

'You don't feel that the scene in the park is a trifle grandiloquent?'

'On the contrary, I thought it remarkably muted, considering its theme,' added Philip confidently, blundering into a trap.

'But what do you really feel *is* the theme? I mean the underlying motif at that point? I have kept it oblique, I think, awaiting the proper moment to develop it more fully; yet it *is* there, all the way through the scene, like an echo to what is said . . . a faint counterpoint to the obvious theme.'

'Ah,' said Philip, looking at Anna helplessly. She only laughed at him, silently.

'The echo I think is the broken statue,' hinted de Cluny eagerly.

'A sense of loss, I should say,' said Philip, gambling everything with a flourish. 'A longing for what will never be.'

'You have it! I *knew* it was apparent but I was afraid it might be lost. You have no idea how relieved I am! Shall I get you more brandy? Yes?' He left the room to find another bottle.

'Where shall we go?' asked Philip, suddenly, when their host was gone.

'Wherever you like, Philip. To the Ida?'

'No, that wouldn't be wise.'

'To your hotel?'

'It's so . . . dark. I don't want that, do you?'

She smiled. 'No, we must have light.'

'Then we leave Paris. Go somewhere else.'

'When?'

'Now . . . tonight.'

'But where?'

'To the sea. What about Deauville?'

'But . . .'

'St Malo? That's better, isn't it? We could stay there.'

'But how . . .'

'You have a car. We'll take that. Please. If we leave right now we'll be there before noon.'

'Before noon,' she repeated, taken aback; then she laughed. 'Do you really want to take such a chance? You hardly know me.'

'I'll take it, if you will.'

'Oh, I will, of course.' Her lack of hesitancy surprised and pleased him.

'But your husband?'

'He won't be in Paris until the end of the month. You are very brave, Philip.'

'Shall we go?'

She nodded.

'Tonight?'

'Whenever you like. It will be a lovely night for driving.'

'Where's the car?'

'At the hotel . . . parked in front. I have the keys with me.'

'Let's not take anything with us. We'll go just as we are.'

'I would like that,' she said, surprising him for the last time.

'This brandy,' said de Cluny, 'has been in my family for fifty years. Look! Cobwebs!' He put the bottle down on the table and wiped his hands with his handkerchief. 'One's voice needs a little . . . lubrication after a long reading, I find. The audience, of course, deserves a stimulant.'

'A sedative,' said Philip gallantly, exuberant, more pleased than he had ever been before. 'After all you keyed us up.'

'Now you exaggerate.' De Cluny's face darkened slightly with pleasure; he poured the brandy.

'You read so well,' said Anna. 'Like an actor . . . your face is very like Jouvet's.'

'Do you think so? Ah, that *is* a compliment, indeed! André Gide was most sympathetic the other day when I paid a call on him at the rue Vaneau. Most sympathetic.'

'Did you read for him?' asked Philip.

'Alas, no. He didn't have the time. He's very old, you know, but he told me he had every confidence that I should maintain my old level . . . he was most encouraging. Such a vigorous man for his age, too. Physically, like a hard, barrel-chested peasant . . . not always kind either: when I made some reference to Claudel he said: who? Imagine! But then I suspect he dislikes discussing in his contemporaries or near-contemporaries. He talked for the most part about a delightful manuscript of pornography, handsomely and primitively illuminated, the work, I swear to you, of a retired Anglican bishop living in Italy. He had sent it to the master with a *dédicace* and, as the master said, it *was* fine but a trifle too literary in tone.'

'He sounds very agreeable,' said Philip.

'A fine manner. And isn't that, on a human level at least, the most important of virtues? Genius exists only in the work, not in the man, or I should say one can only approach it in the work . . . where the man is disembodied, as it were, made pure. Naturalness, of course, is supposed to be one of the most engaging of American virtues, but is it really what one wants? Is it truly civilized? A country of first names! Only the Negroes there have manners. They are most scrupulous in calling one another Mr and Mrs. The white people, especially the ones in business, at their first meeting with a stranger call him by his Christian name, even if he is old enough to be their father.'

Philip made a great scene over the hour. What time did de Cluny's watch say? and the ornate clock on the mantel? the broken Dresden clock in the bedroom? his own often inaccurate watch? Was it really so late? and the evening, was it really gone? Then, the symposium on time concluded to everyone's satisfaction, Philip and Anna said good night.

The false grey-pink Paris dawn had already begun to glow when they drove across the city through dark and silent streets; neither spoke until they were in the open country, the towns of eastern Touraine before them and beyond Touraine, the fields and orchards of Normandy and the northern sea.

'I'm glad I wasn't wearing an evening dress,' said Anna as the day illuminated the dark sky with gold, with rose; then a ghostly yellow sun appeared over the green and misty land and the sky shone blue with morning.

'A few more hours,' said Philip.

'Do you want me to drive?'

'No, I don't want to stop for a minute, until we're there.'

'Neither do I.'

'No breakfast?'

'Nothing . . . until we're there.'

Three miles east of St Malo they stopped and got out of the car. In the distance, partly hidden by the sea mist, they could make out the pyramidal shape of the ancient castle, set far out in the sea. Half a mile away was a stone cottage with a thatched roof, the only building in sight. The land undulated, soft and green, white-dotted with rocks and grazing sheep. The clover-scented air was still and warm as they stood by the side of the car, looking upon the dark blue sea which broke on a dun-coloured, rock-strewn beach at the meadow's edge. Then, without a word, they walked across the coarse turf to the beach and, finding a stretch of sand that was sheltered from the road by tall trees, they paused among the grey, smooth rocks, relics of an age of glaciers and still not speaking, the hot sun in their faces, they undressed. It was noon.

He took her in the cool sea, their lips tasting of salt, blue above and all around them except for the green land they had left behind. Gulls circled slowly overhead. Salt water stopped his watch, holding the sun forever in the centre of the sky: high noon, as they moved to a sea-like rhythm in one another's arms until, at last, the tide drove them back to shore again and the sun fell in the west.

Between two guardian rocks, they lay on the sand, side by side, their bodies touching, creatures belonging neither to the sea nor to the land from which each had come to this beach between earth and water, the air above them and, far below, their own element fire, swathed in sea and air, earth, stone and metal, a smothered sun at the centre of the world.

He sat up on one elbow and looked at her as she lay, white and perfect, upon the sand. He touched her carefully, as though she might melt like the snow princess in the legend. But she was mortal. She sighed and opened her eyes, her dark hair cushioned by seaweeds and shells, crystals of salt glittering like a powder of fine snow on her white skin, dried by the warm air.

'I was asleep,' she said. 'Were you?'

'I think so. Look, the sun is almost down.'

'The day can't end.' She shut her eyes again, her arms crossed upon her breast. He plucked the shells and seaweed from her long hair and, when she opened her eyes again, he half expected to see the pearls that were her eyes. ' "Full fathom five," ' he whispered to himself.

She looked at him a long time, her hand gently stroking his arms and his chest as she gradually followed the line of blond hair to the now limp and childlike origin of life; then they made love again, closer to earth than to sea, once more whole: a double star, a third sun suspended between the other two, the one below and the fiery one which now lingered in the western corner of the sky.

They lay together, joined, until the sun set and the pale grey sky was pierced by a single star, a gleaming point of silver in the nascent evening. 'Ah, there it is,' she said. They separated and got to their feet, unsteadily, like invalids or like children who had just learned to walk. 'Have you made a wish?' she asked.

'I have,' he said, his arm about her waist.

'Have you made the wish?'

'There is only one.'

'Only one,' she murmured, and they dressed at last on the dark beach while, among the trees which bordered the meadow, fireflies gleamed like a swarm of old stars falling.

The room was large with small shuttered windows and rough beams showing; a four-poster bed, square and massive, was set in the centre of the tile floor. Brass gleamed in the fireplace and the room smelled of smoke and linen, wood and roses.

'It is our best room,' said the old man, grumbling and snorting like every French character actor Philip had ever seen. 'Feather.' He punched the thick mattress. 'The *vase de nuit*.' He indicated a blue and white chamber pot beside the bed. 'Only candles. We have no electricity here.' He paused, challengingly, prepared to attack the new age, but they had already surrendered to him and to the room in the stone house, a half mile from their beach.

Since he was always with Anna, Philip had little time to contemplate his own emotions, like a physician taking his own pulse. Yet he was sharply aware that at the centre of those easy days there was a pain equal to the delight of loving . . . the dark side of the love, the parallel emotion without which nothing could be measured or identified: no day without night, no life without death, no love without this cold pain, this separateness. For, at the last, he was a creature of his world, time-haunted and future-loving, obsessed with hours and minutes, terrified by days and years and the loss of youth, the end of the good present in which he now moved, like a man who dreams and knows that he is dreaming in a world all his own, where he reigns a god but, unlike a god, conscious of the world outside his dream, its noises intruding fitfully, unbidden, until at last, half-blind and angry, he awakens, the dream scattered in a hundred fragments by the ruthless light, the significant design forever gone, only the anguish and the sense of loss lingering to mock the day.

But his watch was broken, rusted by sea water, and neither spoke of the hour for many days.

He sat cross-legged on a rock and watched her walk out of the sea wringing water from her dark hair, her body gleaming white in the sun. Birds chattered in the orchards. Grey gulls circled over the sea. The sun burned gold and hot in the sky.

'How brown you are!' she exclaimed joining him on the sand between their two tall guardian rocks, Gog and Magog she had called them.

'And you're still white,' he said, touching her cold wet thigh.

'I never tan. I can't think why. I should like to look like one of those bronze amazons with golden hair. I admire them so.'

'I don't,' said Philip, stretching his legs, the short hairs sun-bleached and glistening on his brown arms and legs, only the lower belly and thighs still white, the line of bathing trunks still marked on his skin. 'It's like going to bed with a man, to go to bed with one of them.'

'Did you ever?'

'Go to bed with one of them? Oh yes. In my college days all the girls were six feet tall and liked to engage the boys in various competitive feats of strength. Fortunately, that was before the days of jujitsu, so all but the slighter boys got their way . . . the weak ones were either thrown back into the sea or else raped by their conquerors. One young man named MacDougall was forced to surrender his virginity to a giantess from Smith College . . . three times in one terrible hour in his room while his two roommates, roaring with delight, watched through the keyhole . . . They had locked the door so he couldn't escape.'

Anna laughed, wondering. 'It sounds like the end of the world,' she said, lying back on the rock, her hair a dark rain cloud against the sand.

One eminent man of letters (whom many think the first among us) once wrote in a novel that when his hero made love to his heroine the earth moved and celestial firecrackers went off in the void where presumably his audience, a benign eternity, applauded rapturously each mighty thrust. A lesser, more superficial man of letters (equally celebrated but less well regarded at the moment) chided his peer, saying that nothing of that sort ever happened when a man and woman made love . . . at best they had a good time. To which the great man responded, '*You* could never understand,' retiring like any good priest into mysteries which cannot be defined in familiar terms: either one *knows* or one does not.

In Philip's case it would be untrue to say that the course of his life was altered by that moment with Anna: it was not . . . at least as far as one can determine which events do affect character and to what degree. He got out of bed the morning after their first night together as he had got out of bed the day before and as he would get out of bed ten years later. He was the same man in the usual sense of sameness: he did not go out into the street and preach the Word; he made no attempt to proselytize; he gave up nothing he had liked before (including promiscuity), nor was he inspired to become a marvellous artist because, as it has been earlier demonstrated, he had no particular talent and, contrary to a certain opinion, vision alone is not enough in the arts . . . although it may serve one handsomely in life. But in one important sense he was changed. Where before he had believed he now knew, and that, as any mystic will attest, is the difference between night and day. And for the rest of a long life, he would glimpse the fire again and again, always reflected, however, in a woman's eyes. Yet never the way it had been the first night when, briefly, his flesh and bone, memory and will had been consumed and he became a part of all that is.

When the Duc de Lyon et Grénoble died, twenty years ago, his vivacious widow, who was then only sixty, moved into a small but stately house on the Faubourg St Germain, selling her husband's hôtel to a speculator who made several apartments of it, in one of which, as we have already noted, Mr Edmond Twill now resides steeped in his own rich atmosphere of drugs and debauched street boys, no trace of the stern Duc or his still handsome Duchesse remaining in that old building . . . even the cobwebs in the cellar have been changed for the Duchesse is very mean, as everyone knows, and she is supposed to have taken the family spiders and mice with her when she moved into that smaller establishment where she has re-created an imperial atmosphere that is the despair of all the Bonapartists, none of whom, not even the Murats, has been able to equal it in grandeur or in authenticity.

Needless to say, the better Royalists have very little to do with her and she, in turn, has nothing to do with any member of the Republican government, excepting always those old friends who have blundered into high office: for those unfortunates, she gives small teas in her boudoir, not allowing them, however, to attend her carefully chosen receptions or those formal dinners where she entertains the relics of the Empire and the older members of that world of high fashion which used always to amuse her before she became deaf and blind. She is, according to Charles de Cluny who insists he knows, a hundred and seven years old. No matter what her age, it is a fact that she was on intimate terms with the Empress Eugénie and dined with her once a week until that lady's death. The Duchesse has had no close woman friends since, although her friendships with men are still much talked of; she is known to have been the cause of a number of duels, suicides, divorce cases, as well as the lifelong love of one lyric poet's short-termed existence. She is now living with her onetime coachman, a portly silver-haired gentleman who is seldom in evidence although early callers report that he brings her breakfast to her each morning on a tray, with a bouquet of fresh violets across the morning paper.

Philip and Anna were led by de Cluny to the centre of a grey and silver drawing room where, directly beneath a chandelier, the Duchesse stood, a straight small figure with bright red hair held in place by a fillet of green velvet, in the style of the 1880's, modified somewhat during the early years of the twentieth century to set off a figure which had once been handsomely proportioned but now had grown thick at one end of the torso and grotesquely frail at the other, where the narrow shoulders were hung with discoloured pearls as filmy and as dark as the eyes which darted this way and that, not seeing, the world shut out by whiteness . . . having attained certain Alpine peaks, thought Philip poetically as he studied those dim eyes, she had been blinded by the glare of light on glaciers.

'Charles?' Her voice was surprisingly full for one so old; loud too from deafness. 'Did you bring me the young people? Ah yes, here are their hands. She is a lovely blonde with white skin and he is a fat American boy. I can always tell by hands. Such a comfort to have some communication with the living since, obviously, I have none with the dead . . . although many of my friends think they can talk to the dead, I don't: all nonsense. Besides, why should one want to talk to an absolute stranger with whom one has nothing in common? "I am Yvette, a midinette, and I died in Seventy-four . . ." ' She mocked in a high voice, still holding the hands of the lovers in her own, her touch as smooth and as dry as old silk.

'Fortunately, everyone I used to know is dead, including the ones who attended séances. They certainly realize *now* what nonsense it all was. Well, go on . . . there are other young people here, I think. Bore one another.' And with a shadow of what must have been a brilliant smile, she let go their hands abruptly and they found themselves in a room full of strangers of whom none were young. They sat in a brocade love seat next to a spinet where a tired-looking man played Mozart with a faded grace, the thin elegant sounds lost in the party's chatter.

Above the mantel was a portrait of the Duchesse as she had looked when Bismarck entered Paris. On the spinet, on every table, were miniatures and photographs of an earlier time: a lock of Napoleon's hair, dark brown and lustreless in a heavy case of gold and crystal, a silver rattle which had belonged to the King of Rome, Murat's spurs and the baton of the first Duc, all preserved under glass with yellowed cards identifying them for those casual visitors who had strayed, like Philip, into his drawing room with no real knowledge of what it meant, of what it had been in other more vigorous days, when ladies sewed gold bees onto handkerchiefs for French boys who were to die far from home.

Anna was finally taken away by an old acquaintance and he was left alone by the spinet with de Cluny, who smiled and bowed continually at figures across the room, talking to Philip at the same time.

'Love of unfamiliar, outworn ways is a weakness, I suppose,' he said genially, bowing very low at a poorly assembled mass of lace which passed close by, exuding a musty odour like a closed room suddenly opened. Philip half expected the ambulatory lace to be attended by reverent outriding moths.

'It's natural,' said Philip.

'On the contrary, most unnatural. Have you noticed the hatred with which lower-class people (and much of the middle class, too) regard the past? One sees it at a cinema where they laugh derisively at the costumes of another time and on those occasions when confronted, in school or in the theatre, with some classic literary work, they respond with confusion and anger, mocking the language not only of the past but, worse still, of all art, since they are as afraid of the new as they are of the old. No wonder one loathes the mob.'

'But why loathe people who don't share your taste? It seems bigoted to say the least.'

'Taste is another thing. No, I don't really mind if the working classes mock Corneille but I do mind when they attempt, as they periodically do, to destroy all art, to reduce the great to their own level. That is the terrible anti-human constant in all our affairs and that is why I, for one, do loathe the mob. The people who deposed Aristides and poisoned Socrates . . .' He kissed a dingy alabaster hand which emerged for one brief moment from yards of faded yellow silk.

'Odd isn't it how each age has its panacea . . . its banner, as it were. In the Middle Ages it was Faith; in the eighteenth century, it was Reason . . . later, it was Progress . . .'

'And what, I wonder, is it now?'

De Cluny smiled. 'I know.'

'What?'

'I don't dare say.'

'That's hardly courageous.'

'Love!' said de Cluny, bringing one long finger down on the keyboard of the now deserted spinet. An eighteenth-century E-flat tinkled faintly, like a derisive echo in the air.

'That has never been the ideal of more than a few,' said Philip sternly.

'I'm not speaking of amity or charity or the brotherhood of man. I am speaking of sexual love. Think for a moment: man is no longer the centre of the universe as he once was, or thought he was, which is the same thing. His displacement began, in modern times, with Copernicus and ended with Darwin. The idea of a personal god who watches over man with a worried eye, giving out marks for deportment and arranging celestial bliss or eternal discomfort for the good and the bad, is dying in the West. While a belief in the universals of Aristotle has been succeeded by a conception of relativity . . . morality is relative and variable, change is constant and the Protagorean conception that man is the measure of all things is, in practice, if not in orthodox belief, quite general. Where, then, is man? The universe in his own image has been succeeded by a universe in its own image *containing* him, and he is now beginning to perceive what two thousand years of Western culture tried to hide: that his race is not the central adornment of the universe and that its control over nature is as pre-carious and as limited as its control over itself. Man is important only to himself. The fiction of a partisan deity has become so transparent that even the most

uneducated are able to see through it, to see the infinite impersonal void beyond
this world, this single particle in an indifferent galaxy . . . child of earth and of
starry heaven indeed! I doubt if even the most eccentric, the most persuasive
mystic will ever again be able to personalize the void, to subordinate it to this
one race as our fortunate ancestors did. Man has nothing except himself; so,
without hope of heaven after death or of Utopia on earth, he is left nothing but
games like art and power, the satisfaction of various hungers and, of all the
games and of all the hungers, the most exalted, the most godlike is the sexual act
since, in human terms at least, it is the most important of all our deeds:
continuation of life, while as sensation, there is nothing to compare with it, in the
vigour of one's youth at least. And of all the old gods of the West, Venus alone is
regnant. Two can face the void with less terror than one. The moment of orgasm
fills the dark with light, or seems to, which is enough, I think. Everywhere in the
West, one sees this sudden preoccupation with sex, in our literature, in art, in
science . . . there's even a new philosophy of sex with men like Lawrence and
Freud attempting to define it, either mystically or empirically. One knows now
that love is the last illusion, the only magic, and unlike other pleasures . . . the
exercise of power, mysticism, the creation of works of art . . . it is physically
possible for nearly everyone while in a spiritual sense (or whatever word one
wishes to use to characterize so tenuous a state of being), it is a challenge to the
few, a proof of virtue, a temporary defeat of the impersonal reality, black magic
in an age of science.'

'That only leaves death to be accounted for,' said Philip, thoughtfully.

'Death accounts for us, not we for it,' said de Cluny, as the room was split in
two by Zoe Helotius.

Philip moved close to the room's centre where Zoe paid court to the Duchesse
and the party paid court to Zoe.

'Darling Hélène, I'm late. I came as soon as I could but I was in the house of
X and you know how difficult it is to get away from them.' The reference to X
was sufficiently lofty to impress even the oldest of the Bonapartists.

'I can't hear a word you're saying, Zoe,' complained the Duchesse which was
obviously not true since Mrs Helotius' voice could have penetrated walls of lead.

'Darling, can you hear me now?' The voice reduced the room to silence.

'Just barely. You must learn to speak without mumbling. When I was a girl,
we were taught elocution by La Meynard of the Comédie-Française. "Speak
up," she used to say. "Speak up!" '

'My childhood was less privileged!' bellowed Zoe, and then, ignoring the old
lady's occasional remarks about her diction, she gossiped and Philip, among
these relics of the first Napoleon, thought of Madame de Staël and her loud
progress through these same drawing rooms a century ago, in search not only of
lions but of ideas.

'She is lovely,' said Charles, admiringly.

'You think so? I think she's terrible.'

'I meant Anna.'

'Oh. I thought you meant Mrs Helotius. Yes, she is.'

'Did you enjoy your trip to the sea?'

'How did you know?'

'I know everything.'

'Yes, very much.'

'I knew in Cairo this would happen.'

'So did I. Do you think she did?'

'Certainly. What do you intend to do now?'

'I don't know. I haven't thought. Go on, I suppose.'

'He'll be coming back.'

'We haven't discussed the future.'

'Sensible. I hope you'll know what to do when the time comes, however.'

'When *what* time comes?'

'The moment of choice. There's always one in every relationship.'

'I don't like generalities. You know, as well as I do, there are no rules to these things.'

'True, but I know better than you the nature of the choice *you* must make . . . if only because I am older and once selected, long ago, impetuously, my own way.'

'Which was not the right way?'

'Right, wrong, it makes no difference; we die in any event. No, I should say one chooses what one must, of course, but I believe there is an instant of free will, a moment when one can assume direction. The trick is to recognize that moment.'

'I'm not sure I follow you.'

'Don't follow me! That's precisely it. There's your answer.'

'There will be war, Hélène!' shouted Zoe.

'More what, my dear?'

'I have it on the best authority . . . within ninety days. Then the end. Pouf! No more Europe. Nothing. Where will *you* go?'

'Know what?'

'I shall die with the world I have loved. I will not desert. Never! I shall be at Antibes, waiting. I shall wear all my jewels and, when *they* come, I shall receive them on the lawn. They will drive their tanks through the boxwood and over the roses, the pink ones named for me, and I shall be drinking champagne with the Duke of Windsor on the terrace when they shoot us down!'

'I haven't been to Antibes in twenty years . . . it was a new resort in those days. I went there with Paul Avril. You remember him? He dedicated his *Titania* to me. They do it now at the Comédie I hear, But I no longer attend the theatre. Crowds confuse me, except here in my own house.'

'No, none of us will survive this war . . . and who will want to? Who?'

'New? What, my dear, is new? You are naïve, but it's your charm, Zoe. Never let them take it away from you.'

'Call me Cassandra! I see what I see.'

'But I love the sea as much as you and perhaps, if these treatments I am taking work, I may be able to visit you at Antibes.'

'I should love that, Hélène.'

'They're giving me the glands of sheep. Imagine! To be a sheep, after all these years.'

'Ninety days, Hélène; that's all we have. Ninety days. One really doubts if there is Someone above.'

'Love? But, my dear Zoe, *who* loves you? And how nice for you. Tell me, I must know.'

'You see,' said Charles, turning to Philip, pausing in their journey across the room, beneath a portrait of Marie-Louise.

'Yes, I think so.'

Through black lace and black broadcloth, he saw Anna at the far end of the room, waiting for him.

CHAPTER TWELVE

'It is fifth night: the moment of revelation . . . the hour of truth!' Glenellen paused, arms outstretched, glowering at the crowded room. The worshippers stood or sat in a dense circle about him, leaving hardly any space around the empty throne before which he now stood. Two young women, hearty in tweed, guarded the Green Door.

There was a sigh of anticipation, a murmur of excitement at this pronouncement. One young man near the bookcase fainted from tension while, in other parts of the room, there were several audible moans of religious fervour, including one resounding 'Hallelujah!' from an American night-club singer, a New York Italian girl who had attempted, with complete success, to pass herself off as a Negress, thus insuring a considerable following among the credulous French.

Then Glenellen, red-faced and tense, stepped to the Green Door and stood, head bowed, in front of it, waiting. The silence was broken at last by the ringing of an alarm clock; then the dinner bell tolled and the Green Door slowly opened, revealing Augusta, completely nude, a tall pale figure with primary and secondary sexual characteristics of unusual variety. With a serene smile the beloved figure moved through the cheering worshippers to the empty throne. But then, before the first Statement of the Day could be made, a dozen gendarmes shouting 'Exhibition! Exhibition!' broke into the room.

The noise was deafening. Most of the young women jumped out the window (the shrine was on the second floor of an eighteenth-century building) while several of the young men fainted and were severely trampled by the panicky worshippers and the no less hysterical gendarmes who rushed this way and that, shouting Republican sentiments, invoking *Legalité* as they tried unsuccessfully to arrest the fleeing Augustans, all of whom, within several minutes, had got out the door, excepting those vigorous young women who had sprained their ankles on the hard pavement below and the young men who had fainted and lay now like corpses after a battle, while the gendarmes hammered on the Green Baize Door behind which Glenellen and Mr Norman together protected the cowering Augusta as she lay on an iron cot, shuddering convulsively, the various articles of worship covered with a torn linen sheet.

'Go away!' shouted Glenellen. 'This is sacrilege! This is a private institution! I shall go immediately to the British Ambassador if you persist! Do you hear me?'

The gendarmes continued to batter at the door, demanding the arrest of Augusta, professing shock at the obscenity of the exhibition they had witnessed.

'You had better let them in, Ayre,' said Mr Norman quietly.

'Never!' shrieked Glenellen, moving an old wardrobe against the door. 'Desecration!' he roared at the gendarmes on the other side, but they were too busy with their hammering to hear the solemn curse which, presently, he thundered at them, leaning against the wardrobe, one hand cluthing his chain of office.

Mr Norman sat down on a three-legged stool, the only furniture in the room besides the cot and the wardrobe. Calmly he lit a cigar and then, exhaling, a model Englishman in a confused moment, he looked about the small airless room curiously, at the shrine which until now none but Augusta had seen. Dust was everywhere and the single window with its dirty panes of glass had obviously not been opened for many years while on the floor, on the bed, on the window sills, lay old candy wrappers and tag ends of food, fragments of stale cake and biscuits while several ominous floor-level holes in the wall suggested that Augusta shared her feats in much the same way the saint from Assisi had shared his.

'That should hold them,' said Glenellen, his curse completed, his last thunderbolt launched at the gendarmes who had found some sort of battering ram and were now, at regular intervals, hitting the door, splintering it methodically as flakes of plaster fell from ceiling and walls upon the motionless figure of Augusta, like a corpse beneath her sheet, and upon the two Englishmen who conversed quietly, pausing only when the regular noise of the battering ram crashed through the shrine.

'What shall we do when the door finally goes?' asked Mr Norman.

'Fight them with our bare hands,' said Glenellen grimly.

'Come now, Ayre. Neither of us could handle an angry child, much less the pride of the gendarmerie.'

'A token resistance, then . . . we will not surrender easily.'

'I suppose they'll book us on some charge or another.'

'Martyrdom!' exclaimed Glenellen, his face transfigured for an instant as he considered grace.

'Should the movement triumph we will of course be included among its first martyrs but should it not prevail we shall have wasted our time in unnecessary humiliation.'

Glenellen looked at his companion sadly. 'You too, Clyde?' he whispered.

'I was speaking realistically, my dear old friend. You know that. I shall never desert you . . . although I have at times disagreed with your methods in the conduct of the Missions . . . especially when you deposed dear Edmond from his post as Bursar, even though I begged you not to.'

'You should never have taken his side.'

'At a time like this . . . a climacteric, as it were . . . I should not think it advisable to be too finicky.'

'Let me tell you, Clyde, since you wish to discuss the squalid affair of Edmond's fraudulency, that you yourself have been, on more than one occasion, accused of selling audiences with Augusta and, worse still, of receiving a retainer from a certain Brazilian for the Privilege of the Braces.'

'*I* sell audiences! It is fortunate indeed that you are my old friend, or I might forget myself.'

'That it is you, dear Clyde, who are the offender, justifies or, rather, ameliorates the deed and precludes penalty.'

'Penalty!' A large section of plaster, shaped like a map of France, fell to the floor at Glenellen's feet. Augusta whimpered and turned her face to the wall.

'Remember Savoy!' said Glenellen furiously. 'The House of Savoy! Remember? Did we desert Umberto, the first gentleman of our adopted country, our rightful lord, for this? That we end by selling audiences to the Incomparable, dirtying our fingers for the sake of ready cash, exploiting our coreligionists . . . Oh, I should rather have remained a Communist and cursed the bourgeoisie than such an Augustan!'

'Don't turn on me, Ayre. I won't have it. I won't! You forget, I am a believer too, more devout than you . . .'

'Stop it, Clyde! You know you're not. You have no vocation.'

'I have.'

'And *I* say you haven't.'

'I shall lose my temper with you, Ayre, if you don't watch your tongue.'

The mirror on the wardrobe came loose and smashed on the floor. There was a shout of triumph from the gendarmes on the other side; they renewed their battering.

'You bore me, Clyde.'

'Is it possible?'

'Listen to me, Clyde. Don't interrupt and stop glowering at me like an idiot.'

'Great heavens! . . . has it come to this?' Mr Norman was genuinely anguished.

'Yes, my dear, all this . . . and more. Fret all you like because from now on I shall be quite serene, undisturbed by these outbursts . . . I find you ludicrous, Clyde. Do you hear? Absolutely ludicrous.'

'Then it is over . . .'

'You say you are more devout that I . . . such insolence. Prove it. Tell me one vision you have had which might substantiate your pretensions.'

'Now you wrong me, Ayre; I'm sorry. I said I was *as* devout as you . . . I didn't say more, did I?'

'I don't care if you did.'

'When we served Umberto you would not have spoken to me like this. You know it. You no longer care for me, Ayre. Augusta has drained you of all humanity.'

'I do not like your faults.'

'If you were a friend you would overlook them.'

'If I were sufficiently insincere, I suppose I could pretend not to see the Eiffel Tower.'

'I am tired,' sighed Mr Norman, with the gesture of one rehearsing for a crucifixion. 'I hope the gendarmes come soon and take us to the station. I can't bear your carping, your hatred . . . this morbid concern with my imagined faults. I'm too weak, too exhausted to bear all this.'

'Oh, Clyde! Clyde!' Glenellen turned to the window as the top panel of the door splintered above the wardrobe.

'I can't bear your contempt, Ayre . . . your indifference.'

'I'm not indifferent, Clyde. I was ill-tempered when I said that.'

Mr Norman rose from his three-legged stool, tears in his eyes. 'I am happy you said that. Give me your hand.'

'Gladly.' They shook hands gravely, too moved to speak, as the wardrobe toppled over and landed with a crash at their feet. Through the shattered upper panels of the door they could see the gleaming vandalous faces of the gendarmes, outlined by shreds of green baize.

'To the barricade!' shouted Glenellen, throwing the stool through the gap in the door. But the shrine was occupied by the blue-uniformed men at whose loud centre Glenellen still struggled, while the recumbent Augusta shrieked like a tropical bird and Mr Norman, wringing his hands, was led away.

Regina returned to Paris on a bitter and lugubrious February day when all alliances seemed purposeless, all motives suspect and the immediate prospect of a war was not only possible but, in the general apocalyptic mood which prevailed, desirable: a fitting climax to the greyness, a last proof of Lucifer's victory so many millennia before in that not so dubious battle on the plains of heaven.

They met in her rooms at the Ida, to Philip's amusement, aware as he was that in the corresponding suite on the floor above Anna Morris occasionally received him, though as a rule they met at his hotel, now nearly empty, the visitors from the West gone back to school, to jobs, to mother and to real life.

As they talked, he could hear the faraway sound of the wind as it assaulted the mansard roof of the hotel.

'Did you get my letter?' she asked.

'No, did you write?'

'Twice . . . to American Express.'

'I never go there. I told you . . .'

'I forgot. I said nothing in particular. Like a good politician I never commit myself on paper!'

'How is your husband?'

'Very well . . .' She laughed. 'I was almost going to say "thank you"! I wonder why we are so formal?'

'Well, we've been separated by quite a few months . . . nearly a year of them.'

'The year is almost over, Philip.'

'Time to go home.'

'To what?'

'I wish I knew. To whatever I was before, I suppose.'

'You feel unchanged?'

'I'm afraid so.'

'You've had no revelation after all?'

'No, and now that the year is gone I see how foolish it was of me to have ever thought I could so arbitrarily resolve all doubts and make a final choice, just like that.'

'That's one discovery, at least.'

'Perhaps, but not much of one. I find it demoralizing to realize that there is no such thing as future time, only a long present . . . that all acts are essentially meaningless, except of course to one's self . . .'

The dialogue proceeded, as it always did between them: from the general to the particular, from the sensibility to the reason and back again. Philip, unknowing, went further in it than he ever had before. If he had gained little in this precious year, he had lost a great deal. What had been only a vague awareness of the long present had at last become a conviction and he was no longer alarmed by this knowledge since it was, finally, the point from which the temporary arrangement of matter that was himself surveyed the material world, without guilt or shame, afraid of death but resolutely concerned with life, preferring harmony to vision.

Snow began to fall. The sky turned black before the sun had set, and the river stopped. Frozen birds fell in the ice streets and shattered like porcelain figurines on the sidewalks. A number of people died of exposure that evening, as they always did when the winter was hard, while one of the energetic philosophers of the day published a novel, produced a play and composed a dozen pamphlets suggesting that although there was no God, no governing spirit, one should still act and, in the act, forget that all was meaningless: constructing not a philosophic system, as the philosopher had hoped, but reporting merely what the majority of the more thoughtful people of the day felt, paradoxically, offering himself as a figure to be believed in and, to an extent, as paradoxically, some did believe, rendering black February less a burden.

'I shall be here for a few months,' said Regina, as the dialogue came to its usual indecisive end.

'Until the first of May?' asked Philip, smiling.

Then, carefully, soberly, they duplicated their former passion and both found it wanting, though Philip as always was attracted to her, against the advice of his reason, and she in her turn, though loving, seemed concerned with something else, something unspoken and as yet undeclared.

The moment ended when a windowpane broke and the room was filled with an ice-cold wind on which, like the white petals of frozen flowers, snowflakes whirled for one brilliant moment; then the wind upset the lamp and the room went dark as the light bulb smashed and the lovers fled.

Jim found his way with some difficulty down the dark hall to his own room where, in the circle of red and blue light from a single paper lantern, his bed was illuminated, like an altar awaiting sacrifice, in this case his own body, pale and lean as, quite naked yet not shivering, not noticing the cold, he did what he had been forbidden to do: he took the long wooden pipe out of its hiding place in the medieval chest and with steady hand lit the blue flame of the burner. There was only one pellet left, he remembered ... almost the only thing he could re- member, he thought, suddenly happy at the familiar odour, redolent of past pleasures, the smoke rising in a pale slender spiral from the blue flame to the faraway ceiling, dark and menacing, where the ghosts and villains and all the unbeloved outrages awaited the extinguishing of the blue flame ... when he would float away from its comforting light to them, to the shadows above, to the nightmare world of the ceiling across which he must journey, occasionally floating, sometimes running, other times struggling to move even a hand, a finger, as the dreary shadows held him tight above the room, embraced his body with a loving greed, draining it of will and memory, even of pleasure, so that when he was released he fell like the discarded husk of a locust from the dark ceiling to the bed below, and what was left of him could hear the dry crackling of the rest, like brown paper rustling in a Virginia kitchen: it was June again and like a faded, cracked movie, sometimes too fast, sometimes too slow, he saw himself speak to this person, speak to that person, saw lips move in question and response ... a silent movie, for the dialogue did not matter since he knew the order of the mass already; and though he might try feebly to exert his will and change the course of ancient events he could never intrude upon that flickering cinematic world which viciously unreeled, over and over again, leading him each time to the same delight and to the same despair as it had done since the first day when there were indeed voices and the trees were green, not grey and white, and he'd been out on location and had accompanied that slim hard figure with its helmet of short wiry curls down to the edge of a river, the camera of memory taking it all in, mercilessly, blackmailing him for life with that one image to which, at last, he came, dry tears in burning eyes, as he saw the bodies touch by firelight and then, with a sense of loss, he moved on in time through a world of faceless men, until the act of violence turned everything about, and he saw with terror that each of the faceless men had now assumed identity, the egg-smooth whiteness of their featureless faces covered with masks: some were vultures, others sheep, others eagles; some were lions, and several apes, while one of them with the monstrous face of a toad nuzzled him until he felt a scream rise like a tide from his groin to his throat, only to die on his lips when he saw himself, as he always did, with terror and eternal astonishment, reflected in the gelatinous globule of the toad's eye, and his own face was as smooth, as white as the shell of an egg: the worst was over then. The film ran backwards at great speed and he blinked his closed eyes, growing dizzy in the flickering light.

'Do you think he'll remember he asked us to come by?' asked Stephen.

'I don't know. He seemed all right to me.' They knocked at the door again. He heard them knocking but he could not speak or move. The good part was next, he remembered.

Stephen opened the door and, followed by Bill, entered the bedroom. The flame still flickered in the rusty burner and by its blue light Jim's body looked as if it had been rolled from some deep sea's bottom to a reef; Stephen almost expected to find seaweed in his hair and the mark of shells upon his skin.

'Is he dead?' whispered Bill.

Dead, dead, dead: what an ugly word it was, thought Jim, contented in his paralysis. Yes, he wanted to say, I am dead. Then, among the soft clouds of his other dreaming, he wondered: am I dead? is this what it is after all? an old movie winding forwards and backwards forever . . . 'I am not dead!' he shouted; but he had no voice. The now caressing clouds held him in their arms and stopped his voice: no sound in a vacuum.

'I don't think so,' said Stephen, and he put his hand on Jim's breast and felt through warm skin the slow thud of the heart. 'No, he's on the stuff again.'

'Didn't the doctor say it would kill him?'

'Sooner or later.'

Not dead, he thought, delightedly. That was a relief, and he viewed the clouds above him spitefully, contemptuously. They were his still; he was not theirs. Lovely Stephen, pretty Stephen, come lie with me.

'I'd better cover him up,' said Stephen. 'He'll freeze to death.'

'He looks all right,' said Bill, as they pulled the blanket over him.

'You'd think he would look worse, considering what he's done to himself,' said Stephen, turning off the blue flame, changing the character of the room, banishing much of the horror as warm red lanternlight replaced blue.

He remembered, as they talked, that he had asked them to come see him that evening but somehow time had got muddled and he now had a distinct recollection of having seen them earlier, that the evening in question had come and gone some weeks (months?) ago and that they had had a pleasant time and the conversation, not to say the circumstances, had been very different from this. He tried to offer them a drink but he was facing in the opposite direction, he discovered sadly, and it would never do to attempt communication with his back to them and all those shadows between. He was grateful for the red light as opposed to the blue: it made all the difference in the world. He felt now as though he was at the warm secret centre of an odourless velvet-leaved rose through whose petals sunlight came, ruddy, diffused, penetrating his blindness like an intimation, a prescience of light to a new-formed eyeless embryo still safe at home.

'Doesn't look like the sanitarium did him much good,' said Stephen.

'Poor kid,' said Bill. 'He was like a ghost this afternoon.'

'No memory. You remember he couldn't think of our names? And he talked so slow, as though he'd forgotten how to talk.'

No memory! At the heart of the rose he chuckled silently, stirred even, like an uneasy foetus anticipating birth. Was it not enough that he *knew*? Was it necessary for him to *remember* as well?

'I don't think those shock treatments do any damn good. You remember . . .'

'That guy in the Army, in the hospital? Shocked his mind clear out of him . . . poor bastard.'

'Do you think he'll die?'

'Who, Jim? I don't know.'

'The doctors all say that if you keep on after a certain point you never get off the stuff, you just dissolve.'

The red stuff of the rose melted about him and he was alone in the dark again, the voices of the two Southern boys, gentle and soft, far below him, as he floated upon a dark tide which transported him quickly away from the viscous carmine puddle where the rose had been. His arms and legs were without sensation; he wondered if they were still attached, or was it only a memory? an odd fantasy that in some other existence he had been a creature with two legs, two arms. Where was he going? he wondered lazily, as layer after layer of darkness opened to receive him.

'Seems funny for a boy like him to have ended up like this,' said Bill, looking at one of the Balzac volumes on the table: '*Louis Lambert.*' He read the title aloud, automatically.

'I know,' said Stephen, considering the melodramatic fate which had so logically, if not tragically, befallen Jim. 'Well, we'd better leave him a note to say we're going back to the States.'

'If he'll remember our names when he sees it.'

'If he can read.' Stephen wrote the note carefully, explaining that they had come, as invited, but that since they had found him asleep they had gone away without disturbing him. And so thia was good-bye, they were going back home to school. 'If you should ever be in Spartanburg, S.C.,' he wrote in big firm letters, 'look us up anytime. Yours truly, Steve and Bill . . .' Followed by their addresses.

'I don't guess there's anything more,' said Bill, looking down at the face of the dreamer. 'Looks like a baby, doesn't he?'

'Well, he's not much older than us.'

'But he's taken it every way, one time or another.'

He was not aware when they left. He had long since ceased even to hear their voices. He was only interested now in trying to recall who and what he was and why, disembodied, he should be caught in all this darkness, with no physical sensation except that of motion . . . forward, outward, away from the tiny red light below.

Then he understood what was happening and he was terrified, preferring any pain, any unpleasurable sensation or anguish, to dissolution, to the enfolding darkness. He tried to speak, to move, to turn back, not wanting to die. He stared fixedly at the red point in space until, slowly, it drew him back to it, grew larger and larger until the leaves of the rose held him once more safe inside. He had a moment of peace, of satisfaction, before the old movie began to unwind once more; and it was June again and his father and mother moved jerkily as the faded strip of memory displayed its images, the light behind as full and as constant as the images themselves were cracked and dim with use.

'We *must* have her, Zoe.'

'But, Julia, she won't fit.'

'You'll have to *make* her fit. You have been at her house twice this year and she's not been to yours *once*.'

'But she can't see . . . she can't hear.'

'She knows, however, that she *is* where she is.'

'Would the Murats come if I had her?'

'The Duchesse always attracts the Bonapartists, you know that.'

'All right, darling, put her name down.' Lady Julia Keen wrote Lyon et Grénoble in her tiny but vigorous hand while her employer, Zoe Helotius, occasionally patted the quart of dry mud which made her face look like a mummy in danger of unravelling. The bed where she lay was shaped like a ship, with an enormous gold Eros for a prow. The remains of Zoe's breakfast (Holland rusk and weak tea) decorated the night table.

'Now, what about the Windsors?'

'Well, what about them, Julia?'

'Will they be in Paris in time for the party, and will they come?'

'They will not be here in time,' said Zoe evenly, like a chief of government who has just lost an important minister in a cabinet crisis.

'I . . . I'm terribly sorry, Zoe.'

'That's all right, Julia. These things must be faced squarely. It never does to cry over spilled figs.' (In moments of crisis she tended unconsciously to relate all things to the source of her wealth, the rock on which her fortress stood.)

'It seems like only yesterday . . .'

'Never look back, Julia. It doesn't pay. Go on, go on: that's my motto. If one were to stop each time fate dealt one an unkind blow one would remain stationary. We will invite . . .'

'*Him?*'

'Yes, Julia.' For a moment the mummy seemed almost to smile with triumph.

'What a thrill! And her?'

'She will come too.'

'But how . . . I mean, well, when?'

'A week ago. It was all arranged. I was saving it as a little surprise for you.'

'And what a surprise! The biggest, absolutely the biggest of all.'

'I know.' The earlier dereliction was forgotten.

'I could not be more thrilled,' said Lady Julia, writing two names under Lyon et Grénoble.

'Back to work,' said Zoe, holding her arms up like a mantis praying, so that the veins in the backs of her capable hands would grow smooth.

'Regina Durham?'

'By all means,' said Zoe. 'Is the husband here?'

'Not until May.'

'Too bad. The politicians one wants always come if Rex Durham is about.'

'Now darling, what shall we do about the young man?'

'What young man?'

'Mrs Durham's.'

'Oh I remember. He's with the Embassy.'

'No. He doesn't work. He was in Capri . . .'

'I know, Julia. I *do* remember things, you know. There are times when you treat me like an utter fool.'

'Zoe!'

'Yes, by all means have him.'

'But there is a complication.'

'I should have known, Julia, from your tone, that you were planning a complication for me. What is it this time?'

'Anna Morris.'

'What about her?'

'And Philip Warren.'

'Who is he?'

'I thought you said you remembered.'

'You mean Regina's friend?'

'I do indeed.'

'And he is Anna Morris's lover now?'

'He is indeed . . . and she is coming to the party too.'

'Now that's very interesting,' said Zoe, waving her arms like a man signalling a ship with flags, exercising the wrinkled wattles of flesh which hung from her sturdy bones, attesting to that age which her face, thanks to certain miracles of quasi-medical science, did not reveal at all. 'You think there might be a scene, Julia.'

'I doubt it.'

'Then we are safe if we have all three.'

'I should think so. I felt you should know, however.'

'But, of course. Now that you mention it, I have heard talk. I must say, he's done well for himself. Is he a gigolo?'

'I don't believe so. He has money.'

'I wonder what his charm is?'

'He's quite good-looking, and young.'

'That combination is easily come by if one has money, if one is Regina Durham.'

'And then I've heard . . .' And Lady Julia lowered her voice although they were alone and, flushing slightly, she whispered something into Zoe's ear. The only word an eavesdropper might have overheard was 'butterfly'. The ladies laughed heartily or, rather, Lady Julia did for because of the mud Zoe could only snort, blowing a cloud of fine dust the length of the bed. Then the telephone, hidden in Madame de Maintenon's chamber pot, rang. Lady Julia answered it. Her eyes grew round with delight and her voice became warm and personal; then she put her hand over the mouthpiece and hissed, 'It's *her*, Zoe . . . the Duchess!'

'My God!' Zoe sat up abruptly and the mud cracked and crumbled about her ravaged shoulders as she seized the telephone.

For three days during mid-April there were violent storms. But when at last the sun shone winter was gone and Philip began to contemplate departure as he read the various letters from home which suggested, mildly yet with an under-lying urgency, that he return to the valley where his life was to be.

'What did you do all winter?' asked Sophia curiously, as they drank coffee on the rue de Rivoli, a glimpse of new green in the Tuileries Gardens across the street, its fence of gold-tipped spears bright in the sun.

'I wonder that myself,' he said. 'When you ask me like that, abruptly, I can't think of a thing. I have an image of myself reading English novels in the bathtub.'

'That's something,' she smiled.

'I have some recollection of having kept a diary.'

'Now that's very interesting . . . Why only a recollection, though?'

'Because I've kept journals off and on all my life, but I continually lose them and I've never written in one more than three days consecutively.'

'What did you write in this one?'

'What would I have written, is more likely. Because the more I think of it the less sure I am that I *did* keep a journal during the winter . . . but if I had I would probably have done what I've always done: commented on whatever I happened to be reading, what conversations I had overheard, what profundities occurred to me while crossing the Place de la Concorde, dodging automobiles, late to an appointment. I've been late recently, to almost everything.'

'Sounds as if you were at least having a social success.'

'I suppose I intended it to sound like that; actually I've seen very few people . . . mostly Americans, at that.'

'Like Mrs Durham?'

'How did you know?'

'I've been here a few days,' said Sophia, with as much malice as her ordinarily serene detachment would allow.

'I've seen a little of her . . . these last few weeks.'

'Poor Regina,' said Sophia.

'Why poor?'

'Her husband is such an oaf.'

'At least he leaves her alone.'

'Perhaps,' said Sophia mysteriously.

But Philip refused to challenge her and they spoke no more of Regina, which did not displease Sophia who was now eager to discuss the character of Anna Morris.

'I like her very much,' said Philip, wondering what had so abruptly caused the usually impersonal Sophia to confront the character of other women with that same intensity which she ordinarily reserved exclusively for facts, for generalities, for the contemplation of those syllogisms which gave her such pleasure.

'I have known her such a long time,' said Sophia, 'such a very long time that I suppose I am too close to her to know what I think.'

'Yet,' said Philip to himself.

'Yet,' said Sophia, unconscious for once of the effect she was having, 'I can't help but feel that she has been somewhat dishonest emotionally.'

'Dishonest?'

'I think that's the word. It's not that one objects to her having affairs. Most women in her position do these days. Rather it's her prodigality. I mean, each time she goes to bed with a man it can't be as earth-shaking, as unique an experience as she maintains it is. Oh, there've been so many! Each time you would think that at last she had found the half for which she had been searching all her life; then, a month later, there's someone else.'

'You make her sound more frivolous than she is.'

'Deluded. No human being could survive that intensity which she claims she experiences each time.'

'She is serious,' said Philip.

'I'm quite sure she is . . . resolutely so. I question only her sincerity . . . or her reason.'

'Not everyone is alike. Perhaps she's exactly the way she seems. Some people are.'

'I remember she loved a general once, a young man, and she followed him about everywhere . . . it was a great scandal.'

'How did it end?'

'The way it always does.'

'And how is that?'

'He lost interest. The man always does. Men aren't constructed for such intensity, simulated or not. Poor Anna . . . she is always deserted in the end.'

'Which proves her sincerity.'

'Or bad judgement.' Then, having said what she had wanted to say, realizing instinctively that she had perhaps gone too far, she spoke of other things, amiably, recalled mutual acquaintances, asked even about Charles de Cluny, as though they had, at one time, all three, been the best of friends.

He told her that he planned to go back in the spring.

'Will you be sorry to leave?' she asked.

'No, I don't think so.'

'But you *have* enjoyed it?'

'Oh very much . . . even if I can't remember what I've done.'

'You'll remember later.'

'I often do.'

'That's right. But a bad habit: not to appreciate the moment except in recollection.'

'I'm not so sure.'

'But I am, for me at least. Do you look forward to going back home?'

'I think so. I don't really know. I have a terrible feeling that nothing matters, that it will make very little difference whether I spend the rest of my life in Egypt poking about in the dirt or whether I have a political career in New York.'

'It seems very different to me.'

'Not when I think of death . . . not when I think there is no reason to be alive . . . but I *am* alive, of course, and don't want to die.'

'Afraid of hell?'

'No.'

'Of pain?'

'Not very.'

'Of what?'

'Of *nothing*. Isn't that enough to fear?'

'One could learn to prefer it,' she said. He laughed at her until he saw that she was serious; he tried then, out of politeness, to present an argument that would support her curious nonsensical announcement, discussing gravely with her the inadequacies of the alien garment of the flesh which they both wore with such distinction, each aware of that day when awareness would be lost in the whole reality: the flesh gone and the breath properly contained in the larger breathing of the world.

He told her about the International Typewriter Company which maintained an enormous factory near his home town of Hudson. The paternalism of this institution (so low has the father fallen in American life that his social function, when recognized at all, is identified with tyranny) has assumed significant proportions. Total security is offered in exchange for total resignation to the order. Wages are high. Company-owned houses, all alike, are sold to workers on easy terms. No union is allowed even to contribute to the delicious harmony which prevails between pater and his children and, when a child wishes to remain home a day to endure or to feign an illness, a registered nurse is sent him post-haste, by broomstick, by magic carpet, to make sure that he is really ill and not playing hooky, as the children of even the very best, the most indulgent fathers will do on occasion. In every lavatory of the new glass-and-chrome factory, in every hall, in every office, there is a placard which enjoins each boy and girl to REMEMBER, signed J. Branson Etting, their father, himself the eldest son of the grandfather of them all: the noiseless International Typewriter. 'Now, more than ever,' quoted Philip to himself, as he discussed the penultimate phase of that eccentric yet occasionally colourful civilization into which he had been born, so near the end . . . yet so near the beginning, he suddenly thought, with some surprise, of still another, of something else again, as yet unknown: I am the alpha and the omega, the first and the last, the beginning and the end. But which? Or did it matter?

Sophia thought not.

The hour of the equinox was celebrated in such a way that what Philip had suspected might be true was proved true, that repetition for the first time in his life became confirmation rather than the familiar boredom which he had inevitably experienced with everyone and everything, more soon than late. Could it be that his body was in some way different from all the others he had known? that this head which he now held cupped in one hand was really so strange: a round globe of bone wreathed in dark hair and containing a mystery which he did not know, would never know . . . thus, through ignorance, was he held by an attraction far more intense than the usual centre, the dark groin where the other mystery resided, the one he had always known, the centre from which he had at last successfully strayed to the true centre, to that unseen mythical altar before which only kings are anointed, adjured and crowned.

'Nor am I jealous,' said Anna suddenly.

'Jealous?' They had been silent for some minutes as their racing hearts quieted in unison and their breathing grew more easy, less quick and harsh. 'I don't know what you mean.'

'Oh, but you do.' She sat up on one elbow, the pale light of early spring across their bodies, across the grey-cold, winter-old city and its gardens and the fields far, far beyond the gates of St Denis. Would there be lilacs soon? he wondered touching her breast carefully, like an unobserved boy in a museum caressing the stone fantasy, the dream lover of a Greek two thousand years dead, the marble evocation of his pain, serene and unbemused among strangers in a distant city, fondled by a boy.

'You mean about Regina?' he asked, falling back upon the crumpled pillows, his arms crossed upon his chest like a Crusader on his bier.

'About Regina. You knew her first.'

'But not as well.'

'She's doing everything she can, you know.'

'Everything?'

'To win you.'

'But why?'

'Don't you know yet?'

'I'm afraid not. I've often thought about it, of course . . . why should she be so interested in me?'

'Because she loves you.'

'Now you're making fun of me. I'm not that vain. Women like that never fall in love, or if they do they would love a completely different sort of man . . . a Rex Durham.'

'And me? What sort of man would I love?'

'I wonder.'

'You?'

'Yes, I think so. For a while.'

She looked away and when she answered she spoke to the pale daffodil light on the wall. 'I never end it,' she said softly. 'I am always there when the other leaves . . . when you go back next month, to your real life . . .'

'This is it, right now.'

'You've made me talk of the future,' she laughed. 'What a bad influence you are! I don't believe in the future. There's no such thing.'

'But there is.'

'There is change in the present and when you leave, the present will change for us both.'

'I could stay.'

'No, you couldn't.'

'I suppose not.'

'But I am vain enough to like hearing you say it.'

'Why can't I see you in America?'

'Because . . . oh, so many reasons. Perhaps you won't want to. Perhaps *I* won't want to. And then, I won't be coming back for some time.'

Philip sighed and wondered what to say, wondered what he should feel . . . it would be nice, he thought, to be able to have definite responses to everything, to know always not only what one should feel but, more important, what one did feel.

'On the other hand,' said Anna sharply, suddenly out of character, 'you will be seeing a great deal of Regina when you go home.'

'I suppose so,' said Philip, almost resenting this display of less than godlike emotion. He had created her, after all, he suddenly realized with some wonder. The body he held in his arms, the perfect response to all his needs on every level, had not existed except in his own imagining. She was not real and he knew it now. The perfect love had been himself, loving himself; the arms of a stranger whom he had never known had held him while his own reflection had come between their two bodies, like a silver mirror or like an old curse: you will never know any other, never walk through the reflecting glass to the true world, to the one outside. Who was she then? he wondered, suddenly frightened at having revealed so much to a stranger: was she a spy? a blackmailer? some sort of saint? or, worse yet, a patient fool who mocked him from behind the smooth implacable glass which separated them. Where am I? He touched the iron bedstead . . . was it iron? Who am I?

'Philip.'

'Yes.'

'What do you want?'

What do I want? 'Knowledge.'

'Of what?'

'Of everything, of someone else, of you.'

'But you know me.'

'Never. You are I.'

She smiled. 'Haven't you always known that?'

'No, no, no.'

'Isn't that what you wanted?'

'To know myself?'

'To know yourself and through yourself to know me?'

'Or the other way around.'

'It is the same.'

'But it shouldn't be.' Not even the iron of the bed was real. 'I want something more than that, more than myself.'

'There's nothing more, Philip. There's only you.'

'No one else?'

'Only when the illusion becomes so intense that you forget yourself...'

'Like St Malo?'

'Like that... and, then, I am dreaming, too, at the same time. You are I... I made it all.'

'But not the same thing.'

'Never the same.'

'That could be unbearable.'

'It could, but it won't be for you, as long as you imagine me.'

'Or Regina?'

The iron was cold and smooth beneath his hand; it chilled his fingers at the same time the warmth of his flesh made the iron less cold. Then the room grew warm with light and through the window he saw the sun.

CHAPTER THIRTEEN

During April the letters began. At first they were wistful; by the end of May, however, they had grown urgent and he knew that the time had come for him to make his choice to return, if he could, to the summer valley and the grey river of home.

Zoe Helotius who had no secrets (other than the central one concerning her obscure birth) had, nevertheless, one peculiarity which none of her intimates suspected, not even Lady Julia. Like most people with a private fancy, a secret life, she was enormously cunning and resourceful and consequently no one was aware that she talked to herself. Most people on occasion will think aloud but Zoe differed from the majority in that she was quite aware that she was talking to herself and since she was essentially a conventional woman, she was ashamed of her habit; even so, whenever she was alone she would address herself, in baby talk, as 'Tiny Tot', an adorable slyboots of a child who was often naughty but always forgiven and indulged. On those busy days when social engagements followed one another too closely, Zoe would grow nervous and irritable, like an addict deprived of drugs, craving desperately the company of Tiny Tot to whom she could confide her latest plan or some bit of gossip, with whom she could share her brilliant triumphs and her glum defeats. When she could bear this separation no longer, she would abruptly leave even the most celebrated of her guests and hurry to the nearest bathroom where, seated on a commode or on the edge of a bathtub, she would commune with Tiny Tot, apologizing abjectly for not having come sooner, for having neglected her darling duck, her fig, her *choux fleur*, her only love.

Needless to say the party for the birthday of the British King (which is celebrated in June) occupied Zoe's every moment for several weeks, enraging the spoiled Tiny Tot who exacted, on the rare occasions when she and Zoe now met, elaborate apologies for her creator's dereliction. On the afternoon of the party, Zoe suddenly broke off a spirited debate with her caterers and hurried to the ladies' retiring room of the Bain de Ligny. Here, alone at last, in front of a Venetian mirror, she crooned to her love, her fig.

'I've been a brute . . . I know, I know . . . a beast . . . you must forgive . . . that's a darling, a true lamb . . . I couldn't endure it another minute . . . five days away from you, I know. Can you ever forgive me? Please . . . please.' And she was forgiven at last, as she always was. Then, briskly, she discussed the arrangements for the fête.

'It will be better than the Eiffel Tower . . . I feel it, I do, Tiny Tot . . . you'll be so proud; just wait and see, my darling. It will be Mummy's best, her very best. It took courage not to rent the Tower this year but nothing lost is nothing gained as they say. It will be an evening like no other! I have done the whole boat like a Byzantine pavilion, like a Venetian palace . . . and there'll be gondolas in the pool and banks of flowers; then, at midnight . . . yes, you've guessed it, darling, your favourites: fireworks! and a portrait of *him* in rockets as the orchestra plays

"God Save the King." There'll never be another party like this in our time . . . my masterpiece: and everyone is coming. Yes, darling, yes, yes! Yes! and she will come, too . . . yes, yes and even her! Imagine! A triumph . . . everyone! And when it's over what stories I shall have to tell my darling Tiny Tot, my own dear . . .' And at this point Zoe Helotius' voice became low and guttural as she murmured endearments in her native tongue, a language which she'd not spoken in thirty years, except in private to Tiny Tot.

Lady Julia put her head in the door of the ladies' room, which had been decorated to resemble an Ottoman hare. 'Zoe, the conductor wants to go over the music with you . . . and also the costumes for the musicians . . . they never arrived.'

'One minute more, Julia, and I'll be done.' She pretended to examine an eyebrow as Lady Julia withdrew: the only person in the world who had even the slightest intimation of Tiny Tot's existence. Zoe was aware of her secretary's suspicions and she often trembled at the effect an exposure might have on her darling who was now listening raptly as she completed the list of those who were to come that evening, the important dozen guests . . . the less important five hundred who were to be scenery, props, supernumeraries.

'Oh, and there may be trouble . . . yes, a marvellous scene, perhaps. Regina Durham – I've told you about her, haven't I? – is coming and her ex-young man who is now Anna Morris's young man, but Anna's husband will be here, too. I hope I shall have time to watch them. Julia will know, in any case, and when she tells me I'll tell you *all*, word for word, my darling, the moment I know. I've already made up my mind that at twelve-thirty, after the fireworks, I will sneak in here for a quick, comfy chat . . . I know how restless you get when there's a party. Now be a lamb while I talk to the musicians, and remember that you are my own love, no matter what anybody says.'

The Bain de Ligny is an enormous barge on the Seine, moored to a quai on the left bank. Inside the barge is a swimming pool of filtered river water with a narrow sun deck on four sides, two storeys of cubicles, a restaurant and a bar. During the summer the Bain de Ligny is very popular with city-bound Parisians and tourists who swim there by the hundreds during the day; at night it is deserted. But not this night, for Zoe had indeed transformed it into a new Venice, a new Byzantium, a new Babylon with glowing lanterns everywhere and burning torches held by half-nude Algerian boys while garlands of flowers festooned *papier-mâché* arches supported by delicate fluted columns of gold-encrusted plaster. In the pool (illuminated from beneath by jade-green lights) gondolas plied languidly back and forth, to the music of a symphony orchestra whose members were dressed, for some curious reason, in early dynastic Egyptian costumes.

At sundown the guests began to arrive. The costumes were exotic though not always Venetian as the invitation had suggested. The moon was full at the black sky's centre and a warm wind made the torches gutter dramatically, a flickering light upon bright jewels and festive eyes.

Philip arrived alone, in Venetian costume, wearing a mask like the other guests. His identity, however, was quickly checked by two non-Venetian thugs who examined his invitation carefully. Then he was allowed to present himself to Lady Julia who stood just inside the gate, by the pool; she greeted him warmly. 'How marvellous you look, Mr Warren! I'm sure you must've been an Italian in another life.'

'You never can tell,' said Philip inadequately, but Lady Julia, a column of scarlet satin, was gone: a pillar of fire by night, thought Philip, moving towards de Cluny who stood near the bar, talking to a massive lady.

'Charles!'

'How did you recognize me? I thought I was invisible.' The heavy lady giggled and retired. The orchestra began the 'Nutcracker Suite.'

'A sixth sense,' said Philip, glancing at the other's spidery legs which black tights did not flatter.

'Lovely party.'

'Very.'

'Lady Julia just told me that she sent to the south of France for a thousand fireflies but they arrived dead ...'

'It might have been too much.'

'Perhaps ... the last impiety: "When the flower of pride has blossomed, death is the fruit that ripens, and all the harvest reaped is tears" ... as the Greeks would say.'

'A grim message for such an occasion.' Then Philip saw Regina; she was seated alone in a gondola which was moving towards them; by torchlight her black gown glowed with tiny pearls and on her head diamonds flashed messages of light in some exotic code.

'Who is that?' asked de Cluny, impressed.

'A friend of mine,' said Philip, excusing himself. Proudly he helped her from the gondola.

'I saw you,' she smiled. 'From the other side.' Beneath her black mask, she smiled.

'Well met by moonlight,' said Philip; and they sat down on a white wrought-iron bench beneath an arch of pink camellias and new ivy.

'What a job she's done,' said Philip conventionally.

'I wonder if the orchestra intends to play *all* the "Nutcracker Suite"?'

Two unidentified couples paid brief homage to Regina. At last alone, Regina said, 'I've seen so little of you these past few weeks. Have you been busy?'

'Oh yes,' he lied. 'I've been seeing all the sights of the city ... places I hadn't bothered to visit before.'

'Are you leaving, Philip?'

He nodded. 'Next week.'

'Then the year is finally over.'

'It seems like only a month ago that I came to Rome, not a year.'

'Are you ready now?'

'For what?'

'Our plan ... I can go back when you do. Rex is expecting me next week.' Philip did not answer.

'It will be so easy, believe me ... and it will happen soon ... if only because I haven't the time Rex and I had when *we* started, years ago.'

'Tell me why you want all this.'

'Because I lost Rex,' she said the truth at last. 'Lost or shed him ... it's hard to say which. Now he lives one life and I lead another, an aimless one. He has no use for me any more: his career is made.'

For the first time Regina had touched him; he took her hand awkwardly and held it, not knowing what to say.

'You wonder perhaps why I don't have a career of my own ... I sometimes wonder that, too. It would make it so easy if I did, if I could be self-sufficient; but

I can't. I can only act through the man . . . I live only through him.' She smiled.
'Don't mistake me, Philip, it's not love I want . . .' And she lost him for good.

'I was the wrong choice,' he said gently. 'We want different things. I want a
private life, not your public one.' And he let go her hand.

'She did this, didn't she?'

'Who?'

'Anna.'

'I don't think so.'

'She did . . . she did,' said Regina, as though her own anger gave her pain, as
though she had, like some furious scorpion, turned on herself. 'Would you give
up the world for someone like her?'

'No,' said Philip coldly. 'I wouldn't. I'm not giving up any world, except
yours . . . one which I never had, in any case. She had nothing to do with it.' But
did she? He could not be sure.

'Don't listen to her, Philip. You'll find she's wrong . . . believe me you will. I
know. I've seen all this before.'

'You don't understand, Regina. You take so much for granted.'

'You'd better go to her then. I understand she's here tonight.'

'I suppose I should.' He got to his feet.

She caught at his sleeve. 'I didn't mean that, Philip. Please stay!' But he
pulled away from her and stepped out of the camellia-decorated alcove onto the
deck. Torchlight made her diamonds burn like a fire of ice. 'Philip!' But he was
gone, separated from her by a band of chattering ladies in harlequin masks.

'A triumph, Zoe! a triumph!' exclaimed Lady Julia.

'I know,' said Zoe, gentle with pride.

'They all came.'

'Are you surprised?'

'No . . . yet I had hardly dared to dream . . .'

'Even our wildest dreams become, on rare occasions, reality,' said Zoe who
was saving this particular line for Tiny Tot but saw no harm in rehearsing it now
with Julia.

'I know . . . I know. Oh, darling, who are those two young men over there?
sitting next to the bar . . . the ones who are wearing old clothes.'

'They are Americans, Julia. Anne brought them. They are writers.'

'Oh . . . how odd they look.'

'We live in a changing world, Julia.' On this philosophic note, the ladies
parted.

The Duchesse de Lyon et Grénoble rode in a gondola, back and forth across
the pool; she was dressed in the wedding gown of the first Duchesse of her name,
an intricate tent of yellowed satin and Brussels lace. Tonight she was enjoying
herself immensely, humming toneless arias from forgotten operas, not always
sure precisely where she was but pleased at being in motion, on water, with a
gondolier to whom she occasionally gave irrelevant commands that he ignored
as he poled their frail bark across the chartreuse pool which reflected, like fire in
an opal, the light of torches, the gleam of rainbow lanterns.

Standing at one end of the dance floor, watching the couples waltz, de Cluny
observed that he seldom minded those tyrants who treated their subjects as
though they were animals since, after all, men *are* animals but he did object to

those new tyrants who treated their subjects like machines, which they were not: the one sin against the Holy Ghost. Philip agreed; then, catching sight of a Tintoretto girl, he deserted de Cluny and danced until the disagreeable scene with Regina had been forgotten, and the girl was claimed by a bearded Moor.

Philip wandered up to the second storey, to a long balcony overlooking the pool, one which had been transformed into an avenue of laurel and adorned with Renaissance interpretations of classic deities, white upon the green which skilfully hid dressing-room doors. At the end of the avenue a figure in grey, a woman, stopped him and said. 'Good evening, Philip.'

It took him a moment to guess who she was for the light was green and dim and, too, he had not expected to find Sophia here.

'I couldn't resist it,' she said, as though apologizing.

'Nor I,' said Philip. 'How have you been?'

Slowly they walked the length of the avenue and then, as slowly, they walked back to the spot where they had met. 'Do you look forward to leaving?' she asked.

'Very much . . . I was getting to the point where I could absorb nothing new here. And then I'm a little homesick, too. There is a lot to be said for living in a country where the people speak your language.'

'I suppose there is.' Sophia paused before a broken Hermes. 'What will you do back home?'

'Practice law . . . in the town where I was born.'

'A quiet life?'

'Who can tell? Perhaps. I don't think of the future any more. Everything is finally here, in the present.'

'I believe that, too. Will you go into politics, do you think?'

'I may,' said Philip, surprising himself a little. 'I think I might like it . . . but who can tell?'

'Who can tell?' sang an American night-club singer, engaged for this one song: 'Who can tell that I'm in hell and not so well and not so swell for the wonder of you and me, the blunder of you and me, the wonder of you you you.'

'Do you know?' she asked suddenly.

'I think so.'

'Is it clear at last?'

'Very nearly.'

'And you? Are you certain?'

'Yes, I know it now.'

'In terms of what?'

'Of people . . .'

'Regina!'

'Not Regina. I never took her seriously.'

'But you take the world seriously.'

'There is nothing else.'

'The idea, each time . . .'

'That, too, but in proportion.'

'Earth smothers fire.'

'Fire comes from earth.'

'Don't!' she said abruptly. 'Don't listen to Regina. The other is more important.'

'I know what I need. No one loses what he needs.'

'But men do.'

'And your way is wrong, too . . . for me, if not for you. I can't tell. No one ever really knows about anyone else . . . and that's the point.'

'What point?'

'Discovery of someone else . . . recognition . . . all that.'

'But you just said no one ever knows another . . .'

'No one does . . . but each should try: and, finally, there is illusion which is so much better than knowledge, as any lover will tell you.'

'I don't understand.'

'I do but I can't explain. But suppose . . . suppose that I was born on an island without people: I should be an animal then, without a language, without words, without reason . . . an animal with a certain instinct for survival, and nothing more. So, in a real sense, I would never exist until I had been identified, until I saw myself as my own kind saw me. But if others should come to the island and give me words and attitudes, I should know who I was, not in ultimate terms of course but in terms of them, the only terms there are. Then, for better or worse. I should exist, created by them; and I would know that some would be attracted to me for my face or my manner and others would be hostile for the same reasons. Of course at the deep centre I should always be the island animal, volatile, instinctive, nameless, but I should have a new, more important life in terms of others . . . and, finally, at some point, if I'm in luck, I would find another like myself, a stranger for whom I would exist in a new and terrible way . . . the way she will exist for me and then, for moments at a time, we shall identify with one another, the true coupling of those island beasts . . . Do you see? do you see what I mean? do you see why I can never go back to the island?'

'You came from the world.'

'No, I am an islander, and I know where the island is even now . . . on dark days I see it clearly, inviting me to return, to lose the myriad faces and all hope of another, to live alone, like Prospero with his dreaming. I am tempted; but I shall not go there now.'

'Is the woman Anna?'

'Yes . . . no.'

'What sort of answer is that?'

'I'm not sure what I mean. She was the first I knew . . .'

'You are a fool!'

'Through her I knew what it could be like . . . isn't that enough?'

'It is all the same.'

'Except where before there was one there are now two; a difference.'

'She'll never leave her husband.'

'Why should she? I may never see her again after tonight.'

'I don't understand.'

'You? – not understand?'

'You tell me she had done a miracle, that you are finally touched, no longer tempted by withdrawal. And then you leave her, too.'

'Strange, isn't it?' said Philip joyously. 'She understands.'

'She always does.'

'Why do you sound so bitter?'

'Only sad . . .'

'Look! The fireworks!' Philip hurried to the end of the avenue of laurel and stood on the upper deck looking down at the pool where, from a raft, fireworks were being set off. The lanterns had been put out and it was dark, except for the light of occasional torches and the fountains of fire on the raft, the exploding constellations in the sky.

In her gondola, the Duchesse heard the noise of fireworks near by, caught a gleam of light through her grey-filmed eyes, and she asked querulously, 'What is it, boatman? don't mumble. What's happening?' But the gondolier, a Paris tough in an embroidered vest, knowing that she was blind and deaf, did not answer, his eyes on the spectacle.

Alone for a moment, Zoe whispered, 'Look at them, my darling . . . look! better than last year, better than the Eiffel Tower. And the rose, see? The rose all in rockets . . . for you, for my own darling Tiny Tot who loves roses and beauty . . . all for you, *mignonne*. Soon I'll leave all these people and we'll talk . . . and what news I have for you! You'll never guess. But here comes Julia.'

When Philip turned to speak to Sophia he found her gone. The avenue of laurel was deserted; one of the marble figures, which had been insecurely fixed to the wall, had fallen face forwards upon the deck, wreathed all in withered laurel, like funeral flowers. He moved down another balcony, one which was light and airy and hung with fern and roses. Here couples made love by the light of rockets. Suddenly, the King's portrait appeared in the sky and the orchestra played his anthem. For a moment there was silence. Then a gondola caught fire, to the delight of everyone, and by its ruddy glow Philip continued his progress down the balcony, watching lovers hide among the fern and rose.

She was waiting for him at the end of the balcony, in a grotto of shell and starfish, of seaweed and mother-of-pearl. She was unmasked, in white, with a summer flower in her gleaming hair. As he looked at her by firelight, saw her smile, the silver mirror dissolved before his eyes, dispelling its ungrieved ghosts like smoke upon the night, and beyond her in the dark, a promise at the present's furthest edge, a dreaming figure stirred and opened wide her golden eyes.

──── MESSIAH ────

For Tennessee Williams

I sometimes think the day will come when all the modern nations will adore a sort of American god, a god who will have been a man that lived on earth and about whom much will have been written in the popular press; and images of this god will be set up in the churches, not as the imagination of each painter may fancy him, not floating on a Veronica Kerchief, but established, fixed once and for all by photography. Yes, I foresee a photographed god, wearing spectacles.

On that day civilization will have reached its peak and there will be steam-propelled gondolas in Venice.

November, 1861: The Goncourt Journals

CHAPTER ONE

I

I envy those chroniclers who assert with reckless but sincere abandon: 'I was there. I saw it happen. It happened thus.' Now I too, in every sense, was there, yet I cannot trust myself to identify with any accuracy the various events of my own life, no matter how vividly they may seem to survive in recollection . . . if only because we are all, I think, betrayed by those eyes of memory which are as mutable and particular as the ones with which we regard the material world, the vision altering, as it so often does, from near in youth to far in age. And that I am by a devious and unexpected route arrived at a great old age is to me a source of some complacency, even on those bleak occasions when I find myself attending inadvertently the body's dissolution, a process as imperceptible yet sure as one of those faint, persistent winds which shift the dunes of sand in that desert of dry Libya which burns, white and desolate, beyond the mountains I see from the window of my room, a window facing, aptly enough, the west where all the kings lie buried in their pride.

I am also conscious that I lack the passion for the business of familiar life which is the central preoccupation of our race while, worse still, I have never acquired the habit of judging the usual deeds of men . . . two inconvenient characteristics which render me uncertain whenever I attempt to recall the past, confounding me sadly with the knowledge that my recollections are, after all, tentative and private and only true in part.

Then, finally, I have never found it easy to tell the truth, a temperamental infirmity due not so much to any wish or compulsion to distort reality that I might be reckoned virtuous but, rather, to a conception of the inconsequence of human activity which is ever in conflict with a profound love of those essential powers that result in human action, a paradox certainly, a dual vision which restrains me from easy judgements.

I am tempted to affirm that historic truth is quite impossible, although I am willing to accept the philosophic notion that it may exist abstractly, perfect and remote in the imagination. A windy attic filled with lovely objects has always been my personal image of those absolutes Aristotle conceived with such mellifluous optimism . . . and I have always liked the conceits of philosophy, the more extravagant the better. I am especially devoted to Parmenides, who was so strenuously obsessed with the idea of totality that he was capable, finally, of declaring that nothing ever changed, that what has been must still exist if it is yet remembered and named, a metaphysical conception which will, I suspect, be of some use to me as I journey in memory back to that original crisis from which I have for so long travelled and to which, despite the peril, I must return.

I do not say, then, that what I remember is all true but I can declare that what I shall recall is a relative truth as opposed to that monstrous testament the one-half world believes, entrenching deep thereby a mission at whose birth I officiated and one whose polished legend has since become the substantial illusion of a desperate race. That both mission and illusion were false, I alone can say with certainty, with sorrow, such being the unsuspected and terrible resolution of brave days. Only the crisis, which I shall record, was real.

I have said I am not given to making judgements. That is not precise. It is true that in most 'wicked' acts I have been able, with a little effort, to perceive the possibilities for good either in actual intention or (and to me more important) in uncalculated result; yet, ultimately, problems in ethics have never much concerned me; possibly because they have been the vital interest of so many others who, through custom, rule society, more agreeably than not. On that useful moral level I have been seldom, if ever, seriously engaged. But once on another, more arduous plane I was forced to make a choice, to judge, to act; and act I did in such a way that I am still startled by the implications of my choice, of my life's one judgement.

I chose the light in preference to the dreamless dark, destroying my own place in the world, and then, more painful still, I chose the light in preference to the twilight region of indeterminate visions and ambiguities, that realm where decision was impossible and where the potentialities of choice were endless and exquisite to contemplate. To desert these beloved ghosts and incalculable powers was the greater pain, but I have lived on, observing with ever-increasing intensity that blazing disc of fire which is the symbol as well as material source of the reality I have accepted entirely, despite the sure dominion in eternity of the dark other.

But now, as my private day begins to fade, as the wind in the desert gathers in intensity, smoothing out the patterns in the sand, I shall attempt to evoke the true image of one who assumed with plausibility in an age of science the long-discarded robes of prophecy, prevailing at last through ritual death and becoming, to those who see the universe in man, that solemn idea which is yet called by its resonant and antique name, god.

II

Stars fell to earth in a blaze of light, and where they fell, monsters were born, hideous and blind.

The first dozen years after the second of the modern wars were indeed 'a time of divination', as one religious writer unctuously described them. Not a day passed but that some omen or portent was remarked by an anxious race, suspecting war. At first, the newspapers delightedly reported these marvels, getting the details all wrong but communicating a sense of awfulness that was to increase as the years of peace uneasily lengthened until a frightened people demanded government action, the ultimate recourse in those innocent times.

Yet these omens, obsessive and ubiquitous as they were, would not yield their secret order to any known system. For instance, much of the luminous crockery which was seen in the sky was never entirely explained. And explanation, in the end, was all that the people required. It made no difference how extraordinary the explanation was, if only they could know *what* was happening: that the shining globes which raced in formation over Sioux Falls, South Dakota, were mere residents of the Andromeda Galaxy, at home in space, omnipotent and eternal in design, on a cultural visit to our planet ... if only this much could definitely be stated, the readers of newspapers would have felt secure, able in a few weeks' time to turn their attention to other problems, the visitors from farther space forgotten. It made little difference whether these mysterious blobs of light were hallucinations, intergalactic visitors or military weapons; the important thing was to explain them.

To behold the inexplicable was perhaps the most unpleasant experience a human being of that age could know, and during that gaudy decade many wild phenomena were sighted and recorded.

In daylight, glittering objects of bright silver manoeuvred at unearthly speed over Washington D.C., observed by hundreds, some few reliable. The government, with an air of spurious calm, mentioned weather balloons, atmospheric reflections, tricks-of-eye, hinting, too, as broadly as it dared, that a sizeable minority of its citizens were probably subject to delusions and mass hysteria. This cynical view was prevalent inside the administration, though it could not of course propound such a theory publicly since its own tenure was based, more or less solidly, on the franchise of those same hysterics and irresponsibles.

Shortly after the mid-point of the century, the wonders increased, becoming daily more bizarre. The recent advance in atomic research and in jet propulsion had made the Western world disagreeably aware of other planets and galaxies, and the thought that we would soon be making expeditions into space was disquieting, if splendid, giving rise to the not illogical thought that life might be developing on other worlds somewhat more brilliantly than here at home and, further, that it was quite conceivable that we ourselves might receive visitors long before our own adventuring had begun in the starry blackness which contains our life, like a speck of phosphorus in a quiet sea. And since our people were (and no doubt still are) barbarous and drenched in superstition, like the dripping 'Saved' at an old-time Texas baptism, it was generally felt that these odd creatures whose shining cars flashed through our poor heavens at such speed must, of necessity, be hostile and cruel and bent on world dominion, just like ourselves or at least our geographic neighbours.

The evidence was horrific and plentiful:

In Berlin a flying object of unfamiliar design was seen to land by an old farmer who was so close to it that he could make out several little men twinkling behind an arc of windows. He fled, however, before they could eat him. Shortly after his breathless announcement to the newspapers, he was absorbed by an Asiatic government whose mission it was at that time to regularize the part of humanity fortunate enough to live within its curiously elastic boundaries, both temporal and spiritual.

In West Virginia, a creature ten feet tall, green with a red face and exuding a ghastly odour, was seen to stagger out of a luminous globe, temporarily grounded. He was observed by a woman and four boys, all of unquestionable probity; they fled before he could eat them. Later in the company of sheriff and well-armed posse, they returned to the scene of horror only to find both monster and conveyance gone. But even the sceptical sheriff and his men could detect, quite plainly, an unfamiliar odour, sharp and sickening among the clean pines.

This particular story was unique because it was the first to describe a visitor as being larger instead of smaller than a man, a significant proof of the growing anxiety: we could handle even the cleverest little creature, but something huge, and green, with an awful odour . . . it was too much.

I myself, late one night in July of the mid-century, saw quite plainly from the eastern bank of the Hudson River, where I lived, two red globes flickering in a cloudless sky. As I watched, one moved to a higher point at a forty-five-degree angle above the original plane which had contained them both. For several nights I watched these eccentric twins but then, carried away by enthusiasm, I began to confuse Mars and Saturn with my magic lights until at last I thought it wise to remain indoors, except for those brief days at summer's end when I watched, as I always used to do, the lovely sudden silver arcs meteors plunging make.

In later years, I learned that, concurrently with the celestial marvels, farm communities were reporting an unusual number of calves born two-headed, chickens hatched three-legged, and lambs born with human faces; but since the somewhat vague laws of mutation were more or less well understood by the farmers these curiosities did not alarm them. An earlier generation would have known instinctively that so many irregularities forecast an ill future, full of spite.

Eventually all was satisfactorily explained or, quite as good, forgotten. Yet the real significance of these portents was not so much their mysterious reality as the profound effect they had upon a people who, despite their emphatic materialism, were as easily shattered by the unexpected as their ancestors who had beheld eagles circling the Capitoline Hill, observed the sky grow leaden on Golgotha, shivered in loud storms when the rain was red as blood and the wind full of toads, while in our own century, attended by a statesman-Pope, the sun did a dance over Portugal.

Considering the unmistakable nature of these signs, it is curious how few suspected the truth: that a new mission had been conceived out of the race's need, the hour of its birth already determined by a conjunction of terrible new stars.

It is true of course that the established churches duly noted these spectacular happenings and, rather slyly, used them to enhance that abstract power from which their own mystical but vigorous authority was descended. The more secular, if no less mystical, dogmas . . . descended variously from an ill-tempered social philosopher of the nineteenth century and an energetic, unreasonably confident mental therapist, a product of that century's decline . . . maintained, in the one case, that fireworks had been set off by vindictive employers to bedazzle the poor workers for undefined but patently wicked ends, and, in the other case, that the fiery objects represented a kind of atavistic recession to the childish world of marvels; a theory which was developed even further in a widely quoted paper by an ingenious disciple of the dead therapist. According to this worthy, the universe was the womb in symbol and the blazing lights which many people thought they saw were only a form of hallucination, harking back to some prenatal memory of ovaries bursting with a hostile potential life which would, in time, become sibling rivals. The writer demanded that the government place all who had seen flying objects under three years' close observation to determine to what extent sibling rivalry, or the absence of it (the proposition worked equally well either way), had affected them in life. Although this bold synthesis was universally admired and subsequently read into the Congressional Record by a lady Representative who had herself undergone nine years' analysis with striking results, the government refused to act.

III

But although nearly every human institution took cognizance of these signs and auguries, none guessed the truth, and those few individuals who had begun to suspect what might be happening preferred not to speak out, if only because, despite much private analysis and self-questioning, it was not a time in which to circulate ideas which might prove disagreeable to any minority, no matter how lunatic. The body politic was more than usually upset by signs of nonconformity. The atmosphere was not unlike that of Britain during the mad hour of Titus Oates.

Precisely why my countrymen behaved so frantically is a problem for those historians used to the grand, external view of human events. Yet I have often thought that much of our national irritability was closely related to the unexpected and reluctant custody of the world the second war had pressed upon the confused grandchildren of a proud, isolate people, both indifferent and strange to the ways of other cultures.

More to the point, however, was the attitude of our intellectuals, who constituted at this time a small, militantly undistinguished minority, directly descended in spirit if not in fact from that rhetorical eighteenth-century Swiss whose romantic and mystical love for humanity was magically achieved through a somewhat obsessive preoccupation with himself. His passion for self-analysis flourished in our mid-century, at least among the articulate few who were capable of analysing and who, in time, like their great ancestor, chose the ear of the world for their confessional.

Men of letters lugubriously described their own deviations (usually political or sexual, seldom aesthetic), while painters worked devotedly at depicting unique inner worlds which were not accessible to others except in a state of purest empathy hardly to be achieved without a little fakery in a selfish world. It was, finally, the accepted criterion that art's single function was the fullest expression of a private vision . . . which was true enough, though the visions of men lacking genius are not without a certain gloom. Genius, in this time, was quite as rare as in any other and, to its credit, it was not a self-admiring age. Critics found merit only in criticism, a singular approach which was to amuse the serious for several decades.

Led by artists, the intellectuals voiced their guilt at innumerable cocktail parties where it was accepted as an article of faith that each had a burden of guilt which could, once recognized, be exorcised. The means of recognition were expensive but rewarding: a trained and sympathetic listener would give the malaise a name and reveal its genesis; then, through confession (and occasionally 'reliving'), the guild would vanish along with asthma, impotence and eczema. The process, of course, was not easy. To facilitate therapy, it became the custom among the cleverer people to set aside all the traditional artifices of society so that both friends and strangers could confess to one another their worst deeds, their most squalid fantasies, in a series of competitive monologues conducted with arduous sincerity and surprisingly successful on every level but that of communication.

I am sure that this sort of catharsis was not entirely valueless: many of the self-obsessed undoubtedly experienced relief when dispensing secrets. It was certainly an instructive shock for them to find that even their most repellent aberrations were accepted quite perfunctorily by strangers too intent on their own problems to be outraged, or even greatly interested. This discovery was not always cheering. There is a certain dignity and excitement in possessing a dangerous secret life. To lose it in maturity is hard. Once promiscuously shared, vice becomes ordinary, no more troublesome than obvious dentures.

Many cherished private hells were forever lost in those garrulous years, and the vacuum each left was invariably filled with a boredom which, in its turn, could be dispelled only by faith. As a result, the pursuit of the absolute, in one guise or another, became the main preoccupation of these romanticists who professed with some pride a mistrust of reason, derived quite legitimately from their own incapacity to assimilate the social changes created by machinery, their particular Lucifer. They rejected the idea of the reflective mind, arguing that since both logic and science had failed to establish the first cause of the universe or (more important) humanity's significance, only the emotions could reveal to us the nature of reality, the key to meaning. That it was no real concern of this race why or when or how the universe came into being was an attitude never, so far as I can recall, expressed by the serious-minded of the day. Their searching, however, was not simply the result of curiosity; it was more than that: it was an emotional, senseless plunging into the void, into the unknowable and the irrelevant. It became, finally, the burden of life, the blight among the flowers: the mystery which must be revealed, even at the expense of life. It was a terrible crisis, made doubly hard since the eschewal of logic left only one path clear to the heart of the dilemma: the way of the mystic, and even to the least sensible it was sadly apparent that, lacking a superior and dedicated organization, one man's revelation is not apt to be of much use to another.

Quantities of venerable attitudes were abandoned and much of the preceding century's 'eternal truths and verities' which had cast, rocklike, so formidable and dense a shadow were found, upon examination, to be so much sand, suitable for the construction of fantastic edifices but not durable, nor safe from the sea's tide.

But the issue was joined: dubious art was fashioned, authorities were invoked, dreams given countenance and systems constructed on the evidence of private illumination.

For a time, political and social action seemed to offer a way out, or in. Foreign civil wars, foreign social experiments were served with a ferocity difficult to comprehend; but later, when the wars and experiments went wrong, revealing, after such high hopes, the perennial human inability to order society, a disillusion resulted, bitterly resolved in numerous cases by the assumption of some mystical dogma, preferably one so quaintly rich with history, so sweeping and unreasonable in its claims, as to be thoroughly acceptable to the saddened romanticist who wanted, above all else, to *feel*, to know without reasoning.

So in these portentous times, only the scientists were content as they constructed ever more fabulous machines with which to split the invisible kernels of life while the anti-scientifics leaped nervously from one absolute to another . . . now rushing to the old for grace, now to the new for salvation, no two of them really agreeing on anything except the need for agreement, for the last knowledge. And that, finally, was the prevailing note of the age; since reason had been declared insufficient, only a mystic could provide the answer, only he could mark the boundaries of life with a final authority, inscrutably revealed. It was perfectly clear. All that was lacking was the man.

CHAPTER TWO

I

The garden was at its best that first week in the month of June. The peonies were more opulent than usual and I walked slowly through the green light on the terrace above the white river, enjoying the heavy odour of peonies and of new roses rambling in hedges.

The Hudson was calm, no ripple revealed that slow tide which even here, miles to the north of the sea, rises brackishly at the moon's disposition. Across the river the Catskills, water-blue, emerged sharply from the summer's green as though the earth in one vivid thrust had attempted sky, fusing the two elements into yet another, richer blue . . . but the sky was only framed, not really touched, and the blue of hills was darker than the pale sky with its protean clouds all shaped by wind, like the stuff of auguries and human dreaming.

The sky that day was like an idiot's mind, wild with odd clouds, but lovely too, guileless, natural, elusive.

I did not want to go in to lunch, although there was no choice in the matter. I had arrived at one o'clock; I was expected at one-thirty. Meanwhile, avoiding the house until the last possible moment, I had taken a neighbour's privilege of strolling alone about the garden; the house behind me was grey and austere, granitic, more English than Hudson Valley. The grounds swept softly down towards the river nearly a mile away. A vista had been cleared from the central terrace, a little like the one at Versailles but more rustic, less royal. Dark green trees covered the hills to left and right of the sweep of lawn and meadow. No other house could be seen. Even the railroad between the terrace and the water was invisible, hidden by a bluff.

I breathed the air of early summer gladly, voluptuously. I lived my life in seasonal concert with this river and, after grim March and confusing sharp April, the knowledge that at last the trees were in leaf and the days warm was quite enough to create in me a mood of euphoria, of marvellous serenity. I contemplated love affairs. I prepared to meet strangers. The summer and I would celebrate our triumph soon; but, until the proper moment, I was a spectator: the summer love as yet unknown to me, the last dark blooming of peonies amid the wreckage of white lilacs still some weeks away, held in the future with my love. I could only anticipate; I savoured my disengagement in this garden.

But then it was time to go in and I turned my back resolutely on the river and ascended the wide stone steps to the brick terrace which fronted the house on the river side, pausing only to break the stem of a white and pink peony, regretting immediately what I had done: brutally, I had wished to possess the summer, to fix the instant, to bear with me into the house a fragment of the day. It was wrong; and I stood for a moment at the French door holding the great peony in my hand, its odour like a dozen roses, like all the summers I had ever known. But it was impractical. I could not stuff it into my buttonhole for it was as large as a baby's head, while I was fairly certain that my hostess would be less than pleased to receive at my hands one of her best peonies, cut too short even to place in water. Obscurely displeased with myself and the day, I plunged the flower deep into a hedge of boxwood until not even a glimmer of white showed through the dense dark green to betray me. Then, like a murderer, the assaulted day part-spoiling, I went inside.

II

'You have been malingering in the garden,' Clarissa said, offering me her face like a painted plate to kiss. 'I saw you from the window.'

'Saw me ravage the flowers?'

'They all do,' she said obscurely, and led me after her into the drawing room, an oblong full of light from French windows opening upon the terrace. I was surprised to see that she was alone.

'She'll be along presently. She's upstairs changing.'

'Who?'

'Iris Mortimer . . . didn't I tell you? It's the whole reason.'

Clarissa nodded slyly from the chair opposite me. A warm wind crossed the room and the white curtains billowed like spinnakers in a regatta. I breathed the warm odour of flowers, of burned ash remnants from the fireplace: the room shone with silver and porcelain. Clarissa was rich despite the wars and crises that had marked our days, leaving the usual scars upon us, like trees whose cross-sections bear a familial resemblance of concentric rings, recalling in detail the weather of past years . . . at least those few rings we shared in common, for Clarissa, by her own admission, was twenty-two hundred years old with an uncommonly good memory. None of us had ever questioned her too closely about her past. There is no reason to suspect, however, that she was insincere. Since she felt she had lived that great length of time and since her recollections were remarkably interesting and plausible, she was much in demand as a conversationalist and adviser, especially useful in plots which required great shrewdness and daring. It was perfectly apparent that she was involved in some such plot at the moment.

I looked at her thoughtfully before I casually rose to take the bait of mystery she had trailed so perfunctorily before me. She knew her man. She knew I would not be difficult in the early stages of any adventure.

'Whole reason?' I repeated.

'I can say no more!' said Clarissa with a melodramatic emphasis which my deliberately casual tone did not entirely justify. 'You'll love Iris, though.'

I wondered whether loving Iris, or pretending to love Iris, was to be the summer's game. But before I could inquire further, Clarissa, secure in her mystery, asked me idly about my work and, as idly, I answered her, the exchange perfunctory yet easy, for we were used to one another.

'I am tracking him down,' I said. 'There is so little to go on, but what there is is quite fascinating, especially Ammianus.'

'Fairly reliable, as military men go,' said Clarissa, suddenly emerging from her polite indifference. Any reference to the past she had known always in-terested her. Only the present seemed to bore her, at least that ordinary unusable present which did not contain promising material for one of her elaborate human games.

'Did you know him?' I never accepted, literally, Clarissa's unique age. Two thousand years is an unlikely span of life even for a woman of her sturdy unimaginativeness; yet there was no ignoring the fact that she *seemed* to have lived that long, and that her references to obscure episodes, where ascertainable, were nearly always right and, more convincing still, where they differed from history's records, differed on the side of plausibility, the work of a memory or a mind completely unsuperstitious and unenthusiastic. She *was* literal and, excepting always her central fantasy, matter-of-fact. To her the death of Caesar was the logical outcome of a system of taxation which has not been preserved for us, while the virtue of the Roman republic and the ambitions of celebrated politicians she set aside as being less than important. Currency and taxation were her forte and she managed to reduce all the martial splendour of ancient days to an economic level.

She had one other obsession, however, and my reference to Ammianus reminded her of it.

'The Christians!' she exclaimed significantly; then she paused. I waited. Her conversation at times resembled chapter headings chosen haphazardly from an assortment of Victorian novels. '*They* hated him.'

'Ammianus?'

'No, your man Julian. It *is* the Emperor Julian you are writing about.'

'Reading about.'

'Ah, you *will* write about him,' she said with an abstracted Pythoness stare which suggested I was indefatiguable in my eccentric purpose, the study of history in a minor key.

'Of course they hated him. As well they should have . . . that's the whole point to my work.'

'Unreliable, the lot of them. There is no decent history from the time they came to Rome up until that fat little Englishman . . . you know, the one who lived in Switzerland . . . with the *staring* eyes.'

'Gibbon.'

'Yes, that one. Of course he got all the facts wrong, poor man, but at least he tried. The facts of course were all gone by then. They saw to that . . . burning things, rewriting things . . . not that I really ever *read* them . . . you know, how I am about reading. I prefer a mystery novel any day. But at least Gibbon got the tone right.'

'Yet . . .'

'Of course Julian was something of a prig, you know. He *posed* continually and he wasn't . . . what do they call him now? an apostate. He *never* renounced Christianity.'

'He what? . . .'

Clarissa in her queer way took pleasure in rearranging all accepted information. I shall never know whether she did it deliberately to mystify or whether her versions were the forgotten reality.

'He was a perfectly good Christian *au fond* despite his peculiar diet. He was a vegetarian for some years but wouldn't eat beans, as I recall, because he thought they contained the souls of the dead, an old orphic notion.'

'Which is hardly Christian.'

'Isn't that part of it? No? Well, in any case the first Edict of Paris was intended . . .' But I was never to hear Julian's intent, for Iris was in the doorway, slender, dressed in white, her hair dark and drawn back in a classical line from her calm face. She was handsome and not at all what I had expected, but then Clarissa had, as usual, not given me much lead. Iris Mortimer was my own age, I guessed, about thirty, and although hardly a beauty she moved with such ease, spoke with such softness and created such an air of serenity that one gave her perhaps more credit for the possession of beauty than an American devoted to regular features ought, in all accuracy, to have done. The impression was one of lightness, of this month of June in fact . . . I linger over her description a little worriedly, conscious that I am not really getting her right (at least as she appeared to me that afternoon) for the simple reason that our lives were to become so desperately involved in the next few years and my memories of her are now encrusted with so much emotion that any attempt to evoke her as she actually was when I first saw her in that drawing room some fifty years ago is not unlike the work of a restorer of paintings removing layers of glaze and grime in an attempt to reveal an original pattern in all its freshness somewhere beneath. Except that a restorer of course is a workman who has presumably no prejudice and, too, he did not create the original image only to attend its subsequent distortion, as the passionate do in life; for the Iris of that day was, I suppose, no less and no more than what she was to become; it was merely that I could not suspect the bizarre course our future was to take. I had no premonition of our mythic roles, though the temptation is almost overpowering to assert, darkly, that even on the occasion of our first meeting I *knew*. The truth is that we met; we became friends; we lunched amiably and the future cast not one shadow across the mahogany table around which we sat, listening to Clarissa and eating fresh shad caught in the river that morning.

'Eugene here is interested in Julian,' said our hostess, lifting a spring asparagus to her mouth with her fingers.

'Julian who?'

'The Emperor of Rome. I forget his family name but he was a cousin, I think, of Constantius, who was dreary, too, though not such a bore as Julian. Iris, try the asparagus. We get them from the garden.'

Iris tried an asparagus and Clarissa recalled that the Emperor Augustus's favourite saying was: 'Quick as boiled asparagus.' It developed that *he* had been something of a bore, too. 'Hopelessly involved in office work. Of course it's all terribly important, no doubt of that . . . after all the entire Empire was based on a first-rate filing system; yet, all in all, it's hardly *glamorous*.'

'Whom *did* you prefer?' asked Iris, smiling at me. She too was aware of our hostess's obsession; whether or not she believed is a different matter. I assumed not; yet the assumption of truth is perhaps, for human purposes, the same as truth itself, at least to the obsessed.

'None of the obvious ones,' said Clarissa, squinting nearsightedly at the window through which a pair of yellow-spangled birds were mating on the wing like eccentric comets against the green of box. 'But of course, I didn't know everyone, darling. Only a few. Not all of them were accessible. Some never dined out and some that did go out were impossible. And then of course I travelled a good deal. I loved Alexandria and wintered there for over two hundred years, missing a great deal of the unpleasantness at Rome, the *unstability* of those tiresome generals . . . although Vitellius was great fun, at least as a young man. I never saw him when he was Emperor that time, for five minutes, wasn't it? Died of greed. Such an appetite! Once as a young man he ate an entire side of beef at my place in Baiae. Ah, Baiae, I do miss it. Much nicer than Bath or Biarritz and certainly more interesting than Newport. I had several houses there over the years. Once when Senator Tullius Cicero was travelling with that poisonous daughter of his, they stopped . . .'

We listened attentively as one always did to Clarissa . . . does? I wonder if she is still alive. If she is, then perhaps the miracle has indeed taken place and one human being has finally avoided the usual fate. It is an amiable miracle to contemplate.

Lunch ended without any signs of the revelation Clarissa had led me to expect. Nothing was said that seemed to possess even a secret significance. Wondering idly whether or not Clarissa might, after all, be entirely mad, I followed the two women back into the drawing room, where we had our coffee in a warm mood of satiety made only faintly disagreeable for me by the mild nausea I always used to experience when I drank too much wine at lunch. Now of course I never drink wine, only the Arabs' mint tea and their sandy bitter coffee which I have come to like.

Clarissa reminisced idly. She possessed a passion for minor detail which was often a good deal more interesting than her usual talks on currency devaluation.

Neither Iris nor I spoke much; it was as if we were both awaiting some word from Clarissa which would throw into immediate relief this lunch, this day, this meeting of strangers. But Clarissa continued to gossip; at last, when I was beginning to go over in my mind the various formulae which make departure easy, our hostess, as though aware that she had drawn out the overture too long, said abruptly, 'Eugene, show Iris the garden. She has never seen it before.' And then, heartily firing fragments of sentences at us as though in explanation of this move of hers, she left the room, indicating that the rest was up to us.

Puzzled, we both went onto the terrace and into the yellow afternoon. We walked slowly down the steps towards the rose arbours, a long series of trellis arches forming a tunnel of green, bright with new flowers and ending in a cement fountain of ugly tile with a bench beside it, shaded by elms.

We got to facts. By the time we had burrowed through the roses to the bench, we had exchanged those basic bits of information which usually make the rest fall (often incorrectly) into some pattern, a foundation for those various architectures people together are pleased to build to celebrate friendship or enmity or love or, on very special occasions, in the case of a grand affair, a palace with rooms for all three, and much else besides.

Iris was from the Middle West, from a rich suburb of Detroit. This interested me in many ways, for there still existed in those days a real disaffection between East and Midwest and Far West which is hard to conceive nowadays in that grey homogeneity which currently passes for a civilized nation. I was an Easterner, a New Yorker from the Valley with Southern roots, and I felt instinctively that the outlanders were perhaps not entirely civilized. Needless to say, at the time, I would indignantly have denied this prejudice had someone attributed it to me, for those were the days of tolerance in which all prejudice had been banished, from conversation at least . . . though of course to banish prejudice is a contradiction in terms since, by definition, prejudice means prejudgement, and though time and experience usually explode for us all the prejudgements of our first years, they exist, nevertheless, as part of our subconscious, a sabotaging, irrational force, causing us to commit strange crimes indeed, made so much worse because they are often secret even to ourselves. I was, then, prejudiced against the Midwesterner, and against the Californian too. I felt that the former especially was curiously hostile to freedom, to the interplay of that rational Western culture which I had so lovingly embraced in my boyhood and grown up with, always conscious of my citizenship in the world, of my role as a humble but appreciative voice in the long conversation. I resented the automobile manufacturers who thought only of manufacturing objects, who distrusted ideas, who feared the fine with the primitive intensity of implacable ignorance. Could this cool girl be from Detroit? From that same rich suburb which had provided me with a number of handsome vital classmates at school? Boys who had combined physical vigour with a resistance to all ideas but those of their suburb, which could only be described as heroic considering the power of New England schools to crack even the toughest prejudices, at least on the rational level. That these boys did not possess a rational level had often occurred to me, though I did, grudgingly, admire even in my scorn, their grace and strength as well as their confidence in that assembly line which had done so well by them.

Iris Mortimer was one of them. Having learned this there was nothing to do but find sufficient names between us to establish the beginnings of the rapport of class which, even in that late year of the mid-century, still existed: the dowdy aristocracy to which we belonged by virtue of financial security, at least in childhood, of education, of self-esteem and of houses where servants had been in some quantity before the second of the wars; all this we shared and of course those names in common of schoolmates, some from her region, others from mine, names which established us as being of an age. We avoided for some time any comment upon the names, withholding our true selves during the period of identification. I discovered too that she, like me, had remained unmarried, an exceptional state of affairs, for all the names we had mentioned represented two people now instead of one. Ours had been a reactionary generation. We had attempted to combat the time of wars and disasters by a scrupulous observance of our grandparents' customs, a direct reaction to the linking generation whose lives had been so entertainingly ornamented with untidy alliances and fortified by suspect gin. The result was no doubt classic but, at the same time, it was a little shocking. The children were decorous, subdued; they married early, conceived glumly, surrendered to the will of their own children in the interests of enlightened psychology; their lives enriched by the best gin in the better suburbs, safe among their own kind. Yet, miraculously, I had escaped and so apparently had Iris.

'You live here alone?' She indicated the wrong direction though taking in, correctly, the river on whose east bank I did live, a few miles to the north of Clarissa.

I nodded. 'Entirely alone ... in an old house.'

'No family?'

'None here. Not much anywhere else. A few in New Orleans, my family's original base.' I waited for her to ask if I ever got lonely living in a house on the river, remote from others; but she saw nothing extraordinary in this.

'It must be fine,' she said slowly. She broke a leaf off a flowering bush whose branch, heavy with blooming, quivered above our heads as we sat on the garden bench and watched the dim flash of goldfish in the muddy waters of the pond.

'I like it,' I said, a little disappointed that there was now no opportunity for me to construct one of my familiar defences of a life alone. I had, in the five years since my days of travel had temporarily ended, many occasions on which to defend and glorify the solitary life I had chosen for myself beside this river. I had an ever-changing repertoire of feints and thrusts: for instance, with the hearty, I invariably questioned, gently of course, the virtue of a life in the city, confined to a small apartment with uninhibited babies and breathing daily large quantities of soot; at other times I assumed a prince of darkness pose, alone with his crimes in an ancient house, a figure which could, if necessary, be quickly altered to the more engaging one of remote observer of the ways of men, a Stoic among his books, sustained by the recorded fragments of forgotten bloody days, evoking solemnly the pure essences of nobler times, a chaste intelligence beyond the combat, a priest celebrating the cool memory of his race. My theatre was extensive and I almost regretted that with Iris there was no need for even a brief curtain raiser, much less one of my exuberant galas.

Not accustomed to the neutral response, I stammered something about the pleasures of gardens. Iris's calm indifference saved me from what might have been a truly mawkish outburst calculated to interest her at any cost (mawkish because, I am confident, none of our deepest wishes or deeds is, finally, when honestly declared, very wonderful or mysterious: simplicity, not complexity, is at the centre of our being; fortunately the trembling "I" is seldom revealed, even to paid listeners, for, conscious of the appalling directness of our needs, we wisely disguise their nature with a legerdemain of peculiar cunning). Much of Iris's attraction for me . . . and at the beginning that attraction did exist . . . was that one did not need to discuss so many things. Of course the better charades were not called into being, which, creatively speaking, was a pity. But then it was a relief *not* to pretend and, better still, a relief not to begin the business of plumbing shallows under the illusion that a treasure chest of truth might be found on the mind's sea floor . . . a grim ritual which was popular in those years, especially in the suburbs and housing projects where the mental therapists were ubiquitous and busy.

With Iris, one did not suspend, even at a cocktail party, the usual artifices of society. All was understood, or seemed to be, which is exactly the same thing. We talked about ourselves as though of absent strangers. Then: 'Have you known Clarissa long?' I asked.

She shook her head. 'I met her only recently.'

'Then this is your first visit here? to the Valley?'

'The first,' she smiled, 'but it's a little like home, you know. I don't mean Detroit, but a memory of home, got from books.'

I thought so too. Then she added that she did not read any longer and I was a little relieved. With Iris one wanted not to talk about books or the past. So much of her charm was that she was entirely in the present. It was her gift, perhaps her finest quality, to invest the moment with a significance which in recollection did not exist except as a blurred impression of excitement. She created this merely by existing. I was never to learn the trick, for her conversation was not, in itself, interesting and her actions were usually predictable, making all the more unusual her peculiar effect. She asked me politely about my work, giving me then the useful knowledge that, though she was interested in what *I* was doing, she was not much interested in the life of the Emperor Julian.

I made it short. 'I want to do a biography of him. I've always liked history and so, when I settled down in the house, I chose Julian as my work.'

'A life's work?'

'Hardly. But another few years. It's the reading which I most enjoy, and that's treacherous. There is so much of interest to read that it seems a waste of time and energy to write anything . . . especially if it's to be only a reflection of reflections.'

'Then why do it?'

'Something to say, I suppose. Or at least the desire to define and illuminate, from one's own point of view, of course.'

'Then why . . . Julian?'

Something in the way she said the name convinced me she had forgotten who he was if she had ever known.

'The apostasy; the last stand of paganism against Christianity.'

She looked truly interested, for the first time. 'They killed him, didn't they?'

'No, he died in battle. Had he lived longer he might at least have kept the Empire divided between the old gods and the new messiah. Unfortunately his early death was their death, the end of the gods.'

'Except they returned as saints.'

'Yes, a few found a place in Christianity, assuming new names.'

'Mother of god,' she murmured thoughtfully.

'An unChristian concept, one would have thought,' I added, though the beautiful illogic had been explained to me again and again by Catholics: how god could and could not at the same time possess a mother, that gleaming queen of heaven, entirely regnant in those days.

'I have often thought about these things,' she said diffidently. 'I'm afraid I'm not much of a student but it fascinates me. I've been out in California for the past few years, working. I was on a fashion magazine.' The note was exactly right. She knew precisely what that world meant and she was neither apologetic nor pleased. We both resisted the impulse to begin the names again, threading our way through the maze of fashion, through that frantic world of the peripheral arts.

'You kept away from Vedanta?' A group of transplanted English writers at this time had taken to Oriental mysticism, under the illusion that Asia began at Las Vegas. Swamis and temples abounded among the billboards and orange trees; but since it was *the* way for some, it was, for those few at least, honourable.

'I came close.' She laughed. 'But there was too much to read and even then I always felt that it didn't work for us, for Americans, I mean. It's probably quite logical and familiar to Asiatics, but we come from a different line, with a different history. Their responses aren't ours. But I did feel it was possible for others, which is a great deal.'

'Because so much is *not* possible?'

'Exactly. But then I know very little about these things.' She was direct. No implication that what she did not know either did not exist or was not worth the knowing, the traditional response in the fashionable world.

'Are you working now?'

She shook her head. 'No, I gave it up. The magazine sent somebody to take my place out there (I didn't have the "personality" they wanted) and so I came on to New York, where I've never really been, except for weekends from school. The magazine had some idea that I might work into the New York office, but I was through. I have worked.'

'And had enough?'

'Of that sort of thing, yes. So I've gone out a lot in New York, met many people; thought a little . . .' She twisted the leaf that she still held in her fingers, her eyes vague as though focused on the leaf's faint shadow which fell in depth upon her dress, part upon her dress and more on a tree's branch ending finally in a tiny fragment of shadow on the ground, like the bottom step of a frail staircase of air.

'And here you are, at Clarissa's.'

'What an extraordinary woman she is!' The eyes were turned upon me, hazel, clear, luminous with youth.

'She collects people, but not according to any of the usual criteria. She makes them all fit, somehow, but what it is they fit, what design, no one knows. *I* don't know, that is.'

'I suppose I was collected. Though it might have been the other way around, since I am sure she interests me more than I do her.'

'There is no way of telling.'

'Anyway, I'm pleased she asked me here.'

We talked of Clarissa with some interest, getting nowhere. Clarissa was truly enigmatic. She had lived for twenty years on the Hudson. She was not married but it was thought she had been. She entertained with great skill. She was in demand in New York and also in Europe, where she often travelled. But no one knew anything of her origin or of the source of her wealth and, oddly enough, although everyone observed her remarkable *idée fixe*, no one ever discussed it, as though in tactful obedience to some obscure sense of form. In the half-dozen years that I had known her, not once had I discussed with anyone her eccentricity. We accepted in her presence the reality of her mania, and there it ended. Some were more interested by it than others. I was fascinated, and having suspended both belief and doubt found her richly knowing in matters which interested me. Her accounts of various meetings with Libanius in Antioch were brilliant, all told most literally, as though she had no faculty for invention, which perhaps, terrifying thought, she truly lacked, in which case . . . but we chose not to speculate. Iris spoke of plans.

'I'm going back to California.'

'Tired of New York?'

'No, hardly. But I met someone quite extraordinary out there, someone I think I should like to see again.' Her candour made it perfectly clear that her interest was not romantic. 'It's rather in line with what we were talking about. I mean your Julian and all that. He's a kind of preacher.'

'That doesn't sound promising.' A goldfish made a popping sound as it captured a dragonfly on the pond's surface.

'But he isn't the usual sort at all. He's completely different but I'm not sure just how.'

'An evangelist?' In those days loud men and women were still able to collect enormous crowds by ranging up and down the country roaring about that salvation which might be found in the bosom of the Lamb.

'No, his own sort of thing entirely. A little like the Vedanta teachers, only he's American, and young.'

'What does he teach?'

'I . . . I'm not sure. No, don't laugh. I met him only once. At a friend's house in Santa Monica. He talked very little but one had the feeling that, well, that it was something unusual.'

'It must have been if you can't recall what he said.' I revised my first estimate. It was romantic after all. A man who was young, fascinating . . . I was almost jealous as a matter of principle.

'I'm afraid I don't make much sense.' She gestured and the leaf fell into its own shadow on the grass. 'Perhaps it was the effect he had on the others that impressed me. They were clever people, worldly people, yet they listened to him like children.'

'What does he do? does he live by preaching?'

'I don't know that either. I met him the night before I left California.'

'And now you think you want to go back to find out?'

'Yes. I've thought about him a great deal these last few weeks. You'd think one would forget such a thing, but I haven't.'

'What was his name?'

'Cave. John Cave.'

'A pair of initials calculated to amaze the innocent.' Yet even while I invoked irony, I felt with a certain chill in the heat that *this* was to be Clarissa's plot, and for many days afterward that name echoed in my memory, long after I had temporarily forgotten Iris's own name, had forgotten, as one does, the whole day, the peony in the boxwood, the leaf's fall and the catch of the goldfish; instants which now live again in the act of re-creation, details which were to fade into a yellow-green blur of June and of the girl beside me in a garden and of that name spoken in my hearing for the first time, becoming in my imagination like some bare monolith awaiting the sculptor's chisel.

CHAPTER THREE

I

I did not see Iris again for some months. Nor, for that matter, did I see Clarissa, who the day after our lunch disappeared on one of her mysterious trips. Clarissa's comings and goings doubtless followed some pattern though I could never make much sense of them. I was very disappointed not to see her before she left because I had wanted to ask her about Iris and also . . .

It has been a difficult day. Shortly after I wrote the lines above, this morning, I heard the sound of an American voice on the street side of the hotel; the first American voice I've heard in some years. Except for me, none has been allowed in Upper Egypt for twenty years. The division of the world has been quite thorough, religiously and politically, and had not some official long ago guessed my identity, it is doubtful that I should have been granted asylum even in this remote region.

I tried to continue with my writing but it was impossible: I could recall nothing. My attention would not focus on the past, on those wraiths which have lately begun to assume again such startling reality as I go about the work of memory . . . but the past was lost to me this morning. The doors shut and I was marooned in the meagre present.

Who was this American who had come to Luxor? and why?

For a moment the serenity which I have so long practised failed me and I feared for my life. Had the long-awaited assassins finally come? But then that animal within who undoes us all with his fierce will to live grew quiet, accepting again the discipline I have so long maintained over him, his obedience due less perhaps to my strong will than to his fatigue, for he is no longer given to the rages and terrors and exultations that once dominated me as the moon does the tide; his defeat is my old age's single victory, and a bitter one.

I took the pages that I had written and hid them in a wide crack in the marble-topped Victorian washstand. I then put on a tie and linen jacket and, cane in hand, my most bemused and guileless expression upon my face, I left the room and walked down the tall dim corridor to the lobby, limping perhaps a little more than was necessary, exaggerating my genuine debility to suggest, if possible, an even greater helplessness. If they had come at last to kill me, I thought it best to go to them while I still held in check the creature terror. As I approached the lobby, I recalled Cicero's death and took courage from his example. He too had been old and tired, too exasperated at the last even to flee.

My assassin (if such he is and I still do not know) looks perfectly harmless: a red-faced American in a white suit crumpled from heat and travel. In atrocious Arabic he was addressing the manager, who, though he speaks no English, is competent in French and accustomed to speaking it to Occidentals. My compatriot, however, was obstinate and smothered with a loud voice the polite European cadences of the manager.

I moved slowly to the desk, tapping emphatically with my cane on the tile floor. Both turned. It was the moment which I have so long dreaded. The eyes of an American were turned upon me once again. Would he know? *Does* he know? I felt all the blood leave my head. With a great effort, I remained on my feet. Steadying my voice, which has nowadays a tendency to quaver even when I am at ease, I said to the American, in our own language, the language I had not once spoken in nearly twenty years, 'Can I be of assistance, sir?' The words sounded strange on my lips and I was aware that I had given them an ornateness which was quite unlike my usual speech. His look of surprise was, I think, perfectly genuine. I felt a cowardly relief: not yet, not yet.

'Oh!' The American stared at me stupidly for a moment (his face is able to suggest a marvellous range of incomprehension, as I have since discovered).

'My name is Richard Hudson,' I said, pronouncing carefully the name by which I am known in Egypt, the name with which I have lived so long that it sometimes seems as if all my life before was only a dream, a fantasy of a time which never was except in reveries, in those curious waking dreams which I often have these days when I am tired, at sundown usually, and the mind loses all control over itself and the memory grows confused with imaginings, and I behold worlds and splendours which I have never known, yet they are vivid enough to haunt me even in the lucid mornings. I am dying, of course, and my brain is only letting up, releasing its images with a royal abandon, confusing everything like those surrealist works of art which had some vogue in my youth.

'Oh,' said the American again and then, having accepted my reality, he pushed a fat red hand towards me. 'The name is Butler, Bill Butler. Glad to meet you. Didn't expect to find another white . . . didn't expect to meet up with an American in these parts.' I shook the hand.

'Let me help you,' I said, releasing the hand quickly. 'The manager speaks no English.'

'I been studying Arabic,' said Butler with a certain sullenness. 'Just finished a year's course at Ottawa Center for this job. They don't speak it here like *we* studied it.'

'It takes time,' I said soothingly. 'You'll catch the tone.'

'Oh, I'm sure of that. Tell them I got a reservation.' Butler mopped his full glistening cheeks with a handkerchief.

'You have a reservation for William Butler?' I asked the manager in French.

He shook his head, looking at the register in front of him. 'Is he an American?' He looked surprised when I said that he was. 'But it didn't sound like English.'

'He was trying to speak Arabic.'

The manager sighed. 'Would you ask him to show me his passport and authorizations?'

I did as directed. Butler pulled a bulky envelope from his pocket and handed it to the manager. As well as I could, without appearing inquisitive, I looked at the papers. I could tell nothing. The passport was evidently in order. The numerous authorizations from the Egyptian Government in the Pan-Arabic League, however, seemed to interest the manager intensely.

'Perhaps . . .' I began, but he was already telephoning the police. Though I speak Arabic with difficulty, I can understand it easily. The manager was inquiring at length about Mr Butler and about his status in Egypt. The police chief evidently knew all about him and the conversation was short.

'Would you ask him to sign the register?' The manager's expression was puzzled. I wondered what on earth it was all about.

'Don't know why there's all this confusion,' said Butler, carving his name into the register with the ancient pen. 'I wired for a room last week from Cairo.'

'Communications have not been perfected in the Arab countries,' I said (fortunately for me, I thought to myself).

When he had done registering, a boy came and took his bags and the key to his room.

'Much obliged to you, Mr Hudson.'

'Not at all.'

'Like to see something of you, if you don't mind. Wonder if you could give me an idea of the lay of the land.'

I said I should be delighted and we made a date to meet for tea in the cool of the late afternoon, on the terrace.

When he had gone, I asked the manager about him but though my old friend has been manager for twelve years and looks up to me as an elder statesman, since I have lived in the hotel longer than anyone, he would tell me nothing. 'It's too much for me, sir.' And I could get no more out of him.

II

The terrace was nearly cool when we met at six o'clock, the hour when the Egyptian sun, having just lost its unbearable gold, falls, a scarlet disc, into the white stone hills across the river which, at this season, winds narrowly among the mud flats, a third of its usual size, diminished by heat.

'Don't suppose we could order a drink . . . not that I'm much of a drinking man. But you get quite a thirst on a day like this.'

I told him that since foreigners had ceased to come here, the bar had been closed down. Moslems for religious reasons did not use alcohol.

'I know, I know,' he said. 'Studied all about them, even read the Koran. Frightful stuff, too.'

'No worse than most documents revealed by heaven,' I said gently, not wanting to get onto that subject. 'But tell me what brings you to these parts.'

'I was going to ask *you* the same thing,' said Butler genially, taking the cup of mint tea which the servant had brought him. On the river a felucca with a red sail tacked slowly in the hot breeze. 'The manager tells me you've been here for twenty years.'

'You must have found a language in common.'

Butler chuckled. 'These devils understand you well enough if they want to. But you . . .'

'I was an archaeologist at one time,' I said, and I told him the familiar story which I have repeated so many times now that I have almost come to believe it. 'I was from Boston originally. Do you know Boston? I often think of those cold winters with a certain longing. Too much light can be as trying as too little. Some twenty years ago, I decided to retire, to write a book of memoirs.' This was a new, plausible touch, 'Egypt was always my single passion and so I came to Luxor, to this hotel where I've been quite content, though hardly industrious.'

'How come they let you in? I mean there was all that trouble back when the Pan-Arabic League shut itself off from civilization.'

'I was very lucky, I suppose. I had many friends in the academic world of Cairo and they were able to grant me a special dispensation.'

'Old hand, then, with the natives?'

'But a little out of practice. All my Egyptian friends have seen fit to die and I live now as if I were already dead myself.'

This had the desired effect of chilling him. Though he was hardly fifty, the immediacy of death, even when manifested in the person of a chance acquaintance, does inspire a certain gravity.

He mumbled something which I did not catch. I think my hearing has begun to go. Not that I am deaf but I have, at times, a monotonous buzzing in my ears which makes conversation difficult. According to the local doctor my arteries have hardened and at any moment one is apt to burst among the convolutions of the brain, drowning my life. But I do not dwell on this, at least not in conversation.

'There's been a big shake-up in the Atlantic Community. Don't suppose you'd hear much about it around here since from the newspapers I've seen in Egypt they have a pretty tight censorship.'

I said I knew nothing about recent activities in the Atlantic Community or anywhere else, other than Egypt.

'Well, they've worked out an alliance with Pan-Arabia that will open the whole area to us. Of course no oil exploitation is allowed but there'll still be a lot of legitimate business between our sphere and these people.'

I listened to him patiently while he explained the state of the world to me. It seemed unchanged. The only difference was that there were now new and unfamiliar names in high places. He finished with a patriotic harangue about the necessity of the civilized to work in harmony together for the good of mankind. 'And this opening up of Egypt has given us the chance we've been waiting for for years, and we mean to take it.'

'You mean to extend trade?'

'No, I mean the Word.'

'The Word?' I repeated numbly, the old fear returning.

'Why sure, I'm a Cavite Communicator.' He rapped perfunctorily on the table twice. I tapped feebly with my cane on the tile: in the days of the Spanish persecution such signals were a means of secret communication (not that the persecution had really been so great, but it had been our decision to dramatize it in order that our people might become more conscious of their splendid if temporary isolation and high destiny); it had not occurred to me that, triumphant, the Cavites should still cling to those bits of fraternal ritual which I had conceived with a certain levity in the early days. But of course the love of ritual, of symbol, is peculiar to our race, and I reflected bleakly on this as I returned the signal which identified us as brother Cavites.

'The world must have changed indeed,' I said at last. 'It was a Moslem law that no foreign missionaries be allowed in the Arab League.'

'Pressure!' Butler looked very pleased. 'Nothing obvious, of course; had to be done, though.'

'For economic reasons?'

'No, for Cavesword. That's what we're selling because that's the one thing we've got.' And he blinked seriously at the remnant of scarlet sun; his voice husky, like that of a man selling some commodity on television in the old days. Yet the note of sincerity, whether simulated or genuine, was unmistakably resolute.

'You may have a difficult time,' I said, not wanting to go on with this conversation but unable to direct it short of walking away. 'The Moslems are very stubborn in their faith.'

Butler laughed confidently. 'We'll change all that. It may not be easy at first because we've got to go slow, feel our way, but once we know the lay of the land, you might say, we'll be able to produce some big backing, some real big backing.'

His meaning was unmistakable. Already I could imagine those Squads of the Word in action through this last terrestrial refuge. Long ago they had begun as eager instruction teams. After the first victories, however, they had become adept at demoralization, at brainwashing and autohypnosis, using all the psychological weapons that our race in its ingenuity had fashioned in the mid-century, becoming so subtle with the passage of time that imprisonment or execution for unorthodoxy was no longer necessary. Even the most recalcitrant, virtuous man could be reduced to a sincere and useful orthodoxy, no different in quality from his former antagonists, his moment of rebellion forgotten, his reason anchored securely at last in the general truth. I was also quite confident that their methods had improved even since my enlightened time.

'I hope you'll be able to save these poor people,' I said, detesting myself for this hypocrisy.

'Not a doubt in the world,' he clapped his hands. 'They don't know what happiness we'll bring them.' Difficult as it was to accept such hyperbole, I believed in his sincerity. Butler is one of those zealots without whose offices no large work in the world can be successfully propagated. I did not feel more than a passing pity for the Moslems. They were doomed but their fate would not unduly distress them, for my companion was perfectly right when he spoke of the happiness which would be theirs: a blithe mindlessness that would in no way affect their usefulness as citizens. We had long since determined that this was the only humane way of ridding the mass of superstition in the interest of Cavesword and the better life.

'Yet is *is* strange that they should let you in,' I said, quite aware that he might be my assassin after all, permitted by the Egyptian government to destroy me and, with me, the last true memory of the mission. It was not impossible that Butler was an accomplished actor, sounding me out before the final victory of the Cavites, the necessary death and total obliteration of the person of Eugene Luther, now grown old with a false name in a burning land.

If Butler is an actor, he is a master. He thumped on interminably about America, John Cave and the necessity of spreading his word throughout the world. I listened patiently as the sun went abruptly behind the hills and all the stars appeared against the moonless waste of sky. Fires appeared in the hovels on the far shore of the Nile, yellow points of light like fireflies hovering by that other river which I shall never see again.

'Must be nearly suppertime.'

'Not quite,' I said, relieved that Butler's face was now invisible. I was not used to great red faces after my years in Luxor among the lean, the delicate and the dark. Now only his voice was a dissonance in the evening.

'Hope the food's edible.'

'It isn't bad, though it may take some getting used to.'

'Well, I've got a strong stomach. Guess that's why they chose me for this job.'

This job? could it mean . . . ? But I refused to let myself be panicked. I have lived too long with terror to be much moved now; especially since my life by its very continuation has brought me to nothing's edge. 'Are there many of you?' I asked politely. The day was ending and I was growing weary, all senses blunted and some confused. 'Many Communicators?'

'Quite a few. They've been training us for the last year in Canada for the big job of opening up Pan-Arabia. Of course we've known for years that it was just a matter of time before the government got us in here.'

'Then you've been thoroughly grounded in the Arab culture? and disposition?'

'Oh, sure. Of course I may have to come to you every now and then, if you don't mind.' He chuckled to show that his patronage would be genial.

'I should be honoured to assist.'

'We anticipate trouble at first. We have to go slow. Pretend we're just available for instruction while we get to know the local big shots. Then, when the time comes . . .' He left the ominous sentence unfinished. I could imagine the rest. Fortunately, nature by then, with or without Mr Butler's assistance, would have removed me as a witness.

Inside the hotel the noise of plates being moved provided a familiar reference. I was conscious of being hungry. As the body's mechanism jolts to a halt, it wants more fuel than it ever did at its optimum. I wanted to go in, but before I could gracefully extricate myself Butler asked me a question. 'You the only American in these parts?'

I said that I was.

'Funny, nothing was said about there being *any* American up here. I guess they didn't know you were here.'

'Perhaps they were counting me among the American colony at Cairo,' I said smoothly. 'I suppose, officially, I am a resident of that city. I was on the Advisory Board of the Museum.' This was not remotely true but since, to my knowledge, there is no Advisory Board it would be difficult for anyone to establish my absence from it.

'That must be it.' Butler seemed easily satisfied, perhaps too easily. 'Certainly makes things a lot easier for us, having somebody like you up here, another Cavite, who knows the lingo.'

'I'll help in any way I can. Although I'm afraid I have passed the age of usefulness. Like the British king, I can only advise.'

'Well, that's enough. I'm the active one anyway. My partner takes care of the other things.'

'Partner? I thought you were alone.'

'No. I'm to dig my heels in first; then my colleague comes on in a few weeks. That's standard procedure. He's a psychologist and an authority on Cavesword. We all are, of course – authorities, that is – but he's gone into the early history and so on a little more thoroughly than us field men usually do.'

So there was to be another one, a clever one. I found myself both dreading and looking forward to the arrival of this dangerous person. It would be interesting to deal with a good mind again, or at least an instructed one, though Butler has not given me much confidence in the new Cavite Communicators. Nevertheless, I am intensely curious about the Western world since my flight from it. I have been effectively cut off from any real knowledge of the West for two decades. Rumours, stray bits of information, sometimes penetrate as far as Luxor but I can make little sense of them, for the Cavites are, as I well know, not given to candour, while the Egyptian newspapers exist in a fantasy world of Pan-Arabic dominion. There was so much I wished to know that I hesitated to ask Butler, not for fear of giving myself away but because I felt that any serious conversation with him would be pointless. I rather doubted if he knew what he was supposed to know, much less all the details that I wished to know and that even a moderately intelligent man, if not hopelessly zealous, might be able to supply me with.

I had a sudden idea. 'You don't happen to have a recent edition of the Testament, do you? Mine's quite old and out of date.'

'What date?' This was unexpected.

'The year? I don't recall. About thirty years old, I should say.'

There was a silence. 'Of course yours is a special case, being marooned like this. There's a ruling about it which I think will protect you fully since you've had no contact with the outside. Anyway, as a Communicator, I must ask you for your old copy.'

'Why, certainly, but ...'

'I'll give you a new one, of course. You see it is against the law to have any Testament which predates the second Cavite Council.'

I was beginning to understand. After the schism a second Council had been inevitable though no reference to it has ever appeared in the Egyptian press. 'The censorship here is thorough,' I said. 'I had no idea there had been a new Council.'

'What a bunch of savages!' Butler groaned with disgust. 'That's going to be one of our main jobs, you know, education, freeing the press. There has been almost no communication between the two spheres of influence ...'

'Spheres of influence.' How easily the phrase came to his lips! All the jargon of the journalists of fifty years ago has, I gather, gone into the language, providing the inarticulate with a number of made-up phrases calculated to blur their none too clear meanings. I assume of course that Butler is as inarticulate as he seems, that he is typical of the first post-Cavite generation.

'You must give me a clear picture of what has been happening in America since my retirement.' But I rose to prevent him from giving me, at that moment at least, any further observations on 'spheres of influence.'

I stood for a moment, resting on my cane. I had stood up too quickly and as usual suffered a spell of dizziness. I was also ravenously hungry. Butler stamped out a cigarette on the tile.

'Be glad to tell you anything you want to know. That's my business.' He laughed shortly. 'Well, time for chow. I've got some anti-bacteria tablets they gave us before we came out, supposed to keep the food from poisoning us.'

'I'm sure you won't need them here.'

He kept pace with my slow shuffle. 'Well, it increases eating pleasure, too.' Inadvertently, I shuddered as I recognized yet another glib phrase from the past; it had seemed such a good idea to exploit the vulgar language of the advertisers. I suffered a brief spasm of guilt.

III

We dined together in the airy saloon, deserted at this season except for a handful of government officials and businessmen who eyed us without much interest, even though Americans are not a common sight in Egypt. They were of course used to me although, as a rule, I kept out of sight, taking my meals in my room and frequenting those walks along the river bank which avoid altogether the town of Luxor.

I found, after I had dined, that physically I was somewhat restored, better able to cope with Butler. In fact, inadvertently, I actually found myself, in the madness of my great age, enjoying his company, a sure proof of loneliness if not of senility. He too, after taking pills calculated to fill him 'chock full of vim and vigour' (that is indeed the phrase he used), relaxed considerably and spoke of his life in the United States. He had no talent for evoking what he would doubtless call 'the big picture' but in a casual, disordered way he was able to give me a number of details about his own life and work which did suggest the proportions of the world from which he had so recently come and which I had, in my folly, helped create.

On religious matters he was unimaginative and doctrinaire, concerned with the letter of the commands and revelations rather than with the spirit, such as it was or is. I could not resist the dangerous manoeuvre of asking him, at the correct moment of course (we were speaking of the time of the schisms), what had become of Eugene Luther.

'Who?'

The coffee cup trembled in my hand. I set it carefully on the table. I wondered if *his* hearing was sound. I repeated my own name, long lost to me, but mine still in the secret dimness of memory.

'I don't place the name. Was he a friend of the Liberator?'

'Why, yes. I even used to know him slightly but that was many years ago, before your time. I'm curious to know what might have become of him. I suppose he's dead.'

'I'm sorry but I don't place the name.' He looked at me with some interest. 'I guess you must be almost old enough to have seen *him*.'

I nodded, lowering my lids with a studied reverence, as though dazzled at the recollection of great light. 'I saw him several times.'

'Boy, I envy you! There aren't many left who have seen *him* with their own eyes. What was he like?'

'Just like his photographs,' I said shifting the line of inquiry: there is always the danger that a trap is being prepared for me. I was noncommittal, preferring to hear Butler talk of himself. Fortunately, he preferred this too, and for nearly an hour I learned as much as I shall ever need to know about the life of at least one Communicator of Cavesword. While he talked, I watched him furtively for some sign of intention but there was none that I could detect. Yet I am suspicious. He had not known my name and I could not understand what obscure motive might cause him to pretend ignorance, unless of course he *does* know who I am and wishes to confuse me, preparatory to some trap.

I excused myself soon afterward and went to my room, after first accepting a copy of the newest Testament handsomely bound in Plasticon (it looks like plastic) and promising to give him my old proscribed copy the next day.

The first thing that I did, after locking the door to my room, was to take the book over to my desk and open it to the index. My eye travelled down that column of familiar names until it came to the L's.

At first I thought that my eyes were playing a trick upon me. I held the page close to the light, wondering if I might not have begun to suffer delusions, the not unfamiliar concomitant of solitude and old age. But my eyes were adequate and the hallucination, if real, was vastly convincing. My name was no longer there. Eugene Luther no longer existed in that Testament which was largely his own composition.

I let the book shut of itself, as new books will. I sat down at the desk, understanding at last the extraordinary ignorance of Butler. I had been obliterated from history. My place in time was erased. It was as if I had never lived.

CHAPTER FOUR

I

I have had in the last few days some difficulty in avoiding the company of Mr Butler. Fortunately, he is now very much involved with the local functionaries and I am again able to return to my narrative. I don't think Butler has been sent here to assassinate me but, on the other hand, from certain things he has said and not said, I am by no means secure in his ignorance; however, one must go on. At best, it will be a race between him and those hardened arteries which span the lobes of my brain. My only curiosity concerns the arrival next week of his colleague, who is, I gather, of the second generation and of a somewhat bookish turn according to Butler – who would not, I fear, be much of a judge. Certain things that I have learned during the last few days about Iris Mortimer make me more than ever wish to recall our common years as precisely as possible, for what I feared might happen has indeed, if Butler is to be believed, come to pass, and it is now with a full burden of hindsight that I revisit the scenes of a half century ago.

II

I had got almost nowhere with my life of Julian. I had become discouraged with his personality though his actual writings continued to delight me. As so often happens in history I had found it difficult really to get at him. The human attractive part of Julian was undone for me by those bleak errors in deed and in judgement which depressed me even though they derived most logically from the man and his time: that fatal wedding which finally walls off figures of earlier ages from the present, keeping them strange despite the most intense and imaginative re-creation. They are not we. We are not they. And I refused to resort to the low trick of fashioning Julian in my own image. I respected his integrity in time and deplored the division of centuries. My work at last came to a halt and, somewhat relieved, I closed my house in the autumn of the year and travelled west to California.

I had a small income which made modest living and careful travel easy for me . . . a happy state of affairs since, in my youth, I was of an intense disposition, capable of the passions and violence of a Rimbaud without, fortunately, the will to translate them into reality. Had I had more money, or none, I might have died young, leaving behind the brief memory of a minor romanticist. As it was, I had a different role to play in the comedy; one for which I was, after some years of reading beside my natal river, peculiarly fitted to play.

I journeyed to southern California, where I had not been since my service in one of the wars. I had never really explored that exotic land and I was curious about it, more curious than I have even been before or since about any single part of the world. Egypt one knows without visiting it, and China the same; but Los Angeles is unique in its bright horror.

Naturally, one was excited by the movies, even though at that time they had lost much of their hold over the public imagination, unlike earlier decades when the process of film before light could project, larger than life, not only on vast screens but also upon the impressionable minds of an enormous audience made homogeneous by a common passion, shadowy figures which, like the filmy envelopes of Stoic deities, floated to earth in public dreams, suggesting a brave and perfect world where love reigned and only the wicked died. But then time passed and the new deities lost their worshippers. There were too many gods and the devotees got too used to them, realizing finally that they were only mortals, involved not in magical rites but in a sordid business. Television (the home altar) succeeded the movies and their once populous and ornate temples, modelled tastefully on baroque and Byzantine themes, fell empty, as the old gods moved to join the new hierarchies, becoming the domesticated godlings of television which, although it held the attention of the majority of the population, did not enrapture, nor possess dreams or shape days with longing and with secret imaginings the way the classic figures of an earlier time had. Though I was of an age to recall the gallant days of the movies, the nearly mythical power which they had held for millions of people, not all simple, I was more intrigued by the manners, by the cults, by the works of this coastal people so unlike the older world of the East and so antipathetic to our race's first home in Europe. Needless to say, I found them much like everyone else, except for minor differences of no real consequence.

I stayed at a large hotel not too happily balanced in design between the marble-and-potted-palm décor of the Continental Hotel in Paris and the chrome and glass of an observation car on a train.

I unpacked and telephoned friends, most of whom were not home. The one whom I found in was the one I knew the least, a minor film writer who had recently married money and given up the composition of films, for which the remaining moviegoers were no doubt thankful. He devoted his time to assisting his wife in becoming the first hostess of Beverley Hills. She had, I recalled from one earlier meeting, the mind of a child of twelve, but an extremely active child and a good one.

Hastings, such was the writer's name (her name was either Ethel or Valerie, two names which I always confuse because of a particularly revolutionary course I once took in mnemonics), invited me to a party. I went.

It seemed like spring though it was autumn, and it seemed like an assortment of guests brought together in a ship's dining room to celebrate New Year's Eve, though in fact the gathering was largely made up of close acquaintances. Since I knew almost no one, I had a splendid time.

After a brilliant greeting my hostess, a gold figure all in green with gold dust in her hair, left me alone. Hastings was more solicitous, a nervous grey man with a speech impediment which took the form of a rather charming sigh before any word which began with an aspirate.

'We, ah, have a better place coming up. Farther up the hills with a marvellous view of the, ah, whole city. You will love it, Gene. Ah, haven't signed a lease yet, but soon.' While we talked he steered me through the crowds of handsome and bizarre people (none of them was from California, I discovered). I was introduced to magnificent girls exactly resembling their movie selves. I told a striking blonde that she would indeed be excellent in a musical version of

Bhagavad-Gita. She thought so too and my host and I moved on to the patio.

Beside a jade-green pool illuminated from beneath (and a little dirty, I noticed, with leaves floating upon the water: the décor was becoming tarnished, the sets had been used too long and needed striking. Hollywood was becoming old without distinction), a few of the quieter guests sat in white iron chairs while paper lanterns glowed prettily on the palms and everywhere, untidily, grew roses, jasmine and lilac, all out of season and out of place. The guests beside the pool were much the same; except for one: Clarissa.

'You know each other?' Hastings's voice, faintly pleased, was drowned by our greetings and I was pulled into a chair by Clarissa, who had elected to dress herself like an odalisque which made her look more indigenous than any of the other guests. This was perhaps her genius: her adaptiveness.

'We'll be quite happy here,' said Clarissa, waving our host away. 'Go and abuse your other guests.'

Hastings trotted off. Those who had been talking to Clarissa talked to themselves and beneath a flickering lantern the lights of Los Angeles, revealed in a wedge between two hills, added the proper note of lunacy, for at the angle from which I viewed those lights they seemed to form a monster Christmas tree, poised crazily in the darkness.

Clarissa and I exchanged notes on the months that had intervened since our luncheon.

'And you gave up Julian, too?'

'Yes . . . but why "too"?' I was irritated by the implication.

'I feel you don't finish things, Eugene. Not that you should; but I *do* worry about you.'

'It's good of you,' I said, discovering that at a certain angle the Christmas tree could be made to resemble a rocket's flare arrested in space.

'Now don't take that tone with me. I have your interest at heart.' She expressed herself with every sign of sincerity in that curious flat language which she spoke so fluently yet which struck upon the ear untruly, as though it were, in its homeliness, the highest artifice.

'But I've taken care of everything, you know. Wait and see. If you hadn't come out here on your own I should have sent for you . . .'

'And I would have come?'

'Naturally.' She smiled.

'But for what?'

'For . . . *she's* here. In Los Angeles.'

'You mean that girl who came to lunch?' I disguised my interest, but Clarissa ignoring me, went on talking as energetically and as obliquely as ever.

'She's asked for you several times, which is a good sign. I told her I suspected you'd be along but that one never could tell, especially if you were still tied up with Julian, unlikely as that prospect was.'

'But I do finish some things.'

'I'm sure you do. In any case, the girl has been here over a month and you must see her as soon as possible.'

'I'd like to.'

'Of course you would. I still have my plot, you know. Oh, you may think I forget things but I don't. My mind is a perfect filing system.'

'Could you tell me *what* you are talking about?'

She chuckled and wagged a finger at me. 'Soon you'll know. I know I meddle a good deal, more than I should, but after all this time it would be simply impossible for me *not* to interfere. I see it coming, one of those really exciting moments, and I want just to give it a tickle here, a push there to set it rolling. Oh, what fun it will be!'

Hastings crept back among us, diffidently pushing a star and a producer in our direction. 'I think you all ought to know each other, Clarissa . . . and, ah, Gene too. This is Miss . . . and Mr . . . and here in Hollywood . . . when you get to New York . . . house on the river, wonderful, old . . . new film to cost five million . . . runner-up for the Academy Award.' He did it all very well, I thought. Smiles gleamed in the patio's half-light. The star's paste jewels, borrowed from her studio, glimmered like an airliner's lighted windows. I moved towards the house, but Clarissa's high voice restrained me at the door: 'You'll call Iris tomorrow, won't you?' and she shouted an exchange and a number. I waved to show that I'd heard her; then, vowing I would never telephone Iris, I rejoined the party and watched with fascination as the various performers performed in the living room to the accompaniment of a grand piano just barely out of tune.

III

I waited several days before I telephoned Iris. Days of considerable activity, of visiting friends and acquaintances, of attending parties where the guests were precisely the same as the ones I had met at Hastings's house.

I met Iris at the house where she was staying near the main beach of Santa Monica, in a decorous Spanish house, quiet among palms and close to the sea. The day was vivid; the sea made noise; the wind was gentle, smelling of salt.

I parked my rented car and walked around to the sea side of the house. Iris came forward to meet me, smiling, hand outstretched. Her face, which I had remembered as being remarkably pale, was flushed with sunlight.

'I hoped you'd come,' she said, and she slipped her arm in mine as though we had been old friends and led me to a deck chair adjoining the one where she'd been seated reading. We sat down. 'Friends let me have this place. They went to Mexico for two months.'

'Useful friends.'

'Aren't they? I've already put down roots here in the sand and I'll hate to give it back.'

'Don't.'

'Ah, wouldn't it be wonderful.' She smiled vaguely and looked beyond me at the flash of sea in the flat distance. An automobile horn sounded through the palms; a mother called her child; we were a part of the world, even here.

'Clarissa told me you've been here several months.'

Iris nodded. 'I came back. I think I told you I was going to.'

'To see the man?'

'Would you like something to drink?' She changed the subject with a disconcerting shift of gaze from ocean to me, her eyes still dazzled with the brilliance of light on water. I looked away and shook my head.

'Too early in the day. But I want to take you to dinner tonight, if I may. Somewhere along the coast.'

'I'd like it very much.'

'Do you know of a place?'

She suggested several. Then we went inside and she showed me a room where I might change into my bathing suit.

We walked through the trees to the main road, on the other side of which the beach glowed in the sun. It was deserted at this point although, in the distance, other bathers could be seen, tiny figures, moving about like insects on a white cloth.

For a time we swam contentedly, not speaking, not thinking, our various urgencies (or their lack) no longer imposed upon the moment. At such times, in those days, I was able through the body's strenuous use to reduce the miserable demands of the yearning self to a complacent harmony, with all things in proper proportion: a part of the whole and not the whole itself, though, metaphorically speaking, perhaps whatever conceives reality is reality itself. But such nice divisions and distinctions were of no concern to me that afternoon in the sun, swimming with Iris, the mechanism which spoils time with questioning switched off by the body's euphoria.

And yet, for all this, no closer to one another, no wiser about one another in any precise sense, we drove that evening in silence to a restaurant on the beach to the north: a ramshackle, candle-lit place, smelling of tar and hung with old nets. After wine and fish and coffee, we talked.

'Clarissa is bringing us together.'

I nodded, accepting the plain statement as a fact. 'The matchmaking instinct is, I suppose . . .'

'Not that at all.' Her face was in a half-light and looked as it had when we first met: pale, withdrawn, all the day's colour drained out of it. Into the sea, the evening star all silver set. We were early and had the place to ourselves.

'Then what? Clarissa never does anything that doesn't contribute to some private design . . . though what she's up to half the time I don't dare guess.'

Iris smiled. 'Nor I. But she is at least up to something which concerns us both and I'm not sure that she may not be right, about the two of us, I mean . . . though of course it's too soon to say.'

I was conventional enough at first to assume that Iris was speaking of ourselves, most boldly, in terms of some emotional attachment and I wondered nervously how I might indicate without embarrassment to her that I was effectively withdrawn from all sexuality and that, while my emotions were in no way impaired, I had been forced to accept a physical limitation to any act of affection which I might direct at another; consequently, I avoided as well as I could those situations which might betray me, and distress another. Though I have never been unduly grieved by this incompletion, I had come to realize only too well from several disquieting episodes in my youth that this flaw in me possessed the unanticipated power of shattering others who, unwarily, had moved to join with me in the traditional duet only to find an implacable surface where they had anticipated a creature of flesh like themselves, as eager as they, as governed by the blood's solemn tide. I had caused pain against my will and I did not want Iris hurt.

Fortunately, Iris had begun to move into a different, an unexpected, conjunction with me, one which had in it nothing of the familiar or even of the human. It was in that hour beneath Orion's glitter that we were, without warning, together volatilized onto that archetypal plane where we were to play with such ferocity at being gods, a flawed Mercury and a dark queen of heaven, met at the sea's edge, disguised as human beings but conscious of one another's true identity, for though our speeches, our arias, were all prose, beneath the usual talk recognition had occurred, sounding with the deep resonance of a major chord struck among dissonances.

We cross the first division easily. She was, in her way, as removed as I from the flesh's wild need to repeat itself in pleasure. There was no need for us ever to discuss my first apprehension. We were able to forget ourselves, to ignore the mortal carriage. The ritual began simply enough.

'Clarissa knows what is happening here. That's why she has come West, though she can't bear California. She wants to be in on it the way she's in on everything else, or thinks she is.'

'You mean John Cave, your *magus?*' It was the first time I had ever said that name. The sword was between us now, both edges sharp.

'You guessed? or did she tell you that was why I came back?'

'I assumed it. I remembered what you said to me last spring.'

'He is more than . . . *magus*, Eugene.' And this was the first time she had said *my* name: closer, closer. I waited. 'You will see him.' I could not tell if this was intended as a question or a prophecy. I nodded. She continued to talk, her eyes on mine, intense and shining. Over her shoulder the night was black and all the stars flared twice, once in the sky and once upon the whispering smooth ocean at our feet, one real and one illusion, both light.

'It is really happening,' she said and then, deliberately, she lightened her voice. 'You'll see when you meet him. I know of course that there have been thousands of these prophets, these saviours in every country and in every time. I also know that this part of America is particularly known for religious maniacs. I started with every prejudice, just like you.'

'Not prejudice . . . scepticism; perhaps indifference. Even if he should be one of the chosen wonder-workers, should I care? I must warn you, Iris, that I'm not a believer. And though I'm sure that the revelations of other men must be a source of infinite satisfaction to them individually, I shouldn't for one second be so presumptuous as to make a choice among the many thousands of recorded revelations of truth, accepting one at the expense of all the others. I might so easily choose wrong and get into eternal trouble. And you must admit that the selection is wide, and dangerous to the amateur.'

'You're making fun of me,' said Iris, but she seemed to realize that I was approaching the object in my own way. 'He's not like that at all.'

'But obviously if he is to be useful he must be accepted, and he can't be accepted without extending his revelation or whatever he calls it, and I fail to see how he can communicate, short of hypnotism or drugs, the sense of his vision to someone like myself who, in a sloppy but devoted way, has wandered through history and religion, acquiring with a collector's delight the more colourful and obscure manifestations of divine guidance, revealed to us through the inspired systems of philosophers and divines, not to mention such certified prophets as the custodians of the Sibylline books. '*Illo die hostem Romanorum esse periturum*' was the instruction given poor Maxentius when he marched against Constantine. Needless to say he perished and consequently fulfilled the prophecy by *himself* becoming the enemy of Rome, to his surprise I suspect. My point, though, in honouring you with the only complete Latin sentence which I can ever recall is that at no time can we escape the relativity of our judgements. Truth for us, whether inspired by messianic frenzy or merely illuminated by reason, is, after all, inconstant and subject to change with the hour. You believe now whatever it is this man says. Splendid. But will the belief be true to you at another hour of your life? I wonder. For even if you wish to remain consistent and choose to ignore inconvenient evidence in the style of the truly devoted, the truly pious, will not your prophet *himself* have changed with time's passage? No human being can remain the same, despite the repetition of . . .'

'Enough, enough!' she laughed aloud and put her hand between us as though to stop the words in air. 'You're talking such nonesense.'

'Perhaps. It's not at all easy to say what one thinks when it comes to these problems or, for that matter, to any problem which demands statement. Sometimes one is undone by the flow of words assuming its own direction, carrying one, protesting, away from the anticipated shore to *terra incognita*. Other times, at the climax of a particularly telling analogy, one is aware that in the success of words the meaning has got lost. Put it this way, finally, *accurately*: I accept no man's authority in that realm where we are all equally ignorant. The beginning and the end of creation are not our concern. The eventual disposition of the human personality which we treasure in our conceit as being the finest ornament of an envious universe is unknown to us and shall so remain until we learn the trick of raising the dead. God, or what have you, will not be found at the far end of a syllogism, no matter how brilliantly phrased and conceived. We are prisoners in our flesh, dullards in divinity as the Greeks would say. No man can alter this, though of course human beings can be made to *believe* anything. You can teach that fire is cold and ice is hot but nothing changes except the words. So what can your *magus* do? What can he celebrate except what is visible and apparent to all eyes? What can he offer me that I should accept his authority, and its source?'

She sighed. 'I'm not sure he wants anything for himself; acceptance, authority . . . one doesn't think of such things, at least not now. As for his speaking with the voice of some new or old deity, he denies the reality of any power other than the human . . .'

'A strange sort of messiah.'

'I've been trying to tell you this.' She smiled. 'He sounds at times not unlike you just now . . . not so glib perhaps.'

'Now *you* mock *me*.'

'No more than you deserve for assuming facts without evidence.'

'If he throws over all the mystical baggage, what is left? an ethical system?'

'In time, I suppose, that will come. So far there is no system. You'll see for yourself soon enough.'

'You've yet to answer any direct question I have put to you.'

She laughed. 'Perhaps there is a significance in that; perhaps you ask the wrong questions.'

'And perhaps you have no answers.'

'Wait.'

'For how long?'

She looked at her watch by the candles' uncertain light. 'For an hour.'

'You mean we're to see him tonight?'

'Unless you'd rather not.'

'Oh, I want to see him, very much.'

'He'll want to see you too, I think.' She looked at me thoughtfully but I could not guess her intention; it was enough that two lines had crossed, both moving inexorably towards a third, towards a terminus at the progression's heart.

IV

It is difficult now to recall just what I expected. Iris deliberately chose not to give me any clear idea of either the man or his teachings or even of the meeting which we were to attend. We talked of other things as we drove by starlight north along the ocean road, the sound of waves striking sand loud in our ears.

It was nearly an hour's drive from the restaurant to the place where the meeting was to be held. Iris directed me accurately and we soon turned from the main highway into a neon-lighted street; then off into a suburban area of comfortable-looking middle-class houses with gardens. Trees lined the streets; dogs barked; yellow light gleamed at downstairs windows. Silent families were gathered in after-dinner solemnity before television sets, absorbed by the spectacle of blurred grey figures telling jokes.

As we drove down the empty streets, I imagined ruins and dust where houses were and, among the powdery debris of stucco all in mounds, the rusted antennae of television sets like the bones of awful beasts whose vague but terrible proportions will alone survive to attract the unborn stranger's eye. But the loathing of one's own time is a sign of innocence, of faith. I have come since to realize the wholeness of man in time. That year, perhaps that ride down a deserted evening street of a California suburb, was my last conscious moment of specified disgust: television, the Blues and the Greens, the perfidy of Carthage, the efficacy of rites to the moon ... all are at last the same.

'That house over there, with the light in front, with the clock.'

The house, to my surprise, was a large neo-Georgian funeral parlour with a lighted clock in front crowned by a legend discreetly fashion in Gothic gold on black: *Whittaker and Dormer, Funeral Directors*. Since a dozen cars had been parked in front of the house, I was forced to park nearly a block away.

We walked along the sidewalk; street lamps behind trees cast shadows thick and intricate upon the pavement. 'Is there any particular significance?' I asked. 'I mean in the choice of meeting place?'

She shook her head. 'Not really, no. We meet wherever it's convenient. Mr Dormer is one of us and has kindly offered his chapel for the meetings.'

'Is there any sort of ritual I should observe?'

She laughed. 'Of course not. This isn't at all what you think.'

'I think nothing.'

'Then you are prepared. But I should tell you that until this year when a number of patrons made it possible for him' (already I could identify the 'him' whenever it fell from her lips, round with reverence and implication) 'to devote all his time to teaching, he was for ten years an undertaker's assistant in Washington.

I said nothing. It was just as well to get past this first obstacle all at once. There was no reason of course to scorn that necessary if overwrought profession; yet somehow the thought of a saviour emerging from those unctuous ranks seemed ludicrous. I reminded myself that a most successful messiah had been a carpenter and that another had been a politican ... but an embalmer! My anticipation of great news was chilled. I prepared myself for grim comedy.

Iris would tell me nothing more about the meeting or about *him* as we crossed the lawn. She opened the door to the house and we stepped into a softly lighted anteroom. A policeman and a civilian, the one gloomy and the other cheerful, greeted us.

'Ah, Miss Mortimer!' said the civilian, a grey, plump pigeon of a man. 'And a friend, how good to see you both.' No, this was not *he*. I was introduced to Mr Dormer, who chirped on until he was interrupted by the policeman.

'Come on, you two, in here. Got to get the prints and the oath.'

Iris motioned me to follow the policeman into a side-room. I'd heard of this national precaution but until now I had had no direct experience of it. Since the attempt of the communists to control our society had, with the collapse of Russian foreign policy, failed, our government in its collective wisdom decided that never again would any sect or party, other than the traditional ones, be allowed to interrupt the rich flow of the nation's life. As a result, all deviationist societies were carefully watched by the police, who fingerprinted and photo-graphed those who attended meetings, simultaneously exacting an oath of allegiance to the Constitution and the Flag which ended with that powerful invocation which a recent President's speechwriter had, in a moment of in-spiration, struck off to the delight of his employer and nation: 'In a true democracy there is no place for a serious difference of opinion on great issues.' It is a comment on those years, now happily become history, that only a few ever considered the meaning of this resolution, proving of course that words are never a familiar province to the great mass which prefers recognizable pictures to even the most apposite prose.

Iris and I repeated dutifully in the presence of the policeman and an American flag the various national sentiments. We were then allowed to go back to the anteroom and to Mr Dormer, who himself led us into the chapel where several dozen people – perfectly ordinary men and women – were gathered.

The chapel, nonsectarian, managed to combine a number of decorative influences with a blandness quite remarkable in its success at not really repre-senting anything while suggesting, at the same time, everything. The presence of a dead body, a man carefully painted and wearing a blue serge suit, gently smiling in an ebony casket behind a bank of flowers at the chapel's end, did not detract as much as one might have supposed from the occasion's importance. After the first uneasiness, it was quite possible to accept the anonymous dead man as part of the décor. There was even, in later years, an attempt made by a group of Cavite enthusiasts to insist upon the presence of an embalmed corpse at every service, but fortunately other elements prevailed, though not without an ugly quarrel and harsh words.

John Cave's entrance followed our own by a few minutes, and it is with difficulty that I recall what it was that I felt on seeing him for the first time. Though my recollections are well known to all (at least they *were* well known, although now I am less certain, having seen Butler's Testament so strangely altered), I must record here that I cannot after so many years, recall in any emotional detail my first reaction to this man who was to be the world's peculiar nemesis as well as my own.

But, concentrating fiercely, emptying my mind of later knowledge, I can still see him as he walked down the aisle of the chapel, a small man who moved with some grace. He was younger than I had expected or, rather, younger-looking, with short straight hair, light brown in colour, a lean regular face which would not have been noticed in a crowd unless one got close enough to see the expression of the eyes: large silver eyes with black lashes like a thick line drawn on the pale skin, focusing attention to them, to the congenitally small pupils which glittered like the points of black needles, betraying the will and the ambition which the impassive, gentle face belied . . . but I am speaking with future knowledge now. I did not that evening think of ambition or will in terms of John Cave. I was merely curious, intrigued by the situation, by the intensity of Iris, by the serene corpse behind the bank of hothouse flowers, by the thirty or forty men and women who sat close to the front of the chapel, listening intently to Cave as he talked.

At first I paid little attention to what was being said, more interested in observing the audience, the room and the appearance of the speaker. Immediately after Cave's undramatic entrance, he moved to the front of the chapel and sat down on a gilt chair to the right of the coffin. There was a faint whisper of interest at his appearance. Newcomers like myself were being given last-minute instruction by the habitués who had brought them there. Cave sat easily on the gilt chair, his eyes upon the floor, his small hands, bony and white, folded in his lap, a smile on his narrow lips. He could not have looked more ineffectual and ordinary. His opening words by no means altered this first impression.

The voice was good, though Cave tended to mumble at the beginning, his eyes still on the floor, his hands in his lap, motionless. So quietly did he begin that he had spoken for several seconds before many of the audience were aware that he had begun. His accent was the national one, learned doubtless from the radio and the movies: a neutral pronunciation without any strong regional overtone. The popular if short-lived legend of the next decade that he had begun his mission as a backwoods revivalist was certainly untrue.

Not until Cave had talked for several minutes did I begin to listen to the sense rather than to the tone of his voice. I cannot render precisely what he said but the message that night was not much different from the subsequent ones which are known to all. It was, finally, the manner which created the response, not the words themselves, though the words were interesting enough, especially when heard for the first time. His voice, as I have said, faltered at the beginning and he left sentences unfinished, a trick which I later discovered was deliberate, for he had been born a remarkable actor, an instinctive rhetorician. What most struck me that first evening was the purest artifice of his performance. The voice, especially when he came to his climax, was sharp and clear while his hands stirred like separate living creatures and the eyes, those splendid unique eyes, were abruptly revealed to us in the faint light, displayed at that crucial moment which had been as carefully constructed as any work of architecture or of music: the instant of communication.

Against my will and judgement and inclination, I found myself absorbed by the man, not able to move or to react. The magic that was always to affect me, even when later I knew him only too well, held me fixed to my chair as the words, supported by the clear voice, came in a resonant line from him to me alone, to each of us alone, separate from the others . . . and both restless general and fast-breathing particular were together his.

The moment itself lasted only a second in actual time; it came suddenly, without warning: one was riven; then it was over and he left the chapel, left us chilled and weak, staring foolishly at the gilt chair where he had been.

It was some minutes before we were able to take up our usual selves again.

Iris looked at me. I smiled weakly and cleared my throat. I was conscious that I ached all over. I glanced at my watch and saw that he had spoken to us for an hour and a half, during which time I had not moved. I stretched painfully and stood up. Others did the same. We had shared an experience and it was the first time in my life that I knew what it was like to be the same as others, my heart's beat no longer individual, erratic, but held for at least this one interval of time in concert with those of strangers. It was a new, disquieting experience: to be no longer an observer, a remote intelligence. For ninety minutes to have been a part of the whole.

Iris walked with me to the anteroom, where we stood for a moment watching the others who had also gathered here to talk in low voices, their expressions bewildered.

She did not have to ask me what I thought. I told her immediately, in my own way, impressed but less than reverent. 'I see what you mean. I see what it is that holds you, fascinates you, but I still wonder what it is really all about.'

'You saw. You heard.'

'I saw an ordinary man. I heard a sermon which was interesting, although I might be less impressed if I read it to myself...' Deliberately I tried to throw it all away, that instant of belief, that paralysis of will, that sense of mysteries revealed in a dazzle of light. But as I talked, I realized that I was not really dismissing it, that I could not alter the experience even though I might dismiss the man and mock the text: something *had* happened and I told her what I thought it was.

'It is not truth, Iris, but hypnosis.'

She nodded. 'I've often thought that. Especially at first when I was conscious of his mannerisms, when I could see, as only a woman can perhaps, that this was just a man. Yet something *does* happen when you listen to him, when you get to know him. You must find that out for yourself; and you will. It may not prove to be anything which has to do with him. There's something in oneself which stirs and comes alive at his touch, through his agency.' She spoke quickly, excitedly.

I felt the passion with which she was charged. But suddenly it was too much for me. I was bewildered and annoyed. I wanted to get away.

'Don't you want to meet him?'

I shook my head. 'Another time maybe, but not now. Shall I take you back?'

'No. I'll get a ride in to Santa Monica. I may even stay over for the night. He'll be here a week.'

I wondered again if she might have a personal interest in Cave. I doubted it, but anything was possible.

She walked me to the car, past the lighted chapel, over the summery lawn, down the dark street whose solid prosaicness helped to dispel somewhat the madness of the hour before.

We made a date to meet later on in the week. She would tell Cave about me and I would meet him. I interrupted her then. 'What *did* he say, Iris? What did he say tonight?'

Her answer was as direct and as plain as my question. 'That it is good to die.'

CHAPTER FIVE

I

This morning I reread the last section, trying to see it objectively, to match what I have put down with the memory I still bear of that first encounter with John Cave. I have not, I fear, got it. But this is as close as I can come to recalling long-vanished emotions and events.

I was impressed by the man and I was shaken by his purpose. My first impression was, I think, correct. Cave was a natural hypnotist and the text of that extraordinary message was, in the early days at least, thin, illogical and depressing if one had not heard it spoken. Later of course I, among others, composed the words which bear his name and we gave them, I fancy, a polish and an authority which, with his limited education and disregard for the works of the past, he could not have accomplished on his own, even had he wanted to.

I spent the intervening days between my first and second encounters with this strange man in a state of extreme tension and irritability. Clarissa called me several times but I refused to see her, excusing myself from proposed entertainments and hinted tête-à-têtes with an abruptness which anyone but the iron-cast Clarissa would have found appallingly rude. But she merely said that she understood and let me off without explaining what it was she understood, or thought she did. I avoided all acquaintances, keeping to my hotel room, where I contemplated a quick return to the Hudson and to the coming autumn. Finally Iris telephoned to fix a day for me to meet John Cave. I accepted her invitation, with some excitement.

We met in the late afternoon at her house. Only the three of us were present. In the set of dialogues which I composed and published in later years I took considerable liberties with our actual conversations, especially this first one. In fact, as hostile critics were quick to suggest, the dialogues were created by me with very little of Cave in them and a good deal of Plato, rearranged to fit the occasion. But in time, my version was accepted implicitly, if only because there were no longer any hostile critics.

Cave rose promptly when I came out onto the patio, shook my hand vigorously but briefly and sat down again, indicating that I sit next to him while Iris went for tea. He was smaller and more compact than I had thought, measuring him against myself as one does, unconsciously, with an interesting stranger. He wore a plain brown suit and a white shirt open at the neck. The eyes, which at first I did not dare look at, were, I soon noticed, sheathed . . . an odd word which was always to occur to me when I saw him at his ease, eyes half-shut, ordinary, not in the least unusual. Except for a restless folding and unfolding of the hands (suggesting a recently reformed cigarette smoker) he was without physical idiosyncrasy.

'It's a pleasure to meet you' were the first words, I fear, that John Cave ever spoke to me; so unlike the dialogue on the spirit which I later composed to celebrate the initial encounter between master and disciple-to-be. 'Iris has told me a lot about you.' His voice was light, without resonance now. He sat far back in a deck chair. Inside the house I could hear Iris moving plates. The late afternoon sun had just that moment gone behind trees and the remaining light was warmly gold.

'And I have followed your . . . career with interest too,' I said, knowing that 'career' was precisely the word he would not care to hear used but, since neither of us had yet got the range of the other, we fired at random.

'Iris tells me you write history.'

I shook my head. 'No, I only read it. I think it's all been written anyway.' I was allowed to develop this novel conceit for some moments, attended by a respectful silence from my companion, who finally dispatched my faintly hysterical proposition with a vague 'Maybe so'; and then we got to him.

'I haven't been East, you know.' He frowned at the palm trees. 'I was born up in Washington state and I've spent all my life in the Northwest, until last year.' He paused as though he expected me to ask him about *that* year. I did not. I waited for him to do it in his own way. He suddenly turned about and faced me; those disconcerting eyes suddenly trained upon my own. 'You were there the other night, weren't you?'

'Why, yes.'

'Did you feel it too? Am I right?'

The quick passion with which he said this, exploding all at once the afternoon's serenity, took me off guard. I stammered, 'I don't think I know what you mean. I . . .'

'You know exactly what I mean, what I meant.' Cave leaned closer to me and I wondered insanely if the deck chair might not collapse under him. It teetered dangerously. My mind went blank, absorbed by the image of deck chair and prophet together collapsing at my feet. Then, as suddenly, satisfied perhaps with my confusion, he settled back, resumed his earlier ease, exactly as if I had answered him, as though we had come to a crisis and together fashioned an agreement. He was most alarming.

'I want to see New York especially. I've always thought it must look like a cemetery with all those tall grey buildings you see in photographs.' He sighed conventionally. 'So many interesting places in the world. Do you like the West?'

Nervously, I said that I did. I still feared a possible repetition of that brief outburst.

'I like the openness,' said Cave, as though he had thought long about this problem. 'I don't think I'd like confinement. I couldn't live in Seattle because of those fogs they used to have. San Francisco's the same. I don't like too many walls, too much fog.' If he'd intended to speak allegorically he could not have found a better audience; even at this early stage, I was completely receptive to the most obscure histrionics. But in conversation, Cave was perfectly literal. Except when he spoke before a large group, he was quite simple and prosaic and, though conscious always of his dignity and singular destiny, not in the least portentous.

I probably did not put him at his ease, for I stammered a good deal and made no sense, but he was gracious, supporting me with his own poise and equanimity.

He talked mostly of places until Iris came back with tea. Then, as the sky became florid with evening and the teacups gradually grew cold, he spoke of his work and I listened intently.

'I can talk to you straight,' he said. 'This just happened to me. I didn't start out to do this. No sir, I never would have believed ten years ago that I'd be travelling about talking to people like one of those crackpot fanatics you've got so many of in California.' I took a sip of the black, fast-cooling tea, hoping he was not sufficiently intuitive to guess that I had originally put him down, provisionally of course, as precisely that.

'I don't know how much Iris may have told you or how much you might have heard, but it's pretty easy to pass the whole thing off as another joke. A guy coming out of the backwoods with a message.' He cracked his knuckles hard and I winced at the sound. 'Well, I didn't quite come out of the woods. I had a year back at State University and I had a pretty good job in my field with the best firm of funeral directors in Washington state. Then I started on this. I just *knew* one day, and so I began to talk to people and they knew too and I quit my job and started talking to bigger and bigger crowds all along the Coast. There wasn't any of this revelation stuff. I just knew one day, that was all. And when I told other people *what* I knew, they seemed to get it. And that's the strange part. Everybody gets ideas about things which he thinks are wonderful but usually nothing happens to the people he tries to tell them to. With me, it's been different from the beginning. People have listened, and agreed. What I know *they* know. Isn't that a funny thing? Though most of them probably would never have thought it out until they heard me and it was all clear.' His eyes dropped to his hands and he added softly: 'So since it's been like this, I've gone on. I've made this my life. This is it. I will come to the people.'

There was a silence. The sentence had been spoken which I was later to construct the first dialogue upon: 'I will come to the people.' The six words which were to change our lives were spoken softly over tea.

Iris looked at me challengingly over Cave's bowed head.

I remember little else about that evening. We dined, I think, in the house and Cave was most agreeable, most undemanding. There was no more talk of the mission. He asked me many questions about New York, about Harvard, where I had gone to school, about Roman history. He appeared to be interested in paganism and my own somewhat tentative approach to Julian. I was to learn later that though he seldom read he had a startling memory for any fact he thought relevant. I am neither immodest nor inaccurate when I say that he listened to me attentively for some years and many of his later views were a result of our conversations.

I should mention, though, one significant omission in his conversation during those crucial years. He never discussed ethical questions. That was to come much later. At the beginning he had but one vision: Death is nothing; literally no thing; and since, demonstrably, absence of things is a good; death which is no thing is good. On this the Cavite system was constructed, and what came after in the moral and ethical spheres was largely the work of others in his name. Much of this I anticipated in that first conversation with him, so unlike, actually, the dialogue which I composed and which ended with the essential lines – or so I still think complacently, despite the irony with which time has tarnished all those bright toys for me: 'Death is neither hard nor bad. Only the dying hurts.' With that firmly postulated, the rest was inevitable.

Cave talked that evening about California and Oregon and Washington (geography and places were always to fascinate and engage him while people, especially after the early years, ceased to be remarkable to him; he tended to confuse those myriad faces which passed before him like successive ripples in a huge sea). He talked of the cities he had visited on the Coast, new cities to him. He compared their climates and various attractions like a truly devoted tourist, eager to get the best of each place, to encounter the *genius loci* and possess it.

'But I don't like staying in any place long.' Cave looked at me then and again I felt that sense of a power being focused on me . . . it was not unlike what one experiences during an X-ray treatment when the humming noise indicates that potent rays are penetrating one's tissue and though there is actually no sensation, *something* is experienced, power is felt. And so it invariably was that, right until the end, Cave could turn those wide bleak eyes upon me whenever he chose, and I would experience his force anew.

'I want to keep moving, new places, that's what I like. You get a kind of charge travelling. At least I do. I always thought I'd travel but I never figured it would be like this; but then of course I never thought of all this until just a while ago.'

'Can you remember when it was? how it was exactly you got . . . started?' I wanted a sign. Constantine's *labarum* occurred to me: *in hoc signo vinces.* Already ambition was stirring, and the little beast fed ravenously on every scrap that came its way, for in that patio I was experiencing my own revelation, the compass needle no longer spinning wildly but coming to settle at last, with many hesitancies and demurs, upon a direction, drawn to a far pole's attraction.

John Cave smiled for the first time. I suppose, if I wanted, I could recall each occasion over the years when, in my presence at least, he smiled. His usual expression was one of calm resolve, of that authority which feels secure in itself, a fortunate expression which lent dignity to even his casual conversation. I suspected the fact that this serene mask hid a nearly total intellectual vacuity as early in my dealings with him as this first meeting; yet I did not mind, for I had experienced his unique magic and already I saw the possibilities of channelling that power, of using that force, of turning it like a flame here, there, creating and destroying, shaping and shattering . . . so much for the spontaneous nature of my ambition at its least responsible, and at its most exquisite! I could have set the one-half world aflame for the sheer splendour and glory of the deed. For this fault my expiation has been long and my once exuberant pride is now only an ashen phoenix consumed by flames but not quite tumbled into dust, nor recreated in the millennial egg, only a grey shadow in the heart which the touch of a finger of windy fear will turn to dust and air.

Yet the creature was aborning that day: one seed had touched another and a monster began to live.

'The first day? The first time?' The smile faded. 'Sure, I remember it. I'd just finished cosmeticizing the face of this big dead fellow killed in an automobile accident. I didn't usually do make-up but I like to help out and I used to do odd jobs when somebody had too much to do and asked me to help; the painting isn't hard either and I always liked it, though the faces are cold like . . . like . . .' He thought of no simile and went on: 'Anyway I looked at this guy's face and I remembered I'd seen him play basketball in high school. He was in a class or two behind me. Big athlete. Ringer, we called them . . . full of life . . . and here he was, with me powdering his face and combing his eyebrows. Usually you don't think much about the stiff (that's our professional word) one way or the other. It's just a job. But I thought about this one suddenly. I started to feel sorry for him, dead like that, so sudden, so young, so good-looking with all sorts of prospects. Then I felt it.' The voice grew low and precise. Iris and I listened intently, even the sun froze in the wild sky above the sea; and the young night stumbled in the darkening east.

With eyes on the sun, Cave described his sudden knowledge that it was the dead man who was right, who was a part of the whole, that the living were the sufferers from whom, temporarily, the beautiful darkness and non-being had been withdrawn. In his crude way, Cave struck chord after chord of meaning and, though the notes were not in themselves new, the effect was all its own . . . and not entirely because of the voice, of the cogency of this magician.

'And I knew it was the dying which was the better part,' he finished. The sun, released, drowned in the Pacific.

In the darkness I asked, 'But you, you still live?'

'Not because I want to,' came the voice, soft as the night. 'I must tell the others first. There'll be time for me.'

I shuddered in the warmth of the patio. My companions were only dim presences in the failing light. 'Who told you to tell this to everyone?'

The answer came back, strong and unexpected: 'I told myself. The responsibility is mine.'

That was the sign for me. He had broken with his predecessors. He was on his own. He knew. And so did we.

II

I have lingered over that first meeting, for in it was finally all that was to come. Later details were the work of others, irrelevant periphery to a simple but powerful centre. Not until that night did I leave the house near the beach. When I left, Cave stayed on and I wondered again if perhaps he was living with Iris.

We parted casually and Iris walked me to the door while Cave remained inside, gazing in his intent way at nothing at all; daydreaming, doubtless, of what was to come.

'You'll help?' Iris stood by the car's open door, her features indistinct in the moonless night.

'I think so. But I'm not sure about the scale.'

'What do you mean?'

'Must *everyone* know? Can't it just be kept to ourselves? for the few who do know him?'

'No. We must let them all hear him. Everyone.' And her voice assumed that zealous tone which I was to hear so often again and again from her lips and those of others.

I made my first and last objection. 'I don't see that quantity has much to do with it. If this thing spreads it will become organized. If it becomes organized, secondary considerations will obscure the point. The truth is no truer because only a few have experienced it.'

'You're wrong. Even for purely selfish reasons, ruling out all altruistic considerations, there's an excellent reason for allowing this to spread. A society which knows what we know, which believes in Cave and what he says, will be a pleasanter place in which to live, less anxious, more tolerant.' She spoke of a new Jerusalem in our sallow and anxious land, nearly convincing me.

The next day I went to Hastings's house for lunch. He was alone; his wife apparently had a life of her own which required his company only occasionally. Clarissa, sensible in tweed and dark glasses, was the only other guest. We lunched on a wrought-iron table beside the gloomy pool in which, among the occasional leaves, I saw, quite clearly, a cigarette butt delicately unfolding like an ocean flower.

'Good to, ah, have you, Eugene. Just a bit of pot luck. Clarissa's going back to civilization today and wanted to see you. I did too, of course. The bride's gone out. Told me to convey her ...'

Clarissa turned her bright eyes on me and, without acknowledging the presence of our host, said right off, 'You've met him at last.'

I nodded. The plot was finally clear to me; the main design at least. 'We had dinner together last night.'

'I know. Iris told me. You're going to help out of course.'

'I'd like to but I don't know what there is I might do. I don't think I'd be much use with a tambourine on street corners, preaching the word.'

'Don't be silly!' Clarissa chuckled. 'We're going to handle this quite, *quite* differently.'

'We?'

'Oh, I've been involved for over a year now. It's going to be the greatest fun ... you wait and see.'

'But ...'

'*I* was the one who got Iris involved. I thought she looked a little peaked, a little bored. I had no idea of course she'd get in so deep, but it will probably turn out all right. I think she's in love with him.'

'Don't be such a gossip,' said Hastings sharply. 'You always reduce everything to ... to biology. Cave isn't that sort of man.'

'You know him too?' How fast it was growing, I thought.

'Certainly. Biggest thing I've done since ...'

'Since you married that brassy blonde,' said Clarissa with her irrepressible rudeness. 'Anyway, my dear, Iris took to the whole thing like a born proselyte, if that's the word I mean ... the other's a little boy, isn't it? and it seems from what she's told me, that you have too.'

'I wouldn't say that.' I was a little put out at both Iris and Clarissa taking me so much for granted.

'Say anything you like. It's still the best thing that's ever happened to you. Oh God, *not* avocado again!' The offending salad was waved away while Hastings muttered apologies. 'Nasty, pointless things, all texture and no taste.' She made a face. 'But I suppose that we must live off the fruits of the country and this is the only thing that will grow in California.' She moved without pause from Western flora to the problem of John Cave. 'As for your own contribution, Eugene, it will depend largely upon what you choose to do. As I said, I never suspected that Iris would get in so deep and you may prove to be quite as surprising. This is the ground floor of course ... wonderful expression, isn't it? the spirit of America, the slogan that broke the plains ... in any case, the way is clear. Cave liked you. You can write things for them, rather solid articles based on your inimitable misreadings of history. You can educate Cave, though this might be unwise since so much of his force derives from his eloquent ignorance. Or you might become a part of the organization which is getting under way. I suppose Iris will explain that to you. It's rather her department at the moment. All those years in the Junior League gave her a touching faith in the power of committees, which is just as well when handling Americans. As for the tambourines and cries of "Come and Be Saved" you are some twenty years behind the times. We have more up-to-date plans.'

'Committees? What committees?'

Clarissa unfolded her mushroom omelette with a secret smile. 'You'll meet our number-one committee member after lunch. He's coming, isn't he?' She looked at Hastings as though suspecting him of a treacherous ineptitude.

'Certainly, certainly, at least he *said* he was.' Hastings motioned for the servingwoman to clean away the lunch, and we moved to other chairs beside the pool for coffee.

Clarissa was in fine form, aggressive, positive, serenely indifferent to the effect she was having on Hastings and me. 'Of course I'm just meddling,' she said in answer to an inquiry of mine. 'I don't really give two cents for Mr Cave and his message.'

'Clarissa!' Hastings was genuinely shocked.

'I mean it. Not that I don't find him fascinating and of course the whole situation is delicious . . . what we shall do! or *you* shall do!' she looked at me maliciously. 'I can foresee no limits to this.'

'It no doubt reminds you of the period shortly after Mohammed married Khadija.' But my own malice could hardly pierce Clarissa's mad equanimity.

'Vile man, sweet woman. But no, this is all going to be different, although the intellectual climate (I think *intellectual* is perhaps optimistic but you know what I mean) is quite similar. I can't wait for the first public response.'

'There's already been some,' said Hastings, crossing his legs, which were encased in pale multicolour slacks with rawhide sandals on his feet. 'There was a piece yesterday in the *News* about the meeting they had down near Laguna.'

'What did they say?' Clarissa scattered tiny saccharine tablets into her coffee just like a grain goddess preparing harvest.

'Oh, just one of those short suburban notes about how a Mr Joseph Cave, they got the name wrong, was giving a series of lectures at a funeral parlour which have been surprisingly well attended.'

'They didn't mention what the lectures were about?'

'No, just a comment; the only one so far in Los Angeles.'

'There'll be others soon, but I shouldn't think it's such a good idea to have too many items like that before things are really under way.'

'And the gentleman who is coming here will be responsible for getting them under way?' I asked.

'Pretty much, yes. It's been decided that the practical details are to be left to him. Cave will continue to speak in and around Los Angeles until the way has been prepared. Then, when the publicity begins, he will be booked all over the country, all over the world!' Clarissa rocked silently for a moment in her chair, creating a disagreeable effect of noiseless laughter which disconcerted both Hastings and me.

'I don't like your attitude,' said Hastings, looking at her gloomily. 'You aren't *serious*.'

'Oh I am, my darling, I am. You'll never know how serious.' And on that high note of Clarissa's, Paul Himmell stepped out onto the patio, blinking in the light of noon.

Himmel was a slender man in his fortieth and most successful year, hair only just begun to grey, a lined but firmly modelled face, all bright with ambition. The initial impression was one of neatly contained energy, of a passionate temperament skillfully channelled. Even the twist to his bow tie was the work of a master craftsman.

Handshake agreeable; smile quick and engaging; yet the effect on me was alarming. I had detested this sort of man all my life and here at last, wearing a repellently distinguished sports coat, was the archetype of all such creatures, loading with a steady hand that cigarette holder without which he might at least have seemed to me still human. He was identified by Hastings, who with a few excited snorts and gasps told me beneath the conversation that this was the most successful young publicist in Hollywood, which meant the world.

'I'm happy to meet you, Gene,' Himmel said as soon as we were introduced. He was perfectly well aware that he had been identified while the first greetings with Clarissa had been exchanged. He had the common gift of the busy world-ling of being able to attend two conversations simultaneously, profiting from both. I hate being called by my first name by strangers, but in his world there were no strangers: the freemasonry of self-interest made all men equal in their desperation. He treated me like a buddy. He knew (he was, after all, clever) that I detested him on sight and on principle, and that presented him a challenge to which he rose with confidence . . . and continued to rise through the years, despite the enduring nature of my disaffection. But then to be liked was his business, and I suspect that his attentions had less to do with me, or any sense of failure in himself for not having won me, than with a kind of automatic charm, a response to a situation which was produced quite inhumanly, mechanically: the smile, the warm voice, the delicate flattery . . . or not so delicate, depending on the case.

'Iris and Cave both told me about you and I'm particularly glad to get a chance to meet you . . . and to see you too, Clarissa . . . will you be long in the East?' Conscious perhaps that I would need more work that a perfunctory prelude, he shifted his attention to Clarissa, saving me for later.

'I never have plans, Paul, but I've one or two chores I've got to do. Anyway I've decided that Eugene is just the one to give the enterprise its tone . . . a quality concerning which you, dear Paul, so often have so much to say.'

'Why, yes,' said the publicist genially, obviously not understanding. 'Always use more tone. You're quite right.'

Clarissa's eyes met mine for a brief amused instant. She was on to everything; doubtless on to me too in the way one can never be about oneself; I always felt at a disadvantage with her.

'What we're going to need for the big New York opening is a firm historical and intellectual base. Cave hasn't got it and of course doesn't need it. We are going to need commentary and explanation and though you happen to be a genius in publicity you must admit that that group which has been charac-terized as intellectual, the literate few who in their weakness often exert enor-mous influence, are not apt to be much moved by your publicity; in fact, they will be put off by it.'

'Well, now I'm not so sure my methods are *that* crude. Of course I never . . .'

'They are superbly, triumphantly, providentially crude and you know it. Eugene must lend dignity to the enterprise. He has a solemn and highly unimaginative approach to philosophy which will appeal to his fellow in-tellectuals. He and they are quite alike: liberal and ineffectual, irresolute and lonely. When he addresses them they will get immediately his range, you might say, pick up his frequency, realizing he is one of them, a man to be trusted. Once they are reached the game is over, or begun.' Clarissa paused and looked at me expectantly.

I did not answer immediately. Hastings, as a former writer, felt that he too had been addressed and he worried the subject of 'tone' while Paul gravely added a comment or two. Clarissa watched me, however, conscious perhaps of the wound she had dealt.

Was it all really so simple? was *I* so simple? so typical? Vanity said not, but self-doubt, the shadow which darkens even those triumphs held at noon, prevailed for a sick moment or two. I was no different from the others, from the little pedagogues and analysts, the self-obsessed and spiritless company who endured shame and a sense of alienation without even that conviction of virtue which can dispel guilt and apathy for the simple, for all those who have accepted without question one of the systems of absolutes which it has amused both mystics and tyrants to construct for man's guidance.

I had less baggage to rid myself of than the others; I was confident of that. Neither Christianity nor Marxism nor the ugly certainties of the mental therapists had ever engaged my loyalty or suspended my judgement. I had looked at them all, deploring their admirers and servants, yet interested by their separate views of society and of the potentialities of a heaven on earth (the mediaeval conception of a world beyond life was always interesting to contemplate, even if the evidence in its favour was whimsical at best, conceived either as a system of rewards and punishments to control living man or else as lovely visions of what might be were man indeed consubstantial with a creation which so often resembled the personal aspirations of gifted divines rather than that universe the rest of us must observe with mortal eyes). No, I had had to dispose of relatively little baggage and, I like to think, less than my more thoughtful contemporaries who were forever analysing themselves, offering their psyches to doctors for analysis or, worse, giving their immortal souls into the hands of priests who would then assume much of their *Weltschmerz*, providing them with a set of grown-up games every bit as appealing as the ones of childhood which had involved make-believe or, finally, worst of all, the soft acceptance of the idea of man the mass, of man the citizen, of society the organic whole for whose greater good all individuality must be surrendered.

My sense then of all that I had *not* been, negative as it was, saved my self-esteem. In this I was unlike my contemporaries. I had, in youth, lost all respect for the authority of men; and since there is no other discernible (the 'laws' of nature are only relative and one cannot say for certain that there is a beautiful logic to everything in the universe as long as first principles remain unrevealed, except of course to the religious, who *know* everything, having faith), I was unencumbered by belief, by reverence for any man or groups of men, living or dead; yet human wit and genius often made my days bearable since my capacity for admiration, for aesthetic response, was highly developed even though, with Terence, I did not know, did not *need* to know through what wild centuries roves back the rose.

Nevertheless, Clarissa's including me among the little Hamlets was irritating, and when I joined in the discussion again I was careful to give her no satisfaction; it would have been a partial victory for her if I had denied a generic similarity to my contemporaries.

Paul spoke of practical matters, explaining to us the way he intended to operate in the coming months; and I was given a glimpse of the organization which had spontaneously come into being only a few weeks before.

'Hope we can have lunch tomorrow, Gene. I'll give you a better picture then, the overall picture and your part in it. Briefly, for now, the organization has been set up as a company under California law with Cave as president and myself, Iris and Clarissa as directors. I'm also secretary-treasurer but only for now. We're going to need a first-rate financial man to head our campaign fund and I'm working on several possibilities right now.'

'What's the . . . company called?' I asked.

'Cavite, Inc. We didn't want to call it anything, but that's the law here and since we intended to raise money we had to have a legal setup.'

'Got a nice sound, ah, Cavite,' said Hastings, nodding.

'What on earth should we have done if he'd had *your* name, Paul?' exclaimed Clarissa, to the indignation of both Hastings and Paul. They shut her up.

Paul continued smoothly, 'I've had a lot of experience, of course, but this is something completely new for me, a real challenge and one which I'm glad to meet head-on.'

'How did you get into it?' I asked.

Paul pointed dramatically to Hastings. 'Him! He took me to a meeting in Burbank last year. I was sold the first time. *I got the message.*'

There was a hush as we were allowed to contemplate this awesome information. Then, smiling in a fashion which he doubtless would have called 'wry', the publicist continued, 'I knew this was it. I contacted Cave immediately and found we talked the same language. He was all for the idea and so we incorporated. He said he wasn't interested in the organizational end and left that to us, with Iris sort of representing him, though of course we all do since we're all Cavites. This thing is big and we're part of it.' He almost smacked his lips. I listened, fascinated. 'Anyway he's going to do the preaching part and we're going to handle the sales end, if you get what I mean. We're selling something which nobody else ever sold before, and you know what that is?' He paused dramatically and we stared at him a little stupidly. 'Truth!' His voice was triumphant. 'We're selling the truth about life and that's something that nobody, but nobody, has ever done before!'

Clarissa broke the silence which had absorbed his last words. 'You're simply out of this world, Paul! If I hadn't heard you, I'd never have believed it. But you don't have to sell *us*, dear. We're in on it too. Besides, I have to catch a plane.' She looked at her watch. She stood up and we did too. She thanked Hastings for lunch and then, before she left the patio on his arm, she said: 'No you boys get on together and remember what I've told you. Gene must be used, and right away. Get him to write something dignified, for a magazine.' We murmured assent. Clarissa said good-bye and left the patio with Hastings. Her voice, shrill and hard, could be heard even after she left. 'The truth about life! Oh, it's going to be priceless!'

I looked quickly at Paul to see if he had heard. But if he had, he ignored it. He was looking at me intently, speculatively. 'I think we're going to get along fine, Gene, just fine,' leaving me only a fumbled word or two of polite corroboration with which to express my sincere antipathy; then we went our separate ways.

III

I met Paul the next day at his office for a drink and not for lunch, since at the last minute his secretary had called me to say he was tied up and could I possibly come at five. I said that I could. I did.

Paul's offices occupied an entire floor of a small skyscraper on the edge of Beverley Hills. I was shown through a series of rooms done in natural wood and beige with indirect lighting and the soft sound of Strauss waltzes piped in from all directions: the employees responded best to three-quarter time, according to the current efficiency reports.

Beneath an expensive but standard mobile, Paul stood, waiting for me. His desk, a tiny affair of white marble on slender iron legs, had been rolled off to one side, and the office gave, as he had been intended, the impression of being a small drawing room rather than a place of business. I was greeted warmly. Hand was shaken firmly. Eyes were met squarely for the regulation length of time. Then we sat down on a couch which was like the open furry mouth of some great soft beast and his secretary rolled a portable bar towards us.

'Name your poison,' said the publicist genially. We agreed on a cocktail, which he mixed with the usual comments one expects from a regular fellow.

Lulled by the alcohol and the room, disarmed by the familiar patter in which one made all the correct responses, our conversation as ritualistic as that of a French dinner party, I was not prepared for the abrupt, 'You don't like me, do you, Gene?'

Only once or twice before had anyone ever said this to me and each time that it happened I had vowed grimly that the *next* time, no matter where or with whom, I should answer with perfect candour, with merciless accuracy, 'No, I don't.' But since I am neither quick nor courageous, I murmured a pale denial.

'It's all right, Gene. I know how you probably feel.' And the monster was magnanimous; he treated me with pity. 'We've got two different points of view. That's all. I have to make my way in this rat race and you don't. You don't have to do anything, so you can afford to patronize us poor hustlers.'

'Patronize isn't quite the word.' I was beginning to recover from the first shock. A crushing phrase or two occurred to me, but Paul knew his business and he changed course before I could begin my work of demolition.

'Well, I just wanted you to know that there are no hard feelings. In my business you get used to this sort of thing: occupational hazard, you might say. I've had to fight my way every inch and I know that a lot of people are going to be jostled in the process, which is just too bad for them.' He smiled suddenly, drawing the sting. 'But I've got a hunch we're going to be seeing a lot of each other, so we ought to start on a perfectly plain basis of understanding. You're on to me and I'm on to you.' The man was diabolic in the way he could enrage yet not allow his adversary sufficient grounds for even a perfunctory defence. He moved rapidly, with a show of spurious reason which quite dazzled me. His was what he presently called 'the common-sense view'.

I told him I had no objection to working with him; that everything I had heard about him impressed me; that he was wrong to suspect me of disdaining methods whose efficacy was so well known. I perjured myself for several impassioned minutes, and on a rising note of cosiness we took up the problem at hand, congenial enemies for all time. The first round was clearly his.

'Clarissa got you into this?' He looked at me over his glass.

'More or less. Clarissa to Iris to Cave was the precise play.'

'She got me to Cave last summer, or rather to Hastings first. I was sold right off. I think I told you that yesterday. This guy's got everything. Even aside from the message, he's the most remarkable salesman I've ever seen, and please believe me when I tell you there isn't *anything* I don't know about salesmen.'

I agreed that he was doubtless expert in these matters.

'I went to about a dozen of those early meetings and I could see he was having the same effect on everyone, even on Catholics, people like that. Of course I don't know what happens when they get home, but while they're there they're sold, and that's all that matters, because in the next year we're going to have him *there*, everywhere, and all the time.'

I told him I didn't exactly follow this metaphysical flight.

'I mean we're going to have him on television, on movie screens, in the papers, so that everybody can feel the effect of his personality, just like he was there in person. This prayer-meeting stuff he's been doing is just a warming up, that's all. It's outmoded; can't reach enough people even if you spoke at Madison Square every night for a year. But it's good practice, to get him started. Now the next move is a half-hour TV show once a week, and when that gets started we're in.'

'Who's going to pay for all this?'

'We've got more money than you can shake a stick at.' He smiled briefly and refilled our glasses with a flourish. 'I haven't been resting on my laurels and neither has Clarissa. We've got three of the richest men in L.A. drooling at the mouth for an opportunity to come in with us. They're sold. They've talked to him, they've heard him. That's been enough.'

'Will you sell soap on television at the same time?'

'Come off it, Gene. *Cave* is the product.'

'Then in what way will you or his sponsors profit from selling him?'

'In the first place, what he says is the truth and that's meant a lot to them, to the tycoons. They'll do anything to put him across.'

'I should think that the possession of the truth and its attendant sense of virtue is in itself enough, easily spoiled by popularization,' I said with chilling pomp.

'Now that's a mighty selfish attitude to take. Sure it makes me happy to know at last nothing matters a hell of a lot since I'm apt to die any time and that's the end of yours truly. A nice quiet nothing, like sleeping pills after a busy day. All that's swell, but it means a lot more to me to see the truth belong to everybody. Also, let's face it, I'm ambitious. I like my work. I want to see this thing get big, and with me part of it. Life doesn't mean a thing and death is the only reality, like he says, but while we're living we've got to keep busy and the best thing for me, I figured about six months ago, was to put Cave over with the public, which is just what I'm going to do. Anything wrong with that?'

Since right and wrong had not yet been reformulated and codified, I gave him the comfort he hardly needed. 'I see what you mean. I suppose you're right. Perhaps the motive is the same in every case, mine as well as yours. Yet we've all experienced Cave and that should be enough.'

'No, we should all get behind it and push, bring it to the world.'

'That, of course, is where we're different. Not that I don't intend to propagate the truth, but, I shall do it for something to do, knowing that nothing matters, not even *this* knowledge matters.' In my unction, I had stumbled upon the first of a series of paradoxes which were to amuse and obsess our philosophers for a generation. However, Paul gave me no opportunity to elaborate; his was the practical way and I followed. We spoke of means not ends.

'Cave likes the idea of the half-hour show and as soon as we get all the wrinkles ironed out, buying good time, not just dead air, we'll make the first big announcement, along around January. Until then we're trying to keep this out of the papers. Slow but sure; then fast and hard.'

'What sort of man is Cave?' I wanted very much to hear the reaction of a practical man.

Paul was candid; he did not know. 'How can you figure a guy like that out? At times he seems a little feeble-minded, this is between us by the way, and other times when he's talking to people, giving with the message, there's nothing like him.'

'What about his early life?'

'Nobody knows very much. I've had a detective agency prepare a dossier on him. Does that surprise you? Well, I'm going far out on a limb for him and so are our rich friends. We had to be sure we weren't buying an axe murderer or a commie or something.'

'Would that have made any difference to the message?'

'No, *I* don't think so but it sure would have made it impossible for us to sell him on a big scale.'

'And what did they find?'

'Not much. I'll let you read it. Take it home with you. Confidential, of course, and, as an officer of the company, I must ask you not to use any of it without first clearing with me.'

I agreed and his secretary was sent for. The dossier was a thin bound manuscript.

'It's a carbon but I want it back. You won't find anything very striking but you ought to read it for the background. Never been married, no girl friends that anybody remembers . . . no boy friends either (what a headache *that* problem is for a firm like ours). No police record. No tickets for double parking, even. A beautiful, beautiful record on which to build.'

'Perhaps a little negative.'

'That's what we like. As for the guy's character, his I.Q., your guess is as good as mine, probably better. When I'm with him alone, we talk about the campaign and he's very relaxed, very sensible, businesslike. Doesn't preach or carry on. He seems to understand all the problems of our end. He's cooperative.'

'Can you look him straight in the eye?'

Paul laughed. 'Gives you the creeps, doesn't it? No, I guess I don't look at him very much. I'm glad you mentioned that because I've a hunch he's a hypnotist of some kind, though there's no record of his ever having studied it. I think I'll get a psychologist to take a look at him.'

'Do you think he'll like that?'

'Oh, he'll never know unless he's a mindreader. Somebody to sort of observe him at work. I've already had him checked physically.'

'You're very thorough.'

'Have to be. He's got a duodenal ulcer and there's a danger of high blood pressure when he's older; otherwise he's in fine shape.'

'What do you want me to do first?'

He became serious. 'A pamphlet. You might make a high-brow magazine article out of it for the *Reader's Digest* or something first. We'll want a clear, simple statement of the Cavite philosophy.'

'Why don't you get him to write it?'

'I've tried. He says he can't write anything. In fact he even hates to have his sermons taken down by a recorder. God knows why. But in a way it's all to the good, because it means we can get all the talent we like to do the writing for us, and that way, sooner or later, we can appeal to just about everybody.'

'Whom am I supposed to appeal to in this first pamphlet?'

'The ordinary person, but make it as foolproof as you can. Leave plenty of doors open so you can get out fast in case we switch the party line along the way.'

I laughed. 'You're extraordinarily cynical.'

'Just practical. I had to learn everything the hard way. I've been kicked around by some mighty expert kickers in my time.'

I checked his flow of reminiscence. 'Tell me about Cave and Iris.' This was the secondary mystery which had occupied my mind for several days. But Paul did not know or, if he did, would not say. 'I think they're just good friends, like we say in these parts. Except that I doubt if anything is going on . . . they don't seem the type and she's so completely gone on what he has to say . . .'

A long-legged girl secretary in discreet black entered the room unbidden and whispered something to the publicist. Paul started as though she had given him an electric shock from the thick carpeting. He spoke quickly. 'Get Furlow. Tell him to stand bail. I'll be right down.'

She hurried from the room. Paul pushed the bar away from him and it rolled aimlessly across the floor, bottles and glasses chattering. Paul looked at me distractedly. 'He's in jail. Cave's in jail.'

CHAPTER SIX

I

Last night the noise of my heart's beating kept me awake until nearly dawn. Then, as the grey warm light of the morning patterned the floor, I fell asleep and dreamed uneasily of disaster, my dreams disturbed by the noise of jackals, by that jackal-headed god who hovers over me as these last days unfold confusedly before my eyes: it will end in heat and terror, alone beside a muddy river, all time as one and that soon gone. I awakened, breathless and cold, with a terror of the dying still ahead.

After coffee and pills, those assorted pellets which seem to restore me for moments at a time to a false serenity, I put aside the nightmare world of the previous restless hours and idly examined the pages which I had written with an eye to rereading them straight through, to relive for a time the old drama which is already, as I write, separating itself from my memory and becoming real only in the prose. I think now of these events as I have told them and not as they occur to me in memory. For the memory now is of pages and not of scenes or of actual human beings still existing in that baleful, tenebrous region of the imagination where fancy and fact together confuse even the most confident of narrators. I have, thus far at least, exorcised demons, and to have lost certain memories to my narrative relieves my system, as would the excision of a cancer from a failing organism.

The boy brought me my morning coffee and the local newspaper, whose Arabic text pleases my eye though the sense, when I do translate it, is less than strange. I asked the boy if Mr Butler was awake and he said that he had gone out already. These last few days I have kept to my room even for the evening meal, delaying the inevitable revelation as long as possible.

After the boy left and while I drank coffee and looked out upon the river and the western hills, I was conscious of a sense of well-being which I have not often experienced in recent years. Perhaps the work of evoking the past has, in a sense, enhanced the present for me. I thought of the work done as life preserved, as part of me which will remain.

Then, idly, I riffled the pages of John Cave's Testament for the first time since I had discovered that my name had been expunged.

The opening was the familiar one which I had composed so many years before in Cave's name. The time of divination: a straightforward account of the apparent wonders which had preceded the mission. No credence was given the supernatural but a good case was made (borrowed a little from the mental therapists) for the race's need of phenomena as a symptom of unease and boredom and anticipation. I flicked through the pages. An entire new part had been added which I did not recognize: it was still written as though by Cave but obviously it could not have been composed until at least a decade after his death.

I read the new section carefully. Whoever had written it had been strongly under the influence of the pragmatic philosophers, though the style was somewhat inspirational, a guide to popularity crossed with the Koran. A whole system of ideal behaviour was sketched broadly for the devout, so broadly as to be fairly useless, though the commentary and the interpretative analysis of such lines as 'Property really belongs to the world though individuals may have temporary liens on certain sections' must be already prodigious.

I was well into the metaphysics of the Cavites when there was a knock on my door. It was Butler, looking red and uncomfortable from the heat, a spotted red bandana tied, for some inscrutable reason about his head in place of a hat.

'Hope you don't mind my barging in like this, but I finished a visit with the mayor earlier than I thought.' He crumpled, on invitation, into a chair opposite me. He sighed gloomily. 'This is going to be tough, tougher than I ever imagined back home.'

'I told you it would be. The Moslems are very obstinate.'

'I'll say! and the old devil of a mayor practically told me point-blank that if he caught me proselytizing he'd send me back to Cairo. Imagine the nerve!'

'Well, it *is* their country,' I said, reasonably, experiencing my first real hope. Might the Cavites not get themselves expelled from Islam? I knew the mayor of Luxor, a genial merchant who still enjoyed the obsolete title of Pasha. The possibilities of a daring plot occurred to me. All I needed was another year or two, by which time nature would have done its work in any case and the conquest of humanity by the Cavites could then continue its progress without my bitter presence.

I looked at Butler speculatively. He is such a fool. I could, I am sure, undo him, for a time at least. Unless of course he is, as I first expected, an agent come to finish me in fact as absolutely as I have been finished in effect by those revisionists who have taken my place among the Cavites, arranging history . . . I had experienced, briefly, while studying Butler's copy of the Testament, the unnerving sense of having never lived, of having dreamed the past entire.

'Maybe it is their country but we got the truth, and like Paul Himmell said: "A truth known to only half the world is but half a truth." '

'Did he say that?'

'Of course he did. Don't you . . .' he paused, aware of the book in my hand. His expression softened, like a parent in anger noticing suddenly an endearing resemblance to himself in the offending child. 'But I forget how isolated you've been up here. If I've interrupted your studies, I'll go away.'

'Oh no. I was finished when you came. I've been studying for several hours, which is too long for an old man.'

'If a contemplation of Cavesword can ever be too long,' said Butler reverently. 'Yes, Himmell wrote that even before Cavesword, in the month of March, I believe, though we'll have to ask my colleague when he comes. He knows all the dates, all the facts. Remarkable guy. He is the brains of the team.' And Butler laughed to show that he was not entirely serious.

'I think they might respond to pressure,' I said, treacherously. 'One thing the Arabs respect is force.'

'You may be right. But our instructions are to go slow. Still, I didn't think it would be as slow as this. Why, we haven't been able to get a building yet. They've all been told by the Pasha fellow not to rent to us.'

'Perhaps I could talk to him.'

'Do you know him well?'

'We used to play backgammon quite regularly. I haven't seen much of him in the past few years, but if you'd like I'll pay him a call.'

'He's known all along you're a Cavite, hasn't he?'

'We have kept off the subject of religion entirely. As you've probably discovered, since the division of the world there's been little communication between East and West. I don't think he knows much about Cavites except that they're undesirable.'

'Poor creature,' said Butler, compassionately.

'Outer darkness,' I agreed.

'But mark my words: before ten years have passed they will have the truth.'

'I have no doubt of that, Communicator, none at all. If the others who come out have even a tenth of your devotion the work will go fast.' The easy words of praise came back to me mechanically from those decades when a large part of my work was organizational, spurring the mediocre onto great deeds ... and the truth of the matter has been, traditionally, that the unimaginative are the stuff from which heroes and martyrs are made.

'Thanks for those kind words,' said Butler, flushed now with pleasure as well as heat. 'Which reminds me, I was going to ask you if you'd like to help us with our work once we get going.'

'I'd like nothing better but I'm afraid my years of useful service are over. Any advice, however, or perhaps influence that I may have in Luxor ...' There was a warm moment of mutual esteem and amiability, broken only by a reference to the Squad of Belief.

'We'll have one here eventually. Fortunately, the need for them in the Atlantic Community is nearly over. Of course there are always a few malcontents, but we have worked out a statistical ratio of nonconformists in the population which is surprisingly accurate. Knowing their incidence, we are able to check them early. But in general, truth is ascendant everywhere in the civilized world.'

'What are their methods now?'

'The Squad of Belief's? Psychological indoctrination. We now have methods of converting even the most obstinate lutherist. Of course where usual methods fail (and once in every fifteen hundred they do), the Squad is authorized to remove a section of brain which effectively does the trick of making the lutherist conform, though his usefulness in a number of other spheres is somewhat impaired. I'm told he has to learn all over again how to talk and to move around.'

'Lutherist? I don't recognize the word.'

'You certainly have been cut off from the world.' Butler looked at me curiously, almost suspiciously. 'I thought even in your day that was a common expression. It means anybody who refuses wilfully to know the truth.'

'Where does it come from?'

'Come from?' Semantics was either no longer taught or else Butler had never been interested in it. 'Why, it just means, well, a lutherist.'

'I wonder, though, what the derivation of it was.' I was excited. This was the first sign that I had ever existed, a word of obscure origin connoting nonconformist.

'I'm afraid we'll have to ask my sidekick when he comes. I don't suppose it came from one of those Christian sects ... you know, the German one that broke with Rome.'

'That must be it,' I said. 'I don't suppose in recent years there have been as many lutherists as there once were.'

'Very, very few. As I say, we've got it down to a calculable minority and our psychologists are trying to work out some method whereby we can spot potential lutherists in childhood and indoctrinate them before it's too late ... but of course the problem is a negligible one in the Atlantic Community. We've had no serious trouble for forty years.'

'Forty years . . . that was the time of all the trouble,' I said.

'Not so *much* trouble,' said Butler, undoing the bandana and mopping his face with it. 'The last flare-up, I gather, of the old Christians. History makes very little of it but at the time it must have seemed important. Now that we have more perspective we can view things in their proper light. I was only a kid in those days and, frankly, I don't think I paid any attention to the papers. Of course *you* remember it.' He looked at me suddenly, his great vacuous eyes focused. My heart missed one of its precarious beats: was this the beginning? had the inquisition begun?

'Not well,' I said. 'I was seldom in the United States. I'd been digging in Central America, in and around Petén. I missed most of the trouble.'

'You seem to have missed a good deal.' His voice was equable, without a trace of secondary meaning.

'I've had a quiet life. I'm grateful though for your coming here. Otherwise, I should have died without any contact with America, without ever knowing what was happening outside the Arab League.'

'Well, we'll shake things up around here.'

'Shake well before using,' I quoted absently.

'What did you say?'

'I said I hoped all would be well.'

'I'm sure it will. By the way, I brought you the new edition of Cave's prison dialogues.' He pulled a small booklet from his back pocket and handed it to me.

'Thank you.' I took the booklet: dialogues between Cave and Iris Mortimer. I had not heard of this particular work. 'Is this a recent discovery?' I asked.

'Recent? Why no. It's the newest edition but of course the text goes right back to the early days when Cave was in prison.'

'Oh, yes, in California.'

'Sure; it was the beginning of the persecutions. Well, I've got to be on my way.' He arranged the bandana about his head. 'Somebody stole my hat. Persecuting *me*, I'll bet my bottom dollar . . . little ways. Well, I'm prepared for them. They can't stop us. Sooner or later the whole world will be Cavite.'

'Amen,' I said.

'What?' He looked at me with shock.

'I'm an old man,' I said hastily. 'You must recall I was brought up among Christians. Such expressions still linger on, you know.'

'It's a good thing there's no Squad of Belief in Luxor,' said Butler cheerily. 'They'd have you up for indoctrination in a second.'

'I doubt if it would be worth their trouble. Soon I shall be withdrawing from the world altogether.'

'I suppose so. You haven't thought of taking Cavesway, have you?'

'Of course, many times, but since my health has been good I've been in no great hurry to leave my contemplation of those hills.' I pointed to the western window. 'And now I should hesitate to die until the very last moment, out of curiosity. I'm eager to learn, to help as much as possible in your work here.'

'Well, of course that is good news, but should you ever want to take His Way let me know. We have some marvellous methods now, extremely pleasant to take and, as he said, "It's not death which is hard but dying." We've finally made dying simply swell.'

'Will wonders never cease?'

'In that department, never! It is the firm basis of our truth. Now I must be off.'

'Is your colleage due here soon?'

'Haven't heard recently. But I don't suppose the plans have been changed. You'll like him.'

'I'm sure I shall.'

II

And so John Cave's period in jail was now known as the time of persecution, with a pious prison dialogue attributed to Iris. Before I returned to my work of recollection I glanced at the dialogue, whose style was enough like Iris's to have been her work. But of course her style was not one which could ever have been called inimitable since it was based on the most insistent of twentieth-century advertising techniques. I assumed the book was the work of one of those anonymous counterfeiters who have created, according to a list of publications on the back of the booklet, a wealth of Cavite doctrine.

The conversation with Cave in prison was lofty in tone and seemed to deal with moral problems. It was apparent that since the task of governing is largely one of keeping order, with the passage of time it had become necessary for the Cavite rulers to compose in Cave's name different works of ethical instruction to be used for the guidance and control of the population. I assume that since they now control all records and original sources, it is an easy matter for them to 'discover' some relevant text that gives clear answer to any moral or political problem not anticipated in previous commentaries. The work of falsifying records and expunging names is, I should think, somewhat more tricky but they seem to have accomplished it in Cave's Testament, brazenly assuming that those who recall the earlier versions will die off in time, leaving a generation which knows only what they wish it to know, excepting of course the 'calculable minority' of nonconformists, of base lutherists.

Cave's term in prison was far less dramatic than offical legend, though more serious. He was jailed for hit-and-run driving on the highway from Santa Monica into Los Angeles.

I went to see him that evening with Paul. When we arrived at the jail, we were not allowed near him though Paul's lawyers had been permitted to go inside a few minutes before our arrival.

Iris was sitting in the outer office, pale and shaken. A bored policeman in uniform sat at a desk, ignoring us.

'They're the best lawyers in L.A.,' said Paul quickly. 'They'll get him out in no time.'

Iris looked at him bleakly.

'What happened?' I asked, sitting down beside her on the bench. 'How did it happen?'

'I wasn't with him.' She shook her head several times as though to dispel a profound daydream. 'He called me and I called you. They *are* the best, Paul?'

'I can vouch for that . . .'

'Did he kill anybody?'

'We . . . we don't know yet. He hit an old man and went on driving. I don't know why. I mean why he didn't stop. He just went on and the police car caught him. The man's in the hospital now. They say it's bad. He's unconscious, an old man . . .'

'Any reporters here?' asked Paul. 'Anybody else know besides us?'

'Nobody. You're the only person I called.'

'This could wreck everything.' Paul was frightened.

But Cave was rescued, at considerable expense to the company. The old man chose not to die immediately, while the police and the courts of Los Angeles, at that time well known for their accessibility to free-spending reason, proved more than obliging. After a day and a night in prison, Cave was released on bail, and when the case came to court it was handled discreetly by the magistrate.

The newspapers, however, had discovered John Cave at last and there were photographs of 'Present-Day Messiah in Court'. As ill luck would have it, the undertakers of Laguna had come to the aid of their prophet with banners which proclaimed his message. This picketing of the court was photographed and exhibited in the tabloids. Paul was in a frenzy. Publicist though he was, in his first rage he expressed to me the novel sentiment that not all publicity was good.

'But we'll get back at those bastards,' he said grimly, not identifying which ones he meant but waving toward the city hidden by the Venetian blinds of his office window.

I asked for instructions. The day before, Cave had gone back to Washington state to lie low until the time was right for a triumphant reappearance. Iris had gone with him; on a separate plane, to avoid scandal. Clarissa had sent various heartening if confused messages from New York while Paul and I were left to gather up the pieces and begin again. Our close association during those difficult days impressed me with his talents and though, fundamentally, I still found him appalling, I couldn't help but admire his superb operativeness.

'I'm going ahead with the original plan . . . just like none of this happened. The stockholders are willing and we've got enough money, though not as much as I'd like, for the publicity build-up. I expect Cave'll pick up some more cash in Seattle. He always does, wherever he goes.'

'Millionaires just flock to him?'

'Strange to tell, yes. But then, nearly everybody does.'

'It's funny, since the truth he offers is all there is to it. Once it is experienced, there's no longer much need for Cave or for an organization.' This of course was the paradox which time and the unscrupulous were bloodily to resolve.

Paul's answer was reasonable. 'That's true, but there's the problem of sharing it. If millions felt the same way about death the whole world would be happier and, if it's happier, why, it'll be a better place to live in.'

'Do you really believe this?'

'Still think of me as a hundred per cent phony?' Paul chuckled good-naturedly. 'Well, it so happens, I *do* believe that. It also so happens that if this thing clicks we'll have a world organization and if we have, there'll be a big place for number one in it. It's all mixed up, Gene. I'd like to hear *your* motives, straight from the shoulder.'

I was not prepared to answer him, or myself. In fact, to this day, my own motives are a puzzle to which there is no single key, no easy answer. One is not, after all, like those classic or neo-classic figures who wore with such splendid monomaniacal consistency the scarlet of lust or the purple of dominion or the bright yellow of madness, existing not at all beneath their identifying robes. Power appealed to me in my youth but only as a minor pleasure and not as an end in itself or even as a means to any private or public end. I enjoyed the idea of guiding and dominating others, preferably in the mass; yet, at the same time, I did not like the boredom of power achieved, or the silly publicness of a great life. But there was something which, often against my will and judgement, pre-cipitated me into deeds and attitudes where the logic of the moment controlled me to such an extent that I could not lessen, if I chose, the momentum of my own wild passage, or chart its course.

I would not have confided this to Paul even had I in those days thought any of it out, which I had not. Though I was conscious of some fundamental ambival-ence in myself, I always felt that should I pause for a few moments and question myself, I could easily find answers to these problems. But I did not pause. I never asked myself a single question concerning motive. I acted like a man sleeping who was only barely made conscious by certain odd incongruities that he dreams. The secret which later I was to discover was still unrevealed to me as I faced the efficient vulgarity of Paul Himmell across the portable bar which reflected his competence so brightly in its crystal.

'My motives are perfectly simple,' I said, half believing what I said. In those days the more sweeping the statement, the more apt I was to give it my fickle allegiance. Motives are simple, splendid! Simple they are. 'I want something to do. I'm fascinated by Cave and I believe what he says . . . not that it is so supremely earth-shaking. It's been advanced as a theory off and on for two thousand years. Kant wrote that he anticipated with delight the luxurious sleep of the grave, and the Gnostics came close to saying the same thing when they promised a glad liberation from life. The Eastern religions, about which I know very little, maintain . . .'

'That's it!' Paul interrupted me eagerly. 'That's what we want. You just keep on like that. We'll call it "An Introduction to John Cave". Make a small book out of it. Get it published in New York. Then the company will buy up copies and we'll pass it out free.'

'I'm not sure that I know enough formal philosophy to . . .'

'To hell with that stuff. You just root around and show how the old writers were really Cavites at heart and then you come to him and put down what he says. Why we'll be half there even before he's on TV!' Paul lapsed for a moment into a reverie of promotion. I had another drink and felt quite good myself, although I had serious doubts about my competence to compose philosophy in the popular key. But Paul's faith was infectious and I felt that, all in all, with a bit of judicious hedging and recourse to various explicit summaries and de-finitions, I might put together a respectable ancestry for Cave, whose message, essentially, ignored *all* philosophy, empiric and orphic, moving with hypnotic effectiveness to the main proposition: death and man's acceptance of it. The problems of life were always quite secondary to Cave, if not to the rest of us.

'When will you want this piece done?'

'The sooner the better. Here,' he scribbled an address on a pad of paper. 'This is Cave's address. He's on a farm outside Spokane. It belongs to one of his undertaker friends.'

'Iris is with him?'

'Yes. Now you . . .'

'I wonder if that's wise, Iris seeing so much of him. You know he's going to have a good many enemies before very long and they'll dig around for any scandal they can find.'

'Oh, it's perfectly innocent, I'm sure. Even if it isn't, I can't see how it can do much harm.'

'For a public relations man you don't seem to grasp the possibilities for bad publicity in this situation.'

'All pub . . .'

'Is good. But Cave, it appears, is a genuine ascetic.' And the word 'genuine' as I spoke it was like a knife blade in my heart. 'And, since he is, you have a tremendous advantage in building him up. There's no use in allowing him, quite innocently, to appear to philander.'

Paul looked at me curiously. 'You wouldn't by chance be interested in Iris yourself?'

And of course that was it. I had become attached to Iris in precisely the same sort of way a complete man might have been but of course for me there was no hope, nothing. The enormity of that nothing shook me, despite the alcohol I had drunk. Fortunately, I was sufficiently collected not to make the mistake of vehemence. 'I like her very much but I'm more attached to the idea of Cave than I am to her. I don't want to see the business get out of hand. That's all. I'm surprised that you, of all people, aren't more concerned.'

'You may have a point. I suppose I've got to adjust my views to this thing . . . it's different from my usual work building up show business types. In that line the romance angle is swell, just as long as there're no bigamies or abortions involved. I see your point, though. With Cave we have to think in sort of Legion of Decency terms. No rough stuff. No nightclub pictures or posing with blondes. You're absolutely right. Put that in your piece: doesn't drink, doesn't go out with dames . . .'

I laughed. 'Maybe we won't have to go that far. The negative virtues usually shine through all on their own. The minute you draw attention to them you create suspicion. People are generally pleased to suspect the opposite of every avowal.'

'You talk just like my analyst.' And I felt that I had won, briefly, Paul's admiration. 'Anyway, you go to Spokane; talk to Iris; tell her to lay off . . . in a tactful way of course. But don't mention it to him. You never can tell how he'll react. She'll be reasonable even though I suspect she is stuck on the man. Try and get your piece done by the first of December. I'd like to have it in print for the first of the New Year, Cave's year.'

'I'll try.'

'By the way, we're getting an office, same building as this.'

'Cavites, Inc.?'

'We could hardly call it the Church of the Golden Rule,' said Paul with one of the few shows of irritability I was ever to observe in his equable disposition. 'Now, on behalf of the directors, I'm authorized to advance you whatever money you might feel you need for this project. That is, within . . .'

'I won't need anything except, perhaps, a directorship in the company.' My own boldness startled me. Paul laughed.

'That's a good boy. Eye on the main chance. Well, we'll see what we can do about that. There aren't any more shares available right now but that doesn't mean . . . I'll let you know when you get back from Spokane.'

Our meeting was ended by the appearance of his secretary, who called him away to other business. As we parted in the outer office, he said, quite seriously, 'I don't think Iris likes him the way you think but if she does be careful. We can't upset Cave now. This is a tricky time for everyone. Don't show that you suspect anything. Later, when we're under way and there's less pressure, I'll handle it. Agreed?'

I agreed, secretly pleased at being thought in love ... 'in love' – to this moment the phrase has a strangely foreign sound to me, like a classical allusion not entirely understood in a scholarly text. 'In love,' I whispered to myself in the elevator as I left Paul that evening: in love with Iris.

III

We met at the Spokane railroad station and Iris drove me through the wide, clear, characterless streets to a country road which wound east into the hills, in the direction of a town with the lovely name of Coeur d'Alene.

She was relaxed. Her ordinarily pale face was faintly burned from the sun, while her hair, which I recalled as darkly waving, was now streaked with light and loosely bound at the nape of the neck. She wore no cosmetics and her dress was simple cotton beneath the sweater she wore against the autumn's chill. She looked younger than either of us actually was.

At first we talked of Spokane. She identified mountains and indicated hidden villages with an emphasis on place which sharply recalled Cave. Not until we had turned off the main highway into a country road, dark with fir and spruce, did she ask me about Paul. I told her. 'He's very busy preparing our New Year's debut. He's also got a set of offices for the company in Los Angeles and he's engaged me to write an introduction to Cave ... but I suppose you knew that when he wired you I was coming.'

'It was my idea.'

'My coming? or the introduction?'

'Both.'

'And I thought he picked it out of the air while listening to me majestically place Cave among the philosophers.'

Iris smiled. 'Paul's not obvious. He enjoys laying traps and as long as they're for one's own good, he's very useful.'

'Implying he could be destructive?'

'Immensely. So be on your guard even though I don't think he'll harm any of us.'

'How is Cave?'

'I'm worried, Gene. He hasn't got over that accident. He talks about it continually.'

'But the man didn't die.'

'It would be better if he did ... as it is, there's a chance of a lawsuit against Cave for damages.'

'But he has no money.'

'That doesn't prevent them from suing. But worst of all, there's the publicity. The whole thing has depressed Cave terribly. It was all I could do to keep from announcing to the press that he had almost done the old man a favour.'

'You mean by killing him?'

Iris nodded, quite seriously. 'That's actually what he believes and the reason why he drove on.'

'I'm glad he said nothing like that to the papers.'

'But it's true; his point of view *is* exactly right.'

'Except that the old man might regard the situation in a different light and, in any case, he was badly hurt and did not receive Cave's gift of death.'

'Now you're making fun of us.' She frowned and drove fast on the empty road.

'I'm doing no such thing. I'm absolutely serious. There's a moral problem involved which is extremely important and if a precedent is set too early, a bad one like this, there's no predicting how things will turn out.'

'You mean the . . . the gift, as you call it, should only be given voluntarily?'

'Exactly . . . *if* then, and only in extreme cases. Think what might happen if those who listened to Cave decided to make all their friends and enemies content by killing them.'

'Well, I wish you'd talk to him.' She smiled sadly. 'I'm afraid I don't always see things clearly when I'm with him. You know how he is . . . how he convinces.'

'I'll talk to him tactfully. I must also get a statement of belief from him.'

'But you have it already. We all have it.'

'Then I'll want some moral application of it. We still have so much ground to cover.'

'There's the farm, up there on the hill.' A white frame building stood shining among spruce on a low hill at the foot of blue sharp mountains. She turned up a dirt road and, in silence, we arrived at the house.

An old woman, the cook, greeted us familiarly and told Iris that *he* could be found in the study.

In a small warm room, sitting beside a stone fireplace empty of fire, Cave sat, a scrapbook on his knees, his expression vague, unfocused. Our arrival recalled him from some dense reverie. He got to his feet quickly and shook hands. 'I'm glad you came,' he said.

It was Cave's particular gift to strike a note of penetrating sincerity at all times, even in his greetings, which became, as a result, disconcertingly like benedictions. Iris excused herself and we sat beside the fireplace.

'Have you seen these?' Cave pushed the scrapbook towards me.

I took the book and saw the various newspaper stories concerning the accident. It had got a surprisingly large amount of space as though, instinctively, the editors had anticipated a coming celebrity for 'Hit-and-Run Prophet'.

'Look what they say about me.'

'I've read them,' I said, handing the scrapbook back to him, a little surprised that, considering his unworldliness, he had bothered to keep such careful track of his appearance in the press. It showed a new, rather touching side to him; he was like an actor hoarding notices, good and bad. 'I don't think it's serious. After all you were let off by the court, and the man didn't die.'

'It was an accident, of course. Yet that old man nearly received the greatest gift a man can have, a quick death. I wanted to tell the court that. I could have convinced them, I'm sure, but Paul said no. It was the first time I've ever gone against my own instinct and I don't like it.' Emphatically, he shut the book.

The cook came into the room and lit the fire. When the first crackling filled the room and the pine had caught, she left, observing that we were to eat in an hour.

'You want to wash up?' asked Cave mechanically, his eyes on the fire, his hands clasped in his lap like those dingy marble replicas of hands which decorate medieval tombs. That night there was an inhuman look to Cave: pale, withdrawn, inert . . . his lips barely moving when he spoke, as though another's voice spoke through senseless flesh.

'No thanks,' I said, a little chilled by his remoteness. Then I got him off the subject of the accident as quickly as possible and we talked until dinner of the introduction I was to write. It was most enlightening. As I suspected, Cave had read only the Bible and that superficially, just enough to be able, at crucial moments, to affect the seventeenth-century prose of the translators and to confound thereby simple listeners with the familiar authority of his manner. His knowledge of philosophy did not even encompass the names of the principals. Plato and Aristotle rang faint, unrelated bells and with them the meagre carillon ended.

'I don't know why you want to drag in those people,' he said, after I had suggested Zoroaster as a possible point of beginning. 'Most people have never heard of them either. And what I have to say is all my own. It doesn't tie in with any of them or, if it does, it's a coincidence, because I never picked it up anywhere.'

'But I think that it *would* help matters if we provided a sort of family tree for you, to show . . .'

'I don't.' He gestured with his effigy-hands. 'Let them argue about it later. For now, act like this is a new beginning, which it is. I have only one thing to give people and that is the way to die without fear, gladly, to accept nothing for what it is, a long and dreamless sleep.'

I had to fight against that voice, those eyes which as always, when he chose, could dominate any listener. Despite my close association with him, despite the thousands of times I heard him speak, I was never, even in moments of lucid disenchantment, quite able to resist his power. He was a magician in the great line of Simon Magus. That much, even now, I will acknowledge. His divinity, however, was and is the work of others, shaped and directed by the race's recurrent need.

I surrendered in the name of philosophy with a certain relief, and he spoke in specific terms of what he believed that I should write in his name.

It was not until after dinner that we got around, all three of us, to a problem which was soon to absorb us all, with near-disastrous results.

We had been talking amiably of neutral things and Cave had emerged somewhat from his earlier despondency. He got onto the subject of the farm where we were, of its attactiveness and remoteness, of its owner who lived in Spokane.

'I always liked old Smathers. You'd like him too. He's got one of the biggest funeral parlours in the state. I used to work for him and then, when I started on all this, he backed me to the hilt. Loaned me money to get as far as San Francisco. After that of course it was easy. I paid him back every cent.'

'Does he come here often?'

Cave shook his head. 'No, he lets me use the farm but he keeps away. He says he doesn't approve of what I'm doing. You see, he's Catholic.'

'But he still likes John,' said Iris, who had been stroking a particularly ugly yellow cat beside the fire. So it was John now, I thought. Iris was the only person ever to call him by his first name.

'Yes. He's a good friend.'

'There'll be a lot of trouble, you know,' I said.

'From Smathers?'

'No, from the Catholics, from the Christians.'

'You really think so?' Cave looked at me curiously. I believe that until that moment he had never realized the inevitable collision of his point of view with that of the established religions.

'Of course I do. They've constructed an entire ethical system upon a super-natural foundation whose main strength is the promise of a continuation of human personality after death. You are rejecting grace, heaven, hell, the Trinity . . .'

'I've never said anything about the Trinity or about Christianity.'

'But you'll *have* to say something about it sooner or later. If – or rather when – the people begin to accept you, the churches will fight back, and the greater the impression you make, the more fierce their attack.'

'I suspect John *is* the Antichrist,' said Iris, and I saw from her expression that she was perfectly serious. 'He's come to undo all the wickedness of the Christians.'

'Though not, I hope, of Christ,' I said. 'There's some virtue in his legend, even as corrupted at Nicea three centuries after the fact.'

'I'll have to think about it,' said Cave. 'I don't know that I've ever given it much thought before. I've spoken always what I knew was true and there's never been any opposition, at least that I've been aware of, to my face. It never occurred to me that people who like to think of themselves as Christians couldn't accept both me and Christ at the same time. I know I don't promise the kingdom of heaven but I *do* promise oblivion and the loss of self, of pain . . .'

'Gene is right,' said Iris. 'They'll fight you hard. You must get ready now while you still have time to think it out, before Paul puts you to work and you'll never have a moment's peace again.'

'As bad as that, you think?' Cave sighed wistfully. 'But how to get ready? What should I do? I never think things out, you know. Everything occurs to me on the spot. I can never tell what may occur to me next. It happens only when I speak to people. When I'm alone, I seldom think of the . . . the main things. But when I'm in a group talking to them I hear . . . no, not hear, I *feel* voices telling me what I should say. That's why I never prepare a talk, why I don't really like to have them taken down. There are some things which are meant only for the instant they are conceived . . . a child, if you like, made for just a moment's life by the people listening and myself speaking. I don't mean to sound touched,' he added, with a sudden smile. 'I'm not really *hearing* things but I do get something from those people, something besides the thing I tell them. I seem to become a part of them, as though what goes on in their minds also goes on in me at the same time, two lobes to a single brain.'

'We know that, John,' said Iris softly. 'We've felt it.'

'I suppose, then, that's the key,' said Cave. 'Though it isn't much to write about. I don't suppose you can put it across without me to say it.'

'You may be wrong there,' I said. 'Of course in the beginning you will say the word but I think in time, properly managed, everyone will accept it on the strength of evidence and statement, responding to the chain of forces you have set in motion.' Yet for all the glibness with which I spoke, I did not really believe that Cave would prove to be more than an interesting momentary phenomenon whose 'truth' about death might, at best, contribute in a small way to the final abolition of those old warring superstitions which had mystified and troubled men through all the dark centuries. A doubt which displayed my basic mis-understanding of our race's will to death and, worse, to a death in life made radiant by false dreams, by desperate adjurations.

But that evening we spoke only of a bright future: 'To begin again is the important thing,' I said. 'Christianity, though strong as an organization in this country, is weak as a force because, finally, the essential doctrine is not accepted by most of the people: the idea of a manlike God dispensing merits and demerits at time's end.'

'We are small,' said Cave. 'In space, on this tiny planet, we are nothing. Death brings us back to the whole. We lose this instant of awareness, of suffering, like spray in the ocean. There it forms, there it goes back to the sea.'

'I think people will listen to you because they realize now that order, if there is any, has never been revealed, that death *is* the end of personality even for those passionate, self-important 'I's who insist upon a universal deity like themselves, presented eponymously in order not to give the game away.'

'How dark, how fine the grave must be! Only sleep and an end of days, an end of fear. The end of fear in the grave as the "I" goes back to nothing ...'

'Yes, Cave, life will be wonderful when men no longer fear dying. When the last superstitions are thrown out and we meet death with the same equanimity that we have met life. No longer will children's minds be twisted by evil gods whose fantastic origin is in those barbaric tribes who feared death and lightning, who feared life. That's it: life is the villain to those who preach reward in death, through grace and eternal bliss, or through dark revenge . . .'

'Neither revenge nor reward, only the not-knowing in the grave which is the same for all.'

'And without those inhuman laws, what societies we might build! Take the morality of Christ. Begin there, or even earlier with Plato or earlier yet with Zoroaster. Take the best ideas of the best men and should there be any disagreement as to what is best, use life as the definition, life as the measure. What contributes most to the living is the best.'

'But the living is soon done and the sooner done the better. I envy those who have already gone.'

'If they listen to you, Cave, it will be like the unlocking of a prison. At first they may go wild but then, on their own, they will find ways to life. Fear of punishment in death has seldom stopped the murderer's hand. The only two things which hold him from his purpose are, at the worst, fear of reprisal from society and, at the best, a feeling for life, a love for all that lives. And not the wide-smiling idiot's love but a sense of community of the living, of life's marvellous regency. Even the most ignorant has felt this. Life is all while death is only the irrelevant shadow at the end, the counterpart to that instant before the seed lives.'

Yes, I believed all that, all that and more, too, and I felt Cave was the same as I. By removing fear with that magic of his, he would fulfill certain hopes of my own and (I flatter myself perhaps) of the long line of others, nobler than I, who had been equally engaged in attempting to use life more fully. And so that evening the one true conviction of a desultory life broke through the chill hard surface of disappointment and disgust that had formed a brittle carapace about my heart. I had, after all, my truth too, and Cave had got to it, broken the shell, and for that I shall remain grateful to him, until we are at last the same, both taken by dust.

Excitedly, we talked. I talked mostly. Cave was the theme and I the counterpoint, or so I thought. He had stated it and I built upon what I conceived to be the luminosity of his vision. Our dialogue was one of communion. Only Iris guessed that it was not. From the beginning she saw the difference; she was conscious of the division which that moment had, unknown to either of us, separated me from Cave. *Each time I said 'life', he said 'death'.* In true amity but false concord, the fatal rift began.

Iris, more practical than we, deflated our visions by pulling the dialogue gently back to reality, to ways and dull means.

It was agreed that we had agreed on fundamentals: the end of fear was desirable; superstition should be exorcised from human affairs; the ethical systems constructed by the major religious figures from Zoroaster to Mohammed all contained useful and applicable ideas of societal behaviour which need not be discarded.

At Iris's suggestion, we left the problem of Christianity itself completely alone. Cave's truth was sufficient cause for battle. There was no reason, she felt, for antagonizing the ultimate enemy at the very beginning.

'Let them attack *you*, John. You must be above quarrelling.'

'I reckon I *am* above it,' said Cave and he sounded almost cheerful for the first time since my arrival. 'I want no trouble, but if trouble comes I don't intend to back down. I'll just go on saying what I know.'

At midnight, Cave excused himself and went to bed.

Iris and I sat silent before the last red embers on the hearth. I sensed that something had gone wrong but I could not tell what it was.

When Iris spoke, her manner was abrupt. 'Do you really want to go on with this?'

'What an odd time to ask me that. Of course I do. Tonight's the first time I really saw what it was Cave meant, what it was I'd always felt but never before known; consciously, that is. I couldn't be more enthusiastic.'

'I hope you don't change.'

'Why so glum? What are you trying to say? After all, you got me into this.'

'I know I did and I think I was right. It's only that this evening I felt . . . well, I don't know. Perhaps I'm getting a bit on edge.' She smiled and, through all the youth and health, I saw that she was anxious and ill at ease.

'That business about the accident?'

'Mainly, yes. The lawyers say that now the old man's all right he'll try to collect damages. He'll sue Cave.'

'Nasty publicity.'

'The worst. It's upset John terribly . . . he almost feels it's an omen.'

'I thought we were dispensing with all that, with miracles and omens.' I smiled but she did not.

'Speak for yourself.' She got up and pushed at the coals with a fire shovel. 'Paul says he'll handle everything but I don't see how. There's no way he can stop a lawsuit.'

But I was tired of the one problem which was out of our hands anyway. I asked her about herself and Cave.

'Is it wise my being up here with John, alone? No, I'm afraid not but that's the way it is.' Her voice was hard and her back, now turned to me, grew stiff, her movements with the fire shovel angry and abrupt.

'People will use it against both of you. It may hurt him, and all of us.'

She turned suddenly, her face flushed. 'I can't help it, Gene. I swear I can't. I've tried to keep away. I almost flew East with Clarissa but when he asked me to join him here, I did. I couldn't leave him.'

'Will marriage be a part of the new order?'

'Don't joke.' She sat down angrily in a noise of skirts crumpling. 'Cave must never marry. Besides it's . . . it isn't like that.'

'Really? I must confess I . . .'

'Thought we were having an affair? Well, it's not true.' The rigidity left her as suddenly as it had possessed her. She grew visibly passive, even helpless, in the worn upholstered chair, her eyes on me, the anger gone and only weakness left. 'What can I do?' It was a cry from the heart. All the more touching because, obviously, she had not intended to tell me so much. She had turned to me because there was no one else to whom she could talk.

'You . . . love him?' That word which whenever I spoke it in those days always stuck in my throat like a diminutive sob.

'More, more,' she said distractedly. 'But I can't *do* anything or *be* anything. He's complete. He doesn't need anyone. He doesn't want me except as . . . a companion, and adviser like you or Paul. It's all the same to him.'

'I don't see that it's hopeless.'

'Hopeless!' The word shot from her like a desperate deed. She buried her face in her hands but she did not weep. I sat watching her. The noise of a clock's dry ticking kept the silence from falling in about our heads.

Finally, she dropped her hands and turned towards me with her usual grace. 'You mustn't take me too seriously,' she said. 'Or I mustn't take myself too seriously, which is more to the point. Cave doesn't really need me or anyone and we . . . I, perhaps you, certainly others, need him. It's best no one try to claim him all as a woman would do, as I might, given the chance.' She rose. 'It's late and you must be tired. Don't ever mention to anyone what I've told you tonight, especially to John. If he knew the way I felt . . .' She left it at that. I gave my promise and we went to our rooms.

I stayed two days at the farm, listening to Cave, who continually referred to the accident. He was almost petulant, as though the whole business were an irrelevant, gratuitous trick played on him by a malicious old man.

Cave's days were spent reading his mail (there was quite a bit of it even then), composing answers which Iris typed out for him, and walking in the wooded hills that surrounded the farm.

The weather was sharp and bright and the wind, when it blew, tasted of ice from the glaciers in the vivid mountains. Winter was nearly upon us and red leaves decorated the wind. Only the firs remained unchanged, warm and dark in the bright chill days.

Cave and I would walk together while Iris remained indoors, working. He was a good walker, calm, unhurried, surefooted, and he knew all the trails beneath the fallen yellow and red leaves. He agreed with most of my ideas for the introduction. I promised to send him a first draft as soon as I had got it done. He was genuinely indifferent to the philosophic aspect of what he preached. He acted almost as if he did not want to hear of those others who had approached the great matter in a similar way. When I talked to him of the fourth-century Donatists who detested life and loved heaven so much that they would request strangers to kill them, and magistrates to execute them for no crime, he stopped me. 'I don't want to hear all that. That's finished. All that's over. We want new things now.'

Iris, too, seemed uninterested in any formalizing of Cave's thought though she saw its necessity and wished me well, suggesting that I not ever intimate derivation since, in fact, there had been none. What he was he had become on his own, uninstructed.

During our walks, I got to know Cave as well as I was ever to know him. He was indifferent, I think, to everyone. He gave one his attention in precise ratio to one's belief in him and the importance of his work. With groups he was another creature: warm, intoxicating, human, yet transcendent, a part of each man who beheld him, the long desired and pursued whole achieved.

And though I found him without much warmth or mind, I nevertheless identified him with the release I had known in his presence, and for this new certainty of life's value and of death's irrelevance, I loved him.

On the third day I made up my mind to go back East and do the necessary writing in New York, away from Paul's distracting influence and Cave's advice. I was asked to stay the rest of the week but I could see that Iris regarded me now as a potential danger, a keeper of secrets who might, despite promises, prove to be disloyal; and so, to set her mind at ease as well as to suit my own new plans, I told her privately after lunch on the third day that I was ready to leave that evening if she would drive me to Spokane.

'You're a good friend,' she said. 'I made a fool of myself the other night. I wish you'd forget it . . . forget everything I said.'

'I'll never mention it. Now, the problem is how I can leave here gracefully. Cave just asked me this morning to stay on and . . .'

But I was given a perfect means of escape. Cave came running into the room, his eyes shining. 'Iris! I've just talked to Paul in L.A. It's all over! No heirs, nothing, no lawsuit. No damages to pay.'

'What's happened?' Iris stopped him in his excitement.

'The old man's dead!'

'Oh Lord!' Iris went grey. 'That means a manslaughter charge!'

'No, no . . . not because of the accident. He was in *another* accident. A truck hit him the day after he left the hospital. Yesterday. He was killed instantly . . . lucky devil. And of course we're in luck too.'

'Did they find who hit him?' I asked, suddenly suspicious. Iris looked at me fiercely. She had got it too.

'No. Paul said it was a hit-and-run. He said this time the police didn't find who did it. Paul said his analyst calls it 'a will to disaster' . . . the old man *wanted* to be run over. Of course that's hardly a disaster but the analyst thinks the old way.'

I left that afternoon for New York, leaving Cave jubilantly making plans for the New Year. Everything was again possible. Neither Iris nor I mentioned what we both suspected. Each in his different way accommodated the first of many crimes.

CHAPTER SEVEN

I

'The tone, dear Gene, has all the unction, all the earnest turgidity of a trained theologian. You are perfect.' Clarissa beamed at me wickedly over lunch in the Plaza Hotel. We sat at a table beside a great plate-glass window through which was visible the frosted bleak expanse of Central Park, ringed by buildings, monotonous in their sharp symmetry. The sky was sullen, dingy with snow ready to fall. The year was nearly over.

'I thought it quite to the point,' I said loftily but with an anxious glance at the thin black volume which was that day to be published, the hasty work of one hectic month, printed in record time by a connection of Paul Himmell's.

'It's pure nonsense, the historical part. *I* know, though I confess I was never one for philosophers, dreary *egotistical* men, worse than actors and not half so lovely. Waiter, I will have a melon. Out of season I hope. I suggest you have it too. It's light.'

I ordered *pot-de-drême*, the heaviest dessert on the menu.

'I've made you angry.' Clarissa pretended contrition. 'I was only trying to compliment you. What I meant was that I think the sort of thing you're doing is nonsense only because action is what counts, action on any level, not theorizing.'

'There's a certain action to *thinking*, you know, even to writing about the thoughts of others.'

'Oh, darling, don't sound so stuffy. Your dessert, by the way, poisons the liver. Oh, isn't that Bishop Winston over there by the door, in tweed? In mufti, eh, Bishop?'

The Bishop, who was passing our table in the company of a handsomely pale youth whose contemplation of orders shone in his face like some cherished sin, stopped and with a smile shook Clarissa's hand.

'Ah, how are you? I missed you the other night at Agnes's. She told me you've been engaged in social work.'

'A euphemism, Bishop.' Clarissa introduced me and the prelate moved onto his table.

'Catholic?'

'Hardly. Episcopal. I like them the best, I think. They adore society and good works . . . spiritual Whigs you might call them, a civilizing influence. Best of all, so few of them believe in God, unlike the Catholics or those terrible Calvinist peasants who are forever damning others.'

'I think you're much too hard on the Episcopalians. I'm sure some of them must believe what they preach.'

'Well, we shall probably never know. Social work! I knew Agnes would come up with something altogether wrong. Still, I'm just as glad it's not out yet. Not until the big debut tomorrow afternoon. I hope you've made arrangements to be near a television set. No? Then come to my place and we'll see it together. Cave's asked us both to the station, by the way, but I think it better if we not distract him.'

'Iris came East with him?'

'Indeed she did. They both arrived last night. I thought you'd talked to her.'

'No. Paul's the only one I ever see.'

'He keeps the whole thing going, I must say. One of those born organizers. Now! what about you and Iris?'

This came so suddenly without preparation, that it took me a suspiciously long time to answer, weakly, 'I don't know what you mean. What about Iris and me?'

'Darling, I know *everything*.' She looked at me in her eager, predatory way. I was secretly pleased that, in this particular case at least, she knew nothing.

'Then tell *me*.'

'You're in love with her and she's classically involved with Cave.'

'Classical seems to be the wrong word. Nothing has happened and nothing *will* happen.'

'I suppose she told you this herself.'

I was trapped for a moment. Clarissa, even in error, was shrewd and if one was not on guard she would quickly cease to be in error, at one's expense.

'No, not exactly. But Paul who I think does know everything about our affairs, assures me that nothing has happened, that Cave is not interested in women.'

'In men?'

'I thought you were all-knowing. No, not in men nor in wild animals nor, does it seem, from the evidence Paul's collected, in anything except John Cave. Sex does not happen for him.'

'Oh,' said Clarissa, exhaling slowly, significantly, inscrutably. She abandoned her first line of attack to ask, 'But *you* are crazy about Iris, aren't you? That's what I'd intended, you know, when I brought you two together.'

'I thought it was to bring me into Cave's orbit.'

'That too, but somehow I saw you and Iris . . . well, you're obviously going to give me no satisfaction so I shall be forced to investigate on my own.'

'Not to sound too auctorial, too worried, do you think it will get Cave across? my Introduction?'

'I see no reason why not. Look at the enormous success of those books with titles like "Eternal Bliss Can Be Yours for the Asking" or "Happiness at Your Beck and Call".'

'I'm a little more ambitious.'

'Not in the least. But the end served is the same. You put down the main line of Cave's thinking, if it can be called thinking. And your book, along with his presence, should have an extraordinary effect.'

'Do you really think so? I've begun to doubt.'

'Indeed I do. They are waiting, all those sad millions who want to believe will find him exactly right for their purposes. He exists only to be believed in. He's a natural idol. Did you know that when Constantine moved his court to the East, his heirs were trained by Eastern courtiers to behave like idols and when his son came in triumph back to Rome (what a day that was! hot, but exciting) he rode for hours through the crowded streets without once moving a finger or changing expression, a perfectly trained god. We were all so impressed.'

I cut this short. 'Has it occurred to you that they might not want to believe anything, just like you and me?'

'Nonsense . . . and it's rude to interrupt, dear, even a garrulous relic like myself . . . yet after all, in a way, we *do* believe what Cave says. Death is there and he makes it seem perfectly all right, oblivion and the rest of it. And dying does rather upset a lot of people. Have you noticed one thing that the devoutly superstitious can never understand – that though we do not accept the fairy tale of reward or punishment beyond the grave we still are reluctant to "pass on", as the nuts say? As though the prospect of nothing isn't really, in its way, without friend Cave to push one into acceptance, perfectly ghastly, *much* worse than toasting on a grid like poor Saint Lawrence. But now I must fly. Come to the apartment at seven and I'll give you dinner. He's on at eight. Afterward they'll all join us.' Clarissa flew.

I spent the afternoon gloomily walking up and down Fifth Avenue filled with doubt and foreboding, wishing now that I had never lent myself to the conspiracy, confident of its failure and of the rude laughter or, worse, the tactful silence of friends who would be astonished to find that after so many years of promise and reflection my first book should prove to be an apologia for an obscure evangelist whose only eminence was that of having mesmerized myself and an energetic publicist, as well as a handful of others more susceptible perhaps than we.

The day did nothing to improve my mood, and it was in a most depressed state that I went finally to Clarissa's Empire apartment on one of the good streets to dine with her and infect her, I was darkly pleased to note, with my own grim mood. By the time Cave was announced on the television screen, I had reduced Clarissa, for one of the few times in our acquaintance, to silence.

Yet as the lights in the room mechanically dimmed and an announcer came into focus, I was conscious of a quickening of my pulse, of a certain excitement. Here it was at last, the result of nearly a year's careful planning. Soon, in a matter of minutes, we would know.

To my surprise Paul Himmell was introduced by the announcer, who identified him perfunctorily, saying that the following half hour had been bought by Cavite, Inc.

Paul spoke briefly, earnestly. He was nervous, I could see, and his eyes moved from left to right disconcertingly as he read his introduction from cards out of view of the camera. He described Cave briefly as a teacher, as a highly regarded figure in the West. He implied it was as a public service, the rarest of the philanthropies, that a group of industrialists and businessmen were sponsoring Cave this evening.

Then Paul walked out of range of the camera, leaving, briefly, a view of a chair and a table behind which a handsome velvet curtain fell in rich graceful folds from the invisible ceiling to an imitation marble floor. An instant later, Cave walked into view.

Both Clarissa and I leaned forward in our chairs tensely, eagerly, anxiously. We were there as well as he. This was our moment too. My hands grew cold and my throat dry.

Cave was equal to the moment. He looked tall. The scale of the table and chair was exactly right. He wore a dark suit and a dark unfigured tie with a light shirt that gave him an austereness which, in person, he lacked. I saw Paul's stage-managing in this.

Cave moved easily into range, his eyes cast down. Not until he had placed himself in front of the table and the camera had squarely centred on him did he looked directly into the lens. Clarissa gasped and I felt suddenly pierced: the camera and lights had magnified rather than diminished his power. It made no difference now what he said. The magic was working.

Clarissa and I sat in the twilight of her drawing room, entirely concentrated on the small screen, on the dark figure, the pale eyes, the hands which seldom moved. It was like some fascinating scene in a skilful play which, quite against one's wish and aesthetic judgement, becomes for that short time beyond real time, a part of one's own private drama of existence, sharpened by artifice, and a calculated magic.

Not until Cave was nearly finished did those first words of his, spoken so easily, so quietly, begin to come back to me as he repeated them in his coda, the voice increasing a little in volume, yet still not hurrying, not forcing, not breaking the mood that the first glance had created. The burden of his words was, as always, the same. Yet this time it seemed more awesome, more final, undeniable ... in short, the truth. Though I had always accepted his first premise, I had never been much impressed by the ways he found of stating it. This night, before the camera and in sight of millions, he perfected his singular art of communication and the world was his.

When he finished, Clarissa and I sat for a moment in complete silence, the chirping of a commercial the only sound in the room. At last she said, 'The brandy is over there on the console. Get me some.' Then she switched off the screen and turned on the lights.

'I feel dragged through a wringer,' she said after her first mouthful of brandy.

'I had no idea it would work so well on television.' I felt strangely empty, let down. There was hardly any doubt now of Cave's effectiveness, yet I felt joyless and depleted, as though part of my life had gone, leaving an ache.

'What a time we're going to have.' Clarissa was beginning to recover. 'I'll bet there are a million letters by morning and Paul will be doing a jig.'

'I hope this is the right thing, Clarissa. It would be terrible if it weren't.'

'Of course it's right. Whatever *that* means. If it works it's right. Perfectly simple. Such conceptions are all a matter of fashion anyway. One year women expose only their ankle; the next year their *derrière*. What's right one year is wrong the next. If Cave captures the popular imagination, he'll be right until someone better comes along.'

'A little cynical.' But Clarissa was only repeating my own usual line. I was, or had been until that night on the Washington farm, a contented relativist. Cave, however, had jolted me into new ways and I was bewildered by the change, by the prospect.

II

That evening was a time of triumph, at least for Cave's companions. They arrived noisily. Paul seemed drunk, maniacally exhilarated, while Iris glowed in a formal gown of green shot with gold. Two men accompanied them, one a doctor whose name I did not catch at first and the other a man from the television network who looked wonderfully sleek and pleased and kept patting Cave on the arm every now and then, as if to assure himself he was not about to vanish in smoke and fire.

Cave was silent. He sat in a high brocaded chair beside the fire and drank tea that Clarissa, knowing his habits, had ordered in advance for him. He responded to compliments with grave nods.

After the first burst of greetings at the door, I did not speak to Cave again and soon the others left him alone and talked around him, about him yet through him, as though he had become invisible, which seemed the case when he was not speaking, when those extraordinary eyes were veiled or cast down, as they were now, moodily studying the teacup, the pattern in the Aubusson rug at his feet.

I crossed the room to where Iris sat beside the doctor, who said, 'Your little book, sir, is written in a complete ignorance of Jung.'

This was sudden but I answered, as graciously as possible, that I had not intended writing a treatise on psychoanalysis.

'Not the point, sir, if you'll excuse me. I am a psychiatrist, a friend of Mr Himmell's' (so this was the analyst to whom Paul so often referred) 'and I think it impossible for anyone today to write about the big things without a complete understanding of Jung.'

Iris interrupted as politely as possible. 'Dr Stokharin is a zealot, Gene. You must listen to him but, first, did you see John tonight?'

'He was remarkable, even more so than in person.'

'It is the isolation,' said Stokharin, nodding. Dandruff fell like a dry snow from thick brows to dark blue lapels. 'The camera separates him from everyone else. He is projected like a dream into . . .'

'He was so afraid at first,' said Iris, glancing across the room at the silent Cave, who sat, very small and still in the brocaded chair, the teacup still balanced on one knee. 'I've never seen him disturbed by anything before. They tried to get him to do a rehearsal but he refused. He can't rehearse, only the actual thing.'

'Fear is natural when . . .' but Stokharin was in the presence of a master drawing-room tactician. Iris was a born hostess. For all her ease and simplicity she was ruthlessly concerned with keeping order, establishing a rightness of tone.

'At first we hardly knew what to do.' Iris's voice rose serenely over the East European rumblings of the doctor. 'He'd always made such a point of the audience. He needed actual people to excite him. Paul wanted to fill the studio with a friendly audience but John said no, he'd try it without. When the talk began there were only a half dozen of us there; Paul, myself, the technicians. No one else.'

'How did he manage?'

'It was the camera. He said when he walked out there he had no idea if anything would happen or not, if he could speak. Paul was nearly out of his mind with terror. We all were. Then John saw the lens of the camera. He said looking into it gave him a sudden shock, like a current of electricity passing through him, for there, in front of him, was the eye of the world and the microphone above his head was the ear into which at last he could speak. When he finished, he was transfigured. I've never seen him so excited. He couldn't recall what he had said but the elation remained until . . .'

'Until he got here.'

'Well, nearly.' Iris smiled. 'He's been under a terrible strain these last two weeks.'

'It'll be nothing like the traumatizing shocks in store for him during the next few days,' said Stokharin, rubbing the bowl of a rich dark pipe against his nose to bring out its lustre (the pipe's lustre, for the nose, straight, thick, proud, already shone like a baroque pearl). 'Mark my words, everyone will be eager to see this phenomenon. When Paul first told me about him, I said, ah, my friend, you have found that father for which you've searched since you own father was run over by a bus in your ninth (the crucial) year. Poor Paul, I said, you will be doomed to disappointment. The wish for the father is the sign of your immaturity. For a time you find him here, there . . . in analysis you transfer to me. Now you meet a spellbinder and you turn to him, but it will not last. Exactly like that I talked to him. Believe me, I hold back nothing. Then I met this Cave, I watched him. Ah, what an analyst he would have made! What a manner, what power of communication! A natural healer. If only we could train him. Miss Mortimer, to you I appeal. Get him to study. The best people, the true Jungians are all here in New York. They will train him. He would become only a lay analyst but, even so, what miracles he could perform, what therapy! We must not waste this native genius.'

'I'm afraid, Doctor, that he's going to be too busy wasting himself to study your . . . procedures.' Iris smiled engagingly but with dislike apparent in her radiant eyes. Stokharin, however, was not sensitive to hostility, no doubt attributing such emotions to some sad deficiency in the other's adjustment.

Iris turned to me. 'Will you be in the city the whole time?'

'The whole time Cave's here? Yes. I wouldn't miss it for anything.'

'I'm glad. I've so much I want to talk to you about. So many things are beginning to happen. Call me tomorrow. I'll be staying at my old place. It's in the book.'

'Cave?'

'Is staying with Paul, out on Long Island at someone's house. We want to keep him away from pests as much as possible.'

'Manic depression, I should say,' said Stokharin thoughtfully, his pipe now clenched between his teeth and his attention on Cave's still figure. 'With latent schizoid tendencies which . . . Miss Mortimer, you must have an affair with him. You must marry him if necessary. Have children. Let him see what it is to give life to others, to live in a balanced . . .'

'Doctor, you are quite mad,' said Iris. She rose and crossed the room, cool in her anger. I too got away from the doctor as quickly as I could. 'False modesty, inhibited behaviour, too-early bowel training,' and similar phrases ringing in my ears.

Paul caught me at the door. I had intended to slip away without saying good night, confident that Clarissa would understand, that the others would not notice. 'Not going so soon, are you?' He was a little drunk, his face dark with excitement. 'But you ought to stay and celebrate.' I murmured something about having an early appointment the next day.

'Well, see me tomorrow. We've taken temporary offices in the Empire State Building. The money has begun to roll in. If this thing tonight turns out the way I think it will, I'm going to be able to quit my other racket for good and devote full time to Cave.' Already the name Cave had begun to sound more like that of an institution than of a man.

'By the way, I want to tell you what I think of the Introduction. Superior piece of work. Tried it out on several high-brow friends of mine and they liked it.'

'I'm afraid . . .'

'That, together with the talks on television, should put this thing over with the biggest bang in years. We'll probably need some more stuff from you, historical background, rules and regulations, that kind of thing, but Cave will tell you what he wants. We've hired a dozen people already to take care of the mail and inquiries. There's also a lecture tour being prepared, all the main cities, while . . .'

'Paul, you're not trying to make a religion of this, are you?' I could hold it back no longer even though both time and occasion were all wrong for such an outburst.

'Religion? Hell, no . . . but we've got to organize. We've got to get this to as many people as we can. People have started looking to us (to him, that is) for guidance. We can't let them down.'

Clarissa's maid ushered in a Western Union messenger, laden with telegrams. 'Over three hundred,' said the boy. 'The station said to send them here.'

Paul paid him jubilantly, and in the excitement, I slipped away.

III

The results of the broadcast were formidable. My Introduction was taken up by excited journalists who used it as a basis for hurried but exuberant accounts of the new marvel.

One night a week for the rest of that winter Cave appeared before the shining glass eye of the world, and on each occasion new millions in all parts of the country listened and saw and pondered this unexpected phenomenon, the creation of their own secret anxieties and doubts, a central man.

The reactions were too numerous for me to recollect in any order or with any precise detail; but I do recall the first few months vividly.

A few days after the first broadcast, I went to see Paul at the offices he had taken in the Empire State Building, as high up as possible, I noted with amusement: always the maximum, the optimum.

Halfway down a corridor, between lawyers and exporters, Cavite, Inc., was discreetly identified in black upon a frosted-glass door. I went inside.

It appeared to me the way I had always thought a newspaper office during a crisis might look. Four rooms opening off one another, all with doors open, all crowded with harassed secretaries and clean-looking young men in blue serge suits carrying papers, talking in loud voices; the room sounded like a hive at swarming time.

Though none of them knew me, no one made any attempt to ask my business or to stop me as I moved from room to room in search of Paul. Everywhere there were placards with Cave's picture on them, calm and gloomy-looking, dressed in what was to be his official costume, dark suit, unfigured tie, white shirt. I tried to overhear conversations as I passed the busy desks and groups of excited debaters, but the noise was too loud. Only one word was identifiable, sounding regularly, richly emphatic like a cello note: Cave, Cave, Cave.

In each room I saw piles of my Introduction, which pleased me even though I had come already to dislike it.

The last room contained Paul, seated behind a desk with a Dictaphone in one hand, three telephones on his desk (none fortunately ringing at this moment) and four male and female attendants with notebooks and pencils eagerly poised. Paul sprang from his chair when he saw me. The attendants fell back. 'Here he is!' He grabbed my hand and clung to it vice-like. I could almost feel the energy pulsing in his fingertips, vibrating through his body; his heartbeat was obviously two to my every one.

'Team, this is Eugene Luther.'

The team was properly impressed and one of the girls, slovenly but intelligent-looking, said, 'It was you who brought me here. First you I mean . . . and then of course Cave.'

I murmured vaguely and the others told me how 'clear' I had made all philosophy in the light of Cavesword. (I believe it was that day, certainly that week, Cavesword was coined by Paul to denote the entire message of John Cave to the world.)

Paul then shooed the team out with instructions that he was not to be bothered. The door, however, was left open.

'Well, what do you think of them?' He leaned back, beaming at me from his chair.

'They seem very . . . earnest,' I said, wondering not only what I was supposed to think but, more to the point, what I *did* think of the whole business.

'I'll say they are! I tell you, Gene, I've never seen anything like it. The thing's bigger even than that damned crooner I handled . . . you know the one. Everyone has been calling up and, look!' He pointed to several bushel baskets containing telegrams and letters. 'This is only a fraction of the response since the telecast. From all over the world. I tell you, Gene, we're in.'

'What about Cave? Where is he?'

'He's out on Long Island. The press is on my tail trying to interview him but I say no, no go, fellows, not yet. And does that excite them! We've had to hire guards at the place on Long Island just to keep them away.'

'How is Cave taking it all?'

'In his stride, absolute model of coolness, which is more than I am. He agrees that it's better to keep him under wraps while the telecasts are going on. It means that curiosity about him will increase like nobody's business. Look at this.' He showed me a proof sheet of a tabloid story: 'Mystery Prophet Wows TV Audience,' with a photograph of Cave taken from the telecast and another one showing Cave ducking into a taxi, his face turned away from the camera. The story seemed most provocative and, for that complacent tabloid, a little bewildered.

'Coming out Sunday,' said Paul with satisfaction. 'There's also going to be coverage from the big circulation media. They're going to monitor the next broadcast even though we said nobody'd be allowed on the set while Cave was speaking.' He handed me a bundle of manuscript pages bearing the title 'Who Is Cave?' 'That's the story I planted in one of the slick magazines. Hired a name writer, as you can see, to do it.' The name writer's name was not known to me, but presumably it would be familiar to the mass audience.

'And, biggest of all, we got a sponsor. We had eleven offers already and we've taken Dumaine Chemicals. They're paying us enough money to underwrite this whole setup here, and pay for Cave and me as well. It's terrific but dignified. Just a simple "through the courtesy of" at the beginning and another at the end of each telecast. What do you think of that?'

'Unprecedented!' I had chosen my word some minutes before.

'I'll say. By the way, we're getting a lot of letters on that book of yours.' He reached in a drawer and pulled out a manila folder which he pushed towards me. 'Take them home if you like. Go over them carefully, might give you some ideas for the next one, you know – ground which needs covering.'

'Is there to be a next one?'

'Man, a flock of next ones! We've got a lot to do, to explain. People want to know all kinds of things. I'm having the kids out in the front office do a breakdown on all the letters we've received, to get the general reaction, to find what it is people most want to hear; and, believe me, we've been getting more damned questions, and stuff like, "Please, Mr Cave, I'm married to two men and feel maybe it's a mistake since I have to work nights anyway." Lord, some of them are crazier than that.'

'Are you answering all of them?'

'Oh, yes, but in my name. All except a few of the most interesting which go to Cave for personal attention. I've been toying with the idea of setting up a counsellor service for people with problems.'

'But what can *you* tell them?' I was more and more appalled.

'Everything in the light of Cavesword. You have no idea how many questions that answers. Think about it and you'll see what I mean. Of course we follow standard psychiatric procedure, only it's speeded up so that after a couple of visits there can be a practical and inspirational answer to their problems. Stokharin said he'd be happy to give it a try, but we haven't yet worked out all the details.'

I changed the subject. 'What did you have in mind for me to do?'

'Cavesword applied to everyday life.' He spoke without hesitation; he had thought of everything. 'We'll know more what people want to hear after a few more telecasts, after more letters and so on. Then supply Cavesword where you can and, where you can't, just use common sense and standard psychiatric procedure.'

'Even when they don't always coincide?'

Paul roared with laughter. 'Always the big knocker, Gene. That's what I like about you, the disapproving air. It's wonderful. I'm quite serious. People like myself . . . visionaries, you might say, continually get their feet off the ground and it's people like you who pull us back, make us think. Anyway, I hope you'll be able to get to it soon. We'll have our end taken care of by the time the telecasts are over.'

'Will you show Cave to the world then? I mean in person?'

'I don't know. By the way, we're having a directors' meeting Friday morning. You'll get a notice in the mail. One of the things we're going to take up is just that problem, so you be thinking about it in the meantime. I have a hunch it may be smart to keep him away from interviewers for good.'

'That's impossible.'

'I'm not so sure. He's pretty retiring except when he speaks. I don't think he'd mind the isolation one bit. You know how dull he gets in company when he's not performing.'

'Would he consent?'

'I think we could persuade him. Anyway, for now he's a mystery man. Millions see him once a week but no one knows him except ourselves. A perfect state of affairs, if you ask me.'

'You mean there's always a chance he might make a fool of himself if a tough interviewer got hold of him?'

'Exactly, and believe me there's going to be a lot of them after his scalp.'

'Have they begun already?'

'Not yet. We have you to thank for that, too, making it so clear that though what we say conflicts with all the churches we're really not competing with them, that people listening to Cavesword can go right on being Baptists and so on.'

'I don't see how, if they accept Cave.'

'Neither do I, but for the time being that's our line.'

'Then there's to be a fight with the churches?'

Paul nodded grimly. 'And it's going to be a honey. People don't take all the supernatural junk seriously these days but they do go for the social idea of the church, the uplift kind of thing. That's where we'll have to meet them, where we'll have to lick them at their own game.'

'I looked at him for one long moment. I had of course anticipated something like this from the moment that Cave had become an organization and not merely one man talking. I had realized that expansion was inevitable. The rule of life is more life and of organization more organization, increased dominion. Yet I had not suspected Paul of having grasped this so promptly, using it so firmly to his and our advantage. The thought that not only was he cleverer than I had realized but that he might, indeed, despite his unfortunate approach, be even cleverer than myself, disagreeably occurred to me. I had until then regarded myself as the unique intellectual of the Cavites, the one sane man among maniacs and opportunists. It seemed now that there were two of us with open eyes and, of the two, he alone possessed ambition and energy.

'You mean this to be a religion, Paul?'

He smiled, 'Maybe, yes ... something on that order perhaps. Something workable, though, for now, I've thought about what you said the other night.'

'Does Cave want this?'

Paul shrugged. 'Who can tell? I should think so but this is not really a problem for him to decide. He has happened. Now *we* respond. Stokharin feels that a practical faith, a belief in ways of behaviour which the best modern analysts are agreed on as being closest to ideal, might perform absolute miracles. No more guilt feeling about sex if Cave were to teach that all is proper when it does no harm to others ... and the desire to do harm to others might even be partly removed if there were no false mysteries, no terrible warnings in childhood and so on. Just in that one area of behaviour we could work wonders! Of course there would still be problems, but the main ones could be solved if people take to Cave and to us. Cavesword is already known and it's a revelation to millions ... we know that. Now they are looking to him for guidance in other fields. They know about death at last. Now we must tell them about living and we are lucky to have available so much first-rate scientific research in the human psyche. I suspect we can even strike on an ideal behaviour pattern by which people can measure themselves.'

'And to which they will be made to conform?' Direction was becoming clear already.

'How can we force anyone to do anything? Our whole power is that people come to us, to Cave, voluntarily because they feel here, at last, is the answer.' Paul might very well have been sincere. There is no way of determining, even now.

'Well, remember, Paul, that you will do more harm than good by attempting to supplant old dogmas and customs with new dogmas. It will be the same in the end except that the old is less militant, less dangerous than a new order imposed by enthusiasts.'

'Don't say "you". Say "we". You're as much a part of this as I am. After all, you're a director. You've got a say-so in these matters. Just speak up Friday.'

Paul was suddenly genial and placating. 'I don't pretend I've got all the answers. I'm just talking off the top of my head, like they say.'

A member of the team burst into the office with the news that Bishop Winston was outside.

'Now it starts,' said Paul with a grimace.

The Bishop did not recognize me as we passed one another in the office. He looked grim and he was wearing clerical garb.

'He's too late,' said a lean youth, nodding at the churchman's back.

'Professional con men,' said his companion with disgust. 'They've had their day.'

And with that in my ears, I walked out into the snow-swirling street; thus did Cave's first year begin.

I was more alarmed than ever by what Paul had told me and by what I heard on every side. In drugstores and bars and restaurants, people talked of Cave. I could even tell when I did not hear the name that it was of him they spoke: a certain intentness, a great curiosity, a wonder. In the bookstores, copies of my Introduction were displayed together with large blown-up photographs of Cave.

Alone in a bar on Madison Avenue where I'd taken refuge from the cold, I glanced at the clippings Paul had given me. There were two sets. The first were the original perfunctory ones which had appeared. The reviewers, knowing even less philosophy than I, tended to question my proposition that Cavesword was anything more than a single speculation in a rather large field. I had obviously not communicated his magic, only its record which, like the testament of miracles, depends entirely on faith: to inspire faith one needed Cave himself.

'What do you think about the guy?' The waiter, a fragile, Latin with parchment-lidded eyes, mopped the spilled gin off my table (he'd seen a picture of Cave among my clippings).

'It's hard to say,' I said. 'How does he strike you?'

'Boy, like lightning!' The waiter beamed. 'Of course I'm Catholic but this is something new. Some people been telling me you can't be a good Catholic and go for this guy. But why not? I say. You still got Virginmerry and now you got him, too, for right now. You ought to see the crowd we get here to see the TV when he's on. It's wild.'

It was wild, I thought, putting the clippings back into the folder. Yet it might be kept within bounds. Paul had emphasized my directorship, my place in the structure. Well, I would show them what should be done or, rather, *not* done.

Then I went out into the snow-dimmed street and hailed a cab. All the way to Iris's apartment I was rehearsing what I would say to Paul when next we met. 'Leave them alone,' I said aloud. 'It is enough to open the windows.'

'Open the windows!' The driver snorted. 'It's damn near forty in the street.'

IV

Iris occupied several rooms on the second floor of a brownstone in a street with, pleasantest of New York anachronisms, trees. When I entered, she was doing yoga exercises on the floor, sitting crosslegged on a mat, her slender legs in a leotard and her face flushed with strain. 'It just doesn't work for me!' she said and stood up without embarrassment.

Since I'd found the main door unlocked, I had opened this one too, without knocking.

'I'm sorry, Iris, the downstairs door was . . .'

'Don't be silly.' She rolled up the mat efficiently. 'I was expecting you but lost track of time . . . which means it must be working a little. I'll be right back.' She went into the bedroom and I sat down, amused by this unexpected side to Iris. I wondered if perhaps she was a devotee of wheat germ and mint tea as well. She claimed not. 'It's the only real exercise I get,' she said, changed now to a heavy robe that completely swathed her figure as she sat curled up in a great armchair, drinking Scotch, as did I, the winter outside hid by drawn curtains, by warmth and light.

'Have you done it long?'

'Oh, off and on for years. I never get anywhere but it's very restful and I've felt so jittery lately that anything which relaxes me . . .' her voice trailed off idly. She seemed relaxed now.

'I've been to see Paul,' I began importantly.

'Ah.'

But I could not, suddenly, generate sufficient anger to speak out with eloquence. I went around my anger stealthily, a murderer stalking his victim. 'We disagreed.'

'In what?'

'In everything, I should say.'

'That's so easy with Paul.' Iris stretched lazily; ice chattered in her glass; a car's horn melodious and foreign sounded in the street below. 'We need him. If it weren't Paul, it might be someone a great deal worse. At least he's intelligent and devoted. That makes up for a lot.'

'I don't think so. Iris, he's establishing a sort of supermarket, short-order church for the masses.'

She laughed delightedly. 'I like that! And, in a way, you're right. That's what he *would* do left to himself.'

'He seems in complete control.'

'Only of the office. John makes all the decisions.'

'I wish I could be sure of that.'

'You'll see on Friday. You'll be at the meeting, won't you?'

I nodded. 'I have a feeling that between Paul and Stokharin this thing is going to turn into a world-wide clinic for mental health.'

'I expect worse things *could* happen, but Paul must still contend with me and you and of course the final word is with John.'

'How is Cave, by the way?'

'Quite relaxed, unlike the rest of us. Come out to Long Island and see. I go nearly every day for a few hours. He's kept completely removed from everyone except the servants and Paul and me.'

'Does he like that?'

'He doesn't seem to mind. He walks a good deal . . . it's a big place and he's used to the cold. He reads a little, mostly detective stories . . . and then of course there's the mail that Paul sends on. He works at that off and on all day. I help him and when we're stuck (you should see the questions!) we consult Stokharin, who's very good on some things, on problems . . .'

'And a bore the rest of the time.'

'That's right,' Iris giggled. 'I couldn't have been more furious the other night, but, since then, I've seen a good deal of him and he's not half bad. We've got him over the idea that John should become a lay analyst. The response to the telecast finally convinced Stokharin that here was a "racial folk father figure" . . . his very own words. Now he's out to educate the father so that he will fulfill his children's needs on the best Jungian lines.'

'Does Cave take him seriously?'

'He's bored to death with him. Stokharin's the only man who's ever had the bad sense to lecture John . . . who absolutely hates it. But he realizes that Stokharin's answers to some of the problems we're confronted with are ingenious. All that . . . hints to the lovelorn is too much for John, so we need Stokharin to take care of details.'

'I hope Cave is careful not to get too involved.'

'John's incorruptible. Not because he is so noble or constant but because he can only think a certain way and other opinions, other evidence, don't touch him.'

I paused, wondering if this was true. Then: 'I'm going to make a scene on Friday. I'm going to suggest that Paul is moving in a dangerous direction, towards organization and dogma, and that if something is not done soon we'll all be ruined by what we most detest, a militant absolutist doctrine.'

Iris looked at me curiously. 'Tell me, Gene, what *do* you want? Why are you still with Cave, with all of us, when you so apparently dislike the way we are going? You've always been perfectly clear about what you did *not* want (I can recall, I think, every word you said at the farm that night), but to be specific, what would you like all this to become? How would you direct things if you could?'

I had been preparing myself for such a question for several months, I still had no single answer to make which would sharply express my own doubts and wishes. But I made an attempt. 'I would not organize, for one thing. I'd have Cave speak regularly, all he likes, but there would be no Cavite, Inc., no Paul planting articles and propagandizing. I'd keep just Cave, nothing more. Let him do his work. Then, gradually, there will be effects, a gradual end to superstition . . .'

Iris looked at me intently. '*If* it were possible, I would say we should do what you suggest, but it would be ruinous not only for us but for everyone . . .'

'Why ruinous? A freedom to come to a decision on one's own without . . .'

'That's it. No one can be allowed that freedom. One doesn't need much scholarship or even experience to see that. Everywhere people are held in check by stifling but familiar powers. People are used to tyranny. They expect governments to demand their souls, and they have given up decisions on many levels for love of security. What you suggest is impossible with this race at this time.'

'You're talking nonsense. After all, obeisance to established religions is the order of the day, yet look at the response to Cave, who is undermining the whole Christian structure.'

'And wait until you see the fight they're going to put up!' said Iris grimly. 'Fortunately, Cavesword is the mortal blow though Cave himself would be their certain victim if he were not protected, if there were no organization to guard him, and the World.'

'So Paul and his – his team, his proselytizers are to become merely an equivalent power, combating the old superstitions with their own weapons.'

'More or less, yes. That's what it has come to.'

'Even though Cave's talking to the people would be enough? Let them use him, not he them.'

'A good slogan,' Iris smiled. 'But I think I'm right. No one would have a chance to see or hear him if it weren't for Paul. You should read the threatening letters we've been getting.'

'I thought all the mail was most admiring?'

'All that came from people who've actually *heard* him, but there's a lot coming in now from religious fanatics. They are very extreme. And of course the churches, one by one, are starting to take notice.'

'I saw Bishop Winston in Paul's office today.'

'He's been trying to see John all week. He finally settled for Paul, I gather. In any case, after the next telecast there will really be a storm.'

'The next? What's going to happen then?'

'John will tell them that there's no need for the churches, that their power derives from superstition and bloody deeds.'

I was startled. 'When did this occur to him? I thought he intended to go on as he was, without ever coming out openly against them.'

'I was surprised too. He told me yesterday; he'd been brooding all day and, suddenly, he started to attack them. It's going to be murderous.'

'I hope not for him.'

'Oh, he'll convince, I'm sure of that. But their revenge . . .' She gave a troubled sigh. 'Anyway, Gene, you do see why we can't, for our own safety, dispense with Paul and his financiers and press agents and all the squalid but necessary crew.'

'It may be too late,' I agreed. 'But I fear the end.'

'No one can tell. Besides, as long as you and I are there with John it will be all right.'

I felt her confidence was not entirely justified, but I determined to defer my attack on Paul's methods until a safer time.

We argued about the wisdom of the coming telecast. Was it really necessary to confront the enemy explicitly? and in his own country, so to speak? Iris was not sure, but she felt Cave's instinct was right even though he had, perhaps, been goaded into action sooner than anticipated by the harsh letters of Christian zealots.

And then by slow degrees, by careful circling, the conversation grew personal.

'I've never told anyone else,' said Iris, looking at me speculatively.

'Don't worry; I haven't repeated any of it.' And, as always at such times, I feel a warm flood of guilt. Any direct statement of personal innocence has always made me feel completely criminal.

'But since I've told you, I . . . it's a relief to have someone I can talk to about John. I don't dare mention his name to my family, to my old friends. I don't think they even know that I know him.'

'I thought it has all been in the papers.'

'I haven't been mentioned but, after Friday, everyone will know. Paul says there's no way for us to duck inquiries. After the directors' meeting he'll issue a statement naming directors, stockholders and so on.'

'But even then, why should anyone suspect you were interested in Cave or he in you? It's possible merely to be a director, isn't it?'

Iris shrugged. 'You know how people are. Clarissa keeps wanting to have what she calls a comfy chat about *everything* and I keep putting her off. Stokharin now takes it for granted that John and I sleep together, that he is the father image to me and I the mother to him.'

It had an odd ring to it and I laughed. 'Do you think that's a sound Jungian analysis?'

Iris smiled faintly. 'Whatever it is, the feeling, such as it is, is all on my side.'

'He shows no sign of returning your affection?'

'None at all. He's devoted to me, I think. He relies on my judgement. He trusts me, which is more than he does anyone else I know of . . .'

'Even me?' Always the 'I' coming between me and what I wished to know: that insatiable, distressing 'I'.

'Yes, even you, dear, and Paul too. He's on guard against everyone, but not in a nasty or suspicious way. He . . . what is the phrase? he keeps his own counsel.'

'And you are the counsel?'

'In a sense, and nothing more.'

'Perhaps you should give up. It would seem that . . . love was not possible for him. If so, it's unwise for you to put yourself in such a position . . . harmful, too.'

'But there's still the other Cave. I love him as well and the two are, finally, the same.'

'A *metaphysique*?'

'No, or at least I don't see a paradox. It's something else; it's like coming out of an illness with no past at all, only a memory of pain and dullness which soon goes in the wonderful present.'

'It?'

'My love is *it*.' Her voice grew strong. 'I've learned that in loving him I love life, which I never did before. Why I can even value others now, value all those faceless creatures whom I knew without ever bothering to see, to bring in focus the dim blurs of all *that* world alive. I lived asleep. Now I am awake.'

'He does not love you.'

'Why should he? It's gone beyond that. I'm no longer the scales most lovers are, weighing the deeds and gifts and treasures proffered against those received or stolen from the other, trying always to bring into fatal balance two separate things. I give myself and what I take is life, the knowledge that there is another creature in the world whose wonder, to me at least, is all-satisfying by merely being.'

'Is it so terrible to be alive?'

'Beyond all expectation, my poor friend.' And then I left her to return to winter, to the snow-filled streets and my old pain.

V

The second telecast had the anticipated effect. The day after, Friday, nearly a hundred thousand letters and telegrams had been received, and Cave's life had been threatened four times over the telephone.

I was awakened at five o'clock on Friday morning by a newspaperman begging an interview. Half asleep, irritably, I told him to go to hell and hung up though not before I'd heard the jeer: 'Thought you fellows did away with hell.' This woke me up and I made coffee, still keeping my eyes half shut in the dim winter light, hoping sleep might return to its accustomed perch; but more telephone calls demoralized my fragile ally and I was left wide awake, unshaven, with fast-beating heart beside the telephone, drinking coffee.

Every few minutes there was a call from some newspaperman or editor requesting information. They had all been shocked by the telecast. When I told them to get in touch with Cave himself, or at least with Paul's office, they only laughed. Thousands were trying to speak to Paul, tens of thousands to Cave; the result was chaos. Shakily, I took the phone off its hook and got dressed. When I opened my door to get the morning paper, a thin young man leaped past me into my living room and anchored himself to a heavy chair.

'What . . .' I began; he was only too eager to explain the what and the why.

'And so,' he ended, breathlessly, 'the *Star* has authorized me to advance you not only *that* money but expenses, too, for an exclusive feature on Cave and the Cavites.'

'I wish,' I said, very gentle in the presence of such enthusiasm, 'that you would go away. It's five in the morning . . .'

'You're our only hope,' the boy wailed. 'Every paper and news service has been trying to get past the gate out on Long Island for three weeks and failed. They couldn't even shoot him at long range.'

'Shoot him?'

'Get a picture. Now please . . .'

'Paul Himmell is your man. He's authorized to speak for Cave. He has an office in the Empire State Building and he keeps respectable hours; so why don't you . . .'

'We haven't been able to get even a release out of him for three days now. It's censorship, that's what it is.'

I had to smile. 'We're not the government. Cave is a private citizen and this is a private organization. If we choose not to give interviews you have no right to pester us.'

'Oh, come off it.' The young man was at an age where the needs of ambition were often less strong than the desire for true expression; for a moment he forgot that he needed my forbearance and I liked him better. 'This is the biggest news that's hit town since V-E Day. You guys have got the whole country asking questions and the big one is: who is Cave?'

'There'll be an announcement today, I think, about the company. As for Cave, I suggest you read a little book called "An Introduction to . . ." '

'Of course I've read it. That's why I'm here. Now, please, Mr Luther, give me an exclusive even if you won't take the *Star*'s generous offer. At least tell me something I can use.'

I sat down heavily; a bit of coffee splattered from cup to saucer to the back of my hand and dried stickily. I felt worn out already, the day only just begun. 'What do you want me to tell you? What would you most like to hear? What do you expect me to say since, being a proper journalist, that is what you'll write no matter what I tell you?'

'Oh, that's not true. I want to know what Cave's all about as a person, as a teacher.'

'Well, what do *you* think he's up to?'

'Me? Why . . . I don't know. I never heard him on the air until last night. It was strong stuff.'

'Were you convinced?'

'In a way, yes. He said a lot of things I agreed with but I was a little surprised at his going after the churches. Not that I like anything about *them*, but still it's some stunt to get up and talk like that in front of millions of people. I mean you just don't say those things any more, even if you do think them . . . can't offend minorities. That's what you learn first in journalism school.'

'There's part of your answer then. Cave is a man who, unlike others, says what he thinks is true even if it makes him unpopular. There's some virtue in that.'

'I guess he can afford to in his position,' said the boy vaguely. 'You know we got Bishop Winston to answer him for the *Star*. Signed him last night after Cave went off the air. I'm sure he'll do a good job. Now . . .'

We wrestled across the room. Since I was the stronger, I won my privacy though muffled threats of exposure were hurtled at me from behind the now-bolted door.

Acting on an impulse, I left the apartment as soon as I was sure my visitor had gone. I was afraid that others would try to find me if I stayed home; fears which were justified. According to the elevator man, he had turned away several men already. The one who did get through had come up the fire escape.

I walked quickly out into the quiet street, the snow now gone to slush as grey as the morning sky. Fortunately, the day was neither windy nor cold and I walked to a Times Square Automat for an early breakfast.

I was reassured by anonymity. All around me sleepy men and women clutching newspapers, briefcases and lunch boxes sat sullenly chewing their breakfast, sleep not yet departed.

I bought a roll, more coffee, hominy grits, which I detested in the North but occasionally tried in the hope that, by accident, I might stumble upon the real thing. These were not the real thing and I left them untouched while I read my paper.

Cave was on the front page. Not prominent, but still he was there. The now-standard photograph looked darkly from the page. The headline announced that: 'Prophet Flays Churches as Millions Listen'. There followed a paraphrase of the telecast which began with those fateful and soon to be famous words: 'Our quarrel is not with Christ but with his keepers'. I wondered, as I read, if anyone had ever taken one of the telecasts down in shorthand and made a transcript of it. I, for one, should have been curious to see in cold print one of those sermons. Cave himself knew that without his presence they would not stand up, and he allowed none of them to be transcribed. As a result, whenever there was a report of one of his talks it was, necessarily, paraphrased, which gave a curious protean flavour to his doctrine, since the recorded style was never consistent, changing always with each paraphraser just as the original meaning was invariably altered by each separate listener as he adapted the incantation to his private needs.

A fat yellow-faced woman sat down with a groan beside me and began to ravish a plate of assorted cakes. Her jaws grinding, the only visible sign of life, for her eyes were glazed from sleep and her body, incorrectly buttoned into a cigarette-ash-dusted dress, was as still as a mountain; even the work of lungs was obscured by the torpid flesh.

I watched her above the newspaper, fascinated by the regularity with which jaws ground bits of cake. Her eyes looked past me into some invisible world of pastry.

Then, having finished the report on Cave's telecast, I put the newspaper down and ate with deliberate finesse my own biscuit. The rustling of the newspaper as it was folded and placed on the table disturbed my companion and, beneath the fat, her will slowly sent out instructions to the extremities. She cleared her throat. The chewing stopped. A bit of cake was temporarily lodged in one cheek, held in place by a sturdy plate. She squinted at the newspaper. 'Something about that preacher fellow last night?'

'Yes. Would you like to see it?' I pushed the paper towards her.

She looked at the picture, carefully spelling out the words of the headlines with heavy lips and deep irregular breaths. 'Did you see him last night?' she asked when her eye finally got to the small print where it stopped, as though halted by a dense jungle.

'Yes. As a matter of fact, I did.'

'He sure gave it to them bastards, didn't he?' Her face lit up joyously. I thought of *ça ira.*

'You mean the clergy?'

'That's just what I mean. They had it too good, too long. People afraid to say anything. Takes somebody like him to tell us what we know and tell *them* where to head in.'

'Do you like what he said about dying?'

'About there being nothing? Why, hell, mister, I knew it all along.'

'But it's good to hear someone else say it?'

'Don't do no harm.' She belched softly. 'I expect they're going to be on his tail,' she added with gloomy pleasure, spearing a fragment of éclair which she had missed on her first circuit of the crowded dish.

I spent that morning in the street buying newspapers and eavesdropping. I heard several arguments about Cave. The religiously orthodox were outraged but clearly interested. The others were triumphant though all seemed to feel that *they*, as the Automat woman had said, would soon be on his tail. Ours was no longer a country where the nonconformist could escape disaster if he unwisely showed a strange face to the multitude.

I tried to telephone Iris and then Clarissa but both telephones were busy. I rang my office but was told by a mechanical voice that if I left my name and address and business Mr Himmell would get back to me as soon as possible. The siege had begun.

I arrived at the Empire State Building half an hour before the meeting was to begin, hoping to find out in advance from Paul what was happening and what we were supposed to do about it.

A line of pickets marched up and down before the entrance, waving banners, denouncing Cave and all his works in the names of various religious groups. A crowd was beginning to gather and the police, at least a score, moved frantically about, not certain how to keep the mob out of the building. When I stepped off the elevator at Cave's floor, I found myself a part of a loud and confused mass of men and women all shoving towards the door which was marked Cavite, Inc. Policemen barred their way.

Long before I had got to the door, a woman's shoe went hurtling through the air, smashing a hole in the frosted glass. One policeman cocked his revolver menacingly. Another shouted, 'Get the riot squad!' But still the crowd raved and shouted and quarrelled. Some wanted to lynch Cave in the name of the Lamb, while others begged to be allowed to touch him, just once. I got to the door at last, thanks to a sudden shove which landed me with a crash into a policeman. He gasped and then, snarling, raised his club. 'Business!' I shouted with what breath was left me. 'Got business here. Director.'

I was not believed but, after some talk with a pale secretary through the shattered glass door, I was admitted. The crowd roared when they saw this and moved in closer. The door slammed shut behind me.

'It's been like this since nine o'clock,' said the secretary, looking at me with frightened eyes.

'You mean after two hours the police still can't do anything?'

'We didn't call them right away. When we did it was too late. We're barricaded in here.'

But Paul was not in the least disturbed. He was standing by the window in his office looking out. Clarissa, her hat and her hair together awry, a confusion of straw and veil and bolts of reddish hair apparently not all her own, was making up in a pocket mirror.

'Ravenous wild beasts!' she hailed me. 'I've seen *their* likes before.'

'Gene, good fellow! Got through the mob all right? Here, have a bit of brandy. No? Perhaps some Scotch?'

I said it was too early for me to drink. Shakily, I sat down. Paul laughed at the sight of us. 'You both look like the end of the world has come.'

'I'd always pictured the end as being quite orderly . . .' I began stuffily, but Doctor Stokharin's loud entrance interrupted me. His spectacles were dangling from one ear and his tie had been pulled around from front to back quite neatly. 'No authority!' he bellowed, ignoring all of us. 'The absence of a traditional patriarch, the centre of the tribe, has made them insecure. Only together do they feel warmth in great *swarming* hives!' His voice rose sharply and broke on the word 'hives' into a squeak. He took the proffered brandy and sat down, his clothes still disarranged.

'My hair,' said Clarissa grimly, 'will never come out right again today.' She put the mirror back into her purse, which she closed with a loud snap. 'I don't see, Paul, why you didn't have the foresight to call the police in advance and demand protection.'

'I had no idea it would be like this. Believe me, it's not deliberate.' But from Paul's excited chuckling, I could see that he was delighted with the confusion, a triumph of the publicist's dark art. I wondered if he might not have had a hand in it. It was a little reminiscent of the crowds of screaming women which in earlier decades, goaded by publicists, had howled and, as Stokharin would say, swarmed about singers and other theatrical idols.

Paul anticipated my suspicions. 'Didn't have a thing to do with it, I swear. Doctor, your tie is hanging down your back.'

'I don't mind,' said Stokharin disagreeably, but he did adjust his glasses.

'I had a feeling we'd have a few people in to see us but no idea it would be like this.' He turned to me as the quietest, the least dangerous of the three. 'You wouldn't believe the response to last night's telecast if I told you.'

'Why don't you tell me?' The comic aspects were becoming apparent: Stokharin's assaulted dignity and the ruin of Clarissa's ingenious hair both seemed to me suddenly funny. I tried not to smile. Paul named some stupendous figures with an air of triumph. 'And there are more coming all the time. Think of that!'

'Are they favourable?'

'Favourable? Who cares?' Paul was pacing the floor quickly, keyed to the breaking point had he possessed the metabolism of a normal man. 'We'll have a breakdown over the week-end. Hired more people already. Whole bunch working all the time. By the way, we're moving.'

'Not a moment too soon,' said Clarissa. 'I suggest, in fact, we move now while there are even these few police to protect us. When they go home for lunch (they all eat enormous lunches, one can tell), that crowd is going to come in here and throw us out the window.'

'Or suffocate us with love,' said Paul.

Stokharin looked at Clarissa thoughtfully; with his turned-around necktie he had a sacerdotal look. 'Do you often think of falling from high places? of being pushed from windows or perhaps high trees?'

'Only when I'm on a top floor of the world's highest building surrounded by raving maniacs do such forebodings occur to me. Doctor. If you had any sense of reality you might be experiencing the same fear.'

Stokharin clapped his hands happily. 'Classic, classic. To believe she alone knows reality. Madam, I suggest that you . . .'

There was a roar of sound from the hallway; a noise of glass shattering; a revolver went off with a sharp report and, frozen with alarm, I waited for its echo. There was none; only shouts of Cave! Cave! Cave!

Surrounded by police, Cave and Iris were escorted into the office. More police held the door, aided by the office crew who, suddenly, inspired, were throwing paper cups full of water into the crowd. Flashbulbs like an electric storm flared in all directions as the newspapermen invaded the office, let in by the police who could not hold them back.

Iris looked frightened and even Cave seemed alarmed by the rioting.

Once the police lieutenant had got Cave and Iris into the office, he sent his men back to hold the corridor. Before he joined them he said sternly, breathing hard from the struggle, 'We're going to clear the hall in the next hour. When we do we'll come and get you people out of here. You got to leave whether you want to or not. This is an emergency.'

'An hour is all we need, officer.' Paul was smooth. 'And may I say that my old friend the Commissioner is going to hear some extremely nice things about the efficiency and good sense of his men.' Before the lieutenant had got around to framing a suitably warm answer, Paul had manoeuvred him out of the inner office; and locked the door behind him.

'There,' he said turning to us, very businesslike. 'It was a mistake meeting here after last night. I'm sorry, Cave.'

'It's not your fault.' Cave, having found himself an uncomfortable straight chair in a corner of the room, sat very erect, like a child in serious attendance upon adults. 'I had a hunch we should hold the meeting out on Long Island.'

Paul scowled. 'I hate the idea of the press getting a look at you. Spoils the mystery effect. But it was bound to happen. Anyway you won't have to talk to them.'

'Oh, but I will,' said Cave easily, showing who was master here, this day.

'But . . . well, after what we decided, the initial strategy being . . .'

'No. It's all changed now. I'll have to face them, at least this once. I'll talk to them the way I always talk. They'll listen.' His voice grew dreamy. He was indifferent to Paul's opposition.

'Did you find a new place?' asked Iris, suddenly, to divert the conversation.

'What? Oh yes. A whole house, five storeys on East Sixty-first Street. Should be big enough. At least for now.' The interoffice communicator sounded. Paul spoke quickly into it: 'Tell the newspaper people to wait out there. We'll have a statement in exactly an hour and they'll be able . . .' he paused and looked at Cave for some reprieve: seeing none, he finished: 'They'll be able to interview

Cave.' He flipped the machine off. Through the locked door, we heard a noise of triumph from the gathered journalists and photographers.

'Well, come along,' said Clarissa. 'I thought this was to be a board of directors' meeting. Cave, dear, you've got to preside.'

But, though he said he'd rather not, Clarissa, in a sudden storm of legality, insisted that he must. She also maliciously demanded a complete reading of the last meeting's minutes by Paul, the secretary. We were able to save him by a move to waive the reading, which was proposed, recorded and passed by a show of hands, only Clarissa dissenting. Cave conducted the meeting solemnly. Then Clarissa demanded a report from the treasurer and this time Paul was not let off.

For the first time I had a clear picture of the company of which I was a director. Shares had been sold. Control was in the hands of Clarissa, while Paul and several West Coast industrialists whose names were not familiar to me also owned shares. The main revenue of the company now came from the sponsor of Cave's television show. There was also a trickle of contributions which, in the last few weeks, had increased considerably.

Then Paul read from a list of expenses, his voice hurrying a little over his own salary, which was, I thought, too large. Cave's expenses were recorded and, with Clarissa goading from time to time, Paul gave an accounting of all that had been spent since the arrival in New York. John Cave was a big business.

'The books are audited at standard intervals,' said Paul, looking at Clarissa as he finished, some of his good humour returning. 'We will not declare dividends unless Mrs Lessing insists the company become a profit-making enterprise.'

'It might not be a bad idea,' said Clarissa evenly. 'Why not get a little return . . .'

But Paul had launched his policy. We listened attentively. From time to time, Cave made a suggestion. Iris and I made no comment. Stokharin occasionally chose to illuminate certain human problems as they arose and Paul, at least, heard him out respectfully. Clarissa wanted to know all about costs and her interruptions were always brief and shrewd.

Several decisions were made at that meeting. It was decided that a Centre be established where Dr Stokharin could minister to those Cavites whose problems might be helped by therapy. 'We just apply classical concepts to their little troubles,' he said.

'But it shouldn't *seem* like a clinic,' said Iris suddenly. 'It's all part of John, of what John says.'

'We'll make that perfectly clear,' said Paul quickly.

Stokharin nodded agreeably. 'After all, it is in his name they come to us. We take it from there. No more problems . . . all is contentment.' He smacked his lips.

It was then decided that Cave would spend the summer quietly and, in the autumn, begin a tour of the country to be followed by more telecasts in the following winter. 'The summer is to think a little in,' were Cave's words.

Next, I was assigned the task of writing a defence of Cave for certain vast syndicates. I was also requested to compose a set of dialogues which would record Cave's views on such problems as marriage, the family, world government, problems all in urgent need of solution. I suggested diffidently that it would be very useful if Cave were to tell me what he thought about such things before I wrote my dialogues. Cave said, quite seriously, that we would have the summer in which to handle all these subjects.

Paul then told us the bad news; there was a good deal of it. 'The Cardinal, in the name of all the Diocesan Bishops, has declared that any Catholic who observes the telecasts of John Cave or attends in person his blasphemous lectures commits a mortal sin. Bishop Winston came to tell me that not only is he attacking Cave in the press but that he is quite sure, if we continue, the government will intervene. It was a hint, and not too subtle.'

'On what grounds intervene?' asked Cave. 'What have I done that breaks one of their laws?'

'They'll trump up something,' said Clarissa.

'I'm afraid you're right. They can always find something to get us on.'

'But can they?' I asked. 'Free speech is still on the books.'

Paul chuckled. 'That's just where it stays, too.' And he quoted the national credo: In a true democracy there is no place for a serious difference of opinion on great issues. 'Sooner or later they'll try to stop Cave.'

'But they can't!' said Iris. 'The people won't stand for it.'

'He's the father of too many now,' said Stokharin sagely. 'No son will rise to dispute him, yet.'

'Let's cross that bridge when we come to it.' Paul was reasonable. 'Now let's get a statement ready for the press.'

While Paul and Cave worked over the statement, the rest of us chatted quietly about other problems. Stokharin was just about to explain the origin of alcoholism in terms of the new Cavite pragmatism when Iris said, 'Look!' and pointed to the window where, bobbing against the glass, was a bright red child's balloon on which had been crudely painted, 'Jesus Saves.'

Stokharin chuckled when he saw it. 'Very ingenious. Someone gets on the floor beneath and tries to shake us with his miracle. Now we produce the counter-miracle.' He slid the window open. The cold air chilled us all. He took his pipe and touched its glowing bowl to the balloon, which exploded loudly; then he shut the window beaming. 'It will be that easy,' he said. 'I promise you. A little fire, and pop! these superstitions disappear like bad dreams.'

CHAPTER EIGHT

I

The six months after the directors' meeting were full of activity and danger. Paul was forced to hire bodyguards to protect Cave from disciples as well as from enemies, while those of us who were now known publicly to be Cave's associates were obliged to protect our privacy with unlisted telephone numbers and numerous other precautions, none of which did much good, for we were continually harassed by madmen and interviewers.

The effect Cave had made on the world was larger than even Paul, our one optimist, had anticipated. I believe even Cave himself was startled by the vastness and the variety of the response.

As I recall, seldom did a day pass without some new exposé or interpretation of this phenomenon. Bishop Winston attacked after nearly every telecast. The Catholic Church invoked its entire repertory of anathemas and soon it was whispered in devout Christian circles that the Antichrist had come at last, sent to test the faith. Yet, despite the barrage of attacks, the majority of those who heard Cave became his partisans and Paul, to my regret but to the delight of everyone else, established a number of Cavite Centres in the major cities of the United States, each provided with a trained staff of analysts who had also undergone an intensive indoctrination in Cavesword. Stokharin headed these clinics. Also, at Cave's suggestion, one evening a week, the same evening, Cavites would gather to discuss Cavesword, to meditate on the beauty of death, led in their discussions and meditations by a disciple of Cave who was, in the opinion of the directors, equal to the task of representing Cave and his Word.

Iris was placed in charge of recruiting and training the proselytizers, while Paul handled the business end, obtaining property in different cities and managing the large sums which poured in from all over the world. Except for Cave's one encounter with the press that day in the Empire State Building (an occasion which, despite its ominous beginning, became a rare triumph: Cave's magic had worked even with the hostile), he was seen by no one except his intimates and the technicians at the television studio. Ways were found to disguise him so that he would not be noticed in the lobbies or elevators of the television network building. Later he spoke only from his Long Island retreat, his speeches recorded on film in advance.

By summer there were more than three million registered Cavites in the United States and numerous believers abroad. Paul was everywhere at once; flying from city to city (accompanied by two guards and a secretary); he personally broke ground in Dallas for what was to be the largest Cavite Centre in the United States; and although the inaugural ceremonies were nearly stopped by a group of Baptist ladies carrying banners and shouting 'Onward Christian Soldiers', no one was hurt and the two oil millionaires who had financed the Centre gave a great barbecue on the foundation site.

Iris was entirely changed by her responsibilities. She had become, in the space of a few months, brisk and energetic, as deeply involved in details as a housewife with a new home. I saw very little of her that spring. Her days were mostly spent in a rented loft in the Chelsea district, where she lectured the candidates for field work and organized a makeshift system of indoctrination for potential Residents, as the heads of the various centres were known.

Iris was extraordinarily well fitted for this work, to my surprise, and before the year ended she had what was in fact a kind of university where as many as three hundred men and women at a time were transformed into Residents and Deputy Residents and so on down through an ever proliferating hierarchy. For the most part, the first men and women we sent out to the country were highly educated, thoughtful people, entirely devoted to Cavesword. They were, I think, the best of all, for later, when it became lucrative to be a Resident, the work was largely taken over by energetic careerists whose very activity and competence diminished their moral effectiveness.

Iris used me unmercifully those first months. I lectured her students. I taught philosophy until, in exasperation at the absurdity of *that*, I told her to hire a professional teacher of philosophy, which she did.

Yet I enjoyed these men and women. Their sincerity and excitement communicated itself to me and I became aware of something I had known before only from reading, from hearsay: the religious sense which I so clearly lacked, as did both Paul and Stokharin. I don't think Cave really possessed it either because, although he believed entirely in himself and in the miraculous truth of his Word, he did not possess that curious power to identify himself with creation, to transcend the self in contemplation of an abstraction, to sacrifice the personality to a mystical authority; none of us, save Iris in love, possessed this power which, as nearly as I can get at it, is the religious sense in man. I learned about it only from those who came to learn from us in that Chelsea loft. In a sense I pitied them, for I knew that much of what they evidently believed with such passion was wrong. But at the same time, I was invigorated by their enthusiasm, by the hunger with which they devoured Cavesword, by the dignity their passion lent to an enterprise that in Paul's busy hands resembled, more often than not, a cynical commercial venture. And I recognized in them (oh, very early, perhaps in the first weeks of talking to them) that in their goodness and their love they would, with Cavesword, smudge each bright new page of life as it turned; yet, suspecting this, I did not object nor did I withdraw. Instead, fascinated, I was borne by the tide to the shore whose every rock I could imagine, sharp with disaster.

Once a week the directors met on Long Island in the walled estate where Cave now lived with his guards. The meetings soon demonstrated a division in our ranks; between Paul and Stokharin on the one side and Iris, Clarissa and Cave on the other with myself as partisan, more often than not, to Cave. The division was amiable but significant. Paul and Stokharin wanted to place the Centres directly under the supervision of the analysts, while the rest of us, led by Iris (Cave seldom intervened, but we had already accepted the fact that Iris spoke for him), preferred that the Centres be governed by the Residents. 'It is certainly true that the therapists are an important part of each Centre,' said Iris briskly, at the end of a long wrangle with Stokharin. 'But these are *Cavite* Centres and not clinics for the advancement of Jungian analysis. It is Cavesword which draws people to the Centres, not mental illness. Those who have problems are of course helped by Stokharin's people but, finally, it is Cave who has made it possible for them to face death. Something no one has done before.' And thus the point was won in our council, though Stokharin and Paul were still able at times, slyly, to insinuate their own creatures into important Residencies.

My own work went on fitfully. I composed an answer to Bishop Winston which brought down on my head a series of ecclesiastical thunderbolts, each louder than the one before. I wrote a short life of Cave in simple declarative sentences which enjoyed a considerable success for many years and, finally, seriously, in my first attempt at a true counterattack, I began the several dialogues in which Cave and I purportedly traversed the entire field of moral action.

I felt that in these dialogues I could quietly combat those absolutist tendencies which I detected in the disciples. Cave himself made to pretence of being final on any subject other than death, where, even without his particular persuasiveness, he stood on firm, even traditional ground. The attacks he received he no longer noticed. It was as simple as that. He had never enjoyed reading, and to watch others make telecasts bored him, even when they spoke of him. After the fateful Empire State Building conference he ceased to attend the world; except for a few letters which Paul forwarded to him and his relations with us, he was completely cut off from ordinary life, and perfectly happy. For though human contacts had been reduced to a minimum, he still possessed the polished glass eye of the world before whose level gaze he appeared once a week and experienced what he called 'Everyone. All of them, listening and watching everywhere.'

In a single year Cave had come a long way from the ex-embalmer who had studied a book of newspaper clippings on a Washington farm and brooded about an old man in a hospital. Though Paul was never to refer again to the victim of Cave's driving, I was quite sure that he expected, sooner or later, that mysterious death would return to haunt us all.

By midsummer, Cave had grown restless and bored, and since the telecasts had been discontinued until the following November, he was eager to travel. He was never to lose his passion for places. It was finally decided that he spend the summer on one of the Florida Keys, a tiny island owned by a Cavite who offered to place everything at the master's disposal. And, though warned that the heat might be uncomfortable, Cave and his retinue left secretly one night by chartered seaplane from Long Island Sound and for at least a month the press did not know what had happened to him.

I declined to accompany Cave and Iris. Paul remained in New York, while Iris's work was temporarily turned over to various young enthusiasts trained by her. I went back to the Hudson Valley, to my house and . . .

II

I have not been able to write for several days. According to the doctor it is a touch of heat, but I suspect that this is only his kind euphemism.

I had broken off in my narrative to take a walk in the garden last Friday afternoon when I was joined by Butler, whose attentions lately have been more numerous than I should like.

'He'll be here Sunday, Hudson. Why don't we all three have dinner together that night and celebrate.'

I said that nothing could give me more pleasure, as I inched along the garden path, moving towards the hot shaded centre where, beneath fruit trees, a fine statue of Osiris stood, looted in earlier days by the hotel management from one of the temples. I thought, however, with more longing of the bench beside the statue than of the figure itself, whose every serene detail I had long since memorized. Butler adjusted his loose long stride to my own uneven pace. I walked as I always do now, with my eyes upon the ground, nervously avoiding anything which might make me stumble, for I have fallen down a number of times in the last few years and I have a terror of broken bones, the particular scourge of old bodies.

I was as glad as not that I didn't have to watch my companion while we chatted, for his red honest face, forever dripping sweat, annoyed me more than was reasonable.

'And he'll be pleased to know I've got us a Centre. Not much of one but good enough for a start.'

I paused before a formidable rock that lay directly in my path. It would take some doing to step over it, I thought, as I remarked, 'I'm sure the Pasha doesn't know about this.'

'Not really.' Butler laughed happily. 'He thinks we're just taking a house for ourselves to study the local culture. Later, after we get going, he can find out.'

'I'd be very careful,' I said and, very careful myself, I stepped over the rock; my legs detested the extra exertion; one nearly buckled as it touched the ground. I threw my weight on my cane and was saved a fall. Butler had not noticed.

'Jessup is going to bring in the literature. We'll say it's our library. All printed in Arabic, too. The Dallas Centre thinks of everything.'

'Are they . . . equipped for such things?'

'Oh yes. That's where the main university is now. Biggest one in the world. I didn't go there myself. Marks weren't good enough, but Jessup did. He'll tell you all about it. Quite a crew they turn out: best in the business, but then they get the cream of the crop to begin with.'

'Tell me, are the Residents still in charge of the Centres or do they share the administration with the therapists?'

'Therapists?' Butler seemed bewildered.

'In the old days there used to be the Resident and his staff and then a clinic attached where . . .'

'You really are behind the times.' Butler looked at me as though I'd betrayed a firsthand knowledge of earth's creation. 'All Residents and their staffs, including the Communicators like myself, get the same training; part of it is in mental therapy. Those who show particular aptitude for therapy are assigned clinical work just as I do communication work in foreign countries. People who get to be Residents are usually teachers and administrators. Sometimes a Communicator will even get a Residency in his old age as a reward for the highest services.' He then explained to me the official, somewhat Byzantine, structure of the Cavites. There were many new titles, indicating a swollen organization under the direction of a Counsel of Residents which, in turn, was responsible for the election from among their number of a unique Chief Resident whose reign lasted for the remainder of his lifetime.

With relief, I sat down on the bench beside Osiris. Butler joined me. 'Dallas of course is the main Residency,' he said.

'It used to be in New York, years ago,' I said, thinking of the brownstone house, of the loft on Twenty-third Street.

'Around twenty years ago it was moved to Dallas by the Chief Resident. Not only did they have the best-equipped Centre there but the Texans make just about the best Cavites in the country. What they won't do for Cavesword isn't worth mentioning. They burned the old churches, you know . . . every one in the state.'

'And one or two Baptist ministers as well?'

'You can't break eggs without making an omelette,' said Butler sententiously.

'I see what you mean. Still, Cave was against persecution. He always felt it was enough for people to hear Cavesword . . .'

'You got a lot of reading to do,' said Butler sharply. 'Looks like you've forgotten your text: "And, if they persist in superstition, strike them, for one idolator is like a spoiled apple in the barrel, contaminating the other".' Butler's voice, as he quoted, was round and booming, rich in vowel sounds, while his protruding eyes gazed without blinking into the invisible radiance of truth which hovered, apparently, above a diseased hibiscus bush.

'I've forgotten that particular quotation,' I said.

'Seems funny you should, since it's just about the most famous of the texts.' But, though my ignorance continued to startle Butler, I could see that he was beginning to attribute it to senility rather than to laxity or potential idolatry.

'I was a close follower in the first few years,' I said, currying favour. 'But I've been out of touch since and I suppose that after Cave's death there was a whole mass of new doctrine with which I am unfamiliar, to my regret.'

'Doctrine!' Butler was shocked. 'We have no doctrine. We are not one of those heathen churches with claims to "divine" guidance. We're simply listeners to Cavesword. That's all. He was the first to tell the plain truth and naturally we honour him, but there is no doctrine even though he guides us the way a good father does his children.'

'I am very old,' I said in my best dying-fall voice. 'You must remember that when you are with me you are in the company of a man who was brought up in the old ways, who uses Christian terms from time to time. I was thirty when Cave began his mission. I am, as a matter of fact, nearly the same age as Cave himself if he were still alive.'

That had its calculated effect. Butler looked at me with some awe. 'Golly!' he said. 'It doesn't really seem possible, does it? Of course there're still people around who were alive in those days, but I don't know of anybody who actual *saw* Cave. You did tell me you saw him?'

'Once only.'

'Was he like the telecasts?'

'Oh yes. Even more effective, I think.'

'He was big of course, six feet one inch tall.'

'No, he was only about five feet eight inches, a little shorter than I . . .'

'You must be mistaken because, according to all the texts, he was six feet one.'

'I saw him at a distance, of course. I was only guessing.' I was amused that they should have seen fit to change even Cave's stature.

'You can tell he was a tall man from the telecasts.'

'Do they still show them?'

'Still show them! They're the main part of our weekly Get-togethers. Each Residency has a complete library of Cave's telecasts, one hundred and eight including the last. Each week, a different one is shown by the Resident's staff, and the Resident himself or someone assigned by him discusses the message.'

'And they still hold up after fifty years?'

'Hold up? We learn more from them each year. You should see all the books and lectures on Cavesword . . . several hundred important ones which we have to read as part of our communication duties, though they're not for the laymen. We discourage nonprofessionals from going into such problems, much too complicated for the untrained mind.'

'I should think so. Tell me, is there any more trouble with the idolators?'

Butler shook his head. 'Just about none. They were licked when the parochial schools were shut down. That took care of Catholicism. Of course there were some bad times. I guess you know all about them.'

I nodded. Even in Egypt I had heard of massacres and persecutions. I could still recall the morning when I opened the Cairo paper and saw a large photograph of St Peter's smouldering in its ruins, a fitting tomb for the last Pope and martyr who had perished there when a mob of Cavites had fired the Vatican. The Cairo paper took an obvious delight in these barbarities and I had not the heart to read of the wanton destruction of works of Michelangelo and Bernini, the looting of the art galleries, the bonfire which was made in the Papal gardens of the entire Vatican library. Later, word came of a certain assistant Resident of Topeka who, with a group of demolition experts and Cavite enthusiasts, ranged across France and Italy destroying the cathedrals with the approval of the local governments, as well as the Cavite crowds who gathered in great numbers to watch, delightedly, the crumbling of these last monuments to superstition. Fortunately, the tourist bureaus were able to save a few of the lesser churches.

'The Edict of Washington which outlawed idolatrous schools did the trick. The Atlantic Community has always believed in toleration. Even to this day it is possible for a man to be a Christian, though unlikely since the truth is so well known.'

'But the Christian has no churches left and no clergy.'

'True, and if that discourages him he's not likely to remain too long in error. As I've told you, though, we have our ways of making people see the truth.'

'The calculable percentage.'

'Exactly.'

I looked at Osiris in the green shade. His diorite face smiled secretly back at me. 'Did you have much trouble in the Latin countries?'

'Less than you might think. The ignorant were the big problem because, since they didn't know English, we weren't able to use the telecasts. Fortunately, we had some able Residents and after a little showmanship, a few miracles (or what they took to be miracles), they came around, especially when many of their ex-priests told them about Cavesword. Nearly all of the older Residents in the Mediterranean countries were once Catholic priests.'

'Renegades?'

'They saw the truth. Not without some indoctrination, I suspect. We've had to adapt a good many of our procedural methods to fit local customs. The old Christmas has become Cavesday and what was Easter is now Irisday.'

'Iris Mortimer?'

'Who else? And then certain festivals which . . .'

'I suppose she's dead now.'

'Why, yes. She died six years ago. She was the last of the Original Five.'

'Ah, yes, the five: Paul Himmell, Iris Mortimer, Ivan Stokharin, Clarissa Lessing and . . .'

'And Edward Hastings. We still use his Introduction even though it's been largely obsoleted by later texts. His dialogues will of course be the basis for that final book of Cave, which our best scholars have been at work on for over twenty years.'

Hastings, of all people! I nearly laughed aloud. Poor feckless Hastings was now the author of *my* dialogues with Cave. I marvelled at the ease with which the innumerable references to myself had been deleted. I began to doubt my own existence. I asked if Hastings was still alive and was told that he too was long dead.

I then asked again about Iris.

'Some very exciting things have come to light,' said Butler. 'Certain historians at the Dallas Centre feel that there is some evidence that she was Cave's sister.'

I was startled by this. 'How could that be? Wasn't she from Detroit? and wasn't he from Seattle? and didn't they meet for the first time in southern California at the beginning of his mission?'

'I see you know more Cavite history than you pretend,' said Butler amiably. 'That of course has been the traditional point of view. Yet as her influence increased in the world (in Italy, you know, one sees her picture nearly as often as Cave's) our historians became suspicious. It was all perfectly simple, really. If she could exert nearly the same power as Cave himself then she must, in some way, be related to him. I suppose you know about the Miami business. No? Well, their Resident, some years ago, openly promulgated the theory that Cave and Iris Mortimer were man and wife. A great many people believed him and though the Chief Resident at Dallas issued a statement denying the truth in all this, Miami continued in error and it took our indoctrination team several years to get the situation back to normal. But the whole business *did* get everyone to thinking and, with the concurrence of Dallas, investigations have been made. I don't know many of the details but my colleague probably will. He keeps track of that kind of thing.'

'If she is proven to be Cave's sister will she have equal rank with him?'

'Certainly not. Cavesword is everything. But she will be equal to him on the human level though his inferior in truth. At least that appears to be the Dallas interpretation.'

'She was very active, I suppose?'

'Right until the end. She travelled all over the world with Cavesword and, when she grew too old to travel, she took over the Residency of New York City, which she held until she died. As a matter of fact, I have a picture of her which I always carry. It was taken in the last years.' He pulled out a steel-mesh wallet in which, protected by cellophane, was a photograph of Iris, the first I had seen in many many years. My hand shook as I held the picture up to the light.

For a split second I felt her presence, saw in the saddened face, framed by white hair, my summer love which had never been except in my own dreaming where I was whole and loved this creature whose luminous eyes had not altered with age, their expression the same as that night beside the western sea. But then my fingers froze. The wallet fell to the ground. I fainted into what I supposed with my last vestige of consciousness to be death, to be nothing.

III

I awakened in my own bed with my old friend Dr Riad beside me. He looked very much concerned while, at the foot of the bed, stood Butler, very solemn and still. I resolved not to die with him in the room.

'My apologies, Mr Butler,' I said, surprised that I could speak at all. 'I'm afraid I dropped your picture.' I had no difficulty in remembering what had happened. It was as if I had suddenly shut my eyes and opened them again, several hours having passed instead of as many seconds. Time, I decided, was all nonsense.

'Think nothing of it. I'm only . . .'

'You must not strain yourself, Mr Hudson,' said the doctor. A few days in bed, plenty of liquids, a pill or two, and then I was left alone with a buzzer beside my bed which would summon the houseboy if I should have a coherent moment before taking a last turn for the worse. The next time, I think, will be the final one and though I detest the thought, these little rehearsals over the last few years – the brief strokes, the sudden flooding of parts of the brain with the blood of capillaries in preparation for that last arterial deluge – have got me used to the idea. My only complaint is that odd things are done to my memory by these strokes which, light as they have been, tend to alter those parts of the brain which hold the secrets of the past. I have found this week, while convalescing from Tuesday's collapse, that most of my childhood has been washed clean out of my memory. I knew of course that I was born on the banks of the Hudson but I cannot for the life of me recall what schools I attended; yet memories from college days on seem unimpaired, though I have had to reread this memoir attentively to resume my train of thought, to refresh a dying memory. It is strange indeed to have lost some twenty years as though they had never been and, worse still, to be unable to find out about oneself in any case, since the will of others has effectively abolished one. I do not exist in the world and very soon (how soon I wonder?), I shall not exist even to myself, only this record a fragile proof that I once lived.

Now I am able to work again. Butler pays me a daily visit, as does the doctor. Both are very kind but both tend to treat me as a thing which no longer matters. I have been written off in their minds. I'm no longer really human since soon, perhaps in a few days, I shall not be one of them but one of the dead whose dust motes the air they breathe. Well, let it come. The fraternity of the dead, though nothing, is the larger kingdom.

I am able to sit up in bed (actually I can get around as well or as badly as before but it tires me too much to walk so I remain abed). Sunday is here at last, and from the excited bustle in the air, which I feel rather than hear, Butler's colleague must have arrived. I am not ready for him yet and I have hung a 'Do Not Disturb' sign on the door, composed emphatically in four languages. It should keep them out for a few days.

I have a premonition of disaster which, though it is no doubt perfectly natural at my age with the last catastrophe almost upon me, seems to be of a penultimate nature, a final *human* crisis. All that I have heard from Butler about this young man, this colleague of his, disposes me to fear him. For although my existence has been kept a secret from the newer generations, the others, the older ones, the chief counsellors are well aware of me. Though I have so far evaded their agents and though they undoubtedly assume that I am long since dead, it is still possible that a shrewd young man with a career in the making might grow suspicious, and one word to the older members of the hierarchy would be enough to start an inquisiton which could end in assassination (ironic that I should fear *that* at this point!) or, more terrible, in a course of indoctrination where my apostasy would be reduced by drugs to conformity. It would be the most splendid triumph for Cave if, in my last days, I should recant. The best victory of all, the surrender of the original lutherist upon his deathbed.

Yet I have a trick or two up my sleeve and the game's not yet over. Should the new arrival prove to be the one I have so long awaited, I shall know how to act. I have planned for this day. My adversary will find me armed.

But now old days draw me back; the crisis approaches in my narrative.

IV

The first summer was my last on the Hudson, at peace. Iris wrote me regularly from the Florida Keys. Short, brisk letters completely impersonal and devoted largely to what 'he' was doing and saying. It seems that 'he' was enchanted by the strangeness of the Keys, yet was anxious to begin travelling again. With some difficulty, I gathered between the lines, Iris had restrained him from starting out on a world tour. 'He says he wants to see Saigon and Samarkand and so forth soon because he likes the names. I don't see how he can get away yet, though maybe in the fall after his tour. They say now he can make his talks on film all at once, which will mean of course he won't have to go through anything like last winter again.' There followed more news, an inquiry into my health (in those days I was confident I should die early of a liver ailment; my liver now seems the one firm organ in my body; in any case, I enjoyed my hypochondria) and a reference to the various things I was writing for the instruction of converts and detractors both. I pushed the letter away and looked out across the river.

I was alone, awaiting Clarissa for tea. I had actually prepared tea since she never drank alchol and I myself was a non-drinker that summer when my liver rested (so powerful is imagination) like a brazen cannonball against the cage of bones.

I sat on my porch, which overlooked the lawn and the water; unlike most other houses on that river, mind had the railroad behind it instead of in front of it, an agreeable state of affairs; I don't mind the sound of trains but the sight of their tracks depresses me.

Besides me, among the tray of tea things, the manuscript of my dialogue lay neglected. I had not yet made up my mind whether or not to read it to Clarissa. Such things tended to bore her; yet, if she could be enticed into attention, her opinion would be useful. Such a long memory of old customs would be invaluable to me as I composed, with diligence rather than inspiration, an ethical system whose single virtue was that it ended to satisfy the needs of human beings as much as was possible without inviting chaos. I had, that morning over coffee, abolished marriage. During lunch, served me by my genteel but impoverished housekeeper (although servants still existed in those days in a few great houses, people like myself were obliged to engage the casual services of the haughty poor). I decided to leave marriage the way it was but make divorce much simpler. After lunch, suffering from a liver-inspired headache, I not only abolished marriage again but resolutely handed the children over to the impersonal mercies of the state.

Now, bemused, relaxed, my eyes upon the pale blue Catskills and the summer green, ears alert to the noise of motorboats like great waterbugs, I brooded upon the implications of what I was doing and, though I was secretly amused at my own confidence, I realized, too, that what I felt and did and wrote, though doubtless unorthodox to many, was, finally, not really the work of my own inspiration but a logical result of all that was in the world. A statement of the dreams of others which I could formulate only because I shared them. Cave regarded his own words as revelation when, actually, they only echoed the collective mind, a plausible articulation of what most men felt even though their conscious minds were corsetted and constricted by familiar ways of thinking, often the opposite of what they truly believed.

Yet at this step I hesitated. There was no doubt that the children and the society would be the better for such an arrangement . . . and there was little doubt that our civilization *was* moving towards such a resolution. But there were parents who would want to retain their children and children who might be better cared for by their progenitors than by even the best-intentioned functionaries of the state. Would the state allow parents to keep their children if they wanted them? If not, it was tyrannous; if so, difficult in the extreme, for how could even the most enlightened board of analysts determine who should be allowed their children and who not? The answer, of course, was in the retraining of future generations. Let them grow up accepting as inevitable and right the surrender of babies to the state. Other cultures had done it and ours could too. But I was able to imagine, vividly, the numerous cruelties which would be perpretrated in the name of the whole, while the opportunity for tyranny in a civilization where all children were at the disposal of a government brought sharply to mind that image of the anthill society which has haunted the imagination of the thoughtful for at least a century.

I had got myself into a most gloomy state by the time Clarissa arrived, trailing across the lawn in an exotic ankle-length gown of grey which floated in yards behind her, like the diaphanous flags of some forgotten army.

'Your lawn is full of moles!' she shouted to me, pausing in her progress and scowling at a patch of turf. 'And it needs cutting and more clover. *Always* more clover, remember that.' She turned her back on me to stare at the river, which was as grey as her gown but, in its soft tidal motion, spangled with light like sequins on a vast train.

She had no criticism of the river when she at last turned and climbed the steps to the porch; she sat down with a gasp. 'I'm boiling! Tea? Hot tea to combat the heat.'

I poured her a cup. 'Not a hot day at all.' Actually it was very warm. 'If you didn't get yourself up as a Marie Corelli heroine, you'd be much cooler.'

'Not very gallant today, are we?' Clarissa loooked at me over her cup. 'I've had this gown for five hundred years. There used to be a wimple, but I lost it moving.'

'The material seems to be holding up quite well,' and now that she had mentioned it, there *was* an archaic look to the texture of the gown, like those bits of cloth preserved under glass in museums.

'Silk lasts indefinitely, if one is tidy. Also I don't wear this much, as you can see, but with the devalued state of the dollar (an ominous sign, my dear, the beginning of the end!) I've been forced to redo a lot of old odds and ends I've kept for sentimental reasons. This is one of them and I'm very fond of it.' She spoke deliberately, to forestall any further ungallantry.

'I just wondered if it was cool.'

'It is cool. Ah, a letter from Iris.' Clarissa had seen the letter beside my chair and, without asking permission, had seized it like a magpie and read it through quickly. 'I admire a girl who types,' she said, letting fall the letter. 'I suppose they all do now though it seems like only yesterday that, if one did not open a tearoom, one typed, working for men, all of whom made advances. That was when we had to wear corsets and hatpins. One discouraged while the other protected.' Clarissa chuckled at some obscene memory.

'I wonder if Paul can keep Cave from wandering off to some impossible place.'

'I shouldn't be surprised.' She picked at the tea sandwiches suspiciously, curling back the top slices of bread to see what was underneath. Tentatively, she bit into devilled ham; she chewed; she swallowed; she was not disappointed. She wolfed another sandwich, talking all the while. 'Poor Cave is a captive now. His disciples are in full command. Even Mohammed, as strong-headed as he was, finally ended up a perfect pawn in the hands of Abu Bekr and the women, especially the women.'

'I'm not so sure about Cave. He . . .'

'Does what they tell him, especially Iris.'

'Iris? But I should have said she was the only one who *never* tried to influence him.'

Clarissa laughed unpleasantly. A moth flew into her artificial auburn hair. Unerringly, she found it with one capable hand and quickly snuffed out its life in a puff of grey dust from broken wings. She wiped her fingers on a paper napkin. The day was full of moths, but none came near us again. 'You are naïve, Eugene,' she said, her little murder done. 'It's your nicest quality. In theory you are remarkably aware of human character; yet, when you're confronted with the most implausible appearance, you promptly take it for the reality.'

I was irritated by this and also by the business of the sandwich, not to mention the murder of the moth. I looked at Clarissa with momentary dislike. 'I was not aware . . .' I began, but she interrupted me with an airy wave of her hand.

'I forgot no one likes to be called naïve. Calculating, dishonest, treacherous – people rather revel in those designations, but to be thought trusting . . .' She slapped her hands as though to punctuate her meaning; then, after a full stop, she went on more soberly. 'Iris is the one to look out for. Our own sweet, self-effacing, dedicated Iris. I adore her. I always have, but she's up to no good.'

'I don't know what you're talking about.'

'You will. You would if you weren't entirely blind to what they used to call human nature. Iris is acquiring Cave.'

'Acquiring?'

'Exactly the word. She loves him for all sorts of reasons but she cannot have him in the usual sense (I found out all about that, by the way). Therefore, the only thing left for her to do is acquire him, to take his life in hers. You may think *she* may think that her slavish adoration is only humble love, but actually it's something far more significant, and dangerous.'

'I don't see the danger, even accepting your hypothesis.'

'It's no hypothesis and the danger is real. Iris will have him, and, through him, she'll have you all.'

I did not begin to understand that day, and Clarissa, in her Pythoness way, was no help, muttering vague threats and imprecations with a mouth full of bread.

After my first jealousy at Iris's preference of Cave to me, a jealousy which I knew, even at the time, was unjustified and a little ludicrous, I had come to accept her devotion to Cave as a perfectly natural state of affairs. He was an extraordinary man and though he did not filfull her in the usual sense, he gave her more than a mere lover might. He gave her a whole life and I envied her for having been able to seize so shrewdly upon this unique way out of ordinary life and into something more grand, more strange, more engaging. Though I could not follow her, I was able to appreciate her choice and admire the completeness of her days. That she was obscurely using Cave for her own ends, subverting him, did not seem possible, and I was annoyed by Clarissa's dark warnings. I directed the conversation into other waters.

'The children. I haven't decided what to do with them.'

Clarissa came to a full halt. For a moment she forgot to chew. Then, with a look of pain, she swallowed. '*Your* children?'

'Any children, all children,' I pointed to the manuscript on the table.

She understood. 'I'm quite sure you have abolished marriage.'

'As a matter of fact, yes, this morning.'

'And now you don't know what to do about the children.'

'Precisely. I . . .'

'Perfectly simple.' Clarissa was brisk. This, apparently, was a problem she had already solved. 'The next step is controlled breeding. Only those whose blood lines seem promising should be allowed to procreate. Now that oral contraceptives are so popular no one will make babies by accident . . . in fact, it should be a serious crime if someone does.'

'Quite neat, but I wonder whether, psychologically, it's simple. There's the whole business of instinct, of the natural desire of a woman to want her own child after bearing it.'

'All habit . . . not innate. Children have been subordinate woman's weapon for centuries. They have had to develop certain traits which in other circumstances they would not have possessed. Rats, whom we closely resemble, though they suckle their young will, in moments of mild hunger or even exasperation, think nothing of eating an entire litter. You can condition human beings to accept any state of affairs as being perfectly natural.'

'I don't doubt that. But how to break the habits of several thousand years?'

'I suppose there *are* ways. Look what Cave is doing. Of course making death popular is not so difficult since, finally, people want it to be nice. They do the real work or, rather, their terror does. In place of superstition, which they've nearly outgrown, he offers them madness.'

'Now really, Clarissa . . .'

'I don't disapprove. I'm all for him, as you know. To make death preferable to life is of course utter folly but still a perfectly logical reaction for these poor bewildered savages who, having lost their old superstitions, are absolutely terrified at the prospect of nothing. They want to perpetuate their little personalities forever into space and time and now they've begun to realize the folly of that (who, after all, are they – are *we* – in creation?), they will follow desperately the first man who pulls the sting of death and Cave is that man, as I knew he would be.'

'And after Cave?'

'I will not say what I see. I'm on the side of change, however, which makes me in perfect harmony with life.' Clarissa chuckled. A fish leaped greyly in the river; out in the channel a barge glided by, the muffled noise of its engines like slow heartbeats.

'But you think it good for people to follow Cave? You think what he says is right?'

'Nothing is good. Nothing is right. But though Cave is wrong, it is a *new* wrong and so it is better than the old; in any case, he will keep the people amused, and boredom, finally, is the one monster the race will never conquer . . . the monster which will devour us in time. But now we're off the track. Mother love exists because we believe it exists. Believe it does not exist and it won't. That, I fear, is the general condition of "the unchanging human heart". Make these young girls feel that having babies is a patriotic duty as well as healthful therapy and they'll go through it blithely enough, without ever giving a second thought to the child they leave behind in the government nursery.'

'But to get them to that state of acceptance . . .'

'Is the problem. I'm sure it will be solved in a few generations.'

'You think I'm right to propose it?'

'Of course. It will happen anyway.'

'Yet I'm disturbed at the thought of all that power in the hands of the state. They can make the children believe anything. Impose the most terrible tyranny. Blind at birth so that none might ever see anything again but what a few rulers, as ignorant as they, will want them to see. There'll be a time when all people are alike.'

'Which is precisely the ideal society. No mysteries, no romantics, no discussions, no persecutions because there's no one to persecute. When all have received the same conditioning, it will be like . . .'

'Insects.'

'Who have existed longer than ourselves and will outlast our race by many millennia.'

'Is existence everything?'

'There is nothing else.'

'Then likeness is the aim of human society?'

'Call it harmony. You think of yourself only as you are now dropped into the midst of a society of dull conformists. That's where you make your mistake. You'll not live to see it, for if you did, you would be someone else, a part of it. No one of your disposition could possibly happen in such a society. There would be no rebellion against sameness because difference would not, in any important sense, exist, even as a proposition. You think: how terrible! But think again how wonderful it would be to belong to the pack, to the tribe, to the race, without guilt or anxiety or division.'

'I cannot imagine it.'

'No more can they imagine you.'

'This will happen?'

'Yes, and you will have been a part of it.'

'Through Cave?'

'Partly, yes. There will be others after him. His work will be distorted by others, but that's to be expected.'

'I don't like your future, Clarissa.'

'Nor does it like *you*, my dear. The idea of someone who is irritable and at odds with society, bitter and angry, separate from others. I shouldn't wonder but that you yourself might really be used as a perfect example of the old evil days.'

'Virtue dies?'

'Virtue becomes the property of the race.'

'Imagination is forbidden?'

'No, only channelled for the good of all.'

'And this is a desirable world, the future you describe?'

'Desirable for whom? For you, no. For me, not really. For the people in it? Well, yes and no. They will not question their estate but they will suffer from a collective boredom which . . . but my lips are sealed. Your tea was delicious though the bread was not quite fresh. But then bachelors never keep house properly. I've gone on much too long. Do forget everything I've said. I am indiscreet. I can't help it.' She rose, a cloud of grey suspended above the porch. I walked her across the lawn to the driveway where her car was parked. The breeze had died for the moment and the heat prickled me unpleasantly; my temples itched as the sweat started.

'Go on with it,' she said as she got into her car. 'You may as well be on the side of the future as against it. Not that it much matters anyway. When your adorable President Jefferson was in Paris he said . . .' But the noise of the car starting drowned the body of her anecdote. I caught only the end: '. . . that harmony was preferable. We were all amused. I was the only one who realized that he was serious.' Dust swirled and Clarissa was gone down the drive at great speed, keeping, I noticed, to the wrong side of the road. I hoped this was an omen.

V

I got through an unusually sultry July without much interference from either Cave or the world. Paul paid me a quick visit to get the manuscript of the dialogues and I was reminded of those accounts of the progresses made by monarchs in other days, or rather of great ministers, for his party occupied four large cars which gleamed side by side in my driveway like glossy beasts while their contents, Paul and fourteen assistants, all strange to me save Stokharin, wandered disconsolately about the lawn until their departure.

Paul, though brisk, was cordial. 'Trouble all over the map. But b-i-g t-r-o-u-b-l-e.' He spelled it out with relish. Size was important, I knew, to a publicist, even to one turned evangelist.

'Is Cave disturbed by it?'

'Doesn't pay any attention. Haven't seen him but Iris keeps me posted. By the way, we're hiring a plane the first week in August to go see him, Stokharin and me. Want to come along?'

I didn't but I said I would. I had no intention of being left out of anything. There was *my* work still to do.

'I'll let you know details. Is this hot stuff?' He waved the sheaf of papers I'd given him.

'Real hot,' I said but my irony was too pale; only primary colours caught Paul's eye.

'I hope so. Got any new stunts?'

I told him, briefly, about my thoughts on marriage, or rather Cave's thoughts. The literary device was for me to ask him certain questions and for him to answer them or at least to ask pointed questions in his turn. Cheerfully, I had committed Cave to my own point of view and I was somewhat nervous about his reaction, not to mention the others'. So far, only Clarissa knew and her approval was pleasant but perhaps frivolous: it carried little weight, I knew, with the rest.

Paul whistled. 'You got us a tall order. I'm not sure we'll be able to handle that problem yet, if ever.'

'I've done it carefully,' I began.

Stokharin, who had been listening with interest, came to my aid. 'In the Centres we, how you say, Paul? soft-pedal the family. We advise young boys to make love to the young girls without marrying or having babies. We speak of the family as a mere social unit, and of course society changes. I am most eager to study Mr Luther's approach. Perhaps a little aid from those of us in clinical work . . .'

But then the dark sedans began to purr; nervous attendants whispered to Paul and I was soon left alone with the fragments of our brief conversation to examine and interpret at my leisure. I was surprised and pleased at Stokharin's unexpected support. I had thought of him as my chief antagonist. But then, my work finished, I tended roses and read Dio Cassius until the summons came in August.

VI

The plane landed on a glare of blue water, more blinding even than the vivid sky about the sun itself, which made both elements seem to be a quivering blue fire in which was destroyed all of earth save a tiny smear of dusty faded green, the island of our destination.

The pilot manoeuvred the plane against a bone-grey dock where, all alone, Iris stood, her hair tangled from the propellers' wind and her eyes hidden by dark glasses. Like explorers in a new country, Paul, Stokharin and I scrambled onto the dock, the heat closing in about us like blue canvas, stifling, palpable. I gasped and dropped my suitcase. Iris laughed and ran forward to greet us; she came first to me, an action which, even in my dazzled, shocked state, I realized and valued.

'Gene, you must get out of that suit this minute! and get some dark glasses or you'll go blind. Paul, how are you? It's good to see you, Doctor.' And, in the chatter of greetings, she escorted us off the dock and across a narrow white beach to a grove of palm trees where the cottage stood.

To our delight, the interior was cooled by machinery. I sank into a wicker chair even as Cave pumped my hand. Iris laughed, 'Leave him alone, John. He's smothered by the heat.'

'No hat,' said Cave solemnly after the first greeting, which, in my relief, I'd not heard. 'You'll get sunstroke.'

Paul was now in charge. The heat which had enervated both Stokharin and me filled him with manic energy, like one of those reptiles that absorb vitality from the sun.

'What a great little place, Cave! Had no idea there were all the comforts of home down here, none at all. Don't suppose you go out much?'

Cave, unlike Iris, was not tanned though he had, for him, a good colour, unlike his usual sallowness. 'I don't get too much sun,' he admitted. 'We go fishing sometimes, early in the morning. Most of the time I just hang around the house and look at the letters, and read some.'

I noticed on the table beside me an enormous pile of travel magazines, tourist folders and atlases. I anticipated trouble.

Paul prowled restlessly about the modern living room with its shuttered sealed windows. Stokharin and I, like fish back in their own element after a brief excursion on land, gasped softly in our chairs while Iris told us of the Keys, and of their fishing trips. She was at her best here as she had been that other time in Spokane. Being out of doors, in Cave's exclusive company, brought her to life in a way the exciting busyness of New York did not. In the city she seemed like an object through which an electric current passed; here on this island, in the sun's glare, she unfolded, petal after petal, until the secret interior seemed almost exposed. I was conscious of her as a lovely woman and, without warning, I experienced desire. That sharp rare longing which, in me, can reach no climax. Always before she had been a friend, a companion whose company I had jealously valued; her attention alone had been enough to satisfy me, but on this day I saw her as a man entire might and I plummetted into despair, talking of Plato.

'Of course there are other ways of casting dialogues, such as introducing the celebrated dead brought together for a chat in Limbo. But I thought that I should keep the talk to only two. Cave and myself . . . Socrates and Alcibiades.' Alcibiades was precisely the wrong parallel but I left it uncorrected, noticing how delicately the hollow at the base of Iris's throat quivered with life's blood, and although I attempted, as I often had before with bitter success, to think of her as so much mortal flesh, the body and its beauty pulp and bone, beautiful only to a human eye (hideous, no doubt, to the eye of a geometric progression), that afternoon I was lost and I could not become, even for a moment, an abstract intelligence. Though I saw the bone, the dust, I saw her existing, triumphant in the present. I cursed the flaw in my own flesh and hated life.

'We liked it very much,' she said, unaware of my passion and its attendant despair.

'You don't think it's too strong, do you? All morality, not to mention the churches, will be aligned against us.'

'John was worried at first . . . not that opposition frightens him and it is *his* idea. I mean you wrote the dialogue but it reflects exactly what he's always thought.' Though in love's agony, I looked at her sharply to make certain she was perfectly serious. She was. This helped soothe the pain. She had been hypnotized by Cave. I wondered how Clarissa could ever have thought it was the other way around.

'In a way we're already on record.' Iris looked thoughtfully across the room at

Cave, who was showing Paul and Stokharin a large map of some strange country. 'The Centres have helped a good many couples to adjust to one another without marriage and without guilt.'

'But then there's the problem of what to do with the children when the family breaks up.'

Iris sighed. 'I'm afraid that's already a problem. Our Centres are taking care of a good many children already. A number, of course, go out for adoption to bored couples who need something to amuse them. I suppose we'll have to establish nurseries as a part of each Centre until, finally, the government assumes the responsibility.'

'*If* it becomes Cavite.'

'*When* it becomes Cavite.' She was powerful in her casualness.

'Meanwhile there are laws of adoption which vary from state to state and, if we're not careful, we're apt to come up against the law.'

'Paul looks after us,' she smiled. 'Did you know that he has nearly a hundred lawyers on our payroll? All protecting us.'

'From what?' I had not been aware of this.

'Lawsuits. Attempts by state legislatures to outlaw the Centres on the grounds of immorality and so on. The lawyers are kept busy all the time.'

'Why haven't I read about any of this in the papers?'

'We've been able to keep things quiet. Paul is marvellous with the editors. Several have even joined us, by the way, secretly, of course.'

'What's the membership now?'

Iris gestured. 'No one knows. We have thirty Centres in the United States and each day they receive hundreds of new Cavites. I suspect there are at least four million by now.'

I gasped, beginning to recover at last from the heat, from my unexpected crisis of love. 'I had no idea things were going so fast.'

'Too fast. We haven't enough trained people to look after the Centres, and on top of that we must set up new Centres. Paul has broken the country up into districts, all very methodical: so many Centres per district, each with a Resident in charge. Stokharin is taking care of the clinical work.'

'Where's the money coming from?'

'In bushels from heaven,' Iris smiled. 'We leave all that to Paul. I shouldn't be surprised if he counterfeits it. Anyway, I *must* get back to New York, to the school. I shouldn't really have gone off in the middle of everything, but I was tired and John wanted company so I came.'

'How is he?'

'As you see, calm. I don't believe he ever considers any of our problems. He never mentions them; never reads the reports Paul sends him; doesn't even read the attacks from the churches. We get several a day, not to mention threatening mail. We now have full-time bodyguards.'

'You think people are seriously threatening him?'

'I don't know how serious they are but we can't take chances. Fortunately, almost no one knows we're here and, so far, no cranks have got through from the mainland. Our groceries and mail are brought in by boat every other day from Key Largo. Otherwise, we're perfectly isolated.'

I looked about me for some sign of the guards; there was none. A Cuban woman vacuuming in the next room was the only visible stranger.

Cave abandoned his maps and atlases long enough to tell me how much the dialogues pleased him.

'I wish I could put it down like you do. I can only say it when people listen.'

'Do you think I've been accurate?'

Cave nodded solemnly. 'Oh, yes. It's just like I've always said it, only written down.' I realized that he had already assumed full responsibility (and credit, should there be any) for my composition. I accepted his presumption with amusement. Only Stokharin seemed aware of the humour of the situation. I caught him staring at me with a shrewd expression; he looked quickly away, mouth rigid as he tried not to smile. I liked him at that moment. We were the only ones who had not been possessed by Cave. I felt like a conspirator.

For several days we talked, or rather Paul talked. He had brought with him charts and statements and statistics and, though Cave did not bother to disguise his boredom, he listened most of the time and his questions, when they did occur, were apposite. The rest of us were fascinated by the extent of what Paul referred to as the 'first operational phase'.

Various projects had already been undertaken; others were put up to the directors for discussion. Thanks to Paul's emphatic personality, our meetings were more like those of account executives than the pious forgathering of a messiah's apostles – and already that word had been used in the press by the curious as well as by the devout. Cave was the messiah to several million Americans. But he was not come with fire to judge the world, nor armed with the instruction of a supernatural being whose secret word had been given this favourite son. No, Cave was of another line. That of the prophets, of the teachers like Jesus before he became Christ, or Mohammed before he became Islam. In our age it was Cave's task to say the words all men awaited yet dared not speak or even attend without the overpowering authority of another who had, plausibly, assumed the guise of master. I could not help but wonder as I watched Cave in those heated conferences if the past had been like this.

Cave certainly had one advantage over his predecessors: modern communications. It took three centuries for Christianity to infect the world. It was to take Cave only three years to conquer Europe and the Americas.

But I did not have this foreknowledge in Florida. I only knew that Paul was handling an extraordinary business in a remarkable way. There was no plan so vast that he could not contemplate its execution with ease. He was exhausting in his energy and, though he did not possess much imagination, he was a splendid improviser, using whatever themes were at hand to create his own dazzling contrapuntal effects.

We decided upon a weekly magazine to be distributed gratis to the Cavites (I was appointed editor though the actual work, of which I was entirely ignorant, was to be done by a crew already at work on the first issue). We would also send abroad certain films to be shown by Cavite lecturers. We then approved the itinerary of Cave's national tour in the fall (Cave was most alive during this discussion; suggesting cities he wanted particularly to see, revelling in the euphony of such names as Tallahassee). We also planned several dinners to be held in New York with newspaper editors and political figures, and we discussed the advisability of Cave's accepting an invitation to be questioned by the House Un-American Activities Committee, which had begun to show an interest in the progress of our Centres. It was decided that Cave delay meeting the committee until the time was propitious, or until he had received a subpoena. Paul, with his instinctive sense of the theatrical, did not want to have this crucial meeting take place without a most careful build-up.

We discussed the various steps taken or about to be taken by certain state legislatures against the Centres. The states involved were those with either a predominantly Catholic or a predominantly Baptist population. Since the Centres had been organized to conform with existing state and federal laws (the lawyers were earning their fees), Paul thought they would have a difficult time in closing any of them. The several laws which had been passed were all being appealed and he was confident of our vindication by the higher courts. Though the entrenched churches were now fighting us with every possible weapon of law and propaganda, we were fully protected, Paul felt, by the Bill of Rights even in its currently abrogated state.

Late in the afternoon after one of the day's conferences had ended, Iris and I swam in the Gulf, the water as warm as blood and the sky soft with evening. We stayed in the water for an hour, not talking, not really swimming, merely a part of the sea and the sky, two lives on a curved horizon, quite alone (for the others never ventured out). Only the bored bodyguard on the dock reminded us that the usual world had not slipped away in a sunny dream, leaving us isolated and content in that sea from which our life had come so long ago. Water to water, I thought comfortably as we crawled up on the beach like new-lunged creatures.

Iris undid her bathing cap and her hair, streaked blonde by the sun (and a little grey as well), fell about her shoulders. She sighed voluptuously. 'If it would always be like this.'

'If what?'

'Everything.'

'Ah,' I ran my hand along my legs and crystals of salt glittered and fell; we were both dusted with light. 'You have your work,' I added with some malice, though I was now under control; my crisis resolved after one sleepless night. I could now look at her without longing, without pain. Regret was another matter but regret was only a distant relative to anguish.

'I have that, too,' she said. 'The work uses everything while this is a narcotic. I float without a thought or a desire like . . . like an anemone.'

'You don't know what an anemone is, do you?'

She laughed like a child. 'How do you know I don't?'

'You said it like somebody reading a Latin inscription.'

'What is it?'

I laughed, too. 'I don't know. Perhaps something like a jellyfish. It has a lovely sound: sea anemone.'

We were interrupted by a motorboat pulling into the dock. 'It's the mail,' said Iris. 'We'd better go back to the house.' While we collected towels, the guard on the dock helped the boatman unload groceries and mail.

Between a pair of palm trees, a yard from the door of the house, the bomb went off in a flash of light and grey smoke. A stinging spray of sand blinded Iris and me. The blast knocked me off balance and I fell backward onto the beach. For several minutes, I was quite blind, my eyes filled with tears, burned from the coral sand. When I was finally able to see again, Iris was already at the house trying to force open the door.

One of the palm trees looked as if it had been struck by lightning, all its fronds gone and its base smouldering. The windows of the house were broken and I recall wondering, foolishly, how the air conditioning could possibly work if the house was not sealed. The door was splintered and most of its paint had been burned off; it was also jammed, for Iris could not open it. Meanwhile, from a side door, the occupants of the house had begun to appear.

I limped towards the house, rubbing my eyes, aware that my left knee had been hurt. I was careful not to look at either the boatman or the guard, their remains strewn among tin cans and letters in the bushes.

Paul was the first to speak. A torrent of rage which jolted us all out of fear and shock. Iris, after one look at the dead men, fled into the house. I stood stupidly beside the door, rolling my eyes to dislodge the sand.

Then the other guards came with blankets and gathered up the pieces of the two men. I turned away, aware for the first time that Cave was standing slightly apart, nearest the house. He was very pale. He spoke only once, half to himself, for Paul was still ranting. 'Let it begin,' said Cave softly. 'Now, now.'

CHAPTER NINE

I

It began indeed, like the first recorded shot of a war. The day after the explosion, we left the island and Cave was flown to another retreat, this time in the centre of New York City where, unique in all the world, there can exist true privacy, even invisibility.

The Cavite history of the next two years is publicly known and the private aspects of it are not particularly revealing. It was a time of expansion and of battle.

The opposition closed its ranks. Several attempts were made on all our lives and, six months after our return from Florida, we were all, except the indomitable Clarissa, forced to move into the brand-new Cavite Centre, a quickly built but handsome building of yellow glass on Park Avenue. Here on the top floor, in the penthouse which was itself a mansion surrounded by Babylonian gardens and a wall of glass through which the encompassing city rose like stalagmites, Cave and Paul, Stokharin, Iris and I all lived with our bodyguards, never venturing out of the building, which resembled, during that time, a military headquarters with guards and adjutants and a maze of officials through whom both strangers and familiars were forced to pass before they could meet even myself, not to mention Cave.

In spite of the unnaturalness, it was, I think, the happiest time of my life. Except for brief excursions to the Hudson, I spent the entire two years in that one building, knowing at last the sort of security and serenity which monks must have known in their monasteries. I think the others were also content, except for Cave, who eventually grew so morose and bored by his confinement that Paul not only had to promise him a world tour but for his vicarious pleasure showed, night after night in the Centre's auditorium, travel films which Cave devoured with eager eyes, asking for certain films to be halted at various interesting parts so that he might examine some landscape or building (never a human being, no matter how quaint). Favourite movies were played over and over again, long after the rest of us had gone to bed, leaving Cave and the projectionist alone with the bright shadows of distant places, alone save for the ubiquitous guards.

There were a number of attacks upon the building itself, but since all incoming mail and visitors were checked by machinery for hidden weapons, there was never a repetition of that island disaster which had had such a chilling effect on all of us. Pickets of course marched daily for two years in front of the Centre's door and, on four separate occasions, mobs attempted to storm the building, only to be repulsed by our guards (the police, for the most part Catholic, did not unduly exert themselves in our defence; fortunately, the building had been constructed with the idea of defence).

The life in the Centre was busy. In the penthouse each of us had an office and Cave had a large suite where he spent his days watching television and pondering journeys. He did not follow with much interest the doings of the organization, though he had begun to enjoy reading the attacks which regularly appeared against him in the newspapers. Bishop Winston was the leader of the non-Catholic opposition and his apologias and anathemas inspired us with admiration. He was, I think, conscious of being the last great spokesman of the Protestant churches and he fulfilled his historic function with wit and dignity, and we admired him tremendously. By this time, of course, our victory was in sight and we could show magnanimity to those who remained loyal to ancient systems.

I was the one most concerned with answering the attacks since I was now an editor with an entire floor devoted to the *Cavite Journal* (we were not able to think up a better name). At first, as we had planned, it was published weekly and given away, but after the first year it became a daily newspaper, fat with advertising and sold on newsstands.

Besides my duties as editor, I was the official apologist and I was kept busy composing dialogues on various ethical matters, ranging from the virtues of cremation to fair business practices. Needless to say, I had a good deal of help and some of my most resounding effects were contrived by anonymous specialists. Each instalment, however, of Cavite doctrine (or rationalization, as I preferred to think of my work) was received as eagerly by the expanding ranks of the faithful as it was condemned reflexively by the Catholic Church and the new league of Protestant Churches under Bishop Winston's leadership.

We sustained our most serious setback when, in the autumn of our first year in the new building, we were banned from the television networks through a series of technicalities created by Congress for our benefit and invoked without warning. It took Paul's lawyers a year to get the case through the courts, which finally reversed the government's ruling. Meanwhile, we counterattacked by creating hundreds of new Centres where films of Cave were shown regularly. Once a week he was televised for the Centres, where huge crowds gathered to see and hear him, and it was always Paul's claim that the government's spiteful action had been responsible for the sudden victory of Cavesword. Not being able to listen to their idol in their own homes, the Cavites and even the merely curious were forced to visit the Centres, where in the general mood of camaraderie and delight in the same Word, they were organized quite ruthlessly. Stokharin's clinics handled their personal problems. Other departments assumed the guidance and even support, if necessary, of their children, while free medical and educational facilities were made available to all who applied.

At the end of the second year, there were more enrolled Cavites than any other single religious denomination, including the Roman Catholic. I published this fact and the accompanying statistics with a certain guilt which, needless to say, my fellow directors did not share. The result of this revelation was a special Congressional hearing.

In spite of the usual confusion attendant upon any of the vigorous old Congress's hearteningly incompetent investigations, this event was well staged, preparing the way politically, to draw the obvious parallel, for a new Constantine.

It took place in March, and it was the only official journey any of us, excepting Paul, had made from our yellow citadel for two years. The entire proceedings were televised, a bit of unwisdom on the part of the hostile Congressmen, who in their understandable eagerness for publicity, overlooked their intended victim's complete mastery of that art. I did not go to Washington but I saw Cave and Paul and Iris off from the roof of the Centre. Because of the crowds which had formed in the streets hoping for a glimpse of Cave, the original plan to fly to Washington aboard a chartered airplane was discarded at the last minute and two helicopters were ordered instead to pick up Cave and his party on the terrace in front of the penthouse, a mode of travel not then popular.

Paul saw to it that the departure was filmed. A dozen of us who were not going stood about among the trees and bushes while the helicopters hovered a few feet above the roof, their ladders dangling. Then Cave appeared with Paul and Iris while a camera crew recorded their farewell and departure. Cave looked as serene as ever, pale in his dark blue suit and white shirt, a small austere figure with downcast eyes. Iris was bright-faced from the excitement and cold, and a sharp wind tangled her hair.

'I'm terrified,' she whispered fiercely in my ear as we shook hands for the camera.

'Paul seems in full command,' I said, comfortingly. And Paul, not Cave, was making a short speech to the camera while Cave stood alone and still; then, in a gust of wind, they were gone and I went to my office to watch the hearings.

The official reason for the investigation was certain charges made by the various churches that the Cavites were subverting Christian morality by champing free love and publicy decrying the eternal institution of marriage. This was the burden of the complaint against Cave which the committee most wished to contemplate since it was the strongest of the numerous allegations and, in their eyes, the most dangerous to the state, as well as the one most likely to get the largest amount of publicity. For some years the realm of public morals had been a favourite excursion ground for the Congress, and their tournaments at public expense were attended delightedly by everyone. This particular one, affecting as it did the head of the largest single religious establishment in the country, would, the Congressmen were quite sure, prove an irresistible spectacle. It was.

At first there was a good deal of confusion. Newspapermen stumbled over one another; flashbulbs were dropped; Congressmen could not get through the crowd to take their seats. To fill in, while these preliminaries were arranged, the camera was trained upon the crowd which was beginning to gather in front of the Capitol; a crowd which grew, as one watched, to Inaugural size. Though it was orderly, a troop of soldiers in trucks soon arrived as though by previous design, and they formed a cordon of fixed bayonets before the various entrances to the Capitol.

Here and there, against the gusty blue sky, banners with the single word 'Cave', gold on blue, snapped. *In hoc signo* indeed!

Then the commentators, who had been exclaiming at some length on the size of the crowd, excitedly announced the arrival of Cave. A roar of sound filled the plaza. The banners were waved back and forth against the sky and I saw everywhere the theatrical hand of Paul Himmell.

The scene shifted to the House of Representatives entrance to the Capitol. Cave, wearing an overcoat but bareheaded, stepped out of the limousine. He was alone. Neither Paul nor Iris was in sight. It was most effective that he should come like this, without equerries or counsellors. He stood for a moment in the pillared entrance, aware of the crowd outside; even through the commentator's narrative one could hear, like the surf falling, Cave! Cave! Cave! For a moment it seemed that he might turn and go, not into the Capitol, but out onto the steps to the crowd. But then the chief of the Capitol guard, sensing perhaps that this might happen, gently steered him up the stairs.

The next shot was of the committee room where the hearings had at last begun. A somewhat phlegmatic Jesuit was testifying. His words were difficult to hear because of the noise in the committee room and the impotent shouts of the chairman. The commentator gave a brief résumé of the Jesuit's attack on Cave and then, in the midst of a particularly loud exchange between the chairman and the crowd, the clerk of the committee announced: 'John Cave.'

There was silence. The crowd parted to make way for him. Even the members of the committee craned to get a good look at him as he moved quietly, almost demurely, to the witness chair. The only movement in the room was that of the Papal Nuncio, who sat in the front rank of the audience. He crossed himself as Cave passed and shut his eyes.

Cave was respectful, almost inaudible. Several times he was asked to repeat his answers even though the room was remarkably still. At first Cave would answer only in monosyllables, not looking up, not meeting the gaze of his interrogators, who took heart at this, professionals themselves. Their voices, which had almost matched his for inaudibility, began to boom with confidence.

I waited for the lightning. The first intimation came when Cave looked up. For nearly five minutes he had not raised his eyes during the questioning. Suddenly I saw that he was trying to locate the camera. When at last he did, it was like a revelation. A shock went through me, and as well as I knew him, as few illusions as I had about him, I was arrested by his gaze, as if only he and I existed, as though he *were* I. All of those who watched him on television responded in the same fashion to that unique gaze.

But the committee was not aware that their intended victim had with one glance appropriated the eye of the world.

The subsequent catechism is too well known to record here. We used it as the main exposition of Cavesword, the one testament which contained the entire thing. It was almost as if the Congressmen had been given the necessary questions to ask, like those supporting actors whose roles are calculated to illuminate the genius of the star. Two of the seven members of the committee were Cavites. This was soon apparent. The other five were violent in their opposition. One as a Catholic, another as a Protestant, and two as materialistic lovers of the old order. Only one of the attackers, a Jew, made any real point. He argued the perniciousness of an organization which, if allowed to prosper, would replace the state and force all dissenters to conform; it was the Jew's contention that the state prospered most when no one system was sufficiently strong to dominate. I wanted to hear more of him but his Catholic colleague, a bull-voiced Irishman, drowned him out, winning the day for us.

Cave, to my astonishment, had memorized most of the dialogues I had written and he said my words with the same power that he said his own. I was startled by this. There had been no hint that such a thing might happen and I couldn't, for some time, determine the motive until I recalled Cave's reluctance to being quoted in print. He had apparently realized that now there would be a complete record of his testimony and so, for the sake of both literacy and consistency, he had committed to memory those words of mine which were thought to be his. At the great moment, however, the peroration (by which time there were no more questions and Cave's voice alone was heard) he became himself, and spoke Cavesword.

Then, without the committee's leave, in the dazzled silence which followed upon his last words, he rose abruptly and left the room. I switched off the television set. That week established Cavesword in the country and, except for various priests and ministers of the deserted gods, the United States was Cavite.

II

The desertion of the old establishments for the new resembled, at uneasy moments, revolution.

The Congressional committee, though anti-Cavite, did not dare even to censure him. Partly from the fear of the vast crowd which waited in the Capitol plaza and partly from the larger, more cogent awareness that it was political suicide for any popularly elected Representative to outrage a minority of such strength.

The hearing fizzled out after Cave's appearance, and though there were a few denunciatory speeches on the floor of Congress, no official action was taken. Shortly afterwards the ban on Cave's television appearances was lifted, but by then it was too late and millions of people had got permanently into the habit of attending weekly meetings at the various Centres to listen to Cave on film and discuss with the Residents and their staffs points of doctrine . . . and doctrine it had become.

The second year in our yellow citadel was even more active than the first. It was decided that Cave would make no personal appearances anywhere. According to Paul, the mystery would be kept intact and the legend would grow under the most auspicious circumstances. He did not reveal his actual motive in Cave's presence. But he explained himself to me late one afternoon in my office.

'Get him in front of a really hostile crowd and there'd be no telling what might happen.' Paul was restlessly marching about the room in his shirtsleeves; a blunt cigar in his mouth gave him the appearance of a lower-echelon politician.

'There's never been a hostile audience yet,' I reminded him. 'Except for the Congressional hearings, and I thought he handled himself quite well with them.'

'With your script in his head.' Paul chuckled and stopped his march to the filing cabinet by way of that television set which dominated every office and home. 'What I mean is, he's never been in a debate. 'He's never had a tough opponent, a heckler. The Congressmen were pretty mild and even though they weren't friendly they stuck to easy issues. But what would happen if Bishop Winston got him up before an audience? Winston's a lot smarter and he's nearly as good in public.'

'I suppose Cave would hypnotize him, too.'

'Not on your life.' Paul threw himself into a chair of flimsy chrome and plastic. 'Winston's been trying to arrange a debate for over two years. He issues challenges every Sunday on his programme (got a big audience, too, though not close to ours. I checked the ratings).'

'Does Cave want to give it a try?'

'He's oblivious to such things. I suppose he would if he thought about it. Anyway it's to our advantage to keep him out of sight. Let them see only a television image, hear only his recorded voice. It's wonderful copy! Big time.' He was out of the chair and playing with the knob of the television set. The screen was suddenly filled with a romantic scene, a pulsating green grotto with water falling in a thin white line; so perfected had the machine become that it was actually like looking through a window, the illusion of depth quite perfect and the colours true. A warm deep voice off-screen suggested the virtues of a well-known carbonated drink. Paul turned the switch off. I was relieved since I, alone in America, was unable to think or work or even relax while the screen was bright with some other place.

'He won't like it. He expects next year, at the latest, to start his world tour.'

'Perhaps then,' said Paul thinly. 'Anyway, the longer we put it off the better. Did you know we turn away a thousand people a day who come here just to get a glimpse of him?'

'They see him at the Centre meetings.'

'Only our own people, the ones in training to be Residents. I keep those sessions carefully screened. Every now and then some outsider gets in but it's rare.'

I glanced at the tear-sheet of my next day's editorial. It contained, among other useful statistics, the quite incredible figures of Cavite membership in the world. Dubiously, I read off the figure which Paul had given me at a directors' meeting.

'It's about right,' he said complacently, coming to a full stop at the files. 'We don't actually know the figures of places without proper Centres like the Latin countries where we are undergoing a bit of persecution. But the statistics for this country are exact.'

'It's hard to believe.' I looked at the figure which represented so many human beings, so much diversity, all touched by one man. 'Less than three years . . .'

'Three more years and we'll have most of Europe too.'

'Why, I wonder?'

'Why?' Paul slammed shut the cabinet drawer which he'd been examining. He looked at me sharply. 'You of all people ask why? Cavesword . . . and all your words too, did the trick. That's what. We've said what they wanted to hear. Just the opposite of my old game of publicity where we said what *we* wanted them to hear. This time it's just the other way around and it's big, ah, it's big.'

I could agree with that but I pressed him further. 'I know what's happened, of course, and your theory is certainly correct if only because had we said the opposite of what they wanted to hear nothing would have happened. But the question in my mind, the real "why", is Cave and us. Why we of all the people in the world? Cavesword, between us and any school of philosophy, is not new. Others have said it more eloquently. In the past it was a reasonably popular heresy which the early popes stamped out . . .'

'Timing! The right man at the right time saying the right thing. Remember the piece you did on Mohammed . . .'

'I stole most of it.'

'So what? Most effective. You figured how only at that one moment in Arabian political history could such a man have appeared.'

I smiled. 'That is always the folly of the "one unique moment". For all I know such a man could have appeared in any of a hundred other Arab generations.'

'But he never did except that one time, which proves the point.'

I let it go. Paul was at best not the ideal partner in the perennial conversation. 'There is no doubt that Cave's the man,' I said, neutrally. 'Not the last of the line but at least the most effective, considering the shortness of the mission so far.'

'We have the means. The old people didn't. Every man, woman, and child in this country can see Cave for themselves, and at the same moment. I don't suppose ten thousand people saw Christ in action. It took a generation for news of him to travel from one country to the next.'

'Parallels break down,' I agreed. 'It's the reason I wonder so continually about Cave and ourselves and what we are doing in the world.'

'We're doing good. The people are losing their fear of death. Last month there were twelve hundred suicides in this country directly attributable to Cavesword. And these people didn't kill themselves just because they were unhappy, they killed themselves because he had made it easy, even desirable. Now you know there's never been anybody like that before in history, anywhere.'

'Certainly not!' I was startled by the figure he had quoted. In our *Journal* we were always reporting various prominent suicides, and though I had given orders to minimize these voluntary deaths, I had been forced every now and then to record the details of one or another of them. But I'd had no idea there had been so many. I asked Paul if he was quite sure of the number.

'Oh yes.' He was blithe. 'At least that many we know of.'

'I wonder if it's wise.'

'Wise? What's that got to do with it? It's logical. It's the proof of Cavesword. Death is fine so why not die?'

'Why not live?'

'It's the same thing.'

'I would say not.'

'Well, you ought to play it up a little more anyway. I meant to talk about it at the last directors' meeting but there wasn't time.'

'Does Cave know about this? About the extent . . .'

'Sure he does.' Paul headed for the door. 'He thinks it's fine. Proves what he says and it gives other people nerve. This thing is working.'

There was no doubt about that, of course. It is hard to give precisely the sense of those two years when the main work was done in a series of toppling waves which swept into history the remaining edifices of other faiths and institutions. I had few firsthand impressions of the country for I seldom stirred from our headquarters.

I had sold the house on the river. I had cut off all contacts with old friends. My life was Cave. I edited the *Journal*, or rather presided over the editors. I discussed points of doctrine with the various Residents who came to see me in the yellow tower. They were devoted men and their enthusiasm was heartening, if not always communicable to me. Each week further commentaries on Cavesword were published and I found there was no time to read them all. I contented myself, finally, with synopses prepared for me by the *Journal*'s staff. I felt like a television emperor keeping abreast of contemporary letters.

Once a week we all dined with Cave. Except for that informal occasion we seldom saw him. Though he complained continually about his captivity (and it was exactly that; we were all captives to some degree), he was cheerful enough. Paul saw to it that he was kept busy all day addressing Residents and Communicators, answering their questions, inspiring them by the mere fact of his presence. It was quite common for strangers to faint upon seeing him for the first time, as a man and not as a figure on a bit of film. He was good-natured, though occasionally embarrassed by the chosen groups which were admitted to him. He seldom talked privately to any of them, however, and he showed not the faintest interest in their problems, not even bothering to learn their names. He was only interested in where they were from and Paul, aware of this, as an added inducement to keep Cave amenable, took to including in each group at least one Cavite from some far place like Malaya or Ceylon.

Iris was busiest of all. She had become, without design or preparation, the head of all the Cavite schools throughout the country where the various Communicators of Cavesword were trained, thousands of them each year, in a course which included not only Cavesword but history and psychology as well. There were also special classes in television production and acting. Television, ultimately, was the key. It was the primary instrument of communication. Later, with a subservient government and the aid of mental therapists and new drugs, television became less necessary, but in the beginning it was everything.

Clarissa's role was, as always, enigmatic. She appeared when she pleased and she disappeared when she pleased. I discovered that her position among the directors was due to her possession of the largest single block of stock, dating back to the first days. During the crucial two or three years, however, she was often with us merely for protection, since all our lives had been proscribed by the last remnants of the old churches, which as their dominion shrank fought more and more recklessly to destroy us.

Stokharin spent his days much like Iris, instructing the Communicators and Centre therapists in psychology. His power over Paul had fortunately waned and he was far more likeable. Paul was 'freed', Stokharin would say with some satisfaction, by therapy . . . and a new father image.

Less than two years after the Congressional hearings, Paul, in his devious way, entered politics. In the following Congressional elections, without much overt campaigning on our part, the majority of those elected to both Houses of the Congress were either Cavite or sympathetic.

III

At last I have met him. Early this evening I went downstairs to see the manager about an item on my bill which was incorrect. I had thought that I should be safe, for this was the time when most of the hotel guests are bathing and preparing for dinner. Unfortunately, I encountered Butler and his newly arrived colleague in the lobby. I suddenly found myself attempting, by an effort of will, very simply to vanish into smoke like one of those magicians in a child's book. But I remained all too visible. I stopped halfway across the lobby and waited for them.

They came towards me. Butler murmuring greetings and introductions to Communicator Jessup (soon to be Resident of Luxor 'when we get under way'): 'And this, Jack, is the Mr Hudson I told you about.'

The Resident-to-be shook my hand firmly. He was not more than thirty, a lean, dark-eyed mulatto whose features and colourings appealed to me, used as I now am to the Arabs; beside him, Butler looked more red and gross than ever.

'Butler has told me how useful you've been to us,' said Jessup. His voice was a little high, but he did not have the trick of overarticulation which used to be so common among educated Negroes in earlier times, a peculiarity they shared with Baptist clergymen and professional poets.

'I've done what I could, little as it is,' I said ceremoniously. Then, without protest, I allowed them to lead me out onto the terrace which overlooked the setting sun and the muddy river.

'We planned to see you when Jack, here, arrived,' said Butler expansively as we sat down, a tray of gin and ice and tonic water set before us by a waiter who was used now to American ways. 'But you had the sign on your door so I told Jack we'd better wait till Mr Hudson is feeling better. You *are* okay now, aren't you?'

'Somewhat better,' I said, enjoying the British gin. I'd had none since I left Cairo. 'At my age one is either dead or all right. I seem not to be dead.'

'How I envy you!' said Jessup solemnly.

'Envy me?' For a moment I did not quite understand.

'To be so near the blessed state! Not to see the sun again and feel the body quivering with corrupt life. Oh, what I should give to be as old as you!'

'You could always commit suicide,' I said irritably, forgetting my role as an amiable soft-headed old cretin.

This stopped him for only the space of a single surprised breath. 'Cavesway is not possible for his servants,' he said at last, patiently. 'You have not perhaps followed his logic as carefully as you might had you been living in the civilized world.' He looked at me with bright dark eyes inscrutably focused.

Why are you here? I wanted to ask furiously, *finally*, but I only nodded my head meekly and said, 'So much has changed since I came out here. I do recall, though, that Cavesway was considered desirable for all.'

'It is. But not for his servants who must, through living, sacrifice their comfort. It is our humiliation, our martyrdom in his behalf. Even the humblest man or woman can avail themselves of Cavesway, unlike us his servants, who must live, disgusting as the prospect is, made bearable only by the knowledge that we are doing his work, communicating his word.'

'What courage it must take to give up Cavesway!' I intoned with reverent awe.

'It is the least we can do for him.'

The bright sun resembled that red-gold disc which sits on the brow of Horus. The hot wind of Numidia stirred the dry foliage about us. I could smell the metallic odour of the Nile. A muezzin called, high and toneless in the evening.

'Before I slip off into the better state,' I said at last, emboldened by gin, 'I should like to know as much as possible about the new world the Cavites have made. I left the United States shortly after Cave took his way. I have never been back.'

'How soon after?' The question came too fast. I gripped the arms of my chair tightly.

'Two years after, I think,' I said. 'I came to Cairo for the digging at Sakharra.'

'How could you have missed those exciting years?' Jessup's voice became zealous. 'I was not even born then, and I've always cursed my bad luck. I used to go about talking to complete strangers who had been alive in those great years. Of course most were laymen and knew little about the things I had studied but they could tell me how the sky looked the day he took his way. And, every now and then, it was possible to meet someone who had seen him.'

'Not many laymen ever saw him,' I said. 'I remember with what secrecy all his movements were enveloped. I was in New York much of the time when he was there.'

'In New York!' Jessup sighed voluptuously.

'You saw him too, didn't you, Mr Hudson?' Butler was obviously eager that I make a good impression.

'Oh yes, I saw him the day he was in Washington. One of his few public appearances! I was very devout in those days. I am now too, of course,' I added hastily. 'But in those days when it was all new, one was – well – exalted by Cavesword. I made a special trip to Washington just to get a glimpse of him.' I played as resolutely as possible upon their passionate faith.

'Did you really see him?'

I shook my head sadly. 'Only a quick blur as he drove away. The crowd was too big and the police were all around him.'

'I have of course relived that moment in the library, watching the films, but actually to have been there that day,' Jessup's voice trailed off as he contemplated the extent of my good fortune.

'Then afterwards, after his death, I left for Egypt and I've never been back.'

'You missed great days.'

'I'm sure of that. Yet I feel the best days were before, when I was in New York and each week there would be a new revelation of his wisdom.'

'You are quite right,' said Jessup, pouring himself more gin. 'Yours was the finer time even though those of us who feel drawn to the Mother must declare that later days possessed some virtue too, on her account.'

'Mother?' I knew of course before he answered what had happened.

'As Cave was the father of our knowledge, so Iris is its mother,' said Jessup. He looked at Butler with a half-smile. 'Of course there are some, the majority in fact, of the Communicators who deprecate our allegiance to the Mother, not realizing that it enhances rather than detracts from Cave. After all, the Word and the Way are entirely his.'

Butler chuckled. 'There's been a little family dispute,' he said. 'We keep it out of the press because it really isn't the concern of anybody but us, Cave's servants. Don't mind talking to you about it since you'll be dead soon anyway and up here we're all in the same boat, all Cavites. Anyway, some of the younger fellows, the bright ones like Jessup, have got attached to Iris, not that we don't all love her equally. It's just that they've got in the habit of talking about death being the womb again, all that kind of stuff without any real basis in Cave.'

'It runs all through Cave's work, Bill. It's implicit in all that he said.' Jessup was amiable but I sensed a hardness in his tone. It had come to this, I thought.

'Well, we won't argue about it,' said Butler, turning to me with a smile. 'You should see what these Irisians can do with a Cavite text. By the time they finish you don't know whether you're coming or going.'

'Were you at all active in the Mission?' asked Jessup, abruptly changing the subject.

I shook my head. 'I was one of the early admirers of Cave but I'm afraid I had very little contact with any of his people. I tried once or twice to get in to see him, when they were in the yellow tower, but it was impossible. Only the Residents and people like that ever saw him personally.'

'He was busy in those days,' said Jessup, nodding. 'He must have dictated nearly two million words in the last three years of his life.'

'You think he wrote all those books and dialogues himself?'

'Of course he did.' Jessup sounded surprised. 'Haven't you read Iris's account of the way he worked? The way he would dictate for hours at a time, oblivious of everything but Cavesword.'

'I suppose I missed all that,' I mumbled. 'In those days it was always assumed that he had a staff who did the work for him.'

'The lutherists,' said Jessup, nodding. 'They were extremely subtle in their methods, but of course they couldn't distort the truth for very long . . .'

'Oh,' said Butler. 'Mr Hudson asked me the other day if I knew what the word "lutherist" came from and I said I didn't know. I must have forgotten, for I have a feeling it *was* taught us, back in the old days when we primitives were turned out, before you bright young fellows came along to show us how to do Caveswork.'

Jessup smiled. 'We're not that bumptious,' he said. 'As for lutherist, it's a word based on the name of one of the first followers of Cave. I don't know his other name or even much about him. As far as I remember, the episode was never even recorded. Much too disagreeable, and of course we don't like to dwell on our failures.'

'I wonder what it was that he did,' I asked, my voice trembling despite all efforts to control it.

'He was a nonconformist of some kind. He quarrelled with Iris, they say.'

'I wonder what happened to him,' said Butler. 'Did they send him through indoctrination?'

'No, as far as I know.' Jessup paused. When he spoke again his voice was thoughtful. 'According to the story I heard – legend really – he disappeared. They never found him and though we've wisely removed all record of him, his name is still used to describe our failures. Those among us, that is, who refuse Cavesword despite indoctrination. Somewhere, they say, he is living, in hiding, waiting to undo Caveswork. As Cave was the Antichrist, so Luther, or another like him, will attempt to destroy us.'

'Not much chance of that.' Butler's voice was confident. 'Anyway, if he was a contemporary of Cave he must be dead by now.'

'Not necessarily. After all, Mr Hudson was a contemporary and *he* is still alive.' Jessup looked at me then. His eyes, in a burst of obsidian light, caught the sun's last rays. I think he knows.

IV

There is not much time left and I must proceed as swiftly as possible to the death of Cave and my own exile.

The year of Cave's death was not only a year of triumph but one of terror as well. The counteroffensive reached its peak in those busy months, and we were all in danger of our lives.

In the South, groups of Baptists stormed the new Centres, demolishing them and killing, in several instances, the Residents. Despite our protests and threats of reprisal, many state governments refused to protect the Cavite Centres and Paul was forced to enlist a small army to defend our establishments in those areas which were still dominated by the old religions. Several attempts were made to destroy our New York headquarters. Fortunately, they were discovered before any damage could be done, though one fanatic, a Catholic, got as far as Paul's office, where he threw a grenade into a wastebasket, killing himself and slightly scratching Paul, who as usual had been travelling nervously about the room, out of range at the proper moment.

The election of a Cavite-dominated Congress eased things for us considerably, though it made our enemies all the more desperate.

Paul fought back. Bishop Winston, the most eloquent of the Christian prelates and the most dangerous to us, had died, giving rise to the rumour, soon afterwards confirmed by Cavite authority to be a fact, that he had killed himself and that, therefore, he had finally renounced Christ and taken to himself Cavesword.

Many of the clergy of the Protestant sects, aware that their parishioners and authority were falling away, became, quietly, without gloating on our part, Cavite Residents and Communicators.

The bloodiest persecutions, however, did not occur in North America. The Latin countries provided the world with a series of massacres remarkable even in that murderous century. Yet it was a fact that in the year of Cave's death, Italy was half-Cavite and France, England and Germany were nearly all Cavite. Only Spain and parts of Latin America held out, imprisoning, executing, deporting Cavites against the inevitable day when our Communicators, undismayed, proud in their martyrdom, would succeed in their assaults upon these last citadels of paganism.

On a hot day in August, our third and last autumn in the yellow tower, we dined on the terrace of Cave's penthouse overlooking the city. The bright sky shuddered with heat.

Clarissa had just come from abroad, where she had been enjoying herself hugely under the guise of an official tour of reconnaissance. She sat wearing a large picture hat beneath the striped awning that sheltered our glass-topped table from the sun's rays. Cave insisted on eating out-of-doors as often as possible, even though the rest of us preferred the cool interior where we were not disturbed by either heat or by the clouds of soot which floated above the imperial city, impartially lighting upon all who ventured out into the open.

It was our first 'family dinner' in some months (Paul insisted on regarding us as a family, and the metaphors which he derived from this one conceit used even to irritate the imperturbable Cave). At one end of the table sat Clarissa, with Paul and me on either side of her; at the other end sat Cave, with Iris and Stokharin on either side of him. Early in the dinner, when the conversation was particular, Iris and I talked privately.

'I suppose we'll be leaving soon,' she said. A gull missed the awning by inches.

'I haven't heard anything about it. Who's leaving . . . and why?'

'John thinks we've all been here too long; he thinks we're too remote.'

'He's quite right about that.' I blew soot off my plate. 'But where are we to go? After all, there's a good chance that if any of us shows his head to the grateful populace someone will blow it off.'

'That's a risk we have to take. But John is right. We must get out and see the people . . . talk to them direct.' Her voice was urgent. I looked at her thoughtfully, seeing the change that three years of extraordinary activity had wrought. She was overweight and her face, as sometimes happens in the first access of weight, was smooth, without lines. That wonderful sharpness, her old fineness, was entirely gone and the new Iris, the busy, efficient Iris, had become like . . like . . . I groped for the comparison, the memory of someone similar I had known in the past, but the ghost did not materialize; and so haunted, faintly distrait, I talked to the new Iris I did not really know.

'I'll be only too happy to leave,' I said, helping myself to the salad which was being served us by one of the Eurasian servants whom Paul, in an exotic mood, had engaged to look after the penthouse and the person of Cave. 'I don't think I've been away from here half a dozen times in two years.'

'It's been awfully hard,' Iris agreed. Her eyes shifted regularly to Cave, like an anxious parent's. 'Of course I've had more chance than anyone to get out but

I haven't seen nearly as much as I ought. It's my job, really, to look at all the Centres, to supervise in person all the schools, but of course I can't if Paul insists on turning every trip I take into a kind of pageant.'

'It's for your own protection.'

'I think we're much safer than Paul thinks. The country's almost entirely Cavite.'

'All the more reason to be careful. The die-hards are on their last legs; they're desperate.'

'Well, we must take our chances. John says he won't stay here another autumn. September is his best month, you know. It was in September that he first spoke Cavesword.'

'What does Paul say?' I looked down the table at our ringmaster, who was telling Clarissa what she had seen in Europe.

Iris frowned. 'He's doing everything he can to keep us here . . . I can't think why. John's greatest work has been done face to face with people, yet Paul acts as if he didn't dare let him out in public. We have quarrelled about this for over a year, Paul and I.'

'He's quite right. I'd be nervous to go about in public without some sort of protection. You should see the murderous letters I get at the *Journal*.'

'We've nothing to fear,' said Iris flatly. 'And we have everything to gain by mixing with people. We could easily grow out of touch, marooned in this tower.'

'Oh, it's not that bad.' To my surprise, I found myself defending our monastic life. 'Everyone comes here. Cave speaks to groups of the faithful every day. I sit like some dishevelled hen over a large newspaper and I couldn't be more instructed, more engaged in life, while you dash around the country almost as much as Paul does.'

'But only seeing the Centres, only meeting the Cavites. I have no other life any more.' I looked at her curiously. There was no bitterness in her voice, yet there was a certain wistfulness which I had never noticed before.

'Do you regret all this, Iris?' I asked. It had been three years since I had spoken to her of personal matters. We had become, in a sense, the offices which we held; our symbolic selves paralyzing all else within, true precedent achieved at a great cost. Now a fissure had suddenly appeared in the monument which Iris had become, and through the flow I heard again, briefly, the voice of the girl I had met on the bank of the Hudson in the spring of a lost year.

'I never knew it would be like this,' she said almost whispering, her eyes on Cave while she spoke to me. 'I never thought my life would be as alone as this, all work.'

'Yet you wanted it. You *do* want it. Direction, meaning, you wanted all that and now you have it. The magic worked, Iris. Your magician was real.'

'But I sometimes wonder if *I* am real anymore.' The words, though softly spoken, fell between us like rounded stones, smooth and hard.

'It's too late,' I said, mercilessly. 'You are what you wanted to be. Live it out, Iris. There is nothing else.'

'You're dead too,' she said at last, her voice regaining its usual authority.

'Speaking of dead,' said Cave suddenly turning towards us (I hoped he had not heard all our conversation), 'Stokharin here has come up with a wonderful scheme.'

Even Clarissa fell silent. We all did on those rare occasions when Cave spoke on social occasions. Cave looked cheerfully about the table for a moment. Stokharin beamed with pleasure at the accolade.

'You've probably all heard about the suicides as a result of Cavesword.' Cave had very early got into the habit of speaking of himself in the third person whenever a point of doctrine was involved. 'Paul's been collecting the monthly figures and each month they double. Of course they're not accurate since there are a good many deaths due to Cavesword which we don't hear about. Anyway, Stokharin has perfected a painless death by poison, a new compound which kills within an hour and is delightful to take.'

'I have combined certain narcotics which together insure a highly exhilarated state before the end, as well as most pleasant fantasies.' Stokharin smiled complacently.

Cave continued. 'I've already worked out some of the practical details for putting this into action. There still a lot of wrinkles, but we can iron them out in time. One of the big problems of present-day *unorganized* suicide is the mess it causes for the people unfortunate enough to be left behind. There are legal complications; there is occasionally grief in old-fashioned family groups; there is also a general social disturbance which tends to give suicide, at least among the reactionaries, a bad name.

'Our plan is simple. We will provide at each Centre full facilities for those who have listened to Cavesword and have responded to it by taking the better way. There will be a number of comfortable rooms where the suicidalist may receive his friends for a last visit. We'll provide legal assistance to put his affairs in order. Not everyone of course will be worthy of us. Those who choose death merely to evade responsibility will be censured and restrained. But the deserving, those whose lives have been devoted and orderly, may come to use and receive the gift.'

I was appalled. Before I could control myself I had said: 'But the law! You just can't let people kill themselves . . .'

'Why not?' Cave looked at me coldly and I saw, in the eyes of the others, concern and hostility. I had anticipated something like this ever since my talk with Paul, but I had not thought it would come so swiftly or so boldly.

Paul spoke for Cave. 'We've got the Congress and the Congress will make a law for us. For the time being, it *is* against the statutes, but we've been assured by our lawyers that there isn't much chance of their being invoked, except perhaps in the remaining pockets of Christianity where we'll go slow until we do have the necessary laws to protect us.'

At that moment the line which from the very beginning had been visibly drawn between me and them became a wall apparent to everyone. Even Clarissa, my usual ally, fearless and sharp, did not speak out. They looked at me, all of them awaiting a sign; even Cave regarded me with curiosity.

My hand shook and I was forced to seize the edge of the table to steady myself. The sensation of cold glass and iron gave me a sudden courage. I brought Cave's life to its end.

I turned to him and said, quietly, with all the firmness I could summon: 'Then you will have to die as well as they, and soon.'

There was a shocked silence. Iris shut her eyes. Paul gasped and sat back abruptly in his chair. Cave turned white but he did not flinch. His eyes did not waver. They seized on mine, terrible and remote, full of power; with an effort, I looked past him. I still feared his gaze.

'What did you say?' The voice was curiously mild yet it increased rather than diminished the tension. We had reached the crisis, without a plan.

'You have removed the fear of death, for which future generations will thank you, as I do. But you have gone too far . . . all of you.' I looked about me at the pale faces; a faint wisp of new moon curled in the pale sky above. 'Life is to be lived until the flesh no longer supports the life within. The meaning of life, Cave, is more life, not death. The enemy of life is death, an enemy not to be feared but no less hostile for all that, no less dangerous, no less wrong when the living choose it instead of life, either for themselves or for others. You've been able to dispel our fear of the common adversary; that was your great work in the world. Now you want to go further, to make love to this enemy we no longer fear, to mate with death, and it is here that you, all of you, become enemies of life.'

'Stop it!' Iris's voice was high and clear. I did not look at her. All that I could do now was to force the climax.

'But sooner or later every act of human folly creates its own opposition. This will too, more soon that late, for if one can make any generality about human beings it is that they want *not* to die. You cannot stampede them into death for long. They are enthusiastic now. They may not be soon . . . unless of course there is some supreme example before them, one which you, Cave, can alone supply. *You* will have to die by your own hand to show the virtue and the truth of all that you have said.'

I had gone as far as I could. I glanced at Iris while I spoke; she had grown white and old-looking and, while I watched her, I realized whom it was she resembled, the obscure nagging memory which had disturbed me all through dinner. She was like my mother, a woman long dead, one whose gentle blurred features had been strikingly similar to that frightened face which now stared at me as though I were a murderer.

Paul was the one who answered me. 'You're out of your mind, Gene,' he said, when my meaning had at last penetrated to them all. 'It doesn't follow in the least that Cave must die because others want to. The main work is still ahead of him. This country is only a corner of the world. There's some of Europe and most of Asia and Africa still ahead of us. How can you even suggest he quit now and die?'

'The work will be done whether he lives or not, as you certainly know. He's given it the first impetus. The rest is up to the others, to the ambitious, the inspired. We've met enough of *them* these last few years. They're quite capable of finishing the work without us.'

'But it's nothing without Cave.'

I shrugged. I was suddenly relieved as the restraint of three furious years went in a rush. 'I am as devoted to Cave as anyone,' I said (and I was, I think, honest). 'I don't want him to die but all of you in your madness have made it impossible for him to live. He's gone now to the limit, to the last boundary. He is the son of death and each of you supports him. I don't, for it was my wish to make life better, not death desirable. I never really believed it would come to this. That you, Cave, would speak for death, and against life.' I raised my eyes to his. To my astonishment he had lowered his lids as though to hide from me, to shut me out. His head was shaking oddly from left to right and his lips were pressed tight together.

I struck again, without mercy. 'But don't stop now. You've got your wish. By all means, build palaces if you like for those who choose to die in your name. But remember that you will be their victim, too. The victim of their passionate trust. They will force you to lead the way and *you* must be death's lover, Cave.'

He opened his eyes and I was shocked to see them full of tears. 'I am not afraid,' he said.

CHAPTER TEN

I

A few days after our disastrous dinner, Clarissa came to me in my office. It was our first private meeting since her return from Europe. It was also my first meeting with any one of the directors for, since the scene on the penthouse terrace, none had come near me, not even Paul, whom I usually saw at least once a day.

Clarissa seemed tired. She sat down heavily in the chair beside my desk and looked at me oddly. 'Recriminations?' I asked cheerfully. The recent outburst had restored me to perfect health and equanimity. I was prepared for anything, especially battle.

'You're an absolute fool and you know it,' she said at last. 'I suppose there are wires in here, recording everything we say.'

'I shouldn't be surprised. Fortunately, I have no secrets.'

'There's no doubt of that.' She glared at me. 'There was no need to rush things.'

'You mean you anticipated this?'

'What else? Where else could it lead? The same thing happened to Jesus, you know. They kept pushing him to claim the kingdom. Finally, they pushed too hard and he was killed. It was the killing which perpetuated the legend.'

'And a number of other things.'

'In any case, it's gone too far. Also, I don't think you even begin to see what you've done.'

'Done? I've merely brought the whole thing into the open and put myself on record as being opposed to this . . . this passion for death.'

'That of course is nonsense. Just because a few nit-wits . . .'

'A few? Have you seen the statistics? Every month there are a few hundred more, and as soon as Stokharin gets going with his damned roadhouses for would-be suicides we may find that . . .'

'I always assumed Paul made up the statistics. But even if they *are* true, even if a few hundred thousand people decide to slip away every year, I am in favour of it. There are too many people as it is and most of them aren't worth the room they take up. I suspect all this is just one of nature's little devices to reduce the population, like pederasty on those Greek islands.'

'You're outrageous.'

'I'm perfectly rational, which is more than I can say for you. Anyway, the reason I've come to see you today is, first, to warn you and, second to say good-bye.'

'Good-bye? You're not . . .'

'Going to kill myself?' She laughed. 'Not in a hundred years! Though I must say lately I've begun to feel old. No, I'm going away. I've told Paul that I've had my fun, that you're all on your own and that I want no part of what's to come.'

'Where will you go?'

'Who knows? Now for the warning. Paul of course is furious at you and so is Iris.'

'Perfectly understandable. What did he say?'

'Nothing good. I talked to him this morning. I won't enrage you by repeating all the expletives. It's enough to say he's eager to get you out of the way. He feels you've been a malcontent all along.'

'He'll have trouble getting me to take Stokharin's magic pill.'

'He may not leave it up to you,' said Clarissa significantly, and inadvertently I shuddered. I had of course wondered if they would dare go so far. I had doubted it but the matter-of-fact Clarissa enlightened me. 'Watch out for him, especially if he becomes friendly. You must remember that with the country Cavite and with Paul in charge of the organization you haven't much chance.'

'I'll take what I have.'

Clarissa looked at me without, I could see, much hope. 'What you don't know, and this is my last good deed, for in a sense I'm responsible for getting you into this, is that you accidentally gave the game away.'

'What do you mean?'

'I mean that Paul has been planning for over a year to do away with Cave. He feels that Cave's usefulness is over. Also he's uneasy about letting him loose in the world. Paul wants full control of the establishment and he can't have it while Cave lives. Paul also realizes – he's much cleverer than you've ever thought, by the way – that the Cavites need a symbol, some great sacrifice, and obviously Cave's suicide is the answer. It is Paul's intention either to persuade Cave to kill himself or else to do it for him and then announce that Cave, of his own free will, chose to die.'

I had the brief sensation of a man drowning. 'How do you know all this?'

'I have two eyes. And Iris told me.'

'She knows too?'

'Of course she knows! Why else do you think she's so anxious to get Cave away from this place? She knows Paul can have him killed at any time and no one would be the wiser.'

I grunted with amazement. I understood now what it was that had happened on the terrace. I felt a perfect fool. Of them all I alone had been unaware of what was going on beneath the surface and, in my folly, I had detonated the situation without knowing it. '*He* knows too?' I asked weakly.

'Of course he does. He's on his guard every minute against Paul.'

'Why has no one ever told me this?'

Clarissa shrugged. 'They had no idea which side you'd take. They still don't know. Paul believes that you are with him and though he curses you for an impetuous fool, he's decided that perhaps it's a good idea now to bring all this into the open, at least among ourselves. He hopes for a majority vote in the directors' meeting to force Cave to kill himself.'

'And Cave?'

'Has no wish to die, sensible man.'

'I am a fool.'

'What I've always told you, dear.' Clarissa smiled at me. 'I will say, though, that you are the only one of the lot who has acted for an impersonal reason, and certainly none of them understands you except me. I am on your side, in a way. Voluntary deaths don't alarm me the way they do you, but this obsession of Cave's, of death being preferable to life, may have ghastly consequences.'

'What can I do?'

'I haven't the faintest idea. It's enough that you were warned in advance.'

'What would *you* do?'

'Exactly what I'm going to do. Take a long trip.'

'I mean if you were I.'

She sighed. 'Save your life, if possible. That's all you can do.'

'I have a few weapons, you know. I have the *Journal* and I'm a director. I have friends in every Centre.' This was almost true. I had made a point of knowing as many Residents as possible. 'I also have Iris and Cave on my side since I'm willing to do all I can to keep him alive, that he *not* become a supreme symbol.'

'I wish you luck,' Clarissa was most cynical. She rose. 'Now that I've done my bit of informing, I'm off.'

'Europe?'

'None of your business. But I *will* tell you I won't go back there. They've gone quite mad too. In Madrid I pretended to be a Catholic and I watched them put Cavites up before firing squads. Of course our people, despite persecution, are having a wonderfully exciting time with passwords and peculiar college fraternity handclasps and so on.' She collected her gloves and handbag from the floor where, as usual, she had strewn them. 'Well, now good-bye.' She gave me a kiss; then she was gone.

II

Events moved rapidly. I took to bolting my bedroom door at night, and during the day I was careful always to have one or another of my assistants near me. It was a strange sensation to be living in a modern city with all its police and courts and yet to fear that in a crisis there would be no succour, no one to turn to for aid and protection. We were a separate government within the nation, beyond the law.

The day after Clarissa had said good-bye, Paul appeared in my office. I was surrounded by editors, but at a look from him and a gesture from me they withdrew. We had each kept our secret, evidently, for none of those close to us in that building suspected that there had been a fatal division.

'I seem to be in disgrace,' I said, my forefinger delicately caressing the buzzer which I had built into the arm of my chair so that I might summon aid in the event that visitor proved to be either a bore or a maniac, two types curiously drawn to enterprises such as ours.

'I wouldn't say that.' Paul sat in a chair close to my own; I recall thinking, a little madly, that elephants are supposed to be at their most dangerous when they are perfectly still. Paul was noticeably controlled. Usually he managed to cross the room at least once for every full sentence; now he sat looking at me, his face without expression.

'I've seen no one since our dinner except Clarissa,' I explained; then I added, earnestly: 'I wonder where she plans to go. She didn't . . .'

'You've almost wrecked everything,' he said, his voice tight, unfamiliar in tension.

'I didn't want to,' I said, inaccurately. I was at the moment more terrified than I had ever been, either before or since. I could get no real grip on him. The surface he presented me was as unyielding as a prison wall.

'Who told you? Iris? Cave? or were you spying?' Each question was fired at me like a bullet.

'Spying on whom?'

'On me, damn you!' Then it broke. The taut line of control which had held in check his anger and his fear broke all at once and the torrent flowed, reckless and overpowering: 'You meddling idiot! You spied on me. You found out. You thought you'd be able to stall things by springing it like that. Well, you failed.' I recall thinking, quite calmly, how much I preferred his face in the congested ugliness of rage to its ordinary banality of expression. I was relieved, too, by the storm. I could handle him when he was out of control. I considered my counteroffensive while he shouted at me, accused me of hostility to him, of deviationism from Cavesword and of numerous other crimes. He stopped, finally, for lack of breath.

'I gather,' I said, my voice shaking a little from excitement, 'that at some point recently you decided that Cave should apply Cavesword to himself and die, providing us with a splendid example, an undying (I mean no pun) symbol.'

'You know you found out and decided to get in on the act, to force my hand. Now he'll never do it.'

That was it, then. I was relieved to know. 'Cave has refused to kill himself?'

'You bet your sweet life he has.' Paul was beginning to recover his usual poise. 'Your little scene gave him the excuse he needed: "Gene's right."' Paul imitated Cave's voice with startling accuracy and malice. '"Gene's right. I never did mean for everybody to kill themselves off, where'd the world be if *that* happened? Just a few people. That's all." And he's damned if he's going to be one of them. "Hate to set that sort of example."'

'Well, you'll have to try something else, then.'

'Why did you do it?' Paul's voice became petulant. 'Did Iris put you up to it?'

'Nobody put me up to it.'

'You mean to sit there and try to make me believe that it just occurred to you, like that, to suggest Cave would have to kill himself if he encouraged suicide?'

'I mean that it occurred to me exactly like that.' I looked at Paul with vivid loathing. 'Can't you understand an obvious causal relationship? With this plan of Stokharin's you'll make it impossible for Cave *not* to commit suicide, and when he does, you will have an international death cult which I shall do my best to combat.'

Paul's hands began nervously to play with his tie, his lapels. I wondered if he had come armed. I placed my finger lightly upon the buzzer. Implacably, we faced one another.

'You are not truly Cavesword,' was all that he said.

'We won't argue about that. I'm merely explaining to you why I said what I did and why I intend to keep Cave alive as long as possible. Alive and hostile to you, to your peculiar interpretation of his Word.'

Paul looked suddenly disconsolate. 'I've done what I thought best. I feel Cave should show all of us the way. I feel it's both logical and necessary to the Establishment he give back his life publicly.'

'But he doesn't want to.'

'That is the part I can't understand. Cavesword is that death is not to be feared but embraced, yet he, the man who has really changed the world, refuses to die.'

'Perhaps he feels he has more work to do. More places to see. Perhaps, Paul, he doesn't trust you, doesn't want to leave you in control of the Establishment.'

'I'm willing to get out if that's all that's stopping him.' But the insincerity of this protestation was too apparent for either of us to contemplate it for long.

'I don't care what his motives are. I don't care if he himself is terrified of dying (and I have a hunch that that is the real reason for his hesitancy), but I *do* know that I don't want him dead by his own hand.'

'You're quite sure of that?'

'Absolutely sure. I'm a director of the Establishment and don't forget it. Iris, Cave and I are against you and Stokharin. You may control the organization but we have Cave himself.' I gathered courage in my desperation. I purposely sounded as though I were in warm concert with the others.

'I realize all that.' Paul was suddenly meek, conciliatory, treacherous. 'But you must allow me as much sincerity as you withhold for yourself. I want to do what's best. I think he should die and I've done everything to persuade him. He was near agreement when you upset everything.'

'For which I'm happy, though it was something of an accident. Are you sure that it is only for the sake of Cavesword you want him dead?'

'What other reason?' He looked at me indignantly. I could not be sure whether he was telling the truth or not. I doubted it.

'Many other reasons. For one thing you would be his heir, in complete control of the Establishment; and that of course is something worth inheriting.'

Paul shrugged convincingly. 'I'm as much in charge now as I would be with him dead,' he said with a certain truth. 'I'm interested in Cavesword, not in Cave. If his death enhances and establishes the Word more securely then I must convince him that he must die.'

'There is another way,' I said smiling at the pleasant thought.

'Another way?'

'To convince us of your dedication and sincerity to Cavesword.'

'What's that?'

'You kill *yourself*, Paul.'

There was a long silence. I pressed the buzzer and my secretary came in. Without a word, Paul left.

Immediately afterwards, I took the private elevator to Cave's penthouse. Two guards stopped me while I was announced by a third. After a short delay I was admitted to Cave's study, where Iris received me.

'I know what's happening,' I said. 'Where is he?'

'Obviously you do.' Her voice was cold. She did not ask me to sit down. Awkwardly, I faced her at the room's centre.

'We must stop him.'

'John? Stop him from what?'

'Doing what Paul wants him to do.'

'And what you want as well.'

'You're mistaken. I thought I made myself clear the other night. But though my timing was apparently bad, under *no* circumstances do I want him to die.'

'You made your speech to force him.'

'And Paul thinks I made it to stop him.' I couldn't help smiling. 'I am, it seems, everyone's enemy.'

'Paul has told me everything. How you and he and Stokharin all decided, without consulting us, that John should die.'

I was astonished at Paul's boldness. Could he really be moving so swiftly? How else explain such a prodigious lie? I told her quickly and urgently what I had said to Paul and he to me. She heard me to the end without expressing either belief or disbelief. When I had finished she turned away from me and went to the window where, through yellow glass, the city rose upon the band of horizon.

'It's too late,' she said, evenly. 'I hadn't expected this. Perhaps you're telling me the truth. If you are, you've made a terrible mistake.' She turned about suddenly, with a precision almost military. 'He's going to do it.'

The awful words fell like a weight upon a scale. I reached for a chair and sat down, all strength gone. 'Stop him,' I said, all that I could say. 'Stop him.'

'It's too late for that.' She took pity on me. 'I think you're telling me the truth.' She came over to where I was sitting and looked down at me gently. 'I'm sorry I accused you. I should have realized Paul was lying.'

'*You* can stop him.'

'I can't. I've tried but I can't.' Her control was extraordinary. I did not then guess the reason for her calm, her strength.

'Then I must try.' I stood up.

'You can't do anything. He won't see you. He won't see anyone but me.'

'I thought he told Paul he agreed with me that he didn't want to . . . to countenance all this, that he . . .'

'At first he took your side, if it is really what you feel. Then he thought about it and this morning he decided to go ahead with Paul's plan.'

I was confused. 'Does Paul know?'

Iris smiled wanly. 'John is reserving for himself the pleasure of doing what he must do without Paul's assistance.'

'Or knowledge?'

Iris shrugged. 'Paul will find out about it this evening, I suppose. There will be an announcement. John's secretary is getting it ready now . . . one for the public and another for the Establishment.'

'When will it happen?'

'Tomorrow. I go with him, Gene.'

'You? You're not going to die too?'

'I don't see that it makes much difference what I do when John dies.'

'You can't leave us now. You can't leave Paul in charge of everything. He's a dangerous man. Why, if . . .'

'You'll be able to handle him.' It was perfectly apparent to me that she was no longer interested in me or in the others; not even in the fate of the work we had begun.

'It's finished, if you go too,' I said bleakly. 'Together we could control Paul; alone, I wouldn't last ten days. Iris, let me talk to him.'

'I can't. I won't.'

I contemplated pushing by her and searching the penthouse, but there were guards everywhere and I had no wish to be shot on such an errand.

She guessed my thought and said quickly, 'There's no possible way for you or anyone to get through to him. Sometime tonight or tomorrow he will leave and that's the end.'

'He won't do it here?' This surprised me.

She shook her head. 'He wants to go off alone, away from everyone. I'm to be with him until the end. Then I'll send the body back here for burial, but he'll leave full instructions.'

'You mean I'm never to see either of you again? Just like that, you both go?'

'Just like this.' For the first time she displayed some warmth. 'I've cared for you, Gene,' she said gently. 'I even think that of us all you were the one most nearly right in your approach to John. I think you understood him better than he himself. Try to hold on after we go. Try to keep it away from Paul.'

'As if I could!' I turned from her bitterly, filled with unexpected grief. I did not want to lose her presence even though I had lost her or, rather, never possessed more of her than that one bright instant on the California coast when we had both realized with the unexpected clarity of the lovers that we were not that our lives had come to the same point at the same moment. The knowledge of this confluence was the only splendour I had ever known, the single hope, the unique passion of my life.

'Don't miss me. I couldn't bear that.' She put her hand on my arm. I walked away, not able to bear her touch. Then they came.

Paul and Stokharin were in the study. Iris gasped and stepped back when she saw them. I spun about just as Paul shouted, 'It won't work, Iris! Give it up.'

'Get out of here, Paul.' Her voice was strong. 'You have no right here.'

'I have as much right as you. Now tell me whose idea it was. Yours? or was it John's? or Gene's? since he seems to enjoy playing both sides.'

'Get out. All of you.' She moved to the old-fashioned bell cord which hung beside Cave's desk.

'Don't bother,' said Paul. 'No one will come.'

Iris, her eyes wide now with fear, tugged the cord twice. The second time it broke off in her hand. There was no response.

Paul looked grim. 'I'm sorry to have to do it this way but you've left me no choice. You can't leave, either of you.'

'You've read . . .'

'I saw the release. It won't work.'

'Why not? It's what you've wanted all along. Everything will be yours. There'll be nobody to stop you. John will be dead and I'll be gone for good. You'll never see me again. Why must you interfere?' She spoke quickly and plausibly, but the false proportion was evident now, even to me. The desperate plan was tumbling down at Paul's assault.

'Iris, I'm not a complete fool. I know perfectly well that Cave has no intention of killing himself and that . . .'

'Why do you think I'm going with him? to send you the body back for the ceremony which you'll perform right here, publicly . . .'

'Iris.' He looked at her for a long moment. Then: 'If you two leave as planned tonight (I've cancelled the helicopter, by the way) there will be no body, no embalming, no ceremony. Only a mystery which might very well undo all our work. I can't allow that. Cave must die here, before morning. We might have put it off but your announcement has already leaked out. There'll be a million people out there in the street tomorrow. We'll have to show them Cave's body.'

Iris swayed. I moved quickly to her side and held her arm. 'It's three to two, Paul,' I said. 'I assume we're still directors. Three of us have agreed that Cave and Iris leave. That's final.' But my bluff was humiliatingly weak; it was ignored.

'The penthouse,' said Paul softly, 'is empty . . . just the five of us here. The Doctor and I are armed. Take us in to him.'

'No.' Iris moved instinctively, fatally, to the door that led to Cave, as if to guard it with her body.

There was a brief scuffle, ending with Iris and myself, considerably dishevelled, facing two guns. With an apology, Stokharin pushed us through the door.

In a small sunroom we found Cave sitting before a television screen, watching the installation of a new Resident in Boston. He looked up with surprise at our entrance. 'I thought I said . . .' he began, but Iris interrupted him.

'They want to kill you, John.'

Cave got to his feet, face pale, eyes glaring. Even Paul was shaken by that glance. 'You read my last statement?' Cave spoke sharply, without apparent fear.

'That's why we've come,' said Paul. He and Stokharin moved, as though by previous accord, to opposite ends of the little room, leaving the three of us together, vulnerable at its centre. 'You must do it here.' Paul signalled Stokharin, who produced a small metal box which he tossed to Cave.

'Some of the new pills,' he said nervously. 'Very nice. We use peppermint in the outer layer and . . .'

'Take it, John.'

'I'll get some water,' said Stokharin. But Paul waved to him to keep his place.

Cave smiled coldly. 'I will not take it. Now both of you get out of here before I call the guards.'

'No more guards,' said Paul. 'We've seen to that. Now, please, don't make it any more difficult than it is. Take the pill.'

'If you read my statement you know that . . .'

'You intend to take a pleasant trip around the world incognito with Iris. Yes, I know. As your friend, I wish you could do it. But, for one thing, sooner or later you'd be recognized, and for another we must have proof . . . we must have a body.'

'Iris will bring the body back,' said Cave. He was still quite calm. 'I choose to do it this way and there's nothing more to be said. You'll have the Establishment all to yourself and I will be a most satisfactory figure upon which to build a world religion.' It was the only time in my experience with Cave that I ever heard him strike the ironic note.

'Leave us alone, Paul. You have what you want. Now let us go.' Iris begged, but Paul had no eyes for anyone but Cave.

'Take it, John,' he repeated softly. 'Take Cavesway.'

'Not for you.' Cave hurled the metal box at Paul's head and Stokharin fired. There was one almost bland moment when we all stood, politely, in a circle and watched Cave, a look of wonder on his face, touch his shoulder where the blood had begun to flow through a hole in the jacket.

Then Iris turned fiercely on Paul, knocking him off balance, while Cave ran to the door. Stokharin, his hand shaking and his face silver with fear, fired three times, each time hitting Cave, who quivered but did not fall; instead, he got through the door and into the study. As Stokharin hurried after him, I threw myself upon him, expecting death at any moment; but it did not come, for Stokharin had collapsed. He dropped his gun and hid his face in his hands, rocking back and forth on the floor, sobbing. Free of Iris's fierce grip, Paul got to Cave before I did.

Cave lay in the corridor only a few feet from the elevator. He had fallen on his face and lay now in his own blood, his hands working at the floor as though trying to dig himself a grave in the hard stone. I turned him on his back and he opened his eyes. 'Iris?' he asked. His voice was ordinary though his breathing was harsh and uneven.

'Here I am.' Iris knelt down beside him, ignoring Paul.

Cave whispered something to Iris. Then a flow of blood, like the full moon's tide, poured from his mouth. He was dead.

'Cavesway,' said Paul at last when the silence had been used up. The phrase he had prepared for this moment was plainly inadequate for the reality at our feet.

'*Your* way,' said Iris as she stood up. She looked at Paul calmly, as though they had only just met. '*Your* way,' she repeated.

In the other room Stokharin moaned.

CHAPTER ELEVEN

I

Now the work was complete. Cavesword and Cavesway formed a perfect design and all the rest would greatly follow, or so Paul assumed. I believe if I had been he I should have killed both Iris and myself the same day, removing at one stroke witnesses and opposition. But he did not have the courage, and I also think he underestimated us, to his own future sorrow.

Iris and I were left alone in the penthouse. Paul, after shaking Stokharin into a semblance of calm, bundled Cave's body into a blanket and then, with the Doctor's help, placed it in the private elevator.

The next twenty-four hours were a grim carnival. The body of Cave, beautifully arranged and painted, lay in the central auditorium of the Centre as thousands filed by to see him. Paul's speech over the corpse was telecast around the world.

Iris and I kept to our separate rooms, both by choice and from necessity, since gentle guards stood before our doors and refused, apologetically, to let us out.

I watched the services over television while my chief editors visited me one by one, unaware of what had happened and ignoring the presence of the guards. It was assumed that I was too shocked by grief to go to the office. Needless to say, I did not mention to any of them what had happened. At first I had thought it best to expose Paul as a murderer and a fraud, but on second thought (the second thought which followed all too swiftly upon the first, as Paul had no doubt assumed it would), I did not want to risk the ruin of our work. Instead, I decided to wait, to study Paul's destruction, an event which I had grimly vowed would take place as soon as possible. He could not now get rid of either Iris or me in the near future and all we needed, I was sure, was a week or two. I was convinced of this though I had no specific plan. Iris had more influence, more prestige in the Establishment, than Paul, and I figured, correctly as later events corroborate, that Cave's death would enhance her position. As for myself, I was not without influence.

I kept my lines of communication clear the next few days during what was virtually a house arrest. The editors came to me regularly and I continued to compose editorials. The explanation for my confinement was, according to a bulletin signed by Stokharin, a mild heart condition. Everyone was most kind. But I was alarmed when I heard of the diagnosis. It meant that with one of Stokharin's pellets in my food death would be ascribed to coronary occlusion, the result of strain attendant upon Cave's death. I had less time than I thought. I made plans.

Paul's funeral oration was competent though less than inspiring. The Chief Resident of Dallas, one of the great new figures of the Establishment, made an even finer speech over the corpse. I listened attentively, judging from what was said and what was not said the wind's direction. Cavesway was now the heart of the doctrine. Death was to be embraced with passion; life was the criminal, death the better reality; consciousness was an evil which, in death's oblivion, met its true fate . . . man's one perfect virtuous act was the sacrifice of his own consciousness to the pure nothing from which, by grim accident, it had come into being. The Chief Resident of Dallas was most eloquent and chilling.

Even sequestered in my room, I caught some of the excitement which circled the globe like a lightning storm. Thirty-five hundred suicides were reported within forty-eight hours of Cave's death. The statisticians lost count of the number of people who fought to get inside the building to see Cave in death. From my window I could see that Park Avenue had been roped off for a dozen blocks. People swarmed like ants towards the gates of the tower.

I sent messages to Iris but received none, nor, for that matter, did I have any assurances that she had got mine. I followed Paul's adventures on television and from the reports of my editors who visited me regularly, despite Stokharin's orders.

On the third day, I was allowed to go to my office, Paul having decided that it would be thought odd if I were to die so soon after Cave. No doubt he was also relieved to discover that I had not revealed to my friends what had happened. Now that he had established the fact of my weak heart, my death could be engineered most plausibly at any time.

I did not see him face to face until the fourth day, when John Cave's ashes were to be distributed over the United States. Stokharin, Paul and I sat in the back seat of a limousine at the head of a motorcade which, beginning at the tower, terminated at the airport where the jet plane which would sprinkle the ashes over New York, Seattle, Chicago and Los Angeles was waiting, along with a vast crowd and the President of the United States, an official Christian but known to incline, as Presidents do, towards the majority. Cavites were the majority and had been for almost two years.

I was startled to find Paul and Stokharin in the same automobile. It had been my understanding that we were to travel separately in the motorcade. They were most cordial.

'Sorry to hear you've been sick, Gene,' Paul said with an ingenuous grin. 'Mustn't strain the old ticker.'

'I'm sure the good Doctor will be able to cure me,' I said cheerfully.

They both laughed loudly. The car pulled away from the tower and drove down Park Avenue at the head of a long procession. Crowds lined the street as we drove slowly by. They were curiously still, as though they hardly knew how to react. This was a funeral, yet Cavesway was glorious. Some cheered. Most simply stared and pointed at our car, recognizing Paul. I suddenly realized why they were so interested in this particular car. On the floor, at Paul's feet, was what looked like a large flowerpot covered with gold foil.

'Are those the ashes?'

Paul nodded. 'Did an extra quick job, too, I'm glad to say. We didn't want any slipup.'

'Where's Iris?'

'I was going to ask *you* that.' Paul looked at me sharply. 'She disappeared yesterday and it's very embarrassing for all of us, very inconsiderate too. She knew I especially wanted her at the ceremony. She knows that everyone will expect to see her.'

'I think she took the idea of Cavesway most illogically,' said Stokharin. His usual sang-froid had returned, the break-down forgotten. 'She should be grateful to us for making all this possible, despite Cave's weakness.'

I ignored Stokharin. I looked at Paul, who was beaming at the crowd, acknowledging their waves with nods of his head. 'What will you do now?'

'You heard the ceremony?'

'Yes.'

'Well, just that. Cavesway has become universal. Even the economists in Washington have privately thanked us for what we're doing to reduce the population. There's a theory that by numerous voluntary deaths wars might decrease since – or so the proposition goes – they are nature's way of checking population.'

'Perhaps you're right.' I assumed a troubled expression as I made my first move of my counteroffensive.

Paul looked away from the crowd to regard me shrewdly. 'You don't think I trust you, do you?'

I shrugged. 'Why not? I can't change Cavesway now.'

Paul grunted. I could see that he did not credit this spurious *volte-face*; nevertheless, an end to my active opposition would force him to revise his plans. This would, I hoped, give me the time I needed. I pressed on. 'I think we can compromise. Short of rigging my death, which would cause suspicion, you must continue to put up with me for a while. You've nothing to fear from me since you control the Establishment and since the one weapon I have against you I will not use.'

'You mean . . .'

'My having witnessed the murder of Cave. If I had wanted to I could have revealed this before the cremation. An autopsy would certainly have ruined everything for you.'

'Why didn't you?' I could see that Paul was genuinely interested in my motives.

'Because it would have meant the end of the work. I saw no reason to avenge Cave at such a cost. You must remember he was not a god to me, any more than you are.'

This twist of a blunt knife had the calculated effect. 'What a cold devil you are!' said Paul, almost admiringly. 'I wish I could believe you.'

'There's no reason not to. I was opposed to the principle of suicide. It is now firmly established. We must go on from there.'

'Then tell me where Iris is.'

'I haven't any idea. As you know, I've been trying to get in touch with her for days. Your people intercepted everything. How *did* she manage to get away?'

'One of the guards let her out. I thought he was one of our boys but it seems she worked on him and he left with her. I've alerted all the Centres; so far no one's seen her.'

Just before Grand Central Terminal, the crowd began to roar with excitement and Paul held up the jar of ashes. The crowd went wild and tried to break through the police lines. The cortege drove a bit faster and Paul set the ashes down. He looked triumphant but tired, as though he'd not slept in a month. One eyelid, I saw, was twitching with fatigue.

'When are we to have a directors' meeting?' I asked as we crossed the bridge which spanned the river. 'We're still legally a company. We must elect a new board chairman.'

'As soon as we find Iris,' said Paul. 'I think we should all be there, don't you? Two to two.'

'Perhaps three to one on the main things,' I said, allowing this to penetrate, aware that his quick mind would study all the possibilities and arrive at a position so subtle and unexpected as to be of use to me if I, in turn, were quick enough to seize my opportunity.

At the airport, a detachment of airborne troops was drawn up before a festooned reviewing stand. Nearby the Marine Band played incongruous marches, while in the centre of the stand, surrounded by cameras and dignitaries, stood the smiling President of the United States.

II

The next day while I was examining the various accounts of the last ceremony, the chief editor came into my office, his face blazing with excitement. 'Iris Mortimer!' was all he could say.

'Iris? Where?'

'Dallas.' He exploded the name in exhalation. Apparently, word had come from our office there that Iris had, a few hours before, denounced Paul for having ignored Cave's last wishes to be embalmed and that, as a result of this and other infidelities to Cavesword, she, as ranking director and with the full concurrence of the Chief Resident of Dallas, was calling a Council of Residents to be held the following week at Dallas to determine the future course of the Establishment.

I almost laughed aloud with pleasure. I had not believed she would show such vigour and daring. I had feared that she might choose to vanish into obscurity, her life ended with Cave. Even at my most optimistic, I had not dreamed she would act so boldly, exploiting a rivalry between Paul and the Chief Resident of Dallas, the premier member of the Council of Residents, a group that until now had existed for purely ceremonial reasons, exerting no influence upon the board of directors which, while Cave lived, was directed by Paul.

I moved swiftly. The *Journal* was at that moment going to press. I scribbled a brief announcement of the approaching Council of Residents, and I referred to Iris as Cave's spiritual heir. By telephone, I ordered a box to be cut out of the first page. I had not acted a moment too soon, for a few minutes after my telephone call to the compositor, Paul came to my office, furious. He slammed the door behind him.

'You knew this was going to happen.'

'I wish I had.'

He paced the floor quickly, eyes shining. 'I've sent out an order countermanding Iris. I've also removed the Resident at Dallas. I'm still in charge of the Establishment. I control the funds and I've told every damned Resident in this country that if he goes to Dallas I'll cut off his Centre without a penny.'

'It won't work.' I smiled amiably at Paul. 'Your only hold over the Establishment is legal. You are the vice president of the corporation and now, at least for the interim, you're in charge. Fine. But since you've become so devoted to the letter of the law you can't act without consulting your directors and two of them will be in Dallas, reorganizing.'

He cursed me for some minutes. Then abruptly he stopped. 'You won't go to Dallas. You're going to be here for the directors' meeting that will cut off every

Resident who attends that circus. We own the damned Centres. We can appoint whom we like. You're going to help ratify my new appointments.'

I pressed the buzzer in my chair. A secretary came in. I told her to get me a reservation on the next plane to Dallas; then, before she had closed the door behind her, I was halfway through it. I turned to look back at Paul, who stood now quite alone in the office. 'You had better come too,' I said. 'It's all over.'

III

The new Establishment was many months in the making. The Council of seven hundred Residents from all parts of the world sat in general session once a week and in various committees the rest of the time. Iris was everywhere at once, advising, encouraging, proposing. We had adjoining suites in the huge white marble Centre, which had now become (and was to remain) the capitol of the Cavite Establishment.

The Residents were an extraordinary crew, ranging from wild-eyed zealots to urbane, thoughtful men. None had been in the least disturbed by Paul's threats, and with Iris and myself as chief stockholders (Clarissa had turned her voting shares over to Iris, I discovered), we dissolved the old company and a new organization was fashioned, one governed by the Council of Residents, who in turn chose an heir to Cave and an administrative assistant to direct the affairs of the Establishment. Iris was unanimously appointed Guardian of Cavesword, while the Chief Resident of Dallas undertook Paul's old administrative duties. From a constitutional point of view the Council was in perfect agreement, accepting Iris's guidance without demur.

I myself was something of a hero for having committed the *Journal* at a crucial moment to the Dallas synod. I was made an honorary Resident (Poughkeepsie was given to me as a titular Centre) and appointed to the Executive Committee, which was composed of Iris, Dallas, two elected Residents and myself.

We worked harmoniously for some weeks. Each day we would issue bulletins to the news services which had congregated in the city, reporting our progress devotedly.

Paul arrived in the second week. He came secretly and unannounced. I have no idea what it was that he said to Iris or what she said to him; all I know is that a few hours after their meeting in the Centre, he took Cavesway of his own free will and to my astonishment.

I had not believed it possible, I said, when Iris told me, shortly after the Centre announced the presence of Paul Himmell among the dead for that week (regular lists were published of those who had used the Centre's facilities to take Cavesway); in fact, so quietly was it handled that very little was made of it in the press, which did not even report the event until ten days after it had taken place.

'We may have misunderstood Paul.' Iris was serene. In the last year her figure had become thick and maternal, while her hair was streaked with premature white. We were alone in the Committee Room, waiting for our fellow committeemen who were not due for some minutes. The August sun shone gold upon the mahogany table, illuminating like a Byzantine mosaic the painting of Cave that hung behind her chair.

'He really did do it himself?' I looked at her suspiciously. She smiled softly, with amusement.

'He was persuaded,' she said. 'But he did it himself, of his own free will.'

'Not forced?'

'I swear not. He was more sincere than I'd ever thought. He believed in Cavesway.' How naturally she said that word which she had so desperately tried to keep from ever existing.

'Had you really planned to go away?' I asked. 'The two of you?'

Iris looked at me, suddenly alert, impersonal. 'That's all finished, Gene. We must keep on in the present. I never think now of anything but Cavesword and Cavesway. It does no good to think of what might have been.'

And that was the most we were ever to say to one another about the crisis in our lives. We talked of the present and made plans. Stokharin had disappeared at the same time Paul flew to Dallas and we both decided it was wisest to forget him. Certainly he would not trouble us again. There was no talk of vengeance.

The committee members, important and proud, joined us and we took up the day's problem, which by some irony was the standardization of facilities for Cavesway in the different Centres. Quietly, without raising our voices, in a most good-humoured way, we broke neatly in half on Cavesway. I and one other Resident objected to the emphasis on death. Dallas and the fourth member were in favour of expanding the facilities, both physically and psychologically, until every Cavite could take Cavesway at the moment when he felt his social usefulness ebbing. We argued reasonably with one another until it became apparent that there was no possible ground for compromise.

It was put to a vote and Iris broke the tie by endorsing Cavesway.

IV

This morning as I finished the lines above I suffered a mild stroke . . . a particularly unusual one since I did not become, as far as I know, unconscious. I was rereading my somewhat telescoped account of the Council of Dallas when, without warning, the blow fell. A capillary burst in my brain and I felt as though I were losing my mind in one last fantastic burst of images. The pain was negligible, no worse than a headache, but the sensation of letting go one's conscious mind was terrifying. I tried to call for help, but I was too weak. For one long giddy moment I thought: I am dying; this is the way it is. Even in my anguish I was curious, waiting for that approach of winged darkness which years ago I had experienced when I fainted and which I have always since imagined to be like death's swift entrance.

But then my body recovered from the assault. The wall was breached, the enemy is in the city, but the citadel is still intact and I live.

Weakly I got up, poured myself a jigger of brandy and then, having drunk it all at once, fell across my bed and slept and did not dream, a rare blessing in these feverish last days.

I was awakened by the sensation of being watched. I opened my eyes and saw Jessup above me, looking like a bronze figure of Anubis. 'I'm sorry . . . didn't mean to disturb you. Your door was open.'

'Perfectly all right,' I said, as smoothly as I could, drugged with sleep. I pulled myself up against the pillows. 'Excuse me for not getting up, but I'm still a little weak from my illness.'

'I wanted to see you,' said Jessup, sitting down in the chair beside the bed. 'I hope you don't mind my coming in like this.'

'Not at all. How do you find Luxor?' I wanted to delay as long as possible the questions which I was quite sure he would want to ask me.

'The people are not so fixed in error as we'd been warned. There's a great curiosity about Cavesword.' His eyes had been taking in the details of the room with some interest; to my horror I recalled that I had left the manuscript of my work on the table instead of hiding it as usual in the washstand. He saw it. 'Your . . . memoirs?' He looked at me with a polite interest which I was sure disguised foreknowledge.

'A record of my excavations,' I said, in a voice which had descended the scale to a whisper. 'I do it for my own amusement, to pass the time.'

'I should enjoy reading it.'

'You exaggerate, in your kindness,' I said, pushing myself higher on the bed, preparing if necessary for a sudden spring.

'Not at all. If it is about Egypt, I should read it. There are no contemporary accounts of this country . . . by one of us.'

'I'm afraid the details of findings in the valley yonder,' I gestured towards Libya and the last acres of the kings, 'won't be of much use to you, I avoid all mention of people less than two millennia dead.'

'Even so.' But Jessup did not pursue the subject. I relaxed a little.

'I must tell you,' he said suddenly, 'that I was suspicious of you.'

Now I thought, now it comes; then I was amused. Right at the end they arrive, when it was too late for them, or for me. 'What form did your suspicions take?' My fear left me in one last flurry, like a bird departing in a cold wind for another latitude, leaving the branch which held it all summer through to freeze.

'I thought you might be the one we have so often heard of . . . in legend, that is. The enemy of Cave.'

'Which enemy?'

'The nameless one, or at least we know a part of his name if lutherist is derived from it.'

'What made you suspect me?'

'Because were I an enemy of Cave and were I forced to disappear, I should come to just such a town in just such a country as this.'

'Perfectly logical,' I agreed. 'But there are many towns in the Arab League, in Asia too. Why suppose one old man to be this mythical villain?'

Jessup smiled. 'Intuition, I'm afraid. A terrible admission from one who has been trained in the logic of Cavesword. It seemed exactly right. You're the right age, the right nationality. In any case, I telephoned Dallas about you.'

I took this calmly. 'You talked to the Chief Resident himself?'

'Of course not.' Jessup was surprised at my suggestion. 'One just doesn't call the Chief Resident like that. Only senior Residents *ever* talk to him personally. No, I talked to an old friend of mine who is one of the five principal assistants to the Historian General. We were in school together and his speciality is the deviationists of the early days.'

'And what did you learn from this scholar?'

Jessup gave me a most charming smile. 'Nothing at all. There was no such person as I thought existed, as a number of people thought existed. It was all a legend, a perfectly natural one for gossip to invent. There was a good deal of trouble at the beginning, especially over Cavesway. There was even a minority at Dallas that refused to accept the principle of Cavesway, without which of course there could be no Establishment. According to the stories one heard as recently as my university days, ten years ago, the original lutherist had led the opposition to Iris, in Council and out. For a time it looked as though the Establishment might be broken in two (this you must remember since you were contemporary to it; fortunately, our Historical Office has tended more and more to view it in the long perspective, and popular works on Cave now make no reference to it); in any case, there was an open break and the minority was soon absorbed by the majority.'

'Painlessly?' I mocked him. Could he be telling the truth? or was this a trap?

Jessup shrugged. 'These things are never without pain. It is said that an attempt was made on our Mother Iris's life during the ceremony of Cave's ashes. We still continue it, you know.'

'Continue what?'

'The symbolic gathering of the ashes. But of course you know the origin of all that. There was a grave misinterpretation of Cave's last wishes. His ashes were scattered over the United States when it was his wish to be embalmed and preserved. Every year, Iris would travel to the four cities over which the ashes had been distributed and collect a bit of dust in each city to symbolize her obedience to Cavesword in all things. At Seattle, during this annual ceremony, a group of lutherists tried to assassinate her.'

'I remember,' I said. I had had no hand in that dark episode, but it provided the Establishment with the excuse they needed. My partisans were thrown in prison all over the country. The government, which by then was entirely Cavite, handed several thousand over to the Centres, where they were indoctrinated, ending the heresy for good. Iris herself had secretly arranged for my escape . . . but Jessup could know nothing of this.

'Of course you know these things, perhaps even better than I since you were alive then. Forgive me. I have got into the bad Residential habit of explaining the obvious. An occupational disease.' He was disarming. 'The point I'm trying to make is that my suspicions of you were unworthy and unfounded since there was no leader of the lutherists to escape; all involved responded nicely to indoctrination and that was the end of it. The story I heard in school was a popular one. The sort that often evolves, like Lucifer and the old Christian God, for instance. For white there must be black, that kind of thing. Except that Cave never had a major antagonist, other than in legend.'

'I see. Tell me, then, if there was no real leader in the lutherists, how did they come by their name?'

His answer was prompt. 'Martin Luther. My friend in the H.O. told me this morning over the telephone. Someone tried to make an analogy, that's all, and the name stuck, though as a rule the use of any words or concepts derived from dead religions is growned upon. You know the story of Martin Luther? It seems that he . . .'

'I know the story of Martin Luther,' I answered, more sharply than I intended.

'Now I've tired you.' Jessup was sympathetic. He got to his feet. 'I just wanted to tell you about my suspicions, that's all. I thought it might amuse you and perhaps bring us closer together, for I'd very much like to be your friend, not only for the help you can give me here but also because of your memories of the old days when Cave and Iris, his Mother, still lived.'

'Iris was at least five years younger than Cave.'

'Everyone knows that, my friend. She was his *spiritual* Mother, as she is ours. "From the dark womb of unbeing we emerge in the awful light of consciousness from which the only virtuous escape is Cavesway." I quote from Iris's last testament. It was found among her papers after her death.'

'Did *she* take Cavesway?'

Jessup frowned. 'It is said that she died of pneumonia, but had death *not* come upon her unexpectedly it was well known that she would have taken Cavesway. There has been considerable debate over this at Dallas. I hear from highly placed people that before many years have passed they will promulgate a new interpretation, applying only to Iris, which will establish that intent and fact are the same, that though she died of pneumonia she *intended* to take Cavesway and, therefore, took Cavesway in spirit and therefore in fact.'

'A most inspiring definition.'

'It is beautifully clear, though perhaps difficult for an untrained mind. May I read your memoir?' His eyes strayed curiously to the table.

'When it's finished,' I said. 'I should be most curious to see how it strikes you.'

'Well, I won't take up any more of your time. I hope you'll let me come to see you.'

'Nothing could give me more pleasure.' And then, with a pat on my shoulder and a kind suggestion that should I choose Cavesway he would be willing to administer the latest drug, Jessup departed.

I remained very still for some minutes, holding my breath for long intervals, trying to die. Then, in a sudden rage, I hurled my pillow across the room and beat the mattress with my fists: it was over. All was at an end except my own miserable life, which will be gone soon enough. My name erased; my work subverted; all that I most detested regnant in the world. I could have wept had there been one tear left in me. Now there is nothing I can do but finish this narrative . . . for its own sake since it will be thought, I know, the ravings of a madman when Jessup reads it, as he surely will after I am dead.

I have tried now for several hours to describe my last meeting with Iris but I find that my memory is at last seriously impaired, the result, no doubt, of that tiny vein's eruption this morning in my brain. It is all a jumble. I think there were several years in which I was in opposition. I think that I had considerable support and I am almost sure that, until the attempted assassination of Iris at Seattle, I was close to dominating the Council of Residents. But the idiotic attempt on her life ruined everything. She knew of course that I had had nothing to do with it, but she was a resolute leader and she took this opportunity to annihilate my party. I believe we met for the last time in a garden. A garden very like the one where we first met in California. No, on the banks of the Hudson . . . I must reread what I have written to refresh my memory. It is all beginning to fade rapidly.

In any case, we met in a garden in the late autumn when all the trees were bare. She was white-haired then, though neither of us was much over forty.

I believe that she wept a little. After all, we were the last who had been close to Cave, heirs become adversaries, she victrix and I vanquished. I never loved her more than at that last moment. Of this I am sure. We talked of possible places of exile. She had arranged for my passage on a ship to Alexandria under the name of Richard Hudson (yes, she who erased my name, in her compassion, gave me a new one). She did not want, however, to know where I intended to go from there.

'It would be a temptation to the others,' she said. I remember that one sentence and I do remember the appearance of the garden, though its location I have quite forgotten: there was a high wall around it and the smell of mouldering leaves was acrid. From the mouth of a satyr no water fell in a mossy pool.

Ah yes! the question and the answer. That's it, of course. The key. I had nearly lost it. Before I left, I asked her what it was that Cave had said to her when he was dying, the words the rest of us had not heard. At first she hesitated but then, secure in her power and confident of her own course, she told me: 'He said: "Gene was right." ' I remember looking at her with shock, waiting for her to continue, to make some apology for her reckless falsification of Cave's life and death. But she said no more. There was, I suppose, no explanation she might have made. Without a word, I left the garden. My real life had ended.

There's more to it than this but I cannot get it straight. Something has happened to my memory. I wonder if perhaps I have not dreamed all this: a long nightmare drawing to its bitter close among the dry ruins of an ancient world.

It is late now. I still live, though I am exhausted and indifferent to everything except that violent living sun whose morning light has just this moment begun to strike upon the western hills across the river: all that is left, all that ever was, the red fire.

I shall not take Cavesway even though I die in pain and confusion. Anubis must wait for me in the valley until the last, and even then I shall struggle in his arms, for I know now that life, *my* life, was more valuable than I knew, more significant and virtuous than the other's was in her bleak victory.

Though my memory is going from me rapidly, the meaning is clear and unmistakeable and I see the pattern whole at last, marked in giant strokes upon the air: I was he whom the world awaited. I was that figure, that messiah whose work might have been the world's delight and liberation. But the villain death once more undid me, and to *him* belongs the moment's triumph. Yet life continues, though I do not. Time bends upon itself. The morning breaks. Now I will stop, for it is day.

THE CITY
AND
THE PILLAR

But his wife looked back from behind him,
and she became a pillar of salt.

Genesis 19:26

For the memory of J. T.

CHAPTER ONE

The moment was strange. There was no reality in the bar: there was no longer solidity: all things merged, one into the other. Time had stopped.

He sat alone in a booth, listening to the music which came out of a red plastic box, lighted within. Some of the music he remembered from having heard it in other places. But the words he could no longer understand. He could recall only vague associations as he got drunk, listening to music.

His glass of whisky and water and ice had slopped over and the top of the table was interesting now: islands and rivers and occasional lakes made the top of the table a continent. With one finger he traced designs on the wooden table. He made a circle out of a lake; formed two rivers from the circle; flooded and destroyed an island, creating a sea. There were so many things that could be done with whisky and water on a table.

The jukebox stopped playing.

He waited a long time for it to start again. He took a swallow of the whisky to help him wait. Then after a long time, in which he tried not to think, the music started. A record of a song he remembered was playing and he allowed himself to be taken back to that emotional moment in time when . . . when? He tried hard to remember the place and the time, but it was too late. Only a pleasant emotion could be recalled.

He was drunk.

Time collapsed. Years passed before he could bring the drink to his mouth. Legs numb, elbows detached, he seemed to be supported by air, and by the music from the jukebox. He wondered for a moment where he was. He looked about him but there were no clues, only a bar in a city. What city?

He made a new island on the table-top. The table was his home and he felt a strong affection for the brown scarred wood, for the dark protectiveness of the booth, for the lamp which did not work because there was no bulb in the socket. He wanted never to leave. This was home. But then he finished his drink, and was lost. He would have to get another one. How? He frowned and thought. A long time went by and he did not move, the empty glass in front of him.

At last he came to a decision. He would leave the booth and go talk to the man behind the bar. It was a long voyage, but he was ready for it.

He stood up, became dizzy and sat down again, very tired. A man with a white apron came over to his table: he probably knew about liquor.

'You want something?'

Yes, that was what he wanted, something. He nodded and said slowly so that the words would be clear, 'Want some whisky, water, Bourbon, water . . . what I been drinking.'

The man looked at him suspiciously. 'How long you been here?'

He didn't know the answer to that. He would have to be sly. 'I have been here for one hour,' he said carefully.

'Well, don't go passing out or getting sick. People got no consideration for others when it comes to doing things like that for other people to clean up.'

He tried to say that he did have consideration for others but it was no use. He could not talk any more. He wanted to get back home, to the table-top. 'I'm O.K.,' he said, and the man went away.

But the top of the table was no longer home. The intimacy had been dispelled by the man with the apron. Rivers, lakes, islands, all were unfamiliar: he was lost in a new country. There was nothing for him to do except turn his attention to the other people in the bar room. Now that he had lost his private world he wanted to see what, if anything, the others had found.

The bar was just opposite him and behind it two men in white aprons moved slowly. Four five six people stood at the bar. He tried to count them but he could not. Whenever he tried to count or to read in a dream, everything dissolved. This was like a dream. Was it a dream?

A woman wearing a green dress stood near him: large buttocks, dress too tight. She stood very close to a man in a dark suit. She was a whore. Well well well . . .

He wondered about the other booths. He was at the centre of a long line of booths, yet he knew nothing about the people in any of them. A sad thought, to which he drank.

Then he stood up. Unsteadily, but with a face perfectly composed, he walked towards the back of the bar room.

The men's room was dirty and he took a deep breath before he entered so that he would not have to breathe inside. He saw himself reflected in a cracked distorted mirror hung high on the wall. Blond hair milk white, bloodshot eyes staring brightly, crazily. Oh, he was someone else all right. But who? He held his breath until he was again in the bar room.

He noticed how little light there was. A few shaded bulbs against the walls and that was all, except for the jukebox which not only gave light but wonderful colours. Red blood, yellow sun, green grass, blue sky. He stood by the jukebox, his hands caressing the smooth plastic surface. *This* was where he belonged, close to light and colour.

Then he was dizzy. His head ached and he could not see clearly: stomach contracted with sharp nausea.

He held his head between his hands and slowly he pushed out the dizziness. But then he pushed too hard and brought back memory: he had not wanted to do that. Quickly he returned to the booth, sat down, put his hands on the table and looked straight ahead. Memory began to work. There had been a yesterday and a day before, and twenty-five years of being alive before he found the bar.

'Here's your drink.' The man looked at him. 'You feeling all right? If you don't feel good you better get out of here. We don't want nobody getting sick in here.'

'I'm all right.'

'You sure had a lot to drink tonight.' The man went away.

He had had a lot to drink. It was past one and he had been in the bar since nine o'clock. Drunk, he wanted to be drunker; without memory, or fear.

'You all by yourself!' Woman's voice. He didn't open his eyes for a long time, hoping that if he could not see her she could not see him. A basic thing to wish but it failed. He opened his eyes.

'Sure,' he said. 'Sure.' It was the woman in the green dress.

Her hair was dyed a dark red and her face was white with powder. She too was drunk. She leaned unsteadily over his table and he could see between her breasts.

'May I sit down?'

He grunted; she sat opposite him.

'It's been an awfully hot summer, hasn't it?' She made conversation. He looked at her, wondering if he could ever assimilate her into the world of the booth. He doubted it. For one thing, there was too much of her, and none of it simple.

'Sure,' he said.

'I must say you're not very talkative, are you?'

'Guess not.' The intimacy of the booth was gone for good now. He asked, not caring, 'What's your name?'

She smiled, his attention obtained, 'Estelle. Nice name, isn't it? My mother named all of us with names like that. I had one sister called Anthea and my brother was called Drake. I think Drake is a very attractive name for a man, don't you? He's in women's wear. What's your name?'

'Willard,' he said, surprised that he was giving her his right name. 'Jim Willard.'

'That's a nice name. Sounds so English. I think English names are attractive. In origin I'm Spanish myself. Oh, I'm thirsty! I'll call the waiter for you.'

The waiter, who seemed to know her, brought her a drink. 'Just what the doctor ordered.' She smiled at him. Under the table her foot touched his. He moved both feet under his chair.

She was not distressed. She drank rapidly. 'You from New York?'

He shook his head and cooled his forefinger in the half-empty glass.

'You sound sort of Southern from the way you talk. Are you from the South?'

'Sure,' he said, and he took his forefinger out of the glass. 'I'm from the South.'

'It must be nice down there. I've always wanted to go to Miami, but I never seem to get away from the city. You see, all my friends are here and I can't very well leave them. I did have a friend once, a man,' she smiled privately, 'and he always went to Florida in the winter. He had beautiful luggage. He invited me to go down with him and I almost went, once.' She paused. 'That was ten years ago.' She sounded sad, and he didn't pity her at all.

'Of course it must be terribly hot there in the summer. In fact, it's so hot *here* that I think sometimes I'll *die* from the heat. Were you in the war?'

He yawned, bored. 'I was a soldier.'

'I'll bet you look good in a uniform. But I'm glad it's finally over, the war.'

He moved his glass around the table listening to the satisfying noise it made as it hit scars and cracks. She watched him. He wished she would go away.

'Why're you in New York?' she asked. 'And why are you getting drunk? You got everything and still you're sitting here all by yourself, getting drunk. I wish *I* was you. I wish I was young and nice-looking. I wish . . .' Quietly she began to cry.

'I got everything,' he said, sighing. 'I got everything, Anthea.'

She blew her nose in a piece of Kleenex. 'That's my sister's name, Anthea. I'm Estelle.'

'And you have a brother named Drake.'

She looked surprised. 'That's right. How did you know?'

Suddenly he felt himself in danger of becoming involved in her life, hearing confessions, listening to names that meant nothing to him. He shut his eyes, tried to shut her out.

She stopped crying and took a small mirror out of her handbag. Tenderly she powdered the pouches under her eyes. Then she put the mirror away and smiled. 'What're *you* doing tonight?'

'I'm doing it. Drinking.'

'No, silly. I mean later. You're staying in a hotel somewhere, maybe?'

'I'm staying right here.'

'But you can't. It closes at four.'

Alarm. He had not thought what he was going to do after four o'clock. It was her fault. He had been happily listening to music, until she came along and changed everything. It had been a mistake, not assimilating her.

She menaced him with reality. She must be destroyed.

'I'm going home alone,' he said. 'When I go home, I go home alone.'

'Oh.' She thought a moment, decided on injury and hurt. 'I suppose I'm not good enough for you.'

'Nobody is.' He was mortally weary of her, and sick at the thought of sex.

'Pardon me,' said Estelle, sister of Anthea and Drake. She stood up, arranged her breasts, and returned to the bar.

Now he was alone and he was glad, with three glasses before him on the table: two empty, one half full with lipstick on it. He arranged the glasses to form a triangle, but then when he tried to arrange them to form a square, he failed. Why? Three glasses ought to be able to form a square. He was distressed. Fortunately, reality began to recede once more. And Jim Willard sat at his table in his booth in his bar room and made lakes, rivers, islands. This was all that he wanted. To be alone, a creature without memory, sitting in a booth. Gradually, the outline of fear grew blurred. And he forgot entirely how it began:

CHAPTER TWO

I

On the warmest and greenest afternoon of the spring, the high school's commencement exercises ended, and boys and girls, parents and teachers, streamed out of the brand-new Old Georgian school building. Separating himself from the crowd, Jim Willard paused a moment on the top step and looked out, searching for Bob Ford. But he could not make him out in the mob of boys in dark jackets and white trousers, girls in white dresses, fathers in straw hats (this year's fashion in Virginia). Many of the men smoked cigars, which meant that they were politicians – this was the county seat and singularly rich in office-holders, among them Jim's father, the courthouse clerk.

A running boy struck Jim's arm playfully. Jim turned, expecting Bob. But it was someone else. He smiled, struck back and exchanged cheerful insults, secure in the knowledge that he was popular because he was the school's tennis champion and all athletes were admired, particularly those who were modest and shy, like Jim.

At last Bob Ford appeared. 'This year me. Next year you.'

'I sure wish it was me who just graduated.'

'I feel like they opened the prison door and let me out into the great big world. So how did I look up there on that stage wearing that black potato sack?'

'Great.'

'Don't you know it?' Bob chuckled. 'Well, come on. We better play while we still got some light.' As they moved through the crowd to the door to the locker room, a dozen girls greeted Bob, who responded with an easy grace. Tall, blue-eyed, with dark red curling hair, he was known throughout the school as 'Lover Man', a phrase somewhat more innocent than it sounded. 'Love' meant little more than kissing. Most girls found Bob irresistible, but boys did not much like him, possibly because girls did. Only Jim was his friend.

As they entered the dim locker room, Bob looked about him with a delighted melancholy. 'I guess this is the last time I'll be coming in here.'

'Well, we can still use the courts this summer . . .'

'That's not what I meant.' Bob took off his coat and hung it up carefully. Then he took off his tie. These were his best clothes and he handled them with respect.

'What do you mean?' Jim was puzzled. But Bob merely looked mysterious.

The two boys walked the half mile to the tennis-courts without speaking. They had known each other all their lives, but it was not until this last year that they had become close friends. They had been on the baseball team together and they had played tennis together, even though Jim always won, to Bob's chagrin. But then Jim was the best player in the county, and one of the best in the state. Games had been particularly important to both of them, especially for Jim, who found it difficult to talk to Bob. The hitting of a white ball back and forth across a net was at least a form of communication and better than silence or one of Bob's monologues.

They had the red-clay courts to themselves. Bob spun a racket and Jim, the loser, took the side facing the sun. The game began. It was good to hit the white ball evenly, making it skim the net. Jim played his best, obscurely aware that this was a necessary ritual enacted for the last time.

They played while the sun set and the shadows of tall trees lengthened, darkening the court. A cool breeze stirred. After the third set, they stopped. Jim had won two out of three.

'Nice going,' said Bob, and gave him his hand briefly, as though they were in a tournament. Then they both stretched out on the grass beside the court and breathed deeply, tired but comfortable.

Twilight and the day ended. Chattering birds circled among the trees, preparing for night.

'It's getting late.' Bob sat up, brushing away the twigs and leaves that had stuck to his back.

'It's still light.' Jim didn't want to go.

'I hate to leave, too.' Bob looked about, again the mysterious sadness.

'What're you talking about! You been hinting around all day. What're you up to?' Then Jim understood. 'You're not going to ship out on a boat, are you? like you said last year?'

Bob grinned. 'Curiosity killed the cat.'

'O.K.' Jim was hurt.

Bob was contrite. 'Look, I can't say anything just now. Whatever it is, I'll tell you before Monday. That's a promise.'

Jim shrugged. 'It's your business.'

'I got to get dressed.' Bob stood up. 'I'm taking old Sally Mergendahl to the dance tonight.' He winked. 'And tonight I mean to do myself some good.'

'Why not? Everybody else has.' Jim disliked Sally, a dark aggressive girl who had been after Bob all year. But then it was none of his business what Bob did.

As they walked through the blue twilight to the school, Bob suddenly asked, 'What're you doing this weekend?'

'Nothing. Why?'

'Why don't we spend it down at the cabin?'

'Well, sure. Why not?' Jim was careful not to show too much pleasure; it was bad luck. The cabin had been the home of a onetime slave, recently dead. It stood deserted now, in thick woods close to the Potomac. Once they had spent a night there; more than once Bob had brought girls to the cabin. Jim was never certain exactly what happened because Bob's stories varied with each telling.

'O.K.,' said Bob. 'Meet you at your house, tomorrow morning.'

An irritable janitor let them into the locker room.

II

Breakfast was invariably unpleasant, possibly because it was the only meal the Willard family always had together.

Mr Willard was already at the head of the table when Jim came into the dining-room. Small, thin, grey, Mr Willard tried to appear tall and commanding. It was the family's opinion that he would have had no trouble at all being elected governor, but for one reason or another he had been forced to allow lesser men to go to Richmond while he remained at the courthouse, a bitter fate.

Mrs Willard was also small and grey but inclined to fat; after twenty-three years of her husband's stern regime, she had assumed the melting look of the conscious martyr. Now wearing a white frilled apron which did not become her, she cooked breakfast in the adjoining kitchen, looking from time to time into the dining-room to see if her three children were down.

Jim, the first-born son, was first to appear. Since this was a special day, he was cheerful, glad to be alive.

'Morning, Father.'

His father looked at him as though he could not quite place the face. Then he said 'Good morning' and distantly started to read the paper. He discouraged conversation between himself and his sons, especially Jim, who had made the error of being tall and handsome and not at all the sort of small, potentially grey son Mr Willard ought to have had.

'You're down early.' Mrs Willard brought him his breakfast.

'Beautiful day, that's why.'

'I don't think a quarter to eight is such an early hour,' said his father from behind the *Richmond Times*. Mr Willard had been brought up on a farm and one of the reasons for his later success had been rising 'at the crack of dawn'.

'Jim, you didn't hear any funny noises around the house last night, did you?' Like Joan of Arc, his mother was always hearing funny noises.

'No, ma'am.'

'Funny, I could've sworn someone was trying to get in the window, there was this tapping . . .'

'I should like some more coffee, if I may.' Mr Willard lowered his newspaper and raised his chin.

'Of course, dear.'

Jim ate his cereal. Mr Willard rearranged his newspaper.

'Good morning.' Carrie came into the room. A year older than Jim, she was pretty but pale, and disliking paleness, painted her face with a bold and imaginative hand which sometimes made her look whorish and infuriated her father. She had graduated from high school the year before, at seventeen, a fact which the family impressed on Jim. Since then, she helped her mother in the house while encouraging the attentive courtship of a young realtor whom she expected to marry just as soon as he had 'put something by'.

'Morning, Carrie.' Mr Willard looked at his daughter with wintry approbation. Of his children, she alone gave him pleasure; she saw him great.

'Carrie, will you come in here and help me with breakfast?'

'Yes, Mother. How was the graduation, Jim?'

'O.K.'

'I wish I could have gone but I don't know why it is, I'm so busy all the time, on the go . . .'

'Sure, sure.'

Carrie joined her mother in the kitchen and Jim could hear them arguing in low voices; they always argued. Finally, John entered. At fourteen, he was thin, nervous, potentially grey, except for black eyes.

'Hi.' He sat down with a crash.

'Glad to have you with us,' said his father, continuing the war.

'It's Saturday.' John was a skilled domestic warrior, master of artillery. 'Everybody sleeps late.'

'Naturally.' Mr Willard looked at John and then, satisfied in some strange way with what he saw, returned to his paper.

Carrie brought her father more coffee and then sat down beside Jim. 'When do you start work in the store, Jimmy?'

'Monday morning.' He wished she wouldn't call him Jimmy.

'That'll be nice. It's sort of dull, I guess, but then I suppose you have to be *qualified* to do more skilled work, like in an office, typing.'

He didn't answer her. Neither Carrie nor his father could irritate him today. He was meeting Bob. The world was perfect.

'Hey, they're playing baseball today over at the school. You going to play?' John struck his fist against his palm with a satisfactory sound.

'No, I'm going down to the cabin. For the whole weekend.'

Mr Willard struck again. 'And who, if I'm not asking too much, are you going with?'

'Bob Ford. Mother said it was all right.'

'Is that so? It is amazing to me why you want to sleep away from your own home which we have tried at such expense to make comfortable . . .' His father slowly unfurled the domestic banner, and charged. Jim refused to defend himself, beyond promising himself that one day he would throw a plate at this bitter old man he was forced to live with. Meanwhile, he simply stared at his future weapon while his father explained to him how the family was a Unit and how he owed all of them a Debt and how difficult a time Mr Willard had had making the Money to support them and though they were not rich, they were Respectable, and Jim's going around with the son of the town drunk did them no good.

During her husband's tirade Mrs Willard joined them, a slightly pained expression on her face. When Mr Willard had finished, she said, 'Well, I think the Ford boy is nice and he does get good marks in school and his mother *was* a friend of ours no matter what we think of the father . . . So I don't see anything wrong with Jim seeing him.'

'*I* don't mind,' said Mr Willard. 'I just thought *you* would mind having your son exposed to that sort of a person. But if you don't, I have nothing more to say.' Mr Willard, having embarrassed his son and disagreed with his wife, ate fried eggs with unusual gusto.

Mrs Willard murmured something soothing and Jim wished that his father were like Bob's father, drunk and indifferent.

'When are you going to the cabin?' his mother asked, in a low voice, so as not to disturb her husband.

'After breakfast.'

'And what are you doing about food?'

'Bob's getting stuff from the store where he works.'

'That's nice,' said Mrs Willard, obviously thinking of something else; she had a difficult time concentrating for very long.

Carrie and her younger brother started arguing and soon breakfast was finished. Then Mr Willard rose and announced that he had business at the courthouse, which was not true. The courthouse never did business on Saturday. But his wife did not question this and with a reserved nod to his children, Mr Willard put on his straw hat, opened the front door and stepped out into the bright morning.

Mrs Willard watched him a moment, expressionless; then she turned and said, 'Carrie, come help me clean up. Boys, you better fix your room.'

The boys' room was small and not very light. The two beds, close together between two bureaux, made the room crowded. Pictures of baseball and tennis players covered the walls, early idols of Jim's.

John had no idols. He was intense and studious and he was going to be a Congressman, which pleased his father, who often gave him talks on how to be a success in politics. Jim had no plans beyond college. It all seemed a long way off.

Jim made his bed quickly; John took longer.

'What're you and Bob going to do down by the river?'

'I don't know.' Jim straightened the patchwork quilt. 'Fish. Loaf.'

'That sounds like a waste of time.' John echoed his father.

'Isn't that too bad?' Jim mocked as he opened the closet and took down two blankets from the shelf, his contribution to the weekend.

John sat on the bed and watched. 'Bob sees a lot of Sally Mergendahl, doesn't he?'

'I suppose so. She sees a lot of people.'

'That's what I mean.' John looked knowing and Jim laughed.

'You're too young to be hearing such things.'

'Like hell I am.' John proved his virility with an oath.

'Sure, you're a real lover and you keep track of all the girls.'

John was angry. 'Well, that's more than you do and you're older than me. You don't ever go out with girls. I heard Sally say once she thought you were the best-looking guy in school and she couldn't understand why you didn't go around more. She said she thought you were afraid of girls.'

Jim flushed. 'She's full of crap. I'm not afraid of her or anybody. Besides, I do my travelling on the other side of town.'

'Really?' John was interested and Jim was glad he had lied.

'Sure.' He was mysterious. 'Bob and me go over there a lot of times. All the baseball team does, too. We don't want to mess around with "nice" girls.'

'I guess not.'

'Besides, Sally isn't so fast.'

'How do you know?'

'I just do.'

'I'll bet Bob Ford said that about her.'

Jim fixed the top of his bureau, ignoring his brother. He was ill at ease and he didn't know why; it was seldom that John could irritate him.

Jim looked in the dusty mirror above his bureau and wondered if he needed his weekly shave. He decided that he could wait till he got back. Absently he ran his hand over his short blond hair, glad that it was summer, the season of short hair. Was he handsome? His features were perfectly ordinary, he thought; only his body pleased him, the result of much exercise.

'When's Bob coming by?' John was sitting on his bed, balancing his brother's tennis racket in his hand.

'Right now.'

'Must be nice down there. I was only to the cabin once. I guess anybody can go there.'

'Sure.'

'They say the guy who owns the land lives in New York and he never comes down here. I'm playing baseball this afternoon and then I'm going to a meeting of the Democratic Party in the back of the drugstore.' John's mind was quick and unsettled.

'That must be a lot of fun.' Jim put his racket in the closet. Then he picked up the two blankets and went downstairs.

Carrie was in the sitting-room, lazily dusting furniture.

'Oh, *there* you are, Jim.'

He stopped. 'Anybody looking for me?'

'No, I just said there you were.' She put the duster down, glad of an excuse not to work. 'Are you going to the high-school dance tonight?'

He shook his head.

'That's right,' she said, 'you and Bob are going to the cabin. I'll bet Sally is jealous of you for keeping him from coming to the dance.'

Jim didn't let his face change expression. 'It was his idea,' he said evenly. 'Maybe you'll find out *why* later.' Mystery was clearly the order of the day.

Carrie nodded. 'I think I know. I've been hearing stories about Bob's going away. Sally said something about it not so long ago.'

'Maybe he is, maybe he isn't.' Jim was surprised that Carrie and Sally knew; he wondered how many people Bob had told.

Carrie yawned and began to dust again. Blankets under his arm, Jim went to the kitchen. His mother was not yet finished with her cleaning.

'Now be sure you're back by Sunday night. Your grandfather's coming over and your father will want you to be here. Are these the good blankets you're taking?'

'No, old.'

Through the kitchen window Jim saw Bob carrying a large paper bag.

'I'm on my way.'

'Look out for water moccasins!'

The morning sun was hot yet the air was cool. The day was green and blue and very bright. Jim Willard was meeting Bob and the weekend was not yet lived. He was happy.

III

They stood on the edge of the cliff and looked down at the brown river, muddy from spring rains and loud where it broke up on the black rocks in midstream. Below them, the cliff dropped steeply to the river, a wall of stone, dark green with laurel and wild grapevines.

'Must be a flood upstream. That old river looks mean,' said Bob.

'Maybe we'll see a house come floating down.'

Bob chuckled. 'Or a privy.' Jim sat on a rock and plucked a piece of long grass and chewed on the white sweet-tasting stem. Bob squatted beside him. Together they listened to the roar of the river and the noise of tree frogs and the rustle of bright new leaves in the wind.

'How was Sally?'

Bob growled. 'Prick-teaser, like all the rest. Leads you on so you think, *now* I can lay her and then, just as you get all hot, *she* gets scared. Oh, what're you doing to me? Oh, stop! You stop that now!' Bob sighed with disgust. 'I tell you it makes a man so horny he could lay a mule, if it would just stand still.' Bob contemplated mules. Then: 'Why didn't you come to the dance last night? Lot of girls asked for you.'

'I don't know. Don't like dancing, I guess. I don't know.'

'You're too bashful.'

Bob rolled up a trouser leg and removed a large black ant which was crawling up his calf. Jim noticed how white Bob's skin was, like marble, even in the sun.

Then, to break the silence, they threw stones over the edge of the cliff. The sound of rock hitting rock was entirely satisfying. Finally Bob shouted, 'Come on!' And they crawled over the edge of the cliff and cautiously worked their way downward, holding on to bushes, finding toeholds in the rock.

The hot sun shone in a pale sky. Hawks circled while small birds flashed between trees. Snakes, lizards, rabbits all scuttled for cover as the boys made their noisy descent. At last they reached the river's muddy bank. Tall black rocks jutted from brown sand. Happily, they leapt from rock to rock, never once touching earth, stepping only on the relics of a glacier age.

Shortly after noon they came to the slave cabin, a small house with a shingled roof much perforated by weather. The interior smelled of rotted plaster and age. Yellow newspapers and rusty tin cans were scattered over the rough wood floor. On the stone hearth there were new ashes: tramps as well as lovers stayed here.

Bob set down the paper bag he had been carrying while Jim put the blankets on the cleanest part of the floor.

'Hasn't changed much.' Bob looked up at the roof. The sky shone through holes. 'Let's hope it don't rain.'

Close to the cabin there was a large pond, bordered by willows and choked with lilies. Jim sat on the moss-covered bank while Bob undressed, throwing his clothes into a near-by tree, the trousers draped like a flag on one branch while his socks hung like pennants from another. Then he stretched happily, flexing his long muscles and admiring himself in the green smooth water. Though slim, he was strongly built and Jim admired him without envy. When Bob talked of someone who had a good build, he invariably sounded envious; yet when Jim looked at Bob's body, he felt as if he were looking at an ideal brother, a twin, and he was content. That something was lacking did not occur to him. It seemed enough that they played tennis together and Bob spoke to him endlessly of the girls he liked.

Cautiously Bob put one long foot in the water. 'It's warm,' he said. 'Real warm. Come on in.' Then, hands on knees, he leaned over and studied his own reflection. As Jim undressed, he tried to fix the image of Bob permanently in his mind, as if this might be the last time they would ever see one another. Point by point, he memorized him: wide shoulders, narrow buttocks, slim legs, curved sex.

Naked, Jim joined Bob at the water's edge. The warm breeze on his bare skin made him feel suddenly free and curiously powerful, like a dreamer who is aware that he is dreaming.

Bob looked at him thoughtfully. 'You got a good tan. I sure look white. Hey!' He pointed at the water. Below the dark green surface, Jim could see the blunt slow-moving shape of a catfish. Then, suddenly, he was falling and there was a rush of water in his ears. Bob had pushed him in. Choking, he came to the surface. With a rapid movement, Jim grabbed Bob's leg and pulled him in. Grappling, they turned and twisted in the water, making the pond foam. As they wrestled, Jim took pleasure in the physical contact. So, apparently, did Bob. Not until both were exhausted did they stop.

For the rest of that day they swam, caught frogs, sunned themselves, wrestled. They talked little. Not until the light began to fail did they relax.

'It's sure nice here.' Bob stretched out full-length. 'I guess there isn't any place as nice and peaceful as this place is.' He patted his flat stomach and yawned.

Jim agreed, totally at peace; he noticed that Bob's belly quivered with the regularity of a pulse. He looked at himself, the same phenomenon. Before he could comment on it, he saw a tick heading towards his pubic hair. He pinched it hard until it popped.

'I got a tick.'

Bob jumped to his feet. Ticks gave you a fever, so they examined themselves carefully, but found nothing. They got dressed.

The air was gold. Even the grey walls of the cabin looked gold in the last light of the sun. Now they were hungry. Jim built a fire while Bob made hamburgers in an old frying-pan. He did everything easily, expertly. At home he cooked for his father.

They ate their supper, sitting on a log facing the river. The sun had gone. Fireflies darted like yellow sparks in the green shadow of the woods.

'I'm going to miss this,' said Bob finally.

Jim looked at him. In the stillness there was no sound but the rushing river. 'My sister said Sally said you were going to leave right after graduation. I told her I didn't know anything about it. Are you going?'

Bob nodded and wiped his hands on his trousers. 'Monday, on the Old Dominion Bus Line.'

'Where you going to go?'

'To sea.'

'Like we always talked about.'

'Like we always talked about. Oh, I tell you I'm fed up with this town. The old man and I don't get along at all and God knows there isn't anything to do around here. So I'm going. You know I never been out of this county, except to go over to Washington. I want to see things.'

Jim nodded. 'So do I. But I thought we were going to go to college first and *then* we would . . . well, you would go off on this trip.'

Bob caught a firefly in his hand and let it climb up his thumb, and fly away.

'College is too much work,' he said at last. 'I'd have to work my way through and that means a job, which means I'd never get a chance to play around. Besides, there isn't a thing they could teach me what I want to know. All I want is to travel and to hell around.'

'Me too.' Jim wished that he could say what he wanted to say. 'But my father wants me to go to college and I suppose I got to. Only I'd hoped we could go together . . . well, team up in tennis doubles. We could be state champions. Everybody says so.'

Bob shook his head and stretched out. 'I got to get moving,' he said. 'I don't know why but I do.'

'I feel the same way, sometimes.' Jim sat beside Bob on the ground and together they watched the river and the darkening sky.

'I wonder what New York is like,' said Bob at last.

'Big, I guess.'

'Like Washington. That sure is a big town.' Bob rolled over on his side, facing Jim. 'Hey, why don't you come with me? We can ship out as cabin boys, maybe even deckhands.'

Jim was grateful Bob had said this, but he was cautious by nature. 'I think I ought to wait till next year when I get that high school diploma, which is important to have. Of course my old man wants me to go to college. He says I should . . .'

'Why do you pay any attention to that bastard?'

Jim was shocked and delighted. 'Well, I don't really. In fact, I'd just as soon never see him again.' With surprising ease, he obliterated his father. 'But even so, I'm scared, going off like that.'

'Nothing to it.' Bob flexed the muscles of his right arm. 'Why, a guy like you with brains and a good build, he can do most anything he wants. I knew these guys, they were sailors out of Norfolk, and they said there was nothing to it: easy work and when you're on shore you have a good time all the time, which is what I want. Oh, I'm tired of hanging around this town, working in stores, going out with *nice* girls. Only they're not really so damned *nice*, they're just afraid of getting knocked up.' Fiercely he struck the ground with his fist. 'Like Sally! Why, she'd do anything to you you want except the one thing you got to have. And that sure makes me mad. She makes me mad. All the girls around here make me mad!' Again he struck the dark earth.

'I know how it is,' said Jim, who did not know how it was. 'But aren't you scared you'll catch something from somebody you meet in New York?'

Bob laughed. 'Man, I'm careful!' he turned over on his back.

Jim watched the fireflies rise from the near-by grass. It was already night. 'You know,' he said, 'I wish I could go with you up North. I'd like to see New York and do as I please for once.'

'So why don't you?'

'Like I said, I'm afraid to leave home and the family, not that I like them all that much, but . . .' His voice trailed off uncertainly.

'Well, you can come with me if you want to.'

'Next year, after I graduate, I'll come.'

'*If* you can find me. I don't know where I'll be by then. I'm a rolling stone.'

'Don't worry. I'll find you. Anyway, we'll write.'

Then they walked down to the narrow boulder-strewn beach. Bob scrambled onto a flat rock and Jim followed him. The river swirled about them as they sat side by side in the blue, deep night.

One by one, great stars appeared. Jim was perfectly contented, loneliness no longer turning in the pit of his stomach, sharp as a knife. He always thought of unhappiness as the 'tar sickness'. When tar roads melted in the summer, he used to chew the tar and get sick. In some obscure way he has always associated 'tar sickness' with being alone. No longer.

Bob took off his shoes and socks and let the river cool his feet. Jim did the same.

'I'll miss all this,' said Bob for the dozenth time, absently putting his arm around Jim's shoulders.

They were very still. Jim found the weight of Bob's arm on his shoulders almost unbearable: wonderful but unbearable. Yet he did not dare move for fear the other would take his arm away. Suddenly Bob got to his feet. 'Let's make a fire.'

In a burst of activity, they built a fire in front of the cabin. Then Bob brought the blankets outside and spread them on the ground.

'There,' he said, looking into the yellow flames, 'that's done.' For a long moment both stared into the hypnotically quivering flames, each possessed by his own private daydream. Bob's dream ended first. He turned to Jim. 'Come on,' he said menacingly. 'I'll wrestle you.'

They met, grappled, fell to the ground. Pushing and pulling, they fought for position; they were evenly matched, because Jim, though stronger, would not allow Bob to lose or to win. When at last they stopped, both were panting and sweating. They lay exhausted on the blanket.

Then Bob took off his shirt and Jim did the same. That was better. Jim mopped the sweat from his face while Bob stretched out on the blanket, using his shirt for a pillow. Firelight gleamed on pale skin. Jim stretched out beside him. 'Too hot,' he said. 'Too hot to be wrestling.'

Bob laughed and suddenly grabbed him. They clung to one another. Jim was overwhelmingly conscious of Bob's body. For a moment they pretended to wrestle. Then both stopped. Yet each continued to cling to the other as though waiting for a signal to break or to begin again. For a long time neither moved. Smooth chests touching, sweat mingling, breathing fast in unison.

Abruptly, Bob pulled away. For a bold moment their eyes met. Then, deliberately, gravely, Bob shut his eyes and Jim touched him, as he had so many times in dreams, without words, without thought, without fear. When the eyes are shut, the true world begins.

As faces touched, Bob gave a shuddering sigh and gripped Jim tightly in his arms. Now they were complete, each became the other, as their bodies collided with a primal violence, like to like, metal to magnet, half to half and the whole restored.

So they met. Eyes tight shut against an irrelevant world. A wind warm and sudden shook all the trees, scattered the fire's ashes, threw shadows to the ground.

But then the wind stopped. The fire went to coals. The trees were silent. No comets marked the dark lovely sky, and the moment was gone. In the fast beat of a double heart, it died.

The eyes opened again. Two bodies faced one another where only an instant before a universe had lived; the star burst and dwindled, spiralling them both down to the meagre, to the separate, to the night and the trees and the firelight; all so much less than what had been.

They separated, breathing hard. Jim could feel the fire on his feet and beneath the blanket he was now uncomfortably aware of small stones and sticks. He looked at Bob, not certain of what he would see.

Bob was staring into the fire, face expressionless. But he grinned quickly when he saw Jim watching him. 'This is a hell of a mess,' he said, and the moment fled.

Jim looked down at himself and said as casually as he could, 'It sure is.'

Bob stood up, the firelight glittering on his body. 'Let's wash up.'

Pale as ghosts in the dark night, they walked to the pond. Through the trees they could see the light from their fire, yellow and flickering, while frogs croaked, insects buzzed, river thundered. They dived into the still black water. Not until they had returned to the fire did Bob break the silence. He was abrupt.

'You know, that was awful kid stuff we did.'

'I suppose so.' Jim paused. 'But I liked it.' He had great courage now that he had made his secret dream reality. 'Didn't you?'

Bob frowned into the yellow fire. 'Well, it was different than with a girl. And I don't think it's right.'

'Why not?'

'Well, guys aren't supposed to do that with each other. It's not natural.'

'I guess not.' Jim looked at Bob's fire-coloured body, long-lined and muscular. With his new-found courage, he put his arm around Bob's waist. Again excited, they embraced and fell back onto the blanket.

Jim woke before dawn. The sky was grey and the stars were fading. The fire was almost out. He touched Bob's arm and watched him wake up. They looked at one another. Then Bob grinned and Jim said, 'You're still going Monday?'

Bob nodded.

'You'll write me, won't you? I'd like to get on the same boat with you next year.'

'Sure, I'll write you.'

'I wish you weren't going . . . you know, after this.'

Bob laughed and grabbed him by the neck. 'Hell, we got all day Sunday.' And Jim was satisfied and happy to have all day Sunday with this conscious dream.

CHAPTER THREE

I

Bob wrote one letter from New York: things had been tough, but now it looked as if he'd be shipping out on the American Export Line. Meanwhile, he was having a swell time and had met a lot of girls, ha-ha. Jim replied promptly, only to have his letter returned, 'Addressee Unknown'. There was no second letter. Jim was hurt but not entirely surprised. Bob was not much of a letter writer, particularly now that he was absorbed in that new life which they would soon share, for Jim had already made up his mind that once high school was done with, he would follow Bob to sea.

On the greenest and the warmest day of the next June, Jim graduated from high school and began a two-week battle with his father. Jim won. He would go to New York for the summer and work, with the understanding that in the fall he would return to Virginia and enter college. Naturally, he would have to work his way through the university, but it was not every father who was willing to offer his son that opportunity. And so, early one bright yellow morning, Jim kissed his mother, shook his father's hand, said a casual good-bye to his brother and sister, and got on the bus to New York with seventy-five dollars in his pocket, more than enough, he reckoned, to keep him until he found Bob.

New York was hot, grey, dirty. Jim found it astonishing (where did all those people come from? where were they all hurrying to?) and oppressive in the summer heat. But then he was not a tourist. He was on a quest. After renting a room at a Y.M.C.A. he went to the Seamen's Bureau, where he learned that there was no record of a Bob Ford. For a moment he experienced panic. But then one of the old-timers explained to him that men often shipped out using other men's papers. In any case, the best thing for him to do was to apply for a berth as a cabin boy. Sooner or later, he and Bob would meet. The sea was surprisingly small; paths always crossed. Jim was put on a list. There would be a wait, perhaps a long one. While his papers cleared, he visited bars, got drunk twice (and disliked it), saw dozens of movies, and became an interested spectator of the life of the street. Then, just as his money ran out, he was signed on a freighter as cabin boy.

The sea was a startling experience. It took time to get used to the constant throb of engines beneath steel bulkheads, the slap and fall of a ship going full-speed into the wind, the close confinement in the fo'c'sle with thirty strangers, foul-mouthed but for the most part amiable. He ended by enjoying the life. In Panama he learned that a deckhand named Bob Ford had recently passed through the port, on his way to San Francisco. Jim's luck was improving. He transferred to a cargo ship bound for Seattle by way of San Francisco. But the trail ended in San Francisco. He could find no trace of Bob. Disconsolately, he roamed the city and visited waterfront bars, hoping for a sudden glimpse of Bob. Once he thought he saw him at the far end of a bar, but when he approached, heart beating fast, the figure turned towards him and showed a stranger's face.

Jim signed on as cabin boy aboard the Alaska Line and spent the rest of the year at sea. Entirely absorbed in his new life, he no longer wrote to his parents. Only the absence of Bob shadowed the full days he spent aboard ship during that first snow-bright winter of his freedom.

On Christmas Day the ship was off the coast of southeastern Alaska, headed for Seattle. Jagged mountains rose from black water. The sea was heavy, the wind rising. Those passengers who were not sick were having breakfast in the dining-saloon. They sat at round tables and made brave jokes about the motion of the ship and their fallen comrades, while the messboys hurried back and forth between galley and saloon, carrying heavy china plates of food.

Only one of Jim's passengers had come to breakfast. She was a plump, small woman with bad skin. She was very jovial. 'Good morning, Jim,' she said brightly. 'Nasty weather, isn't it? I suppose all the landlubbers are sick.'

'Yes, ma'am.' He began to clear away the remains of her breakfast.

'Me, I've never felt better.' She inhaled the close cabin air. 'This weather agrees with me.' She patted herself and glanced at Jim as he picked up his tray. 'When are you going to fix that porthole thing of mine, the thing that's broken and keeps rattling all the time?'

'I'll try, when I make up your cabin.'

'That'll be fine,' said the plump woman and she left the table, swaying slightly as she walked, using what she called her 'sea legs'.

Jim took the tray back to the galley. Breakfast was over. The Steward dismissed him. Whistling to himself, Jim walked down the companionway to a small cabin aft where he found Collins, a short, square young man of twenty with dark curly hair, blue eyes and a love of himself which was surprisingly contagious. On his left arm he had an intricate vein-blue tattoo which pledged him for ever to Anna, a girl belonging to the dim past, when he was sixteen and living in Oregon, not yet a seaman. Collins was sitting on an upright box smoking.

'Hello, boy,' said Collins.

Jim grunted and sat down on another box. He took a cigarette out of Collins's shirt pocket and then lit it with his own match.

'Only two more days,' said Collins, 'and then . . .' He rolled his eyes and made obscene designs in the air. 'Can't wait to get back to Seattle. Hey, what've they got planned for today? You know it's Christmas.'

'Sure, I got a calendar, too,' said Jim callously.

'I wonder,' said Collins more specifically, 'if we'll get any liquor. This is the first time I ever been to sea at Christmas. Some ships, foreign ships mostly, serve liquor to the men.'

Jim exhaled sadly. 'I don't think they will,' he said, watching the smoke fade. 'But we ought to get some truck from the passengers.'

'Hope so,' Collins yawned. 'By the way, how you doin' with the hog?' The messboys enjoyed kidding Jim about the plump woman at his table. Her interest in him was hardly secret.

Jim laughed. 'I keep her in deep suspense.'

'Wonder if she's got any money. You might pick up some extra change there.' Collins was serious, and Jim was disgusted but he didn't show it because Collins was his best friend aboard ship. Also, Jim was never sure if Collins really did the things he said he did or not.

'I'm not that hungry,' said Jim.

Collins shrugged. 'I always need money. All the time I need it and now we going to Seattle I'll need a lot more than I got. Well, maybe somebody rich'll die and leave it to me.' Collins was essentially a thief, but it was good policy to appear to have illusions about shipmates. Besides, Collins was guide as well as friend. He had made Jim's life easier aboard ship by showing him different ways to avoid work, as well as places like this cabin to hide in.

Jim stretched. 'I got to start making beds.'

'Plenty of time. Steward won't be looking for you for a while.' Collins stamped out his cigarette butt and quickly lit another. Jim finished his own cigarette. He disliked smoking. But aboard ship it was important to keep your hands busy when there was nothing to do, and in his months at sea there were days on end when there was little to do, except listen to the men talk of women and ships' officers, of good ports and bad. And once each man had said what he had to say he would promptly repeat himself, until no one listened to anyone else. There were times when Jim could conduct an entire conversation with Collins and at the end not remember a word that either had said. It was a lonely time.

Suddenly he was aware Collins was talking. The subject? He waited until he caught the word 'Seattle'.

'I'll show you around. I really know that town like nobody's business. Show you these girls I know, Swedes, Norwegians . . . you know, *blonde*.' His eyes shone. 'You'll be real popular. I was when I was your age. Oh, they all used to make a fuss over me. They used to roll dice to see who was going to go with me. I was something, I guess. You'll be the same way because they like young guys.'

Jim was going to ask more, but they were interrupted by the Steward, a tall lean Scot with no sense of humour. 'Willard, Collins, why're you not working?'

They fled.

On deck the wind was cold and sharp and full of spray. Jim squinted in the wind as he made his way to the plump woman's cabin.

He rapped on the door. 'Come in.'

His admirer wore a pink silk dressing-gown that made her look somewhat heavier than she actually was. She was cleaning her nails. A strong smell of salt and gardenia perfume was in the air.

'Late today, aren't you?'

He mumbled agreement as he took the broom out of the locker and began to sweep, quickly, self-consciously. She watched him.

'Have you been a sailor long?'

He kept on cleaning. 'No, ma'am.'

'I didn't think you had. You're not very old, are you?'

'Twenty-one,' he lied.

'Well, you had me fooled. You certainly look younger than that.' He wished she would stop talking. She went on. 'Whereabouts are you from?'

'Virginia.'

'Really? I have relatives in Washington, D.C. You know where that is, don't you?'

He was amused and irritated. She obviously thought him simple. But he played the desired role. Nodding vaguely, he opened the cabin door and swept the dirt out onto the deck. 'Where did you learn such housekeeping?' She was endlessly inventive in her lust.

'Just came natural, I reckon,' he said, mouth slightly ajar, idiot boy catching flies.

'Oh, really?' She was unaware that he was giving a performance. 'I'll bet you never did that back home, did you?'

He said oh, yes, and began to make the bed, first brushing out the cigarette ashes. She continued to babble. 'My friends in Washington say Virginia is lovely. I went to see the Blue Ridge Mountains once. You know where they are, don't you?'

This time he said no, and looked bewildered. She was informative. 'I went all through those caverns underneath the mountains and they were very interesting, with all those stone things growing down and the others up. Is your mother alive? Are your family living in Virginia?'

He replied accurately.

'My, but your mother must be almost as old as I am,' said the plump woman, making her first tentative move.

'I expect she is,' he said evenly, taking the round on points.

'Oh.' She was silent. He worked quickly; there were other cabins to be done.

'This is my first trip to Alaska,' she said at last. 'I have relatives in Anchorage. You've been to Anchorage, haven't you?' He nodded. 'It's very civilized for Alaska, don't you think so? I mean I always thought of Alaska as being like the North Pole, all ice and snow. But Anchorage is just like a small town anywhere and they've got trees and beauty parlours, just like in the States. "Outside", they call the States. Isn't that a funny way to refer to the rest of the world? "Outside"? I enjoyed myself very much visiting my relatives and so on. But you've travelled around a lot for someone so young, haven't you? I'll bet you've had some interesting experiences.'

'Not so many.' He finished making her bunk. When she saw he was ready to leave she said quickly, 'Oh, you're going to fix that porthole thing for me, aren't you? It keeps rattling all the time and I can't sleep at night.'

He looked at the porthole cover and saw that a screw was loose. With his thumbnail he tightened it. 'I don't think it'll bother you any more,' he said.

She got up, pulling her silk dressing-gown tight at the throat, and joined him at the porthole.

'Aren't you clever! Why, I tried all night long last night to fix that thing and I couldn't.'

He moved towards the door.

She spoke again, quickly, as though to prevent him from leaving by her talk. 'My husband used to be good at fixing things. He's dead now, of course. He's been dead since 1930, but I've a son back home. He's much younger than you. He's just starting college . . .' Jim felt as if he were being pushed to the edge of a cliff. With a son his age, she was trying to seduce him. Suddenly homesick, lost, he wanted to run away, to hide, to vanish. She was still talking as he opened the door and stepped out onto the wet, shining deck.

But he had no time to be lonely that evening. There was a party for the passengers and it was a hard evening for the messboys.

The saloon was decorated with imitation holly and shedding branches of pine which the Steward had thoughtfully brought from Anchorage. Not until two in the morning did the last passenger leave the smoky saloon. Then the Steward, red-faced and sweating, congratulated the messboys and wished them a Merry Christmas and told them that they could have their own party in the saloon.

Tired as they were, they managed to drink a good deal. Jim drank beer and Collins drank Bourbon from a bottle given him by a young girl passenger. Then some of the men started to sing and soon everyone sang loudly, to show what a good time they were having. As Jim continued to drink beer, he felt a certain affection for the others. Together they would sail for ever back and forth between Seattle and Anchorage until the ship sank or he died. Tears came to his eyes as he thought of this beautiful comradeship.

Collins was drunk now. 'Come on, boy,' he said, 'stop being so gloomy.'

Jim was hurt. 'I feel fine,' he said. 'I'm not gloomy.' Then he did become sad. 'But I never thought that I'd be 'way up here last Christmas, be here on Christmas Day one year when a year ago I was home.' He was not sure if this made sense but it had to be said.

'Well,' said Collins happily, 'I know I never thought I'd go to sea, back in Oregon where I lived. Old man was in the lumber business. Outside Eugene. Wanted me to go in the business, too, but I had to go places and so I went. But some time, maybe, I'll go back. Settle down. Raise a family . . .' His voice trailed off, bored with what he was saying. Then he stood up shakily and together they left the saloon. The night was cold and clear. The clouds were gone and across the shifting black water the peaks of Alaska were visible, defined by starlight.

Exhilarated, Jim breathed the cold air deeply.

'Some night,' he said. But Collins was only interested in keeping his balance as they walked forward to the fo'c'sle.

The fo'c'sle was triangle-shaped with double-deck bunks and bare light bulbs overhead, and heavy with the smell of too many men living in too small a place.

Jim had an upper bunk; Collins slept below him. Groaning to show how tired he was, Collins sat down on his bunk. 'I'm wore out.' He took off his shoes and stretched out. 'I can't wait to get to Seattle. You never been there, have you?'

'Just passed through.'

'Well, I'll show you 'round these dives I know. They know me at all the waterfront places. And I'll get you a girl. A real good one. What do you like?'

Jim was uncomfortable. 'I don't know,' he said. 'Almost anything.'

'Hell, you got to be *particular* or you'll catch something awful. Me, I never caught anything . . . yet.' He touched the wooden side of his bunk. 'Get you a blonde, they're best. Natural blondes, I mean. Swedes, that kind. You like blondes?'

'Sure.'

Collins pushed himself up on his elbow and looked at Jim, suddenly alert. 'Hey, I'll bet you're a virgin.'

Jim flushed and couldn't think of anything to say; the pause was enough.

'I'll be damned.' Collins was delighted. 'I never thought I'd find a guy who was. Well, we'll be real careful about the girl. How come you waited so long? You're eighteen, aren't you?'

Jim was embarrassed. He cursed himself for not having lied as all of them did about their affairs. 'Oh, I don't know,' he said, trying to dismiss it. 'There wasn't much chance back home.'

'I know just the girl for you. Name's Myra. Professional but nice, and clean. She don't drink or smoke and because she don't drink she takes care of herself. She won't give you no dose. I'll get you and Myra together.'

'I'd like to meet her,' said Jim, and the beer he had drunk made him excited at the idea. He dreamed occasionally of women, but most often he dreamed of Bob, which disturbed him when he thought about it.

'I'll show you around,' said Collins, undressing. 'I'll show you one good time. Yes, sir, I know my way around.'

II

It was already evening when Collins and Jim left the ship. Collins wore a brown suit with red checks. Jim wore a grey suit that was already too tight in the shoulders. He was still growing. Neither wore a tie.

They took a street car to the theatre district. Jim wanted to see a movie but Collins told him there was no time for that. 'First we find us a room.'

'I thought we were going to stay with these girls you been telling me about.'

Collins gestured. 'How do I know if they're in town, or if they ain't already booked for tonight? We'll get us a room; then we'll have a place to take whoever we find.'

'You know a place like that?'

'I know a lot of places.'

They found what they were looking for not far from the waterfront, in a street where the buildings were red brick and dingy and there were many bars, crowded with seamen prowling.

A bald wrinkled man sat behind a desk at the top of a long flight of flimsy steps. He was the proprietor of the Regent Hotel.

'We want a room for tonight,' said Collins, and he put his lower jaw out to show that he meant what he said.

'Double room?'

Collins nodded and so did Jim.

The bald man said, 'Pay in advance, two dollars apiece.' They paid in advance. 'I don't want no loud noise or drinking or bringing women up here. You know the law, boys. You from a boat?'

'Yeah,' said Collins, his jaw still out.

'I was a sailor myself once,' said the bald man mildly. 'But I don't follow the sea no more.' He led them up two flights of steps, then down a dark, damp-smelling corridor to a small room. He turned on the light. The room was fairly clean, though the paint was flaking off the walls. A large iron bed was at the centre of the room. A single window looked out upon the side of another brick building.

'Leave the key at the desk when you go out,' said the bald man. He looked around the room a moment, pleased with what he saw. Then he left.

'Isn't this something?' Collins sat down on the bed and it creaked.

Jim was depressed. Though he had slept in worse places, he did occasionally wonder if he would ever again live in a room like his room in Virginia, a clean place with familiar walls.

'Come on,' said Jim, turning to the door. 'I'm hungry.'

'Me too!' And Collins winked at Jim to show what he was hungry for.

They walked the dark streets, looking tough whenever they saw seamen, whistling boldly when any girls gave them the eye. It was good to be in Seattle on a clear winter night.

They stopped in front of a restaurant-bar. A neon sign announced spaghetti. 'Here it is,' said Collins. 'This is the place.'

'Where the girls are?' asked Jim.

'What else?' They went inside. The restaurant was large but only half filled. A dark-haired waitress led them to a booth.

'So what've you got, honey?' Collins twinkled.

The waitress handed him a menu. 'That's what I got,' she said flatly and walked away.

'Stuck-up bitch,' commented Collins, and Jim saw that his charm was not infallible. 'Women shouldn't work anyway. Not with the Depression and all. They ought to stay home.'

Jim looked around the restaurant. Red booths, brown walls, yellow-shaded lights: a cavern somewhere in hell.

After spaghetti, Collins belched and then announced, 'We'll stay here a while. Over there, at the bar. Then, if we don't see nothing we want, we'll go over to the Alhambra, this dance place where I know everybody.'

The bar was not crowded. They ordered beer. 'Swell place,' said Collins, with a self-congratulatory air.

Jim agreed, adding somewhat maliciously, 'Of course, they got hundreds of places like this back in New York.' Collins had never been to the East Coast.

Collins frowned at his beer. 'Well, I'll stick to little old Seattle.' He took a drink of beer. 'I'll bet,' he said, making a point, 'that *Hollywood* has got New York beat a mile.' He knew that Jim had never been to Hollywood. 'Yes,' he went on, pleased at his own tactic, 'I'll bet they got more pretty girls and crazy people and queers in L.A. than any other town.'

'Maybe so.'

Then the girl came up to the bar. Collins saw her first and nudged Jim. She was a slim girl with khaki hair, grey eyes, large features, large breasts. She sat down at the bar, smiling slightly. Red lips.

'What do you think of that?' murmured Collins.

'She's pretty.'

'Real class, too,' said Collins. 'Probably works in an office.' Apparently the bartender knew her because he said something to her in a low voice and they both laughed. He gave her a drink and she sat with it in her hand, watching the door.

'Here goes,' said Collins, and went towards the men's room. On his way, he paused at the end of the bar. He looked at the girl, pretending to be puzzled by what he saw. He spoke to her. Jim couldn't hear what he said, but he could see her frown, then smile. They talked a moment. She looked at Jim. She smiled again. Collins gestured for Jim to join them.

'Jim, this is Emily.' They shook hands.

'It's a pleasure to meet you,' said Emily, and her voice was husky and ladylike. Jim muttered a greeting.

'Don't mind him. He's real shy. We're on the same ship. We only got in today.'

Emily was impressed, as she was supposed to be. 'But you ought to be out on the town celebrating.'

'We plan to. But the night is young, like they say.'

'And so are we.' Emily took a tiny sip of her drink. 'Is this your first visit to Seattle?'

Collins shook his head. 'I been in and out of Seattle most of my life. I know this old town backward and forward. In fact, I was thinking of showing Jim here some of the sights.'

'Where are *you* from?' When Jim told her, she gave a little cry. 'Oh, a

Southerner! I love Southerners. They have such good manners. So you're from Virginia.' She said Virginia as though it were Vur-gin-ee-ah. 'But you haven't got much of an accent, have *you-all?*' Emily and Collins laughed at her mimetic skill.

Jim smiled. 'No,' he said, 'I guess not.'

'By the way,' Emily turned to Collins, 'what sort of sights had you planned on seeing tonight?'

'Well, I thought maybe we'd go over to the Alhambra . . .'

'Why, that's my very favourite place! My girl friend and I go there a lot to dance. You meet such nice people there. Not the rough gang you get in some places.'

'Oh, you live with another girl?' Collins was on the scent.

Emily nodded. 'We work in the same office and sometimes we go out on dates together. Tonight she was supposed to meet me here. Two boys she knows are coming into town (we think) and she was going to bring them here.'

'Oh, hell.' Collins scowled and looked unhappy. 'And here I was hoping maybe you and your friend could join Jim and me. You see, the only girls I know in town happen to be away right now, so I was hoping maybe . . .'

'Well,' said Emily thoughtfully, 'I *could* call her up and find out whether they are definitely going to come tonight or not and if they aren't . . . well, I think she would be *glad* to join us.'

And so it was that Emily went to the back of the bar to telephone her room-mate.

'How's that for operating?' asked Collins.

'Good.' Jim was genuinely impressed. 'Do you think her girl friend will really come?'

'Are you kidding?'

'She's pretty,' said Jim, watching the blonde girl through the glass door of the telephone booth. He appreciated her handsomeness but he was not moved by her in the way Collins was. He wanted to be excited by her. But it was no use, at least not while he was sober. It was very odd.

Emily joined them at the bar, red lips smiling. 'My friend, Anne, is going to meet us in a few minutes at the Alhambra. She said that our two friends are *not* coming after all. You know, some people are so undependable that way. So, as I said to her, it's a lucky thing for us to have such a nice invitation from two boys just in town after such a long time at sea. Anne's just crazy about the sea. Once they gave an office party, a picnic out on the Sound, and Anne went sailing with one of the fellows and they could hardly get her back to shore she liked it so much.'

'I guess,' said Collins with a wink, 'that Anne will be Jim's date. If that's all right.'

Emily laughed and both of them watched her breasts shake. 'Why, if it's all right with you, it is with me.' And she looked at Collins, lips parted seductively. Then she turned to Jim. 'I'm sure you'll like Anne. She's a lot of fun.'

The Alhambra was a large dance hall on a side street, with a bright neon sign which flashed on and off above the mock-Moorish door.

Inside, the hall was crowded and dim. A small band played swing.

A grey-haired woman in a black evening dress led them to a table. Collins greeted her warmly. She looked at him blankly and left.

'Old friend of mine,' said Collins. 'I used to come in here a lot last year. She always remembers me.'

A waiter came over and after a short discussion they ordered rye. Meanwhile, Emily made an unconscionable amount of conversation. 'I expect to see Anne any minute now. She's the fastest dresser I've ever seen for a woman. And then we live just a few blocks from here.'

'Yes?' Collins was alert.

'Just a few blocks,' repeated Emily. Then: 'Anne is really such a clever girl. Why, she even used to do modelling work.'

'She must be real pretty,' said Jim, forcing excitement.

Emily nodded. 'Anne *is* good-looking. She's one of the most popular girls in the office. She and I date together all the time and I'm sure that the fellow with me is always wishing he was with Anne.' This was an excellent opening for Collins to protest. He protested. Emily continued. 'She's younger than I am. She's twenty and I'm twenty-two. How old are you, Colly?'

'Twenty-five,' lied Collins, and he pulled his chair nearer hers.

Emily looked at Jim. 'I'll bet you are not a day over twenty,' she said with a grin.

Jim nodded solemnly. 'That's right.' Now that false ages had been established all around, the evening assumed direction.

Finally, Anne arrived. She was small and thin and she wore a brown dress. She looked about her uncertainly until she saw Emily. Then she hurried over, smiling, posing. Emily introduced everybody and then, as she was a little drunk, she introduced everybody a second time. This proved funny.

While Anne laughed, Jim decided that she was indeed pretty, though nearer thirty than twenty. Not that it made the slightest difference to him.

'And so you're Jim,' said Anne after she had taken a drink and the excitement of her entrance was gone.

'That's right. Emily's been telling us a lot about you.'

'Flattering, I hope?' At times Anne sounded like an English movie actress. Like her friend, she had a good deal of small talk.

'We work in an office in a department store. I file things and Emily types and does things like that. Are you from the South?'

He nodded and she made up a funny sentence with 'you-all' in it and everybody laughed and then Emily and Collins got up from the table and announced that they were going to dance. So Jim invited Anne and all four of them went out onto the dance floor. Jim made an effort to dance well. There were so many things to be proved this evening.

Anne pressed close to him, her cheek against his; he could smell powder and soap and perfume. Once he looked down at her and saw that her eyes were closed.

Collins came by with Emily. 'Hey, Jim,' he said. Anne opened her eyes and Jim moved a few inches away from her.

'Yes?' said Jim.

'Emily here's suggested we go over to their place for a while. They've got liquor over there and a radio and we can dance where it won't be so crowded.'

'That's a good idea, Emily,' said Anne brightly.

They went back to their table, paid the bill, gathered coats and left the Alhambra. Though the night was cold, Jim was sweating from whisky.

In a side street they stopped before a small apartment house. Emily opened the door. At the top of two flights of clean and carpeted stairs, Emily showed them into an apartment consisting of a sitting-room, a small kitchen and a bedroom. The door to the bedroom was open and Jim could see twin beds inside.

'Home,' announced Emily, turning on the radio while Anne disappeared into the kitchen, returning a moment later with a bottle of rye and some glasses. 'Get some ice, will you, Emily?'

Emily went into the kitchen, followed by Collins. Anne put the glasses down on the table and Jim stood beside her, awkward, unsure of himself.

'Let's dance,' she said, when she had arranged the glasses on a table. He held her away from him, but she pressed close. He was ill at ease. He wanted desperately to be carried away by the music and the whisky and this girl, but all he could think of was the flecks of dandruff in her hair.

He heard a laugh from the kitchen. Then Collins and Emily came into the sitting-room. Both were flushed and Collins's eyes were bright. Emily put a bowl of ice cubes on the table and Collins produced a bottle of soda water.

'Let's all have a drink,' said Emily. They all had a drink. Collins proposed a toast to Emily and she graciously proposed one to him. Jim and Anne toasted each other. Jim was drunk now. His eyes refused to focus. Everything was suddenly warm and cosy and intimate. Boldly he put his arm around Anne and they sat down on a couch, side by side, and watched Collins and Emily dance.

'You really dance well,' said Anne. 'You must've taken lessons. I never took any lessons but I picked up a lot from the girls I knew in school. I went to a secretarial school and we used to have a lot of dances. I enjoyed them so much. And that's where I learned how to dance.'

He wanted to keep her talking. 'Did you always live in Seattle?'

She scowled to show that this was a question which troubled her. 'Yes, I've always lived here but I don't like it. You see, I want to travel. I've *always* wanted to travel. That's why I envy you men on ships, you get to travel so much and see so many things.'

'Where would you like to go?' As Jim held her, he was pleasurably astonished at his own bravery. She moved close to him.

'Everywhere,' she said. 'But mainly I want to see Southern California. I want to go to Hollywood. You know, I think I'd like to be in the movies.' She said this in a low voice, confidingly.

'I guess a lot of people do.' Jim had read a few movie magazines and he had been impressed by the difficulties movie stars encountered in becoming movie stars.

'I know,' said Anne. 'But I think I'm different. No, really. I'm serious. I think I'm going to be famous. Why, even when I was a little girl and saw people like Jean Harlow on the silver screen I knew that would be me one day. But for now I got to work in an office and I don't know when I'll be able to get to Hollywood. But I'll get there some day. I just know it.'

'You've certainly got ambition.'

'Oh, I've got plenty of that! Just think what it'd be like to wear all those pretty clothes and have men with moustaches and tweed suits take me out to eat in those expensive places with palm trees.' She stared into space, her mouth open with longing for this other life.

Jim muttered soothing things, aware that Collins and Emily had disappeared. The door to the bedroom was still open, and he could see Collins in his shorts approaching Emily, who lay naked on one of the beds. Emily giggled. Jim looked away, blushing.

'What's the matter?' Anne abandoned her Hollywood vision. Then she saw what was happening in the bedroom. She giggled; an echo of Emily.

'You're only young once,' she said. Jim looked at her and saw that her eyes were bright, shiny, bestial. He had seen the same look in Collins's eyes, in Emily's eyes, yet not in Bob's eyes. He was repelled. But Anne, unaware of his response, put her face so close to his that he could smell the whisky on her breath. 'My, but they're having fun!' Her body was against him now and he could feel the rapid pounding of her heart.

'I'll bet they're having a good time,' she repeated. 'You're only young once, that's what I say.' She kissed him. It was a wet and tongue-involving kiss. He pulled away. Aware of his withdrawal, she started to cry. 'I used to be in love, too,' she said, missing the point. Between small actress-sobs, she said that she understood the way he felt and she knew that what she was doing was terribly bad but she was lonely, without anyone to care for her, and – God knows – they were only young once.

He made himself kiss her, his mind full of memories and half-forgotten fears. With an effort of will, he tried to melt the fear in his stomach. Gradually, desire began. He was startled but pleased. Soon he would be ready. But suddenly she stood up and said brightly, 'I better take my dress off. Don't want to get it rumpled.'

She went into the bedroom. He followed her to the door and stood watching Collins and Emily on the bed. Neither of them seemed to care if they were observed or not. They were involved in the intricate act of becoming one. Fascinated, Jim watched them. They made primitive noises and writhed blindly, according to the mindless ritual of the sexes. Jim was frightened, unready for this.

Anne appeared, and posed for him without her clothes. He stared, fascinated. He had never seen a naked woman before. She walked towards him. She put out her arms. Involuntarily, he backed away.

'Come on in, Jimmy,' she said, and her voice was high-pitched and artificial. He hated her then. He hated her passionately. This was not what he wanted.

'I got to go,' he said. He went into the sitting-room. She followed him and he found himself staring at her again and this time he compared her with Bob, and found her wanting. He no longer cared whether or not he was different from other people. He hated this woman and her body.

'What's the matter? What did I do wrong?'

'I got to go.' He couldn't say anything else. She started to cry. Quickly he went to the door and opened it. Just as he left, he heard Collins shout to Anne, 'Let the queer go! I got enough for two.'

Jim walked a long time in the cold night and wondered why he had failed so completely in what he had wanted to do. He was not what Collins had called him. He was certain of that. Yet why? At the moment when what should have happened was about to happen the image of Bob had come between him and the girl, rendering the act obscene and impossible. What to do? He would not exorcise the ghost of Bob even if he could. Yet he realized that it would be a difficult matter to live in a world of men and women without participating in their ancient and necessary duet. Was he able to participate? Yes, he decided, under other circumstances. In any case, the word Collins had shouted after him was hardly apt. It couldn't be. It was too monstrous. Yet because it had been said, he could never see Collins again. He would jump ship and go . . . where? He looked down the dark empty street, searching for a sign. Just opposite him was a movie house. 'Yesterday's Magic, starring Ronald Shaw', proclaimed the marquee in unlit light-bulbs. He thought of Hollywood, recalling Anne's voice droning on wistfully about the movies. That did it. At least he would get there before she did. Obscurely pleased at this small vengeance, he returned to the hotel.

The bald-headed man was still behind the desk. 'You're a sailor. I can tell. Me, I was a sailor but I don't follow the sea no more. No, no more of that for me.' Jim went to his room and tried to sleep, tried to forget what Collins had called him. He slept and he forgot.

CHAPTER FOUR

I

Otto Schilling was half Austrian and half Polish. He was blond with a brick-red face, much lined from weather. He was tennis instructor at the Garden Hotel in Beverly Hills.

'You were a sailor, yes?' Otto's accent was thick, though he had been in America half his life.

'Yes, sir.' Jim was nervous. He needed this job.

'When did you leave ship?'

'Last December.'

Otto looked thoughtfully out the window at his kingdom, the eight clay courts which adjoined the hotel pool.

'That was six months ago. You have been in Los Angeles since then?'

'Yes, sir.'

'You have been what?'

'Working in a garage mostly.'

'But you play tennis, yes?'

'Yes, sir. I used to play back home at school.'

'How old are you?'

'Nineteen.'

'You think you know enough to help around here? Roll courts, be ballboy, string rackets . . . you can do this?'

'Yes, sir. I talked to the guy who was here before and he told me what the work was and I know I can do it.'

Otto Schilling nodded. 'I take you on trial. That boy was here before was lazy. You better not be lazy. You get twenty-five a week but I make you work hard for all that money. If you're any good, you help me give lessons. Maybe I let *you* give lessons, if you play good. You play good?' His wide blue eyes looked at Jim.

'I was pretty good,' said Jim, trying to sound both modest and informative.

Otto nodded approvingly. He did not share the American passion for modesty. When he had been singles champion of Austria, there were those who had thought him conceited. But why not? He had been a great player. 'You will live in the hotel,' he said finally. 'Go see Mr Kirkland, the manager. I call him on the phone now. You start in the morning, seven-thirty o'clock. I tell you what to do. Maybe I play with you and see what you know. Go on now.'

Jim murmured 'Thank you' and left the tennis house. On his right was a large swimming pool edged with imported beach. Prosperous-looking men and women sat beneath umbrellas, while several young girls were photographed by a sinister-looking cameraman. Jim wondered if the girls were movie stars, and if so, who they were. But they all looked alike, with white teeth, bleached hair, slim brown bodies. He recognized no one.

Jim climbed the steps to the Garden Hotel, a large rambling white stucco building set among palm trees. After six months of uncomfortable rooming houses, he was delighted at the thought of living here, if only temporarily. He was quite used by now to being transient. He took it for granted that this travelling would not end until he found Bob. Then they would work out some sort of life together, though precisely what that life would be he left deliberately vague. Meanwhile, he took what work he could find, and lived happily in the present. Except for the golden image of Bob beside the river on that sunshine day, he was without history. In memory, his father was a dim blur; his mother, too; both grey, shadowy. The sea was dark and vaguest of all. Everything forgotten except Collins and the two girls in their Seattle apartment. Only that night was vivid in his memory. With an effort, he tried not to think of it as he hurried up the steps to the Garden Hotel.

Mr Kirkland's office was large and modern and looked much more expensive than it actually was. So did Mr Kirkland. He was a short man whose real name was probably not Kirkland. He affected a British accent, while his clothes and manner were exquisite and discreet, except for the large diamond he wore on the little finger of his left hand, an outward and visible sign of sudden rise and of unfamiliar affluence.

'Willard?' The voice was sharp.

'Yes, sir. Mr Schilling sent me to you.'

'You're going to be ballboy, I understand.' Mr Kirkland pronounced the title as though it were an accolade. 'As such, you will be paid twenty-five dollars a week. Quite a large amount for a young boy, but I trust you will work for it to the best of your ability.' Jim recognized a speech that had been made before. 'We here at the Garden Hotel like to think of ourselves as a family, in which each one must do his part, from myself,' he smiled tightly, 'on down.' He looked at Jim. 'You start work as of tomorrow morning. I suppose you gave your references to Mr Schilling. Ask the housekeeper in the servants' wing to assign you a room.' With a nod, Mr Kirkland ended the interview and Jim departed.

The lobby of the hotel was large with square marble pillars which pretended to hold up the lozenge-patterned ceiling. The floor was carpeted in a royal red. Behind a plywood desk simulating mahogany, clerks in formal clothes received guests, simulating welcome. Bellboys in livery lounged on a bench at the front door, waiting to carry bags and run errands. The lobby was usually a busy place, for there was always someone arriving or departing. Jim found the magnificence awesome and the bored air of the bellboys infinitely sophisticated. Perhaps one day he would be as casual.

Jim crossed the lobby, conscious of his shabby suitcase. He approached one of the bellboys and asked uncertainly, 'How do I get to the employees' wing?'

The young man looked at him with slow boredom. Then he yawned and stretched. 'I'll take you back.' They went from the lobby to the famous tropical garden which gave the hotel its name. Dazzled by colour, Jim followed his guide through the artificial jungle.

'What's your job?'

Jim told him.

'An outdoor boy! So where you from?'

Jim decided to be impressive. 'Nowhere. I been to sea.'

The young man was respectful but inquiring. 'To sea *where?*'

Jim was offhand. 'Caribbean, Pacific, Bering Sea, all over. I been around.'

'I guess you have. So what're you doing here?'

Jim shrugged. 'Killing time. What else?'

The young man nodded and thoughtfully scratched one of a number of pimples.

Jim was assigned a small room overlooking the parking lot. The housekeeper was pleasant and the bellboy promised to show him the ropes. The thing was done. He now had a small place in the world of others.

In Southern California, September was not much different from any other month. The weather was clear and bright and there was no rain. According to the newspapers there was a war in Europe but Jim was not quite sure what it was all about. Apparently there was a man named Hitler who was German. He had a moustache and comedians were always imitating him. At every party someone was bound to give an imitation of Hitler making a speech. Then there was an Englishman with a somewhat larger moustache and of course there was Mussolini but he didn't seem to be in the war. For a while it was very exciting, and there were daily headlines. But towards the end of September Jim lost interest in the war because there had been no battles. Also, his days were now occupied teaching tennis to rich men and women who were not very interested in the war either.

Schilling liked Jim, and after they had played together several times, he allowed him to instruct. He also encouraged him to go into tournaments, but Jim was satisfied to continue as he was. The life was easy and healthy. He gained weight; his body thickened with muscle. He was popular with the people who used the courts, particularly the young girls who lived in the hotel. They flirted with him, and he always responded politely, if evasively, which made them think him sensitive as well as handsome.

He was now used to the sight of famous actors and actresses playing tennis and sunning themselves beside the pool. In fact, one brilliant old actress (almost forty) took tennis lessons from him every day, swearing obscenely whenever she made a bad shot. He thought her most impressive.

Jim had also begun a social life. Several times he had gone on parties with the bellhops. Most of them wanted to be actors, which explained the somewhat detached air with which they did their jobs around the hotel. Several took a fancy to Jim because he didn't want to become an actor; also, he seemed sincerely to admire them. Jim was not without social guile. Yet his new companions puzzled him. Their conversation was often cryptic, their eyes quick-moving, searching. Ill at ease with outsiders, they were quarrelsome with one another. The one thing they had in common was the desire to move in narcissistic splendour through the lives of others, to live forever grandly, and not to die.

They had many rich friends who gave parties, consisting largely of middle-aged women, widowed or divorced, and plump men with unpleasant habits when drunk. The women, particularly, took a fancy to Jim and he was often told that he was a 'real person' and not like the others, whatever that meant. The plump men were also nice to him, but when through ignorance he did not respond to the suggestive ritual of their conversation, they left him alone.

Otto Schilling warned Jim about the bellhops. He explained that since they were not normal young men, they would try to corrupt him. Otto was stern as he explained these matters to Jim, who managed to look so shocked and unbelieving (he *was* surprised) that Otto spared him the full explanation of what he meant.

Jim went through several stages after his discovery that there were indeed many men who liked other men. His first reaction was disgust and alarm. He scrutinized everyone carefully. Was he one? After a while, he could identify the obvious ones by their tight, self-conscious manner, particularly when they moved, neck and shoulders rigid. After a time, as the young men grew used to Jim they would talk frankly about themselves. Finally, one tried to seduce him. Jim was quite unnerved, and violent in his refusal. Yet afterwards he continued to go to their parties, if only to be able to experience again the pleasure of saying no.

Late one afternoon, a bellhop named Leaper entered the tennis house just as Jim was finishing his shower. Leaper peered into the shower room. 'Hey, Jim.'

Jim rubbed soap out of his eyes. 'Hi!' Though Leaper was one of those he had refused, they had remained on good terms.

'You want to go to a party?'

'Where?' Jim turned off the shower, picked up his towel and joined Leaper in the locker room. As he dried himself, he knew that he was being examined with passionate interest. He was more amused than irritated.

'At Ronald Shaw's. In Beverly.'

Jim was surprised. 'The movie actor?'

'The very same, and they say he is quite *sympathetic*.' Leaper made a feminine gesture. 'He asked a friend of mine to collect some beauties so I thought of you. Of course you may be the only straight guy there but then you can never tell, there might be some girl with red hair hanging onto the fringes.' Jim had developed a mythical reputation for liking girls with red hair. Leaper chattered happily about Ronald Shaw while Jim dressed.

'It's really something to go to one of Shaw's parties. He's an honest-to-God Movie Star, with all the girls everywhere mad for him! That's a joke, isn't it? Why, when I worked in a picture with him at Metro . . .' Like most of the bellhops, Leaper had done extra work in the movies and he spoke often of stars he had 'worked with'. 'These Girl Scouts came around to give him some sort of prize and he said: "Will you please take these pubescent monsters and lay them end to end on the back lot." Of course they covered it all up, just like the time he was knocked down in a bar at Santa Monica by this Marine from Pendleton. Oh, that guy is *something!*'

'He's pretty young, isn't he?' Jim parted his wet hair in the mirror.

'Thirty, maybe. You can't tell about those guys. Anyway, you better be warned, he'll make a pass at you, which I bet you wouldn't mind one bit.'

'Just let him try,' growled Jim into the mirror, aware that his sun-tanned face made him resemble a South Sea movie islander. 'Sure I'll come,' he said, ready for adventure.

II

At thirty-five, Ronald Shaw was disturbingly handsome, with features of such ordinariness that they were, paradoxically, unique. Dark curly hair tumbled over a classic low forehead to give him a look often described as 'impish' by admirers, 'Neanderthal' by detractors. With his light blue eyes, he seemed typically 'black Irish', a type which occurs most often among Jews. Ronald Shaw had been born George Cohen. At one point he had thought that to be taken for George M. Cohen might be rewarding, but it was not, and so George Cohen became Ronald Shaw, a handsome fiery young Irishman whose films made money. George Cohen of Baltimore had been very poor, but now that Ronald Shaw was wealthy neither was going to be poor again. Shaw was notoriously mean, except with his mother in Baltimore. As every reader of movie magazines knew, his mother was his 'best girl' and the reason that he was still a bachelor, which was exactly right, as any Freudian would agree.

Although Shaw had been a star for five years, he had never bought a house in Hollywood. He preferred to rent large impersonal houses where he could give parties for young men behind thick walls and an elaborate burglar-alarm system. In this way, he was discreet. Yet everyone in the homosexual world knew that he was one of them. Naturally there were rumours about other actors, but where in other cases there was often some vestigial doubt in the minds of even the most passionate apologists for Socratic vice, there was none in Shaw's case. He was always mentioned by the great fraternity with pride, envy, lust. Fortunately, the women of America remained in ignorance, regarding him as a satisfying love object, unattainable but useful as a companion in dreams, the boy-man of advertising come alive thirty times life-size upon the screen.

Ronald Shaw had it made, and since he was nothing if not human, he found most human relationships disappointing. His sexual partners were selected for a combination of physical beauty and hard masculinity. Each affair began as though the creation of the world was to be re-enacted, and each usually ended in less time than it took the Old Testament Creator to put up the sky. No one could please Shaw for very long. If a boy came to love him (and to disregard the legend), Shaw was affronted and endangered; yet if a lover continued to be dazzled by the idea of him, he soon grew bored. Nevertheless, Shaw was a happy man and if he had not been told about romantic love, it would never have occurred to him to take coupling seriously.

Jim was much impressed by the magnificence of Shaw's house. An interior decorator had done it for nothing: unfortunately, the affair had ended before the bedrooms were done. Nevertheless, the downstairs was a success, a riot of Spanish baroque with a huge drawing-room whose windows looked down upon Los Angeles, glittering to the west. Over a cavernous fireplace hung a portrait of Ronald Shaw, half again as large as life. The original of this glamorous work of art stood at the centre of the room, graciously directing the party's traffic. It was an odd group. For one thing, there were three times as many men as women. Jim recognized several character actors: Ronald Shaw needed only the flimsiest support. The women were all elegant, with high voices, large jewels, towering befeathered hats. They were not, Jim was assured by the knowing Leaper, lesbians. They had simply passed the age of being able to attract normal men and so, still craving attention, they were drawn into the world of hairdressers and couturiers. Here they could gossip and make stage love and avoid boredom, if not despair.

'Isn't this swell?' murmured Leaper, in his awe forgetting his role as sophisticate and guide.

Jim nodded. 'Where's Ronald Shaw?'

Leaper pointed to the centre of the room. At first, Jim was disappointed. Shaw was smaller than he had expected. But he was handsome, there was no denying that. In contrast to the others, he wore a dark suit which gave his slim figure dignity. At the moment he was surrounded by women. The young men were more circumspect; they held to the periphery of the party, waiting.

'You better meet him,' said Leaper.

They crossed to the group of women and waited until Shaw had finished telling a story. Then, during the sharp, loud laughter, Leaper said hurriedly, 'You remember me, Mr Shaw, don't you?' Shaw looked blank but Leaper kept right on talking. 'It was Mr Ridgeway who asked me to come tonight, and I brought this friend of mine with me, Jim Willard. He's real keen to meet you ...'

Ronald Shaw smiled at Jim. 'How do you do?' His hand was cool and hard.

'I ... like you in the movies,' said Jim, to Leaper's horror. This was impossibly bad form. With movie stars, one was supposed to appear unimpressed.

But admiration never offended Ronald Shaw. He grinned, showing white teeth. 'That's nice of you to say so. Come on, let's get you a drink.' Gracefully, Shaw extricated himself from the women and together they crossed to the far end of the room.

Acutely embarrassed, Jim was conscious of many eyes watching him. But Shaw was serenely at ease as he stopped a waiter and took a glass from the tray. 'I hope you like Martinis.'

'Well, I don't drink very much.'

'Neither do I.' Shaw's voice was low and confiding, as if the only person in the world whose company and good opinion he sought was the bedazzled Jim. And though he asked only the usual questions, his warm voice made those familiar phrases sound significant, even the inevitable 'Are you an actor?'

Jim quickly told him what he was.

Shaw grinned. 'An athlete! Well ... You look too young to be an instructor.' They were standing now at one of the large windows. Out of the corner of his eye, Jim noticed that his fellow guests were preparing to close in on Shaw and recapture him. They did not have much time. Shaw sensed this, too. 'What's your name again?' Jim told him. 'You must,' said Shaw, looking thoughtfully down at the city, 'come see me some day. When are you free?'

'I'm not working Thursday afternoon,' said Jim, startled at the speed of his own response.

'Then why don't you drop by here Thursday. If I'm still shooting, you can swim until I get back. I'm usually through at five.'

'Sure. I'd like to.' Jim felt his stomach contract with fear and expectancy.

'See you Thursday.' Then Ronald Shaw, with a distant polite nod calculated to deceive his audience, allowed the young men to surround him.

Leaper joined him. 'Well, you're in.' His eyes glittered. 'He fell for you like a ton of ...'

'Shut up, will you?' Jim turned away angrily.

'Don't con me. You hooked him. Everybody saw you. They want to know who you are. So I've been telling them you're straight as a die, which just makes their mouths water all the more. You're a hit, boy. Look at them all staring at you.' Jim looked but caught no one staring. 'So what did Shaw talk to you about?'

'Nothing.'

'Oh, sure! Well, you better put out this time. He can do a lot for you.'

'Sorry, I got no plans to shack up with him. Or anybody else.'

Leaper looked at him with genuine surprise. 'So maybe you're not queer, but *this* is an exception. Why, this is something people dream about. You could make a fortune out of him.'

Jim laughed and moved away. He tried to appear relaxed and at ease, but he was neither. Soon he would have to make a decision, on Thursday to be precise. What to do? Mechanically he moved through the evening, his heart pounding.

When it came time to say good-bye, Shaw smiled and winked. Blushing, Jim turned away. He said not a word to Leaper as they rode home in the bus.

III

Jim Willard's erotic life took place almost entirely in dreams. Until that day with Bob beside the river, he had dreamed of women as often as of men, and there had seemed no set boundary between the two. But since that summer day, Bob was the constant dream-lover, and girls no longer intruded upon their perfect masculine idyll. He was aware that what he dreamed of was not what normal men dreamed of. But at the same time he made no connection between what he and Bob had done and what his new acquaintances did. Too many of them behaved like women. Often after he had been among them, he would study himself in a mirror to see if there was any trace of the woman in his face or manner, and he was always pleased that there was not. Finally, he decided that he was unique. He was the only one who had done what he had done and felt the way he did. Even the elegant, long-haired youths all agreed that he was probably not one of them. Nevertheless, women expected him to make love to them, and when he didn't (he could never quite explain to himself *why* he didn't) they felt that it was they who were lacking, not he. None suspected that he dreamed every night of a tall boy by a river. Yet as Jim got more and more involved in Leaper's world, he found himself fascinated by the stories they told of their affairs with one another. He could not imagine himself doing the things they said they did. Yet he wanted to know about them, if only out of a morbid desire to discover how what had been so natural and complete for him could be so perfectly corrupted by these strange womanish creatures.

In a mood of indecision, Jim went to see Ronald Shaw, and what he suspected would happen did happen. He allowed himself to be seduced, impressed by Shaw's fame and physical beauty. The act was familiar except that this time he was passive, too shy to be the aggressor. With Bob he had taken the initiative, but that was a different occasion and a more important time.

The affair began. Shaw was in love, or at least he talked of love, and how they would spend the rest of their lives together ('like those two ancient Greeks – you know the ones, Achilles and so-and-so – who were such famous lovers'). Not that there was to be any publicity. Hollywood was a merciless place and they would have to be extremely discreet. But for those who did know about them, they would be worshipped as a dazzling couple, two perfect youths, re-enacting boyhood dreams behind the stucco walls of the house on Mulholland Drive.

Although Jim was flattered by Shaw's protestations of love, the older man's body did not excite him. Jim was oddly reluctant to touch a mature man's flesh, no matter how handsome he was. Apparently only those his own age had the power to attract him. Yet when he shut his eyes he enjoyed himself, for then he would think of Bob. And so the affair began, or the relationship, as those who had undergone analysis would say. It was a new experience for Jim and not entirely a pleasant one.

The first skirmish with the world occurred when Jim told Otto Schilling that he was going away.

Schilling was surprised. 'I don't understand,' he said. 'I don't understand why you want to leave here. You get more pay somewhere else?'

Jim nodded.

Schilling looked at him sharply. 'Where? How?'

Jim was uncomfortable. 'Well, you see, Ronald Shaw, the actor, and these other people' (he added vaguely) 'want me to teach, you know, on their courts, and so I said I would.'

'Where will you live?'

Jim could feel the sweat trickling down his side. 'I'll stay at Shaw's place.'

Schilling nodded grimly and Jim kicked himself for not having lied. Everyone knew about Shaw. Jim felt ashamed. 'I didn't think you were like that,' said Schilling slowly. 'I am sorry for you. There is nothing wrong with seeing a person like Ronald Shaw, there is nothing so wrong with being that way, but to be a kept boy, ah, *that* is bad.'

Jim wiped his forehead with the back of his hand. 'Is there anything you want me to do before I go?'

'No,' said Schilling wearily. 'Tell Mr Kirkland you're leaving. That's all.' He turned away.

Shaken, Jim went to his room and started to pack. Leaper joined him. 'Congratulations!' he exclaimed. 'Beginner's luck, you can't beat it.'

'What're you talking about?' Jim packed furiously.

'Come off it. It's the talk of the circuit how you're going to live with Ronald Shaw! So what's he like?'

'I don't know.' Jim felt his façade of normality crumbling.

'So what're you going to be, his cook?'

'I'm going to teach him tennis.' This sounced idiotic even to his own ears. Leaper brayed contempt. But Jim stuck doggedly to his story, explaining how Shaw was to pay him fifty dollars a week, which was true.

'Ask me over some time,' said Leaper as Jim finished packing. 'We could play doubles.'

Jim merely glared. Yet in all of this one thing surprised him: Leaper, believing that Jim was heterosexual, took it for granted that any normal boy would live with a famous actor, given the chance. In Leaper's world all men were whores and all whores were bisexual.

Shaw was sitting beside the swimming pool when Jim arrived. The swimming pool was set like a navel in a red brick terrace flanked by two bath-houses resembling the turreted pavilions of a medieval knight. Shaw waved as Jim approached.

'Did you make a clean break?' The deep voice was mocking.

'Clean enough. I told Schilling I was going to teach you and some other people tennis.'

'You mentioned me?'

'Yes. I wish I hadn't. I'm sorry. Because he knew exactly what was going on. He didn't say much but I felt like dirt.'

Shaw sighed. 'I don't know how the hell they know so much about me. It's the damnedest thing.' Like most homosexuals, Shaw was astonished that anyone saw through his mask. 'I guess it's because so many people are so bloody jealous of me.' Shaw sounded both sad and proud. 'Because everyone knows who I am and because I make a lot of money, they all think I must be terribly happy, which they resent and which isn't so. Funny, isn't it? I've had all the things I ever wanted and I'm not . . . well, it's an awful feeling not having anybody to be close to. Oh, I tried to get my mother to come out here but she won't leave Baltimore. So here I am, all alone, like the song says. At least until now.' He gave a flashing smile. Jim smiled back, in spite of himself. He couldn't help thinking that the man did have everything, and if he hadn't found a lover by now it was doubtless his own fault.

Jim unbuttoned his shirt. The day was warm and the sun was pleasant. He sat very still, trying not to contemplate the sadness of the life of Ronald Shaw. But Shaw was persistent. 'You know,' he said, 'I don't think I've ever known anyone like you. Somebody so natural and . . . well, unscheming. I also didn't think you could be made. You don't seem the type.' Jim was pleased to hear this, faith in his own manhood momentarily restored. Shaw grinned. 'But I'm glad things turned out the way they did.'

Jim smiled, too. 'So am I.'

'I hate those others, those lousy queens.' Shaw lifted one shoulder and gave a curiously feminine shake to his body, mocking in a single gesture the entire legion.

'They're O.K., some of them.'

'I'm not talking about them as people,' said Shaw. 'I mean for sex. If a man likes men, he wants a man and if he likes women he wants a woman, so who wants a freak who's neither? It's a mystery to me.' Shaw yawned. 'Maybe I ought to be psychoanalysed.'

'Why?'

Shaw examined his biceps muscles critically: his appearance was his livelihood. 'I don't know. Sometimes I . . .' But he did not pursue the thought. The arms went slack. 'Bunch of fakes, every last one of them, telling you stuff you already know. No, what matters is being tough. You *got* to be tough in this world. There's no place for the weak, like Mamma used to say. She was right, too. That's how I got where I am, being tough and not feeling sorry for myself.'

Jim was impressed by the sternness of this speech. He was also reminded of his own situation. 'That's O.K. for you,' he said, 'this being tough. You had talent. You knew what you wanted. But what about me? I'm just a better-than-average tennis player. So what do *I* do? Toughness isn't going to help me play any better.'

Shaw looked at him obviously making an effort to consider the case. 'Well, I don't know.' The beautiful eyes went slightly out of focus. 'Would you . . . uh, like to act?'

Jim shrugged. 'Me? Why?'

'Well, that's not what I'd call burning ambition. No, you've got to *want* this thing so much it hurts.' And Shaw resumed the monologue which pleased him most, the chronicle of his own rise in the world, aided by no one except Mamma. Within the circle of his own self-love Shaw was content, and Jim did not in the least resent being at the periphery of that self-absorption. Jim accepted Shaw completely and uncritically. After all, their affair was but a temporary halt on a long voyage whose terminus was Bob.

When Shaw had finished his hymn to achievement, Jim said, with an admiration not entirely false, 'I guess I haven't got it,' he said. 'I don't want anything that bad.'

Shaw fondled the vertical line of dark hair on his own chest. 'We could certainly get you work as an extra. Then who knows?'

'Who knows?' Jim rose and stretched. Shaw watched him, pleased and aroused.

'Put your bathing trunks on,' he said, and he led Jim into the knight's pavilion.

IV

Two months passed peacefully. Jim enjoyed the large house with its rooms like movie sets. On the days when Shaw was at the studio, Jim would play tennis with various friends who wanted to meet Shaw's new lover, as well as improve their backhand. Jim was agreeably surprised to find himself something of a celebrity, at least in this one world, and the interest he inspired compensated somewhat for the shame he had felt with Schilling.

Jim enjoyed Shaw's parties and he quickly made himself useful. He learned how to cope with drunks, mix drinks and discreetly cue Shaw if there was a story he wanted to tell. Jim was much impressed by the beautifully dressed people who drank heavily and talked incessantly of their sex life. Their harsh candour both shocked and pleased him. They feared nothing, at least behind the high stucco walls of Shaw's estate.

Jim found Shaw not only an agreeable companion but, more important, informative. He showed him the secret Hollywood where, so it was said, nearly all the leading men were homosexual and those few who were not were under constant surveillance. A number of women acted as outriders to the beautiful legion, and they were often called upon to be public escorts. They were known as 'beards'. But they were not always reliable. One evening a drunken outrider tried to make love to Shaw and when he pushed her away, she shouted obscenities at everyone present; then she was led away and no one ever saw her again.

For purposes of publicity, Shaw appeared regularly at night clubs with girls, often rising actresses. He did this to satisfy the head of the studio, a nervous businessman whose nightmare was that scandal might end the career of his hottest property.

Jim liked Shaw, though he never believed him when, together at night, he would tell Jim how much he loved him. For one thing the speeches flowed so easily that even the inexperienced Jim recognized that the actor was play-acting. Nor was Jim disturbed. He was not in love with Shaw, nor did he pretend to be. For one thing, the idea of being in love with a man was both ludicrous and unnatural; at the most a man might find his twin, like Bob, but that was rare and something else again.

One day, Shaw took Jim to the studio. As a rule they never went out in public together, but today Shaw thought it time Jim saw him work.

The studio was an immense enclosure of white sound stages, resembling mammoth garages. As Shaw drove through the studio gate, he was saluted respectfully by the gateman, while a pack of girls gave shrieks of recognition and waved autograph books at him.

Beyond the gate was another world, peopled with costumed extras, executives, technicians, labourers. Twenty films were being made simultaneously. Nothing else on earth mattered here.

They parked in front of a bungalow framed by hibiscus.

'My dressing-room.' Shaw was already beginning to get businesslike. Inside, stretched on a sofa, was a small bald man.

'Baby, you're late. I got here half an hour ago, like we agreed. And so far I've read *Variety*, the *Reporter*, and even the script.'

'I'm sorry, Cy.' Shaw introduced Jim to the man on the sofa. 'Cy's directing my picture.'

'If that's what you can call what I'm doing in this miserable place,' Cy moaned. 'Why did I ever leave New York? Why didn't I stay with the Group Theatre?'

'Because they didn't want you, baby.' Shaw grinned as he shed his jacket.

'There he stands. Pound for pound, the worst actor in America.' Cy turned to Jim. 'All he's got is that adorable smile and those obscene pectorals ... or pector*i*als, as they say out here.'

'Jealous, baby?' Shaw stripped to his shorts and flexed his celebrated pectorals. Cy groaned with disgust and shut his eyes.

'I can't stand it!' He pointed to a door. 'Get your costume on. Make-up's been waiting since seven.'

Shaw stepped into the next room, leaving the door ajar. 'So what's the schedule?'

'A new scene, that's what. The writers were at it all night. They wrote this wonderful new scene on a menu at the Cotton Club. You'll love it.'

'Am I terribly brave?'

'What else? They've given you a stiff upper lip, a tight sphincter ... *everything*.'

'A tight what?'

'I'll say one thing, if they ever educated one of you dopes it'd be the end of the American Dream. You agree, baby?' Cy gave Jim a sharp look.

'Sure,' said Jim.

'Sure,' mimicked Cy. 'What am I doing here?' he asked the ceiling.

'Making fifteen hundred a week,' came Shaw's voice from the next room, 'and that's nothing for a good director, but for you ...'

'Is this my reward for coming here to try and help you with this crucial new scene so that when you face the Big Brownie you'll know what you're doing? Yes, this is my reward, and you'll just wing the words like always, and another money-making bagel will drop into the laps of the American moviegoers. I guess you want to be an actor, too?' Again the sharp eyes turned to Jim.

'Well ...'

'Well, *of course*! Where else in the world can a guy with no brain and no talent get to be rich and famous all because ...'

Shaw entered in full eighteenth-century costume. 'All because I am a Sex Symbol,' he said happily. 'Look at those legs, baby. Drool at the thought.' Shaw patted a muscular thigh with obvious affection. 'That's what they want out there in the dark and I got it.'

'Keep it, please.'

Jim had never seen an actor in full make-up. He was awed by the transformation. This was not the man he knew but someone else, a glamorous stranger. As usual, Shaw was conscious of the effect he was making. He gave Jim a conspiratorial grin.

'What sort of picture is it?' asked Jim.

'Shit,' said Cy quietly.

'Popular entertainment,' said Shaw. 'Which will gross four million domestic. It's a remake of this classic French novel by Dumas *fils*,' he added in a rehearsed voice, suitable for instructing interviewers in the commissary.

'Dumas *fils* was the Ronald Shaw of his day, God help him.' Cy stood up. 'So let's get down to the set. The Bitch Goddess is already there.'

Shaw explained to Jim that the Bitch Goddess was his co-star, a famous lady whose presence in a film guaranteed success. The combination of Shaw and this lady was considered especially potent.

'She hung over?' asked Shaw as they stepped from the bungalow into the main street of the studio.

'At dawn, her eyes were like two rubies,' said Cy, dreamily. 'And her breath was reminiscent of a wind in summer over the Jersey Flats.'

Shaw grimaced. 'We got a love scene?'

'Kind of.' Cy handed him two pages. 'That's it. Straight from the back of the menu of the Cotton Club. You'll love it.'

As they walked, Shaw studied the two pages intently. Jim noticed that all the marvellously dressed people who crowded the studio street stared enviously at Shaw, and Jim took vicarious pride in this attention. Just in front of the sound stage, Shaw handed Cy the script. 'I got it,' he said.

'You mean you learned it, which isn't exactly getting it.'

'Quickest study in the business.' Shaw turned to Jim. 'I've got this photographic memory. I can see the whole page in my head when I'm acting.'

'And that's just about what comes across.' Cy was mocking. 'Shaw even gives you the typos. Remember that time you said, "But where is your husband"?'

'Knock it off,' said Shaw, and all badinage ended as they stepped onto the sound stage where he was in his proper kingdom. The Bitch Goddess, looking extraordinarily beautiful, lay on an incline board in order not to crush her elaborate costume. When she saw Shaw, she shouted in her celebrated hoarse voice, 'Hiya, Butch!'

'You got the new scene?' Shaw was flat.

His co-star held up the pages. 'It's even worse than the old scene.'

'Academy Award time,' said Shaw lightly.

'Academy Award? We'll be lucky not to end up in radio when this turkey hits the nabes.' She threw the script down.

Then Cy came over. 'Ready, folks?' Obediently, they followed him to the centre of the set. He then talked to them in a low voice, rather like a boxing referee before a bout. The rules understood, Cy yelled 'Places!' The extras fell into position, some talking in groups of three or four, some ready to walk slowly from group to group when the action started. A buzzer sounded and Cy shouted, 'Start moving, children! Let it roll!' There was silence on the sound stage. As the camera approached the female star, she turned, smiling; then, seeing Shaw to her left, she looked surprised.

'Why did you come?' Her voice was clear, the question vital.

'You knew I would.' Shaw's voice was resonant and warm. Jim barely recognized it.

'But ... my husband ...'

'I've taken care of him. Get your cloak. Quickly! We must leave tonight for Calais.'

'Cut!' yelled Cy. The room became noisy again. 'Let's take that over again. Shaw, remember to keep your left shoulder down when you walk into range. Darling, try and remember to show surprise when you see him. After all, you think that your husband has had him locked up. O.K. We'll take it again.'

Jim watched them do this scene for several hours. At the end of the day he was no longer interested in acting.

V

December came and Jim found it hard to imagine that it was winter, for the sun continued warm and the trees green. And he was able to play tennis every day. He was beginning to make money and acquire a reputation as a teacher. When a magazine photographer came to take pictures of Shaw's house, he also took pictures of Jim. These were published in a fan magazine. As a result, Jim got many offers to give lessons, which he accepted. Offers of another sort he sternly rejected.

Although Shaw approved of his earning money, he disliked it when Jim left the house. One night when Jim didn't come home until after dinner, Shaw accused him of being ungrateful and thoughtless. They shouted at one another until Jim went to his room, angry at being treated like a possession. It was even worse later when Shaw came to his room to say that he was sorry, and to make love, and to tell Jim how great the love was he had to give but how hopeless it all was, knowing that such deep feeling could never be returned. Jim could not help but think that perhaps Shaw had less to give than he suspected.

As Jim lay very still in the dark, his arm beneath Shaw's head, he wondered if he should at last speak up and say that he wanted to be free to go wherever he pleased and see the people he wanted to see without giving excuses to a lover who was not in love. But Shaw divined his mood.

'I'm sorry I'm so jealous, Jimmy, but I hate to think of your being out with anybody else. I depend a lot on you when I'm tired and want to get away from all these hangers-on. You're different from all the others. You really are. God, I'd love to quit this whole racket one of these days. Get out of this town of fakes and go off somewhere in the country and buy a farm maybe. Then Mamma could come live there with us. Of course we'd have to be a little careful with her around, but we could manage. Yes, I'd like that, wouldn't you?'

Jim moved uneasily in the dark. His arm was beginning to go to sleep beneath Shaw's head: he clenched his fist, trying to restore circulation.

'I don't know, Ronnie. I don't know if I'd like to settle down just yet.'

'Oh.' Shaw's sigh was bitter and stagey. 'You really don't give a damn, do you? It's the same old routine: upward and onward. Whores of the world, unite. Because of me, you can now make a living with those tennis lessons, if that's what they are. So I'm nothing to you.' Shaw moved over to the other side of the bed and Jim was relieved to feel the blood circulating again in his arm.

'That isn't true, Ronnie. I like you a lot but I haven't had an awful lot of experience with this sort of thing before. I'm still pretty new at it' (he had never told Shaw about Bob) 'and I don't think you're being very fair. You can't expect me to give up my whole life when I don't know but what you might find another guy you like more than me, and where'd I be then?'

'What would you do if you did leave me?' Shaw's voice was distant.

'I'd like to start a tennis school, maybe. That's what I'm saving for.' Jim realized that he had said too much: he had not wanted Shaw to know that he was carefully saving money, three thousand dollars so far.

'You're not really planning to leave?' Shaw was plaintive.

'Not until you want me to,' said Jim simply, making up for his blunder.

After breakfast Christmas morning, Shaw telephoned his mother in Baltimore and talked to her for half an hour, regardless of the cost. Then he gave presents in front of the tree. Jim received an expensive Australian tennis racket. Next came dinner at one o'clock, the high point of the day.

Shaw had invited a dozen guests, old friends, men without families who had no place to go at Christmas. Jim knew them all except one, a sandy-haired young man who was talking intensely to Cy. Through the window, Jim caught a glimpse of a palm tree. No, it was not really Christmas, he thought as he said hello to Cy, who looked like a Persian vizier from one of his own pictures. Drunk and merry, he introduced Jim to the sandy-haired man.

'Jim Willard, this is the great Paul Sullivan.' They shook hands and Jim wondered why Paul Sullivan was great. Then he excused himself and helped Shaw serve egg nog. Shaw's face was flushed; he was in a good mood.

'Lovely party, isn't it, Jimmy?'

Jim nodded. 'Who is this guy Sullivan? Should I know who he is?' Shaw was usually careful to let Jim know who people were and what they did so that he could treat them accordingly. That was Hollywood procedure. In the hierarchy of money, each man was treated with the deference his salary called for.

'He's a writer who writes books and he came out here to work with Cy on a picture. He's a real highbrow, which means he's a real pain, always bitching about Hollywood. These guys take the industry's money, then they complain. He's typical.'

At dinner, Shaw carved the turkey. Champagne was served. The guests were happy. And to Jim's inattentive ear, the conversation sounded brilliant. Even though most of it was about movies: who was being signed for what picture, and why.

Sullivan sat beside Jim. He was a quiet man, with dark eyes and a slightly upturned nose. His mouth was too full and his ears were too large. But he was attractive.

'You're a writer, aren't you?' Jim spoke respectfully, wishing to make a good impression.

Sullivan nodded. 'I came out here to work on a picture but . . .' The voice was light and boyish. Deliberately he left the sentence unfinished.

'You don't like working for movies?'

Sullivan glanced at Cy who was sitting across from him. 'No,' he said in a low voice, 'I don't like it at all. Are you in this business?'

Jim shook his head. 'You write books, don't you?'

Sullivan nodded.

'Novels?'

'Novels, poetry. I don't suppose you've read any of them.' This was said sadly, not defensively.

'I don't expect so.' Jim was truthful. 'I don't seem to find time to read.'

'Who does in this damned town?'

'I guess they like their work,' said Jim uncertainly. 'They think about pictures mostly.'

'I know.' Sullivan ate a stalk of celery and Jim watched him, wondering if he liked him. Most of the people who visited Shaw seemed all alike. They said what they thought about everything, including themselves, and usually they liked themselves rather more than other people did. Sexually they were obvious, unlike Sullivan, who appeared perfectly normal.

'Are you from the east?' asked Jim.

Sullivan nodded. 'New Hampshire originally, but I live in New York.'

Then Sullivan asked Jim many questions and Jim answered most of them truthfully. It was a bit like a cross-examination. Jim had never known anyone to ask so many questions. By the time dessert was served Jim had told Sullivan most of the facts of his life. As for Sullivan, he was twenty-eight (Jim thought that was old), married once and divorced, an impressive achievement which explained why he was not like most of the sensitive young men who visited Shaw. Obscurely Jim was glad.

Dinner over, the guests gathered in the drawing-room. As usual, a group gathered about Shaw. But Sullivan was not one of them. He sat alone in a window seat, his large hands playing idly with a silver matchbox. Jim joined him. him.

'A beautiful place,' said Sullivan.

'You mean this house or . . .'

'The whole thing. It's idyllic. Like going to Heaven before your time. Perfect climate, bright colours, fantastic houses. And beautiful people with suntans, white teeth, empty heads.'

'Like me?'

'Yes. No!' Sullivan laughed. Suddenly he was a boy, and Jim was captured. 'Like our host,' said Sullivan. 'I'm sorry. I shouldn't have said that. You live with him, don't you?'

'Yes.'

'Then he must be all right.'

'He is,' said Jim, realizing that he should say more but not able to.

'You give tennis lessons on the side?'

'That's how I make my living.' Jim tried not to sound kept. But it was no use. The thing was plain enough.

'What would you like to do eventually?'

'Set myself up as a teacher. Buy some courts. But that takes money.'

'And *otherwise*, do you know what you want?'

'No,' said Jim accurately. 'I don't know what I want.'

'Neither do I.' Sullivan smiled, reminding Jim of Bob. Then he rose to go.

'Would you like to play tennis sometime?' Jim was bold. They made a date and Sullivan left. Not until then did Jim realize that Shaw had been watching them.

CHAPTER FIVE

I

Jim and Sullivan met every day, unknown to Shaw, who suspected but did not know for certain what was happening. The lovers would meet at Sullivan's hotel each noon, the only time during the day when Sullivan was able to leave the studio lot. Since Jim was usually the first to arrive, he would go straight to the room and wash up after the morning's tennis. Then he would lie on the bed and wait for Sullivan, heart beating fast, surprised to find that he was not only excited by their lovemaking, but also by Sullivan as a person. He was intrigued because Sullivan never mentioned their affair, destroying Jim's theory that all homosexuals talked continually of love, like Shaw. Reticence was a relief, while it lasted. But eventually words became necessary. Sullivan's contract with the studio was ending. Soon he would leave California. That meant they needed to understand one another before plans could be made, *if* plans were to be made.

'How many times have you done this?' Sullivan was abrupt. Jim hesitated, then he told the truth. 'Three times. Three different people.'

Sullivan nodded. 'I thought so.'

'What do you mean?' Flattery or insult?

'Just that you haven't followed the usual pattern. I could tell right off. So could Shaw. I expect that's why he wanted you to live with him.' This was the first time Sullivan had mentioned Shaw.

'So what's the usual pattern?'

Sullivan lay back on the bed, his eyes on the ceiling. 'It starts in school. You're just a little different from the others. Sometimes you're shy and a bit frail; or maybe too precocious, too handsome, an athlete, in love with yourself. Then you start to have erotic dreams about another boy – like yourself – and you get to know him and you try to be his friend and if he's sufficiently ambivalent and you're sufficiently aggressive you'll have a wonderful time experimenting with each other. And so it begins. Then you meet another boy and another and as you grow older, if you have a dominant nature, you become a hunter. If you're passive, you become a wife. If you're noticeably effeminate, you may join a group of others like yourself and accept being marked and known. There are a dozen types and many different patterns but there is almost always the same beginning, not being like the others.'

'I'm pretty ordinary,' said Jim, almost believing himself.

'Are you? Perhaps. Anyway you started late and I don't think you're much involved with others. I don't think you could ever love a man. So I hope you find the right woman for yourself.' Sullivan stopped. Jim did not answer. He had not told Sullivan about Bob, and yet Sullivan had revealed him to himself as just like the others, varying hardly at all from what must be a familiar pattern. With self-knowledge came alarm. If he was really like the others, then what sort of future could he have? Endless drifting, promiscuity, defeat? No. It was not possible. He was different, Bob was different. After all, hadn't he been able to fool everyone, even those like himself, even Sullivan? Deliberately he banished the unsought revelation to that part of his brain where he disposed of unpleasant memories and then, truth disposed of, he found that he was hurt by something Sullivan had said. Was it true that he was so unfeeling in his relationships? Perhaps with Shaw and Sullivan, but not with Bob. Certainly no one had ever felt as desperate and as lonely as he when Bob had left. Yes, he was perfectly capable of love, at least with someone who could be his brother. And though Sullivan was hardly this longed-for twin, at least he was wiser than Shaw and less demanding and Jim felt easy with him, if not candid, and even affectionate.

'I think you're the unluckiest type.' Sullivan rolled over on his stomach and looked at Jim. 'You'll attract everybody, yet you won't be able to do anything about it. Not really. Oh, maybe some day you'll find a woman who'll suit you, but not a man. You're not like the rest of us who want a mirror. It's exciting in a way but it's also sad.'

'I don't know what you mean,' said Jim, who knew exactly but chose to maintain his secret: a memory of a cabin and a brown river. Some day he would relive all that again and the circle of his life would be completed. Meanwhile he would learn about the world and please himself and scrupulously hide his secret from those who wanted him to love.

In February Sullivan's option was not renewed. A few days later, coincidentally, Shaw took a new boy. Jim tried to avoid the obligatory scene of parting, but Shaw had waited two months for this moment and so it was played through to the end.

Knowing what was coming, Jim packed his bags that morning and tried to leave the house but Shaw had insisted that they have a 'last supper' together, with Jim in the role of Judas. So Jim remained.

Shaw was silent during most of dinner, crown of thorns resting heavily on his brow. Not until after coffee did he speak. He started in a low voice, more in sorrow than in anger. 'I suppose you and Sullivan are going to leave town?'

Jim nodded and Shaw smiled gently. 'It's such a shame, Jim. I really was counting on you. I really felt that *this* was the one, the big one that would last. In a funny way, I'm kind of innocent. I thought you were different, and you weren't. Not that I'm blaming you,' he said quickly, eager to seem fair. 'I know it's tough living with somebody like me, and all the people around us trying to break things up. I know, God knows I know, what the temptations are. Only an awfully strong person could resist, a really strong character – or else someone in love. Which you weren't. Not that that was your fault. I don't blame you. How could I?' Not wanting to be interrupted, Shaw was careful to give both sides as he went along. 'After all, love is something which few people are capable of. You were too young. And I should have realized that. You can only love yourself, and now that you've gotten the most out of our relationship, you're ready to move on to this writer, this misfit who's just as incapable of feeling as you. Yes, I've heard a lot of things about Sullivan,' said Shaw darkly. '*You* wouldn't believe what I've heard, of course. You must find them out for yourself. I'm only telling you this now because I'm still very fond of you, in spite of what you've done, and to show you that I'm not bitter. As a matter of fact, I'm happy because I've found Peter, who's coming to live with me.' He paused, ready for the defence. But there was none. Jim stared at him politely, wondering when he could decently go.

Disappointed, Shaw tried walking on water. 'I'm sure Peter can return the affection I give. At least I hope so. My bad luck has *got* to end some day. Oh, I hate to sound as if I'm accusing you, Jim. I'm not. I know how difficult it must have been for you. You never really cared for me, and at least you were honest;

you never *said* you did. But then since you never said you *didn't*, I hoped and even believed sometimes that you did care a little. It's only now that I have Peter that I can regard what we had together, our affair, detachedly and with *complete* understanding. I see that you weren't mature enough, and that's probably my fault for trying to attain the impossible.' Jim recognized this last line from one of Shaw's recent films. Tag-ends of scripts tended to work their way into his conversation.

'I hope,' Shaw continued, turning the other cheek, 'that you will realize these thing about yourself before you hurt Sullivan, too. Yes, I admit I've been hurt, terribly hurt by you, but I don't hold it against you. Which is the one quality I have that you will never find in anyone else. I always forgive. Will Sullivan?' Jim tried to appear interested in this new question, which he knew would soon be answered. It was. 'You see, Paul Sullivan is an unusual person. There's no doubt about that. They got him here for snob appeal, or so they thought. He's an *intellectual*, and I suppose in Greenwich Village the left-wingers think he's wonderful, though he's never written a real bestseller or anything anybody has ever read. I certainly haven't. Not that I have much time for reading but at least I've read all the classics – Walter Scott, Dumas, Margaret Mitchell, all that crowd, and *they* were popular . . .' He stopped, aware that he was making too much of a case for the popular. 'Anyway, it's not important whether he's a good writer or not. The important thing is whether he is capable of feeling, whether he has the maturity to overlook your shortcomings. He was quite cruel to one boy, I'm told. But I'm sure you'll have better luck. I want you to be happy. I really mean it. I do.' Shaw's radiant smile almost disguised the hatred in his eyes.

There was a sound in the hall and a dark-haired youth appeared in the doorway.

Shaw rose from the dead. 'Come in, Peter, and have some coffee. Jim was just saying good-bye.'

II

Sullivan was the first person Jim had ever met who found obscure pleasure in his own pain. Obsessed by failure, professional and private, and unable to relieve himself in scenes like Shaw, Paul's only outlet was to write. Yet even in his work he was so studied and inhibited that all he could ever convey was a light bitterness, a casual anger at a world which, all in all, had done well by him. A doting family, until he ceased to be Catholic at sixteen. There was much argument then, but he would not budge. Even the family priest gave him up at last, perfectly bewildered by this unlooked-for apostasy. None suspected that he had forsaken the Church because he was homosexual. For a long time he had tried to exorcise the unnatural spirit, demanding furiously of God that he be freed of this terrible inclination. He prayed continually. But in the end God failed him, and he turned to Hell. He studied a book of witchcraft, celebrated a Black Mass, tried to sell his soul to the devil in order to be free of lust. But the devil had no use for him either, and so Paul Sullivan abandoned all religion.

For a time Paul was happy. If only in this one act, he had at least demonstrated that he could be free. But his happiness did not last long. At school he fell in love with a young athlete. It was months before he summoned up the nerve to speak to him. During this time he could do nothing more than sit near him in class, watch him play football, and wait. Finally, late one afternoon when everyone else had gone home, they met in front of the school. The boy spoke first. It was easy after that. Though Paul was thin and shy, he had always been accepted as one of the boys. Since he was admired because he was known to read a lot, an athlete would not lose caste by being his friend. So it began. Together they experimented with sex and Paul was as happy as he would ever be again in his life, and perfectly pleased that Heaven and Hell had forsaken him.

But the next year everything changed. The athlete liked girls and they liked him, and so Paul was abandoned and suffered accordingly. He became shyer, more aloof than before. He made no friends. His parents worried about him. His mother was certain that his unhappiness came from the denial of God and Church. He let her believe this, unable to tell her what it was that set him apart from others and made him feel obscurely superior to all the heterosexual world, if only because he had a secret that they could not guess and an insight into life that they did not have. Yet simultaneously he hated himself for needing the body of another man to be complete.

Women were attracted to him, particularly older women; they were kind to him and as a result Paul learned a good deal about women at a time when his contemporaries were learning only about girls' bodies. But this knowledge had its price. Imperceptibly, these amiable companions would begin to presume that conversational intimacy might lead to something else. When that happened, flight was in order.

At seventeen Paul went to Harvard. For the first time in his life he found himself in a tolerant environment. He soon made a number of friends all of whom were going to write books. Spurred by them, he concentrated on writing. When his father suggested that perhaps he should prepare for the Business School, he reacted so strongly that the subject never came up again.

In college Paul wrote his first novel, about a young man who wanted to be a novelist. (Thomas Wolfe was popular that year.) The novel was rejected by every publisher he sent it to. He also wrote poems: several were published in little magazines. Confident that he was a poet, he left Harvard without a degree, went to New York, broke off all communication with his family, did odd jobs and wrote a novel about a bitter young man who did odd jobs in New York. The prose was crude, the politics Marxist, the dislike of Catholicism authentic. The book was published and he found himself with the reputation of a person of promise, living in New York with other persons of promise.

One day, in a spirit of rebellion against his nature, Paul married a girl his own age. The marriage was not consummated. He loathed the bodies of women. He liked their faces but not their bodies. As a child he remembered watching his mother undress and being horrified by her sagging body. Since then all women were associated with his mother, not only taboo but unaesthetic. His wife left him and the marriage was annulled.

Paul had many affairs. Some for physical relief, some as the result of boredom, a few for love or what he thought was love. These all ended badly, he never knew exactly why. Of course the men that he liked were usually simple athletic types, bisexual, who preferred the safety of family life to the edgy pleasures of a homosexual affair, and so he turned to those bars where he could always find a boy who would spend the night with him, in cold blood as it were, through callousness giving him the pain he had come to expect and secretly need. He lived alone and saw few people. He travelled a good deal and he wrote novels. He put everything into his novels. Yet the result was disappointing. His books were praised but not taken seriously. He made enough money to live but he was not a bestseller. He had an honest contempt for the bad novels that sold well and yet he secretly envied their authors, damned by reviewers but wealthy. Nevertheless, he continued to write. There was nothing else to do, no other life for him but the surrogate one of putting words on paper.

As Paul got older, he deliberately opened himself wide to suffering, and he was not disappointed. He even gained strength. But the bitterness never left him, and at heart he remained the same furious boy who had performed the Black Mass. He was secretly convinced that sooner or later the devil would grant him complete and reciprocated love, whether man or woman made no difference. He would exchange his soul for that.

After a time, Paul became so used to his loveless estate that he had to discover new and more subtle tortures for himself. So he decided to follow in the wake of all those legendary damned souls who had deserted their art for a rich suffering among the orange groves of California. After a long negotiation (it is never easy to sell out), a movie studio agreed to give him the price his agent had demanded and he moved to Hollywood, where he was depressed to find that he really rather enjoyed himself. But fortunately he met Jim and found that he was still vulnerable. Their affair looked to be most promising, with endless possibilities of disaster.

After the break with Shaw, Jim and Sullivan went to New Orleans. Here they stayed in a large hotel in the modern part of the city, while they explored the French Quarter with its narrow dirty streets, low buildings, iron galleries, long shuttered windows, and of course a thousand bars and restaurants, particularly along Bourbon Street, which echoed day and night with jazz and blue music, as everyone prowled: men from ships and men from the country, looking for dark, wiry-haired girls who giggled and looked at them impudently and hinted at 'the good time' to come.

In spite of the heat, night in New Orleans was stimulating. So much promise in the air, so much pleasure to be had. One by one, like the Stations of the Cross, Jim and Sullivan visited the bars, listening to Negro singers, observing the men and the whores. It was a pleasant way to pass time, without guilt or any sense of future.

In the mornings Sullivan would work on a novel (a story of unreciprocated love told with light bitterness) and Jim would go sightseeing. In the afternoons they would go to the Y.M.C.A. to swim.

In the evenings they would visit queer bars, pretending to be innocent tourists and fooling no one.

A bar called Chenonceaux particularly intrigued them. On the edge of the Quarter, in a quiet street, it occupied all of an old stone building from whose walls most of the plaster had fallen. At one end of the room a small fire burned on a stone hearth, while candles burned and the jukebox played soft popular songs. The result was so soothing that even the wildest of the patrons tended to behave themselves at the bar, their cries muted, their sibilants hushed, their cruising become demure.

Jim and Sullivan always sat near the fire, where they could watch the men and women come and go, acting out their various rituals of courtship for the benefit of strangers.

As Sullivan watched the menagerie, he would talk in a low voice, saying many things that he would not say in other places, and Jim listened to him, waiting as always to learn something new about himself. But Sullivan spoke only of others.

In March Jim was twenty, and he found himself brooding on the many things he had done and seen since he left Virginia: it was almost as if he had been deliberately courting odd experiences in order to be able to tell of them when he was an old man, sitting in a Virginia store with other old men, none of whom had had so many adventures. Not of course that he would be able to tell everything. At times he wondered if Bob was leading the same sort of life. Was Bob like himself? He hoped not. Yet if they were proper twins, he would have to be the same. It was not easy to sort out. But one day he would know the answer. Now he gave himself up to experience.

Jim's birthday was celebrated at Chenonceaux's by the owner, a fat motherly man who had once been a decorator in New York but was now 'reformed'. Though he knew only their first names, he suspected that they were wealthy or important or both, but he was far too discreet to ask for information which was not volunteered. Besides, these two young men were much admired by the other patrons, and that was good for business.

'Paul, Jimmy, how're you tonight?' He smiled at Jim, his favourite, and Jim smiled back. He liked the owner despite the motherly ways.

'What'll it be?' They ordered beer and he brought it to them himself. Then he sat down at their table.

'What's the gossip?' asked Paul.

'Well, you'd never guess it, but that tall pale boy, you know the one who used to make such eyes at Jim . . . well, he's gone off with a *Negro* truck driver! It's the funniest thing to see those two together. They're quite wrapped up in each other and I understand the Negro beats him regularly. Really, it's the funniest thing!' They agreed that it was indeed funny, and Jim wanted to know if many Negroes were that way; he had always supposed that they were not.

The fat man rolled his eyes. 'Loads of them, literally loads of them! Of course, I expect being a Negro in America is enough to make anyone neurotic. So this added bit, this extra kick, is nothing to be surprised at. Then of course many of them are truly primitive, and primitives don't seem to mind *what* they do if it's fun.'

'We should all be like that,' said Sullivan.

The fat man frowned; thought of any sort was an effort. 'But we have to have *some* conventions, some order, or everyone would be running around wild, committing murder and everything.'

'I meant only the sexual taboos, which shouldn't be the business of the law.'

'Maybe they shouldn't be, but they certainly are! The times I've been picked up by plainclothes-men who made *all* the advances, just awful. Sometimes it costs you a hundred dollars or more to pay off. They're such crooks, especially here.'

'Which is all wrong!' Jim could see that Paul was angry. 'Why should any of us hide? What we do is natural, if not "normal", whatever that is. In any case, what people do together of their own free will is their business and no one else's.'

The fat man smiled. 'But do you have the nerve to tell the world about yourself?'

Paul sighed and looked at his hands. 'No,' he said, 'I don't.'

'So what can we do, if we're all too frightened?'

'Live with dignity, I suppose. And try to learn to love one another, as they say.'

'Fair enough,' said the fat man. 'I have to get back to the bar.' He left them.

'Do you really care?' asked Jim. 'Do you really care that much about the rest of the world?'

Paul shrugged. 'Sometimes, yes. Sometimes I care very much.'

They drank their beer and watched the people.

In many ways, the women were the most pathetic. Particularly one old woman who was known as the Major. Grey hair cut like a man's and dressed in a skirted suit with a sombre tie, she made a great fuss over the pretty girls, particularly the ones who were shy and clinging.

'There,' said Jim, motioning to the Major, 'there's somebody honest. You want to be like that?'

'That isn't what I meant. I just want a little simple honesty, and acceptance. Why anyone is anything is a mystery, and not the business of the law.'

Jim changed the subject. 'How long do you want to stay in New Orleans?'

'Why? Are you bored?'

'No, but I've got to go to work one of these days . . . that tennis deal, I told you about it before.'

'Relax. You've got a lot of years to do all that in. Save your money. Have a good time. Wait.'

Jim was relieved that neither he nor Sullivan pretended they were going to live together for ever. But it did not occur to him how much it hurt Sullivan, who was almost in love, to be so casual. Since they did not understand one another, each was able to sustain an illusion about the other, which was the usual beginning of love, if not truth. They were joined by a handsome blonde lesbian girl who looked not unlike the Apollo Belvedere, reproduced in plaster. She was much in demand.

'Hiya, boys! Got a drink for your best girl?' They had the drink.

III

The days passed quickly and Jim enjoyed living without purpose. He was happy to get up in the morning; he was happy to go to bed at night with the thought of a new day to look forward to. He knew his life was aimless, and he could not have been more content.

Suddenly the war in Europe occupied even the attention of the people in Chenonceaux's bar. They discussed whether or not Britain would be invaded and it seemed that everyone had some sentimental reminiscence about Stratford or Marble Arch or the guardsmen in Knightsbridge. Rather self-consciously, people became absorbed by the bit of history through which their century was passing.

By the end of May, New Orleans had begun to bore them. Jim spoke of going to New York to work, while Paul thought they should go to South America; but he was not insistent: he merely indicated that he would like to continue with Jim for a while longer. Then, unexpectedly, their course was set for them.

One night at the Chenonceaux, while talking to the owner, Jim saw a woman enter the bar, quite alone. She was dark, exotic, well dressed, impossible to classify. Diffidently she ordered a drink. She attracted the owner's attention. 'Oh, dear!' he looked distraught, 'this one's come to the wrong bar. I can tell a mile off!' He got to his feet. 'We'll lose our reputation, if civilians start coming here.' He crossed to the bar, scowling. Then Sullivan recognized the woman at the same time she recognized him.

'Paul!' she exclaimed, and she took her drink from the bar and joined them. Whoever she was, Paul was delighted to see her. When he introduced her to Jim, she gave him a genuine smile, showing interest but not curiosity, for which he was grateful.

Jim watched her face as she talked, thin eyebrows arched naturally, hazel eyes, dark hair. Slim with an unobtrusive figure, she moved like a dancer.

She spoke of Amelia, Sullivan's ex-wife. 'Where is she now?' asked Paul.

'Still in New York, I think.' Maria's accent was all her own, delicate and evocative.

'Do you think she'll get married again?'

'I doubt it. But who knows? She works for a magazine. I saw her just a week ago. She's now developed a large . . . *world*-consciousness. She's interested in nothing so small as the marriage of two human beings. She thinks only of the masses and the spirit of history. At the moment she is violently against the Russians because they are pro-Hitler. Ten months ago she was a Stalinist. I'm afraid she's abandoned all thought of a private life. She is entirely public, and most formidable.'

Jim listened with interest. Sullivan seldom mentioned his brief career as a married man. 'Poor Amelia,' said Sullivan finally, 'she hasn't had a very happy time of it. Is she making money?'

Maria nodded. 'I should think so. In that world she's quite well thought of.'

'What have *you* been doing, Maria?'

She laughed. 'Nothing, as always. But it keeps me busy. I was in France until the war started and I came back to New York, where I was very proper.'

'Do you ever hear from Verlaine?'

She frowned slightly and made sketches on the table with her long fingers. 'He's in the Army, I understand. No, I haven't heard anything from him. I haven't seen him in years.'

'Are you painting still?'

'No,' she said. 'How was Hollywood?'

Paul grinned. 'It was perfect, until they asked me to write something for them and then of course I had to go.'

Maria laughed. 'Still Don Quixote?'

'I'm afraid so.' Sullivan was obviously delighted at being thought impractical yet pure of heart.

They were silent. Jim studied the smooth, well-cared-for face of Maria Verlaine, aware that the more he looked at her the more beautiful she became. Finally Sullivan asked her what she was doing in New Orleans.

'I'm *en route*.'

'To any place, or just in general?'

'In general. But most immediately to Yucatán.'

'What a curious place.'

'I have a reason. My father died last winter and left me a plantation where they grow whatever it is you make rope out of. Now I have an offer to sell the place. They need me there.'

'Is it civilized?'

'No, but it's near Mérida, which is a proper city.'

Sullivan turned to Jim and saw that he was looking at Maria Verlaine. He frowned, but neither noticed. 'And you,' Maria asked, 'are you *en route?*'

Sullivan shrugged. 'No destination that I know of. Jim and I just drift.'

'I see.' And it seemed that she did. Then: 'Why don't you drift with me. They say Mérida's fascinating, full of ruins, and if sightseeing gets dull, you can always fly up to Mexico City. Oh, do say you'll come! It will save my life.' And so it was decided that they would travel together.

In their hotel room Jim asked Sullivan about Maria. Sullivan was unusually communicative. 'She was married to a Frenchman, a bit of a gigolo. They were divorced. She's had a number of affairs, usually with artists, always doomed. Of course she's the Isolde sort. Also, she's attracted to difficult men, particularly homosexuals, and they usually find her attractive, too. Don't you? I do, I even went to bed with her years ago.'

Jim wondered if this was true. 'She seems very nice,' he said cautiously.

'You'll like her. That's a promise.' They got into bed. Sullivan was enormously pleased with himself. He had now endangered his affair with Jim. He had deliberately brought him into contact with the one woman who might appeal to him. There was now an excellent chance that he would lose Jim, and the thought gave him a profound and bitter pleasure. He would suffer. He would know pain. With infinite care and patience, he set about destroying his own happiness.

CHAPTER SIX

I

Yucatán is a flat land of low scrub jungle and sisal fields. The capital city of Mérida is close to the Gulf of Mexico. Sisal plantations surround the city and, from the air, travellers can see the white pyramids of Chichen Itzá and Uxmal, the ancient Mayan cities. So much for the guide-book.

As they drove from the airport to a hotel in the centre of town, the driver pointed out the cathedral, a baroque church with many cracks in its stucco walls, overlooking a great plaza filled with shade trees. Here the natives sat on stone benches, small and brown with faces more Indian than Spanish. Ragged boys scurried about, shining shoes and playing games with tops.

Once a private house, the hotel was a large square pink building whose interior smelled like the inside of an ancient cigar box, musty and stale. A tall bandit with a thick moustache welcomed them. He was the manager and had known Maria Verlaine's father. He treated them like royalty as he showed them their rooms.

Jim and Sullivan were given a three-room suite decorated in French provincial bordello, with a smoky glass chandelier, a tile floor and two great beds shrouded in mosquito netting. 'You will like, yes?' Yes, they would like. And they did. Jim even got used to sleeping in the middle of the day. As for Maria, she was at last removed from a world that had come to bore her; also, she enjoyed being with Jim, aware that a flirtation was now inevitable. He in turn was attracted to her but he was not sure in what way. The game was new to him. He had to learn the rules as he went along. Meanwhile the opening moves had been made.

Sullivan knew with a curious prescience exactly what would happen. He was like God. He had arranged a set of circumstances, and now all that he needed to do was to wait for the expected climax.

After the first week of sightseeing, they did not go about much in the town. Men would come in the morning to talk business with Maria. Sullivan would read and Jim would go swimming at the mineral baths. Nothing more strenuous was possible, the heat was too enervating.

Then Sullivan began to drink heavily. Jim was shocked. Sullivan had seldom drunk before. Now he drank steadily through the day so that by dinner time he was ready for bed. Politely if shakily, he would excuse himself, insisting that Jim stay with Maria and keep her company.

One evening after Sullivan had gone to bed, Jim and Maria sat down together in the patio. A crescent moon shone white and clear in the black night, and a breeze rustled the fronds of the palm trees.

'I know how difficult it is.' Maria guessed his mood. 'Paul's a strange man, so bitter about everything. Everyone. When you praise another writer, it hurts him, even if you're praising Shakespeare. If you say you like people with dark hair, he'll be hurt because his hair isn't dark. And now he has turned completely away from people. I don't know why. In the old days he was different. He was more . . . alive. He felt that he had been given great insight, greater than anyone else's, and he regarded it as a sacred gift, which it is, though perhaps the gift was never so great as he thought.'

'But he's very good, isn't he?' Jim wanted to know.

'Yes,' said Maria quickly, 'he's very good. But not good enough. Not as good as he wanted to be. I think that hurts him.'

'Is it so important, being a great writer?'

She smiled. 'It's important to those who think it's important, who've given up everything to be great.'

'Has Paul given up so much?'

'Who can tell? Is he capable of love?'

The question was direct, and Jim blushed. 'I . . . I don't know. I think so.' But Jim was not at all certain that he knew what love was. He assumed that it must be something like what he felt for Bob, an emotion which, as he grew older, became even stronger, as though absence in some way preserved it pure. Also, what he felt had the virtue of being unstated, a secret all his own. He smiled, thinking of this, and Maria said, 'What amuses you?'

'I was just thinking how far I am from Virginia, from the town I was raised in. I was thinking how different my life is from all the rest of them back there.'

She misunderstood. 'Do you mind it very much, being different?'

It was the first time she had made direct reference to the affair with Sullivan, and he hated her for mentioning it, furious at being marked. 'I'm not as different as all that.'

'I'm sorry.' Aware of her mistake, she touched his arm. 'I was clumsy.'

Jim forgave her, but not completely. Obscurely, he wanted to hurt her, to throw her on a bed and take her violently against her will, to convince himself and her and everyone that he was not like the others. A pulse beat in his throat. He was afraid, even as they talked lightly of other matters.

Sullivan was reading when Jim came upstairs. He looked a ghostly figure beneath the mosquito netting. 'Have a nice time?'

'What do you mean by that?' Jim was ready for battle.

'With Maria, you know what I mean. She's attractive, isn't she?'

'Sure. Sure.' Jim let his clothes drop to the floor; the night was hot; he was suddenly weary.

'Wait till you know her better. She's a marvellous lover.'

'Shut up.'

'Just wait. That's all. Just wait.' He grinned drunkenly. Jim cursed him. Then he turned out the lights and got into his own bed. It was several hours before he could sleep.

II

Maria Verlaine was a curious woman, subtle, not easily apprehended. At forty she seemed a girl, slender, expectant, dreamy, her whole life devoted to that desire and pursuit of the whole which obsesses the romantic and confounds the rest. She moved from affair to affair, drawn to the sensitive, the delicate, the impossible. Her imagination could transform the most ordinary of men into dream lovers, if the occasion were right and his response sufficient. But in time imagination flagged. Reality intruded and the affair would end, usually in flight. Yet she continued like some gallant warrior committed to a losing cause; after all, her favourite legend was that of Don Quixote and the impossible quest. Believing this, she had made it her life. But as time passed, she found herself drifting more and more towards men younger than herself, to youths whose delicacy was almost feminine. Adolescents could often give gentleness for gentleness, heightened awareness for heightened awareness, and of course they too believed in love. But she usually stopped short of homosexuals. She had lived too long in Europe. Too many of her contemporaries had been captured by the league of dressmakers and decorators, and she had vowed that she would not be trapped by them, though they amused her, made her laugh, treated her as confidante. Yet out of kindness, not malice, they tried to unsex her and make her one of them. Fortunately, she had a genius for flight. She knew when to leave without inflicting pain. So they allowed her a temporary visa in their world, and she enjoyed being a tourist.

Now she was attracted to Jim. He was exotic to her. Never before had she been attracted to an ordinary man, much less a boy. Aesthetically he pleased her. She had always been drawn to the Nordic gods. Blue eyes, blond hair, pale skin intrigued her. Did they feel anything at all, these silvery northerners? Were they quite human? But more to the point, he touched her. He was so completely locked in himself, inarticulate, without means of communication, with nothing to offer but his body, which he used almost as a sacrifice to propitiate some dangerous god. She wanted him. If there was some silver Nordic mystery, she wanted to partake of it. She hesitated only because of Paul. At a signal from him she would withdraw. But the signal never came, and she took this to mean complaisance.

One afternoon she drove with Jim in a horse-drawn carriage to a pool where they often swam. Sullivan had stayed at the hotel.

'How long do you think it'll be before your business is done?' asked Jim.

'I don't know. I really don't know. They're so slow here. In a few weeks, perhaps. You must be terribly bored.'

'No, I'm not bored. Not yet, anyway. I even like hot weather. But I want to go to New York before the fall.'

'And start playing tennis again?'

'Yes. I like to work.'

'Will you live in New York with Paul?' The question was asked.

Jim paused. 'Maybe. But I'm on my own.' The question was answered.

'What did you do in Hollywood?'

'Taught tennis. Not much.'

'Hollywood must be interesting. I've never been there for very long. Did you know . . .' She mentioned names and he answered 'yes' or 'no'. Then, subtly, she asked names of homosexual figures; he answered 'yes' to many of them. They talked, finally, of Shaw.

'I met him once in New York. I thought he was a vain little man.'

'He's not so bad when you know him.' Jim was loyal. 'He isn't very happy, God knows why. He has everything.'

'Except what he wants.'

'I don't think he knows what he wants, like the rest of us.'

Maria was amused: she had underrated Jim. 'I expect you're right. Not many people know. And even when they do, it's not easy finding it.'

'I think I'd like money,' said Jim. 'Enough to live anyway.'

'Is that all?'

'Well, there's one other thing.'

'And that?'

'Is my secret.' He laughed.

The summer passed. Maria's business was done but they did not leave. Sullivan drank. Jim swam with Maria and looked at ruins. The heat was almost palpable. To cross a street left one wet with perspiration. But they remained, and no one spoke of leaving, not even Jim.

All three were waiting.

One day they visited the ruins of Chichen Itzá and stayed overnight in the adjacent inn, where they were picked up by a couple from Seattle named Johnson. The Johnsons were young, lively and innocent. Mrs Johnson ('I read everything') was thrilled to meet Sullivan. Actually, she had read only one of his books and had forgotten what it was about. Even so, she was excited at meeting a genuine author.

That night, after dinner, they sat outside among the palm trees and Mrs Johnson did most of the talking. They were all pleasantly drowsy. Maria sat with her hands folded in her lap, looking at the ruins in the distance: pyramids and square ornate buildings monstrous by starlight. Jim tried to hide his yawns. He wanted to go to bed. Sullivan drank tequila and Mrs Johnson's praise.

'I really do envy you writers. You have such a good time going around from place to place. You know, I used to think I'd be a writer. You know, somebody like Fannie Hurst. But I guess I had more important things to do.' She looked fondly at her husband.

'Yes,' said Sullivan. 'I'm sure you did.'

'Are you married, Mr Sullivan? if you'll excuse me being personal.'

'I'm divorced.'

'Oh, now that's a pity. This may surprise you, but I didn't really *live* until George and I were married. But I expect you'll be getting married again, Mr Sullivan. I mean a distinguished man like yourself and still young . . .'

'I don't think so.'

'That's what they all say!' Mrs Johnson chattered gaily about marriage and its heady pleasures.

Jim always felt oddly superior when he was with normal people who assumed that everybody shared their tastes. If they only knew, he thought, smiling to himself in the dark. He glanced at Maria and saw that she was sitting still as the statue they had seen that day among the ruins, a goddess with a skull mask. Paul had laughed when he saw the stone figure; he found it significant that the only goddess in the Mayan hierarchy was Death.

'Are you a writer, too, Mrs Verlaine?' The Johnsons had decided that these three people were a bit unusual, travelling together, but that they were probably *all right*. If they weren't all right, then it was even more interesting.

'No,' said Maria. 'I am nothing.'

'Oh.' Mrs Johnson turned to Jim, but then decided not to question him; he looked too young to have done anything worth talking about.

'Don't you find the Indians here absolutely charming, Mr Sullivan?'

'In what way?'

'Well, they're so basic and yet . . . inscrutable. I think they're probably quite happy even if they are poor. Certainly it'd be a mistake to educate them. They'd just be miserable, that's all.' She talked a while about Indians. Then, inevitably, they spoke of the movies.

Mrs Johnson saw almost as many movies as she read books. She was happiest when she was seeing a movie made from a book that she had read. She always remembered every character and she disliked unfaithful representations. 'Of course my favourite actor is Ronald Shaw. He's so *forceful*. I happened to be reading in a movie magazine – I see them at the hairdresser, they always seem to have them – and I read where he was going to marry that Spanish actress Carlotta Repollo who is years older than he is. Such a pity, don't you think?'

Sullivan glanced at Jim, who blushed. Maria was also amused. Three people in disguise were performing a play for an audience that could never know or appreciate the quality of the performance.

'I should like to see the ruins,' said Maria suddenly.

'By starlight?' Sullivan was mocking. 'Well, why not? You take her, Jim.'

'Well . . .' he looked at Maria.

'I think we should all go,' she said.

'No. You two go. You're the romantic ones.'

The Johnsons looked at the trio, aware of undertones. Then Maria left the table and Jim followed her. They walked out of the small square of electric light and into the darkness. The starlight made no shadows in the cool night. Like disembodied spirits, they walked down an avenue of cropped grass and then, at the same instant, without words, they sat down side by side on the shattered stone remains of a forgotten god.

Jim looked up at the stars, brilliant and white in the black sky. He breathed deeply. There was the scent of sage in the air as well as the dry odour of sunburned stone.

He turned to Maria and saw that she was waiting. He was surprised that he was not afraid.

'One feels dead here.' Her voice was distant and remote among the ruins.

'Dead?'

'In a peaceful way. All things finished, inevitable, like one of these stones: there is to be nothing else.'

'*If* death is like that.'

'It must be.'

They did not speak for a long while. At last Maria spoke. 'We've been play-acting.'

'Yes.'

'And dishonest.'

'With Paul?'

'With Paul. Ourselves.' She sighed. 'I wish I knew more about people. I wish I could understand why things are as they are.'

'Nobody knows.' Jim was amazed to find himself playing at wisdom. 'I don't know why I do what I do or even who I am.'

'I don't know who you are either.' They looked at one another, faces white and indistinct.

'Myself. That's all. Limited.'

'Limited? Not really. Actually you're everything, man, woman and child. You can be whatever you choose.'

'What am I now?'

'Until a few moments ago a child.'

'What am I now?'

'I don't know.'

He began to tremble; he began to hope. Perhaps it could happen.

'Are you afraid?'

'No. Not afraid.' Nor was he at that moment.

'Could you kiss me?'

'I could kiss you,' he said, and he did. He kissed the Death Goddess.

Everything was different afterwards; different and yet the same, for nothing finally happened. Jim failed. He could not perform the act. He was inadequate. Yet in its way his relationship with Maria was a love affair. They were with each other as much as possible. They were confidantes. Yet when it came to physical contact, except for that first kiss, Jim could not bear the softness and smoothness of a woman. Maria was baffled. Because he was both masculine and drawn to her, she found his failure all the more mysterious. There seemed nothing to be done except to continue as lovers who never touched. Sullivan, however, accepted the surface affair for an actual one, and the agony it gave him was exquisite.

November came and still they did not move from Mérida.

Jim and Maria were together most of the time. Sullivan refused to join them during the day. He had begun to drink after breakfast; by early evening he was often vivacious and amusing but by the end of dinner he was inevitably heavy and bitter. Their lives stopped until December when the United States went to war with Japan, and they were once more part of the world. Sullivan stopped drinking. Plans were made as they sat in the patio after dinner. Both Sullivan and Jim were excited, brought to life. Maria was sad. 'I don't like to think about it,' she said. 'All my life there has been a war, just begun, just finished. There seems to be no escape.'

Sullivan paused in a nervous turn about the patio. 'We'll have to go back,' he said to Jim.

Jim nodded, caught up in the drama of new things. 'I want to enlist before I'm drafted,' he said, pleased at the words if not the thought.

'It's so senseless.' Maria was vehement. 'If I were a man I'd run away, hide, desert, turn traitor.'

Sullivan smiled. 'Five years ago I would have done just that.'

'Why not now?'

'Because this is . . . something to do.'

She turned to Jim. 'Do you feel the same?'

'It solves a lot of things.'

'Perhaps.' She seemed unconvinced.

'We should go back as soon as possible,' said Sullivan.

'What will you do?' asked Maria.

'Be a soldier. Or a correspondent. Whatever I can get.'

'It looks,' said Maria, 'as if our Mexican vacation is at an end. I've enjoyed it.'

'So have I.' Jim looked at her and felt a sudden warmth; threat of war and parting drew him closer to her.

'And so have I.' Sullivan's voice mocked them. 'I've enjoyed every minute of it. We've made an interesting trio, haven't we?'

'Have we?' Maria was bleak.

It was decided that they return to the States by way of Guatemala City.

They rode comfortably above clouds, mountains, dark green jungle. It was pleasant to sail over the hot steaming land as though they were no longer earth creatures but something more than human, elemental, with no difficulties that could not be overcome by rigid silver wings.

Jim had bright visions of himself in the Air Corps, flying across continents and oceans, able to move rapidly over the earth and leave no scar. He longed for flight.

Guatemala City was a relief after Yucatán. The city was cool with streets which looked as if they had been recently scrubbed. The people were cheerful, the air good. And wherever one looked, volcanoes loomed, sharp, veined blue with shadow, topped by rain clouds.

At the hotel, Sullivan sent cables to various newspaper friends who might help him to get an assignment as war correspondent. Then, communication with the real world established, Jim and Sullivan went to their room.

'It's almost over.' Sullivan stood at the window, looking at mountains. Jim unpacked.

'The trip?'

'The trip, of course.'

'Yes,' said Jim, who knew what he meant. 'I guess we'll split up when we get to New York.'

Sullivan smiled. 'I doubt if the Army would send us to war together.'

'Everything ends. I wonder why.'

'Don't you know?' Sullivan was scornful. 'Don't you know?'

'Do you?'

'Certainly. When you fall in love with someone else, that automatically ends the original affair, doesn't it?'

'You mean Maria?'

'Yes, I mean Maria.'

'It's . . . a very complicated business, Paul. It's not what it seems to be.' But Jim failed to tell the whole truth; it was too humiliating.

Fortunately Sullivan was not interested in facts; his intuition was quite enough; whatever the details were, the result was bound to be the same. 'Anyway, I knew all along that this would happen. I let it happen.'

'Why?'

But Sullivan could never admit to anyone why he was driven to behave as he did. 'Because,' he said, and he knew he was not convincing, 'I thought it would be the best thing that could happen to you. She's a wonderful woman. She can get you out of this world.'

'Why should I get out?' For the first time Jim admitted what he was.

'Because you're never going to fit into this sort of relationship, and so the sooner you find your way to something else the better it'll be for you.'

'Maybe.' Jim looked at Paul. The dark circles had gone from beneath his eyes. He was still attractive to Jim, even now, when everything was over. They spoke kindly to one another. Yet finally, each was so perfectly dishonest that neither was able to feel the slightest regret at what was ending.

On the last night they dined in a restaurant particularly recommended for those who wanted native food without diarrhoea. Walls bright with primitive scenes of volcanoes, conquistadores, flowers, lakes. Rooms loud with the noise of a small marimba band. Tourist couples danced.

All during dinner Jim felt reckless and glad, like a child let out of school.

They drank Chilean wine and even Maria was gay. But towards the end of dinner when the music grew sad and sentimental and they had all drunk too much white wine, they became sad and sentimental, too. But it was the sort of sadness that is closely related to happiness. Each was now secure in his own failure. Doubt was gone. Boundaries had been drawn and accepted.

'It's too sad,' said Maria as the band rattled 'La Paloma'. 'We've lived such a long time together. And played so many games.'

'True.' Sullivan was moody. 'But it's also a relief to have things end.'

'Some things.' Maria twirled her wine-glass in her hands. 'I think love is always a tragic thing, for everyone, always.'

'But that's what makes life interesting. How can we value anything until it's gone?'

'No light without dark?'

'Yes. And no pain without pleasure.'

'What a curious way to put it.' She looked at him, almost aware of his secret.

'Even so,' he said quickly, 'there are other things in life than being in love. Look at Jim. He's never in love, are you?'

'Of course I am. With what I want.' Jim thought of Bob.

Maria was puzzled. 'What do you want?'

Sullivan answered for him. 'What he cannot have, like the rest of us.' He turned to Maria. 'Have *you* ever found what you wanted?'

'For a time, certainly.'

'But not for long.'

'No, not for long. I've failed, like everyone else.'

'Why?'

'I suppose I may want more than any man cares to give. And sometimes I give more than any man wants to take.'

'Shaw was like that,' said Jim suddenly. 'I mean he *thought* he was that way.'

'Shaw was an idiot,' said Sullivan.

'We all are,' said Maria sadly, 'at the end.'

They were silent. The marimba clattered in the room. They drank more wine. At last Sullivan got up and went to the men's room. For the first time since they had come to Guatemala, Jim was alone with Maria. She turned to him. 'I'm leaving tomorrow.'

'You're not coming with us?'

'No. I'm not strong enough. You know, sometimes I believe that there *is* a God, a vindictive self-righteous God who punishes happiness. I was happy with you when I thought . . .' She could not finish. 'Anyway, it will be years before you can love a woman. I haven't the time to wait.'

'But you know how I feel about you.'

'Yes,' she said, and there was no more emotion in her voice. 'I know how you feel.' She stood up. 'I'm going back to the hotel.'

He stood up too. 'Will I see you before you go?'

'No.'

'In New York?'

'Perhaps.'

'I'll be able to see you then. I'll want to see you. I don't want to lose you, too.'

'When I'm happier, we'll see each other. Good night, Jim.'

'Good night, Maria.' She left the restaurant quickly, the black lace of her dress rustling about her legs.

Sullivan came back. 'Where's Maria?'

'She's gone to the hotel. She was tired.'

'Oh? Well, let's have another drink.' They drank.

Though sad, Jim was relieved to have a temporary end to emotion. He had been exhausted by these two people, taken out of his depth. Now he looked forward to freedom. Released by the fact of war, he would soon be resolved by action. He could not wait for his own life to begin.

CHAPTER SEVEN

I

Jim and Sullivan arrived in New York in mid-December. Almost immediately Sullivan obtained a job with a news syndicate, while Jim enlisted in the Army. Neither saw Maria Verlaine; she had disappeared.

Jim went first to a reception centre in Maryland where he was put to work tending fires while the Army decided what to do with him. Bad weather and petty tyranny kept him so angry that he had no time for self-pity, as he moved stolidly through the black days, acknowledging the existence of no one else.

Waking up late one afternoon, after an all-night vigil at the coal furnaces. Jim wandered into the recreation room of the Company barracks. A dozen new soldiers watched the afternoon pool game, played by two members of the permanent Company. Lonely, Jim decided to break his long silence. He turned to the soldier next to him, a man of forty, hopelessly civilian, with a small moustache and sad eyes.

'How long you been here?' asked Jim.

The man looked at him, gratefully, a little surprised. 'Why, almost a month.' The voice was educated, unlike the guttural barks of so many of the new soldiers, recruited from slums and deep country. 'And you?'

'Two weeks. I enlisted in New York. Where are you from?'

'Ann Arbor, Michigan. I was with the University.'

Jim was impressed. 'A teacher?'

The man nodded. 'Professor of history, associate professor.'

'Then what're you doing here? I thought people like you got to be Majors.'

The professor laughed nervously. 'So did I. But I was wrong. In the age of Demos, only yokels like our First Sergeant rise to the top.'

'Did you enlist?'

'Yes. I'm married, have two children, but I enlisted.'

'Why?'

'I had some strange idea that I'd be useful.'

For the first time since Jim had enlisted he was able to feel sorry for someone else. He was pleased at this manifestation of good character. 'Rough deal,' he said. 'What do you think they're going to do with you?'

'Classify me as a clerk. That seems to be my fate.'

'Won't you get to be an officer?'

'Perhaps. I have friends in Washington. But I seem to've lost all faith in this business. Of course things were even worse in the Army of the Potomac. The Civil War,' he added apologetically.

'Worse in combat now, too.' They had all heard horror stories about the Philippines, where American troops had been so badly defeated.

'Perhaps,' said the professor, 'but I find it hard to believe. This seems like hell, in a way, or a nightmare with no way out of it. We are governed by madmen.'

Two large red-faced country boys approached. They were clumsy and good-humoured. 'Hey there, Professor, you look like you shot your wad. They gettin' you down?'

'Hello, boys. No, they haven't got me down just yet. I'm simply converting from peace to war at my own slow pace.'

One of the boys made a joke about the word 'peace' and the professor laughed as loudly as they did, eager to be their butt. Jim was sad to see him play the buffoon. It was important to remain oneself. Even though he could not acknowledge what he was, he refused to pretend that he was just like everyone else. It hurt him now to see another man sacrifice his pride, particularly when it was not necessary.

The professor kept the red-faced boys laughing by telling them funny stories about his trials on twenty-four-hour K.P. They occasionally glanced at Jim to see if he was laughing. But he did not respond and they disapproved. Fortunately, he was larger than they.

The First Sergeant, a short man of fifty, came into the room and there was silence except for the click of billiard balls. 'I want two men,' he said. 'I want two volunteers to clean out the goddam latrine. Some son of a bitch fouled it up and I want two men.' Suddenly he swooped down on Jim and the professor. 'You two,' he said.

'Certainly, Sergeant,' said the professor, jumping to his feet. 'Always happy to volunteer!'

It took them two hours to clean the latrine, during which time Jim learned a good deal about American history and the tyranny of democratic armies.

II

In February Jim was transferred to Georgia. For the next three months he was busy with his basic training. The physical side of Army life appealed to him; he enjoyed being active, although the minor humiliations continued to annoy him.

In May he was sent to the Air Corps as a general duty man (the usual classification for the unskilled), and shipped out to an air-base in Colorado, where he was assigned to the headquarters of a Wing which in turn was part of a Command which in turn was part of the Second Air Force, devoted largely to training pilots and bombardiers. Of the two hundred men in his unit, most were headquarters personnel. Older than the average soldier, those of non-commissioned rank usually lived off the post with their wives in Colorado Springs.

Jim and his fellow infantrymen were received by the First Sergeant, a tall emaciated man who had once been a salesman of household appliances.

'You're in the Air Corps now.' He tried to sound ominous. 'You may have heard stories that we aren't as tough as some branches, but that's just a crock. You hear me? You hear what I say? We got discipline here, a lot of it. Because this is a pretty important headquarters, and don't ever forget it. We got a tough General. So you keep on the line and do your job and you'll be O.K.'

But the Air Corps was by no means as tough as the infantry. Discipline was spasmodic. The clerks were just like clerks anywhere and Jim was contemptuous of them. Though the wooden tar-papered barracks were gloomy and the food was bad, the life was not unpleasant. For the first months he and the other infantrymen did not associate with the Air Corps clerks; they kept their identity proudly, but inevitably they were absorbed.

One day was very like another. In the early morning a record of reveille was played over the loudspeaker. As the men yawned and swore, the First Sergeant charged through the barracks, bellowing at those still asleep. Then they ran through the icy air to the latrine twenty yards away: then came breakfast in the mess hall. Jim downed the greasy food perfunctorily, unaware of what he was eating. Afterwards the First Sergeant would have a number of jobs for the general duty men to do. The work was often hard – building barracks, loading garbage trucks, repairing runways. Hard work but not much of it. Jim often had whole days to himself when he would go down to the long runways and watch the B–17s and the B–24s take off and land. The bomber crews were obviously fascinated by what they were doing, unlike the rest of the men, who were listlessly engaged in pointless tasks. Jim was particularly struck by one of the pilots, a roaring boy with blond hair who was particularly popular with the ground crews. He sang popular songs in a loud toneless voice, indulged in horseplay and generally gave pleasure. Once Jim found himself face to face with him. Jim saluted but the pilot only grinned and clapped him on the shoulder and said, 'Hi!' One boy to another. Jim was dazzled. And that was all. Rank separated them. It was sad.

Jim made no friends. He avoided the nightly bull sessions in the barracks. Instead he saw movies and read books, among them a novel by Sullivan which seemed to him to be the work of a perfect stranger; no doubt it was. Occasionally he visited Colorado Springs, where he was very much aware of those alert-looking soldiers, for ever searching for a response. But Jim ignored them; he had no interest in sex.

Eventually Jim was reclassified. One of the Personnel Officers, noting that he had been a tennis instructor, put him in Special Services as a physical-training coach. His life improved. He got along well with Captain Banks, the Special Services officer, a football player who had been a pilot, grounded for reasons of health. Captain Banks moved dreamily about his office, signing necessary papers, unaware of what he was doing. Like so many base officers, he had abdicated all authority to his Sergeant.

Sergeant Kervinski was a slim dark man who wore a large diamond ring on his little finger and talked quickly, blushing often. His delight when Jim was added to the section was plain even to an innocent eye. Trouble ahead, thought Jim.

The Special Services detachment consisted of those who ran the Post Theatre and Library, staged plays and radio programmes, edited a newspaper. Along with these mercurial types there were a half-dozen quiet youths who were physical-training instructors. But since all efforts at group discipline were invariably sabotaged by the clerks, Jim had a very easy time of it. Hardly anyone reported for callisthenics, and the instructors had the gymnasium to themselves, which suited them well since they were all dedicated body-builders.

Agreeable though the life was, Jim longed to be sent overseas, even though he knew that in modern armies there is seldom much action except for line troops and combat pilots. Nevertheless, he was excited by the thought of danger. He wanted release. A few of the general duty men longed for the same thing. They too hated routine and inactivity, but they were not in the majority. Each headquarters clerk had at least one officer friend pledged to keep him from being sent overseas or, if sent, shipped to a reasonably safe place like England. The clerks were not heroes and they were honest about it. Only Sergeant Kervinski was different. It was his dream to be sent to a languorous island of white beaches and no women. When Jim asked to be put on the first overseas shipment list, Kervinski told him of this Paradise, adding, 'I know what you mean, honestly I do, and I'll put you on the list. Perhaps we'll ship out together, to the South Seas. Come on, let's go to supper.'

They stood in line together to collect the usual heavy food. Then they sat down at one of the long wooden mess tables. A calendar with a picture of a heavy-breasted woman hung just above Kervinski's head. He glanced at it with distaste. Then he turned to Jim and made an exploratory move. 'Some woman!'

'Some woman,' Jim repeated flatly.

'I guess you never had the time to get yourself a woman, a wife,' said Kervinski brightly. 'I mean with your travelling around so much.' He knew something of Jim's story.

'No, I never had time.' The approach was made even more depressing by the Sergeant's unattractiveness.

'Well, they say there's nothing like a wife. But not for me. After all, it's a lot cheaper to buy milk than keep a cow! Isn't it?'

Jim grunted.

'What was Hollywood really like?' Kervinski looked at him eagerly.

'Just like any place else.' Jim had once shown some of the clerks the movie magazine with his picture in it. They had been sufficiently impressed to dislike him afterwards; he had learned his lesson and now never mentioned the past.

'I understand,' said Kervinski, blushing, 'that you knew Ronald Shaw and a lot of other stars. What was *he* like?'

The entire underworld knew about Shaw. 'I didn't know him well.' Jim was evasive. 'I just played tennis with him a few times.'

'Well, I hear a lot of strange stories about him but I don't see how they could be true.'

'Oh? What sort of stories?' Jim was malicious.

The Sergeant turned scarlet. 'Oh . . . just stories. The kind you always hear about Hollywood people. I don't see *how* they could be true.'

'People always talk.'

'By the way,' said Kervinski, examining a piece of green watery cabbage, 'I understand that ratings will be open this month.'

'That so?'

'I've recommended you to the Captain for a P.F.C. stripe.' The Sergeant put the cabbage in his mouth.

'Thanks a lot,' said Jim, fearing the worst.

Kervinski chewed thoughtfully. 'We should have dinner some evening, in town. I know a wonderful restaurant out near the Broadmoor. We bachelors should stick together,' he added with a little laugh.

'That would be fine,' said Jim, hoping that when he eventually said no Kervinski would not be too upset.

'Then,' said Kervinski, 'there are some girls I know. They're very nice and I'm sure you'd like them. Do you know any girls in town yet?'

Jim shook his head.

'Well, you certainly haven't given these Colorado girls a break! Where's that Southern chivalry?'

Jim played Southern idiot. 'Well, I just don't go out much at all, I reckon.'

'Just between us, neither do I. These girls here aren't half as attractive as the ones back home.' He winked and Jim was disgusted. Although it was impossible for anyone in the Army to be honest about such things, at least there were more straightforward ways of going about a seduction. At his present rate, it would take the Sergeant weeks to come to the point, probably just as well. Jim promised the Sergeant that he would have dinner with him soon; then he excused himself and went back to the barracks where he found a group of men sitting on his bunk. Most were clerks and not young; a bull session was in progress. Though Jim made a friendly motion, the men moved to other bunks. Jim took off his shirt and lay down. He said nothing. The bull session continued. As always, the dominant note was one of complaint. Apparently, each was losing an extraordinary amount of money while in the Army; and of course all officers were unjust and all women unfaithful.

Jim lay back on the coarse brown blanket and looked at the dark rafters. The barracks was always dark; there never seemed to be enough light or heat. He turned towards the coal stove and saw that there was a new man in the barracks, a young Corporal, who sat on the bunk nearest the stove, listening politely, obviously aware that if a man wants to be accepted by a barracks, he must listen to a great deal of talk about a very few subjects, and he must accept as a law of nature that whenever a point is made, it will be repeated a hundred times, often in the same words, rather like part-singing.

One of the more important Sergeants (secretary to the Personnel Officer) was telling them about the General. 'He's a real Section Eight case. Why, the other day he came into our office and he said to me, "Sergeant," he said, "how many men've we got at Weatherley Field?" "None," I said, "we lost them all to the Fighter Wing yesterday." He didn't know that one of his own bases had been transferred the day before. Well, he tried to get out of it by saying he thought the transfer hadn't taken place yet. But that gives you some idea how his mind works, if it works. He's always thinking up ideas to discipline the men. As if we didn't have enough work running his Wing for him. Didn't know about Weatherley being transferred!'

The others agreed that the General was too tough and not particularly bright. Or as another Sergeant, whose past was mysterious with unspecified success, put it, 'I'd like to see *him* hold down a job in civilian life. I'll bet he couldn't make thirty-five a week.'

The others agreed solemnly that in their world the General would be far less than they, unable to make thirty-five a week.

Then the conversation turned to women.

Some liked plump women; some liked small women; some liked blondes, others brunettes, and a few liked red-haired women. But all were agreed that they liked women and as they talked their eyes brightened as they recalled wives, lovers, dreams. Jim was amused and puzzled: were these clerks really successful with women? None was attractive physically. They were either too fat or too thin, and he wondered how any woman could care for them. Yet they talked incessantly of conquests, boasting in order to impress men who boasted – proof of what they said must be true. Even so, the thought of clerks in love was depressing.

Then one mentioned fairies. As far as Jim knew there were none in the barracks, except possibly the soldier who had started the conversation. He was small and thick, with a flat unpleasant voice. 'Just the other day this queer came up to me in the can in the movie house in town and wants me to go with him. Me! Well, I told the bastard what I thought of him. I told him if he didn't get out of there quick I'd break his neck, that's what I told him, and boy, he got out of there fast!' The others nodded solemnly when they heard this story, and each told an identical story, although in some instances the outraged man had indeed slugged the fairy. Jim tried not to laugh. It was always the ugliest and most suspect of the men who was invariably propositioned.

Jim glanced at the young Corporal. He was a dark-haired boy with grey eyes and a small slim body that looked strong. Watching him through half-closed eyes, Jim felt desire. For the first time in months he wanted sex. He wanted the young Corporal. Mentally, he raped him, made love to him, worshipped him; they would be brothers and never parted.

'This town is full of those damn queers,' the bald soldier droned on. 'A guy can't be too careful.' But since another conversation had started, no one except Jim heard. The soldier looked to Jim for support. 'Isn't that right?'

'That's right,' said Jim, continuing to look at the Corporal, who yawned sleepily.

Jim was soon a friend of the Corporal, whose name was Ken Woodrow, from Cleveland, aged twenty-one, in the Army a year and a half. He was a graduate of a secretarial college, and his ambition was to work for an important industrialist. Preferably in the Midwest, 'where the people are real'. Ken told him everything about himself and Jim listened intently, infatuated, unable to think of anything except how to get Ken to bed. Not since Bob had anyone so excited him. But with Bob there had been a sense of identity, of twins complementing one another; with Ken what he felt was absolute lust. He must have him.

They saw each other daily. Yet Ken seemed serenely unaware of what Jim wanted. Leading questions were invariably deflected by innocent answers. It was hugely frustrating. Meanwhile Sergeant Kervinski observed them darkly and suspected the worst: he was particularly angry with Jim, who continued to refuse to have dinner with him in town.

At last, unable to bear the waiting another moment, Jim talked Ken into going with him to Colorado Springs. It was a sharp November night. They had an overnight pass. They would sleep at a hotel. Something would have to happen.

Colorado Springs was crowded with soldiers. They came not only from the air-base but also from a neighbouring infantry camp, crowding the streets, bars, movie theatres, pool rooms, bowling alleys, looking for sex and a good time.

Jim and Ken had dinner at an Italian restaurant. At the next table two girls dined alone.

'See that girl staring at me?' Ken whispered, delighted. 'You think we ought to ask them to join us?'

'Oh, no,' said Jim as though the thought tired him. 'I'm not up to it. I worked hard today. And I'm beat.'

'Gosh, you never go out with girls, do you?' said Ken, as though the thought had just occurred to him.

Jim had been waiting for this question for weeks. He had a lie ready. 'Well, I got this one girl here in town, and I see her regularly, alone.'

Ken nodded wisely. 'See what you mean. Keep it to yourself. I figured you must have a set-up like that, because you've been here quite a while and it wouldn't be natural not to have a chick somewhere.' Ken nodded several times. They ate their spaghetti. Then Ken said, 'She doesn't have any friends, does she? You know the kind I mean.'

'Does who?'

'Your girl in town, does she . . . well, have friends?'

'Oh, no. At least I don't think so. That is, I'd have to ask her. She doesn't go out much.'

'Well, where'd you meet her?'

Jim was irritated by the necessity to invent. 'I met her at the USO, but like I told you she doesn't go out much. She works for the Telephone Company,' he added, attempting verisimilitude.

'Oh.' Ken was silent for a moment, his long fingers playing with a fork. 'I met a girl last week. She was really stacked, and she had this apartment out by Pike's Peak. But I got so drunk I couldn't remember where it was when it was over, and she didn't tell me her name, so I don't know how to find her. Boy, I'd give anything to see that chick again. It's awful being in a town full of G.I.s and not knowing anybody.'

'It's rough.' Jim realized that he was getting nowhere. With each piece of new evidence Ken's normality became more and more established. From the beginning, Jim had known that Ken was engaged to a girl in Cleveland, and that as soon as the war was over they would be married. But despite the engagement, Ken enjoyed talking about other girls and more than once he told Jim, solemnly, that he wondered if maybe he wasn't over-sexed because he couldn't stop thinking about women. Since there was no evidence that Ken was interested in men, Jim's only hope was to trust in the ambivalence of a young man who liked him.

'Well,' said Ken at last, eyes straying again to the two girls, 'I guess we better go somewhere and get drunk, if you're sure you don't want to pick up something.'

They toured the bars. Jim was careful not to get drunk. He had one drink for every two of Ken's. Wherever they went, Ken invariably struck up a conversation with a woman, but because Jim had said that he was tired Ken did not make a date for himself; he was going to be a 'good buddy' and get drunk.

Shortly after midnight Ken was indeed very drunk, slurred speech, eyes glazed; he clung to the bar for support. The moment had come. 'Maybe we better stay in town tonight,' said Jim.

'Sure, sure . . . good idea,' mumbled Ken.

The night air was reviving. Jim helped Ken to walk without stumbling. They went to a hotel frequented by soldiers with overnight passes.

'Double bed or two singles?' asked the desk clerk.

'Which is cheapest?' asked Jim, who knew.

'Double.' They registered. The room was like all other rooms in similar shabby hotels.

'Jeez, but I'm drunk.' Ken stared at his own reflection in the mirror, face red, sweating, dark hair tangled over bloodshot eyes.

'So'm I.' Jim watched him, wishing that he *was* drunk enough to do what he wanted to do.

'Jeez.' Ken sat down on the large bed which sagged in the middle. 'I sure wish I had a date. I mean that I had a date with one of those girls we saw, and you had a date, too. That'd be something, wouldn't it? Four in a bed. I had a buddy once who liked to do that. He tried to get me to do that with him and a couple of girls, but not me, I like it private. I'd hate to have somebody watching, wouldn't you?'

'I sure would.'

Ken stretched out on the bed, fully clothed, and shut his eyes. Jim shook him. He mumbled incoherently. Boldly Jim pulled off Ken's shoes, then the damp socks; Ken did not stir. But when he started to undo his belt, Ken opened his eyes and smiled; he looked like a corrupt choir boy. 'Now that's what I call service,' he said, wiggling his bare toes.

'I thought you'd passed out. Come on. Get your clothes off.'

They both undressed down to their olive drab shorts. Then Ken flung himself again on the bed. 'You sure sleep good when you're drunk,' he said happily, and shut his eyes once more, and seemed to sleep.

Jim turned out the light. The darkness was complete. His heart beat rapidly. He was conscious of the warmth of Ken's body close to him. Slowly he moved his hand beneath the covers until he touched Ken's thigh; he waited, fingers resting lightly on the firm flesh.

Ken moved away. 'Cut that out,' he said in a clear sober voice.

A pulse beat furiously in Jim's temple. Blood rushed to his head. He turned over on his side. In the morning he would have a hangover.

III

The winter was cold and bitter. Snow came and went but the desert remained dry, and dust was forever in the wind. Jim was cold most of the time. During the day he spent as much time as he could in the hot sun, out of the wind. But at night he was always cold.

Neither Ken nor Jim acted as if anything untoward had happened but Ken was plainly embarrassed, and Jim was furious. They avoided one another and now Jim found himself disliking the boy who had once filled his dreams with such intense passion. It was a lonely time. He had no friends. Even Sergeant Kervinski had proved fickle, transferring his affections to another physical-training instructor, newly arrived.

During the hard winter, Jim surrendered himself to an orgy of self-analysis. He thought continually about himself and his life and what it was that had made him the way he was. He pondered his early life.

Jim had disliked his father; he remembered that more clearly than anything else. His first memory was one of bleakness and unfair punishment. On the other hand he had liked his mother. Yet he found it strange that he could not recall her face although he could remember her voice: soft, Southern, tired. Far back in memory, he could recall a wonderful safe time when he was held in her arms while she kissed and fondled him. But all that ended when his brother was born, or so he supposed. She had never been demonstrative again.

School memories were vague. Jim had once been attracted to girls. When he was fourteen he was very interested in a heavy-breasted girl named Prudence. They exchanged valentines and the other children giggled that they were in love. He had sexual fantasies involving Prudence, but they stopped when he was fifteen and became interested in athletics and Bob. From that time on no one existed in the world except Bob.

Then came life at sea. He still shuddered when he remembered the night with Collins and the two girls in Seattle. He marvelled now at how little he had understood then. Yet even now he wondered what might have happened if he had gone through with that adventure. He still half believed that should he ever have a woman he would be normal. There was not much to base this hope on, but he believed it.

Memories of Shaw were pleasant and he smiled whenever he thought of him, despite the drama of their parting. He had learned much from Shaw; and through him he had met interesting people who might still be useful to him. Also, he found himself pitying Shaw, always a gratifying emotion, since it pleasurably diminishes the object.

Sullivan and Maria Verlaine were still too close to him for analysis. But he was aware that each had been important to him. Of the two he cared more for Maria, even though he now realized that he would never be able to make love to her, if only because they had talked too much about it. Words had taken the place of the act. Sullivan, too, had tended to vanish behind a screen of words, of emotions overstated yet undefined.

As for Bob, he had vanished. No one knew where he was, according to Mrs Willard, who wrote Jim irregularly, giving him news of his father's illness, Carrie's marriage, John's admission to the State University. Yet Jim was positive that one day Bob would appear and they would continue what was begun that day beside the river. Until then his life was in suspension, waiting.

Unable to bear the winter cold any longer, Jim went to Kervinski. He was at his desk, surrounded by the theatrical Sergeants, soft young men who knew a thousand unpleasant stories about famous people.

'Well, Jim, what can I do for you?' Kervinski smiled brightly.

'I was wondering, Sergeant, if there's any chance of my going overseas.'

Kervinski sighed. 'Really, Jim, you don't know when you're well off. As it is, according to current orders, you'll be shipped out in April. But who knows? Anyway, there isn't a thing I or anybody can do. It's up to Washington.'

'I was wondering if maybe I could get assigned to one of the bomber outfits they're forming here.'

'Possibly. But they're not going overseas until spring. Anyway, why do you want to leave?'

'It's too God-damned cold. I'm freezing to death.'

The Sergeant laughed. 'I'm afraid you'll just have to rough it with the rest of us. You Southern boys are so . . . sultry,' he added, amusing the Sergeants. That was that.

Christmas came and with it a blizzard. For two days wind and snow raged about the base. It was impossible to see more than a few feet in any direction. Men were lost going from building to building. Day was like night. When the blizzard stopped, the base had become a white lunar land with snowdrifts higher than buildings and craters that glittered in the sun.

In the club for enlisted men, a Christmas tree had been set up and the men gathered around it to drink beer and speak bitterly of past Christmases. Jim, bored, wandered over to the piano where a Corporal was picking out a tune with one finger. Not until Jim was at the piano did he realize that the Corporal was Ken.

'Hello,' said Jim. The moment was awkward.

'Hi.' Ken was flat. 'Kind of dull.'

Jim nodded. 'And I don't like beer.'

'I remember. You been busy?' Ken continued his one-finger piano playing.

'Just trying to keep warm.'

'I thought you were in Alaska once.'

'But since then I was in the tropics, I hate cold weather.'

'Why don't you transfer to Louisiana? We got a new base there.'

'How?'

Ken was now playing the Marine Corps Hymn. 'Well, if you want me to, I can fix it up with the Sergeant in Personnel. He's a good buddy of mine.'

'I wish you would.'

'I'll ask him tomorrow.'

'Thanks.' Jim was grateful, also suspicious. Why was Ken so willing to help? Did he want him to leave Colorado?

The next day, by accident, Jim met Sergeant Kervinski in the post library. The Sergeant was reading a movie magazine.

'Hello, Jim.' Kervinski blushed. 'I expect we're both goldbricks today. By the way, Ken told me he spoke to you about Louisiana.'

'That's right.' Jim was startled. 'I didn't know you knew him.'

'Oh, yes!' Kervinski beamed. 'As a matter of fact, we're going into the Springs for dinner tonight. Why don't you join us?' The invitation was put in such a way that it was perfectly clear that the last thing in the world Kervinski wanted was for Jim to join them.

'No, thanks. Not tonight. He's a good guy, Ken.'

'I think so. I first noticed him when you and he used to go around together when he first arrived, remember? Such a sincere person.'

'Yes.' Jim was suddenly angry. 'Yes, he's O.K.' He paused, searching for a way to wound his successor. The best he could do was: 'I guess Ken's going to be married soon.'

Kervinski was serene. 'Oh, I don't think there's any *immediate* danger. He's having too good a time. Besides, it's a lot cheaper to buy milk than keep a cow.'

Jim looked at Kervinski with perfect loathing. But the Sergeant gave no sign that he was aware of Jim's dislike. 'You know that we'll be shipping quite a few men down to Louisiana.'

Jim got the point at last. 'Yes, Ken's going to see if I can be one of them. Do you think it'll be all right with Captain Banks?'

'Of course it'll be all right. We'd hate to lose you, naturally.' Jim was baffled. He had failed with Ken. Kervinski had been successful. It seemed impossible, yet obviously something had happened and both were now eager for Jim to be shipped out.

'Thanks,' said Jim, and left the library, contemplating murder.

But Jim was not transferred to Louisiana. On New Year's Day he caught a chill. He went to the hospital and was put to bed, with a streptococcic infection of the throat. For several days he was delirious, tortured by memory, by certain words and phrases which repeated themselves until he swore aloud and twisted in his bed. He dreamed of Bob, of a menacing, subtly distorted Bob who retreated when he tried to touch him. Sometimes the river was between them and when he tried to swim across, he would be dashed against sharp rocks, Bob's derisive laughter ringing in his ears.

Then he would hear the voice of Shaw talking and talking and talking of love, saying the same things in the same way, until Jim knew how each sentence would end by its first word: yet there was no way of silencing the voice; it was literally maddening.

Then there were memories of his mother, holding him in her arms; the face no longer grey and lined but young, the way she had been when he was a child and secure. Then his father would approach and he would slip from her arms and his father would beat him, while the river roared in his ears.

The pain in his throat was sharp, like a knife-blade probing, underscoring his nightmares. He remained in this dream-haunted state for what seemed years. But on the third day, chronologically, the fever broke and the dreams ended, and he woke up one morning, tired and weak; the worst was over.

Jim was in a small room in the base hospital. Through the window he could see snowy mountains. He was conscious of being quite alone and for a moment he wondered if he might not be the only person left in the world, but then the muffled sound of voices reassured him and the nurse entered the room.

'I see we're better today.' She took his pulse and put a thermometer in his mouth. 'You know, you were quite sick for a while there.' Her tone was accusing, as she removed the thermometer from his mouth. 'Normal at last. Well, we stuffed enough sulfa into you.'

'How long've I been here?' Jim's voice was weak; it hurt him to talk.

'This is your third day, and don't talk. The doctor will be around soon.' She put a glass of water beside his bed and left.

The doctor was cheerful. He examined Jim's throat and nodded with satisfaction. 'Good. Good. You'll be out of here in a few weeks.'

Apparently Jim had nearly died. This did not surprise him. There had been times in his delirium when he would have been glad to depart. 'Anyway, it's over now. But it may be weeks before you can go back to active duty.'

The days passed quickly and pleasantly. It was the most comfortable period of Jim's Army career. He read magazines and listened to the radio. In time he was transferred to a ward with twenty other convalescents. He was perfectly content with life, until the pains began, first in his left knee, then in his left shoulder, a constant aching, like a bad tooth. After a number of tests, the doctor sat on Jim's bed and talked to him in a low voice while the others in the ward tried to hear.

'Are you absolutely certain that you've never had these pains before?'

'No, sir, never.' Jim had been asked this particular question a dozen times.

'Well, I'm afraid that you've got what we call rheumatoid arthritis.' He sighed. 'Contracted while in the Army.'

The ward boy had already given Jim the same diagnosis and so he was prepared for the verdict. Even so, he manged to look alarmed. 'Is that bad, sir?'

'Not in this stage, no. It'll be painful, of course. Not that we know much about arthritis, though I'm willing to bet your throat infection had something to do with it. Meanwhile, you'll be sent to a warm, dry climate. Does no good, of course, but it'll make you feel better. Then they'll probably discharge you with a pension, because the calcium deposits show up in the X-rays, and it all happened to you while serving your country in time of war, and you've got a swell racket from here on out.'

'Where will I be sent, sir?'

'California Desert, maybe Arkansas, Arizona. We'll let you know.' The doctor stood up slowly. 'I've got the same thing as you.' He chuckled. 'Maybe they'll discharge me, too.' He left, and Jim wondered if there was anyone in the world he liked so much as this particular doctor.

'You going to be shipped out?' asked the Negro soldier in the bunk next to his. Jim nodded, hiding his great happiness.

'Man, you're lucky. I'd sure like to be shipped out of here, to anywhere.'

'It's tough.'

The Negro then talked about intolerance and discrimination. He was certain that even if he were dying the white officers would not take proper care of him. To cite an example, he told a long rambling story about a Negro soldier who had gone to an Army doctor a number of times for backache and the doctor had told him that there was nothing wrong with him. One day when the soldier was sitting in the waiting room and the nurse went in to tell the doctor that he was there, he heard the doctor say distinctly, 'Well, send the nigger in.' White doctors were racially intolerant. Everyone knew it. But some day . . .

As the Negro talked about the miseries of his race, Jim thought only of his own happiness. He had long since given up all idea of going overseas. From the stories he had heard it was hardly more exciting than duty in the States. He was now eager to leave the Army. He had been no use at all to the war. Soon he would be free. Meanwhile the thought of his pending release made him want to resume relations with those who had been important to him. He borrowed writing paper from the Negro soldier and slowly, laboriously, in his awkward childish handwriting, he began to write letters, using them as a net in order to recapture his own past.

CHAPTER EIGHT

Ronald Shaw was tired and there was an uncomfortable pain in his duodenum which he was convinced was an ulcer, if not cancer. His death took place before his eyes, beautifully lit and photographed, with Brahms playing on the sound track. Then there was a slow dissolve to the funeral cortège as it moved through Beverly Hills, escorted by weeping girls, carrying autograph books.

Tears in his eyes, Shaw turned into the green oasis of Bel-Air. It had been a bad day at the studio. He disliked his new director and he hated the part he was playing. For the first time he was supporting a woman star. He wished now that he had turned down the part, or at least had it rewritten, or retired from the screen before he died of overwork and cancer. The bright cheerful sun made things worse; his head ached; perhaps he was going to have sunstroke.

But the house was cool and he gave a weak sigh of relief as the butler held the door open for him.

'A bad day, sir?' The butler was sympathetic.

'Terrible.' Shaw picked up his mail and went out to the swimming pool where George was taking a sun bath. George was a sailor from Wisconsin with hair so blond that it was white. He had been with Shaw for a week. In another week he would go back to sea. Then what? Shaw asked himself bitterly.

'Hi, Ronnie.' The boy pulled himself up on one elbow. 'How's the salt mine?'

'Rotten.' Shaw sat down beside the pool. 'The director's an untalented, lousy, professional kike.' Shaw had begun lately to make anti-Semitic remarks, which amused rather than distressed those who knew him.

'I guess they're pretty lousy, some of them out here.' George was a happy youth who believed everything that he was told. Shaw tousled the blond hair idly. They had met in a bar in Hollywood. Shaw had started to frequent bars, a dangerous pastime, but he was bored and restless, and morbidly aware of time passing, and of the fact that his hair was quite grey beneath the dye and that his stomach was bad, and life was ending even though he was hardly forty. Why? Too much had happened to him, he decided; his career had burned him up and of course he had been unfortunate in love, cheated and betrayed.

George stretched out again beside the pool while Shaw read his mail. He opened Jim's letter. The handwriting was unfamiliar and at first he thought it was a fan letter. Then he saw that it was signed quite formally, 'Jim Willard'. Shaw was pleased, flattered, suspicious: if Jim wanted money, he would not get it. That would be Shaw's revenge as well as a good lesson for Jim, who had deserted a truly genuine human being for a self-centred writer. Shaw was slightly disappointed to find that the letter was friendly and nothing more.

Jim wrote that he was in the Army hospital but no longer sick. He expected to be discharged soon and he would like to see Shaw again. It was puzzling and yet in character. Jim had always been direct. Shaw experienced a sudden ache of sexual memory. Then he saw that George was watching him. 'What you got?' asked George. 'A fan letter?'

Shaw smiled dreamily. 'No, it's from a kid I used to know, Jim Willard. I showed you his picture once.'

'What happened to him?'

'He went into the Army,' Shaw lied glibly. 'He writes me often. I suppose he's still in love with me, at least that's what he says. But I don't feel anything any more. Funny, isn't it?'

George nodded, impressed. Then Shaw sent him into the pavilion for a drink. As the late afternoon sun shone in Shaw's face and a soft flower-scented wind cooled him, his unhappiness turned to a detachment that was not at all unpleasant. He was utterly alone in the world. This knowledge thrilled him. Of course there was his mother in Baltimore and a few friends at the studio, as well as the millions who knew of him and would doubtless be honoured to be his friend; yet having conquered all the world, he was still very much alone and it struck him that there was something magnificent in being a prisoner of fame. He allowed a brooding look to come into his eyes. What a waste, he thought, contemplating the inability of others to reciprocate the love he had to give. None could equal his intensity. A tragic figure, he sat with the western sun in his eyes, perfectly content.

George approached with two glasses. 'Here you go.' He gave Shaw his drink. Shaw thanked him very gently.

'You feeling O.K., Ronnie?'

'Oh, yes, thank you.' The gin was cold. Suddenly a spasm went through his stomach. For an instant he was panicky. But then he belched and the pain went away: it was only wind.

Mr Willard was dying and Mrs Willard wished that he would die soon. Apparently years of bad temper had damaged his liver and weakened his heart. The doctors were able to keep him from pain with great doses of morphine.

Mrs Willard grimaced as she entered the sickroom; the odour of medicines and dying was overpowering. Mr Willard lay on his back, breathing noisily. His face was yellow and sagging and the once commanding mouth hung loose. His eyes were like grey glass from the morphine.

'That you, Bess?' His voice was hoarse.

'Yes, dear. How're you feeling?' She arranged the pillows.

'Better. The doctor said I was better.' The evening before, the doctor had told Mrs Willard that her husband would not live another week.

'I know, he told me the same.'

'I'll be up and around soon.' Mr Willard would not admit to himself that he was going to die. He asked his wife about the courthouse.

'They're doing fine, dear. Mr Perkins is doing your job until you're ready to go back to work.'

'Perkins is an ass,' said Mr Willard.

'I'm sure he's doing his best. After all, he's only filling in.'

Mr Willard grunted and shut his eyes. Dispassionately his wife looked at the sunken yellow face, and wondered where the insurance policy was. She had not been able to find it anywhere in the house, but of course the Will would tell, and the Will was at the lawyer's office. Mr Willard's eyes shut, and he seemed to sleep. She left the room.

On the floor in the hall were several letters. As she leaned over to pick them up, she groaned. The older she got, the more she disliked bending over. But then she forgot her pains: one of the letters was from Jim.

She read it slowly. He was in the hospital and that alarmed her, but he reassured her that he was now well and would soon be getting out of the Army. He promised to come home and visit her as soon as he was free. Her heart beat more quickly as she read this.

She thought of her eldest son, and wondered what she felt about him after such a long separation, much of it without communication of any sort.

She had not wanted him to leave home. She had wept the night he left even though she realized that he could never live in the same house with his father. In her quiet way, Mrs Willard had hated her husband from the first day of their marriage. During family quarrels, she had sympathized with Jim and longed to tell him that she felt as he did but that they both had to bear those things which could not be changed. Unfortunately, she had never spoken frankly, and because she had not, Jim left home. Now, of course, it was too late. Jim would never belong to her again. She wanted to cry but she could not.

Mrs Willard sat erect, the letter in her hands, wondering what had happened to her life. Soon she would be alone, without even a husband to hate in the last years of her life. Where had all the time and all the promise gone to? She pitied herself, but only for a moment. After all, Carrie and her husband lived near by and so would John once he was a lawyer.

The thought of Jim's return cheered her considerably. She wondered how he looked now that he was a man. She had no clue except the photograph in the movie magazine which she had shown to everyone, creating an impression that Jim was a movie star, an impression she had never entirely corrected.

Mrs Willard daydreamed pleasantly of the future. There were several nice girls who would make Jim the kind of wife who would be glad to share him with his mother. As for a job, Jim could take over the physical-training post at the high school. She knew enough politicians to make this possible. Yes, the future could be good, she decided, putting the letter away and returning to the sickroom to find that her husband's eyes were open. He was staring at the ceiling.

'I've a letter from Jim.'

'What does he say?'

'He's been in the hospital – it's not serious – and he thinks he'll be discharged from the Army soon. Then he'll come home.'

'Probably broke.' Mr Willard scowled briefly; his features were too weak to hold even a scowl for long. 'Wonder what he'll do when he gets out? Can't go on playing games for ever.'

'I thought perhaps he could get a job at the high school. I . . . we could get him something, don't you think? I'm sure Judge Claypoole would be glad to arrange it.'

Mr Willard's skeleton hands fumbled with the white sheet. 'How old's the boy now?'

Mrs Willard thought a moment. 'Twenty-two come April.'

'He's grown.' Mr Willard was gloomy.

'Yes,' said Mrs Willard happily. Jim would take care of her. 'He's grown.'

'Don't know why he wants to wander all over.'

'But the experience is good for him, and anyway you know what they say about wild oats.'

Mr Willard shut his eyes. Conversation tired him. Mrs Willard went to the kitchen, where she found Carrie. 'How is he, Mother?'

'It's almost over. A few more days at the most. Thank the Lord he feels no pain.'

'That's something to be grateful for.' Of them all, Carrie was the only one truly sorry about her father's approaching death. They had been fond of one another. But her sorrow was somewhat assuaged by the fact of pregnancy. Inclined to plumpness, Carrie was now round and contented and looked exactly what she was, a comfortable housewife fond of her husband. Mrs Willard gave Carrie Jim's letter.

Carrie was delighted. 'I do hope he comes back and lives here!'

'So do I.'

'I wonder what he's like now.'

'We'll know when we see him. Now I expect you better go in and see Father.'

Carrie left the kitchen and Mrs Willard began to fix broth for her husband. It would be a great relief to her when he died. She wondered idly if he might not have left the insurance policy with his friend Judge Claypoole. But of course the Will would tell them everything.

London was chilly and damp and Sullivan was depressed as he walked past St James's Palace on the way to his hotel in Mount Street.

He had been to dinner with H. G. Wells, whom he admired as a figure if not as a writer. The evening had gone well; Mr Wells had been in good form. Yet Sullivan was obscurely irritated by the perfectly plain fact that not only had the great man never read one of Sullivan's books, he had never heard of him either. Naturally Wells was an old man, but even so it was disquieting and Sullivan was again reminded of his literary failure.

The night was dark and the blackout made it even darker. A cold wind blew through the streets. Shivering, he fastened his trench coat at the neck. He would have a strong drink when he got back to the hotel bar, even if it meant running into Amelia, who was now in London. Aggressive, bustling, eager for bygones to be bygones, his ex-wife was unbearably cheery.

And of course there she was, thin and untidy, enthroned in the hotel bar, surrounded by correspondents (she herself was covering the war for a left-wing magazine).

'Paul dear, come on over!' He did.

The other correspondents greeted Sullivan respectfully. At least they knew he was an author. They were impressed by novelists, though they did not take his journalism very seriously, for which he could hardly blame them.

Sullivan shook hands all around. He knew most of them by reputation. Those who were not Stalinists were crypto-Trotskyites. Sullivan was apolitical. But Amelia was totally engaged. She talked rapidly, maintaining herself as group leader. 'Paul's such a dear. Really, I always think one should be nice to one's ex-husbands, don't you?' The question was asked at large and no one answered. 'I believe if we're to be really civilized we should have no bitterness when we fail at marriage or anything else, except perhaps politics.' She was a little drunk. 'Does that sound like that lovable old cynic La Rochefoucauld? Everything else does!' She laughed gaily, then turned to Sullivan. 'Where've you been this evening?'

'I had dinner with H. G. Wells.' Sullivan won that round. Immediately everyone asked him about Wells and for a moment Amelia ceased to be the centre of attraction; even when she loudly demanded a drink for her ex-husband, he still retained his lead. 'He was very pleasant. We talked about writing mostly. He'd read one of my books and so I was quite flattered by that. Not that I supposed he liked it, but even so . . .'

'Here's your drink, Paul.' Amelia thrust the whisky at him. He took a swallow and Amelia filled the brief silence. 'I think,' she said to the table at large, 'that it will be years before there is a Labour government in England. The Churchill–Cliveden set are too well entrenched and, just between us, I shouldn't be in the least surprised if they created some sort of dictatorship that could *never* be thrown off without a revolution, and you know how slow these English are at revolting against anything! A nation of masochists.'

Paul was surprised to find that people took Amelia seriously. He could hardly be critical: he had married her. But when they first met she was different. A quiet, thoughtful girl, she had worshipped him until it was plain that a physical relationship was impossible. Then, defensively, she had grown masculine and aggressive. It was all his fault, he decided, or at least the fault of the way he was, and this racketing woman was the result. Did nothing turn out well?

Sullivan finished his drink and stood up. 'If you'll excuse me, Amelia, I must cut class.' Though he said this amiably enough, he was pleased to see that he still had the power to hurt her. She stopped in mid-sentence: the needle had been lifted from the record. He said good night to the correspondent and left the bar. As he entered the lobby, he could hear Amelia beginning again.

At the desk Sullivan got his mail and took the lift to his room, hoping there would be no air-raid warning to break his sleep. He was weary. Not until he was in bed did he notice Jim's letter on the night table. He read the letter twice and was both disappointed and pleased. Jim was going to be discharged from the Army and he would like to see him again. Nothing more. No mention of Maria. Did that mean their affair would continue, if it was an affair? During the months Sullivan had been in England, he had thought of Jim often, dreamed of him, wanted him. Could they resume? That was the question.

It was morning before Sullivan fell asleep. During the long night he thought mostly of the books he had written, and was filled with gloom. He had succeeded at nothing. He had no lover, no family, and H. G. Wells had never heard of him. But then as he grew sleepy, he comforted himself. After all, he was young and there was still time left in which to write a masterpiece, as well as to recapture Jim. Meanwhile, first thing in the morning, he would send Mr Wells one of his novels, autographed.

Jim's letter made Maria Verlaine sad and somewhat embarrassed. She had been a fool to love a child incapable of response. She had deserved to suffer, and she had, for a time. Now she wanted only normal men and uncomplicated attachments.

In New York, despite the austerities of wartime, she dined out often, met strangers, made love. In constant motion, she ceased to think of herself as a tragic figure. Now this unexpected letter reminded her of that strangely lowering season she had spent in Yucatán with a boy and his lover. Did she want to see him again? She thought not. She was at an age when she did not care to be reminded of old defeats. Yet at the same time she was sorry for Jim. More to the point, was it not a proof of her own power that he had again turned to her? and of her own maturity that she could receive him as a friend? Yes, she would write to him. They would meet when he came to New York. After all, she had nothing to fear, nothing to gain. The worst had happened.

* * *

Everyone agreed that Bob Ford looked remarkably handsome in his
Merchant Marine uniform. First Mate aboard a Liberty ship, of all the home-
town youths at war he was considered the most successful. Of course the
Merchant Marine was not exactly the Army or Navy, but still it was quite an
achievement to be a First Mate and not yet twenty-five. His homecoming was
something of a triumph, although, properly speaking, he had no home since his
father had been committed to the insane asylum the year before, and the family
home was now a boarding-house. The new owner, however, was willing to rent
him his old room at half-price, and here he stayed during the two weeks of his
leave, while he wooed Sally Mergendahl, the reason for his return. They had
written one another for five years. During that time, Sally had grown into a
quiet pretty woman, no longer 'wild'. As a child, she had made up her mind that
she was going to marry Bob, and nothing had ever caused her to change her
mind. Now her patience was rewarded. One evening, while walking her home
from the movies, Bob spoke of marriage.

'Are you sure that you really *want* to be married? Could you be married and
still be a sailor?'

Bob looked at her. They were standing beneath a tall elm tree; his face was in
darkness, hers in the light from a near-by street lamp.

'I'm sure I want to marry you. But I love the sea. It's the only thing I know.'

'I talked to Daddy,' said Sally slowly, 'and he thought you would do very well
in the insurance business, in his business, and he thought it was a shame that
someone with your personality was away at sea all the time when you could be in
business with him, selling insurance, as a partner.'

'You think he'd give me a job after the war?'

Sally nodded. She had already won that battle.

'Then if it's all right with you, let's get married right away.'

'I think,' said Sally Mergendahl, 'that that would be a very good idea.'

The morning of the wedding was a Sunday. Church bells rang, and most
people slept an hour late. But Bob was up early. He shaved carefully, put on his
newest uniform, and went downstairs for breakfast. His landlady was ecstatic:

'What a lovely day for a wedding! Though any day's a good day to get
married. I made pancakes. There's nothing like a full stomach to start you off
with. Oh, by the way, here's a letter for you. It came Friday, but in the
excitement I forgot all about giving it to you. I'm sorry. It was addressed to you
in care of old Mr Ford here, which means it's from somebody out of town. Well,
enjoy your breakfast. I'll see you at the church. I wouldn't miss this for
anything!'

Bob opened Jim's letter. He was surprised to hear from him after so many
years; he also felt a bit guilty for not having answered those early letters Jim had
written him. Sally occupied what little talent he had for correspondence.

The letter was simple enough. Jim was getting out of the service and he hoped
to see Bob soon, perhaps in New York. That was all. Something disturbed Bob as
he crumpled the letter. He frowned and tried to remember what it was. But his
mind was a blank. As he tossed the letter neatly into a wastepaper basket, he
made a vow that he would answer Jim's letter the moment he got back to ship.

CHAPTER NINE

I

Jim was not discharged immediately. Instead he was sent to a hospital in the San Fernando Valley of California where he was treated and observed. In the hot sun his arthritic condition improved but because he was now eager to get out of the Army, he said nothing of this to the doctors. He continued to limp in a most distinguished way.

Jim visited Hollywood often, but he did not go to see Shaw since he had received no answer to his letter; he assumed that Shaw was still living with Peter and not interested in a reconciliation. But he did meet the director named Cy, in a bar, sitting too close to a sailor, drunk. When Cy saw Jim he shouted, 'Well, if it isn't the tennis boy!' He was exuberant. 'So what's new? In that butch uniform yet! Been to see America's Sweetheart?'

'No. Not yet.'

'Where you stationed?'

Jim told him.

'A hospital? What's wrong? A rosy chancre? The dread disease that dare not tell its name?'

'No, arthritis.'

'Serious?'

'Not very.'

'Well, let's have a drink.'

Jim shook his head. 'I'm not drinking.'

'Then I'll have one.' Cy ordered himself gin. 'So why haven't you been to see Shaw?'

'Because I don't think he wants to see me, do you?'

Cy took a swallow of his new drink and wiped his mouth with a hairy paw. 'Oh, you know Shaw. He's such a ham. Who was the one who came after you? I've forgotten.'

'Peter, an actor.'

'That one!' Cy beamed with malice. 'Well, I'm responsible for that break-up. In a way. I put the kid in a picture and, believe it or not, he was good. So the studio offers him a term contract, he takes it, and walks out on Shaw who, by the way, got me to put him in the picture in the first place. Isn't that a hoot? But hell, I don't blame the kid. After all, he wasn't even queer. He's shacked up with a broad at this very moment, at Malibu. Saw them myself this afternoon, on the beach.'

'Who's with Shaw now?' The story of Peter was not entirely surprising.

'Everybody. Nobody. He hunts the bars and the studio is worried as all hell. And ... oh, by the way, he's going in the Navy. Now that's a *real* hoot!'

'But I thought he was supposed to be too valuable or something to go.'

Cy chuckled. 'You got to go to war if you want to make pictures. He'll be commissioned and sent overseas to maybe Honolulu and we'll take a lot of pictures of him being one of the boys and then, if the Navy doesn't lock him up for raping their personnel, he'll come home with a couple of ribbons and a new contract from the studio. Last few months they've been working him hard, so there'll be plenty of Shaw pictures while he's gone. The idiots won't be allowed to forget him.'

'When's he going in?'

'As soon as the Navy gets the go-ahead from *Life*.'

'Nice deal,' said Jim. The bartender began to move ominously towards him: non-drinkers were unpopular. 'Well, I'll see you around.'

'Why don't you come on up to my place tonight . . .' Cy began.

'No, thanks.'

'Suit yourself.'

The routine of the hospital was a relief after Colorado, and Jim enjoyed himself. He played tennis for the first time in two years. He gained weight and soon his illness was a barely-remembered nightmare, like the cold white mornings on the Colorado desert.

In April his mother wrote to tell him that his father had died. Jim felt no regret. Almost the contrary: a weight was lifted in his mind, a hatred ended. Jim sat in the sun and looked across the green lawn where patients in maroon Army dressing-gowns were wandering back and forth.

Death seemed impossible in the sunlight. Yet Jim wondered what it was like. He himself had been close to death but he could recall nothing. Now, in the sunlight, he pondered death and his father. He did not believe in heaven or hell. He thought it most unlikely that there was a special place where good people went, particularly when no one was certain just what a good person was, much less what the final repository was like. What *did* happen? The idea of nothing frightened him, and death was probably nothing: no earth, no people, no light, no time, no *thing*. Jim looked at his hand. It was tanned and square, and covered with fine gold hairs. He imagined the hand as it would be when he was dead: limp, pale, turning to earth. He stared for a long time at the hand which was certain to be earth one day. Decay and nothing, yes, that was the future. He was chilled by a cold animal fear. There must be some way to cheat the earth, which like an inexorable magnet drew men back to it. But despite the struggle of ten thousand generations, the magnet was triumphant, and sooner or later his own particular memories would be spilled upon the ground. Of course his dust would be absorbed in other living things and to that degree at least he would exist again, though it was plain enough that the specific combination which was he would never exist again.

The hot sun warmed him. The blood moved fast in his veins. He was conscious of the fullness of life. He existed in the present. That was enough. And perhaps in the years ahead he would have a new vision, one which would help him, somehow, to circumvent the fact of nothing.

In May Jim went before the medical board. Since X-rays showed a mineral deposit in his left knee-joint, it was the decision of the board that James Willard be medically discharged from the Army of the United States, with a pension for disability. To his delight, all this came to pass. Papers in order, he was given a railroad ticket to New York. On the train he read in a newspaper that Ronald Shaw, the actor, had enlisted in the Navy.

In New York Jim rented a room in Charles Street in Greenwich Village and looked for work. After some time he found what he wanted. Near the East River there was a vacant lot which had been converted to tennis-courts. Here Jim met

Wilbur Gray, who, with his partner Isaac Globe, owned the courts. Eventually a new building would go up on the lot but, according to Mr Globe, that was at least five years away, and in the meantime, business was excellent.

Jim visited the courts every day. He became friends with both Gray and Globe. Finally, he offered to buy part of their business and to be an instructor as well. After many conferences and much examining of books, the men, who knew nothing about tennis, agreed to allow Jim, who knew nothing about business, to become their partner.

Jim worked for the rest of the year, giving lessons on good days, and since there were an unusual number of good days that summer and fall, he made money. Except at work, he saw very little of his partners. They were both devoted family men and had no interest in the outside world. Neither did he while he was working. He saw no one. He did call Maria Verlaine's hotel once, but she was not registered.

One winter afternoon, on Fifth Avenue, Jim saw Lieutenant Shaw looking rather wistfully at a display of Christmas toys in the window of F. A. O. Schwartz's.

'Ronnie!'

'Jim!' They shook hands warmly. Shaw had been at sea in the Atlantic. He was now on leave, living at the Harding Hotel. Would Jim like a drink? Yes.

The suite in the Harding was vast, with rococo mirrors and spindly gold-encrusted furniture. Shaw ordered a bottle of Scotch and then they stared at one another, each wondering how to begin. At last Shaw remarked that a lot of water had gone under the bridge since they last met. Jim agreed. Then the conversation stopped for a long time until Shaw said, 'Are you living alone?'

Jim nodded. 'I worked pretty hard all summer, I don't really know anybody yet.'

'You're better off playing the field. I know I am. Ideally, of course, a relationship is best, but then how many people are capable of deep feeling? Practically none.'

Jim put an end to that familiar dirge. 'How's the Navy?'

Shaw shrugged. 'I've had to be careful. But then I've always had to be careful. By the way, what're you doing tonight? I've been invited to a faggot party, very chi-chi. I'll take you. It can be your coming-out party in New York. They'll all be there.'

Jim was surprised at how little Shaw seemed to care for appearances. In the old days he would never have gone to such a party. But now he was indifferent, even defiant.

The party was given by Nicholas J. Rolloson, heir to a notorious American fortune. Rolly, as he was known, had two passions, modern art and the military. Both were well represented in his apartment overlooking Central Park. Paintings by Chagall and Dufy hung on stark white walls. Mobiles tinkled from the ceiling. A huge Henry Moore nude dominated one end of a long drawing-room in which at least one chair resembled a wrecked armadillo. Through these startling rooms a full company of soldiers, sailors and marines wandered, awed by their surroundings if not by Rolly and his friends, who were perfectly familiar to them.

There was a hush when Shaw entered. Although there were other famous men at the party, painters, writers, composers, athletes, even a member of

Congress, Shaw was most glamorous of all. Eyes watched his every move. He was a legend here, and that made him entirely happy.

Rolly welcomed them enthusiastically. He wore a scarlet blazer with a crest; as he moved, breasts jiggled beneath a pale yellow silk shirt. The handshake was predictably damp. 'My dears, how lovely of you to come! I was so afraid you wouldn't, Ronnie, and I would have died of disappointment, but now my evening is made, but absolutely *made*! Now come with me. Everybody's just about out of their minds to meet you.' Shaw was borne away, and Jim was left on his own. A waiter gave him a Martini. Cocktail in hand, Jim went exploring, somewhat excited by the servicemen, conscripts in Rolloson's army.

In a corner of the dining-room, Jim was hailed by an effeminate man with a hairpiece. 'Come on over, baby. Join the party.' Without alternative, Jim sat down on the couch between the hairpiece and a set of bifocals. Opposite sat a grey-haired man and a bald young man. They had been talking earnestly and both the grey-haired man and the bifocals were irritated at being interrupted.

'You came with Shaw, didn't you?' asked the hairpiece.

Jim nodded.

'Are you an actor?'

'A tennis player.' Jim ground out the phrase in his deepest voice.

'Oh, how thrilling! An athlete! I adore body men,' said the bifocals. 'Teutonic and primitive, not like those of us who are simply frustrated and inhibited by a society grown too complex to understand. This young man is the true archetype, the original pattern of which we are neurotic distortions.' The bifocals examined Jim as if he were some sort of moderately interesting experiment.

The grey-haired man objected. 'Why are the rest of us necessarily the result of a distortion? In any case, you are being taken in by an appearance. We don't know his reality. He could be most neurotic of all. By the way,' he turned to Jim with a smile, 'we speak of you not as yourself but as a symbol. We're not being impertinent.'

'But there is something,' said the bald man, 'in this Teutonic theory. In Germany, isn't it the army, the athletes, the most virile men, who are homosexual, or at least bisexual? And God knows Germany is primitive enough. On the other hand, in America and in England we find that effeminacy is one of the signs of the homosexual, and of course neurosis.'

'Five years ago we might have thought that true,' said bifocals. 'But I'm not so sure now. Of course there have always been normal-appearing men who were homosexual but never or seldom practised, while the other type (what you call Teutonic) was not so much in evidence and we knew very little about them and thought they were just trade, you know, the truck driver who enjoyed being had but pretended that he was really interested in women and money. But I think the war has caused a great change. Inhibitions have broken down. All sorts of young men are trying out all sorts of new things, away from home and familiar taboos.'

'Everyone is by nature bisexual,' said the grey-haired man. 'Society, early conditioning, good or bad luck – depending on how you were told to look at it – determine the result. Nothing is "right". Only denial of instinct is wrong.'

Across the room, Shaw motioned for Jim to join him. Jim excused himself.

Shaw and Rolly were surrounded by sailors who regarded Jim jealously as he joined them.

'I thought you looked bored with those intellectuals,' said Shaw.

'Who are they?' asked Jim.

'Well, the grey-haired one is a professor at Columbia and the one with glasses is a journalist – you'd know his name if I could remember it – and the other one is a perfect bitch,' said Rolly, patting his thick lustrous hair. 'They were probably talking politics. So dreary! I say, why worry? Let them eat cake and all that sort of thing. I mean, after all, really, isn't live and let live the best policy?'

Jim agreed that indeed it was and Rolly pinched his thigh. Shaw was suddenly carried off by the sailors and Jim was left with Rolly, trapped.

'I understand from Ronnie that you're a tennis player. Now I think that's terribly exciting . . . I mean to be an athlete and work out of doors. I've always thought that if I had my life to live over, which fortunately I haven't, I would have spent more time *al fresco*, doing things. As it is, I do nothing. You know I do nothing, don't you? I hope you don't hate me. Everyone's so snobbish about working these days. It's the Communists, they're everywhere, saying people must *produce*. Well, I say that there must be somebody who knows how to appreciate *what's* produced. Which is why I'm really quite a *useful* member of society. After all I keep money in circulation and other people get it and I do so believe in everyone having a good time . . . Oh, there's that butch marine, isn't he something? He was had five times last Sunday and still went to Mass, so he told me.' Jim looked at this celebrity, who turned out to be a rather tired-looking young man in uniform.

'You know, I loathe these screaming pansies,' said Rolly, twisting an emerald and ruby ring. 'I have a perfect weakness for men who are butch. I mean, after all, why be a queen if you like other queens, if you follow me? Luckily, nowadays everybody's *gay*, if you know what I mean . . . *literally* everybody! So different when I was a girl. Why, just a few days ago a friend of mine . . . well, I wouldn't go so far as to say a *friend*, actually I think he's rather *sinister*, but anyway this acquaintance was actually keeping Will Jepson, the *boxer*! Now, I mean, really, when things get that far, things have really gone far!'

Jim agreed that things had indeed gone far. Rolly rather revolted him but he recognized that he meant to be kind and that was a good deal.

'My, isn't it crowded in here? I love for people to enjoy themselves! I mean the right kind of people who appreciate this sort of thing. You see, I've become a Catholic.'

Jim took this information in his stride.

'It started with Monsignor Sheen, those *blue eyes*! But of course I needed Faith. I had to know just where I'm going when I shuffle off this mortal thing, and the Catholic Church is *so* lovely, with that *cosy* grandeur that I adore. One feels so *safe* with the rituals and everything and those robes! Well, there just isn't *anything* to compare with them. They have *really* the most beautiful ceremonies in the world. I was in St Peter's once for Easter – I think it was Easter – anyway, the Holy Father came riding in on a golden throne wearing the triple tiara and the most beautiful white robes you've ever seen and the Cardinals all in red and the incense and the beautiful marble and gold statues . . . absolutely *yummy*! Anyway, then and there I became a Catholic. I remember turning to Dario Alarimo (he was a dear friend of mine of an extremely old Neapolitan family, his father was a Duke and he would have been a Duke, too, but I believe he was killed in the war because he was a Fascist, though all the best people were Fascists in those days, even though we all realized that Mussolini was hardly chic). What was I talking about? I was about to make a point. Oh, yes, about becoming a Catholic. So I turned to Dario and I said, "This is the most splendid thing I've ever seen," and he turned to me and said, "Isn't it, Rolly?" All my

friends call me Rolly. I hope *you* will, too. So, right after that I took instruction.
Oh, my poor head! It was so difficult. There was so much to memorize and I've
a perfectly wretched memory, but I did it. I don't like to seem carping or to be
finding fault with the Church but if they would only cut out all that memory
work, things would be a lot *simpler* and they might pick up all sorts of really nice
people, not that I'm implying they don't already have the best people. Good
evening, Jimmy, Jack, Allen. Enjoying yourselves? But as I was saying, except
for that awful memory work at the start, it's been thrilling. I go to confessional
once a month and I even get to the Sunday morning Mass, the one at ten, and
really I think I'm something of a model convert.

'Of course it will probably be years before I die. I certainly *hope* it will be
years. But when I go, I want to be prepared. I've picked out the nicest crypt at
the Church of St Agnes in Detroit. That's where my family makes those awful
motor-cars. And I shall be buried there. I expect the Cardinal will officiate at
the funeral. He better, considering the money I'm leaving them in my will.
Going so soon, Rudy? Thank you, good night. I understand that the Pope is
thinking quite seriously of giving me a decoration for the good deeds I've done.
I've given them rather a bit of cash, you know. It's the only way to defeat
Communism.

'I do hope I'll go to heaven after doing so many good works on earth. I think
sin is *terribly* fearsome, don't you? It's practically impossible not to sin a little, but
I think the *big* sins that are the ones that can't be forgiven, like murdering
people. A few lies, white lies, and an occasional infidelity, that's really the extent
of my personal falls from Grace. I have such hopes for the afterlife. I see it as a
riot of colour! And all the angels will look like marines. Too gay! The party is
going well, don't you think?'

Jim agreed, weary of the flood of talk.

'If you'll excuse me I must make my rounds. The work of a hostess is never
done. You wouldn't like to spend the night, would you?'

As Jim started to say no, Rolly giggled. 'So few people do any more, that's one
of the horrors of age. Well, I've enjoyed this little chat with you *immensely*, and I
hope you'll come by some evening when we can have a *quiet* dinner together.'
Rolloson patted Jim on the buttocks and plunged into his menagerie.

Jim found Shaw drunk and surrounded by sailors.

'I'm going home.'

'But it's early. Come on, what you need is a drink.'

'I'll call you up in a day or so.' Jim departed. It was a relief for him to breathe
the fresh air of the street.

Winter passed swiftly. Jim saw Shaw occasionally and Shaw was friendly
and amusing and introduced him to a number of people who had money and
nothing to do. There were many different homosexual worlds in New York, and
each usually had some knowledge of the others. There was also the half-world
where hetero- and homosexual mingled with a certain degree of frankness; this
was particularly true of theatrical and literary groups. But in the highest society,
the homosexual wore a stylized mask in order to move gracefully, and often
unconvincingly, among admiring women who were attracted to him because his
understanding was as great as his demands were few. Occasionally two homosexuals might meet in the great world. When they did, by a quick glance they
acknowledged one another and, like amused conspirators, observed the effect
each was having. It was a form of freemasonry.

From all over the country homosexuals had converged on New York. Here, among the indifferent millions, they could be as unnoticed by the enemy as they were known to one another. Yet for every one who lived openly with men, there were ten who married, had children, lived a discreet, ordinary life, only occasionally straying into bars or Turkish baths, particularly at five o'clock, that hour between office and home when the need for relief is particularly urgent. These masculine, rather tense men appealed to Jim, who disliked the other sort he met through Shaw. Yet he learned a great deal from the bold homosexuals. Like jazz musicians and dope addicts, they spoke in code. The words 'fairy' and 'pansy' were considered to be in bad taste. They preferred to say that a man was 'gay', while someone quite effeminate was a 'queen'. As for those manly youths who offered themselves for seduction while proclaiming their heterosexuality, they were known as 'trade', since they usually wanted money. Trade was regarded with great suspicion; in fact, it was a part of the homosexual credo that this year's trade is next year's competition. Jim was thought to be trade by most of Shaw's friends, and inaccessible trade at that.

All during the winter Jim saw a good deal of the Rolloson world. Though he was repelled by the queens, he had no other society. Furtive encounters with young married men seldom led to anything. For a time, he hoped that if he saw enough of the queens, he might begin to like their society and be happy in it. But this was not possible, and so when Shaw went back on active duty, Jim dropped out of the gay world, preferring to haunt those bars where he could find young men like himself.

On an impulse one afternoon, Jim telephoned Maria Verlaine's hotel and to his surprise he found her in. She invited him to come to see her. Maria embraced him at the door: 'You look so well!' She led him into the sitting-room. Her eyes were luminous; she was vivacious; she laughed often. Then Jim noticed that her hands shook as she smoked her cigarette, and that she was ill at ease. He wonderered why, but she gave him no clue. 'Where have I been? Well, let me see. Everywhere. Nowhere. The summer in Maine. Then Jamaica. But New York is the centre where I touch base between excursions.'

'You haven't been happy, have you?' Jim was direct.

'What a question!' She laughed, eyes not meeting his. 'It's hard to say *what* being happy is. Absence of pain? In that case, I have been happy. I suffer no pain. Feel nothing.' But she mocked herself as she spoke.

'Then you still haven't got what you want?'

'No, I haven't. I live entirely on the surface, from day to day.' She was suddenly grave.

'Will you ever find him?'

'I don't know. Perhaps not. I'm not young. I won't live for ever. I simply go on. And wait.'

'I wonder if any man wants the complete thing that you do. I don't think men are capable of so much feeling; that's why so many prefer one another to women.' He was immediately sorry that he had said this. Yet he was convinced that it was the truth.

Maria laughed. 'You don't leave us much hope, do you? One must be what one is. Besides, at times I have been very happy.'

'Maybe we'd all be better off just having friends and forget about lovers.'

Maria smiled. 'That seems like such a waste, doesn't it?'

They talked then of other things until it was twilight and Jim got up to leave. Maria had told him that she was expecting a friend at five.

'I'll see you again. Soon,' she said.

'Soon,' said Jim. They did not embrace when he left.

Jim went straight to a Times Square bar frequented by soldiers and sailors. He studied the room carefully, like a general surveying the terrain of battle. Then he selected his objective: a tall Army Lieutenant with broad shoulders, dark hair, blue eyes. Jim squeezed in beside him and ordered a drink. Jim's leg touched the Lieutenant's leg, a hard muscular leg which returned the pressure.

'You in the service?' asked the Lieutenant. His voice was slow, deep, Far Western.

'Yeah, I was in the Army, too.'

'What outfit?'

They exchanged information. The Lieutenant had served with the infantry during the invasion of North Africa. He was now stationed in the South as an instructor.

'You live around here?'

Jim nodded. 'I got a room downtown.'

'I sure wish I had a place. I got to stay on a sofa with this married cousin.'

'That sounds pretty uncomfortable.'

'It sure is.'

'You could,' said Jim, as though he were thinking it over, 'stay at my place. There's plenty of room.'

The Lieutenant said no, he couldn't do that: they had another drink together and then went home to bed.

II

In the spring, Jim returned to the courts. According to his partners, it might be ten years before the lot was built on; meanwhile, it was a gold-mine and Jim worked hard, and he made money.

New York was full of servicemen, coming and going. Jim moved to a larger apartment, though still in the Village. He now knew a number of people but none well. It was easier to have sex with a man than to acquire a friend.

Jim saw Maria Verlaine once or twice, but since it was obviously painful for her to be with him, he stopped telephoning her.

That summer Sullivan returned and Jim went to meet him at his club. They greeted each other in a gruff off-hand manner. Sullivan was thinner than Jim remembered and his sand-coloured hair was beginning to go grey. He wore civilian clothes. 'Yes, I'm through with being a correspondent.' He grinned. 'I quit before they fired me. I just don't have the vulgar touch, unlike my angel wife.'

'Amelia?'

Sullivan nodded. 'She's a great success. She started out by telling the *Ladies' Home Journal* what it was like to be a British housewife during the Blitz, and now she's graduated to the higher politics. Everyone quotes her. The Dark Ages continue.' Sullivan ordered another drink for himself. 'Have you seen Maria?'

'A few times. Not much. She's out of town.'

'Too bad. I wanted to see her. You know she's almost the only woman I've ever really liked as a person. She's so un- . . . pressing.'

'I think she's all right now.' Jim was tentative.

Sullivan waited.

'Interested in some man or other. I don't know who,' Jim continued doggedly, not certain why he was lying except that he did not want to hurt Sullivan again.

'Well, that's nice for her. She deserves good luck.' He changed the subject. 'What about your business?'

Jim was proud to be able to tell him how well he was doing. Boasting to a friend is one of life's few certain pleasures.

'That's good news.' Sullivan paused. 'Are you alone, are you living alone?'

Jim nodded. 'I just play the bars. I like strangers, I guess.'

'It's better to have one person . . . isn't it?'

'Maybe for some people. But not for me,' he lied. 'Sometimes I never even know their names. Sometimes we never say more than a few words. It all happens so natural, so easy.'

'Sounds lonely.'

'Isn't everything?'

Sullivan sat back in his chair and looked about the old-fashioned bar with its dark heavy wood. Several club members sat drinking quietly at a corner table. 'You've changed,' Sullivan was casual.

'I know.' Jim was as casual. 'When you almost die, you change. When you've been a soldier, you change. When you get older, you change.'

'You seem a little more . . . *definite*, now.'

'About some things. But I still don't know how to get what I want.'

Sullivan laughed. 'Who does? Change is the nature of life.'

'But that's not true,' Jim continued, intent on his own thought.

'What?'

'There's someone I knew in Virginia. Someone I grew up with.' It was the first time Jim had ever mentioned Bob to anyone. He stopped immediately.

'Who was he?'

'It was a long time ago.' Jim said no more. But it gave him a sense of power to realize that he could one day recapture his past simply by going home. He made a vow. As soon as the work of the summer was done, he would go back to Virginia and find Bob, and complete what was begun that day by the river.

Jim was conscious that Sullivan had asked a question and was waiting for an answer. 'What? I'm sorry.'

'I said,' Sullivan was awkward, 'that I was alone, too, and if you wanted to, we might . . . again.'

Jim was flattered but not greatly moved. He responded amiably. Their affair was resumed. And since it was no longer of much importance to either of them, their life together was rather more pleasant than it had been the first time around.

In June, Paul's new novel was published and his publishers gave a cocktail party for him. The day was hot. Jim was bored and ill at ease, but Sullivan, immaculate in a new gabardine suite, was almost happy.

In the stifling room, the talk was loud as the flower of New York publishing got drunk together. Jim drifted from group to group, eyes smarting from cigarette smoke, puzzled by what conversion he did hear.

'Henry James revival? It won't last. It's the British, you know. They're responsible. During air-raids, people need to be comforted, so they read James and Trollope. Return to a safe golden self-contained world, with no bombs in it.'

'I suppose there will be war novels. The real horror of war is the novels which are written about it. But don't expect anything good for at least a decade. I wouldn't publish a war book for the world. Harry Brown of course is an exception. John Hersey, too.'

'Carson McCullers? Yes. And of course Faulkner. The Agrarians, yes. A lot of Southerners seem to be writing. Perhaps it was the Civil War. One must have a tragedy to have a literature. Also, Southerners are not forced so quickly into business. That makes a difference. And then they talk so awfully much.'

'Is the *Partisan Review* really, truly Trotskyite?'

'The Jews can't write novels. No, I'm not anti-Semitic. And Jews do make excellent critics. But they are not creative. It has something to do with Talmudic training. Of course Proust was a genius but he was half French and all social climber.'

'Henry Miller is almost as boring as Walt Whitman, and a good deal less talented.'

'I adore *For Whom the Bell Tolls*. I read it twice. Obscenity of an obscenity but it was beautiful and good and true.'

'Scott Fitzgerald? I don't think I know the name. Is he here? Does he write?'

A lean young man in need of a shave asked Jim if he was a writer and when Jim said no, the young man was relieved. 'Too many writers,' he mumbled. He was drunk.

'What do you think of Paul Sullivan?' Jim was curious to know. But he found the answer unfathomable: 'I don't like Aldous Huxley either.'

Across the room Sullivan was signing a book. Jim departed.

It was a busy summer. The war continued. Jim's work was hard but rewarding. He particularly liked Mr Globe, who knew nothing about tennis. 'I'm in this for the money, Jim,' he said one day. 'I used to have this secondhand shop and that closed in the Depression. And then I was a clerk until I got into this for the money. I say you can make money easy if you're in things for the money, but you need a little help sometimes. You know why we let you buy in the business?'

Jim shook his head, though he knew.

'Because you're not in this just for the money. You like what you do and there's always got to be a few people who know something to help the ones who're in it for the money to make money.'

That summer they made money, and Jim was happy.

When Maria Verlaine returned to New York that autumn, Jim and Sullivan visited her at the Harding. She was in good form, Jim thought, and told her so.

'I've been in Argentina.'

'Is that an answer?' Sullivan laughed.

'I thought you were in Canada,' said Jim.

'Yes, to both of you. I'll get you a drink. I thought we'd have dinner here in the room.' Her movements were swift and graceful. 'It's a very simple, a very familiar story. I met an Argentine in Canada. He invited me to visit him in Buenos Aires. I did.'

'Was that wise?' Paul was oddly conventional.

'Dear Paul! He's a rich poet and quite indifferent to what people say. As a matter of fact, he told everyone I was a famous literary figure from Mexico and I was worshipped. It was delightful.'

'And now?'

'I'm back, as you see, and we'll be here for the winter.'

'*We?*' asked Jim.

'Yes, Carlos is here with me. But in a different suite. We must be hypocrites in New York. We don't want to corrupt the Anglo-Saxons.'

'Is he published in America?' asked Paul.

She shook her head. 'I don't think he's ever really written anything.'

'But you said he was a poet.'

'That doesn't mean he has to write poems, does it? Actually, he does nothing at all and that's his poetry, to do nothing, with imagination of course.'

'Are we going to meet him?' asked Paul.

Maria was evasive. 'Of course. But not today. Perhaps later. Now tell me about your new book.'

Jim listened and wondered why he felt betrayed instead of pleased for Maria, who seemed to have found what she had been searching for. But he was not pleased. He was furious with her – and with himself for being unable to give her anything except a friendship and a candour she could get as easily from others quite as understanding as he. Yet he was hurt; it was as if she had indeed been a lover who had deserted him.

Dinner was brought them in the room, and Jim drank pre-war Burgundy, hoping to get drunk, but his mind was too sharply focused in its outrage.

During dinner Paul described his London meeting with Amelia. Maria was not surprised. 'I was afraid she would become an Amazon.'

'Now don't blame it on me.'

'Never! It was not your fault, nor hers. It's just this terrible country.'

'Terrible?' Jim was startled from his self-pity. He had never heard anyone be quite so vehement about God's Country.

'Maria's a Nazi,' Paul chuckled. 'Or a Communist.'

'The Russians are our allies.' Maria was light. 'But I'm not political. Just a woman. A rather hard thing to be in your country. Either I meet men who have been . . . wounded, or I meet those who think only of women as a kind of relief, rather like aspirin.'

'Latents are lousy lovers,' Paul grinned. He had never been impressed by Maria's hymns to Aphrodite.

'You are perfectly right.' Maria chose to take him seriously. 'Everything in this country is calculated to destroy both sexes. Men are told that their desires are dirty and unwanted. Women are told that they are goddesses and that men are fortunate to be able just to worship them at a distance . . .'

'It's the fault of advertising,' said Paul. 'Since women buy the most things, the advertisers flatter them the most, tell them they have more taste than men, more sensitivity, more intelligence, even more physical strength because they live longer. The advertisers of course are men.'

'Well, they have a lot to answer for.' Maria was uncharacteristically grim.

'Are Europeans so much better?' asked Jim.

Maria shrugged. 'At least the men know who and what they are, and that is the beginning of sanity.'

Paul agreed. 'Americans tend to play different roles, hoping that somehow they'll stumble on the right one.'

Jim turned to Maria. 'When the war is over, will you go back to Europe?'

'Yes. For ever!'

'With the Argentine?' Paul was amused.

'Who knows?' She smiled. She had never seemed quite so lovely to Jim. 'I live in the present.' She looked at Jim and because he saw affection in her eyes, he looked away, pondering the betrayal, cursing its cause.

III

Sullivan's new book was not a success. He wrote articles for magazines and wondered if he should try his luck in the theatre. Jim found him easy to get along with. From time to time one or the other would bring home a stranger and neither was in the least jealous or envious. From Jim's standpoint it was an ideal relationship; only the intense experience with Bob could be more satisfactory that his life with Sullivan.

Jim saw Maria Verlaine occasionally; the Argentine was never present. Their old intimacy continued but he was aware, now more than ever, that it was not enough. He found it unbearable that she should be happy and that he was not the cause.

On New Year's Eve Rolloson invited Jim and Sullivan to a party: 'a congenial group, my dears, just a little gathering' of what turned out to be the same group that had been there at the time of Jim's first visit. Rolloson wore a light grey suit pulled in tightly at the waist, a mauve shirt gorgeously monogrammed, and a sea-green crêpe de chine ascot at his rosy throat. He greeted them at the door, smelling of violets.

'How lovely of you to come, Mr Sullivan. May I call you Paul? Paul, there are loads of people here *dying* to meet you and I'm sure you'll find a lot of old friends, too. I think literally *everybody* is here, and I did so intend to have an *intimate* party. Ah, well.' He thrust Sullivan at a group of literary-looking men, among whom was the grey-haired professor from Columbia. With Sullivan safely put aside, Rolly took Jim about the room, introducing him to various people, all the while chattering. 'First Shaw and now Sullivan. Aren't you the one, though! How do you do it? Or should I say, *what* do you have?' He gave Jim a lightning grope. Jim shied away, irritated.

'It just happens that they're the only people I know.'

'But *where* did you know them?'

'In Hollywood. Did you get your Papal thing, that decoration?'

Rolly frowned. 'My dear, the Church is riddled with politics, literally riddled. As a matter of fact – don't repeat a word of this to *anyone* – I think I shall take up Vedanta. I've met the most wonderful swami. At least I think he's a swami. He's here tonight unless I forgot . . . no, I remember I saw him at the Van Vechtens' and I invited him . . . or was that the prince? I've got the most wonderful Hindu prince here, too. You'll just love him. He looks like Theda Bara. *He's* here, I know, because I remember complimenting him on his turban. But I'm not so sure about the swami. You know, he's got millions of dollars in rubies and emeralds right here with him in New York – the prince, I mean, not the swami. I don't think *he* has anything but he's terribly high-*minded*. Read Gerald Heard if you don't believe me. Where's Shaw now?'

'Who? Oh, Shaw. Well, I think he's back in Hollywood by now. He's been discharged from the Navy, or so it said in the papers.

'Papers? Don't you ever hear from him?'

'No, we don't write.'

'What a pity! You know, he broke so many hearts when he was here. Good evening Jack, Jimmy, Allen. Lovely of you to come. I think he's terribly handsome – Shaw, I mean. He has such an *air* about him.' Rolly looked about the room at his guests. Jim noticed that he was wearing make-up. 'It's very gay, don't you think so? Oh, here comes Sir Roger Beaston, the perfect *camp*! Do excuse me.' Rolly darted across the room to meet a pale little man with yellow hair.

Jim found Sullivan at the centre of a group of people, not all literary. They were drinking champagne and talking animatedly about a certain European king who had taken a new boy who was supposed to be extraordinarily handsome and charming, even if he *had* begun his career hustling in Miami. Jim listened, no longer surprised at hearing revelations about people he had never suspected before. At first he had disbelieved all the stories on principle, but too often they had proved to be true. Obviously the world was not what it seemed. Anthing might be true of anybody.

Jim ambled away. In the hall he found a telephone, cradled in a piece of driftwood. Without thinking he picked it up and telephoned Maria. She answered. He could hear music behind her voice and the sound of voices.

'Jim! Where are you?'

'At a dull party.'

'Then come here!'

Maria wore an evening dress of silver and a red flower in her hair. Her eyes sparkled and she seemed drunk, although she never drank. She simply became charged with energy and enthusiasm when she was with those she liked. They embraced and she led him into her apartment. Maria introduced him to a dozen handsome couples, most European émigrés. Then she gave him champagne and they sat in front of the mock fireplace.

'Whose party did you desert for me?'

'A man named Rolloson.'

She made a face. 'I've known Rolly for twenty years. He's harmless, I suppose, but he alarms me. It's like seeing oneself in a distorted mirror.'

'We only went . . . well, because we were asked to come.' He felt awkward because she had not invited him originally to her party. Sensing this, she said, 'You know why I didn't ask you?'

'Carlos?'

She nodded.

'Is he here now, in this room?'

'No, he's gone downstairs to order more champagne. It won't hurt you to see him, to meet him?'

'No, of course not. I'd like to.'

Then the bells began to ring and over the radio came the noise from Times Square and everyone exclaimed, 'Happy New Year!' and Carlos returned and kissed Maria. 'I was almost too late,' he said. She turned to Jim. 'This is Carlos.'

They shook hands. 'Happy New Year,' said Carlos.

'Happy New Year,' said Jim. In a few minutes he went home.

CHAPTER TEN

In the spring Sullivan received an advance from a publisher to write a book about Africa. 'And that means six months of travelling, all expenses paid. If I don't take it, you'll have to support me.'

'Not if I can help it,' Jim was guiltily pleased at the thought of living alone again.

'Funny thing about travel, once you start, it's hard to stop. Like being an alcoholic. I really want to go.'

'So do I. But I've got work to do.'

'And someone else to find.' This was flat.

'I'm not exactly looking.' Jim was sharp.

'I know.' Contrition. 'I'm sorry. Anyway, there is something wrong with two men living together, a man and a woman, too, for that matter. Unless they have children, it's pointless.'

'We're too selfish, I suppose.'

'And separate. Perhaps a good thing. I don't agree with Maria's high romantic view of love. We affect one another quite enough merely by existing. Whenever the stars cross – or is it comets? – fragments pass briefly from one orbit to another. On rare occasions there is total collision, but most often the two simply continue without incident, neither losing more than a particle to the other, in passing.'

So they separated, with a metaphor involving stars.

The next day, as if by further celestial design, there was a letter from Mrs Willard, full of news.

'You remember Bob Ford, don't you?' she wrote. 'He was such a friend of yours in school. Well, he's in the Merchant Marine now and he was home on leave for a few days last week. He asked after you and so did his wife. I don't know if I ever wrote you that he married Sally Mergendahl last year, and they have a baby. You know that job with the school is still open and if you want to come back . . .'

There it was. Bob had returned. But he was married. Not once had it occurred to Jim that Bob could ever in any way be different from the way he had been that day beside the river. Yet he must have changed. He had married Sally. Jim experienced a sudden panic. Was it possible that he had waited years for a reunion with a man who cared only for women? No. He rejected the thought. Bob was obviously bisexual, if only because no one could have been so perfect a lover on that unique occasion and then change entirely. Jim reassured himself, and because he wanted to believe that nothing had changed, nothing changed, in his mind. Meanwhile, he made plans to go back to Virginia as soon as summer ended and take up his life at the precise point where it had left off that green summer evening seven years before.

During the summer Shaw came to town for the première of someone else's picture and Jim met him in a restaurant where the food and service were bad but where many people who were famous came not only to look at one another but also at themselves in the mirrors which lined the dining-room.

Jim was startled to find that Shaw was grey at the temples; he was moving with unusual dispatch into middle age.

'You're looking handsome, Jimmy,' said Shaw, 'really handsome, I must say. Of all my graduates, you're easily the best-looking.'

'That's like winning the Davis Cup. Thanks.' Jim smiled. 'Who're you living with now?'

'Nobody. I was with a perfect son of a bitch, from Detroit, a diver, of all things – you know, Olympic Games stuff. He had a wonderful build but stupid! My God, I don't think I've ever known anybody so stupid. All he wanted to do was drink beer and sit up late in gay bars. I kicked him out. Anyway, he had a wife and two children so I really think I did the right thing, don't you? Nobody wants to break up a home. What have you been doing?'

'Working.'

'Sullivan?'

'Gone to Africa.'

'Hope they eat him.' Shaw was sour. 'He's such a pretentious bastard. I saw where his new book got bad notices. Not that critics mean a thing. When they pan my pictures I make money, and when they praise them we lose it. After all, entertainment is entertainment.'

Jim noticed that everyone in the room was aware of Shaw, but for once Jim disliked the attention; particularly when he noticed several men he had met at Rolloson's party: each accompanied by a woman, for this was enemy territory.

'Are you making a picture?'

'No. It's hard to get the right roles nowadays. I'm sitting it out. The studio thinks the war is going to be over and they'll get the old stars back and to hell with us who've been selling the tickets for them. Well, they'll find out. Gable means nothing now.'

Jim wondered if Shaw was finished. It was a harsh business, as everyone liked to say.

'They'll come back to me in time. But it'll be too late.'

'Why?'

Shaw looked about him; then he whispered, 'I'm quitting the movies, retiring.'

'And do nothing?'

'Not quite. I'm going on the stage. I start rehearsing in September.'

'That's wonderful.'

'But tough. I've never been on a stage, but I've got to do it.'

'How's your mother?'

'Still in Baltimore. It's a funny thing, she brags about me, of course, but sometimes I think she resents my success. Imagine a mother being competitive! I guess people are people, first. Anyway, she's happy about me being married.'

'Married?'

Shaw nodded. 'It's the studio's idea. They think too many people are catching on. Maybe they're right.'

'Who's the girl?'

'Calla Petra. Hungarian actress. Kept by the head of the studio, lost a hundred thousand dollars one night gambling at Vegas. A real tramp. But I won't give her a penny. He'll have to. We've signed a pre-nuptial agreement, ironclad. No money from me. She's a dike, anyway, and she needs the publicity as much as I do.'

'Sounds real cosy.'

'Sounds awful.' Shaw groaned.

They saw each other often during the summer. The day Shaw's play opened, he announced that he was retiring from the screen; a week later the play closed, and Shaw went back to Hollywood. His wedding to Calla Petra was the most glittering of the season.

After Shaw left New York, Jim returned to the bar life. He particularly liked one Eighth Avenue bar where both men and women gathered and some of the men were available and some were not, which gave a certain excitement to negotiations. He most liked the innocents who would say the next morning, 'Gee, I was sure drunk last night!' and pretend not to remember what had happened.

One heavy summer night, Jim stood at the bar nursing a beer, examining the inmates. He had almost settled on a young marine with blue eyes and buck teeth when a voice behind him said, 'Ain't you Willard?'

Jim looked around and saw a fat bald young sailor. 'That's right, and you're ... ?' He couldn't recall.

'Collins, Alaska. Remember?'

'Sure. Come on. Have a drink.'

Collins squeezed in beside him at the bar. 'I'm Navy now. I was a petty officer but I got busted.'

'What happened?'

'I got pissed and told a commander off. My usual trouble. Were you in the service?'

'Army. I been out a year.'

'What're you doing now?'

Jim told him.

'Coining money?'

'Fair. You in town long?'

'No, we're sailing soon. This is my last liberty. Boy, you got a good deal, living here, with your own business. I wish I was in your shoes.'

'What're you going to do when you get out?'

'Me? I'm a sailor. What else? I don't know anything else. Once I tried to work in this machine shop, but I couldn't stand being in one place so long, so I quit, left my wife, went back to sea.'

'You're married?'

'Divorced. I knew her since I was a kid in school and she always wanted to marry me but I wouldn't until I got drunk one night and knocked her up and she said I'd *have* to marry her and so I did. We got a kid who lives with her, that's in Eugene, Oregon.'

'Too bad,' Jim tried to sound sympathetic.

'I guess some guys just aren't meant to be family men and I'm one of them. I got this chick in Seattle now who's panting to be married but I told her I been stung once and I'm not going to get stung again. You married yet?'

'No,' said Jim. 'Not yet.'

'You're smarter than me. But I'll bet you got a girl in New York?'

'Kind of.' Jim was noncommittal.

Collins took a long swallow of his drink and said, 'You know any girls around town?'

Jim shook his head. 'Just one. You see, I've been working pretty hard and . . .'

'I know how it is. Say, where did you go after you skipped ship?'

'L.A.'

'Man, that's *my* town! Wide open. Where all the chicks want a good time, like us, and no talk about marrying or any of that shit. You ever see any movie stars?'

'Some.'

'Like who?'

'Calla Petra.'

'No kidding! She must be something the way she's stacked. You get to talk to her?'

'Oh, lots of times.'

'No kidding! You bang her?'

'No, I just played tennis with her.'

'I'd sure like to play tennis with her.' Collins leered. 'And that ain't all I'd like to play with her.'

Jim ordered another beer. Usually he could keep the same beer going for an hour but Collins made him nervous and he found himself actually drinking the beer, an unusual gesture.

'You like the Navy?'

Collins shrugged. 'They don't know nothing about the sea, that's for sure. Wished I was back in the Merchant Marine.'

'Why aren't you?'

'I was on land with my wife and I was going to be drafted. So to get out of the draft, I joined the Navy, because I didn't want to be in no Army where I had to walk.'

As they drank together, Jim looked about the bar. The marine had gone. There was no one else who appealed to him. At the opposite end of the bar an old man was trying to make a sailor who in turn was trying to make a soldier. It was very funny. Collins, perfectly unaware of the comedy, suddenly asked, 'Hey, why did you leave the ship in such a hurry?'

It was a question Jim had been waiting for. He spoke slowly, simulating ease. 'I wanted to see California and I didn't want to have to argue with the Steward, so I just skipped out.'

'I figured it was something like that.' Collins finished his drink. 'How come you left those girls in that apartment? That was one thing I never been able to figure out.'

Jim shrugged. 'I didn't like the one I had, that's all.'

'Well, she was madder than hell, but you was smart to leave when you did.'

'Why?'

'They both had clap. And I caught it and had a hell of a time getting cured.' They both laughed and Collins told Jim about the man who had had clap twenty times and been cured every time except the first. At last they parted and Jim was relieved that Collins's liberty was almost over and they would not meet again.

One cold day when the winter sky was bitter orange and grey and a chill haze hung over the city, Jim went home for Christmas.

Mrs Willard stood on the porch as her son came up the path to the house. He was startled at her appearance. White hair, untidy as always, face pale and lined; she had grown old while he was away. They embraced and she clung to him, holding him tight, saying nothing, only holding him. Then they went into the house where, at least, nothing had changed. The parlour was as depressing as ever, despite a Christmas tree glittering with small buzzing lights. Jim felt oddly displaced in time. He turned to his mother and they looked at one another without speaking, two strangers with a common memory.

'You've grown up, Jim,' his mother said at last. 'You've changed.'

'We all do, I guess.' He was inadequate.

'You look more like my side of the family. You don't look like your father any more. You used to.'

Jim saw in his mother's face his own features grown old and he was frightened at the thought of age and death.

'You haven't changed much,' he lied.

She chuckled. 'Oh, yes, I have. I'm an old woman now. But I don't mind. If you haven't got beauty in the first place, age makes you better-looking, they say, gives you character.'

He looked at her face in the light of the Christmas tree and he agreed with her. She had improved with time. She had achieved a face of her own, something she had lacked before.

'Are you going to get married, son?' It was strange to be called son again. 'Some day.'

'The older I get the more I think people should be married early. I sometimes think that the reason your father and I never got along as well as we should was because we married so late. You're just the right age to settle down.'

'Perhaps.'

'There're some nice girls growing up here. They'd make fine wives. You'll meet them while you're home. You should marry a nice girl here rather than one of those New York girls, not that it's any of my business.' Jim smiled: New York people were not very well thought of in the South.

She asked him about his work and he told her about it. She was pleased. 'I'm glad you're making money. Nobody in this family ever has before and it's about time somebody did. But money's not everything, is it? I mean sometimes marriage and settling down and enjoying life are more important, don't you think so?' Sooner or later she would suggest that he stay home for good.

'I don't know, Mother. I really haven't thought much about settling down yet. I've got a good business in New York and as long as it's good I better stay with it.'

Sensing resistance, she changed the subject. 'Your brother is a Second Lieutenant now. He's in the Air Force and he's going overseas any day. Why, I don't know, since the war's almost over, or so the papers say.'

'Will he be here for Christmas?'

She nodded. 'He's got a few days' leave. He's a very bright young man.' Jim wondered if perhaps she disliked her younger son. His mother was definitely changed. Anything was possible.

'You're taking in boarders now?'

She had written him this news. 'Just a couple, a man and wife. You'll meet them at dinner. Carrie and her husband are coming to dinner, too.'

'How's my nephew?'

'Nice and fat.' She paused. 'I can't get over how you've changed,' she said finally. They were silent. Jim idly kicked his suitcase and his mother said, 'You'd better take your things up to your room.'

'Which one?'

'Your old room.'

'Does John stay there when he's on leave?'

'Yes. Nothing's changed. I try not to change anything if I can help it. I know that's maybe living too much in the past but I think the past was pretty nice, in some ways. I think maybe the future can be even nicer.'

'You mean since Father died.' Jim was blunt.

She nodded placidly. 'Yes, since your father died. I always believed if you make a bad bargain, you just have to keep it. But when it's over, there's no use pretending that it was the best thing that ever happened.'

'Why did you marry him?'

'Lord, son, why does anyone marry anybody? If I ever knew why I married him I've forgotten. Probably because he asked me. I wasn't in much demand. Now take your bag up and get ready for dinner.'

Everyone was at table when Jim came into the dining-room. His mother introduced him to the boarders; then he shook hands with his brother-in-law and kissed his sister. Carrie had grown stout. Her breasts and hips seemed ready to burst her clothes. Without make-up, she looked tired but good-humoured, and obviously she was pleased with her husband, an amiable sort who did whatever she asked him to do.

'Well, Mother, he's as beautiful as ever.' Carrie looked at her brother admiringly. 'He sure got all the looks in this family.' Her laugh was like an explosion and only stopped when her husband told her what she wanted to hear: that she was beautiful, too.

During dinner, they spoke of Jim's work and whether or not it was profitable, and if he came home, as they all desired, could he do as well as he had done in New York? And of course Carrie asked the inevitable: 'When are you going to get married, Jim?'

He shrugged. 'When some girl asks me.' Everyone laughed at that.

'You were always shy with the girls,' said his sister, her mouth full. 'You really ought to settle down. There's nothing like it, is there, dear?' Her husband agreed that there was nothing like it. Jim found the masquerade depressing. He tried to change the subject and failed.

'Jim will marry when he's ready to settle down,' said his mother tranquilly. 'I think he's been wise not to have gotten married while he was traipsing around the world.'

They talked of marriage, secure people whose lives followed a familiar pattern, the experience of one very much like that of the other. But when they tried to advise Jim, none suspected that their collective wisdom was of no use to him, that the pattern of his life was different from theirs. This fact made him sad, as well as annoyed at the never-ending masquerade. He was bored by his own necessary lies. How he longed to tell them exactly what he was! He wondered suddenly what would happen if every man like himself were to be natural and honest. Life would certainly be happier for everyone in a world where sex was thought of as something natural and not fearsome, and men could love men naturally, in the way they were meant to, as well as to love women naturally, in the way they were meant to. But even as he sat at the table, pondering freedom, he knew that it was a dangerous thing to be an honest man: finally he lacked the courage.

'By the way,' said Carrie, 'you know Bob Ford married Sally Mergendahl, didn't you?'

'Mother wrote me. Where is he . . . where are they now?'

'She's living here with her family, and he's at sea but I think he's due back in a few days. He'll be here for the Christmas party the Mergendahls are giving. You're invited. And they have the cutest baby girl, with dark red hair just like Bob's.'

'Why, Jim, I would never have recognized you, so grown up and everything! Isn't he, dear?' Mrs Mergendahl turned to Mr Mergendahl and got his agreement. She continued, secure in her audience. 'Well, he's a grown man now. They all are. Seems like only yesterday when you played in all those tennis tournaments at school. Now look at you! And all the other boys in the Army, married, and our own little girl a mother!'

Mr Mergendahl winked at Jim. 'You better let him go, Mother, so he can meet the young girls who are dying to meet him. Got a whole new crop of 'em, too.' Jim excused himself and went into the crowded old-fashioned living-room. Carrie took him by the arm. 'I'll introduce you around.

Many of the people he recognized; some he had known in school, others from the town. Everyone remembered him and they seemed genuinely glad he was back, recalling events that he had forgotten. As in a dream, he moved from group to group, toward a central point where he knew Bob must be.

Then he saw Sally Mergendahl, now Sally Ford, and he broke away from Carrie to talk to her. Sally was now a tall and graceful woman with dark hair braided about her head. They shook hands warmly, each scrutinizing the other, looking for signs of change.

'Congratulations!' said Jim.

'On the baby? or marrying Bob?'

'Both.' Jim sounded blithe; yet she was his rival.

'That's sweet of you, Jim. Here, let's sit down. There's so much we have to catch up on.' They sat on a horse-hair sofa, their conversation broken regularly by newcomers who wanted to say hello to Jim.

'See how popular you are? Oh, you really ought to settle down here with the rest of us.'

'You heard I wasn't going to?'

'Well, not exactly, but you know how everybody knows everybody else's business around here. We spend all our time prying, even though there's never anything very interesting going on. We all know each other too well.'

'Where's Bob?'

She frowned. 'Newport News, with his ship. He won't be in until tomorrow. When he does get there, why don't you have dinner with us, just the three of us.'

'I'd like to. Bob's a First Mate now, isn't he?'

'Yes. But he's quitting when the war's over.'

'How come? He loves the sea.'

'But Daddy needs him in the insurance business, and everybody thinks Bob will make a wonderful salesman, and Daddy says that when he retires Bob can have the company.'

'That'll be nice for him.' Jim saw the kindly noose being dropped over Bob's unwilling shoulders. But were they unwilling? Could he have changed? It was possible.

'He's roamed around long enough. After all, there's just so much world to see and then where are you? Anyway, all his friends are here and he can have a good job. I think everything will be just grand for us. I can't wait for you to see the baby.'

'Is Bob a good . . . father?'

'Well, he hasn't had much practice. At the moment he thinks a baby is something to play with until it starts to cry, when he wants to wring its neck. Then he says that I care more about the baby than I do about him, so I tell him that, after all, the baby *is* him, which it is.'

'Does he understand that?'

'Well . . . yes, at times. You know how he is.'

'I don't know if I do any more.'

'It *has* been a long time, hasn't it? And he is different. Of course he looks about the same. But he laughs a lot more than he used to. He was rather grim when he was a boy. And of course he was girl-crazy then. He still gets letters from girls all over the world. He lets me read them and they're really pathetic. But I'm not jealous. I don't know why, I guess it's because he came back to me, when he didn't have to.'

As she talked, Jim wondered if Bob had ever been attracted to men. From what she said – and what he suspected – it seemed unlikely, which meant that their experience had been unique. And that meant Bob had made love with him not out of a lust for the male but from affection. The fact that he now preferred women to men could only make their relationship all the more unusual and binding.

Jim did not deceive himself that his return would mean an end to Bob's marriage. Their boyhood dream of going to sea together was no longer practical. Too much had happened. Each was now part of the world. Yet there was no reason why the affair could not continue, particularly if he returned to Virginia and took the job at the high school. Proximity would do the rest. He wondered about the old slave cabin by the river. Was it still there?

Sally was still talking. 'I don't like to be old-fashioned. And I really don't think I am. I believe a man should have lots of affairs with women before he settles down with one. I told my mother that and I thought she would explode. She says she never *will* be able to understand the younger generation.'

'When do you think Bob will be out of the Merchant Marine?'

'When the war with Germany's over. So they say. Daddy has a friend in Washington who can fix it if there's any problem. Jim, would you get me some punch? I'm parched.'

Jim crossed the crowded living-room, smiling at all the people who wanted to talk to him. He was surprised that he was popular. If only they knew. At the punch bowl he found himself face to face with his brother.

John was tall and dark and he looked trim in his uniform. Jim disliked him as much as ever. He was astonishingly self-confident and everyone said that he was going 'to make his mark' and he believed it, too. Politics was to be his career.

'What's up, Jim? It's been a long time.' John's voice was rich and deep; he had been drinking too much, Jim noticed. They exchanged greetings and perfunctory compliments. Then John indicated Sally. 'She's very nice, isn't she?'

'Yes. I like her.'

'Shame Bob missed the party. You must be looking forward to seeing him again.'

Jim wondered if John knew about him. His brother was shrewd and he obviously remembered how much Jim had seen of Bob when they were boys. But

was that enough to make him suspicious? Or did it take one to know one? Jim
smiled to himself at the thought. It often ran in families, they said. He gave his
brother a speculative look.

'What's the matter?'

'Oh . . . nothing. I was just thinking. Well, I better get Sally her punch.'

'Don't get caught under any mistletoe,' said John in his deep mocking voice.

'What took you so long?' Sally was pleasant. 'I was afraid you'd deserted me.'

'No, I was just talking to my brother.'

'It must be wonderful to be back,' said Sally Ford.

The day of the dinner came and Jim was nervous. He snapped at his mother
when she told him that he should wear an overcoat, and he lost his temper with
his brother, whose fountain pen in a bureau drawer had leaked all over his last
white shirt. After a satisfactory row with John, Jim left the house.

With pounding heart, Jim knocked on the door of the Mergendahl house. Bob
opened it.

In a daze, Jim shook hands, hardly able to speak.

'How the hell are you?' Bob was saying. 'Come on in and have a drink.' He
led Jim into the living-room. 'The old folks are out for dinner and Sally's
upstairs doing something or other to the baby. Gosh, but it's good to see you.
You look the same. How've you been?'

Jim's voice was hoarse when he finally spoke. 'Fine. I've been just fine. You
look good, too.' And Bob did.

Jim was surprised that he had forgotten what Bob looked like. He had always
thought his mental picture of him was accurate, but apparently his memory was
emotional, not literal. He had forgotten how dark Bob's red hair was, and that
he had freckles and that his mouth curved up at the corners and that his eyes
were as blue as the Arctic Sea. Only the body was as he recalled it, long and slim
and heavy in the chest. He looked good in uniform.

They sat in front of the fireplace and Bob forgot to get the drinks. He too was
taking inventory. Did he remember everything?

'You just disappeared,' said Bob at last.

'Me? You! I wrote you and wrote you but you were never where I sent the
letters.'

'Well, I was on the move a lot, like you.'

'We both were.'

'Hey, you met Sally yet? Since you been back?'

'At the Christmas party.'

'That's right. I forgot. She invited you for tonight.'

'She's a wonderful girl.' Jim wanted to establish that at the beginning.

'I'll say! I'm glad you like each other. You didn't really know her back at
school, did you?'

'No. But I remember you used to go around with her even then.'

'So when are *you* getting married?' That question again.

'Not for a while.'

'You think you might come back here to live?'

Jim nodded. 'I think I might. You'll be living here, won't you?'

'So they tell me. It looks like I'm going into the insurance business, with
Sally's father. Everybody thinks I'll be good at it.'

'But you'd rather be at sea?'

Bob moved uneasily in his chair, crossing and uncrossing his long legs. 'Well,

I've been at sea almost ten years now and I've made a place for myself. It won't be easy changing to land. But if Sally wants it . . .'

'She wants it. But you don't?'

'Yes, I do.' Bob was defiant, even petulant. Then he shifted. 'Well, maybe not.'

'I don't see what's wrong with being a sailor, especially since you're making good money. Why wouldn't Sally like that?'

'You know women. They want you where they can look at you all the time. She says she just doesn't feel she's married when I'm gone.'

'So you'll settle here.'

Bob nodded gloomily. 'I'll settle here. Oh, I'll get used to it, all right. And I like the idea of being a family man.'

'So I guess I'll be moving back, maybe.'

'That'd be swell, just like it used to be. Funny, I knew all kinds of girls here but I never did know any of the guys very well, except you. It'd be nice having at least one buddy in town. To play tennis with.'

'Yes.'

'But you're too good for me. You're a pro and I haven't played for years. But it sure would be nice to play again.' He was nostalgic and Jim felt an instant of triumph. Bob would return to him, as easily, as naturally as he had gone with him the first time.

'We had some good times when we were kids,' said Bob dreamily, looking into the fire. Jim looked, too. Yes, this was the way it had been: fire and the mood of firelight. It was going to happen again. He was certain of that.

'We had a good time.' Jim vowed he would not mention the cabin first.

'I wish sometimes that we had gone to the university together. The sea was probably a mistake, though fun. You only went because I did, didn't you?'

'That was one of the reasons.'

'Do you think I . . . we made a mistake?'

Jim studied the fire. 'No,' he said finally. 'We did what we were meant to do. I think it was natural for you to be a sailor and me to be a tennis player. We were never like the other people around here. We weren't housebroken. We got away. They hate that. Only now we're coming back.'

Bob smiled. 'You're the only person who understands why I had to go to sea. Yes, we did do the right thing. But now is it right to come back? *Can* you come back to living in the same house, with the same people day after day? Is it possible?'

'I don't know. I just don't know. Of course it's easier for me. I can teach tennis here but you certainly can't be a seaman on land. I guess you ought to do what you feel you have to do.' Jim spoke with something else in mind.

Bob sighed. 'I can't make up my mind.'

Jim wanted to help but he could not. 'Wait,' he said. 'Wait until something happens. Something always does.'

They were silent before the fire. Jim could hear the muffled sound of a baby crying upstairs, Bob's baby.

'How's your father?' asked Jim finally.

'Dead. Last month.'

'Did you see him before he died?'

'No.'

'Didn't he want to see you?'

'He was crazy, they say. He'd been crazy for the last five years. It wouldn't

have done any good. Besides, I didn't want to see him. I didn't care if he died or
not.' Bob was matter-of-fact, all bitterness gone. 'You got a girl, Jim?' he asked
suddenly.

'No.'

'That sounds like you. Still shy with women. But you ought to find yourself
one. Changing around wears a guy out.'

'Maybe I'll find somebody when I come back here.'

'And then we'll be two married men. Gosh, we never thought of ourselves
being that old, did we?'

'No, never.'

'And in a few years we'll be middle-aged and then old and then dead.'

'Morbid, isn't it?' They both laughed. Then Sally came into the room.

'Hello, Jim.'

'How's the baby?' asked Bob.

'Asleep. Thank God! Bob! you haven't given Jim a drink.'

'Sorry. What do you want?'

'Nothing, thanks.'

'Then we'll go in to dinner,' said Sally.

The dinner was good and they talked of the townspeople and their families
and about the war in France. In the intimacy of the family dining-room, Jim
was completely at peace. He would not have to make a move. The thing was
happening of its own accord. Soon Bob would be with him. And, sure enough, it
was Bob who manoeuvred their lives into conjunction. 'I think I'll be up in New
York during May. Let's get together then and have one last fling before the old
prison doors shut!'

Sally smiled indulgently.

Jim said, 'That'd be wonderful. I'll give you my address and you call me soon
as you get to town.'

That spring Jim tried to exhaust himself in work so that he would not think of
Bob. But it was difficult. Nor did matters improve when May came and went
and there was no word from Bob. Finally he wrote Sally, who told him that Bob
was still at sea and wasn't it just awful? But at least the war was finally over and
the Merchant Marine could not keep him much longer.

A year later, Bob appeared at Jim's apartment. They shook hands as though
they had seen each other only the day before.

'Swell place you got.' Bob looked approvingly at the apartment. 'Won't you
hate to give this up for Virginia?'

'I haven't given it up yet.' Jim smiled.

Bob sat in a chair and stretched his long legs. He still wore uniform. 'Swell
place,' he murmured again.

'When are you getting out?'

Bob frowned. 'Damned if I know. I have a chance now to get master's papers.
That's something at my age, and I hate turning it down.'

'But Sally?'

'That's just it . . . but Sally. I don't know what I'm going to do. She wants me
home.'

'And you don't want to go?'

'No.'

'Well, don't. It's your life. If you're happy at sea, stay there. Sally isn't the
first woman to marry a sailor.'

Bob nodded. 'That's what I said to her but she's so damned set on my staying put. Her family, too. Sometimes I think it's her family more than her. She seems happy enough with the baby. I don't think she'd miss *me* all that much.'

'You'll have to make up your own mind,' said Jim, who preferred Bob to be at sea. They would be separated for long periods, but then he would be separated from Sally too. 'How about dinner?'

They went to an Italian restaurant and drank a flask of Chianti between them. Soon the circle would close.

'Where do you want to go?' asked Jim when they had finished.

'I don't care. Any place I can get drunk.'

'There's a bar I know.'

They walked through the warm night air to a bar where men hunted men. Jim was curious to see how Bob would react. They took a table and ordered whisky. There were enough women present to disguise to the casual observer the nature of the place.

Bob looked about him. 'Not too many women here,' he said at last.

'No, not so many. Do you want one?'

Bob laughed. 'Hey, I'm a married man. Remember?'

'That's why I brought you here. No temptation.'

They drank and talked. Their old intimacy was resumed, which meant that Bob did most of the talking, while Jim listened and waited. While Bob talked of life at sea, Jim watched the comedy at the bar. An Air Force pilot would squeeze in beside a sailor. They would talk, legs pressed together. Then they would leave, faces flushed, eyes bright. Youth drawn to youth, unlike the sad old men, eager but unattractive, who tried first one boy, then another; inured to rebuff, they searched always for that exceptional type which liked old men, or money.

'That's sort of a queer-looking crowd,' said Bob suddenly, motioning to the bar.

'Just New York.' Jim was a little frightened. Suppose Bob panicked? Had he overplayed his hand?

'I guess that *is* New York. Full of queers. They seem to be everywhere now. Even on board ship. Once I had a skipper who was, but he never bothered me. He liked niggers. I guess it takes all kinds. Want another drink?' Bob ordered another round.

Jim was relieved at Bob's display of tolerance.

'You know any women?' asked Bob finally. 'I mean just to talk to. Sally'd kill me if I ever did anything else. That's why, believe it or not, I've only shacked up with one other woman since I married, which is a pretty good record. No, I just mean girls for company.'

'Yes. But they'd all be tied up this late.'

'I guess it's pretty short notice. Of course I know a few numbers. Maybe I ought to call them.'

Jim thought it wise to make no protest.

'Let's go over to my hotel.' Bob stood up. 'I'll call from there.' They paid for their drinks and left the bar. Envious eyes watched them depart.

They crossed Times Square. Hot windless night. Lights flashing. People everywhere. The mood jubilant, post-war. Bob's hotel was in a side street. They went straight to his room. As Jim stepped inside, he was suddenly overwhelmed by Bob's physical reality. Clothes were strewn about the floor, a damp towel hung from the bathroom door, the bed was a tangle of sheets, and over the harsh odour of disinfectant and dust, Jim was aware of Bob's own smell, to him erotic.

'Kind of a mess,' said Bob mechanically. 'I'm not very neat. Sally always gets mad at the way I throw things around.' He went to the telephone and placed several calls. No one was home. Finally, he put the receiver down and grinned. 'I guess I was meant to be good tonight. So let's get drunk. Might as well be drunk as the way we are.' He took a bottle from his suitcase and poured two drinks. 'Here's how.' He drank his shot at a gulp. Jim merely tasted the whisky. He had to keep clear-headed.

As they drank beneath the harsh unshaded light of a single electric bulb, the room became stifling with summer heat. They took off their shirts. Bob's body was still muscular and strong, the skin smooth and white, not freckled, unlike most redheads.

The duet began pianissimo.

'You remember the old slave cabin?' asked Jim.

'Down by the river? Sure.'

'We had a lot of fun there.'

'I'll say. There was a pond, too, wasn't there? Where we swam?'

Jim nodded. 'Remember the last time we were there?'

'No, I don't think I do.'

Could he have forgotten? Impossible. 'Sure you remember. The weekend before you went North. Right after you graduated.'

Bob nodded. 'Yeah, I kind of remember.' He frowned. 'We . . . we fooled around quite a bit, didn't we?'

Yes, he remembered. Now it would happen. 'Yes. Kind of fun, wasn't it?'

Bob chuckled. 'Kids always do that, I guess. Though it's funny, I never did, except that one time.'

'Neither did I.'

'So I guess we were just a couple of little queers at heart.' Bob grinned.

'Did you ever . . . well, do *that* again, with anybody else?'

'Any other guy? Hell, no. Did you?'

'No.'

'Let's have another drink.'

Soon they were both drunk and Bob said that he was sleepy. Jim said that he was, too, and that he had better go home, but Bob insisted that he spend the night with him. They threw their clothes on the floor. Wearing only shorts, they tumbled on to the unmade bed. Bob lay sprawled on his back, arm across his face, apparently unconscious. Jim stared at him: was he really asleep? Boldly, Jim put his hand on Bob's chest. The skin was as smooth as he remembered. Lightly he touched the stray coppery hairs which grew below the deep-set navel. Then, carefully, like a surgeon performing a delicate operation, he unbuttoned Bob's shorts. Bob stirred, but did not wake, as Jim opened wide the shorts to reveal thick blond pubic hair from which sprouted the pale quarry. Slowly his hand closed around Bob's sex. He held him for what seemed a long time. Held him, until he looked up to find that the other was awake and watching him. Jim's heart stopped for a full beat.

'What the fuck are you doing?' The voice was hard. Jim could not speak. Obviously the world was ending. His hand remained frozen where it was. Bob pushed him. But he could not move.

'Let go of me, you queer.'

Plainly a nightmare, Jim decided. None of this could be happening. But when Bob struck him hard in the face, the pain recalled him. Jim drew back. Bob leapt to his feet and stood, swaying drunkenly, fumbling with buttons. 'Now will you get the hell out of here?'

Jim touched his face where he had been struck. His head still rang from the blow. Was he bleeding?

'Get out, you hear me?' Bob moved towards him, menacingly, fist ready. Suddenly, overwhelmed equally by rage and desire, Jim threw himself at Bob. They grappled. They fell across the bed. Bob was strong but Jim was stronger. Grunting and gasping, they twisted and turned, struck out with arms, legs, but Bob was no match for Jim and at the end, he lay face down on the bed, arm bent behind him, sweating and groaning. Jim looked down at the helpless body, wanting to do murder. Deliberately he twisted the arm he held. Bob cried out. Jim was excited at the other's pain. What to do? Jim frowned. Drink made concentration difficult. He looked at the heaving body beneath him, the broad back, ripped shorts, long muscled legs. One final humiliation: with his free hand, Jim pulled down the shorts, revealing white, hard, hairless buttocks. 'Jesus,' Bob whispered. 'Don't. Don't.'

Finished, Jim lay on the still body, breathing hard, drained of emotion, conscious that the thing was done, the circle completed, and finished.

At last Jim sat up. Bob did not stir. He remained face down, clutching the pillow to his face while Jim dressed. Then Jim crossed to the bed and looked down at the body he had loved with such single-mindedness for so many years. Was this all? He put his hand on Bob's sweaty shoulder. Bob shied away from him: fear? disgust? It made no difference now. Jim touched the pillow. It was wet. Tears? Good. Without a word, Jim went to the door and opened it. He looked back once more at Bob, then he turned out the light and shut the door behind him. He left the hotel, not caring where he went. For a long time he walked aimlessly, until at last he came to one of the many bars where men looked for men. He entered, prepared to drink until the dream was completely over.

CHAPTER ELEVEN

It was late, very late. He had begun to forget again. Only by great effort had he been able to remember what had happened to him. Now he felt no sorrow. Nothing. Bob was finished and that was the end of that.

He called to the bartender. The man came over. 'Another one?' Jim nodded. His head felt strangely heavy. If he nodded too hard it might fall off. 'Another one.'

Then a little man with a dark moustache and quick-moving eyes came over. 'May I sit down? Could I buy you a drink?'

'If you want to.'

'It's certainly been warm weather, hasn't it? I'm from Detroit myself. Where are you from?'

'I forgot.'

'Oh, I'm sorry if I'm intruding. I didn't mean to pry.'

'All right.' Jim was glad to have someone sitting opposite him. Someone who liked to talk. The sound of words was peaceful if one didn't attend to their meaning.

'Isn't this a big town, though? I've been here maybe two weeks and still don't feel I've seen a thing. It's much bigger than Detroit and there seems to be everything here. I've never seen so much of *everything*. Do you work here, if I'm not being too personal?'

'Yes.' Jim wondered how long it would take the waiter to bring him his drink. He could make no contact with reality or even unreality until he had another drink. Suddenly there was a glass in front of him. Jim took a swallow: cold, hot, cold, hot. That's the way it should be. He looked at the small man. He had a feeling that a question had been asked for the little man sat looking at him. He wondered if he had heard the question and forgotten it or whether he had never heard it at all. 'You say something?'

'I only asked if you lived here in town.'

'Yes.' Now the next question. The catechism never changed.

'Do you live with your family?'

'No.'

'Then you're not married?'

'No.' Jim decided that he would play for a while. Lead the man on and then pretend anger and frighten him. It would be amusing.

'Well, neither am I. You know, I've always said it's a lot cheaper to buy milk than keep a cow.' He paused as though expecting either laughter or agreement. He got neither. 'I'll bet they've got some good-looking girls around here.' The little man winked at Jim. 'I'll bet you have a girl here.'

'I don't have a girl.' Jim offered hope.

'Now that's strange, a young fellow like you. Were you in the Army?'

'Yes.'

'Overseas?'

'Yes.'

'The Pacific?'

'Yes.'

'What were you in, what branch?'

'I was a pilot,' Jim lied. He enjoyed inventing new personalities for himself.

'That certainly must have been dangerous. I've always said we've really got to hand it to those Air Corps boys because they took all the risks. I say anything they get they deserve. Yes, sir, if I was going to be in the service (I've got only this one kidney) I'd pick the Air Corps any time. I guess there were a lot of nurses and so on out in the Pacific.'

'Yes.'

'Some of those nurses are pretty cute, I expect.'

'Yes.'

'I'll bet it was awful in the places where there weren't any women. I knew a soldier once who said he was on an island with a bunch of soldiers and no women for a year. He said they used to look good to each other, the men, I mean.' The little man looked at Jim, expectantly.

'Yes,' said Jim, and he took another swallow. Everything was pleasant and warm inside his stomach. But his knees felt odd, disconnected. Then the little man put his foot next to his. Deliberately Jim picked up his own foot and, after a long thoughtful minute, brought it down hard on the little man's foot.

'Ouch!'

'Sorry.' Jim was happy that he had caused pain.

'That's all right,' said the little man. They were both silent. Jim drank and the little man nervously chewed the ends of his dark moustache. 'I guess you live alone.'

'Yes.'

'That must get pretty lonely. Back in Detroit I live with my mother. I'm a C.P.A. – an accountant – and of course it's nice at the office, going to the office. I've been ten years with this firm and so I know everybody and I try to like everybody. The head of the firm calls me Walter – my first name is Walter. What's yours, if I may ask?'

'Herbert.'

'That's a very nice name,' said Walter. 'I like names . . . beginning with "H". So at the office I know a lot of people but when the work is over I think it would be terribly lonely to go home and not have *anybody* there. That's why I like living with Mother. She's seventy-two but she's terribly active. I only hope I'll be as active when I'm her age. How old are you, Herbert, if I'm not prying?'

'Twenty-one.'

'My gracious, you're still terribly young. I wish I was that age again, I really do – but know the things I know now. Of course you've been around a great deal for your age. I didn't go around much when I was your age. You probably know what the score is, eh?'

'What is it?'

'What is what?'

'The score.'

'Well, that was just a figure of speech. I meant you had a lot of experiences probably, in the Army and so on.'

Jim drank the rest of his drink and the little man offered to buy him another and Jim allowed him to.

'You've certainly had a lot to drink,' said Walter.

'How can you tell?'

'I mean ... well, you seem to have had a lot to drink.' Walter paused uneasily. 'By the way,' he said, 'I've got a bottle of real Scotch up in my room at the hotel. If you'd care to ...'

'I like it here.'

'I just thought maybe you might like to come up for a little while, that's all. We could have a friendly chat and it's certainly much nicer there than it is here.'

Jim glared at Walter. 'You think I'm trade maybe? You think maybe I'll go home with a little fag like you, maybe? Or do you want to get me drunk in case I'm straight, and screw me?'

Walter stood up. 'Now, really, I think you've gone far enough. If you weren't drunk you wouldn't say such things to me. Such a thought never entered my mind. If you'll excuse me ...' Walter went away and Jim started to laugh. He laughed loudly for several moments and then he stopped, wanting to cry or sob or shout. But the bartender put an end to that. He came over and told him that the bar was closing and it was time to go.

Unsteadily, Jim walked out into the damp air of early morning. It was very dark. There were no stars; no moon; only street lamps shining in the blackness. Then he was sober.

The edges of the buildings became sharp and clear. He knew exactly where he was and who he was and there was nothing left to do but continue, as though nothing had happened. But even as he made this vow, he recalled firelight and heard again the river's roar. No vision ended except in something vivid and new, and there was nothing new for him. The lover and brother was gone, replaced by a memory of bruised flesh, tangled sheets, violence. Panicky, he contemplated flight. He would return to sea. Change his name, memories, life. He turned west towards the waterfront where great ships were moored. Yes, he would ship out again and travel in strange countries and meet new people. Begin again.

Then suddenly he was on the docks, with silent ships all about him. The air was cool. The morning near. At his feet the waters rose and fell slowly, gently, like the breathing of some vast monster. Once more he stood beside a river, aware at last that the purpose of rivers is to flow into the sea. Nothing that ever was changes. Yet nothing that is can ever be the same as what went before. Fascinated, he watched the waters shifting dark and cold against the stony island. Soon he would go on.